FIVE SMOOTH STONES

IN EACH GENERATION, ONE BOOK CAPTURES THE POIGNANCE AND PASSION OF ITS DAY.

Mirroring and magnifying life, exploring and provoking emotion, telling a tale of today with enduring power and compassion . . . **FIVE SMOOTH STONES** IS THE NOVEL FOR OUR TIME!

"RARE UNDERSTANDING AND MAGNIFICENT FEELING . . . FASCINATING."

—**Book Week**

"A MOVING AND POWERFUL PIECE OF WORK!"

—**Book-of-the-Month Club News**

"THIS IS A NOVEL—A STORY—TO REMEMBER!"

—**Associated Press**

"EVERY SO OFTEN ALONG COMES THE BIG BOOK THAT DEFIES CATEGORIZATION . . . It has real size, stature . . . Above all, it rings true . . . You may put it down, but you can't forget it. You have to come back. Such is the case with **FIVE SMOOTH STONES!**"

—**Springfield Daily News**

"A POWERFUL STORY . . . **FIVE SMOOTH STONES** is big physically . . . More significant is its awareness of the world in which we live; by present literary standards, that awareness is very large indeed!"

—**Minneapolis Tribune**

"SCENES THAT BLAZE WITH BITTER TRUTH . . . The central character of this long and richly realized novel is David Champlin . . . a man of dignity, capable of love, of hurting and being hurt. The obstacles he overcomes demand inborn fortitude, wry humor and simple raw courage . . . the numerous people characterized so clearly in this novel are, with few exceptions, 'mortal humans.' That is rare enough in any fiction dealing with one of the bone-deep issues of our time!"

—The New York Times

"NO MATTER HOW LARGE ANN FAIRBAIRN'S AUDIENCE IS, IT WON'T BE LARGE ENOUGH . . . Technically Miss Fairbairn is flawless . . . David Champlin is a great tragic hero in a memorable story!"

—Denver Post

FIVE SMOOTH STONES

A novel by Ann Fairbairn

BANTAM BOOKS
TORONTO • NEW YORK • LONDON • SYDNEY • AUCKLAND

*This low-priced Bantam Book
has been completely reset in a type face
designed for easy reading, and was printed
from new plates. It contains the complete
text of the original hard-cover edition.*
NOT ONE WORD HAS BEEN OMITTED.

FIVE SMOOTH STONES
*A Bantam Book / published by arrangement with
Crown Publishers, Inc.*

PRINTING HISTORY
Crown edition published December 1966
2nd printing . . . January 1967
Literary Guild edition published June 1967
Bantam edition / July 1968
41 printings through April 1985

*For information address: Crown Publishers, Inc.,
One Park Avenue, New York, N.Y. 10016.*

ISBN 0-553-25203-8

Published simultaneously in the United States and Canada

Bantam Books are published by Bantam Books, Inc. Its trademark, consisting of the words "Bantam Books" and the portrayal of a rooster, is Registered in U.S. Patent and Trademark Office and in other countries. Marca Registrada. Bantam Books, Inc., 666 Fifth Avenue, New York, New York 10103.

PRINTED IN THE UNITED STATES OF AMERICA

H 50 49 48 47 46 45 44 43 42 41

FOR MY FATHER

And Saul armed David with his armour, and he put an helmet of brass upon his head; also he armed him with a coat of mail. And David girded his sword upon his armour, and he assayed to go . . . And David said unto Saul, I cannot go with these; for I have not proved them. And David put them off him. And he took his staff in his hand, and chose him five smooth stones out of the brook, and put them in a shepherd's bag which he had, even in a scrip; and his sling was in his hand: and he drew near to the Philistine.

I SAMUEL 17:38–40

FIVE SMOOTH STONES

I

THERE WAS A TEN-DOLLAR BILL IN JOSEPH CHAMPLIN'S pocket on an evening in early March in 1933. Few Negroes in New Orleans during those days of a paralyzed economy could boast as much. With the ten-dollar bill was a fifty-cent piece; this he had made on a four-hour cleaning job. The ten dollars he attributed to the direct intervention of the Almighty in his troubled affairs. He budgeted his windfall in his mind as he walked along the banquettes of the Vieux Carré on his way home: coffee, coal, beans, rice, salt meat, oil for the lamps, something held back for his mother, and something to pay on the overdue rent.

Geneva would be happy, he thought; Geneva would sure be happy. He planned to keep quiet about the ten dollars at first, giving her the four-bit piece when he came in, giving her chance to blow off steam because he'd worked fcr so little. He knew by heart what she would say, and he would not give her the opportunity to say all of it.

"Don't come crying to me, Li'l Joe Champlin!" Her voice would be sharp with worry, and there would be desperation behind it. In the early days of their marriage the sharpness had been less, more a thing of tone than of emotion. These days it sliced at his nerves. "Don't come crying to me. You think they gonna pay you good if you don't have no understanding first? Or even if you got an understanding. But you got no understanding at all, they going to take all they can get even if it's blood. They gonna take it and expect you to say 'thank-you-*suh.*' "

"You don't understand. Things is different. Things is bad, real bad. Even they got it rough."

"That ain't our fault."

"Sure as hell ain't, but there ain't nothing we can do about it. You knows damned well, Neva, I never done no job in my life till now I didn't have an understanding first how much I'd get. Li'l Joe Champlin got his price or he didn't do no work."

"That's because they knew you was the onlies' man could turn out the work like you do. Working like a pint-sized mule, half killing yourself."

"I'll get me my own price again, you wait and see, better times come."

"Better times ain't coming."

"They say they is. Seen it in the paper. Everything's going to be better now they got them a new President." Joseph Champlin laughed without sound. "You does a lot of talking, but I don't see as how you've had no better luck getting more'n a dollar a day washing dishes in that restaurant where they gets five dollars just for putting the water and bread on the table. That and maybe some beef ribs to tote home. What kind of a dog you tell them folks you was taking them bones home to?"

Then it would go on, Li'l Joe Champlin's voice quiet, soft; Geneva's rasping. It hadn't been like that when they'd first started living together, after he and his first wife, Josephine, had separated, or after he'd made her his married wife. Now the nagging was wearing him down.

Usually, after a few hours of it he would leave the house, sometimes slamming the door, more often letting it close quietly behind him. Then he would walk, legs laden with fatigue, the meal Geneva had somehow managed to scrape together a burden in his stomach. Most of the time he wound up at Hank's Place and sat slim and straight at the counter, drinking his coffee slowly, making it last until he knew Geneva would be in bed. Sometimes he had a little money he'd held back, and then he would have a drink of bootleg or corn whiskey. If he didn't have the money even for coffee, Hank would trust him, winking at him to say nothing.

When Li'l Joe went home, it would not matter how harsh the words had been earlier. He would move quietly, as he always did, undressing in the dark, slipping into bed beside the tired woman who was his wife. Just as he felt sleep creeping on to obliterate the ache of living, one slender brown hand would reach out almost without volition, and he would grasp a fold of her nightgown, holding it tightly. If he woke up through the night and found it no longer in his grasp, he would reach out again, and return to sleep with its folds in his fingers.

Tonight there would be no need to leave the house, no preliminary quarreling or nagging. He would not let it get to that stage before he pulled out the ten dollars. He thought of telling Geneva he had earned the ten dollars, and then decided against it. She wouldn't believe him. He would tell her the truth—that he had found it, wadded into a ball, on the floor of the men's toilet in the Creole Club when he was finishing his job of mopping.

Joseph Champlin was forty-two in that year when the economy of the country had reached its nadir. He was a slight, brown-skinned man, quiet in his ways. He was respected and loved by his own people and in considerable demand by the whites as a worker, because he had the capability and drive to turn out more work in a day than most men twice his size. His top weight was one hundred and twenty-five; on the night Providence had led him to the ten-dollar bill it had dropped to one hundred and nine. He could not remember the time when he had not been known as "Li'l Joe" Champlin.

When the economic rigor mortis of the depression settled over New Orleans, it had been hard for him to take whatever came his way. Not that there had ever been work he was too proud to do. His mother had taught him that, speaking as often in French or Creole as she did in English. But there had been jobs he had refused to return to because he did not like the treatment he received as a Negro. He had always resented the patronage of householders more than he did the sometimes abusive, always profane, attitude of the white straw bosses on the docks or other manual jobs. He resented the "boy" of the genteel white far more than the "nigger" of the straw boss.

He did not make all his money by manual work. He could play banjo and guitar with the best New Orleans had to offer, and when times were good he was always able to make extra money playing.

He looked with contempt on his own people who talked "poor mouth," whose voices changed when they talked to whites. He had no more scruples than the next man when it came to lying to whites as a means of self-preservation or to please them and keep them in a good mood. Lying to whites was a fact of life; it was like keeping your head up and your eyes up when you worked on the docks around the cranes, because the cranes could mean a horrid death. But if he gave his word to any man, colored or white, he kept it. If they did not keep theirs, his was not given again.

Now hunger and want were threatening to strip his dignity from him as a vulture strips flesh from the bones of the dead; they were not unfamiliar, he had known them all his life, but not in quite the guise he knew them now. He had worked before his seventh birthday, and with the pennies bought salt meat to surprise his mother. Now hopelessness was added to hunger and want. That had not been there before. There had always been hope before, within the narrow, circumscribed world in which the color of his skin required him to live.

During his adult life he had never failed to stop at his mother's room on St. Peter Street on his way to a job, to drink a cup of coffee with her. He did not change the habit now; the difference was that he was not setting out on a job, but to walk God only knew how far before dark in search of one.

Irene Champlin was a small woman, almost tiny; it was from her the man called Li'l Joe inherited the delicate look, the slender bones, the slight frame, and the hidden strength. Her skin was as blue-black as her mother's had been when she had been brought to America as a child, eight years old, straight from Africa on a slave ship. Irene spoke precise and nearly perfect English because she had taken the fancy of the woman she had been put out to work for when she was a child and had been taught to read and write and speak properly along with her employer's children. She spoke Creole and French fluently because those were the languages spoken by her own family.

She was waiting for her son the morning of the day he found the ten dollars, coffee hot on the tiny stove, the strong black coffee of New Orleans, bitter with chicory. As Joseph Champlin drank the coffee, he knew he did not want to leave the little room, wanted to sit there quietly with her, drawing from her strength. He felt dead inside, and dreaded what he must face when he walked down the worn stairs and into the streets.

She waited until she saw the shadows of his face lighten a little, and said: "It's near your birthday, son. Pray to St. Joseph. He'll help you. And when the work comes, offer it to God."

He tried to speak lightly. "Looks like God don't need no work, Ma."

There was no softness in her eyes when she looked at her son, her first and only child, but behind them there was pain.

"God never made the mouth he wouldn't feed." She spoke in French.

He was silent a moment, did not answer directly; he had seen too many mouths in need of food these past months. "You need anything, Ma?"

"Nothing, son. I worked three days last week. You know that. Stop by tonight and I'll give you some rice and some sugar for Geneva. She likes plenty of sugar for her coffee."

He did not tell her they had used the last of their coffee that morning. He had not yet told her of the real poverty of his home these days. What must she have made last week? Two dollars? Some to put up for the rent, some for the coffee she loved herself, some for rice and beans and what she could pick up at the French Market for a few pennies—filleted fish backs, chicken backs—and she would make them taste better than some of the junk Geneva brought home from the restaurant where she sometimes worked. If he told her of their need, she would wait until he had left her room and go to their house, and if Geneva was not there she would open the door with the key they had given her and leave something in the icebox or on the kitchen table.

She sat at the little table by the window opposite him. "They're waking Ruth tomorrow night," she said. "Will you be there?"

"If I ain't working."

"It's the wake for your son's wife."

"I know, Ma, I know. I'll be there, I tell you, if I ain't working. If I gets a job, no matter what time of day or night it is there ain't nothing going to keep me away from it. Reckon John would understand."

It had been six months, almost to the day, since his second son, John, born to him and Josephine twenty years before, had died under the wheels of the freight train he was hopping north to find work. John had been big and strong, with skin almost as black as his grandmother's, and had laughed a lot. "He laughs like his grandfather," Irene Champlin said. "Like my husband did."

Then John's wife, Ruth, had died in a little room on the other side of town just twenty-four hours after giving birth to their son. There was sick sadness in Joseph Champlin's heart that morning as he sat with his mother.

"Ain't never thought I'd envy the dead," he said, and stood quickly, wanting to get away, to take his sadness outside where it would not worry his mother.

She went into the hall with him and said, "God's blessing, son," as he turned from her and started down the stairs, shoulders straight and thin under the clean, starched khaki shirt. She watched him from the top of the staircase, eyes on the nappy black hair kept as she had trained him to keep it, close cut and gleaming, and she put out her hand to him as he went from her. He did not see her, only felt along the back of his neck a prickle of warmth, for he knew without seeing it that she had made the gesture.

By ten o'clock that morning he could sense there would be no work. He was far more tired than he ever remembered being at the end of a day's work with pick and shovel, deep in a ditch; more tired than he had ever been after ten, twelve hours wrassling coffee sacks on the docks. He walked endlessly, without a dime in his pocket. His belly was beginning to cramp, as it always did when it was empty, but he could not bring himself to go home. He went to numberless restaurants, offering to wash dishes, and found no takers. One woman laughed sympathetically. "We've got a waiting list," she said. "Come back tomorrow afternoon. Maybe then." Something in the straightness of his shoulders as he turned away prompted her to call him back. "I'll send someone out with a cup of coffee," she said.

The coffee stopped the cramping for a while and chased the giddiness of hunger from his head. When there was no place left to go on that side of town, he turned toward Canal Street, heading for the depot and the area back of it. Ahead of him he saw a white man he knew, unlocking the door of a small nightclub where he had played gigs with Kid Arab's band in the good days when there was music to be played all over, and the streets of the Vieux Carré were alive and swarming with people. The man was Tony Guastella, and the club was called the Creole Club. It was a white club, a bootleg joint, and he stood now in the open doorway through which Guastella had disappeared, and knocked on the jamb.

Ten minutes later, equipped with dusting cloths, pail, mop, and broom, Joseph Champlin was attacking two weeks' accumulation of dirt. He had not asked what the pay would be; Guastella had not told him. He wrinkled a fastidious nose at some of the dirt, but went after it in the only way he knew how, as though the devil were riding him.

Stale coffee was in a pot on a battered electric plate on the shelf beneath the bar. The bartender had washed the glasses last night, but had left the coffee to grow stale in the pot. He asked Guastella if it was all right if he had a cup, and was told to take all he wanted, and help himself to the pretzels in a bowl on the bar. These and the knowledge he would not be going home that night with completely empty pockets gave him strength to make the job a good one. Do it good enough, he thought, mebbe I can get me a little work here now and then.

When he saw the end of the job in sight, could see in his mind's eye a can of coffee on the shelf, salt meat in the icebox, and enough rice and beans to last them a while, he began to sing. Singing was not one of his accomplishments; his musical talent was strictly instrumental. His voice was rougher, stronger than his size would indicate, and he let it out now, the rhythm helping his arm with the mop:

> " 'Oh, Mary, don't you weep, don't you moan—
> Oh, Mary, don't you weep, don't you moan—
> Pharaoh's army got drownded—
> Oh, Mary, don't you weep—
>
> " 'When we get to Heaven, gonna sing and shout—
> Can't nobody in Heaven throw us out—
> Pharaoh's army got drownded—
> Oh, Mary, don't you weep—' "

He sang this song because it was on his mind. He had sat alone in his kitchen the night before, listening to a church "sing" in Conservation Hall, just behind their back window, in the next street. Emma Jefferson was playing the piano, anyone could tell that, playing it with a force so compelling, a touch so sure, and a sense of beauty so perceptive that her chording breaks made his flesh prickle, brought out gooseflesh on his arms. After they had sung about Pharaoh's army until he could see it, and the Red Sea swallowing it up, he waited hopefully for "He's My Lily of the Valley." It came finally, and as soon as he heard the opening chords he began to smile. In a little bit Geneva's voice would break away from the others and take off alone, take off and travel, not strong, but clear and high and sweet. The ensemble would be strong and close—" 'He's my lily of the valley, everybody knows—' "; then Geneva's voice would soar like the exultant song of a solitary bird flying high above its companions—" 'Everybody don' know—everybody don' know—what Jesus means—' " And then the ensemble would come under her voice and cradle it, and then it would break away again, soaring and swooping—" 'What Jesus means, what Jesus means —' " He could listen to it over and over, but it was the hymn about Pharaoh's army that lived with him for two or three days after he heard it.

The owner of the club left before Joseph Champlin finished his job of cleaning. Guastella could do that because he had known Li'l Joe ever since Joe had been a spindle-shanked, brown-skin boy in short pants doing odd jobs wherever he could find them. Guastella had learned through the years that if you gave Li'l Joe a job to do he'd never quit until it was finished, really finished.

"There's money for you on the back bar, Joe," he said as he left. "Take a beer from the icebox when you finish."

Joseph Champlin smiled. "Sure will."

"Leave the key next door in the barbershop. Anyone comes in before you leave, tell 'em I'll open up at eight. O.K., boy?"

"Sure. Sure. I'll tell 'em." He was not smiling now.

You never could tell with niggers, thought Guastella. Never could tell, even with the good ones like Li'l Joe Champlin. One minute they'd be smiling, and the next they'd be looking at something over your shoulder while you talked, eyes blank, and if there was a smile it would be teeth and that's all, and damned if anyone could tell what made them change. It was the first time Li'l Joe had not discussed the price of a job with him before he started it. It had been evident when the thin, anxious man had knocked on the door that he'd been looking for work all morning. The city was full of them these days, but he'd never trust a nigger he didn't know, and he always sent them away. Li'l Joe he could trust.

Joseph Champlin gave Guastella a few minutes after he left, then walked to the bar and looked over at the shelf behind it. He saw the gleam of a four-bit piece, looked for green and did not find it, not even after he walked behind the bar and searched the floor and the surface of the shelf inch by inch. "Sweet Jesus!" he muttered. "That what he's giving me for all this work?" He dropped the coal from his mental budget. He wanted to leave the fifty-cent piece on the bar. He'd damned well quit now, he thought. The hell with the men's room and the rest of it. All Guastella cared about was what showed. But he walked back to his pail and mop, muttering, "Four bits. A stinking four bits," and kept on with the small unmopped area in the main room, then started for the men's room, dragging the mop after him, tired now in the late afternoon with miles of walking behind him, and then the work here, and nothing in his stomach but coffee and pretzels.

He did not see the crumpled bill in the far corner of the room until he pushed his mop toward it. Even though he knew he was alone in the club, he picked it up with the quickness of a cat stealing a piece of meat from a plate, shoved it in his pocket, then hooked the door and took it out. He had thought it was a one; instead it was a ten, crumpled the way a gambler crumples a bill. Some of the men had told him there'd been a bunch of gamblers from Chicago around New Orleans lately; there was one gambler poorer by ten dollars.

He forgot his anger at Guastella. He was shaky with relief, and wished he dared pour a drink. He knew where Guastella kept the stuff but he was afraid to touch one of the bottles because as sure as he did someone from the neighborhood would come in and then tell Guastella he'd caught the nigger clean-up boy stealing liquor.

He settled for the beer Guastella had told him he could have, and took it into the back room where the colored musicians were forced to sit between sets. He had already cleaned that room, but no amount of cleaning could change the air, could make it anything but rank and fetid.

He sat down with the opened bottle of beer and a glass and relaxed for a minute, feeling the ten-dollar bill in his pocket with long, grateful fingers, thinking of Geneva's face as it would be when she had finished giving him hell about the four bits—he'd have to give her a chance to do that—and she saw him take the ten dollars out and lay it on the kitchen table.

Because there were no other ears to assault but his own, he sang out loud and strong as he walked to the front door to leave, " 'Pharaoh's army got drownded—Oh, Mary, don't you weep—' "

2

AS HE APPROACHED THE HOUSE on St. Philip Street where he and Geneva lived, Joseph Champlin thought that he must be sure and remind his wife to save enough out of the ten dollars to buy rat poison. It would do little good but it was an effort; it was better than giving in to the rodents—aggressive, obscene, and dangerous—that swarmed through the houses of the French Quarter. He had met them on the stairs, and had them face him and not run; he had battled them in the outdoor privy that was the only toilet he and Geneva had, had awakened in the night to the feel of a rat running across his shoulders. He pitied his neighbors with babies and small children; theirs was a battle that never ended.

He sighed, and thought that he could have spent fifty dollars and still not had enough with which to buy the things they needed to make life more bearable: a decent stove to keep them warm in winter, oil to burn in it, a fan for the humid, breathless nights of summer, a decent cookstove for Geneva. Or maybe take the fifty and pay up the back rent and move across the river, or over the lake, rent a shack with room enough for his mother, raise their own vegetables and chickens. God knows, he thought, I don't want much. And then felt guilty that he had even wished the ten dollars was more. His mother would give him hell if she knew what he was thinking, right after God had met a present need.

When he walked into what passed for the living room of their small quarters, he stopped. The night was not unreasonably cool, was, in fact, pleasant and springlike, but the tiny apartment felt like an oven. He could see Geneva in back, in the kitchen-alcove, bending over something on the table. There was a sudden wailing, and he stopped in stride, then moved forward quietly, not speaking. He stood just behind his wife until the shock had worn off, then said: "Neva. You has to put your finger under the pin where it goes through.

You don't do that you're going to pin that pore chile's skin right into the diaper."

Geneva jumped, startled, then turned to him, her face wrinkled with anxiety. There was a sound from the baby on the table, and she turned back and picked the child up, holding it against her breast, rocking it gently. "You ever seen a sweeter baby, Li'l Joe? You ever seen a sweeter?"

"You better get that diaper on that chile, woman, or you're going to be sorry. Who's that baby belong to? Who you taking care of it for?" Then, when she laid the baby on the table, "Sweet Jesus! That baby ain't more'n two, three days old."

"It's your grandbaby, Joe. Can't you see? That's Ruth and John's pore little motherless chile. Can't you see?"

"Lawd Gawd!" said Li'l Joe. "What's he doing here?" He moved closer, took the powder can from Geneva's hand, dusted expertly, and then with quick, deft fingers secured the diaper, spare safety pins in his mouth. The baby made a contented sound, and Geneva, standing by silently, said, "He said something, Joe. You hear him?"

"That chile didn't say nothing. You lost your senses, woman?" He stood looking down at the infant, smiling into its vague, unfocused eyes. "Sure a fine baby," he said. "Sure a fine boy. Look at them shoulders."

"Now can you see?" asked Geneva. "Now can you see he's your grandbaby? Shoulders just like John's. And long hands like yourn."

He had forgotten the ten dollars in his pocket, and the fifty cents, and even his hunger. He eyed his wife warily. "Where'd you get him, Geneva? Why'd you-all bring him here?"

"Listen, Joe, I ain't saying this because Josephine was your first wife, because she was your wife before you and me married up. That baby stays at Josephine's he's going to die sure as he's an inch long. All them kids there, handling him like he was a puppy or a kitten or something, crying his little heart out, all wet, and Josephine so fat and lazy she can't do nothing but sit on her fat butt and carry on about Ruth and John. And this pore little chile like he ain't never been born."

"Josephine's his grandma."

"And you're his grandpa."

"Jesus have moicy!" Like many New Orleanians of both races, there was, in certain syllables, an accent close to Brooklynese in Li'l Joe's speech. "Jesus have moicy!" he said again, and backed away from the table. "What you saying? What you *saying?*"

Geneva picked the baby up, wrapped a worn piece of blanket around him, and carried him to the chair beside the stove. There was a carton on the chair, and Li'l Joe could see that it had been lined with another piece of the same blanket so that the folds hung over three sides and could be brought over to cover the baby. He let out a long breath. "You planning to have that baby smothered for supper, like an old hen? My Gawd, it's hot enough in here to kill him. We ain't got all that kind of coal. Speck of air never hurt a young un. He's no incubator baby."

Geneva laid the baby in the carton without answering, turned to the stove and took a nursing bottle from a pan of water. She handed the bottle to her husband. "You understands about this better than what I do. You done raised three, and the Lord only let me have one but a few hours. You test this, see is it all right."

He took the bottle, shook a few drops of milk on the inside of his wrist, and gave it back to her with a nod. "You giving that baby straight milk? You want it to get colic?"

"It ain't milk; it's formula. They give it to me at the clinic at the hospital, *and* showed me how to fix it. They give me the talcum powder too; the sister did."

"You went to—Neva, what you been doing?" His voice grew husky. "Neva, what you going to *do* with that chile?"

She bent over the carton, put the nipple of the bottle in the baby's mouth, then looked up at her husband over her shoulder. "You mean what *we* going to do with that chile," she said. "We going to *raise* him, Li'l Joe. We sure as the devil going to raise him."

Joseph Champlin heated up the supper that night, red beans, rice, some leftover greens, eggs. "Where'd them eggs come from?" he asked.

"Tant'Irene give them to us."

"My ma? She been here?"

"I been there. We went to Josephine's to see could we help, and to find out about the wake. Lady your mamma works for left word at the store across the street she wanted your mamma to work tomorrow. Lady what keeps the store says your mamma could have credit for what she needed. Your ma give us them eggs, and a little coffee and some sugar."

Li'l Joe had not yet told her of the ten dollars. He felt vaguely cheated that the excitement over the baby had pushed the miraculous finding of ten dollars into the background. He knew that if he had found a hundred dollars it wouldn't bring the look to Geneva's face the sight of the baby brought, wouldn't erase the edge from her voice as the presence of the baby had.

He had not argued with her at first when she said, "We sure as the devil going to raise that chile." He never argued with Geneva when she said they sure as the devil were going to do anything. Sometimes he lost out when he eventually got round to opposing her; sometimes he won. He knew Geneva had lost a baby right after its birth years before, when his and Josephine's babies had been coming along so fast, and that there had never been another; he thought he knew how she must feel about this one.

He drew a deep breath. "Geneva, we too old to start raising a child, let alone try to feed one, times like these. Ruth's got folks, real good people, up there in Mississippi. They got a little farm; they'd probably be happy to take the chile, and take better care of him than what we can."

When they had first been married, the police had come to the house one night and, without warning, broken the lock of the door and thundered in, looking for a man Li'l Joe had never heard of, let alone been harboring. The fear he had seen in her eyes that night, when she had thought the police were after him, had been as great as the fear he saw in them now. He could not look at her, looked instead at his empty plate.

"We send that chile away, it's flying in the face of Providence," said Geneva. "God sent him to us."

"God never done no such thing, Neva. Way you tell it, you walked clear across town and fetched him your own self."

"God don't have to leave no baby on a doorstep to mean He wants it taken care of." She stopped, listening. "You think he wants another bottle?"

Li'l Joe sighed, and walked to the chair by the stove, stood looking at the sleeping baby. The shadow of a look of his son was there, and more than a shadow—and he did not know this—of a child who had been born more than sixty years before, just a few blocks away. He heard Geneva saying: "Tant'Irene say he's like your boy John was. She say he don't look a bit like you when you was born. But she says more than anyone he looks like his great-grandaddy must have looked when he was a baby, only his skin's going to be lighter, like Ruth's. She says she can sure see your daddy in him. Tell me, you think he needs another bottle?"

Li'l Joe came back to the table. "You want the chile to bust? Along with smothering? He wants feeding he'll let you know. Long about the time you just beginning to get a good sleep, he'll let you know."

"We kept 'em in the dresser drawer, me and Josephine did, when they was real little. Makes a fine crib."

"We ain't putting that baby in no dresser drawer, Joseph Champlin. What about them rats? I'll keep him with me, right in the bed with me."

"You fixing to finish that chile off before he even gets a good start. You can't keep him in the bed. You'll overlay him sure. You roots, woman."

"Maybe I does. God knows you don't. You sleeps like a co'pse. Sometimes you so quiet that if I wakes up I puts out my hand to tech you and see is you really breathing."

"Better watch them hands, girl. No telling what you'll find."

Suddenly Geneva Champlin laughed, and her husband turned to her and saw the young woman he had married. He had not seen her for a long time.

"You comfortable, Joe, laying on the inside?"

"Reckon I'm all right if you don't turn over."

"I ain't all that big."

"You big enough, girl. You big enough so's I don't stand no chance if you start rooting me up against the wall."

"You sure he don't need another bottle?"

"I keep a-telling you, Neva, that baby wants another bottle he sure as hell ain't going to be backward about letting you know. Mebbe he won't want one till morning. You get you some sleep, girl."

"Funny. I done all that walking and I ain't tired."

"You tired all right. You just ain't got sense enough to know it."

"You sure you fixed them ropes good around that carton so's it'll stay on that chair?"

"It's right beside you. Jiggle it and see."

"Seems all right."

"That's the way my ma kept me when I was born. . . . Gawd sake, go to sleep, woman."

"Joe . . . Joe . . . *Joe!* You awake?"

"Lawd! I am now. What you want?"

"You get a job of work today?"

"Yeah. Made me a little piece of change. Worked for Guastella, cleaning out that club of his. Sure was dirty. Made me four bits."

"How long you work for a four-bit piece? . . . How long?"

"Three, four hours."

Sometimes when Joseph Champlin described his wife's reactions to anger he would say, "Geneva's a mighty fine churchgoing woman. But she can sure cuss like a grown-up, she puts her mind to it."

She put her mind to it now. The mildest she came up with was "ofay bastard." Li'l Joe gave her her head, smiling in the darkness. When she had finished he said: "I done better than that. Found me ten dollars. On the floor in the men's room."

"Ten dollars! And you never said nothing to me about it!"

"Gawd sake, Neva, you ain't give me chance. I was fixing to tell you in the morning when you wasn't so excited about the chile and all."

"Ten dollars! Joseph Champlin, you'd oughta be ashamed. I swear you ought. If that ain't proof God sent us this chile, I don't know what is."

"It ain't proof of no such thing. If it's proof of anything it's proof of what my ma was always telling me—you has good luck, you has to pay for it, somehow, some way or another. How's it proof? You think we can raise a chile on ten dollars? You think we going to live on air, and cook on paper fires, and put water in the lamp 'stead of oil, and pay the rent and insurance with cigarette coupons?"

"It's going to tide us over, that's what it's going to do. Your ma, she'd call it 'signs of land.' Better times coming."

"You said yestiddy better times never coming."

"That was yestiddy," said Geneva.

"Joe!"

"Jesus!"

"Joe, I can't sleep for thinking that chile's got no name. They ain't never bothered to give him no name."

"Worry about it in the morning. He ain't going to fret about it for quite a spell."

"Ruth didn't pick no name because she say she wanted to wait and see. She wanted a girl real bad."

Silence, the silence of hope that if one doesn't answer the voice will go away.

"Joe . . . Joe."

"Gawd sake—"

"Joe, your ma, she looked at that chile, and the first thing she said was 'David.' She didn't say nothing else, just 'David.' You hear what I'm saying, Joe?"

The silence was different now. The woman could feel the difference; she could not see her husband, but she had shared his bed for a long time. "You hear me, Joe?"

"I ain't deaf. David was my daddy's name."

"I knows that. But ain't no one in your family ever had that name since him. It's a good name, 'David' is. Tant'Irene says there never was a better man than your daddy. It don't seem right never having a chile come from him carry his name."

She waited a long time for an answer that did not come.

"Joe—Joe, you thinking 'bout how your daddy died. You thinking you don't want a little chile to carry his name; you thinking it'll bring him bad luck. It says right in the Bible that God loved David. What you thinking is foolish. Tant'-Irene don't think that way."

"She didn't name me 'David.'"

"That's because your daddy was a good Catholic. You knows that. He made your mamma promise before he went away she'd name you Joseph if you was born on his day. And you was. You got a birthday coming up soon."

"I ain't studying 'bout no birthday."

"I seen your mother's face when she looked at that baby, first time she seen him, this morning. 'David' she says, just like that; not 'ain't he sweet' or anything. Just 'David,' and her face all lighted up. Your mamma's past sixty, and when she said that, she looked like she wasn't no more'n sixteen."

After a long time the quiet man beside her spoke. "All right," he said. "All right. My mamma wants it, you wants it, I reckon that's what it will be. David. David Champlin."

3

JOSEPH CHAMPLIN WAS NEARING his sixth birthday when he learned a little of the circumstances of his father's death. By that time his playmates and most of his relatives called him "Li'l Joe Champlin," always giving the surname the French pronunciation. His mother always called him "Joseph."

Whenever he asked his elders why he did not have a father as the other children had, he sensed a wall of concealment in their answers. About his father he knew a great deal because his mother talked about him often; about his father's absence he knew little, because the talk stopped there. "An accident," his mother said. "An accident." For a while the answer was enough.

It was his grandmother, Gran'Cecile, who brought his quiet child's doubts into the open. He was always a little afraid of his grandmother, of her wandering, sometimes wild, speech, of her "spells," and was never tempted to disobey his mother's orders that he stay away from the old lady unless she was with him, although Gran'Cecile was kind and given to buying ice cream and candy and licorice whips.

The day that Gran'Cecile filled his mind with questions he kept his own counsel until his mother came home from work. He had learned not to question that tired, harassed woman when she first entered their little room after a day's work, or when she picked him up at Miz Jefferson's, where he was often left to play with the Jefferson children, especially Abraham, a year older. He would follow Irene Champlin quietly around the room, watching with round eyes as she unpacked her big bag, looking hopefully for something a small boy could eat, seldom disappointed, hoarding his day's store of troubles or joys until she sat down for a moment and took him on her lap, rubbing her cheek against his head, saying, "Have you been a good boy, son?"

But on this day the story of Gran'Cecile's "spell," of the words that had poured in a moaning scream from her mouth, was of such magnitude that he could not hold it back, must rid himself of it as soon as the door closed behind his mother. When he finished she stood in stony, frightening silence, speaking at last—as she always did when she was upset—in French. "How many times have I told you, my son, Gran'Cecile does not know what she is saying? That she is not to be believed. *Mon Dieu!*" She broke into Creole. "You have been a bad boy. You have disobeyed me. You have gone to Gran'Cecile's—" her voice was rising.

"No, Ma! No! I didn't go to Gran'Cecile's! Don't lick me, Ma! I didn't. Not really. She took me, Ma. She met me on St. Claude Street and—and bought me a licorice whip and held my hand and took me to her house and we sat on the step."

"And then? And then, son?"

He told her again of the clanging of the great brass bell atop the fire engine, how it had seemed to come closer and closer as they sat on the step, and then how the sound had faded as the horses carrying the engine turned down the street above them. "Then she had a spell, Ma. Gran'Cecile had a spell."

He told it as best he could within the limits of his vocabulary. Gran'Cecile had begun to moan and rock—"like this, Ma," and his thin arms hugged his chest and he rocked back and forth—and then Gran'Cecile had cried out. "They're going for David!" she cried. "They're going for our David!" Her voice had become a crazed keen, a wail. The child, staring at her in fright, knew that she had forgotten his presence, had lost him somewhere in the dark terror that was filling her mind. "They can't get to him! They can't get to our David! Jesus ride with them! Jesus put out the fire!" She keened aloud in French now. "They're burning David; they're burning our David! They're burning my baby's David, and she is carrying his chile!"

Then she stiffened and screamed without words, and Joseph Champlin turned and ran in blind fright, to be caught at the courtyard entrance by Miz Jefferson and carried to the banquette. "Run," she said. "Run to my house, chile. Abraham's waiting for you." The hand with which she hit him across the small buttocks was hard and strong; he felt its sting, and it acted as a counter to his fear and he ran as she had told him, to her house. Behind him, in the courtyard, Gran'Cecile was still screaming, and he heard other voices now, and though he could not see he knew that she was being carried inside.

"Ma," he said now. "Ma, Gran'Cecile's crazy, ain't she? She don't know what she's saying, do she, Ma?"

"You mustn't say such things about your grandmother. And try not to say 'ain't'—or 'do she.' "

Irene Champlin stood at the stove quietly, speaking to her son in even tones, correcting him—but not fooling him, only deepening his fear.

"Ma! Mamma!"

"Son." She turned to the stove without looking at him. "Look in Mother's bag. There are pralines."

He did not move. "Ma. Ma! My daddy didn't burn. Did he, Ma? Gran'Cecile is crazy, ain't she, Ma?"

"She has notions, son. Crazy notions."

It was not enough. "Ma, he didn't burn, did he? He didn't! It was a naccident. You told me he got hurted in a naccident!" Suddenly he was on her like a small brown fury, thin hands reaching for her, pulling at her clothing, thin feet stomping on the floor, thin voice rising, rising. "Mamma! Mamma! *Mamma!*"

Irene Champlin turned and held him with a grip so strong it hurt the tiny shoulders. "Yes! Yes, I told you! Be quiet. It was an accident!" She looked down at her son, and knew that for the first time he recognized the lie for what it was.

He was screaming now, and she caught him roughly into her arms, a hand at the back of his head, pressing his face into her breast to stifle his crying. "Be still. Be still, baby. Mother will let you go if you'll be quiet. Mamma will tell you. It is not so bad."

She picked him up in her arms and sat in the only chair in the room besides the two broken kitchen chairs. She rocked him gently as she talked. "You must listen," she said. "Mamma cannot talk to you while you cry like that. Your daddy was a good man. Do you hear me? He was a great and good man. Everyone for miles around knew and loved your daddy. I have told you this often. He loved you. Even before you were born, he loved you although he never saw you. He loves you now. Baby. Hush. Be quiet. For the love of God, be quiet."

With a movement so quick she could not forestall it, he twisted the upper part of his body free of her arms, caught her blouse in a tight fist, almost pulling it from her shoulder.

"They didn't!" he cried. "They didn't burn my daddy! My daddy never done nothing bad. He never!"

"No," she said. "No, baby. He never did anything bad." She caught the fist in one of hers, held it tightly. "Never in his life. It was a mistake. They—they thought he did. It was a mistake, Joseph. Do you understand? It was as I told you —a mistake, an accident."

She kept him in her bed that night, holding him close. When she felt the small body was still awake, felt it shaken by tremors, she got up and fixed him laudanum she had bought for a toothache, and he slept at last, one hand holding a fold of her nightgown so tightly she dared not turn for fear of waking him, knowing if he did his first thoughts would be of the horror he had learned.

She blamed herself for the shock he was suffering. She had made David Champlin live for his son. There had been only one photograph of the man who had died on a bonfire on the eve of his son's birth, and he had carried that wedding picture with him when he left home. But she had painted a picture of him on the canvas of her son's mind that was more real than any photograph could have been. A big man, she told her son, and very dark, almost black. Joseph would not be so big when he grew up, she said; he would be more as she was, slight and small-boned, and his skin would be lighter. She told Joseph how she and his father had grown up together under the same roof, how her mother, Gran'Cecile, had taken him when he was only a few weeks old, and raised him and loved him as she would the son she had never had. And because he liked to hear the story, she often told him how she and his father had played along the riverfront when they were children and how one day they had promised solemnly that they would never be separated; that when they grew up they would be married in the Church of St. Augustine, and she would wear a long white gown and veil.

"Did you?" her son would ask each time she told the story.

"Yes, Joseph. In a white gown and a long white veil. We had a picture taken, but your daddy had it with him when he went away, looking for work. He—he carried it with him always."

"Was he big, Ma?" The boy would always ask this question too.

"Yes, son."

"Big, big, big like this, Ma?" The child's hand reached as far above his head as he could hold it.

"Big, big, big like that. So big he used to pick me up like this!" She would bend and catch the boy up in her arms, the moment he had been waiting for, and bring him to her shoulder. "We didn't have any baby for a long, long time, and when I used to cry about it he would hold me like this and say *he* had a baby if I didn't. He was always smiling. And when he laughed you could hear him two courtyards away. And kind and gentle; he was always kind and gentle."

Round eyes looked at her with solemn assurance. "My daddy wouldn't have spanked me."

She would laugh, speak in Creole. "Oh, but he would, or I would have known the reason why. If you were a bad boy, or impolite, or unkind, he would have spanked you, just as I do."

"I'm not, Mamma; I'm not."

"No, dear, you are not. You will be like your daddy. Not big, as he was, do not expect that. But kind and gentle."

Now, lying in the narrow bed with her son's body close to her, not moving for fear that any movement would waken him to a terror newly found, she wished she had never done these things, never taught him to love a man dead before his birth; never given him a dead father to cherish; never brought, by her words, the sound of that father's voice and laughter, the sight of his smile, into their room.

It would have been better never to have given the child the knowledge of his father's kindness and goodness; long ago she should have forgotten, or pretended to forget, the man who had been so close to her that he was like a part of every atom of her being—mind, body, and soul. It would have been better if she had married any one of the half-dozen men who had wanted her after David died, and given the boy a father. She knew herself for a selfish woman, loving a dead man so much she could not bring herself, even for her son's sake, to go to another; bringing the dead alive because it gave her comfort.

The child she held now would have learned the truth someday. If his father had been a dim, shadowy figure, never mentioned, if he had never lived in his son's imagination, it would have been easier for the boy to accept the truth. Now it came as a shattering thing, filling his small world with nightmare horror.

Her arms grew numb from holding him, and when he stirred they tightened round him, and when he whimpered she lay still as death, holding her breath, releasing it at last with a whisper so intense it sounded like a loud cry in her own ears.

"Mother of God!" she whispered. "Blessed Mother, help me with this child!"

4

THE BANK HOLIDAY OF 1933 found Joseph Champlin and his wife with seventy-five cents left from the ten dollars he had found a few days before. They had spent their windfall almost immediately, a few dollars to a clamorous landlord, a funeral insurance premium, a small supply of coal, rice, beans, staples, and a dollar that Li'l Joe proudly gave his mother.

On the morning of March sixth he learned of the bank closings from a friend he met on the street, when he was setting out to find work. When he returned to the house and told Geneva, she said, "My Gawd! What they trying to do!"

"I don't know," answered Li'l Joe. "Swear I don't. Pete, he told me he's been working for a white family stays over by Metairie, and they told him it was going to save the country from bankruptcy, some dam-fool thing like that."

"Locking everyone's money up going to save the country? Going to make *every*one bankrupt, that's what it's going to do. *Every*one, white *and* colored. What we going to do? What's everyone going to do if they gets a day's work and there ain't no money to pay 'em? You going to hold still for doing a day's work and no money? How we going to feed that chile?"

"We ain't," said Joseph Champlin. "You going to have to see can you get more of that formula stuff by the hospital, and me, I reckon all I can do is walk around some when what we got's gone and see can I find someone, mebbe someone I done work for, can lend me some. If things keeps on like they is, we're going to have to get that chile to the country somehow, by Ruth's folks—Gawd knows how—and let them take care of him. They got cows and chickens and a little piece of truck garden. They can feed theirselves and him, too."

The fear he had seen in Geneva's eyes the first time he had made this proposal was not there now. The baby had been with them three days, and already her husband was fussing at her about the way she fixed the bottles, getting up in the night, climbing over her to get to the stove and ready the formula when the baby woke up crying. The sounds that came to her as he gentled the child and fed him would have been familiar to his first wife, Josephine. "So-so," he would say. "So-so, little man." Geneva had agreed to the dresser-drawer crib in the daytime, and he had found packing casings to stand endwise under it and make it firm, and it was Li'l Joe who made it up, constructing a mattress from an old blanket and a piece of sheet.

Geneva watched him when he did things for the baby, and let him instruct her, and when his back was turned winked at the occupant of the dresser drawer, saying to him, when his grandfather was out of hearing: "I can't do nothing with him. Hardheaded as a mule. But you just keep working on him, David. You just keep working on him, we got nothing to worry about."

The chaos that followed immediately after the bank closings made even Joseph Champlin realize the futility of looking for work. From their friends and from the newspapers they learned of unbelievable situations among the whites: millionaires caught with only a few dollars in their pockets, talk of paper scrip being printed, people making fantastic offers just for cold cash. Some stores were good about credit to a limited extent, but it could not be offered for long. On the second day Hank beckoned him mysteriously to the back of his barroom, and slipped him a paper bag with a quart bottle of homemade wine in it, because now more than ever he dared not be seen serving anyone on credit.

It was Geneva who suggested that he appeal to the Professor.

"I ain't going to do it, Neva," he said. "That man's probably no better off than what we are. We are all in the same boat, rich *and* poor. Where's he going to get cash any more'n anyone else? It ain't like he worked in a store. He's a professor in a college. I know he's rich, but I don't want—"

"You fixing to say you don't want to ask no favors," Geneva snapped. "That's what you're fixing to say. Since when's a colored person in this town got so Goddamned proud he can't ask no favors of a white? Ain't nothing no white gives you any favor anyhow. You knows that."

Joseph Champlin did not answer, then wished he had. Silence on his part often irritated Geneva to the point where she would talk until it seemed she'd forgotten how to stop, prodding him to answer, then not giving him a chance.

She was always particularly talkative on the subject of the Professor. Li'l Joe had known him for three years. Odd and different people were common in New Orleans, a seaport whose docks knew the feet of men from every country, whose restaurants and bars and waterfront dives knew as many tongues as Babel had, but even in New Orleans the bristling red beard and hair, the vivid blue eyes, the huge bulk and booming voice of Bjarne Knudsen were conspicuous. Li'l Joe had been playing a gig in a small club when he saw the big man for the first time. It was a Negro club, and Li'l Joe and the other musicians were uneasy and uncomfortable at the presence of a white man. It could, and often did, mean trouble with the law. The man was with Kid Arab, who was without a job that night. Kid's assurance that the bearded stranger was O.K. was enough to admit him, but there were still uneasiness on the stand, and an attitude composed in almost equal parts of downright hostility and reserved, suspicious friendliness in the audience.

During the course of the evening the big man worked his way forward in the smoky, crowded room until he sat directly in front of Li'l Joe. Li'l Joe remembered watching him from the corner of his eyes, thinking he had never known a white man to respond to the music as this man did, hearing it not as something just to tap a foot to, bob a head to, clap hands to, but almost the way his own people heard it—as a tale to be told, a feeling to be passed on for other men to share. When Woodenhead Pete gave a mocking, laughing answer on the clarinet, the man would laugh aloud, throwing his head back until the throat beneath the red beard showed. When the instruments drew together, trumpet, trombone, and clarinet, blending tone and heart, when they moaned about it, told the folks about it, let go with the sadness and ache of it, the fire left the blue eyes of the man in front of him and they clouded, and when the band played a blues that had no name but came from their memories alone the eyes were shaded by a huge hand so that they could not be seen at all.

When the band turned loose with a stomp or march, Li'l Joe, watching the big man's feet and hands, thought, Sure make a fine drummer, that white man would; make a fine drummer.

Between numbers Kid told them the man was a professor at the university, that he came from over the water, a country called Denmark, and that he was wealthy. "He's all right," said Kid. "He's all right. He ain't been here long, but it wouldn't make no difference if he stayed here all his life, he'd still be all right."

The second time he came he asked Li'l Joe to give him banjo lessons. Li'l Joe could still remember the feel of the delighted thwack on the shoulder the big man had given him when he consented, a thwack that almost catapulted him out of his chair. "I am sorry!" the Professor had boomed. "I am sorry! You are so small and I am so big and I do not always realize how big I am. You will forgive me, no? And come to my house—when?" They agreed upon a time, and that night planted the seeds of a friendship Li'l Joe admitted he would once have said was impossible. He tried to discuss it with Geneva, and she was mocking and incredulous. He knew that none of his friends would understand it, not even Pop Jefferson, whose given name of Abraham had disappeared years before in the nickname "Pop." The friendship did not grow rapidly; Li'l Joe was hard put to remember just when the time came that he knew he could use the word "friend" in speaking of the Professor; it must have been a year or more.

From the beginning drinks were always ready to be served when he arrived at the old house on the edge of the French Quarter that the Professor had bought when he first came to New Orleans. For the first time in his life a drink was mixed for him and served to him by a white man; he didn't count the beers he'd been given by employers, and had stood in kitchens or on galleries to drink. For the first time in his life he saw a white man upset when, at the beginning, he would not sit down in a chair by the fire and talk, and then sat, when it was insisted upon, at the edge of the chair, nervous and ill at ease. At first the man he now called "Prof" as often as he called him "Professor" did all the talking, and gradually Li'l Joe grew easier. Man's nervous, thought Li'l Joe, that man's nervous. And gradually the understanding came to him of the reason. When at last Li'l Joe began to talk, not as he had always talked to white men but as he would talk to a friend, the Professor listened with an interest so intense Li'l Joe knew it had to be real. The Professor sought his friendship, he could tell that, and sought what he had to offer, not as a musician but as a person, and, finding what he sought, was—in a way that puzzled Li'l Joe—almost humble in his pleasure.

But there was no making Geneva understand. On this troubled day at the start of the bank holiday, she pressed her argument with dogged persistence: "You don't have no feelings about going to folks you've done work for, asking them. But when it's the Professor, you suddenly got feelings about asking favors. You're all the time talking about how he's your friend, how he's different. You knows damned well ain't no white man a friend to colored, not a *friend.* What we call 'em 'ofay' for? Don't it mean foe? And even if he was a friend, wouldn't he be the first to go to? Answer me that, Joe Champlin. You think just because he has you there in his house, sitting with him and drinking beer with him, and talking, that he's your friend. Shucks! He's just picking your brains, that's all he's doing, picking your brains, learning about how the colored people—us 'darkies'—lives and talks. They's a lot like that, a whole lot, coming down here, coming down South, setting around talking to us, not doing a God-damned thing for us, just using us."

They had been over this before. Things had improved, though, in the short time the new baby, the second David Champlin, had been with them. All he needed to do now, when he thought Geneva's tired, frustration-born nagging was going to get out of control was to say, "That chile's fussing, Neva. You sure he ain't wet?" He had to admit that since the night he had walked into the house and found her trying with inexperienced, fumbling hands to diaper a squirming baby, her nagging had been cut in half. Joseph Champlin loved his wife with a quiet, undemonstrative intensity that no amount of nagging lessened, nor did it detract from the feeling of warm security her presence gave him. Their quarrels had never been bitter ones, never so serious that, when he drifted off to sleep, he did not hold in his fingers a fold of her nightgown.

He tried the diversionary tactic now, on the second day of the bank holiday, saying this time: "You got that chile's bottle ready, Neva? The pore little thing's going to be setting up asking for it, you don't give it to him pretty soon."

She was at the stove, bustling, talking to the baby. "You wait now, David. Y'all wait. Grandma's coming right now." A pan rattled. "Anything I hates to see is a hungry chile," she said to her husband.

"I been seeing plenty of them these days," he said. "Too Goddamned many." He was sitting at the table in the little alcove kitchen off the bed-sitting room. He stopped speaking suddenly, his head cocked like a wary chipmunk's, listening.

"Someone's coming," he said. "Someone's coming 'cross the courtyard."

Although Li'l Joe had been half expecting it, the knock on their door was so loud and peremptory that he jumped with a nervous start. Geneva's pan rattled again as she dropped it to the stove, then caught it before it tipped over. "Gawd sake!" she said.

She started to speak again, stopped when she turned and saw the man standing in the doorway, filling it from side to side, head almost at its top. She did not need to be told who it was. Her husband had described the Professor too often for her not to recognize him—the big frame, the startlingly blue eyes, the red hair and beard, the tremendous voice and the lilting, singsong accent so different from the French and Italian accents to which her ears were accustomed.

She glanced quickly at her husband. Joseph Champlin was standing with the knob of the open door in his hand. His thin face was split by a wide smile that turned the vertical lines in his cheeks into half-moon brackets. He was looking up at the man in the doorway; even Pop Jefferson, six feet and some, would have had to raise his eyes to this man.

"*Ja!*" the big man said. Geneva saw her husband's slight, small hand disappear in the other's grasp. "I have found you. It was not easy. I knew only that you lived on this street. They lied to me, those I asked. They knew where Joseph Champlin lived but they would not tell me. Only when I said I was searching for you to offer you work did they tell me."

She saw him throw an arm around her husband's shoulder, and then he saw her where she stood by the stove, and walked over to her, smiling. When he came opposite her he stopped, feet together on the worn boards. The heels did not click but seemed to, and he made a bobbing bow with his head and held out his hand. Her own was drawn to it as by a magnet and she felt it engulfed in warm, muscular hugeness.

"Mrs. Champlin! Your husband hides you," he said. "He talks of you much of the time, and now we meet after all these years. I am delighted."

"Yes, sir," said Geneva, because she could think of nothing else to say, and was overwhelmed and bewildered.

Her husband came to her rescue, pulling forward Tant'-Irene's old rocking chair, their only chair with arms. He set it beside the center table with some misgivings.

"Sit down and rest yourself, Professor," he said. "You sure surprised me. Heard someone walking 'cross the courtyard and thought to myself, That's a mighty big person walking 'cross our courtyard. Didn't figure it would be you. Neva, why'n't you fix us some coffee? The Professor likes it strong. Real strong."

"No!" said the Professor. "No, no! In times like these coffee is too precious to share."

"We got enough," said Geneva.

"Then you are fortunate." He turned to Li'l Joe. "How is it with you, my friend? That is why I am here. Do you have money?"

Joseph Champlin laughed. Only on rare occasions did he laugh aloud; usually he laughed as he did now, with little sound. "You ever seen anything like what's going on?" he asked. "There ain't no one, near's I can make out, has any money. Few days ago I got aholt of a little piece of change, and we spent it for stuff we needed and all, and then we wakes up one morning and there ain't no money at all, no place. You all right for cash, Professor?"

Knudsen, who would not sit until Li'l Joe had pulled up one of the straight chairs from the kitchen and sat across the table from him, leaned back in the rocker and did not hear Geneva's gasp of apprehension as its ancient frame creaked with fierce complaint at his weight.

"Yes!" he said. "For once Bjarne Knudsen becomes lucky. On the first of the month I receive a check from the university. I cash it instead of banking it because I have things I must buy and people I must pay and many of them do not trust checks, even Bjarne Knudsen's checks, people who like the look of green. And after I have done these things I have money left and do not put it in the bank. This morning I woke up with the thought of my friend Joseph Champlin in my mind. I think, Perhaps he has no money, and so I come here. With cash I come. Bah! Man is a selfish animal. I should have come yesterday."

"That's sure fine of you, Professor." Joseph Champlin spoke softly. "That's sure fine. But you needs your cash. No telling what's going to happen, how long things will be like they is." Behind him kitchenware rattled significantly. He ignored the sound. "Reckon we're no worse off than most folks, and not as bad as some."

Geneva was at the table now with cups and saucers and a pot of coffee. Knudsen was on his feet. "I will not drink unless you join us." He seemed at home already in the cramped quarters, and walked around her to the kitchen alcove, bringing the other straight chair back to the bed-sitting room. Before he could set it down, young David Champlin made his presence known with a loud, hungry wail. Knudsen stopped, holding the chair in midair. It looked like a toy in his hands. His eyes were wide and startled under the bristling brows and heavy mop of hair. "My God!" he gasped. "What is that!"

Geneva brushed past him without ceremony. "That's David," she said. "That's our David. I'm late feeding him." Her tone was accusing.

Knudsen set the chair down. "Why did you not tell me?" he whispered.

Li'l Joe chuckled. "Can't see's you've given me much chance, Prof," he answered. "That's my boy John's son; my boy that was killed. The chile ain't more'n a week old. His mamma died birthing him, and we taken him for a while."

"You should have told me, Li'l Joe." The Professor was still whispering. He walked to Geneva's side, watched her as she picked up the baby and cradled it on one arm, putting the nipple of the bottle in the eager mouth. "I am terrified of babies. They are so weak and helpless, which is a strange reason. Children baffle me, but babies terrify me."

"Ain't no need to whisper." Li'l Joe's smile was wide again. "He's awake now. He ain't going to pay no mind to us now he's got that bottle. And they ain't as weak and helpless as you think. They speaks up for theirselves, and they can stand a lot more'n you'd think. Lots of 'em has to."

"I suppose so," said the Professor. He no longer whispered, but his voice was lower by several decibels. "I suppose so."

Joseph Champlin was watching his wife covertly, thinking of the many times he had wanted to ask the Professor to his home for a meal, red beans and rice, gumbo, stuffed crab. He was not ashamed of their home. They were poor people, but they offered no less than the rich—the best they had. It would have delighted this big man from over the water. But Geneva had refused. She was not, she said, cooking for no whites in her home unless she had to, unless it was an emergency. "When I cooks for the whites," she had said, "I does it for pay, and I does it in their house. And when I walks out of their house I walks out. I mean *out*."

Li'l Joe wished, now that his wife had been so unexpectedly confronted with the Professor, that he could read her mind. He had not missed the expression on her face when the Professor had stood before her and bowed with Old World courtesy, because she was a woman and he was a man of politeness and breeding. He had boomed at her, "Mrs. Champlin!" Li'l Joe knew it was the first time in her life she had ever been called "Mrs. Champlin" by a white person. Joseph Champlin himself had never been called "Mister" by a white person, even by the Professor, but their manner of meeting had precluded it. Identified by Kid Arab as "Li'l Joe," it was as that the Professor addressed him, although he always remembered that the big man had said, "Do you mind if I presume on such short acquaintance and call you by your k-nickname?"

He wondered, as he watched Geneva feed the baby now, if she was remembering some of the things she had said about the Professor. "I don't know nothing about Denmark, and no Danes," she had said. "But I sure don't think they're all that different. White's white. He just ain't heard what they calls people like him down here. You just wait. Some day someone's going to call that man a 'nigger lover' and that day come he's going to be learning banjo from a white musician, drinking his beer with an ofay player."

"He's been called that," said Li'l Joe. "He's been called that plenty times. Told me so hisself."

"What's he say about it?"

"He laughed, just at first, when he told me. Then he cussed." Li'l Joe shook his head in reminiscence. "Cussing sure sounds mean in Danish."

Was she remembering these things now, he wondered, and maybe coming round, just a bit, to his way of thinking about the Professor?

Now Knudsen rose and walked toward Geneva and the baby, looking down at them nervously. He reached out a huge paw and touched the baby gently on the cheek. Like a lion patting a kitten, thought Li'l Joe. The big man smiled a fearsome smile at the baby and Li'l Joe, looking at his wife's face, saw it as he had seen it often these last few days, soft and young. He wished again that he could read her mind, know what she was thinking of the man he called his friend.

Geneva answered the question for him. Cradling the baby in both arms she held it out to the Professor, smiling.

"You-all want to hold the baby a minute?" she said.

As they sat over their coffee, Li'l Joe thought of the wine in the cupboard, Hank's donation. He put down a momentary twinge of selfishness and watched Geneva a little fearfully as he took it down. There was no sign of displeasure on her face when he brought the bottle and glasses to the table.

They sat drinking companionably, talking about the nightmare that the country was living through, and the Professor explained the situation so clearly Li'l Joe thought that even a little child could have gotten an understanding of it. "Maybe now they got a new President, things will be better," Li'l Joe said.

"I have no doubt they will," said the Professor. He looked at the man opposite, lids narrowed over searching eyes. "You do not say 'we,' Li'l Joe; you say 'they.' Bah! How can one teach the history of civilization as I am supposed to do in this country! My God! How can one teach the history of something that has never been realized fully by those whom one teaches!"

Li'l Joe poured more wine, and Knudsen leaned back, exhaling mightily, and said, "Whatever happens when the pendulum swings back—and it will, my friend, because it is a law of nature—there must always be wine and fellowship or we are truly lost! Eh, Li'l Joe?"

"Reckon so," said Joseph Champlin. His tone carried no conviction. Knudsen leaned across the table and wagged an enormous finger at him. The first time he had done that, in the days when Joseph Champlin had first known him, the small brown man had drawn back nervously. Now he smiled. The Professor boomed: "I know what you are thinking, my friend. You are thinking of your people. You are thinking there can be no fellowship in a world where one must teach a child fear, *teach him fear*. It is a terrible thought, that a child must be taught to be afraid, must be trained to be afraid of doing certain normal things, must be taught not to look into the eyes of another person because the other person's skin is white. You see, I know how you must raise your children, Li'l Joe. It is one of the things I have learned since I came to this country. They are civilization? No!"

For the first time since they had started talking, Geneva's

voice was heard. She had moved into the kitchen alcove and sat in one of the straight chairs, cradling the baby in her arms, rocking it gently. Now she spoke. "You saying the truth," she said. "You saying it *right.*"

Knudsen went on. "As for your people"—again the finger shook menacingly and again Li'l Joe smiled—"I tell you there is more hope for your people than for those who oppress them. Believe me, it is so. There will be changes. That baby your wife is holding, he will see them, and his children will see them. But the changes will not come because your people have sat still and waited for them, Li'l Joe, sat and waited and hoped and accepted their lot. But oppression does not remain static. It carries the seed of its own destruction." He sighed gustily, then said, like a child: "I am hungry. Li'l Joe, may we use some of our precious cash for the things that are needed for a meal? And would Mrs. Champlin—"

Geneva stood quickly, the baby in her arms. "Lawd!" she said. "I been mighty rude. Professor, I'd be happy if you'd have a bite with us. We ain't got a lot but we got beans and rice, and if I had me some chicken and some shrimp and a little crab, I've got filet and other things for a gumbo. You like gumbo, Professor?"

While Li'l Joe was at the store, Knudsen said: "Mrs. Champlin, I talk too much. I talk too much because I am an angry man, and an impatient one. You understand? Anger can be good, very good, but it must be coupled with patience."

"Yes, sir," said Geneva. It was not the "sir" of subservience. "I think I knows what you mean."

"And for that patience, Mrs. Champlin, I turn to your people. And perhaps to God, if there is such a being, such a force. I do not know. Your people have never failed me when I have turned to them for patience. God—" he shrugged. "God baffles me. I have said that I am afraid of babies and that children baffle me. God does not frighten me, but He baffles me, as children do. Why is it, Mrs. Champlin, that God does not baffle you and your people, who have known a dark crucifixion all your lives? For He does not."

Geneva was bringing things from cupboards, setting them on the table. She spoke slowly. "We're ignorant people," she said. "And most of us poor. Dirt poor. We got nothing to come between us and God. No book learning, no things like a pile of money brings. Maybe we sees Him plainer. We been kept ignorant. You knows that. Ain't no colored person I knows of what ain't praying his children get an education like he never was let to have. I mean, *praying* for it. I knows."

She was silent for a long time, coaxing the fire in the stove to a hotter blaze. Then she said: "What they going to do with that education when they gets it? They going to let it come between them and God?"

Knudsen drew a deep breath. "I had not thought of that." His voice, low, rumbled like a train. "I had not thought of that," he repeated. "When your people come into the light of learning, Mrs. Champlin, they must drive their learning and their God abreast, yoked together? That is what you mean?"

"Yes," said Geneva. "I reckon that's what I means. We got God here now, with us; we got Him close because we needs Him so bad. He ain't never far from us. Just so long as we keeps Him and keeps His son, Jesus, near us, we ain't plumb lost."

Knudsen watched her without speaking, without answering her. He must not, he thought, speak what was in his mind, for this above all things she would not have understood. Behind her, he told himself, there were generations that had been taught the belief of "no cross, no crown," generations inculcated with the doctrine that through suffering they would find happiness in some vague hereafter. That doctrine had come from the whites, their masters and their owners, who had known the way, diabolically had known the way, to keep an oppressed and enslaved people from revolt, perhaps without even realizing that they knew the way. Yet if that faith had brought them thus far, who was he to say that, with learning, it would not bring them entirely out of the darkness and into the light?

When at last, in midafternoon, they finished dinner and he stood at the door just before leaving, there were two ten-dollar bills on the table and a five-dollar bill on David's blanket. "With your permission, Mrs. Champlin?" he had said when he laid it there, and she had nodded, smiling but not speaking.

To Li'l Joe he said, "You will come with your banjo tomorrow, my friend?"

"Sure will. You knows that. And don't go forgetting, Professor, these next lessons are on me. You done paid for 'em today."

As he strode across the cobbles of the courtyard, the Professor was muttering, addressing himself, as he often did, in Danish, bad though it might be for his English.

"In a dresser drawer. Kind God in Heaven, in a dresser drawer. And You in there with him. That is what they believe, what they *know* with every atom of their being. What they *know*. Bjarne Knudsen, you are an ignorant man. There is a dull knife in your kitchen. Go home and cut your throat with it."

5

A CHILD'S MIND DRIFTED in the midst between waking and dreaming. In the dream part of the mist, behind sleep-heavy eyelids, there was a shimmer of silver light on wide, dark water, and sleep-dulled ears heard the voices of many people singing beside the water. Although it was night and his eyes were closed, the child could see the people, all black, all singing, all somehow known to him. There were no words to the song, only the great sound of the voices mingling with the sound of flowing water and a nearer song, that of the woman who held him. His head rested on her shoulder. The softness of her breast and thighs cradled his small body, and the dark sweetness of her voice was in his head: " 'Oh, Mary, don' you weep, don' you moan. . . . Pharaoh's army got drownded. . . . Oh, Mary, don' you weep. . . .' " Then the voices on the banks of the dark, shimmering river were singing the same song, and the sound swelled inside his head and became one with her voice.

He stirred, and the lids weighted with sleep fluttered as he felt strong, thin arms lifting him, heard gentle words: "I'll carry the chile home, Neva." Then he no longer heard the woman's song, only the warm soft sound of all the many black people that were the dream part of the mist, all singing on the banks of the dark, shimmering river; then there was the nothingness of the sleep of a tired child.

David Champlin murmured sleepily, opened, then

squeezed his eyes closed against light, tried to, but could not, follow his grandmother's words as she knelt beside his cot: " 'Our Father, who art in Heaven . . .' " He sighed tremulously and slipped again into nothingness at " 'Give us this day.' "

There had never been a day like it before; it had been the most exciting, the most satisfying, the happiest day of his short life. For the first time bare feet had run through grass with no one to call out, "No!" For the first time bare brown toes had curled into country dust and dirt; small, long-fingered hands had picked flowers that grew wild and undisciplined, and a small body just outgrowing chubbiness had rolled in rough undergrowth. There had been a fat brown dog that came and rolled with him, a dog that came from nowhere just to play with him and then returned to nowhere. There had been a solemn, skinny black boy who crossed a bumpy, ill-paved road and watched, then shared a licorice whip with him. Then there had been a time of racing through the empty rooms of a half-finished house, crowing, laughing, shouting.

His happiness had been marred only once that day, when his grandfather, smiling, had said, "You reckon you'd like to live here, son? Reckon you'd like to move over the river and stay in this house? Have your own room and all?"

He stood motionless, looking up first at Gramp, then at Gram. The dark eyes widened as he rolled them, looking around at walls whose unplastered lath framework gave a vista of every room from where they stood. Tears spilled over, the round face crumpled. Gram picked him up quickly. "Baby!"

He fought back sobs. "Where'm I going to sleep? Where's David going to sleep?"

"With us, baby," said Gram. "Just like it is now. Don't you fret. We fixes your cot like it is now, at the foot of our bed."

His grandfather said, "Shucks, you knows we ain't going to turn you loose to sleep by yourself, son. Least, not till you learns to stay in the bed and not keep falling out. Gets mighty cold some nights for an old man like your Gramp to go traipsing around into another room to pick you up every time you falls out of bed."

That had made it all right, and happiness came rushing back. Gramp and Gram had never lied to him. If, in this new place, Gramp would be as near as he had always been to pick him up from the floor to which he fell so often with a soft "Plop!" in the night, there was no need for fear. Some day he would be older and wouldn't fall out of bed and waken with a wail of fright. Gramp had told him that. But until then he could go to sleep without fear, knowing that should that startled wakening come in the dark there would be, almost at the same moment, the quiet slap of Gramp's feet on the floor, the sleepy murmur, exasperated but without reproof, "Jesus have moicy! There he goes again!" and the feel of Gramp's arms, and Gramp's voice very close. "So-so, little man, so-so." And then the safety of his cot again with the covers tightening over him as Gramp tucked them in firmly.

Geneva Champlin gave full credit to the Almighty for her husband's good fortune when disaster and tragedy were common fare for almost everyone. She was also sure she knew the reason for His kindness: that she and her husband would be able to take care of the child He had placed in their care. Tant'Irene said only, in her high, quick voice, "I told you, Joseph. God never made the mouth He wouldn't feed. See you thank Him, hear?"

Sometimes, in Jones's Funeral Home, working over an eviscerated, post-mortemed cadaver from Charity Hospital or the city morgue, Li'l Joe found it hard to make his thanksgiving without reservations. He had done a kind and thoughtful thing one morning and stopped in to see Zeke Jones, who had broken his collarbone a few days before. He didn't suppose God had too many rewards to pass out in those bad times, and tried to be duly grateful when Zeke offered him the job of helper, working under Zeke's own expert guidance. "You do a good job, Li'l Joe," Zeke said, "maybe you can stay on permanent. That man I got ain't a bit of good no more. Shucks, he's taken to drinking so bad I even watches the embalming fluid. You dependable, Li'l Joe; you always been dependable." With an unspoken prayer to the Almighty not to hold it against him if he didn't stay permanent, what with the various unpleasantnesses of the job, Li'l Joe agreed. "Times is bad," said Zeke. "Still, folks keeps on dying. Seems like there's more dying now than ever. Most folks got a little piece of insurance to bury theirselves with. I'll be fair with you, Li'l Joe. You knows that."

"Lawd!" he said to Geneva, a few nights after he started the job. "Anyone told me a while back I'd be helping an undertaker lay out co'pses, I'd have said they was crazy. It's going to take a heap of getting used to."

"You got a lot to be thankful for," said Geneva sternly.

"You think Zeke's any prize to work for, you got another think coming, woman."

"He ain't white," said Geneva. "He ain't white. That's the main thing."

Her husband did not answer. Didn't do any good with Geneva to point out that their own people could cheat and chisel and underpay and overwork their help as bad as any white. Didn't matter to Neva. She'd rather get a bad deal from one of her own people any day than say "thank you" to a white. He understood and sympathized and, in principle, agreed. It just wasn't practical, that was all.

Didn't do any good either to try and make Neva admit that there were a lot of colored wouldn't stack up so good come Judgment Day. She knew as well as he did that there was a whole different world of Negro life from the one they lived in, a world of violence and drinking and bad things happening all the time, but she would push the knowledge to the back of her mind. When word came to them of bad things happening in the Quarter or over on the other side of town, her lips would set tight and she'd shake her head, but she never got self-righteous about it the way most did. Once when a friend of his had been knifed by a jealous woman in a barroom fight, he'd said, "Scum—" and she'd jumped him.

"Ain't no one born bad," she'd said. "Man or woman. But they's some as goes bad under trouble. It's the way they's made, but it don't mean they was born plumb bad clear through."

Li'l Joe didn't agree with her, but he always kept his arguments to himself on a point like this there wasn't any proving of. Instead he had teased her.

"Whites, too?" he said.

"Don't ask me nothing 'bout no whites. I ain't studying 'bout no whites. I ain't even trying to figure out if they bad or what. Don't matter, do it?"

Almost immediately after he went to work for Zeke, Geneva decided their grandson would do well to go to embalming college. "That way he ain't ever going to have to work for whites," she said. "He gets his education and he goes to embalming college, and he ain't never going to be broke. Right now everyone's out of work, everyone's broke, and Zeke Jones, he's doing so well he can hire hisself a helper when he gets hurt."

"Time enough to worry about that when the chile gets his

education. That's the first thing, that's the very first thing," said Li'l Joe, but he had to admit there was merit in her idea. There sure as the devil was security in the funeral business. There wasn't any worry about supply and demand. Competition was the only menace.

When the WPA began putting people to work as laborers, Li'l Joe augmented what he made at Zeke's with pick-and-shovel work when things were slow at the funeral home, and occasionally with a "little piece of change" from a music gig or parade when there was one to be played. Everything that he and Geneva made, over and above what they needed for themselves and their grandson, was carefully saved. Never overly trustful of banks, and with the memory of the bank holiday still vivid, they put paper money under the rug, while coins were hoarded in all manner of unlikely places. Only for their grandson were these hoards ever broached for anything but necessities. They disciplined the child, but with more gentleness than they themselves had been disciplined by parents of another generation. "Mebbe he's spoilt," said Geneva. "But he ain't spoilt rotten."

When David outgrew the carton beside the bed and the dresser drawer, they moved. The new rooms were only a block away, and no great improvement on their previous cramped quarters, except for an anteroom that might once have been a trunk closet. Into this they managed to squeeze a bed, a dresser and, first, a borrowed crib, then a borrowed cot that they managed to fit at the foot of their bed. On the days when Li'l Joe and Geneva both worked, they took the boy to Ambrose Jefferson's house, next door to Pop Jefferson, his brother. the Abraham Jefferson of Li'l Joe's childhood.

Joseph Champlin could not remember when there had not been a lot of Jeffersons in his life. They were scattered through the French Quarter in an ever-growing and progressively more intricate pattern of brothers, sisters, aunts, uncles, cousins, grandparents, and small sons and daughters. It was the first Abraham Jefferson who had been with Li'l Joe's father, David, when that doomed man had died on a pile of blazing logs in a nearby state. Abraham had managed to escape somehow, and by blind instinct found his way to New Orleans, but had never been coherent enough again to tell all that had happened on that spring afternoon when his friend had died in flames, with the howling laughter of a mob in his ears. "Abr'am just never did come to hisself," said Gran'Cecile.

It was the sight of a white doctor, sent for by Cecile, that had sent the half-crazed Abraham running from the house, a mad, screaming black man no one dared stop, a man who ran like the wind, with bulging eyes and wide-open mouth, ran through the streets of the French Quarter straight and fast as an arrow to the docks, crying "Jesus! I'm coming, Jesus! Take me Jesus!" until the kind waters of the river filled the screaming mouth, closed over the frenzied eyes, and did not give him up for three days. There were old people still alive in the French Quarter who remembered that day.

When Li'l Joe and Geneva were both working and they took David to Ambrose Jefferson's house, Geneva fretted. "They got a lot of white children coming in, playing in that neighborhood," she said one morning.

"You can't help that, Neva. Chile's got to know there's whites, got to learn what they're like. Can't wrap him up in cotton wool all his life."

"Onlies' white he knows now is the Professor. Suits me if he don't ever have to know no more."

"You talking foolishness, Neva. He's going to think all whites is like the Professor, way it is now."

"He ain't going to think it long."

She nagged her husband to keep after Zeke Jones about their grandson's future.

"Gawd sake, Neva, the chile ain't even walking yet, and already you wants him to start laying out co'pses."

The Professor, admittedly hazy about the mental working of the very young, gave them a set of alphabet blocks when the boy was four. To Geneva, whose scant knowledge of reading and writing had come long after she was grown, some of it with the help of her husband, alphabet blocks were not playthings. They were means to an end, and to Li'l Joe they represented the same opportunity—to start his grandson on the right road. He spent hours on the floor with the child whenever he could, making a game of the alphabet, using pictures of dogs and cats and cows and horses until at five David could spell out simple sentences.

It did not bother the child that the only plumbing in their home was a single cold-water faucet, his only playground the cobbled courtyards and banquettes. He was, in the words of his grandfather, "just as happy as if he had good sense." When he was very small he would stand, jigging up and down with excitement, at the kitchen table, his eyes just over its top, while his grandfather cleaned and repaired the broken, secondhand toys they managed to get for him. Gramp could make them work, he knew that; Gramp could make them shine and gleam, and if an old tap washer had to replace a missing truck wheel it made no difference.

Geneva tried to keep the acrid envy out of her eyes and heart in those days when she saw the train sets and fire engines and shiny toy trucks on the floors of the families she cleaned for now and then; tried to keep the bitterness out of her eyes when she took her employers' children to play on park grass where her grandson would not be allowed to set foot.

There were always plenty of books and pictures in the house. The Professor saw to that. The books the Professor brought were new, with no pages missing or defaced by crayons like the ones Geneva brought home, and David learned that if he marked them up or did not take care of them retribution would be swift. At night after Li'l Joe came home he would hold his grandson on his lap and as far as his own limited education would allow he read aloud, the light of the oil lamp, soft and yellow, mellowing the outlines of the shabby furniture. The Professor never missed a chance to pick up a book or magazine with stories about Africa, or with pictures of wild animals, and sometimes Li'l Joe would become so engrossed in the tales of Africa his voice would trail off and David would have to prod him back to reading aloud. "There's where your people comes from, son," Li'l Joe would say. "Don't you never be like some of these colored, shamed your people comes from there. Can't no white say they comes from the same part of the world as King Solomon and the Queen of Sheba. Wouldn't be surprised but what Moses and a lot of them couldn't ride in the front of the bus was they down here."

Both Gramp and Gram would bring home toy animals, some of them cloth, some of them china or pottery, all of them damaged but new and exciting to him. They joked about the damage. "See," Gram said once. "It's a three-legged dog. Reckon he got in a bad fight. That's what happens, baby, when you gets in fights."

"Gramp'll fix it."

"Can't fix this. Nope. Reckon that other dog he got messed up with runned off with his leg."

They cleaned and mended and restuffed the cloth animals. One tiger defied them, and at last they re-covered the tattered beast with bits and pieces of calico, adding green glass button eyes and drooping yellow wool whiskers. Tant'Irene was there the Sunday afternoon they finished it, and when her great-grandson shouted aloud with laughter she said, "David," and her stern face frew soft. Li'l Joe, looking at her, knew she was not speaking of her grandson but of her dead husband.

"Mane," said David. "Where's its mane?"

"Shucks, tigers don't have no manes, son."

"This one do, Gramp, this one do."

And so they made a tiger's mane for him of loops of wool of many colors, red, green, yellow, blue, and cut the loops, and Gramp gave one look and said, "Lawd! Set that pore thing down in the middle of Africa he'd be one lonesome tiger. All the other tigers'd run like five hundred minute they seen him."

To David it was the most wonderful tiger in the world, and he slept with it every night.

David Champlin was a shy child with those outside his immediate environment, and less aggressive than most of his playmates. The first time he ran afoul of the neighborhood bully he came sobbing to his grandfather, who withheld sympathy.

"You let that boy see you crying?" asked Gramp. "Did you?"

David shook his head, dislodging tears. He was stunned that the usual ready comfort was not there.

"Then you get on back out there. He bullies you again, you stand up to him, y'hear!"

"Jimmy—he said he was going to hit me." David was still sniffling, engulfed in self-pity.

"Ain't no law says you can't hit him first."

Silence.

"Well, is there?"

"No—no, sir."

As he left the room slowly, reluctantly, he heard his grandmother's voice raised shrilly: "You crazy, Joseph Champlin? That Jimmy's twice as big as him—and bad." And his grandfather's slow, quiet, "Chile's got to learn sometime. Chile's got to learn there's coming a time won't no one stand up for him but his own self." But he heard soft footsteps, and knew that Gramp was following him, then was standing at the door, quiet, alert.

David went to bed that night nursing his first black eye.

Several times, after he had been guided through his prayers by Geneva, he climbed out of his cot and over the foot of his grandparent's bed, looking at his bruises in the mirror, seeing himself as a hero in the dim light that filtered in from the kitchen. He had not followed his grandfather's implied advice to hit first. Instead he had marshaled his strength, and at the first taunt from the bully—a light-skinned boy, overloaded with soft, flabby flesh—had taken a running start and, goat-like, butted the soft belly with his head backed by all the momentum he could muster. The results were even more than Gramp could have hoped for. He was not clear in his mind how he had gotten the black eye, because the sight of the neighborhood scourge lying winded on the banquette had started a free-for-all.

The fight had taught him something, though, and it was his first real secret, a something he could not share with Gramp, something only he would know: He did not like to fight. All that he could tell Gramp and take pride in was that he was not afraid to fight and that he could fight. Gramp had been, according to his own stories, which Tant'Irene acknowledged to be true, "One helluva fighter" when he was young. "Used to go out looking for 'em if they didn't happen natural," he'd say, and usually add, "Ain't but two things makes me want to fight now I'm older and come to my senses—that's seeing somebody hurt a young un or an old person."

The process of teaching David Champlin to live in a divided world was begun when he was still too young to walk down the street without holding the protecting hand of Gram or Gramp. It was the first order of the business of upbringing. That he had white playmates with whom he romped on terms of equality only made it more urgent. He was told to take off his hat to all adults and call them "sir" or "ma'am" whether they were white or colored, but in dealing with white adults he was to keep his eyes to himself and never on them, and he must never look a white woman squarely in the face. Once his business with any white person was over he was to get out of their company, even though at that age the business might be no more than the purchase of an ice-cream cone. He learned early that lying to Gram or Gramp or those entrusted with his care was a bad thing and brought a stinging whipping; lying to a white, except the Professor, was glossed over, and therefore it was not a bad thing as lying to his own was a bad thing. The inevitable "why" of childhood's logic was never adequately answered.

"What's a nigger bastid?" he asked his grandparents at supper one night.

"Lawd!" said Geneva. "Lawd!" There was the sound of keening in her voice.

Joseph Champlin finished flavoring his stew with hot sauce, and carefully replaced the bottle in the cruet stand. "Why you ask, son?"

"Tommy Lucido called me a nigger bastid."

It was not the "bastid" that made the muscles of Li'l Joe's jaws set; it was the lisp of childhood in the epithet. "What you do?" he asked.

"I hit him," said his grandson. "I hit him and he runned away. I didn't want to hit him but I did."

"You should of come home, baby," said Geneva. "You should have come home. Don't play round with him no more, y'hear! How many times I got to tell you—stay in your own courtyard; nev' mind what the white kids do."

David paid no attention. He was looking at his grandfather, the source of all wisdom.

"Is there white bastids?" he asked. "Is there?"

"They's plenty," said Li'l Joe, and David heard an abrupt laugh from his grandmother.

"And we the ones what knows it," she said. Then, "Lawd! his folks going to tell all their friends how their lily-white chile got beat up by colored. Going to use it to show why their kids is too good for us. I wish God would strike 'em dead. I wish they was all dead and rotting in hell."

"They bound to be someday," said Li'l Joe reasonably. "They bound to be. Ain't no God I ever heerd about going to find no places for 'em too close to Him. The whites is lots of things, but there's one thing they ain't—that's Christian." He frowned at his wife. "Ain't no use getting all upsetted. God don't work in no hurry. He'll catch up with 'em, give Him time. Ain't nothing you can do about it, not if you wants to keep on living." He looked across the table into the dark, round puzzlement of his grandson's eyes, and flinched as from a blow. "Next time some white calls you bad names, don't go to fighting, and—"

"But—but Gramp—you said when Jimmy—"

"That's different. He's colored. Some white lays a hand on you, you fight back, but don't get in no humbug over bad names. You going to be hearing bad names from whites all your life. Ain't nothing but bad comes from fighting 'em. They ignorant."

"What's iggerant?"

"They don't know no better. You getting old enough to learn now how it is. You gets in trouble with the whites, I'll tan your hide so good you can use it for shoe leather. You let 'em alone, y'hear!"

David nodded, his eyes seeming to be all that there was of his face. He had never heard that tone in Gramp's voice before; had always known that threats to "tan his hide" were joking, that the worst he would get was a right smart switching. He had never been afraid of Gramp before, and now, suddenly, he was. It was a shattering thing—to be afraid of Gramp, to see a real and bitter threat in Gramp's eyes, hear a harsh promise in Gramp's voice of fearful punishment for disobedience to an order he could not comprehend. The foundations of his small world rocked, threatening to disintegrate. He sensed something else behind that harshness. Gramp was no longer Gramp, gentle, loving, kindly; Gramp was a being to fear and yet Gramp, too, was afraid.

He was sobbing now, and Gram held him close and rocked him fiercely in her arms. "You got no call to cry, baby. All the love you got, you got no call to cry." Her voice was edged and sharp as she spoke over his head to her husband. "You stir yourself, Joseph Champlin, and get down to Antonelli's and get us some ice cream and some of them frosted cookies they got the baby likes."

Gramp's hands were under his shoulders, setting him on his feet, but Gramp's tone was still strange. "Stop it, son! You going to be crying all your life, you keep on like this. There ain't nothing you can do about it. Reckon me'n' Gram's got to teach you about God some more. Come on, li'l man, right now we gets ourselves some ice cream."

At Antonelli's he had a peppermint, and Gramp bought ice cream and some cookies to take home. Later, at the table, he warily approached a question he had to ask, a question that came from the depths of a new bewilderment.

"Gramp." There was a ring of ice cream on the smooth brown of his lips, and the cookie in his hand had a half-moon bite in it.

"Don't talk with your mouth full, son."

David swallowed ice cream and the bite of cookie and tried again. "Gramp, when I says my prayers I says 'God bless Gram and Gramp and Tant'Irene and Ol' Miz Jefferson and the Professor and little colored children everywhere.' Don't I, Gramp?"

"Sure do, baby."

"Ain't the Professor white, Gramp?"

Li'l Joe had been expecting this one eventually. "Sometimes they's what they call exceptions, son. The Professor, now, he comes from over the water, where they got all different kinds of countries. They even speaks different languages. I mean different from what we speaks and the Creoles and French and Eyetalians speaks around here. And the people is different, way different."

David carefully put a heaping spoonful of ice cream into his mouth, the last in the plate, smoothing it, rounding it off with his lip, leaving some in the bowl of the spoon so it would last longer.

"You mean the Professor's white, but he ain't *New Orleans* white. That what you mean, Gramp?"

Li'l Joe sighed, then smiled at the boy. "Reckon you could say that, son." He pushed his half-eaten plate of ice cream across the table. "Here, baby. Finish it for me. My teeths can't stand no more of that cold."

6

BJARNE KNUDSEN HAD KNOWN for a long time of the dream that sustained Joseph Champlin, that made his job with Zeke Jones bearable, that sent him out to play a gig on nights when his body ached with fatigue because he had worked at hard labor since dawn. The Professor tried to slow him down, to show him that the human body can absorb only so much without harm, but Li'l Joe would only smile and say, "Reckon I'm just hardheaded like my ma says." It was why happiness and relief brought the big Dane storming across the room to envelop his friend in a bear hug and pound him on the back when the little man said: "Looks like I found it, Prof. Looks like I found me the house and the li'l piece of property where me'n' Geneva and the chile can live, with room for my ma as long's she's alive."

Sipping beer, seated across from the Professor, Li'l Joe

said: "It ain't no great shakes. And it ain't finished. Just the outside walls and the inside framework. Fellow that owned it, he's in the penitentiary. His lawyer, he's trying to get the property for his fee, but I got me a real-estate agent and we're going to work it out somehow so's I pays a down and then something every month, and after a while I gets title. I got friends'll help me work on it, musicians, fellows scratching for a dime when they ain't playing. They'll help for whatever I can pay 'em." His thin face almost vanished in a smile. "It's got gas connections and drains all in it, so's someday when I got the money we can have an inside bathroom. You want to know something, Prof? All the years of my life I been living in the great city of New Orleans, that's something I ain't *never* had."

Later he said: "Fellow what owns the house, he put an old piano in it. They calls him 'Cat.' Cat Masterson his name is. He's a real fine musician. I've heard him plenty times. It's about all he lives for, his music and his daughter. She's near fifteen but she ain't real bright. Guess they calls 'em retarded, but she's a real nice girl. That piano's the onlies' thing in the house. Ain't even no walls on the inside, but he got him a second-handed piano and put in it."

"Are you sure, Li'l Joe, he won't want it when he gets out?"

"Ain't sure of nothing except it's going to be a mighty cold day in hell the day he gets out."

"What did he do? Why is he there?" Knudsen was sorry he had asked the question the moment the words had crossed his lips. He knew now, always, the kind of answer he would get to a question like that by the way the spirit, the essence, of Li'l Joe Champlin withdrew behind a blank brown mask, behind eyes grown dull and without expression.

"Didn't do nothing you could fault him for really. Nothing more'n what any man would do. Lost his head and went after a guy for trying to force his daughter, guy what ran a laundry next door; he caught him trying to get in the bed with his daughter one night when he come home early. Heerd her screaming when he come in the courtyard. Cut the guy bad. Didn't know what he was doing, I guess. Onlies' trouble is the guy was white. They tells me, them what's got friends in the penitentiary up there, he's going queer in the head. He's got—he's got—I can't call it right, but it means he can't stand to be shut up in no small place. Now they got him in solitary."

"Claustrophobia," said the Professor. His voice was dull

and sick-sounding. He ran a hand through his hair, tugged at his beard. "All right," he said. "All right, Li'l Joe. No more. For God's sake, no more. You tell me of these things that are a stench in the nostrils of humanity as though you spoke of the price of sugar. I hear what you are saying, but I cannot know what you are thinking. Perhaps I should thank God for it."

"You-all don't believe in God, remember? That's what you been saying."

"*Ja*. If I could believe in the God I learned as a child, with a long white beard who rewards the good and punishes the evil—"

"He do," said Li'l Joe. "He do. But he don't do it right now. He takes His time. He sure takes His time."

The Professor was quiet for a moment. "*Ja*," he said at last. "*Ja*. He does."

They discussed the work to be done, and Bjarne Knudsen relaxed and felt warmed and better as his friend rambled on happily about his plans.

"Kid Arab, he's a good plasterer," said Li'l Joe. "And Bob John—he plays trombone *and* piano—he's a pretty fair carpenter if you can keep him away from a bottle, and my son, Evan, when he ain't in trouble, works for a roofer. Far's that goes, I could do most of it myself in the evenings, but it would take a helluva long time, and then the short days coming on and all. These men all scratching when they ain't working. If we keeps that down payment low, I got enough put by to pay 'em, long with what I makes."

They worked as fast as they could, with Li'l Joe breathing down their necks and outworking them all during his off-work hours. Evan Champlin got the better part of the roofing work done at the start of the job. Now that John was dead, Evan was the only living child of Joseph Champlin's first marriage; a daughter had died in childhood. "He ain't a bit of good," Li'l Joe would say morosely, speaking of his son. "He ain't a bit of good. His mother done ruint him." When word came that Evan would be unavailable because he was doing thirty days, Li'l Joe cursed roundly and wound up saying, "Damfool woman." When Bob John commented that there wasn't nothing surer than a woman to get a man in trouble, Li'l Joe said: "It ain't like you mean. Evan never was one to get hisself in trouble over no woman. He's got a good wife, a real good wife. It's his ma. If I says it myself, that boy's a helluva boxer. He won more fights than any boxer in his class round here. Didn't he whup Sammy Nelson twice—and he's champeen now? But it ain't no good sticking round New Orleans if you going to get any place fighting. Ain't no future round here where a colored boy can't fight a white boy. They too scared the colored boy's going to whip the white boy, knock him out maybe, then they won't be soopreme no more. Evan, he got a fine chance to leave from here and fight up North, and his mother raised such a sand he didn't go. Carried on and had herself heart attacks and Gawd knows what. Now he ain't going no place but the jailhouse, doing his fighting in the bars and on the street."

The night the house was finished to the point that it was judged fit to live in, Li'l Joe came home in no state to go into details. Geneva did not nag. Before he fell asleep he managed to tell her how he had slipped on the roof and hung, dangling, kicking wildly, cussing like five hundred, until Bob John and Kid rescued him. After that they had celebrated. Which was obvious.

The next day was Sunday, and Geneva let him sleep late, shushing David, running him out into the courtyard to play. At late breakfast Li'l Joe told her how the house looked, how it was finished except for the inside doors and a window here and there still boarded up. He had not wanted her to see it until it was ready, and she had not pressed him to take her over. Now he said:

"You get that chile ready, Neva, and fix us some sandwiches. We going over there so's you can see the place. I'll get us some beer. Ain't no stove yet to fix coffee on."

"We got the Thermos."

Li'l Joe winced. He had always contended that Geneva stole the Thermos, and Geneva always denied it, then contradicted herself by saying: "They away over the water. You think they going to miss it when they come back? You needs a hot drink or some soup, working on them docks in the cold and rain. They'da give it to me anyway." She would laugh her quick, abrupt laugh. "After one of them kids broke it and it didn't work good no more, they'da give it to me then."

"How you like it, Neva? Suits you, I'm satisfied."

Geneva had not spoken since they had walked up the path to the front door and stepped inside. "Everything's fine," she said. "Everything's just fine."

There were no more words to say; she had said all she

could from a full heart. As she walked through the empty house, the long narrow front room, the small dining room behind it and the big kitchen beyond, turned and walked back into the little hall off the dining room with its small bedrooms at each end and what would be the bathroom in its center, she was remembering the first time she had lain all night with the man who was now her husband, remembering waking in the night and reaching for him, not seeking passion but just his presence. I was happy that night, she thought. First time I'd been real happy since I'd growed up. And I'm happy now like I was then.

"You got the privy built?"

"Shucks, we done that first thing."

Li'l Joe had never been demonstrative, but now he put his arm around his wife's waist and, holding her body close to his, led her to the back porch.

"See?" he said, pointing to the far end of the backyard. "Can't no wind blow that down. And you just looka there. Bob John, he scrounged some used brick and I laid us a path so's we won't have to walk through no mud and wet to get to it like we does now. But you wait. We keep saving and I gets some used tile. I know where I can get it real cheap. Mebbe I can even get it free if I does some work for the man. Then I lays it in the bathroom. Later we can get us a tub and a basin and a toilet. I can get them secondhanded real cheap too from the same guy."

He looked down at the wide-eyed child who had followed them and who stood now holding his hand.

"That day come and we has a tub, you'n' me going to have a time, li'l man; we going to have a *time.*"

Geneva was looking at the new privy and at the clean brick path that led to it, and her throat was tight.

"Everything's fine," she whispered again. "Everything's just fine. Just the way it is—"

Now grass and brown earth were under David Champlin's bare feet every day; there were flowers to pick and bring to his grandmother, and she showed him what peppergrass looked like and where it grew, and he brought it to her to cook. The fat brown dog came almost every day, and they rolled and played together in the grass and undergrowth. There were so many children in the old frame house across the road that David thought it must be a school, like the big building near where they had lived in the French Quarter. After a few days they straggled over, one by one, and did what Gram called "made themselves acquainted." Their name was Timmins, and there were as many different complexions as there were children, from the jet-black, skinny boy who had come over the first day Gramp brought them to the house, to the youngest girl, whose skin was creamy and whose brown hair curled loosely, softly, not in tight kinks. Miz Timmins, their mother, who had brought a pot of coffee over the first day they moved in, was tall and as skinny for a woman as Gramp was for a man, with black skin and big teeth that stuck out in front, and a way with her with a child that soon placed her next to Pop and Miz Emma Jefferson in David's affections. David puzzled for a while about a conversation he overheard one night, between his grandparents, after he'd said his prayers and was supposed to be asleep.

"Sure an ugly woman," said Gramp.

"She's real friendly," said Gram defensively.

"That's a fact," said Gramp. "That's sure a fact. Wonder which one of them kids' daddies was named Timmins."

"Angelina's," said Gram. "She the oldest. Miz Timmins said that was her *first* husband's name. Them other kids carries the name, too."

Gramp said something David could not catch; then Gram said, "Can't see as it makes much difference."

"I ain't saying it does."

"She's a mighty kind woman. She going to get David in Sunday school with her chilren and she's going to take me to church with her next Sunday. She says they got a fine choir for singing. That's what I likes in a church, plenty singing. Don't seem real somehow without the singing, letting out with the way you feels."

The only furniture in the house was the piano, tuned now by a friend of Gramp's and moved into the dining room, and what they had brought from the rooms in the Vieux Carré: Tant'Irene's old rocking chair, the two kitchen chairs, and the two rickety tables, the big bed and David's cot, and a battered wooden icebox. They had been there a year before Li'l Joe could have the house wired for electricity, and the pride of his life was the small overhead light in the front room with the pink glass shade Geneva had brought home from a secondhand store.

On the days when Geneva worked she took David with her

and left him with Pop and Emma Jefferson or with the Ambrose Jeffersons. If they both worked late, David slept at Miz Emma's, and she took care of him as she would have taken care of the child she had never had. On the way home on the ferry at night with Gram and Gramp, he usually slept. Most nights, as he drifted into sleep there would be the half-dream first, of the wide water with silver light shimmering over its dark surface and the sound of many voices on its banks, singing.

There were other houses along the ill-paved street. Just below the Timminses' a battered shabby house with sagging porch and broken steps housed a man and woman and Ol' Miz Specks, the woman's mother. Between that house and the Timminses' a one-room cabin sat back from the others, and David hated to see the couple who lived in it come home because the sound of their shouted quarrels and banging furniture frightened him.

Right after the Champlins moved in, a man and his wife and little girl came over one Sunday and walked around the lot next to theirs, and Gram and Gramp wondered if they'd be neighbors. The girl, Gram said, must be at least five years older than David. "Pretty as can be," said Gram, "and born to trouble. The devil's own, my ma would have said if she'd seen her."

Tant'Irene came over often, but would not move in with them. She had never lived away from the French Quarter in her life and its sounds and smells, its sights, its crowded streets, the cries of its vendors, were a part of her and she could not give them up.

One of the windfalls that came their way was a huge overstuffed divan, upholstered in a fuzzy blue material that tickled David's skin when he lay on it. The divan opened into a bed, and had been given to Geneva—with the stipulation that she arrange to have it carted away—by one of her employers. "They coulda sold that," said Geneva with grudging gratitude. "Sure is beautiful even if it do take up most of the room."

Irene Champlin knew it to be hideous but praised it heartily for Geneva's sake, slept on it those nights when she came over the river, and crocheted antimacassars for it, making them stiff with starch.

The day Li'l Joe borrowed a truck to carry the divan home he noticed a used electric refrigerator in the lot of the second-hand dealer who owned the truck. He wavered briefly, then signed up for it. It was hard for him to believe sometimes that he was buying something for his own home, but Geneva's quiet happiness was a sure reality.

7

TWO YEARS AFTER they moved over the river, Joseph Champlin and his grandson were alone. On a night when Tant'Irene was staying with them, David awakened to the sound of strange voices, and called out, and Tant'Irene came in and lifted him from his cot and carried him to the kitchen with surprising strength. He had been sleeping in his own room for almost a year and was, in his own opinion, much too big to be carried. In the kitchen she held him on her lap and sang to him in French and Creole, rocking him gently. The door to the dining room was closed, but through it he could hear voices, and then Gramp came in by the side door from the hall and looked in and shook his head, his face as hard and cold as the black marble bust of George Washington Carver on the Jeffersons' mantel. Behind him David saw a man in a white coat, and then Gramp turned, his face terrible in its stillness, and as he started down the hall David broke from Tant'Irene's arms and ran after him, screaming, but Tant'Irene caught him as he reached the hall and held him with fierce strength.

God had sent His angels for Gram in the night, Tant'Irene said, but David did not believe her. Not even when he saw Gram in her coffin did he really believe it. It was not so much the sight of Gram in her coffin that made him cry as Gramp and Gramp's face, set and still, his eyes not looking like eyes at all, a man who did not speak in the church and who later sat in the front room without speaking, like a dead man sitting in a chair.

David had almost always wakened in the morning before Gram and Gramp, and had stood in the doorway of their room, not daring to make a noise but willing them to wake, shouting in his mind: Gram! Gramp! Wake up! I'm hungry!

David's hungry! One morning an uncontrollable giggle broke from him as he stood there, and he clapped a hand over his mouth, but it was too late. Gramp, who always slept more quietly than what Tant'Irene called their *chat-sans-queue,* Stumpy, had heard him. "Fix yourself some cereal, son," he said sleepily. "You big enough now." Later, at breakfast, he asked, "What were you laughing about, standing in the door?"

David giggled again. "You looks like a mouse when you're asleep, Gramp. Like the little brown mouse I seen on the back porch. You told me a story 'bout him, 'bout the wise brown mouse."

After the frightening night when they took Gram away, Gramp was never asleep no matter how early he went to the door; instead he would be lying quietly, his eyes open, the pillow that Gram had always slept on gone, used now on the divan-bed Tant'Irene was sleeping on. It was about a week after Gram had gone when the full realization came to David that Gram would never be lying beside Gramp again when he came to the door in the morning. He didn't mean to slam the door when he ran into his own room, but it crashed behind him. He tried not to cry too loud, lying face down on his cot. The sobs were so hard that they hurt him, deep inside. Then Gramp was sitting on the edge of the cot in pajamas and slippers, talking to him, but what he was saying didn't help, only made it worse. At last Gramp said: "All right, son. All right. You cry it out. Seems like it's better that way. Makes a person sick, all that grief inside 'em, never coming out, like poison." He felt Gramp's hand on his head, roughing his hair, heard him say, "Going out and fix us some hot biscuits for breakfast, son. Time you feels better they'll be ready."

That night the feeling of loss woke him, even though Gramp had come back, had been Gramp again, talking more than he had since Gram had been with them, even playing a game with him after supper, and it was Gramp instead of Tant'Irene who heard his prayers that night. Ever since Gram had gone, Tant'Irene kept the light on in the hall, with dark blue cloth carefully draped over it to cut the glare. Now, in the dark and no-time of the night David got up and padded to Gramp's door and opened it softly. The dim light from the hall showed Gramp's eyes open, gleaming.

"Gramp."

"You all right, son?"

"Gramp, if I bring my pillow can I sleep in your bed?"

"Sure can, little man, sure can."

The sad feeling was not so big with Gramp beside him, warm and still and as quiet as the little brown mouse he had seen on the porch. As he drifted into sleep he wondered about the mouse and where it slept at night, and hoped Stumpy the cat wouldn't catch it. In the morning he-would-tell-Stumpy-not-to-hurt-the-wise-brown-mouse.

They took Tant'Irene to the big hospital in the heart of the city. The buildings were so huge and sprawling David was sure she would never come out, and wondered how Gramp could ever find her when he went there to see her. There was a hazy, lonely period while Tant'Irene was in the hospital when he and Gramp stayed with Pop and Miz Emma, sleeping together on the divan-bed that was like their own. Gramp was very still and quiet all the time, the way he had been after Gram died, and David begged to stay with the Timminses, but Gramp said there were too many young uns there already and it would be too crowded. "We'll be back soon," said Gramp.

"Stumpy don't want us to go," he said desperately.

"Sure don't," said Gramp. "But them Timmins chilren, they'll take care of him. After the trick the Prof played on that pore animal, he ain't going to be doing no tomcatting around."

David giggled, remembering when Stumpy had come to them, a bedraggled yellow wisp of half-grown cat with a stub of a tail no longer than his own thumb, and remembering how one day when Stumpy was bigger the Prof had carried him off in a basket, and how Gramp had roared and raised a sand when he got home that night.

"They ain't going to hurt him," Gram had said. "The Professor says they puts 'em to sleep and when they wakes up they don't know what happened."

"The hell they don't!"

"The Prof says he's going to be a better pet for David; says he won't be off getting in fights and losing an eye and all; says he'll be kind and gentle 'stead of mean."

"What'd they *do?*" asked David. "Huh, Gramp? What'd they *do* to Stumpy?"

"Never you mind, son. Took his manhood, that's what they did. Lawdgawdalmighty! Dirtiest trick I ever heard of. You wait till I sees the Prof. You just wait."

But when the Professor drove up to the door with Stumpy

and carried him inside, Gramp was smiling as he always was, and the Prof ate with them that night, and as David was going to sleep with Stumpy curled beside him and his calico tiger on his pillow, he could hear the Prof's voice rumbling like a train and now and then the soft purr of Gramp's voice answering.

8

THERE WAS A PAIN, a big one, only it was a long way off; it was a pain happening to someone else and he was whimpering with it. There was something touching his face and his forehead, but when he opened his eyes there was only a blur. He closed them again, and a jillion years later opened them and the blur was gone and Gramp's eyes were just above him, filled with tears. Gramp was touching his forehead and cheeks with the back of his fingers. "You all right, son." Gramp was whispering. It was not a question; he was saying it, "You all right, little man."

He said, "Gramp," and then the pain came back, happening to him now, happening to him in a high bed in a strange place, happening to a foot and leg that wouldn't move. He whimpered again, and Gramp took his hand. "I *hurt*." There was a crackling sound, and a woman was there, all in white, with starched coif and bib, holding a pill to his lips. He clenched them tightly closed and turned his head away, and Gramp said sternly, "You do like the sister says, y'hear, boy! It's going to help that hurting." He took the pill, but the water from a cup dribbled down his chin, and Gramp wiped it off gently, held the cup so he could swallow the water and the pill.

He closed his eyes and in the darkness through the pain heard Gramp saying in a shaky voice, "He was playing in the street. I done told him so often—"

"I know," said the woman. "They will do it. I think I can find Doctor now, and he can tell you just what's happened."

David opened his eyes. "You ain't going?" he whispered.

"You going to sleep now, son. You do like they tells you, understand. I don't want to come back and hear nothing about you being bad. You do like they says."

He nodded dumbly.

"Gramp's got to go over the river and feed Stumpy. You knows that." Gramp leaned over and put a moist cheek against his and whispered: "Pray to Jesus, son. He's helping you. You pray to Jesus like Gram taught you. I'll be back. You take your rest—"

There wasn't anybody there then, and the pain grew bigger and he began to cry. He remembered now. He had been spending the day in New Orleans, and playing duck-on-a-rock in the street. He remembered hearing Abraham Jefferson scream, remembered a terrible noise and a blinding crash. There had been a bed that was moving and a man sitting beside it; then the bed was lifted and carried, and then he had awakened here.

The pain began to go farther away, and he clung to Gramp's last words: "I'll be back." He fought sleep off because maybe Gramp had meant right away, to take him home, but sleep was too strong for him. He knew he'd be asleep if Gramp came back because he saw the wide, dark water, saw the people on its banks and heard them singing.

Joseph Champlin followed the sister down the corridor, shaky with relief. Less than half an hour before he had walked along that corridor, shaking with fear, and as he had approached the ward where his grandson lay, his lips had been moving. "Lord! Lord Jesus! Don't let there be no screen around his bed. I can't take no more, Jesus; I can't take no more."

There had been no screen, but his heart had almost stopped at the stillness of the child's face in the high bed, the lavender tinge that paled the lips and underlay the tan-brown of his skin. The bedclothes were tented over his legs. "A rather bad leg injury," the sister said. "The doctor will tell you about it." Now they were seeking the doctor, and he followed respectfully, just behind her, and when she turned into a small room near the end of the corridor he stood outside its threshold.

The thin young man in a white uniform who faced him from the center of the room had dark hair, small dark eyes, and was pale from fatigue. His speech was quick, southern, impatient. He said, "Well? You're here about the Champlin boy?"

Like I was doing something wrong, thought Joseph Champlin; like I was doing something wrong, being here about the Champlin boy; like he was God Almighty chewing out the Philistines.

He said, "Yes, sir," politely when the doctor snapped, "Come in."

The doctor turned from him and walked rapidly to a desk against the wall and sat down. Li'l Joe remained standing. He felt a consuming anger when the doctor said, "Why in hell do you people let your children play in the streets! You're lucky the boy's alive."

Li'l Joe did not speak. His lids dropped over his eyes to hide the rage in them, and he looked at the floor. Behind him his hands were gripped so tightly he could feel the knucklebones grinding together, bone on bone. At last he spoke. "They got no place else to play." In his mind he saw green parks with white children running over grass, and playgrounds with colored children running past, stopping to look and watch, then running on, eternally shut out. God, don't let me do no wrong thing, he prayed. God, don't let me do or say nothing that will hurt David.

"All right," said the doctor. "All right." He swept the subject away like a sloppy housewife sweeping dirt under a rug. He was looking at a typed report, and Li'l Joe shifted the weight on his legs, cramped by the tension of his anger. "The boy has a crushed ankle and foot," said the doctor. "As bad as I've seen. The wheel of the truck must have passed clear over it. I don't see how we can hold out any hope."

"You means—the chile's going to die?"

"Of course not. He had a slight head injury, nothing serious. I mean I don't see how we can hold out any hope of saving the foot and ankle." He looked up, saw the man before him sway, and said, "Sit down."

Li'l Joe shook his head. The doctor was saying, "As his father, his legal guardian, we should have your written permission."

Li'l Joe's mind was working in darting flashes. "His father" the doctor had said; he didn't know that David didn't have a father, that he was the child's grandfather. And Li'l Joe didn't know whether a grandfather was a "legal guardian" or not. What he did know was he wasn't signing no paper, wasn't signing no paper that said this smarty pants ofay boy could lay a hand on David, could cut off his foot.

"I'll study 'bout it," said Li'l Joe, and when he looked at

the doctor his eyes were as dully black as an old shoe button.

The doctor began to talk, illustrating the talk with sketches on a pad of paper, and Joseph Champlin did not hear a word. The doors of his mind and ears were on well-greased hinges, and he closed them easily, from long practice. The doctor, when he had finished, looked up and said, "You see—what's your name?"

"Joseph. Joseph Champlin."

"You understand, Joe? It's the only—"

"I has to study 'bout it. You ain't—you ain't going to do nothing tonight?"

"Not unless infection sets in. You better be here early in the morning, boy. Tell them at the desk to page me—Dr. Carson." He scribbled the name on a piece of paper, wrote a quick memo under it. Li'l Joe took the paper and put it in his pocket without looking at it, and started from the room. Behind him he heard the doctor's voice, sharp, impatient, "We're trying to save the boy's life—" but he did not turn back, and found his way somehow to the street.

There didn't seem to be the sound of anything in the streets, and the faces of the people passing were blurs. He knew only that behind him, close to one of a thousand windows, a little boy lay in a high bed surrounded by strangers, in pain, lonely. If David had to lose his foot, he had to, and there wasn't anything anyone could do about it, but Li'l Joe didn't believe he had to; didn't believe God would do it to a li'l chile, yet knew He could and had and that David Champlin was no dearer in God's sight than Ambrose Jefferson's grandson Henry, who had lost both his legs under a trolley car. For the first time in his life he bumped into a white man on the sidewalk. The man snarled, "Watch where you're going, nigger!" but it did not snap him out of his preoccupation.

He did not know where he was going, only that he was seeking help and advice. He headed for the French Quarter because his friends were there, but he did not know to which one of them he could turn. His old friend Isaiah Watkins might be the best. Isaiah knew something about the law; Isaiah had more education than most, and at night, when he had finished his work on the docks, he was trying to start a little insurance business. Ever since it had started he had worked with the N-double-ACP, and along with that he was trying to found a local chapter of a new group, the American

League for Equal Citizenship, ALEC, they called it. He had even been to Boston several times to national headquarters. Geneva had not been optimistic about the activities of Isaiah and the others who were working with groups to help their people. "Fat lot of good it'll do 'em," she would say. "All these N-double-A's and ALEC's. Ain't nothing going to change the whites but a slow fry in hell."

"Meantimes," Li'l Joe had said, "Meantimes, till they fries, I can't see as it hurts us none to try." Still, Neva had paid her dues and he had paid his and taken out a membership for David in each when he was still crawling over the floor in diapers.

Li'l Joe knew he wouldn't be able to see Isaiah until nightfall, and his need was urgent.

Suddenly his steps quickened, and when he reached Rampart Street he turned left instead of going on into the French Quarter. He'd never liked to ask favors of the Professor, but this was one time, he thought, he'd have walked barefoot to Washington and asked the President.

Bjarne Knudsen saw Joseph Champlin walking down the path that led to the rear of the house as he drove his car up to the front door. He bellowed, bull-like, and the slender figure halted, turned quickly, and retraced its steps to meet him. Together they entered the house, and as he closed the front door behind them Knudsen realized that it was the first time his friend, Joseph Champlin, had entered by this door. In the study he laid his portfolio on his desk and turned on Li'l Joe.

"So! What is it? For God's sake, Li'l Joe, what is it that makes you look like death?"

Li'l Joe, his knees giving way, sank into the big chair by the fireplace. "It's David," he said. "And he's hurted, real bad."

Knudsen had not expected this; had expected some "worriment" or financial difficulty that could be solved by advice or other help. His voice sank, became low and gentle. "Tell me about it, Li'l Joe. It cannot be as bad as you think."

At the end of his halting story Li'l Joe said: "I ain't signing no paper says they can cut David's foot off. I'd rather carry him out of there unless somebody more'n that little piece of something what calls hisself a doctor says it's right. He ain't more'n a chile hisself."

Knudsen thought: I never before saw that black head bent, the shoulders bowed, not even after Geneva's death. He tried to find words, and knew that the ones he heard himself saying were stupid and poor comfort. "Perhaps, Li'l Joe, it must be done to save the boy. It is not so bad today, to lose a foot. In one of my classes I have a young man with both legs paralyzed."

Li'l Joe looked up at him, and what might have been a smile flickered across his face. "He ain't David," he said.

After a moment Knudsen spoke softly. *"Ja,"* he said. *"Ja,* you are right."

His voice changed, became the more familiar half-roar. *"Ja!"* he said again. "We must try. We must try, Li'l Joe." His hand was on the telephone, and he did not miss, as he waited for his call to go through, the sudden relaxation of Joseph Champlin's body, the letting go of taut muscles as though an invisible rubber band had snapped. He felt like God, and hated the feeling because he was not; if he had been God, he thought, he would be a most disturbed and unhappy man. When he said into the telephone, *"Ja,* I would like to speak to Dr. Fricke, if you please; you will tell him Professor Knudsen is calling and it is an emergency." His eyes were still on the man in the chair, and he saw the body freeze, every fiber listening as a small woods animal in its den would freeze and listen at a strange sound.

Li'l Joe heard only one side of the conversation that followed, but even in the midst of his worry what he heard brought a smile: "There is a boy you must see in the hospital, Joel. . . . *Ja,* I know, but he is badly hurt. There is talk of amputating his foot. . . A truck crushed his ankle. . . *Ja, ja, ja,* he is colored. . . I have *no* chip on my shoulder. . . . I know he is getting good care, but he must be seen by you. . . . The hell with your regulations! You must examine him. If you do not I will raise . . . I am not excited, not yet. . . . What can you do! What can you *do!* What can the great Joel Fricke do for a boy who may lose his foot? You can save it. . . . Bah! You know what the hospital can do with its regulations. . . . You are the great bone man, the great Joel Fricke; they will be honored at your presence. . . ." Li'l Joe heard the voice change, lower, become almost wheedling, but it was a wheedle with a menace. "You would do it if I were lying there, Joel. You would do it then, no? Then pretend it is I. . . . *Ja!* Good! I will be at your office in twenty minutes. . . . No! You will not go alone. . . . I will go with you. . . . I trust no one, Joel, and I must see the boy, too, and I must know quickly, very quickly, what can be done. . . . You will wait for me, my friend."

Knudsen looked down into the face that had turned to him as he hung up the receiver, then quickly looked away. There was too much nakedness in it. He clapped his hands together briskly, said loudly: "So! We go together, my friend Joel Fricke and I, and we see. He is the best, the very best. He teaches at the university and he is a consultant on the staff at the hospital. If he has not the guts to take over the boy's care, like Sampson I will pull the hospital down about his ears. Where will you be so I may call you later? At home?"

"Lawd, no! I can't go that far away, not now. You call me at the Jeffersons'. I'll stay there till I hear."

When Joseph Champlin left the Professor's house that evening there was some difficulty with legs that seemed to belong to someone else. He had finally let himself be persuaded to drink schnapps with his beer. Schnapps had always held, in his eyes, great peril, ever since his first taste, but this evening had been a real occasion, and the Prof had been like a child in his pleading that he try Denmark's favorite drink. "The news is good, Li'l Joe," he said. "It is not perfect but it is better than the news you brought to me earlier. The odds are good that your boy will not lose his foot, but he will be lame. You must face that. He will be lame. And there must be surgery. Not once but several times. He must be patient, and you too. He is a good boy. They let me see him, even though it was not visiting hours. Oh, I raised a sand, I tell you!"

Li'l Joe chuckled. He always did whenever the Prof's Danish accent accommodated itself to one of the colloquialisms of Li'l Joe's people. He felt a relief that came close to making him sick, and he drank the schnapps in haste to account for gathering tears.

Three days after his grandson's first operation Li'l Joe went to the Professor's house again. It was late evening, damp and drizzly, and he knew that there would be a fire in the little grate in the study and that the Professor would have a drink ready, because he had called and asked if he might come over.

He stood in front of the fire for a minute, warming his legs, and apologized for his work clothes, then sat in the big chair beside the grate, rubbing his palms together nervously.

"You are upset, Li'l Joe?" said the Professor. "You are not sure about your boy? He is doing splendidly. I have it from the great Fricke himself."

"I ain't worrying about the leg now, Prof. Not anymore. I trusts what you say."

"You are still worried about something, Li'l Joe. You come in here looking like a troubled chipmunk; you forget the drink I have so carefully prepared. That can only be worry."

Joseph Champlin twisted uneasily in his chair.

"How long the doctors say that boy's going to have to lay up there in that bed?"

"Several weeks."

"Then he's going to come out with his leg in a cast?"

"I'm afraid so, Joe. That is the way it was explained to me. And, as the doctor told you, he will have to return for more surgery."

"And each time he goes back in there for this surgery, he's going to be there like he is now, mebbe weeks? Two, three times for the next two, three years? With casts and all?"

"Yes."

Joseph Champlin was quiet for a long time. The drink remained untouched. Knudsen shuffled papers on his desk, rumbled in his throat, wished himself in Denmark. When the small brown man in the big chair finally spoke, there was despair in the low voice.

"He ain't going to get his schooling. He ain't going to get his education right. I'd most rather he'd lost both his feets than lose that."

Knudsen whirled, glared at Li'l Joe, drew in a deep breath and roared when he spoke.

"That's it! That is what is worrying you!" The roar died, the eyes softened. "You are being a damned idiot, my friend. Of course he will get his schooling. Perhaps a little late, but he will get it."

Joseph Champlin shook his head. "No. You don't understand. Chile like that, he needs schooling when he's young. That boy thinks all the time; I mean, *all* the time. Thinks too damn much for a young un his age. Worrying me all the time about stuff I can't explain good to him because I only had a little bit of education. I ain't going no place now, but mebbe he could have, thinking the way he does, quick like he is."

"Is he doing well in school, Joe?"

"He's doing fine, just fine. I tried to teach him a little myself, best I could, before he even went to school. I taught him his alphabet and how to spell little words like 'cat' and 'dog' and 'God.' "

Knudsen's lips twitched. "In that order?"

"Sort of. A chile knows a cat and a dog, chile just learning about God. Seemed like if I could make him see a cat and a dog had names you could spell out, then seemed like if I could make him see God did, too, why then God would be more real." He smiled apologetically. "He caught on quick. My mamma always said I caught on quick, too; only in them days schools for colored weren't as good as they are now, and Gawd knows they ain't much now. And she was working all the time, and I had to start rustling up money before I even got out of the fourth grade." He hesitated and went on: "They tells me my daddy was like that. Taught himself to read and write, with my mamma helping him."

"Do you remember your father, Joe?" Knudsen was sparring for time, trying to get the other man's worry into some kind of perspective, trying to find an answer to the problem, knowing it was not nearly so great a problem as Joseph Champlin believed it to be, but respecting Li'l Joe's concern over it.

"No," said Joseph Champlin. "No, I don't remember my daddy. Ain't no one alive now remembers him excepting one or two of the real old folks in the Quarter, ol' Miz Jefferson, folks like that."

"He died when you were small?" It occurred to Knudsen that he had never heard Joseph Champlin mention his father before. He did not know what drove him to ask further questions. He pressed the questions as he would have with no other Negro but Joseph Champlin, and he could sense that even with him he was endangering a friendship that must always remain fragile.

"He died before I was even small," said Li'l Joe. "He died before I was born, while my mamma was carrying me. He died away from here, not even in Louisiana." There was no sound in the little room except Knudsen's breathing. Joseph Champlin did not seem to be breathing at all. "My daddy's name was David, too. He was a real good man, but they burnt him; burnt him alive on a pile of logs in the middle of a field. Made them a bonfire out of David Champlin."

Bjarne Knudsen felt the room sway around him, could for a moment see nothing, not even the man in the chair in front of him. He tried to speak, but emotion clogged his throat. He choked on his own horror. He felt the house in which he sat, with its high ceilings, its classic grace, its perfect proportions, fall away from him and leave him alone and shuddering at the edge of something unknown.

It was Joseph Champlin's voice that came to him, called to him, brought back the walls of the room, set his house around him again with its galleries and lacy ironwork, its staircase, its grace, its slave quarters in the rear. He knew it would never be free again of the evil he had just glimpsed.

"Prof," said the gentle voice of Li'l Joe, "Prof. I'm sorry. Swear to Gawd I didn't mean you to get upsetted like that. You asked me, Prof. I thought you knew till you asked me."

He had spent years in the United States, but now Bjarne Knudsen's adopted language failed him. He spoke in Danish briefly, profanely, not to Li'l Joe or to himself, but to what was in the room, and then, in English, said, "You have lived with it. All your life you have lived with it."

"Wasn't nothing I could do about it," said Li'l Joe reasonably. "It's in the past now, Professor. Don't do no good thinking on it too much. Things like that happened. Still happening, here and there, if you wants the truth."

"Always, Joe? Do you believe they will always happen?"

Joseph Champlin did not answer at first; then he shrugged. "Always will, I reckon, less'n we gets help, less'n we gets educated, learns how to fight it with law and stuff. Far as I can see, ain't nobody going to help us but ourselves, and we ain't got what it takes. Not here, not now."

"That is why, Li'l Joe, you want your David to have an education. Underneath that is why. Because of the first David Champlin."

"Mebbe so. Mebbe way back in my mind that's it."

Knudsen moved so quickly Joseph Champlin did not have time to stop him or offer help. He took their glasses, and in the kitchen poured out the stale drinks, and pulled open the refrigerator door with ill-controlled violence. He ran warm water over the ice-cube tray and wished he had never come to Louisiana. It would have been better if he had taken a professorship in the Northeast—or as his brother Karl had done, in the Midwest. The evil in some form would have been there too, but it would not have been an evil sanctioned and somehow made holy by tradition.

He had not asked his friend why the first David Champlin had died on a bonfire in a far-off field. He did not need to; there was always and eternally the One Reason, the Big Fear.

"Prey from the day they are born," said Knudsen aloud. He had often thought how every male Negro born in the South was marked for hunting. Even after he had been domesticated, he must be tamed like a pet lion cub, caged at maturity because of fear of its strength. Their maleness was an unsigned death warrant, its signature, the inadvertent glance, the mischance of being in the wrong place at the wrong time, or merely the tinder of suspicion sparked by nothing more than the flint of hate and fear. Let a white woman, be she whore or housewife, maiden or crone, strip herself naked before him, crawl into his bed, lay the white skin of her body against the brown of his, let her do it in fact or with her eyes and the movements of her body that her blood's heat dictated, then let her cry rape and he was for burning. Let a white man violate her and let her cry out the truth—that he had been white—yet a black was marked for burning because rape was abroad in the land.

Bjarnè Knudsen thought: If I were a Christian I would think of the fear in the minds of the burners; I would pity them. But I am not a Christian. I am a nothing, yet I must stand before upturned white faces and try to teach them something they have never known, and will never know until their minds and hearts are changed—civilization.

When he returned with the drinks, he crossed the room to Joseph Champlin's chair, placed a hand on the other man's shoulder when he started to rise, and put the drink on the low table before the fireplace. He carried his own drink to the desk, but did not sit down; instead stood looking at the man almost lost in the big chair.

"You will believe me if I tell you something, Li'l Joe?"

"I always does," said Joseph Champlin.

Knudsen thought: You will not commit yourself utterly, not even to me, not even if committal imposes no obligations; the habit of noncommittal is so strong it is almost a reflex.

"Then believe me now. I promise you our boy in the hospital, your grandson, the great-grandson of the man who died so horribly, shall have his schooling. But it must be planned. We Danes are a methodical people, for all some call us overgrown pixies. He will not, in the long run, lose an inch of ground, I promise you. I do not know children, but I feel today I know this boy of yours, this David, *par coeur*. No child will have better tutoring—if he is up to it. Tell him this. But he must be up to it, Li'l Joe."

"He's up to it, Prof; he's sure up to it." The smile on the thin face drove some of the evil from Bjarne Knudsen's room. "You tell me what you wants done, Prof, and I'll do it. Means working day and night, it don't matter. I'll do it."

9

THE PORTER ON THE HUMMING BIRD watched the tall boy with the straight shoulders and gimpy leg settle himself into the seat by the window of the Jim Crow car. He had smiled at the boy when he boarded, but the smile had faded quickly. There was that in the boy's eyes that did not take to smiling, that did not smile back, although the lips formed a smile and the white teeth showed strong and clean in the tan face. The porter, Henry Sampson, puckered his forehead as he watched the youth make his way to his seat. Damn, it had to be Li'l Joe Champlin's grandson. He'd been seeing him around Beauregard for a helluva long time; lots of times when he went over the river from his home in New Orleans to visit his mother he'd see the boy, and he'd always be smiling, pleasant as you please; a polite boy, anyone could tell that, well brought up by his granddaddy. What was he doing on the Humming Bird headed for Cincinnati, not even getting on in Louisiana? Plenty of reason for him to get to Cincinnati—everyone knew the boy was planning to go to some college up that way—but why was he getting on here? Henry Sampson figured he could give a guess, he could give a helluva good guess after seeing the boy's face. "Them buses," he said to himself. Them damned Crow buses. The boy took hisself a bus and run into trouble. Lawd! It was plain as day the boy'd never been on a train before. Henry Sampson went over to the seat.

"Lemme show you how these chairs work, sir," he said, and saw the boy's eyes widen, the red anger in them die away a little. He showed him how to let the seat back, and how the leg rest came out. "Ain't quite long enough for them legs of yourn," he said, smiling. "Better'n nothing, though. Lemme get you a pillow so's you can relax good and res' yourself. Come night I'll fetch a blanket. Anything you wants, you ask for, y'hear?" He kept up a low murmur of conversation, brought the pillow, saw the boy's face soften, and thought, Ain't right, boy as young as that, looking like he done when he got on.

In a few minutes Henry Sampson returned. He had gone back to his own seat but had been unable to sit there, thinking of the boy. He put a hand on the back of the seat in front of David, leaned over the empty aisle chair, and said in a hoarse whisper, "How about a cup of coffee, son?" Not "sir" now. Boy needed gentling. "Man just been through here with the coffee and sandwiches; he ain't coming back for a while. I got me some coffee and a sandwich or two back here. You feeling peckish?"

Wasn't no doubt about who the boy was, now that he was smiling. Henry Sampson had been knowing the Champlins for a long time; he'd known Li'l Joe since they were boys, and known Evan and John, before John got killed, and it would be John who was this boy's father. He knew that Champlin smile good as a book.

When he brought the coffee and two sandwiches—that was a *big* boy—he smiled at the boy's thanks and said, "Shucks. Couldn't let Li'l Joe Champlin's grandson go hungry on my car."

The boy was grinning now. "How'd you know?" Then he glanced down at his feet. "Guess this gimpy leg gave me away."

"Never took no notice of that. Seen you in Beauregard lots of times. Knowed your granddaddy in New Orleans 'fore you was born. Knowed your Uncle Evan and your daddy, too. Thought I knowed you when I seen you get on. Soon's I seen you smile I was sure. Stretch out now, son, and take your rest—"

David Champlin stretched out as best he could, but he wasn't tired, just sick, the sickness he had come to know would always follow anger. It was a nausea, a gagging in the throat. He'd been subject to it ever since he was a kid, and the only thing he could do was ride it out.

Eventually the sickness slipped into the background in the novelty of train travel. All that remained was a determination not to go through with this business of a scholarship to Pengard College in a town called Laurel, Ohio, even if the Prof and his brother did have their minds set on it, even if the Prof's brother was a nice guy and one of the big shots there. He thought of the Prof's disappointment if he backed out now, and stopped thinking about it as quickly as he could. Maybe he wouldn't pass anyhow, on this trip up there; maybe he'd flunk the tests and not have to go there next fall. The Prof had said he was ready for second-year Latin, but he was lousy in math, and he supposed you had to be good in everything. "Not a white college." That was what the Prof and his brother had said. They'd said it was a college for everyone who wanted learning more than anything else; that there were students from Africa and Thailand and China and Japan—what the hell, it was still a white college, and he didn't want it.

Gramp had told the Prof and him that his grandmother had wanted him to learn to be an undertaker, and the Prof had blown up a Danish gale. "Better watch out for them windowpanes, Prof," Gramp had said, and laughed, and never mentioned the subject again. Now David wished Gramp had stood up to the big man. There wasn't anything, not a damned thing, wrong with being an undertaker. Maybe it was backing out on being a lawyer, what he'd wanted to be ever since he was a kid, but it would sure do what Gram had said: keep him away from the whites, even the dead ones.

There weren't many people on the bus, not even many colored in the back with him. He'd had two cups of coffee before he left home with Gramp in the morning, and two cokes on the ferry crossing and another cup of coffee in the bus station. By the time the bus slowed for the first "rest stop" he was gritting his teeth against the urgency of a full bladder. It was rough waiting for the whites to get off, and he didn't even notice that none of the Negroes he was sitting with stood up to leave. He heard one of them say, "Wait, son—" as he started down the aisle, but his discomfort was so great he paid no attention. Then just as the last white person, a man, stepped to the ground the driver said: "Get on back there and sit down, boy. Ain't no facilities for colored here —" and the bus doors closed.

"Jeez!" he gasped. "Look, I've *got* to get off—"

"Ain't no nigger on my bus *got* to do anything he ain't allowed to. Get back there like I said. You don't, you'll be using the can in the jailhouse. You make any trouble, boy, I'll call the police."

He turned from the door, dizzy with rage and discomfort. The driver was not looking at him, was counting change. David thought: "I'll kill you. Someday, you white son of a bitch, I'll catch up with you and kill you." No one in the back of the bus was going to help him. Trouble was stirring and they were all middle-aged and older people, and they did not look at him until he made his way back; then there were murmurs of protest and sympathy, but they were low and cautious, wouldn't carry to the front of the bus. David looked toward the front and saw the driver's face in the rear-vision mirror. It was a face with small, close-set eyes and a mouth so narrow the outer corners seemed even with the nostrils, and the face was smiling. He felt as though he had been touched by, smeared with, something inexpressibly filthy.

Twenty agonized minutes later, the bus began to slow down, and ahead of them David saw a railroad crossing. He saw nothing else, not even the little town off to the right or the railroad station at its outskirts, a quarter of a mile away. He knew only that the bus would have to stop at the crossing, and when they were almost there he was standing behind the driver, overnight bag in hand.

"You better let me off here." His voice was low. "You *better* let me off. I'm standing right behind you and I can't hold out much longer." He saw the back of the driver's neck redden, and the bus lurched as brakes were applied with vicious force. The doors opened, but closed again when he had only one foot on the ground, and he leaped forward, his game leg failing him at the last moment so that he sprawled headlong, hearing the driver's words, "Get out, nigger!" He knew the driver was saving face, making the passengers think he'd ordered a troublemaking nigger off his bus.

He relieved himself when the bus left, and, half sobbing with rage, limped toward the railroad station in the distance. But when he entered the station he was composed, the dirt from the highway brushed from his clothes, lips tightly set. At the ticket window he said, "I'm going to Cincinnati. Can I get there from here?"

"Humming Bird'll be along in about an hour. One way or round trip?"

"One—no. I want to go to Cincinnati, then back to New Orleans."

"Sell you round trip from here, boy, one way to New Orleans on the return." The wizened old man behind the ticket window might have been talking to a five-year-old, and he was kindly in the same manner he would have been to a five-year-old.

David paid for the ticket, thankful he'd won out in the humbug the night before between him and Gramp. He had said he was going to take most of his money with him, all he'd saved from jobs during fall and winter, and Gramp had objected strenuously.

"S'pose you loses it? Then what you got?"

"I won't lose it. Then if anything happens or I have to stay longer or something, I won't have to send for it."

He picked up his change—a ten and a one and some loose coins—and tucked the bills in his wallet. There better not be any more trouble, he thought: he'd never make it. He walked out to the platform, a tall boy with skin the color of light milk-chocolate, a small, well-shaped head with close-cropped hair that was well cared for and frequently disciplined by stocking caps, straight shoulders, slender hips, seeming to be relaxed, except for his eyes. He was wearing gray slacks and a blue pullover, with a fresh blue shirt open at the neck, the collar turned back over the sweater, and brown loafers. He looked as though he could run the mile in good time, snake a football through a line, pull them down from outer space in center field—until he walked, one leg a little shorter than the other, the foot and ankle stiff, but still covering ground with long strides, straight-backed, square-shouldered, somehow graceful in spite of the limp.

10

THE PROFESSOR HAD SNEAKED up on him, thought David; as far as education was concerned he had sure sneaked up on him. It had begun way back when he was in the hospital the first time, right after the accident. The Prof had brought him picture books with just enough text within his power of reading to make them intelligible, then brought him harder ones to make him curious. There were rewards and surprises when he learned to put words together by letters and meaning. Some spelling he learned by rote so that he memorized "height" and "weight" and was roared at in an inside-a-hospital roar when he couldn't understand why "wait" and "weight" sounded the same and "late" was pronounced like both, while height was something else again.

Damned smart, these Danes, thought David, and smiled, there in the train heading toward his examinations for the scholarship he had been maneuvered into over the years.

He remembered that after he left the hospital at last, his leg straight and stiff in a cast, Gramp beside him in the back seat of Ambrose Jefferson's taxi, the Prof let up for a while, giving him time to adjust and be happy with Stumpy and the Timmins kids across the road and, at night, with Gramp. The cast was shortened gradually, and when his knee was freed and a metal peg set in the sole of the shorter cast he was able to go back to school, but by that time the term was nearly over and he was ahead of his classmates. Except in arithmetic. Everyone, even Gramp, had sweat with him in arithmetic.

He started going to the Professor's house for lessons the first summer after the accident. It was the first time he had ever been inside a white person's home. He did not like it much, he decided. Only the staircase with its long curving banister appealed to him. It would be better to slide down than the rickety old metal slide in the school playground.

Shyness paralyzed his tongue that first morning in the high-ceilinged study on the first floor, and he sat, straight and scared, on the edge of the chair by the Prof's desk, his good leg wound around the chair's leg. This big man sitting at the desk was never, never, never the man whose beard he had pulled irreverently, crowing with laughter at the howls of mock anguish. This man was a stranger in a strange world, and he, David Champlin, wanted to go home. Fast.

The Professor had roared his refusal of money or of services in exchange for his teaching; but David knew, when he was older, that the sessions had cost Gramp just the same, because Li'l Joe had paid Ambrose to pick him up each day at Pop and Emma Jefferson's house where he had been left by Gramp in the morning, and where he was picked up by Gramp in the evening. He did not know when or how he had absorbed the knowledge that you took anything a white offered, but meticulously paid your own people; it was something you just knew. But always there was the exception: the

Professor. One day the Prof had said to him: "You said once when you were very small, while your grandmother was still alive—your grandfather has told me of it—'The Prof is white, but he's not New Orleans white.' For that, young David, you will always be loved."

Gramp didn't baby him in those days. Gramp sure as hell didn't baby him because he was hurt. Heck, sometimes it seemed like Gramp was tougher on him then than he had ever been, but there were times when he would see something in Li'l Joe's eyes that brought him thump-thumping across the room to climb on the thin knees and scrootch close to the thin hard chest as he had done when he wasn't any more than what Gramp called "nothin' but a li'l piece of a chile."

Uncle Evan came over often in those days, almost a stranger at first because before the accident they had seldom seen him. Uncle Evan fascinated him, brother to the father he had never seen. Everyone told him Evan and his father were as different as two brothers could be. Evan was black, almost jet black, heavy-shouldered, bullnecked, short, his face sullen and unsmiling most of the time, marred by two evil-looking scars. John, they said, had been tall and brown-skin, with wide shoulders and a fine figure, and had laughed and smiled a lot. Evan was in trouble most of the time, John seldom, because, they said: "John, your daddy, he got along with everyone, black *or* white. He didn't fight with no one less'n they got on to him real bad, rather walk away from a fight; but John he never *run* away from no fights; he could take care of hisself if he had to. Evan, now, seems like he's always sticking his neck out, getting hisself on spots he's got to fight to get off of."

Evan was clumsy looking, the muscles of a boxer beginning to lard up with fat, but he was quicker than a cat with his fists and even quicker with a knife. There must have been a couple of times he hadn't been quick enough, David would think, looking at the scars on his face. David knew, but never told Gramp that he knew, of the knife Evan carried with him; he'd seen it one day when his uncle brought out the contents of a pocket, searching for something. He slid it back so quickly David scarcely saw the movement, but after that he was always conscious that the knife was there.

The old punching bag Uncle Evan brought was hung on the back porch. When Evan showed up with a pair of boxing gloves for him, Gramp displayed rare emotion toward his only living child. "Sure nice of you, Evan," he said. "Them gloves is new." Then his eyes clouded. "Where'd you get the money?"

"I got 'em honest," said Uncle Evan. "I got 'em honest. You got no call to look like that. We got no kids of our own and if we wants to do it, ain't no one's business, even yourn."

When Evan shadowboxed for David, the heavy clumsiness disappeared. He was as quick and fast with his feet and hands as Stumpy when he was playing with a wad of paper, throwing it into the air, catching it. When his uncle used the punching bag, David watched in awed silence as it became blurred and formless under the speed of the black fists. The first time David tried, the bag knocked him down, and Evan showed him how to use it, starting easy as a beginner, and how to compensate for the lack of balance his stiff ankle caused. "Ain't nothing too bad about a gimpy leg," he said. "You get them shoulders strong, get that little belly good and hard, and you learns to react quick, shucks, boy, you ain't never gonna have to worry. You going to be a fine big man like your daddy was. Ain't no one gonna be able to pick on you, nossir!"

As his leg grew stronger he pitched on the five-man Timmins baseball team—the Timmins Terrors they called themselves—and when it was his turn at bat, the oldest Timmins girl ran for him. Gramp used to watch them on Sundays, and when Gramp was watching he pitched as hard and mean as he could, and for a long time his nickname around the house was "Satch."

Now, an aging seventeen, he thought he must sure have been a trial to Gramp, always wanting something, usually getting it, but getting his share of discipline too. He remembered one Sunday when his leg was still in a cast he had begged Gramp to take him to the movies. "Gramp, can I go to the cartoon? Can I, Gramp? Huh? Can I go to the Mickey Mouse?" And Gramp, tired and wanting to rest, had finally said, "Reckon so, boy. Reckon Gramp can carry you up them stairs."

"I can walk 'em, Gramp. Honest. Please, Gramp. I can walk 'em."

"Mighty long flight, boy. Nev' mind. Gramp'll take you, you wants to go all that bad."

Later, at the theatre, when he had struggled up the first few steps on the way to "nigger heaven," refusing help, Gramp said: "Don't act foolish, son. Let Gramp take you up them steps. You gonna hurt yourself, you don't let Li'l Joe help you." Then suddenly he found himself in the air, picked up by strong big arms, looking into a smiling black face he had never seen before. The man almost ran up the stairs with him, and David remembered laughing aloud at something the man said about "li'l black angels *as*cend up." Gramp had thanked the man, who laughed and went away, and they never saw him again.

Kids were selfish, he thought now. But when Gramp took him fishing and hunting in the country back of Mandeville where Li'l Joe had gone to stay with his auntie sometimes when he was a kid, Gramp enjoyed it as much as he did. Gramp showed him crab netting, and shrimping, and they came home with rabbits and possums, and river catfish with meat as sweet and white as any fish in the world. He'd bet there wasn't anything as good anywhere in any city in the world as river cat the way Gramp fixed it.

The white world, except for that part of it inhabited by the Professor, was remote, and without much interest to him. The white family who had lived down the road when he was little moved away, and Zeke Jones's relatives moved in, and then the neighborhood was all his own people. Sometimes some white family would call Gramp to do a job of work, and if Gramp felt like it he'd do it if he had the time. He took David along now and then in the little piece of a car he'd picked up from one of the men who used to come "visit" Miz Timmins, one of a succession of visitors David had given up trying to keep track of. All he knew then was that things picked up at the Timminses when there'd been a visitor around; sometimes there was steak and the kids blossomed out in new suits and shoes and dresses, and the oldest, after one visitation, got braces on her teeth. Now, a sophisticated seventeen, he smiled at the memory, thinking of the visitors and at the same time of the parade of Timmins children, starched, scrubbed, marching two by two to Sunday school. When Gramp took him with him on the jobs he did for whites now and then, the whites always went out of their way to be nice to a little lame black boy, smiling, patting his head, making him squirm as his own people never did. These were foreigners.

"Don't you never let me catch you asking for nothing," Gramp said. "I catch you begging or asking for something I'll whup you good; I'll tear you apart if I catch you."

"Yes, sir."

The dimness of the train became less as a man several seats in front snapped on the reading light above him, picked his way carefully over the feet of his seat companion, then came sleepily down the aisle toward the men's room. The man's eyes were half closed, and David thought he smelled liquor. He could hear a low, hoarse, half-awake humming: "Gloryland." Miz Timmins sang "Gloryland" all the time around the house until the kids made fun of her. He remembered the first time he'd ever heard it. He and Gramp were in church, Gramp on Gram's insistence. Miz Jones, old Zeke Jones's daughter-in-law, was at the piano and Gram was in the choir, really letting out. They sang "Gloryland," and he could see the little brown boy that had been himself sitting beside Gramp, black head bobbing, small body bouncing in time to the music, feet that couldn't quite make the floor knocking together to the beat, thin hands clapping. Then suddenly the boy had been way up there over everyone's head, in Gloryland itself, like a kite on a golden cord, and the cord was the music and Gram's voice.

When they got home from church he was still in Gloryland, still singing, and Gram said, "Tell 'em 'bout it, baby!" and he walked around the kitchen singing it with Gram and Gramp clapping it out for him. After dinner Gramp got out his banjo, and Gram played piano and they sang hymns until Miz Timmins and the whole Timmins tribe came from across the road to sing with them.

After he got out of the hospital Gramp taught him basic chords on the banjo, and also on the guitar that he sometimes played, and later on the old piano that still stood against the wall in the dining room. He learned rapidly, and then Miz Jones from down the road took over and gave him piano lessons. After a year he and Gramp were really swinging, Gramp so small and gentle in every way except for his touch on the banjo, a hard, insistent, running touch that could drive a band like a good drummer's beat. Listening to him a few nights before he left, David thought, It's as if everything inside of him only comes out when he plays.

He was restless by midnight, and got up and went toward the rear of the car, looking for the porter, for someone to talk to, and found Henry Sampson in the drawing room of the car, head tilted against the window, mouth half open, snoring gently. David sighed in disappointment and meandered down to the men's room, where he washed his face and peered closely into the mirror. He decided he didn't need a shave, and grinned derisively at his reflection. "You're sure an optimist," he told it. "Long about Wednesday you can start worrying."

He almost wished now, swaying in the dimly lit, fusty men's room, that arrangements had been made for him to travel to Pengard with Nehemiah Wilson, instead of the plan to space their visits two weeks apart. The Professor had told him four weeks ago that Nehemiah also had been chosen as a candidate for a Pengard scholarship. "Do you know this boy, this Nehemiah Wilson?" the Professor asked.

"Ne'miah? Sure. Him and me—"

"David."

A grin, then, "He and I was in—"

"David!"

The grin became a laugh. "Shucks, Prof, I was kidding. Just getting you upsetted, like Gramp says."

"*As* Gramp says."

"That's what I said."

"No, you did not. You said 'like Gramp says.'" The Professor's eyebrows were twitching balefully.

"Oh. Well, gosh, maybe I did. 'As Gramp says.' O.K.?"

"O.K."

"Gee! Even Gramp gets on me. He keeps saying, 'You ain't saying it right. Maybe I don't talk like I should, like your Tant'Irene tried to teach me, but that don't mean you can't learn better."

The Professor's finger shot out. "Remember," he said, "always remember that the way your grandfather speaks is a good way; it is not bad; it does not make him any less a man, and the way he speaks is often clearer, more meaningful because it is the speech of a folk who have learned to handle words as they do musical notes, in their own way. Do you understand?"

"Yes, sir. Sure I do."

"I 'get on' you, David, because I am thinking of the future. You have not changed your mind? You must still study law, become a lawyer?"

"Yes, sir. Why? You think now I shouldn't?" He was nervous; it would be a real bring-down if the Prof withdrew approval now of the career he'd chosen.

"No! No! For God's sake, no! You should, you must. It is something of which I am very proud, that of your own accord you have chosen law. It means I have done my work well. You were young, David, very young, when you made the choice; young and round-eyed and scrubbed."

David remembered. The Professor had taught him history, not by dates and detail, but by stories and anecdotes, weaving them together in what he saw now was a well-planned pattern. "The first man to be shot in the war that freed your country was a Negro, David. Your people do not think of it as 'our country' the way the whites do. But it is, David; it very much is. And some day it must give to you—to your people—their birthright. But you will have to fight first. It will not be a pretty fight; it is never a pretty fight when a man must battle for what is rightfully his."

"But look—look—" David had said, sitting as tall as he could in the straight chair by the desk. "The Constitution. You done shown me—I mean, you showed me what it says 'bout citizens and how they all got—all have a voice, and how they have rights. If it's the law, like it says there, why we have to fight?"

That had been the beginning, and out of that had grown the realization—nurtured, coaxed along by the Professor like a budding plant—that the battles must be fought on many fronts but that only the battle fought and won on the front of the law would be a lasting victory. The Professor said he had "made the choice." It hadn't been a "choice," he thought that day when they discussed Nehemiah; it hadn't been of his choosing, it had been the only thing, and he never gave a thought to any other calling.

The Prof had been curious about Nehemiah, and brought the conversation back to him. *"Ja!"* said the Prof. "Now we go back to where we were. He of whom we were speaking—"

"Hey, Prof! No fair. You gave me a little book, remember? On English. And it kept saying 'keep it simple.' Gee! 'He of whom—' "

"Just getting you upsetted. Now. Back to Nehemiah."

"Well, he and I were in school together till they moved back over the river to New Orleans. His daddy's a preacher, a real ripsnorting gospel shouter. He starts to preach real low and slow, quiet as anything; then the first thing you know he's sort of singing it, and then everyone starts answering and clapping their hands and stomping and joining in. I mean he's really swinging, up there in that pulpit. Does what Gramp calls 'carries a man.' Ne'miah's kinda like him."

"That is so?" Knudsen's red-gray, bushy eyebrows arched.

"I have not seen the boy. It is not what I would have expected of a prodigy in mathematics. What does he look like?"

"He's a monkeyman. Black. I mean real black. Small. Gets real excited over things. Got a sort of high, squeaky voice like his daddy's until he gets worked up. Then he really lets out."

"You were good friends?"

David shook his head. "Not exactly. I mean we never did run around together much. I see him now and then."

What he did not tell the Prof was that Nehemiah's bitterness was deep and corrosive, and Gramp had said of him: "He's bound for trouble, that boy, if'n he don't learn to get along. Man don't have to crawl on his belly to get along but he's got to learn to take things as they is. He sure as hell ain't gonna change 'em none, popping off like he does, not down here. They's other ways of getting back at 'em."

David knew the wellspring of Nehemiah's bitterness. Gramp told him recently. Ne'miah's daddy was a musician years ago, a bass player, and he and Gramp played gigs together sometimes, back in the Cajun country where the kids jigged in front of the band while the men were tuning up, crying, "Play, nigger! Play, nigger!" and where once, at the end of the night when the band was leaving, a bunch of drunken dancers—"wimmens, too"—threw the bloated, decayed body of a dog into the truck as it started off—"laughing like a bunch of Goddamned hyenas"—and where earlier that same evening someone had snatched the trumpet player's new Panama from his head and stomped it into the mud, yelling, "Ain't no nigger going to wear a hat as good as mine—"

"Me," said Gramp, "I never did go back there no more. Some of the others did, when they needed money real bad. I been hungry, son; I been really hungry, gone hungry so's my kids could eat, but I ain't never been that hungry."

He told David that Nehemiah's daddy had been one of those who had gone back now and again, and sometimes taken his handsome black wife along because she had relatives living in the town where they played the oftenest and she could visit with them while the band was working. The third time he brought her she took the fancy of the sheriff in the town, and he "enticed" her into the jailhouse on the excuse of a phone message for her husband. "She hadn't more'n got inside the door when she caught on," said Gramp.

But when she turned to run, the sheriff dragged her inside and into a cell, then beat her into frightened silence and raped her. "She's a real good woman," said Gramp. "She didn't want no part, not *no* part of that red-neck ofay bastard, but it didn't make no difference. That bastard, he told what he'd do to Nehemiah's daddy did she tell him; told her how he'd fix her husband so's he wouldn't be no good to her or any other woman, so's she'd come crawling to him for what her husband couldn't give her. Said he'd fix it with the New Orleans po-lice to get him back up there on some charge or other. Every time they went up there after that the sheriff was waiting for her. The other mens in the band, they knew, but they didn't dast say anything, and Ne'miah's daddy he didn't catch on for a few times. When he found out he didn't blame her none, but he mighty near went out of his mind thinking how he'd been standing there playing his bass all night and what was going on in the jailhouse." Gramp had paused in telling the story, shaken his head slowly, said, "Lawd!" and then gone on. "You seen Ne'miah's big brother? So damned light he could pass most anywhere. Don't know how Ne'miah found out about it less'n he heard his folks or some big-mouth talking about it."

The night following the Professor's news that Nehemiah was being considered for a scholarship, Nehemiah called him and they met the following afternoon over Cokes in a juke joint. "How come you're even thinking about a white college?" asked David.

Nehemiah shrugged shoulders too wide for the short body. "You know a better way to be as smart as they are, learn how to cut 'em?"

"Never thought about it just like that."

"Start thinking, man. Don't see how being smart in math's going to help, but there'll be a way. Those ofays ain't going to be on top always."

David wondered why he left the ofay epithet unqualified. It had always been a mystery to him how anyone as filled with evangelistic fervor as Preacher Wilson's son could fall so easily into the biological obscenities so common among others of his people. Nehemiah, thought David, knew more damned dirty, really dirty, phrases than anyone else his size and weight, and bigger, in all New Orleans. Yet Nehemiah, once the spirit got hold of him, could outpreach and outshout his own daddy. David had heard him do it, even when he was a kid in Sunday school, and then, after it was over, the little boy, the blackest kid in all the Sunday school, would break up and cry like a crazy girl.

"I'm taking everything the bastards will give me," he said the afternoon they met. "And what they ain't giving me, I'm getting somehow. They want to educate me, that's fine. Just fine. Time's going to come they'll wish they hadn't. What you going up there for? What you planning to do?"

"Law."

"Yeah? Jeez, man, that's the stuff. That's the stuff to yense 'em with. By the time you get it all down, get through law school, the bells will be ringing; yessir, they'll be ringing."

"For church?" David had learned how to needle Nehemiah along.

Nehemiah's teeth flashed white in the deep blackness of his face. "Yeah, for church." He slapped an open palm on the table-top in rhythm to his words: "Come-to-Jesus-and-*git*-yo'-guns—"

"Your old man feel like that?"

"My daddy? Hell, no. Or if he does he buttons his lip about it. He's got nonviolent ideas, my old man has, most of the time. Maybe it was different when he was young. That's what we got to do, David."

"What?"

"Stay young. Don't ever let ourselves get old and beat and scared like they are."

Rudy Lopez was really the cat he wished was with him on this trip. He and Rudy had done just about everything together since they were kids, everything but study, because all Rudy wanted to learn was the insides of motors. Lying back there in his chair on the train, he could see Rudy plain as day: tall, thin, with light reddish skin peppered with freckles, and reddish hair as nappy as David's black hair, and the features of his white father. Rudy was the grandson of Miz Jones, the great-grandson of old Zeke Jones. Miz Jones had raised him. No one knew where his mother, Miz Jones's daughter was, but everyone knew where his father was: all over the damned place, a big shot in parish politics, always making speeches, pulling strings, always talking about how he loved the "good niggers," how much he was doing for them ("free paint for their privies," Gramp said), screaming for tighter segregation, screaming for the laws to be strengthened that separated black from white, laws David knew were fashioned on the old Bienville Black Code—screaming, screaming, screaming. And the silent, hating screams, the loud, obscene screams—David knew them now as fear.

Thinking of Lopez, he could hear Rudy saying, "That's my pappy, that's my daddy, that's my old man, that's my li'l ol' daddy, and I wish to God they'd cut his balls off before he was ten." Without that nappy hair, the tinge of brownish red underlying the freckles, Rudy could have passed. And wouldn't, he said. "Not if you was to string me up by the thumbs and pull my toenails out one by one, I wouldn't. It's bad enough being half white, looking like 'em. If I got close as passing maybe I'd start acting like 'em, thinking like 'em. Then I'd go to hell for sure."

He and Rudy discovered sex at about the same time, and David supposed that all kids when they found out about sex—really found out about it, not just fooled around—thought they'd discovered it. "It's been going on a long time," Gramp said, and smiled, and David had the feeling Gramp knew a hell of a lot about it, even if he did look as innocent as a li'l ol' lamb. Gramp said: "Had a white doctor I done some work for say a funny thing to me once. Asked me why it was colored could start in so young and keep going so long. 'How come?' he sez, and I told him I didn't know. He said he was damned if he could figure it out, speaking as a doctor." Gramp shook his head. "Them whites worries theirselves sick about us and sex. Had their way they'd de-ball us all, only then there wouldn't be no new generation coming along to do the dirty work for 'em, no new colored they could teach their kids to feel soo-preme about."

Edna Mae, the girl next door that Gram had called "the devil's own," was mistress of ceremonies at David's initiation. Looking back on it, he had to admit she'd been a good one, slipping in and listening, quiet, while Miz Jones was giving him a piano lesson, sticking around after Miz Jones left, drinking lemonade with him, one leg over the arm of Gramp's chair, no pants on, showing everything she had while he sat on the divan, averting his eyes at first, then finally doing what he was being invited to do—enjoying it. He couldn't understand what a nineteen-year-old girl wanted with a shy fourteen-year-old; but when he confided in Rudy he found that Rudy's mentor had been a grown woman in New Orleans—near forty, Rudy said, and what *she* knew was a shame. Man! he was glad he hadn't picked himself some rabbity li'l ol' girl his own age, he said; man learned something, really learned something with a real woman, and listening to him David felt chagrined and brought down, and didn't brag as much after that when they compared notes.

There was a twinge of remorse now when he remembered how sex had messed him up for a while. Lawd! It had been all he could think about. The Prof had been understanding about his neglecting his studies, even tried to straighten him out some. Gramp had known about it just by being around without being told anything, and had raised a sand. Not because he was carrying on—"You a man now; been worried if you hadn't"—but because the carrying on was with the girl next door. "That's too close for comfort," Gramp said. "Too damned close. Spose she gets herself knocked up—"

"She won't." David wasn't able to keep the pride from his voice, felt every inch the man Gramp said he was. "She knows how to take care of herself."

"Goose balls!" said Gramp. "Ain't *no* woman all that smart. You find yourself someone else, y'hear! Don't go messin' with the neighbors."

Edna Mae and he had split up, not because of anything Gramp said but because she got a job over the river in New Orleans. He had it rough for a while with jealousy because someone told him she had taken up with a gambler, a big shot, way older than she was. She got herself a car and new clothes and a wristwatch, and came over to Beauregard only now and then to see her mother. Then she was home all the time for a while; then she took to staying away over the river again. Every time she was in Beauregard she came over to the house, even when Gramp was there, but David didn't want any part of her now. "There's plenty more," Rudy had said. "Tail's one thing New Orleans is plumb full of." And been right.

He wished again that it had been Rudy instead of Nehemiah who'd been the one to go to Pengard. Probably the other colored guys there would be a bunch of uppity northern Negroes, and sometimes, going by those he'd met, he couldn't say but what they were damned near as bad as whites, maybe worse, and all the time the real colored, the down-home colored, were laughing at them.

It wasn't that Nehemiah wasn't a good guy, but he got so damned excited about everything. Wore a man out. And you couldn't talk about anything with Nehemiah it didn't end up in race. Not that sooner or later every conversation with anyone didn't wind up in race, only it got there quicker with

Nehemiah. But with everyone, from sex, from music, from car engines, no matter what, talk always wound up in race. It was the same with the old folks; only difference was, they talked about it in an accepting kind of way. Even Gramp and his musician friends dwelt on incidents that wouldn't have happened, wouldn't have lived in their memories if race hadn't accounted for them.

He didn't remember his grandmother too well, the woman Gramp still talked about as though she had just stepped into the next room, but he did remember her bitterness and some of the things she used to say, and the memories of her bitterness and the love she had wrapped around a small boy were somehow intermingled, as though the bitterness grew from the love and the love from the bitterness.

He knew it wasn't just the kids, the little kids like he had been the first time a white boy called him a "nigger bastard" and he'd asked "Why?" The old folks asked it too. Isaiah Watkins—David could hear him now, sitting in the front room, talking to Gramp—said once, "Why in hell we got to get so much hate, Li'l Joe? We ain't got all that hate, at least, most of us ain't. Good Godalmighty, Li'l Joe, I ain't got the stren'th to tote it round. You coming to the ALEC meeting, Li'l Joe?"

"Have to see has I got a gig, 'Saiah."

"Damn it, y'all ought to come, gig or no gig. We needs everyone we can get, Li'l Joe. We got a lot of young folks coming along. We needs the older folks too."

"Let you know, 'Saiah. Man has to make his bread. I pays my dues."

"Takes more'n money, Li'l Joe. And one of these days, and it ain't too far off, it's going to take a hell of a lot more'n money."

"Blood," said Gramp.

"You saying it, Li'l Joe. You the one saying it."

"Seen a lot of it in my time, 'Saiah. Seen plenty. Seen my own cousin when he wasn't more'n eleven year old shot dead on purpose by a white boy. Over back of Mandeville it was, and no one moved a hand against that white boy, nary a hand. Seen the blood that day. Seen it since. Came damned close to killing me a white boy that day, but they helt me back. Red blood on brown skin. It ain't pretty."

"Sure ain't." Isaiah was walking around now: David could hear him, the heavy, limping step. Isaiah was younger than Gramp by a few years, a big man, heavy set, almost fat, with a congenital hip defect. When he walked the defect made him swing his protuberant, oversized buttocks in almost a complete half circle. He spoke again, and David could tell he was talking from behind the cigar that was his trademark all over New Orleans. "Sure ain't. And green grass in a public park can't no brown-skin child set foot on is downright ugly. That blood goes away, and the man it run out of mebbe he dies or gets better and it's all forgot. But there ain't no forgetting li'l black kids being held down, ev'ry day, ev'ry day, *ev*'ry day. You don't want to get busy for yourself, you better get busy for that boy, Li'l Joe."

The "Why?" was never answered, whether it was asked by the kids or the older folks. Maybe, thought David, the reason the question "Why?" bothered him so much was that "Why?" was one of the Prof's big things in teaching him. "Why—why—why!" Knudsen would thunder. "Ask it of everything your mind touches, and let your mind touch everything!"

He couldn't remember when it was Gramp had said, "You a lucky boy. You got any idea how lucky you is?"

"I—well—I guess so—"

"You know what it means, David, colored boy like you learning from a famous Professor? Having him to help you? I ain't saying there ain't other colored jes as smart as you are, mebbe smarter. I'm jes saying you lucky. The brains they got going to rot down here like mine done."

"Gramp!" He always hated it when Gramp ran himself down.

"Shucks, ain't no sense not saying it. Me, I been working ever since I was in the third grade. Never did make it through the next. My ma tried to teach me, but Lawd, you Tant'Irene, she was working seven days a week, sunup to sundown, sometimes half the night, making twelve dollars a month. She tried, tried her best, but she never could get me to even speak good like she done." There was sternness in Gramp's face when he added, "But you been lucky. You take care, y'hear!"

"What you mean?"

"Man pays for his luck, son. Man pays for it, one way or another. Your Tant'Irene say, 'You pays for your pretties.' You be mighty sure you let the good Lord know you thanks Him. Ain't many had it lucky as you. . . . And don't go to looking at that cast on your leg. That ain't nothing. That ain't nothing compared to having a cast on your mind like us colored has had since we was born down here. And still having.

Ain't no gimpy leg gonna hold a man back has he got education and learning." The sternness left Gramp's face. "Ain't no black skin gonna hold him back neither if'n he gets outa here —less'n he lets it." David could remember, even now, the gleam of the moisture in Gramp's eyes. "You gonna go way from here one of these days, son."

"No, I ain't, Gramp. I mean, no, I'm not."

"Yes, you is, baby; yes, you is. I knows that."

Gramp almost never called him "baby," only when love and fear crowded him and it slipped out.

"You wrong, Gramp. You sure wrong about that."

After that he didn't take things for granted so much. Gramp's words stayed with him. What was he going to have to pay, and when? He looked around and saw the truth of Gramp's words, realized them, young as he was, and felt a strange, abstract guilt. Remembering it, he knew it was not the solid guilt he'd feel for playing hooky to go swimming, or staying away from a session with the Prof for a toss in the hay with Edna Mae, but guilt for something that just was, and for which he had no responsibility. He mentioned it to Gramp, who said: "You ain't got no call to feel guilty. That's foolishness. Ain't no man guilty for something he can't help. I didn't mean you was to feel bad about it. Reckon if it wasn't right for you to have it, the good God wouldn't have give it to you. Jes you keep it in mind things ain't always gonna be like this. Get yourself ready to pay up. Shucks! Ain't no call to feel guilty."

He did, though, no matter what Gramp said.

11

LOOKING BACK, DAVID COULD SEE that the Professor had sneaked up on him in the matter of the scholarship just as he had in the matter of preliminary education and that the scholarship to Pengard had always been the big man's goal for him.

He was ten years old the first time he met the Prof's brother, Dr. Karl Knudsen, head of the Mathematics Department at the Ohio college. The Prof explained that the "doctor" was an academic degree and had been used at first only to avoid confusion when there had been yet another, unrelated, Knudsen at Pengard. "It has stuck," the Prof said. "Now I am afraid he is 'Doc' to them all."

David tried to describe the Prof's brother to Gramp. "He's so *little,"* he said. "I don't believe he's the Prof's brother, honest I don't. I never seen—saw—two people so different." He struggled for a comparison, came up with: "You know that li'l piece of a dog the Joneses got? They calls it a wired hair? That's what he's like, Gramp, except his hair stands up straight all over and grows every whichaway." As David grew older and met Karl Knudsen on subsequent visits, he understood better what the Prof meant when he said, "Overgrown pixies, that is what some people call the Danes."

The summer he was eight, David fixed himself a shoeshine kit, working on it secretly so he could surprise Gramp with his first money earned away from home. The first day he took it out, after Gramp had left for work, he went to the corner of Petra and St. Anne streets in Beauregard, instead of to the Timminses. It was close to the ferry slip bus stop, and he knew there would be a lot of people. He made two dollars that day, shining shoes, doing it right, the way Gramp had taught him to shine his own. That night he showed the kit and the money to Gramp, proud. Gramp's face broke in two the way it always did when he smiled, and then, suddenly, the smile was gone and Gramp took the kit away from him and put it on a high shelf in the kitchen.

Surprise and disappointment silenced him for a minute. When he spoke his voice was high and querulous with hurt. "Why'd you take it away, Gramp? Why?"

"We finds you something else—"

"Gramps! You done it! You told me you was shining shoes when you was five. And I'm *eight!"* Newly learned grammar was washed away in the tide of emotion.

"I know, son, I know. I done a lot of things to make a penny."

"But I *likes* it, Gramp! And you said, you said a jillion times about earning money. Gimme back my box, Gramp!"

"You ain't gonna get a right understanding of this, not now, not till you grows up and maybe has a chile of your own. But I never was one to tell a chile 'no' and not tell him 'why.' Ain't no job a man should feel shame for doing if it's honest and he does it good as he knows how—"

"Gramp, lemme do it for a while. Please, Gramp."

"If you'd asked me could you go to shining shoes I'd of said 'sure'—"

"I wanted to sur*prise* you, Gramp."

"I knows that, David. I ain't faulting you for not asking. I'd of said 'yes' if you'd asked. But when I seen you with that shoeshine box something ris up in my insides. I ain't going to argue, son."

"It was *fun*—"

"Said I ain't going to argue. How many colored you shine shoes for?"

"A couple. The first was Bucky Harris from 'cross the road. He said he'd start me off. He give me two bits."

"The rest was whites?"

David nodded. "I—I guess so."

"How many of them whites rub your head?"

David ran long, thin fingers over hair cropped close to his scalp. "I—I don't remember. Maybe three—four—"

"Sure, sure," said Gramp. "Figured it'd bring 'em luck, like finding a pin or seeing a white horse. And you smiled real big, and I bet they tipped you good."

Again David nodded. "They was O.K., Gramp—"

"I dunno, David. Seems like the good Lord's waking me up too late for breakfast. But you ain't getting down on your knees and shining whites' shoes, and you ain't gonna do what I done when I was a kid, kissing white asses for a nickel or a dime. I never done it when I got bigger; you ain't gonna do it no time. You got to work for 'em; hell, a man can't be a damned fool and starve to death, but when you works for 'em it'll be because they *needs* what they pays for, not because they want to rub a li'l black boy's head and see him grin. Your gram was what they calls extreme, but she wasn't wrongheaded all the way."

A day or so later David knew that his grandfather was trying to soften the disappointment when he said, "I know one guy you can fix up with a nice shine, son. Your gramp."

"Shine 'em your own self."

Quick anger flared in Gramp's eyes. "You ain't so big you can't still get a good licking, not showing respeck—"

David turned, sulking, and scuffled his way to the back door, not slamming it because Gramp gave a licking the way he played banjo—hard. He sat on the back steps watching the chickens Gramp was too mush-hearted to kill and eat, scratching Stumpy's head, feeling sorry for himself.

As time went on, he found other jobs to do in the summer and on weekends: delivering finished wash for Miz Emma's sister, helping one of Gramp's friends, Slim Sims, in his little grocery store near the house, and, when he was older, working as helper on a laundry truck. If any of the work he found to do threatened to take time from his studying, Gramp raised such a sand he had to quit. He gave a large share of the money he made to Gramp, and God only knew what Gramp did with it; that he "put it up" somewhere David was sure. When he could he bought his own clothes, and Gramp taught him to smell out a bargain, and tried to keep him from buying flashy, foolish things.

One thing he and Li'l Joe always managed to find time to do was what Li'l Joe called "make music." Lately Li'l Joe had sometimes taken him along on playing dates at the clubs, and during the last year or two, when there wasn't anyone from the union around, he had played a little solo piano between sets, fumble-fingered with stage fright at first, then letting the music carry him over his nervousness. Most of the time he played as Gramp and Miz Jones had taught him, but sometimes he worked it over differently, like the music he and Rudy listened to on records and in juke joints, fooling with the chords, making them say something different, until Gramp got on him. "You young uns wants to mess with stuff like that, showing off, all that stuff they calls 'far out,' that's your business. Gawd knows, it sounds like hell to me, all them chords, thirteenths and Gawd knows what—getting so far away from a good tune can't no one tell what it is after the intro. But that ain't what the folks come to this place to listen to."

When Bjarne Knudsen first started mentioning Quimby scholarships with a sort of fierce casualness, David shied away. He didn't know a great deal about scholarships, except that they were something you had to be a near genius, maybe a full genius, to get and he knew for sure he wasn't either of those. It scared him when the Prof said, "Once you are at college, David, you will be glad I have been hard on you in Latin—" Actually, thought David, the Prof hadn't been hard on him in Latin; he had made ancient history of such absorbing interest that an ancient language became easy because the desire to learn it was strong. He didn't say this; might as well let the Prof feel apologetic if he wanted. He told the Prof he wanted to learn Greek, too, and the Prof grinned wolfishly into his beard and said, "Ah! That is good," and added that usually Greek was not permitted in the first year, but because of his grounding in Latin they might make an exception. With his eyes blazing with indignation, the Professor told him that Pengard was one of the few colleges left in the country where ancient Greek was taught and where students were encouraged to study it.

It was during one of Dr. Knudsen's visits to his brother that he got the real information about Quimby scholarships. A "Quimby," he learned, was confined to Pengard college, and was reserved for Negro students of marked intellectual promise.

"Why Negroes, sir?" he asked.

The Professor's roar came before his quieter brother could reply. "Chips!" he said. "My God, chips! How often must I say it, David! Keep the chips from your shoulders. There are those, many of them, who will not take up the challenge to knock them off!"

"Do not shout at the boy, Bjarne. You have chips on your own shoulders about the chips on his shoulders." The doctor turned to David. "Horace Quimby is an old man, a very old man. His father founded Pengard and gave it his mother's family name. In fact, Dr. Quimby is president emeritus, but we still call him president. He is a wealthy man, a very wealthy man, through the death of his wife. It is unfortunate that wealth should be so important. President Quimby is a great man in his own right, and much loved by faculty members. The actual president is a young man, and must think of things like science buildings and a new lab building and modern dormitories. And always, I am sure, the directors and the young president must carry in their minds the picture of an old man living in a big house on the edge of a lake, a very old man who controls millions of dollars. But Quimby believes that a college, even his own, must, like a person, earn what it receives, must receive money from outside sources as well, in recognition of worth. He gives what you call 'cagily.'" The little professor smiled. "It is a fine college, David. I know of no better this side of the Atlantic for freedom of thought, of action, for the questing mind to find its answers for itself, yet be guided by gentle discipline. You will like it. For prelaw work it cannot be equaled."

David squirmed nervously. "I—I'm not there yet." It

would be nice if these two guys would let him decide for himself. They hadn't really answered his question, and now he said: "Has he given anything to Negro colleges? They need it, they really need it, they're scratching for pennies—"

"Perhaps he has," said Dr. Knudsen. "I do not know. I do know he dislikes very much the terms 'white' and 'Negro' colleges. He feels it is almost a sacrilege to differentiate institutions of learning by such labels. I agree. Learning must be universal or it is not true learning."

David smiled politely, knowing it was a smile that always irritated the Professor because he recognized it as a mask, and knew that behind it a mind was working on things with which the smile had nothing to do.

It was all right, he thought, it was fine, just fine, for these two men to talk. Next to Gramp he supposed he liked the Professor better than anyone else he knew. Sometimes the liking came close to love, and the Professor was the only white person with whom he had ever discussed race. Not with any other white would he talk as he had talked with the Prof, but there were doors that were closed even to the Prof, dark vaults in his mind that this man he came close to loving could never enter. Even a brown-skin boy not yet in college, thought David, knew the difference between the world of theory and principle in which the Prof and his brother lived and the world his own dark face confronted.

"You must decide for yourself, David," the Prof was saying. "Remember, if you will, what I have tried to teach you: the long view, the view that takes in generations, not just years."

"Yes, sir," said David. "I see what you mean." And did not see, not then, but now, in a train on the way to Pengard, was just beginning to see.

When Li'l Joe was told about the scholarship, he did one of his double takes, the quick, wide smile, then the concerned frown. "It's up to you, son. Like I say, you a man now. But you sure you wants to go up there? Go to a white college? Trying to study and learn among them white boys, all the time wondering, worrying about 'em, what they going to do? You sure you wouldn't be happier, do better with your own? You needs to study 'bout it, boy, before you decides."

"I been studying about it, Gramp. A scholarship means it's free, mostly."

"We ain't broke. I got a few pennies put up."

"I can get a job; I'm sure I can. The Prof says a lot of the guys have jobs."

"You ain't gonna get no job if it's gonna mess up your studying, learning. I told you, we ain't broke."

"It won't. First thing, I guess, is to find out if I'm smart enough to get accepted."

"You smart enough. Thing is, you sure you wants it?"

"I can handle it, Gramp. Been living with a white world all my life, haven't I?"

They were eating supper. David had cooked it because he was starving, and wanted to eat as soon as Gramp came home. There were stuffed crabs and stuffed artichokes, red beans from the day before, rice. Now Gramp, comfortably full, leaned back and patted his stomach appreciatively. "Taking my job away from me, son." He lit a cigarette, spooned prodigious amounts of sugar into his coffee, tasted the coffee tentatively, added a little more sugar, and went on. "You been living *with* a white world all your life, but you ain't been living *in* it. They's a difference. We lives in one world; they lives in another. Never could go all the way with your gram, not wanting you to even have to work for 'em. Hell, that don't make no sense at all; they got all the money, all the jobs, all the power. Thing is, though, you moving right *into* their world. And that's something they don't want. Nohow. How many colored they got there in that collidge?"

"The Prof says maybe a dozen or a little more. That's in all classes. They want more. And the Prof says there's no segregation. Not in the dormitories or the classes or even in the town."

"You colored boys going to look like a bunch of lonesome fleas floatin' in a pan of milk. How many head of kids they got there, all told?"

"Maybe couple of thousand."

Gramp was quiet for a moment, then elaborately casual. "They got wimmens up there?"

"It's co-educational."

"You ain't answered my question."

"It means they've got girl students too."

Suddenly Li'l Joe Champlin's voice sharpened. "You steer clear, y'hear!"

David gave an involuntary start at Gramp's quick sharpness. "My gosh, Gramp! Did I say I wouldn't? Don't get so excited."

"It's no good."

"What's no good?"

"Pork meat," said Gramp bluntly.

David's sideways glance was sly and amused. "You speaking from experience?"

"I ain't saying I is and I ain't saying I ain't. What I'm saying is I ain't never knowed one of us what hasn't had the chance was he damn fool enough to take it. You ever hear Kid Arab tell about how they goes after them mens of his when they travels? How they entices 'em? You ever hear them mens of his braggin' about how the white wimmens throws theirselves at 'em?"

"Sure I have. Plenty of times. And I didn't need Kid Arab or any of 'em to tell me. Learned a thing or two myself, right down here. There's a woman where I used to deliver laundry, couple of months ago—I told you about it. See-through nightgowns and negligees, managing to get her hand on me when she took the package—"

"You'd have touched her and someone come along she'd have screamed rape. You'd have been seeing striped moons the rest of your life. *If* you lived—"

"That's what I knows. Shucks, what you think I am? Some kind of a li'l chile? Who wants it? Me, I always thought it would be like messing around with a half-dead fish." Now David's smile was open and wide. "Is it?"

Gramp ignored the smile and the question. "Mebbe you ain't no chile, mebbe you a man now, but you young yet." Obviously his fears were not quieted. "They sure funny people. All the time worried and screaming 'bout their lily-white southern wimmens, scared as a cat in a kennel full of bulldogs. All the time saying they has to keep segregation on account of mixed marriages, getting a lot of mongrels around. Sweet Jesus! What they got now! People passing whose grandaddies were a hell of a lot blacker'n me, and way blacker'n you. Got 'em in high places, too. You never seen your ma, but she was near as light as Rudy. Had freckles, too. Them white men making the most noise, they the ones shacking up with colored wimmen all the time, and their kids running wild being called niggers. Somebody, I disremember who, said all a white woman had to do if she didn't want to marry colored was to say 'no.' "

"Langston Hughes. Colored author. He's the one who said it."

"Well, he saying it right. He sure saying it right. What they scared of? I knows. You knows. Their own wimmens. That's what they scared of. Marriage ain't rape, and the rape they hollering so loud about ain't a thing in the world but what comes of segregation. And there's damned little of what they calls rape that's really rape. I knows."

David stood up and pushed his chair back, still smiling. "Bet you do, Gramp. Bet you know a hell of a lot more'n what you're saying. But for gosh sake, quit worrying. I keep telling you, I'm not interested. Period. Look, I'll do the dishes when I get back. I got a movie date with a girl. She's green with red spots. That O.K.?"

"Be better was she black," grumbled Gramp, unsoothed.

The Professor's advice, the day before David took the bus for Cincinnati, was different. "You must not be like the old maid who looks under the bed every night, David."

"Say that again, Prof?"

"I have never known whether the old maid hoped she'd find a man or was afraid she would. You know what I mean. Do not look so puzzled. You must not see prejudice, which you live with every day in New Orleans, everywhere. It will be in many places, even there, but it will not be everywhere. Do not look under the bed for it when something happens or something is said that would have happened or been said whatever your color."

"O.K., Prof, I'll try. But like—as—Gramp says, it's better to be safe than sorry. I'm not pushing myself."

"My God! This I must see. *Ja!* This I must see. David Champlin pushing himself. You are damned near as shy today, my boy, as the first time you sat over there, one leg in a cast and the other wound around the chair leg like a rubber band. You remember? You are still that boy grown only a little older. When the great day comes, David, that you push yourself, you must let Bjarne Knudsen know."

Now, in the train with sleep catching up with him, David thought: "I wasn't shy in that Goddamned bus, not after I got my senses back after that minchy-mouthed red-neck wouldn't let me off."

The Professor had walked to the door with him the day before, and repeated his earlier words. "Remember, you are not to see things under the bed. They will not always be there."

That, thought David just before sleep obliterated his thoughts, that I have to see; that they gotta prove.

12

When he left the train at Laurel, he stood for a moment on the platform, movement arrested by the scent of a spring he had never experienced. Spring did not come like this to New Orleans: cold crispness with warmth beneath it, new grass a faint green mist over open ground, trees not quite budded yet showing pale promise, defying the patches of gray snow that lay in the crooks of their trunks and on the ground in shady places, the sap of the trees restlessly stirring. The feel of its stirring was in his own body, disturbing and exhilarating.

And then Dr. Knudsen was there, bustling, talking, his hair rising in islands of spiky disorder, triumphant over brush and comb and water. David had called him from the Cincinnati station and explained his early arrival by saying that he had changed his mind and taken a train instead of a bus. Knudsen had told him there was a train to Laurel in a matter of minutes and, miraculously, he had made it.

When they were in the car and driving off, the doctor said, "We had planned that you would stay with us: *Ja.* But our niece arrived yesterday. With a broken arm." He clucked and shook his head. "She was alone because her father is on a trip and she called us and we told her to come at once. It is not a bad break but there is a cast. She lives outside of Chicago."

David was sorry for anyone with a broken bone, anyone, white or colored, but he felt a surge of relief over not staying at the doctor's. How in hell would they have worked it? Have him eat in the kitchen with the cook or maybe go out to meals? Now that he had arrived he felt dubious about all this talk about integration in the town and college. There was bound to be a Negro boardinghouse somewhere in the town where he could relax and feel at home. As they drove he could see Negroes working in yards, maids shaking dust mops from windows and porches, men in a work crew repairing the road.

"You will stay at the Inn." The words penetrated his thoughts slowly, then left him disturbed and fearful. What in hell was the "Inn"? It sounded white, and he wondered if the doctor knew what he was doing. It also sounded expensive, and his money would just barely hold out for three days in a cheap boardinghouse. The car slowed and stopped. *"Ja,"* said the doctor. "We are here. I will go in with you."

You'd better, thought David. Sweet Jesus! You'd better go in with me. Or stay on the porch and catch me on the way past when they heave me out.

He followed the other up broad steps, across a wide porch, and through massive, graceful doors. The lobby had once been the central hallway of a converted mansion, and there was still the aura of another age about it. He was walking very straight and tall, eyes masked and wary, defenses bristling.

Karl Knudsen was talking to a man behind a counter in the far left corner of the lobby beyond a wide, arched entrance to a lounge. The man swung a book toward David, looking at him coolly with no welcome in his eyes. He did not speak. David signed the book and wondered, smarting under the clerk's cold disapproval, if he ought to write "Colored" after his name, then heard a voice beside him that warmed and strengthened him. He turned and saw a youth of about his own age, and of his own complexion, wearing tan slacks and a light-blue, brass-buttoned uniform jacket. "I'll get your bag upstairs, show you the way," the boy said.

"Ah, Randall!" Dr. Knudsen gripped the boy's shoulder, shook it gently. "You did not go home for vacation?"

The boy called Randall smiled. "No, sir. Needed the bread."

"Slang!" barked Knudsen, then turned to David. "A fellow Pengardian, David. Randall, this is David Champlin— Randall is a sophomore, David. Only slightly retarded."

David shook hands with Randall, heard Knudsen saying, "Straight A's. *Ja.* Straight A's. Only one A-minus to show his weakness."

"Can't win 'em all," said Randall. "You coming up with us, Doc?"

"We are going to eat first, if there is food."

"It can be arranged." The man behind the desk did not

smile. "I do what I'm paid to do," the narrowed, cold eyes seemed to be saying.

"See you later, Champlin," said Randall.

Throughout a gargantuan breakfast—its probable cost making David shudder inwardly—the little doctor talked almost without stopping. David learned that if he was accepted he would be known as "Champlin," although, Knudsen said, he himself would probably call him "David" because he had known him first as a leggy ten-year-old. He also learned that the college kept a loose rein on students and that students were aided in finding jobs if they needed them, either on or off campus. There were no restrictions on weekend leaves, but there was an eleven-o'clock week-night curfew, Monday through Thursday. Liquor was not allowed on campus, but a strange astigmatism prevailed where beer was concerned. "We can do it like this because we are so small," said Knudsen. "And because we are so careful. Our students come to learn. If they do not—there are other colleges and universities—"

Many of the things Dr. Knudsen said did not sink in. David was nervous and edgy. They were alone in the smallish dining room except for a middle-aged white couple sitting across the room at a table against the wall. Whenever he glanced at them they were either eating or talking, but David felt that, whenever he was not looking at them, their eyes were fixed on him. It was a real bomb that Dr. Knudsen tossed when he said: "You see that couple sitting across the room? She is on the board of directors of our local NAACP chapter. Her husband is vice-president. He holds the chair of anthropology. If you are lucky you will be in his class next year. I will see what I can do."

I'll be damned, thought David. I mean, I'll really be damned, a couple of honest-to-God white northern liberals like you read about. And with only one head apiece, yet. He looked over at the doctor, saw that he was smiling, and surprised in the blue eyes the same warmth that so frequently animated the eyes of the Prof in New Orleans. "See?" said the doctor. "As my brother said—'chips.' I saw them. Wear them for the stupid clerk. Discard them for others."

"Yes, sir—" said David, and tried to smile, then was distracted when the waitress presented the check and Dr. Knudsen scrawled his signature across it. "When you eat your meals here, David, sign your name to the check. Your room, of course, is paid for. You did not know? *Ja.* My brother was to tell you. We have an arrangement here for scholarship applicants during our remodeling period, while we are short of dormitory space."

David was thankful his room was paid for, but he was damned if he'd walk into that dining room alone, NAACP directors, anthropology professors or not. For every one of those, there could be ten fuming racists, and he wasn't about to take any chances.

In the lobby the doctor said, "At four, either my wife or I will pick you up. This morning I arranged your first interview for four thirty. Latin. Afterward you will have dinner with us."

"I will? I mean—thanks, only I don't want—"

"At four."

He followed Randall to a small room under the eaves on the top floor. When they were inside, he said, "What kind of a place is this?"

"Good," said Randall. "It's O.K. most of the time. Hell, for a cat just coming out of the South, it'll seem like getting out of jail."

"Where you from?"

"Philadelphia. And that place doesn't smell like roses, either. I had some adjusting to do. Look, take it easy. Some of the colored guys hole up and don't have anything to do with anyone, and some of them throw their weight around, and either way it's not good. Most of the students are all right. Some of them stink. Where would you find it different? The faculty's O.K. Most of it. You have to feel your own way."

"What about the town? Man, that dining room gives me fits. Suppose I want a sandwich or a Coke or something?"

Randall shrugged. "Any place you want. This Inn was Crow for years. I guess ever since it opened way back when. Then the faculty boycotted it; most of the students went along and had their parents stay at the hotel across the square. The Inn saw the light. Same with the Coke and juke joints and hamburger places. Enough of the students gave 'em a bad time to make 'em change their minds. A real quiet cash register's a mighty moving thing. Influencing."

This guy must know what he's talking about, thought David. But he wasn't taking too many chances. There were bound to be, had to be, what Gramp called "traps for the unwiry."

The doctor's wife was walking through the front doorway

of the Inn just as David reached the bottom of the wide curving staircase that afternoon. Her first words were a commonplace greeting, and David felt surprise because he had taken it for granted that she would be Danish. But hers was a strictly American accent, of a region he could not identify, and his guard went up instantly. She was a tall woman; must be, he thought, a good two inches taller than her husband, with curling light brown hair touched with gray, and clear, direct, gray-blue eyes. She was wearing a short Mackintosh-type jacket and plaid skirt. Her handshake was crisp, firm, and unavoidable. The car she led him to was an elderly Plymouth four-door. She went to the far side, slid beneath the wheel, and reached across the front seat to release the lock of the right-hand door.

David wondered if she had noticed that his hand had been on the handle of the rear door. *Act like you would was you down here. That way you can't get in no trouble. Smell out the land first.* Gramp had said that to him. Still, he couldn't ignore the door to the front that she had pushed open. "Best car we ever had," she was saying. "We won it in a raffle and it makes us practically the only two-car family in the faculty."

They swung away from the Inn and she drove first around the central square of the town, pointing out buildings and landmarks he knew he'd forget as soon as they were left behind. They passed the Inn at the end of the circuit and continued on a broad tree-lined street from which they did not turn and which, after the first mile, became less thickly lined with houses, until finally it was almost a rural road with mailboxes at the sides.

"My husband told you that we're expecting you for dinner?"

"Yes, ma'am. It's sure nice—"

"Nonsense. You'll be company for Sara. That's our niece. Not our real niece, our courtesy niece. Her mother and I were childhood friends and then roommates at Smith. She died three years ago. We claim Sara gladly. She has a sister living in Brazil, and her father flew down there a few days ago. On the way home from the airport her taxi was in an accident and she broke her arm, poor pet. She'll be entering Pengard when you do, next fall."

He could feel his guard lowering, not all the way, just enough so that his replies were made in normal tones. The car slowed and she said, "On your right—" and he turned and saw a big white house of turn-of-the-century vintage. A sign hanging from the roof of the porch proclaimed MOM'S.

"When we can't find a student anywhere on campus, we inquire at Mom's first. Fried chicken and spareribs. They raise their own chicks and I don't know where they get the ribs, but they're the best you've ever tasted. And inexpensive. It's closed now for spring vacation."

He could see ahead, on their left, the cluster of buildings that must be the campus, and behind the buildings there were glimpses of blue water through the trees. "Laurel Lake," said Mrs. Knudsen. "And very beautiful. Some of the hardier swim in late spring."

David had poured over so many pictures in Pengard catalogues that he had little trouble identifying many of the buildings: the Infirmary just inside the entrance to the campus, on their right; the dormitories lining two sides of a quadrangle whose far end was framed by the recreation hall and student dining hall. He knew that beyond the main quadrangle was another, smaller one formed by classroom buildings and the administration building. On this day scaffolds hung against the walls of several dormitories, piles of brick and lumber obstructed the sidewalks, and in two places, one on each side of the main quadrangle's broad, grassy center, new buildings were going up.

"We're trying desperately to expand without enlarging," said Mrs. Knudsen. "It's a neat trick if you can do it. There will be two new dorms in the fall, and remodeling of the old ones. The place is an architectural hash, but we hope to improve it gradually."

In the classroom-building area they stopped in front of a gray two-story fieldstone building. "Here we are, David Champlin. Your first interview. Room Ten. Don't let it worry you, please. Andrus is a pet, truly. From all I've heard you'll be what my husband calls 'right out of his kitchen cupboard.' We live over thataway and we'll be expecting you any time at all." She gave him explicit directions, then stopped quickly and said, "We'll pick you up," and David knew she had remembered his gimpy leg.

"No, ma'am. You forget about me until I get there. That's no walk at all."

When he left Room Ten more than an hour later, he felt drained and empty, and recognized the feeling as relief. Randall had said to him, "Don't let this interview with Andrus spook you. He's O.K. If you walked in there with three heads, each one a different color, he wouldn't be anything but happy as long as each head knew Latin."

Half an hour after entering Andrus's study, some of the meaning of a remark by the Prof began to sink in, not wholly accepted, yet not totally rejected as it had been when the Doc first made it. "There is only one color in which most of your instructors will be interested: gray. *Ja!* Gray. The gray of that unpleasant-looking, spongy material within your skull." Before the interview was an hour old, David had been given a cup of tea, which he was too nervous to drink, and some pretty God-awful cookies, had discussed some hitherto unexplored reasons for the decline of the Roman Empire, and had translated without too much difficulty a short essay in Latin that the tall, pale, angular professor had himself written. At the close of the translation, which he was required to do verbally, Andrus said, "Professor Bjarne Knudsen was your tutor, was he not? The brother of our Dr. Knudsen?"

"Yes, sir."

"Of course." Andrus's smile was a thin and reserved one, but it had its own peculiar warmth. "A young man from our Deep South who speaks Latin with a Danish accent. No matter. This can be easily corrected. You will be well ahead of your class, Champlin." Andrus sighed. "Well ahead. Is there a subject you'd like to add?"

"Well, sir." David hesitated. He didn't want this guy to think he was showboating. "If I could, I mean if it's all right, I'd like to take Greek."

"Greek, eh? Do you know the language at all?"

"No, sir. Just the alphabet. I learned it for kicks once."

"Learned it for kicks! Good God!"

David felt ill at ease, embarrassed, his cheeks hot. "I—I'm not a freak, sir. You know, a—a prodigy. Only, I had a lot of time every now and then because I had to be in the hospital a lot and all. I'm lousy—very bad—in math, and, well, I'm not too good in physics, and I was lazy and so I guess I did what came easiest."

When he rose to leave, Andrus came to the door with him and laid a thin hand on his shoulder. David sensed the gesture was an unusual one for this man. "Don't worry about Greek, Champlin," said the professor. "I'm sure it can be arranged. I will talk with Dr. Knudsen. He will be your faculty adviser, I understand. The dean's approval must be obtained, of course. It can all be arranged, I feel sure." He shook his head, and again the thin smile appeared. "And to think, to think, you did not quote at me once. I suffer excruciatingly at the hands of would-be students who quote at me. I say 'at me' advisedly. Most of them could not translate adequately what they quote, but quote they must. Until later, Champlin. Tell Dr. Knudsen I am pleased."

As he walked to the Knudsens', David kept telling himself: "Take it easy, Champlin; take it easy. They won't all be like that one. Don't get cocky—"

The Knudsen home was an undistinguished gray frame house with white trim and a wide, old-fashioned porch. There had to be large, shabby, comfortable rooms inside, both upstairs and down, and it was not until he reached the door that David felt the inner withdrawal, the fear and the resentment at the fear, and the simple, sick perplexity of the question: Should he have gone to the rear?

As he stood uncertain and wavering, the door opened so suddenly that he took an involuntary step backward. A clear, rather high voice said, "You're David Champlin. Hello—" He looked down toward the source of the voice and found it in a small girl whose short, close cap of gleaming brown hair came to a spot well below his shoulder and whose dark, intense eyes were wide in a stare of unabashed and unashamed curiosity. His own eyes widened in surprise. He had thought the Knudsens were childless. Then he noticed that the splash of kelly-green silk he had taken for a scarf was actually a sling for a forearm in a plaster cast. This must be the niece, and if it was, she looked a long way from being old enough to go to college. The hand she held out was so tiny the palm of his own could bound it, and when he closed his fingers only a small thumb showed, pink and white against the brown of his skin.

"Come in, for goodness' sake. I'm Sara. Sara Kent, and we've been waiting for you, just busting with curiosity." In the background he heard Mrs. Knudsen's voice. "Is he alive and well, Sara? Bring him in."

He followed the small figure with the ridiculous kelly-green arm sling across a wide hall covered with soft-toned throw rugs toward an arched doorway on their right. Although the girl ahead of him was actually walking, it seemed to David that she was half running, half skipping, like a child, and he quickened his step.

Bookshelves lined the open spaces of the living-room walls; there was a pleasing clutter of miscellaneous objects on the flat surfaces of tables; some of the chairs were ancient and of wicker, with cushions covered with faded chintz. A huge old-fashioned divan faced a fire of just the right intensity for a cool early spring night.

"Sherry, David?" Dr. Knudsen had appeared from a room under the stairway at the rear of the entrance hall and was holding out a small tray of sherry-filled glasses. David stifled a sigh. He loathed sherry. It turned his stomach; there wasn't anything that came out of a bottle he hated more than sherry, but he'd seen enough movies and read enough books to know that it was some damned ceremonial sort of thing with a lot of people like these, and he forced a smile and said, "Yes, sir. Thank you."

"It went well, David? Your interview with Andrus?" asked the doctor.

Sara was sitting, legs curled beneath her, in a corner of the divan, and now she leaned forward and tugged his jacket gently. "Sit," she said. "For gosh sake don't just stand there. Sit and tell us about it."

Dr. Knudsen had turned to place the tray on a table near the fireplace, and Mrs. Knudsen was arranging two chairs so they would all be facing one another. He lowered himself gingerly to the edge of the divan, and as he did so thought fleetingly of Gramp. He'd die, he told himself; Gramp would plumb die if he saw me; probably grab me by the ear and haul me out. Then Sara Kent's hand, small as a child's, reached out and gently took his sherry glass from him. "I can tell you loathe it," she whispered, and he turned and grinned down at her gratefully, started to speak and found silence clogging his throat, something smothering his mind. He looked away quickly.

Dr. and Mrs. Knudsen were seated now, the doctor leaning forward, hair and eyes both seeming alive with interest. "Come, David. Tell us of it." Then when David finished, "He is human our Andrus."

"Yes, sir. At least, I thought so. I was sort of nervous—"

"He offered you tea and cookies? Did you eat them?"

"One, sir."

"Good. Good. More and we might not have had the pleasure of your company. His wife makes them. Probably from an ancient Roman recipe. Dreadful things, but offered only to those whom he likes. You are hungry now. Nerves plus relief spell hunger for a young stomach. Eve, shall we eat?"

The doctor led the way to the dining room across the hall,

and Sara walked beside David and again he had the feeling that though her feet were going through the motions of walking something inside her was running, skipping, something so vital and electric her small body could not quite contain it.

Soup came first, from an old-fashioned tureen in front of Mrs. Knudsen. There was a tureen just like it, or nearly so, on their sideboard at home; only, Gramp used it for spare safety pins, thumbtacks, and Scotch tape; and an old rubber ball and some jacks were in it that he had played with when he was a kid. He was waiting, from habit, for someone to ask the blessing when he realized Mrs. Knudsen was ladling out the soup and there would be no blessing. As he started to eat he thanked silently and with fervor his Tant'Irene for teaching her son, Li'l Joe Champlin, the manners she had learned, the manners she had taught the white children in the homes where she had worked throughout her life, and he thanked with equal fervor her son for passing those lessons along to his grandson. Right now he could feel in retrospect the sharp rap of a knife or fork handle on his knuckles, and he carefully spooned his soup away from him as he had been taught.

Then, for no reason he could find, his complacency cracked and then shattered. In place of the memory of Gramp's teachings he heard Nehemiah and Rudy and a half-dozen others of his friends, heard in his mind what they would be saying if they saw him now, and could have read his mind a second ago. "Bootlicking, ass kissing—Uncle Tom, Jr.—white man's pet puppy, ain't you now—" Hell, those were mild. Nehemiah would have reached down into that store of biological oddities he had in his mind and come up with some beauts. Almost defiantly he tilted his soup plate the wrong way and spooned the last mouthful toward him and then wished he hadn't been childish. Damn, he wasn't any of those things; not any of them, yet misery took hold of him because of the knowledge that he might be and not know it.

A question from Dr. Knudsen brought his attention back sharply. It was about food and the proper preparation of it, and was a continuation of discussions held a long time ago in the Prof's study, when Gramp had been there. He was in definite disagreement now with the doctor, and found himself arguing with intensity, and in a hidden corner of his mind was surprised at his own temerity. "Not thyme?" said the doctor. "*Not* thyme," said David firmly. "Bay leaf."

When they finished the meal David felt well fed and almost relaxed; would have felt completely relaxed were it not for the ghosts of Nehemiah and Rudy and the others peering from the corners of the room. It had been a good meal; not, thought David judiciously, as interesting as one of Gramp's, or even one of his own, but passable.

Sara pushed back her chair and stood up. "Dishes," she said. "It's one of the rewards of being young. David will help, won't you, David? He can wash; we'll stack 'em in the drainer and pour boiling water over 'em. I'll put them away later."

Mrs. Knudsen turned to David. "I'm sorry, David. She's overcompensating for her plaster cast."

"I'd like to. Honest. Honestly, Mrs. Knudsen."

David scraped and Sara rinsed, holding the dishes under scalding water from the faucet; then David took over, hands and forearms deep in suds.

"Want to bet Uncle Karl went rushing to the study to call Professor Andrus?" asked Sara.

"To call—oh, gosh!"

"You mustn't worry. I'm not scholarship but I took regular entrance exams early—last Christmas. I was interviewed by scads and scads. And Andrus just sort of glared at me and said my declensions were very poor and he 'hoped' I'd do well. As though I had some incurable disease or something. Do you know any of the other students?"

"No. Yes. One. From New Orleans. He's a mathematics whiz kid."

"Wait. With an odd name—from the Bible—"

"Ne'miah. Ne'miah Wilson."

"Uncle Karl told us. He's coming up later. I won't be here. I don't know a single one, not one except little Tommy Evans; only, he hates to be called 'little Tommy.' So I don't because I think it's mean if someone doesn't like a nickname to use it, even if you grew up together. Have you got a nickname, even if you don't like it?"

"No. Everyone's always called me David. Even my grandfather." He grinned, remembering. "Once in a while, when I was growing up, someone would call me 'Dave' or 'Davey,' and Gramp would say 'Chile's named David.' "

"Even your mother?"

"I don't have a mother. She died when I was born. My father died before I was born."

He was holding the gravy boat under the hot-water faucet,

and when he turned off the water the room was so quiet he could hear the clock ticking over the sink. He looked down at Sara, into a small, unhappy face, eyes wide and dark with distress.

"David! Oh, David— Gosh, that's—that's awful. You were an—a *full* orphan when you were born, and I've been a half-orphan for three years and feel sorry for myself. David, that's terrible."

She's not phony, he thought; whatever else she may be she's not phony; she's hurting inside; she's honest-to-God hurting inside thinking about it, feeling it. "It's not all that bad," he said. "My grandfather and grandmother brought me up; at least until my grandmother died. After that it was just Gramp."

"He's super."

"Who?" It was hard keeping up with this pint-sized kid.

"Your grandfather. Who else? Uncle Karl told us about him."

"He's just a li'l guy, just an ordinary li'l guy. Maybe a hundred pounds with his pockets full of nails. He's sure been good to me, though. All hundred pounds. Sure been good."

Then she was singing. She had a high, clear voice, not strong, but true in pitch and tone and rhythm, and David turned, hands still in sudsy water, and stared as she sang: " 'Lord, Lord, Lord, you sure been good to me! Lord, Lord, Lord, you sure been good to me. . . . Saved my soul from sinandshame—' "

It was white singing but it was good. He let her finish the first verse. "Where'd you learn that? My gram used to sing it."

"My father. He's got, I'll bet you, just about every record that ever was made of every Negro spiritual and blues and early jazz. I mean *every*. Bessie Smith and Ma Rainey and Chippie Hill and King Oliver and—oh, gosh, all of them."

"You like it? It's sort of old-fashioned now—I mean—"

There you are again, David, there you are again, off by yourself, a brown boy in a white world where people just love you to pieces because you're a Negro or hate you to death because you're a Negro and they collect the records of your people and the songs you went to sleep by because you're—what the hell are you?—a folk, maybe. Because you're a folk and different, your people were different. But the songs they collect are the songs of another generation that wasn't going anywhere because it couldn't, and maybe that's why they like the songs, because they reassure them. But it wasn't true now, not like it used to be—

Sara was saying: "You mean you think I ought to like bop and Kenton and progressive—stuff like that? Well, I do. I really do, only I like the older music better because it sort of says something and you can sing it. You know what my father says? He says the young generation of Negroes is making a terrible mistake, turning away from what was beautiful in the greatest art form, the only real art form—that's what *he* calls it—America ever had. So there."

It was always better when a white came right out and acknowledged you as a Negro, didn't skirt around the subject and try to pretend you weren't, the way some people, even his own, tried to pretend they didn't know he had a gimpy leg.

"Maybe he's right," said David, thinking of Rudy and how Rudy sometimes low-rated his piano playing. "But I guess every generation has to have its say," he added sententiously.

"Tom Evans agrees with father and me. He comes over to the house all the time to play records."

David let a handful of silver slide very slowly into its groove in the dish drainer. He let it slide slowly because he wanted to throw it in with all his strength. Who in hell was this guy Tom Evans? Some ofay kid who must live in her town and who goes to her house and listens to records and raves over "Negro art forms." God damn him and her and her record-collecting old man to hell and let him, David Champlin, get back home as quick as he could. "Little Tommy Evans." Probably some pasty-faced brat, white as a biscuit, with a crew cut and horn-rimmed glasses and an earnest handshake and earnest moist eyes who could tell you what Jelly Roll Morton's first words had been in the cradle and who, when he came to New Orleans, liked to come to the back rooms of the clubs and meet the musicians; and as far as he, David Champlin, was concerned, he hoped they'd all do what Gram was always wishing for 'em, fry in hell forever. Sara was still talking, and he wished she'd shut up. He smiled. "I'll just put the drainer in the sink and pour boiling water over them. Then I'll dry."

"Nope. Just pour the water and leave 'em lay." She smiled up at him. "That's what we always do. Basically, Aunt Eve and I are lazy."

After that, until they finished, he let her do the talking, and in his present mood he couldn't see that what she said amounted to anything. As they entered the living room they surprised Dr. Knudsen in a yawn, and it gave David what he was looking for: the chance to say he'd better be leaving.

"To be rested for tomorrow, eh?" said the doctor. "There is one interview you can omit from your list. The dean. Dean Goodhue. His wife just called, and he was taken to the hospital this afternoon for an emergency removal of his appendix. You must wait to talk with him until after you enter. He will accept the combined judgments of your interviewers."

The doctor drove him back to the Inn and he spoke his piece, said his "thank yous" prettily, as Gramp and Gram had taught him, then hurried up the stairs without looking back.

He closed the door of his room softly, in case there were others sleeping on the same floor. It was all too mixed up and confusing. Whether it was bad or not, he'd be one of the students Randall had said "holed up." That was the best way. What in hell was he there for anyway? To get his hand compulsively shaken by more whites so far than he'd just about met in his whole life, or to prepare for a law course? A guy didn't have to bother about Crow in New Orleans because it was always there, but here you had to sniff it out, go round like a damned ol' houn' dawg with your nose twitching. There hadn't been much of it so far, he'd hand 'em that, except for an occasional student and the day clerk on duty at the Inn desk who made him feel when he and the doctor went into the dining room, as though he were a typhoid carrier walking into a nursery full of kids.

Then, because the Professor had taught him that no matter how much he lied to anyone else he could never lie to himself, because to do that killed the intellect, he faced the truth: that he was sick, angry, and brought down, misery bound and disgusted, because of a guy he'd never seen in his life, never heard of until tonight, who lived a thousand miles from New Orleans and spent a lot of time listening to race records at a dame's house he, David Champlin, would never get to see inside of. A white dame, and as far as he was concerned if he never saw her again or any other white chick all the time he was at Pengard it would be all right with him. Her and her sympathy and her "David! Oh, David, that's terrible—" and why in hell was Gramp so worried about it anyway? Couldn't he give his own grandson credit for having a little sense, just a *little* sense?

After the ease of the Andrus interview some of the others made him feel as he had when he was a kid and fell out of bed in the middle of the night: shaken up. After they had talked a while and he'd done some verbal translations, Andrus hadn't bothered with a written examination; the others weren't so trusting. He took his mathematics examination with two white boys in Dr. Knudsen's classroom, and was thankful that one of the others was as bad as he was. After it was over and he was ready to crawl under a desk, Knudsen said, "Don't worry, David. As Randall said—you can't win them all."

Because he realized his money wasn't going to hold out forever, he finally started eating breakfast and dinner in the hotel dining room, gritting his teeth every time he walked in, getting up way early in the morning so there wouldn't be anyone else there, and eating dinner early in the evening for the same reason.

On the day he left, Mrs. Knudsen drove him to Cincinnati. Sara Kent sat between them, talking, thought David, like a damned parakeet chit-chittering away in a cage. Mrs. Knudsen had called and said she and Sara were going into the city to spend the night with friends and do some shopping the next day. He tried unsuccessfully to back away from the invitation.

"It's a poky old train," said Mrs. Knudsen. "And you'll have another poky old ride to New Orleans on top of it. Say four thirty?"

They were on a cutoff road that wound through low, tree-studded hills, when Sara finally stopped talking and asking the questions he had been trying to answer politely and briefly. All this "interest" was just so much crap, he thought, and the less he responded without being rude, the better. Mrs. Knudsen was saying: "Things are so different after classes start. Everything is in such dead earnest; at least, for us. We don't dare see too much of any one student because there mustn't be any playing favorites. That's why we're so delighted to have these in-between visits."

"I don't see why things should be all that different," said Sara. "Not with David, anyhow. Gosh, he's practically a relative."

She'd better have left the crack unsaid, thought David. "Practically a relative!" He almost snorted out loud. She was another one of these whites who gushed and palavered and sweet-talked you to death because you were a Negro, who went to the other extreme. Mrs. Knudsen's remark about "playing favorites" could sure as hell be just a polite way of saying, "Look, boy, it's all right in vacation, when the college is practically empty, but, well, during the rest of the time it won't quite do. Negro students for dinner and driving around with us and all that. So don't expect it." Not that he gave a damn. Did they think he wasn't in "dead earnest" too? He wasn't going to have any time, not any time at all, for what Gramp called "socializing." Particularly not with any damned whites.

Sara was talking again, and a phrase, a word, knifed into his thoughts. ". . . and you'll like Tom Evans even if he does look as though he ought to be playing with alphabet blocks instead of studying. When he and Gwen get married—and I guess they will someday because they've been planning on it ever since they both really were playing with blocks—the minister will probably pat his head, Tom's head, and—"

Mrs. Knudsen broke in. "Sara, you must try and realize that other people don't know always what or whom you're talking about, and explain things as you go along. Gwen, David, is Sara's oldest and best friend; Tom Evans, as you must have gathered, is Gwen's 'steady.' They all grew up together. Tom will be in your class. Gwen is going to her mother's college, Vassar. Sara would have gotten to all this eventually, but it might have taken us into Cincinnati."

David hoped, almost prayed, that they hadn't heard that breath leave his lungs. He'd tried to hold it back. It couldn't make all that much difference, the difference between a silly, chattering parakeet of a silly little dame, and a girl who was so alive and vital and sort of reaching out, running in her mind toward something, feeling things so strongly that she was somehow inside you when you talked to her. Just the knowledge that another guy in another city was going steady with a girl named Gwen—it couldn't make all that difference—

He turned to look out the window on his right, not turning just his head but his shoulders and body as well, to free them from the soft, warm feel of her cashmere coat, the sense of flesh beneath it. He pointed to a gleam of silver-gray in the distance. "Is that another lake?"

"No," said Eve Knudsen. "That's the first glimpse of the river. We'll be driving along beside it now for three or four miles."

What had been a gleam and then a sliver of silver-gray grew broader now, could be seen in length, was a wide gray ribbon unwinding. The Ohio. And on the other side, Kentucky. To eyes used to the Mississippi it was not a wide river. Wide enough, he told himself; it's wide enough, Champlin; over here you're "Champlin"; over there you're "David" and "boy"; . . . *'Tis summer, the darkies are ga-a-y.* But it doesn't make any difference, it doesn't matter, he thought desperately; it doesn't matter if you're "Champlin" here and a damned darky over there; the shells of the eggs you're walking on are just as thin here as they are everywhere, and if you forget it you're in trouble, you're sure as hell in trouble; take it easy, Champlin, take it easy and get on home. There's more than a river to cross.

At the station, after David left the car, Eve Knudsen and Sara waited, Eve bent forward, hand on ignition key, Sara leaning from the window. When the tall figure of David Champlin reached the doorway to the terminal, Sara touched the horn button gently and David turned. She waved one small hand frantically and, smiling, he returned the wave; then the doors of the terminal closed behind him and the car started off.

Sara leaned back, stretching slender legs out straight. After a moment she said, "He's nice."

"Isn't he, though! His grandfather must be all that Karl says he is, to bring up a boy like that almost unaided, at least for most of the time."

"I wish I could draw him."

"Why can't you, dear? You have more crayons and paper than a Paris art supply store."

"Because—well, just because I don't think I can. Yet . . . Aunt Eve, why can't I take art first year? It's not fair. It's all I want. It's every blessed thing I want to do."

"We've been over this before, my dear. Because your father wants you to go to Pengard. And he's quite right. I don't believe any artist has ever been severely damaged by a liberal-arts education. And there's no reason why you can't go to summer classes in Chicago. Or Cincinnati."

"I know, but—"

"You can take art, the history of art, art appreciation, all those courses, for three years. A first year devoted to mental groundwork isn't going to hurt you. Why don't you make a sketch of David when we get home? It should be a good practice exercise, even with only one hand available."

"Yes." Sara closed her eyes, her head against the back of the seat. She couldn't explain, even to Aunt Eve, who was a super sort of adult with a super sort of understanding, why sketching David Champlin wouldn't be just a good practice exercise. Because she didn't want to just sketch David Champlin, his features and body, the set of his head and shoulders. She wanted to catch and put on paper (canvas, that was what she really wanted to do, put on canvas) what she had seen when she opened the door the night he came to the house: a tall figure silhouetted against a gray world slipping into the darkness of night, light from the hall behind her falling on the quiet, dark face, the dignity of it, the depth of the wide, dark eyes, wary, perplexed and—and? That was what she wanted to know and catch, that other thing she had seen that was not fear, yet somehow was fear, was not belligerence, but contained belligerence within it, was somehow allied with the dignity. She could find no word for it, yet might, given the training, the skill, be able to capture it so that someone—David—would say, "That's how it is."

Eve Knudsen was saying, "Quite often it's difficult even to remember the features of people we see every day, when they're away. Do you think you'll be able to remember David's?"

Sara did not open her eyes, was silent for a minute.

"Easily," she said. "Easily."

13

UNLESS THE WEATHER WAS subfreezing, the study of Merriwether Goodhue, dean of men at Pengard College, always depended on its open fireplace for heat. The rest of the house depended on an oil furnace, and was warm and comfortable. Goodhue was an Anglophile. "Oppressive," he said of the warmth of the rest of the house. "Stultifies the mental processes." Of his English setter, who usually lay before the fire warming old bones, the students said, "Barks with a British accent."

The room's temperature was bearable to Goodhue because of the shaggy tweeds and pullover sweaters he affected. He still wore Norfolk jackets with leather elbow patches, and his trousers were without creases. His shoes were sturdy and British made. A pipe was seldom more than an arm's length from him, and invariably, when with someone newly met, he drew attention to a patched burnhole in his jacket, caused by absentmindedly placing a still glowing pipe in the pocket.

The only jacket he owned that did not show evidences of having harbored a pipe, by either bagginess of pocket or patched burnhole, was his dinner jacket. When he wore the dinner jacket, the pipe was always in the pocket of his topcoat. Students in attendance at the few combined faculty-student functions where a dinner jacket was called for never failed to find him on a side porch or in the shrubbery, smoking. And being young and filled with wisdom, knew that they had been meant to find him doing just that. "I like a pipe," Goodhue would say with a deprecating smile. "Don't tell on me."

The first student to hit upon his nickname had long since gone on to greater things, but the nickname itself found its way into the vocabularies of both students and faculty members, and he was seldom referred to as anything but "Cozy." He knew of this, and could only be thankful it was no worse; was not, for example, the obvious play on his first name. Better, he told his wife, that it be "Cozy" than "Merry." She had sniffed angrily. "Neither one shows any respect," she said. His wife's voice was syrup laced ever so lightly with acid. She had left Alabama when she was twenty-two, but she clung to every vestige of her origins as though without them she would disintegrate.

The Goodhues, in 1950, had been married twenty-three years. They met at 'Bama. They always called it 'Bama. Their marriage took place two days after graduation, and they left immediately for the North. In the years that followed, neither of them mentioned the stricken horror of her family when their only daughter had married the son of a tenant farmer.

Merriwether Goodhue had been a student of slightly above average ability. He had entered the University of Alabama on a scholarship, and then elected to try for a Master's in English history at Yale. His wife's money financed it. At twenty-one Elacoya Goodhue had come into a trust-fund inheritance. Its income was more than sufficient for a young childless couple, and they spent the first year of their marriage in England, where Goodhue's gradual transformation from the son of a tenant farmer to folksy don began. After they returned, two years at a college in northern New England and indefatigable maneuvering resulted in the post at Pengard.

The Pengard appointment had been made soon after Horace Quimby's retirement to the status of an extraordinarily influential president emeritus, while he was vacationing in Europe, and there was still talk among board members and higher echelon faculty groups of the ex-president's wrath when he heard of it.

There were numerous Pengard faculty teas and get-togethers throughout the year. Two of them came under the heading of what Dana Brooks, professor of English, called "tribal ceremonies." These were the fall and spring teas, the fall tea at the Quimby residence at the edge of the lake, the spring tea at the Goodhue home. The latter was always held on Friday and had been distinguished for a number of years by a certain fish-paste sandwich served for the benefit of Catholic faculty members unable to eat the thinly sliced ham and chicken salad sandwiches.

"There are always cheese and olive. Mine are scrumptious. They do it on purpose." Eve Knudsen was speaking to her husband, Dr. Karl Knudsen, as they walked across the campus on their way to the Goodhues' spring tea.

"Do what?" he asked.

"Have the tea on Friday so Elacoya can serve those abominations and show how broad-minded and understanding they are. If I hear Elacoya Goodhue say one more time 'Those are fish' I shall eat one and then throw it up. On the hooked rug, because that's the hardest to clean."

"This year you may have to throw up twice," said her husband. "We now have the Gottliebs and Steins with us. Elacoya will be saying to the Gibbonses and the Kerrys and Aiellos, 'Those are fish,' and to the Gottliebs and Steins, 'Those are fish and these are chicken.' "

"I can manage," said Eve. "Never think I can't. And without the aid of mustard water yet."

She tightened the knot of the scarf she wore over her short hair with an irritated jerk. "I don't suppose the Beanie Benfords will be there. And I do like them so."

"What makes you think they won't be there?"

"Would you? Would you want to feel that the teacups you drank from were going to be boiled after you left, while the others were just washed with soap and water?"

"You exaggerate, Eve. True, Goodhue's a phony, but—"

"You're naïve, Karl. You've always been naïve. Perhaps it's because you didn't grow up in the land of the free and the home of the brave. It's something one senses like—like—oh, I don't know—a dead mouse in the woodwork."

Although Dean Goodhue spent at least an hour in the process of dressing before the annual spring teas, to make certain the right degree of casualness was obtained, he always managed to carry with him the spirit of the tweed Norfolk jacket and its leather-reinforced elbows, as some military men carry with them, when they are in mufti, the spirit of their medals and decorations. On this day the casualness was perfection itself, even to the lock of hair that straggled almost, but not quite, over one eye.

If, thought Dr. Knudsen, Eve was going to make good her promise to throw up the fish sandwiches on the hooked rug, the least he could do was hold his end up by handing Goodhue a pocket comb. His own bristling hair was beyond help, but Cozy's forelock would comb back nicely. It would, of course, leave him looking like nothing so much as the gangling, big-boned proprietor of a small-town variety store, but Knudsen could not see that this would necessarily be any worse.

This thought sustained him through the hall and into the already crowded living room. He glanced at the door of the study and wondered if, with Cozy's permission, he could manage to slip through it. Goodhue had some rather good first editions in there, and had told him recently of some new ones. Goodhue bought first editions on the advice of a dealer, managing always to give the impression that they were the fruits of long and arduous personal search.

Knudsen heard the rasp of Elacoya's accent near him, like the sound of a file heard through velvet. "Those are fish, my dear. I took special care with them. I hope you'll like them." He turned quickly to throw a cigarette into the fireplace, then poked vigorously at a fire already burning nicely. He would not, actually dared not, look at his wife.

He heard Cozy's voice beside him. "Thanks, old boy. We've had the devil of a time with that chimney this year. Can't think why. Seems to be working splendidly now. I do like a proper blaze." He lowered his voice to a whisper. "Let's pop off to the study. No one will miss us."

As soon as they entered the study Goodhue made a long-armed grab for the pipe that lay in an oversized ashtray at the edge of the eighteenth-century table he used as a desk. While he loaded the pipe, lit it, puffed at it, lit it again, and then tried it out, Knudsen looked with delight at the first editions, held them gently in his hands, then replaced them carefully in their places. He glanced through the text of an early nineteenth-century history of the thirteen original colonies; it was not a first edition, merely an old book, and dry and dull. Goodhue said: "Interesting volume, that. Might be a splendid book to put in the hands of some of our less promising students. Might give them a sense of the real idealism of our founding fathers, change their viewpoint, awaken their interest."

"It is doubtful," said Knudsen. "It is very doubtful. I would fear the opposite effect. Flight, in fact."

Goodhue took the book from Knudsen, caressing it gently with large, bony hands, and Knudsen tried to erase all expression from his face. The book was of no value and was excruciatingly boring.

For a time they discussed common problems concerning students. Of a student who might be forced to drop out before the end of the year because of ill health, Goodhue said, "Pity. A great pity if it happens. I am sure he has many potentials, particularly with that background. I believe there are unsuspected potentials in all young people, if we can but use the right divining rod to find them. It is worth a try at any rate, worth the attempt at salvage."

He was busy with his pipe for a moment, then said: "What about our new Quimby, due in the fall? The protégé of your brother. The boy who came up for interviews when I was in hospital."

"Ja!" said Knudsen. "A find, Dean. A real find."

"You are really impressed?"

"Definitely. I saw the lad for the first time when he was just a child, and then last fall I flew to New Orleans and talked with him twice. I was much impressed. And so were the other faculty members who interviewed him here. There is something about him—something eager. Dedicated, perhaps, although that is a poor word for an untried scholar. But I felt it. *Ja.* I felt it."

"Is he a New Orleans boy? A native-born Louisiana Negro?"

"He was born just across town from my brother's home. Bjarne saw him first when he was only a few days old."

The stem of Goodhue's pipe was directly in the center of his smile and made it unreadable. "He sensed this—this eagerness then?" He removed the pipe so it would not obstruct his quiet laughter at his own wit.

Knudsen did not laugh. "I am quite serious. You will see when he comes here. He is a find. He will bring honor to our gray hairs—and to Pengard—in the years ahead."

"I hope you are right," said Goodhue. "What is his name?"

"Champlin." Knudsen gave it the French pronunciation, as had his brother, and David, and David's grandfather.

There was a sucking, gurgling sound as Goodhue drew on his pipe. His eyebrows were raised in interrogation. "He has another name, no doubt?"

Knudsen frowned. "David," he answered. "David Champlin."

"I grew up with those people," said Goodhue. "I find it hard to adopt the more formal usages." He smiled. "We understand these things better. I am glad he is from the South. The Negroes from the North seem somehow unnatural to me. Negroes from the South, if they are the right sort, have more charm as a rule, more malleability."

Knudsen, who had perched himself like a small, enthusiastic bird on the arm of one of the chairs that flanked the fireplace, did not speak for a moment. His eyes were not on Goodhue when he answered, and his voice was flat and uninflected.

"Ja," he said, and stood. *"Ja.* Well." He walked to the door. "I must find Mrs. Knudsen. I must help her dispose of some of those delicious fish sandwiches your good wife prepares."

14

David Champlin did not hear his grandfather's step coming up the walk. He was sitting in the dining room reading, the heel of his good foot cocked on the edge of the table. He dropped the foot hastily to the floor because Gramp was already on the porch when he heard him, and when Li'l Joe got to the screen door he would be able to see in, through the sitting room to the dining room and kitchen beyond, and would be vexed at the sight of a foot, even his grandson's, on the dining-room table. The light was in David's eyes as he turned and faced the front door. Only after his grandfather had entered the living room was he able to see that there was something in his hands besides his lunch pail, a square something with a handle. He started toward his grandfather, but Li'l Joe brushed past him and went to the kitchen where the tabletop was clear. He put his burden carefully on the table and stood back. "You better shut your door when you use it, son," he said. "I needs my sleep."

David stood without speaking, beyond speech. Beside him a soft voice said: "Ain't you going to open it, son? Don't you want to look and see is it all right?"

David unlatched the cover, raised it gently, and the keys of the portable typewriter seemed to smile up at him. He reached out and touched one, but the carriage did not move, and one of Gramp's long, slender fingers reached out, touching a lever pridefully. "Now try it, son."

David touched another key, then pulled his hand back. It wouldn't be good for the platen, letting the keys hit it without paper in the machine. It would work, he could tell that.

"Gosh, Gramp," he said at last. "Gosh. It's—it's super. It's—it's an awful lot."

"Lawd!" said Gramp. "I can do it. I got a little put by. I could have bought it all at once, only I got it on payments. They're not much. Not enough to hurt. You want to try it?" He moved forward and looked down at the keyboard in frowning concentration, his eyes searching. "That man showed it to me just as plain." He was talking half to himself. "Just as plain as can be, and now I can't find it. It's got—it's got tab—taber—"

"Tabulation," said David. "A tabulator key." He pointed it out. He did not turn his head. He knew his grandfather's eyes were shining so brightly that he would not trust himself to look at them. "They're the best kind, Gramp. The deluxe kind." He paused, then added, "Most expensive kind, too. You—you shouldn't have—"

"Ain't no sense in spending money for something half good," said Joseph Champlin. "Not if you can help it. Figured you might need that tab—taber—that key there. All my life I've had to put up with things half good—or worse'n that, secondhanded. I figured to start you off with something all good, bran-new." He grinned. "Damned near the only real good, bran-new thing ever come through that door. You happy with it, suits me."

"Happy with it!" David was whispering. "Gee, Gramp." He couldn't think of anything to say, hoped Gramp somehow could feel the gratitude, the warmth, the love—but not the lump in his throat.

He closed the lid as gently as a mother covering a sleeping baby and carried the typewriter into the dining room, clearing a place for it on the table. Joseph Champlin went to the sink in the kitchen and started washing up. Through the splashing David could hear the low voice.

"Thought mebbe I'd surprise you and carry it to the train, the day you left. Then I thought"—there was a pause, a louder splashing, a "brr-rr-rr-" and the voice went on—"then I thought that wasn't no good. You going to be mighty busy once you gets up there. You're not going to have no time for fussing and learning anything except your lessons. Did you see, David? It's got a book goes with it, how to teach yourself. You got most all summer to learn when you ain't working or studying. You see it, son? In the cover?"

"I seen it—saw it, Gramp. It's swell. And they've got a night class at the high school. Mostly all girls, but that doesn't matter." He walked to the screen door and looked out. Gramp would know he couldn't talk, couldn't find words.

It could hardly be called air, the heavy, humid outside atmosphere that was coming through the screen door. Behind him there was the quiet whir of the big fan in the window over the kitchen sink. Outside, the little street sweltered, still weighed down with the burden of stale heat from the breathless day that was ending. David walked out on the porch and stood on the top of the steps, hands plunged deep into his pockets.

Across the roadway, which would be soft and sticky from the merciless assault of the earlier sun, the Timmins twins tumbled and played, fat brown bodies dusty from the ground. Their mother would be out in a minute, or one of the older kids, to pick them up, dust them off, scold, paddle plump bottoms briskly but with love. On the porch of the old gray house next to the Timminses', ol' Miz Speck sat, rocking. She would be half asleep, David thought, like a tired child. When her daughter came out and spoke to her gently, she would waken quickly, pretending she had not been dozing. Her daughter would help her to her feet, supporting her into the house, and inside would feed her as Gramp and Gram must once have fed him, with a spoon and coaxing words.

But this evening ol' Miz Speck was more alert; David had been mistaken to think her dozing, for as he looked at her he saw her head crane forward, knew the dark eyes with the gray rings around the irises were trying to focus. He saw one black, gnarled hand raised toward him, could tell the lips were moving over the toothless gums, knew she was saying, "Evenin', evenin', son!" He waved back and called out. "Evenin', Miz Speck! You feeling good this evenin'?" The old head bobbed delightedly, and he could hear her cackle of laughter and the words, like the echo of a strong voice, "Doin' fine, son. Doin' fine for a young un," and the cackle of laughter again.

In a little while Bucky Harris would be coming up the street, bowlegged, heavy with muscle and fat, sweaty, and more than likely roaring drunk; mean drunk and cursing, and there would be another fight in the little shack in the back, between Miz Timmins's house and ol' Miz Speck's house. And, just as probably, the police again. "What's she stay with him for, Gramp?" he had asked Li'l Joe Champlin. "What's a woman want to stay with a man like that for?" Gramp had shrugged. "Gawd knows, son. No telling what makes a woman stay with a man. She ain't no better than what he is, though. I can tell you that. She drunk most of the day, he drunk most of the night. Hard to say what makes folks do like they do. They been together a long time, and drunk most of it."

The slam of the screen door of the house next to the Champlins' was like a rifle shot in the quiet sultriness, and the rat-tat-rat-tat of Edna Mae's heels like shots from a machine gun. David heard them go down the steps and along the walk. He did not turn his head or his eyes. He knew without looking, when the rat-tat stopped, that she was fixing her white gloves, worrying with a belt, killing time, waiting for him to turn. The sound of the high heels was louder, sharper, when it came again, going down the street, the sharp crack of the high heels of a frustrated woman.

Across the street a fat Timmins twin wailed, and there were loud voices from inside the house. A lanky girl, all arms and legs, her skin almost pure black, ran through the screen door that had plugs of newspapers in its holes. She gathered up both fat brown bodies, one under each arm, both twins wailing now. The wails faded, stopped when she went in the door and it closed behind her. In a few minutes, David knew, the whole Timmins tribe would be sitting at the kitchen table, the twins dusted off and bibbed, round brown faces smeared with food, gurgling with happiness. All the Timmins kids, when they had been babies, had looked like the twins. David couldn't have counted how many times he had picked how many Timmins babies off the floor or off the ground when he had been spending every day over there; how many times he'd heard their mother yell shrilly at them, then seen her pick them up and gentle them, feed them.

He couldn't have remembered, either, how many times he'd heard her say, there at the kitchen table, as she was probably saying right now, "It's Joey's (or Ginnie's or Stella's or David's) turn to ask the blessing. Y'all be quiet, *y'hear!*" He remembered that when it had been his turn all during the short time he was solemnly (Mrs. Timmins would not stand for a hurried blessing) saying the blessing, there would be the soft thump-thump of various bare Timmins heels on chair rungs. He would peek up from under his eyebrows and see Mrs. Timmins frowning; then after he had said, "for-Jesus-sake, Amen," the frown would be lost in her frenzied efforts to keep all the dishes upright on the table as a half-dozen pairs of hands grabbed for them.

Bucky Harris had come home now, even drunker than usual. You could hear both Bucky and his wife cursing and yelling. Next door Edna Mae's mother had turned up the volume of the radio so she could hear it when she was in the kitchen, and the strident voice of a blues shouter drowned the quiet sounds of Gramp in the kitchen making supper.

Gramp hadn't raised any objections when he'd been accepted by Pengard, although under the little man's quiet pride David had sensed the worry, and something more—apprehension. And there was the knowledge of how lonely Gramp would be after he left. He tried not to think of Gramp's loneliness when that day came, and he wished for the ten-thousandth time that he could be like some of the other kids, his friends, who didn't much care how their parents or the older folks felt as long as they got their own way. Me, I've always got to be worrying about how somebody else feels, thought David. Always knowing how they feel, especially Gramp.

Gramp's voice behind him made him jump. "Don't you want supper, David? You better get in here and get washed up."

When he walked through the dining room he stopped at the table, picked up a piece of paper, and ran it into the machine. Gramp turned in the kitchen doorway. "I asked the Prof about it, David. He said you oughtn't to use it much till you learn touch system. He says the more you uses your own hunt-and-peck system, the more you messes yourself up for learning touch system."

"Gramp," said David. "Gramp, did I say thank you?"

Joseph Champlin smiled, eyes as bright as black diamonds. "Sure, son," he said. "Sure, you said thank you. You get yourse'f a plate now and start dishing up the rice while it's hot. Wash up first."

After supper David said, "Gramp, you want to go to the show? It's Saturday."

"Ain't you got no place to go, David?"

David laughed. "Sure. Sure, I got lots of places to go. Only, I sort of wanted to go to the show. My treat."

"Getting mighty rich all of a sudden; where'd you get all that kind of money? Never mind, son. That's your money. None of my business."

"It's an animal picture taken in Africa. *Tiger, Tiger.* You've been reading about it. They've got it at the Lyceum."

Li'l Joe's eyes lighted, and the slow, wide smile came, then faded.

"You go on, David. Go on and take one of them girls that's always calling you up every night, talking for a couple hours, never leaving me in peace to enjoy my programs."

"You feeling all right, Gramp? I said it was an animal picture. From Africa. Rudy says it's the best he ever saw. You *like* those."

Gramp pushed his chair back, picked up his dishes and walked to the sink, his grandson trailing after him, towering over him. "Don't think so, son." He spoke quietly. "Last time I went I got took real bad at the top of them stairs. Had me a right sharp pain and couldn't get my breath good. Reckon when colored starts getting old they ain't supposed to go to no good movies. 'Nigger heaven,' they calls it. I sure as hell thought it was going to be heaven for me, just for a few minutes there, top of them steps."

David stood for a long moment without speaking. His spine felt cold, and the skin on his body prickled with fear for Gramp, while a searing flame of sick rage started at the pit of his stomach and seemed to consume him. He tried to stop his legs from shaking, fought to keep his hands steady. "Sons of bitches," he said.

Joseph Champlin turned to him. "Ain't no use talking like that, David. No use at all. There's nothing you can do about it."

"I can get out! So can you! Gramp, come with me. Huh, Gramp? You can get work in Laurel. I know—I've been there. There's colored working all over. Easy work. And if you can't get work, I can take care of you. I'm going to work. How bad were you sick, Gramp? How bad? Whyn't you tell me when you came home? Whyn't you *tell* me! I'd have taken you to a doctor. I'd have *made* you see a doctor!"

"So-so, David, so-so. You was up there in Ohio. Go in and turn on the radio so's it'll warm up. I wasn't took too bad. Just a pain, and I had the shorts for a few minutes, trying to breathe. That's all it was. Mygawdalmighty, David, I wouldn't of told you if I'd known you was going to raise a sand like this."

"Answer me, Gramp! Why can't you come with me?"

"You going to do them dishes, boy?"

"Later. I'll do 'em later."

David's anger was turned on his grandfather now. He was infuriated by the implacable stubbornness of this little man who wouldn't give a straight answer, would only shunt him off. Gramp had always been able to anger him this way, irritate him to the point of shouting. It was as though the old man didn't hear him, but David knew he did. Sooner or later he would answer, but David knew it would not be until Li'l Joe felt his grandson's temper had cooled.

Gramp, the dishes stacked and rinsed, said, "You turn on the radio?"

David shook his head, still angry, still irritated, and limped to the radio in the living room. As he switched it on, he muttered under his breath, "Stubborn old goat, stubborn old goat."

He emptied the ashtray on the end table beside his grandfather's chair, wiping it out with a Kleenex from a box beside it. Gramp's got the sniffles again, he thought.

Li'l Joe came in, as he always did, carrying a bottle of beer in one hand, glass and opener in the other. He put them beside the radio on the table and before he sat down took his cigarettes and lighter from the pocket of his shirt and laid them beside the ashtray, on a spot carefully calculated to need the least reaching. "Always make it easy for yourse'f," he'd say. "Ain't nobody else going to do it for you." He sat down, and with the sides of his feet maneuvered the battered old hassock into the exact position that would give him maximum comfort. He glanced at his watch. "Too early for the news," he said. He started to unfold the evening paper.

"Gramp," said David. "Gramp, did you think I was kidding when I said why didn't you come with me to Ohio?"

"Didn't think you was kidding. Just thought you was talking foolish."

"Why! Why was I talking foolish?"

Joseph Champlin sighed and laid the paper half unfolded back on his knee. "Look, David. You know Jim Stacey? Stays over by St. Anne Street?"

"Sure I know him. What's that got to do with anything?"

"Him and me went to school together. Near where the Ursuline Convent is now. Every morning his ma would bring him to the school, and every evening she'd come and get him. My own ma told me how all during the first week he was there she used to stay round the school-house all day till going-home time. Us kids gave him a bad time. Had to have his mamma bring him to school and take him home. What you-all think those other boys up there at that collidge going to think? Big lummox like you bringing your grandaddy with you! You just ain't got real good sense, boy."

David, standing by the mantel, looked down at his grandfather's face and said: "You've been studying about it,

Gramp. Even before I said anything, you'd been studying about it."

"S'pose I had?"

"Then I wasn't talking too foolish."

"Mebbe so, mebbe not." The long wrinkles on Li'l Joe's cheeks bracketed his mouth as he smiled. "Besides, who'd take care of them chickens?"

"Chickens! Sweet Jesus, Gramp! Chickens! You could sell those chickens! You're too chicken yourself to kill 'em and eat 'em. You could sell 'em. Sell the house, too."

"Reckon I could, son. Sell them chickens, I mean. Lots of good dinners out there in that yard. Smothered. They too old for frying. Still, I makes a pretty fair piece of change out of them eggs now and then. But I ain't going to sell no house, David. You're mighty young, son, to try and tell an old man coming on for his social security to sell a house he saved pennies for. You'll see someday, David. You're going on for a grown man now, but some ways you still ain't nothing but a chile."

"But suppose you got sick? You're too damned hardheaded and stubborn to call a doctor. If you had a heart attack or something, you'd rub yourself with b'ar grease and think you were O.K., I swear you would. Look what you just told me. Getting the shorts climbing those Goddamned Jim Crow stairs. And a pain. How do you know you haven't got heart trouble? Hard as you've worked all your life, it's a wonder you've *got* a heart. What were you telling me the other day about that foreman who keeps wanting you to quit grading and come back on the unloading gang? One of these days you're going to be just stupid enough to say 'yes.' What you weigh now? Hundred and ten?"

"Look, son—"

"You just let *me* talk. 'Ain't nothing but a chile!' You know the Bible a hell of a lot better than I do . . . . you know where it says out of the mouths of babes and stuff. All right, you just listen to *this* babe."

Gramp laughed. "I'm listening, son. Swear to God I am."

"But you're not *hearing* me. You don't *want* to hear me. What did you tell me the guys say on the docks about mules and niggers? Kill a mule, buy another; kill a nigger—"

"It's just a saying, David. Just an old-time—"

"Saying! Shit! It's true and you know it. If I ain't nothing but a chile, you ain't nothing but a nigger—a two-legged mule—on the docks. Now you've got a chance, now in your old age, to be something besides just a two-legged nigger mule on the damned New Orleans docks—"

"Nigra, son. You ain't got it quite right."

David slammed his fist down on the mantel so hard that pain shot up his arm. "One way they're right. One way they're right! You're a mule!"

Joseph Champlin laughed again, not unkindly but with genuine amusement. David tried to hold his anger and his irritation back, to keep calm for a final spurt of entreaty. Gramp might be softening.

"Look, Gramp, look. It makes sense, it does make sense. It's not foolishness."

Gramp leaned forward, ran a long finger under the vamp of one leather house slipper, eased his foot out, then slipped it back in. "Getting me a blister," he said.

"Oh, God!" said David. "Oh, sweet Jesus!"

15

HE DID NOT REALLY HEAR the slam of the front door behind his furious charge to the street until he was on the ferry. Then the sound of the door and the memory of the typewriter came all at once, and he was sick with shame. He wondered what the little man sitting in the house in Beauregard had that could fill him with shame for slamming out in a fit of anger. Perhaps it was because he could still remember, young as he had been, the sound of a low voice that said "So-so, little man, so-so—" when he had awakened frightened and crying in the dark.

On the New Orleans side he did not leave the ferry, but turned in his ticket and remained on board. On the upper deck, on the colored side, he stood leaning on the rail, watching a big Negro down below as he directed the cars that came aboard. Funny, he thought, a white man will take orders from a Negro when the Negro is doing something like that; obey like a heeling dog the "This way, that way," the directions of an imperious black hand, no time for "sirs" or "ma'ams."

When the cars were all parked, the gates closed, and the ferry groaning reluctantly away from the slip, the man below leaned for a moment on the rail, looking across the wide river. The cars seemed like well-trained circus animals, quiet in the places allotted to them. David looked again at the big man below, and wondered if he had seen the animal picture at the Lyceum or if he, like Gramp, got "the shorts" when he climbed the Jim Crow stairs to nigger heaven. Or if maybe he was planning to go to the late show when his shift was over.

There was a glow on the town they were leaving, and ahead of them a brighter glow was drawing closer. David had not known where he was going when he had stormed out of the little white house. *Part yours now, boy, part yours.* Gramp had sounded proud when he said that. He knew he wasn't going to that movie. *Seems like when colored gets old they ain't supposed to want to see no good movies.* It was the last time he'd spend his good money, money he'd worked for, to help a damned son-of-a-bitching Jim Crow movie house get rich.

Under his feet the ferry groaned and complained. People were saying there'd be a bridge over the river one of these days. What kind of a bridge? Bridge a colored man could walk across? Bridge a colored man could drive across? It would have to be a long bridge, thought David, an almighty long bridge, and there would have to be an almighty lot of men working on it, white and black, to make a bridge across the river that would take a colored man and his grandson to a good seat in a movie.

"It's coming," said David. "It's *gotta* come."

"You speaking to me, son?"

He whirled, the blood hot in his cheeks because he had been caught talking to himself when he had thought he was alone, leaning on the rail of the ferry, watching the dark water, listening to his own thoughts, and trapped into talking out loud to himself.

The man leaning on the rail beside him was a man about Gramp's age, wearing work clothes. On the deck beside him was a lunch bucket just like Gramp's. The smell of liquor was strong on his breath, but his eyes were as bright and alert as a squirrel's.

"No, sir. I'm sorry, sir. Guess I was talking to myself. Got to be crazy to do that."

"I don't know," said the old man. "I don't know 'bout that. Go crazy if you don't sometimes."

"Hope I didn't scare you."

"Me? Scare me? Lawd, son, it'd take more than Li'l Joe Champlin's grandbaby to scare Henry Clay. Now, if you'd been one of these here delinquents, these here teens, all hipped up, smelling of weeds, mebbe I would of been scared. Soon hit an old man or cut him and take everything he's got as spit. But I ain't scared of Li'l Joe's grandson."

"How come you know me?"

"Seen you with your grandaddy, plenty of times. I been knowing Li'l Joe more'n forty years. Worked with him plenty. Just never happened to meet you. He said you was a fine boy. And I sez, 'You saying it, Li'l Joe; you the one saying it.'" He laughed. "Damned if he wasn't right."

David squirmed. It always made him squirm when people said things like that, unless it was a girl. There was quiet for a moment, the boy and the man leaning on the rail of the boat, looking across the widest river on the continent, and David remembered his childhood's half-waking, half-dreaming fantasy of a wide, flowing river, its banks lined with people, all black, all singing. The banks were lined with people now, he thought, in broken-down old houses with slave quarters in the rear, in rat-ridden rooms, in shacks, and he wasn't a child anymore and they weren't singing.

He forgot the old man, began to hum, patting his hand on the rail in time. "Oh, Mary, don't you weep—" In a moment the old man took up the tune, singing the words while David hummed. The old man can sing, thought David. That old man can really sing. When David joined the other in the words, the big Negro below heard them and looked up and smiled, teeth showing strong and white and clean in the dark face.

David had finally convinced his grandfather that the overhead light with the pink glass shade wasn't enough to read by. Protesting every inch of the way, Joseph Champlin had bought a gooseneck lamp at a secondhand store. It was on the end table now, its light coming over his left shoulder the way David said it should. He had read the paper from front to back, trying to dispel the small devils of worry that dwelt in the back of his mind those nights when his grandson was away from home. He had lingered over the sports news, wishing again that his first wife hadn't been the ruination of their son Evan, thinking that if she hadn't, Evan's name might have been in the sports pages, and he wouldn't have to look for it, half fearfully, in the crime roundup.

The rattle of the paper as he was folding it covered the sound of David's entrance. The soft click of the latch as the boy closed the screen door made him jump. "Lawd, David! Might as well shoot a man to death with a gun as scare him to death! Wasn't looking for you. Not till way late."

David turned his eyes away from the shining relief in his grandfather's. Now that he was home, there was a lot he wanted to say, nothing that he could say.

"You forget something?" asked Gramp.

"Nope. Just didn't want to go anywhere once I got started. I got a lot of studying to do."

"You already done that, David. Young fella like you can study too much. You going to get up to that collidge with your mind all tuckered out. Get yourse'f a beer and set a while. Does a man good just to set sometimes. Too damned hot setting outside, listening to Bucky and that woman of his fighting. They still fighting when you come up the street?"

"Some. Didn't sound too bad."

" 'Bout time they got to bed. Reckon that's what they fight for. Going to bed's better for some after a good fight."

David laughed. The shame was gone now; he was easy, relaxed. "You sure know a lot for a little guy," he said.

"Watch yourse'f, boy! Watch what you're saying. I ain't so little I can't take you on."

"Aw, come on, Gramp." David was in the kitchen now. The muted slam of the refrigerator door sounded good, and the chill of the bottle of beer felt good in his hand. "You wouldn't hit a guy with a gimpy leg." He was walking toward the living room.

"I'd give him a whupping," said Li'l Joe Champlin. "Sure would if he was my bigmouth grandson."

David stopped in the dining room and stripped off his shirt, laying it across the back of a chair. He walked into the living room and sat on the overstuffed divan, balancing beer bottle and glass on its arm. He stretched out long legs, feet wide apart, and held the bottle of beer high, looking through it, smacking his lips, then opened it and poured it carefully into the glass, tilting the glass to control the collar. Li'l Joe had not spoken again, did not speak until his grandson had taken a deep swallow of the beer, sunk his long body lower on the divan, pushed wide brown shoulders against its back, and crossed his ankles. Then Li'l Joe smiled, just widely enough to deepen the long wrinkles in his thin cheeks, etch finer ones at the corners of his eyes.

"You sure a lot of boy," he said. "You sure one hell of a lot of boy."

"I'm a man now," said David. "At least that's what you're always saying: 'You a man now, son.'"

"Look, David." Gramp's voice was so low it scarcely carried across the room. "I'm sorry I got you so riled up."

David's eyes grew round. He hadn't expected that. He sure as heck hadn't expected that. He opened his mouth to say something, he didn't know what, but Gramp was talking:

"When you gets older, David, you forgets sometimes what it was like, how you thought when you was young. Then it comes back. Yessir, it comes back. Someday, son, you're going to find out fifty-nine ain't so old. Gawd knows, I feels a hundred and nine sometimes, but fifty-nine ain't so old. But when you're young, fifty-nine seems like the grave's yawning."

Li'l Joe Champlin straightened the square ashtray so that its edge was true with the edge of the end table beside him, and leaned back. "Well," he said, "the grave ain't yawning yet for Joseph Champlin. But it ain't right for an older man to brush off a young un, not paying any attention to what's troubling him. Because things troubles young uns worse'n they does us older folks. Wouldn't want you to think the old man didn't understand what was worrying you."

"Sure, Gramp," said David. "Sure. I know you understood. Only it seems as if things like—well, things like that damned Jim Crow balcony don't make any difference to you folks, seems as if they don't bother you. And they're bad."

"I knows that, son. Lawd, don't no one knew it better than what we does! You going to see changes, son. You can feel 'em coming. But there's going to have to be a coupla generations, yessir, a coupla generations white and colored die off before they's any *big* changes."

David sighed, took another long swallow of beer. Any way you looked at it, it was bad. It was bad talking about it too much, because that way you were like a chicken getting its neck rung, just squawking. It was bad not doing anything about it, because that way meant you'd given up hope. The only thing that wasn't bad was doing something about it.

Gramp went on. "But seems like there's a difference now, some. Ain't no one hardly in my generation didn't have someone got lynched or treated bad. Like my daddy, burned alive. You can't fault the colored, David, if they was a frightened people, and they was. Wasn't no crime, wasn't nothing, to kill a nigger. Ain't no bad crime now. But it still seems like there's a difference, a feeling coming up that ain't fear, among the young folks. But it ain't different for us."

When David didn't answer, Li'l Joe went on, his voice soft as silk in the warm room. "It's like this," he said. "All your life you remembers what you was taught by your mammas and daddies, and you keeps hold of yourself. You knows what you got to take and you takes it. Then one day something comes along and you can't keep hold no longer. You're a human being and you ain't no color, and you acts like a human being. And the whites don't like that. Lots of colored gone to their Maker many a time because they acted like a natural man. It ain't right to be too hard on us older folks, son; we got memories of bad things, and bad things still happening."

Without speaking David got up and went into the kitchen for more beer for them both. A license to kill, he thought. That was what the whites had been handed in their cradles. And not only a license to kill; a license to rape, to rob, to break into a man's home, a license to ease their lust on a black woman's body and abandon their bastards like Rudy, half-Negro, half-white, all Negro in the eyes of their world. It was a license that said for everyone to read: "Know ye by all these presents that this man is in no way bound by any laws of decency, written or unwritten, and is free to go his way of evil without let or hindrance insofar as his relationships with those of the Negro race are concerned."

Gramp was right, though, when he said there was less fear; he could feel it, an undercurrent of something stronger than fear flowing deep, deep under the darkness of their lives, but a felt and real thing.

When he came back from the kitchen he sat again on the divan, legs outstretched, shoulders squared against its back, head on one of Tant'Irene's antimacassars. When he finally spoke, it was a single word: "Jungle," he said.

"That's what the whites think," said Gramp. "Really think,

down deep. We nothing but jungle critters who can talk. Talking animals."

"That's not what I meant. I meant it the other way round. The Negro's not the critter from the jungle. Nope, it's the white. They're closer to it than we are. Way closer. Living off the weak. The lion on the veldt, he's got 'em all scared. That's why they call him the King of the Beasts. Living off the flesh of little animals. Getting fat on it. Teaching the cubs to kill."

Li'l Joe was quiet. When his grandson talked like that he listened, not always agreeing, but always with pride. Boy sure can study a thing out, he thought.

"But that's only half true," said David. "There's more. A lion's not scared of—oh, say an antelope. Not one bit scared. He doesn't know enough to know that when he's fattening himself up on a nice young antelope, the other antelopes could get together and kill him. They could tramp him to death in five minutes." David poured beer in his glass, watched the collar settle. "Hell of it is," he said, "the antelope doesn't know it either."

Joseph Champlin uncrossed the ankles he had propped on the hassock, eased the leather house slipper off one foot with the toe of the other, let the slipper drop to the floor. "Reckon so," he said.

"And," said David, head back again, "there's the difference. Right there's the difference. The white man has a different brain from the lion. The lion doesn't know the antelopes could kill him, but the white, he knows. The lion's the King of Beasts, he never doubts it; the white man wonders, worries—he sure as hell isn't going to give the antelope—the colored—a chance to find out that he's not. See what I mean?"

Joseph Champlin saw what his grandson meant; he had been seeing it for half a century. He had never defined the insight with words, because he did not have the facility with words. Those things were known the way it was known that rain was hovering, the way it could be told by the look of a stream that fish would rise to the bait. Now a seventeen-year-old who had, it seemed to Joseph Champlin, stood by his bed only a few nights ago and said, "If I bring my pillow, Gramp, can I sleep in your bed?" was putting these things in words, was defining instinct and insight, and a knowledge so hidden as to be almost arcane.

They couldn't answer it, the boy and the man, sitting

together in the sweltering heat of a New Orleans summer night. But Joseph Champlin, whenever he talked like this with his grandson, had a feeling that there was an answer and that it was coming. He did not know why he had this feeling, but it was there.

Later in the evening Li'l Joe said to his grandson: "Never did get a chance to tell you what I started to say before we went lion hunting. I never said I wouldn't come away from here to see you, David. Never did say that. I wants to come see you. But I sure as hell ain't going with you. There's a difference. Lawd, boy, after you been there a while and settled in, I can get me a bus—"

"Train, Gramp. F'Gawdsake, train!" David had never told his grandfather how he had been Jim Crowed on the bus.

"You think train's best, I'll take the train. Always did like being on a train. Maybe a plane. Now *that's* something I *really* wants to do. We'll see how the money is. Plane or train, it don't matter." Gramp started to hum, then sing. " 'Tell 'em I wuz flyin'—Tell 'em I wuz flyin'—' " He looked at his grandson hopefully. "Feel like making a little music, son?"

16

TWO MONTHS LATER, Bjarne Knudsen stood before the tall window in his study, looking down at the boy in the big chair as he so often had looked down at Li'l Joe Champlin. But where Li'l Joe had been almost lost in the chair's depth, David Champlin filled it. "Your grandfather is a small, stubborn man," said Knudsen. "And you are a large, stubborn boy."

David, who had not looked directly at the Professor since he had come in twenty minutes earlier, clasped and unclasped his hands for the hundredth time and said, "Yes, sir."

"David! Stop saying 'yes, sir,' like a parrot that knows nothing else! What did the doctor say to you about Li'l Joe?"

"That—that he'd have to be careful. That he might have another—"

"Wait! He said, did he not, that the heart attack was not a major one? A critical one? That many people have had far more severe attacks and lived for many years? Did he not say this? Do not lie to the Prof—"

"Well—yes, sir—"

"So! He is not a fool, your grandfather."

"Yes, he is too. A hardheaded old fool. That's—that's what I'm saying. Going back to the loading gang on the docks, doing work he'd no business doing, little and old as he is—"

"Bah! Not quite sixty and you say he is old! And he will not do it again. Believe me, I am sure of this. A heart attack of that kind leaves a residue of fear. An instinctive thing. The doctor will tell you. Men will go back again and again to hazardous jobs on which they have received serious injuries. Few will court a second heart attack. Did the doctor not tell you that many people who have had such attacks actually live longer than those who have not because they do take care?"

"Something like that. But—"

"But! But! And you call your grandfather hardheaded!"

Knudsen felt the same pitying anger and frustration shake him inwardly that had shaken him so often with his friend Li'l Joe. He looked down at the boy who had grown to mean so much to him, at the bent head. They would turn to him for help, Joseph Champlin's people, even Joseph Champlin himself, in those things that were of life's exterior, never for help in those troubles of the inner world in which their inmost beings dwelt, to which they withdrew, as David had withdrawn; a world that no man with white skin might enter into, no matter how great his love, how strong his yearning to help.

His tone became gruffly wheedling. "David, there is something else the doctor told you. That your grandfather should not become emotionally upset. That he must be spared things that might upset or anger him. Yes?"

"Yes. Gramp's not excitable—"

"No? He gets what he calls 'upsetted,' does he not? And easily. Have you thought, David, how upset he will be if you tell him you are not going to Pengard because of his illness? Have you thought about that?"

David was quiet for a long time, then rose, hands in pockets, to walk to the fireplace and stand looking into the empty blackness of the grate. "He—he wasn't ever too happy about it. It worried him, me going away and all, to a—to a college like that."

"No. That is not so. At first, yes. But not now. Now he is proud. I meet his friends, the musicians, and they tell me how he brags about you—"

"Gramp doesn't brag—"

"I used the wrong word. How he talks about you. About the fine grades you made in the tests last spring. If you do not enter now, he will blame himself."

"He can't do that—"

"Be quiet! He will blame himself for the rest of his life. Upset! My God! David, there is nothing—nothing, I tell you—that could upset him more. And you would deliberately do this thing?"

"I'll—I'll have to study about it—"

Knudsen's sigh was so deep it might have stirred the heavy drapes hanging beside the tall windows. He looked at David, his brows drawn together in a fierce frown. "We have talked, you and I, about how countries are governed, and laws are made, about compromises. Study about this, my boy: it is a compromise I offer you. Listen carefully. I will write my brother, or better, telephone him, and I will tell him you must enter late. In a large university you could not do this, but Pengard is small and personal. Be quiet until I finish. He has told me how you impressed them all last spring. He will gain the support of the other professors; he carries weight, my brother, small as he is. The dean cannot refuse them all. Then he will—"

"Please, Prof—"

"Quiet! Then he will send me outlines of the work of the first semester, and we will go over them, study them, you and I. When Li'l Joe is strong again, in a month or so, then you will go—"

"Prof, it's too much. I—I'll think—"

"No! For once in his life, just once, Bjarne Knudsen says 'Do not think!' "

And then the boy before him was smiling. "Gosh, Prof, do I have to do all the compromising?"

David was David again, and Knudsen turned away to hide his relief, to keep from the boy any thought that he had been triumphed over.

"I'm going back to work on the laundry truck tomorrow," David said. "We'll need the money."

"You will not need—"

"Wait."

Suddenly Bjarne Knudsen laughed, *"Ja!* It is I who am interrupting now. And you are too polite to roar at me. I will be quiet."

"O.K. I'll go to work, and then when Gramp comes home next week—that's when the doctor says it will be—I'll take care of him and see how he gets along. And—and sort of feel my way. But I can't leave him, Professor; I can't leave him all alone if he's not all right."

"Stop clucking over me, son! Gawd's sake, you're worse'n a broody hen—"

"Doctor said you ought to keep your feet up whenever you could, didn't he?"

"He didn't say I *had* to."

"Said it was better, didn't he? *Don't pick that hassock up!* I'll carry it over there—"

"Jesus have moicy! I ain't going to have no peace till you gets up there in Ohio. Then mebbe me'n Stumpy can settle down—"

David looked sideways at his grandfather, seated now in his chair by the mock fireplace, feet propped on the hassock, and for the first time realized fully what the Professor had meant. To tell Gramp he wasn't going to Pengard because he thought there was need of him at home would send the little man into cat fits, pure cat fits. David was almost scared to tell him he had permission to enter late; he'd let the Prof do that; Gramp wouldn't fly off the handle with the Prof.

He prayed as he had when he was child, not so much that Gramp would get well, because he seemed to be doing that, but that he would show sense. Look God, he prayed. Look. Make him have sense. Make him do what the doctor says so's he won't have another attack. Ever. Please. Until the night Gramp had been rushed to the hospital David hadn't prayed for a long time, except on the surface. Once in a while, after he'd asked the blessing at mealtime, Gramp would say, "You still say your prayers, son?" and David would answer, "Sure, Gramp. Sure do."

But the night Gramp had the attack, it was all David could do—pray. He'd never seen pain like that in another human being; to see it contorting Gramp's gentle, quiet face into a twisted mask of agony was almost more than he could take. Sitting on the edge of his bed after he got home he kept saying, over and over, "Help him, Jesus! Help him. Help

Gramp, Jesus!" He did not want to close his eyes because when he did all he could see was the twisted face, feeling at the same time the tight clutch of the slender hand on his own in the taxi, hearing the gasping whisper in his ears.

The Professor had been swell. The night it happened, just after supper, the Professor was out, but David reached him after he returned from the hospital, and the big man's deep assurance quieted him down, got him breathing regularly again. The next morning he went to the Knudsen house. "If he hadn't done it, Prof, hadn't let them talk him into going back on a loading gang just because they wanted a workin' fool—".

"It is past, David; it is past. Think now of when he will be well and home again—"

And now that Gramp was home, David had to admit that the Prof had been right; Gramp didn't seem to have the slightest intention of going back to any heavy work, talked only of going back to grading coffee, or maybe even doing what he had done years before, help out in Zeke Jones's funeral home. "Onlies' thing about that," said Gramp, "the hours is too irregular." Another time he said: "Lucky I knows how to do some of these other things. Mighty lucky. Ain't too many of us could make a dime was they told they couldn't use their backs. Reckon there's a many of us ain't around no more, jes for that reason."

David had a long cord put on the telephone so Gramp could take it with him wherever he went, but when he came home one afternoon and found Gramp napping in the bedroom and the telephone on the kitchen table, he had a bedside extension installed. He made elaborate and careful arrangements with the neighbors to check daily on Gramp, warning them against being too obvious about it, giving them the doctor's and the Professor's telephone numbers. He knew that all the Jeffersons, the Professor, Isaiah Watkins, others, would be checking too.

After he came home one afternoon in late September, he realized the Prof must have been at the house, talking to Gramp.

"I don't want no foolishness out of you about not going up there to that collidge," said Gramp. He spoke very quietly.

"I haven't said—"

"Not to me, son. You did to the Prof. He explained it to me. Anyone had told me you was going to enter late on account of me, I'da raised a sand, but no one told me. The Prof says it's all arranged and there ain't nothing to do about it now. But you going up there when the time comes long about November. They got it all arranged. Seems like you all mighta said something to me—"

"You were too sick, Gramp."

"Mebbe so. The doctor says I ain't to get upsetted. Lemme tell you one thing: Li'l Joe Champlin's going to get plenty upsetted you does a damfool thing like not going to that collidge. I'll be all right. You think I'm crazy? You think I wants another bad spell like that? All them pains? Your Gramp ain't exactly teched in the head, not yet, less'n you makes me that way, r'aring back, not taking that scholarship—"

"All right, Gramp, all right."

But there was unease within him, a deep worry, the first of his life, and he carried it wherever he went, a burden that could not be lightened by sharing, a burden that was his alone, and its weight became part of his maturity.

17

David Champlin's second train trip brought him into Cincinnati on the Humming Bird early Sunday morning. He had slept little during the night. His legs were too long for comfort in the coach seats, his mind too full for tiredness to quiet. At Gramp's insistence they had arrived at the terminal in New Orleans more than an hour before train time. Half an hour later they saw the Professor enter, hatless and wearing a long shabby raincoat. Rain gleamed on his hair and darkened the shoulders of the coat. He came directly to them, and Gramp said, "You knows better than that, Prof. This the colored section." They had walked to the doorway then, and stood talking. The Professor, more than either David or his grandfather, seemed at a loss for words. He stood looking at David, then into the terminal, then back at David, and now and then down at Li'l Joe. At last he took a package from a capacious pocket in his coat and gave it to David.

"I know it will please you," he said. "It is what I would like to give my son if I had one. So I give it to you, the son of my mind. No—no. Do not open it now. Open it on the train if you must."

David stumbled over words, and heard his grandfather saying, "You've given the boy so much. We sure thanks you."

The Professor threw an arm around David's shoulders, heedless of stares. He tightened the muscles so that David smiled at the strength, then released him. "I must go now," he said. "Tell my crazy brother to write to me, David. Do not try to remember everything I have taught you. Only some of the things."

"Yes, sir," said David.

Before the Professor could reach the taxi stand, David was at his side. "Professor!" The big man whirled. *"Ja?"*

"Professor—could you—I mean, would you keep an eye on Gramp? Let me know if he's not all right? Please."

Bjarne Knudsen was standing looking down now, not at the face of an eager college-bound student, but into the eyes of a small brown boy standing behind a battered kitchen table, earnest, trusting, solemn, watching an adored grandfather repair a toy picked up in a secondhand store. "I will watch the stubborn old fool, David," he said brusquely. "You are not to worry. He is my friend."

The Professor's hand touched his shoulder for a moment. David could scarcely hear the words—"God bless"—and the big man vanished into a waiting cab.

On the train David opened the package. It was Vergil's *Aeneid* in the original. It was the same beautifully bound, expensive edition he had seen and admired in the Professor's library, the book from which the Professor had read to him, and from which he had used passages in teaching him Latin. He opened it, and on the flyleaf, in the Professor's strange handwriting, were the words: *Homo Vitae commodatus non donatus est.* Below it in—drat the man—Danish was an inscription he could not read, and the signature, *Bjarne Knudsen.* The Latin quotation was as close to a sermon as the Professor had ever come: "A man is lent, not given, life."

After he left the train he drank two cups of black coffee and ate two stale doughnuts at a stand in the terminal. He did not dare tackle the counter in the restaurant until he could ask one of the colored porters if it was all right, and they were all busy. His mind was still full of the countryside he had seen from the train window, a world white with quiet snow. Even as early as seven o'clock people had been on porches and front walks clearing the soft, shallow white drifts away. If the weather was like this all winter, he thought, here was one way of earning a few dollars.

He stood in the doorway of the terminal, looking out at a scene as strange as Venice or Baghdad would have been. The red brick of the old houses, the brown branches of the trees, bare except for the light fall of snow, the quietude that snowfall brings were like a dream scene. Even a taxi that made a skidding turn into the side driveway, the driver's face showing red against a gray woolen scarf, was part of the dream.

He wondered, on the train to Laurel an hour later, what it would be like to be in the North. He hoped he was not fool enough to count on it being much better. He had listened too many times to stories his grandfather's friends told of poverty and slums, jobs withheld, crime and evil among his people up North to have great hope that it would be much different. He remembered one of the Professor's better diatribes, when he had said: "But remember, no matter how bad it is—and as long as the darkness in the white man's heart equals the darkness of the black man's skin, it will be bad—remember it is not the law. Here, in the South, the oppression of your people is sanctified and made holy by the law.

"In the North you may be looked down upon by the blind; many will not rent you a home or let you buy one where you will; you may be refused service in restaurants, but remember, *it is not the law*—it is the darkness of the heart of the individual. The darkness and the greed.

"In a city in New York little children are taken to the home where Harriet Tubman lived out her latter years as though to a shrine; I could take you to a house in New Hampshire with false walls and hidden closets where they harbored runaway slaves on their way to Canada. Here in New Orleans they will show a thousand tourists old homes with slave quarters in the rear, show them with pride, and take them up the river to see old plantations that thrived and grew wealthy on slave labor."

The Professor had waggled a huge forefinger at him, and David had bitten his lip and lowered his eyes to keep from smiling at the ferocity of the man. "Here there are laws," he said, "evil laws to keep alive oppressions they must perpetuate to save their way of life. In Virginia, the first to emancipate its slaves, they have never removed from the statute books the laws designed to keep down slave revolts. Do you wonder I say: Where is the God, what is the God this people pretends to worship?"

David remembered it all now, between Cincinnati and Laurel, in the little train that smelled of hot dust and old plush. He remembered, too, and smiled at the memory, what the Professor had said when they had stood by the taxi and the big man had touched his shoulder gently. "God bless—" the Professor had said.

The station was small and bleak-looking in the gray November light, different from the way it had looked in the spring, when there had been buds on the trees and pale green grass had been hesitantly testing the warmth of the sun before pushing all the way to life. This must be a part of the change of the seasons in the North, the different faces common things like stations and houses and trees put on, bleak and dour for winter, warm and glowing for summer, soft and young for spring. He heard voices behind him, farther down on the platform, toward the end of the train, and turned and saw a group of young men sprinting toward a battered taxi that stood at the edge of the asphalt that bordered the station. He wanted to shout, to call out to them to wait, but checked himself. He knew nothing of the taxis in this strange town, whether they had separate ones for white and colored as they had in New Orleans, knew even less of the reception he might receive from the students if he asked to share the cab with them.

He watched the cab drive off, and limped down the platform, its pavement cold through shoes not made for northern climates. He had almost reached the entrance to the baggage room, at the side of the station building, when he heard running footsteps and his name: "Champlin! Hey, David Champlin!" A rotund, breathless young man skidded to a stop beside him. A small hand that just escaped pudginess was held out to him, and he took it. The face that looked up at him was round, and the cold made two red spots on the cheeks stand out against a skin paler than average. The eyes were blue, and from under a knit cap pulled well over the ears a strand of nondescript hair straggled. David judged him to be about his own age. The boy let out a gusty sigh of relief and said: "Nearly missed it. I thought you might drive off in that cab. My name's Sutherland. Clifton Sutherland, but I keep quiet about the Clifton. Actually, the name's Sudsy. Incidentally, I'm glad to see you. I'm here to drive you to the campus."

"I'm sure glad to see you," said David. "Looked like a long walk if I couldn't get a cab."

"Four miles," said the rotund youth. "Four long, lonesome miles. You could have gotten a cab all right, in an hour or so. Hell of a way to hit school, though."

They were in the tiny baggage room, and the stationmaster swung David's suitcase to the counter. The boy who claimed "Sudsy" for a name took it, and David said, "Hey!"

"Make the most of it, man," said Sudsy. "It won't happen again. Standard treatment for midterm newcomers. Next time carry it yourself."

That was good, thought David; that was very good. No hint the other had taken it because of his lameness. He was skeptical about the "standard treatment" remark. He did not believe new students, even midtermers, were met at trains; believed it to be at the instigation of the Prof's brother, a way of lessening the bewilderment of a new Negro student.

David's suitcase weighed the other youth down and threw him off balance, but David did not insist further; met tact with tact. They walked to a waiting car, and Sutherland slid the suitcase into the luggage compartment. The car was a yellow so bright it screamed, and as they climbed into it Sudsy said, "Three guesses what they call this jalopy."

David smiled, settling himself in the seat. "Yellow Peril," he said.

"Yeah. Damned unoriginal bunch here. Too many brains. No imagination. Driving around town I hear 'em yelling 'Cab! Hey, cabbie!' I knock 'em down when I can. Painted the damned thing myself, too. Do you drive?"

"Yes. But I never drove in weather like this. Snow and ice, I mean."

"The snow's not so bad; it's the ice that'll kill you. But you'll learn," he said. "A lot of the students have some kind of beat-up four-wheel vehicle. We have to keep them off campus most of the time. I garage this with a family about half a mile away from the campus." Then, abruptly, "Hear you're a brain."

The sudden change of subject threw David off for a moment; then he laughed. "Who, me? I'm no brain."

"You've got to be to be a Quimby. Or any other scholarship student here, as far as that goes. The grapevine has it you're a brain and a half."

"Shucks," said David. "You know how big things can grow on a grapevine."

"We heard you buy your cigarettes in Latin, and order Cokes in Greek. According to the grapevine, Einstein was a kindergartner just learning his numbers compared to you."

"Sweet Jesus!" gasped David. "I've even got trouble with the multiplication table."

"Then you better start learning, man. Our math professor, old Beanie Benford—" he shuddered.

"Tough?"

"Tough like a bullwhip. They say he's the best in the country, but he's rough to get along with if you don't happen to think higher mathematics is the answer to everything from the immaculate conception to the atom bomb."

David shuddered even more violently than Sudsy had. His shudder was genuine. God knew, he was scared enough without having to face the toughest professor in the college in his weakest subject. And it was required, not elective. He sighed. "And me starting in late."

"Maybe he'll give you a break on account of that. If he does, you'll be the first Quimby he ever gave a break to. He's rough on 'em. Rougher than on anyone else."

Like that, is it? thought David. Like that. Sutherland said, "Hey, I didn't mean that the way it sounded. He was the first Quimby, fifteen years ago. Graduated with every honor this academic sweatshop can hand out."

"You mean he's a Negro?"

"Compared to Beanie, you're an outstanding example of the true Nordic type. After he was graduated here, he went to Cambridge—Cambridge, England, that is—and got a degree there the way I'd go in and buy a candy bar. Then they got him back here to teach. He's next in line for head of the department. He's about six four, and we've got bets up he wouldn't weigh in at 125 soaking wet. Don't let it worry you too much. After a while you find out he's a hell of a teacher. For some reason light dawns. I don't even have to think now when someone asks me what seven times nine is."

David was silent. The surprise of learning that one of the key professors was a Negro was lost in the realization that apparently neither the Prof nor his brother had thought it of sufficient importance to tell him of it. Or had deliberately kept quiet about it.

"This is the town," Sudsy was saying. "You better look quick or you'll miss it."

"I saw it last spring. It's sure pretty."

"Say that after a few weekends stuck in it."

18

As they passed through the town and on to the road leading to the college, David became increasingly curious about where he would be housed. He hoped they wouldn't put him with a white roommate. That would be what Gramp called "crowding the mourners." But he also hoped they wouldn't put him with Nehemiah Wilson. Nehemiah was all right, but a steady diet of that nervous drive and intensity would be hard to take.

Almost at the end of the main quadrangle they turned into a short dead-end street. Sutherland drove to its end, made a U-turn, and returned almost to the corner to park in front of an old-fashioned house that was big and many-gabled, with bay windows and dormers, and a wide, deep porch.

"This use to be the president's house," said Sudsy. "Old Man Quimby's. Then, when he built himself a place on the lake, he gave the house to the college. No one dares tear it down while he's alive. It's a kick inside. Obviously, it's called Quimby House. But I think you're the first Quimby to live in it."

Sudsy was unlocking the trunk of the car, and David was beside him, reaching for the suitcase before the other boy had chance to take it. He stood looking up at the house for a moment until the other joined him. It's sure different, he thought. Sure different from 3020 St. Augustine Street.

When they closed the heavy front door behind them and passed through the small entrance foyer to the main hall, David looked around and whistled. It was not like any house he had been in down home. It seemed huge, the ceilings high and remote. At the left a lounge looked vaguely cluttered and more than vaguely comfortable, with big chairs and old-fashioned divans. Ahead a wide staircase curved upward, its ascent interrupted twice by landings.

"The architect who planned the place was raised on Tinkertoys," said Sutherland.

David followed the other up the stairs, almost bumping into him when he stopped on the first landing and turned left. A short flight of steps, recessed and invisible from the main hall, led to another small landing. Sutherland opened the door at its back that faced them.

"You lucky character," he said.

"Gee!" said David. His eyes traveled round the room. "Nice."

"Super," said Sudsy. The room was good-sized, must once have been a study or a library. A small fireplace with coal-burning grate was in the wall opposite the door. It was flanked by two windows. Under one window was a built-in desk, and bookshelves ran between the window and a wash-basin set in the wall on the left. A couch of the type called "studio" was beneath a window in the right-hand wall. There were a large, old-fashioned armchair, a smaller occasional chair, and two straight chairs. To their right, as they stood in the doorway, a short flight of steps led to another door.

David knew that he was grinning like a four-year-old at the sight of the room. "Why me?" he asked. "Just a freshman."

"Just a lucky break," said Sudsy. "They're tearing down one of the older dormitories. Everyone's crowded. Actually, this used to be the study for the room up there." He gestured toward the door beside him at the top of a short flight of stairs. "Couple of upper classmen in there now. Pretty good guys. You were slated for one of the regular dormitories. Then the guy who had this room had to drop out and here you are. You haven't any study, but by God you've got a fireplace. The only damned fireplace in the only damned student's room on the whole damned campus."

David walked further into the room. "I suppose I shouldn't ask," he said. "Do you suppose I can keep it? I mean, all the time, next year and all?" He'd envisioned bare, cold-looking dormitories; this room could come to seem like home.

"Put in a bid when you leave this summer."

Sutherland was standing in the center of the room, looking at the suitcase David had tossed on the couch. He had not missed the ease with which David had handled a piece of baggage he, Sudsy, was convinced was full of lead ingots.

Being small and not possessed of great physical strength, he always felt a faint twinge of envy when he encountered it in others. The envy never lasted long. He had taken off the knit stocking cap, and now he rumpled his hair with a nervous gesture.

"Look, Champlin," he said. "Look, you want to unpack now?"

"Guess I'd better. Those clothes've been in there since Thursday night, and I don't suppose I can get 'em pressed anywhere today. What wrinkles won't shake out may hang out by morning."

"We've got an iron," said Sutherland. "And an ironing board. Actually, they're my roommate's, but he won't care if we use them. Harry's a pretty good guy for an old maid. He's having dinner with some town chick and going in to the city for a symphony or some damned thing later."

"Well—if it's—"

"Sure it's O.K." David heard something like appeal in the other's voice, and could not analyze it. "Look, a few of us did the town last night—I mean Cincinnati—and we wound up in Fountain Square buying chicken and French fries at a rotisserie. To eat today. There's enough for a mob, and the other guys seem to have taken off. Whyn't you give me a hand with them? The food at the hall is sudden death on Sundays, slow death on weekdays. You can bring whatever clothes you want to press."

David had opened the suitcase, and he stood now looking down at its neatly folded contents. *No, David, no. You don't fold a coat like that. You take it so—tucks the arms in so—* His mind was working rapidly. He was sure Dr. Knudsen had asked Sutherland to meet him, make him feel at ease. Whether it was because he was a new Negro student or whether it was actually the custom to meet all new students arriving in midterm he could not tell. If it was because he was a new Negro student, Sutherland had done his duty nobly. There was no need for further coddling. But the guy had sounded sincere, almost anxious, in some queer way. *Play in your own courtyard; never mind what the white kids do.* Nothing, not one solitary thing, since he had arrived had smelled of Crow. It was the first time he could remember anything like this, except for the foreigners and some of the students from the North who had sought out the bands in the smelly back rooms of the clubs when Gramp had taken him along on a gig. And of course the Prof, who was in a class by himself.

Perhaps it was all the more reason for wariness. What the hell. What if he was wrong. It wouldn't matter. You'd think he was scared of Crow, and he'd lived with it all his life. And he was as hungry as a bitch wolf with pups.

"Well—you sure you got plenty?"

"Plenty! Man, I tell you, I've got enough for three dinners for each of us! O.K.—you coming?"

"I've got to get cleaned up. Then I'll come over. You tell me where it is."

Sudsy drew him to the side window over the couch. "Go back to the main quadrangle, at the corner there. Cross this street, and it's the second dormitory building. Emory Hall. Want me to wait for you?"

"I'll be along. Thanks."

He went to the landing after Sutherland left. Somewhere there had to be a shower or a tub. They wouldn't be downstairs. He climbed to the next landing, heard splashing, and located its source. He returned to his room and gave the present occupant of the bath time to finish, then padded down the hall in bathrobe and slippers, feeling like a college man and reveling in it. Twenty minutes later he was pulling on the rubbers he had known damned well Gramp would sneak into the suitcase, grateful for them, remembering the feel of the snow and slush-covered pavement.

When he started down the path from Quimby House, he told himself he would have to learn a new technique of walking. He remembered a remark of Pop Jefferson's about a man who wouldn't eat raw oysters because he didn't want to put his teeth into anything he couldn't control.

He limped gingerly to the corner, and stopped, trying to accustom himself to the sight of the campus. He could see other students going in and out of buildings, some of them running. He decided they must be wearing spikes. A whole gaggle of women students emerged from a dormitory on the other side of the wide quadrangle, and were joined at the corner opposite him by a group of male students. He saw a colored student among the girls, her face dark against a bright green scarf, teeth showing white, wearing glasses that he could tell, even from where he stood, had heavy rims. He wondered if she was a Quimby. Even from this distance she looked awfully damned academic.

It was when he turned to step from the sidewalk that the icy footing betrayed him, and he crashed down, arms and legs flying, the suit he was carrying landing in the low bank of shoveled snow at the edge of the sidewalk. He sat there a minute, half laughing, amazed at the quickness of the fall, his helplessness to save himself; then he swore briefly and prepared to get up.

"Did you break any bones? Interesting ones, I mean?"

He looked up, startled. A solemn young face framed in a red balaclava helmet was looking down at him, a face so young he thought the boy a campus visitor—someone's younger brother or the son of a professor. "I don't think so," he said. He pulled himself upright, and turned to pick up the suit. The boy had the coat in his hands and was shaking it vigorously. "A really good fall could be good for two days in the infirmary," he was saying. He put the coat over his arm, started on the trousers. "I've made it twice. There's a knack to it. Actually, you almost have to sustain a head injury. Here's your suit. If you're interested, my name's Evans, Tom Evans."

"Mine's David Champlin."

"The brain. The new Quimby. We're classmates." Evans held out a hand as small as a child's, but strong and firm. This must be the Tom Evans who lived near Sara Kent. David thought he had never seen a face so young on a boy old enough to be in college. Evans had the red cheeks and general overall look of a magazine-cover baby. David felt a paternal desire to call him "son."

"Is it any of my business where you're headed for?" asked Evans.

"I don't see why it isn't." David smiled down at him. "One of—" (What did they call themselves here? Students? Men? Boys?) He decided on "student," and started again "One of the students who lives in Emory Hall asked me to come over. He met me at the station. He said his name's Sutherland."

"If he said it is, it is. Did he by any chance mention anything about fowl—chicken—edible birds?"

"Well—"

"He did." Evans took David's elbow in a cupped hand. His head was only a little above David's shoulder. "Onward, friend Champlin. A goodly portion of those chickens are mine. A fact that has no doubt slipped his mind. We'll refresh it."

Sutherland's room was on the second floor of the new dormitory building. They passed a lounge on the first floor whose modern furnishings did not look nearly so comfortable, David thought, as the over-stuffed period pieces in the Quimby House lounge. From open doors in the second-floor corridor, as he followed Evans, he heard radios, voices, laughter. Sutherland's room was at the end of the corridor. Evans rapped perfunctorily, then opened the door, standing back for David to enter. Sutherland greeted David loudly. "Man, what happened to you? This isn't white tie and tails—" He caught a sight of Evans behind David. "Cripes! Where'd you pick it up?"

"He didn't," said Evans. "I picked him up. And I speak literally." He walked into the room, his nose wrinkling, looking more absurdly young than ever. He took off the knit helmet and the mackintosh he was wearing, tossed them on the bed, and roamed the room, sniffing expectantly. Sudsy took David's light coat, said "God, one of these nature boys."

Evans was still sniffing around the room. "Look, Suds," he said severely. "Chicken?"

"You said you were going to the city."

"That's got nothing to do with it. Four chickens. Four lovely brown chickens and two large bags of French fries. Purchased last night in a moment of alcoholic intelligence. One-half of the purchase price being put up by one Evans."

"Beer?" said Sudsy.

"Certainly."

"Stoopid! I'm not asking you to have a beer. I'm asking you have you *got* beer."

Sudsy, pudgy young face earnest and intent, was wrestling with a card table. David took it from him, thankful for something to do with his hands. Evidently he would have to wait until after they had all eaten before pressing his coat and trousers. He felt awkward and out of place. He could not follow the quick banter of Sutherland and Evans, could not have joined in if his life had depended on it. Only the shyness he had felt the first day he sat in the Professor's high-ceiling study equaled the shyness he felt now. He could evaluate human relationships in the South; had known no shyness with any white he had known in the South, because, however friendly, there was beneath the friendliness a nonacceptance, an adherence to a double standard, a willingness to wait till Judgment Day, if need be, before putting any concept like the brotherhood of man to any test. Knowing this, he had felt no shyness, only inner contempt.

Today he felt acceptance, and did not know what to do with it. The talk between the two boys in the room was like a foreign language, different from the humor of his own people. This cross talk was barbed, open, not soft and subtle like that of the Negro with its hundred different meanings left unspoken, yet clearly understood.

The antennae of his mind searched for Crow, expected it, and did not find it. He was conscious for the first time that there was another side to the gulf that stretched between white and colored. If—and today he felt it might be true—there were actually whites who sought and wanted friendship with his people, they must find it difficult because they must not only bridge a gulf but must then climb a wall on the other side of the gulf even higher and more forbidding than the wall that surrounded them.

He set the table in the center of the room, heard Sudsy call "Catch!" and made a backhanded grab at a tablecloth.

"No!" Evans groaned. "Not a tablecloth!"

"Company," said Suds.

"This guy's just a student, for cripe's sake. Just a li'l ol' student like you and me."

"Look, my sainted mother sent me this tablecloth. If I don't send it home dirty with the laundry she'll think"—he shuddered—"I eat off bare tabletops. I hope you cats spill something on it."

They were no longer calling him "Champlin," by the time they sat down, but "David." When they said "Champlin" they used the flat, Anglicized pronunciation, not the French pronunciation of New Orleans. Evidently it was last names by the faculty always, and last names by fellow students until they became better acquainted. It was plain that the "Stoopid" he heard so frequently was a campus catchword, to be repeated *ad nauseam* until something else was found.

They ate with their fingers, in spite of the tablecloth, and talked little. Sudsy made instant coffee from water boiled over an electric plate, and a second pan of water was simmering when Sudsy called out in response to a low knock. The knock had been so gentle that David was unprepared for the appearance in the doorway of a mountain of blond student, taller than he by at least two inches, with wide, heavy shoulders, the open and inviting countenance of an old-fashioned kitchen clock, and a shock of tow-colored hair that grew much like Dr. Knudsen's, without let or hindrance or visible signs of discipline.

"Y'all eating?" The voice came from deep inside the massive chest, and the accent came from Georgia. Or, thought

David, it might be Alabama, but Georgia was more likely. I'm glad I got that chicken in me first, he thought. Hope to hell I can keep it down.

Sudsy was introducing the newcomer. "Martin," he said. "Chuck Martin—David Champlin."

A big-knuckled hand was held out to David, who fumbled with his napkin, then took it. "Sure glad you finally made it," said Martin.

David thought: I'd sure be glad if you hadn't. Mighty happy if you hadn't. Even happier if you'd drop dead. The wall between him and this cracker would shut out the others, too; leave him alone on one side of it, not wanting to embarrass Evans and Sutherland, angered and resentful at what he was certain would be the newcomer's attitude, in spite of the handshake.

Sudsy's next words arrested his thoughts abruptly. "You belong to ALEC, Champlin?"

"I—why—sure."

"This character who just came in was elected chairman of the campus chapter last week. If you're already a member you don't have to pay anything. If you aren't he'll get money out of you before you can put that chicken wing down."

He had thought when Chuck first shook hands with him that this was another of the many whites met in the South who are insistent they have no prejudices. Now he wasn't sure. Those whites used to come to the stinking, fetid back rooms where his grandfather and the other musicians were required to sit between sets; they meticulously, almost ritualistically, shook hands with every man in the band, not just the leader; they didn't ask who wanted a drink, had usually ordered drinks sent back before they came in, and more often than not it was gin, because there was a hoary legend that all colored people liked gin.

After the drinks came they usually took a chair and sat in attitudes of such relaxed and self-conscious familiarity that, even when he was a child, David had smiled at the phoniness. Their accents were usually syrupy-thick and drawling like Chuck's, depending on where they came from. And they talked. Judas Priest! how they talked! On and on, palsy-walsy as all hell. But they sure as hell didn't recruit members for ALEC.

Most of the other whites who came back of the stand, the foreigners or students from the North, were different. They usually stood until asked to sit, shook hands with the leader, and always asked first who wanted a drink and what kind before they ordered it, seeming embarrassed, many of them, at finding themselves in a situation that was humiliating to others.

Only the Prof and a few other whites from the North had such a gut-twisting hatred of the customs of New Orleans that they never came to the back rooms, but instead sought out the musicians in their homes, almost pathetically grateful when sponsorship of some responsible Negro gained entrance for them to Negro clubs, often foregoing that pleasure when they found the police could—and probably would—make trouble for the club if they were found there.

Now David tried to fit Chuck into one of these categories and found that he could not, and he waited warily for some word or action that would guide him. He could see now that the youth with the cracker accent was older than the others, perhaps by two years. Something else was becoming evident about the big, blond youth, and David recognized it for what it was because he himself had felt its discomforts all his life. It was shyness. This lumbering, straw-haired student from some small southern town was shy, and the shyness, David sensed, was because of him. Suddenly David thought longingly of his room, of his fireplace, and the unpacking he must do, and the peace without worry he would find there. He had enjoyed his time with Sutherland and Evans; now there was a Problem, and its face was as familiar as the face of his wristwatch, and he did not want, just now, to be worried with it.

Tom Evans had moved to the studio couch, and was leaning back on his elbows, happy surfeit on his face. Chuck was sitting in the vacated chair, looking sadly at the ruins of four chickens.

"Skeletons," he said. "Nothing but poor, picked, li'l ol' skeletons. I've seen pictures of steers' skulls on the desert that had more meat on 'em."

"If you'd come with us last night you could have had you a chicken all to your li'l ol' self," said Tom.

"I told you why I couldn't." His "I"s were "Ah"s, and most of his intermediate "r"s and final "g"s were missing.

"There's no law says you can't bone up on geometry on Sunday."

"What y'all think I've been doing all day? Playing tiddleywinks? There's a law known as diminishing grades that says Martin's got to bone up on math every time the good Lord sends him a free weekend."

Sudsy turned to David. "There are half-a-dozen chicks on campus plotting against this character. No free weekends for Chuck. It's his age gets 'em. He's practically senile."

David pushed his chair back, stood up. "I sure appreciate the chicken dinner," he said. "Can I help clean up before I go?"

"You aren't going?" Something in Martin's tone swung David's eyes away from Sudsy and toward the big student. The other's eyes were direct and friendly, and there was an expression in them that matched the tone that had halted David.

"What about your suit?" said Sudsy.

"It looks pretty good since its been hanging there by the door," said David. "Maybe I don't have to—"

"Oh, Lawd!" Chuck's voice was low. "My damned mealy-mouthed cracker accent is sending you off." Chuck was shaking salt on a limp sliver of French-fried potato, not looking up now. "I sure wish I didn't have to go round explaining myself. They won't let me take public speaking and diction until junior year. Meanwhile I've got to watch every colored student comes into this place shy away from me, while I sweat to talk different." He turned to Tom appealingly. "I'm getting better, don't you think?"

"We-e-l-ll," Tom looked thoughtful. "You don't say 'haid' anymore. And I haven't heard you use a houn'-dawg analogy for a couple of weeks. As Beanie says, by the use of some effort and a little imagination I think I can detect a slight improvement."

"That's like saying somebody's an advanced case of adult infantilism."

Even if David had known what to say, he would not have had a chance. There was a sharp knock at the door, and he saw it open and a student lean against its frame.

"Well, hi-yah." Chuck's voice did not commit him to a welcome. "Come in, young Clevenger. We were just about to start talking about the likes of you."

"Whatever you mean by that," said the youth in the doorway. He was only slighter shorter than David, but he gave an impression of smallness, of bones under a thin layer of flesh that were delicate, almost fragile. His hair was darker than blond, lighter than that called honey-colored; his eyes were dark, set in a face whose framework was sharply defined, and over which the pallid skin was beginning to tauten in the pattern of maturity. He looked older than the others, but the petulant mouth was that of the perpetual adolescent. David estimated that the trench coat, sweater, slacks, and shoes he was wearing could well represent at least a semester's tuition.

Even without Chuck's greeting, which had contained a warning that David had picked up as quickly as it had been tossed out, he knew he would have felt the tightening in the pit of his stomach, felt that certain crawling of flesh over inner heat.

"I'm sure I don't know what you mean by the 'likes of me,' " the newcomer said. His speech was soft, not slurred, like Chuck's, but low and well articulated. Virginia, thought David. Or maybe Maryland. He glanced toward Chuck, but the raw-boned student's face was blank. The boy in the doorway ran his eyes around the room, fixed them on David. "Our new Quimby?" he said.

"Champlin," said Chuck. "David Champlin—Randolph Clevenger."

A remote smile appeared on Clevenger's face. "Sorry you had to start in late, David. We heard you were ill and couldn't make it."

"No," said David. "It was sickness in the family."

"From what we've heard of you the delay isn't going to hurt much." There was no sarcasm in the words; the words were innocent, but the tone, thought David—the tone was guilty as hell.

"Are you looking for food? Because if you are we have a nice paper bag full of chicken bones." Sutherland tossed in the remark quickly. David looked at Chuck again. "—the likes of you" Chuck had said. It was the first time any white person had ever done anything like that. Things were coming too fast; again he felt the urge to leave, to go back to his room, the only damned student's room in the whole damned college with a fireplace, Sudsy had said; the only room in the world where there was a suitcase full of clothes belonging to David Champlin; the only room in the world where there could be, in a moment's time, a row of stuffed and ceramic lions and tigers belonging to Li'l Joe and David Champlin ranged on a mantel, and a typewriter bought by Li'l Joe Champlin open on a desk.

He decided that this time, much as he wanted to, he would not give way to the urge to get the hell out. Behind him he knew Tom was setting up a collapsible ironing board.

Sudsy spoke again. "If it's food you want, you can go home. And why doesn't anyone think to bring beer?" he complained. "Do I hoard? No. Sudsy shares. Do my friends hoard? Yes."

"I haven't got any beer," said Clevenger. "You could have it if I did. The way I feel today the sight of a glass—" He shivered. "What I came for was to beg an Alka-Seltzer."

"You will do it," said Tom.

Clevenger ignored him. "You have any, Sudsy?"

"Why would I have Alka-Seltzer? A temperate—"

"Stow it. What about Harry?"

"Harry, as you well know, is near teetotal."

"Champlin," drawled Chuck, "did y'all bring the necessities of life with you? Or did you just pack the nonessentials like clothes? Can you help this poor damned soul out?"

"Sure sorry," said David. He had plugged the cord of the iron into an outlet, and was laying the leg of a pair of trousers on the ironing board in the best Gramp-approved fashion. He accepted a wrung-out damp towel from Sudsy, smiled his thanks, then spat on a finger and tested the iron. There was no sizzle, and he stood waiting, holding it up. He glanced at the youth in the doorway and surprised him in what was close to a stare. David thought suddenly of the driver of the bus he had boarded in New Orleans in the spring. The driver had been trash, semiliterate white trash, and this youth was what David supposed some people would call an aristocrat. Gramp could have told him, right now, whether the boy came from Virginia or Maryland. *The knife them folks cuts your throat with's so sharp you don't even know what happened till you're bleeding to death.* Yet, catching Clevenger's eye now, he remembered the bus driver.

"Too bad we don't go in for sports here, David." He was smiling. David did not miss the fact that it was first names right off the bat with this character, no "Champlin" to a Negro. "I was just thinking you'd make a fine back for a varsity squad."

"I doubt that," said David. He did not return the smile, although he knew it was expected of him, and hated the knowledge. "Left leg's gimpy."

"Sorry. I didn't notice." Clevenger's voice sounded sincerely sympathetic. Which was in character, thought David.

"You couldn't very well. I've been standing back here. It's nothing much. Just a stiff ankle joint."

"Champlin." Clevenger gave the name the French pronunciation, and his voice was thoughtful. "Champlin. Two 'a's?"

"One," said David shortly. "I guess it used to be two."

"I'm sure it did," said Clevenger. "My grandmother was a Champlain from down your way. It's an old southern name."

"Meaning?" Chuck spoke quietly. David would not have to have asked the meaning, and he knew Chuck did not. Former slaves carried their owners' names even until today.

Chuck didn't wait for a reply. "Run along and get your Alka-Seltzer," he said, and David's muscles tautened at the raw anger in his tone. "We were breathing real fine wholesome, healthy air until you came along."

If I've got to get mixed up in a fight the first day I'm here, thought David, if I have to do that, I'm flyin'. But there was no answering anger in Clevenger's face as he looked at Chuck; instead there was a contempt that, thought David, if it had been directed at him he would have wiped off with a fist, much as he hated to fight. Clevenger did not speak, turned to leave, but before he was well into the hallway he stopped and turned back, his eyes on David. "You'll find a fellow Quimby in this building, David. And two in Justin Hall." He closed the door, and they heard his footsteps on the uncarpeted floor of the corridor.

The strained silence in the room after Clevenger had left made David more acutely uncomfortable than he had ever been in his life. There was no sound except the thud of his iron. He glanced at Chuck covertly, and saw what had been the dull, brick-red flush of anger gradually subsiding. It was Sudsy who broke the silence with a high-pitched, wailing protest. "What's the matter with guys like that! What's the *matter* with them!"

"Me," said Evans, and, unlike Sudsy's, his voice was unexpectedly strong, far more mature than the troubled, boyish face. "Me, I think a lynch mob's a cleaner proposition."

"Look," said David. "Look. You fellows shouldn't get all—"

Chuck took over. His face had returned to its normal pink. He spoke slowly, his accent exaggerated, the voice pitched somewhere behind the nose.

"Y'all don't understand," he said. "Y'all just don't understand. David knows how it is. We've got a Problem. With a big capital 'P.' Our nigras understand this. Ouah nigras have been happy for a hundred years. No one was any happier than what we was to free the slaves. My grandfather freed his slaves long befo' Abe Lincoln come along, messin' with ouah way of livin'. My grandaddy even gave his slaves a little piece of ground all their own, those he'd had a long time.

Ouah nigras know we understand them and take care of them. Ouah *good* nigras don't want no interferin' nobodies from up No'th comin' round messin' up a relationship that's been so good and beautiful so long."

David had quietly set his iron down at the end of the board at the beginning of Chuck's speech. Now he looked quickly at Sudsy and then at Tom, who was back on the couch. There was sheer horror on Sudsy's face, set cold anger on Tom's. He looked at Chuck, whose eyes met his squarely. Suddenly he put both hands on the ironing board and leaned forward, laughing the deep clear laughter of the man of whom Irene Champlin had said, "You could hear him laughing two courtyards away." When it was spent he said, "I don't know why you're wasting your time on liberal arts, Chuck; I swear I don't. Why didn't you go to one of those big dramatic schools in the East?"

Chuck stood up. "Forget about that character Clevenger," he said. "You must have known we'd have 'em like that. They've got 'em everywhere, nearly as I can tell." He turned to the others. "I've got beer." He sighed gustily. "I'm ashamed, plumb ashamed to admit that I was saving it for next weekend. And I know where I can get more. I'll break it out now I'm a repentant sinner."

19

"Lawd! What you moaning about? The boy ain't dead." Li'l Joe Champlin spoke aloud with only the yellow tail-less cat to hear. There was a great loneliness within him and an emptiness in the little white house that changed it from a cottage warm with life to a vast echoing hall, as chill and empty as a disused auditorium. It had not been like this even after Geneva died; then there had been a small boy and an old woman to silence the echoes.

He pushed his supper dishes and coffee cup back and stood. "You just griping because now you has to wash the dishes," he told himself, and smiled at the liar he was talking to. This would be David's first night at the college, and he wondered what sort of room, in what kind of bed, his grandson would be sleeping.

David had brought home some lamb liver for Stumpy the day before he left, and Li'l Joe began cutting it up in small pieces for the cat's ancient teeth. "Going over the river," he said to Stumpy. "Going to get that belly of yours full before I leaves."

Perhaps somewhere over the river he would find one of the groups he played with and could sit in for a while. If not, there were plenty of warm, smoky places he could go and be greeted loudly by friends, where he could have a friendly drink or two. The doctor had said that one or two were O.K., but he wished he could get drunk; it had been a long time since he'd been good and happy drunk.

He didn't suppose he'd feel a hell of a lot better even if he did go over the river. He'd still miss the boy because David had been going over with him often lately, playing piano sometimes. Playing it good, too, thought Li'l Joe, even if he did have to get on the kid now and then for some of that "far-out" stuff he'd work in. No sense in it, good as the boy could play the real stuff. "Uncle Toms" was what the younger musicians were calling men like himself and Kid Arab and other older men, but they were wrong. Li'l Joe forced his mind to stay on this track, away from the boy's absence. People were asking for the old-time stuff these days, and it was coming back, professors and writers, all different kinds of whites, writing books about it, collecting records, asking ten thousand damfool questions a minute. Speaking for himself, he couldn't see anything Uncle Tom about it. Give the people who were paying their money what they wanted, don't bite off the tongue in your cheek; give 'em "Dixie" then come on strong with "Gettysburg March," and the hell with them; the kitty stayed full and you didn't have to scrape too hard to pay your ALEC and your N-double-A dues.

Even some of the young whites were calling them "Uncle Toms," and Li'l Joe thought about it a lot, wondering what they'd have been like if they'd grown up the way the folks they criticized had grown up. A man's got to survive, he'd think. What they didn't know, what they didn't know at all, was that the guys who put on the biggest show of Uncle Tom-ing were the ones who hated the whites the most, men like Papa Ballantine and Bob John. Sometimes Papa Ballantine was enough to turn a man's stomach, capering around up there on the stage, talking to people sitting at the tables in the club where he'd played for years. "Lawd! Lawd 'a' mercy!" he'd say. "If there ain't Miss Betty So-and-So! Sho' glad to see you, Miss Betty. Folks, I been knowin' Miss Betty ever since she wasn't nothing but a baby. Been knowin' her mamma and her daddy, too. Lawd! Lawd! My mamma, she nursed Miss Betty's mamma way back there, way back, an' here's Miss Betty, pretty as a picture and got a baby herself! What you-all want Papa Ballantine to play for you, Miss Betty?"

He knew, Li'l Joe knew, and so did the others in the band, that the little notes Bob John blew on his trombone before they started on "Miss Betty's" request were retches. And there didn't any of the whites, not any of them, know the things Papa Ballantine said when there wasn't anyone around but his own people. Lawd! Some of 'em wouldn't even know the meaning of the words.

Li'l Joe sat in the big chair in front of the mock fireplace, feet propped on the hassock, and reached to turn on the radio beside him. He stopped, hand on knob, at the sound of a heavy thud-thud of feet on the porch. When he opened the door the Professor was standing before it, red-gray beard jutting over the top of the brown paper bag he held in his arms.

"Ah! My friend—" The Professor pushed past Li'l Joe and went directly to the kitchen. "You are lonely. Do not lie to me and say you are not." He was opening the refrigerator. "Bjarne Knudsen is lonely with the boy away, and I know Li'l Joe must be also. So I come. With beer. Good Danish beer. The shot glasses, Li'l Joe! The shot glasses. What have you done with them?"

"Lawd!" Li'l Joe, just behind him, was looking at the bottle the Professor had placed on the table. "You brought them schnapps. I dunno, Prof—"

"There is no law that says you must drink schnapps with beer." The Professor was carrying a tray laden with bottles and glasses into the living room. "But there should be. To-night you will have some, yes?"

"No. I mean sure. Sure, Prof. Mebbe one or two."

Later, sitting in a corner of the blue divan, the Professor shook a finger at him, a small shake, without menace. "Two grown men; two grown men and we sit consoling each other because one young boy has gone a short distance. Do not tell me your heart is not heavy. It is true that there is a feeling, no? A feeling that he has gone a long way."

"I done told the boy, long time ago, I done told him he'd be leaving this place one of these days. Said he wa'n't, but I knows better. Lawd, Prof! That boy's been lucky. I *mean,* he's been lucky! I looks around and I sees these other boys around here and the way they going, and I thinks about it all the time. Not that I ain't had no problems with him; reckon just being a teen like he is, that's a problem all by itself. But still I wonders what I done the good Lord should make it so fine for David. I keep a-telling him there ain't nothing free; sooner or later a man pays for his luck."

"You must not say that to him. He owes nothing. Except to his people. And this he will know, or I am a stupid man."

Li'l Joe grinned. "You ain't stupid, Prof." He sobered. "Y'all think he'll make it? Y'all think he'll measure up?"

"With—how do I say it?—with no sweat he will measure up. Without sweat he will make it. He is no prodigy, thank the good God, but he has what I call a wide intelligence."

The Professor smiled at Joseph Champlin, and there was a sweetness in the smile Li'l Joe had never seen before, not in all the years he had known the Prof.

"Something within you almost hopes he will not make it, no? It is natural."

"My Gawd, Prof! I ain't all that selfish! I ain't like—"

"You are human, Li'l Joe, and you love the boy. He is your life. He is—what is it your people say?—your 'heart.' " Knudsen picked up his glass of schnapps, downed it in one gulp, and followed it with beer. "He will go far, our David. But not from you, Li'l Joe. I know this. You do not understand? You will remain with him, Joseph Champlin, you and your wife and this house and the Timminses and the Jeffersons and the bureau drawer in which he was cradled. And, I hope, the Prof. Good God, yes! I hope the Prof! A man cannot cast aside his childhood, Li'l Joe, though he run from it as he would run from the devil. He may make of it a burden under which to stumble and fall, or a shield to hide behind, or he may make of it a tool." He sighed. "I do not make myself clear?"

"Sure." Li'l Joe was looking into his glass. "Sure you makes yourself clear. You always does when you puts your mind to it."

Knudsen found himself in the unfamiliar position of being

without words. He knew Li'l Joe understood what he had said. He also knew that there was in Li'l Joe's mind a dark land as unknown to Bjarne Knudsen as the surface of a far planet, a land that his words would never reach, or if they reached would never lighten. Of that land he knew only that its prevailing wind was fear.

He rose quietly and went to the kitchen, opened two more bottles of beer, and brought them back. He handed one to Li'l Joe, and said: "From your own life, you have given him courage. Do not worry about him. Where he goes, you go too." Picking up the bottle of schnapps, he said: *"Akvavit,* Li'l Joe? Three? Bah! It is nothing. Will you let a Viking outdrink you?"

Li'l Joe was quiet for a moment, then he said, "Lawd! Ain't no—what you always calling it? Wiking?—what can't outdrink me. Reckon all of you was weaned on that stuff. Where y'all going with that bottle? You didn't hear me say I wouldn't."

The outstanding feature of "Margie's" Coke and hamburger dispensary was noise. Its booths seemed made of elastic siding, capable of expanding to accommodate anywhere from one to eight young people. The day after David Champlin's arrival at Pengard, the woodwork of the back booth was creaking under the weights and against the pressures of Suds Sutherland, Tom Evans, Chuck Martin, and three girls, one of them Sara Kent. At the end of the booth's table Randolph Clevenger sat, chair pushed back, legs crossed, hands clasped around one knee. The other two girls were Carol Babcock, who had come with Chuck, and Lou Callender, Tom Evans's current companion in off moments. Randolph Clevenger had been drinking coffee at the counter when they entered, and had now attached himself to their table. They were talking about Goodhue, from whom Tom, earlier that day, had received a sternly tolerant lecture on curfew violations. Tom's mimicry of the dean was subtle but sure in touch.

" 'Cozy,' " said Carol. "Whoever thought that up—"

Sutherland protested. "He's too big. Man, he's got bones like a dinosaur."

"I don't care. I think he's dreamy," Lou answered him. It was an adjective current at the time, and Lou used it as though she was afraid it would go out of style or vanish from the vocabulary before she had exhausted its possibilities.

"Distinctive. That's the word for Cozy," said Sara. "You can take it two ways—"

Clevenger lighted a cigarette, extinguished the lighter with a quick snap. "You're talking like adolescents," he said. "I'll agree that in some ways he's not all he cracks himself up to be. But at least he has standards you people don't seem to appreciate. Unfortunately, they're vanishing—"

Sudsy made a rude noise, said, "Like the dinosaurs—"

"And good riddance," said Tom. "They sure did mess up the campus."

"I tried taking one home," said Chuck. "I wanted him for a pet. Never could housebreak him." He shook his head sadly. "My old man made me have him put to sleep."

"No understanding of today's Young," said Sudsy. "That's the trouble with parents. We all, I'm telling you, we all have to have something to love. It says so in the books. But do they know it?" He threw an arm around Carol, nuzzled her hair with his nose.

Clevenger stood, ground out the cigarette that was only a third smoked, said something about studying, and left.

"What's about him?" asked Suds. "What's *about* him?"

"Don't y'all know?" Chuck was drawling. "Cain't y'all see? He's a suth'n gentleman."

"He's a fink," said Tom.

"What's a fink?" asked Carol.

"Something dirty?" Lou's tone was hopeful.

"No! For gosh sake! A fink is really a low form of life known as the boss's man. Most prevalent among white-collar workers. Only nowadays everybody uses it and it means something different. When I was a kid—"

"How does it happen you know so much, baby?" asked Carol.

"Because my old man's Bull Evans, that's how. And I bet you never even heard of Bull Evans."

"I have so heard of him. Only—gosh, it was a long time ago, wasn't it? I mean, isn't he, well, kind of old for a parent?"

"Yup. Old as most people's grandparents."

"There's more," broke in Sara. "My grandfather got Tom Evans's father out of prison. It must have been"—she frowned—"it must have been before any of us were born."

"It was," said Tom.

Lou said, "You mean poor Tom's father was in prison and all?"

"You don't need to sound so damned sympathetic and patronizing all of a sudden," said Tom. "We're damned proud of it around our house."

"I didn't even know about all this," said Chuck. "I mean, I never even heard of Bull Evans, and I apologize. I really apologize, but I can't help being ignorant. I was born that way—"

"Listen," interrupted Sara. "Bull Evans was a great labor leader. I've known him ever since I was a baby, and he's super. Isn't he, Tom? He was a labor leader when being a labor leader was something, really something, when it took —it took—"

"Guts," supplied Tom.

"Yes. And way back in the old days when a strike was really something and people got hurt and killed, Bull Evans got thrown in jail, and they dragged out some old law and dusted it off and were trying to send him to prison for life or anyhow a long time. Right, Tom? And then my grandfather heard about it and raised a terrible ruckus and took over his defense—"

"Your grandfather being a lawyer?" asked Suds.

"Of course, Stoopid. And my father, too. All three of them still get together at our house and talk and argue all night."

"And he got out of prison? Tom's father?" Lou's eyes were wide.

"I'm here, aren't I? Gosh, Lou, I wonder." Tom shook his head. "Sometimes I wonder. I really wonder."

Chuck half rose. "If you all would stand up so I can slide out of this booth, I'll fetch Randy back. It's a downright shame not to have Clevenger here to learn all about your father being in prison—"

"He'd die," said Sara. "He'd die utterly."

"Sure would." Chuck was seated again. "And did you all know the new Quimby's finally arrived?"

"The boy from New Orleans?" asked Lou.

Suds answered her. "Yes, I met him and fed him. Knudsen asked me to meet him. The feeding was my own idea. Tom and Chuck helped."

"What's he like, Sudsy?" asked Carol.

"O.K. He's a real swell person—"

Sara broke in. "He's a livin' doll—"

"Sara!" Lou's shock was obvious. "What a thing to say!"

Sara turned to her, face flushing. "Don't be like that. Why shouldn't he be?"

"How'd you know, Sara?" asked Chuck.

"Last spring. Remember? I'm the one with a courtesy aunt whose husband's faculty. I was here with them when he came up for interviews. He came to dinner. And if Lou will stop acting like a southern belle, I'll say it again. I will anyhow. He's a livin' doll."

Carol asked, "Not another Simmons or Dunbar?"

"No. Gosh, no," Sudsy answered. "He's a real guy. He was —well"—Sudsy hesitated—"sort of standoffish and shy at first—"

"Poor thing," said Lou.

"Stop being like that, Lou! Can't you educate your dames, Tom? Anyhow, you kept wanting to tell him to snap out of it. Gosh, no, he's not like Simmons or Dunbar. Those two guys bug me, I mean, really bug me, and if I say anything I'm talking against a Negro and I've got leprosy."

"What about me?" asked Chuck plaintively. "You all think I haven't got leprosy every time I open my big mouth? I swear—" He ran big-knuckled hands through the tow-colored hair. "There's nobody in this whole cotton-picking, evil, li'l ol' world hates the way the South treats the Negro worse'n I do. And listen to me. Every time I open my mouth somebody calls out the N-double-ACP and the American Civil Liberties Union and ALEC. On the double."

"Never you mind, Chuck," said Sara. "Never you mind. You don't say 'nigra.' That's one good thing."

"First time I meet a colored person up here and just say 'Howdy' or something I feel like a one-man lynch party. What'm I supposed to do? Tell 'em I got kicked out of two southern colleges just for talking about civil rights and integration? Walk up and tell 'em my old man caught me in the basement of a church with a bunch of kids trying to start an interracial group and if the minister hadn't been there the old man would have horsewhipped me?"

"Hush yo' mouth, Chuck," said Tom. "You're spitting on your grandfather's grave. You know that, don't you? Right on the green grass of his grave."

"Oh, stop it!" cried Lou. "None of you know what you're talking about—"

Tom Evans picked up Lou Callender's tightly clenched fist, began trying to pry the fingers open. "Quit sizzling, sweetie. Simmer down. . . ."

"Look," said Carol, who was large, phlegmatic, and who disliked arguments. "Look. Let's change the subject—"

"No!" Lou pulled her hand away from Tom's. The thin, almost transparently pale skin of her face was flushed.

"Lou—" said Sara, and Tom interrupted, "Let her go, Sara. She's got opinions, too."

"I certainly have! I most certainly have! The way you-all talk people would think everyone in the South went around smelling magnolias and calling for a slave to—to peel a grape." Lou's chin was trembling. "You just don't understand, that's all. Chuck Martin, you know better than to talk the way you do. You know better. You're—you're nothing but a traitor!"

There was an uncomfortable silence. Chuck's voice, when he spoke, was quieter and more serious than any of them had ever heard it. "To what?" he asked. "My country or the Confederate slave states?"

"For gosh sakes!" Sudsy's voice was pleading, and Lou turned on him.

"You just be quiet, Clifton Sutherland! You just hush! You come from New England, and everyone knows what they're like. Smug and—and know-it-all and trying to run everyone's business in the country, getting rich on the slave trade and being self-righteous about the South—"

"Hey! Swear to God I never shipped a slave in my whole life! All my people were doctors, and that's what I want—"

"It doesn't make any difference. I like Negroes. I was brought up to respect and be kind to them. Why, everyone knows, everyone *knows* Margaret Benjamin's my friend. Everyone knows I'd—I'd jump in the lake through the ice before I'd do anything to hurt her because she's a Negro. When I see the new Quimby—what's his name—"

"David Champlin," said Sara.

"When I see David I'll—I'll go out of my way to make him feel welcome. Just like I did Margaret. The way you-all talk—"

"He won't buy that," said Chuck. "Not if you marked it down to ninety-eight cents and threw in your lily-white body he wouldn't buy it. He'd rather you crossed over and walked on the other side of the street. Margaret doesn't buy it."

"I don't now how you figure you know so much about it, Chuck Martin. You're talking—"

"Maybe it's because he thinks, honey chile," said Tom. "Try it some time." He curled a lock of her hair around his fingers, then slipped an arm through hers and pulled her to her feet. "Come on, sweetie. Let's go. Your head's going to start aching—"

Sudsy parked his car in the garage he rented from a family living near the campus, and he and Sara walked together toward the college. "You always act like you're running somewhere," he complained. "Even when you're walking. You have to run? Can't you ever just sort of amble along? I bet you'd run to the dentist."

She didn't answer, didn't speak until they were almost at the college gates. Then she said "Why?"

"Why what?"

"Why do people have to fly at each other's throats over other people just because the other people's—other person's—well, anyhow, because their skin's a different color? We're all having a nice time together, then all of a sudden we're fighting the Civil War. It's stupid!"

"I can't see that it's exactly stupid, Sara. If your dad's a lawyer and mixed up in labor cases, I'll bet when you were a kid you met Negro lawyers and, well, Negroes like that. The only ones Lou's ever known are the ones the whites have manufactured—"

"You mean down there in what Tom's always calling the murder belt?"

"Yes."

"Well, it's all lousy. Chuck's right. Margaret Benjamin hates Lou. Honestly she does. I can see it. Sometimes she isn't even nice to her, and Lou tries so—so damned hard she makes you just plain sick."

They were quiet for a few moments, walking along the center strip of the quadrangle; then Sara said, "If David Champlin had walked into Margie's while we were talking, we'd have all shut up and then we'd have started gushing all over the place and he'd have known, he'd have *known,* and it's awful."

"We had a swell time together yesterday. Except when Randy was there."

"I'm glad Chuck jumped him. Glad! And that's something else. Chuck's from as far south as Lou. So it can't all be just early environment and influences."

"I dunno. I've wondered myself. I've got a sneaking hunch it's something that happened when he was a kid. Maybe he's got what my father talks about—a low threshold for pain, only with him it's for other people's pain."

"And maybe he's got a low threshold for ideas, too." They had reached the upper third of the quadrangle, and as Sara turned to leave she said, "And it could be Tom's right. That Chuck thinks—"

She headed for Rainsford Hall, really hurrying now in the gray light of late afternoon. She thought of the sketch of David Champlin she had tried to do last spring. It lay hidden now in the bottom of her suitcase because it wasn't good enough. She had made it after she returned home to Lakeside Heights, completed it after more than a score of false starts, and then almost destroyed it because she knew it was the best she could do then, and it wasn't good enough; it was so far from good enough that a jagged tear in an upper corner showed where she had started to tear up even that final copy.

Still, she might show it to him even now, she thought; she would if he called her and let her know himself that he'd arrived. He ought to, she told herself; it would only be polite. After all, they'd had dinner together and washed dishes together and she'd been sort of junior hostess, and he must know, just couldn't help knowing, that they liked him and were interested in him. Actually, he should have called her yesterday, he really should; it would have been the right thing to do; and not having called yesterday, surely today, this evening he would.

Then as she reached the sidewalk on the women's dormitory side of the quadrangle she knew with deadly certainty that he could never have called her yesterday, would never call her now, not if they boiled him in oil. She felt sickeningly helpless in the face of that knowledge, cornered by an enemy she could neither touch nor fight off.

"It's not going to be like that. It's not, not, *not*—" She was running up the steps of Rainsford Hall, really running now across the hallway to the telephone booths, stopping only briefly to read the directory of extensions thumbtacked to the bulletin board. Two "Q"s, Quentin Hall and Quimby House. Three-seven-three-five; three-seven-three-five; she repeated the figures over and over as she entered the booth. One hand was already on the telephone receiver while the other was closing the door.

20

You colored boys going to look like a bunch of lonesome fleas floatin' in a pan of milk. That was what Gramp had said, and although for years David had been far from agreeing with Gramp on everything, he was willing to admit, at the end of his first two weeks at Pengard, that Gramp's batting average was pretty high.

Ever since he'd settled in at Quimby House on Sunday, he'd waited with subconscious anxiety for the summons to the dean's office for an interview. Doc—he was calling him that in his mind now—Doc Knudsen had said it would probably be the day after his arrival, and when, late that first Monday afternoon, the buzzer in the hall sounded one long and two shorts, indicating a phone call for him, he hurried downstairs to the booth in the main hall, relieved that the call had come at last. He was so sure that if not the dean it must be Doc Knudsen to notify him of the interview that when he picked up the receiver his first words were an interrogatory "Yes, sir?"

"Oh, no! Not 'sir'! How are you, David Champlin? This is Sara. Sara Kent."

First there was the gone feeling in the pit of his stomach, then the very definite prickle at the back of his neck, then the odd sensation that his circulation had gone into reverse, that he was in the throes of what Gramp called "a revolution of the blood." He could hear the croak in his own voice when he answered. "Oh, I—hello—I'm fine. I mean, I'm O.K."

"That's wonderful, David. I'm—we're so glad you got here. I looked and looked for you at the beginning of term, and then Uncle Karl told me about your grandfather. Is he all right now?"

"My grandfather?" How did she manage it? How did she manage to sound as though it made all that difference to her if Gramp was all right?

"Of course, Stoopid. No one else's—"

"He's—he's pretty good. The doctor says he'll be all right if he takes it easy. I mean—thanks for asking—"

He'd gotten well into his halting, embarrassed reply before he realized he'd been called "Stoopid" by someone he'd met only once, a white at that, and had felt not even a flicker of resentment.

"We were scared. Honestly we were. Not just about your grandfather but that you wouldn't make it this year. Uncle Karl was having conniptions all over the place."

He could find no answer, and even had he found one he had no confidence that his voice would be up to delivering it. Sara broke into a pause that was becoming almost audible. "David—what time is your sitting?"

"My sitting—"

"In the dining hall. At dinner."

"Six o'clock."

"Oh, damn. Mine's six thirty. Look, we'll see you after dinner? In the rec hall? Everyone goes in then for a candy bar or something. You just have to after those puddings—"

"Well, gosh, I've got an awful lot of studying and, well, sort of straightening out to do on my schedule and assignments and all—"

"Pooh! You'll do it all the better. Everyone has a lot of studying to do. Don't be difficult. That's what my mother used to say—"

"Well—I'll try. And—and thanks for calling—"

He walked back upstairs slowly. For all his kidding around with Gramp, he knew the last thing he wanted was to start out his college career with some damned girl entanglement, any girl, but especially a white one. It wasn't that good here; a guy only had to walk his black self across the campus two or three times, only had to catch a few of the stares, a few of the big, phony smiles—smiles that would have been casual if he'd been white—and listen to some of the accents to know it wasn't all that good. He sure as hell wanted to see Sara Kent again; more, he guessed, than he'd ever wanted to see anyone. And there it was, staring him right in the eye: his own dark face, trouble, danger, loneliness, staring him right in the eye.

He didn't go to the recreation hall. Instead, he battled furiously with the problems Benford had assigned, then restored his self-confidence by whipping through Andrus's assignment in Latin. Maybe this was what the guy at the hotel, Randall, had called "holing up," and had said wasn't good. Let it be that way, then; let it be.

He had learned a lot about some of the students the day before, in Sutherland's room, after Clevenger left and they all settled down to digest their chicken and drink Chuck Martin's beer. Sutherland was the son of a famous doctor in Boston, the grandson of the doctor who had founded the Sutherland Clinic. David had read about the clinic in news magazines, and about the royalty and famous people from all over the world who came there. Sudsy was headed for Harvard Medical—he hoped. "Hey!" he said. "Maybe you'll make Harvard Law the same time I make the med school and—"

"Gosh, I hadn't figured on Harvard—"

"Hell, man, you've got to. You're going to be the first Negro Justice of the Yewnited States Soopreme Court, and Harvard's the first rung—"

Some whites saying that would have offended him. Now he just grinned and said, "You saying it. Not me."

To Tom Evans's obvious pleasure, David knew all about Bull Evans. The Prof had considered Bull Evans one of the greatest leaders American labor had ever known. Tom said: "Kinda hard for a guy who looks like me to live up to. The old man's always telling me if I ever forget my father was a labor man and got his arm broken by a labor cop, and did time in prison, he'll break my neck." He sighed. "I look awful funny making muscles."

"You'll meet Hunter Travis," said Chuck.

"Travis—Travis—you mean—"

"Yeah. Son of Lawrence Travis."

"Gosh."

"Hell of a swell guy. And he's almost as blond as I am—"

David wondered if this Travis guy was passing, then realized he couldn't be, his father was too well known.

"He writes," said Sudsy.

"Already?"

"Well, gosh!" said Tom. "You have to be able to if you want to get in here. Read, too."

"Don't be so damned smart," said Sudsy. "Champlin means does he already write and get published. And he does. In the little magazines."

"I tried reading one of his things once," said Chuck. "Too highbrow for me. I couldn't reach that far."

David made a mental note to give Travis a wide berth.

They didn't know, as he did, what a pain in the neck an uppity, near-white northern Negro could be. Some of them could give lessons to any ofay red-neck in any southern town. And Travis probably wasn't the only Negro at the college it would be well to go easy with at first. He had already learned, by way of a surprisingly long letter from Nehemiah, about two other characters, Negroes, and Nehemiah's adjectives had prompted him to destroy the letter in case Gramp got hold of it. Gramp was no kindergartener when it came to cussing, but Nehemiah qualified for a degree.

"And you've already met the scourge of my childhood," said Tom. "Sara. Little Sara Kent."

"Well—sort of. Last spring."

He wanted Tom to go on, but the smaller youth only sighed, said "Oh, well. Our relationship goes back to prehistoric times. She's all right, I guess—" and the conversation veered to the peculiarities of various professors and the dearth of entertainment in Laurel. Sara wasn't mentioned again until Tom Evans walked back to Quimby House with him, invited himself upstairs, and stood for a moment looking out the window over the couch. "That's Rainsford Hall, directly across the quad. Sara's there and a girl I go out with sometimes named Lou Callender. Kinda stupid but sexy. And there's a girl there from down your way, colored, named Margaret Benjamin. You could spot her even if she wasn't colored because she's one of the dead-earnest kind, and it's all you can do to see her for textbooks. She even studies in the rec hall and looks at the rest of us like we were a bunch of incorrigible delinquents."

He turned from the window and saw David, who had started to unpack, and his eyes widened like a child's. "What in hell you got there, Champlin!"

"Oh, my God!" said David. "Sweet Jesus!" He looked at the object in his hand, felt that he must be changing color with embarrassment. Never, never, never, if he lived to be ten thousand, would he let Gramp mess with his packing again. The cloth lions and tigers, the ceramic and ivory elephants and giraffes he and Gramp had collected as a sort of hobby, were all right; he'd packed a few of those himself, and put them on the mantel. But *this*—this was a battered calico tiger with yellow wool whiskers and multicolored mane of yarn, made for him so long ago he couldn't remember, although he remembered sleeping with it almost until he got into high school, remembered that the night he came home from the hospital the first time, it had been on his pillow, where Gramp had put it, and that he had gone to sleep with it feeling good in his hand, while Stumpy had lain curled beside him, purring.

Evans was laughing now. "Relax, Champlin. I'll bet if I hadn't hidden it, my mother would have packed my old Teddy bear. I guess they figure these things are sort of symbols. If they can get us to hang on to 'em, we'll keep on looking innocent and cute when we're asleep. That tiger's a work of art. Put it in the center of the mantel and punch the first guy in the nose who laughs at it. It's got real character."

David saw Nehemiah the first time on Monday morning, walking down the steps of the dining hall, swaggering a little, squinting as he searched with small, dark eyes the hurrying groups of students crossing the campus on their various ways to classes or breakfasts. David whistled, and Nehemiah turned, grinned, and hurried across the grass. "Hey, man! Looking for you! You made it—"

"Yeah. How you doing?"

"Somewhat. Somewhat."

It was an expression that was exclusively Nehemiah's, and it sounded good to David. Then, for the first time, he realized the truth of Gramp's remark about the fleas in a pan of milk.

"Hi, flea!" he said, and chuckled at Nehemiah's puzzlement. It was plain that Nehemiah thought this was a new slang phrase he should be up on.

"How's Li'l Joe? He all right now?"

"Seems to be. I wouldn't have left if he'd been too poorly. He's a stubborn old goat, though. Sure hope the doc stays on his back—"

"How you like it so far? I went to Columbus over the weekend. Next weekend I'm going to Dayton. Man, you know I got uncles and aunties and cousins all over this damned state? Man, you gotta make that Columbus scene with me. They got girls there—you just don't know. You got to make it with me—"

"O.K., O.K. Give me time, man. Right now I've got to go eat, then pick up my schedule, then go to nine o'clock class."

They talked for a few minutes, the questions David wanted to ask going unspoken. Nehemiah wasn't the guy to answer them. Nehemiah didn't just see things under the bed; if they weren't there, he put them there. From the talk of the New Orleans musicians who had traveled outside the South, David knew the technique of finding the way. If you traveled by train and the porter didn't know, you found a redcap or a clean-up man in the station and you asked him "What kind of a town is this?" The question had only one meaning; it had nothing to do with weather or the cost of living or the possibilities of a good time. Let the whites worry about those aspects of a city; when a Negro asked the question it meant just one thing. Before the conversation was over he'd know what hotels would take colored, where he could eat, where he could go, and—most important of all—where he could not go.

If a town was entered by car, a guy kept his eye out for the poorer streets, the slum areas, those places where only Negroes were seen on the sidewalks, or mostly Negroes.

As far as Pengard and the town of Laurel were concerned, the boy at the Inn last spring, Randall, had answered most of his questions. He had learned a lot yesterday, too, albeit from whites, although he hadn't quite digested it yet. Nehemiah's answers to further questions were bound to be diatribes and would only be confusing.

"Y'all meet a couple of colored guys named Simmons and Dunbar yet?" Nehemiah was asking.

"No. They the two cats you wrote about?"

"Yeah. You'll know 'em. Light-complected, nappy. They both wear solid gold threads, swear they do. They aren't in the same dormitory, but that's the only time you'll see 'em apart. Got no time for anyone, either of 'em. Don't rush up to speak. They'll put you in the deep freeze right now. Make you feel like you never was born."

"Where they from?"

"New York. Chicago. Dicty! Man, they invented it. If you come from the South or you talk like it, they got you down for a handkerchief-haid Uncle Tom, no matter do they even know your name. You'll meet 'em; can't miss 'em."

"I'll watch out. See you later?"

"Sure. You got a buck and a quarter to spare?"

"I—I guess so." He was surprised. Nehemiah was too proud to borrow.

"Been saving. Thought maybe we'd get us some ribs tomorrow night. Place called Mom's. Closed Mondays."

"Sure." One thing was certain: Gramp wouldn't blame him for spending part of his small hoard on ribs.

When he walked into the dining hall his defense went up

automatically. It was a defense that had served him well all his life; it was like a modern glass window in a door: those behind it could see out, but to those on the outside it was opaque. The Prof had spotted it, had growled once, "What I am thinking you know, but what you are thinking—bah! I will never know."

He told himself that most of the stares when he walked into the room were reactions to be expected. Even a bunch of kids in grade school stared at a newcomer, even if he was the same color. The room was filled with long tables, and the wall on his right was taken up by a cafeteria-style counter. Through an archway opposite the entrance he could see more long tables with women students eating at them. He saw no faces that were not white, were not strangers, and it was like walking into winter. Then he heard someone call, "Hey! David! Champlin!" and, searching for the source, saw Chuck Martin at the rear of the room hurrying toward a side door. The big ungainly youth waved to him, called, "Gotta rush! See you later!" and was gone.

He turned to go toward the cafeteria counter, and a tall, good-looking, rather elegant youth rose from the table directly in front of him and came over, hand outstretched. "Sit anywhere you can find a seat, Champlin," he said. Then, looking back over his shoulder, "There's one next to me now. Fellow just left."

David said, "Thanks," and followed, took his seat and said "Thanks" again when someone handed him a filled coffee cup. He sugared it and listened as the slim young man who had greeted him said, "This is the routine: get the motor started at the table with coffee and juice, then fuel up at the counter. Tilt your chair against the table when you go—"

There was something about this guy, thought David, something familiar that he couldn't be quite sure about, but was pretty damned sure. In New Orleans, when they were as light as this guy, they rode in the front of the bus, drank at the tables in the nightclubs or at the white end of the bar in saloons, used the white toilets, and married white women—or men—if their own ancestry wasn't too well known. If that was the case they usually moved north. Gram's first cousin, a woman named Ella something-or-other, wouldn't even speak to Gramp when she saw him on the street, usually crossed over, yet she'd had the same grandparents Gram had.

He finished his coffee, started to rise and go to the counter, when the fair-skinned young man beside him said: "My name's Travis. Hunter Travis. Glad you made it O.K., Champlin. Doc Knudsen told me about you."

"Yeah?" He shouldn't be surprised, should have known, after what Chuck had said the day before. He remembered that he'd decided to give this Travis guy a wide berth; now the decision flickered and went out. Travis's speech, though it was warm and friendly, was precise, the speech, almost, of a foreigner who had complete mastery of English. Hadn't someone said that Travis had received most of his education in Europe? And here he was, David Champlin, sitting next to a guy whose father was just about one of the most famous statesmen in, well, just about in the world.

"Get your breakfast," said Travis. "The sleep-in nine o'clock classes will be here any minute. You'll get trampled in the rush."

When David came back to the table with his tray, Travis was just finishing. "I have to go," he said. "What house are you in?"

"Quimby."

"I'll drop in if it's O.K. with you. Maybe tonight. Seen the dean yet?"

"Not yet. Not even this spring. He was in the hospital then. I'd thought I'd probably have to see him this morning. Maybe he's forgotten me."

"No such luck, sonny boy. He'll get around to you. Luck and all that—"

"Thanks. I'll need it."

"Not to worry—" and then Hunter Travis was walking toward the door, not fast, but moving with a sort of controlled hurry. His tan slacks and darker jacket over a yellow cashmere pullover were tailored, David could tell, to the last ten-thousandths of an inch, yet they managed to look casual, unostentatious. David thought, with some envy, that there was a guy who would look just as well dressed in sweatshirt and Levis. Lawrence Travis's son; that was something for the books, something to write home to Gramp about. Gramp would be impressed, even Gramp, who had no illusions about anyone, black or white.

The rest of that day was a blur of classrooms that all looked alike, professors who all looked different, and students he didn't have time now to worry about. The professors, especially Andrus, were friendly, although some of them, he decided privately, were a little on the screwy side. He approached his mathematics class, the last of the morning, with a nervous quiver in his belly. Chuck Martin walked with him, and David said, "Like going to the dentist." Chuck answered, "He's not all that bad. He doesn't expect miracles."

"Maybe not. But he expects something I sure as hell don't have."

"Sure you have. He'll find it."

Benford's appearance was anything but reassuring. Well over six foot, thought David, maybe six three or four. He was as thin as a lath, and his face seemed composed of hollows and the rims of hollows, the dull black skin tight-stretched over the bones, eyes so deep set their expression couldn't be read. He said, "Ah, Champlin," when David entered, then appeared to forget his new student's existence. He posted a problem on the blackboard, smiled at the class with what seemed to David to be pure ferocity, then called David to his desk. For half an hour they reviewed David's previous work, David apprehensive, Benford inscrutable. At the end of the half hour he handed David a list of books. "These will be of help to you, Champlin. You can get them at the college library. Or at the bookstore. Look for used ones. If they happen to be out of any of them, let me know. I'll lend them to you."

"Thank you, sir," said David. He looked longingly at the French window behind Benford's desk, then walked to his seat, his mind, he thought, a blank, just a damned vacuum no one would ever be able to pour mathematics into, least of all a character made purely of black ice.

Sara's call came late that afternoon after he returned from the library and bookstore and was thinking it was a sobbin' shame that the only Negro professor he'd seen so far had to be a sour-faced scarecrow who must have been weaned on persimmons.

When he came back to his room from the telephone booth, he sat looking at the pile of books on the too small desk. He'd have to get a card table, he thought, something with more surface to it. He was fighting his mind, battling to drive from it the thought—any thought—of Sara Kent's voice, of a rendezvous in any old "rec hall" where he'd get himself—and her—stared at, whispered about. Maybe there'd even be a humbug; plenty of mealymouthed southern accents around, and a white boy could be all right, he could be friendly as a pup, all smiles and buddy-buddy talk—until he saw you even looking at a white girl. David Champlin hadn't come to any college to show any damned white he was as good as they were, not him; he knew he was, and for now that would have to do. Didn't this pint-sized chick have any sense, any sense at all?

Suddenly his subconscious mind threw to the surface something she had said the first night they met when he wasn't listening much because he was all jarred up by her reference to a "Little Tommy" Evans. Now he heard it in his mind: "My father says anyone who'd do that"—what it was David couldn't remember—"didn't have good sense, and I said that sometimes I just didn't think you ought to have good sense. That if you had a lot, an awful lot, of sense you didn't have any fun, and couldn't get a lot of things done that ought to be done and that maybe 'sense' is a sort of, well, hindrance—"

That answered his question. She didn't have any sense at all, and he knew that he was going to have to remember it and watch out.

And he knew, too, that careful, careful, careful as he must be, he would be doing every day what he had been doing ever since Suds Sutherland's car had gone through the entrance to the campus yesterday: looking, listening, waiting with something deep inside himself that functioned independently of mind or body for the glimpse of a small figure that walked outwardly and ran inwardly, the sound of a high young voice tumbling out words in a freshet of sound that sparkled and glowed from the warmth beneath it. This he knew he would be doing, and there could be no stopping it.

21

TWO WEEKS AFTER DAVID entered Pengard, Dr. Karl Knudsen sat in the little office adjoining Dr. Andrus's classroom, talking with the Latin professor. He started to refuse the proffered cookies that Andrus was passing across his desk, then, fearing to appear rude, took one and held it fearfully. He had often considered the possibility of slipping one into his pocket and taking it to the Geology Department. One of the instruments used to determine the age of fossils and rocks might be tried with interesting results.

Andrus, munching contentedly and somewhat noisily on his own cookie, disposed of its residue with a swallow of tea and said, "So you threw your protégé to the wolves, eh?"

"Benford will be good for Champlin. The boy will never be outstanding in mathematics, true, but he should manage a 'B' once he learns to discipline his mind. You agree with me and the others that there is no objection to Greek?"

"Certainly. Haven't you made your recommendation to the dean yet?"

"I was waiting until I had talked with you. I will call him this afternoon. I mentioned Champlin's desire to take Greek in my report—"

Andrus pushed the telephone that was on his desk across to Knudsen. "Why not do it now?"

"Why not?" Knudsen dialed a number well known on campus because of the dean's habit of singing it whenever he gave it out—"Ein, zwie—" one-two-three-four. It was a separate line to the dean's study. In a moment Goodhue's voice was audible even to Andrus. "Goodhue here—"

"Yes, Dean Goodhue. Knudsen here . . . I know, and I apologize. . . . I have been busy but that is no excuse. . . . But now I am pardoned, I hope. . . . It is about young Champlin that I am calling. . . . I have been talking with his instructors. . . . They see no reason why he should not add Greek to his curriculum, even though he has started late. . . . But, Dean . . . there have been exceptions in the past. . . . We are not a rigid . . . you were favorably impressed when you interviewed him, no? . . . You have not? It has been two weeks! . . . One moment, Dean, one moment. . . ."

Knudsen lowered the receiver, cupped a hand over the mouthpiece, and looked across the desk at Andrus, who sat quiet and unsmiling. There was a look of tiredness in the Latin professor's eyes. Knudsen's eyes were wide, seemed a deeper blue than when he had placed the call, had fire behind them. "He has not interviewed David Champlin! Two weeks the boy has been here, and the dean has not interviewed him. Yet he refuses Greek. Incredible!"

"No," said Andrus. "Not in the least incredible. Get back to him, Knudsen. He'll be suspicious."

Knudsen spoke again into the telephone. "When do you plan to interview him? . . . This afternoon? Do not crowd yourself. . . . I am not being sarcastic. I try only to point out that the boy is worth taking time with. . . . You will call me after you have seen him? . . . Good—"

Knudsen replaced the receiver on its bracket with exaggerated gentleness. "My wife says I am naïve," he said softly. "It is possible. *Ja.* She says it is because I did not grow up in the land of the free." He sighed. "I should have followed through when the boy first arrived. There was an inkling last spring, at the dean's tea—"

"Don't blame yourself," said Andrus. "You have been in this country how long? Ten years? And you came directly to Pengard. What can you be expected to know of the prevalence of an evil we take for granted? Some of us fight the evil, a few of us, but feebly. Feebly. Goodhue is angry because he did not dare veto Champlin's delayed entrance. We would all have been lined up against him; it would have reached the old man by the lake—I will personally guarantee that it would—and there would have been hell to pay."

"He need not take it out on the boy."

"Human nature in any case. With the boy's color, the situation is inevitable. For years Goodhue has been quietly imposing his own quota system."

"A 'quota'? For Negroes? This is—is odious. The old man—"

"We can't prove it. But of twelve Quimby applicants for entrance this year, all apparently well qualified and able, only six received the dean's approval: Champlin, the Benjamin girl, Wilson, Simmons and Dunbar, and Travis."

"Travis? You're confusing him with someone else—"

"You didn't know that Hunter Travis is the son of Lawrence Travis?"

"Good God, no! I was not aware even that he was—is—a Negro!"

"You know, of course, who his father is?"

Knudsen's voice was testy when he answered. "Naturally. I read the papers. A great international statesman."

"Possibly one of the greatest your adopted country has produced. Of mixed ancestry, ethnically speaking. But definitely a Negro in the eyes of his countrymen."

"Well!" said Knudsen. "Well." He sighed again. "My wife will not be happy with me."

"Travis's mother is an Englishwoman. Much of his education has been received in Europe."

"The latter I knew, at least." Knudsen was silent a moment, then asked, "Why did Goodhue accept Nehemiah Wilson without argument? Except for mathematics his preliminary showing was less than mediocre—"

"One can only guess," said Andrus. "It is my theory only, and wholly empirical. Wilson is not going anywhere."

"Don't make me feel more ignorant than I obviously am."

"Wilson is a prodigy in mathematics. Very well. But that alone will not carry him far. He must do better in other areas. The dean is no fool. He is a Southerner and he knows, not the Negro mind—no white Southerner gets below the surface of that—but the Negro stereotypes. In Wilson he sees a sort of freak. And he is shrewd enough to recognize Wilson's hatred and antagonism. It is my theory that Champlin represents to him the hated symbol of Negro intellectual equality, possibly superiority. He has heard of your brother's tutelage, knows his high opinion of the boy's mind. Wilson's hidden psychological scars have already deformed his mind to such an extent that he poses no threat to us."

"Andrus! Do not say to 'us'—"

"It's true, is it not?"

"That we are white? Yes. That we are all of a piece? No! Bah! How do you know so much, my friend?"

"You forget. If I believed in reincarnation I would say that in some past life I fed great numbers of early Christians to the lions, and for that I taught for ten years in a college in the Deep South."

"It was bad?"

"I suppose I exaggerate. It was not that bad. There were many fine and sensitive minds. But. But. Knudsen, I cannot put a name to it, cannot fully explain it, except to say that in the South the white mind is as crippled, in its own way, as the Negro mind. Not in every instance, mind you, but in most. There is a something that is not direct, is devious. Perhaps it is because they know subconsciously the evil of their own thinking. My God! How can they help but know it! Yet they will not face it, and in not facing it their minds become like, let us say, someone with a 'wry neck.' I used to call it, to myself, the 'wry mind.'"

"There is Martin. The boy they call 'Chuck.' A fair student, and one who has been twice expelled for interracial activities in southern colleges."

"Ah, yes. The Martins. There were a number of them, and they were the leaven in a bitter, sodden loaf. In the Martins perhaps the South will find salvation. And in some of its writers who have achieved objectivity. But I doubt that their numbers are great enough."

"That may be good."

"Why do you say that, Knudsen?"

"Because even I can see that the Negro, if he is to achieve his proper status, will have a far firmer foundation if it comes through his own efforts, without the patronage of whites."

"This will mean violence."

"You believe this?"

"I am almost certain of it."

Knudsen sighed, stood. "I am not happy, Andrus. No, I am not happy. I am far more unhappy than when I came in. Now I must go home, and my wife will make me more unhappy. She will say 'See? That is what I have been trying to make you understand.' "

"Before you leave—one question. In Nehemiah Wilson we also face the problem we have faced so often with Negro students from the Deep South: the problem of the cultural lag; the problem presented by inadequate, segregated schooling, often illiterate or only semiliterate parents with no background of learning or even simple schooling. Champlin was fortunate. Few of them are so fortunate. His injury exposed him mercilessly to your brilliant brother. But Wilson—like so many others—did not have such an advantage. Why wasn't he given precollege brush-up courses in the summer, as we have done for others?"

"It was offered, Andrus. I assure you it was offered. But he would not. And I felt we could handle it after he entered. Perhaps I was mistaken. There were economic reasons, valid ones. There is poverty, and there are many children. They needed what little he could earn. It was a real sacrifice for them to send him up here."

Andrus was silent for a long moment; then, for the first time in their years of friendship, Knudsen heard Hugh Andrus, head of the Department of Ancient Languages at Pengard, swear.

"God damn," said Andrus. "God damn to hell a world in which the human mind is at the mercy of those who hate the color of the body that houses it!"

22

THE SUMMONS FROM DEAN GOODHUE came on David's second Friday at Pengard. "Four thirty at the Dean's residence," it read. From Sanders, one of the upper classmen in the big room that adjoined his in Quimby House, he received directions for finding the house. "He likes to have the interviews there," said Sanders. "Cozier."

It would be shorter cutting through the outer quadrangle, and David was halfway across when he saw Dr. Knudsen emerge from one of the buildings and come toward him. For the first time since David had known him the little professor looked worried, but his face lightened when they met. "Ah, David! You are headed for the dean's?"

"Yes, sir."

"Have your ears burned? Professor Andrus and I have been talking about you. Don't look so concerned. What we said was good. If the dean does not keep you too long, come and have coffee with us. We are close by. I shall be interested to hear what is said, and my wife also. She asks about you constantly."

"Yes, sir. Thanks. I'll be glad to—"

Perhaps Sara would be there; that would be something he couldn't help. Meeting her there would be different from seeking her out, looking for her, knowing he was looking for trouble at the same time. He had stayed away from the recreation hall, knowing he was doing what Randall had warned against, that he was "holing up," but seeing no alternative that wasn't worse. He and Sara took no classes together, but he knew that sooner or later there would be a meeting; only the need for intensive study these first two weeks had prevented it so far.

A semicircular drive swept in front of the dean's brick-and-timber house, and the French door to his study opened directly on it, set between mullioned casement windows. Sanders had described it to him. He knocked, making it a firm knock, and when he heard the summons to come in he carefully scraped the mud from his shoes on the old-fashioned iron scrapers beside the door and took off his new knit cap before entering. He had been downright shocked by the manners of some of his fellow students: caps on in the house, not saying "sir" or "ma'am" to an older person or a teacher, things like that. Gramp would give 'em hell, he had thought, pure hell. If these were white manners—

When he entered he found himself looking directly at the top of the dean's head, bent over papers on a desk in the center of the room. He didn't know how he knew, but he knew; the minute the dean raised his head and reached for the pipe resting in the heavy ashtray, David knew. It wasn't ever something seen or heard; it was something smelled with a mental olfactory apparatus. He wondered why Nehemiah hadn't tipped him off, but Nehemiah saw Crow everywhere he looked, and the dean would be part of Nehemiah's general picture of the world, no better, no worse, than any other white.

"Ah, David," said Goodhue. Andrus had said "Ah, Champlin" that first day in class. Doc Knudsen was the only faculty member who called him "David." From the Doc, "Champlin" would have sounded forced.

You wants to keep breathing in and out you has to take it. Jes remember how ignorant they is. Gramp had said that once, but a hell of a lot of good it did in a spot like this. Gramp had said something else, too, and that did help sometimes. He guessed it was from the Bible. *"Does it matter that they know thee not? I knows thee—"*

Now, in this spot, the best thing to do after saying "Yes, sir" was to keep quiet, say nothing. Even if someone had held a gun at his head he wouldn't have smiled, and that was what this ofay character was looking for, hoping for; a nice wide, white-toothed nigra smile. Son of a bitch, he thought. You'll be dead and smelling even worse'n you do now before you see li'l David's teeth.

He sensed and grimly enjoyed that his own impassiveness had put the dean momentarily at a loss, made him flounder.

The dean looked down at his desk again. "Your reports," he said, indicating the papers before him. Now that he spoke as an authority he was in possession of himself again.

"Your reports," said the dean again. "They are surprisingly good."

David inclined his head slightly, said nothing.

"Surprising, I mean, when one considers that you entered late. You had help, no doubt?"

"From Professor Bjarne Knudsen in New Orleans. He tried to keep me caught up."

"Ah, yes. Well, I can find no fault with them, except your mathematics report. I have discussed this with Professor Benford. He does not seem concerned."

Was there an ever so slight accenting of the "he"? An intonation that said plainly, "*He* does not seem concerned, but what could one expect? *I* certainly am." Whether or not this was true, the knowledge that Benford had not expressed concern was the best news he'd received since entering.

The dean shuffled through the papers. His pipe was resting in its accustomed niche in one side of his mouth, and small puffs punctuated his phrases. "There is a recommendation here—no—here—no—this is it—" He separated one paper from the others and leaned back, reading it, but not aloud, frowning as he did so. "About Greek. That you be permitted to add it to your first-year courses. It is submitted by your faculty adviser, Dr. Knudsen, and"—puff-puff—"apparently has the"—puff-puff—"approval of some of your instructors."

This bastard was lying, sure as hell was lying; David was certain the recommendation carried the approval of all of his professors, even Benford. The dean's sigh was commensurate with his size, and he removed his pipe from his mouth to give full vent to it. "I regret that I must disagree with these faculty members. But this seems ill-advised at the present time, and it is definitely a departure from established procedure. No, I cannot consent to this. Any spare time you have, any spare energy, should be devoted to strengthening your weaknesses, not on added studies." He laid the paper down gently. "You may, of course, elect it in your sophomore year."

David was not particularly disappointed, had begun to have doubts himself about carrying an additional subject. He had the textbooks with him; if he had time he could keep on fooling around with it unbeknown to anyone. But he'd fry before he'd tell this man that. He remained silent behind his one-way wall, neither smiling nor scowling, eyes set and still.

The dean replaced the pipe in his mouth, leaned back again, and said expansively: "So much for the details, David. You are doing well otherwise?"

"I think so."

"Do you have any problems?"

Now he could feel a smile coming on, coming on so strong

he had to fight to keep it from showing. It wasn't the kind of smile the dean would like at all; it was a smile he'd probably be lynched for in some places. It said, "Problems! Yes, you son of a bitch, you!"

He drove his hands deep into his pockets and looked directly into Goodhue's shallow, slate-colored eyes, saw the wince and quick inner withdrawal he had seen in other whites when a Negro looked them directly in the eyes, measured them, hated them, knew them. Above all, knew them.

"No problems." He kept his eyes on the dean's face. "Not right now," he added.

Goodhue did not rise and go to the door with him, although David felt sure that this was one of his cozy customs following an interview. When David's hand was on the door handle, Goodhue said: "Don't hesitate to call me any time, David. My extension is one-two-three-four"—a throaty chuckle—"Ein-zwei-drei–vier—"

Now David smiled without opening his lips, nodded, said, "Thank you. I hope I won't have to bother you."

"My *raison d'être* is to help, to advise. I try to keep in touch." A brief pause. "With everyone."

There was no point in answering, thought David; no point in wasting energy on this man. Doc Knudsen, Andrus, even Benford, a fellow wanted them to like him. This ofay son of a bitch? Let him alone. Let him hate and stay happy. *Do your business and get away. Don't mess with 'em more'n you has to. Tip your cap and get away.*

He pulled his knit cap over his ears, closed the door gently, and limped down the drive, shoulders straight, erect. The sound of his parting "Good evening, Dean" had been almost inaudible even to his own ears.

Karl Knudsen stood beside the desk in his study listening to Goodhue's blandly deep voice on the telephone. The little professor was frowning fiercely, but his own end of the conversation was in quiet monosyllables. Goodhue said, "I will be frank with you, Knudsen. I've always found it best."

"Of course."

"I fear I cannot share your enthusiasm—and the enthusiasm of the others—for your protégé."

"No?"

"No. He is a type certain to create difficulties."

"Why do you say that? We have not found him so."

"Permit me, Knudsen, to say that I am better equipped to

judge these people. They are, after all, our people in the South. . . . You said?"

"Nothing, Dean. Nothing."

"He appears uncooperative, and is uncommunicative to a point that borders on sullenness—"

"Champlin?"

"Yes."

"He is shy—"

"It is not shyness I am speaking of. No matter. There is no fault to be found with him from the scholastic standpoint, of course. Your brother did an excellent job. There is, of course, your own subject, in which he does not shine, but Benford appears confident this will be overcome, and I am not in a position to quarrel with his opinion."

"I am seeing Benford this evening."

"Good. Good. I called you, however, concerning the matter of the boy taking Greek. Really, Knudsen, it's out of the question. Quite out of the question. I explained this to him."

"I see."

"I hoped you would, old boy—"

"I do. Quite clearly now—"

"Good. Good. I only hope this boy won't let your side down. It's always a gamble—"

"*Ja.* Thank you, Dean. I must go. Our doorbell is ringing. It was good of you to telephone so promptly."

"Quite all right. We should always talk these problems out together. That has been my policy—"

"*Ja.* My wife is calling. I will see you no doubt at the faculty breakfast tomorrow. Goodbye—"

Eve Knudsen's greeting was warm and gracious. Man would be a fool, thought David, to doubt her sincerity; she just wasn't phony, not in any way that he could see. He was smarting with anger and resentment after his interview with Goodhue, and had tried to think of an excuse to stay away from the Knudsens' but could find none that would hold water. He didn't give a damn what that country son of a bitch with the fake English accent thought about him, not one damn. He knew. Nigger. He was a nigger again. It wasn't easy, he thought bitterly, being a human being on Thursday, a nigger on Friday, maybe a human being again on Saturday and a nigger again on Sunday. That was one of the darkest spots in the night of a colored person's life when he came away. A guy's guard was up all the time at home; up here he got conned into letting it down, and the knife was in him before he could see it.

He wondered about Goodhue and Benford as he walked to the Knudsens'. It must kill that white bastard's soul, just kill his soul, to have to look at a face as black as Benford's at faculty lunches and breakfasts, to have to call him "Professor," to know—this must be real pain, real hurtin' pain—that inside that black skull was a brain that had racked up degrees all over, even from Cambridge, a brain that made his own look sickly and puny.

Mrs. Knudsen led him into the living room and turned to him, laughing. "David! Would you be insulted if I said you've grown? Sometimes, after seventeen, young people resent being told that."

"No, ma'am. My grandfather says I'm plumping out—"

"Plumping out? Heavens, no! Filling in would be better. And"—she paused, became grave—"and, David, growing up. Definitely growing up."

"Yes'm. Guess we all do, sooner or later—"

"My husband will be here in a minute. He's on the telephone—" Before he could stop her she had gone into the hall, and he heard her call "Karl." He heard a telephone hung up, heard Knudsen say, not loudly but with an intensity obvious even to someone out of sight, "I am learning. *Ja!* I am learning now, Eve. You have been—"

Mrs. Knudsen's voice interrupted quickly. "David's here. We're waiting for you so we can have coffee—"

"Ah!" Knudsen hurried into the room, grasped David's arm with surprising strength. "Ah! Glad you came, David. I would not have blamed you had you stayed away."

"Why?" Eve Knudsen was frowning. "Why do you say that, Karl?"

"He has been with the Dean of Men. As I have just said, Eve, I am learning. Sit down, my boy, sit down; our coffee is not so strong and bitter as the Creole coffee—brr-rr!—but it is excellent. My wife has a certain touch with coffee—"

David sat on the deep wide-armed sofa where he had sat with Sara the first night he came to Laurel. He realized now that ever since he entered the house it had seemed somehow empty, that he had been listening for the sounds that would mean Sara was there, quick steps, a tumble of words.

The doctor sat down, then bounced up again, coffee cup in hand, and stood now before the fire. "I should not say it, not to a student, and tomorrow I will be sorry, but now I am ashamed and angry, so I say it. Damn the dean. I am sorry about the dean."

"Don't worry about it, Doctor. I mean, well, there's lots like him, all over—"

"The Greek—"

"Shucks, that doesn't matter. Honest, Doctor, I mean, honestly, I wasn't all that disappointed. Gosh, I've got an awful lot on my hands right now. Next year's time enough."

"Goodhue was nasty?" Eve Knudsen was looking at her husband, her voice low enough to hide any emotion that might lie behind it.

Knudsen shrugged. "I do not know. Was he, David?"

"Nasty? No, sir. He—he just said he wouldn't let me take Greek." How in hell could you explain to people like the Knudsens that characters like Goodhue were never nasty—in their sense of the word—to Negroes? That to be nasty or subtly unpleasant would be to put the Negro on a basis of equality. One was nasty and unpleasant to one's peers; to a Negro one was condescending and patronizing, dictatorial or violent, or even kind and gentle, but never, never nasty or sarcastic as one would be to a fellow white. David put his coffee cup down on the low table in front of the sofa and said, "Only, you see, I knew why. That was all."

"All! All! It is too much!"

"Karl." Eve Knudsen's voice was still low. "Karl, my dear, there is nothing to be done at this point. We will only make it harder on David if we—if you—press it."

This woman sure has sense, thought David; sure has sense and understanding both.

"It is hard," snapped Knudsen. "It is very difficult. One wants to fight—"

"Fight what? A set, shallow, stupid mind that nothing will ever change, not even righteous Danish indignation?" She turned to David. "We're being rude, David, talking as though you weren't here, but you do seem like one of the family, you know."

This time he didn't resent the "one of the family" remark as he had the earlier one about "almost a relative."

The doctor was still fuming. "I suppose you are right, Eve. When I cool down it is possible I will know it." His voice was without conviction. He turned to David. "We wish we could have invited you to have dinner with us, but we are dining with the Benfords tonight."

David, gratified that the subject had been changed, grinned. "I hope I live through it," he said.

The doctor looked puzzled, but his wife laughed until a breeze of fresh air seemed to have swept through the room. The doctor, whose laughter had joined his wife's, said, "We will leave a few shreds of you, David." Then added, "But soon, David, you will dine with us. We will have our niece Sara and perhaps young Evans. My wife has known him also since he was a baby." He looked almost wistful. "They tell me you play piano. We could have music, real music, as well as records, if you did not mind—"

"Me? Mind playing piano? Gee, no. I've been scared of getting rusty—"

23

WHEN DAVID WENT HOME for summer vacation, he felt full of years and wisdom. It was his first trip home since Christmas. There had been too many unexpected expenses, books, warmer clothing, for him to go home in spring vacation. He felt himself bridling when Gramp, meeting him at the station, said, "My Gawd, boy! You've growed!" He felt that he was well past the growing stage, was in the full maturity of manhood, then lost the feeling abruptly when, looking for Stumpy, Gramp told him the tail-less cat was dead. He wouldn't let even Gramp see the tears in his eyes; instead he made a great to-do about unpacking, thinking, not only of Stumpy who had shared his bed every night, but of Gramp without Stumpy's company, Gramp who hadn't told him about Stumpy because he didn't want him upsetted up there at the college.

Seeing Gramp again took some of the worry off his mind. Li'l Joe looked fine. He had never wholly believed Gramp's letters that always ended, "I am feeling O.K. Yrs. truly, your grandfather, Joseph Champlin," and had taken to calling home, collect, every couple of weeks, and Gramp had never objected to the expense.

Li'l Joe's happiness at having him home was quiet, controlled, and warmly deep. The Prof's was outspoken and boisterous, his great hug rib-cracking. The hardest part of the return was the realization that he could not communicate to either man anything but the surface features of his life at Pengard. To David's near bewilderment the Prof did not ask immediately about his grades but, eyes fiercely twinkling under the bushy brows, said, "My brother writes me of jam sessions! He says he is becoming quite a drummer. Tell me about them—"

It would have been better if the Prof had asked the question when Gramp wasn't around, instead of in the little house in Beauregard with Gramp's nose twitching like an inquisitive chipmunk's. Li'l Joe Champlin was pure murder when it came to knowing what was going on. David knew he wouldn't have to mention Sara Kent's name, any girl's name, but what Gramp would catch on and by some sort of psychic osmosis know damned well whether she was white or colored.

Remembering that first session was like living it again, covertly watching Sara clap hands no bigger than the palms of his own while they listened to records; Sara feeding him song titles as he sat at the piano in the little room off the Knudsen living room; she and Tom both singing, then the Doc disappearing and coming back from somewhere in the depths of the house with an old set of drums, grinning like a kid. The Doc wasn't bad on drums, but Tom was terrible, and David coached him at this and other sessions until he became, as David told Gramp and the Prof, passable. Nehemiah had been invited, but said he was spending the weekend with relatives in Cincinnati, and David knew this to be a barefaced lie. David did not need to ask why Lou Callender, the girl Tom dated every now and then, wasn't there. Tom had introduced them one day, and she shook hands and gushed, and David wondered, as he did so often, what some whites saw in the women they picked. Maybe Tom was making out with her, but David doubted it. She looked like a teaser to him.

Suds Sutherland and Chuck Martin came to some of the sessions after that first one, and a couple of girls whose faces David couldn't even remember very well the next day, although Sara could be in the room with him now, as close as she had been then, so clear was his memory of her face.

When at last they broke up the first session to go back to the dormitories, Sara, walking from the little music room into the living room, went into a quick Charleston step, and a shoe flew across the room. She reached out and grabbed his arm, and instinctively David bent it at the elbow, stiffening the muscles of his forearm for her to grip. Even with her full weight on it while she put the shoe on, the grip had been as light as a bird's or a kitten's. Yet he was still feeling it when he reached the quadrangle and walked across it to his room.

After that he didn't stay away from the recreation hall, although he kept in the forefront of his mind the knowledge that the dull red blocks that made up the floors were, for him, not tiles but eggs. Clevenger was there often, aloof and elegant, yet showing a patronizing friendliness that, thought David, was enough to make a guy puke. The youth from Virginia made a great point of tipping him off about the food at the snack bar, showed him the billiard room and library-study, and the room off the main lounge where there were a record player and records, as well as an old upright piano. David's eyes had gleamed at the sight of the grand piano in the main lounge, but he stayed away from it, partly from sheer awe at its magnificence, partly because he didn't want to call attention to himself.

The Negro student, Margaret Benjamin, who lived in Sara's dormitory, was in his history class, but they didn't seem to be able to hit it off together. There wasn't any question about her being a dedicated scholar, but, damn it, so was he, and there sure as hell must be something a fellow and a girl could talk about besides the Federalist Papers.

It was Margaret who switched the subject one morning in his second week and said: "What do you plan to do when you graduate? Or haven't you decided? I think making decisions is important."

"Law," said David. "Never thought about anything different."

She had chosen teaching, she told him; hoped for a Master's after Pengard. "Teaching and law," she said. "Those are the areas where we are most needed, don't you think?"

"Well—I guess so—" No need to ask what she meant by "we." Educated Negroes, and somehow she managed to sound condescending about it.

She said, "I haven't seen you at an ALEC meeting yet. You know about them, don't you?"

"Yeah. What they do besides talk?"

"Well, goodness, talk and discussion bring understanding—"

He shrugged. "I'll go along on law and teaching, but if

there's one thing we don't need it's more talk. Jesus! Yak-yakity-yak! What's it going to get us?"

"Oh, really now! Understanding—"

"Understanding!" He almost said, "Understanding, shit!" when a shaft of watery sunlight struck her heavy-rimmed glasses and made them gleam with an even brighter earnestness than usual, and he smothered the epithet. All the talk in the world wasn't going to bring about "understanding" between a Clevenger and a Nehemiah, or between a Goodhue and, say, himself. Or a red-neck bus driver and a Negro passenger.

His first real encounter with Simmons and Dunbar came in the recreation hall. There had been nods and greetings in class and on the campus, but they were distant and without warmth. On this day he was alone, playing piano softly in the small music room off the main lounge, running over blues chords, noodling around, relaxed, half humming, half singing one of Li'l Joe Champlin's favorites, *I'm the winin' boy—don't deny my name—Mamma, Mamma, won't you look at Sis*—when he turned quickly, flustered and thrown off by the feeling that someone was watching him. They were standing together in the doorway, Simmons, light-skinned, whip-slender, cat-graceful, his impassivity an ineffectual covering for cool contempt; Dunbar, shorter, darker, also slender, eyelids too heavy for a small face half covering the eyes in a concealment more revealing than a wide-eyed stare. After what Nehemiah had told him of these two, David had decided there would be no speaking first on his part, but now he was at a disadvantage, embarrassed, half angry, and before he could stop himself he said, "Hi—"

"Yeah." From Simmons it was half-greeting, half-contemptuous comment.

"Having fun?" asked Dunbar, and added, "Don't let us spook you."

"You're not spooking me," said David evenly. "Just fooling around, practicing."

"What?" asked Simmons.

"Nothing in particular. Music, blues—"

"Oh," said Simmons.

"Now we know," said Dunbar. They turned together, moving, it seemed, as one person, and crossed the main lounge. David saw them stop, with no apparent communication between them, at the grand piano by the big side window. He knew Simmons's laugh was coming before he heard it, then saw the tall youth slither onto the piano bench with the uncanny, jointless movement of a snake. There was the sound of the piano's fine tone, then one and then another slashing, dissonant chord, then the theme of "Tea for Two" was established, and from there on things happened musically that held him quiet and intent. The hands on the keyboard were skilled, subtly rhythmic, their owner passionately involved in what he was playing, and David thought: Bastard knows, that bastard really knows that piano. But he's never going to get out of that one; he's never going to make it home from way out there, serves him right, showboating—

Simmons, without ever getting home, with obviously no intention of getting home, stopped on a series of progressions that seemed to David to be going nowhere. His playing was a long way from the music David had learned from Miz Jones and Gramp.

He watched the two cross the lounge to leave through the snack bar, and felt cut off and alone. He had heard the message in Simmons's piano, knew it was meant for him, and it had come from across a gulf wider than the gulf that lay between him and the whites who surrounded him.

On Friday and Saturday nights the recreation hall was crowded. He never intended to go, yet usually found himself there, standing against a wall or sitting cross-legged on the floor with Sutherland or Martin or Evans, listening to the impromptu music, watching the dancing because—and he had stopped trying to deny it to himself—Sara Kent was usually on the floor, light and quick and laughing. Often she danced with either Simmons or Dunbar, and he fought down jealousy, knowing that it was she who had nicknamed them "The Ineffable Twins," knowing she would probably have danced with the devil himself if he turned out to be a good-enough dancer. It took Sara and Hunter Travis, with an assist from Chuck Martin, to persuade him finally to play the grand piano in the main lounge; then what had been genuine reluctance vanished when the small group standing around it when he started enlarged until students were three and four deep in front of and beside him.

Toward the end of the term, at Sara's urging, he attended a few ALEC meetings, held in the basement community room of a church near the campus, under the leadership of the rector of the church, a Father McCartney. He had been right; they talked—ethnic cultures, economic problems, psychological pressures, the whole routine. A frequently discussed subject was the bright day that would dawn when the Supreme Court outlawed school segregation, and during these discussions David had a rough time keeping his peace.

Walking back with Suds one night he said, "You-all honestly, I mean honestly, think that when the Supreme Court acts to desegregate schools it's going to make all that difference?"

"Well, gosh, isn't it? I mean if kids go to school together they can't grow up with all that hate and prejudice—"

David pushed his cap back, scratched his head, thought it wasn't possible that anyone, even a white, could be that stupid about race relations. Only Chuck Martin, he thought, would have known what he was talking about when he answered: "Look, Sudsy, it's going to be worse. Man, it's going to be a hell of a lot worse. For a hell of a long time. You want to bet?"

"How much?"

"A reasonable sum. Maybe a dime. But I'm stealing your money."

"O.K. Have it your way. But I don't get it—"

"Look, comes the time the government orders school desegregation, there are going to be so many, so damned many, new segregation laws passed by individual states, so damned much maneuvering to avoid compliance, it'll take a couple of generations to unravel 'em all. And I'll bet you a hell of a lot more than a dime that there's going to be bloodshed and riots the first time anyone tries to make integration work. And it won't stop. You ask Chuck Martin. He'll agree with me."

"You've got to be wrong. You've got to be—"

"I'm not, Suds. That's how it is."

It came to an end almost before it began, that first school year, with nothing left but memories of long hours of study, of worry over grades, of a growing sense of belonging to the world at large and not just a dark portion of it when he was with certain people, and of sharply defined alienation when he was with others; memories of occasional weekends with Nehemiah's relatives in Cincinnati; and church services there that reminded him of home and made him feel, briefly, no sense of being away. And a memory of Sara Kent. And this was a different kind of memory because it was a single one, weaving itself in and out of all the others, never absent, continuous, and it brought him a kind of pain he had never known before, and sometimes he wished to God he did not have to go back, and other times he told himself that by fall it would be better, might even go away, and knew that it would be no better, would never go away.

24

THE KENT HOME IN LAKESIDE HEIGHTS, just outside Chicago, was too big for one young girl and her father. It had even been too large in the days when Helen Kent had been alive and lived there with her husband and two daughters. Sara Kent, the younger, had always loved it. There was room for a child to run in; there were banisters to slid down. Later, the small and almost secret rooms that hid behind and between larger rooms had been a delight to a teenage urge for privacy. A huge third-floor room under the eaves, once a nursery, was her own now, a place where she could draw and paint and read and be Sara Kent, alone with herself.

During her first summer home from Pengard she drove to the city each morning with her father for art classes. They tried, these two, to assuage each other's loneliness, and worried, each of them, about the other. Only in the past year had Sara felt that she could reach across and touch her father in the world of grief and loneliness in which he lived.

Now Ellis Kent said, "Sara, are you sure you don't want to fly to Rio and see Martha?"

"I've been there. Let Martha visit us for a change."

"With three children? God forbid, if I do say it of my own grandsons."

"And that husband? God forbid, if I do say it of my own brother-in-law."

They laughed together. They had laughed together more often lately. Kent said, "How's it going in art class, chick?"

"Just lousy, thank you. And I know why, so please don't tell me to be patient. My anatomy instructor keeps at me and at me about having to crawl before I can walk, and walk before—"

"You can run. And you're running with crayon and paint as fast as you do with everything else."

"Would—would you like to see—"

"Some of your work? Immediately!" He followed her up the two flights of stairs to the top-floor room with a step almost as quick as her own. He stood in the doorway of the room and said, "Is it permitted to enter the artist's studio?"

"If you don't muss things up and leave a clutter—"

"Leave a clutter!"

"Just close your eyes and I'll lead you."

"I'm not like your mother, babe. I don't know a damn thing about art."

"You might as well finish it: but you know what you like, and that's just fine because I can't see why anyone paints or draws or writes or composes or stuff like that if it isn't for people to like, even if they don't like it for the right reasons and even if it makes 'em squirm because it's true—"

"Slow down. You'd give a jury fits, you would. Let me look in peace."

After a moment he turned from the sketches and smiled down at her. "For God's sake, daughter child, breathe! My opinion isn't worth a bean."

"It is, too. Of course it is—"

What he saw in the sketches before him was good; true and meticulous. There were sketches that even he could tell had been disciplined with some pain and much effort; they were like the music of a young jazz musician forced for an evening to play it sweet; there was a sense of straining at the leash about them.

"They're good, chick. They're very good."

"Wait. There's more. Paintings yet—"

She left him to cross to a cupboard on the far side of the room, and he flipped idly through the contents of a smaller portfolio that lay on the drawing board. He stopped suddenly and looked for a long moment at a sketch before him, then picked it up and held it for a closer view. A bust only, showing a young, dark face and strong, muscular neck on broad, sloping shoulders. Dark eyes that were—that were—what the hell were they? Wary? Angry? Pleading? Not pleading, not with that dignity, that poise, that massive, dark silentness.

Ellis Kent felt his daughter's presence beside him again and did not look up from the sketch. "Sara. Sara, this is a little more than good. It's yours?"

"Yes. That's—well, that's the steenth million try—"

"From life?"

"Sort of. Not exactly. I mean it wasn't posed or anything—"

"He wasn't a model?"

"Oh, my gosh, no! He's in my class at Pengard. I'd sketch when he wasn't looking. The first ones I did from memory."

He laid the sketch down slowly, the dark eyes in the young face seeming to look directly at him. Or at Sara, beside him? Or beyond them both? He could not tell. All right, Kent, all right, he told himself. Keep it easy. You're one of America's great liberals, you are; one of America's fighting liberals; take it in stride; if it's true it's only a phase, it's got to be only a phase of youth. Christ! Why was my youngest left motherless and vulnerable! Yet if Helen were alive, if her mother were here, who's to say that it would change things; who's to say that, now her daughter was beyond influence, her mother's presence would do more than worsen the situation? Hypocrite. Lousy, stinking hypocrite, Ellis Kent. A merchant, a tailor, a butcher—my God, you should have been one of those and never developed the intuition of a good trial lawyer, an intuition that's telling you something now that you must run from. But keep it easy; try, for God's sake, try, to know how a young girl thinks, how she feels. Don't crush, don't hurt, let it pass; it's a phase, for Christ's sake, it's only a phase.

His daughter was standing beside him still, a sheaf of watercolors in her hand, and between them on the drawing board, the eyes of a Negro youth were like dark weapons aimed at his heart. His daughter's cheeks were flushed, and he felt the same pain and anxiety he would have felt if the flush had been that of a consuming, mortal fever.

Sara was saying, "Actually, I did a lot of them from memory, last summer. I kept one and then tore it up when I finally finished this one."

"From memory? Last summer?"

"He was at Aunt Eve's when I stayed with them in spring vacation. He was up for scholarship interviews and exams."

"You didn't say anything—"

"Well, gosh, just for dinner, that's all. I guess I didn't even think of it."

Didn't even think of it. He looked away from her. Didn't even think of it? Yet you did a lot of sketches of him from memory after you'd seen him once. Just for dinner, that's all.

He kept his tone level when he asked, "He has a name?"

"His name is David. David Champlin. From New Orleans.

He's well, he's a real great person. He's one of Tommy Evans's best friends there. He's going to be a lawyer."

"Sara." Forget the tricky courtroom maneuverings, Kent, the subtleties. With your daughter, with this child, they won't work.

She was straightening the sketches in the portfolio now, stooping over, and a brown wing from the dark cap of her hair had fallen across one cheek, hiding her eyes. She was so small, he thought, so young, yet he feared her at this moment, and reached deep for the courage to say again, "Sara."

"What, Father?" She was tying the tapes of the portfolio.

"You know this boy, David, very well? He's certainly handsome."

"No. And yes. I mean: no, I don't know him well, and yes, he's handsome."

Her voice sounds natural, he thought. Her voice sounds natural and nonconcealing. Relief swept over him and was gone with the suddenness of a switched-off light when he turned and saw her eyes. "Good God, Sara—" She turned her head away, and he prayed for wisdom to the hazy, now-you-see-him-now-you-don't God he had never quite accepted, never quite rejected.

"Like that, Sara? Like that, chick?"

"I—I didn't mean for you to see it. You shouldn't have—have snooped."

"I didn't snoop, Sara. Want to tell me about it?" He didn't want to hear. God in heaven, He didn't want to hear what had passed between his daughter and this dark and lonely-looking boy.

The tears he had seen had not fallen, were still imprisoned by her lids. Now she drew a deep breath, then gulped. Like a baby. Christ! Like the baby he remembered on his wife's lap. "I wasn't crying. I don't know why I puddled up. I guess it was because I, well, I guess I thought I'd never be able to talk about it, never, never, never. And then we were talking about it. And there's nothing to talk about, nothing to tell." Again she drew in her breath unevenly. "Perhaps that's why, too."

"You're so young, chick—"

"Don't! Don't spoil it, Father! Don't spoil it. Don't say I'll get over it. Please. Please, I haven't. Not since that night at Aunt Eve's. And I won't. It's something you *know*—"

"Sara, is it because he's a Negro that you puddled up? Because there's nothing—"

She had turned away from him; now she whirled and faced him, her eyes wide, free of tears, direct. "Of course not. Of course not. You couldn't think that, Father. You brought us up, didn't you, to know right from wrong. Didn't you? You shouldn't even have asked."

He stood looking at her, not speaking, one phrase echoing in his mind: "You brought us up, didn't you—" God, yes! I brought you up, you and your sister, to know that if there be such a thing as a sin against the Holy Spirit it is to give to any man or woman less of your respect than you give another. Any man or woman.

"What's the matter, Father? Were you faking? Were you?"

She was slipping away from him, and he called out to her silently, "Sara! Come back. Come back, child!" Then he gave back her own words of a moment before.

"You shouldn't have asked, Sara," he said.

"It's all right, then?"

"Nothing's all right, Sara. Nothing's what you call 'all right' that means the trouble and sorrow you're asking for."

"It—there won't be. Because he doesn't know I'm alive, even. Except when I'm right there, in the same room maybe. He's all hidden and secret inside and he doesn't know I exist. I—well, actually, really actually, I guess that's why I almost cried, too. Because I don't guess there'll ever be any trouble or sorrow or—or anything good either and I'll *have* to get over it."

"You will, Sara, I'm sure. Sara, would you like to leave Pengard and concentrate on art? You could go abroad—" Say "yes." For God's sweet sake, say "yes." Because I won't force you; I haven't the guts and I've got a little too much sense.

She hesitated for a long enough time for Ellis Kent to feel the burden of many years not yet lived. Then she shook her head.

"No." She was looking at him directly again. "No. Why?"

She had called him "Fader" when she was a child. He could hear that child now, insistent, exasperating. "Why, Fader? Why? Why? Why is a bear brown? Why is the rain wet?" She did not need to go on now; he knew this "Why?" for what it was: a simple, childlike questioning of his integrity. Yet he heard himself say, "If I insisted, Sara?"

"You wouldn't. You couldn't. Not now. You couldn't pull the heavy parent act now. And go back on everything you taught us and believe and—and then don't believe all of a sudden because it's me. I've got to go back, Father. Maybe you're right. Maybe I'll get over it. I mean people do, don't they?"

"Yes, Sara. Often. Almost always."

"So. So you see. I'll go back and I'll get over it—" Her voice quavered, and Ellis Kent, facing his daughter, felt like a man without bones or muscles or sinews. "Because," she was saying, "because I'll have to get over it, even if I think I can't. Or—or hate myself for not having any pride when someone doesn't even know I exist—"

"Let's go back downstairs, chick. Suppose I call Bull and Lois Evans—they're at the lake cottage—find out if they have any guests, and if they don't we'll run out there, get out of this hellish heat till Monday morning. There's no statute that says I have to be a damned fool and go to the office Saturday mornings. Or that you have to go to one lousy class. Would you like that?"

All summer, he thought, almost all summer, and Sara hadn't had a date; except one with Tommy Evans and Gwen and a friend of Tommy's. And he'd been too blind to notice.

"I'd love it. And I know the only guest they have is Gwen. We can take some records—"

He wasn't expecting the quick, almost shy kiss, but it did not elate him. It was, he knew, not so much love for him as a gesture of gratitude that he had given her no censure because she was in love with a dark and, to him, unknown boy from New Orleans named David Champlin.

She went down the stairs ahead of him, and Ellis Kent followed slowly, a man who felt that he had fought two battles and lost them both.

25

WHENEVER THE SNOW WAS NOT so deep on road and footpath that a man could not walk in it, David Champlin ignored the ache that cold and dampness brought to his stiff ankle, and walked for the joy of it, wondering at his own inner response to the alien white and secret stillness, a stillness broken only by the crunch-squeak of his galoshes on the earth's soft carpet. He timed his "Hey!" of greeting to synchronize with a snowball's splattering high between Suds Sutherland's shoulders. Suds, on his way to the campus from the garage where he kept his car, turned and waited for David to catch up.

"I'd smother you, only I'm too bushed," Suds said, and shook his head wonderingly. "You sure get a charge out of this stuff, don't you? Me, I grew up in it and it gives me fits."

They walked together toward the campus entrance a quarter mile distant, and David said, "I think I got me a job."

"Doing what?"

"Laundry truck. Three hours, three afternoons and all Saturday afternoon."

"Swell. That is, if you need it."

"Sure do."

"There goes my B in Latin. I gotta go down to the C again."

"Jeez, how low can you get! Anyhow, I can keep on coaching you. What you think about me? You think I can get by Beanie with better than a C without you? We'll keep on with the skull sessions. We'll work it out."

"You sure you got the job?"

"Pretty sure. I'm going to see 'em again day after tomorrow. I'll have to see what I can do with my schedule."

"That means Cozy."

"Maybe. Maybe not. Not if I can work it out some other way."

"You can't."

"I can try. Because if I have to work it out with him, I might as well call 'em and say I can't take the job."

"Honest, David, you think he'd louse you up that bad?"

David walked on without answering. He was learning—had already learned—the blind spots in the minds of the whites of goodwill who could not, literally could not, comprehend the dark depths that harbored hatred in the minds of others of their race. He said lightly, "No point in finding out. That is, if I can work it out without him."

Ahead, a group of children were plodding up a hill that rose from the roadway across from the entrance to the campus, dragging sleds behind them. "Those kids are rushing the season," said Suds. "There's not enough snow yet for real good coasting." He turned to David. "Know what a Flexible Flyer is?"

"A rubber airplane?"

"Gosh! You're not even high enough up to be in the ignorant class. It's a sled. We used to get 'em for Christmas presents, under the tree, taking up all the room. We couldn't wait to get out on 'em and do belly bumpuses—"

"Do what, for gosh sakes?"

"Of all the wasted childhoods! That's what I call really underprivileged. No snow, no belly bumpuses—see those kids up there? They'll be doing belly bumpuses in a minute."

David watched, then grinned. "They aren't all kids. One of 'em's Sara Kent."

"Yeah? . . . . Damned if it isn't. Same difference."

While they stood there, Sara reached the bottom of the low hill flat on her stomach on a child's sled, then got to her feet, waving to the children at the top of the hill. One of them picked up a sled, ran forward a few steps, then flung sled and self forward and coasted down to her. The child took her sled from her, and she started toward the roadway. Sudsy took off a woolen glove, put two fingers in his mouth, and a shrill whistle sliced through the raw air.

Sara was running now, red cap and sweater bright against the white background, waving, calling to them as she ran. "Hey! Wait! Wait you guys! Wait for me!"

When she reached them, panting, cheeks flushed, Suds said: "Wait for you, girl? No point waiting for you. You'll catch up."

She did not answer, stood looking up at David as a child looks up at mother or father, ignoring outsiders.

"David, I'll bet you've never been coasting. I'll bet you've never done a belly bumpus on a Flexible Flyer. I'll bet you don't even know what a Flexible Flyer—"

"It's a sled. Yaa-ah, there. . . ."

"You've been cheating, Champlin."

She tucked a mittened hand under his arm.

"Let's get coffee and hot dogs in the rec hall."

He wanted to pull away from her hand, to say, "Look—please—" and at the same time wanted to put his own hand over hers and draw her closer. Hell of a fix, he thought; hell of a fix I'm in. There were plenty of guys, he knew, who wouldn't be in any fix, who'd do something about it, wouldn't hold back, but knowing that didn't make it any more possible for him to act differently.

She was speaking again. "David. Listen, will you please come down to earth and just listen. Because I've got news. Have you talked to Tommy Evans?"

"Not since yesterday."

"He's looking for you."

"What'd I do?"

"Nothing, Stoopid. I mean, it's what you're going to do. Maybe. If you want to. It's the super answer to a problem."

What problem? he wondered. There wasn't any answer to the problem that confronted him whenever Sara Kent was near, or even when she wasn't, no "super" answer to that problem, not for David Champlin, and now it was the only problem in his mind, all others were forgotten—scholastic, economic, whatever—and there was only this problem with its knife-sharp edges, its hurting weight.

Sara was saying: "You wait. You'll find out. I won't say a word, just let him tell you. I think he's in there now."

Suds groaned. "Women! Drive a man nuts."

They found Tom Evans and Chuck Martin in the billiard room, bought coffee and hot dogs, and commandeered the fireplace in the little room off the main lounge. Then Tom said, "Listen, David. You got a job yet?"

David did not even try to hide a smile. Tom Evans looked so much like some damned kid, mustard on his face, solemn and earnest as all hell. But he evaded a direct answer, and was put out with himself for evading it. There was nothing wrong, absolutely nothing wrong, with working on a laundry truck. He hadn't minded telling Suds. It was better than waiting on table like a lot of the guys, white ones at that, yet he answered only, "Could be. Why?"

"Know the Calico Cat in Cinci? Piano bar."

"I've heard of it." Didn't Tom know the place was Crow?

"I know what you're thinking. But I had to tell you. The piano player, a cat named Chick Sands, is leaving. In fact, he's already left."

"I heard he might, but not this soon. I met him a couple of weekends ago at Nehemiah's uncle's house. He plays a lot of piano."

"No more than you."

"Oh, for gosh sake, Tom! He's ten, fifteen years older than I am. Maybe more. I mean, he's good, man. I mean, he can *really* play."

"All right, all right. But the guy that owns the Calico Cat wants to audition you. Tuesday—that's tomorrow—afternoon, if you can make it. I mean, it's the only place in town for that kind of music now. And that's only Fridays and Saturdays. Dear old Cinci and its blue laws. Everyplace else is progressive or bop, or a band and dancing. They get a big crowd weekends from all over, people who like the regular stuff."

"How'd he hear about me? Who told him?"

Tom grinned. "Some of the students from here. And Chick Sands himself. Nehemiah says his uncle can get you fixed up quick with the union, and an I.D. card's no problem. Except for me, damn it."

When David didn't answer Tom went on. "This character runs a quiet joint; the law doesn't get around there much. Too busy at the other spots. You could get away with the age bit."

David carefully inspected the remaining one-third of his hot dog on a bun, keeping his eyes from the others, knowing his look would reflect the sudden upsurge of resentment, making his face feel hot. All arranged, wrapped in a package, and handed to him as though he were a helpless fool; no waiting to tip him off that the job was available now, along with a suggestion that he go see the man. He didn't resent Sands's action; that was O.K., that was swell, one musician giving another, younger, musician a boost, letting him have a crack at a job he was quitting. One Negro helping another Negro over a rough spot maybe, but Sands wasn't the kind to do that if he didn't think the other cat could cut it; that would be a black mark against himself if he ever wanted to come back. But these guys, well meaning as hell, finding out about the union from Nehemiah, getting the appointment for the audition, taking it all into their own hands—white hands—making it easy for him because—why? Because he was a Negro, their "favorite Negro," or because he was their friend? He hadn't expected it from Tom or Chuck, had thought both of them possessed of more understanding. The paucity of their understanding was made even clearer when Tom said, "Look, David, I know it's a lousy Crow joint—' Was that why they thought he'd fallen silent? Because the place was Crow? What place wasn't that he could play in? Who else wanted his music these days but the whites, and so few Negroes they wouldn't keep a colored joint in the black for even a weekend?

He turned to Tom and said evenly, "It's Crow. So what?" He felt his anger fade in spite of himself at the troubled perplexity on Tom's face, the perplexity of someone who has hurt another and does not know how, a look that says "Tell me what I've done and I'll go shoot myself if it will help." He couldn't live with these guys—and he had to—if he faulted them for every deed that grew out of their Negro-white relationship; all he could do was ride it out with them, recalling now with a kind of desperation the Prof's words, "You must not see prejudice, which you live with every day in New Orleans, everywhere. . . . Remember, you are not to see things under the bed. They will not always be there." Centuries of alienation—you couldn't bridge them in a year, but you could make that alienation utter and complete in a minute.

Sara said: "Tommy! I didn't know that was the place. All you told me was that it was a job playing piano. It's Crow as —as Crow can be. They wouldn't serve Simmons one night. None of us, I mean our crowd, will go there. I won't."

David saw the trouble in her eyes, and smiled. "Listen, Sara—" He always wanted to call her "Smallest," wanted to say, "Listen, Smallest—" but instead repeated, "Listen, Sara. A fellow could starve to death, just one guy, waiting for that kind of Crow to die. Now if every piano player—I mean, every one of us, black *and* white—was to rare back and refuse to play in a Crow dive, it would do some good."

Tom, obviously relieved, was smiling again. "I know what my old man would do. He's a stinker, Bull Evans is. He'd say take the job, wait till you've built up a real big following, you know, crowd the place every weekend; then if he refused to serve some Negro friend, leave him cold."

Chuck spoke for the first time, drawling: "The mouths of babes, that's what it is. You all listen to ol' Chuck. That's the way it's coming, eventually."

"It's—it's sort of sneaky—" said Sara doubtfully.

"Sure is. Like killing a rattlesnake."

David had now, as he so often had since moving into a new world, the uncomfortable feeling that his mind was outstripping the inhabitants of that world by great leaps, that his mind was taking ten-league strides beyond them. Now he thought of Tom saying "some of the students" had talked up his playing to the owner of the Calico Cat. It hadn't been Tom or Suds or any of the others in what Sara called "our crowd." Sara was right; none of them would spend money in a place if they knew beforehand that it had a Jim Crow policy. So it had to be the other students who had heard him at college, had wanted to keep on hearing him, and hadn't given a damn about a Crow policy, those who didn't care about color bars if they could hear what they wanted to hear, or, if it was a restaurant, eat what they wanted to eat. Their recommendation had been based on his music, not his color. And maybe this was good, very good, because Tom or Suds or some of the others would have recommended him if he'd only been able to stumble through "Chopsticks."

He needed the job, that was for sure. He wasn't certain he could cut it, but he could sure as hell try. And it meant no fooling around with his schedule. And that meant no fooling around with Cozy. To be able to keep away from that character was worth damned near anything. He didn't know what scale was for a job like that, but scale plus the kitty, which was sure to be there, ought to equal or better what he'd get driving a laundry truck. Gramp always figured on the kitty supplying a good part of a night's pay—and that was for one member of a trio or maybe a quartet.

He looked at Sara, ignoring the trouble still in her eyes, and said, "You all going to drum me out of ALEC if I take the job? Providing it's offered."

Sara shook her head, but her eyes darkened. "No-o-o. Of course not. Only it's terrible. You playing there and we can—we could—go and hear you and you couldn't. I mean, you couldn't go in if someone else was playing there, and—well, it *stinks*, that's all."

Chuck Martin said, "He's right, Sara."

"That's crazy."

"Sure it's crazy. And wrong. But David's got no hold on this character. Al Savoldi—that's his name—couldn't care less about hiring a guy he never heard of. David would be biting his own nose off. And David needs the dough. Right, David?"

"Sure."

"So he plays in a Jim Crow club in a border city. And he makes his bread."

David was looking at Sara, and he saw her cheeks flush before she spoke. "You damned Southerners—"

"Whoa, Sara." He leaned forward in his chair. "Chuck's O.K. And he's right. There are other ways to fight, as Tom said. I'll see this Al Whatever-his-name-is tomorrow."

Suds, who had remained in unaccustomed and dubious silence, spoke up. "I'm agin it. How the hell we going to get anywhere, I mean, anywhere, if we don't take a stand—"

David was on his feet. "More coffee? Sara? Chuck? Anyone?" He wanted to move away until this second surge of anger spent itself. Who the hell did they think they were? Even Sara, running his life for him, deciding whether or not he should make money anyway he chose because he needed to take some of the load off a little guy named Li'l Joe Champlin who had gone too far overboard already to help him. Chuck was the only one who knew what the score was. Someday he'd solve the riddle of Chuck Martin. Tom knew the score, but not the way Chuck did; Tom knew it, but had not yet united the knowledge to understanding. Suds didn't seem to know, really know, any score. Suds was just a friendly guy. He either liked you or he didn't like you, without much thought about it. There were no complexities in Sudsy's makeup. If he liked you he didn't like people who disliked you, and he'd go to bat for you. It was that simple.

David came back from the snack bar balancing four cups of coffee and another hot dog for Tom. As he sat down he asked: "You using your car tomorrow afternoon, Suds? Think I could borrow it?"

"I'll take you. Tom and Sara want to go too."

"Stay outside, then." There was no fighting this compulsion to take care of him. The main thing was the job and the money. Again Chuck Martin came to his rescue. "Nuts. He'd better go alone. The owner's going to think it's pressure—"

"Not if we—" Tom stopped speaking suddenly, bit into his hot dog, mumbled, "Yeah. Mebbe you're right."

David and Suds called their joint Latin-mathematics coaching plan The Sutherland-Champlin Self-Help Project for Partially Retarded Pengardians, and had decided, after the first month, that it was going to work out fine. David knew he could never give Suds what the Professor had given him, a driving urge to learn Latin, and Suds knew he could not give David what had been inculcated in him—a curiosity about what happens, abstractly, when you move from simple arithmetic to algebra, to geometry, to trig, and so on forward. That had been a bit of magic worked by Benford, which hadn't worked for David. Each knew the other had to have the subject pounded into him, learned by a combination of faith and rote.

That night, following the talk in the recreation hall, Suds said in the middle of a Latin session: "You have real strong objections to my going with you tomorrow? I sort of got the idea you didn't want anyone."

David looked across the card table that was now a fixture in the center of his room, and caught something close to wistfulness on Sudsy's plump face.

"Hell, no. Come on. I just didn't want a whole gang." With Suds it so obviously was not an intent to nursemaid him. Which was one of the reasons, he thought, that he was so fond of Suds. No one had warned him before he came out of New Orleans that some of the whites would have an attitude so damned protective it made a man feel like a fool, increased his divisive race consciousness fully as much as any outright or overt insult. It was as though the color of his skin was like the plaster casts he had worn as a child that had made people want to help him up and down steps he'd rather tackle alone. Suds at least didn't make him feel that way.

On the way to Cincinnati the next afternoon he thought that if the owner of the Calico Cat turned out to be a stinker, well, he was a stinker and that would be that, and the only thing to do about it would be to play the hell out of the piano and stay out of his way. It wasn't anything he could talk about with Suds because this was a roadway in his life not even Suds, much less any of the others, could ever walk with him. To these white kids, stinkers didn't come along very often, and when they did, the kids weren't particularly involved. Hate and fear were bad things they read about in books, or apprehended as forces exterior to themselves.

Crow in the North, what David had seen of it, seemed to him more repugnance than anything else, a drawing away, a man saying, "O.K., O.K., so a squid has nice tender meat—but you still can't pay me to eat it." Except in the industrial areas; there, he always thought, the toughest fight would come because in the industrial centers Crow really was fear, a dollar-and-cents fear that made a black skin not only repugnant but menacing, a threat to full bellies and car payments and mortgages. But Gramp had said, "Hell, a man's got to trust someone. Man can't quit living."

A fellow had to accept the friendship of whites like Tom and Suds and Chuck, but holding back a little because sooner or later there would come a time when the ground on which he was walking would not be the ground on which they were walking and between them there would be a bottomless chasm.

He sighed, turned halfway round in his seat beside Suds, and said, "Hey, Stoopid. How about a little review? *Verendus, verenda, verendum*—"

"Oh, gosh!" groaned Suds. "They made Simon Legree the wrong color."

When he met the owner of the Calico Cat David thought it was too bad you couldn't see the color of his eyes for the dollar signs in them. Small eyes, set close together, a small mouth; a small man, he thought, just a plumb small man in every way. The club, larger than what is usually called a "piano bar," was dim, almost deserted in the hour before cocktail and predinner drink time, with a smell, real or imagined, of last night's smoke and stale drinks. Three men were standing at the bar, drinking; a fourth was sitting on a stool nursing a drink and a protracted hangover. The piano, a baby grand, faced the bar, and small tables lined each wall and were clustered along the center of the room. Suds came in with him but slipped quietly into a chair at a table just inside the entrance.

"You the piano player?" It was the owner's only greeting as he walked toward them from the bar.

What if I'm not? What if I said, "No. I just came in for a drink?" David's hand closed tightly over change in his pocket; he felt the muscles along the back of his shoulders tense and threw his shoulders back, squaring them, easing the tightness.

"Right. You wanted to hear me."

"Yeah. Chick said you were O.K. You know the kind of place this is? If you don't, lemme tell you. We've got a reputation all over the state—all over the Midwest, as far as that's concerned—for barroom piano. Blues, boogie, ragtime. We've had Meade Lux, Johnson, cats like that. Something square now and then for the tourists if they ask for it, but nothing fancy. None of this new stuff. It's O.K., and I like it, but we'd lose our clientele, our regulars. Understand?"

"Yes." David looked at the piano. "Nice instrument."

"See what you can do with it."

David slid along the bench, went through the usual routine motions of a man trying out a piano for the first time, striking A, hitting a B-flat chord, then others. He swung into a boogie, gently at first, muting it, then gradually built it up until he was rocking it, and the man who was sitting at the bar looking like a hung-over mummy began to come to life, and the bartender stopped whatever he had been doing and stood still, listening. Before he went into a blues, David looked down the room at Suds, saw the round face grinning encouragement, and caught the circled thumb and forefinger of approval.

He struck the first chords of "Michigan Water," and began to hum. He wished now he'd picked some other number besides this Morton favorite, because for the life of him he couldn't play it without singing it, and he didn't want to showboat: " 'Michigan Water . . . hmm . . . tastes like sherry wine—' "

The boss of this place might be a drip, but he knew the kind of piano music he wanted. David could tell that by the numbers he asked for after "Michigan Water." One of the men standing at the bar had been getting ready to leave when David entered. Now he turned back and ordered another drink, and stood, back against the bar, drinking slowly. That would do it, thought David. Any time a musician or a band could hold 'em in the place, keep 'em drinking, they were set. But he wasn't giving this guy an afternoon's bar profit. After ten or fifteen minutes, he stopped playing and waited quietly.

The owner came toward the piano, jerked his head in the direction of a door at the back of the room. "Come into the office." David followed him into a small room that held an unbelievably cluttered desk and two chairs. The wall behind the desk seemed to be almost completely covered with glossy prints of musicians, some of whom David recognized.

"Have a drink?"

David shook his head. "Thanks, no."

"Teetotal?"

"Not quite."

"You'll drink Coke or Seven-Up here if you order during working hours. Too bad you're so young. But you look old enough, so I think we can get away with it. You fixed up with the local?"

"I will be if you need me. At least for part-time work on a transfer."

"O.K. You get scale and half the kitty. I'm taking a chance."

The muscles of David's face stiffened, and he broke the stiffening with a smile. "Scale and the kitty," he said, and wondered at himself. No one had ever tried this on him before; an employer didn't bargain with a punk kid over what he'd get for driving a laundry truck or mowing a lawn or waiting on customers in a neighborhood grocery store. That had been Gramp talking: *Mebbe they ain't going to treat you like a man, but don't you never forget you is one.* He could hear Gramp on the phone: *I'm sorry, I'm sure sorry, but I can't do no job like that for no money like that.* And, another time, exploding to him at dinnertime: *Uncle Toms! Hell, it ain't the bigmouths and the poor mouths and the crazy acting fools that's the real Uncle Toms. It's the guys trying to get in good with the whites by selling theirselves cheap, splittin' scale under the table, stuff like that. Man has to do it sometimes. Man has to live. I done it. Don't never think I hasn't. But I never done it jes for Li'l Joe Champlin. And I never done it jes so's some white would think good of me.* A man stood alone in a white world, alone in a circle drawn around him by white hands, but if he stood tall enough and firm enough, the time would come when the circle wouldn't hold him. Gramp hadn't known that; Gramp's circle had been forever, but no circle was forever.

Now David, remembering Gramp, waited.

"Scale and all the kitty, eh? That's not the way we do it here, boy."

The "boy" might have been just because he was young, might have been used even if he'd been white; the guy wasn't a Southerner; by his speech he was a New Yorker, but it bolstered David's determination.

"Sorry. That's not the way I do it. Kitty's the musician's."

He could feel the man's eyes on his face, met them squarely with his own, and smiled again. "Nice piano," he said. "Nice place. Sorry we can't get together."

He had crammed his scarf into his pocket when he sat down to play; now he pulled it out and put it around his neck, turning to leave. Suddenly the other man laughed, a short, staccato bark.

"I'll be damned. I'll be Goddamned. O.K. Scale and the kitty, and give me a 'Michigan Water' like that once a night. Get a contract from the union and bring it in Thursday night. You'll play Fridays and Saturdays. You going to get independent about the hours?"

"If they suit the union, they'll suit me."

The owner followed him out, stopped at the bar. "Sure you won't have a drink?"

David shook his head. "Thanks, no," he said again. He couldn't have walked in and up to the bar and ordered a drink even if he'd been older, not without trouble, and he wasn't drinking with the boss, accepting a temporary-customer status as a special favor. The hell with the guy. Just let him get at that piano and then let him alone and they'd get along fine. There was a hollow white-black-yellow ceramic cat crouched on top of the piano, winking one green eye, and as he passed it, David winked back. Suds was standing at the door, waiting for him, his plump face as furrowed as its contours would allow.

Outside, David said: "It's all set. I start Friday. Mind if we look up Nehemiah's uncle? So I can get straight with the local? It may take some finagling."

"The guy give you any trouble?"

"They always do. Wanted to split the kitty. My grandfather has a saying, 'You can't fault a man for trying.' "

"Was he—" Suds stopped, embarrassed.

"Sure. Sure, Sudsy. It's standard. But no more so than most. Look, let's eat first, huh?"

Suds was getting close to that ground on the edge of the chasm, and it was ground white feet could not tread safely, ground on which he did not want to linger, not with Sudsy. He liked the guy too well, and the reason he liked him, he guessed, was that Sudsy never seemed to be making a big fat effort to be friends, trying hard, like most of them did. Eventually, thought David, it was their damned trying that got a man down.

26

THE FIRST NIGHT THEY PLAYED at the Calico Cat, David drove to Cincinnati with Hunter Travis beside him in Sutherland's car, leaving Suds sniffling morosely in his room with what David called a "fresh cold."

"It's not 'fresh,' " snapped Suds. "It's the same one. It just gets coy and goes into hiding every now and then."

"If it was me and I didn't check in at the infirmary it would be O.K.," said David self-righteously. "But your old man's a doctor, and that makes it stupid."

"I went this afternoon. They gave me a shot and some stuff and told me to come back Monday. I'll wait till I go home Thanksgiving and the old man can check me through the clinic." He blew his nose, said "Aa-ah, hell!" and began coughing. When the spell was over he said: "Maybe I'll get to stay home a few extra days. Anyhow, if I stay on campus I can study tonight and tomorrow. Andrus has been giving me the business. And Beanie called me 'Clifton' after class today, and that's bad."

"It's not right. Gosh, you push me uphill in math and slide down yourself."

"Don't ever make a real good grade for Beanie. Stay mediocre because it's murder if you slip."

David was glad of Hunter's company on the trip. He was always glad of Hunter's company at any time, although he was just beginning to shake off the feeling that Hunter was, somehow, in a class by himself, not above but beyond him. The gradual discovery that Hunter Travis was warmly human, that he was not aloof or withdrawn but merely self-contained, had been one of the most satisfying experiences of his freshman year. "Sure taught me not to jump at conclusions," he told the Prof during summer vacation. "He's a brain, a real brain, but he doesn't make any big thing about it."

On this Friday of David's first night of playing, Hunter was catching a lift to Cincinnati for a night train to New York to meet his mother and father, due the next day from Europe. David wondered if he should envy that. No, it sure as hell was better to have a home to go to that you knew was always there and a family that stayed put, even if that family was only a grandfather.

"Are you jittery?" asked Hunter when they were halfway to Cincinnati.

"You mean about playing tonight? Gosh, no. Hadn't thought about it. Guess I should be. I've been too busy worrying about that phony I.D. card, and afraid of losing out."

"Mind if I write a story about you, chum?"

"Just don't call me by my right name."

"You're an interesting character. Could be you're an anachronism."

"Lay off—"

"Well, you are." Hunter stretched his legs out under the dashboard, plunged his hands in his pockets, looking, thought David, like a damned ad for college clothes for the modern young man. "For one thing," Hunter went on, "you're all Negro. Or mostly."

David laughed. "Just call me lucky."

"Luckier than I am, anyhow. That's what I mean, though. You were being sarcastic when you said that about being lucky. But you weren't being, well, fed up and bitter."

"And that makes me interesting?"

"Definitely. Guys like Simmons and Dunbar are a dime a dozen among us, David. If you don't know that by now, you'll learn it every year you stay away from home."

"You sound ninety years old."

"Perhaps I am. I guess it's one of the things that happen to you when you're born and grow up with a foot on each side of the fence."

"Suppose I was what you call 'fed up and bitter.' Wouldn't change anything, would it? I'd still be a Negro here and a nigger at home—and here, too, sometimes. You've got the wrong slant, buddy. I don't aim to relax and enjoy it, like the gal who gets raped. I just figure that the good Lord wanted David Champlin in a black skin for some reason. If He hadn't I'd have a white skin. Sooner or later I'll find out the reason."

After a minute Hunter said, "You really still believe all that stuff, don't you? God and all."

"Oh, gosh—here we go again. I keep saying to you how the hell can you help believing?"

"That's no problem. I suppose your grandfather instilled—"

"Crap! What I keep trying to pound into that thick skull of yours is that Gramp wouldn't believe if there wasn't something to believe in that it's God that makes faith, comes first, not after. Even primitive people who hadn't had a damned thing instilled in 'em had it."

"So we have to stay primitive?"

David's face was somber; then suddenly he broke into a wide smile and took his eyes from the road to look over at Hunter. "You ought to start being all nigger and do a little believing yourself."

Hunter shook his head slowly. "Can't," he said. "Just can't make Godsville."

What David later described to Suds as "jitters, minor type" caught up with him when he started to play that night. At first he wisely paid no attention to requests, concentrating on numbers he knew best and had worked over the most, mixing them up nicely, rags, blues, stomps, and finally a little boogie. When he felt that he was easy and relaxed, he began playing requests.

The whole evening shook down to normal when he saw a party of four couples come in, and recognized two of them as habitués of a club in New Orleans where Gramp often played and where he himself had sometimes played during intermission. They greeted him with loud and slightly alcoholic shouts of delight. He gave a quick, sideways glance at Al Savoldi, standing at the bar, and could tell that the owner was definitely impressed. Nothing like a following, thought David, with an inner grin, even if it was only eight people. They stayed most of the night, drank copiously, and fed the kitty generously. At the end of the job David was dog-tired, and acknowledged then that he must have had more inner tension than he had realized, but he was reasonably certain the job was secure.

He had arranged to keep a small room to sleep in at the home of Nehemiah's uncle, a man named Zack Charles, in case he couldn't make it back to Laurel at night. He knew he would be staying in town some Saturday nights because he had promised the Charles family he would go to church with them and sing, if there was a special occasion.

On Saturday night the two New Orleans couples showed up again, and there were several other repeaters, and he remembered some of their requests and played them. He wouldn't admit to anyone that he got real pleasure out of playing numbers people obviously liked. A lot of guys he knew would call it Uncle Tom, but he couldn't see it that way. He played his own way, and if they liked it, that was a pleasant feeling.

But it was more than a surface pleasure when, waiting for Al to pay him after the place closed Sunday morning, he sat at the keyboard, tired and relaxed, running through blues chords, and heard from close at hand a low voice. "I hear you, man. I hear you—" He looked up to see the Negro janitor and clean-up man standing quietly beside the piano, leaning on a mop, old eyes bright with understanding. What he felt now was not the simple satisfaction of pleasing customers; the sound of that voice, the light in the old eyes, were the reasons for music, the source of the only real joy to be found in making music; they were the evidence of communication, the certain proof that the feeling within yourself had broken its bonds of flesh and reached out and found and awakened the same feeling in another, as two people will talk in darkness, understanding.

David smiled. "What you want to hear, old man?" he asked softly.

" 'Yellow Dog'? That other fellow, he never played it. Heered Bessie sing it once, long time ago, back home. You know who I mean?"

"Sure I do. Got every record. 'Yellow Dog'—" and started it slow and easy, singing it low and rough, did not stop until he had played it out even though Al, the owner, was standing, money in hand, waiting at the far edge of the piano.

Talking to Suds, Tom, and Chuck on Sunday, he said, "Only one gruesome incident last night. Clevenger showed up for a while."

"Yeah?" said Suds.

"He would," said Tom. "I suppose we have to give the bastard credit for something. He likes the music. And knows jazz. He's got a keen collection of records, all kinds."

"You think I don't know!" said David. "That cat's been bugging me to come and listen all year so far. And last year, too."

Suds laughed. "Wonder he doesn't invite you to take a run up to dear old Richmond on vacation. He's got a sister going to have a coming-out party. You could play, special added attraction."

"Sure could," said Chuck. "I reckon they'd have a nice room over the garage for you."

"With bath," said David. "Gotta be with bath."

For quite a while now he had stopped being surprised at the casual, almost unthinking way he could join in with this type of kidding with whites; until his first day at Pengard, he had never discussed race with any white except the Professor. All through his freshman year, and so far in his sophomore year he had shied away from ALEC meetings, knowing how hard it was for him to participate in biracial discussions of a gut issue. The few meetings he did attend only confirmed his attitude; he got so damned sick of talk, and so more than damned sick of the well-meaning, well-intentioned, but utterly uncomprehending minds of the whites. Only Sara Kent's repeated urgings and, he admitted, the knowledge he would be near her for a whole evening, got him out to a meeting occasionally. But the kidding of a Suds or a Tom or a Chuck was far different; it was an open hand of fellowship, instinctive and sincere, far different from the self-conscious intellectual approach of the white ALEC-ites. Excluding Sara, he thought; always excluding Sara.

Sudsy's voice broke into his thoughts: "I don't dig that guy. I just don't dig him. The first day David's here, way back last year, he goes out of his way to be obnoxious—"

"He didn't need to go far," said David.

"O.K., so he was just doing what comes naturally. Then after that he starts getting in your hair, being nice."

"Not nice," said David. "You don't understand. Helpful. Friendly. Kind."

"He's a southern gentleman," said Tom. "Not same like Chuck."

"Gave him fits the other day, young Champlin did," said Chuck. "Pool."

"Aw, shucks," said David. "That wa'n't nothin'. Jes a li'l ol' practice game."

"Lawd, lawd," said Chuck, "deliver us from evil. I saw it. You guys haven't heard about it?"

Tom and Suds shook their heads.

"Champlin here wanted a little solitude. Said he had to do some thinking on the multiplication table—"

"Liar," said David.

"Mebbe it was subtraction. Anyhow, he moseyed along to the billiard room in the rec hall and starting knocking some balls around, easy like. Randy saw him go and waited a few minutes; then he moseys along too, and me, I get curious and go and stand in the doorway. Randy watches David, then he ups and suggests playing. I could tell David was riled, but he just said, 'O.K.'" Chuck began to laugh, until at last David joined in. Tom said, "Well, you baboons, what happened?"

"The slaughter of the whites, that's what happened," said Chuck. He shuddered. "It was right-down pathetic, it was."

"We got some of the best pool players in the country down my way," said David. "You gotta be good or stay home."

"I thought you'd tell him to get lost when he asked for a game."

"When I knew I could lick the damned pants off him? You think I'm nuts or something?"

"And young Champlin was so-o-o kind," said Chuck. "Yessir, he was real kind. 'You're just off today, Randy,' he says. 'Better luck next time.' And Clevenger, he doesn't say anything. Just crawls out, thinkin' black thoughts about white supremacy."

It was Chuck Martin who talked David into an ALEC meeting the week after he started work at the Calico Cat, although in all fairness he couldn't say he'd been "talked into it," because Chuck didn't operate that way. There was something compelling about Chuck's sincerity, and if he caught a guy in a weak moment there was no resisting.

Martin puzzled him: Why had a guy whose roots were so deep in the soil of southern thinking turned his back on a way of life that must have been damned close to a religion for his family? There was a concrete reason, and Chuck had told him about it one Sunday afternoon, sitting on the small beach beside the lake. Yet it had not entirely satisfied him. Revulsion against that way of life—yes, it would have brought that. But would it have brought dedication to the cause of fighting it?

The story had been a simple one. David knew what the outcome would be before Chuck was well into it. Chuck's best friend as a child had been a Negro boy, Jimmie Thornton. They had played together when they were very small, and Jimmie's father had brought his son along when he did gardening work for the Martins. Later, when they were old enough, Jimmie's father had taken them hunting and fishing. "He was the most wonderful guy with kids I've ever known," Chuck said. "Patient—Lord, I never heard him raise his voice or say an unkind word, and I never saw a little kid come up to him he didn't have a smile. But he got results. I couldn't get Jimmie to do anything hardly, unless his daddy said it was O.K. But he was strict. Really strict, rock-ribbed Baptist strict. Heck, I got more moral lectures from Jimmie's daddy in a year than I ever heard from my own in all my life."

Thornton had been a handsome man, Chuck said. A far-off Indian ancestor had given him high cheekbones and a high, proud nose, and Africa had bequeathed him grace and symmetry of body. "And sing!" said Chuck. "He could sing the hair right up straight on your head."

One of the town's most notorious "loose women"—that's what they called them in front of children, Chuck said—had been much taken by the charms of Jimmie's father. She was a white woman, and as nearly as Chuck could remember not much to look at, not enough to impress her image on him, which was vaguely of someone plump and blonde. And Jimmie's father, with his Puritan ideas, wanted no part of her.

Somehow, maybe only a Southerner could understand just

how, Chuck said, the rumor started that he had entered her home one night—object, rape.

David interrupted. "You know, don't you? How the rumor started?"

"Hell, yes. Now. I think even then, young as I was, I suspected. She started it."

"And they lynched him."

"Of course. Only they didn't kill him. They finally had to take him to the state insane asylum. He died there, I think. I don't know. I guess I don't want to know."

They were both silent until David, poking deep holes in the sand with a stick, said, "What happened to the kid—Jimmie?" Then he looked at Chuck, and what he saw made him add, "don't tell me if you don't want to—"

"I do. It's—well, this is the first time I've told it to anyone. Maybe it'll be good to get it off my chest, after all this time."

"Suit yourself, Chuck. I mean, I don't want you getting all riled and upset over something that happened years ago—"

"And still happens. That's it, David. And still happens. You see what's bad—hell, it's all bad, but I mean what's really been eating me inside all these years is that my old man could have stopped it. He knew Jimmie's daddy couldn't have been at her house then because he saw him himself, my old man saw him, ten miles away when it was supposed to have happened. And Jimmie's daddy didn't have a car. He couldn't have made it. My father didn't take part in what happened. All he did was not lift a finger to save the guy. That's all. That's damn all."

After that, Chuck said, no one saw Jimmie for a long time. He hadn't dared go to the house where the sick man lay, raving, but he roamed the woods and up and down the streams where he and Jimmie had been together, looking for his friend.

"When I finally found him he tried to kill me."

David, somehow, hadn't been expecting that, the stark simplicity of the statement, the quiet way Chuck said it, all emotion stifled but there, underneath. After a moment Chuck went on: "He had a hunting knife. I was bigger than he was, but he was quicker. Before I got it away from him he got me on one ear. You can see the scar if you look close. I told my family I got it from broken glass. I got the knife away from him somehow, and we had a fight. And then all of a sudden we were both crying, holding on to each other. All I cared was that Jimmie didn't hate me any more."

David's stick broke, hitting rock under the sand. "Is he still down there?"

Chuck shook his head. "I don't know where he is. I never saw him again. His mother managed somehow to scrape up a little bit of money and get him to St. Louis to an aunt. His mother—she wouldn't let me in the house. I never was able to find out what happened. I've even been to St. Louis to try to find him, but I can't. Someday maybe I will."

"I hope so," said David. "I sure hope so." It wasn't much to say, after a story like that; it was lame and faltering but it was something. Keeping silent made the whole thing unbearable.

On their way back to the campus, Chuck told him that it was then he knew that he was going to break away some day. "I stuck around for my mother's sake, went to the colleges they picked—and got kicked out of them both, as you know. Then that little legacy came along—"

"What little legacy?"

"I thought I'd mentioned it. Had an uncle, my mother's brother, who lived in Rochester, New York. He left me something, and that's how come I'm independent now. I got the income when I was eighteen. It's not much, but it means I can get an education, and stay the hell away from home. And that's O.K. by my old man. Mom knows where I am—she could come up here, but I guess the old man has her sold on the idea that I'm past redemption or something."

Chuck's story explained a lot, but not all. There was something else that drove him, something more than a dreadful wrong remembered from childhood. One of these days, if he kept his senses alert, maybe he'd be able to spot what that something was.

He tried to explain his liking for Chuck to Nehemiah once, and immediately wished he hadn't. Nehemiah's reaction was violent and profane. He wound up his tirade with: "You going to get yourself so Goddamned messed up, futzing around with these ofays. You want to kiss-ass the profs, O.K.; that'll get you somewhere. Mebbe. Just mebbe. But you never gonna make it with these other whites here. You think they like you? Sure they like you. It makes 'em feel good to like you. And that's why they like you, because it makes 'em feel good to like a Negro. Especially guys from cracker country, like this here Martin. You don't see any of 'em putting their money where their mouths is, do you?"

"They contribute—"

"Pee on their contributions! You don't see none of 'em down around our way, do you? Down in the South trying to do something for the wonderful, wonderful Negro? Scholarships! Why they got to have scholarships just for us? Why can't they just have scholarships, period? You know enough, you get 'em; you don't know enough you don't. But hell, they got to send scouts out, like houn' dogs, smelling us out. Go find us a smart Negro so's we can show how good we are."

"Look, you dope! You just said—"

"Don't make no difference what I just said. I don't know why in hell I got sucked into coming here, why I didn't go to Howard or Dillard or some other college. Or maybe no place. All this shit here, trying to be white, trying to act like whites, imitating the whites—"

"Oh, for cripe's sake! Speak for yourself. I'm not imitating any whites. Grew up around 'em, didn't we? Wore the same kind of clothes when we were kids, didn't we? Wear the same kind now, don't we? I mean, in general. Pants, shirts, shoes. Talk the same language—"

"Live under the same laws? Look the same to a cop? You're fixing to walk right into a trap, arguing like that."

"O.K. What do you want? Go get yourself a lion skin and some white paint. Go ahead. Wear a lion skin and paint stripes on your face. I'll take you back to New Orleans, and they'll run you out of every colored place in town. Negro colleges! You think you'd be any better off? That's where they really imitate the whites! Sororities and fraternities and class distinctions and color distinctions. Man, black as you are you wouldn't be anywhere! That's where they're really messing up, lots of 'em. You ask Rudy Lopez. You ask a lot of 'em. You aren't making sense, Ne'miah. You want two worlds—"

"What the hell we got now? Two worlds, that's what we got now; only, we haven't got the sense to keep it that way till we're stronger."

David sighed. "You go round and round and you don't come out anywhere. Why don't you just try for a while to stop worrying yourself with it all and try and catch the rest of your schedule up with your math? You got more going for you than any guy on campus and you're standing still on it—"

Nehemiah's eyes grew flat and lusterless, anger smoldering behind them. David didn't give the anger chance to flare up, said quickly: "What the hell, man. Who knows? Maybe you're right. I don't know. I'm going along with things. You said it once: Law, that's the thing to yense 'em with. And I'm not messing up; not till I get what I came for."

Flare up, give in, take a stand—and then retreat. You couldn't do it differently with guys like Nehemiah because there was a fire inside them that burned your words up, destroyed your reasoning before it reached their minds and their own reasoning faculties.

David was surprised when Nehemiah said he was going to the ALEC meeting too, but he was sure Nehemiah was going out of a certain bitter curiosity and, perhaps, looking for a reason to say "I told you so."

The meetings were held in the "social hall" of St. John's Episcopal Church, almost directly across from the garage where Suds kept his car. The rector of the church, though named James McCartney, was known to parishioners and students as "Father Mac," a nickname in which he found great satisfaction. David had commented to Sara once, "Sure seems funny to call a man with a wife and three kids 'Father.' " Sara had explained carefully that the church was of the "high" persuasion, and he had answered, "I know all about that. I still wonder what would happen if I called him 'Preacher.' "

"He'd love it," said Sara.

"Sure would," said David. "He'd think it was quaint as all hell—"

"David—" and then she had fallen silent.

On this night David was delayed, and told Nehemiah and Chuck to go on. As he reached the entrance to the campus, he saw Margaret ahead of him, and whistled softly to her. After the first half of freshman year Margaret had shown refreshing symptoms of being a human being after all, the shell of her scholasticism cracking when she was with David. They had dated a few times, and after the first one David found himself looking forward to kidding her into laughter and a quick, relaxed humor that answered his own. Tonight, however, the shell was around her again, and they walked solemnly along—as though, thought David, they were going to a funeral.

When they reached the hall Nehemiah had already settled down to an attitude of exaggerated ease, one leg thrown over the arm of his chair, his quick, small eyes darting around the room, taking in everything. He was ill at ease, thought David, hostile, and showboating to cover it up. His voice was resentful, high, when he called out, "Where you been, man?"

"I got held up."

Father McCartney came forward, shook hands with David, and said, "Glad you persuaded Wilson to come, Champlin."

The damn fool; in the first place, he hadn't persuaded Nehemiah to come, but even if he had, this man should have let Nehemiah keep on giving the impression he had come of his own accord. Maybe someday he'd grow to like this minister the way everyone else seemed to, but it was going to be tough going. The closest he could come to pinpointing his reasons for disliking him was that the minister kept harping on how race relations were God's business, that race prejudice was a spiritual shortcoming, instead of getting at the crux of the situation. David knew that people didn't give a damn whether God liked prejudice or not or whether it was a sin or not—they knew damned well it was. The crux of the situation was that the maintaining of a second-class citizenry was uncivilized, illegal, an economic crime, and just plain stupid. He didn't go along with all this yuk-yuk about changing men's hearts first. Let the kids go to school together, get in fights together at recess, share gripes at teachers together, sit together in a library, laugh together in a movie, and let their hearts take care of themselves; don't go messing around with the people's damned little lily-white souls and hearts, because the only way you could change 'em was to bring about a sharing of common experiences. And besides, Father McCartney didn't know the first thing about what he talked of so glibly. An illiterate Negro riding in the back of a New Orleans bus could give him cards and spades on God and what He thought of backs of buses for His people—any of 'em.

Sara Kent came in from the kitchen, carrying soft drinks. She saw him and called, "David!" then distributed the bottles and sat down, patting the chair next to her. When David took it, she said, "I'd rather you sat over there—" and pointed to an upright piano standing against the wall near the door.

"Fine thing. Ask a guy to sit next to you and then tell him you wish he was across the room."

"Dames." Tom Evans was seated now on his other side. "We've been fighting all evening. She's hard to get along with. Always was. You know what she used to do when she was a kid?"

"Shut up, Tom. David likes me and he didn't know me when I was a kid—"

"That's why he likes you. Fiend, that's what she was—"

"Pipe down," said David. Father McCartney's voice could be heard now, over the others, calling the meeting to order informally. David glanced toward Nehemiah and saw that he was talking to Margaret, saw Margaret nudge him and direct his attention to Father McCartney, who was straddling a chair in the center of the room, arms crossed on its back. Earnest as all hell, thought David, and for gosh sake, Champlin, quit disliking the poor bastard because he honest-to-God wants to help. Again he glanced at Nehemiah, and immediately wished he hadn't. Nehemiah wasn't having any of this, least of all Father McCartney.

Chuck Martin caught his eye, raised a hamlike hand, palm out, grinned and said "Peace" with his lips, and David grinned back. Sitting on the floor beside Chuck was Suds, and he glared at David balefully and David's grin broadened. Suds was going to give him hell later for the Latin exercise he'd given him to translate.

David heard the words "tonal" and "Africa," and sank lower in his chair. He glanced at the blackboard, saw that someone had drawn a complicated percussion pattern, sighed heavily, and didn't care who heard him. They were off again, buckety-buckety, riding the good reverend's favorite hobbyhorse: the links of the chain that bound modern popular music to Africa. By this means everyone was supposed to arrive gradually and happily at their destination: the problems of Negroes in today's world, arrive relaxed and easy, and it was, to David—and, he was sure, to several of the others—a stupid, self-indulgent approach. It didn't have a Goddamned thing to do with some poor devil of a taxpaying black man whose kids couldn't take books out of a tax-supported library, or cool their brown bodies broiled by a southern sun in the waters of a tax-provided swimming pool.

He wanted to say "Oh, balls!" out loud, and didn't even dare mutter it because Sara was so close. He crossed his ankles and wagged his good foot back and forth, noting morosely a tiny V-shaped tear in the toe of one shoe, hoping he could get the loose scrap of leather stuck back down. He was debating between just plain spit or some kind of thin glue when he heard his name. He started guiltily, drew up his legs till his feet were flat on the floor, pushed himself upright, and tried to look bright.

"Wouldn't you, David?" Father McCartney was looking at him from under unevenly raised eyebrows, a mannerism that never failed to irritate David.

"I—I'm sorry, Father McCartney. I was thinking— What is it I wouldn't?"

"The piano, David? And, maybe, if we can induce someone to take over on the piano in a while, perhaps some drums?"

"Piano. Period." He stood and started forward, working his way around chairs. "I'm no drummer."

"Liar!" called Tom, from behind him.

He spun the stool to the right height and struck a few chords, wishing he was in his room, even though Sara wouldn't be nearby. He started a boogie rhythm with his left hand, knowing it wasn't what McCartney wanted, but not wanting to just sit. Father McCartney came over to the piano, tall, reflective. "That's fine, David," he said. "But along the lines of our discussion perhaps you'd dig down in your memory and give us some of the spirituals and hymns you heard as a boy, the ones you were telling us about earlier in the year."

Old loose-lips Champlin, he thought; what'd you do that for? Let yourself be conned into talking about church music. "Needs singing," he said, and knew he'd done it again before the second word was out.

"I don't hear any symptoms of laryngitis in your voice tonight, David. Come on, that's a good chap—"

Margaret. Hers was the voice Father McCartney wanted, and didn't know he wanted because he had never heard it. David remembered the first time he had listened to her in chapel, her voice like a muted bell, a voice with chimes in it, only held back, muffled. It was a voice like Gram's had been, but instead of letting it carry her she reined it in taut, tight, as though she were afraid of it. As far as he was concerned, at this point ALEC could get 'em another boy. It wasn't the songs dear old Grandma and Grandpa used to sing that should be taking up ALEC's time; it was the songs their li'l ol' gran'chilren were learning. Different songs, with different meanings, their message clear as crystal, a message to the world and a challenge, a threat to those whose ears could not hear. But Father McCartney wanted the songs of a folk, the songs of sorrow and despair and of faith triumphant. Beyond those, David doubted he could hear.

He started off with "Lord, Lord, Lord, you sure been good to me—" knowing that if no one else did Sara would start them off. He remembered his surprise the first time he heard her sing it, and on his first night in Laurel.

Sara didn't disappoint him. She was humming it, then singing, and Father McCartney was humming, off key, and in back of him someone's hands—probably Tom Evans's—were clapping softly. He said to Father McCartney, "Get Margaret Benjamin up here, Father, and you'll hear a real voice." If McCartney wanted a damned singsong session instead of intelligent discussion, let him have it. Nehemiah was sure to join in, wouldn't be able to help himself. Nehemiah didn't have too bad a voice, a little thin, high, almost falsetto, but compelling.

Father McCartney had come back to the piano now with Margaret. She stood where the rector had been standing, beside the piano, facing the room. She was fussing and holding back, saying, "Really, Father. I'm not a soloist—" and David said, "The hell you aren't—" then "Oops! Sorry, Father." As Father McCartney moved away, David looked up at Margaret. "What'll it be?"

She smiled self-consciously, poked at the bridge of her eyeglasses with a forefinger, said, "Something everybody knows, don't you think? Like 'Abide with Me'—"

"Cripes!" He played louder, striking random chords, to cover his voice. "Y'all know better than that, sugah. That ain't what the man wants. We going to give 'em what the man wants." That would rile her, really rile her, especially "the man." And that was good, because maybe she'd turn loose and sing.

He let the chords run naturally into the opening of "He's My Lily of the Valley," singing it himself with a low, soft insistence. " 'He's my lily of the valley,' " stopped singing to say under his breath, "Come on, Margaret. You know it; you have to know it, coming from where you do. It's a good one. You can sing the devil out of it—'. . . everybody don't know, everybody don't know, what Jesus means, what Jesus means . . .' Come on. I'll start her over again." He brought it into a key her voice could handle better, confined his own voice to low humming answers to the phrases, then heard her really take hold of the melody, knew by the sureness of her attack that he had been right when he said, "You got to know it"; knew she had heard and sung it in childhood in some little church or hall in Louisiana, a piano behind the voices, breaking the melody up, rippling beneath it, stating it with a voice of its own. He upped the tempo a little, transposed to a slightly higher key, and had his reward: Margaret's voice soaring, as Gram's used to, over everyone's head, then beyond them, through the walls and the windows, soaring over the endless expanses of the world. Now Nehemiah's voice came from behind him, piercing, poignant, and he gave them both the support of his own voice, rich and strong, and they rode it out together.

While he searched his memory for another spiritual or hymn, he found himself striking the opening chords of one of Gram's favorites: "Were You There When They Crucified My Lord?" and suddenly Nehemiah was taking it away from him, and his own hands were hurrying to keep up. Now Margaret's voice was the answering one, letting Nehemiah's make the statements, ask the burning question, "Were you there?" knowing so unerringly when to step down, to give over to another's message, strengthening it, yet not appropriating it.

Small chills ran up and down his spine and back, and he could almost feel the muscles over his ribs twitching. Something made him turn his head to bring Nehemiah into his line of vision, and the chills transferred abruptly to his belly and became the gripping cold of apprehension. Nehemiah was off and he'd be running without a bridle if someone didn't stop him. David slowed his tempo against the insistent drive of Nehemiah's voice, broke the rhythm down into solid beats and let the chords signal a ride-out. He sighed with relief when Nehemiah's voice stopped with the piano; Margaret's had stopped a few bars earlier. But it was only Nehemiah's singing voice that had stopped. He was talking now.

"That what you wanted, Father?" he was saying. "That what you wanted? Or did you-all want just the music, not the words? Just to study the music? The beats and the harmonies, compare 'em? Music's not going to tell it all. You got to listen to the words, man; hear the words. What's the difference if the beat and the harmony are out of Africa? The words are out of hell—"

"Nehemiah." Father McCartney's voice was low and gently reasonable. "We need it all, the whole story. Music *and* words. To make us feel—and to make us think. Think, Nehemiah."

"Think! You want me to think! There's more harm done just thinking than you knows of, Father."

David turned on the piano stool to face the room, catching a glimpse of Margaret's face while his body was in motion. She looked sick. Sure as hell looked sick, and about five sizes smaller. He knew that if she thought she could do it without calling attention to herself she would make it through the cluster of seated students in front of the entrance and be long gone. Margaret knew what was coming just as he did. He could stop it; he could get up now, quickly, and walk over to Nehemiah, give him a reassuring whack on his shoulder, take him into the kitchen for coffee. Every muscle in Nehemiah's body seemed rigid; he was standing still, steady, yet David knew that inwardly his whole being was trembling and that the force of that trembling must and would break through the rocklike immobility of his body. But right now, right at this preclimactic moment David knew that he could stop it. He gathered his muscles to rise, then suddenly released them, and remained seated on the piano stool. Let him go; let Nehemiah have his head—and his heart. Perhaps that was what these noble-thinking liberals needed, what Father McCartney needed—to see a man's soul wide open, to hear a man beyond the control of cool reason tell of things in which reason had no part. Let them listen and squirm.

"The words, Father. You hear 'em? 'Were you there—were you there when they crucified my Lord?' You wasn't there, Father; you wasn't there. They crucifies my Lord every day, every day in the night and in the day. Every time a white man go to a black woman, every time a little black boy hears 'nigger.' You wasn't there—but my daddy was there, and my mother and that black boy sitting on that piano stool yonder, they was there—that black boy was there when he wasn't nothin' but a child and an ofay kid called him a nigger bastard. 'Were you there—were you there'—" Nehemiah's body rocked gently now, backward and forward, in rhythm with his words. Now it was coming, now it was really coming; Nehemiah was headed into a singing sermon, the kind his daddy did, the kind his daddy was still doing—"Singin' Preacher Wilson."

David clenched his fists until he could feel his nails, short as they were, digging into the palms. He thrust his hands into his pockets and stood up, because if he had not he would have whirled on that stool back to the piano, giving Nehemiah a solid platform of chords from which to speak, keeping his beat intact, adding to it. The chills had gone now; he could feel sweat on his forehead, on his ribs and under his arms. He moved forward a step, caught Nehemiah's eye, and suddenly wanted to weep with remorse for having let him continue. Nehemiah couldn't help it once he got started. *You ever see his older brother, son? White as a biscuit.* As he walked toward Nehemiah now, he felt a surge of warmth, of love for the small, taut black youth. He wanted to spread his arms as he could to a child, gather Nehemiah up, hide him, carry him off and away from any laughter, any hurting thing —Nehemiah, whose wounds were deep as Christ's.

He was beside Nehemiah now, a hand gentle on the boy's arm. "Take it easy, man," he said softly. "Take it easy."

"Y'all know what I'm saying, David. Y'all know!"

"I hear you. I hear you good." His fingers became firmer, and he spoke in a tone so low no other but Nehemiah could distinguish the words. "I hear you," he said again. "But we're alone, man. We're all alone. . . . Let's get us some coffee. . . ."

Nehemiah turned, and beneath his fingers David felt some of the tenseness leave the boy's body. Together they walked to the kitchen. On their way David glanced sideways and saw Chuck Martin seated on the floor against the wall, legs drawn up, arms wrapped around them, one big hand, the knuckles white, clasping the other wrist. His forehead rested on his knees, and his face was invisible.

At the kitchen door David turned and called, "Sara. Sara Kent! You and Tom rustle up the cups and saucers from the cupboards out there and set 'em up—"

He and Suds left the hall together. Suds made no inquiries about Nehemiah, and David was grateful. In the kitchen, after they left the main room, he had poured coffee into Nehemiah, wondering if the overwrought youth would do as he used to when he was a child—burst into sobs. Apparently he had not worked himself up to that point, although as David stood at the outside entrance to the kitchen and watched him walk away into the darkness he could not be sure. There was a faint glow from the doorway of the church —St. John's Church, Father McCartney was fond of saying, never closed its doors, night or day, to those who sought peace and prayer—and Nehemiah's figure was silhouetted suddenly against the surrounding darkness, and then he was gone; yet David did not turn away immediately. "God," he muttered. "Keep Your eye on Your boy Nehemiah." He turned back into the room, feeling a loneliness he had never known before, an alienation, a setting apart, feeling there in the warm kitchen like a man in the middle of a vast desert in which there was no life but his own.

The feeling was still with him when he left the hall with Sudsy. He waited while Suds, sniffling again with a cold, found and put on his galoshes, and as they walked through the door Suds said: "Fine thing. Now Sutherland has to think. Sutherland has to start thinking about not thinking, like Nehemiah said—"

David did not answer, and as they reached the end of the concrete walkway to the sidewalk Suds said, "Where's Chuck? I forgot him—"

A movement in the darkness caught David's eye, and he turned his head to see it better. A tall, awkward figure was walking slowly, its back to them, toward the church. The hands were in the pockets, the shoulders bent forward, the head low. At the bricked path to the church entrance the figure turned, the light catching the tow-colored hair, the troubled face, and in a moment Chuck Martin had passed through and into the light.

Now it was becoming clearer, the riddle of Chuck Martin. First there had been Jimmie Thornton and two boys crying in the woods, clinging together, and Chuck caring only that Jimmie didn't hate him any more. And it all had to do with something Chuck must have been born knowing—feeling—about God and love—and that something led him away from his fellows tonight, into the light from the church's open door. David wanted to follow him, to pray beside him in that little building, apart from the others, lighten by his own presence the burden Chuck carried on his shoulders, share with him the presence of a love that knew no differences.

"He didn't wait for you, Suds," said David gently to the boy walking beside him. For the first time the key to the puzzle of Chuck Martin was in his hand.

27

A COUPLE OF WEEKS AFTER he had started his job, David sat at the piano in the Calico Cat winding up a medley of ballads. He wasn't making anyone particularly happy by his choice of music except a couple in late middle-age, celebrating their thirtieth wedding anniversary, who had been begging for things like "Embraceable You" and "Tea for Two" and "Alice Blue Gown," and he figured their money was making Al prosperous just as much as the money from the blues lovers, and it certainly was making the couple happy. He was wondering how long he'd have to keep it up when he heard a voice directly in his ear. "What the hell," it said. "What the *hell* are you playing?"

He turned and found himself looking directly into Hunter Travis's face. Hunter was hunkered down on his heels to bring his head just below David's. David grinned, kept on playing. "Clear-the-room music," he said. "You no like?"

"Christ, I thought I'd wandered into a Lawrence Welk audition by mistake. Look, David, did you drive in?"

"Yeah. Sudsy's car. Want a lift?"

"No. Meet me outside when you're through."

When he met Hunter outside a little later, they took a cab to the lot where David had left the car, and as he started the motor, David said, "Why'd you ask me if I drove in?"

"A couple of your classmates are stranded at Lou's Place. With a problem child named Clevenger. They drove in with him. He was a little high when they left Laurel, and he had an accident just outside town. No one hurt, but the car's in a garage. They came in by taxi. I'm staying in town—if I can."

"Oh, hell, Hunter! Not Randy. Not that bastard. Take him somewhere, huh? Let him sleep it off. I'll take the other fellows."

"He's not that kind of drunk."

"Who all's with him?"

"Tom Evans and Bob Witherspoon. Nobody gives a damn what happens to Clevenger; it's just that the others want to get back. And we can't just leave the son of a bitch here."

"All right. Cripes! Clevenger drunk."

They found Clevenger and Witherspoon at a table at Lou's Place. Clevenger was slumped back in his chair, watching with glassy-eyed disgust the gyrations of a singer, the bodice of whose sequine-spangled gown covered no more than the nipples of her breasts. Witherspoon was soberer than Clevenger, and so was Tom, standing at the bar, ostensibly drinking a Coke.

The proprietor was coming toward them, and David had no trouble getting the message: Colored not served. When Hunter said, "My friend is going to take that guy home," and indicated Clevenger, the proprietor smiled broadly and retreated.

David expected an argument from Clevenger when they approached him, but there was none. "Always the little gentleman," said Tom as he and Witherspoon left the club, Randy between them. Outside, Clevenger pulled away from them, and started for the front of the car.

"Here, man, get in back," said Tom.

"No," said Clevenger. He was swaying. "Not going to get in back. Get carsick in back. Going to ride in front with David."

David said: "Sure, Randy, sure. Get in front and take a nap. Go on, you guys, get in back." He opened the door, and as Clevenger clambered unsteadily into the car, muttered to the others, "Food? Coffee?"

"We tried that," said Witherspoon under his breath. "He won't eat, and he says coffee makes him vomit."

Clevenger was quiet as David drove along the riverfront and out of town. It was the first time he had been around when Randy had been drinking to any extent. It didn't look as though he was going to make any trouble, and David relaxed, squaring his shoulders against the back of the seat, getting his hands easy on the wheel. Every now and then Clevenger would say something, but David didn't bother to listen. The moon was nearly full, and the highway, although free of snow, had a ghostly sheen to it. He was tired, as he always was on Saturday nights, but he knew he wouldn't start feeling sleepy until they reached Laurel. He could tell from the broken snatches of conversation in the back that both the others were sobering up. Sometimes he wished he didn't have a good head for liquor; it was always guys like him who wound up taking everybody home. He was relieved that the distasteful task of rescuing Clevenger had come off so smoothly; that they hadn't had to strong-arm him to get him into the car or anything like that.

When he felt Clevenger's hand on his knee the first time, he thought it was an accident, that Randy had been dozing and wakened, muzzy in his mind.

"Take it easy, Randy," he said. "I'm driving."

Clevenger said something David did not even try to catch. They had turned from the main highway and were on the two-lane back road that cut across to the approach road to Laurel. The silence in the back seat indicated that the other two might be napping. The second time Randy spoke he caught the words.

"Lef' the others behind," he said. "Lef' other fellows behind." There was a giggle. "Poor devils. Lef' behind. Jus' me an' David."

David said, "They're back there all right," then felt the hand on his knee again, on his thigh, moving back and forth, stroking. At first he did not take in what was happening; then suddenly his stomach churned violently, and he reached for Clevenger's wrist, closing strong fingers around it in a bone-crushing grip, and thought even as he did it that the wrist was so small it felt like a woman's. "Jesus Christ!" He tightened his fingers, heard in response another insensate giggle.

"Strong," said Clevenger. "Davey-boy's mighty strong."

What the hell was he going to do? He was still stunned and close to incredulous. He loosed his grip on Clevenger's wrist, threw the other's arm away violently. "Keep your hands to yourself, you damned fool. You want to crack us up?"

"Don't be cross, Davey. Davey—"

They were still twenty miles from Laurel, with the long slow grade ahead of them where he would have to shift Sudsy's old car into second. He couldn't drive twenty miles holding this bastard's arm, and it was clear he couldn't let it go.

The jerk of the car as he slammed on the brakes and brought it to a jarring stop off the roadway brought a "Hey, man!" from Witherspoon and a "What's the matter, Stoopid? Forget to get gas?" from Tom.

His answer was a concise, expressive curse as he flung the door open on his side of the car and ran around the front to the door beside Clevenger. When he opened it Clevenger was leaning away, one hand groping across the driver's seat, saying, "Tha's fine, David. Tha's fine. Nice and quiet here—Davey—"

His hand went inside Clevenger's collar, and the feel of the bare neck against the back of his fingers made his skin crawl. When he jerked, Clevenger came out backward, stumbling, off balance. He spun him around, caught shirtfront and tie in one fist, clipped him once, just hard enough, on the point of the jaw, then let him slump to the ground.

He turned and saw Tom standing beside him, eyes round and bewildered. "What—what happened?"

Witherspoon came forward, looked down at Clevenger, then at David. "Made a pass?" he asked.

"Passes," snapped David. Tom, looking at the youth on the ground, drawled in a voice that might have been Chuck's:

"Reckon we-all got to do something with the body. Cain't just leave it lay. It's sho a mighty purty sight, though."

David stooped and put his hands under Clevenger's shoulders. "Get his feet, someone. Throw him in the back seat. Stay in there with him."

Tom said, "Wonder if he'll remember when he comes out of that fog in the morning."

David shivered. "I hope not," he said. "I hope to God not."

Tom was closing the rear door when David stepped on the starter and swung back to the roadway with a whirling skid. "All I've got to say," he muttered as they picked up speed, "is that for a peaceable guy this has been a helluva night."

28

RANDOLPH CLEVENGER GAVE NO indication in the following days that he remembered the incident; it might never have happened. David told Sudsy about it, and laughed at Sudsy's nearly popeyed incredulity.

"Look—that guy—I'll be damned—"

"It's not all that unusual, Suds. F'gosh sake, you never heard of queers?"

"Well, sure, of course, only—hell, I mean for Randy to—"

"Make a pass at me. Yeah. He was drunker than we thought. He was sort of, well, I guess you'd call it disoriented. All of a sudden he thought the guys in the back weren't there."

"I had an uncle—still got him—who can't drink because when he does he gets hallucinations. Once he went into a police station and reported all sorts of imaginary characters in the back of the car—in Boston, yet. Randy gets hallucinations in reverse, huh?"

"Something like that, I guess."

Sudsy sighed. "I wish I'd been there. I never get to have any fun. Why'd you only hit him once?"

"Look, all I wanted to do was knock him out. That's all. No sense beating a guy up for something I guess he can't help."

"All I have to say is, better luck next time."

David remembered the revulsion he had felt when his fingers touched the skin of Randy's neck. But he said, "Jeez, Suds, if I thought that—don't say things like that, man."

Nehemiah's reaction was different. When he said "I told you—" David jumped him.

"Don't give me that 'I told you so' stuff. You never told me anything like that."

"Told you to stay clear of being so palsy with the whites, didn't I? Said they'd cut your throat?"

"Listen, Ne'miah, if there was one thing that bastard was not trying to do it was cut my throat. You've got it wrong end up. And for gosh sake, you think we haven't got queers? First time anything like that happened to me, I was ten years old. And the guy was a big truck driver with nine kids. And blacker than you. I ran like hell for home."

"Well," said Nehemiah, "if you're going to get buggered you might as well stick to your own."

The next time he saw Hunter, he said: "Don't come barging in again asking me to be a Good Samaritan. Next time drive your queer friends home yourself. Just come in and listen."

"No. Maybe I'm nuts. If there's someplace I want to go real bad, and can't go because I'm a Negro, I'll pass. I've got to want to go damned bad, and I'm ashamed of doing it, but I will. But I won't do it there. I won't go in there and sit and drink and know if you didn't work there you couldn't sit with me, know damned well the only reason they let you sit at the tables during intermission is because it sells more drinks."

David decided against going home for Thanksgiving, much as he wanted to, because if he did it would cut into the money he'd been saving for Christmas. Nehemiah was spending the holiday with relatives in Dayton; Tom was going home and taking Chuck with him, and Sudsy planned to go home too. Sara was spending the holiday with the Knudsens.

On Tuesday, Beanie Benford asked Sudsy to stay after class. David waited just outside the door of the classroom, leaning against the corridor wall, trying to catch Benford's words. He hoped Suds wasn't going to catch hell for low grades. Suds had been feeling lousy for a long time; one cold after another, sniffling and coughing, turning down trips to the city unless he had a date with a girl. David hoped Beanie would lay off the guy until after the holidays, and the first words he heard made him tighten his jaw muscles in exasperation.

"I've never singled you out as a student with any great potentials as a mathematician," Benford said. "My despairing hope has been to make it possible for you to work out the simple problems you'll encounter in your chosen profession."

The sarcastic bastard, thought David, then straightened and edged closer to the door at the next words. "But I cannot, with a clear conscience, give a sick student the grades you've been earning this fall. I'd like to think it would be impossible for a healthy, literate young man to make such a poor showing." Through the crack in the door David saw a bony black hand flick out, rest for a second on Sudsy's forehead, heard Benford say: "You're running a fever right now, Sutherland. I'm calling the Infirmary. You'll go there from here. I'll notify the dean's office."

David could not see it, but he knew Sudsy's mouth had set in the familiar stubborn line, so at variance with the plump. boyish face. He heard a mumbled phrase, "Going home tomorrow," and then Benford's voice. "All the more reason, Sutherland." He raised his voice. "Champlin!" and when David entered he said, "Go to the Infirmary with Sutherland. Take his books to his room if they keep him there, and follow through."

"Yes, sir," said David, and grinned at Sudsy. "Come on, Stoopid." He turned to speak to Benford, but the professor had already disappeared through the door behind the blackboard.

Half an hour later he stood beside Sudsy's bed in one of the cubicles in the contagious ward of the Infirmary. The nurse had said "probably flu," and put in a call for the doctor. She silenced Sudsy's protests by threatening to undress him herself, and looked quite capable of doing it.

"If you'd done what they told you to a long time ago—come back here for a checkup when you had that cold—you wouldn't be here now," said David self-righteously.

"Go to hell," said Sudsy.

David picked up the books on the dresser, asked, "Need anything?"

"Cigarettes."

"Will they—"

"The hell with 'will they.' Shove 'em through the window."

David walked to the window, found himself looking over a small parking circle in the rear, and beyond that to the main roadway just before it branched at the entrance to the quadrangle. Emory Hall was catercorner across from him. He tossed a half-empty package of cigarettes on the bed, said, "O.K., leave it unlocked."

Dean Goodhue was coming up the walk to the main entrance as David left. The dean's pipe was in his mouth, and he did not remove it; said around it, "Good morning, David." He slowed down as he drew opposite. "We have a sick student, I hear. Sutherland. Too bad. How is he?"

"The doctor's been sent for," said David. "The nurse thinks it's probably flu. She made him go to bed. I guess he's got a fever."

"Pity," said Goodhue. "Just at the holiday. I'll see what I can do for him." He continued up the steps, dismissing David, giving the impression that he was taking over now and all would be well.

The day after Thanksgiving, Clifton Sutherland walked past Emory Hall and did not see it. There was no sun, and the small, circumscribed area of the world through which he moved was gray sky and white snow, the dark brown of barren trees, and the dull, cold-looking red brick of the campus buildings. Snow was piled on the balustrades of their steps, and their cornices were coifed in white, like nuns. He smelled woodsmoke and knew that in the lounges of some of the dormitories fires were crackling. The cold nipped through his duffel coat and the heavy sweater beneath it. He cut through the passageway between Emory Hall and the corner dormitory building, but before he reached its end he began to cough, and stopped until the paroxysm passed. He stood for a moment, looking at a patch of unmelted snow beneath a tree beside the walk, and at the irregular red spot that stained it. It was not the dull red of the brick walls around him but a red that, like a paste jewel's, glistens but does not glow.

He did not knock at David's door in Quimby House because he did not want to be told to "Come in!" He wanted to open a door without knocking, to walk in without waiting, and find someone there; specifically, David.

David was sitting behind the card table in the center of the room, face hidden behind a wide-open newspaper. Sudsy said, "David," and the newspaper lowered abruptly, then dropped as the dark surprised face was above him, smiling.

"Sudsy! What're you doing here? When'd you get sprung? Don't just stand there. Come in and sit."

He was taking books from the seat of the big leather chair, but before he could finish Sudsy sat suddenly, abruptly, on the edge of the couch.

"O.K., O.K., have it your own way. Why don't you stay in out of the cold, man? Want a nip?"

"No," said Sudsy. "Not a nip. Not a lousy little nip."

"Baby want a bottle?"

Sudsy's eyes lighted. "Where'd you get a bottle?"

David nodded to the door to the upper room. "My neighbors. They went home for the holiday. Left it on my bureau with a note—'Get lost.' Mighty fine college spirit, I call it."

He was opening the bottle now, eyes on Sudsy's face, the beginning of a puzzled frown on his forehead. When he had the cap off he held the bottle out to the other, but Sudsy shook his head. "Got a glass?"

"What the heck!" David went to the washstand, rinsed a glass, and poured whiskey into it with a generous hand. He watched Sudsy drink, then shudder violently, and his frown deepened. "It's not *that* bad," he said. He put the bottle to his own lips, took a moderate drink, and waited for the other to speak.

Sudsy crossed his arms over his chest, hugging himself, then leaned forward so that his forearms rested on his knees. He looked at David's feet, at the leather slippers and dark socks with the diamonds of bright colors woven into them, and knew he would never forget the pattern. When he spoke at last his head snapped back as though controlled by a spring.

"I've got TB," he said. "David."

David had often said to Sudsy, in telling anecdotes about New Orleans friends, "Man, he changed color right now!" Sudsy had always thought it a manner of speaking; now, looking at David, he saw it happen. He saw the eyes change, too, and the pain in the eyes was in the voice when David spoke.

"So-so, Suds," he said. "It's all right. For Chris'sake, man, it's all right. It's nothing today. Nothing. Where's your head, man? You know that."

Sudsy said, "I've got to pack, David."

"Now? You've got to pack right now? Right now?"

"Right now. I just walked out of the Infirmary. They said I had to stay till they telephoned my dad in the morning. But I walked out the back door when no one was around. I'm going home."

"Listen! Suds, listen! We've got to talk first. You shouldn't have walked out like that. You crazy? You should have waited until they released you."

"You scared of me?"

David slammed the bottle he was holding down on the table. "Big-mouth!"

"Sorry, David."

David walked around the table to sit where he had been sitting when Sudsy came in, tilting his chair back, hands in his pockets. He looked big and competent, and relaxed, all except his eyes. The eyes were darker than Suds had ever thought of them as being, and there were circles under them he had not noticed before. David said, "Pour another drink and rest yourself, Sudsy."

Sudsy took the bottle, raised it halfway to his lips, then lowered it abruptly and picked up his glass from the floor.

"Lawd!" groaned David. "Lawdalmighty! We've been drinking out of the same bottle for more than a year. Now he has to have a glass." He took another glass from the shelf beside the washstand and walked over to Sudsy. "Keep pouring, man. I've got me a thirst, too."

"I've just been told," said Sudsy. "Drinking glasses. Eating utensils. Dishes. You'd think they'd know that a guy with a famous doctor for a father would know about these things, wouldn't you? But no, they had to spell it out for me. Somehow, you never think you'll be the one with the plague."

"Going a long way back, aren't you, pal?" asked David quietly. "Plague! No one's called tuberculosis the plague since long before you were a fat little something in diapers. My grandfather would say it: 'You're talking foolish, son. You're talking downright foolish.' "

He was seated again now, and he leaned forward across the table, elbows splayed out, shoulders hunched around his ears, hands clasped, his chin almost touching them. His eyes brooded on Sudsy.

"My grandfather has a good friend drives a colored cab. Just before I came back here this fall he asked me and Gramp if we wanted to drive out to the airport with him when he went to meet someone—some friend. Colored can't ride in the airport limousines in New Orleans. That would be getting *too* damned cosmopolitan. When we got there the plane was late and we stood around, and Ambrose—that's Gramp's friend—decided he wanted a drink. He said the bar wasn't segregated and he went in, but Gramp wouldn't go. Gramp wouldn't ever go anywhere, or let me go anywhere, he thought there was a chance of being humiliated. I mean more'n you are just breathing in and out. Know what happened?"

"They wouldn't serve him. David, *will* you—"

"Yeah. They served him. Finally. When the bartender had worn the bar top down a couple of inches polishing it off, he came over and said, 'Waddyawant?' Just like that. Growled it. Ambrose said, 'Whiskey straight; water back.' And he put five dollars on the bar. You know what that red-necked bastard did?"

"Threw it in his face. *David*—"

"How you talk! They not like that in N'Awlins. They loves their nigras. Don't y'all know that in N'Awlins we their people? 'Ouah people'—that's what they calls us in N'Awlins. Threw it in his face? Hell, no! That wouldn't be kind, Sudsy. You got to be *kind* to the nigra. You come to the South now, you remember that, y'hyah? Don't you go round calling their nigras names like clever son of a bitch or handkerchief-haid bastard. He didn't throw that whiskey in Ambrose's face. He walked down to the end of the bar and he got him a paper cup—yes, suh, a nice, clean, li'l ol' paper cup—"

Sudsy, interested in spite of himself, said, "Dixie cup, no doubt."

David continued: "Must have been. Anyhow, he poured a slug of whiskey in that li'l ol' Dixie cup and he gave it to Ambrose, and poured water in another Dixie cup and he gave it to him—"

"And spit in 'em?"

"No! Sudsy, you've got to learn about these things. They're things like unwritten laws. No, he didn't spit in 'em. He waited till Ambrose finished his drink; then he picked up the money in one hand, and the water cup in the other, and crumpled up the water cup and threw it in the trash basket—hard. Like it was some kind of filth. Then he picked up the other cup, and he did the same thing with it; only, he threw it in harder. Then he walked over to the cash register and made change. You see, if he'd made change before he showed Ambrose how upset he was about having to serve him, Ambrose might have left before he had chance to see him throw those cups away that a nigger had drunk from. It'll be a long time before I forget the look on Ambrose's face when he walked out of there. How you talk! Throwing whiskey in the face of a poor thirsty nigra, spitting in his drink."

David straightened his shoulders, sat erect now, and his voice changed and became the familiar voice Sudsy knew, only lower and more gentle. "And you're talking about the plague, Sudsy? There's millions of us were born with it."

The warmth of the room, the two stiff drinks, the stillness of a deserted dormitory on a holiday weekend were getting to Clifton Sutherland. His eyes were moist, as they always were after the second drink. The knuckles of the hand that held the bottle were no longer white as they had been when he had clutched it as though it were going to save him from drowning. He held up the bottle, looked through it at David, said, "Yea, verily," and poured more whiskey.

When he had finished the drink and the inevitable shudder, David looked at him, and smiled. "I don't know why," he said, "I swear to God I don't know why you drink when you suffer like that."

The quirk of Sudsy's lips might have passed for a smile.

"Son of a bitch," he said. "Clever son of a bitch."

David leaned across the table, took the bottle, and drank from it. "Yes, oh, yes." he said. "Be kind. Let us be kind. Let us all love one another. Quit looking at that bottle, man. You can have it back." He sloshed the whiskey around in the bottle, gauging the amount left. "Brethren, let us be kind," he said. "Yea, brethren, let us love one another." He took a swallow of the whiskey, began to sing. " 'Take this *bot*tle, Carry to the *cap*tain'—"

He reached out a long arm, held the bottle out to Sudsy. "Going to get you drunk, Sudsy," he said. "Going to get you real stinking drunk. Boxed out, that's what I'm going to get you. Tell me now, while you can still talk, brother, what you want me to do for you while you're drunk?"

It did not take long for David to realize that his goal of getting Clifton Sutherland sufficiently drunk to get him back into the Infirmary, or at the worst into bed in his own room, was not likely to be achieved. Sudsy appeared to be well aware of his intent, and developed a caginess that liquor would not dim. David made another attempt to appeal to reason. "They'll be sending you home on Sunday at the latest, Suds. Come on. Use your head. If you go back now they may not even have discovered you're out. That wouldn't be too bad a rap—just coming over here."

"I told the nurse I was going to sleep. I *gotta* be out of this place before they bring the supper trays around."

David poured another drink, offered it to him, but he shook his head. "Later," he said. "Later, man."

"Listen to reason, Suds. What good's it going to do to get a bad mark against you? Besides, you aren't fit to travel."

Sudsy's eyes were glazed, the round cheeks beginning to look flushed, and his speech slurred slightly. He stood up and shrugged into his duffel coat. "I didn't come here for a lecture," he said. "What the hell did you think I came here for?"

"Help," said David.

Sudsy's hand was out to push David aside, on his way to the door, but one of David's big ones spread out on the smaller youth's chest. He pushed, not hard, and Sudsy went back a few steps, and the edge of the couch struck the back of his legs. One arm flailing, he lost balance and wound up, half lying, half sitting, on the couch.

"Cut out that crap, Sutherland. Have it your own way." David looked down at the other boy, and suddenly his half-angry exasperation left him. He saw a friend, achingly homesick and troubled, judgment warped by illness and shock. What in hell difference did a lousy rule make? Sudsy wasn't trying to do anything bad; he just wanted to go home, like a hurt child.

"So-so, Sudsy," he said. "So-so. I'll pack for you, and get you ready to go. How'll we get you there? You're not going to drive, that's for sure."

"Who said I was going to drive? Going to get prain or tlane—train or plane."

"Where? Where are you going to get this prain or tlane?"

"Cinci. We've got time, David."

"On a holiday weekend?"

"Train. Then we don't have to go to Covington. Listen, David." Sudsy had the top off the bottle and was peering into it with one eye closed. "Listen, David, old friend. I'll pour us another drink. Then you go downstairs and telephone, see. You telephone that li'l ol' railroad station and see if you can get me on a train for Boston. Get me a roomette. You got credit at that switchboard."

When David came back, Sudsy was lying across the bed, feet on the floor.

"Sick," he said when David entered. "I feel so damned sick."

"So-so," said David. "So-so, little man. You're going to feel sicker. All they had was a bedroom, and that's out of Columbus."

"You get it, David?"

"Sure, I got it. You have any money?"

Sudsy snickered and rolled his head from side to side on the bed. "Money! Sure I've got money! All kinds of—" Suddenly he sat up. "My God! Money! Three dollars! Three lousy li'l ol' dollars!"

"I told you you were going to feel sicker." David stood over the other boy, looking down at him. Sudsy waggled a forefinger at him. "Drive," he said. "We can drive. We can drive to New York and I'll get a train there. You call the station again and you tell the man what he can do with his big ol' bedroom. You tell him to be glad it's not a pineapple."

David walked to one of the windows beside the fireplace. Snow had begun to fall again, big flakes mingling with small ones, drifting past. It did not look like the start of a heavy fall, but he'd give it an hour to cover the roads. He did not relish the idea of driving so far in a snowstorm, however mild, and there was no telling what the weather would be doing between Laurel and New York. And somewhere between the two places they would have to stop. And Suds would get hungry; he always did when he had been drinking, and there would be places where they wouldn't serve him—David Champlin—because he was colored. He would have to go in and get the food and bring it out, perhaps go around back and get it. If that happened he knew he wouldn't be able to keep Sudsy in the car because Sudsy would know why and would make a scene sure as hell. They might even wind up in jail.

All David knew of tuberculosis was the general knowledge he'd picked up from reading, and what he knew of Gramp's friends in New Orleans who had died of it—and there had been plenty. There had been Big Red Harris, who, Gramp said, had played drums every night with a coffee can beside him, coughing and spitting up blood, and who had died on the stand coughing blood so that it filled the coffee can and ran onto the stand. For all his brave words to Sudsy, "It's nothing today," he was afraid. He couldn't see how pneumonia or a night in jail could be anything but bad on top of TB; very bad.

He turned away from the window. "I've got money, Suds. You take the train."

"Not all that kind of money, pal? More'n a hundred dollars?"

"It's only sixty something. And I can let you have some for taxis and meals and stuff like that."

"But that's—" Sudsy looked at David, and the face crumpled like a baby's, then set; the flush left it, and it was doughy and pale, opaque, a surface on which no emotion could reflect. "That's one-way," he said. "That's a one-way ticket."

"Sure it is. Round trip's only good for six months. Look, Suds, it's tough—but they won't let you back this year. Next year. Come on, fella—"

Sudsy did not move for a minute, then rose slowly. "I wanted to be a doctor," he said.

"Jesus have moicy!" said David. "Jesus have moicy! How can one sorry little piece of a guy have so much stupidness in him! And your old man a doctor. You grew up with doctoring. You must've learned *something*. My grandfather still doesn't believe in germs, not really. No one ever taught him any better. Gramp still thinks if somebody faints or has a bad spell it's a 'revolution of the blood.' But even Gramp's not *that* ignorant. You'll be a doctor—but I'll be darned if I think you'll be a good one!"

Sudsy was rolling the whiskey bottle between the palms of his hands, still sitting on the edge of the couch. "Takes a hell of a long time to be a doctor," he said. "A year's a hell of a long time."

"And we're messing around talking for a hell of a long time. Come on, let's move the bodies over to Emory."

They slipped out the side door of Quimby House, and David's reconnoitering showed him no signs of life on the campus. They hurried down the side path, over gray slush under a powder of new snow. A cold wind met them at the corner, and Sudsy stopped, buffeted not by the wind but by a paroxysm of coughing.

David's arm was around his shoulder, holding him upright. Sudsy felt the warmth of the other's blood through his coat, the strength of his body, thought he could feel the steady, strong rhythm of the heart. He tried to speak, but the coughing stopped him, and its sound was horrible in his own ears.

Through it he heard David's voice: "Lawd! Lawd! Warm sun! Arizona! You've got it made, man. You tell your old man you've got to take me with you." Then the coughing stopped, and he tried to laugh, clearheaded for a minute in the gray cold.

"Tell my old man I've got to have the first Negro Justice of the SOO-preme Court of these YEWnited States with me?" He was still shaken, weakened by the paroxysm, but he started across the roadway. "That takes a hell of a long time, too. And a hell of a lot of brains. You going to write to me, David?"

"I'll study about it," said David. "I don't see why I should worry myself writing to an ornery little creep without any more sense than you have, but I'll study about it."

"Bastard," said Sudsy. "Handkerchief-haid bastard."

Inside the rear entrance of Emory Hall, David stopped and brushed the snow from his head, then rubbed his scalp until it tingled. Gramp had always made him do that when he'd been out in the rain without a hat. "Brings the blood back to the head," Gramp said. "Keeps away a cold."

Sudsy went up the back stairs ahead of him, was halfway down the second-floor corridor when David reached it. Sudsy called out sharply: "Come on, come *on,* David. You've been dragging your ass all afternoon."

David heard a sound behind him, turned his head as Suds was speaking, and saw a slender figure in a blue bathrobe cross quickly from the showers to a room across the hall. He recognized it as Clevenger, and swore under his breath. There were no other signs of life in the dormitory.

The rule about cars on campus had been unofficially repealed during the holiday weekend, and Sudsy's was parked behind the dormitory. David packed the essentials quickly, promising to send the rest of the stuff the following week. As David stowed the suitcase in the luggage compartment, Sudsy said: "The money. I'll get the money back to you. My dad'll send it Monday."

"You better," said David. "Gramp's saying he's picked up weight, mighty near a hundred and five now, he says. He'll take me on if I don't get that money. That all? We got everything you want?" He was wearing a green stocking cap borrowed from Suds, and now he pulled the cuff down over his ears and climbed behind the wheel. "Better get your head down till we clear the campus, chum," he said.

As they neared the driveway that led to the parking circle behind the Infirmary, David swore loudly at a noise from the rear of the car. He glanced at Sudsy to make sure he still had his head below the level of the window and windshield, and stopped the car. "Damned trunk lock," he said, and ran to the back of the car. He raised the lid of the luggage compartment, slammed it shut with enough force to engage the catch, locked it and tried it carefully before returning to his seat. Sudsy laughed. "You scared the whey out of me," he said. "I thought you were going to try and get me back in."

"You're not drunk enough. I tried. I know when I'm licked."

"Listen, David." They were on the highway now. "When the stink comes, you tell 'em you didn't know I'd sprung myself out of the Infirmary, see? Tell them I came to your room and said they'd released me. You mind lying?"

"Cripes, no! It's my neck, too. You came to my room—*with* that bottle."

"Right. No one saw us."

"Clevenger did."

"Randy? He went away for the holiday."

"Then he got back. I saw him, upstairs in the corridor in Emory."

Since David had given up hope of keeping Sudsy on campus, he had only pretended to drink, wanting a clear head for the driving he had no taste for, and there was still some whiskey in the bottle that Sudsy had tucked tenderly under his coat, along with two paper cups. He poured a generous slug into one of the cups, offered it to David, who refused, then drank it quickly himself. David said, "Take it easy, Suds; tomorrow's coming."

David knew the ride to Columbus would never leave his memory. There were no special incidents to fix it in his mind, nothing outstanding to ensure its life through the years, just a long ride on a gray winter afternoon, through grayer dusk, the snow falling at first and then stopping, with darkness coming on long before they reached the lights of the city.

It was still dusk, and they were a long way from Columbus when Sudsy said, "The car. You keep the car, huh?"

"I never thought about the car," said David. "How could I get it to you?" He started to say he could sell the car for Sudsy, but decided it was too much like talking about funerals to someone who was dying.

Sudsy leaned his head against the back of the seat. "Sick," he said again, as he had in David's room. "I feel so damned sick."

"So-so," said David. He felt Sudsy's sickness in his own bones and nerves and muscles and belly. "Sure you do. You'll feel better. Swear to God you'll feel better, Sudsy."

He heard the gurgle as Sudsy sat up and poured more whiskey. "Listen," said Sudsy. "Listen. You take the car. Keep the darned old car. You can have the li'l ol' car. Give you the li'l ol' car."

"Stop talking foolish. We'll leave it the way it is. Until you want it I'll use it to get back and forth to the job weekends. Don't worry about a thing. Just let me know what you want when you feel better."

They drove without speaking for a long time. David began to hum, then to sing. He didn't know why he sang, except that somehow singing released the tautness that the sorrow within him had brought on.

"Blues," said Sudsy. "Hell of a thing to sing. Why'd you want to sing blues? Lesh—lesh—let us be gay."

"What d'you want? Old English madrigals? That what you want?"

"Something square, David. Shomething real cubed. Shomething Shquare for Shimmons." He giggled. "I'm not that drunk."

David laughed, then started to hum again, then to sing, his voice soaring, driving like a lead trumpet, Sudsy's following, faltering, like a badly tuned clarinet at the lips of a tone-deaf youth.

"Ever tell you I was tone deaf?" said Sudsy.

"You think you need to tell me? Man, that's not something you ever have to tell a guy. Come *on*, man, get your back in it. . . . 'Pharaoh's army got *drown*ded. . . . *Oh*, Mary . . .' "

The man at the gate to the train platform in the Columbus station let David through without a ticket because of Sudsy's noticeable unsteadiness and because the stairs were long and steep. He watched them as they went down, the tall Negro impassive, unsmiling; the white boy flushed and sick-looking. "Damned jigs," he muttered automatically. "Steal the gold outa his teeth." He told himself he was no damned southern cracker; it was none of his business, none of his business at all; he was just a white man, just a good white American; but right's right, he said to himself, and wrong's wrong, and damned if it wasn't wrong—decent white boys getting drunk with niggers.

Behind dirty spectacles and pursed mouth, he debated with himself as to the advisability of following the white boy and his companion, thought about going down the stairs and tipping off the conductor, while below him, on the platform beside the door of a Pullman car, David Champlin drew a five-dollar bill from his pocket and gave it to the porter.

"Keep your eye on that boy," said David. "He's sick."

"He's mighty *high,*" said the porter.

"Yeah. But he's sick, too. See he gets coffee in the morning—lots of it. In his room, y'hear. He won't be feeling too good. He may get feeling hungry—"

"I'll find him something," said the porter. "Sure will. And I'll look after him in the morning. I knows them bad feelings, morning after." He turned to help a passenger, and when he turned back to speak again the tall youth was no longer beside him. He was—damned if he wasn't—thumbing his nose at the window of Bedroom C, waving, then limping off, long-legged, big, quiet-seeming. Gonna be a powerful man, that colored boy, thought the porter. Fine boy. Fine-looking boy. He saw David reach the steps, get a third of the way up, then flatten himself against the stair rail to let a man pass. The man hurried by him, not saying "thank you," not acknowledging the courtesy. "Um-um," murmured the porter. "Um-ummmm."

29

DAVID PROWLED THE WAITING ROOM of the station uneasily. In an obscure way he sensed that Sudsy had done more than just go home because he was sick; he was leaving David's world for another planet where David could not follow him even in his thoughts. If it had been Nehemiah, David would have known what was happening, would have been able to see Nehemiah's folks when they heard the news, know what they would do and what they would say, hear the cadence of their voices. Nehemiah absent would still have been as much a part of his life as Nehemiah present.

He did not like to think of Sudsy getting off the train in the morning, sick as he was bound to be, with no one to meet him, yet he shied away from calling Sudsy's father, in spite of Sudsy's frequent reiteration that for a parent the famous Dr. Sutherland was a pretty regular guy. You didn't know these things just because somebody told you. You didn't know anything just because somebody told you. The ice was always thin, and no one could test it but you. He said "Hell!" under his breath, and reached into his pocket for his wallet. He had ten dollars left, two fives. It couldn't cost more than five, station-to-station, after six, to call Boston. If the doctor wasn't there he would leave word. Someone ought to meet a guy as sick as Sudsy would be in the morning. Until he had taken care of that, Suds was still in sight, still had one foot on the world they inhabited together; after that he would be gone.

The newsstand attendant, clearing shelves before closing up, watched David covertly. He was sliding the glass panels over the upper part of the stand when David came up to him. Over the tall Negro's shoulder he could see, leaning against the wall opposite, the man who had been at the gate to the train platform. The gate attendant was looking across at him, unsmiling, wary, like a mangy, protective terrier.

It startled David when, after a seemingly endless succession of bong-bongs as coins dropped into slots, a man's voice said, "Why not make it collect, Cliff?" He had been hoping the telephone would be answered by a servant—he was sure the Sutherlands must have servants—and that he could say, "Clifton Sutherland's arriving—" and let it go at that.

Now he said, "It's—it's not Cliff, sir."

The voice sharpened. "Has something happened to Cliff?"

Sudsy had said his father was shaped like an egg. This voice did not sound as though it belonged to a man who was shaped like an egg, thought David. It sounded as though it belonged to a man who might be very tall, and pleasantly thin, with a firmly kind face, but he supposed a fellow would say his father was shaped like an egg if he wasn't.

"No, sir. He's all right. I mean, well, nothing really bad."

"This is David Champlin, isn't it?"

"Yes, sir."

"We've heard a lot about you, David. Is my son in some kind of trouble?"

"No, sir. No, Doctor. It's just that, well, he's been sick,

and he wanted to come home and, well, I thought if someone could meet him—"

"Signal your operator, David. Tell her to reverse the charges."

"It's all right—"

"Please, I can talk more easily."

Sutherland père might look like an egg, thought David, but he spoke with unanswerable authority. David obeyed, and when the lengthy and complicated process of reversing the charges on a call already put through had been completed, the doctor said: "Ah. Now. Give me the story. He was in the Infirmary on Tuesday with what he said in his wire was influenza. There's been a lot of it this fall. You take it from there."

David, more at ease now, took it from farther back than the preceding Tuesday. He told the story from the beginning: Sudsy's repeated colds, the persistent cough, the tiredness, the fever. All he omitted was the diagnosis. At the conclusion of the story he said, "He decided he wanted out, sir. Wanted to come home."

"Yes," said the doctor. "Yes, I see. Don't beat around the bush, David. What you are trying to tell me is that my son was told he had pulmonary tuberculosis?"

"Well—yes, sir."

The silence that followed was so long David thought they had been disconnected. "Dr. Sutherland?"

"I'm here. Very much here. Why didn't they take X rays, do skin tests, before?"

"I couldn't say about that, sir. The last time he went there, and that was almost two months ago, he just had a cold. They told him to come back for a checkup, but—well, he never did."

"Why didn't they follow through!"

David knew the anger in the doctor's voice was not directed at him, not directed even at the authorities at the Infirmary, but at himself. Dr. Sutherland and his wife had been in Europe most of the previous summer, David knew that, and had not returned until after Sudsy had left for college. David knew what the man on the other end of the telephone was thinking: If he and his wife had been there, or had insisted that Sudsy go with them, the symptoms would have been uncovered long before.

"I'm surprised they released him from the Infirmary," the doctor said.

The telephone booth became smaller, hotter, more airless. He took off the green stocking cap with a nervous yank. "Well, sir, they didn't. Not exactly."

"He just walked out? Damned young idiot."

"I tried to stop him, sir, but there didn't seem to be any way. I really tried."

"I'm sure you did. Will you be in trouble over this?"

"It will be all right, sir."

"Where did he get the money for the ticket? The wire I received asked for money. Did you give it to him?"

"Well, I just happened to have some put by—it was just luck."

"I'll mail a check in the station when I meet Cliff, special delivery. Thank you, David."

"That's O.K., Doctor. He'll be all right now."

"We'll see. But will you? You shouldn't have done this. David, I want you to let us know if you are in any kind of serious trouble over this—this incident. Cliff has made you seem one of the family, you know. You're to write. That's an order."

"All right, Doctor. And, please, will you ask Sudsy—Cliff, to let me know how—well—how things are going?"

"We both will. And thank you again, David. His mother and I will meet the train."

When David left the telephone booth, the platform guard was standing opposite it, the newsstand attendant with him. It was obvious they had been watching the booth and their eyes followed him as he crossed the waiting room. They'll know me next time, he thought. They sure as hell must have seen a guy with a gimpy leg before, even a Negro with a gimpy leg.

He felt both relieved and sad. He knew now what he would do. Park the car in some safe garage, and then try and find the girl Nehemiah had introduced him to a few weeks before, a girl who was so good she might be able to make him forget that Sudsy had TB.

When David returned to Pengard the next day just before noon, he felt better than he had expected to, but still not good. There were messages in his mail rack. He stood looking at them morosely, then took them out and without looking at them went up to his room. There he heated water, made coffee, and splashed cold water on his face. As he sat, coffee mug in hand, at the card table, he read the messages. Two of them read "Call the Infirmary." These he crumpled and threw away. It was too late now. Two others read "Call Dr. Knudsen," and the fifth read "Call Dean Goodhue."

He finished his coffee, made another cup and drank that, then went downstairs to the telephone. His conversation with Dr. Knudsen was brief, consisting of: "This is David Champlin"—"Be here immediately"—and "Yes, sir."

He was glad he had Sudsy's car, and he thought as he drove to Professor's Knudsen's that Sudsy's offer of the car had not been the result of whiskey; stone sober, Sudsy would have done the same thing. It would be a godsend on weekends to get him back and forth to his job in Cincinnati. He just wished it didn't seem so damned empty without Sudsy in it.

Eve Knudsen opened the door, smiled warmly, and said, "He's waiting for you, David."

"With a club?"

She laughed. "No, no. Not with a club. Never a club for you, David."

She had turned and started down the hall, and David felt his eyes drawn upward, perhaps by a sound, but if it had been a sound it had been a very small one. Sara was standing halfway down the stairs, not moving, her face solemn and troubled. He smiled up at her. "Hi, Sara!" He had stopped himself just in time from saying "Hi, smallest."

She smiled, like a child who has been reassured. "Hi, David." She wrinkled her nose, and in a stage whisper said, "It's all right. Don't worry." Then, without moving a hand, or pursing her lips, without changing her position, she blew a kiss to him.

He told himself as he followed Eve Knudsen, "You're out of your mind, Champlin; she couldn't have. You're-out-of-your-ever-lovin'-mind."

At the study door Eve stopped, knocked, and said, "It's David Champlin, dear." Before she turned away she patted his shoulder. "He's not angry," she whispered. "Just upset. An upset Dane is a fearsome thing—but not lethal."

He was grateful for her reassurance when he entered the room. Dr. Karl Knudsen's eyes were a blazing blue; every hair on his head seemed crackling with emotion. He was sitting facing the door, in a swivel chair behind a flat-topped desk.

"Where have you been?"

"Columbus, sir." David sat in the modern Danish armchair opposite Knudsen.

"Have you called Dean Goodhue?"

"No, sir. Just you."

"Sutherland. Where is he?"

"I don't—he's at home, sir. In Boston. By now."

"Why is he at home? Is he at home because you took him out of the Infirmary and drove him to the train?"

"No, sir!" It had not occurred to David that this interpretation would be placed on the incident of the day before. "I took him to the train. But he walked out of the Infirmary himself and came to my room." There was something in the wind; he could smell it.

"You are sure about this? Quite sure? We have been told differently. We have been told that Sutherland's car was seen stopped just near the rear entrance to the Infirmary. And that you were driving."

It had to have been from a window, thought David. The campus had definitely been deserted. There were no windows affording a view of the rear of the Infirmary except those on the south side of Emory Hall. To the best of his knowledge only Randolph Clevenger had been in Emory Hall the afternoon before. And his room was on the south side. But Clevenger had seen him in the upper corridor, must have heard Sudsy urging him to hurry, saying "Come *on*, David; you've been dragging your ass all afternoon."

He answered Knudsen now. "We went from my room to his, and I helped him pack. We drove from Emory Hall, and when we got near the Infirmary the lid of the trunk began to bang. I got out and locked it."

Some of the blaze left Knudsen's eyes.

"You have a great responsibility," he said.

David's breath did not even quicken when the wall closed round him, a wall transparent to those on one side, opaque to those on the other. He thought, behind his wall: Why? Why do I have a great responsibility? The whites have no responsibility because they are human beings, but I am a Negro and not a human being; therefore I have a great responsibility?

To Knudsen, he said, "Yes" in a flat tone, while his mind raced on: Every damned one of you whites, you carry your race on your shoulders just as we do; what about your responsibilities to your race? It doesn't matter, it doesn't matter a Goddamned bit that you degrade it every time you put a Negro on a spot because he is a Negro? The hell with my responsibilities—what about your responsibilities to the human race, you guys with the whip hand?

He was conscious that during the silence Knudsen had been looking at him closely; was conscious, too, of an almost plaintive note in the other's voice when he said, "I do not know what you are thinking."

David wanted to answer, "No, but I know what you are thinking, and it will always be that way, and that is why someday the loss will be yours." Instead, he remained silent. Knudsen would think he was sulking. It didn't matter.

"Will you at least tell me what happened, David?"

"Yes, sir." He gave Knudsen the story of the previous afternoon. When he finished, he said: "I admit I tried to get him drunk. I figured they wouldn't be rough on him if he'd just sneaked out and gone back to his room and gotten drunk. And I thought for a while that I could get him back into the Infirmary before they missed him. But he was too cagey. I don't see how I could have stopped him—outside of force. He was—he was like a stubborn homesick kid."

Knudsen sighed. "It makes sense." He pushed the telephone across the desk to within David's reach. "Call the dean. Call Goodhue."

As he dialed Goodhue's number David could hear that fruity voice in his mind, speaking to a student, any student: "Don't hesitate to call me, any time." Then the singsong "One-two-three-four—Sometimes I wish there were more—Ein, zwei—" and the pipe-distorted chuckle. Then he heard Goodhue's voice, "Dean Goodhue here."

He was a little surprised that he felt no fear, surprised at the quick realization that Goodhue could not hurt him; that none of the brass at Pengard could hurt him. Sudsy could hurt him by being sick and unhappy and away, but the others could not. They could hurt Gramp; that was what mattered, but even as he said, "This is David Champlin," he realized they could not hurt Gramp either, because Gramp would be expecting it; would always and forever, as long as he lived, be expecting something like this when his grandson was away, was charting a course over the perilous, uncertain seas of the white world where no compass ever pointed true North for a colored navigator.

Goodhue was saying something now about calling Quimby House and not being able to reach him. "I must have a talk with you," he said.

"Whenever you say, Dean."

"Two thirty would be best."

"I'll be there at two thirty."

"Right." There was a click as Goodhue hung up, and David looked at the receiver in his own hand and said, "And right to you."

Knudsen made no comment, but stood, and then walked with him down the hall to the front door. The blaze had gone entirely from his eyes, and they were troubled now. As he opened the door he said: "Don't worry too much, David. I am sure it will work out."

David looked at him, eyes without expression, voice low and courteous. "I'm not worried, Dr. Knudsen. Whether it works out or not. I'm not worried."

Merriwether Goodhue turned from the telephone and walked to one of the armchairs that flanked the fireplace in his study. As he sat he looked at Randolph Clevenger, opposite him. "That," he said, "was David Champlin."

The attempt at humor was sententious and unfunny, but Clevenger rewarded it with a smile. "So I gathered, sir."

Goodhue picked up his pipe and spoke in jerky phrases as he went through the ritual of getting it going. "You are sure" —puff—"Clevenger, that"—puff—"it was"—puff—"David?"

"I could hardly be mistaken, Dean."

"True"—puff—puff—puff—puff—"Ah!—And that the car was stopped? I'm sorry, Randolph, to appear to be giving you a third degree, but we must be certain of these things."

"The car was stopped, sir, and David was closing and locking the trunk. Presumably after stowing something in it. A suitcase, perhaps."

"Ah. Yes. Precisely. Sutherland is still driving that monstrous yellow car?"

"Yes. I couldn't have been mistaken about that."

"Appalling color," said the dean. "Appalling."

Clevenger started to rise. "I think I'd better be going, Dean Goodhue. You can send for me if you need any more—"

"No, Randolph. Sit down, bear with me for a few moments. There is plenty of time." He puffed reflectively on his pipe, leaned forward and poked the fire; then, leaning back again in the chair, he said: "There is a question, Clevenger, I feel I should ask. Yet it is one I dislike asking, for reasons that should be obvious. You are one of the few students I feel will understand why I must ask it. What can you tell me of this boy—David's social life, both on and off campus?"

"Hardly very much, Dean." There was a faint expression of distaste on Clevenger's petulant lips. "It is not too active

—but he gets around, as the saying is." He hesitated, then went on: "I think I know what you are getting at, sir. He does, of course, see quite a bit of the other students of—er —both sexes."

"And both races? In each instance?"

"Yes, sir. Aren't we supposed to pride ourselves on that at Pengard?"

"Some may, Randolph; some may. I have, of course, heard rumors. One does. But even if they were more than rumors —and, as you are no doubt aware, these rumors involve just one person—one's hands are tied by the standards that prevail here. I am talking to you very frankly, Clevenger; far more frankly than I would to any other student. I feel"—he smiled—"shall we say 'at home' with you; feel that we speak the same language."

"Thank you, Dean. I think we do."

"To return to yesterday's incident. Would you be willing to repeat what you have told me to other—er—authorities at the college if it becomes necessary?" In the dean's mouth the word became "nec'ry," and might conceivably have baffled an Englishman.

"I—well, yes, I believe so, sir."

"Don't hesitate to say 'no,' Randolph. I would quite understand a certain amount of apprehension on your part."

The thin, pale skin of Clevenger's face flushed. "I am not in the least afraid of David Champlin. But he has a great many champions here. They would take a dim view of any student who voluntarily 'put the finger on him.' That's underworld slang for—"

Goodhue's laugh was deep and reassuring; it was one of the things that had earned him his nickname. "I am quite familar with the expression, There is no reason to fear that any student will learn how David was—er—fingered. Now bear with me just a little longer, if you will. You did not actually see Sutherland in the car with David?"

Clevenger hesitated before replying. "No, sir. But I saw David turn and look down at something—or someone—in the seat beside him."

"You could actually see him do this?"

"Easily. I had a side view of the car. David was wearing a green knit cap—I think it was Sutherland's. I saw him look down at something in the seat beside him—or someone in the seat who might have been scrooched over."

The dean's pipe was going nicely now. He spoke around it:

"Is it your opinion that Sutherland would go along with any story David chooses to tell to—er—extricate himself?"

"Oh, definitely, sir."

"It is your opinion that their friendship is strong enough for that?"

"What does Sutherland have to lose? I think he'd go along with David out of gratitude. The friendship part . . ." His voice trailed off. He looked oddly, unnaturally mature at that moment, the mouth firmer, thinner.

Goodhue's eyebrows went up. "Yes, Randolph?"

"Well—that's about it, sir. Friendship isn't a word I'd use, if you don't mind. I mean, isn't friendship—I mean among adults—a thing of common background, common interests? Something more than just—I don't like to say this, Dean. I can't say it, really. The consequences could be too serious—"

Goodhue took the pipe from his mouth at last, holding it away from his lips. Clevenger's eyes met his directly, and suddenly the room was filled with the warmth of a dark understanding.

Beside them the fire flickered unevenly. The log in its center, burned through now, disintegrated with a hissing crash.

"I see," said the dean softly. "I see."

Clevenger glanced nervously at the ship's clock over the mantel, and rose. "I think I'd really better leave, Dean Goodhue."

Goodhue stood beside him, his arm across his shoulders. He could not have noticed the involuntary movement of withdrawal, because his arm remained across the student's back. "One of the drawbacks of my position," he said, "is that it is so difficult to become really acquainted with the students as individuals, without being accused of favoritism. One tries, of course. One of these afternoons—soon—perhaps you'll come in for a cup of tea? My wife would be delighted."

"Thank you, sir. So should I."

Dean Goodhue stood watching Randolph Clevenger as he crossed the narrow brick terrace to the driveway, slim, casually elegant in slacks and cashmere sweater, the feet—even in heavy shoes—delicate, picking their way as a cat's would, around the patches of slush in the driveway; the head with its darker than blond but lighter than honey-colored hair tilted characteristically, ever so slightly, to one side.

The knuckles of the dean's hand, which was still holding

the handle of the door, whitened; the rise and fall of his breathing was uneven, hurried.

David braked the yellow car to a stop outside the double French doors of Goodhue's study. Through the glass of the doors he could see Goodhue at the eighteenth-century mahogany table that served as a desk. He appeared to be writing. There was no percentage in doing what he wanted to do, which was sit in the car and think it out some more. He had done all the thinking he could do in a hot-and-cold shower and while he was shaving, after he returned to Quimby House from Knudsen's.

Goodhue did not look up when David knocked, but David heard the "Come in!" As he entered, Goodhue said, "Ah, David," continued writing for a few moments, then said, "Sit down, David."

David took the chair opposite and the dean reached for his pipe. "I regret this whole incident," he said. "Regret the necessity for calling you in here."

David thought: What the hell am I supposed to say? What the hell? That I regret it, too? Goodhue didn't regret anything, not anything at all. Why couldn't he have opened the interview as Knudsen had, with a direct, angry question?

There was only one answer David could make, an answer that must have been made by hundreds of students, at one time or another, sitting where he was sitting now. "Yes, sir," he said.

"You have let everyone down, David. Everyone."

"I don't see that, sir. I didn't have much choice."

"Choice?" Goodhue lit a match with a quick, impatient gesture, applied the match to his pipe. "What 'choice' was involved in aiding a fellow student—and a very ill one at that—to break college regulations and—er—escape from the Infirmary?"

"That's not what I did, Dean Goodhue."

"Suppose you tell me your version of what occurred."

"Your version of what occurred"! Not "what occurred." What are you wasting your time for, David Champlin? Get up and get out. Get back to your room and start packing. Don't sit there like a damned sheep waiting to get its throat slit. *Tell 'em I wuz flyin'*. Neither Gramp nor the Prof would fault you for it. He stopped his thoughts in midflight. He wasn't going to make it that easy for this lily-white bastard.

"I remained on campus over the holiday to—" he started to say "save money," but that wouldn't do; that would sound like a poor-mouth bid for sympathy. Instead he continued, "to do some catching up. On Friday morning—yesterday—I went to the Infirmary to see Sutherland. They wouldn't let me see him because the doctor was with him. I had a sandwich at the rec hall and went back to my room." As he talked he heard his phrases and his tone becoming more formal and stilted. He left out any mention of the bottle, and, when he finished the story, said: "The only recourse I had was force. I couldn't have done that. He was determined. And sick."

"And drunk."

How had this son of a bitch known that? There was no question in his tone; it was a flat statement of fact.

"A little," said David.

The dean's pipe was making bubbling, sucking sounds. He took it from his mouth and said, "There is a rule about liquor in the students' rooms. As you well know. It must be obvious to you, David, that either someone brought liquor to Sutherland while he was still in the Infirmary—possibly slipping it through the window—or he became drunk with you. We know that Sutherland boarded the train in a very unsteady —a drunken—condition. And that you were with him when he boarded. You must have realized that as soon as his absence was noted a most extensive inquiry would be made. We checked airports and railroad stations—both Cincinnati and Columbus. The least, the very least, you could have done was notify me or some faculty member of the circumstances."

He hadn't thought of that. Goodhue was dead right there. He'd been too upset, too sick in his mind over Sudsy's trouble, to do the sensible thing. "Yes, sir," he said. "I realize that now."

"A little late," said Goodhue. "Yes, David, a little late."

"But, Dean. I did not take liquor to the Infirmary, and I did not help him to get out of there. The first I knew of his being out was when he showed up at my room."

"If that story is true, he must have done his drinking with you."

"He did." He was damned if he'd tell Goodhue the liquor had been left in his room by a couple of guys in the adjoining room.

"Then what was Sutherland's car, with you driving, doing at the rear entrance of the Infirmary late in the afternoon?

You were obviously putting something in the luggage compartment."

I'd lie to you, thought David. I'd lie to you with no more compunction than I'd have in lying to any white man in New Orleans who'd put me on a spot. But the truth is so damned simple. He told Goodhue, as he had told Knudsen, the reason for the stop.

"I can prove that Sutherland was in Emory Hall before that," he said when he finished.

"I hope so, David."

"Clevenger saw us. Randolph Clevenger saw us when we were walking down the upper hallway to Sutherland's room. He was coming out of the showers."

A quiet hung between them that was different from the voicelessness of previous pauses in their conversation. He looked into Goodhue's face and saw that the slate-colored eyes were looking over his head, fixed, without expression. When the dean spoke at last he made no reference to David's statement of having been seen by Clevenger in Emory Hall. The damned red-neck phony, thought David; he's taking it for granted that I'm lying, and why in hell would I tell a lie I could be caught out in so easily?

Goodhue went on. "All of the Quimby scholarship students have a grave responsibility, a responsibility to improve in every way possible the image of their race—"

That's how your great-grandaddy died, son, my daddy, and you're better off getting it from me. . . . Died on a fire like a roast of meat. . . . Young Abr'am Jefferson, he went crazy, he went plumb crazy. . . . That white doctor come near him and he went screaming crazy . . . ran out of that house of theirs and down the street . . . and there wasn't no one could catch him . . . screaming all the way . . . "Coming, Jesus. I'm coming, Jesus!" . . . And when he got to the riverfront he threw hisself in the water and drownded. . . .What a pretty image, what a pretty, pretty white image it was when the sight of a white doctor coming toward him could send a Negro out of his mind. . . . What a pretty image, what pretty, pretty images those white men must have made standing round the fire that burned David Champlin like a roast of meat.

"David. You weren't listening."

"I'm afraid not, Dean." He stood up.

He realized now there was no point in staying longer. The picture was clear. Clevenger hadn't seen them; Clevenger, walking across the hall just behind them, hadn't heard Sudsy's loud "Come on, come *on*, David. You've been dragging your ass all afternoon." The hell he hadn't! David turned toward the door, and a sharp voice halted him.

"One moment, David! I have not dismissed you yet. There is one other—er—factor involved in this situation. I shall not go into it, except to say that I am aware of it. These problems are not strange to us, or to any college. However, when they become known, steps must be taken. We do not condemn; we try to understand; however, our duty is painfully clear."

David looked down at the man behind the desk. His bewilderment was so great he could not keep it from his eyes. What was the old fart getting at? What in the name of God was he talking about? He wouldn't—he couldn't—give him the satisfaction of asking. Whatever it was, it couldn't be true, but—*What the hell you want to do a damfool thing like that for . . . argue with 'em? . . . It don't do no good. . . . They ain't going to believe you was Jesus Christ to be standing side of you swearing to it.* He told himself: Keep your mouth shut, David. This is evil, white evil; don't mess with it.

"You appear puzzled, David, You will, I am sure, understand what I am talking about if you give the matter some thought. I believe you do now." Goodhue rapped his pipe sharply on the edge of a heavy ashtray, then picked up a knife and began scraping at the bottle. "The next thing is Sutherland's car."

"Sutherland asked me to keep it. He told me to use it for the remainder of the term."

The slate-colored eyes looking up at David were bleak. "I hardly think Sutherland was in a position—condition, I should say—to exercise sound judgment. I shall notify Clifton's family that the car is in storage. The key, please."

The leather key container lay on Goodhue's desk when David left the room. He had not spoken. Outside, a raw wind was rising. Because Sudsy's car had a heater and was warm, he had worn only a light pullover sweater, and the shoes he had put on were lightweight. He knew depressions and faults lay below the gray slush of the driveway. Behind him, he was certain, Goodhue would be sitting at his desk, the full length of the driveway within his range of vision. The soft ground at the edge of the driveway would be wet, soggy, but it would give better footing, would not trap him into a treacherous hole. He felt the cold ooziness of the slush and mud through his shoes, felt it seeping inside, but he limped along the unpaved edge without fearing a sudden slip, the humiliation of a fall with Goodhue watching.

30

DAVID'S FIRST CLASS ON Monday was Benford's, at ten o'clock. It was the only day he did not have an early class, and he usually made trite and corny cracks to the students he met on campus who were leaving their first and second classes, like "Why don't you stay in bed and get more sleep?" He didn't make any remarks to anyone this morning, not only because he did not feel like it but also because something in the faces of his hurrying classmates stopped any greeting before it could cross his lips. What was the matter with these self-righteous characters? Hadn't any of them ever broken a college regulation? Were they so damned full of rectitude and piety they'd shy away from a guy just because he was in a jam?

In class he was more inept and prone to error than he had ever been, even in his first semester. He cringed inwardly in expectation of Benford's sarcasm, but it did not come. In fact, Beanie was unusually tolerant and patient. He had taken a seat beside Chuck, whose attitude seemed no different than it had ever been. Ella Denslow, a white femme student whom he had always disliked heartily was sitting a few chairs away, and light from the window's big single pane was falling directly in her eyes. Just as Beanie came through the doorway back of his desk she walked to the window and lowered the Venetian blind. On her way back to her seat she glanced at David, and he almost gasped audibly at the repugnance in her eyes.

There was a letter to Gramp in his pocket, written the night before, not making excuses, just saying that he was coming home and that he hoped Gramp would understand. It didn't mean he had given up college, the letter said; just that he was coming home and would then seek entrance to another college and cram so that he could finish in three years instead of four, and go on to law school. It might even be that he could beat the letter home, if Dr. Sutherland's check was in the noon mail at the rec hall, and if he spent most of it by taking a plane.

He was doodling in the margin of his notebook, fierce-looking lions and tigers, an elephant, a snake wearing horn-rimmed glasses, and did not hear Beanie's dismissal of the class, only heard him say: "Champlin. Please remain for a few minutes. Unless you have another class immediately."

"Yes, sir," said David. He did have another class: Burbridge's in ancient history, but the hell with it. He had learned all Burbridge was teaching now in the Prof's study in New Orleans.

He sat quietly while the others filed out, only one or two of them able to keep from looking at him curiously. He felt Chuck's big fist punch his shoulder, said, "Hey!" half-heartedly.

He had expected Benford to call him back into his office behind the classroom. Instead the Professor nodded his long, skull-like head at his student, then inclined it toward the doorway that led to a small bricked balcony overlooking the inner quadrangle, more of a terrace than a balcony, with three steps leading down to a narrow paved walk. He thought that the whole lousy situation was a nightmare, and of all the persons who could make it more of a nightmare no one was better equipped than Beanie, with his whiplash phrases and razor-edged sarcasm.

A sun too bright for winter, too pale for summer, was behind Benford as he walked to the brick wall that surrounded the balcony, threw a sweater he had brought with him over it, and perched on it like a giant bird, long, thin legs swinging, teeth showing white in the black gauntness of his face. He laid a bony hand over the wall beside him. "Sit down, David Champlin," he said. "Relax." Then, when David hesitated, added, "Res' yo'self."

It was like misjudging the number of risers in a flight of stairs, coming to the top and thinking there was another, stepping on it and jolting to a stop when it wasn't there. "Res' yo'self" wasn't New Orleans or Atlanta or Birmingham or Richmond—it was just colored, gentle, kindly older-generation colored; and not older generation, either, because he used it himself instinctively when he was home and friends came to the house. Beanie had sounded—damned if he hadn't—like Gramp. He didn't think Beanie would use it as a mockery, as Simmons or Dunbar would. But he didn't know; he didn't know anything anymore, either about his own people here or the people of the other world he had elected to thrust himself into. He didn't know anything for sure, and he felt lost and sad and rebellious. He wanted to run, run as fast as his bandy leg would let him and, running, call over his shoulder to the man on the wall: "Don't worry yourself, you hear? Don't worry yourself about David. David's gone—he's long gone!"

He did not run. Instead he obeyed Benford's gesture, hoisted himself to the wall beside the Professor, throwing his duffel coat over it first.

"Almost warm enough to go fishing," said Beanie. "More like baseball than football weather."

"Yes, sir," said David. And waited.

"Used to play baseball," said Beanie.

David could not stop the surprised turn of his head. "Yeah?"

"Outfit called the Black Pelicans. In Georgia, where I was born. You're learning mathematics, David, from a man who once pitched against the great Satch Paige."

"Yeah? Well—I mean—gosh, did you win?"

"He shut us out. The concept of jet propulsion was inspired by Satch's arm."

Even in his bewildered aloneness David wanted to ask questions. Satch Paige was Gramp's hero. It would be fun telling Gramp that he knew someone who had pitched against him. He was finding it hard to adjust to this bit of information, trivial though it was. Beanie had been Beanie since the day he was born, as far as his students were concerned. He had certainly never been a pitcher on a Negro baseball team, and before that a skinny youngster playing in the red dust of Georgia. Now Beanie had hooked a heel over the edge of the wall and wrapped long arms around his knee.

"I keep my secrets," he said. "Especially the secret that, in spite of all evidence to the contrary, I'm a human being." Benford tightened his arms around the knee, waited a moment, then said abruptly, "Did you pack last night?"

David was silent, kicking a heel against the bricks, rubbing a hand along their roughness.

"None of my business, of course," said Benford. "None of my business at all. But the reason I asked the question is because I packed a number of times myself. Six, to be exact."

"Yes, sir," said David. Here it comes, he thought—the lecture. "It's not going to take long to do that. Pack, I mean."

"Two hours at the most," said the man beside him.

David slid to his feet, plunging his hands into his pockets, facing Beanie from an angle so the sun would not be in his eyes. He'd forestall the lecture. There was nothing to lose now.

"You didn't run away," he said. "That's what you're trying to say—that you didn't run away. I'm not running away. They're going to kick me out anyhow. I'm just not giving them the chance. It's better to leave, isn't it, than be expelled? Better on your record when you enter another college? You think they'll ask me at Howard or Tuskegee or Dillard why I quit? You think they won't know? But if I get expelled, then they'll think I'm a troublemaker, breaking rules, all that—in a white college, yet. All this talk about 'this isn't a white college' is a lot of crap. I shouldn't have come here in the first place."

"You should have listened to your grandfather? That's what you're trying to say?"

"No—I—well—what do you mean?"

"Just that. And I wish you'd sit down. You didn't listen to your grandfather when he said, 'Don't mess around with the whites, son. You'd be better off getting yourself an education with your own. You want to be worried all the time, fighting the white's prejudice, trying to study and learn, worried all the time about the way they going to act?' "

The smile came so quickly, spontaneously, David could not control it. "You might have been there," he said. "How'd you know?"

"Because my father said the same things to me. I don't know how things were for you, David. Of course, I know something of your background; all the faculty know the backgrounds of the students, it's part of our job; but just how things were for you in another sense, I can't know. A Negro boy growing up in the South—they can't have been good. But I think, at least from a material standpoint, they were better for you than they were for me, for most Negroes in the rural South. Not that they don't stink, everywhere."

"I've been lucky," said David. "Awfully damned lucky. Too damned lucky, I guess, for it to be right."

"Nonsense. So was I, if you want to put it that way. People do hit jackpots. Are you going to walk off and leave your jackpot in the machine? The odds against another one are mighty long."

When David did not answer, Benford went on: "The odds, for that matter, are against us all the way. They're against us if we stay where the whites have put us; they're against us if we make it in their world. You know that, for God's sake."

"Sure. Sure, I know it."

"If you quit now it will not lessen your troubles. They will come to you no matter where you find yourself. You've heard, 'Woe succeeding woe has made us torpid.' The weariness of misfortune, Cicero argues, makes grief lighter."

David could find no answer. This was not what he had squared off mentally to meet. Benford turned so that he was facing him directly, and David remembered Sudsy saying that on those rare occasions when Beanie smiled he looked like a benevolent death's-head.

"Shall we get down to cases?" said Benford. "Torpidity is not for us any longer, David. Nor weariness of misfortune. Those were for the generations before us. My generation, perhaps; your grandfather's, yes; yours—no. My God, no! Do you think you'll escape one iota of what's in store by running from this? Three years of peace of mind in a college with your own people. That's what you're thinking. And after that?" When David did not speak, he prodded. "And after that? Why in hell do fighters spend so much of their time in training with sparring partners? And a good fighter wants a good sparring partner. What you're doing—what I think you're doing, because you've told me nothing—is to take the comparatively mild punches of a sparring partner and decide you don't want any part of a real fight if it's going to be worse than that. And it is, David. Compared to other places the academic world in the North is duck soup, especially in the professional fields. After all, the whites do realize that there have to be colored people in the professions. All they hope is that the Negro will practice his specialty among his own people. You're going on—Harvard Law, isn't it?"

"Am I?"

"Don't be so damned young, David. A Negro boy—youth—trying to make it in the white world can't afford adolescence."

David listened as Benford's voice went on with a gentleness there was still unbelievable, coming from this man of acid.

"I repeat, for a young Negro in a white world, adolescence is a luxury beyond his means. He must jump from marbles and roller skates to maturity—all at once."

At the cost of appearing to be the adolescent that Benford was trying to drive out, David said: "I can't roller-skate, but I play a mean game of marbles. I guess I should have stayed with them. What'd I do that was so damned criminal? What'd I *do?* Helped a guy who was my friend. Sure he's white; sure, I let him talk me into breaking a rule because I was sorry for him. If Cozy's been looking for something to pin on me, to use to get rid of me, he sure picked a petty little something, a real petty little something. Hell, if I'd been accused of cheating or stealing or something like that I wouldn't quit under a cloud. But if he wants me out so bad he'll push it through on a damned petty little something like this, I figure it's best to give him what he wants."

"David!" Benford spoke so sharply that David turned to look at him, and he saw a face that didn't seem to be Beanie's at all.

"David, don't you know?"

"Don't I know what? All I know is they've got something in their stinking little minds I can't get. Can't get at all."

Benford slid to his feet and walked a few nervous paces to the door to the classroom, then turned back. He hoped his face did not show the pain within him, pain that had been strong before, but was more piercing now that he realized he must be the one to look into the deeply troubled eyes of this boy while he told him of the evil that was spreading through the campus. He felt a momentary wave of self-pity. "And it has to be me—" he said, and tried desperately to smile. Then in quiet, somber tones he told David what was going on, and when he was finished he said, "Lynching, you see, isn't civilized."

He turned away again, looking across the inner quadrangle of the distant lake, because he could no longer look at the sticken face of David Champlin. He had thought to see anger, but did not. There was incredulous horror, and the sick look of a man who has been hit without warning, violently, in the wind, changing color, fighting nausea. Professor Benford knew the students disliked him, knew the Quimby scholarship students in particular resented his classroom attitudes, and he accepted their resentment because those attitudes were born of the drive within him that goaded him to torment them into excellence. If he relaxed these attitudes for even the space of a breath, he would become outwardly what he was inwardly, a man at times made almost physically weak by his own compassion. His students, the children of his people God help them all, would be lost, these boys and girls who were the hope of the future, if he let that compassion—a compassion so great it could turn his guts to water at times—take over to gain even a foothold. Better, far better, to lash them with the whip of sarcasm, anger them with unreasonable demands, force them—as the white overseers on the plantations generations ago had forced their ancestors—past their endurance, knowing they would, somehow, endure.

He did not turn back to David until he heard his voice.

"No!"

The incredulous horror was still on the boy's face, but the look of sick shock was gone, and the eyes showed healthy anger.

"No!" he said again. "It can't be. It *can't*. They're saying that about me? That I'm a homo? A queer? Who's saying it? *Who's saying it?*"

Benford laid a hand on David's arm, took it away quickly. "I don't know, David. I intend to find out."

David was picking his duffel coat off the wall, folding it carefully, as though a wrinkle might ruin its disreputableness forever. Quiet now, he did not look at Benford when he said, "Thanks, Professor. I'll be going back to my room now."

He turned to walk away, and Benford shot out a long arm and sank bony fingers into the boy's shoulder. "Wait. Wait, David."

He did not loosen his grip until David turned and stood waiting for him to speak. He put his hands on the brick wall, leaning on them, looking toward the lake, the sun in his eyes. Why, he thought, why, why, *why* did an unkind God constitute me so that I must always and eternally be seeing, in the faces of these students, small brown children with round, dark eyes, standing in warm kitchens with a cookie in one hand and a ring of crumbs around soft defenseless mouths? Just once, just *once*, God, let me see them as I see my white students, with no past and a future about which I care little. When he turned back and leaned against the wall, his voice was tired. "You don't have to stay, David. I'm not trying to hold you here, to make you listen to me."

"It's all right," said David. "It's O.K.; I mean, I wasn't going to rush off and do anything crazy."

"If I had thought you were I wouldn't have tried to stop you. You must see now—now that you have the whole filthy story—why I would hate to see you leave the college?"

"I suppose so. I—I've got to think about it."

"Then let me talk. Perhaps something I say will mingle with your thinking, color it a little, help." Benford smiled. "We have to do such a hell of a lot of thinking. Small wonder that when we make it in the white world we so often surpass them." He hoisted himself to the wall again. "I've given you—given all the Quimbys—a rough time. If you don't know why, you haven't the intelligence I credit you with having."

"I guess—I think I know why. Now."

"You should. Have you ever thought, David, that those of us whose beginnings were in the South—not all of us, but so very many of us—share something inexpressibly good? That we hold in common emotional memories that the whites can never know?" He paused, and when he saw David was listening, he went on: "I was a country boy, you were not; that makes no difference. Within the four walls of whatever place we called home there was a security of love that passeth the understanding of those who have never known it. I've heard well-meaning, well-intentioned whites wonder out loud how the Negro has managed to stand up under more than a century of oppression and humiliation, not only stand up under these things but stay spiritually strong. Perhaps I don't have all the answers, but I think I have one. It's love.

"Negroes like you and me—and our fathers and mothers and grandfathers and grandmothers—carry it back, David, to the slave mother who knew her child might be taken from her arms and sold at any time—I say, Negroes like these were cradled in a fiercely strong love. Money we did not have; hope we did not have; decent schooling was denied; we were not very old before we learned what the word 'nigger' meant in a white mouth, though we used it ourselves. But we had in our homes a love so protective, so great, that it created a world of its own in which we lived, walled off, a love like the love of the God our parents tried to teach us about. It was within the world of that love that we grew up, that our spirits developed, expanded. Within the microcosm of some of those ramshackle southern homes we learned something of the macrocosm of the universe, of God, if you will. Abiding love, swift and sure punishments, infinite understanding.

"I doubt that the Simmonses and the Dunbars of our people grew up in homes like that. And perhaps, for the future of our people, this may be good. Perhaps we need the Simmonses and the Dunbars, too. But they are not, mark my words, David, the hope of our race, its saviors.

"Do you know Browning? It's fashionable to laugh at Browning today, but the math professor I lived with during my high school years was what you youngsters call 'hooked' on Browning. In Saul, Browning puts in the mouth of David —by God, that's an odd one, in the mouth of David—the words: 'Do I find love so full in my nature, God's ultimate gift—That I doubt his own love can compete with it?' My mother and father, your grandfather, would have bogged down trying to read that. But never doubt they knew its meaning."

Benford looked at the boy standing beside him, tall, straight, with strong, wide shoulders and dark head silhouetted against the sun. "You're wondering, aren't you, why old sourpuss Beanie Benford is talking like this? I'm not doing it to keep you from thinking about what has happened. I couldn't do that. But, David, there are two things I fear above all others for our people: pity for themselves as individuals, and pity from the whites. God deliver us, David, because we won't be able to do it for ourselves, if we let self-pity take over. And God deliver us ten times over from a white world that feels 'pity' for us, as I define the word. Pity for the sick, the hurt, the lost in mind or soul, yes. But we are not sick, not hurt, not lost in either mind or soul. If we were not the spiritual masters of those who oppress us, our race would have been wiped out long since in countless bloody revolutions. And in my opinion, our mastery is at its height in the people we sprang from, and its cradle was the passionate, fiercely protective love of millions of mothers and fathers, grandmothers, grandfathers, all of whom saw the dark future of their children in their eyes and held it off as long as they could."

Benford drew a package of cigarettes from his pocket, accepted a light from David. "Boring you, son?" he asked.

"No, sir." David smiled, and Benford was glad to see the smile reach the eyes and warm them briefly. "But you're sure surprising the hell out of me."

Benford's face became again the benign death's-head. "Don't give me away," he said. " 'I spoke as I saw—I report, as man may, of God's work—.' When I came here there were several restaurants in Laurel that would not serve me. Once when a group of students went into a lunchroom in Laurel, I overheard one of them say—I was just in back of them on the sidewalk—'What's that poor devil Benford going to do? Where's he going to eat?' That was the first time I packed. No one, but *no one,* was going to feel sorry for Oscar Benford. Hate him—O.K.; feel sorry for him? No! I think that was the inception of my lousy disposition."

He saw David smile again. "Is it all right, Professor, if the other students in your class—the white ones—feel just a little sorry for the poor Quimbys you have?"

Benford laughed. It was a laugh that belonged to a man with heavy shoulders and a deep chest, not a long, gaunt, black heron of a man. "You can take it," he said. "You can all take it. They stop feeling sorry for you when they watch your grades."

He stood, stretched, wanted to put a hand on David's shoulder but put it deep in a pocket instead. "I'm not sure what all this has to do with your situation, David, not sure why I went into it, except that I wanted to help. Certainly I had no intention—have no intention—of trying to pull the old familiar line of how much you'd be hurting your grandfather if you quit, stuff like that. I think I know your grandfather as well as I knew my own father. It wouldn't hurt him. He might even feel relieved."

"Yes," said David. "He—well, he worries."

"I know," said Benford quietly. "I know. So do I. About all of you."

He looked at David and saw that the sickness had gone from his face and that it was impassive now. "It's not my business, David," he said. "You don't have to tell me now, but will you let me know, as you would a friend, what you plan to do?"

"Yes, sir," said David. "Of course. But I'm not going to pack, if that's what you're thinking. I'm not going to pack. And—well—anyhow, thanks; thanks a lot." He turned and limped across the brick of the little balcony, down the three shallow steps to the paved walk and away from the building, his back to the tall, thin man with the skull-like head and the black skin.

Benford watched him, seeing with the eyes of his memory the inside of a tiny shack in Georgia as it had looked years before; seeing his baby brother held close in their mother's arms, sobbing on her shoulder over some childhood's grief.

And he saw his father broken and weary beyond all complaining, looking down at the mother and son.

His own lips formed the words he had heard his father say then. "Lord Jesus, he'p him. He ain't nothin' but a chile."

31

WHEN DAVID REACHED HIS ROOM he shot the old-fashioned bolt on the door behind him. The campus, as he had crossed it, had been almost deserted. In a few minutes it would be full of students hurrying to lunch. He met no one in the outer or the main quadrangle except three freshmen, two girls and a boy, who looked at him with impersonal curiosity, no knowledge in their eyes that he was anything but another student loose before lunch for some reason. Evidently the rumor had not yet escaped from the confines of the sophomore class. One of the girls had a pink-and-white face and china-blue eyes. She was as blond as a Norse goddess is supposed to be, and David thought Wisconsin, and then found himself hating her, although he could not remember even speaking to her before, and only remembered seeing her from a distance. Then the hatred extended beyond her, became all-encompassing, took in every aspect of his life at Pengard for the past year and a half, concentrated on no one thing or person, but seemed to swirl around him until he was like a man in the eye of a tornado, in a still, small place made quiet and secure by invisible walls of deadly force and power.

When he was alone in his room, the door locked behind him, he felt that this was good: to hate with such intensity removed him from the hostile world to a place where nothing could hurt him, where nothing could reach him. He had been living in a foreign country, and now, at last, in the eye of his tornado, he was at home. He spent the day in his room, cutting classes. He tore up the letter to Gramp. He couldn't put his finger on any particular thing that Benford had said that had kept him from going to the rec hall and mailing it. All he knew was that something had changed and that he was going to play a waiting game. Time enough to write to Gramp when he was expelled. He ate cold luncheon meat, and crackers and cheese in his room, washed down with black coffee.

Peace, thought David. Peace, it's wonderful. It was a bitter peace, but a safe one.

He reached for his math notebook and flipped it open to the problem of that morning's class. He had made no effort to work the problem in class. He scanned it now, took a pencil from the beer mug on the card table, and resolved it quickly, easily. After that, still working in that eerie inner quietude, he organized his history notebook and started to make an outline from the paper Burbridge would expect at the end of the week. Three times, while he was working, there was a knock at the door; twice it was followed by a voice calling his name; the first time it had been Chuck's, the second time, Tom's. He did not know who had knocked the third time.

When he was two-thirds of the way through organizing his paper, he stopped, wondering at the exhaustion that swept over him, not recognizing it as delayed reaction. He found that he could not fight it, and stretched out on the couch.

Half an hour later he was still awake, wondering why he could not nap. How could he be so deadly tired, so sleepy, yet not sleep?—he who had always bragged that he could stretch out any time he wanted to and cork off for five, ten minutes, half an hour—and wake up wide-eyed and bushy-tailed.

He knew he shouldn't try to think the situation out now; that it needed perspective. *You got to take things like they come, son. There ain't nothing you can do about it.*

Sweet Jesus! How did you go about proving a negative like this? Screw every chick on the campus and find out how fast lynch law could become civilized? Of all the accusations that could be brought, this was the one that could not be laughed off. He remembered the times he and Sudsy had locked the door of the room he lay in now, and he had labored until past midnight to pound Latin into Sudsy's head. "No, Stoopid! A deponent verb is *not* the same thing as a transitive verb. It just *acts* that way. Now, *look*—" If one of the knocks on the door that afternoon had been Sudsy's familiar rat-tatat, he would have opened the door, but that didn't mean—Who in hell? Who in the *hell* could have started that rumor? He thought of some of the students who had found it difficult to hide their dislike of matriculating with Negroes. There weren't many: a girl from Alabama, two boys from Georgia, a few others. There was a girl from Louisiana whose green eyes had always made him wonder how far back in her ancestry the dark woman was who had been impregnated by white lust. She made it a point never to walk alone with him across the campus or be seen alone with him talking, even in the rec hall. As a suspect she made sense, until he remembered someone saying she had gone home for Thanksgiving and had been operated on for acute appendicitis last Friday, must even now be convalescing in some mossy Louisiana town. This rumor had to have started sometime during the weekend.

He sat, finally, on the edge of the bed, swearing, elbows on knees, rubbing his head violently with strong, hard fingers. If he could not nap perhaps he could wake himself up enough to do some more studying. He did not hear the door open at the top of the little flight of stairs before he heard Chuck's voice.

"There's more'n one way to skin a cat, as my granmaw used to say, a puffin' on her ol' clay pipe."

David turned his head. Tom Evans, ahead of Chuck, was already on the lower step of the short flight, with Chuck looming behind him. Chuck looked at David and stopped with a suddenness that was almost recoil. Tom Evans did not look directly at David but walked without speaking to the chair behind the card table and sat down, picking up a ball point pen, twirling it in his square, small boy's hands.

"Look, David," he said in that surprisingly deep voice. "Look, you can't just hole up—" He let his eyes go to David's face, then stopped speaking.

David did not greet them or stand. "Which one of you guys," he said, "is chaperoning the other?"

"Stow it!" Chuck's exclamation was sharp, loud. He repeated it. "Stow it, David."

David did not answer, and Tom spoke again, inspecting the pen in his hands with the care of a foreman in a missile factory inspecting a crucial part. "Look, David, you can't just hole up. We were here earlier, separately. So was Travis, he says. Finally Chuck got the bright idea of trying the back way."

"If you were all that damned smart," said David, "you ought to be smart enough to figure out that if I'd wanted to answer the door I would have."

"Sorry," drawled Chuck. He walked toward the shelf that

ran between washbasin and bookcase. "You-all got any coffee?"

"Plenty."

"Reckon it's all right if I make some for me and Tom?"

"Do anything you damned please."

"Only get the hell out and leave you alone?" Tom's eyes were extraordinarily adult in the childlike face.

"Right," said David.

Tom did not move. The flame of the Sterno was sputtering beneath the pan. Chuck was standing over it, watching it as intently as though it were a laboratory experiment. David watched him and smiled suddenly, but it was not a smile either of his companions would have recognized.

"You're both having a tough time, aren't you?" he said. "I'll give you a hand. Everything's just fine. For the first time since I came here I know where I stand. Right where I belong—in my place. It's going to be a hell of a lot easier from now on. One hell of a lot easier. You guys stay out of my backyard and I'll stay out of yours, and nobody'll get hurt."

Tom slapped the pen on the table and started to speak, but Chuck was ahead of him. "Yeah," said Chuck. "That's what I thought you'd say. You think I grew up in Georgia for nothing?"

He stirred coffee in two mugs, handed one to Tom, said, "You're welcome to some of your own coffee, young Champlin. I'll fix it in your toothbrush glass. Mugs are for company."

David stood for the first time since they had entered. "Look," he said. "Look, you guys. Get lost, huh?"

"How you talk," said Chuck.

"I'm not going to get lost," said Tom. "I'm lost already. A little lost sheep, that's me. Chuck now, he's not as lost as I am because I guess he's more conditioned to it." Suddenly Tom exploded verbally, and the unexpected spate of invective penetrated even the quiet spot in the center of the tornado where David was dwelling. David looked at him with awe. The words, coming from a youth who would not have looked out of place playing sand lot baseball with a bunch of eighth-graders, had a breathtaking impact. Bull Evans's son knew his way around in Anglo-Saxon. When he had finished, David could not hold back the comment: "Congratulations."

"Yeah," said Tom. "Sure. Congratulations. I've heard my

old man, when I was a kid, tell strikers about scabs and finks."

"And what, if I may be so bold, did he say to the scabs and finks?" asked Chuck. "If I'm not too young to hear."

"He didn't say anything to them. He just smiled. Like a wolf smiling at a lamb. He used to tell me he didn't want to catch me swearing unless I meant it; he said otherwise it was just obscene."

"My old man—and a fine old southern farmer he is, and meaner than they usually come—cusses the way he breathes, natural like, all the time," said Chuck.

"Look, David." Tom pointed the pen at him. "Now, look. I've been listening and watching my old man trying to fight discrimination all my life. So far he's lost, as far as the unions are concerned. And that's one hell of a note."

Chuck said: "Prejudice is the same difference, anywhere you find it. It doesn't have to be a rope or a fire or a knife. You want us to get lost, David. We're not going to get lost. Maybe we shouldn't have come here. Maybe we should have gone about our business first."

Something in his tone brought a sharp question from David. "What business?"

"They aren't going to get away with it. That's what he means," said Tom.

"Who's 'they'?" snapped David. "Who in hell knows who 'they' is—are. Just drop it. Drop it right now." He walked past the table where Tom was sitting to the window beside the fireplace, stood looking out, his back to the room.

"David," said Chuck, "I couldn't drop it. I humbly suggest that you come down out of that ivory tower and give us a hand. Of course there's no law says you have to. You can just shack up here in your li'l ol' room with your li'l ol' fireplace and hire you a li'l ol' freshman to bring you your meals, and you don't even have to speak to li' ol' us again. And all through the cold winter nights you can sit in front of your li'l ol' fireplace and think of us out there fighting your big ol' battle for you."

David heard a sharply indrawn breath, and knew it was Tom's, and that Tom was afraid Chuck had gone too far. He had, thought David, too damned far. He felt his hands ball into fists in his pockets, felt anger crawling up his belly, fought it, waiting for the calm he knew would follow. From the window he saw a world grown dark enough to bring out the pale lights in the main quadrangle. He felt a lifetime older than the two boys in the room with him. When, for Christ sake, had the whites fought the Negroes' battle on any front except argument and words? He turned back to the room with an abrupt laugh.

"All right, John Brown," he said. "All right. And when your academic body lies a-moldering in the grave I'll put flowers on it every Grand Army day. And I'll tell my little black pickaninny grandchildren what a good fight you put up. For the last time—Chuck—Tom—will you drop it? Drop the whole Goddamned stinking mess!"

"No," said Tom. "We won't drop it, David. You can do whatever you want, and if it's nothing, then do that. But we aren't going to drop it. We sort of hoped you'd give us a hand, help us find a starting point, but if you won't, we'll have to find it ourselves."

"There isn't a starting point. That's what I'm trying to tell you guys; there isn't a starting point. Not one you'll ever find. A thing like this is like some—some self-generating poison gas."

"I know that," said Chuck. "I know that too damned well. You can't ever track down where the rumor came from that starts a lynch mob gathering." He stopped, ran a hand through the tow-colored stubble that was his hair, finally spoke hesitantly, almost appealingly, ignoring Tom, looking directly at David. "You'd understand, David, you'd recognize the words, if I said 'A man's got to trust someone.' " His eyes met and held David's, and the somber fire in David's seemed to die out a little, and he dropped his eyes first and turned away.

Tom had taken the pen apart and reassembled it. He held it up and looked at it closely, one eye squinting. "Maybe so there isn't any starting point," he said. "But I've got a nasty, dirty little suspicion running around in my mind. Have to do some research before I say anything. You had supper?"

"I've got enough here. I'm stuffed now."

"We thought we'd get some ribs." There was still hope in Tom's voice, but when his eyes met only the impassive darkness of David's face he joined Chuck at the door. "See you in class tomorrow?"

"How the hell do I know? Maybe they expel you in the middle of the night here, give you an hour to leave town. If I'm not there, it's been nice knowing you."

David saw Tom's face flush with anger, and looked away.

"O.K.," said Tom. "O.K., dad, if that's the way you want it."

Chuck's hand was inside Tom's coat collar. "Come on, young Evans, come on."

"Wait," said David slowly. "I'm—I don't want you to think I'm not grateful. I guess I was rude. Anyhow, thanks."

"That's all right," said Tom. "But you sure as hell can make me see red. Be seeing you—"

David looked at the clock on his desk—a few minutes past six. He could call New Orleans collect and it wouldn't cost much. Calling every so often made Li'l Joe happy, and also took the pressure off him to write his weekly letter. When he heard Gramp's voice accepting the charges, he could always hear the undertone of happiness. He wanted to hear Gramp's voice now and called himself a damned baby for it. But he hesitated; there had never been any way to keep anything from Gramp for long. No matter how hard he might try to keep his voice normal, he knew how the conversation would go: "What's worrying you, son? . . . Nothing, Gramp, nothing. Just thought I'd call. . . . You lying, son. . . . No, Gramp. . . . Yes, you are. You feeling all right?"

Beanie was right. Gramp would probably be relieved if he quit, not even mind too much if he was expelled. But David knew that Gramp would be so damned proud if things went all right, if his grandson made it all the way through. It was going to be one hell of a thing to explain, not only to Gramp but to the Prof.

He decided against calling, and thought of something he had heard Kid Arab say when Kid returned to New Orleans after playing an engagement in a northern city. "Least you knows where you stand down here. Maybe it's in the muck, but you got no worries about being kicked out of the muck. You can settle in and make yourself at home. There's no way of telling up there. You gets your hand shaken one day and your ass kicked the next. There's just no knowing."

For the second time that day he did not hear the door of his room open. He had not thought to lock it after Chuck and Tom left. Now at the sound of a step he turned from his desk at the window to face the newcomer, on the defensive. Then abruptly he was on his feet, no longer in a vacuum, no longer dwelling alone. He was smiling when he said, "Hi-ya, Ne'miah." He pulled back the chair Tom had been sitting on. "Where you been, man? Sit down. Res' yourself."

Nehemiah Wilson sat, folding his arms on the table, looking at David with no expression in the simian-like eyes. "I've just been talking to Evans and Martin," he said. "First I knew about all this stink."

"Where've you been?" asked David again. "Where the devil you been? It's all over the place. I mean all *over.*"

"I didn't get back till late last night. I heard about you being in trouble over helping Sutherland get home. You asked for that, man. I mean, you got up on your hind legs and you asked for that. But that's not a hell of a big beef. I figured you get a slap on the wrist, maybe. *And* you had it coming. *And* I wasn't fixing to offer sympathy. What you didn't learn in eighteen years in New Orleans I guess you got to learn here. Fact is, you asked for the whole damned mess."

"All right. Cut the lecture."

"Evans and Martin thought I'd heard about this other. Why would I? Who the hell would tell me? I'd be the last to hear. You had enough, David? You had enough ofay bitching up?"

"Yeah. Yeah, Ne'miah, I've had enough. Heck, I'm on the way out. I'm pretty sure of that. But at least they're going to have to kick me out."

"Cozy's gotten rid of us before," said Nehemiah. He looked with astonishment at David's puzzled face, and said: "What the devil's the matter with you, man? You think you're something special? That trash hates us all, only he's too smart to move unless he thinks he can win. He's letting me alone because I've kept my nose clean. You been fooling around with whites. And if there's one thing that bastard can't stand it's a white face and a black face side by side. And if the white face's female—"

"But—"

"Don't give me any 'buts.' You think he doesn't know what's going on? You think he hasn't got half-a-dozen minchy, mealymouthed spies coming to him and getting taken in by his—coziness? Telling him things?"

"There's nothing going on? What the hell can anyone tell him about me?"

"Oh, *shit*, David." Nehemiah made no attempt to conceal his disgust. "Don't be a starry-eyed ass all your life. You do, you're going to wind up swinging in the breeze—and it's going to be a mighty high tree."

David did not protest. He had been stupid, he thought, to

even pretend ignorance of what Nehemiah was talking about. Sara. Little Sara Kent, Sara of the mittened hands and the shining hair, who walked beside you like a child skipping; Sara, with the dark eyes that could be as bright as a bird's or as soft as a young puppy's; Sara who cares so Goddamned much about everything and everybody you could feel the caring, like electricity.

"Man," Nehemiah was saying, "where he comes from they cut a guy's nuts off for just *thinking* about it. And you know it. His old man was poor white. But somewhere along the line a little piece of a brain got into Cozy's head by mistake and he wound up at 'Bama University. The whites he comes from are so damned stupid, and you know that, too, that I think there must have been a little mix-up somewhere. That southern moon when it's full can be a mighty moving thing."

David was quiet for a moment, and then spoke slowly. "What you said about cutting a guy's nuts off for just thinking about it. This thing about me—"

"Now you're talking, man," said Nehemiah softly. "Now you're *really* talking. He's just doing it gentle-like to you."

It was dark now. The only light in the room was the gooseneck lamp on the desk by the windows. Downstairs someone had lighted a fire in the big fireplace in the lounge, and a trick of the breeze outside brought its pungent friendly smell into the room through the window that was always kept open a crack. David looked down at the small, compact figure, drawing comfort from its presence. "You hungry, Ne'miah?"

Nehemiah gave a quick start. "Hungry? Me? I'm always hungry. Why? You got food?"

"That li'l piece of a car you got running all right?"

Nehemiah was on his feet. "Running like a rabbit. Where you want to go?"

"Mom's. Swear to God I can't talk anymore till I get some ribs in me. I've been starving for the last two hours. Let's go, man."

Tom Evans's voice sounded like that of a child who has discovered his father has lied to him. "That was David, Chuck," he said. "Sitting at the table in the window with Nehemiah Wilson. He said he wasn't hungry."

"Tom." Chuck, seated beside his friend in Evans's car, sounded like a kindergarten teacher trying earnestly to explain some natural phenomenon to a five-year-old. "Tom, if you and me—you and I, were on Mars, and we were living among a bunch of Martians and they didn't speak our language, and they looked different, and they thought different, and one of us got in bad trouble—where the hell would he run to?"

After a moment Tom said, "The other one." Then, pounding his fist on the steering wheel, "And that's what's so *wrong*."

"There ain't nothin' you can do about it," said Chuck. "Not right now. Just keep driving, young Evans; just keep going. We'll eat someplace in Laurel."

32

IF HE HADN'T WRITTEN "GLASSES" on a card in black crayon and clipped it to his math notebook, David would have forgotten his appointment with an ophthalmologist in Laurel the day after his dinner with Nehemiah. He saw it that morning, and swore. The appointment had been made for him through the Infirmary after Doc Knudsen had seen him holding a book too far from his nose, and he'd broken down and confessed to headaches. Now if he didn't go it would be more hot water. Not that he could see that it made much difference when you were drowning in the stuff already.

The appointment was at four, and there were no buses to Laurel between one and four. He'd get there as best he could —on foot. He had told no one of Cozy's final humiliation of him, and he wasn't about to ask favors of anyone, or accept them either. In the drizzly rain his ankle would hurt like hell before he got there, but he'd survive. The ache in his ankle on bad days and after long walks was a clean one; there was good and sufficient reason for it; it wasn't like an inner ache that was not clean, and for which there was no good and sufficient reason.

The wind from the lake was raw and damp as he walked through the main gates of the campus, then turned right toward Laurel. He saw no students he knew more than by sight, and they spoke casually, the way any half-stranger would speak, and common sense told him the rumor hadn't had time to spread throughout the entire college.

He didn't see how he could do much more thinking; he'd thought himself into exhaustion. There wasn't a damned thing to be done and the sensible thing was to face the fact. Right now the guy he wished he could talk to was an old man in a big mansion on the lakefront, a man named Quimby who, according to Doc Knudsen, didn't like the terms "white college" and "Negro college." He apostrophized him *in absentia*, feeling his circulation smarten up in the process. "You better wake up, Mr. President Emeritus Quimby. You better believe that what you've got now, like it or not, is a 'white' college. You've just been kidding yourself, Mr. Pres, just kidding yourself, and you haven't got one dollar or one million that will make it—this one or any other—any different."

Whites were so damned stupid, he thought; even the ones he liked, the good guys like Suds and Tom and Chuck who came on sincere as hell and meaning it, not giving a damn about what color a guy's skin was, and you let yourself get taken in and you quit thinking. Right off the bat, that made you even stupidier. Then something happened, as it always had and always would, and they had their hackles up and were mad and horrified because they hadn't known the gun was loaded.

The sound of a horn was so unexpected that he jumped sideways, then turned and saw a florist truck draw up just ahead. When he drew alongside, the door was open and a young man about his own age was leaning across the seat. "Ten degrees warmer inside!" he cried. "Want a lift?"

David climbed in, slammed the door shut, and said "Thanks" before he remembered his resolve to neither ask nor accept favors. The boy was saying: "I'm only going as far as Abington, just this side of the library. Want me to drop you off there? Or you can come along with me—"

"Drop me," said David. "Got a doctor's appointment." He glanced at the boy. "Seen you on campus or the rec hall or somewhere, haven't I?"

"Yes. I'm just a freshman."

"Don't apologize. We all were once."

"You're—you're David Champlin, aren't you?"

The muscles at the back of David's neck stiffened. "Yes. So?"

"Well—nothing. It's just that—well, I've heard a lot about you."

Don't go on, thought David; just leave 'er lay, kid; leave 'er lay.

But the boy was continuing: "How you're a brain, and yet you're a helluva piano player. I listen to you all the time in the rec hall."

"You're the guy who's always eating an ice-cream cone? Now I recognize you."

Was this all the kid knew about him? He waited as the boy rattled on in a half-embarrassed, friendly way, seeming more than a little awed. "You got Benford in math?" he asked.

"Yeah," answered David. "Good man."

"Holy cats! You think so? In math maybe, but—"

"He's a good man. He's O.K.—" But you'll never know it, thought David; you'll never know the kind of good man Beanie is. And it's your loss. Your loss.

"We-ell, maybe. Perhaps I just don't know him—"

"That's right. You just don't know him."

As David left the truck at Abington, the boy leaned across the seat again, ducked his head the better to see David through the opened window. There was an almost wistful note in his voice as he said, "Hey, look, mind if I drop in and see you sometime? Have a talk—"

David checked himself this time, bit back the impulse to say, "Sure kid, come on. Any time." The boy was lonely; he could tell that. And for some reason he had a pretty inflated idea of David Champlin. But the gun's loaded, kid—he said this to himself, and to the boy said—"I'm damned busy these days. After Christmas maybe—" and turned away quickly from the hurt in the boy's eyes. Damned kid wouldn't know till he heard the story that David Champlin had done him a favor, turning away like that.

His mood was hot and bitter as he neared the library. He'd never done anything like that before in his life, to anyone, white or black—been deliberately and cold-bloodedly hurting rude to someone who didn't deserve it. This thing's making a sonofabitch out of me, too, he thought. He crossed the street just before he reached the library; too much chance of meeting someone he knew coming out of it if he didn't. His ankle was pure murder now, but he walked as fast as he could.

He felt the quick touch on his arm almost as soon as he heard the running feet, a soft, light touch like a kitten's gentle pass at someone loved.

"David!" Sara was panting. "David, for gosh sake, slow down! I've been running like crazy to catch up!"

He did not want to look down, not at a red knit cap with a pompon on top, at shining dark hair and eyes he knew would be looking directly into his. He said "Hi!" and kept walking, not slowing down, wishing to God she'd take her hand off his arm. Dames ought not to touch guys. Not unless they were asked. A woman ought to keep a hand in a red mitten off a guy's arm unless—

"David, aren't you going to say more than that? Slow down. Gosh, please slow down."

"I've got an appointment. Eye examination."

"I told you, Stoopid! I told you if you couldn't borrow Sudsy's car to let me know if you were coming into town. Where is the Yellow Peril?"

"In—in a garage."

The hand was gone from his arm, and that was better. That was altogether good. Now if she'd just get gone herself —get lost—be missing—

"You didn't want to, did you? Drive with me, I mean—"

Why'd these people have to be so damned direct? That was one of the little things, just a little one of the many things about whites, so damned direct, so damned "yes" and "no."

Sara said, "What's the matter? It's this mess, isn't it? This awful rotten, rotten mess."

"Nothing's the matter. What mess?"

"Please, David. Don't be all nasty and prickly."

"Me nasty? How you talk."

"Yes, you are, and I don't wonder. But—but I want to talk to you about—about things. I've—well, I've got some ideas."

This did not seem to call for an answer, and he remained silent. The Medical Building was just ahead now, and he tried to think of something to say that would be off the subject.

"David! Answer me! Talk. Talk. For heaven's sake, talk! *Communicate.*"

He hoped she hadn't heard his under-the-breath laugh. There was no reason to laugh; there wasn't anything funny to laugh at, but she'd wrapped it up so perfectly, put it in a word so neatly, and not even known she'd done it. Communicate. She might as well have said, "Make your ankle stop aching. Make your anklebones normal—" She hadn't meant to but she'd hit on the key to the whole damned thing between them. Communication was something that didn't exist, not between him and Sara Kent, not between him and others like Chuck and Tom and even Suds, and now he didn't want it to exist, didn't want the impossible, could content himself with the possible—clear and complete and without need of words, the communication that existed between him and his own people, a heritage from a distant day when such communication was necessary for survival. It was a communication that existed even in a snarly way between him and the Simmonses and Dunbars he'd met in this world he'd entered.

"David."

"What?"

"If I wait for you while you get your eyes examined, will you have a cup of coffee with me afterward? And let me drive you home? My car's in the library lot."

"Look, Sara, why? Talking's no good. It's happened and that's that. There's nothing we can do about it—"

"Will you, David? You're going to be blind as a bat when you come out—"

"I am not. The nurse told me on the phone that they put drops in your eyes afterward to counteract the dilation—"

"Oh, pooh! Nurses—doctors. They'll tell you anything."

"Look, Sara, I can't stop you. If you want to wait you're sure as heck going to wait. You're the damnedest dame I ever did know that way. And if you wait you'll be cold and wet and I'll feel like a jerk or something if I don't get you a cup of hot coffee."

"I'll stand out in the rain and cold and sell matches on the corner until I am all goose-pimply and blue. No, I won't. I'll shop for stockings and paints and crayons and stuff and meet you right here in the doorway. If it's too cold I'll come up to the office. Then I'll lead you up the street—"

"You better not, Smallest. You better not lead me up any street. We'll go to that fancy bakery place next door and have coffee, and you can eat an eclair while my pupils contract—"

He'd done it. Damn it, he'd done it, and he almost let the heavy door of the office building slam in an old lady's face. He'd let Sara get through to him, called her "Smallest," given in to the something vital and electric and warm that was Sara Kent, and he wished to God he'd canceled the appointment and not come to town at all. How many weeks till Christmas? Three. Too many.

Sara was waiting for him when he came down, her face framed by the packages she held. He wasn't blind as a bat, he told her, although he admitted to considerably less than twenty-twenty vision, and also to the fact that he was going to have to get reading glasses. He didn't tell her that in the pleasantly blurred world inhabited by those with dilated pupils she was beautiful; that she was not small and piquant and gaminesque, but soft and lovely and downright beautiful. Her hair, disciplined somewhere while he had been inside, was a misty nimbus around her face, her eyes soft and dark and mysterious, not Sara's eyes at all, which could be soft and dark but were never mysterious. He looked down at her, smiling. "Cold?"

"Freezing. Are you all right? Can you really see?"

"Fine. Give me some of those packages. You want that coffee and an eclair?"

She nodded vigorously. Now, his eyes clearing rapidly, Sara Kent was emerging from the misty outlines of the girl who had been waiting for him. Yet something of that misty beauty remained, and he knew it always would. He knew there would be times when he would remember that beauty, long after he had seen Sara Kent for the last time. Thinking of those times as they entered the bakery-cum-coffee shop, he lost all sense of where he was, the warmth and brightness of the place, the ornate pseudo-Viennese décor, the cases filled with pastries and breads, the smell of it, the sight of the Laurel housewives standing in front of counters pointing to displays with hungry fingers, the students agonizing over gooey choices to take back to dormitories—and he was alone without Sara, with no one but David Champlin projected into a future as bleak and barren as a distant planet. In that future there would be only stabbing thoughts of the sudden beauty that had been waiting for him in a cold doorway.

He reached and took her arm, holding her back as she started toward a display case. "Wait. Let's go to the drugstore for a quick cup at the counter and then go to Mom's for dinner."

"David! That's the superest idea you ever had. Sometimes I wonder how you carry that brain around. Dutch."

"No."

"Dutch."

"No!"

"Yes, sir. O.K., sir." She tucked her hand under his arm as they went into the street. "The car's across from the drugstore. I had time to go get it. You're not the only brain—" He could have sworn she was skipping, but when he looked down he saw that her feet were progressing normally, first one, then the other in front of it.

Not until they drew into the clearing beside Mom's did he realize that two hours before he had crossed a wet, puddled street rather than take a chance on meeting someone he knew coming down the library steps; now he was going into a place where there probably wouldn't be more than a few people he didn't know. And that was Sara Kent's fault; that was a woman for you. Make you forget your whole damned life if you weren't careful, didn't stay clear. It was too late to back out now, and he followed her inside, wary and defensive.

Mom's was already nearly full; the only table for two left was one in the rear, next to the swinging doors to the kitchen. As they walked toward it he noticed Simmons and Dunbar seated at a wall table, and to his surprise both raised a hand in greeting accompanied by what, for them, passed as smiles. Racial solidarity, thought David, intellectual type.

He was quiet after they sat down, looking over a menu he knew as well as he knew the Lord's Prayer. The waitress stood over them, fat and short-breathed. "You want ribs again tonight?" she asked David.

"Yes, please. And chicken for the lady with French fries on both, and coffee. And garlic bread."

"Why are some people fat and some people thin?" asked Sara. "And probably eat the same things. Like that waitress and the baneful Beanie."

"Beanie's all right." For the second time that day he found himself defending Benford. "He's O.K."

"You crazy or something?"

"I know he's sort of difficult as a teacher—"

"Difficult! He's murder. I know he goes to church, because I've seen him, but I'll bet you my new paints, David, that when he says his prayers he says 'em to Euclid and Einstein, his only begotten son. Didn't he eat you out yesterday. After class?"

David's eyes widened, then narrowed. "Eat me out? Beanie? No. Who says so?"

"Oh—everyone—"

"Tell 'everyone' for me to go take a big fat jump in the lake." He could not go on and explain, because this was in one of those important areas in life where there was no communication. There could be no telling Sara about Beanie Benford who had been revealed yesterday on the balcony outside the classroom. There could be no telling Sara about so many things. They could share only the surface of life, the things that had to do with life and not its wellsprings—not, certainly not, a Beanie Benford saying ". . . for a young Negro in a white world, adolescence is a luxury beyond his means . . ."

He said, "Just because a guy who has to sweat in math has a talk after class with his professor doesn't mean he's being chewed out. People like 'everyone' ought to mind their own business."

Ella brought the chicken and the ribs, but they did not silence Sara. "David, let's talk."

He smiled across at her. "That's like saying 'be funny.' "

"Well, I'm going to anyhow. If you don't want to listen you can walk out, and I'll just sit here and talk to a plate of cold ribs."

"All right, Sara. You do the talking because I haven't got anything to say."

"You ought to have, David. Honestly, you ought. You can't just—just sit and let people lie about you and tell dreadful stories—"

"Eat your chicken, Smallest—"

"Oh—the—the *hell* with my chicken. And put that rib down and listen."

"I'm not putting any rib down, woman."

"Then eat it and listen. David, I think there's an answer. I honestly do."

"Fine. You'll go down in history as the only person who had the answer."

"David, stop. There's a girl in the administrative office that I grew up with. You've heard me mention her. Dolores Mathewson. We're good friends—and she's getting a list, sneaking it, of the names and addresses of every Quimby and every non-Quimby Negro student who's left Pengard or been expelled in the last five or six years. She thinks she can give me the list in the morning."

David had finished his ribs. At Mom's, French fries were eaten with the fingers, and he sat now, a sliver of potato in one hand, a salt cellar in the other, not moving, forgetting he held them.

"What are you two going to do with it? With this list?" He hoped he was keeping the rising anger out of his eyes as he looked at her.

"It's not just we two—well—" She stumbled over the words, her eyes on his face. "David, for gosh sake! Are you angry? It's as plain as the nose on your face what we're going to do with it. Track them down. Get them to tell what really happened. And then—"

"Tell who?"

"Whoever we decide to have write to them, of course. There'll have to be a sort of spokesman, anyhow. Maybe some of them could even be reached by telephone. Maybe—"

"Maybe you'd better let it alone, Sara—"

"David, you stubborn mule! Can't you see how important it is? Look, David, I was, well, all starry-eyed and stupid about things until this happened—"

"You mean you aren't now? Look again—"

Something apart from his anger told him he was well into his first free-swinging quarrel with Sara Kent, and it had the effect of bringing their relationship into the realm of reality. He hadn't thought he'd ever permit himself to get closely enough involved to quarrel with her; certainly he hadn't intended to; now, with every contrary, angry word the involvement was becoming deeper.

He spaced his words slowly. "Sara, I appreciate it. I honestly do. It's swell of you to go to the trouble. But let it alone. And don't drag other people into it." He wanted to go on, but knew it would be useless. He couldn't explain to her that this was his fight, that this was white against black in a mess that was different only in kind from any other white-against-black fight, different only in weapons from a rock-throwing street fight.

He looked over at Sara, and saw that by now her anger matched his own.

"Don't you want to straighten this out? Not just for yourself but for the others? You like it the way it is? Don't you ever think of anyone besides yourself and your own—your own damned pride!"

He laid his big paper napkin down slowly, wondering how a guy could feel such anger at a girl who hadn't done anything but be herself. He laid change under his plate and pushed his chair back deliberately.

"Come on, Sara," he said softly. "Come on. Let's go."

"David." He could scarcely hear her. "I'm sorry. I didn't mean—"

"Let's go, Sara. They need this table. There are people waiting now—"

He walked ahead of her as they left, stopping at the cashier's desk to pay the check. Sara did not speak again, but he felt her eyes on his face as they walked through the rain to the car. He had picked up the packages she had piled by the umbrella stand in the hall and now he took the car keys from her and unlocked the trunk of the car, moving slowly and deliberately so as not to give in to the impulse to throw the packages into the trunk and slam the cover shut. Instead he stacked them slowly and carefully, closed the trunk gently, testing it to make sure the catch was engaged.

When he came forward, Sara was still standing outside, hair wet against her cheeks now, the pompon on the knit cap sodden and limp. He opened the right-hand door and said: "Get in, Sara. You'll catch cold. I'll drive. My eyes are O.K. now." She looked like a wet and bedraggled kitten as she slid into the seat. Twice before they reached the campus she started to speak and stopped, red-mittened hands opening in an unfinished gesture, then closing on each other tightly.

He stopped at Quimby House and got out, closing the car door quietly. Looking through the half-opened window on the driver's side as she slithered across the seat to the wheel, he felt his breath go and his muscles become limp. For the first time he saw that her eyes were a dark, wet blur, her cheeks streaked with their overflow. He cleared his throat, but his voice still came out hoarse.

"O.K., Sara," he said. "Everything's going to be all right. Don't worry about a thing. Take it easy—" and he turned away to limp into the house with the sound of the car's turning wheels in his ears.

When he got to his room, he pulled back the cover from the couch, stacked pillows against the wall at its head, and sat against them, legs stretched out. Another time when study was impossible he would have gone through the rain and slush to the rec hall where he could play the piano, listen to records, knock balls around on the pool table in the game room, even find someone to talk to, but not tonight, not to face the question he would see in the eyes of those who had heard. If those eyes asked, "Did you cheat—did you steal—" it would be easy. But not when the question started with the words "Are you—"

Tom Evans had implied the afternoon before that he had a good idea of the person who had started the rumor. David hadn't gone along—but now he was sure, damned well knew that it had to have been Randolph Clevenger. And if he did what he wanted to do, which was cold-bloodedly and deliberately beat Clevenger to a pulp, that would be the ballgame as far as Pengard was concerned. Or he could just ride it out, and if he was expelled that would be it and if he wasn't he wouldn't come back after Christmas. And if he followed either of these courses all but a handful of students at Pengard during his term there would be convinced that he was a queer. And probably that Sudsy was too. And maybe the others in the group—Hunter, Tom, Chuck. And that kind of thing could r'ar up and hit you in the teeth twenty years later.

Hell! He snatched a small, hard pillow from the couch beside him and threw it in the general direction of the grate, followed it with a heavy, oversized glass ashtray that hit a corner of the mantel and shattered. After that, he felt childish but somehow better. Mixed up in it all, mixed up in the decision of going or staying, or coming back, or giving a guy a well-deserved working over, was a small, dark-haired girl named Sara Kent, whom he must love because you had to be in love with a woman to get as angry as he had been at her this afternoon and an hour later want her so bad your teeth damned near rattled.

The knock on the door was followed by the crisp sound of Hunter Travis's voice: "David. Open up. Now."

He was at the door in spite of himself, unlocking and opening it a short way, but Hunter widened the crack without ceremony, shouldering his way in, and David fell back without speaking. Then Chuck Martin's big figure loomed behind Hunter and he followed his companion into the room.

"Ah! Fire!" said Chuck. From his lips it sounded like "Faahr!" He walked toward the grate, rubbing his hands together. "Sure feels good. Cold outside." He looked at David, and shivered. "Colder in here." He smiled. "My distinguished friend here, Mr. Hunter Travis, he figures to do the talking. Ah told him it wouldn't do no good—"

"Cracker," said Hunter. "Try and speak English. Or American, anyhow."

"Snob," said Chuck. He dropped the accent, and the open, homely, country-boy countenance was suddenly serious. "This time you're going to listen, Stoopid," he said to David. He nodded toward Hunter. "That's why he's here." Some of the lightness of tone returned. "He can talk up a storm when he's a mind to—even if that's not very often. They just put him on the debating team."

"It's late—" said David lamely.

"Not as late as it will be in about ten days or two weeks," said Hunter. David did not bother to ask a question he knew the answer to: What are you talking about? He went to the wall shelf, lifted the alcohol stove, set out mugs, and started measuring instant coffee into each. He'd tried to get rid of well-meaners the day before, and now they were back and he might as well accept it. After a while, if he stayed at Pengard, they'd let him alone. Everyone would let him alone. He noticed that a wind had risen since he came in, and its gusts were shaking the windows. "Lousy outside," he said.

"Lousy inside," said Hunter, and David turned from where he was standing at the wall shelf, his eyes angry.

"Finish with the coffee before you slug him," said Chuck.

Why couldn't they let him alone? He was conscious of an unexpected twinge of pain, and realized that it was the first evidence of what would be a continuing sense of loss at Sudsy's absence. He gave his own big chair to Chuck, and sat on the edge of the bed, cradling his coffee mug in his hands. Hunter remained standing, tall and slim and elegant looking in trench coat over tweeds and a pullover sweater, even his heavy galoshes managing to look like Bond Street. He bent now to take them off. "Seen Sara Kent?" he said as he struggled with them.

"She spotted me on the way to the eye doctor's this afternoon. We had dinner." He wouldn't mention that she'd given him a lift home; one of them might ask about Sudsy's car.

"Did she tell you what's been cooking?" Hunter walked over and put his wet galoshes on the square of linoleum in front of the washbasin.

"She mentioned an idea she had—"

"She wouldn't have told you that the rest of us have been hashing it over too," said Chuck. "You being a mite techy about other people messing in your affairs."

"Who isn't?" snapped David.

"Quite a few intelligent people," said Hunter quietly. "And 'messing' isn't the right word. Now listen. And keep quiet. You aren't the first Negro to be Jim-Crowed here—or anywhere else. You know that. I've felt it—here and a lot of places. As soon as they learn my father's identity."

"God damn it, Hunter, you're just beating your gums together. You're being stupid. Of course I know it. I've lived with it all my life. You haven't. And while we're on the subject, what bright boy or girl suddenly realized there was a nasty thing like prejudice involved? How come all of a sudden someone wakes up?"

Hunter shrugged. "I don't know, dad. Those things just happen."

Chuck said, "Andrus."

David turned to him. "Why Andrus?"

"Because he had me in his private den feeding me jawbreaker cookies for an hour yesterday. He'd heard about it from God knows who. He just might have inadvertently said something to shut them up that indicated he suspected prejudice. And they were off and running. He asked me not to say anything about being there. Don't ever trust li'l ol' Chuck. Here I am with my big mouth flapping."

"Flap it some more," said David. "Hunter said something a minute ago—about my not being the first to be Jim-Crowed here. You mean by that maybe some of the other Negro students got eased out quiet-like, got the same deal?"

"I'm damned sure of it," said Hunter. "You probably gave Sara such a bad time for trying to map out a plan of action you didn't give her chance to tell you."

David wriggled uneasily. "She hinted at it. Suppose you tell me."

"I haven't got details. I don't happen to be thinking about you entirely. And I don't think the rest of us are, either. You're the immediate object of attack, of course, but we're also concerned with whether or not there have been others. It happens to be our fight also. Mine and Chuck's and Sara's and Tom's. And God knows, it's Sudsy's. And after we've exhausted that list we have about eighty percent of the rest of the students. We're all either going to receive a diploma from a scholastically exclusive, supposedly liberal college that in the past has eased out half a dozen or so colored students on trumped-up reasons, or we're going to be graduated from a college that woke up and vindicated those guys. And at the same time we are incidentally going to vindicate a student who is still here."

David was watching Hunter, discomfiture forgotten in his surprise. "You!" he said. "Hunter Travis—the nonparticipant —the objective—the no-stand-on-anything guy—the debater on either side with equal ease—"

"It's probably the first and last time," said Hunter. "I'm not going to muff it."

"If you can't whup us, join us," said Chuck. "And you sure as heck can't whup us."

"And you can't do it alone, you big ape," said Hunter.

David stared into his half-empty mug, said slowly, "I probably won't be around long enough. I don't mean I'm going to quit—"

"You'll be around long enough. I spent the afternoon finding out, among other things, how an expulsion works around here. Unless you're caught in the act of cold-blooded murder in the middle of the quadrangle or spit in an instructor's eye in class—and I'm not sure even then—it takes time to kick a student out of these halls of learning. Meetings, conferences, and opportunity for the student to be heard, then a meeting of the board and, of course, consideration of the dean's recommendations."

"Democratic as all hell, aren't they?"

Chuck said, "Among other things that Hunter found out was that in a couple of these other cases the dean recommended against expulsion."

"But," said David. "But. The guy quit anyhow—"

"That's what really stinks," said Hunter.

"All right," said David slowly. "All right. I guess it's different if it's a policy you're fighting. So who writes the letters? Sara says that's the plan."

"I will, if it's all right with everyone," said Hunter. "Then they'll have an authentic Negro pedigree. If you write you'll have to make a point of it. I'll try making a few telephone calls, too. We won't be able to track them all down; we don't need them all."

David kept his eyes down, not looking at the others. He thought of what Hunter had just said—that the whole college was involved. It was an argument that left him cold and unconvinced, even though he had agreed to go along. He was surprised that Hunter had even advanced the argument. To him, as a Negro, a liberal tradition was something the whites talked about and the Negro kept still about because if he said anything it would be a dirty word. It was all very high-sounding and noble but it didn't get to him at all. It was northern white tradition, and what had it ever done, liberal as all hell though it might have been for a hundred years, for the Negro as a race, the Negro he knew and had grown up with? Not a Goddamned thing. He'd lived under a white tradition, too, a different kind—one that worked.

Chuck's voice broke into his thoughts. "We think we've spotted Cozy's little helper."

He shrugged. "Hell, so have I. I wasn't sure yesterday, but I've thought it over. It's got to be Clevenger. Who else? He's the only one who was in Emory that afternoon; he's the only guy who's made a pass; and he's the only guy here I've punched in the jaw. And besides all that he's a natural-born son of a bitch. So why don't I just beat the shit out of him and take whatever comes?"

"You can't—" Hunter broke in quickly.

"I don't see why not. But I'm not going to. Sure be a hell of a lot simpler, though. Solve a lot of problems."

"Sure enough would," said Chuck. "So would shooting Senator Joe McCarthy. It's the new problems that would hurt—"

David stood up. "O.K., Hunter. Get going. I'll type the damned letters. I'm faster than any of you. And I'll have a say about what goes into them. But get this: they have to be out soon. Because if they throw me out, I'm staying out. They can get down on their cotton-picking knees and they won't reinstate this boy. No, man!"

"You halfway hope they will, don't you?"

"Yes," said David. He picked up the coffee mugs and started for the basin, his back to them. He was achingly conscious of a girl named Sara Kent, who had no life, no existence for him outside Pengard and, as far as he could see, never would. "Yes," he repeated over the sound of running water as he started rinsing mugs. "Halfway."

"Tom's now," said Hunter as he and Chuck walked down the steps of Quimby House. From the corner they could see a light in the window of the study Tom shared with Bob Witherspoon. When they knocked, Tom greeted them in paisley print pajamas that rocked Chuck back on his heels and made Hunter say, "Too old for you, son. You should stick to Dr. Denton's."

Tom's study was as chaotic and disordered as David's room had been neat, and Hunter said: "You guys only have two choices in life. Stand up or go to bed. Where's to sit in this mess?" Tom emptied a chair by the simple expedient of tilting it forward and letting its burden of books and notebooks slither to the floor. Hunter slid into it, legs extended. "Been standing for an hour trying to pound sense into young Champlin."

"Get anywhere?" Tom's eyes were eager.

"Sure did," said Chuck. "I won't go so far as to say we got wholehearted support, but we got him out of his shell far enough to say he'd cooperate to a certain degree."

"That's enough," said Tom.

"Tom, what about Witherspoon?" asked Hunter. "After all,

he's the only other person who was there the night David laid Randy out. How far will he go?"

Tom was silent for a moment, his face solemnly concerned. "Not far enough. He's the type who doesn't like involvement."

"He won't lie, will he?"

Tom sighed. "I don't know whether he's lying or not. I sort of worked his conscience over. If it comes to a showdown, he'll say he was asleep; that the first thing he knew the car was stopped and Clevenger was out cold on the ground. Maybe I can work him over some more and come up with something better. But don't count on it."

"So right now it's just your word?" Hunter sounded doubtful.

"Look, dad, Clevenger knows. That rat knows I'm telling the truth. I didn't see any actual pass, but I sure as hell heard what he said. What I don't know is how in hell he's been spreading the word."

"I think I do," said Chuck. "Part of it, anyhow. I think he asks the question first—'Is the rumor true—' and all that. Then he says—and I heard him say this just after supper—that he feels these things shouldn't be talked around if they aren't true—but, of course, one can't tell—it's pretty well known that homosexuality is almost a way of life with the Negro—of course he couldn't say about Champlin; he seemed a very clean-cut type—although he and Sutherland *had* been closer than usual—I got in on the act then and tried to shut him up. Made things worse, I suppose."

"Why, God damn his stinking little soul to hell," said Hunter slowly. "I didn't think even that guy could get that low. Now—what do we do if we pin the story on Clevenger? This is a separate deal from finding out about these others. After we pin it on Clevenger—you'll never be able to pin it on Goodhue, even if we do think he's encouraging it or something."

Chuck, who had been half sitting on the edge of the desk, stood up, running a big hand through hair already standing upright in random spikes and tufts. He lumbered to the window and back, to stand in the center of the room, hands in the pockets of his corduroys. "Look," he said. "I reckon it's time I said what I've been wondering whether to say or not. I don't like shooting off my face about a guy unless I have proof, and I'd be the last to be able to come up with proof in this case. But I'll tell you flat what I think—I said 'think'—and that is that Cozy's as queer as our Randy. Queerer."

Tom's eyes widened. "Yeah? No kidding? You aren't—"

Hunter interrupted, leaning forward in his chair. He spoke slowly, thoughtfully. "Wait. Wait. You could be right, Chuck."

Tom said, "Cripes! If this is true it complicates things—"

"Sure does," said Chuck. "And I might as well go on, now my big mouth's open. I've got another hunch that complicates the complications. Right now I think our boy Randy is his pride and joy—"

"What gives you that idea?" asked Hunter.

"I don't know. I just plumb don't know. I see them together a lot. It's just—heck, I suppose it's something you sort of smell, like a hound dog smells a rabbit. And Randy was with the dean the day David came back after Thanksgiving weekend, back from putting Suds on the train. I saw him leaving Cozy's study. And he's asked Randy to tea. Randy told me that just before the stink came up—"

"All last year he kept asking me, but I never went because—" Tom stopped abruptly, moaned softly. "Oh, my God, no!"

Hunter was laughing now, and Tom said, "Shut up, damn it!"

"I'm remembering," said Hunter. "You're the type. I'm remembering the guys he's been especially nice to. The ones that got invitations to tea and had no trouble switching courses and stuff. Let's see—last year, Parsons, Anderson, Cramer, Holt; this year—Sessions and Terhune. Now Randy. He's a little different in type. Maybe Cozy's getting old enough to need variety—"

"How many of these guys do you think he made it with?" asked Tom.

"Why ask me? Offhand—Anderson and Cramer. And Terhune. Then Terhune got hurt in that car wreck on his way back from Chicago one weekend—whether Randy's been any active consolation, who the hell knows? Who gives a damn whether he made it with any of them?"

"We ought to," said Chuck. "I mean we ought to give a damn."

"He doesn't carry a gun," said Hunter. "Don't be so damned moral and Christian about it. It's their business. Tom didn't fall for it, did he?"

"Look," said Tom pleadingly. "Let's change the subject,

huh? I'm sort of in shock. You know what I'm going to do? My folks are having an anniversary celebration this weekend. I'm going to give 'em a thrill and go home. Then I'm going to tell the old man about this and see what he has to say. He's an outsider, and it's a long way out of line, but you'd be surprised what he can come up with in the way of ideas. And there's something else I haven't told you. David say anything about the car—Sudsy's Yellow Peril?"

"No."

"Cozy took it away from David. Nehemiah Wilson told me."

"What?" Hunter was on his feet now.

Chuck ran a hand through his hair again. "You surprised? I'm not. David needs that car. When Suds was here he could almost always borrow it to get to the city and back weekends. This way if he can't get a lift he's stuck with the walk to and from the bus. In bad weather that's rough. He's lame—I mean he can make it but—where you going, Hunter?"

"To see Nehemiah, get him out of bed, and get the real dope from him. You're going home to Chicago this weekend, Tom? I'm going to Boston. It happens that Sudsy's grandfather took care of my mother's family until he died, and then Sudsy's father took over. He put casts on me, stuck needles in me, warned me of the dangers of promiscuous sex—" He was belting his coat. "The name Sutherland packs weight in more than medical circles. If we can't lick it with our own troops, maybe we can bring up some reinforcements."

"I'll stay behind and mind the store," said Chuck.

33

DR. KARL KNUDSEN WALKED FROM garage to house in the glare of a floodlight beside the back door, operable from the garage. His gait was the slightly stiff-legged one of a terrier advancing on a hated foe, and Eve Knudsen, watching alone from the kitchen window, murmured, "Oh-oh. He's heard—" and hastily carried coffeepot and cups into the living room.

She was waiting there to greet him as he entered the room, a little apprehensive. He had been known to break things.

If he heard her greeting, he made no reply, glared at her a moment, then said, his accent thickened by anger, "Why was I not told?"

She was used to being expected to be a mind reader. "Because I only learned about it myself an hour ago. I assume that question concerns David?"

"Who else—and what else!" Suddenly the stiffness of his body relaxed and he walked over to her, kissed her quickly on the cheek. "You always understand. I did not mean to frighten you."

"Karl, my love, you couldn't. Where did you hear about it?"

"Andrus." Karl sighed. "Andrus has tried to educate me before. Tonight it was all very clear. He charges that what is happening to David is prejudice and that it is deliberate. And that this, or something similar, has happened to others before David. David is one of his favorite students. Favorite persons, would be a better phrase—" Knudsen was rattling on, and his wife did not interrupt him; it was doing him good. "He has had David in his office often, having tea and petrified cookies. God help the boy, I think they make Latin puns together. If I did not know the boy better I would think he was polishing the orange—"

"Apple, dear."

"Apple. Whatever you say." The expected change of mood came explosively. "Good God, Eve, what are we going to do? Where did you learn about it?"

"Sara, of course. She's upstairs in bed. Probably crying. I decided to say she was coming down with something and called the dormitory and lied."

"Good, good."

"Really, Karl—"

"Her roommate is thoroughly stupid. Better Sara should sleep in a snowbank than have to be with that female if she is upset." He took a swallow of coffee, then frowned at his wife. "Crying, did you say?"

"Very probably."

"It is like that, Eve?"

"Like that, Karl."

"Damnation." He spoke without heat.

"That's about it, Karl. Damnation. We've got to help them—"

Karl Knudsen drew a deep breath and did not look toward his wife. Thank God, he thought, thank the good God for a wife who could say "them" under these circumstances. He would not have judged her harshly had her attitude been different; she was not a European with the universal standards of the European, but it was a warm pleasure that in this situation their minds and hearts would not be traveling separate roads.

"Tell me about it, Eve—"

She had been putting away dishes, tidying up the kitchen, when Sara came in without knocking. Eve insisted that wet outer clothing be stripped off, and held the red knit cap by its pompon, at arm's length, saying, "I-i-ick! I'll put it on the radiator in the dining room—"

When she came back, Sara was still standing. "Sit down, for goodness' sake. You look like damp death. I'll fix cocoa." She had seen Sara look like that once before, when she was very small and had learned that the aged family setter had been taken to the vet for merciful euthanasia. She wanted to do now what she had done then, put her arms around the child and try to comfort her; but as she had no idea why she would be offering comfort, she waited quietly, preparing cocoa, making Sara sit down to drink it.

The wait was not a long one. The cocoa, she thought, must have been the homey touch that unlocked Sara's emotions.

"Aunt Eve, people stink."

"Of course they do, dear. Every once in a while I look around and say the same thing. Then I think—Well, here you are, Eve Knudsen, right in the midst of them, and what can you do but hold your nose—"

"Please, Aunt Eve—"

"Sweetie, I'm not being facetious. Suppose you tell me specifically who stinks and why."

"It's about David—"

"Sara, he doesn't—"

"No, Aunt Eve, no! It's other people—" and slowly, with an occasional prod from Eve, the story came out. Eve already knew the incident of the Infirmary; she and Karl had discussed it and dismissed it as being unfortunate and probably calling for some discipline but of no real importance. Her first real interruption came when Sara haltingly told her of the rumor that was slowly creeping through the campus—

"Sara Kent! No one, but no one, in their right mind is

going to believe any such nonsense. I'm ashamed of you for letting it upset you."

Sara nodded slowly. "Yes, they are. They—some of them are going to *enjoy* believing it. Maybe you just don't know how it is on a campus."

"I spent four years on one," said Eve a little tartly.

"Then you do know."

Eve did not answer. On second thought, of course she knew.

"And—"

"Wait, dear. You seem to feel prejudice is involved in this."

Again Sara nodded. "Yes. And we've got a plan, only I can't tell you about it. And—and David—" She stood abruptly and carried her cocoa mug to the sink. There had been no hint in the straight back and resolutely squared shoulders of what Eve saw when Sara turned and faced her: a small, dead-white face, lip muscles stiffening with the effort at control, eyes brimming.

"Sara—dear—"

"David hates me. He's furious with me. I—I don't suppose he'll ever speak to me again—"

"Sara, you idiot—"

Eve held the small body close, let Sara cry it out against her shoulder, said, after a while, "I didn't really know, my dear—wasn't really sure—now, now." She put two fingers under Sara's chin. "Sara, it's not all that bad. David couldn't in a million years stay angry with you for very long. He couldn't possibly. You know that. So stop this." She held Sara away from her, shook her gently. "It's going to be all right, my dear. It has to be. For you and David. It's not the end of the world. Honestly, it isn't."

When Eve Knudsen finished her story to her husband, he was silent for a few moments, then rose and went into the hall. He reappeared in the doorway, struggling into his raincoat.

"Karl, where in the world—"

"Oscar Benford's—"

"At this hour?" She followed him back into the hallway.

"He never goes to bed."

"Sits up all night working on theorems or whatever you mathematicians do work on in the silent hours?"

"No." He kissed her absent-mindedly and picked up his hat. "Mystery stories."

In Benford's living room a short time later, Knudsen spread his square, strong hands to a welcome blaze, walked to the table beside the chair Benford had been sitting in, and picked up a book. "I wish I could learn the secret of being diverted by these—"

"It's a big help," said Benford. "Although it's gone back on me at the moment. I was on page one twenty-nine last night. I was on one thirty-one when you came in, and weakening."

Knudsen gave a short bark of laughter. "*Ja.* I can well imagine. You know why I am here?"

"Of course, Actually, I think I was waiting for you."

"This is a bad thing. A vicious thing."

"Yes."

"You seem damned calm about it, Benford."

"Would it help if I raved?"

"No. But you seem to treat it as though it was routine—"

"Isn't it, Doctor? Sit down, man—"

"Oscar—" It was the first time Knudsen had ever called his immediate subordinate by his first name. Benford's face still showed the slight smile, a smile Knudsen could not interpret; it was not an unpleasant smile, it was—Knudsen searched for a word, found it: disturbing. He forgot what he had started to say originally, and said the thing that had been in the back of his mind since leaving his house. "Quimby."

Benford's smile was replaced by a thoughtful frown. "If you want to do that, there is nothing to prevent it."

"I do not 'want to.' I merely present it as the only answer I can find."

"Karl." Without effort Benford swung from "Doctor" to "Karl." The time for title was long past. "We all know about that famous skunk at the picnic. That would be you if you go over the heads of all involved—the board, the president—to the power behind the throne. Remember, it's a power that's resented in some quarters."

"I know. And the quarter in which it is the most resented is the quarter from which this foul wind has sprung. This is a frame-up, pure and simple. I would swear to it."

"So would I. It was the surest weapon under the circumstances. Champlin is too well liked to make a more specific accusation stick."

"But there has to be an accuser! One cannot, even Goodhue cannot, act on suspicion alone. Certainly he is not going to say that David Champlin made advances to him!"

Benford laughed, the same surprisingly deep laugh David had heard the day before. "I'm glad you said that, Karl. I needed the laugh. Now—to be serious. Did you know that David Champlin knocked out a fellow student not long ago? Cold-cocked him, on a lonely spot in the road between here and Cincinnati, in the small hours of the morning? The victim of the knockout is not of the breed that takes kindly to liberties taken by Negroes. And I assume being knocked out would come under the heading of taking liberties."

"Probably. Probably. But David isn't the kind who goes about taking that particular kind of liberty with anyone! White or colored!"

"Wait. I had better add that, from something I've overheard, the aforesaid victim is not equally averse to taking liberties with Negroes. Certain kinds of liberties."

At last Knudsen sat, heavily and with a great gust of outgoing breath, in Benford's big chair.

"I had planned on telling you as soon as I had more to go on," said Benford. "I'm glad now I didn't wait."

"Was it Clevenger?"

"Yes. You're quick—"

"No. Just a hunch. He's a pet of Goodhue's. Would you tell Andrus?"

"Yes. If we—you and I—agree that I should."

"Can you dine with us tomorrow? With Andrus."

"Certainly. Do you still favor seeing Quimby?"

"Yes." Knudsen had forgotten his drink, finished it now.

Benford said, "You can see why I have never been to him. Even a man of Quimby's idealism could be forgiven for thinking that it would be special pleading. I've had to content myself with waiting until I saw an opportunity to move in, defending certain students before the board, and warning them when I saw storms ahead. I did manage on one occasion to completely exonerate a Quimby on a charge of cheating. Damn it, Karl!" For the first time Knudsen saw anger, red and violent, flare in Benford's eyes. "A man can fight a lynch mob. Or outright persecution. How in hell can he fight complacence? The damnable, intangible fog of liberal complacency that surrounds those who are so sure of their liberality they cannot see the festering sores within their own establishment! Liberal! Negroes do not love the word. It implies generosity, a giving of something that should be possessed by right."

"I do not know," said Knudsen slowly. "I do not know—

about anything. Yet we dare to call ourselves learned. We dare—" He stood and walked to the table, poured himself a drink from the decanter. "Another drink, Oscar, for the walk home."

"Another drink, sure. But I'll drive you home."

"No. I shall walk. And think. And decide."

"Your job could be at stake if you go to Quimby, tenure or no—"

"I know that, and I will not say that I like knowing it." Then Knudsen laughed, and this time there was real mirth in the sound. "You have met my brother. Half again my weight, nearly a foot taller. David Champlin is the apple of his eye. But that is not why I would do it—although it would give any man pause. Can you see Professor Bjarne Knudsen if David Champlin is expelled on trumped-up charges and malicious innuendos?"

Benford laid a bony black hand on Knudsen's shoulder. "When you go to Quimby, I'll go with you. I think Andrus will also. We can all of us always make a living as tutors."

Dr. Sutherland stood back from the examining table on which Hunter lay clad only in his shorts, and turned to the basin to wash his hands. "Put your clothes on, Hunter, and come into the office."

"Yes, sir."

"I'd like to see a bit more weight on you. A pound here and there—"

In the office the small, rotund man who fitted his son's description of "egg-shaped" so well that some people who saw him only sitting down wondered about his lower extremities looked across at Hunter and smiled.

"You're a humbug, Hunter."

"No, sir—I—"

"You are not here to have me tell you that you could gain a few pounds, but that it is not of major importance whether you do or not."

"My mother says a yearly examination—"

"Fiddlesticks. What's bothering you?"

Hunter hesitated only a moment, to marshal his story, then told it succinctly and clearly; he had been well chosen as a member of the debating team. Dr. Sutherland interrupted twice with a brief question; otherwise he listened without speaking. Hunter finished, spread his hands wide, and said, "That's the story, Doctor Sutherland. Why I'm here."

Sutherland frowned, looking like a troubled Humpty-Dumpty. "Have you talked with Clifton?"

For a moment Hunter was lost. Who was Clifton? Some one of the brass at Pengard he hadn't heard about? Then he choked and said, "You mean Sudsy?"

"An abominable nickname—"

"No, I haven't. Grandmother tells me he's in a sanitarium in upper New York. I wouldn't have called him for any reason without asking you."

"I'm glad. It's hard enough keeping him there as it is. He'd really—what is it? flip—if he heard this. He's doing very well, by the way. Should be on his feet by summer, back in college by fall."

"Pengard?"

"No. California, possibly. Then premed and medical at Harvard."

A buzzer sounded on the doctor's desk, and Hunter pushed back his chair, but Sutherland checked him, cold anger in his blue, usually mild eyes. "Thank you, Hunter. I shall do something. What, I don't know. But let me think."

Tom Evans had never experienced more than minor difficulties in communicating with his father. He had never bothered to analyze this situation, but if asked would probably have said it was because his father had never knocked himself out trying to communicate, never made a big thing of the father-son relationship, as he knew the parents of most of his contemporaries had done. He had often thought that Bull Evans was an opinionated old tyrant, but he did not deny to himself, though he might to others, a carry-over of hero worship from his childhood. Bull Evans, for his part, would have laid their mutual understanding to the fact that he had no mystical fear of youth as such; he remembered his own with great clarity, and was far more concerned with his two children's attitude toward life than with their actions.

Tom tactfully delayed mentioning his problem until Sunday morning, after the confusion of the anniversary celebration had subsided. Then he said, at breakfast, "You got a little time this morning, Pop?"

"Sure. Want to play some cribbage?"

"And get licked? No. I want your advice."

"The hell you do—" There were people who said that on several occasions Bull Evans had frowned and his eyebrows had become tangled, and he had been forced to continue frowning until they were untangled.

Tom grinned at the frown now. "After breakfast." Members of the Evans household didn't disturb its master during his favorite meal.

Later they sat facing each other across the table in the breakfast nook of the big old-fashioned kitchen. The nook had been built in years before when union meetings had overflowed into the dining room. Bull was leaning on heavy, hairy forearms, the massive shoulders that had given him his name hunched forward. He was frowning again, his eyes on the astonished face of his son. "Sometimes you have to go at it that way, Tom," he said.

"But Pop! I've been telling the other guys we shouldn't go to the brass. We ought to handle it ourselves. I thought you'd agree—"

"When the plant catches fire you don't go looking for the shop steward. And you don't run back and forth to the cooler with paper cups of water to put it out."

"You think this is all that bad?"

"I think it's a rottenness that goes way deeper than you kids can get at. Half the battle, son, is to know your weaknesses. And the other guy's."

"I was thinking you could give me some pointers on how to get the fellows—and the girls—sort of together; you know, a sort of student-protest thing, once we get answers to those letters."

"If you couldn't do that without my advice you'd be someone else's son."

"Well, we've got ALEC and all—"

"And rub this thing into the boy by making a big public stink out of it? You've got something going that's more than just a snide attack on one student. What were you planning on? Picketing the dean with signs, 'Champlin isn't a fag! Goodhue is a fag!' You going to write on fences with chalk 'Goodhue loves Clevenger'? With no proof one way or the other?"

"How you going to get proof? Jeez, Pop, it's hard as hell to prove a negative like that, or a positive either."

"Tom, we never struck a plant in our lives we didn't know what we were striking for. Even the wildcatters had grievances that would make a saint throw rocks. You've got a creeping fire there. Not something clear-cut like starvation wages and a seventy-hour week with no overtime. Would all the students back you?"

"Well, probably not all. Did all the workers back you guys?"

"Damned near."

Tom sighed heavily. This was rougher going than he had anticipated. He'd thought the old man would come up with a battle plan. "But, Pop, this isn't a union beef—"

Suddenly the kitchen was filled with Bull Evans's bellow, and his wife, washing dishes in the old-fashioned pantry, jumped, then smiled. She hadn't heard that particular sound since—when? It had to have been when Vlad Petrosky was killed in a mill accident because of lack of safety equipment. "Sic 'em, Bull!" she said under her breath. She was small and slight, with softly curling brown-gray hair and freckles. At fifty-seven she looked forty, and her son was a male replica of her.

The bellow died away as she translated it: "That's just my point, you dumbhead!"

"Now, look, Pop, damn it—" her son's voice was rising now.

In a minute both voices subsided to a rumble, and she smiled again. She would learn what it was all about later; that night when she and Bull were comfortably propped up in bed, planning to read, ending up as they had for twenty-five years, talking. Meanwhile, Bull had the situation in hand.

"We didn't rely on violence—direct action—all the time, Tom," said Bull. "They had spies, but we had our methods too. There were other moves, behind the scenes." He laughed. "I remember one old fellow I knew way back when. He was an I.W.W. organizer even before my time. One jump ahead of the law all his life. He spent most of his time on the West Coast, with the Wobblies in the fruit. He used to tell about going around hanging signs on the trees for the workers: 'DON'T hammer nails in the fruit trees. It ruins the crops.' That old boy taught me a lot."

"I don't see how it applies. I honestly don't."

"It doesn't, except in a very general way, as an example of indirect action."

"Yeah, but—"

"Pick your weapons, Tom. You don't use the same kind of ammo to destroy a fighter bomber you do for an aircraft carrier." Bull Evans reached across the table and laid a huge fist along the side of his son's head, pushed it roughly, affectionately. "As long as you're fighting, kid; that's what it's all about. As long as you're fighting—"

Tom grinned in spite of his misgivings. "O.K., Pop—"

"Now, first thing we have to do is get proof. Or a reasonable facsimile of it—"

Tom leaned back in his chair and sighed with relief. He realized he had been subconsciously waiting for that "we."

"Listen, Tom. Even in the worst days, before my time, when they were shooting labor men down like mad dogs, they let the bosses know what they wanted. Gave 'em a chance to prove they were sons of bitches. They were—and they did. Could be all those guys at Pengard aren't. That's what I'm getting at. Don't go flying off in all directions like a bunch of apes swinging through the trees, making a suffering martyr out of one boy, until you're sure you haven't got a chance otherwise. The very way this character Goodhue is going at it proves he knows he's got opposition. Find out where your strength is. You don't think the brass in that place would be real overjoyed, do you, if they knew the dean of men was—" Bull fell abruptly silent, then said thoughtfully: "Keep your shirt on till after Christmas, son. Keep in touch with me. I think—I think, by God, that maybe I've got something—"

Stu Prentiss rolled over on the couch where he had been taking an insomniac's late-afternoon nap, and picked up the receiver of the ringing telephone. "Prentiss speaking."

"The hell you say. How you been, gumshoe?"

"Chris'sake! Bull Evans!"

"Yup. You busy these days?"

"Just waiting for you to call, old man. Been waiting more'n a year. What's the matter—no dirty work for Stu all this time?"

"We're all going to hell in a handbasket of sweetness and light—"

"Not with you around—"

"Look, Stu, I'm at O'Hare. If you aren't busy thought I'd drive by and chew the fat with you for a while. Got something on my mind. It's sort of out of your line, but you never know—"

Bull Evans had told his wife a hundred times that Stu Prentiss was the only man he'd ever known who'd been a convert from the other side, and right in the middle of the bloodiest steel strike. No one had trusted him for a long time, least of all Bull. Prentiss had been jailed four times and hospitalized twice before he was grudingly accepted; then Bull had yanked him out of the front ranks and put him to work doing what he'd been doing for the company—investigating, although Bull kept a wary eye on him for several years. When the thick smoke of labor battles dwindled to a wisp here and there in a clear sky, Prentiss had developed a business of his own that prospered so well he was now semi-retired.

Prentiss was tall, his face pallid, yet with a bony, rugged strength. Snow-white hair was the only indication of age. He carried an ugly scar that ran from the center of his forehead to the corner of one eyebrow. It had been Bull Evans's hand that had held the flap of flesh in place over the frontal bones on the way to the hospital after a riot. It had been years ago; now each man considered the other both friend and moral creditor.

After he hung up the receiver, Prentiss yawned, stretched in a series of catlike movements, and went into the kitchenette to start coffee. It was always good to see Bull, to talk over old times, and to do whatever he could for him. Maybe there was something cooking in the mills he hadn't heard about. He sniffed battle, and liked the smell.

Three hours later Prentiss said: "Look, Bull, call your wife and tell her you're having dinner with me. I think I can help you out. This isn't as far out of my line as you think."

"How come?"

"Two or three months ago I spent several weeks in a town in Indiana. Never mind which one now. There was a mess like this involving more than just one guy. The chief of police was an old friend. He asked me to give 'em a hand because I wasn't known in the town. We nailed the president of the Chamber of Commerce, a bank manager, a minister, and two scoutmasters. Poor devils."

"Save the sympathy."

"All right, Bull. Put that damned checkbook away. I'll bill you for out-of-pocket expense. That'll be it. If I was as lucky as you are, you old goat, I'd maybe have a kid there myself—"

34

MERRIWETHER GOODHUE CAME INTO his study every Monday afternoon after lunch to light the fire before interviewing students. On the Monday following Hunter's trip to Boston and Tom's to Chicago, the matches were in his hand and he was headed for the fireplace when the buzzer sounded, signaling a call on their outside line. He answered the telephone with a clipped, "Goodhue here," then admitted to the operator that it was, indeed, "Dean Goodhue speaking." So unnecessary, he thought, when he had already identified himself so properly. At the sound of the unknown voice that came on the line next, he sank into his desk chair, sighing.

"Am I speaking to Dean Goodhue?" It was a bleak voice and a cold one, a Yankee voice, a parent voice if he had ever heard one. The caller he conjured up mentally was a bleak, cold man, like his voice, with lean features and a hatchet-type face. Parents who called him in that tone were the frequent crosses he was called on to bear, and he tried to bear them bravely; usually before the conversation ended there was mutual warmth, even well-bred, guarded laughter. He sensed that this might not happen today. At the caller's second sentence he was sure it would not: "This is Dr. Maynard Sutherland speaking."

He had been able to forget many of the former conversations; this one he suspected he would, unfortunately, have to remember.

The opening question was to the point. "What are the medical facilities at Pengard, Dean?"

He explained graciously and, he hoped, clearly, that there was an excellent Infirmary, modern and well equipped, with a registered nurse on duty twenty-four hours a day, a doctor there every afternoon for two hours, and a doctor always on call.

"Is the Infirmary equipped with X ray?"

He tried not to grit his teeth audibly as he informed the

doctor that the Infirmary was equipped with the newest and most modern type of X-ray machine, that it had, in fact, been one of the most expensive items installed.

"Then why is it not used?"

From then on the conversation sent him tobogganing from uneasiness to nightmare. No, he did not know why X rays had not been ordered in the case of a chronic cold and cough, or tuberculin skin tests performed when a history was so obviously suggestive of respiratory disease. He would take it up immediately with the medical director. He had not been aware—certainly, he would expect Dr. Sutherland to talk with President Vidal, but he could assure him that he, Dean Goodhue, would take every possible step to find out what had occurred in the case of Clifton Sutherland. Indeed, he did realize that others were involved, had been exposed—of course, it might be better if Dr. Sutherland took it up directly with their medical director, Dr. Hathaway. Microscope? (Dear God, why did it have to be Maynard Sutherland's son who had contracted tuberculosis? Why couldn't it have been a lawyer's son or an investment broker's?) He could not imagine that there would not be so fundamental a piece of equipment as a microscope in the Infirmary; blood counts, urinalyses, he was sure these were done. Sputum? Of course, if there was— (He was becoming confused. Had he already said there was a microscope or not?) Certainly, when believed necessary, various specimens were sent to pathological laboratories in Laurel or even Cincinnati. The doctor's sarcasm nipped lightly, then sank sharp teeth in deeply.

And all the time the bleak, cold voice was talking, Merriwether Goodhue had the feeling that this part of the conversation was a prelude; that there would be more, and perhaps worse, to follow. When it came it took him a moment to adjust his thinking.

"There is another matter, Dean, which I must take up with you. You are, I believe, the person in authority closest to the students."

"I try to be."

"I'm certain you do." There was more than acid in the tone now, something other than sarcasm, and Goodhue fumbled in his pocket for the comfort of his pipe. "About my son's car."

"Ah, yes. It is quite safe, Doctor. I have seen to that. We have been waiting for your instructions. I had planned to call you tomorrow if we did not hear. I hated to trouble you during this unfortunate time—"

"Thoughtful of you. The car. It is to remain in the possession of David Champlin. He is now the legal owner. Transfer of ownership was taken care of this morning by my attorney, and the papers sent airmail. I believe Champlin has been driving it?"

"Er—I believe he did—while Clifton was here. But not since he left us. It seemed wise—er—to ask him to relinquish the keys until we received word."

"You have received it."

Goodhue could have told the doctor politely that he was encroaching on territory where he had no right; that for certain good and valid reasons it was considered unwise to permit Champlin to have a car on campus, but he did not. The college was in the soup already; it was his job to get it out, not push it in further by antagonizing this thoroughly aroused man.

"Thank you, Dean. Now if you will be kind enough to give me the name and telephone number of your medical director —Dr. Hathaway, did you say?—and tell me how to reach President Vidal as quickly as possible—"

Goodhue cradled the telephone finally, muttered, "And God have mercy on their souls—" then picked up the matches and started again for the fireplace; the room was like a tomb.

Two envelopes were in David's mailbox when he came back to Quimby House for lunch Wednesday, and he carried them upstairs without opening them. He ate in his room most days now, at least at noon. When he didn't he always wound up wishing he had, unless Nehemiah or Chuck or someone like that was around. And it wasn't too good then, either, because he was worried about the connotation others might put on any student's close association with him. One thing that was good about it, he kept saying to himself, was that he could brush up on study for the first afternoon class—and if that wasn't pure rationalization, what was?

One envelope, marked "Airmail," bore in discreet type in its upper left-hand corner, the name "Maynard Sutherland, M.D.," and the address of the Sutherland Clinic in Boston. The other proclaimed itself in lower case as being "from the office of dean goodhue" and contained some hard, oblong object. He opened it first, and smiled as the leather container for the keys to the Yellow Peril slid to the table. He opened the half-sheet memo that was also inside the envelope. The note it contained was brief and in longhand. There was no salutation:

Because it is never my intention to work undue hardship on any student in disciplinary matters, I am returning to you the keys to Clifton Sutherland's car. I understand that you are employed in the city on weekends. I suggest that in the future, as long as you are at Pengard, you guard against impulsive actions that, however well meant, constitute a definite breach of regulations and are detrimental to the college as a whole.

MERRIWETHER GOODHUE

The car is in stall #5 in the faculty garage behind the Administration Building.

David murmured, "Um-*ummmm.* The old bastard. The ofay bastard." He looked at the note again, read, ". . . as long as you are at Pengard . . ." I'm still here, you son of a bitch. What's holding you up? Want to be sure I'll flip, waiting for the other shoe to drop?

He slipped the keys into his pocket, made a sandwich and coffee, and sat down, feet cocked up on the table, munching cheese on rye as he opened the other envelope. There was a document in the envelope, but he concentrated on the letter. It was typed, dated Monday, and glancing at its conclusion he saw that it had been dictated to someone whose initials were EG. He slid further down into his chair and began to read:

DEAR DAVID CHAMPLIN,

Saturday afternoon Mrs. Sutherland and I drove to the sanitarium where Clifton must remain for a few months, and returned with many messages for you and his other classmates. The gist of them all was "best wishes." He is lonely and wanted me to thank you for the humorous cards you have sent him. They have been good therapy, as has been the knowledge that he is not forgotten. Unhappily, patients in sanitariums sometimes tend to feel that they are, and I hope you will continue, and ask his other friends to continue, to keep in touch.

Chatty old boy, thought David; sounds nice. The letter became more formal:

> We discussed the matter of the car, which he calls the Yellow Peril. From what he has told me, it appears to be well named. It is our unanimous decision—and I include his mother—that you retain the car, not merely physically but legally. Therefore I instructed our attorney to draw up a bill of sale, which I enclose. (You will pay no attention to the "consideration" therein referred to.) I am also enclosing my check to cover transfer fees and insurance. I was shocked to learn that Clifton had been driving it for more than a year with no insurance. Please attend to this detail immediately.

Yes, sir, thought David. Yes, *sir*. Right now. He was grinning. The tone of the letter changed again:

> We hope that you will find time one of these vacations to come to Boston and visit with us. You probably will not want to leave your grandfather at this season (you see, my son has told me a good deal about you), but should you feel free to do so we would be delighted to have you spend some time with us, and go up with us to visit Clifton. If not at Christmas, then perhaps later in the year?
>
> Mrs. Sutherland joins me in extending our most sincere wishes for a happy holiday season and a bright New Year.
>
> Sincerely,
>
> MAYNARD SUTHERLAND

He had stopped eating the sandwich halfway through the letter, and sat now, looking straight ahead. He was six feet and a bit, a man now, and a desire to bawl like a five-year-old meant he had to be slipping fast. Gramp was fond of saying, "Things'll be made clear, you'll see. Up yonder things'll be made clear." He figured he was going to have a hell of a long wait, healthy as he was, before he made it up yonder. He started fixing another sandwich; sure would be nice if the problems of life, death, God, and the hereafter, were as simple as Gramp saw them to be.

Crossing the campus to class after lunch, he gave way to

relief that the Yellow Peril would be in his hands now. It had been rough getting back from the city Sunday. Going in hadn't been so bad, because Chuck had been with him on his way to a date with a UC girl. Tom and Hunter had headed for parts unknown. "Where'd they go?" he asked Chuck after they were on the bus. "First thing I knew I saw 'em hightailing it down the road with overnight bags to catch the bus before this one."

Chuck, sitting next to the window, kept his face turned away, gazing intently at familiar countryside. He'd never been a good liar, but they had all agreed not to tell David that Tom was seeking advice from his father, Hunter from Dr. Sutherland. "Where'd they go?" he said. "Who knows? Who knows where those two characters take off to for weekends? Maybe it's better if we don't. Maybe we're too young. That Tom—"

"Yeah. If that girl—what's her name? Gwen?—really knew—"

"They'll come back peaked and wan, and we'll be bright-eyed and rosy-cheeked."

"I'd sure look a mess with rosy cheeks—"

They laughed together as the bus rumbled through a dusk that became night before they reached the city, David remembering a ride less than two weeks before, Sudsy beside him, singing off-key along with him: *Come on, man! Put your back in it—"Pharaoh's army got drownded—Oh, Mary, don't you weep. . . ."*

Special permission had to be granted for private telephones in students' rooms, a restriction made necessary by the number of unpaid phone bills at term end in previous years. Hunter Travis was one of the few who had sought and obtained permission at the start of his second year. Now, on this Wednesday afternoon, three days after he returned from Boston and his talk with Dr. Sutherland, Tom Evans sat at the telephone, cheeks flushed, eyes glistening. Hunter sat cross-legged on the floor, an unfailing sign of complete absorption in the matter at hand, while Chuck sat on the extreme edge of the couch, elbows on knees, big hands clasping and unclasping nervously.

"Relax, Tom," said Hunter. "Stay loose."

Tom dropped the receiver back into its cradle, and said, "Line's still busy." He felt like a man who has just received a time bomb in the mail and doesn't know how to deactivate it.

Three quarters of an hour ago a long-distance operator had traced him down through the college switchboard to the billiard room in the rec hall. When he went to the telephone Bull Evans's voice greeted him, a circumstance so unusual he was certain for a moment that their house had burned to the ground with all hands except Bull in it.

"Everything all right, Pop?"

"Fine. Fine. Your sister just won some kind of intercity swim meet—"

"In this weather? Hope it was indoors. That what you called about, for gosh sake?"

"No. This line goes through a switchboard—"

"Yes."

"O.K.; so don't talk. This is about the matter we discussed Sunday. You're to go to a pay telephone or a private line and call the number I give you, collect. It's Stu Prentiss's place. I'm there now."

"Good ol' Uncle Stu? Jeez, Pop, you got him in on this—on what we talked about?"

"Yes. If you've got a couple of friends you can trust, O.K.; we may need their help. I'd keep the boy who's most involved out of it. Now. Take this number down—" Bull articulated it carefully, while Tom wrote it on the back of an envelope. "Now get going, son, and call back as soon as you can. We'll be at this number for a couple of hours."

It took half an hour to round up Chuck and Hunter, another ten minutes to give them a rundown on Bull's instructions and Prentiss's identity on their way to Hunter's room. Now they sat waiting, Hunter apparently unmoved except for a darkening of the skin around his eyes, Chuck not even trying to hide his excitement.

Tom dialed the operator again, and Hunter laughed softly. "Damnedest thing—"

Tom glared at him. "Shut up, will you, for gosh sake, I can't—Hello? Uncle Stu? Hi! This is Tom—"

"Howya doing, boy!"

Hunter and Chuck crept nearer, crouching with their heads close to Tom's so they could catch Prentiss's words.

In Chicago, in the combined office and living room of Stu Prentiss, Bull Evans, massive head on one side, sat with one huge hand nursing the ankle that was cocked up on his knee in a characteristic posture thousands of labor men would have recognized. He learned all he needed to know from Prentiss's end of the conversation.

"Good to hear you, Tom. . . . Listen, I'll be down there one of these days. . . . Yes, in Laurel. But take it easy. You never saw me before. . . . No, you didn't. . . . And I don't want so much as a blink out of you if you see me on the street. Got it? . . . Now I want you to find out the names of the kids this man Goodhue has been most friendly with. . . . For as far back as you can get them. . . . No, no, Tom. They won't be in any trouble. . . . No. . . . All right, all right. Then do it this way: don't give me their names but find out how many of them have been away from the college on weekends and when. Where, too, if you can . . . No, Tom, you will not be getting them in a jam. I'll guarantee it. . . . Now listen. Sometime soon someone who will be doing a magazine article on why culture is moving into the Midwest will show up and be in touch with you. . . . Have him interview these boys if you can. . . . How can it be anonymous? . . . Figure something out. If you can't, then drop that angle. He'll interview one of the faculty too. . . . Call me when you get anything. . . . And give me a number where I can reach you, pay phone or private line. . . . Where is it? . . . Travis. Hunter Travis? . . . Trust him? . . . O.K., boy. Got everything? . . . Repeat it. . . . Right. Be talking to you. . . ."

Tom hung up and looked at the others with something like panic in his eyes. "My God, what've we done?"

Hunter had straightened up and returned to his cross-legged position against the wall. "Nothing, Tom. I think I know what he's after. None of those poor, misguided blokes will be publicly involved." He smiled, the sharp planes of his face softening. "You guys'll have to give up reading private-eye paperbacks. You're living one."

Tom's eyes were troubled. "We don't want to stink as bad as Cozy does."

"We won't."

"I don't think I like it. I should of stood in bed."

"And let Cozy kick David out—and any other guy whose complexion he doesn't happen to like? Another thing—one of these days his fun and games with the kiddies is going to backfire. Some apple-cheeked laddie"—he grinned at Tom's wince—"is going to turn out not to like the rules of the games and run home and holler bloody murder to Papa. Cozy's just been lucky. When that happens it could mean the law and all kinds of crap and corruption—for all concerned.

If your friend Prentiss says these kids'll be protected, it's good enough for me."

Chuck said: "I couldn't hear it all, but I can't see now that you've got much to say about it, daddy-o. You and I and Hunter could drop dead right now, and it sounds like this guy would keep right on going. It might take longer, but it'd get done."

Tom sighed. "Why can't we get into simple trouble, huh? Like busting into the women's dorms or something? No ethics involved—just good ol' red-blooded, All-American collegiate lust—"

35

PENGARD COLLEGE HAD BEEN one of the first to eliminate semifinal and final examinations. Instead, at the end of each semester there was a period of what was called, informally, "scholastic appraisal." During the year the standard system of grading was used.

Dean Goodhue was of two minds about the merits of the system. There could be no doubt of its advantages, but nevertheless the "appraisal" periods were invariably marked by two or three weeks of unrest and jitters among the students, and his counsel and advice were sought to an exhausting degree. To these frequent counseling sessions were added faculty conferences. By the Friday before winter vacation he was edgy and irritable, and had established a custom of solitary reading and relaxing in his study on Saturday and Sunday.

On this particular weekend before Christmas he was more than edgy; he was disturbed. There had been a call from the old man in the big house by the lake the previous week and a disquieting interview with him. The old fool should long since have relinquished any hold on the reins of college affairs, but he still persisted in meddling, sitting in that echoing mansion of his like a withered old eagle in its aerie, worrying about racial discrimination. The day Goodhue was summoned, Quimby had his damned scholarship students on his mind; that was clear after his first words; and as Goodhue looked at the almost fleshless face, the domed head with its thin white hair, the sunken, hooded eyes, he wondered uneasily what had brought about this fresh concern. That Quimby was as dedicated to integrating the campus as he himself was to keeping it untainted he was well aware. He was also uncomfortably aware, as he sat there in that quiet study, that the old man seemed in possession of information that he, Goodhue, did not have.

He lost the first part of a sentence by Quimby that ended ". . . a reinvestigation." He listened carefully and uneasily to what followed. "I should like your thinking on this, Dean. It will be done in any event. President Vidal assures me of that. He has asked certain of the faculty members to instigate it. Please give them any cooperation you can." He had stood up then with surprising alacrity for a man whose age no one dared guess at. "Thank you for coming to see an old man, Dean Goodhue." And he had been dismissed, like a student who has just been cautioned about a misdemeanor.

For this reason he listened to his wife's breakfast chatter on the Saturday before Christmas with only half his attention. He had been forced to cancel his request for a faculty committee meeting on the subject of the Negro David Champlin, and the knowledge that he had taken this backward step rankled. The meeting now would have to wait until after Christmas, by which time he hoped the old man's senile concern might evaporate. This would be a more comforting thought, he told himself, if he or anyone else really believed the old man had a senile cell in his brain.

His wife's voice broke in on his thoughts. "Merriwether, you're not listening."

"Sorry, my dear. What was it? Something about New York—"

"I said that the next time you take off on a trip to Chicago or New York, you may find me tagging along with you. And it will be free. Plus hotel expenses. Wouldn't that be nice?"

He stared at her, a forkful of scrambled eggs halfway to his mouth. "Have you been going through a 'scholastic appraisal' too, my dear? What on earth are you talking about?"

"Last week—I didn't want to bother you then, and besides I haven't seen much of you—a really charming gentleman came here to talk with you, but you were out and he said I'd do just as well. He was from one of the airlines, and they are doing some sort of survey in cities and towns that connect by train and plane to Chicago and New York. Various classifications of people; you know, businessmen, professional men, academic—"

"Do come to the point, Elacoya."

"I am, dear. It's a bit complicated. The ones in each category who have traveled exclusively by plane, or have the most mileage—I've forgotten which exactly—will be the guests, with their wives, of the airline—for a weekend in Chicago. Or New York, my dear. Imagine! If we win wouldn't you rather go to New York?"

"Win! Elacoya, did you give this man any information?"

"Of course, dear. How often you went, whatever dates I could remember—where you usually stayed—that sort of thing. What in the world is wrong with that?"

"Do you want to be—my God!—the winner in a cheap commercial scheme to promote an airline? Your name in paid advertisements? Even pictures. On the radio, perhaps television commercials—don't think there won't be those kinds of strings attached—the whole bit? I'm astounded that you even gave him five minutes' time. He must indeed have been charming."

Elacoya Goodhue's face flushed and she squared plump shoulders defensively. "He was. Not the crass commercial type at all. An older man with white hair and the most interesting scar on his forehead." She looked at her husband's shocked face. "Oh, dear, I'm afraid I didn't give any thought to that part of it—the advertising and publicity and all. Maybe I was rather stupid—"

"You were. What was his name and what was the airline? I shall call them and tell them to take our names off the list immediately."

"The airline was the Midwest-Northern. And his name was—let me think, it was a common name with something uncommon about it—Anderton. That was it."

"Let me have his card."

"Card?" She flushed again, this time with embarrassment. "He said he had run out of cards. He apologized very nicely. He's writing us, he said, to verify the interview."

"Elacoya, this is inexcusable. You let this man in the house, permitted him to take up your time, answered his questions, and didn't even insist upon credentials? Never mind. I don't need the card. I'll give the airline his name."

Half an hour later he was talking to Midwest-Northern's account executive at their advertising agency in Chicago. "No one by that name? You must have. You must know something about this business. Someone must. The airline people don't. Isn't that your job?"

"Certainly. But I assure you we know nothing of any such survey. My advice, Dean Goodhue, is that you notify the police and the Better Business Bureau in your city immediately. Meanwhile, we will investigate at this end. We cannot have our name—"

Dean Goodhue's hand suddenly gripped the telephone with convulsive strength, the knuckles whitening. Fear knotted his stomach, swept through his blood in icy waves, made him physically sick, paralyzed his lips so that he had difficulty forming his words. "No. Wait. My wife could have been mistaken about the airline. She—she often is about names. Let—let me make certain there's been no mistake—"

"I'm sure there has been. But we are very much at your service. Will you let us know—"

"Yes—" Without saying goodbye he let the receiver drop into its cradle, saw that sweat from his hand was beading its blackness. Elacoya had not been alone in her stupidity. Her words came back to him now on the shock waves of fear that had followed his realization of what this might mean. *How often you went. Whatever dates I could remember—where you liked to stay—that sort of thing*—Last week, the week before—oh, God, when had it been?—there had come to his office in the Administration Building a youngish man with crew-cut hair and black-rimmed glasses who had said he was doing an article for a magazine, something about the cultural growth of the Midwest. For what magazine? For what—Goodhue feverishly searched his mind.

He remembered the questions now, and each one was like a tom-tom beat of fear in his mind: the proximity of the college to cultural centers, the frequency of trips by students to worthwhile cultural events, ballets, symphonies, special lectures, the ability of students to pay for these trips, because "of course it was known that Pengard was not a rich boy's college, unless the riches were of the mind." And he, Merriwether Goodhue had talked, had prattled, on and on. Then—oh, God! then he'd seen the young man on campus, talking to Cramer. What had Cramer said? He was home in New Jersey by now. Who else had he talked to? Parsons? Holt? Sessions? Thank God, he'd get nothing from Sessions; he had not left the campus this semester. The card—the name of the magazine—he did not know why it was important, but all at once it was the only thing that mattered.

He had risen to his feet and was standing on legs in which the muscles quivered uncontrollably, when Elacoya came in.

"So nice to be able to just bounce in on you these vacation days—"

"What do you want?"

"Nothing important, dear. Just something I forgot to tell you. That nice young Virginian, Clevenger, is marooned on campus until Monday. Family away or something like that. Are you ill, Merriwether?"

"No! I'm going out. I'll be back shortly—"

"Let me finish, dear. I hate knowing any student is lonely at this season and I know he's one of your favorites, so I've asked him—Merriwether, you're certainly ill—I can tell—"

"No! I'm perfectly all right, I tell you! Just leave me alone, for God's sake—I'll go out this way—"

David sat on the top step of the porch of the Beauregard house, chin in hands. It was Sunday afternoon, warm even for a New Orleans Christmas season, and the late sun touched his shoulders gently. Weeks before, he had made a plane reservation for early Sunday morning, saving his money carefully to make it possible because he did not want to give up a weekend's work at the Calico Cat.

There was a good-sized Christmas tree in the center of the dining-room table in the house behind him, decorated by Gramp, who had set its lights blinking as soon as they entered the house, showing them off. Under the tree were assorted packages, which Gramp pointed out pridefully before going into his room to nap. David showered, took out the presents he had brought for Gramp, wrapped them, and put them with the others under the tree. One was a soft tan cashmere cardigan, the other a beautifully carved black panther that David had seen in a secondhand store and bought for what he knew must be a tenth of its value. Gramp would put it on the mantel as soon as he opened it, where it would lead the parade of lions, tigers and elephants that already marched above the mock fireplace.

Uneasy, needing sleep but not wanting it, he had gone out on the porch and sat on the steps in the winter sun. He answered Miz Timmins's wave from across the way, and hoped she wouldn't come over; he also hoped the kids were at a Sunday-school Christmas party or something and wouldn't come over either. His mind felt as though it were made of a million springs, all coiled too tightly. Now that he was away from the pressures and worries of the last three weeks at Pengard, he was finding that the perspective of distance wasn't helping any, that coming home hadn't brought the relaxation he'd hoped it would.

Had any one guy ever had so damned many things to worry about all at once? Right now he sure doubted it. Beanie Benford had been right. *Perhaps something I say will mingle with your thinking, color it a little, help. . . . We have to do such a lot of thinking, don't we, David? Small wonder that when we make it in the white world we so often surpass them.* Bits and scraps of Beanie's words that day on the balcony had come back during the past weeks, and while they had helped a little, they hadn't solved a damned thing.

Probably the best thing to do would be to go at it the way you would a history paper. Line up the facts and the dates and what happened and why and what effect it had on things in general. The hell with that. It wouldn't work. It hadn't started when Sudsy quit the Infirmary and came to his room, or any other special time; it had started when Randolph Clevenger's great-grandfather bred slaves in Virginia, a state known throughout the South for the get of its studs. It had started when Goodhue's tenant-farmer grandfather—he could smell the cracker under the tweed if no one else could—had feared and hated Negroes because the upper-class whites had fostered that fear, had told him if he didn't watch out the freed blacks would take over, get his land. It had started a long time ago, and now he, David Champlin, a black student from a supposedly liberal white college sat on a porch step in the Deep South and looked at disgrace, and you couldn't work that one out like a history paper. He sat there, unlynched, un-spat-upon, unpersecuted as many of his race were persecuted, yet so damned close to becoming a pariah it made his head swim to think about it, just as much a victim as his great-grandfather had been, just as much the target for prejudice as any Negro whose body had swung from a tree, who had been broken by police, who had been drowned in a river or tortured in prison.

On the step below him a wisp of silver rain from the Christmas tree glistened in the sunlight, and he reached down and picked it up, twisting it around his fingers. He had to keep reminding himself—he knew that—that there were islands of common humanity in the white world, the Chucks and Toms, Knudsens and Andruses, and a few others, because if he didn't he'd turn into a Nehemiah type, wouldn't sleep at night for shadowy critters under the bed. He had to go along with Gramp, who said there wasn't any gain in hating all the whites because it got in your way; try and forget 'em; then when you found one like the Prof, hate didn't stand in the way between you; be a helluva thing, Gramp said, if a man was so full of hate he couldn't see the occasional good one, now and then, for the bad.

He would have to talk the whole mess out with the Prof, he supposed. The Prof had left early that morning for Laurel to spend Christmas with his brother. If David knew Doc Knudsen, the Prof would have the whole story after he'd been there ten minutes. At least when the Prof come back David would have the chance to say "I told you so—and they weren't under the bed." It would be good to hear the Prof explode again. He couldn't mention it to Gramp or Rudy, because in a case like this Rudy would probably react like Nehemiah. Which he supposed almost any Negro with any sense would do. Rudy would think he had been taken in, but it had been a lot more subtle than that. There wasn't a Negro he'd ever known who'd really been taken in by a white; that was part of the game of living in the same world with them, outguessing them. The whites, especially the New Orleans whites, were so damned certain that you accepted their patronage gratefully. Fooling them could become an end in itself.

But there was something else he had to face, and that was the biggest something of all. The wisp of silver rain broke in his fingers, and he rolled it up and tossed it to one of the neighborhood cats who was meditating in the sun on the bricked path below him. A fellow could study all his life, he supposed, cram his mind with knowledge and facts and other men's thoughts and conclusions and philosophies, and never come up with the answer to the questions a Negro faced every time he walked down the street, applied for a job, or just plain tried to be a human being. And never, never the answer to the question David Champlin faced when he found himself hooked, gaffed, helpless and flounderingly in love with a white girl. It wasn't enough that he had to get talked into going to a white college; he had to wind up in the Goddamnedest fix anyone could think up—and on top of that he had to really mess up and fall in love with a white girl, and the best thing he could do was stay where he was, right on his own front porch, or pick himself a Negro college and get the hell out of where he had been. He knew a lot of mixed couples had already broken the ice in a lot of places outside of the South, and then they'd usually fallen through that ice into the cold depths below. Unless it was an exceptional case like the Travises, he'd never heard of a mixed marriage that hadn't turned out anything but lousy. Besides, he wasn't the ice-breaking type. Already, just showing his black face in a white college had blown up a storm. And life was going to be like that, just like that, like it always had been and would be for a long time—a mess-up; he couldn't ask a half-pint-sized kid who didn't know what it was all about to join him in the mess-up. It wasn't that he had any fool idea he wasn't good enough for her; he was, and he knew it. It was that after a couple of years of rock-throwing she'd wish she'd never heard of him, and he'd rather never see her again than have that happen.

He thought of the first time he'd met her after their big dustup at Mom's. She had seen him walking toward her in the inner quadrangle and stopped for just the fraction of a second, then come forward more slowly, and he had grinned self-consciously, feeling like a kid. "Sara," he said when she drew closer. It was hard enough to say that, but it was harder still to say what he knew he must. "Look—I didn't mean—I guess I was pretty stinking—"

She had looked up at him, eyes shining, mouth laughing. "You were. Oh, David, my darling, you were. And it doesn't matter. Honestly it doesn't because when I want to be mean I can—well, I can out-mean you and anyone else—you wait—"

"I don't think I want to—" He had been trapped then in her eyes, her laugh, her whole vibrant body; he could not look away, and it was only the heavy thud of Chuck Martin's running feet, Chuck's heavy handclap on his shoulder, and "Come on, Stoopid—we're late now for Beanie—" that brought him back to earth.

For a long time after that, he forgot he was beginning to feel like a pariah, that by now there were quick glances his way and equally quick ones away from him, and the quick whispered comments between students were beginning to have a meaning he did not want to think about. And even after the problem came back to ride on his shoulder, "Oh, David, my darling" made it lighter to carry.

The Prof came back at the end of the week, not roaring, to David's surprise, but with a sort of sustained rumble in his voice, like distant thunder. "Say it, my boy," he commanded. "The Prof has deserved it. 'I told you so'—and that these things were not under the bed."

David laughed as heartily as he had for a long time. "How'd you know, Prof? You picked the words, the same identical words, I was all set to say. Dirty trick, not giving me the chance."

The Prof did not go into any detail about what his brother had told him at Pengard. On that score he said only: "David, I cannot urge you. A man must make up his own mind to stay or run. I urged you when your grandfather was sick, and you followed my urging then. Now you must follow your own. But wherever it takes you, David, I think you know Bjarne Knudsen is with you."

"Yes, sir. Thanks."

The day before New Year's a package came, with Sara Kent's return address in Lakeside Heights in the upper left-hand corner. David thanked what luck was left to him that Gramp was out when it arrived. A card was Scotch-taped to the gleaming gold of the Christmas wrapping, and he opened it and read: "Am sorry to pieces this is so late but I thought I could get it finished. Only I couldn't because I was too busy being appraised. If it doesn't fit, blame Chuck. I used him for a model. Please like it. And please call me as soon as you get back. A Happy New Year to all—Sara."

The present was a sweater, a heavy green one in cable stitch that he had seen her working on for weeks before Christmas vacation. It was high in the neck for warmth, with long sleeves. For her brother-in-law, she'd said. It fitted perfectly, long and snug around the hips with a cuff that could be turned up waist high if he wanted it that way, snug at the wrists, shoulders and neck easy and right.

After he took it off he sat for a long time on the edge of his bed, holding it in his hand, turning it over and over, looking at the careful, beautifully even work, not seeing much of any of it, knowing that into the stitches there had to have been knit thoughts, because you couldn't knit a big sweater like this without thinking of the guy you were knitting it for. And damn it, there he was again, and he wished life would let him alone just long enough for him to get on his feet emotionally, know where he was going, or at least how he wanted to get wherever it was he was headed.

There was the sound of the front door closing. Gramp was back. He started up guiltily, folding the sweater back into the tissue paper quickly, kicking the box under the bed, and then pulling his suitcase out of the closet. He threw it on the bed and opened it, put the sweater carefully in the shirt compartment, and buckled the flaps over it. Then he locked the suitcase. That was one thing Gramp mustn't see. Gramp knew something was wrong, he could tell that; and Gramp was worrying about him. If he showed him a sweater knit by a white girl—Jesus have moicy! David didn't even want to think about it. And if he lied and said she was colored, Gramp would be so happy and relieved he'd start picking out names for his great-grandchildren right then and there.

But even though the sweater was well out of sight, he could still see the girl who had made it for him. He stood looking at the suitcase, while in the kitchen there were the sounds of Gramp stirring round. "Sara—Smallest—". He knew now. It would take guts to go back and face that situation—but it would take more guts to stay away from wherever Sara was, and he didn't think he had them.

36

PRESIDENT JOHN VIDAL WAS Pengard College's answer to the youth movement that was becoming evident in the academic world through the appointments of young and progressive men to head many universities and colleges, including some of the most conservative. He was still only forty-seven when he was faced with one of the stickiest problems he supposed he'd ever have to deal with. Crew-cut, ruddy-complexioned, of medium height and stocky build, his general appearance of Kiwanian bounce and vitality was so deceptive that there was scarcely a faculty member who did not bear psychic scars acquired in encounter with a broad and penetrating mind that was balanced nicely between objective intellect and subjective humanitarianism. Vidal made no fetish of comradely relationship with his students, although he did not hesitate to fall in step with one, on or off the campus, and say, "I'm John Vidal. What's your name? Tell me about yourself." When Benford had jokingly commented on it once, Vidal had grinned at him and said, "With professors like you around, I feel I have to show them that Someone Cares." His greatest weaknesses were an occasional naïveté in his relationships with his fellows, and a real belief in a basic goodness inherent in all men. This naïveté and belief explained the presence of Goodhue and several assistant professors the students were forced to suffer, not often gladly. He was a widower, with twin sons at Exeter and a daughter at a preparatory school in New York.

His selection had been accomplished without any discernible pressure from the then president, Horace Quimby, yet the opinion prevailed among the faculty that he was "Quimby's man." The opinion was correct. On Thursday of the final week of a midterm vacation that Vidal knew he would always remember as one of the most troubled periods of his academic career, he faced the prospect of meeting with his full board, once in the afternoon and again in the evening. There was little comfort in the thought that facing his board could be no worse than the job of facing himself had been for the past four weeks—ever since Horace Quimby had called him to the house by the lake on the Sunday following Thanksgiving weekend. He had not known at the time, but he knew now that on that same Sunday Tom Evans, troubled and perplexed, had talked with his father in the Evans home, and on the day before Hunter Travis had sought counsel from Dr. Maynard Sutherland in Boston.

He had been curious but not concerned on that Sunday as his car jounced over the unpaved shortcut to the lake road, a shortcut forbidden to student cars except on special occasions. When he rounded a curve that would bring the lake into full view, he saw two students walking ahead of him. One student was the tall, good-looking young Negro from New Orleans, David Champlin, whom he had talked to several times and liked better each time; the other was the bony, rugged-looking chap from Georgia with the unruly blond hair and candid face. Vidal remembered him well because of circumstances connected with his admission. He blew his horn, and drew alongside them. "Lift?" he called when he had lowered the window. "It's cold out there!" Charles Martin had answered. "Sure is, but we're getting our exercise. Thanks, sir —" And Champlin had smiled. (Good God thought Vidal now, was it only four weeks before? He could still feel the warm charm of a smile lighting a face that always appeared almost somber in repose.) "Thank you, sir," Champlin had said. "There's no place to lift us to. We don't know where we're going." Vidal remembered laughing. "That's scarcely an attitude we encourage at Pengard, Champlin, but it's sure as the devil the best one to have when you start out on a walk. Take care—and good luck!" And he had driven on, to Quimby's home, and the start of the unhappy four weeks climaxing today in the meeting of the board.

Only Horace Quimby, for whom Vidal had more affection than for any older man he had ever known, could have cooled his anger when he learned that three faculty members had gone over his head to the former president with a strange story of racial discrimination and bias, a story that held certain other unsavory implications as well. Quimby had said, "Would you have been able to receive their story open-mindedly, John? All three ran a certain risk in coming to me, but they did so because they had no proof—yet. They believe, and so do I, in the truth of the story. But to have come to you with nothing definite to go on would have seemed like gossipmongering, particularly as all of them are known to be anything but supporters of Goodhue. They came to me for counsel solely; after all, I have no real power—"

A good measure of Vidal's anger was expended in his laughter at Quimby's last words. Quimby responded to the laughter with a dry chuckle. "Do what you can, John. What seems right. My advice was that they put the entire problem in your lap. I think your secretary will tell you that you have an appointment with them tomorrow."

"Should I say, 'Thank you'?"

Again the dry, aged chuckle. "You're getting your lumps at last, John. I believe that's the expression. My advice—and please understand that it is advice only—is that you start with the current problem, the one that involves David Champlin, and work back."

"I just saw him, on the way up here. It's incredible. I could wish, though, that he hadn't attacked a fellow student."

"I've told you what the circumstances were. He had reason enough, in my judgment."

"Of course, under those circumstances, it seems to have

been expedient. And it could explain, possibly, the origin of a malicious rumor."

"Possibly?" said Quimby.

He remembered that interview well, standing at the window of the board room, watching the members arrive, listening to the rumble of talk in the hallway and waiting room. Ordinarily he would have been out there, greeting them. Today he did not feel like the amenities. As they came into the board room he sensed their surprise at his expression, but he could not lighten it. One member said, as they shook hands, "It's quite apparent, John, that we aren't here to discuss an unexpected ten-million-dollar endowment."

"Not even one million, Henry."

Pengard's governors had been chosen through the years for their mental flexibility, their ability to think and make decisions within the framework of current thought and problems; it was not, therefore, what is known as "well balanced." During his years as president, Quimby had snapped at a well-intentioned adviser: "I'm not in the least interested in balance for its own sake. I'd rather see us go overboard and have to rescue ourselves than never get wet at all."

Vidal announced the plan of the meeting when they were all seated at the big oval table in the center of the room; there would be an informal, and probably lengthy, session first, then dinner at the Laurel Inn, followed by a formal session for action later. In anticipation of the length of the afternoon session a long table against a side wall held a coffee urn and cups and saucers.

He sat at one end of the table, not the relaxed, smiling figure they were accustomed to, but straight, almost stiff, eyes cold, one hand resting on a stack of folders in front of him, the other holding his dark-rimmed reading glasses. Without comment he passed one of the folders to each man, then leaned forward, holding his eyeglasses delicately in both hands as though afraid that if he permitted himself to grasp them firmly he would shatter them.

"The contents of the folders you have just been given will be easier to understand after I have told you something about them. You will find, when you open them, photostatic copies of records pertaining to certain students who were either asked to leave the college during the past few years or who left of their own accord. There are six of those. You will also find, attached to the records of some of these students, letters recently received setting forth their views of the reasons they are no longer students. Naturally, these are for the most part subjective in tone, although far from entirely so. In almost every instance careful reading cannot help but result in the suspicion that these expulsions and voluntary quits were—and it is painful, very painful, for me to say this—quite probably rigged."

Dr. Edward Sampson, a dark, intent man, medical director of one of the country's largest research institutions, and chairman of the board, waited until the rumble of shocked comment died down, then asked, "John, why were these letters written? I mean, at this late date? And to whom?" He picked up a stapled sheaf of documents from his folder. "This letter, for example, is not addressed to any of the college personnel. At least, any that I know of—"

"No. It is addressed to a student, one of a group that took the action, on their own initiative, of tracking down these former students to protect a classmate they believed was about to get the same treatment, differing perhaps in kind but not in intent. If you'll be patient, Sam—"

"I'll try," said Sampson grimly. "But something smells to high heaven."

"It does. Now—" For almost an hour Vidal reviewed in detail the cases that lay before them, adding to what was documented the information he had been able to gather personally.

At the conclusion he leaned back in his chair for the first time. "These cases have one significant similarity—"

"Don't beat around the bush, John," said Sampson. "They're all Negroes. With one exception. The student"—he flipped through his folder quickly—"the student—Meadows—who became engaged to a Quimby scholarship girl while he was here—and married her later. Damned clever of you to tack that pertinent bit of information on the end, like an afterthought."

Vidal, turning to him almost angrily, spoke bitterly: "I'm not clever. Not even particularly discerning, as I should be in this job. I let these things happen, do you understand? These things happened right under my eyes. Which I did not know were quite so astigmatic."

A man halfway down the table, Dr. Henry Parrish, whose reputation as the Midwest's leading psychiatrist had begun to spread nationwide, said quietly: "Relax, John. We're equally to blame. More than one thing is evident in these reports. The role played by Goodhue sticks out a mile. One can't escape him. Suppose you stop blaming yourself and give us the story of the student these young people are concerned about."

"David Champlin is the student's name," said Vidal. "I am sure none of you has heard of him. I've met him, of course, and been much impressed. Since this broke I have asked for special reports on him from such of his instructors as I could get hold of, and am even more impressed. Now, this story must, of necessity, get into some very unsavory details—"

"Unsavory?" The newest member of the board, a young scientist named Patterson, walked to the side table for coffee, spoke over his shoulder, eyebrows raised.

"Unsavory. And it will be climaxed by another story, and grave charges."

Vidal told them of what he had learned about the incident involving David and Clevenger, and then of the apparently unrelated incident of Sutherland's unofficial departure from the Infirmary and trip home on Thanksgiving weekend. "It was in my opinion a minor, very minor, infringement of rules under the circumstances. The pressures involved in an impulsive action like that must be taken into account. It most certainly was not grave enough to prompt the dean to call a committee meeting to consider Champlin's expulsion. Unless some additional charges could be brought forward." Vidal sighed, his first evidence of nervous fatigue. "No charge was forthcoming, at least then, but a rumor popped up that was rather startlingly coincident with the Sutherland episode. And that was a rumor that Champlin was a homosexual. If enough substantiation could be found for it, it would, of course, have justified a quiet request that he leave. Or expulsion, if he proved uncooperative. I, for one, place absolutely no credence in the rumor and am definitely suspicious of its source. We have pretty well established the fact that Clevenger was in a position to clear Champlin of a charge of sneaking Sutherland out of the Infirmary. Also, of course, Clevenger was in a position to spike any homosexual rumors, although he could hardly be expected to do so. In fact, there is evidence that the rumor might have originated with him, possibly in retaliation for the physical rebuff he received at Champlin's hands.

"You would all be justified in thinking that, after all, a situation like this is unfortunate but hardly justifies a full board meeting; that it could and should be handled by the authorities here. The matter of the expelled students requires further and more detailed investigation, and under ordinary circumstances consultation with the dean. What you have heard so far explains in part why this has not been done. What you will hear in a moment explains it fully." He knew there was only one way, both practically and morally, to lay the full story of Goodhue before them, and that was to support it with the proof that had so horrified him two days before at a meeting in Chicago with the elder Evans.

He looked at his watch. "If he has been prompt, a man named Stewart Prentiss is waiting to make a report to us. When I was in Chicago on Tuesday I read this report. Mr. Prentiss is a semiretired private investigator of excellent repute. He is a friend of Bull Evans. It is not easy for anyone in my position to admit that there has been any kind—any kind whatsoever—of espionage going on in his own domain. In fact, it's damnably humiliating. My resignation is yours for the asking—"

"What the hell! Cut out that kind of talk, John—" The exclamation came from a stormy and unorthodox academician whose fame rested on his devastating attacks in print on most current theories of human behavior.

Vidal stood and walked to the door, called, "Miss Ames—" and when his secretary appeared, asked, "Is Mr. Prentiss here yet?"

"He just arrived, Mr. Vidal."

"Ask him to be kind enough to wait just a few moments. I'll call him shortly."

When he returned to the head of the table he did not sit down, but stood behind his chair, his hands grasping its back. "So far," he said, "we've been more or less formal. Now I want to be informal. Unlike many colleges, Pengard has chosen its governors, not for wealth or influence, but because of their acknowledged positions in the vanguard of human thought. We let the wealthy in on the less-important jobs. They're just as pleased. After you have heard what Mr. Prentiss has to tell you, it's my hope that each one of you will forget his vanguard position, so to speak, and become, mentally, an old-fashioned parent, with an old-fashioned concern for the moral and psychological welfare of a well-loved son. I am conversant with the modern theories of psychiatrists, doctors, and psychologists in the field of homosexuality. I am in accord with many of them. However, at this point I choose to ignore all of them because I am emotionally involved in the welfare of young men—all young men. The future of the students who are involved in what you are about to hear is a problem we must approach prayerfully, and with all the understanding, compassion, and knowledge that we possess. This problem can be considered later. The problem of the faculty member involved is one that I, for one, cannot approach with objectivity. Perhaps it will come later. Right now, though, let's forget if we can the joy and peace of objectivity and become involved."

He walked to the door again, nodded to his secretary, and when Stu Prentiss entered, placed a chair beside his own at the head of the table. He introduced each man individually to the newcomer, certain in his own mind that Prentiss would remember them all.

Stu Prentiss talked well, was awed by no one, knew all mankind to be frail and full of faults, including members of college boards of governors, trustees, regents, or overseers. He had never minced words with any client, and he did not mince them now; he merely tailored them, as he always had, to fit the minds of his audience.

He took a folder from his briefcase and laid it on the table in front of him. "That is a long and very detailed report. There are only two copies of it, this original and a carbon. I retain the carbon, President Vidal has the original. When you learn what it contains I am sure you'll agree with us that it wouldn't do to have multiple copies of it floating around. Because of its length and detail I am not going to read it. I prefer to tell the story in my own words, and refer to the report for answers to any questions."

Prentiss leaned back in his chair, legs crossed, apparently relaxed and very much at ease. He might have been discussing a survey of weather conditions in the Appalachian Mountains during the spring months. Only a marked reddening of the scar on his forehead showed any emotional involvement in the subject matter of the report.

"During the first week in December the father of one of the students at Pengard College, a man I have known for many years, called on me to investigate what appeared to be the homosexual activities of the dean of men, Merriwether Goodhue." He had known his opening statement would set off a tumult of comment, like firecrackers on a string, and he waited for it to die down. "I hope none of you gentlemen feel inclined to blame the authorities here for not spotting it before. This accusation, particularly in a place like this, is about as vicious a weapon as a man can wield. You don't toss it around carelessly. And like so many things, those closest to it are often the last to know. Like the wronged wife. It is not an accusation that a parent can make on the basis of a 'hunch' by his son, based on some trick of the accused's personality or some vaguely suspicious circumstance. Proof is needed, and proof is damned hard to get. I shall tell you how I went about securing proof, and if you are interested in exact dates, times, that sort of thing, you will find these details in the written report."

He gave them a broad outline of how he had gathered his information, how he learned from Mrs. Goodhue of the trips to Chicago and New York, of their dates and frequency, and the hotels her husband preferred to stay in when she did not accompany him.

"Good God!" said Patterson. "The man's own wife—"

Prentiss looked at him impassively. "I'm afraid we live in different ethical climates, Mr. Patterson. No matter what the source of my evidence, it cannot be ignored. Constitutional rights or any other kind don't mean much in a case like this, at least as far as getting information is concerned—"

He told of persuading a young friend, a former newspaper reporter and now a free-lance photo-journalist, to help him tie the dean's out-of-town visits to the absences from the campus of certain students, and then of the final routine steps of checking with hotel detectives. "The dean was under a common misapprehension—that you can lose yourself in a large hotel. Actually, the house detectives in a large hotel are much more observant and inquiring of mind than those in the smaller, family-type hotels. For one thing, they are better trained, with better backgrounds; for another, they are usually on the lookout for the very people I mentioned—those who think they can lose themselves. My writer friend was able to get several candid pictures of the dean on campus. He was readily identified in several places as the man who had been traveling with, in some instances, his son; in others, his nephew. In one New York hotel, and one Chicago hotel, we were fortunate enough to get an identification of the boys, also using photographs that were taken without the subjects' being aware of it."

"How did he explain to his wife that he stayed in a different hotel when he was traveling without her?" asked Patterson, who seemed to be the only man at the table able to formulate words.

Prentiss shrugged. "I have the impression that he has her pretty well under his thumb. The trips, ostensibly, were to meet some professor friend or attend some special lecture, something like that, and the other hotel was more conveniently located. And, of course, he convinced her that he could not afford to take her. As for his companions—they attended concerts, stage presentations, were escorted around art galleries—the bait, as you can see, specially chosen to appeal to their individual enthusiasms. Even major-league baseball."

The specialist on human behavior gave a short bark. "He'd have had a ball if he could have wangled half a dozen tickets to the World Series." He looked around at his fellow governors. "This is a helluva thing," he said. "I don't mean to be flip about it. It's a sort of cockeyed reaction to shock, I guess—"

Prentiss said: "I'm almost through. There's a clincher, however. It's a situation that I think would have resulted in his exposure even if I had not been called in. My investigator tipped me off to a youngster here named Sessions, who lives in Detroit. Something the boy said about passing up a number of chances to go to Chicago and New York to attend some concerts—he's majoring in music—made my man suspicious. I talked to the boy myself. He's a nice kid. He was leery of me at first, but with young people you have to be honest. You can fool an astute businessman, but it's hard to fool that astute adult in the formative stages. Eventually he seemed relieved to have someone to talk to about it. He and his family, or at least his father, apparently aren't very close. The boy told me Goodhue finally gave up on him and seemed to be concentrating on a student named Clevenger. This was after Sessions had shied away from Goodhue's discreet and indirect advances."

Prentiss did his work well. There were few questions to be asked when he finished; all that remained was the need to adjust to the shock of his revelations, and to plan future action. When he left them, declining Vidal's invitation to dinner on plea of taking an evening plane to New York, he had performed the minor miracle of being a bringer of bad tidings who had made friends. After the door had closed behind him Sampson said, "Who's paying him?"

"Bull Evans," said Vidal. "He told me Prentiss was an old friend and a sort of courtesy uncle to his son. Prentiss refused a fee, agreeing only to accept actual expenses. I'm certain the other two men have insisted on sharing that."

"We pay it," said Sampson. "Plus whatever his fee would have been. This isn't entirely generosity. I want it on the record that Pengard hired him, not outsiders, even if they are parents. Will you make arrangements, John?"

"I was hoping someone would say that. I would have proposed it later if no one had. It will take a formal motion at the after-dinner meeting."

"You'll have it."

The men were moving about the room now, refilling coffee cups, talking aimlessly around the subject, letting off steam generally. Dr. Parrish made his way to Vidal's side. "Take the weekend off, John. Get up in the mountains. Get away from the mess for a couple of days. You'll function better for it."

"Run away? You should be the last to advise that, Henry."

"I have a few old-fashioned theories."

"I wish I knew what steps to take with the Clevenger lad. There's nothing to pin anything on, only a moral certainty that he's taking petty revenge in a far from petty way."

"It's more than a petty revenge, John. It's a bitter, sick thing, and his inner unhappiness is in direct ratio to the bitterness and sickness. If there is nothing to be done—that's what I would advise doing. I doubt that he will continue with this, and I think the other boy's friends and the boy himself will ride out the rumor."

"Leave Clevenger to the not so tender mercies of his classmates?"

"It could be a harsh sentence, but I think at the moment it's the best. I'd hesitate to advise expulsion or even asking him to leave. You only martyr him and quite possibly make it tougher on Champlin."

"Thanks, Henry. I'll take your advice to the extent of adopting a wait-and-see policy. Wait a moment and drive to the house with me. We're having cocktails there before dinner—" Vidal walked to the table, rapped it with his knuckles for attention. "Before we break up, gentlemen, one final word. You might be keeping in mind our agenda for this evening. We must consider ways and means of clearing the records of such students as in our judgment were wrongfully expelled, reinstating them if they desire it. Then we must take care of the matter of payment for Mr. Prentiss. As for the third, at nine o'clock Dean Goodhue will appear before us. He has already been confronted with the evidence. I did this myself, as a sop to my self-respect. I told him we would, of course, listen to his side of the story if he cared to present it. He made no comment, merely stated that he would appear. Now—shall we leave all this behind for a short period?"

Dean Goodhue, crossing the inner quadrangle on his way to his office in the Administration Building, saw a tall stranger leaving the small, Swiss-cottage type of building that housed the office of the president, the board room, and a small dining room for informal faculty luncheons. As the stranger came closer, Goodhue looked away and quickened his step. Elacoya had been right in her description, even to the scar on the forehead. Goodhue felt no fear now, no apprehension about what this man had been doing in the president's domain. He knew. In less than four hours he would go into that building and face the board of governors. He slipped a hand inside his coat, felt the envelope in the inner pocket. After the past four weeks he was drained dry, exhausted by fear; it would be a relief to lay that letter on the table before them and walk out, no longer dean of men at Pengard College. He had no doubt that they would accept his resignation.

37

JOSEPH CHAMPLIN REMEMBERED that his mother had always been very firm in her admonitions against pride, either in self or in possessions. It was one of the graver sins, she said, but on David's graduation day he succumbed to pride without a struggle. If it was a sin, then he was going to sin like five hundred on this day because there could never be one like it again.

Bad weather during graduation week and predictions of worse for commencement day resulted in all final-week festivities at Pengard being carried on indoors, the final ceremony being held in the auditorium instead of the traditional location—a grassy slope just north of the lake. Quimby Auditorium was a comparatively new building, Mrs. Horace

Quimby's last gift to the college before she died, not completed until after her death. The architect had given to modern form an atmosphere of cathedral-like spaciousness and grandeur. The wide, deep balcony seemed to float above the lower floor without visible support except the shallow staircases ascending on each side. At its rear similar staircases descended to the inner lobby. Today the balcony was a sea of black gowns and mortarboards rising gently from the front row to high, vaulted windows where an unpredictable summer sun threw its rays across them and down to the auditorium below.

Joseph Champlin, on the main floor, sat beside his friend Bjarne Knudsen, a few rows back from the front seats reserved for faculty. He sat quietly, without stirring, almost lost to sight between the bulk of the Professor and the figure of a fat stranger on his right. Above, from the first-row seat, David Champlin could see his grandfather and the Prof clearly. Gramp looked so damned tiny, especially from this distance, thought David, and so straight and proud. The small, dark head, level with the Prof's shoulders, never turned, and David knew Li'l Joe's eyes were dutifully fixed on the stage where an eminent modern philosopher was giving what might be an inspiring address if he paid attention to it, which he wasn't doing. He knew Gramp was paying even less because Gramp's thoughts were damned near visible, even with only the back of the carefully groomed, close-cropped head to be seen.

Li'l Joe was not only not paying attention, he was grateful for the respite the commencement address gave him, the chance to collect his thoughts and get set for seeing David walk up there and get his diploma. He had been in Laurel two days, and it seemed like he hadn't had a minute to breathe. Without moving his head he directed his eyes to the third row back on the other side of the aisle where Lawrence Travis sat beside that fine-looking white wife of his. Lord, Lord, who'd have thought that Li'l Joe Champlin would ever be having lunch with a great man like that the way he and the Prof had done the day before? And that this man's son would be one of his grandson's best friends. And you couldn't fault the man, not anywhere. Li'l Joe supposed Lawrence Travis must have eaten with kings and queens maybe, and presidents and big shots all over the world, and just yesterday he'd been eating ribs with Li'l Joe Champlin in a place called Mom's, and laughing fit to kill over some of Li'l Joe's stories about home, telling a lot himself; he'd been a Louisiana boy, country Louisiana boy, and he'd never forgotten.

Li'l Joe was glad this wasn't his first trip to Laurel. He had spent two weekends there in David's third year and another one earlier this year, and met all of David's friends, and had a chance to become accustomed to the way things were. David's friends had treated him like royalty, and they were all nice kids, every one of them, colored *and* white. The second time he came up, that little boy who didn't look like much more'n a child, named Tom, saw him walking through the gate with David, and let out a regular war whoop—"Hey! There's Gramp!" and ran up to them, then stopped, pink and blushing. "Gee, sir, I'm sorry. Bet I sounded fresh. Only, that's the way we all think of you—" It had been hard to take in, a white boy apologizing to him for calling him something like "Gramp" and calling him "sir" and all.

He wished he could have met the boy David called Sudsy, and his father, the big doctor up in Boston. David had been way up there to visit them two or three times. The first time he went was at the end of his second year, and the doctor sent him a round-trip plane ticket, because he wanted David's visit to be a surprise birthday present for that sick boy of his. David had been up in Chicago, too, had driven up in that God-awful yellow car with Tom, met his folks. The Prof told him about Tom's father, all he'd done for the workingman, but it didn't impress him too much; there were workingmen and workingmen, and they came in different colors and no one knew it better than the unions down where he lived. Still, he guessed from what the Prof said that this man, Bull Evans, was trying, and he sure was a well-met man, friendly, a little like the Prof.

Li'l Joe resolutely tried to keep his mind from dwelling on Sara Kent. She was all girl, all woman, li'l piece of a thing she was, and as sweet and nice as they come, but whenever she and David were together Li'l Joe felt as worried as a mother cat with kittens in a kennel full of dogs. Maybe the dogs didn't mean no harm, but— He'd be relieved when David got up north there in Boston where he'd be so busy learning law that he wouldn't have time for a little girl who could come mighty close to worming her way into even Li'l Joe's affections if he'd let her. He'd met her father the night before, shaken hands with him, and sensed the same worry in him.

Of them all, thought Li'l Joe, it was the big, awkward

white boy they called Chuck he took to the most. That accent had thrown him off at first, but David told him not to pay it any mind. And he'd been right. He felt sorry for the boy, too. He knew from David how Chuck's family wouldn't have anything to do with him and why. These past two days Chuck had stuck with him and David and the Prof, which was fine; time like this a young fellow wanted to feel he belonged somewhere with someone.

All around him were folks who were there for the same reason he was: to see their young ones graduate. Yet only those few who were of his own people could be feeling the way he was feeling. A lot of those folks around him would be taking it for granted; they'd known that sooner or later they'd see their kids graduate from college. But the son of the first David Champlin sure hadn't known any such thing, scrambling to make a dime when his own son, John, was born. That Li'l Joe Champlin could never have known that someday he'd be waiting in a big, beautiful building like this, waiting to see John's son get a diploma from a famous college; couldn't even have thought it, wouldn't dared have thought it. He wished John could see this, that big, quiet son of his who hadn't lived to know his own baby. Maybe he did. Geneva—Lord, Lord, he knew Geneva could see it. He could feel Geneva right there, close as the Prof's big shoulder beside him. And Tant'Irene, too, who said so often, "Never forget your 'thank-you's,' son." She was close by, too. Li'l Joe's lips moved without sound. Seemed like he shouldn't just think it; seemed like he should say it with his mouth, even if no one could hear—"Thank you, Jesus."

Above and behind there was a sustained rumble, and every head in the auditorium turned back and up. The graduates in the first two rows were standing, men on one side of the center aisle, women on the other. They filed slowly to the staircases on each side and then down and along the side aisles, while the next two rows stood, ready to fall in behind. The Prof's brother had told him the plan. They would approach the stage, mount its side steps; then a girl student would advance and receive her diploma and a handshake from the president, walk to the temporary steps in center stage, descend into the body of the auditorium and march up the center aisle, while her male opposite number, just behind her, followed the same procedure. The procession of black-gowned young people would then pass into the inner lobby to ascend its stairways to the balcony again.

Li'l Joe began to worry about David. Would he leave, like he did every now and then, a blob of lather on his earlobe after shaving? Would he have been fussing with his tie up there in the balcony, nervous, and spoiled the knot? And then, abruptly, there was David, walking up the steps at the far side of the stage, taller than anyone in front or behind, tall, tall—and straight and scarcely limping at all, eyes dead ahead, face so solemn it looked almost sad. Feeling all that responsibility, thought Li'l Joe, then caught his breath, held it while David received his diploma and shook hands with the president, heard the microphone pick up the words, "Well done, Champlin—" then let the breath out in a long sigh. His eyes were too moist to see David coming down the steps and start up the aisle, but he blinked frantically so that when the boy passed his row of seats he caught the wide grin and the wink.

His eyes cleared completely and suddenly at an unexpected and loud "Harrrrumph!" from the seat next to him. It startled him so that he jumped and then edged over in his seat when the Prof's elbow jostled him as the big man fumbled in his pocket for the handkerchief into which he blew his nose with controlled violence. After that the Prof looked straight ahead, very stiff, shoulders squared, as though he'd been caught doing something he shouldn't and was trying by his attitude to deny any knowledge of it. Li'l Joe smiled. If the Prof could blow his nose to cover up, he could, too, and he did so, only quietly and gently. He felt the Prof's shoulder shake, looked up to find the bearded face and blue eyes turned to him, and the two men laughed together, at each other, silently and happily.

The loud "Harrrumph" that had so startled Li'l Joe had also startled its perpetrator. It had been as involuntary as a sneeze. Like his companion, Bjarne Knudsen had been caught unawares when David Champlin had appeared on the stage in front of him. The man selected to speak at the commencement was an old friend, but Knudsen had never dreamed he could be so dull. He recalled uncomfortably that he himself, when asked for comment by his brother, had heartily recommended him to deliver the commencement address.

He sighed, and deliberately detached his mind from what was being said onstage. He was very conscious of the wisp of a man who sat beside him, and equally conscious of the presence of that man's grandson somewhere above them. Unlike

Li'l Joe, he had no misgivings about pride; he rejoiced in it and knew, with Li'l Joe, that there would never be a day more filled with it, no matter what heights of achievement were reached by the dark boy in mortar board and gown waiting now to be formally graduated from Pengard College —*summa cum laude*.

Bjarne Knudsen had learned, some from his brother, a little from David, of what the boy had faced at college, although it was not until the end of David's junior year that he had been able to sit down with his brother Karl and really discuss David's career. Karl and Eve had spent the previous summer in Europe; there had been no time for visiting during the bulk of the following year, and letters, especially Karl's, were unsatisfactory.

He remembered that first really informative discussion now, while he waited for the climax of the commencement ceremonies. He had arrived at his brother's late in the afternoon. David was not mentioned either before or during dinner. When Karl suggested inviting friends in after dinner, Bjarne said, "No. Tomorrow perhaps. Tonight I want to talk." Eve Knudsen touched his shoulder in a quick gesture of affection and said, "This is news?" and he roared at her. "Woman! You speak with a forked tongue, like the serpent! Karl, you should not permit your wife to abuse your brother—"

" 'Not permit'? If you had possessed the courage I did, and married, you'd know that you are talking nonsense."

"But they made only one Eve. What could I do? I must content myself with variety—"

"A lecherous, promiscuous old man—that's what you'll be when you grow up," said Eve.

"Ah, I hope so, Eve, I hope so. I am trying—"

After dinner Eve set out schnapps and Danish beer, with cheese and crackers, and he sat on the big couch, Karl and Eve facing each other across the fireplace in front of him. He had not been content, because he had been troubled, but he remembered the comfort of that room that night, and his realization that this was the only place in which he felt a deep loneliness, this room with its fire and its man and woman.

Before Eve started knitting she said, "Do you want me to leave? Or sit and knit and gather wisdom at your feet?"

"Stay, Eve," said Bjarne. "You are always welcome. And you do not gather wisdom; you dispense it."

After they were served and beer foamed in long slender glasses, Bjarne said, "About my boy, David. I do not want to ask questions, Karl. I want you to tell me your thoughts, without my leading or prompting you."

"Are you asking about him as a scholar? He will make the honors list, undoubtedly a *cum laude*. But—" Karl shrugged. "Almost any student of his ability and brains could do the same if he devoted himself almost wholly to study and classwork."

"It's not right. Not what I hoped. He would make honors without doing that. I know the boy."

"I agree. What is your impression of him when he is at home? Allow me a few questions also."

"I do not want to talk about my impressions; I want yours. And Eve's. But I will say this. He is quieter, yes, and it is not just the quietness of added maturity. He has many reticences. All his people, we realize, have many reticences, too many, and too tragic. But he has new ones he did not have before."

"Ja." Karl Knudsen was silent for a moment, then sighed deeply. *"Ja."* He refilled his brother's glass and resumed his seat. "He has been lonely, although he has good friends, many of them. Perhaps he has not even known that he was lonely. Or perhaps he has preferred loneliness to exposing himself to further possible hurt. Yet by the end of his sophomore year I believe the rumors and talk had almost entirely subsided. Goodhue's resignation—you must have known this would happen—set off a terrific buzz of talk on campus. It could be that some of the students with whom he was involved and who did not go along with his—er—ideas felt free to talk. I don't know. Our students are well able to do the simple mathematical problem of two plus two. Goodhue now exposed as a homosexual—it got around with fantastic speed, Bjarne—his bias toward David, his liking for Clevenger, and David's action in knocking Clevenger out when he made a pass. That, too, swept through the campus like a forest fire. All these things helped discredit any malicious rumor. Our students aren't fools; they examine. And I believe certain of David's loyal friends had a good deal to do with all of this, and with, I believe, getting Clevenger to assist them—"

Eve spoke quietly from the depths of her wing chair. "We more than 'believe,' Karl. We know."

"Yes. Well. David must have been aware of all this, yet it made no difference. It was as if he feared another attack from ambush and walked very quietly."

"What have his outside activities been, Karl? He says nothing at home except that he's been so loaded with studying there hasn't been much time for anything."

"Bah! Much of this loading he has done himself. Plenty of less able students than David Champlin will also graduate high in their class and yet will have found time for the activities I would have liked to see him take part in. Drama, poetry readings and discussions, music, many recreational activities. Do you know we have an intercollegiate chess champion in our junior class? Laugh, but that is good. David plays chess now and then with Andrus. A promising player, Andrus tells me."

"No social life at all, Karl?"

"Little, on campus. While Wilson—Nehemiah—was here he spent a good deal of time with him. He spends some time with the two students Simmons and Dunbar, now, although at first there was real antagonism between them. Now there seems to be only friendly and pleasant wrangling. Then there are Evans, Travis—whom he also plays chess with—Martin. They are together quite a bit. But they too are good students, not group-minded, and spend considerable time studying. You have met them. Evans is planning on a master's in English, so that he may teach, odd though it may seem. Travis wants to write. I hear he has already started a book. Martin—"

"David. David. It is David in whom I am interested."

"He continues to earn money playing piano weekends at the Calico Cat—he must have told you—and the club recently moved to larger quarters. Not because of David, but I believe it has been of financial help to him. He works out on a punching bag and on the rings and bars in the gymnasium several times a week. Andrus says he is working off his aggressions. I have watched him. He is a magnificent specimen. I understand that every so often he goes over to Laurel on a Wednesday night to a Negro church there and sings. Sometimes he does this on Sundays at a church in Cincinnati where Nehemiah Wilson's aunt and uncle go. Occasionally he stays with them weekends when he remains in the city. He attends some of the ALEC meetings here, but not regularly. I have been to some of the meetings myself—I learned a great deal last year. I cannot say that I wonder at David's lack of interest. It is not well administered here. The guiding light is the minister of our Episcopal church down the road, who likes to be known as Father McCartney. He reminds me of nothing so much as a kind and optimistic angel flapping around the edges of a stinking swamp, searching for the pretty flowers that grow there so that he may pick them and talk about them. Of the swamp itself he knows nothing."

Bjarne Knudsen laughed, scattering cracker crumbs. "May I tell this to David?"

"I have already expressed my opinion to David. He is in complete agreement."

"He is a realist, like all his people."

"Sara." Eve Knudsen dropped the word quietly into the conversation between the two men, and their talk stopped.

"Ah, yes," said Bjarne at last. "Sara."

"They're in love." Eve spread her knitting over one knee, began counting rows, and could have been remarking on the number of them.

Her husband said, "You are right, Eve, to bring it up." He turned to his brother. "It is true."

"I know, I know!" Bjarne Knudsen bristled visibly. "You think I am a fool? It is very clear, even to a bachelor. And difficult."

"Not for Sara," said Eve. "The difficulties seem to be in David's thinking."

Bjarne said: "I have known Sara almost as long as you have, Eve. Or at least as long as Karl. There would be no difficulties for Sara if she loved. But with David it is different. He sees not only the difficulties and pressures the world will present to them, but the difficulties and pressures from within themselves, their own hearts and minds. He is very much a man of his people. He will always be. And he is an extremely intelligent one, and a farsighted one. One does not see David Champlin forgetting, in the happiness of the present, the picture of what the years ahead could bring. And what he has been through here has only sharpened his awareness. Or so I believe."

"Karl and I are unhappy about it," said Eve. "Not because they are in love, you understand, but because neither one of them seems to have very good sense. Sara has no patience, and David no 'give'—it doesn't make sense—"

"It makes sense, Eve," said Bjarne. "It makes a sad sense. Yet it may work out. It may—if we let them alone, if we do not force our middle-aged romanticism upon them. Harvard, the North, his career—they may give David a different perspective, a deeper understanding, more courage—"

"Perhaps by then," said Karl, "they will be over it."

"No," said Bjarne, quietly for him when in a contradictory mood. "No. They will not. I can promise you this."

Today, more than a year after that conversation with his brother, remembering it, Bjarne Knudsen was conscious not only of David sitting, unseen, behind them, but also of Sara, both looking serious and proud in their gowns and mortarboards. He wanted to reach out a hand to each, draw them together, say, "Take what life has given you and be thankful, and take the suffering with it and be thankful, too. . . ."

He suddenly realized that the man who was a stimulating friend and such an unforgivably boring speaker had stopped talking and that President Vidal was standing at the long table with its twin cases of diplomas just behind it, prayerfully arranged and watched over so that the proper one would be handed to him just as the student for whom it was intended approached. The possibility of a slipup in this procedure fascinated Knudsen. He remembered one such nightmare ceremony at his own university—there was a rumbling behind, and he and Li'l Joe looked back and saw the first row of students filing across the balcony to the upper staircases—then he watched carefully and saw with relief that things were going smoothly for the first eight students. He drew in a breath sharply, because there was David just coming onto the stage—the David he had seen first cradled in a bureau drawer with Geneva Champlin standing over him knowing her God was in there with the child, knowing it; the David of the round dark eyes and the soft mouth rimmed with ice cream, playing with battered secondhand toys; the David looking very small and brown in a hospital bed trying to fight back tears of pain and fright, saying, "Prof—Prof—where's my Gramp? Isn't my Gramp coming back?"

David's diploma was in his hands now and he was turning smartly and coming forward to the head of the steps in the center of the stage. He was looking straight ahead as he limped, no slower than the others, down the steps and up the aisle, very solemn and intent. It was the unexpected smile that lightened the dark face, the broad wink that took in both him and Li'l Joe that brought on the loud and startling "Harrumph!" and the embarrassing flood of moisture to his eyes. He reached for his handkerchief, amazed at his own weakness—he had thought better of himself—and blew his nose. In a minute there was the gentle sound of Li'l Joe doing the same, and Knudsen's feeling became one of amusement. Two grown men, side by side—it was a wondrous disgrace. He glanced down and was looking into Li'l Joe's face, into his eyes that were still moist, and then Li'l Joe's soundless laughter joined with his. He knew that they could not share again just this particular, private happiness, and he wanted never to forget it.

Now, in less than an hour, it would be all over, thought David, and it hadn't been too bad; it hadn't been what you'd call exactly good, but it hadn't been too bad and he supposed that if he could say that about all the experiences of the lifetime that lay ahead, he would be more fortunate, far more fortunate, than most. The mess of his sophomore year had done other things besides sharpen his wariness; it had built a wall around him that not even Joshua's army, blowing every horn in New Orleans, could topple, and from behind that wall had come *summa cum laude*. There were a few, seated behind and around him, who had climbed over the wall and visited with him there, and they'd been welcome because finally they understood that this was where he wanted to be. And there was Sara, always. And God give him strength now to think of it as "was" and not "is."

But even if it had been all bad and there had been no Sara, the sight of two men easily discernible in the auditorium below him would have made up for it. Gramp had not understood about *summa cum laude*, and the Prof had explained, not talking down but making it clear, and Gramp had been without words to express his pride. When he did speak he grinned and said, "That ain't luck, son. That's you." David knew that he could get every degree the world of law had to offer, sit on the bench of the U.S. Supreme Court, and there would never be happiness and pride such as he saw now in Gramp's face.

Meanwhile, he was Pengard, *summa cum laude;* it was all over, thank God, and maybe someday when he heard the college song he'd feel nostalgic and maudlin, but he doubted it.

Graduation night was a time of well-bred, well-educated bedlam on the Pengard campus. The larger of the residence halls put on elaborate buffets, overseen by undergraduates, and relatives and faculty roamed the campus in the tow of gowned sons and daughters, from buffet to buffet, on a sort of progressive supper party, except for a select few of the students who preferred to give small parties in their rooms. By tradition graduates kept on their gowns.

He had finally agreed, after pleading that was close to tearful from Chuck, to prepare red beans for the Quimby House buffet. It was the only one of the small residence halls serving buffet, and he sent Chuck up town for the necessary ingredients. As he watched the awkward blond boy drive off in baggy slacks and sweater, he wondered how he'd look in a dark suit and clerical collar with that mop of no-color hair and that earnest, country-boy face, standing in a pulpit. He couldn't picture it, yet he had not been in the least surprised when Chuck had told him of his decision to enter a theological seminary in New York after graduation. They had been changing the Yellow Peril to a car thereafter known only as the Peril, spraying it a dark blue. The paper shielding a side window became detached, and spray from Chuck's gun hit the glass full force. Chuck had said—"Doggone—" and David had laughed. "One of these days, you're going to cuss real bad and the world's going to come to a shrieking end. You and Tom. Only, he can do a good job of it if he's stirred up enough. What it is usually, you two sound like a Boy Scout handbook."

"Too late to start now, dad. I'm going to enter a seminary, study for the ministry, if I get out of here with a diploma in my hand—"

"The hell you say!"

"Father McCartney's recommending me. It looks like it's going through O.K.—"

"You have to have that? A recommendation?"

"Yes. I know you're not exactly crazy about him—"

"He's O.K."

"He's helped me a lot. And I talked with the dean yesterday about realigning my schedule and—well, that's it. O.K. with you, Papa Champlin?"

David grinned at him over the hood of the car. "It's fine with me, Chuck. I—well, honestly, I'm not surprised. It doesn't shake me up or anything. Maybe I've sort of expected it ever since—" he hesitated, awkward with the words, and started again—"ever since that night at the ALEC meeting when Nehemiah sounded off. I saw you afterward—"

"I guess I made up my mind, sort of, that night. Only, I didn't know it. Seemed as though it came gradually, but I don't think it did. Sometimes I think we make decisions in our subconscious minds and don't know it, like going into the ministry or committing murder or something. Then for a long time our conscious mind fights 'em and then one day something comes along and the conscious mind gives up and there's the decision—all made and ready for action. Maybe Nehemiah was what did it."

David inspected the shields over the headlights intently, not looking at Chuck. Just talking about Nehemiah made him half sick with a kind of frustrated anger, and it didn't do any good. There was a rage inside and nothing to rage at, nothing to hit out at. Nehemiah, just nineteen, dead someplace in Korea after the Army took him. And the hell of it, the damned hell of it, was that the Army hadn't really taken him; he'd walked in like a damned fool and said, "Here I am." Nehemiah!

He'd done everything but get down on his knees to the crazy ape. "Man, you're out of your mind!" He'd almost been yelling. "I'm telling you, man, telling you—hell, I've been telling you for two years—that I'll work with you all summer and in vacation, help you catch up. God damn it, you ought to have known that just math wouldn't do it, should have studied more! It's not too late. Who told you you'd flunk out?"

"Beanie."

"Oh." David's face fell. "You're his favorite guy as far as math is concerned. He must have felt bad about it himself—"

"I guess he did—"

"But didn't he tell you if you'd catch up on the other stuff you could come back in the fall—get deferred if your grades were good enough then? I'll do everything I can, man—"

"Cool off. It's too late anyhow. I already put in for the Army."

"Oh, my God! Oh, Chrisalmighty! How crazy can you act! I'm asking you—why!"

Nehemiah shrugged, sank lower in his chair in David's room and looked up at David under lowered eyebrows. "Because I'm just plain sick of the place, that's one reason. Look what happened to you. If I never see another Goddamned ofay face I'll be too happy to stand it. Anyhow, I started too late; I couldn't make it anyhow. It's not a bad deal, the Army. They train you. Hell, man, I'm a hot mathematician. You think they won't use that? They got a lot of soft jobs in the Army, technical jobs and stuff, for a guy who can handle mathematics like I can. And this way I'm not flunked out.

And the Army's waiting until the end of the term, till I get in two full years here. The Army's got its little khaki tongue hanging out, waiting for Nehemiah. Come a war, don't matter how much they hate us, they gotta have Sam—"

"Why the Army? Why not the Air Force? That's a helluva lot better deal—"

"Maybe they'd put me in a plane—"

"You no like? And Gramp's going to be wing-walking next trip. They fly you everywhere in the Army, man. Everywhere—"

"They doing it, not me. Anyhow, it's too late now. It's Army—"

"You've gone out of your mind, you've flipped, you're—you're—what the hell, you some kind of a patriot or something?"

"Christ, no! Are you?"

"No. But I'm not saying if I live long enough and things change I couldn't be. I mean I'll take a crack at making things so I could be. As I said, if I live long enough—"

"Long enough to see a white man swing for killing a Negro? You'll be living so long you'll be tired of living. You think it'll hurt to know how to use a gun?"

"You were going to be some kind of technician a few minutes ago."

"I still am. But I hear everybody learns how to shoot. Look, blabbermouth, what would you do, huh? I mean would you join up, I mean if it wasn't for your ankle and your damned A-plus grades?"

"You think I'm stupid or something? Why the hell should I? If they drafted me, sure, I'd go. It's a lot better than five years in jail or whatever. And I'd wind up killing Koreans and Chinese and people who never did a damned thing to me—"

"Compared to what the whites in your own country have done—"

"Well, yes—"

"To you and yours, daddy-o. You and yours. And me and mine. Hell, you know anyone down our way hasn't had two or three in the family what hasn't caught it? Strung up or shot or thrown in jail or some damned thing like that just because they're black? Do you? Or someone who can't tell you about a grandmother or an auntie or a sister didn't have something happen like—like what happened to my mother?

Your Gramp—what about his daddy? And it wasn't enough just what happened to my mother. Long before that happened they found her own brother floating in the river upstate with a rope around his neck. Didn't anyone even bother to find out was he strung up or drownded. Her baby brother what she brought up—"

"You're going in circles again! And still you joined up, you knucklehead?"

"Like I said, it ain't going to do any harm to learn how to fight scientific. And besides, they'd of had me two weeks after I flunked out. This way I get a better deal. Get out faster—"

"If it's too late, I suppose it's too late. But look, people get dead real fast in the Army—"

"Hell, man, they get dead real fast, our people, in Natchez and Bogalusa—and anywhere at all, just anywhere at all, in Plaquemine Parish. And they going to finish off this war before they get around to sending Nehemiah over. I'm telling you, I'm as safe in the Army as I would be in Plaquemine Parish—"

But he hadn't been. On July first he went to basic training. David had three postcards and a couple of letters. The last letter said, "They haven't waked up yet to the fact that the great man's in the Army. They sure take their time—" A card two weeks later said he might be taking a trip soon.

The first week in October, Gramp called him on a Saturday just as he was leaving Quimby House for work, and told him Nehemiah had been killed in action. His family, Gramp said, were upsetted real bad.

That night after work David got drunker than he'd been since the night after he put Sudsy on the train for Boston. And drunk or sober, it didn't make sense.

The next morning he pulled himself together and took Nehemiah's aunt and uncle to church, and sang, standing by the piano, three of the hymns Nehemiah had always liked. And all the time he was singing he was seeing Nehemiah in the recreation room of the church, hearing him: . . . *Were you there? . . . The words, Father. You hear 'em? . . . You wasn't there, but my daddy was there . . . Were you there?* . . . remembering how he'd walked toward the tense, half-hysterical boy, suddenly wanting to pick him up as he would a child and carry him away from any hurts that he had suffered, was suffering, and the hurts that lay ahead as surely as life and the living of it lay ahead.

When church was over and he drove toward Laurel, still nothing made any sense, nothing, not a Goddamned thing, made any sense.

Now as he sat waiting, back in the balcony again, for the ceremony to end and the V.I.P. bishop to pronounce his benediction, Nehemiah had been dead for almost two years; Chuck was all set for the ministry; he, David Champlin, was all set for Harvard Law; Hunter Travis had finished a book; Tom Evans and Margaret Benjamin were both taking their Master's at the University of Chicago next year; Simmons and Dunbar were headed for some kind of literary venture; Clevenger said he was going in for scientific farming, which was all the funnier because he kept saying he wanted to take graduate work at Oxford first—with a B-minus average. And Sara Kent was leaving for Paris to study art. For how long? David didn't know, told himself it had to not matter for how long, or even where, because Sara Kent was Pengard, and Pengard was finished, and he and Sara had known that more than just four college years were over, last week after their last talk together. At least he had thought she knew, but something kept telling him that perhaps she didn't.

When he came out of the auditorium, Gramp and the Prof and Doc Knudsen were ahead of him, talking to Hunter and his mother and father near the auditorium steps. He walked over to them, slid an arm around Gramp's shoulders and gave a strong squeeze, so that Mrs. Travis said, "Gracious, David, I heard bones crack!" He held out his hand to take the Prof's, then hit Hunter's shoulder with a fist. "All over, man!" And Lawrence Travis said, "All God's children got diplomas—"

They talked for a moment, and David said, "I have to run and make sure they aren't letting the beans stick—" and Gramp frowned in worry.

"You sure they going to be all right? You ain't forgot nothing?"

"Always been all right at home, haven't they?"

A quiet voice said with exaggerated formality, "Are you referring to red beans, David Champlin? Louisiana style? Red beans and possibly rice?"

"Sure am, Mr. Travis. At Quimby House."

Lawrence Travis turned to his son. "Is there any law that says we have to eat a cold buffet at your hall, Hunter?"

"Only unwritten. Want to break it?"

"I most certainly do. Marcia, my dear—Dr. Knudsen, Professor, shall we follow David and his grandfather? I promise manna—"

All through the evening, with people coming and going and confusion in all directions, David's eyes went time and again to the door, looking for Sara, not seeing her. He blamed himself for hoping she would come; she had said she wouldn't, said that when they said goodbye at the auditorium that would be it. She wasn't waiting until morning to leave the campus; she and her father and Bull and Tom Evans were driving partway to Chicago that night, the rest of the way the next day. They were going to start right away after the ceremonies. Just when he saw them, in his mind, driving into Cincinnati, he looked toward the doorway to the main hall, and she was there, and Chuck was calling, "There's baby! Beans, Sara, but you'll have to hurry!" She was all in blue, blue coat with a little round collar, fitted over the small perfect bust to the tiny waist, flaring below, darker blue shoes and bag, and a little blue hat with a sailor brim that made her look like a schoolboy straight from a print in a Victorian novel. David did not care whether anyone, anyone at all, thought that he was staring, even Gramp, because this was the way he was going to have to remember her after tonight and he wanted the image clear, down to the last button. She made a quick round of the room, kissing Mrs. Knudsen, hugging Doc and the Prof, was kissed soundly on the cheek by Chuck and Hunter, hugged Gramp, who looked startled to the point of shock, and when Lawrence Travis said, "I'm sorry we've just met—" hugged him and Mrs. Travis also. Then Tom Evans was in the doorway calling, "Sara! Your life's ahead of you—that's what the man said this afternoon—you going to spend it here? We're waiting—" and Sara was standing in front of David, hat askew—Sara, Sara, always with your hat askew—her hand out, but when he took it she did not shake hands but drew him after her into the hall. "Go tell them I'm on the way, Tom—"

In the hall she looked up at him, and one small hand banged the top of her hat and it miraculously straightened, making her the Victorian schoolboy and a Vogue model of the well-dressed modern child all in one. Her eyes were intent and dark, fixed on his. "I'm not going to kiss you, David. That would embarrass you. But you heard what Tom said, and the man said—our lives are ahead of us and stuff. Mine isn't. Mine's here. Mine isn't ahead of me without you. And yours isn't ahead of you without me. And you know it. David, will you write—"

"Sara, it won't be right—Sara, please—"

"I'll see you, David. I don't know when or anything, and I'm not being corny, but I'll see you—maybe you won't even know it—"

And then she was running, really running and not just seeming to, across the hall to the door, forgetting to close the inner door so that through the outer screen door he could see Tom leaning out of a big car, see him pull her in with comradely roughness, then heard the door slam and saw the car drive off.

He dreaded going to his room, stripped and bare now, and going to bed this last night at Quimby House. He went into the Laurel Inn with Gramp and the Prof and sat talking with them over a drink in the cocktail lounge until Gramp yawned abruptly and, eyes watering from the yawn, apologized. He left then, after arranging for the drive to Cincinnati the next day where they would board a train and, to Gramp's twinkling delight, share a bedroom suite to New Orleans. He would follow in the Peril. It wasn't a trip to which he looked forward.

He'd had the foresight to leave a paperback novel out to read, but it might as well have been in Sanskrit. He should have left something out to translate, so he'd have to concentrate, and a hell of a lot of good that would have done either. Sara would have been there—no concentration could have banished her—just as she was there now, in every corner of that empty, bare room, looking at him, laughing, maybe crying. As, God damn it, he wanted to do.

For a long time he'd thought that if he hadn't taken that walk the Sunday he returned from Christmas vacation in sophomore year none of it would have happened. Now he knew it would have because nothing could have stopped it. For some damned, contrary reason known only to an unfeeling God the whole thing had had to be, starting with Sara catching up with him that day on one of the paths to the lake.

It had been late in the afternoon, the winter sunset a pale gold farewell to what warmth there had been in the day that was dying. He had arrived in Cincinnati on Friday from New Orleans, going directly to the home of Nehemiah's uncle, where he had left his car. Friday and Saturday night he remained in Cincinnati, playing at the Calico Cat, and on Sunday morning drove to Laurel. Saturday night, at work, he learned of Goodhue's resignation when a classmate who lived in Cincinnati came into the club with a party and made directly for the piano, grinning, saying, "Let me be the first to congratulate us—"

"Hi, Paul! What're you passing out congratulations about?"

"We no longer have a dean named Goodhue. He's quit. Resigned. Gone from us. It happened Thursday night."

David's hands hit the keyboard in a resounding, crashing chord. "You're kidding!"

"Honest to Gawd."

"You've got to be!"

"I'm not. It so happens that my mother and Mrs. Goodhue belong to the same regional chapter of something or other, and Mrs. Cozy called her and told her. They serve champagne here?"

"Sure do. Order it, but I'm splitting the check with you—"

When he got to Pengard the next day there wasn't anyone around he knew well. Chuck and Tom weren't back yet, nor was Hunter, and he wasn't going to be bothered with anyone else. Except Sara, and he called her at both the Knudsens' and Rainsford Hall and missed her at each place. He unpacked, then took a pair of heavy boots from the closet and put them on over thick wool socks, tucking trouser legs in, turning the tops of the socks over the boots, then put on the green sweater Sara had knit for him. He might run into her, and he wanted her to know he wasn't just being polite when he said it was a perfect fit. A heavy mack left in his room by Chuck, and Sudsy's green stocking cap ought to keep him warm even if he walked down along the lake. It had been snowing a little, and he wanted to be out in it, to feel the strange calm of it, the peace that seemed to lie hidden under its white covering of the land.

He had not reached the lake when Sara caught up with him. He heard her calling to him while she was still a long way off, and by the time she reached him he had unbuttoned his mack and was holding it open so that she could see that he was wearing the sweater.

"It fits!" She was laughing and patting the sweater, tugging it here and there, critical of her own handiwork.

"Sure does, Sara. But you shouldn'ta oughta—"

"I loved doing it, David. I loved every minute of doing it. I drove poor Chuck just about round the bend with fittings.

Button up, idiot, it's not fur. You'll catch cold. Where are you going? Can I go? May I go, I mean. Please?"

"Nowhere." He took her hand and tucked it under his arm, and lost it because it was so small he could not feel it. "You can come if you promise not to skip. I can't skip."

She ignored him, managed to skip anyhow without outstripping him in speed, and said, "David, the news! It's wonderful. Cozy—"

"I know. Paul Cameron told me last night at the Cat."

"Damn you! I wanted to be the first."

"I don't know why or anything. Neither did Paul—"

"I do! I do! I know all about it. David, let's go down to that boathouse, the last one in the row, where they keep the canoes. There's an oil stove there and we can be warm while I tell you. I heard about it late Thursday night. President Vidal called Tom's father, and Tom called me and woke me up and the next day Bull told us all about it. He said we deserved to know." She pulled her hand from under his arm, fumbled in the outsize pockets of her coat. "I've got two sandwiches—and there's always a jar of instant coffee there —come on, David? We never have a chance to really talk—"

He knew that, knew it well, because he'd tried to work it that way. Being alone with Sara in a confined space was something he always avoided. A guy could take so much, and he wasn't any damned marble statue and for a long time he'd known that would spell trouble. Or something.

He tried to pry information out of her as they walked, but she shut her lips tightly and shook her head. "When we get there and my feet get warm. This blasted cold. Why did you pick today for a walk?"

"Nothing else to do. No one here. I called you—hey, the boathouse is locked. There's a padlock—"

"I know. But there's a window, too. Margaret Benjamin and I found it last fall when we got caught in a thunderstorm."

"I'm afraid there's too much of me to get through that window—"

"I can. There's a back door that unlocks from the inside—"

She wriggled through the window, trim legs kicking as though she were swimming, and in a minute he was inside with her, lighting the stove and the oil lamp, pouring water into a pan to heat. She unbuckled storm boots and took them off, revealing wool socks over nylons. He unlaced his boots, then took them off, because his ankle was beginning to ache and he wanted the heat from the stove to get to it.

Sara said, "I brought these sandwiches from Aunt Eve's to eat later tonight, and then when I saw you out the window—"

"Saw me?"

She nodded. "Certainly. You don't think I'd be idiot enough to go to walk when I'd just gotten into the hall after vacation unless I had reason? You want a sandwich now or you want to take it back with you? No food on campus till tomorrow."

"I've got a whole chicken and French fries and pie; brought them from Cincinnati. My problem is to get 'em eaten before Chuck and Tom get here. Look, Sara, food's fine, it's wonderful, it's necessary, but for God's sake—why did Goodhue resign? Why has our Cozy left us?"

When she finished he was leaning forward in the canvas chair, elbows on knees, fingers digging at his scalp. "Damned," he said. "I'll be damned. I'll be Goddamned—"

"You certainly will if you keep talking like a profane parrot."

"What's he going to do? You mean he quit Thursday night and—and isn't even around anymore? How'd he do it?"

"I don't know what he's going to do. Drop dead, I hope. And I suppose he knew he was quitting long enough ahead of time to be all packed and everything. Uncle Karl said the moving people were there Friday. And he said he'd heard they were going to Europe."

David shook his head in bewilderment. "The poor bastard," he said. "That poor, stupid bastard. Stupid. Just plain stupid—"

"David, you're not sorry for him!"

"No. I don't suppose so. I'm damned glad he's gone, and I'm glad he got found out. So he's a queer, and that's his business. But he shouldn't have tried to drag other people along with him—only, I'm all over being mad at him. That's all. What's the use of staying mad at a guy who's as far down as he is now?"

"Clevenger—" said Sara.

David looked up quickly. "What about him?"

"Tom and Hunter say they're going to make him work just as hard to counteract that rumor as he did to start it. David, *don't* get all prickly again! You couldn't do it. Not under the circumstances."

"Maybe I could, but I wouldn't. I'm not getting prickly, Sara. If they want to, I can't stop them. I wish they'd let it alone, but I know 'em well enough now to shut up. If Clevenger had sense he'd quit, and I wish he would. I'm not fond of the sight of him—"

"He won't."

"O.K., so we'll try and forget him. It's not going to be easy—squelching that kind of a rumor—"

"No-o-o. But in time, David. Things work out."

He smiled and stood up, and looked down at her where she sat on the edge of the camp cot. "You sound like my grandfather." He walked to the window. "Hey, it's pitch dark out! How long we been here?"

"Hours and hours. Maybe we'll get lost walking back—"

She was standing beside him, and he could see her reflection in the window by the yellow glow of the oil lamp that softened and made mysterious the corners of the room, the cupboards, the canvas chairs, the camp cot, the boating gear—everything beyond the perimeter of its glow. He turned away from the window and found that she had stepped back and was facing him now. He tried to smile, and said: "My ears are getting cold just thinking about it out there. And it could snow, know that? We'd better be moving along—"

He did not draw away when her hands touched his cheeks, crept along them softly, covered his ears like small, warm earmuffs. "Your ears, David. They mustn't be cold. I've always loved your ears. Not just as me but as an artist. They're just right. They're not big like Chuck's or little tiny things like Dunbar's. They're—they're just right—"

"Sara, Smallest, you better let go of my ears—" He couldn't have moved now if his life had depended on it; his muscles were like mush, and there seemed to be no messages going from brain to feet or hands or legs to galvanize them. All the messages were clearly coming from someplace else.

"I love you when you call me 'Smallest'—"

"What—what're you saying?"

"I mean—I meant—I love it when you call me 'Smallest'—that's what I meant to say."

"It's not what you said, Sara; it's not what you said."

Suddenly she dropped her arms to her sides and stood very still, her eyes, looking into his, enormous and dark over cheeks flushed from the warmth of the room.

"David."

"Sara, we have to go—we—"

"David. We're in love."

Now, tossing in bed on the last night he would ever spend at Pengard, it was easy to say that he should have run, have bundled her into her coat and cap and boots, and run, telling her not to be silly. And, after that, stayed away, stayed the hell away. His brain had come alive at the shock of that outright statement, but it hadn't sent the right message.

"Sara—baby—"

"David, we're in love. We have been. Always. I—I guess I've known since the very first night when you came to Aunt Eve's—"

A man ought to be angry at a woman who took the initiative like that, ought to lose his interest in her. Interest, hell! When it wasn't interest but was your breath and your heartbeat and every hidden cell of your being, there couldn't be any losing of it just because she had been the one to put it into words, half frightened, half defiant, yet all love in the glow of a foul-smelling oil lamp in a dim boathouse with the black of a moonless night crowding in, the faint night sounds of a lake and a forest clear in the silence.

He sat up in bed in his room at Quimby House and snapped on the lamp beside it, and the room sprang into light, but Sara did not go away. If he'd known then what he knew now, been able to see ahead to the heartache that was inevitable— Yet he had known, even then he'd damned well known there were storms ahead, known it, *known* it—he slammed a fist into a pillow—yet he had reached out and put his hands on her waist, almost spanning it with his fingers, and she had put her hands over his, holding them closer; then she had relaxed her pressure. "Not your hands, David. Your arms—"

Their first kiss had been very gentle, like the kiss of two strangers taking part in some solemn ceremony. There had been more greeting than passion in that first kiss, more a drawing together of two people who had been separate for a long time and wanted first to savor slowly the joy of union. The next had been different. It had been David Champlin and Sara Kent, male and female since time began, wanting each other to the ultimate limits of wanting, very young and impatient and wanting what no man or woman ever had, utter possession, finding a storm, a tumult, and then a singing silence of love.

"Sara—little love—"

"David—"

David supposed, in the self-conscious maturity of twenty-one years and a college degree, that if anyone asked him "When did you really grow up?" or if he had asked himself when Gramp's often repeated remark "You a man now, son," became truth he would have begged the question with an outsider, but to himself would have answered that it was on that night in the boathouse. Because if being a man meant feeling whole and complete and fulfilled, he had become one then.

Until that time a girl had been just a girl; she was nice or she wasn't; you could have fun with her or you couldn't, and you could lay her or you couldn't—and he'd always been glad that most of the time he'd known the difference, that he hadn't been like a lot of guys who had the motto "no harm in trying." Maybe they liked being put down; he didn't, and he was always very cagey about testing the ice before he walked on it.

He'd known, of course, for a long time that with Sara it was different. He was in love. He thought she was too, but he tried to make his thinking stop there. It didn't always. And the farther afield his thoughts traveled, the more scared he became that in spite of himself he'd make a wrong move and find out she wasn't in love with him at all. A rebuff from any other girl could be laughed off; from Sara Kent it would be a mortal hurt.

Maybe if she had just said "I'm in love with you," he could have handled it somehow, but that wouldn't have been Sara. Instead, she had said "We're in love." As simply as that—and that had been Sara. Saying what she knew to be true, not letting him run away from it or from her without facing it.

He remembered their quarrels, most of them no more than spats, and how she had grown to know the attitudes and things that made him flare up, although she had never learned them completely because every once in a while she'd forget and say something and they'd be off again. He remembered, too, the time she had insisted, in an excess of honesty, on telling him about a boy she'd known before.

"David, you knew, didn't you—that night—"

"All I knew was that I loved you, baby. I mean, that's *all*. It's all I wanted to—"

"Don't put me off. The—the other time, David, I didn't like it—it wasn't—well, it wasn't what I know it really is now—"

"So now do you feel better? Now will you forget about it? Because I know a lot of things about you I don't think you even know about yourself, and that's why I don't give a damn what happened before I ever saw you. You don't hear me making a big lot of confessions—"

"You better not! David, don't you dare! I can't even stand *thinking* about it—"

He had thrown his head back and laughed then so that a bird skimming the lake a long way off veered and took flight high and fast, and Sara laughed with him, and the echo that lived in the lake near where they stood bounced their laughter back and forth. After that every time he walked there he thought that he could hear that laughter, still echoing.

That summer Sara went to Europe with her father, and he came down to earth. He came home broker than he dared tell Gramp and headed for the laundry where they usually had a job for him driving a delivery truck, and was taken on immediately. The man who owned the laundry said: "What in hell you want to go way up there for? You're the best driver I ever had, and what's more I can tell you so and you won't get swellheaded. What they got up there you ain't got here? Those books teaching you how to earn a living?"

"Not here," said David, and smiled, hating the man but needing the job. Hell, what an old story. Hating the man but needing the job. A hundred-year-old story.

"Here's the key to the truck. Pick it up at the garage, seven thirty in the morning. You're just lucky. Next time you got time on your hands may not be a job open. Get smart, boy—"

David stood very still, looking at the key case the man was holding, not touching it. His eyes rose to the man's eyes, looked into them directly, and he knew that what he felt must show in his face. He smiled and knew that when he smiled the blaze of anger in his eyes grew hotter, and he saw the man step back.

"Keep the keys. I could tell you what to do with them, but you know already. I've changed my mind." He walked away slowly, deliberately, fighting back the rage, the almost uncontrollable desire to go back and feel white flesh spread under his fist, hear teeth crunch.

Gramp said that night: "You a bad nigger now, son. That's what he'll be saying. Now you been up north you're a bad nigger." But Gramp was smiling. "Calls for a beer, son. You set 'em up for three. The Prof said he'd come by."

That was when he came down to earth. Isaiah Watkins put him to work mornings collecting insurance premiums, and afternoons he drove a delivery truck for a grocery store in Beauregard. Evenings when he was home he sat on the porch with Gramp until the mosquitoes drove them inside, not talking much, thinking, traveling slowly to an inevitable conclusion, backing away from it, facing it again, growing nearer each time; finally, just before he returned to Pengard, accepting it.

It hadn't even been too hard telling it to Sara. It was Sara's reaction that had been hard. She refused to take him seriously at first. She didn't exactly laugh at him because Sara wouldn't do that, would be afraid of hurting him, but she said: "David, you don't mean it, you know you don't. It's—oh, for gosh sake, David—it's not all that important."

"Yes, it is, Sara. You don't understand. You don't know, Smallest. You can't. Sara, in my state the law—the *law*—wouldn't let you marry me. As though I was—was unclean—"

"But who cares! Who in hell *cares* about your state? We don't have to live there."

"I—I don't care about my state, Sara. I do about my people."

"Of course you do! You should. So do I."

"And I care about you. Sara, you don't know what the world does to your people when they're too—too friendly with my people. And if they marry them—Sara, it's hell. It's—it's—Sara, you'd grow to hate me. You'd learn things you never even knew existed—up north, too. Things about living and—Sara, if I didn't know what would happen—"

"You don't know any such damned thing, David Champlin! And I don't want to talk about any such damned nonsense anymore. You—you haven't any guts!"

They hadn't talked about it much after that. In the summer she went to Brazil to visit her sister, and he worked as he had the year before. In Beauregard the Champlin house was one of the first on the mailman's route, so he usually got her letters out of the box on the way to work, and Gramp saw only a few of them—and said nothing. But David could tell he was troubled.

Back at Pengard when he saw her for the first time it was the way it had always been—as though he'd just started to live all over again, not having really lived since the last time he saw her.

And then, incredibly, graduation was only a few weeks away, and then only a few days, and she was standing before him just as she had in the boathouse, in the woods near Laurel, the spring sun bright on her face and hair, dappling them with shadow when the new green leaves of the tree above them stirred. "David. We're still in love."

"I know."

"We always will be. It won't make any difference if we make a project out of saying goodbye. It won't change anything. We'll still be in love. We'll still love. And that's even more important. We'll still love."

"Sara—I know—I know—"

"You won't give me a chance, David. And it wouldn't be 'chance.' It would be good and right, no matter what happened, no matter how rough it might be. You're wrong, David. You're so wrong, wrong, wrong—"

"How can a guy know that? Know it, I mean. Your family wouldn't think so—"

"My family! David, it's *my* family. I'd have to worry about that, not you. And I know my father knows. He's—he's great, David. I'd have to live with whatever my family think—"

"I'd be living with it too, Sara, with you, or it wouldn't be a marriage. And your father's not so great it isn't breaking him up. I met him, remember. He tried, he sure tried, but—well—a guy knows these things somehow. You don't understand—"

"David, look. We couldn't afford to get married anyhow, could we? Not with you sure to be all stiff-necked about my having any money—"

"No. Gosh, no—"

"So lots and lots of couples have to wait until they can afford to get married. So let's make it that way, David. That we have to wait. I won't say goodbye. I won't. Not for any such crazy reasons."

"It's better—"

"Don't I have anything to say about it? Not anything? Someday you'll have pots of money—"

He had laughed then. "How you talk—"

She moved closer, and as it had been that night in the boathouse her hands touched his cheeks, crept along them—"That's what I'm waiting for, David." She grinned up at him, gamin now. "For you to make those pots of money and be famous. Marrying you for your money and fame, that's what I'm doing—"

"Sara—you birdbrain—"

Her hands drew his head forward, and he put his own over them. "Sara—"

"A week from now we'll be gone from here, from the boathouse and this place in the woods and the lake and—and everywhere. You can say goodbye if you want to. I won't. Not now or ever. And I won't see you again like this, just David and Sara. Only on campus and at the auditorium—and I'll never really mean goodbye because, David, it would be some kind of a—dreadful sin. David, come closer—kiss me —because I know it will be a while—it may be a long while—"

"Sara—please—Smallest—" He picked her up bodily, fiercely, held her so tightly she cried out, "David—David! You're squashing me to pieces—"

"Sara—little love—you always win, don't you, baby—"

She had won that afternoon, and she would win again and again if he let himself see her. It might take him all summer and most of next year to strengthen his will to the point where she couldn't win a final time.

He turned the bedside lamp off and slept, on his last night in Quimby House. But Sara was still there.

38

As he walked up Third Street in East Cambridge, David tried to tell himself that he was too old to feel like a kid going to the circus for the first time. It was no way to approach his first day in a courtroom, just as a spectator. He wouldn't be doing this at all, would be doing what was more sensible—looking for a room—if he had not read the feature article in the Boston paper on the train the day before, an article about an attorney named Bradford Willis. There had been a familiar sound to the name; then he remembered hearing it mentioned by Sudsy's family and, after reading the article, he felt what he knew was a childish pride that he had rubbed shoulders, even remotely, with this man. The article had led off with: "Opposing counsel call him the green-eyed monster; his clients for the most part regard him as one of the best defense attorneys of our time. Last week he did it again—saved another man from a little room in State's prison, the last room many men have ever seen in their lifetime." The article had not been a long one, had detailed a few of the trials in which he had appeared for the defense, most of them trials for murder, most of them apparently hopeless. He had not won acquittals in all of them, but not one of his clients had received the death penalty.

David had three days in which to find a place to live; he would cut it to two, and if this man was appearing in any court nearby would try to hear him. That morning, feeling like an idiot as he did so, he had called the office of Bradford Willis and asked the girl who answered the telephone if Mr. Willis was going to be in court that day. She not only replied that he was, but furnished the name of the court—Middlesex County Superior Court. And did he want Mr. Willis to return his call, because she expected him to call in? "No, ma'am," said David hastily. "It's all right. Thank you." He hung up hurriedly, feeling uncomfortable even about having troubled the switchboard operator in the offices of the great Bradford Willis. Perhaps all Willis would be doing would be filing a demurrer or something, but David was under the impression such routine tasks were performed by underlings and juniors, and he might strike it rich and find Willis was trying a case; he'd been too flustered to ask the switchboard operator. "You'd be a hell of a trial lawyer," he told himself. "Getting butterflies just from the idea of watching a trial."

The conductor on the streetcar had told him how to recognize the courthouse. Now he saw it, a red brick building with a central entrance flanked by two wings, the main doorway overlooking an open, paved clearing centered by a flower bed and flagpole. It was obviously very old, and gave an impression of being none too clean, of hiding mustiness behind its doors and windows. When he entered he smelled, along with cigar, cigarette, and pipe smoke, the blue, thick smell of politics; a smell, he supposed, that permeated every courthouse in the country. He waited while a deputy sheriff carrying a long white staff and followed by a column of people passed. That had to be a jury, he thought. The deputy sheriff looked weighed down with a half-century of boredom, and the members of the jury looked self-conscious. He noted three Negroes on the jury, a woman and two men. No one paid any attention to him, and he felt shy about asking someone to tell him where Bradford Willis could be found. He decided to follow the jury.

He was behind them as they went up a flight of stairs beside the entrance but was not quick enough to arrive at the top before they had disappeared. Standing outside a pair of double doors was an old man, not much bigger, David thought, than Gramp. Brass buttons on a dark blue coat indicated he had something to do with some court proceeding, and David walked up to him diffidently. He said, "Excuse me," politely, and then, "Is there a trial going on in there?"

The old man looked at him with rheumy eyes. "Parsons versus Bay Indemnity. You a witness?"

"No, sir."

Something stirred in the faded eyes. The old man evidently appreciated politeness. "Interested party?" David shook his head. "Just a spectator. A—a student."

The "party" had become "pahty" and "Parsons" was "Pahsons" in the old man's mouth. It wasn't the soft dropping of an "r," to which David's ears were accustomed, not the "mo'nin" and "fo'" of his people; there was a metallic clang to this speech up here, and there was no inflection in the tones. His own voice, he thought, must sound affectedly soft.

"I'm just a student," he said again.

"You picked the right place," said the old man. "This one's a pretty good one. Good enough to bring Brad Willis on it himself. If it wan't good to start with, he'd make it good. Brad Willis—you ever hear of him?"

"Yes, sir. I read all about him on the train coming over from New York. He's the one I came to hear."

"You watch Brad Willis, you'll learn more about how to try a case in court than ten years in a law school. Sharp as a tack, Brad Willis."

Did people still say "sharp as a tack"? Evidently they did up here.

"Go on in." The old man opened one of the swinging doors. "Get yourself a good seat down front, over on this side." Then, instead of letting him go in alone, the old man followed him, picking out the most advantageous seat, not in the center but on the side of the front row of seats. "See everything better here," he said. "That weazened-up old geezer pawing through his briefcase—looks like a squirrel—he's the attorney for the defendant. He's a big shot. Probably be a judge someday. Willis ain't come in yet. Young blond feller in glasses, that's his assistant."

The old man rambled on, and David thought of the people who had told him he would find cold unfriendliness in New England. One of the people who had warned him had been a white man in New Orleans, for whom he had done some work the previous summer. He thought of a white-haired, middle-aged woman of whom he had hesitantly inquired directions when he had been lost in midtown Boston on the first day of his arrival, remembered how she had walked with him to the corner so that she could make her directions clearer by pointing out the way. And he remembered, even as the old man was talking, the old lady in the French Quarter he had heard Gramp and his friends talk about; he heard Gramp saying: "That old lady must have been nigh ninety year old. Blind as a bat. Used to stand on the curb, and when she heard someone walking close she'd say, 'Walk me across, please,' and when they got to the other side she'd say, 'White or colored?' and if they said 'Colored,' she'd shake 'em away and say 'Turn me loose, nigger.' I helped her across a coupla times, but after that I didn't do it no more; I didn't want no more insults even from a blind old lady." Maybe things were as bad in the North as they were anywhere else, but the ratio of insults to people met was a whole hell of a lot lower.

There was a short wait after the old man left, and then a stir as the jury entered. As they filed into their seats, David noticed a tall man entering through the double doors. The man walked with an ambling stride that seemed casual, but covered the ground between doorway and one of the counsel tables with surprising swiftness. His skin was the color of coffee well laced with rich cream; the hair was dark and nappy, but not so dark and nappy as David's; the face was thin, the lines appearing to be more those of worry and lack of flesh beneath the skin than those of age. He had been looking at his wristwatch when he entered, but now his eyes swept the well of the court, and David saw them clearly: the nearly true green eyes of some mixed-blood Negroes, so common in New Orleans and throughout Louisiana one did not look twice on seeing them, but here, in Cambridge, Massachusetts, he stared, and did not even realize he was staring. This must be, had to be, Brad Willis, whom the feature article had described with special emphasis on the green eyes, and who was unmistakably a Negro. When he had heard the name mentioned at the Sutherlands', there had been no reference to his being a Negro. David was chagrined at his own surprise; he had thought himself well up on the accomplishments of those of his people who had made it in the white world, but this was one he had missed.

David watched the tall man as he greeted his assistant, saw the blond young man turn to him and smile warmly, watched them as they talked briefly and then turned to stand in respectful silence while the judge entered and an ancient cracked voice intoned, "Oyez—Oyez—" and finally, "God save the Commonwealth of Massachusetts." There was a rustle as the people in the courtroom sat down, and he realized he was still staring at the man who seemed, after he entered, to dominate the room so effortlessly.

He judged Willis to be a man who did not smile often, and after noting his greeting to his assistant thought him wise to reserve the smile. The lawyer favored the jury with it now as they squirmed and settled into their seats, running his eyes along front and back rows, including each man and woman in a silent greeting, commiserating with the women in a sort of silent communion because they were not at home tending to what must be tended to, and with the men because they were not at desk or wheel or wherever they belonged in the economic scheme of their lives, thanking them wordlessly for being there and helping him.

David glanced quickly at Abbott, the defendant's attorney, saw him trying to emulate his opponent's attitude, his smile an effort, behind it all too painfully evident the feeling that this was needless fol-de-rol to which he was stooping. Thinks he's better than any of them, thought David. Willis is saying, "Sit down. Res' yo'self."

When Willis conferred with the judge he was polite without undue deference; when he turned from the judge to Abbott he was gracious; a graciousness, David decided, he would trust only as far as he could sling a man-eating tiger. He was saying to the judge now: "The plaintiff is ready, your Honor, but because of the unfortunate illness of the next witness we planned to call we must change our procedure slightly. However, rather than try the patience of the court by further delays, we ask permission to call this witness at a later time, possibly out of order, when she is feeling better."

David drew a deep breath. How did he do it? In a few sentences David had been made to feel sorry for some unfortunate, unnamed female who meant nothing whatever to him, suffering on a bed of pain with what was probably only a head cold; he had been made aware that during the preceding days the attorney for the defendant had messed things up generally by uncalled-for delays, and he was also conscious of having been appealed to for tolerance and sympathy in an unavoidable situation that might give rise to a special request for a favor later. And the statement had been such a simple one, drawing only a nod from the judge, and an impatient slap by the opposing counsel of a yellow legal tablet on an oak table.

David leaned forward, arms on knees, knowing he had been trickled into a partisanship that had nothing to do with coffee-colored skin or the nappiness of close-cut hair. At that moment he succumbed to his first attack of hero worship since his childhood when he had collected baseball pictures, regarding baseball players as without color, as he did the gods of Olympus the Prof had told him tales about.

He sorted out the issues of the case quickly: a suit for heavy damages growing out of a crippling back injury. Someday, he thought, the maneuverings of people in a squared-off area in front of a judge—like a prizefight ring—would be as clear and familiar to him as the strategy of a baseball game, but now he was like a spectator seeing that game for the first time, not knowing what to watch for, missing a stolen base, bewildered by a double play. By midmorning he was hoping desperately that the case of *Parsons* vs. *Bay Indemnity* would be over before classes started next week so he could hear all of it. If a simple suit for damages could be, in the hands of Bradford Willis, as all-absorbing as this, what would a murder trial in the same expert hands be like? He was glad he had decided to concentrate on civil and constitutional law; he strongly doubted his own capabilities in the rough-and-tumble of trial law, disliking open conflict as he did, preferring strategic battles, but whether it was civil or criminal law, he knew he was watching a master this day in the Middlesex County Courthouse.

During a pause in the proceedings, while a witness was sought, Willis and his assistant moved away from the counsel table, toward the railing in front of David. They spoke in low tones, Willis half facing him. David realized he was staring rudely, and looked away from the pair in front of him, but not before Willis's eyes had flicked to him and away, the glance so quick it was felt more than seen. Lord! thought David. Lord, Lord! He knows my height, weight, previous condition of servitude, the size of my collar, where I bought my suit, and the size of my shoes he can't see. And that I've got no more manners than an untrained pup.

When noon recess was called, David went downstairs—once again behind the jury—and into the paved area in front of the building. He realized the jury, like sheep, must be driven to pasture somewhere. He continued to follow them, up Third Street, although he was not particularly hungry.

At the counter of a little restaurant on Cambridge Street he lit a cigarette and ordered a grilled cheese sandwich. He had not had such a good time, he reflected, since he had been to his first major-league ball game, a thousand years ago on a warm spring day in Cincinnati. He realized he had gone three hours without missing Sara, but now he missed her so achingly that when he put his cigarette out he ground it to a shredded mess in the ashtray.

The restaurant was crowded, the tables along one side filled, and there were standees behind him waiting for a seat. When the girl sitting next to him finished her coffee and left, the man who edged in to take her seat brushed his shoulder, and said, "Sorry." Glancing sideways David saw long, firm, coffee-colored hands with short well-trimmed nails pick up a menu, and sat, motionless, his coffee cup halfway to his lips. Willis was talking over his shoulder to someone behind him, on the side farthest from David. He heard the words "sure as hell talk over their heads," and heard the other person say, "How about making him draw a diagram on the blackboard?"

"I'd thought of that." It was sarcasm, but not wounding or unkind.

"There's a seat down below. I'd better grab it."

David swallowed coffee to moisten his throat, turned and said: "Excuse me. You two gentlemen are together. I'll go down to the other seat."

Willis turned to him and smiled. "Most certainly not. Stay where you are. Actually, this young man is sick of the sight of me." He spoke over his shoulder again. "Scram. Down the line. Forget it for a while. Go dream of Ella in Iowa."

Willis folded long arms, waiting to be served, turned and looked directly at David. "Did you enjoy the session?"

"I—it was—" David swallowed a youthful "Gosh," and went on, "It was about the most interesting morning I've ever spent."

The older man's eyebrows went up. "Not exactly a *cause célèbre*. Rather run of the mill."

"I don't know about that, sir. It didn't seem that way to

me. I suppose it's because it's the first time I've ever watched a real trial. I thought—well—I thought you were great."

Willis smiled broadly. "Well, thankee, young sir. But wait till you hear me expound on the human spine. At this point I think I know more about the human spine than our expert medical witness."

"Will you do that soon?" He tried not to sound too eager.

"Probably this afternoon. Are you curious, just killing time, or an interested party?"

"None of those, sir. I'm a student. Harvard Law. Or will be next week."

Willis's eyebrows went up again. He poured quantities of sugar into his coffee, said, "Energy," then turned curious eyes on David again. "Are you telling me that you have completed all the academic courses required for entrance to Harvard Law School? My own, incidentally. You're not old enough."

"Yes, sir. I mean yes, I have, and yes, I am." He cleared his throat and smiled. "I'm older than I look. When I wear my glasses I look my age."

"I'll bet. Anyhow, you'll look older than your age when they get through with you up there. But it was nice of you to drop in. I was watching you. Even lawyers need the stimulus of a rooting section sometimes."

Bradford Willis had been watching him! David could have sworn the lawyer had not even known he was there until that quick glance when he and his assistant had been standing near the railing. He looked down at his sandwich and saw that it was cold, soggy, and greasy, a fact that bothered him not at all. Willis was struggling with a well-stuffed hamburger, and David applied himself to the sandwich before him. He hoped Sudsy would be at home that night. It was going to be quite pressingly necessary that he talk to someone. Sara. No. Not Sara. She was back from Paris; Tom Evans had told him this in a letter. But even if he had a hundred dollars in his pocket for long-distance calls to Chicago, not Sara.

Sara had probably never heard of Bradford Willis, but Sara would be as excited as though he had told her he had lunched with the President at the White House. As he talked to her he would be able to see her—as he always could—bouncing like a child with happiness for him, saying: "David! David, that's wonderful! Oh, David I'm so thrilled. Tell me about it, sweet—" No! Not Sara.

He finished his sandwich, decided against pie after a mental check of his resources, and accepted more coffee. Willis's assistant, who must either have bolted his lunch or settled for pie and coffee was back, standing behind Willis. The lawyer stood, and David looked up at him. He started to say "Thank you—" and saw that the tall man was looking at him expectantly. "Drink your coffee, and come along," he said.

"I—gosh—" he wasn't able to swallow the "gosh" this time. "I don't really want it." He grabbed his check and followed the two men to the cash register, paid for his lunch, and when he left the building found them standing on the sidewalk outside.

"This is my assistant, Bill Culbertson," said Willis. "Bill this is—who?"

"Champlin. David Champlin."

Willis seemed to take it for granted he would walk with them to the courthouse. At the corner he said, thoughtfully, "Champlin—Champlin—I have a feeling I should know the name—"

"Suds—Clifton Sutherland and I were at college together. We're still pretty good friends. I've been up here visiting them a couple of times. They've talked about you—"

"Hold on—Champlin—automobile—I made out a bill of sale for a car of Clifton's—you were the second party—I remember."

"Yes, sir."

"You're from New Orleans, aren't you?"

"That's right—"

"My father came from New Orleans. Near there, anyhow. Mandeville Parish."

"Right across the lake."

"You know it?"

"Know it well. My grandfather used to take me hunting and fishing over there when I was a kid. You know back of Mandeville there, where—"

"Never been there," said Willis. "If God is good, I never will be."

"No, sir," said David, feeling rebuffed. "Guess you're smart not to."

"Someday we'll go into it, Champlin—David. The Willis family and New Orleans. Meanwhile, you are aware that the human spine has never adapted itself to the comparatively recent upright posture of the genus we whimisically call human?"

"Yes, sir." David laughed, and the laugh surprised him because it broke through his shyness and came out easily and naturally. "I know it, and you know it, but what's going to happen if you've got a couple of people on the jury who don't believe in evolution?"

"Ah—those are the things you think of when you select a jury. Although I must say it appalled me to have to take it into consideration in the mid-twentieth century. My opponent was snorting with impatience."

Inside the courthouse Willis left them, walking with that deceptive amble down the main corridor. As he left he said to Culbertson, "Set up the blackboard, please." And to David: "Enjoy yourself, David. Make notes if you want, and I'll be glad to go over them with you after it's over."

Culbertson walked upstairs with David, accommodating himself unobtrusively to David's slower ascent. "He's great," he said. "He's the greatest."

"He's just about got to be," said David. "Why—he never even saw me before."

As they stood outside the courtroom, Culbertson said, "Let's see—blackboard—chalk—Oh, God! Chalk!"

"If they have a blackboard here they must have chalk."

"He'll want colored. Three colors anyhow. Hell!"

When David brought the chalk back from a variety store on Cambridge Street, he felt something like the man who brought the message to Garcia whose name no one—certainly not he—ever remembered.

The old man who had shown him where to sit that morning was nowhere in sight. There was a conference going on at the bench, and when Willis turned away to return to the counsel table and saw David in the doorway with his package, he made a quick beckoning gesture. David, feeling now like Clarence Darrow, fumbled with the hinged gate in the low-railed barrier, finally got it opened, and crossed the well of the court to Willis.

"Good." Willis checked the chalk, saw that it was varicolored, and smiled with pleasure. He touched David's shoulder briefly, said: "Get back to your grandstand seat and learn about the spine. And thanks. See you again, I hope."

39

Before David left for Cambridge, Li'l Joe Champlin predicted, "You going to be res'less, working like you has all summer outside and all, then jes setting on your rear studying—"

After two weeks of classes he would have welcomed a spell of restlessness. At Pengard he had learned what was meant by a "trained mind," but not until he reached Harvard had he known what it was to be surrounded by them, in students as well as faculty. At Pengard he had felt the concern of his instructors; at Harvard he learned that excellence was not something to work toward, that it was expected and taken for granted, and he approached both classwork and study with tense apprehension. He was not aware of any problems created by his race; if they existed, he was too preoccupied to care or notice.

Isaiah Watkins had sent him to see a cousin who, with her husband, lived just off Massachusetts Avenue in Boston, near the subway, and who rented rooms. They had available a two-room-and-bath basement apartment, with separate entrance. The rent was more than he could afford, but a gas plate and small refrigerator meant he could prepare his own meals and save, and he took it thankfully. Nevertheless, he knew he was going to have to find a job to augment his money, but in those first weeks he did not worry about it; there was too much else to worry about. Gray by Christmas, he thought. That's what I'll be, gray by Christmas.

Late in the afternoon on Friday of his third week, someone hailed him as he came down the steps of the library. He turned and recognized Bill Culbertson, the young assistant he had met with Bradford Willis at the East Cambridge courthouse. He smiled broadly, and waved; here at last was someone to talk with; he had begun to doubt that he would ever make friends at the law school; even among his own people no one had time, not even, he admitted, David Champlin.

They shook hands, and Culbertson said, "Where in hell have you been?"

"Living in a book," he answered. "Living plumb in the middle of a book. Not always the same one—"

"God, I know! Murder, isn't it? Brad Willis sent me bird-dogging for you."

"Bradford Willis? For *me?*"

"Don't look so shocked. How about a drink?"

"Hell, yes!" Three weeks of self-imposed loneliness began to recede.

"I've got Brad's car," said Culbertson. "I know a good place where we can get a drink and eat, both."

David hesitated. Money was involved in eating out. In the refrigerator were filet gumbo, red beans, and a bowl of rice, made the day before. He hadn't skimped on the quantity; there was plenty for two. Should he ask this white boy to eat with him and risk an effusively concealed snub? He told himself not to be a supersensitive fool. The boy was working for a Negro lawyer; there had been no slightest smell of Crow when they had first met. He said: "Let's have the drink first. If you like real New Orleans gumbo I have it and I'd be glad—"

"You haven't given New England food a chance? This place is right in town: broiled mackerel, scrod, lobster, steamed clams. I'm a Catholic and it's Friday, so it has to be fish. Do you good to eat out. The Abernathy, Willis and Shea office is picking up the tab."

They were in the car now, and David turned and looked at his companion in astonishment.

"You've got the wrong guy. I'm not a client. Why should they?"

"Relax. You'll find out."

Two hours later Culbertson sat in an ancient Morris chair in David's room, nursing a beer, waiting while David showered and shaved. He knew he would always cherish the memory of Champlin's face at the words: "If you haven't anything important to do after dinner, we're going to the Willises' house. Brad wants to talk to you." He wondered as he waited about this man called David Champlin who, if he wanted, would succeed him, Culbertson, in Brad's office. He had not always felt about Negroes the way he felt now. It had taken a state university and law school—and Bradford Willis—to change an attitude of "I'll fight for your rights, but stay where you belong," an attitude halfway between the prejudice and patronage of the South and the wordy liberalism of the Northeast, a Midwestern attitude of "You're O.K., but just stay out of my living room, away from my job, and we'll get along fine."

Now he sat in the room of a New Orleans Negro, envying him the experience that lay ahead, if he chose it: that of working under Bradford Willis, whose mind had made Culbertson cringe more than once. He himself would be back in Iowa, married to Ella, practicing law with his father, a most worthy gent but no Bradford Willis. He had no doubt about Champlin's accepting Brad's offer, was sure the kid would probably go into shock, as he had nearly done. A nice guy, he thought, a nice, gentle, quiet guy, but wary, most definitely wary, and behind the gentle quietness a mind that Culbertson sensed was never still. From the vast distance of four years away, Culbertson told himself that Champlin would make out fine in law. He might never have the dash, the courtroom flair of Brad Willis, but his would be a different gift, perhaps equally telling, equally forceful. They would make a good pair.

Culbertson sighed, nostalgic already, just as David, in shorts and undershirt, came out of the bath. Nothing wrong with that guy, he thought, nothing at all. Wide shoulders, smooth muscles, small waist, only the scarred and stiffened foot and ankle spoiling a near perfect body.

David caught the sigh, said, "Gee, I'm sorry to have kept you waiting—"

"O.K., O.K. I'm as full of food as an Iowa hog—which I guess I was at dinner—and there's no rush."

When David was dressed and they were leaving, Culbertson said, "Want to stop for another beer?" His breath was already indrawn to add, "We won't get anything at the Willises'," but he stopped and let the question go untagged. It might bring queries, and he did not feel that it was up to him to explain Peg Willis to David Champlin. David would find out about Brad's deeply loved Peg soon enough, she of the warmth and generosity and deep, understanding humor—when she was not drinking. The time would come when David would see, just as he had, the hell Brad Willis faced almost constantly. Just being around a mind that was dull and blurred was hell on Brad; add to that Peg's constant telephoning—"an emergency" she would tell the switchboard operators—to both office and courts, her spells of deep melancholia, her terrifying habit of going for long drives when her step was so unsteady she could barely make it to the car, and Brad's patience seemed, to an outsider, close to saintly.

Culbertson remembered dinner invitations that never came more than twenty-four hours in advance, then Brad at the office the next day saying, after a telephone call, "Do you mind a rain check on the dinner?" Finally the invitations had come at the last minute, with always a quick check by phone before they left the office.

Even now, driving to the Willis home in the suburbs, Culbertson dared not be too optimistic, although Brad had sounded cheerful and confident when he said: "I've been hoping I'd hear from the Champlin boy. How about trying to track him down? Bring him out to the house tonight."

David asked, "Has Mr. Willis always been a defense attorney? Criminal defense, I mean?"

"Not always, but he has for quite a while. He started out with Shea and Abernathy in corporation law and civil stuff. They had a few criminal cases, but not many. One of them was a murder charge. He saved the client from the chair. After that, he was off and running. He still handles civil cases, of course. Does a neat job on them too, believe me."

Culbertson was almost giddy with relief when he saw Peg Willis at the door. By now he could tell at a glance if she had been drinking. He introduced David, and then Brad was behind her, throwing an arm across her shoulders, holding out his hand to David. From here on in, thought Culbertson, it was Brad and David's baby, and he ruefully fought down an unmistakable pang of jealousy.

Warm greens and browns dominated the Willis living room; the furniture belonged to an era of deep comfort, was cleverly spiced with modern touches. There were lamps whose lights were focused for reading, not imprisoned in cylindrical monstrosities. David tried to overcome his nervousness, or at least any show of it, and knew that in doing so he would probably give an unfortunate impression of dark and silent immobility.

He and Culbertson entered the room together, Willis and his wife behind them, and he heard her say, "Find chairs, boys," and when he did so, "Nothing will break, Mr. Champlin. Especially that chair. Lean back and relax." Her voice was deep, the kind of voice that would be mistaken for a man's during the first few moments of a telephone conversation. She placed an ashtray on the end table beside his chair, and he had his first close look at her. A full figure, deep breasted, with slender waist and a long line of leg and thigh that, he thought, exceeded standard specifications for grace. Her eyes were as dark as his own, her hair a reddish-brown, more red than brown, its deep waves obviously natural. Not until she said to Culbertson, "Sit on the couch beside me, Bill. Then you'll know we aren't plotting against the whites," did he realize that she was of his own race. Then it was so obvious he was surprised at his slowness in detecting it.

She must be many years younger than her husband, he thought; certainly she was far too young to have those deepening lines from nostrils to lips, too young not to be able to relax, as she had told him to do, to have to sit forward on the edge of the couch, twisting a bright handkerchief in her hands until he wondered how the fabric held out. She sat there only a moment, jumped up to inspect ashtrays, sat again, and then was up and bringing coffee, and, before they had time for more than two swallows, on her feet once more, coffeepot in hand to replenish their cups.

Willis searched the pipe rack beside his chairs, said, "Hell! I must have left it in the study—" then held up a quieting hand. "Please, Peg. Sit still. I'll get it." As he passed the divan he touched his wife's shoulder and smiled down at her, and David, seeing the smile, felt the ache of Sara's absence reawaken. He did not know how long the Willises had been married; he could only guess by the settled, lived-in atmosphere of the house that it had been a number of years, but there was no guesswork about the feeling between this man and woman. Then why, he wondered, the nervous tension of the woman on the couch, the inner anxiety that her husband could not quite conceal?

When Willis returned, pipe in hand, and sat down, Culbertson said: "I'm suffering from a sort of benign jealousy. I'm remembering when I sat here for the first time myself."

Brad smiled, turned to David, and without speaking welcomed him as he had welcomed the men and women of the jury that morning in court, and David, warming now, less nervous, wondered why a verdict ever went against this man. "What's happening to you up there in Cambridge, David?"

"Lord! Everything."

"It's not easy. A trite remark if I ever made one—"

They talked for an hour of Harvard, its law courses and professors, until David found himself leaning back in his chair, legs stretched out easy and less nervous, laughing at Peg Willis's abrupt husky interruptions, relieved that she, too, seemed more relaxed. She'd be a hell of a swell person, he thought, a hell of a swell person if she'd just untie those knots.

Then, as unexpectedly as David had heard him switch a particular line of questioning that day in court, Brad Willis said, "Wondering why you're here, young man?"

"Well—yes, sir, I guess I am—"

"Can you type?"

"I'm fair at it. Taught myself touch system. My grandfather gave me a portable when I left home for Pengard—"

"How fair?"

"About fifty, I'd say. Sixty's tops for me."

"My God! Fair, you said? And I've no doubt you're accurate."

"Well—"

"Our office is swamped. A good law office always is. We have space problems, too, when it comes to hiring additional help. Someone who can work at home is a godsend. And I prefer a law student to an ordinary stenographer any day. And they usually need the money."

"You lie," said Culbertson. He turned to David. "What he means is, he'd rather give a leg up to a promising student, even if the guy is a two-finger typist."

"Well, I'll be damned," said Brad. "Now he knows he's leaving, he calls the boss a liar. Does it interest you, David? Routine stuff at first."

"Interest me! My God, sir—Mr. Willis—you don't know—"

Peg Willis's husky voice barely penetrated the haze that was obscuring any rational thought in David's mind as she said: "Brad always knows. Never think he doesn't. He knows how he felt when someone made him the same offer."

"Back in prehistory," said Brad. "Well, David?"

"But you don't know me—"

"Didn't my wife just say I always know? She neglected to add 'everything.' You think it's a snap judgment? If you become a trial lawyer, David, you'll have to make snap judgments constantly; witnesses you may never have seen—or even heard of—before, and opposing counsel you've never faced, a new judge, others; and a man's life or freedom depending on that judgment. One might say you formed a snap judgment of me, in spite of things you may have heard or read, which might or might not be true. Or might be biased."

"I"—he stumbled over his reply—"I—well—how do I know I can do it?"

"We'll change that attitude, young man, as soon as possible. I know, and that's enough. Think about it."

David was leaning forward now, elbows on knees, the heels of his palms pressed against his forehead. *You a lucky boy. You got any idea how lucky you is.* This time he had more than an idea; this time he knew; it was like being hit in the wind; he had almost the same physical reactions as when Beanie Benford had told him of the homosexual rumor that was being spread about him.

When he looked up, Bradford Willis was looking at him, smiling, and for some damned reason this light-skin attorney with the green eyes made him think of Gramp.

"I don't need to think about it, sir," he said, quietly. "Not for even a minute. It's—there's nothing in the world I'd rather do. I don't even know how to begin to say 'thank you'—"

"Don't. For God's sake, don't thank me. Wait till next year when you start helping on briefs. You may be sorry you jumped so quickly."

"Guess I'm not very good company," he said to Culbertson on the drive home. They were his first words since leaving the Willis home ten minutes before.

Culbertson laughed. "Don't give it a thought. I went into the same kind of trance. There's a final-year student there now. He'll come up into my spot for a year if he wants. He hasn't come out of his trance yet." After a moment, Culbertson said, "Know what Brad said about you after that day in East Cambridge? Said he liked the way you laugh."

"The way I laugh! Sounds like hell to me. My grandfather says it raises the roof six inches. Runs in the family. My great-grandmother used to say you could hear my great-grandfather's laugh two courtyards away. And they tell me my father laughed the same way."

"I know why Brad liked it. You will, too, after a while. He doesn't get too many laughs himself. Look, David, take care of that character; keep your eye on him. I'll give you my address before I go. Keep in touch, huh?"

At two o'clock in the morning David, who had planned for a good night's sleep, climbed out of bed, took the one remaining can of beer from the refrigerator, and sat in the Morris chair by the round, old-fashioned table in the center of the room. If he couldn't sleep, he ought to study; he knew that, but study was out of the question. He felt as he had at the lunch counter that day in East Cambridge: that it was almost a necessity to find someone to talk to, and that was out of the question too. Sudsy would be good-natured about being waked up, but it would be impossible to communicate his inner excitement to him. After all, Sudsy was studying to become a doctor; Sudsy's father was the founder of a clinic that had become a Mecca for sick from all over the world; Sudsy had no money problems that a careful hint or two at home wouldn't solve; he couldn't be expected to know what it meant to a law student, only three weeks at Harvard, to be taken under the wing of a famous attorney and at the same time have the burden of worrying about money lifted from his mind.

It would be unkind to call Gramp in the middle of the night, unkind and maybe dangerous. Nothing the doctor said about his heart being in good shape, all things considered, would erase from David's mind the memory of the pain-racked little body, the agonized clutch of thin fingers over his hand, the night of Gramp's attack.

Sara. Sara would understand, yet Sara's position was as dissimilar as Sudsy's. But Sara would know how he felt, would catch the glow that was warming him, the "My God it can't be true" feeling. And that, he supposed—hell, he knew—was because she loved him.

He sat there, very quietly, the beer forgotten, only an occasional street sound heard dimly through the fog of loneliness that now, slowly, inexorably, dimmed the glow that had warmed him. Lately on the streets, in the restaurants, in classes, he forgot that he was Negro except when an occasional rude stare from a passerby, a withdrawal in a fellow student reminded him. Now, alone, he knew it in every fiber of his being, knew it, damned it, and raged at himself for damning it.

Was what he had done about Sara just a damfool mistake? Would it be better to be like some, jump at the chance to marry a white woman whether you gave a damn about her or not, just to show you could; jump at the chance to take whatever she offered, using her as balm for old and aching wounds? How many kinds of a fool had he been to listen to the voice of Gramp, and what would have been the voice of

Gram if she were alive? How stupid had he been to make his first consideration that of what marriage to him would mean for Sara, the trouble, the humiliation, the almost inevitable estrangements, knowing in honest moments that most of this consideration was selfish, because he could not face a future where he would be the instrument that would bring these things about, could not face a future that might change what was in her eyes now to something so different it chilled his blood to think of it.

Man pays for his luck. Was this it? Was this the payment? He shook his shoulders in a violent shrug. Logic. Philosophy. He had done well in them. Was what he had learned going to degenerate in a matter of months to the simple myths of a small brown man in New Orleans, whose goodness was greater than he had ever known in any other man but whose life was governed by superstitions passed from generation to generation by an oppressed, untaught people?

He knew that when he told Gramp what had happened tonight the old man would say: "That's fine, son. That's fine! Been praying for you. Ain't it like I been telling you ever since you was a chile? Jesus always hears." Whenever Gramp said something like that, David always wanted to point out that Tant'Irene must have prayed, too, for the young husband who died in flames, wanted to say, "Where was Jesus then? Out for coffee?" But he never voiced the questions; it would have hurt Gramp, and Gramp would have had an answer, damned if he wouldn't. Li'l Joe Champlin would have an answer if God himself was on trial and Bradford Willis was the prosecutor.

Now, sitting alone and chill with loneliness, he closed his eyes, tired at last, and rested his head against the back of his chair. *Man pays for his luck.* Li'l Joe Champlin gave credit to God and Jesus in one breath and warned against "luck" in the next, and right now in the darkness of early morning David could not reason. He knew he had been fortunate, probably more fortunate than any other member of his first-year class; and, lonely for Sara though he might be, aching unbearably from the loss of her, he must acknowledge this good fortune. Crutch for a lame ego or not, faith was what had been placed in his hand before he could walk, and he could not discard it now, could not take for granted the opportunity that, unsought, lay ahead of him, accept it as his due, and he murmured, because he could not help himself, "Thanks, God." It might make the payment less.

40

Bradford Willis sat across from his wife in one of the deep armchairs that flanked their living-room fireplace. Peg was knitting with dizzying speed, a means, he knew, of working off the tensions built up during a week of sobriety. He sometimes wondered whether these weeks—if the spells of sobriety stretched into weeks—were any harder on her than they were on him. His own tensions seemed to build vicariously; he had the feeling during these periods that her surface equilibrium was a fragile, brittle fabric stretched over a framework of nerves equally fragile and brittle, a framework that vibrated at the slightest impact and could shiver suddenly and then splinter into sharp fragments whose sharp pain knew only the one anodyne. He also wondered at times whether it was harder to come home knowing what he would find, or to come home during one of Peg's dry spells and feel the sickening dismay, the inner lurching of his stomach when the evidence was plain that the drought was over.

Yet in spite of the knowledge of their mirage-like quality, he treasured these oases of companionship and understanding, stored up for the future the memories of evenings like this one, when they could sit and talk, when the depth of understanding that was so vital a part of Peg could encompass his ideas and strengthen them; when, by God, even a discussion, such as they were having now, of tree roots clogging their house's sewer pipe could be enjoyable because it was intelligible. One drink, he thought, just one, and she would be a million miles away, untouchable, her mind a centrifuge whirling, whirling, yet never succeeding in its purpose of precipitating the self that was Peg into a definable substance. The ache of wanting to help her at times was unbearable, the knowledge that he could not, at least in any way known to him, more than unbearable. Because he loved her, it never occurred to him to leave her.

She disposed of the sewer-line problem with a simple:

"The hell with the roots. I won't part with that tree, Brad. We'll just have to figure de-rooting into our expenses."

"It's all right with me, my dear, if you like it that much."

"Such a lovely tree, Brad. And it's peaceful. There's a certain permanent peacefulness about it."

"The tree stays. We de-root."

She was quiet, counting stitches; then she asked, "Young Champlin, hon. How's he doing?"

"Fine. Really fine, Peg. Naturally, he's doing what I knew he would, going at it too hot and heavy. I bawled him out the other day, but he just grinned and said, 'Yes, sir.' I doubt it did any good. I called him a brat and told him to go home and relax."

"I'm not talking about his work. I'm asking about him as an individual. His possibilities."

Brad leaned forward, fussed with the fire. "It's early to say. Two months. One could be wrong."

"One seldom is. When it's you."

"Nonsense. I've been wrong a number of times. But—I don't think I am in this instance. Right now he's a bit of an enigma. Very damned quiet. Shy. Naïve to a certain extent. And wary. I don't know that I'd use the word 'brilliant' yet, but he has a fine, searching mind. And sense enough to know that the law has been around a long time, longer than he has, and he's willing to take a step at a time. And that, my love, makes for a good lawyer."

"I know. How does he stack up against Baker?"

"Hell, they don't talk the same language." He was silent for a moment, thinking of the slender, acidulous young Negro, Baker, a final-year law student who might conceivably take his first year's practice with Abernathy, Willis and Shea after Culbertson left in the summer. Brad was not looking forward to the possibility. He supposed one could apply to Baker the adjective he had temporarily withheld from Champlin—brilliant. But he was also bitter, frustrated, and so racially oriented that the attaining of any objectivity in the conduct of a case seemed, at this point, an impossibility. Brad had discussed it with Peg often, had said before what he said now: "There are cases, you know, that go through our office involving Negroes in which the Negro is in the wrong. I can think of a number where we represented the plaintiff and the defendant was a Negro. That he was in the wrong because of character flaws brought into being through psychic trauma suffered as a Negro is not, I'm afraid, something a New England jury swallows too easily. True though it so often is."

"And Champlin?"

"David would understand son-of-a-bitchery in one of his own race, just as Baker does. But I don't see him letting it cloud his judgment. For a youngster he has what I can only call great compassion, which is something else again. He brought in a résumé of a case the other day that he'd typed, and said if his pay was coming out of the client he'd be glad to pass it up and do more work on it in his 'spare time.'" Brad smile. "That's what he said—'spare time.' He also said, 'That poor guy's had a rough time, Mr. Willis.'"

"Was the client a Negro?"

"Yes. Baker might have been as generous. But not out of compassion or a sense of outrage at injustice as such. It would have been out of a desire for revenge. He would have seen himself in the client, would have seen in the case every wrong our race has ever suffered. David would probably win the case before a jury; Baker would lose it before it ever got to a jury."

"You walk on eggs, don't you?"

"That's an odd remark. Yes, I suppose I do. Most of the time."

"I didn't mean it to be an 'odd remark.'" Her husky voice was beginning to show tension. "You've traveled a fur piece on eggs. And objectivity."

"That's hardly fair. If I had more, had even enough objectivity, you'd be wearing mink."

"I don't want mink." Her tone warned him, and he sought frantically for a change of subject. He did not know what she wanted of him; not mink, that was certain. Her material wants were few and moderate. There was doubt in his mind that she herself knew exactly what she sought for in him—and apparently could not find. When he had tried to question her, there had been bitter, illogical quarrels; he would not try again. He knew only this much: that she would be happy to see him tackle the problems of their people on a full-time basis—yet she had followed with tense interest his defense of a young Polish boy accused of rape, had gone to court the final day and wept real tears of joy at the acquittal. And that night had started a month-long drinking bout.

All of his work as a consultant to ALEC's Boston-located national headquarters he gave unstintingly and without fee.

But he would not, he told her once, become in his private practice what he called a "professional Negro." There had been no quarrel, although he had feared one the moment the words were out. There had been only the familiar journey into unreality, culminating on that occasion in a wrecked car and a broken ankle.

She was rolling up her knitting now, preparing to stand, and he felt the muscles of his belly tighten with dread, but she said only, "Coffee?"

When she brought the coffee back he said, "I'm inclined to think some of young Champlin's emotional maturity stems from an incident in college. More than an incident, really."

"What incident? You didn't tell me."

Peg, he said silently; Peg, Peg. You hadn't been sober for three weeks, and if I'd told you then, you probably wouldn't even have remembered. Aloud he said: "Dr. Sutherland told me about it. David's best friend his first year and a half at Pengard was Dr. Sutherland's son, Clifton. 'Suds' he's called —God knows why. I think they are still close friends. David is at their house a lot, and they seem very fond of him. Anyhow, the boy had a damned nasty time for a while—"

He told her the story, as Sutherland had told it to him, finishing with, "The dean resigned."

"God!" said Peg. Her eyes were wide and so dark they seemed pure black. "Oh, God! The poor kid. The poor damned kid—"

"He weathered it, Peg. He weathered it and stayed seaworthy. And didn't become—let's say—Bakerized."

"What makes people react, Brad? Why does one man become a Baker and another a Champlin? This damned generalizing—this 'they, they, they—' This 'The Negro is this—*they* are that—' "

"Our own people are guilty of it, too, Peg. I swear every Negro who gets his opinions in print becomes immediately the spokesman for the race. 'We Negroes hate whites—we Negroes love everyone—we this—we that.' They moan because they have no identity, yet they destroy their individual identities by burying them alive in a race identity of their own invention." Thank God, she was in agreement with him, the tensions of a half hour ago lessening. "In David's case I think the credit goes to his grandfather. And a Danish professor named Bjarne Knudsen who lives and teaches in New Orleans. From what I've heard, Knudsen is a big wheel in the academic world, and he took David under his wing when the kid was only about seven or eight. But I would say his grandfather did the most."

"I envy him."

"Who? The grandfather? Or David?"

"His grandfather. It must be pretty damned great to grow old and watch a boy like David growing up and know you had a part in what he is."

"As I said before—it's early yet, Peg. Things can happen. He's still nothing but a brat."

"A nice brat."

"A nice brat."

"I wish—if we'd had a son—"

"Peg, my dear, to have a son David's age you would have had to marry in kindergarten."

"I know. I—I guess it doesn't do any good thinking about it—" She stood up and began gathering ashtrays and glasses.

Brad walked over to her, put an arm around her shoulders, and drew her closer so he could rest his cheek against the glow of her hair. "Thinking never did a damned thing in the field of procreation. You know that, don't you?"

She laughed, then turned her head so that it rested on his shoulder, the long strong fingers of one hand digging into his arm. "I know. Brad, I'm a bitch. And you've been so damned, so Goddamned good. But Brad, if I'm a bitch it's not because I don't love you. Not ever. I do love you, Brad—"

"Of course, Peg." And wished he did not feel as though she had left a phrase unsaid, a phrase that would have begun, "in spite of—"

On the same night that Brad and Peg Willis were discussing him, two months after he entered Harvard Law, David sat with Suds Sutherland in a dim and ancient Boston fish house surveying a mound of empty clamshells. He sighed deeply and said "Whew!" and Sudsy said, "Courage. There's more coming. Mackerel."

They ate contentedly and when the meal was over sat drinking beer and talking. David was conscious now and then of stares, but he reflected that it had been a long time since he had known the acute discomfort of those meals in the Laurel Inn on his first trip to Pengard. He had been trying, whenever he could spare the mental effort from his studies, to assess the racial climate of this city, to compare it with Chicago and Cincinnati, and so far had not been able to arrive at any conclusive opinion. He lived within blocks of what could only be described as a Negro ghetto, a ghetto rapidly encroaching on his own neighborhood, and whenever he walked its streets to barbershop or restaurant he felt again the sting of guilt at his alienation from his people, the feeling that what he had should somehow be shared, that he had no right to it. He had compared with a sort of bitter wonder the outspoken defense of the Negro made by various prominent citizens in print, in the letters-to-the-editor columns of the papers, and from public platforms, with the ill-equipped schools and the all-black hordes of children romping in their asphalt-paved schoolyards at recess.

Without thinking he said now, "I like this town. But it's phony as hell just the same."

Suds' eyes became round and questioning. "What brings that crack on?"

David shrugged. "Sorry if I riled you. But I'll tell you, chum. Look at me. No one's given me a bad time since I've been here. Anyplace. I don't go in places I'm not sure about, but I don't suppose there are any I couldn't if I looked like a student or a big shot—professional, that is—and wore the right clothes. But suppose I was married and wanted to rent?"

"Hell, we've got integrated suburbs all around—"

"Maybe. If you're a doctor or a lawyer and have the dough to buy. But last Sunday I went to a little church on the edge of Roxbury—"

"How in God's name did you get over there?"

"Got to talking with a guy on the subway. He said they had good singing. I'd been hankering for some—well, anyhow, I could have been at home. And if those aren't segregated schools I've been seeing—"

"Yeah, I know, but—"

"You think something isn't going to crack now that the Supreme Court has acted? Here in the North, too?"

"Yeah, but—"

"Lay off the 'yabbut' routine. You think they'll do anything about it here?"

Suds was quiet for a minute, then said slowly: "No. Not here. I mean voluntarily. You haven't been here long enough to get the true picture. The politics. The apathy. We New Englanders will fight, yes, man, we'll fight for the poor downtrodden Negro in the South. But, by God, we Bostonians won't stoop to dirty our fingers to clean out the rotten politics, overcome the apathy, that stymies any fight here. And, David, so help me—and you can hit me over the head with that beer bottle if you want—your own people around here aren't exactly what you'd call activists. I'm no student of the situation, but I swear they act as though they'd invented the *status quo* concept."

"That's what Willis says. I'm beginning to get it."

"We argued once about what would happen when the Supreme Court decided, didn't we? Mildly. I didn't believe you then—that things would just get worse. I'm beginning to now. Chuck Martin said the same thing. And you seemed to know—"

"Hell, man, the white racist isn't exactly unpredictable. My grandfather can tell you every time one of the public ones is going to sneeze. But I can't predict, damned if I can, what these half-assed so-called liberals in the North will do. Only that whatever they do when the chips are down I don't think I'm going to like it." David looked at his watch. "Your daddy told me to get you home early."

"Oh, my God! He'll never stop feeling guilty because somebody else found out I had TB."

"You feeling O.K.?"

"Fine. Gosh, I feel fine."

Driving to David's rooms Sudsy said: "Onc thing about this city, phony or not, it's a small town. Everyone's mixed up with everyone else. You're doing some work for a firm that handles my father's legal affairs, and Hunter Travis's old man uses it too, for some of his stuff—"

"Abernathy, Willis and Shea? Lawrence Travis? I didn't know—"

"Yup. Mrs. Travis's family were Boston's best. Related somewhere along the line to the Abernathy clan. Everyone here is related somewhere along the line. Anyhow, her mother took a trip to England and married an English title. She sent her daughter—that would be the present Mrs. Travis—back to the States to stay with her grandparents and go to prep school and college. Since her father died, her mother lives here most of the time. Marcia wound up in Radcliffe." Suds laughed. "Don't get any preconceived ideas. Mrs. T. is swell. Anyhow, that's how she met Lawrence Travis. He was working his way through Harvard. Waiting tables, janitoring, anything he could get. My mother told me all this after I left Pengard when she found out I knew Hunter. The Travises were married after Lawrence went into practice."

"Did the grandparents raise a sand?"

"You mean about Travis? No-o-o." Suds squirmed almost visibly. "I mean, they—"

"Took it like Spartans? Breeding and all that?"

"No, damn it! They, well, just didn't raise any sand—"

"Probably thought it was a sort of mark of distinction. If it had been an Irish bartender they'd have raised hell."

"Don't be prickly."

"I'm not being prickly. I've been here long enough to sense a little bit about how some of their minds work. Some things are so far out they come full circle. If you can't marry another Brahmin, don't marry into the middle class. Marry a Negro. Thereby carrying on the great tradition of—of—damned if I know of what."

"Oh, for God's sake! Sometimes you can't find a good word to say for anyone, can you?"

"Nope. And sometimes I can. I'm an ambivalent anachronism, according to Hunter."

"I'll ask him what he meant when he gets here. He'll be over here soon. Something about his book."

David felt a glow of pleasure. There was no one from Pengard he would rather see, he thought; his fear that time and the distances Hunter traveled would make their friendship a part-time thing began to recede. And he was glad Hunter's book was going well. It had made quite a splash—a first novel written while the author was still in college. He loyally declared aloud and to himself that it was a great book and tried to smother the memory of his puzzled boredom as he read it. But critics had waved banners; he knew that the book was well written, and if nothing happened in it, well, life was probably like that for the people about whom Hunter wrote.

When David let himself into his apartment, he looked at the law books on his desk, and groaned. Ten nights out of eleven the pile of books and notebooks was a challenge; on the eleventh night it became a torture. The sheer weight of the books, the realization of the vast quantities of printed matter within their covers, all of it to be digested and assimilated eventually, brought a great blankness to his mind. What he studied on those nights was a blurred and fuzzy recollection in the morning. He knew he should take Dr. Sutherland's advice and knock off more frequently. "Go out on the town now and then, my boy," Sutherland had said, and David had withheld the obvious comment that going out on the town cost money. He had made friends at the church in

Roxbury, mentioned briefly to Sudsy, but it was a long way to go at the end of the day and then return to the mountains of textbooks. The Sunday services he attended now and then were anaesthesia for a loneliness he could not always fight off. The singing did what Gramp called "carry him," as it had in his childhood; it laid a stilling hand on inner turmoil.

Tonight he knew study was out. Somewhere behind the pile of books there were some magazines and a science-fiction paperback. He didn't want anything weightier. By the time he had fixed coffee for morning, undressed, hung trousers and coat carefully, each on its own hanger, and tossed his shirt in the laundry hamper for a Sunday scrub session, he began to look forward to the evening. He put on pajamas, slid bare feet into slippers, and belted around him the robe Gramp had given him for his nineteenth birthday. He put an opened can of beer on the table, settled down into the room's only good-sized armchair, and cocked his feet up on chair opposite. As he was adjusting the lamp on the table beside him to exactly the right angle, he laughed softly. "Damned old maid," he muttered. "Fussing around like a broody hen. What'll I be when I'm sixty!"

After an hour he knew if he didn't get up and go to bed he would fall asleep over the book and waken after midnight stiff and cramped. He decided to hold out to the end of the chapter and then go. The third time he heard what he had thought was the rattling of a light wind he realized that it was a knock on the door, and sighed, damning himself for not having turned out the light and gone to bed ten minutes before. With no light on and no answer to the knock, whoever it was would have gone away. Now he would have to answer it.

At first he did not see her standing small and quiet in the dark. It was her voice that brought his eyes down to hers.

"Look down here, David. I'm way down here—"

"Sara—"

She stood outside the circle of light cast by the table lamp, all dark intent eyes and soft dark hair. He had not found words yet to follow that first "Sara—" and stood foolishly looking at her, trying to fight back the surge of joy, the choking tightness in his throat that wanted release in a shout.

"Can't you say anything, David? Not anything? For an awful minute I thought you weren't going to let me in—"

Words came finally, halting and inane. "I—well, I guess I was surprised."

"You shouldn't have been. You should have known." She smiled, and he plunged his hands into the pockets of his robe to keep them from her shoulders, her waist, her face, from anything that was Sara.

"How—how was Paris?"

"Pooh! Paris." She turned away, into the circle of light, slipping her coat off, then faced him again, handing it to him. After a moment she said, "Don't just hold it, Stoopid. Do something with it!"

He fitted it across the back of a straight chair, taking a long time, and when he looked at her again she had walked to the desk and was touching his books, his yellow legal pad, his pencils, fingering each object lightly, then going on to the table, then across the room and into the small bedroom beyond and the bath and out again to gas plate and refrigerator.

"You wonder," she said. "You lie awake at night and wonder where someone you love is sleeping, and waking up, and reading, and missing you. And when you get there—it's like coming home."

She crossed to the big chair and sat in it, cross-legged. "Was this where you were when I knocked?"

"Yes. Almost asleep. Sara, why did you leave Paris? You came back early in September. I had a letter from Tom. I—" He stopped. He had started to tell her that he wanted to call her one day, the day he had met Bradford Willis. But he couldn't tell her that, couldn't let his guard down that far. Instead he finished the sentence by saying, "I always thought Paris was a sort of Mecca for young artists."

"Not for this one. Not right now. Next spring, perhaps. Paris, London, and then maybe I can exhibit."

"But—but why Boston?"

"Because you're here. And the Boston Art Museum. And some of the best instructors anywhere."

"In that order of importance?" Words were coming more easily now; he no longer felt short-winded and as though he were choking.

"Of course." She grasped her ankles and rocked gently back and forth, like a child. "I got here late this afternoon. I called Sudsy's house, and his mother said he was having dinner with you. She gave me your address. So I waited until I thought you'd be home, and walked over from Copley Square. Like—like a homing pigeon."

"You shouldn't have. I mean, it's not a very good neighborhood."

"I didn't even think about it. I came back from Paris because—because—well, anyhow I was coming here as fast as I could, as soon as I knew you'd be here for classes. And then the first of September my sister in Rio had twins. They hadn't had a baby for seven years and then they have twins. Isn't that marvelous! Think of it, David—two babies at once! It's super!"

He was glad that his laugh sounded natural, at least to himself. "Could be. It would scare hell out of me." He began to relax. "How about coffee? Beer?"

"Coffee. If it's made."

"I can make instant coffee. Or plug in the percolator. It's all set up for morning."

"That's good."

"What—" He cast an almost frightened glance back at her over his shoulder as he walked toward the back of the room. What had she meant, "That's good"?

While he put water on and measured coffee, she said: "When we got the cable from Rio my father decided to go down there. He was positively psycho about having twin grandsons. So we took off—just like that. And then three days after we got there my brother-in-law had word from the home office that he would be recalled and promoted all at once. So I stayed to help. I just got back last week."

"And came to Boston."

"Of course."

He handed her the coffee without saying anything. She looked up at him as she took it and said, "David. Your eyes are shining. They're shining like—gosh, like streetlights or something. Aren't you going to say it, David? I mean, really say it and not just look it?"

He spoke almost crossly. "Say what?"

"That you're happy? That you're happy to see me? Because you are, David. You know you are."

He sat in the occasional chair, rays from the lamp on the table beamed away from him and illuminating Sara, making her a glowing idol sitting cross-legged in his chair.

"Yes," he said almost inaudibly. "Yes, of course I'm happy. I—I'm so damned glad to see you I guess I haven't got good sense. But—I wish you hadn't. It was rough, but it was easier too—the way things were. Because nothing's changed. Nothing ever will."

"David! You're—you're stupid and dense and hardheaded and stubborn and—and blind. And you're wrong, and I love the hell out of you, David."

When he didn't answer she leaned forward, her face no longer in the light. She had spoken, in spite of the words, softly, slowly, in quiet measure, not tumbling her thoughts out, sounding like someone else, not like Sara Kent at all. It will be all right, thought David; it will be all right if she stays in that chair. If she just doesn't get out of that chair and come over here and touch me, I can make it. But she did not move, just said softly, "David."

He fussed intently at an almost invisible hangnail on one thumb, not looking up. "Maybe I am all those things you called me. But I'm not blind."

"Perhaps not to everything. Only to what's good."

"What do you mean by that?"

"David, can't you see! Oh, my darling, can't you see? There's a great good, I mean *good* when two people love each other! It's just us, Sara and David, male and female, and we love each other and it's good because it doesn't mean hurt to anyone else. It's wrong, wrong, *wrong* to turn our backs on it—just because there'll be trouble and—and talk, and nastiness and stuff. Isn't it for me to decide? Whether I can take it or not? Whether I love you that much or not? Isn't it? What do you want, David? Perfection? It doesn't exist." When he didn't answer, she gave an exasperated sigh. "David Champlin, you're the only person in the world who can make me grit my teeth, I mean literally grit my teeth. Suppose I'd married that—that drip I told you about? Suppose I had? That would have been real trouble. That would have been awful—"

"Why? Is he in jail or something?"

"No!" The word exploded. "No, he's not in jail. He's in San Francisco with a scraggly red beard and sandals, living in some kook artist colony—"

David swallowed hard, trying to hold back a laugh, then gave way to it. "I'm supposed to be flattered?"

"David. Please. We can't quarrel. Not now—"

"Sara, I don't want to quarrel. Not now or at any time. A spat with you leaves real honest-to-God wounds. Only—"

"Only what?"

"Only, I guess, that I wish you wouldn't put me on a spot. Perhaps everything I think is right is wrong—and vice versa. I don't know. I just don't know. But I *think* it's right, at least for now, and I can't see how I can ever think differently. Not in the world we live in, anyhow. And, well, it's just damned tough, that's all."

Slowly she unfolded her legs and lowered her feet to the floor. When she stood and reached for the coffee cup on the table there was a fine tremor in her hand. She drank deeply, then said quietly: "All right, David. I wasn't going to leave tonight. Not if I had to sleep in a chair or on the floor or standing up, I wasn't going to leave. A lot of people would think I didn't have any pride. But you know better. All that long time at Pengard when I first knew you and was in love with you and didn't think you knew I existed I never made a move. It wasn't till I knew, really *knew* that I said anything. And I had to be the one to say it because you'd have let them boil you in oil before you'd have opened your stubborn mouth. Then all this summer in Paris and then in Rio I kept thinking of you getting further and further away, getting to be just a damned memory, someone to reminisce about. And I thought of the years and years—and—and I made up my mind that if I was ever with you again I wasn't going to leave." Now she put the cup that she had been cradling in her hands back in its saucer, carefully, slowly, precisely. "But now I will, David. Now I will leave. You've won. Damn it, you've won again—with your blasted righteousness and damned noble self-sacrificing stupidity—"

"Sara!" He was on his feet, anger flaring.

"Don't touch me, David. Get my coat. Just get my coat."

He stood looking down at her, realizing at last what he had known subconsciously since he had seen her standing at his door: not that she wasn't going to leave, but that this moment would come when he would not have the strength to let her leave.

He crossed the few steps between them and threw an arm around her shoulders, turning her around, holding her close.

"David. I said don't touch me, David. Don't touch me. And for God's sake, don't comfort me!"

His arms slid lower on the body until one was at her waist, the other under the small rounded hips, and he lifted her clear of the floor so that her face was close. He cradled her head with one hand—"Sara—Sara—little love—"

When his mouth left hers at last, he said, "That wasn't comfort, little love. That wasn't comfort—"

"No—oh, God, no, it wasn't. . . . David . . . put me down. . . . I feel so—so small and—and inadequate—"

His face was buried in her throat between the soft edge of the dark hair and the smooth curve of her shoulder, and he was half laughing, his words indistinct.

"Inadequate! . . . Sara. Smallest . . . You're as inadequate as—as an earthquake. . . . Stop wiggling, little Sara . . . I'll let you down . . . in a minute . . . just a minute. . . ."

41

When Sara came into the bedroom the next morning carrying percolator and mugs for coffee David was sitting up, arms wrapped around his knees, eyes on the door.

"Don't do that to me, Smallest," he said softly. "Don't ever do that—"

"Do what?" She put the tray on the table beside the bed.

"Sneak out of bed and not tell me. Nudge me, honey; say 'Hey dear, I'm getting up for two minutes—' I woke up and you were gone—"

"Idiot! Couldn't you hear me banging around out there? Couldn't you smell the coffee?" Mug in hand, she perched at the end of the bed, back against the footboard. She had done what she could to adapt David's robe to her small frame, without noticeable success.

"For a split second I couldn't. The longest split second of my life. Smallest, what are you doing way off there?" He leaned forward quickly, a long arm reaching for her, but she evaded his hand.

"You have to get up," she said. "You have to, David. Classes. You-just-have-to-get-up."

"I do?"

"You know you do. Please, David. That's something I don't ever—I mean ever—want to do. You know, hold you back—"

He grinned. "How come you've got the strength to be so stubborn? After last night. Me, I haven't. I'm going to class.

Only, don't you think we could hold hands, that's all, just hold hands while we drink our coffee?"

"David—" She moved closer, slipped a hand into his. "I don't trust you. And I don't trust me. And David—in case you forget—I love you."

"I won't forget—" With his free hand he took her coffee mug away from her, put it on the table, then drew her into his arms. "Damn it to hell," he murmured. "Damn it all. Why've we both got to have good sense—"

After they had dressed and eaten breakfast and were finishing their final cup of coffee at the card table, she said, "Should we leave together?"

"Why don't you leave about nine thirty? Both the Perreiras—my landlords—work on Friday. There won't be anyone upstairs."

"I'll do the dishes." She made a face at him across the table. "And they won't all get back in the right places and maybe there'll be egg on a spoon, but I'll do my best."

"Rinse 'em and stack 'em, sweet. We'll do them tonight."

"I forgot! We're invited to dinner at the Sutherlands'. When I called there last evening Mrs. Sutherland asked me to tell you."

"And you said 'yes'?" His face was serious and unsmiling.

"No, David. Don't look like a trod-upon male. I said I'd ask you and let her know. I'm not all that bad, making decisions for you even about a dinner date."

He stood up and walked over to her and lifted her from her chair, picking her up and holding her against his shoulder as he would a child, "Only about more important things, baby—"

"David! Put me down and get going!"

He let her slide to the floor, bending to kiss her quickly. "I'm gone, Smallest. I'll call you at the hotel at five thirty. Right?"

"Right—"

For the next few days David reveled in his own defeat, fighting off the knowledge of an inevitable reckoning, crowding it into the background of his thoughts, letting his love for Sara possess him, trying not to recognize the sadness in it. Yet something within him waited, something that was only completely quiet when Sara was in his arms. He would watch her walk across the room and feel that his body must be shaking visibly with the force of his love and desire, and then, unbidden, there would come a cold foreboding, a voice of dread that seemed to say, "This isn't your life; this is a detour, a side-road trip to happiness—the main road is back there, waiting for you—" And only Sara's small, warm, immensely vital body, only its responses, could still the voice.

It was after one of these episodes that Sara, lying spent and quiet in his arms, said: "You frighten me, David. Sometimes you frighten me."

He tightened his hold gently. "I'm sorry, little love. I'm sorry. I think it's because sometimes I'm frightened myself—"

"Of what?"

"Us, Sara—"

"Ah, David, please—not now. Let's not talk about it now—let's sleep now, David—let's sleep now—"

"All right, little love, all right—"

On the sixth evening after Sara's appearance at David's door, his landlord telephoned. David had just come in from walking part of the way to Copley Square with Sara. "I'm going home early," she had said. "So you can have one whole long evening for studying. And missing me. Can't let you get too used to me—" He had said "Stoopid!" but she had stuck to her word. It was not quite eight o'clock when Perreira called, his voice sounding nervous and worried, and David wondered if he had been drinking.

"You got a minute?" he asked.

David cast a desperate look at the books on his desk. "Yeah, but only a minute. Why?"

"The old lady wants to see you."

David put the receiver down slowly. What in hell! After he and Sara had finished eating, he had found the usual after-dinner lack of hot water. He filled the teakettle now and put it on the gas plate for the dishes. Besides, it would give him an excuse to break away from upstairs—"Got something on the stove—" He felt uneasy. Was Perreira's "old lady" going to bawl him out because she'd heard a woman's voice in his apartment? He reviewed what he knew of Lessie Perreira and what he had surmised after some uncomplicated adding of two-and-two following a few slips of her tongue when she'd had a beer or so too many.

If his estimate of her age was right, based on these slips, she could quite easily have participated in the World War I hegira from Storyville. She knew a hell of a lot about that particular era of New Orleans history and that particular area as it had been in those days. And, she had told him, the best friend of her youth had been a blues singer with whom David was well acquainted and whom Gramp had known for donkey's years. The blues singer was a pious individual now, attending Mass daily, refusing to sing in any but the most respectable places, preferring to display her talents, whenever possible, at college jazz concerts, where she was much in demand. Of her, Gramp had once said: "Lawd, Lawd! Who's she think she's fooling! She ain't fooling no one. Been a spo'tin' woman most all her life. First time she married she married a gambler, and the next time she married a pimp. Still got him. I ain't faultin' her for what she's been, but she sure as hell ain't got no call to put on all them airs, treating the rest of us like we wuz a bunch of gin-soaked sinners."

And she'd been Lessie Perreira's good friend, or so Lessie Perreira claimed. Lessie had never struck him as being too damned righteous. She'd taken up with Joe Perreira and moved away—and whether they were married or not David didn't suppose anyone knew or cared—but she could and would still tell a salty story in the language it was meant to be told in. He remembered now the telephone invitations he'd had, when he first moved in, to come up and have a beer, always on the nights Joe played pool. He shivered reminiscently, remembering his revulsion when he realized what she intended "a beer" to mean.

Joe Perreira opened the door for him and led him into the kitchen at the rear. Mrs. Perreira was scrubbing the drainboard as though her intention was its annihilation. When he entered she put the scrub brush in the sink and turned on him, hands on fat hips. "Listen here, Mr. Champlin."

David recoiled inwardly from the "Mr. Champlin." He'd thought it might be a rent raise; but this was no rent raise.

"I don' know what you-all think you're getting away with down there, but I'm standing here telling you you ain't getting away with anything. We ain't renting no apartments to no dicty young student to carry on in like you been carrying on down there. And don't say you don't know what I'm talking about because you know damned well."

He did. It was a woman coming to his apartment. Lessie Perreira must spend more time snooping out the front window than he'd thought. The Goddamned old hypocrite!

"I'm not stupid, Mrs. Perreira. But I didn't think when I rented that apartment that I was going into holy orders, entering a monastery."

"And you wasn't. Women's one thing. A man's a man, and you young and hot-blooded. But white women's something else. And don't tell me that's some blue-vein Negro you been laying up with down there because it ain't. She's whiter'n a fish's belly. And that I ain't standing for—"

He heard her out, through a long tirade, until, short of breath, she turned to her husband. "Joe, you tell—"

But Perreira was having no part of it. He backed away until he was leaning against the sill of the rear window, and said: "You leave me out of this. I got nothin' to do with this. I ain't seen nothin—"

"I'll be gone within two hours." David wished now he'd shut her up after her opening attack. The sound of her words was hanging in the air like poison gas. As he started out, Joe skittered nervously around the side of the room, keeping the kitchen table between himself and his wife, and followed David to the front door. "Look," he said. "Don't rush off. Your rent's all paid up to the first. Always did say Ma sees red when she sees white—"

"It's O.K., Joe. Forget it—"

Back in the apartment he stood in the center of the room, more disgusted than angry, and mentally inventoried his possessions. Too damned many for a taxi. He went to the telephone and dialed Suds, who answered his greeting with, "Hey, man! Where you been?"

"Busy." He thought he heard a low chuckle, but he was in no mood to call Sudsy on it. He was sure Suds knew the score as far as he and Sara were concerned; knew and, miracle of miracles, seemed to take it for granted. "Suds, I need a hand. I'm moving."

"Why? I thought you liked that place."

"Never mind why. Can you lend a hand?"

"Sure. Anytime. Tomorrow evening?"

"Tonight."

"My God! What's happened? Where you going?"

"Damned if I know. Can you keep my stuff till tomorrow? I'll find a place then and get a room tonight. Maybe the Y—"

"Don't be a drip. You'll come here—"

"Look, I don't want to be a nuisance. I'll find—"

"Shove it. Get busy. I'll be there—"

When David and Suds entered the Sutherland house in Back Bay, Dr. Sutherland came to the door of his study at the rear of the front hallway, egg-shaped and benign.

"Ah, David! Clifton said you were coming to us for a while. Nice to see you. We don't see enough of you, my boy."

David laughed nervously. "And I was afraid I was wearing out my welcome."

"Not in this household, David. Come in, both of you, and have a nightcap. Mrs. Sutherland is out, and I've been feeling deserted."

David followed Suds into the softly lighted, book-lined room. "Do you mind if I use the telephone, sir?"

"Good grief, no! Use the one in the living room. Clifton can fix us a highball while you're calling."

He telephoned Sara first because she might call him and then imagine all sorts of things when there was no answer. When he told her he was at the Sutherlands', bag and baggage, she cried, "David! What's happened!"

"Nothing, Sara. Can't a guy move—"

"No! Not in the middle of the night, for heaven's sake. Tell me—"

"Later, Sara. Meet me at Hennessy's at six tomorrow? We'll have dinner—"

He'd have to dream up something to tell her before tomorrow night; right now he had to call Gramp, collect. Only once since he had left home had he failed to leave word where he could be reached if Gramp was sick or needed him. That had been the night in sophomore year at Pengard when he had taken Sudsy to the train.

"Where you been, son? You behind in your letterwriting. I was hoping you'd call."

"I've been busy, Gramp, real busy." He told Li'l Joe that he had moved, not saying it was less than an hour ago, but Li'l Joe was not accepting the story without question.

"What's the matter, son? You in trouble, some kind or another?"

"No! For gosh sake. I didn't like the place, so I moved."

"Without having no other place to go? That don't make sense, son. You been cutting up?"

David sighed. Perhaps someday, just once, he'd be able to fool Gramp. It didn't seem probable, and only barely possible.

"I haven't been cutting up. I'll write you about it."

"You been staying by Joe Perreira's, ain't you? 'Saiah's cousin."

"Yes. I wrote you."

"That's a worrisome woman he's got."

"You know her?"

"Been knowing her. Been knowing her a long time. She ain't nothing but trouble. Reckon you had your reasons. Long as you ain't in no fix."

"I'm not, Gramp. Honestly. Here. You take this address and phone number. I'll write when I find a place—"

"Lawd, boy! You sure worries—" There was a wait while Gramp sought pencil and paper. For a man who was careful about his money, Gramp sure was free and easy when it came to long-distance calls. He heard the sound of Gramp's voice some distance from the phone, and when Li'l Joe came back and said, "All set—" David said, "You got company?"

"Just Chop-bone."

"Chop-bone! Who in hell is Chop-bone?"

"It ain't who, it's what."

David grinned into the receiver. "We've got us another cat, I'll bet."

"Sure has. Black and white, and no bigger'n a minute. Seen him out back the other day, 'most starved to death, chomping on a chop bone he got out on the garbage. That's how come I named him."

"Tell him I said to keep an eye on you. And, Gramp, tell the Prof thanks for his letter, and I'll answer it next week."

"See you do. You ain't got time to write to both of us, you write to the Prof. He sets a lot of store by them letters of yours—"

Later, punching a pillow into submission in an upstairs guest room, David had time to reflect on the complexities of life. He wondered if any black man anywhere in the United States, whatever his status, had ever gone through a twenty-four-hour day without devoting some of the minutes or hours contained in it to thinking of the complexities, the paradoxes, that were a part of being black.

It could be, he thought now, that Nehemiah had been right all along. Which in itself was a strange conclusion to arrive at under his present circumstances: a welcome guest in the home of a prominent white family where even his supersensitive antennae of mind and spirit had been unable to detect any sign of patronage, condescension, or superiority. Yet his very acceptance could be, unless he was careful, one of Gramp's "traps for the unwiry."

David had wondered, sitting in Sutherland's study a little earlier, how long the Sutherlands' cordiality, the adult Sutherlands' acceptance, would last if the doctor and his wife knew the real story of what had happened tonight, if he had told the truth instead of a plausible lie. Tolerant toward sex he knew Sutherland to be, and thought he sensed the same tolerance in Mrs. Sutherland; tolerant toward sex between the races he did not know them to be.

Hunter had spoken once of the difficulties of having been born with a foot on each side of the fence. Why hadn't he, David Champlin, had sense enough to keep both feet on his own side of the fence? Life would be *one* whole hell of a lot simpler and more relaxed. It was almost as though the words were spoken aloud in the room: "Without Sara?" And the answer had to be: "Yes, without Sara."

Below there was the sound of the heavy front door closing, then the sound of footsteps on the stairs. Mrs. Sutherland must have come home. Dr. Sutherland had come upstairs when he and Suds did, and now the footsteps were in the upper hall, near his door; then from just beyond the room where he lay, he heard a door open, and Dr. Sutherland's voice.

"Dorothy?"

"Yes, dear."

Now Mrs. Sutherland must have entered their bedroom and the door must still be open. In the night quiet of the house their voices were clear and distinct.

"Good meeting? It's late—"

"Grim. And interminable. Honestly, Jim, sometimes I despair of human progress." A pause. "There's a suitcase in the front hall."

"Yes. Young David Champlin's. Clifton brought him home here for a few days. He's in the green room."

Shut the door! For God's sake, shut your damned door! I'm awake and I can hear and I don't want to hear.

Her response came quickly, without reservation, without knowledge that the subject of their conversation was an unwilling listener:

"Really? How nice! I wish Clifton would bring him oftener. Remind me about clams tomorrow, dear. I know he likes them."

Hell!

When he met Sara the next night at the inexpensive restaurant they had found near his old apartment, he knew, before she even saw him approaching, that she was excited and happy about something.

After they found a booth in the rear and were seated, he said, "You're bouncing."

"I know I am. It's disgusting to be so transparent. But I've found a studio, a real attic one with a big skylight and a gas plate and refrigerator, and a bath and shower on the same floor and it's perfect, absolutely perfect! I moved in this afternoon, only I couldn't get hold of you to have you come there instead of here. Isn't it super, David!"

"Where is this place?"

"It's near here. And it's close to the subway—David, come back with me and see it—"

He hesitated. How long would she last in this new place if her first guest was a Negro? Sara caught the hesitation and pounced on it. "Stop seeing things under the bed!"

He grinned. "O.K., Prof—"

"What—"

"Never mind. Go on."

"Well, it's a sort of fantastic place. An old rebuilt house, and it's full of students, art students, music students, every kind. There are two Chinese girls and two boys from Pakistan, and a colored couple—he's doing graduate work at Boston University, and she's taking a library course—and a funny old lady who likes to think she's offbeat but who really writes greeting-card verses; only, she tells everyone she's a modern poet. And, let's see—"

He shook his head. "How do you do it! Find all this out so soon?"

"The landlady or manager or whatever she is. She liked me. I think she's a bit of a lush, she smelled that way, but she's nice and made a point of telling me she didn't mind anybody's business but her own—"

"In a place like that she'd go nuts if she did—"

"Anyhow, it's clean, and the rent is the best part of it next to the skylight. Please, David, come back with me."

"Sure. For once it seems as though I can fade into the background atmosphere."

"David, I've been an egocentric pig! *My* studio—*my* find. What happened to you? Why did you move out?"

"Later. Let's eat. And I'm looking at the right-hand side first. I lost half a month's rent."

After they arrived at the house, David made the three flights of stairs only a little behind Sara, conscious that she had held her pace down. This was the only aspect of his lameness that really bugged him—the knowledge that there were times when others had to adjust to his handicap.

Tonight there was something elaborately casual about her; he knew her well enough to know that eventually the casualness would break down and matters of grave import would be revealed. Her delight in the studio was like a child's delight; he would not have indicated by so much as a look that to him it had all the charm and appeal of a deserted barn.

After he had lifted suitcases to strategic spots for unpacking and moved the few pieces of heavy old-fashioned furniture to more convenient locations, she suddenly became serious.

"David—"

"What? You've been worrying something around in your mind all evening."

"Not worrying, just holding back because I'm afraid you'll scream and yell."

"David Champlin? Scream and yell? You're out of your mind."

"Well, I mean be difficult and hold-offish—"

"You propositioning me? Because if you are, honey child, I can get that suitcase off that couch in one-half second flat."

"Later. As you said when I asked about your move. And you haven't answered yet. David, listen, two flights down, on the second floor, there's a vacancy."

"Oh."

"Yes, and it's, well, just about perfect. It's on the front and it was two rooms; only, there's been a partition knocked out so it's one big room and a good-sized alcove. And there's a fireplace even if it is bricked up, and there's a real apartment-size stove, with an oven, and a little refrigerator. And a shower and toilet. There are only three apartments in the whole place with that. Plus—it's five dollars a month less than you were paying—"

"You'd better hold up a minute and take a breath—"

"David, wouldn't you like it? Wouldn't you? I have the key. And the lights are connected."

He was quiet for a moment. He remembered feeling like this that day at Pengard when they had all taken over for him, and practically gotten him the job at the Calico Cat. Finally he said, "Thanks, Sara."

"David, you're cross."

"Not at all. Let's look at it."

"You are. The only reason I have the key is because the landlady's going to be out, she said, and she let me have it to—to—"

"Show the apartment to me."

"Yes. What's wrong with that?"

"Nothing. Let's go. Two flights down, on the front?"

"On the right-hand side. David, please—" But his steps were already sounding unevenly on the uncarpeted stair treads, and she followed slowly, wondering if she would ever understand, fully understand.

David had to admit to himself that the apartment was all —in some respects more—than he had hoped to find. That there would be no racial difficulty was obvious from the glimpses he had caught of other tenants in the hallways. After he had overcome the deficit of giving up a half-month's rent he could put another five, with some sacrifice, with the five-dollar saving and rent the piano one of the members of the church in Roxbury had told him about. But he was still half angry and resentful, acting, he knew, like a mule, but unable to give in.

"I'd need a desk. They moved one in for me from another apartment at the old place—"

"Isn't that long, hideous table over by the wall big enough? It's got twice as big a top. And there are three, actually three, floor outlets for lamps. And two—*two* comfortable chairs. Plus those beat-up diningroom-type ones—"

"Sure old."

"For gosh sake, what do you want? Swedish modern!"

He walked to the big bay window that overlooked the street. Its width was filled by an old-fashioned bed-divan, like the one at home. With a decent rug and his own things around, the place could be homelike and livable. And there would be sun, something he had never seen inside the place he had just left. He realized now that his mood comprised more than resentment at once again being taken over; he recognized fear in it, a fear of being drawn inexorably into a predicament that, sooner or later, must be resolved, a fear that he was traveling faster and further on that side road and that the journey back to the main road could be made only in pain. He wished Sara would go away, go back upstairs, until he could work his way out of this mood, leave for a while and save him from making her the target of his feeling of frustration and helplessness.

"David?" She was unable to keep the anxiousness from her voice.

"I guess it's all right. I have to live somewhere."

"But—but—David. Aren't you glad that we can be so close? . . . All right. Be difficult."

"I'm not being difficult. Or if I am I've got cause. You want to know why I moved?"

"Of course. I've been waiting hours and hours to find out."

"I'll relieve your suspense. My previous landlady is a reformed whore. Or nearly reformed."

"You're not all that prudish! Oh, you mean she made passes?"

"So who cares if she made a pass or two? You never saw her. I was safe. She gave me hell because I'd had you down there."

"Oh, David! I'm sorry! But if she's what you say I'd think she'd be surprised if you didn't have women—"

"It wasn't women. I could have had a dozen of those. If they'd been the right color."

That had done it—transformed the resentment in his own mind to a hurt in hers. He could see it in her eyes, in the barely perceptible droop of the slim straight shoulders, the half-opened lips that sought words. Yet he could not comfort or explain. This was the way things were; he had tried to tell her and she had brushed him off. This was a trivial incident compared to what could lie in store. She would have to learn by experience—first the little things, then the big ones, the ultimate rejections.

"Does that surprise you, Sara?"

"I—I—perhaps."

"Perhaps? Perhaps, Sara?" He spoke slowly, the words coming out crisply with a clean-cut, almost pedantic bitterness. "Do you think you whites are the only ones who don't like to see the races mixed? Don't you know that there are black people—people as different as Lessie Perreira and my grandfather—who resent it as deeply as your lily-white friends? Or did you think that a Negro who entertains a white woman in his apartment acquires a certain distinction, a kind of prestige, from the association?"

Dear God, what's happened to his eyes? thought Sara. "You're—you're—David, you've never been like this. Never talked to me like this before. You've no right to—to put things in my mind—"

Why didn't she flare up, lash back at him, give him hell? It appalled him suddenly to realize that he had taken out on her a perverse, resentful mood brought on not by recent events alone but by God knew how many other things in which she had no part, memories that were stored within him and had been stored within him since long before he had even known her. Yet, even in remorse, he found himself unable to speak or make a move toward her.

At last he turned away and walked slowly to the door. Hand on the knob, he looked back. "Tell the landlady she's got a new tenant. Wait." He drew his wallet from his pocket, took a ten-dollar bill from under the flap where he kept his reserve. "Will you give her this as a deposit? Please. Suds will bring me and my stuff tomorrow night, and I'll give her the balance then. Thanks."

Sara nodded, eyes still wide and deep with hurt. She folded the bill, nervously, over and over upon itself until it was a tiny wad. David turned from the door and walked toward her slowly, reaching a hand to touch her cheek with his fingertips.

"I told you, baby," he said. "That's the way it is—like this." Then he was gone.

Sara did not move, except for her fingers, which unfolded the bill then started refolding it. After a while her lips moved, and she half whispered, "Sara. Sara Kent. He was right. He's always right. He's—he's like a mirror. That was what you thought. Way down deep, that was what you thought. And that's why you're hurt. Because he was right. You've got to understand. How—how—*how* do you understand what can't be understood? Because love isn't enough. It isn't enough. And if you don't understand there won't be any David, now or ever. God! How do you understand when you're blind and all you have is love?"

During those first few months at law school David found his relationship with Brad Willis slipping into one of friendly relaxation. He was no longer in awe of the older man, although he strongly suspected the change from awe to respect to have been brought about deliberately by Willis—a man obviously as adept at handling most ordinary human beings as he was at handling witnesses. He was as accessible as a busy man could be, more so than David would ever have dared hope. His office opened off the main hallway just past the reception desk, and often when David came by early in the morning or late in the afternoon to leave or pick up work there would be a quick voice through the intercom on the receptionist's desk: "Is that young Champlin out there? . . . Ask him to wait if he can. . . . I'll be free in a minute. . . ."

The work he was given to type changed also. It was rougher, with fewer corrections, and David was sure he was getting Willis's first notes on a case. Instead of being sequential there would be occasional paragraphs of facts appearing far down in the notes, obviously learned after a first interview with a client. The first time it happened, he said "Damn!" and went back to the beginning, retyping the entire draft, inserting the belated paragraph where it belonged. He was careful to bring it to Willis's attention when he brought the work in. "I thought I'd take a chance, sir, and rearrange it. But I've kept the original typing, in case it was intended—"

"Fine. You did absolutely right. Thanks."

There always seemed to be coffee brewing somewhere in the mysterious back regions of the rambling, spread-out suite of rooms, and on late afternoons when Willis was still in the office and had no client with him David would just have time to obey Willis's "Sit down, David. Relax," before the receptionist appeared with coffee. It was only a short time before he was talking to Willis with more ease than he had ever known with any older person since his days with the Prof.

During one such coffee session Willis clasped his hands behind his neck, tilted his high-backed chair, and stretched long legs along the side of his desk, turning his head so that his eyes were on the darkening sky beyond the window.

"You were fortunate, David. My God! Have you any idea how fortunate?"

"Yes, sir. It's not something you forget. It scares me sometimes. Especially when I go home and see—well—"

"The waste."

"Yes. I mean—look, Mr. Willis"—he leaned forward, suddenly earnest, and sounding, even to himself, very young—"I'm not all that smart. I've got friends down home, lots of them, just as smart as I am. Some of them, I bet, would be smarter if they had the chance—only, I got the chance and they didn't. And what are they doing?"

"I don't think I want to know."

"You do know, Mr. Willis. If they're too proud to lick the whites' boots they're driving trucks—like I do in the summer

—or working on the docks or doing day labor or janitoring. And if they like the taste of shoe polish—"

"You don't have to be delicate with me, David."

David grinned. "That's my grandfather. He can cuss like a grown-up when he wants to, but he says there's a time and place for it. Anyhow, if these guys like the taste of shoe polish and they can stay adjusted long enough to finish school, maybe they can wangle a fair job. Maybe they can get a civil service job, in the post office, for instance. But not behind a window. No, *sir.*"

"Is it true, David, that a Negro who is known to be a troublemaker—and I don't mean that in any derogatory sense—let's say a Negro with influence among his own people, someone who is trying to help them actively, is frequently quieted by a good job handed out by the city or parish politicians? A job with enough money and security to make it decidedly unprofitable for him to continue his work for his people?"

"It's pretty standard procedure."

"And that, of course, gives the whites a rebuttal argument when Northerners and civil-rights groups accuse them of denying job opportunities to the Negro."

"Exactly."

"Nasty."

"Yes. And it's one of the reasons I think—I'm sure—that help for the Negro in the South is going to have to come from outside sources. I don't mean we haven't got some strong leaders there. We have. But not enough. And the pressures are too close. Isaiah Watkins and the ALEC people—they've got guts. But you know yourself, Mr. Willis, they have to call on headquarters here."

"David, would you like to lend me a hand in vacation time with some of the ALEC work here? They have a crack legal staff, but they still need help on routine stuff. They don't come any more devious or more brilliant or more dedicated than Klein, and his doctor has ordered him on a six-hour day. He's working fourteen. I try to help out. We could use you."

"Anything. I'll do anything at all I can." He looked into his coffee cup, stirred it absently. "I don't know," he said slowly. "I don't know whether I'm being noble and dedicated or trying to justify my own damned luck."

Willis laughed. "Bothers you, doesn't it? What you call your luck."

"Yes. Maybe it's because my grandfather used to say to me 'Man pays for his luck.' "

"I hope you'll get your grandfather up here one of these days."

"I'm planning on it. But he'll only come for a visit. I know that. He won't stay, damn it."

"Sometimes roots grow stronger in hostile surroundings."

"His do."

"But you mustn't let yourself become hipped on this 'luck' thing. You're too intelligent for that. I've never been a religious man. I have no religion. Let's say I'm an agnostic." He smiled. "Although I must admit, with due immodesty, that on a number of occasions I've managed to convince a jury that it was God's personal and heartfelt desire that my client be acquitted. Still, I've been forced to one conclusion: that there is some sort of cockeyed plan working somewhere for some persons. Certain circumstances that seem at the time to be a result of general cosmic chaos turn out, viewed in retrospect, to have been the only set of circumstances, that could bring about—do bring about—great good. Such as your grandfather playing banjo in an obscure New Orleans club the night a Dane named Bjarne Knudsen dropped in. We could pursue it endlessly, back to your grandfather's choice of banjo as an instrument—and beyond. Let's forget this 'luck' business, and figure there's some pattern in what has happened."

"I'll try," said David. He paused, conscious of Willis's eyes on him. "But—you ever been on the South Side in Chicago, Mr. Willis?"

Willis sighed. "Yes. God, yes!"

"That's what I mean. I've never been in Harlem, but I don't see how it can be much worse. And there are places here—it makes a guy feel guilty—"

"If you let these things do that to you, David, you're emasculating yourself, in a certain sense. You can't change things single-handed, trite as the observation may be. I can't. No one can. But you sure as hell can't help the situation any if you let anything so stupid as a feeling of guilt rule you. Would it do our people any good if you gave up and became one of the hundreds of thousands in our city ghettos—frustrated, trapped? Or one of the millions of our people in the South?"

"No-o-o. I know you're right, of course. At least, my mind knows it—"

"That's all that counts at this stage, David. Absolutely all. Your mind—"

Brad watched David leave the office, a smile softening the tan leanness of his face. His secretary came in, laid papers on his desk. "You ought to go home, Mr. Willis. You're tired."

He smiled up at her. "Speak for yourself. I didn't know you were still here." He glanced quickly through the papers. "These can wait until morning. Did you see young Champlin?"

"I make a point of having a word with him when I hear him come in. I like the boy."

"Yes." His eyes, thoughtful and remote, were on the door through which David had left a few minutes before. "I had hoped—I suppose I still hope—that one of these days he'd be here with us."

"I'm rooting for it. I've never seen a better candidate. And," she added grimly, "I've seen a muckle of 'em in my time."

"I don't know, Lucy. I don't know." He drew in his breath sharply, tapped the papers on his desk into order, laid them in the basket marked "Current." "I think he's the person I've been seeking—subconsciously—for years. To stand beside me. But there's a chill feeling in my bones that something stronger than the law firm of Abernathy, Willis and Shea is going to take over one of these days."

"Not something better, Mr. Willis. For a young lawyer this would be the opportunity of—"

He did not let her finish. "Something better? Again—I don't know. But—" There was a long pause. "Probably, Lucy. Probably."

"I don't believe—"

"Who said 'go home' first?"

"What—oh, I did."

"Then scram. And take some time off in the morning. I won't need you before eleven."

42

Late on a Friday afternoon a few weeks after his move into the new apartment, David braced his back against the cross seat next to the door of a subway train and wondered why Boston people bothered to take their kids to the beach to ride roller coasters when the Boston subway system was so close at hand. He took a copy of *Jet* from his pocket and flipped casually through its pages. Reading the compact little magazine was one way of keeping up with some of the prominent people of his own race in the country. As the train began to slow for his stop, the word "Boston" in one of the gossip paragraphs caught his eye. "What prominent Boston attorney," the short item read, "is due for gray hairs before his time if his wife doesn't cut down on the sauce? Friends are worrying."

He ran over in his mind the names of Negro attorneys he knew of or had been introduced to by Willis, then forgot the item as he came out into Boylston Street, the nip of the late fall afternoon making him turn up the collar of his topcoat.

He was in good time to leave the work he had done for Willis at the office, then subway to his apartment to shower and fix dinner for Sara, Sudsy, and Sudsy's new girl friend, Rhoda Sherman.

After they had met Rhoda the second time Sara said: "Let's don't be trite and say 'What does he see—' and all that junk. After all, she's nice and I do like her, even if she is—well—"

"Uninteresting?" supplied David.

"Well, in a way. And perhaps—"

"A little slow on the uptake?"

"All right. Poor dear. She won't have a shred of personality left when we get through with her. You're simply jealous because she's probably going to marry your best friend. All men are."

"Hey, wait! No one's said anything about their getting married, for gosh sake."

"Pooh! Want to bet they won't?"

"Make a bet like that with a woman? No."

"It's this way, David. Young men just don't spend all that time and attention on the Rhoda type if they aren't serious. And she'll be a super doctor's wife. Uncomplaining, patient, understanding—"

"The poor devil. No fun. He's too nice a guy for all those intangible virtues. Drive a man crazy after a while."

"And she's a comfortable person—"

"Jesus have moicy! I'd rather marry a Teddy bear."

"Anyhow, I repeat, she's nice and I like her and she does fit in. Sometimes I wish Hunter wouldn't give her such a bad time—"

"Don't worry. She doesn't even know he's doing it."

"Kitty—kitty—" said Sara.

Dora Moore, the receptionist in the Abernathy, Willis and Shea offices, was not at her desk when David entered. Just beyond Willis's office a door stood open, and from behind it Dora's voice called, "Who is it?"

"David Champlin."

She came into the hallway, lipstick in hand, a pertly competent young woman with Irish blue eyes, freckles, and a small, impudent nose. He had already been around the office enough to know that she had all three partners and the juniors nicely wrapped around her finger.

"Didn't you meet Mr. Willis on your way up? You must have crossed each other in the elevators. He just left and I'm leaving. Everybody's gone—"

"So soon? No business? Nobody suing anybody or anything?"

"Just a lucky break, I guess. Can you wait two minutes while I finish my face? I'll be right out—"

She disappeared into the dressing room, and the telephone in Willis's office began to ring stridently.

"David! I've put the night lines up. Will you catch it? Tell them he's gone home, and get a message—"

He lifted the receiver in mid-ring. "Mr. Willis's office."

There was a pause before a husky voice answered him, one that could be male. "May I talk to Mr. Willis?"

"He's gone for the day, sir. Will you leave a message?"

The abrupt laugh was a woman's; the caller obviously was not male. "Oh, dear. And it's not 'sir.' This is Mrs. Willis."

A lot of people sounded different on the telephone; there

was no reason to be uneasy at the difference in Mrs. Willis's voice. She continued, "Who is this?"

"David Champlin, Mrs. Willis."

"David! How nice to hear you. My husband and I talk about you so much. He's so proud of you, David. You're to come to dinner soon. Let me talk to him for just a minute, David—"

"He's gone, Mrs. Willis. There's no one here. He should be home soon."

"David, tell him to stop at Miller's Garage—"

"I can't, Mrs. Willis. He's left—"

"My car's there. A stupid" (had she said "shtupid"?) "man shmashed" (there was no doubt about that one) "in a fender. Silly old man, he was. It's so nice to talk to you, David. My husband's so proud of you. . . ." There was no stopping her. In the space of the next two minutes David figured she must have repeated herself at least six times. *What prominent Boston attorney is due for gray hairs before his time. . . .* This woman wasn't just a little high; she was close to being boxed out. Way out. And David was sure she hadn't been what Tom Evans use to call "taken suddenly drunk." There was a quality of saturation in her speech: the repetition, the inability to take in—or drunken refusal to accept—the simple statement that her husband had left, the obvious belief that no one could possibly suspect she had been drinking. She was saying again, "Let me talk to him, David. I'd better tell him about the car myself—"

"He should be home soon—"

There was a quick step behind him, the low words, "Give me the phone, David—" and Dora's hand took the receiver from his.

"Mrs. Willis? This is Dora. Your husband has gone home." She spoke slowly, distinctly, as though she were speaking to a foreigner with a limited knowledge of English, in a tone of kindly finality. ". . . No, Mrs. Willis. He should be there soon. . . . I have a call on the other line, Mrs. Willis. You just be patient and he'll be there. Goodbye."

She cradled the receiver quickly, drawing her hand away from it as though it burned her, then looked up at David's troubled face.

"You didn't know?"

He shook his head, feeling as though he had witnessed a scene of shame and humiliation he should not have seen, feeling sick at the thought that within a short time Brad Willis would walk into his home to face the woman who had just been on the telephone. "Is it—does it happen often?" he asked.

Before Dora could answer, the telephone rang again and he instinctively moved toward it. Dora's hand caught his arm. "Let it ring. That will keep up till he gets home." She took a large Manila envelope marked "David Champlin" from the desk and drew him out of the room, closing the door behind them. The unanswered summons of the ringing telephone was a lonely sound, and followed them, stayed with them as they stood at Dora's desk. She added another typescript to the nearly full envelope, then said, "Damnation!" David thought he detected something close to tears in her voice. "It's not fair. It's not fair. And she's so swell. She's such a swell person. When she's—all right."

"Then this isn't all the time?" He remembered the handsome, warm, friendly woman sitting on the edge of the big divan twisting a bright-hued handkerchief into a shapeless wad, tearing at it, drawing it back and forth through long, restless fingers, then getting up a dozen or more times during the evening on trivial errands, remembered his own puzzlement at her tense nervousness.

"Not all the time. Sometimes she's all right, and then Mr. Willis is like a different person. You can tell the minute he comes in. He's so wonderful to her, David, and so patient. It just isn't fair." She slammed the center drawer of her desk shut with a bang. The ringing of the telephone had stopped a moment before; now it started again. "Let it alone," she said. "You'd have found out about it anyhow, David, after you'd been around a while. But it's sort of a jolt, getting it that way —one of those phone calls. She calls everywhere—even courthouses and clients' offices sometimes. Everyone knows about it and everyone's so fond of them both. Only, no one will talk about it. I guess I'm just letting off steam." She handed him the envelope. "Walk me to the subway?"

"Of course."

After they left the elevator and could not be overheard she said, almost fiercely, "Peg Willis is one of the grandest people I know. Do you know what she did after my mother got a fractured pelvis in a fall? After Mom got out of the hospital Mrs. Willis sent a practical nurse—wouldn't let me say a word—to take care of Mom while I was working. For a whole month. Mom's the one who had to insist she didn't need one anymore because she was better off taking care of herself. Mom and I have prayed to just about every saint we know about, and I've made Novenas. Perhaps they'll work in time. Perhaps it has to be this way for a while—"

They reached the subway entrance, and as they went down the stairs Dora said, "I've talked your arm off."

"It's been good for you."

"Anyhow, now you'll understand. Once in a while Mr. Willis is nervous and fractious—"

"My God, who wouldn't be!"

"It's easier for him if people understand. You'll say a prayer for him? And her?"

"Sure will. You can count on it, Dora."

She smiled up at him. "Funny, isn't it, how we know the people we can say things like that to and not be laughed at? See you next week—"

The following Sunday Hunter Travis arrived at David's apartment just after Sara, in paint-smeared smock, had appeared for breakfast. He had just arrived at the airport an hour or so earlier, he said, checked in at a hotel and come directly up there.

"Phones, man, phones!" said David. "It's the twentieth century—we've got all kinds of gadgets."

"I never make local calls. Only long distance. Coffee?"

"Sausage and eggs—"

"Just toast and coffee."

"Your book, Hunter," said Sara, pouring coffee. "I just got around to reading it last week. It's well, it's not very cheerful, is it?"

"Cheerful!" Hunter set the coffee mug that was halfway to his mouth back on the table with an audible thud. "Cheerful! Sara, for God's sweet sake when are you going to grow up? Acquire even a surface layer of sophistication? No! It wasn't cheerful. What a word! 'Cheerful.' "

"Stop being superior and putting everyone on the defensive, Hunter. Maybe it is a lousy word. Maybe I meant something a little different. Perhaps I meant 'hopeful' or something like that. I'm not a writer. I just paint."

"Pretty little flower baskets?"

"Stop it, you two!" said David. "You're headed for another one of your knock-down and drag-outs. If Hunter wants to be desolated and gloomy, let him. And if Sara wants to be nonconformist and square, let her. Brethren, love one another—"

"We do manage to have at one another," said Hunter. "But always remember, Sara, I love you dearly. God knows why."

"I know why." She flashed a quick grin across the table at him. "I'm the voice of your better nature—"

"Sara, there'll be violence in a minute," said David. "Hunter admits to no better nature. What's wrong with the one he has?"

"I like it." said Hunter. "Easy on the eggs, chum. I'm having a sort of midafternoon dinner. At your boss's house, incidentally."

"Bradford Willis?"

"Yes. Known to me in my extreme youth as Uncle Brad." He looked at David, and frowned. "What's the matter? You look dubious—"

"You're seeing things—" Before David could continue, the telephone ringing from its place on the mantel stopped him. When he answered it he did not at first recognize the voice that said, "David?"

"Yes—"

"This is Brad Willis."

"Oh—good morning!"

"David, I need help in locating the only hard-working dilettante I know of. He was due in town this morning—"

"Hunter Travis. He's right here drinking coffee."

"Good! May I talk to him?"

David handed the telephone down to Hunter. It was impossible not to hear Hunter's end of the conversation.

". . . Just got here, Brad. . . . Two or three days, I hope. Have to check up on David and Sara among other things. . . . A very charming young lady, if naïve . . . I'll tell him. . . . That will be perfectly all right, Brad . . . Not a bit. Forget it. . . . We'll make it anytime you say. Actually, it probably would be better if I came to the office. Mother wants me to ask you about drawing up a deed of gift for her property in Chestnut Hill. Some kind of nursery-school project . . . Two o'clock tomorrow's fine. . . . I can have a yak with my publishers in the morning. . . . Making a start on one, yes. . . . Father? He's fine. He's in Istanbul at the moment. . . . I'll do that. . . . See you tomorrow. Cheers."

Hunter replaced the receiver and put the telephone back on the mantel with exaggerated care. Sara broke the silence. "What's the matter, Hunter? No dinner?"

"No dinner." He came to the table, took a cigarette from

the pack in front of David, and looked at the other over the flame of a lighter. "You're not surprised."

"No," said David.

"You've found out?"

"Yes."

"Brad tell you?"

"No, he's never mentioned it. I was in the office late Friday after they'd all left. There was a phone call—"

"Oh, God, one of those—"

"From what the receptionist tells me, they're almost routine—"

Sara leaned forward. "What is it, you two? What's wrong, Hunter?"

"Just the cheerful circumstance of Brad Willis's wife on another bender."

"'Another' bender?"

"She's an alcoholic. A periodic."

Sara turned to David. "I didn't know—"

"I know you didn't, Sara. I'd have told you eventually. I was just so damned upset I didn't want to talk about it. Brad's the kind of guy you grow fond of—"

"And Peg's that kind of a woman," said Hunter.

"The poor man! I've never even seen him, but I feel sorry. Can't they do anything about it, Hunter? Doctors, psychiatrists—"

"It's not all that simple, Sara. I suppose they've tried. A psychiatrist would have a field day with Peg. And probably be useless. For every one good reason the average alcoholic has for drinking, she has three or four. You know the background, David?"

David shook his head. "No."

Hunter sat down, picked up his refilled coffee mug, and said, "In fairness to Peg I'm going to give it to you."

"Perhaps Brad wouldn't appreciate our talking about it."

"I think in one sense he'd be grateful. Sooner or later he'd have to tell you himself. He very desperately wants people to understand. There aren't many who can. You can—and God knows, I can."

"All right—"

"Remember, David, our friendship—that is the family's—with Brad goes back to the time when Brad was a student in law school. My father met Brad by chance, liked him, did what Brad's doing with you—took him under his wing. When

Brad got his degree my father was the one who arranged for him to go with Abernathy. Right after that the State Department tapped my father on the shoulder. And Brad, of course, more or less skyrocketed; a few, damned few lawyers, go ahead as fast as Brad did without stepping on toes. Abernathy—he's my mother's maternal uncle, by the way—wasn't too well, and he loaded a lot on Brad's shoulders. I'm telling you all this, even if you happen to know some of it already, so you'll see how close to the situation my father and mother were, and why I happen to know so much about it. . . ."

43

After his talk with Hunter, Brad Willis walked slowly from his study to the chill, gray loneliness of a Sunday-morning living room before shades have been raised, ashtrays emptied, the untidy residue of a previous day's life cleared away. It had been stupid to ask Hunter to dinner when he had called yesterday. He had extended the invitation on a flimsy hope born of the circumstance that Peg, that morning, had "seemed" to be snapping out of it.

He stood staring into the dead ashes in the fireplace. You're too old to be hopeful, he told himself grimly. He passed a hand over his face, trying to wipe the tiredness from his eyes. "And too young to give up," he added aloud.

He wondered idly who the "Sara" was that Hunter had mentioned, obviously under the impression that David had told him about her. He hoped she was a vegetable, brought up on a farm, illiterate, and with no psychological complexities. It might be dull for the boy, but it wouldn't mean long wakeful hours at night and a prodding, subconscious worry all day like the throb of an aching tooth.

Two ashtrays on the coffee table overflowed and he threw the butts into the fireplace, then picked up and folded the soft woolen blanket that trailed crazily from divan to floor, and plumped the pillows into shape. Oblivion had hit Peg suddenly last night, before she could make it into the bedroom. He could only take her shoes off gently, loosen her dress, and cover her warmly with a blanket. Later, he knew, she would wake up, go to the kitchen for another drink, and then manage to undress and get into the bed beside his before it knocked her out.

He managed to sleep in brief fidgeting naps before he heard her come into the room and get into bed. He covered his face with his hands, as though even there in the dark the pain could be seen, when he heard her mumble, just before she fell into a stuporous sleep, "Brad—Brad—"—a cry in the night he could not answer because she had gone beyond hearing any answer.

Now, this morning, everything was quiet; it would be an hour or more before she would waken. When she did, she would go into the kitchen and pour a glass of milk. There was a poignant hurt to Brad in her pathetic confidence that he did not know the milk would be liberally laced with whiskey, that he was unaware that the bottle out of which she would pour this morning drink was hidden in some one of a half-dozen places he had long since discovered. For a long time he had brought coffee to her bed those mornings when he was at home, but stopped the practice when he realized there was real cruelty in making it necessary for her to try to hide the fine tremor of her hands, the swollen eyelids, the sniffles and choking hoarseness that were invariable symptoms of one of her hangovers. "Hay fever" she would say, and use her handkerchief or a cleansing tissue as an excuse to turn away from him. Nowadays he waited until the alcohol in the milk had taken hold and stilled the tremors that he knew shook her inwardly as well as outwardly, and when he could—on mornings when he did not have to go to the office—he waited for her to seek him out.

He drew back the draperies and raised the shades, letting a thin sliver of early sun cross the floor. After he had laid and lighted a fresh fire, he decided he felt better, then smiled wryly. "I can put a stop to that," he muttered. "I can end this 'feeling better' just by wondering what in hell I'm going to do." He dreaded these periods of reappraisal, of sending his mind back into the past, searching for some answer that might lie there, trying to find the causes or reasons, finding plausible ones but finding no way to overcome them, no way to replace them with new causes and new reasons that would make reality a bearable burden for Peg, instead of something she could carry only a short time before laying it down and fleeing.

What would have happened if he had said "No" that afternoon years before when Lawrence Travis, just before leaving for Switzerland on his first State Department assignment, had called him at the office and said, "Can you drop in at the apartment after work? We'll give you sandwiches and a drink. We're in a mess. The movers come in the morning, and we're going to Marcia's mother's for a few days before leaving for Switzerland."

A man didn't say "No" to someone who had done what Lawrence Travis had done for him. He laughed and said, "Dropping in on moving day usually means work."

"This will," said Lawrence. "But not the kind you mean. I have a problem I'd like to leave in your hands. Nothing backbreaking, but it concerns someone of whom Marcia and I are very fond."

"I'll be there as soon as I can get away."

The Travis's apartment door had been unlocked when he got there, and when no one answered his knock he walked into the chaos of the day before moving. He picked his way gingerly over cartons, packing boxes, piles of books, and around furniture that had been pushed into unfamiliar locations to facilitate the rolling up of rugs. He found Marcia Travis in the dining room wrapping chinaware and packing it into a barrel. Her hair, shorn down to short, fair curls, fell over her forehead, smooches of dust were scattered over her face, and her eyes, clear blue under brows darker than her hair, held a look of near panic. "We'll never make it, Brad. We'll have to postpone the van." She had a brusque, clipped manner of speaking; her accent showed clearly the childhood and girlhood spent in England.

"One of the spheres of hell that Dante overlooked was moving day," said Brad.

"Of course. I never thought of it before."

"Where's the boy?"

"At my mother's. Out of the way, thank God."

"And Larry?"

"In his den, sorting books. There comes a time in moving when one has to stop sorting and start packing, sorted or not. Do go explain this to him."

He found Lawrence Travis in blue mechanic's coveralls,

bent over a case of books, and said, "Your wife says pack, don't sort."

Travis straightened up. "Thank God, you're here. Now I can stop for a while. Marcia on moving day is not the woman I thought I'd married. Sit down." He cleared books from the seat of a chair. "How would a drink go?"

"Down—and good."

At that time Lawrence Travis had been a slender, light-skinned man, shorter than Brad, his eyes dark and deceptively soft and guileless. His speech, unless sparked by emotion, was slow, and the gentle cadences of the South of his birth were still evident in it. Today he was heavier, black-ribbed glasses lending a solemnity not quite deserved; behind them the eyes were sharper and gave clearer evidence of the comprehensive intelligence, the lightning-quick workings of his mind. But to Brad Willis he remained the man who had given him his first break—the slender, quiet man of that winter dusk in a cluttered den.

On that day he had gone out and returned with long drinks, than sank into a chair, groaning loudly. He took a long swallow, groaned again, and said, "I'd better get down to the meat of this thing before my client gets here."

"Here?" Brad looked around the disordered room.

"By design. She'll eat sandwiches from the drainboard with us—you will too, I hope—and if she twists our arms we'll let her pitch in and help. It's what she needs. Right now one more law office, one more breath of legal stuffery, and she'd probably crack."

"I see."

"You will in a minute, at any rate. Do you remember the Montgomery case of three months back?"

"Yes. I read about it. I don't suppose anyone in New England missed it. I even recall that they dusted off the standing type of a routine lead—'Mystery surrounds the death of a Boston couple,' etcetera, etcetera."

"You recall the pictures?"

"Yes. He was a Negro; she was white. And there was a daughter."

"My client. Our client, I should say. A particular favorite of Marcia's and mine since she was in diapers. Curt Montgomery, the father, and I come from the same part of the country, northeast Louisiana, right in the heart of the murder belt. My family came out of the galleon first, when I was very young, by the grace of God and relatives in the North. Curt and I didn't know each other, but when he was on the run—and he was—a mutual friend gave him our address. He didn't have a dime, not a crying dime, when he got here. We took him in—he got what he called a 'li'l piece of a job'—and after we made him go to night school for a year he was O.K. and stuck it out until he had full high-school credits.

"He was always clever with his hands, and he talked himself into a job with one of the best known manufacturers of prosthetics in the country—Addison and Hyatt, near Medford. He also had a clever, inventive mind and he came up with something unusual for an artificial foot and ankle joint. When the firm claimed he had invented it on their time—he had, of course—and wouldn't give him royalties, he quit and started in business for himself, and took, on the side, the agency for another manufacturer. He never became wealthy, but he prospered." Travis paused to rattle the ice in his glass and take another swallow of the drink. "Meantime he had married."

"This is the cliff-hanger?"

"In a way. I know very little about the woman he married—and what I do know I don't like. He met her when he went to her home to fix an artificial limb for her father, and train him to use it. The marriage was a mistake from the start. And obviously to the finish. Neither one of them was equipped for the rigors of a mixed marriage in this country.

"Their little girl, Margaret—Peg—was a lovely child. She's a lovely young woman. The mother was a domineering, possessive, ambitious hellcat."

"If she was ambitious why did she make the one marriage calculated to hold her back?"

"Who knows, Brad? Perhaps she felt that by marrying a Negro she was assuring herself of the upper hand."

Brad laughed. "It just ain't so, Larry."

"I know." Travis chuckled, then sobered. "Anyhow—to get back to the Montgomerys. Curt was light-skinned, about your complexion, only with dark eyes. The mother had red hair, fair skin, blue-green eyes. One is forced to admit her beauty. The child reversed the usual pattern and inherited all her mother's physical characteristics except the eyes. Her eyes are Curt's. She could pass—and did pass, at her mother's screaming insistence—when she entered Smith College."

"And then—Oh! Good God!"

"Yes. But by the time she entered college, life in the Montgomery household was pretty much constant hell. Curt was drinking; so was the mother. Perhaps not habitually, but too much. There were epic quarrels, I gather, just short of actual violence. At least, when the child was around—"

"Why didn't he leave the bitch?"

Travis shrugged. "Again—who knows? For one thing, he adored the child. For another, there may have been a certain ego-satisfaction in having a white wife. Good God, Brad, who knows what holds thousands of couples together? When I first started in practice I worked like hell on a divorce for one couple, and I'd no sooner get it set up for court than they'd reconcile and it would start all over."

"Abernathy won't handle divorce, thank God."

"That's not all to the good. It's graduate work you'll never get in a university. Back to our client. Curt was a sweet man. I mean, in the true sense of the word. Gentle under ordinary circumstances, kind, and there wasn't a child he didn't love, didn't identify with. I've seen him after he had been to a hospital and fitted some youngster with an artificial limb. He'd glow with happiness, skip around, do a little dance step to show how well it would work in time. He never lost his southern speech. 'Lawd!' he'd say. 'That was a mighty happy chile. A mighty happy chile.'" Travis was silent for a moment. "Curt was my link with the past, my 'lest we forget.' When his wife heard little Peg use one of the Deep South idioms she had picked up from her father, she'd slap her across the mouth."

"May I interject something here, Larry?"

"Certainly."

"The child adored her father."

"Of course. He told me that one time when he returned from a business trip—she was still very small—instead of jumping up and down with joy or laughing, she climbed into his arms, and sobbed. She hated her mother, I'm sure, although she may not have recognized that hatred. But, like Curt, she was helpless. That woman, Brad, was like a juggernaut—"

"I know. I've run into them."

"To get to the time when Peg was due to enter college. Peg had been an outstanding pupil, straight A's, all that. Smith accepted her—and her mother insisted that she go over the line."

"Parents visit students who are in colleges that close at hand. How did she manage that?"

"The story to the college was that Peg's parents were separated. The mother came up on special occasions: Curt didn't. But she came close to making one fatal mistake. Her first plan was to say that she was a widow, that Peg's father was dead. Peg went into a screaming, hysterical rage, rushed out of the house, and went to her father's shop. At first, she refused to go back, but he 'gentled' her into it. 'You got to get that education, honey,' he told her. 'You just be patient. Life ain't easy, but you just get that college education; then mebbe you and me can find us a place together. Mebbe we can take off together. You do what your mother says and keep things peaceable. You stick with it, honey; then you'n me'll see about things.' Her mother backed down on the widow story."

"And that's what pulled her through?"

"Yes. Give Curt the credit. She was in her senior year lightning struck. Thank God for our friends. One of a newsman on the *Globe*, got hold of me before the story the papers and radio and I was able to get hold of authorities at Smith on the telephone, and they kept her incommunicado on some excuse until Marcia and I got th

"Give me the details, Larry. Was it a killing and suicide?"

"No one will ever know. A neighbor came to the door to borrow something. There was no answer, and when she looked through the glass of the door she could just see Curt's legs sprawled on the stairs. She called the police. When they broke in, they found Curt sprawled along the bottom steps, his head on the floor, dead of a broken neck. Upstairs they found the mother dead of a bullet wound. She was also on the floor. The gun was nearby. There had been a struggle. There was a mishmash of prints on the gun—both his and hers—which was almost impossible to interpret. Was he leaving after a quarrel, and did she come up behind him and push him down the stairs? Then go back and shoot herself? Or did he shoot her, start to run down the stairs, trip and fall? They had both been drinking."

Brad finished his drink, got up and walked the length of the room and back, then sat again. "My God, Larry! What do you want me to do?"

"Just keep an eye on things, help Peg if she needs it. Curt and his wife made separate wills; I drew his up six weeks before he died. There's no difficulty in either case. Both wills name Peg as principal beneficiary. The mother left what she had—not a great deal—in trust until Peg is twenty-five. Old Colony is trustee. Curt's is also in trust until Peg is twenty-one. Which she will be in a few months. That is when she will need help and counseling."

"Will she want me to take over?"

"Brad, haven't you any idea how shot to hell she must be inside? If I advise it, she'll do it."

"Is she back at Smith? Is she going back?"

"No. She tried. She lasted two weeks. Remember—she had passed for almost four years. Suddenly she's the central figure in a sordid tragedy involving her parents—a white mother and a Negro father. I thought it would help her if she talked it out, and I asked her point-blank what the attitude at college had been. All she would say was, 'They were very kind. They were very kind.' "

"Christ almighty!" Shivers crawled up Brad's back, around his ribs, into his belly.

Travis, watching his face from across the desk, said: "Yes. I thought you'd react that way. It would have been better if they'd been cruel, called her a nigger, enraged her, given her cause to identify with her dead father, the only person she really loved. Instead, they were 'very kind.' God bless them all—they meant well."

Brad was leaning forward, arms on knees, eyes on the cigarette lighter he was turning over and over in his fingers. "She must have known damned well what they were thinking, what they stopped saying as soon as she came into a room, started up with the minute she was out of hearing. Known they were trying to be big and enlightened about an unfortunate fellow student with a beautiful white mother and a probable beast of a Negro father, who did just what you might expect. What else could come from that stage of development in a group of young sheltered white girls?"

"And she's been eaten up, almost destroyed, by a feeling of guilt—the feeling that she let her father down by giving in to pressure, by denying him," said Travis.

"Where is she living now?"

"With Curt's sister. She got out of the galleon, too. Curt sent for her. She's down-to-earth, basic, rock-bottom good, and almost as black as we come. Peg has always been fond of her. She chose Auntie Tuttle's household as the place she wanted to go."

"If it was anyone but you, Larry, I'd start out of here on a dead run."

"I don't know that I'd blame you." Travis reached for Brad's glass, then stopped, hand extended. "That's a cab door closing. I think she's arrived."

They heard voices in the hall, Marcia's high and clear, and another that was deeper, huskier. Then Peg was there, standing in the doorway in the circle of Marcia's arm, tall and, in spite of her youth, commanding—until one saw her eyes, dark pools that cried, without tears, against the pain within her. The gold-red hair lay in heavy waves held down by a bandeau. Her figure was already mature, full-breasted, small-waisted, with well-rounded hips and a long, clean line of thigh and leg. But young, thought Brad, so very young, whatever she might have gained of adulthood seared from her by the flames of grief and shock.

He rose to step back and stand quietly by the window, watching her as she crossed the room to Lawrence Travis and kissed him gently on the cheek. "Uncle Lawrence"—she looked around the chaos of the room, "Uncle Lawrence—don't go away." In that quick survey of the room her eyes had touched Brad and then gone on as though he did not exist. To her, thought Brad, I don't.

It was Marcia who answered her. "If we don't, Peg, how are we going to get you to Europe for that visit?"

Travis took her hand. "It won't be long, sugar, before that happens." He drew her forward, into the center of the room. "And I'm leaving you in good hands. Brad—"

Brad came forward, not smiling, knowing any gratuitous friendliness on his part would only heighten her sense of loss over the Travises' leaving.

"Bradford Willis, my dear—" Travis was saying.

She looked at him directly now, unsmiling. "In your hands?"

"If you'll accept their help—"

"What—what else can I do? I—I suppose it will be all right." She took a quick, shallow breath. "I'm sorry. I don't mean to be rude."

"Of course you don't, my dear." Marcia spoke crisply. "You and Larry and Brad can talk, and I'll fix coffee and sandwiches. We'll send Larry to the Square for dessert, and gorge on chocolate-marshmallow-sundaes-to-go." As she left she kissed Peg's cheek. "Be nice to Brad, dear. He's really a pet. The only green-eyed man I've ever known I'd trust with my life. And yours."

He had never been sure afterward just when it was that he

knew he loved her. It might have been that first night or it might have been a day in the office weeks later, after he finally convinced her that in the fall she should make up her credits for a degree. He suggested Boston University as the most convenient; his real reason—that it would be most impersonal—he did not mention.

When at last she agreed and they were standing together at the doorway of his office, she looked up at him and said, "I'm going to call you Brad."

"Of course!"

"Thank you, Brad, for everything. No one except my father and Uncle Lawrence has ever been so good to me before. Perhaps you can't understand what it means. When you're hurt and bruised all over because the whole world's fallen on top of you, and you hate yourself besides—"

"I think I can understand, Peg. Give me marks for trying."

"The highest—"

They were married a little more than a year later. He hadn't known how to propose. Juries were no problem compared to this. One night, driving back from a shore dinner on the Cape, he said, "I don't suppose twelve years difference in age is an insurmountable obstacle."

She had not been in the least puzzled. "Insurmountable? I don't consider it an obstacle at all."

They spent their honeymoon in Europe, much of it with Lawrence and Marcia. "You wanted to run, remember?" said Lawrence the day they arrived, and Brad answered, "Yes. But I didn't know then in which direction."

Even before they were married, he had noticed that one cocktail before dinner always called for a second, often a third, and that after dinner a highball glass was seldom out of her hand. One night on the ship, crossing over, he said, "You've a strong head, my girl."

"I have, haven't I? Sometimes I wish it weren't quite so strong. I don't seem to get half so much fun out of it as most people. It just unties me."

"Then why bother?"

"Because I like the feeling of being untied."

She waited hopefully for signs of pregnancy, fumed when they didn't appear.

"Peg, dear, be patient! We've only been married a year."

"That's what that doctor said. 'Go home and forget about it. It will happen when you least expect it.' Which is more than reasonably dense, because I'm expecting it all the time."

The approximate date when her drinking became clearly recognizable as a problem was one he could pinpoint. After they returned from Europe she threw herself headlong into the work of every active Negro and biracial organization in the area, even when the organizations were battling among themselves. After some of the meetings and get-togethers, she would come home and rage futilely: "What's the matter with our people, Brad! What's the matter with them! They don't do anything, They not only don't, they won't! Except squabble among themselves. And if you say another word, one word about the time not being ripe, I'll divorce you!"

For a time she wrote fiercely on racial problems, completing a magazine article that was accepted enthusiastically by a prestigious monthly literary magazine. She started two others, but left them unfinished. The half-finished third she tore into scraps and threw across the living-room floor. "Words! Words!" she cried. "And a damned lot of good they'll do!"

"Without words this country would still be a British colony," Brad said patiently. "They always precede bullets."

At first he noticed that when he came home at night there would be times when her cheeks would be flushed, her eyes unnaturally bright, her talk repetitious. For a little while he joked with her about it, and she returned the jokes. It was when she started denying it that the seeds of real worry were sown. She always brought their coffee cups into the living room after dinner, and they lounged companionably on the divan. On a night when she had left the room to answer the telephone he stubbed out a cigarette, looked into his coffee cup for a final swallow and, finding it empty, picked hers up, too comfortable and lazy to go out to the kitchen for more. The bite of raw liquor thinly diluted with coffee had made him wince.

He called her on it when she returned, and she flared up angrily; then, for the first time since he had known her he saw slyness in her face.

"Sorry I blew up, Brad, but I hate being lectured. Hate it! I'm drinking it for cramps. Satisfied?"

"I would be, Peg, if you hadn't had cramps ten days ago."

"Oh—those. These are intestinal."

"Who told me to lay off lettuce and roughage when I had the same trouble a while back? That was a big salad you had tonight."

"Let me alone, Brad! Let me alone! Stop nagging me!

You'd think I was some sort of damned alcoholic or something!"

And then, because he knew, sickeningly and without doubt, that she was, he called upon what wisdom he had and remained silent, saying only: "Just don't sneak it, Peg. Just, for God's sake, dear, don't sneak it."

But she had continued to sneak it, while still firmly denying it, apparently getting a perverse pleasure from the secrecy until what he had believed at that time to be the first break came in the guise of a critical double pneumonia that hospitalized her for three weeks. "Lobar type," said the doctor. "Both lungs a mess. Be thankful for modern drugs, Brad. I don't think she would have pulled through without them."

When she got home Brad arranged for her aunt to take care of her during the day. He tried to get the old lady to live with them during that time, but she refused. "Them gran'chilren of mine," she said. "Peg, she's all right oncet you gets home. Sets a heap of store by you, she does."

"And I by her, Auntie Tuttle."

"I knows. I ain't blind. You been powerful good to her, powerful good. An' you've had plenty trouble."

He was afraid that even under the watchful eye of Auntie Tuttle the weakness and depression of convalescence would start the drinking again, and he felt weak with relief when, sitting with him in front of the fire one night, she said: "I think I've learned my lesson, Brad. I know I was hitting it too heavily before. I'll admit it now. But I like it this way better—wobbly in the legs, maybe, but clear in the head."

When she started again, a year later, the pattern had changed. The drinking became periodic, and he knew she was licked when she said: "I can control it, Brad. A beer now and then, a drink before dinner occasionally, wine with dinner." He watched the now-and-then beers and the before-dinner drinks, and the wine with dinner pyramid—sometimes over a period of days, sometimes over a period of weeks—into protracted bouts of heavy drinking that were terminated only by her body's eventual and violent rejection of the abuse she heaped upon it. But if there were sobriety and a relatively good state of physical well-being during those interim periods, there was no inner stability or peace, only that precarious surface equilibrium.

The only lay person with whom he discussed the problem in any detail was Michael Shea, the firm's junior partner whose open, apparently guileless Irish countenance had lulled scores of opposing counsel into complacency, only to find themselves all but blown out of the courtroom before the case was finished. If his brogue had been assumed at one time, it had become part of his personality by the time he entered the firm, and had long ago stopped irritating Brad. Mike, everyone knew, was a member of AA, and made no bones about it.

Brad had prowled restlessly around Mike's office a few weeks before this Sunday morning when he sat before the fire trying tiredly for the thousandth time to find a solution, a path that would lead both Peg and him to peace.

"She doesn't want to quit, Brad." Mike pushed the papers on his desk away and leaned back.

"How could anyone help but want to? Mike, one, just one of those hangovers and I'd run screaming for a cure."

"Because there's something—rather, some *thing*, she can't face. What it is you don't know. Sure, and I don't think she does either."

"Last year she went to a psychiatrist. It was one of those rare periods when she admitted to a problem."

"And it didn't work."

"She went three times. It set her off again. She refused to go back—asked me if I'd ever had a dentist fool with a live nerve without using novocaine."

"The poor darlin'. I'd feel the same way. If you'd asked the old pro here, I'd have told you to save your money."

"Save my money? She won't use my money, either to buy liquor or for something like a psychiatrist or that brief spell in the sanitarium."

"When hers runs out she'll use any money—for the liquor, that is. That's a cruel thing to be saying to you, Brad. I wish to God I could help you. What happened after the sanitarium bit?"

"She didn't stay long enough for anyone to find out what the end result would have been."

That was something he could not discuss with Mike or anyone else. How Peg, at eight o'clock on a Sunday night, three hours after he had finished his visit to her, had managed somehow to elude the nurses and come home. She had been given her clothes to wear outside in the gardens of the institution, three days before. For ten days he had known rest and a sort of desolate peace of mind, and freedom from worry. He was at his desk in the study going over the final draft of a rebuttal argument when he heard her voice. "Brad

—" She was standing in the doorway, clear-eyed, sober—and he saw the hurt and lonely child of that first meeting in Lawrence Travis's home. When he jumped to his feet and took her in his arms, she did what she had not done that first day—wept, clinging to him. "Brad, don't be cross with me. Don't be cross. I was so lonely—after you left, Brad—so damned lonely—"

He looked down at Shea. "I thought you knew. She didn't stay long enough to finish the treatment. After about a week or so at home, she started drinking again. And refusing to admit it."

"You've the patience of a saint, man. It's as I said, she doesn't want to quit. And never has, if you ask me. She'll not stop to please you, Brad, no matter how much she loves you. And she'll not stop for fear of a hangover or any physical results. She'll stop when sobriety means more than being drunk. To put it bluntly."

"There has to be some way—"

"It will come—if you've faith—"

Damn, that was the trouble with the Irish like Shea, and it still irritated Brad. When you wanted a clear-cut, objective appraisal of an apparently hopeless situation you were apt to wind up in the fuzzy, abstract realms of what he called faith. "Thanks, pal," he said. "That's a tremendous help."

"Don't be hardening your heart now. There's a priest in our group. I'll be seeing him tonight and I'll ask him to pray for her—"

"You and Dora and the priest—" He smiled at the open, ingenuous face. "You're a good man, Mike Shea. I'll say that."

Mike laughed. "There's times when I'm thinking you're nothing but a sunburned Irishman yourself. You big dope—don't you know that what you're doing—which is trying—is faith? In a cockeyed sort of way? Go on now, go home and get some rest. You've a tough one in the morning."

Brad stood up, stretching, squaring his shoulders to relieve the tension. He walked to the fire, stirred it into indifferent life, then returned to the divan. He picked up one of the pillows and tossed it to one end, then stretched out, covering his eyes with the crook of an elbow. There it was—full circle, that journey into the past in which he was like a man lost, without compass, in a dense forest, returning always with nightmare regularity to the point from which he had first set out for home. And he was no closer to the true course than he had been that revealing night when he had taken a swallow from Peg's cup and felt the darkness closing in.

There could be no running away from it, no insistence—even legal coercion—that Peg remain under medical and psychiatric supervision. It would do no permanent good. *Don't be cross. I was so lonely—after you left, Brad—so damned lonely.*

Then he was back in the darkness of their bedroom, and Peg, searching blindly, suicidally, for oblivion, was calling out to him from the edge of the abyss of that oblivion, "*Brad—Brad—*"

Hunter Travis, during the course of his story to David and Sara about the problems of the Willis marriage, had worked his way from standing position to chair and from chair to floor, where he sat now, cross-legged, with his back against one of the fluted columns that supported the mantel.

"That's the way it has been," he said. "And apparently that's the way it still is. Judging by that phone call a while ago."

"Dora expressed it," said David. "It's not fair."

"What is?" said Hunter. "If it's unfair to Brad—and what in hell do you think life is, anyway, a cricket game?—it's equally unfair to Peg. She didn't ask for her parents. Didn't handpick them. Only some chaotic, cosmic chance handed her a good man for a father and a shrew for a mother. Of different races, yet."

He walked over to Sara, who was sitting stiff and unsmiling, still at the table, kissed her lightly on the top of her head. "And you, my jolly little crumpet, want me to write cheerful books? 'Hopeful,' wasn't it? Hopeful is the word for Hunter." He patted her shoulder, said, "Cheers, kiddies—" and was gone.

After a long silence Sara said, "I don't like prophets of doom."

"No," said David quietly. He did not look at her. "They're not popular. But the odds that they're right are so damned high, Sara. Too damned high to fool with."

44

Joseph Champlin was singing, a little flat and enough off-key to have distressed his grandson, but with considerable verve. He finished "Move the Body Over" and slipped into "What a Friend We Have in Jesus" with no apparent strain. Now and then he stopped to taste the turtle stew he was cooking for dinner or to peer through the windows over the kitchen sink at darkly threatening skies, shaking his head in distress each time. Being a lawyer, he thought, hadn't put a lick of sense in that young limb of a grandson when it came to carrying an umbrella. Wouldn't do it when he was growing up, wouldn't do it now; wouldn't even do it up there in Boston when the snow had been coming down as Li'l Joe Champlin had never thought it ever could come down except in moving pictures. Hardheaded as a mule, and sure to catch a fresh cold it he didn't use some sense.

Li'l Joe deliberately tried to keep his mind on his cooking and on his grandson's imminent danger of getting soaked to the skin if he didn't get home from the Prof's soon. He had arrived home the day before for a visit and taken off that afternoon to see the Prof. Li'l Joe's mind had been troubled ever since the boy had arrived, but now he was trying not to let his thoughts wander in the worrisome area of his grandson's evident unhappiness.

And definitely he didn't want to let his mind dwell now on what he was sure was the reason for it. You can help a young un before something happened, he told himself, by trying to tell him about trouble; after it had happened a man couldn't do much about it, and it sure wasn't right to make it worse by saying "I told you so." God knew, he'd tried to tell David, and the boy had heard and agreed. But that had been a long while back. Li'l Joe reflected that it had been a long time since he himself had been young; he'd had a mother to help him, but no daddy. He had tried to be both to David. But a man could talk himself hoarse for all the good it would do with a young un, when the sap was just beginning to rise and a woman with the right combination came along. Only, it shouldn't have been a white woman. No, Lawd! That was all wrong; that was trouble, and there wasn't anything he had he wouldn't give to make it different. Maybe she wasn't what you'd call a woman when David had met her, but she was by the time Li'l Joe Champlin had met her, up there in the North, visiting his grandson. Just a little piece of a woman at that, no bigger'n than the twelve-year-old Timmins girl across the street, but a woman just the same, and white as the Timmins girl was black. I knew, he thought now, I knew the minute she walked through the door how things were and how they'd been. When she was just standing there, inside the door, looking at David and David looking at her, I knew. And I've been knowing ever since that there was trouble coming, trouble coming and nothing to do about it, like standing on a sidewalk watching a truck come down on someone when you couldn't stop it, like it would have been standing on the sidewalk seeing the truck coming that crushed the boy's leg.

Not that she wasn't a fine young woman, for all she was white. There wasn't anything to fault her on as a woman, anything at all. Excepting that David loved her, she'd have been as fine and pretty a piece as a man could want, but now there wasn't anything to do but wait for the trouble the boy'd been asking for. And some of it must have come already. He could see it in the boy's eyes and hear it in his voice; smell it as he watched the boy walk down the path, just as tall and straight and fine as ever, but different, somehow. He could smell it, too, in the boy's silences around the house, and sense it in the click of a lamp being turned on, sounding loud in the dark silent hours after midnight.

Li'l Joe sighed. He had stopped singing, had let his mind go where he didn't want it to go, and he moved quietly around the kitchen, sampling the stew, cocking his head on one side like a sparrow to listen to the rice and make sure that it was done before uncovering it. Dinner was almost ready, and he picked a saucer from a shelf, took a piece of kidney from the refrigerator and cut it expertly into small pieces. "Time to feed the stock," he said, and went to the back door, whistling softly until a black-and-white cat appeared from nowhere and bounded past him into the kitchen. "Where y'all been, Chop-bone? Seems like you old enough to be bringing something home, 'stead of having to be fed.

Three years—that's a good age for a cat." He put the dish on the floor, grinned at the cat's soft mew, said, "You're sure welcome," and walked into his living room just as his grandson and the rain arrived simultaneously.

"Hi, Gramp! You and Chop-bone save me some dinner?"

"Chop-bone ain't saving nothing except for hisself. You been running ahead of that storm? Go close them windows in your room. You ain't never going to learn, is you? What you think umbrellas is for?"

"Keep the sun off, Gramp. What else? Made it, didn't I?"

At dinner David said, "Gramp, am I imagining things or does the Prof look bad? Thin and all?"

Li'l Joe hesitated, then said: "No, son. I don't think you're imagining. I been seeing it. When you see a man two, three times a week you don't take so much notice. But when he come back from that trip over the water, that's when I seen it. You notice it when he stopped off there in Boston?"

David shook his head. "No. Or at least not much. Thought he looked tired, but he'd been doing a lot of traveling. And we kept him pretty busy there."

"He told me. He was mighty happy when he come back, seeing you there, meeting Mr. Willis and all. And seeing what was left of his folks in Denmark. Had himself a time, the Prof did. Sure glad for him."

David grinned, remembering Knudsen's arrival in Boston several weeks before. He had burst without warning, like a summer storm, through the Abernathy, Willis and Shea door, sending Dora into a wide-eyed bolt to the cubbyhole that had been David's temporary office since receiving his degree. "David! There's a man out there twelve feet tall with a red beard and he wants you!"

"My God, the Prof! I thought he was in Denmark—" And David had followed her into the reception hall, and for a few moments there was a loud chaos of greeting and questioning; then from behind them a voice had said, "Professor Knudsen?" and David turned to see Brad hurrying toward them from his office.

"*Ja!*" said the Professor, and bowed. "This is Mr. Willis. I know him well," and their hands met, both men laughing.

The Professor had unknowingly timed his visit for the right moment. Peg Willis was not only sober but less nervous than usual; Chuck Martin was in town for a few days, staying with David. Even Tom Evans was there, taking a summer course at Harvard, looking no older than he had at Pengard in spite of a master's degree and two years of teaching at a women's college in Vermont. And Sara. She had been there, and then she had been gone.

"We all had ourselves a time," said David now. "We ate, drank, and were merry as hell for almost a week. He loved it. And I took him to the church in Roxbury the day before he left." He laughed suddenly. "He stopped the show with 'Yesus Knows My Name.' Made me mad every time I thought about you only being gone a few days before he got there."

"Next time," said Gramp, but he said it without conviction. More than most men, more than his young grandson, he knew the look of finality, could recognize a face and eyes eternity was touching. When a man was growing older, he thought, seemed like the good Lord didn't spare him none. Seemed like his grief was multiplied, seeing his friends who'd been beside him on the road forge ahead toward the horizon, while he'd still be hearing the young uns coming up behind, stumbling, sometimes crying out in pain, and he couldn't turn back. All he could do was warn 'em of the drop of the cliff at the roadside, and the steep places waiting around the turns. He couldn't walk with them and steady them, and that was a grief.

After the dinner dishes were washed, David stretched out on the divan, feeling lazy. Gramp came in, dressed for the street. "You going out, Gramp?"

"Got a job of work, son. Playing at a dance."

"Gramp, you shouldn't. Damn it, the doctor said a good night's rest every night. We don't need money that much."

"Shucks, son, far as money goes I got no worries. 'Specially not now, you finished school and all set. How much you think me 'n' Chop-bone can eat, all by ourselves here? And the house free and clear. I puts away more'n half of what I makes every week. Been doing it. How you think I been able to come up there and see you and all? You want to know something? I ain't even applied for my social security yet."

"Be damned. I thought you had."

"Man can only earn so much is he getting social security. I'm doing way better than that. And that doc's O.K. and I ain't saying different, but he don't know that playing a gig a couple, three times a week's keeping me young. You ought to know that. You're a musician, too."

"Yes," said David. "Sure. I can see it, when you put it that way. But if you're all that rich you can lay off work for a day after you've played at night. I'll settle for that."

"I does, son. I does. When I feels like it."

After a minute David grinned. The years hadn't changed things much. Gramp could still rile him. Hardheaded old character.

"O.K., Gramp. O.K. Just take it easy." He raised his voice. "Wear your rubbers and take an umbrella, y'hear!"

When Brad ordered him to take a vacation, David wondered if the older man had been motivated solely by his concern for a young junior's "rest," or if he had sensed more than the normal fatigue and letdown after intensive study and examinations. Looking back over it now, David supposed he'd been part of the firm ever since the first time he'd stopped in to pick up work, right after the evening he and Culbertson had spent at the Willis home. Yet when Brad said: "We've only got that little room where we keep the old files, David. Think you can make out in it until the firm next door moves and we can expand?" David felt his knees go rubbery, knew he was grinning like a five-year-old at the circus who's just been given a horn of cotton candy. Ever since that first student year there had been more and more work to do, and when he graduated from clerical work to precedents he had used the big law library at the office, with its rich smell of law and leather and its huge Oriental rug, a present from Mrs. Abernathy, sixty years before. Later still they moved a small desk in there for him. Now when he returned there would be—Jesus have moicy!—an office of his own. Brad had told the Prof about it. "The next time you visit us, Professor," he said, "your boy's name will be on that door."

There had been something suspiciously like moisture in the Prof's blue eyes. Perhaps that should have tipped him off that the big man was under par. The Prof was due for a sabbatical next year. David decided to make a stab at getting him to spend some of it in Boston where he could keep an eye on him, see that he got some rest, even put him through the Sutherland Clinic.

When David came to the office the day before the Prof left for New Orleans, he was greeted by Dora's statement: "Your Wiking is with Mr. Villis." Probably, David thought, instructing Brad on the care and feeding of David Champlin, and smiled at the knowledge of how angry he would be if it were anyone but the Professor.

Waiting at the airport the next day for a delayed plane to New Orleans, Knudsen said: "It is a good feeling for me, David. From Li'l Joe to Knudsen to Willis—a double play. I am proud of you and at ease in my mind. I have no worries."

"It's not from Knudsen to Willis," said David. "You're the one who started it; you and Gramp are still top dogs."

"First the apprenticeship, eh? First you learn how to apply the law that is in your head, to make it work. After that?"

"Well, I've been thinking for a long time, ever since my first year in law school, that sometime I'd like to take a year off and read political science and international law at Oxford. Hell, I know it sounds crazy—"

"Did it not sound crazy when I first said you would go to college?"

"Yes. But this sounds even crazier. And I think, I hope, the firm would keep my chair warm for me. And I have to save enough money—"

"International law? This I did not expect. But crazy—no—it is not crazy if you want to do it. I will help—" David remembered that he had stopped then, in midsentence.

"I think I can make it. But if I can't, I'll ask. Now that I've got an income and can pay back. So keep your blood pressure down, Prof. I won't refuse help if I need it. And it's still just an idea."

But this afternoon, the first time David had seen the Prof since that day at the airport, he did not bring up the matter of Oxford. He was quieter than David had ever known him to be, his talk reminiscent, oddly gentle. Only when he was leaving did David see the old, explosive Prof. At the door, an arm around David's shoulder, Knudsen had boomed: *"Ja!* I know now why those who have children say death is not so bad, because there is continuity. My friend, Joseph Champlin, lives in you, and I live in your mind—and we will both live in your children: There does not have to be a blood relationship. You will name one of them Bjarne, no?"

They had laughed together. "A brown 'Bjarne,' Prof? My God!"

David was relieved that the Professor had not brought up the matter of Oxford and further studies in international law. He was glad to be off the hook of explanation. Because, had the Prof probed, as only he could, his probe would have opened wide a wound—and revealed Sara.

It had been a small wound at first, a surface thing, like the initial incision of a surgeon over an operative site, made a week before Christmas the first year he was at law school. Sara was going home to spend the holiday with her father and her sister and the twin nephews. David had wanted Gramp to come to Boston, but the first heavy fall of snow had changed his mind. He could see Gramp, a small brown icicle, probably frozen immobile on a street corner, and decided to go home instead. Gramp had assured him there would be enough money if he ran short. There seemed to be some inexhaustible hoard somewhere that Gramp could always tap if it was a case of a reunion or a long-distance telephone call, but which suddenly dwindled to a few pathetic pennies at a too high gas bill or an assessment. He didn't argue about it anymore. If he refused the extra money to come home on, Gramp would just spend it on a ticket north to visit him.

A few days before he left, he went up to Sara's studio. She was sitting on the couch, wrapping packages. "David. If there was more money you could fly to Chicago first, on the way home, and see my twins." She looked around her at the gaily wrapped gifts, and moaned. "Where am I going to *put* them all!"

"I don't suppose the twins would mind."

She was too engrossed to catch his emphasis on "twins" immediately. He wondered why in hell he had said it; he ought to steer clear of those shoals. Then, a pink-and white plush rabbit in her hand, she had looked around quickly at him.

"What do you mean—the *twins?*"

Let it lie, Sara; for God's sake let it lie, but then he heard himself going ahead, heard his own voice say, "Only that they're young enough to be color blind." It would always be like this, always, this involuntary transference of pain. And that she could not see, or did not want to see, the existence of any problem was one of the goads that set him off. It was kind to call it naïveté, more honest to call it blindness.

She let the rabbit drop to the couch where it lay, flop-eared and ridiculous, among the gay wrappings, the bright ribbons and rosettes. "That doesn't speak well for the rest of my family."

"Do you think they'd hire a band to welcome me?"

"They didn't hire a band to meet my sister's husband, either, when he was still her financé. Took a damned dim view of him, they did."

"Oh, for God's sake, Sara! Face facts, just once."

"David, I told you, last spring at Pengard, that my father knew I was in love with you even before you knew it."

"You didn't tell me then when I asked you, and you won't tell me now, but I am going to ask anyhow. Was he happy about it?"

"No, Stoopid! And I did tell you. He wasn't happy and he wouldn't have been if you'd been the Prince of Wales. No father is 'happy' about a daughter's boy friend. Especially if he thinks it's serious."

"You begged the question then and you're begging it now. Suppose I said, 'O.K., Sara. I'll go to Chicago and be introduced to your family. I'll even spend Christmas there.' Suppose I did? What would your reaction be? Your first move? Want me to tell you?"

"All right. You know so damned much about it. Suppose you tell me."

"To warn them."

"*Warn* them?"

"Yes. To write a letter and say, 'Dear Daddy—' "

"I don't call my father 'Daddy.' I call him Father—"

"O.K., a minor point. 'Dear Father—here I come, ready or not, with my Negro boy friend, and please be nice and tell the rest of the family and the neighbors to be nice—' "

"That's ridiculous and childish! You know who my father is—what he's done—"

"I've even met him. At graduation."

"And he liked you! He thought you were great!"

"Maybe he did. But let's suppose we went back there all married up, as Gramp would say. And we come down the first morning. And your dad—father—looks at you, and the rest of 'em look at you, and then they all look at me, and start thinking that all night long you and I have been sleeping in the same bed in that house, and probably not sleeping all the time, either. What room would we have? Your room from the time you were a wide-eyed innocent child, where your mother and father used to tuck you in every night and hear your prayers? And the only brown thing near you was probably a Teddy bear? So, little Sara? What then? Be honest, baby, for God's sake be honest."

She was quiet for so long he thought she wasn't going to answer. She had picked up the rabbit again and was flip-flopping its pink-lined ears over her fingers nervously. At last she said slowly: "I'll be honest, David. Just as honest as I can be. But I won't say that they'd be horrified and outraged and all that. Or that they'd be pleased, either. Because I don't know. I just don't know. Wait. Please. Let me finish. I let you. In the first place, David, families aren't all that important."

"I've got to interrupt, Sara. They are to you. And they are to me. You've got to realize that any general problem sooner or later has to be particularized. Must be viewed through the eyes of an individual facing it. We've both got roots. I don't mean just geographical roots or the shallow roots of custom. I mean deep roots of mind and heart. What happens to them if we tear them up? Do we let them dangle? Bleeding."

Her words still came slowly: "So they bleed, David. Can't we stand to have them bleed?"

"Not when they're bleeding the life away from the plants they nourished—"

Now her words came faster, tumbling out, sounding more like Sara Kent: "Why did you start all this! Why! It happens all the time. We're happy and everything's going just fine and then all of a sudden you're off. I—I never know what silly little thing will start you off, and suddenly we're—we're fighting and miserable. Isn't all this—this stupid business about *my* father and *my* family after all *my* problem? Isn't it? If I'm willing to face it—and I don't admit it's a big one because it isn't, David, it isn't—"

"Sara, where did you say your brother-in-law comes from?"

"Virginia. My God, David, every Virginian isn't a Clevenger!"

"No? I'll take an ex-cracker like Chuck Martin any day. He's revolting mentally and spiritually against violence and murder and stupidity. There are as many kinds of prejudice in the South as there are kinds of people. Know what they called Virginia in the old days? The 'mother of slaves.' It should have been the 'father.' Know why? Because that was where they had the best slave studs. Stud farms, actually. Slaveowners used to bring slave women there from hundreds of miles around to be bred."

"What's that got to do with my brother-in-law! What in *hell* has it got to do with him! *He* didn't! Who's always making a big thing about not generalizing? You. Now listen to you!"

"Yeah, I know. Don't say all the rattlesnakes in a basket are poisonous, because one of 'em may have had its venom removed. How you going to know which one? That's when the general comes down to the particular. You want to bet that if I went back home with you, your brother-in-law wouldn't make life hell for your sister? And for your father? In a quiet, well-bred, aristocratic way—the same way they make life intolerable for a self-respecting Negro in that state? And never raise his voice—just like they don't have many lynchings in that state? Sara, the sorrow isn't just for the interracial couple. It spreads, like poison, to everyone involved, whatever color—"

"Color, schmolor! It wouldn't be sorrow, David; it wouldn't be sorrow! Trouble, maybe. I can see that. I'm not an imbecile. But sorrow—no! Trouble I can take. Didn't you say last spring that it's total commitment for a white woman who marries a Negro? I know that! I *know* it. And you throw that commitment back in my face! David, will you answer the same kind of question you asked me a few minutes ago? And be as honest as you wanted me to be?"

He hesitated, then said, "Go ahead. But be careful."

"Suppose I said to you, 'David, I'm going to go home with you, stay a while in New Orleans, meet Gramp and your friends, maybe spend Christmas with you.' Suppose I said that? What would your reaction be? Your first move?"

That had been three and half years ago, and even now, in the quiet of the little house in Beauregard, David flinched from the memory of his rage at the questions. Flinched, too, from the realization that had come later: that his anger had been unfair. What could Sara Kent, who had never been a part of the world in which he grew up, know of the hands slimed with hate that had rocked the cradle of his being, the humiliations and spirit-destroying pressures that had given him and all his people hidden scar tissue that pinched the nerves of heart and mind so that it took only the lightest touch to bring those nerves to quivering, throbbing life? How could she have realized that what she had done was to ask him to expose himself in the light of his home environment, a light that debased every member of his race it touched; to ask to be a witness to a debasement that would deny him the right to walk beside her down the street, to eat across from her in a restaurant, that made their love a mockery and perversion, a gutter-dirty aberration that could send them both to penal servitude. He knew that she was aware of the facts of life in the South, yet could not, perhaps would not, accept them as conditions of being and survival, saw them as abstractions, could not believe that it was impossible to equate them with the normal, whites-only problems of manners and mores.

And so, unwittingly, she had forced him to a confrontation of his own separateness in a way no Negro-hating, Negro-baiting white of the deepest South could have bettered for cruelty.

He had risen slowly from the hassock on which he was sitting, anger and frustration knotting his guts, shaking with inner tremors, frightened of what he might say, frightened of what he might do. Not until afterward had he recognized, in retrospect, the fear in Sara's eyes as she looked up at him, her actual physical drawing away. His voice was not shaking when he spoke at last because he had raised it to steady it.

"For Christ's sake! *For Christ's sake!* How can you be so God-damned stupid!" And then, because he could not face her any longer across the abyss that had opened between them—an abyss he knew now must always have been there but whose true depths he had never glimpsed until that moment—he had turned and left her.

In midafternoon of that day he called Hunter Travis, and at five-o'clock boarded a train for New York. Two days later he went directly to New Orleans from Pennsylvania Station.

He had run from that first hairline incision of the scalpel, he thought now, to the undemanding, understanding Hunter Travis. When he arrived Hunter said: "What brought you up here, man? Six invitations you've had, and you finally show up for no reason."

"Mind? I mean, you sure you've got room?"

"See that couch? It bears young. Underneath there's another one that rolls out. All the room in the world, chum."

"No prior claims?"

"None. Where's your suitcase? How long can you stay?"

"Just a couple of nights. I checked my suitcase through to New Orleans. I already had my train ticket. Got my razor and etceteras in this little one."

"Want me to stop asking questions?"

"Yeah. For now. How're you making it?"

"Great. I went on my father's payroll a couple of weeks ago. Secretary. Aide. Some such."

"Then why aren't you with him in Timbuctu or wherever? I mean, aren't secretaries and aides supposed to stick with the boss? Hand out Kleenex or important documents, whichever is needed at the moment?" David put his small overnight bag on the couch, beginning to feel self-conscious, beginning to see his unexpected stopover in New York as Hunter was probably seeing it, yet knowing that he could not have gone direct to New Orleans and Gramp's omniscient gaze. And he had dreaded the three days and two nights on the train without some chance to pull himself together, somehow change the churing, roiling current of his thoughts.

Hunter was explaining that his value as a secretary lay, at this time, more in his absence than in his presence. "Right now the great man's in Cyprus, and probably will be for several months. I'm here with one ear on what's going on at the UN and the other glued to a telephone, being cued what to watch out for and report on. Don't be misled by my appearance. I'm no dilettante. I'm having a ball. And working."

The apartment was below sidewalk level, its windows giving a view of feet and portions of legs only, its kitchenette a curtained-off alcove. The furnishings were Hunter's, and included an antique captain's chest with an exquisite, glowing Oriental scarf on its top, Benares brass, French prints, a silky Persian rug, a hand print from India serving as a throw for the couch. There were color and warmth, where David had expected severely cold modernity. Only the desk and typewriter and the comfortable chairs were things of today. He looked around admiringly, and as Hunter handed him a drink and a plate of dark bread and cheese, said, "Any old time you want to move out, man—"

"Any old time at all, David. When I'm here or if I'm away, it's all yours. No kidding. If you ever want to come over—don't go anywhere else. I'll give you a key."

"I'll call first."

"That's considerate, but I don't bring any women here. I know what you're thinking. Perfect setup. But I've got a sort of feeling for this place, David, and the stuff in it. And to tell you God's truth, I haven't found any one of them yet I wanted to share it with. I try to pick 'em with apartments of their own. A man needs sanctuary. But you—that's different."

They talked until the drinks ran out, Hunter letting David

ask the questions, asking none himself, then went to bed, the pain of the scalpel deadened by more Scotch than David could ever remember drinking at one time before.

The next day he tagged along after Hunter through the vast complexity of the United Nations building. After the first hour he stopped asking questions, unable to phrase intelligent ones under the successive waves of new impressions, of dawning concepts of a world that before had existed for him only in the columns of the newspapers, the phrases of a news announcer's broadcast. He met and shook hands and drank coffee with two correspondents whose names and voices were household words. With a third, Christopher Barkeley, Gramp's favorite, he drank beer while Hunter put in a transatlantic call. Barkeley had just returned the day before from West Germany, and David found himself answering questions about the Supreme Court decision on school desegregation, and its impact on the South.

From sheer panic when Hunter left them alone together he slipped without realizing it into complete ease and relaxation, a feeling that this slight, quiet-eyed, dark-haired man had been a drinking-and-talk companion of long standing. He was almost disappointed when he saw Hunter crossing the room toward them. Barkeley stood when Hunter reached the table, and said: "I have to leave, much as I dislike it. I've enjoyed talking to you, Champlin—maybe our paths will cross again."

"I hope so, sir."

David watched him as he walked away from them, then turned to Hunter with a puzzled frown. "Damn it, Hunter, I wanted to ask him a mess of questions about the government in West Germany—and I never asked one."

"That's the way it is with Chris. A grand guy, probably one of the best friends I have."

They returned to the apartment late in the afternoon, and David, leg-weary and quiet from sheer exhaustion, sat on the edge of the couch rubbing his stiff ankle, unaware that he was doing it until Hunter said, "My God, I've run you ragged. Almost walked your bad leg off."

"It was worth it." He gratefully accepted the drink Hunter offered. After a minute he said: "They're right next door, aren't they? I mean all those countries. Next door to each other and next door to us. Right damned next door. When any one of them dumps garbage on his lawn we can smell it. And if we dump garbage on our lawn they can smell it. Man,

I've got a whole set of brain cells working that never worked before."

"Know what you did not see today? Wouldn't have seen even if the Assembly had been in session? It's something you'll be seeing four, five, ten years from now."

"I can't think offhand."

"I'm not pontificating, just stating what is generally taken for granted. Black. Black faces, white robes, nappy black heads with keen minds inside them. Bush babies, some of them, with master's degrees from great universities all over the world." Hunter laughed quietly. "The inferior savage, you understand. They'll be moving through that building, David, and moving with authority. They've been sending my father everywhere except Africa, but Africa is his private study project. Think it over."

After a while David said: "Those inferior savage types with master's degrees will be living next door to us then. Wonder if they'll like the smell of our garbage?"

"Nobody else does, certainly not the other Caucasian nations, and certainly not the Oriental nations. The black nostrils will be even more sensitive."

"Opens up all kinds of areas for speculation, doesn't it? There'll be a whole new dimension to our problems then."

"Let's hope."

David took a swallow from his drink. "Let me dream a minute, Hunter. Just let me dream. An entente—I suppose you'd call it that—of free African nations challenging the voice of the United States in the United Nations on the grounds that we don't have free elections, that many members of our legislative branch of government hold office by virtue—or vice—of illegal elections."

"When you dream, you really take off, don't you?"

"Yes, and is that so far out? We go haring off in all directions screaming freedom and democracy, don't we? Moving into the affairs of smaller countries, telling them how to run their governments the way we want them to, even if their majority doesn't want it that way? What's so crazy about somebody—or a group of somebodies—moving in on us? The centuries of white dominance are numbered, that's for sure."

Hunter grinned. "Come the take-over, what happens to me?"

David stood up, stretching. "So-so, little man, so-so. Don't you worry yo'se'f about nothin'. David'll take care of you. Yes, sir, big, black, conquering David'll tell 'em to put out the fire because you're just as black a cat as the rest of us."

45

DAVID REMEMBERED THAT the trip to the United Nations had not only activated formerly inactive brain cells but had also succeeded in bringing into saner focus the scene with Sara of the day before. The familiar loneliness he always knew without her was back, but with it there was the feeling of having turned away from the detour, the byroad trip to happiness, and of being once again on the main highway of his life, the highway he had walked since birth. It was a road too steep, too full of peril for Sara's quick, childlike steps and gentle faith, and when the thought came to him "But not for Sara's love" he tried desperately to put it from his mind. Self-immolation should be a quick, an instant thing, not a lifetime experience; he could not believe that the day would never come when Sara would not run from its pain. When he returned to Boston he would move. This time, so help him God, there would be no detours or byroads.

Hunter had a date that second night in New York and David, restless and uneasy, roamed the streets until he tired, and then returned to the apartment understanding better what people were talking about when they called New York a lonely city.

The next morning the ringing of Hunter's telephone awakened him. He looked over at the other couch, saw that it had not been slept in, and reached sleepily over his head for the instrument on the desk.

"Hunter?" It was a man's voice answering his "Hello."

"No. Hunter isn't here. Would you like to leave your number?"

"Who is this?"

"A friend. Just visiting—"

"David! Hiya! This is Chuck! Couldn't miss that voice—"

David woke up completely now, swinging his legs over the side of the couch. "Hey, man! Where you calling from?"

"Never mind. What are you doing up here?"

"Sleeping—till you called. Sure good to hear—"

"Well, quit sleeping and put the coffee on. I'll be there in twenty minutes—"

He had made it in fifteen. "Why didn't you let me know you were here, you big dope? Did you think I was in a monastery under vows of silence or something?"

"I didn't have time yesterday and I forgot to ask Hunter where to reach you last night."

Chuck looked thinner, David thought, and when he remarked on it, Chuck said: "I'm working. All my misspent life at Pengard when I didn't study goes through my cotton-picking mind every time I crack a book. I don't know about law, but theology's murder on the unaccustomed mind."

"You still like it? Still glad you picked it?"

"Yes, without qualification. But I hope I can do what I want to—"

"I thought the idea was to do what the Almighty wants—"

"It is. But the real idea is to try and synchronize. If my bishop is still around when I'm ordained, I think I can. I pray for his health and well-being daily, believe me."

David saw a quiet figure seated on the floor of the recreation hall of a church in Laurel, knees drawn up, face hidden, while the agonized words of Nehemiah Wilson still rang through the room; saw a tall, ungainly figure with bent head walking slowly through the nighttime snow, and saw the light from an open church door shining on a troubled, unhappy face.

"Say, I forgot. Gramp gave me a message for you the last time I saw him."

"Well, give—"

"He said, 'Tell that young fellow, Chuck, that I prays for him all the time—' "

"Yeah?" Chuck's face lighted, then sobered. "You tell Gramp I'd rather have his prayers going for me than the presiding bishop's."

They talked over coffee, later over bacon and eggs, then later over more coffee.

"Hunter out tomcatting?" asked Chuck.

"How you talk! And you damned near being what Gramp calls an Episcolopian preacher."

"Have to face facts, my boy, have to face facts. I tried to call last night, but no one answered."

"Hunter was out and I was restless so I went wandering around. I even thought of going up to Harlem."

"See the promised land, eh?"

"You've been up there?"

"We've got some missions there. I go up in my spare time to help with the kids. The twentieth century's answer to the fundamental belief in an actual hell. A hell here, not hereafter. Speed everything up, why wait for death to show you? Trains leave every five minutes on the West Side subway—"

"Chuck, you turning into a blasted do-gooder? Like handing out goodies to the poor damned souls on the grids?"

"Not entirely. We've got a lot of things going. But it's like the sparrow in the Arabian legend. A horseman found him lying on his back in the middle of the road, feet up. When the horseman asked him why he was doing it, he said he'd been told the heavens were going to fall that day. The horseman laughed and asked him if he thought his puny little legs could hold the heavens up, and the sparrow said, 'One does what one can.' "

"Sure, sure. Big deal."

"You're a plumb contentious man. Besides, while I'm not low-rating faith, your hope for survival is better if you have a carton of milk in your hand."

"He who gives the milk away lives to fight another day?"

"That's pretty lousy, son, pretty lousy, but there's a germ of truth in it."

Chuck walked over to the gas plate, poured more coffee and came back cradling the cup in both big hands. "If you want to punch my head in, David, you can—notice I don't say 'haid' anymore?—but how come you haven't mentioned Sara? Hunter's told me what the score is. Or should I say 'was'?"

"Theology makes personal questions O.K., eh? Four months and you're already a confessor."

"All right, Stoopid. I just happen to like you both. I reckon your answer takes care of the question."

David, sitting on the couch, leaned forward, elbows on knees, hands twisting the belt of the robe he had borrowed from Hunter. "It's all right, Chuck. I shouldn't have blown. I guess I'm glad you asked. For some reason I can talk to you. Although I couldn't have yesterday."

"Couldn't have talked to anyone yesterday. Right?"

"Right." He was silent for a long time, then said, "Listen, Chuck, there's nothing wrong with the mixed marriages I've seen or heard about that divorce won't cure."

"That's the first completely puerile, adolescently cynical remark I've ever heard you make. Besides being stupid. What about Hunter's folks?"

"That's no answer. They're not even an exception. That's a mixed marriage in another world. Look. I keep saying 'look' when I should say 'listen,' but maybe that's what I mean: look. How can two people, no matter how much they love each other, stick it out when there's a great gulf between 'em they can't walk across and they can't talk across, so they wind up shouting across it, and that doesn't mean communication because they're shouting in different languages? And it's there for a lifetime. And where do the kids grow up? In the bottom of the gulf?"

"I'm supposed to answer that little dilly?"

"If there was an answer there wouldn't have been a question. Maybe I just wanted you to listen."

"To you talk a lot of plain and fancy hogwash?"

"It's not, Chuck. It's not."

"That's what you think." Chuck stood, walked slowly across the room, and came back to stand in front of David, looking down at him. "Did you want sympathy? Because you're not getting it. Not from Chuck Martin. 'If I can't be captain you can't use my ball and bat.' And then when there isn't a ball game you feel sorry for yourself. I don't get it. I just don't get being in love with a champion like Sara all this time, and not having any faith in her. Nobody's going to hold a gun at her head and make her marry you. She'd be doing it with her eyes open."

"Well, well, listen to ol' sweetness and light! No problems. Everything's for the best in the best of all possible worlds."

"Problems? I didn't say there weren't any problems. There'll be a problem every time you turn around. And I'm not saying that it wouldn't be easier in time if you called the whole thing off now, that she wouldn't forget. . . . That got to you, didn't it? But one thing's for dead sure, David: you can't go on like this. It's certain trouble, and I'm not talking about the moral aspects of it, although I suppose I should be."

"That's what I know."

"And I don't think cutting your hearts out is the answer, either. Give her a chance! Don't make her live as a half-woman. Give her a chance to do what she must do if she's to stay alive spiritually—commit herself. Who are you, you self-righteous idiot, to look God's gift in the teeth? To say, 'Thank you very much, God, but I don't believe I care for any.' Sometimes, young Champlin, you make me sick!"

Now the little house was very quiet, its windows closed against the rain. A radio was playing next door where Edna Mae's mother still lived, its sound muffled. David let out a sudden gasping "Whoosh!" as fourteen pounds of black-and-white cat landed unexpectedly on his stomach. He pushed gently so that Chop-bone lay between him and the back of the couch, a loud insistent purr the only sound inside the room.

It had been three years—a little more—since Chuck had spoken what were, for him, explosive words. And David had taken them, not protesting too much because it had been Chuck Martin and he knew, without analyzing how he knew, that whatever David Champlin and Sara Kent chose to do with their lives either individually or jointly, Chuck would always be able to tap on an inexhaustible well of understanding, his occasional explosions but a symptom of that understanding.

That first Christmas home David had watched Gramp covertly, wondering if the little man, who still looked like a wise brown mouse when he was asleep, was picking up anything of his grandson's inner turmoil. And came to no satisfactory conclusions.

When he had returned to Boston there was no way of knowing if Sara was back; her studio was too far from his apartment for him to be able to pick up sounds, and he would not ask the other tenants he saw in the halls.

The first morning there he cleaned his apartment quickly, laid out books and note pad on the table for study, then decided to pick up the work that must be waiting for him at the office so that both study and work would be under his hands. He was slipping a woolen pullover sweater on when the knock sounded, the door opened, and a small red beret sailed into the room. He stood staring foolishly, one arm through one sleeve, the other arm halfway through the other sleeve, his face and head emerging from the neck of the sweater.

"I—I can't throw it back," he said. "I'm hung up."

Sara's small and anxious face appeared around the edge of the door. "Champlin's plumbing establishment?"

He pulled the sweater down around his hips and stood, arms akimbo, looking at her, his world reassembling itself in a series of jarring jolts. "Yes, lady. You have plumbing troubles?"

"David, it's the same thing. That damned round thing on a spike that's supposed to drop into a hole and stop the water running—"

He fought the grin he felt spreading over his face. "The ten-year-old across the street from us at home fixes theirs."

"I know, David. Only I'm—well, I suppose I'm not even ten yet—"

He rolled the sweater up over his rib cage, raised his arms, ducking to pull it off over his head, then began rolling up the sleeves of his shirt. "Lead on, Smallest."

Halfway up the first flight of stairs she stopped so abruptly, just in front of him, that he almost lost balance, grabbed the bannister to steady himself.

"I've got English muffins, David. I was going to toast one—"

"Sure I'll have one." He smiled up at her, drinking in the glow of her eyes at his words, the flushed cheek. "Sure, baby. And on the way back from the office this morning I'll pick up the makings for a gumbo."

"Dutch, now—"

"Dutch if you insist, if it's the only way you'll eat it—"

And that had been that until late spring when Sara left on her preplanned study trip to Europe.

46

THREE AND A HALF YEARS had passed since the red beret had sailed through the door of David's apartment in Boston. During that time he and Sara and the other tenants had been forced to move because the house was marked for destruction to make way for a new building. David found a single apartment not far from the first one he had occupied, and Sara took over a studio near the Art Museum vacated by an artist friend. It had been David's last move. The apartment was waiting for him now, and he would return to it when he left Beauregard and reached Boston a full-fledged lawyer with his name on the door of his own office, the most junior member of the Abernathy, Willis and Shea staff. And, as far as his personal life was concerned, a loner.

The hell of it was, he was as much a loner in Beauregard as in Boston, he thought. The feeling of loss brought by the last and apparently final break with Sara two weeks ago was a living entity that traveled with him in airplanes and on buses, on city streets and in subways, not to be banished this time, as it had been banished several times in the past three years, by the sight and sound of Sara herself, coming to him, coming back—"Coming home. David, my darling, coming home. Don't send me away."

And in the end he had not sent her away; she had gone away saying: "You see, David, you're unhappy inside. Always now. I can feel it, and it's wrong, but you're all torn apart and I can't stand knowing I am the reason. But—but David, my darling, if you ever, ever see how wrong you are—"

"Sara, Smallest. I've got to know I'm wrong. And I'm not. How can I—"

"David, I love you. That won't change. It can't ever. David, if you ever need me—"

"I'll always need you."

"This is silly. And it's hell. Goodbye, my love."

Two hours later she had been on a plane to London. There had been no further word.

Chop-bone had returned sneakily to sleep on David's stomach again, and now David eased him off. "Fourteen pounds, cat! I'm not in condition." He sat up, wondering if the pain of that final break with Sara would lessen if he went out, looked up Rudy Lopez, and got reacquainted with Rudy's family—a wife and two-year-old son. He looked at his watch. It was too late; Rudy had become even more domesticated than Chop-bone.

He would have been in the same situation in Boston, with

Suds and Rhoda starting their second year of marriage and Rhoda into her fifth month of pregnancy. They had been married at Rhoda's home in Walla Walla, Washington, and Suds had moaned: " 'The voice that breathed o'er Eden'—I can hear it now. Jeez, David, I wish you were going to be there. Man, I need you! Like when I sprung myself out of the Infirmary."

"I just help my friends out of trouble pal, not in."

"You understand, after all the red tape of the wedding is over, everything's going to be fine."

"Sure, sure."

"Oh, go to hell!"

After the young Sutherlands' return, Suds returned to his classes, and Rhoda accepted a teaching position. Sara and David admitted that although Rhoda might seem a little on the dull side, Sudsy seemed content.

"Medical studies are demanding," said Sara somewhat pedantically. "It's just as I said it would be. Rhoda's the perfect answer."

David answered grudgingly, "Yeah. I suppose so."

All through the three and a half years that followed the first break with Sara at graduation, David lived with the nagging feeling that the end of his detour from the main highway would face him at the end of his law studies at Harvard, that the day of reckoning and decision would come simultaneously with his degree. Just what that decision would be was not always crystal clear. That life without Sara would be a major hell for a long time and a minor hell for a lifetime he knew. And that for Sara marriage to him could mean—would mean—an equal hell he felt equally certain. And that there was within her the toughness, the resiliency to take it, once the bravado and defiance had worn off, he doubted. "It ain't good to say you'll never do something," Gramp had said once. "You always has to prove it."

Chuck Martin had said, "But one thing's for dead sure, David; you can't go on like this." That had been more than three years ago, three years of months of happiness broken suddenly by quick, explosive quarrels, then a week, two weeks, of separation, and then always there had been Sara—coming back, "Coming home, David, coming home."

And so, when the reckoning came in one brief, clean-cut session brought about by Sara, it left him stunned and unbelieving, remembering wide, dark eyes in a small white face, words coming slowly that usually tumbled out in quick freshets of phrase.

"I'm going to London, David. And after that to Paris."

They were at Sunday breakfast, and he looked across the table at her. "For the summer?"

"For good, David. Unless you ask me not to. I'll come back for visits, of course. But not here."

"Sara! What a hell of a spot to put a guy, any guy, on!"

"How many times have we broken up, David? Three—four—five? And I've always come back, David, you were so close, so near. But I can't come back from over there, because I won't be able to afford it. And I—I couldn't go after a quarrel, David. I had to do it this way. With no—no horrid memories—"

"They've been my fault—"

"I know. I know they have. Because you've been afraid, David."

"I'm not afraid, Sara! I just know what lies ahead."

"And it terrifies you, because you think I can't stand up under rough weather—and I can't prove you're wrong unless you give me a chance. And you won't. And so I'm going over there and study and paint and try to stop hurting. Perhaps I'll —I'll be a good artist. Now. I haven't been so far."

"Your stuff is great!"

"Pretty little flower baskets. Unless I'm drawing you." She stood. "The coffee's all gone. I'll put some more on, but I won't be able to stay and drink it with you."

He was on his feet now. "What in hell do you mean?"

"My plane leaves in two hours. I'm all packed. All I have to do is go back to the studio for my luggage and call a cab."

"Sara!" He felt as though he had run a mile on a hot day and had fallen without warning into a pool of icy water.

"Yes. Suds and Rhoda may be hurt because I didn't let them know. You tell them it was unexpected. Please?"

"I—of course. But—but what about me?"

"I don't know, David. What about you? You see, David, my darling—"

And then at last she had said, "This is silly. And it's hell. Goodbye, my love—"

Now, back in Boston after ten days in New Orleans with Gramp, David stood in front of a door that bore on the opaque glass of its upper panel the name DAVID CHAMPLIN.

Someone behind him said, "Is that why you're here so early? Couldn't wait to see it—" and he turned and smiled at Dora, who was taking off a rain bonnet, grinning up at him.

"Not really, Dora. Couldn't sleep."

"Ha!" said Dora. "And a couple of 'ha's.' You don't know what insomnia is yet. You've got Mr. Wu."

"Mr. Wu? . . . Mr. Wu? . . . Wait, now . . . I have a dim memory. . . . Oh, my God, no!"

"Yup. All the papers are on your desk."

"Don't ever call me teacher's pet again, mouse. I'll throttle you."

"Yes, sir. Give me a shout if there's anything you need." She made a face at him and trotted around the corner and down the hall to the dressing room.

David had suspected that Brad was well aware of his state of mind after Sara left, and had meant more than was indicated by his kindly, "You're fagged. Take a two-week rest. My graduation present." If Brad wanted to guard against the continuation of that state of mind, he had picked a good means of doing it by handing him Mr. Wu's suit for damages against a truck driver. Everyone in the firm, in particular the three juniors, had been ducking it.

Mr. Wu was a cherubic, myopic Chinese importer of transcendent charm and considerable vanity who refused to wear the eyeglasses prescribed for him except in cases of dire necessity. On one occasion he had been visiting a widow in whom he was interested and had removed his glasses, putting them in the glove compartment. Other things had been on his mind when he left, and his eyeglasses had remained in the glove compartment. Within a very few minutes he had driven in front of a large truck at an intersection, with resultant serious injuries, including a compound fracture of a leg.

In addition to an appealing charm, Mr. Wu also possessed a sense of scrupulous and hair-splitting honesty. He and Brad Willis had been friends for years.

David thought upon these things with dark misgivings as he flipped back the cover of a virgin yellow legal pad and wrote at the top of the first page, *Wu* vs. *N. E. Indemnity*, and beneath that, *Action for damages—personal injuries.* He was staring glumly at the blank remainder of the page when Brad came in and said, "Welcome back, David."

"You and Mr. Wu!"

"It's salutary to lose your first case, my boy. And maybe you won't. And honest to God, there's no one else free."

"Maybe by the time it gets on the calendar?" said David hopefully.

"It's on the calendar."

"Jesus have moicy! O.K., Chief."

"Believe me, I tried to talk him out of it. Mr. Wu's attitude is that when a man gets hurt in an accident he receives large sums of money. He reads about these things in the paper. He likes large sums of money. He is hurt in an accident. Ergo, he will receive a large sum of money."

"Because he was hurt in an accident. As his due."

"Precisely. Lots of luck—"

For the next two weeks David dedicated himself to the lost cause of Mr. Wu, emerging baffled and exhausted from each interview with the cheery little man, interviews that Mr. Wu had to be urged to attend with all the persuasiveness David could muster. Mr. Wu quite evidently saw little point in them. David managed to extract the opinion from him that the truck might—just might—have failed to come to a full stop at the boulevard stop sign, but when David learned that Mr. Wu had been unaware until the accident that a stop sign even existed at that intersection he went on to other things. Mr. Wu was equally vague about what he had said to the insurance adjuster who had visited him in the hospital, except that he had refused a small settlement, offered more to abate a nuisance than because it was just. David had a mental picture of Mr. Wu, a benign and bandaged little Buddha, smiling bravely and myopically at the adjuster from his bed of pain, and turned from the picture, shuddering.

The case went, as was expected, with great rapidity, and Mr. Wu's testimony was due before David was quite ready. Later, Brad reprimanded him: "You should have asked for time. A short adjournment; your client suffering, sick, in great pain, nervously exhausted, in danger of apoplexy."

"The day that character has apoplexy I'll have twins."

"David, don't you find yourself feeling a certain affection for the little man?"

"Affection!" Then, cooling off, he said, "You know, I do. In an enraged sort of way."

When he stood to question Mr. Wu he knew his case was in shreds and tatters. This knowledge, coupled with the shredded and tattered state of his nerves, faced as he was by his first live client on a witness stand, seemed to affect his vision, and Mr. Wu was a far-off statue, inscrutable and unpredictable. David's voice was firm, but he could not trust his hands.

He started to fold them behind his back, decided it looked pompous, and compromised by putting them in his pockets, although he had been brought up on the teaching that this was sloppy. It might be sloppy, but it was also comforting.

He took his client carefully through the details of the accident, bringing out the fact that he had indeed seen the truck, but too late, stressing the possibility that the truck driver might have failed to come to a full stop at the stop sign, knowing almost certainly that he had made the stop. The man had a record of twenty years without accident or citation. Leaving that phase of the questioning behind with an inner sigh of relief, he began on the sufferings and sorrows of Mr. Wu as a result of the crash.

"You were in the hospital a long time, were you not, Mr. Wu?"

"Yes. Very nice hospital."

"Please, Mr. Wu. Just the question. You suffered a great deal of pain, didn't you?"

"Sometimes. Nurse give medicine. Pain go—"

"Mr. Wu, please. You're a brave man. I've had broken bones, and I know the pain is bad most of the time—"

"Maybe then they not have medicine so good—"

Behind him there was a choking sound he knew came from the defendant's attorney. He couldn't be surprised. If he was sitting where that attorney was, he'd be in hysterics. Not even Brad could have known Mr. Wu would be this difficult.

"You lost a lot of time from your work, your office, didn't you, Mr. Wu?"

"Yes."

"This meant loss of money—"

"My business family business. My sons good sons, smart; they take care—"

David glanced at the judge and wished immediately that he hadn't. That usually dour individual was pink to his hairline, his mouth compressed. If he had given way to the smile he was holding back, thought David, it would be the first time in history, from what he'd been told, anyone had ever seen him do so. And it would be at David Champlin's expense. David squirmed miserably; he and Mr. Wu had been over these points carefully, and he had thought Mr. Wu understood.

"When you left the hospital, what was the condition of your leg?"

"In cast."

"Of course." David lowered his voice to one of tender sympathy. "For a long time?"

"Yes. Long time."

Now he felt on safer ground. "And after the cast was removed, Mr. Wu, you were quite lame, were you not?"

"Yes." Mr. Wu smiled, looking more like an Oriental cherub than ever, and started to elaborate, but David jumped in before he had a chance.

"Are you still lame?"

"Just a little. Doctor tell me all O.K. now. Soon, not be lame at all."

David stopped him somehow just before the judge mercifully called noon recess. The defendant's attorney came up to David and put a consoling hand on his shoulder. "My God!" he said. "The slaughter of the innocents."

David looked at the other man with bleak despair. It was bad enough to watch your client throw his case out the window, weak though the case might be, but when opposing counsel offered sympathy before the jury was even out it had to be the zenith of frustration.

Mike Shea had dropped in to watch the proceedings just before recess and insisted on taking David to lunch. They revised and attempted to strengthen David's presentation to the jury, and Mike said: "Don't lose your sense of humor. It's what gives perspective. So help me, another five minutes and I'd have been rolling on the floor. But not laughing at you, son. You're doing a fine job. Brad's pleased as a mother cat with a new kitten."

"He was there?"

"He came in a couple of times. You were too busy to notice."

"I was too busy to notice anything. Can't we drop the damned case?"

"Sure, you know better than that. Not without your client's permission. Or a settlement out of court."

"They'd have to be certifiable to offer that, even five dollars."

He was dry-mouthed and blank-minded when the time came to present his case to the jury. A few weeks ago, at home, he had told Gramp he knew he'd be tongue-tied from stage fright the first time he addressed a jury, and Li'l Joe had said, "Ain't nothing to worry about; just relax and God'll send you the words."

God wasn't going to send him any today; it would be an imposition on the Almighty even to ask it. Suddenly he found himself smiling at a picture of an amused Deity, saying, "Man, you're licked. Don't bother me. Come round next time and I'll see what I can do." The foreman of the jury returned the smile with the wrinkles at the corners of his eyes, keeping his mouth straight and set. David could not tell what the smile meant, but it gave him courage and started him off on his opening sentences. Before he was well into the presentation of his case he discovered that he was becoming downright involved emotionally with a charming and honest little Chinese whom, a few hours before, he would gladly have shot. He remembered Brad's advice: "Identify with your client. And try to make each juror believe you're talking to him personally, appealing to his or her—especially her—sense of fairness and compassion."

It was a warm day, but not warm enough to account for underthings soaked with perspiration when he finished. As he turned away to go to the counsel table, he saw Mike Shea standing by the doorway grinning, David thought, like a damned Halloween pumpkin.

Two hours later he stood in stunned disbelief by the side of his client, too shocked even to move forward and shake hands with the jury foreman, who had just finished announcing that Mr. Wu, as a result of being banged into by a truck because without glasses he hadn't been able to judge its distance, would be the richer by fifteen thousand dollars.

Eventually he revived enough to thank the jury and return to glare at his client. "You were lucky, Mr. Wu."

His eyes suddenly wise and smiling, Mr. Wu said, "No. You good lawyer. I not think we win."

David gasped. "*You* not think we win!" The tension gone, he began to laugh so that the few people left in the courtroom turned to look at him, smiling themselves. He had misjudged Mr. Wu. The award was less by many thousands than the suit had asked, but Mr. Wu was happy. He had had his accident and been paid for it, and his conscience was as unsullied as the conscience of the newborn.

Mike Shea greeted him on the sidewalk. "A drink, my boy."

"I need it."

At the bar Shea ordered a soft drink, and David a bourbon. "Why?" he said. "Why?" and Shea said, "Didn't we tell you to be loading the jury with Irish and women?"

"Ye-es, and I did my best. But Mike, you're Irish and you're no damned fool. You're a smart cookie."

"I'm Irish and I like a good fight. And the underdog, boy, the underdog. The little guy."

"But his eyesight, man! His eyesight."

"He said he saw the truck, didn't he? Sure and everybody knows what a truck driver's like. And they'd no witnesses that the truck driver *didn't* jump the light. And the judge was so sure you'd lose he didn't bear down. It was no handsome award. It wasn't much more than he'd have grossed if he'd been at his desk all those months—"

"His sons! His blasted, bloody smart sons!"

Shea shrugged. His eyes were still bright with amusement. "If they'd thought you'd anything going for you on that score, Dennis might have been making a thing of it. Let what happened to your opponents be a lesson to you. When you've got your man on the ropes swing harder. They laid back—"

After he returned to the office David sat contemplating his new briefcase, a present from the Prof, lying unopened on his desk. He had won his first case, and there was a vague taste of dust and ashes in his mouth. He heard footsteps in the hall, and then Brad thrust head and shoulders around the half-open door. "Don't get carried away. You won't win 'em all."

"For gosh sake, come in! Why'd I win that one? It's all wrong. It's haywire. The man's a menace on the highway. I'm not even going to tell you what his vision test was."

"Don't. I already know. I don't want to dwell on it." Brad came in, stood looking down at his troubled protégé. "I'll tell you what really happened. And it won't be easy to take. Not for you, anyway. That verdict was in favor of two babes in the woods. Let's admit it, Counselor; to have found against you would have been downright unkind. And by and large, the American jury is kind where large sums of money are concerned—especially if possessed by large corporations. It's their way of embracing a share-the-wealth principle while remaining loyal to the capitalist concept. It cost them nothing to make our Oriental cherub happy; he was obviously a good and honest man. They should be so honest! At the same time they could give a boost to an unhappy young lawyer with a personality equally winning in its own way. And they were unquestionably aware that it was your first case. These things get around."

"Jesus have moicy! And he a Chinese and me a Negro!"

David looked around the room. "You want to buy a mess of thirdhand lawbooks, marginal notes included free?"

Brad's smile broadened. "Go on home. You'll lose a few, too. Console yourself with the thought that they'll reverse us on appeal."

The next weeks, except for one break, were filled with dry, routine work that increased rather than decreased the pain of day-by-day living without Sara. He saw Sudsy and Rhoda infrequently, not enjoying time spent with them as a couple, able to see Sudsy for lunch or a companionable drink only occasionally because Suds was spending most of his time at the clinic preparing for the grind of fourth-year medical. The break in the monotony came ten days after the Wu award, while he was still smarting and embarrassed over the hollowness of his victory, when Chuck Martin unexpectedly appeared at the office late one afternoon.

David was inordinately glad to see him, and urged him to come out to the apartment and stay with him.

"Can't," said Chuck. "I got in late last night and I'm already booked into the hotel. Telegrams and mail and stuff will come there—"

"Well, you can eat at my place, can't you?"

"I wasn't going to ask outright, just hint. Thanks."

There would be, thank God, a few meals not eaten alone or with friends who carefully and noticeably stayed clear of the subject of Sara Kent. Peg Willis was on a drinking bout, and Brad was remote and what Dora called "fractious."

For the first time since Sara had left, he hummed as he prepared dinner, felt for the first time a sense of pleased anticipation of what the next few hours would bring.

The "few hours" stretched into a full night, and as the apartment windows showed a gray prophecy of dawn Chuck yawned, stretched, and said, "I should have known better than to pay for that room in advance."

"Anyhow, we got a fair amount accomplished," said David.

"Not enough," said Chuck. "We've been talking about Harlem for two hours now, and we still haven't got the kids out of it before it gets 'em." He got up and began to walk slowly up and down the room. "Now and then some of them make it, David. But they don't leave it behind, anymore than you've left the South behind. You've brought with you certain attitudes, certain reflexes. So do the ones who break out of Harlem. And I contend that their attitudes are harder to shake, their reflexes more basic. By the time a Harlem kid is eight years old he's seen a killing or two, and a cutting is routine. Half of them don't even know what a father looks like, and a lot of them aren't too sure about a mother. Even those with stable homes—give me a week and I could name two or three—don't have much of any place to go except the street. A kid doesn't always steal because he needs the money—he steals because it's more fun than earning it, and it gets you accepted by your peers. Isn't that the big thing today? The peer group? And when the standards of that peer group are petty thievery and skill with a knife, and being able to outrun a cop—it plays the devil with the optimism and the hope of people like me."

"You think there is hope?" asked David.

"I say 'yes' but I think I mean 'perhaps.' One thing I believe—there's more hope for the Negro in the South than for the Negroes in Harlem or South Chicago or East Philadelphia, or Los Angeles—"

"Why do you say that? There's more hate among the whites in the South—"

"Man, that's why! Wait now, before you start asking questions. Your people can fight the whites down there, and eventually you will. And you'll have a lot of white bleeding hearts on the barricades with you. Why? Because it's more dramatic, man! The scene down there has everything. Slave descendants who never were freed, their rights denied, expected to fight for their country but not allowed to vote—name it, man! To arms! Charge! Come the call, and the so-called liberals will be singing 'We're coming, Father Abraham' and marching down there in regiments. But how many are going to march against filth and vice and unemployment and lousy schools and crooked, brutal cops? How many are going to fight for the kids who are gangsters at ten, addicts at fourteen, killers at seventeen, dead inside at twenty?"

"Damned few," said David slowly. "Very damned few. It sort of opens up a new area of thought. No one seems to get too jittery about a Harlem riot—except temporarily. It's like a riot in a prison. Who gives a damn about a riot in a prison except the prisoners and the warden and guards? That's what a Harlem riot is, really. Or any other ghetto race disturbance."

"That's what I'm trying to say. The Negro in the South actually has the hatred of the southern whites going for him, in one sense. All the white liberals here shudder about it, go all clammy thinking about it. It's something they get all het up about, think they've got to do something about it. But who really hates the Negro up here, David? I mean, the way they are hated down there—except, of course, for those Southerners who love their Negroes like pets. But up here—who gives enough of a damn about you as a Negro to bother hating you? Any more than who gives enough of a damn about convicts rioting in Sing Sing. Actually, most of the whites up here have it all figured out that the Negro in the North asked for it; nobody forced him to come up here, did they? He can vote, can't he? He can send his kids to a white school legally even if he can't actually; he's out of the galleon, isn't he? What's he squawking about? And when someone tries to tell them, to make them understand, they shy away. This is their part of the country, and it makes them feel good to criticize the South. I've heard some of them make a big, inconsistent point about wishing they could go down there and show those uncivilized red-necks a thing or two about a man's rights."

David stood up, shook the coffeepot, and found it empty. Chuck said, "Don't make more, not for me, anyway." David set the pot down, stretched and said: "All night, by God, all night we've talked, and all we've got to show for it is a coffeepot empty for the third time and the well-known conclusion that nobody loves us black boys. And that unfortunately nobody up here hates us either."

"I think that unless something gives pretty soon you'll have some of that hate, because you'll have fear. And come fear, come hate. The walls around Harlem aren't going to hold up forever, not with what's inside them."

"They'll build higher ones next time," said David.

"No," said Chuck. "From what I've seen at first hand, there's so much hell bottled up, so much howling, hidden hell that it will break down any wall, and enough of it will spew out to scare the pants off the people on the outside."

"We need a Joshua."

"Amen, brother," said Chuck. "Amen. Amen." He was standing now, straightening clothes mussed from long sitting. His face was frowning and troubled. "You know the other name for Joshua? There was another Joshua—called Jesus—and no one paid much attention."

"The world was smaller then by a few billion," said David. "Suffer little children—love thy neighbor—hurt the least of these and you're hurting me. How long did the words last except in print? And how much more than print are they to the people outside the walls?"

"'I hear their gentle vo-oi-oices calling'—" As Chuck laughed, David said: "That's just an intro. What I've heard 'em singing, a long time ago, was 'Pharaoh's Army Got Drownded.' It used to be my favorite hymn, when I was a brat, before I started figuring out that somebody either made a mistake or they weren't talking about us—"

"You mean the song, 'Oh, Mary, Don't You Weep,'" said Chuck.

"It doesn't matter, nit-picker. Any old way you name it, that army's a long time drowning—"

The last week in August, Isaiah Watkins arrived in Boston to confer with ALEC officials at headquarters on the crisis that was building rapidly in Little Rock. He brought with him a jar of fresh filet powder from Gramp, as well as a number of admonitions and warnings. David's conscience hadn't let him tell Li'l Joe that he'd won his first case; he was still smarting with chagrin, and if he was going to brag he'd wait till he had something to brag about that would be to his credit as a lawyer.

Several weeks before, Brad had asked him to pinch-hit for a while at ALEC meetings. "I'm up to here in work," said Brad. And added, "As well as trouble." There was no necessity now for Brad to mince words with David. Both David and Sara had answered late at night "emergency" calls when Brad was out of town, and, fearful of mistaking a real cry of distress for a cry of "Wolf, Wolf!" had hurried to the Willis home and sat with a Peg Willis they scarcely knew: talkative, repetitive, tearful at times, progressing to incoherence and finally to a submissive somnolence, letting them put her to bed as they would a child. Then weeks would pass before they heard from her. Eventually there would be an invitation to dinner, either out or at home for the filet gumbo or deviled crab David had taught her to cook, and no mention of their last meeting; it might never have happened.

Recently Brad had hired a housekeeper. "Peg doesn't want it," he said to David. "But what else can I do? How else can I dare go out of town? And I often have to. This woman—Peg doesn't know this—was a practical nurse in a sanitarium. I'm paying her the national debt monthly, but it's worth it in peace of mind."

During the week Isaiah was in town, there were several

ALEC meetings, and the break in routine was a welcome one. Joseph Klein, ALEC's executive secretary and attorney, was back at his desk after an enforced six-month absence for health reasons, trying to hold himself to a reduced work schedule. He was a driving, intense man, one of the few whites David had ever known who had the complete trust of every Negro who knew him with no vaguely suspicious hold-outs. When there were night sessions David briefed him informally the next day. "You're the only one gives me an objective account," Klein said. "I have to sift out everyone else's personal likes and dislikes for this one or that one."

David and Isaiah had just attended a meeting and were cutting across Boston Common to Boylston Street in midafternoon on a day toward the end of Isaiah's visit, when Isaiah said abruptly, "When we gonna git up off our fat black asses and do something, David?"

After a moment David said, "I suppose 'Saiah, when someone fills 'em with buckshot."

"You think you're kidding? You ain't. But first we got to expose 'em to the buckshot. It's hard to hit a man in the ass when he's sitting down even if you got good aim."

"A few tacks in some chairs, maybe?"

"What we trying to do if it ain't that?"

Walking across the Common had been Isaiah's idea. It was easier on his gimpy leg, he said, than "Them sub stairs." Now he pulled a large cigar from his pocket, lighted it, and puffed vigorously for a minute. Suddenly he chuckled from behind it.

"So?" asked David.

"These whites," said Isaiah. "These whites you got up here. Lawd have mercy! I ain't sure we ain't better off without 'em down there."

Starting at Pengard, David had come by his knowledge of the starry-eyed liberal of the North gradually, those well-meaners who wouldn't even give a Negro a chance to be a son of a bitch even if he happened to be one. Those dewy-eyed characters were hard to deal with, just waking up, as they were, to the sins of their own people, looking on every Negro as a potential saint just because he was a Negro, seeing in every brown skin a mantle of persecuted righteousness. And it was so damned easy to fool these fledgling liberals, so damned easy to take them down almost any path you wanted them to go. His people had done it countless times.

Take this woman they were talking about, this Mrs. Hubbard, to some of the places he knew in New Orleans or Chicago or New York, tell her how Negroes themselves were afraid to walk the quiet side streets of Harlem, afraid of their own, show her the violence, expose the trickery they practiced among themselves even as the whites did—how would she react? She'd recoil, and in her recoil might in all likelihood take away her support. Or she'd become defensive about her own position, and rationalize and justify these manifestations of Negro life and character as being the results of pressures and persecutions and denials. He was sure she wouldn't turn out to be one of those rare whites who actually saw the Negro as a human with balanced capacities for good and evil. Somehow the dewy-eyed liberals could manage to deprive a Negro of his identity with the human race as effectively as any white supremacist. They were the ones he feared, damned if he didn't, because you could never be sure of them, never know how they'd react when the truth hit 'em—that the poor, downtrodden Negro their hearts bled for weren't just Negroes—they were mortal humans.

They had reached Boylston Street, and David steered Isaiah to a small restaurant. "I've just got time for a cup of coffee and a piece of pie before I get back to the office." When they were seated he said, "Go on, 'Saiah. Don't stop there. What do you mean, 'better off without 'em'?"

"I ain't talking about guys like Joe Klein. He's a fine man. A good man, every way. Can't fault him for anything except he's killing hisself." He chuckled again. "But you take a woman like this here Miz Hubbard—"

"Yes, Lawd, take her—"

"Now there's a good woman. Don't matter what color she is, she's a plumb good woman. And she got no more idea of what the score is—man! She don't even know what teams are playing or who's pitching."

"Hell, we know that!" said David. "Sure we know it. But she's got energy enough for ten people, and she'll do anything, even if it's only licking stamps for a mailing. And she's loaded, 'Saiah, loaded. And generous. And her husband's one of the most powerful politicians in the state. Except when he's at home, and then she is."

They sat drinking coffee, smoking, talking of the meeting they had just left. It had been an informal meeting with Klein keeping it on the track, finally letting it relax into a general talk session. Klein was an opportunist and a brain-picker without equal when it came to furthering the cause of ALEC, and he rode his ethics with an easy rein when he felt that the savage injustices against those whom he represented called for it. With Mrs. Hubbard, a new member of the executive committee, he was in public most earnestly and tenderly cooperative. In private he had said to Brad and David: "Half the time I don't hear what she's saying. She is, however, almighty useful."

Brad had stirred uneasily. "One of these days she's going to back out."

David added: "Brad could be right. Someday some Negro is going to shoot some white in the back of the head, and that poor soul is going to be plumb sick-a-bed with disillusionment. To her, if you're black you are, per se, a Jesus-on-the-cross type. Get down off the cross and bop your persecutors over the head and you're something else again. I don't think her convictions would survive a fighting Jesus."

Klein shrugged. "So what? Our budget is in better shape because of her, our 'image'—if you want to use that word—is enhanced, and every once in a while she comes up with a good idea."

She had come up with an idea that afternoon. It was, she said, high time some thought was given to the education of the Negro in the South in the political field, how to use the vote once the crusading armies of ALEC and the NAACP had won their battle. She brushed aside Klein's gentle reminder that any such battle would have to be fought with guerrilla tactics. In spite of his doubts about her staying powers once she was face to face with the Negro as a human and not a symbol, David always had to make an effort to keep from smiling when she took over. Other members of the committee were less tolerant and fidgeted noticeably.

"How would you go about this educational program, Mrs. Hubbard?" asked Klein.

What had been a gleam in her eyes became a bright and shining light. "By recruiting young workers to go into the South to start what I have called 'citizenship classes.' It is a terrible commentary on our country that such large numbers of its people should need such instruction, but—there it is." She was, thought David, Facing Facts Bravely. "When the present situation in the South is abolished and all our citizens are granted their rights, they must be prepared to use their powers in the most constructive fashion possible. In other words, they must be armed against corrupt political pressures from the outside."

David started to speak, caught a silencing flick of a finger from Klein.

Mrs. Hubbard continued, head bobbing vigorously to emphasize her points: "My thought is that we could set up a separate division of the League under strong leadership. Send the workers everywhere, into the cities and the small towns and the rural areas, to organize these study groups. I've given the matter a great deal of thought. We could call such a movement the Citizens' Army for Political Enlightenment. CAPE."

Dear God! thought David; she must have lain awake nights for a month to think that one up. It was so far removed from reality that it silenced him completely.

Isaiah was not so easily made speechless. He removed the unlighted cigar from his mouth and inspected it carefully. "You fixing to get a lot of people killed, Miz Hubbard," he said.

"You're understandably pessimistic, Mr. Watkins. But I believe we could enlist the help of our government in such a movement." She made it "Our Government," and David heard Klein make a low, involuntary sound of protest.

"You don't agree?" Mrs. Hubbard's bright eyes pinned Klein down.

"I agree absolutely that the need for such education exists, Mrs. Hubbard. But inasmuch as we are currently having trouble persuading the administration to take a moral stand on the desegregation of secondary schools, don't you think it's a bit overly sanguine to expect help on a project such as you suggest? I think it would be well to wait for a change in political climate."

Mrs. Hubbard's political toes had been stepped on, and the pain showed in her face. "The administration is taking a firm—a *very* firm—stand in support of the Supreme Court. Really, Joe Klein—"

"Mrs. Hubbard." David did not look at Klein because this time he did not want to be silenced. He spoke slowly and distinctly, feeling that he was trying to put over an abstract philosophical argument to a child. "In the South the Negro is expendable. He is as expendable as a possum in the woods or a nice fat catfish in the river. And he shares a common peril with them—it's always open season. In short, Negroes would be murdered in large numbers if they encouraged or engaged in such activities. Have you ever been in a community during a rabid dog scare? Every loyal, trusted pet becomes suspect.

If such a movement started openly in the South, not only would Negroes be murdered in cold blood, but those who survived would be bombed, beaten, jailed, deprived of their jobs, their credit cut off, and their welfare funds withdrawn. Whether they were participants or nonparticipants."

"Surely not!"

"Surely yes."

Isaiah broke in. "David, you saying 'the Negro would be —*if*.' What you talking about, man! It don't take any big movement for them things to happen."

"It seems incredible," said Mrs. Hubbard. Her lips set in a determined line. "It only serves to make the fight that much more challenging."

"When has it ever seemed far short of impossible?" asked Klein gently.

"All I'm trying to do, Joe," said David, "is point out to Mrs. Hubbard that human life, if it happens to exist inside a black skin, comes cheap in the South. Except, of course, to the owner of the black skin. He sort of wants to keep on living. Sometimes a fellow wonders why."

"Hope," said Mrs. Hubbard brightly. And, undaunted, "Faith."

"I'll grant you the faith, Mrs. Hubbard. Not the hope. But the faith the average southern Negro has—except the younger generation—is not a faith that freedom will come to him in any future that he can foresee, in which he will live to participate. His faith is in the future of another world, after death. What we must try and do is build a new kind of faith on a concept of more immediate freedom, an 'in-this-lifetime' concept of freedom."

"But, Mr. Champlin—David—isn't that just what this type of program would do? Especially if we could enlist government aid and protection? We could stress the American-way-of-life approach. Surely the Southerners would not retaliate against that? Perhaps we might design an emblem, have banners made and fly them with the American flag over our headquarters buildings or in the windows. After all, the American flag—"

David felt a near hysterical urge to roar with laughter, followed by an equally strong urge to explode with a single four-letter word and walk out. It was like being confronted by a responsible and otherwise intelligent adult who sincerely believed in Santa Claus. Or that the world was flat. He carefully avoided looking at Isaiah while mentally passing the ball to him, praying that he'd get the unspoken signal. Klein was either too stunned and chicken, or too amused to tell her she was nuts.

Isaiah must have gotten the signal, because he picked up the ball and now proceeded to make a few yards with it. "I tell you what, Miz Hubbard. You design that there emblem you talking about and you fly it with the Confederate flag down there and you got something. And you teach just the whites. The whites down there needs education in citizenship worse'n the colored do, anyhow. Ain't no American flag flying over a place where they teaching citizenship to colored going to get you anywheres but in a jail or a grave. But you figure out a way to use the stars and bars and you got yourself a real idea."

David stood and started for the door. "We'll teach 'em all the rebel yahoo—I have to get back to the office. Let us know about the next meeting, Joe?"

Klein said, "Wait a minute, David." He turned to the others. "Mrs. Hubbard will understand, I'm sure, when I say that she hasn't taken into consideration certain conditions of which she could have no personal knowledge. In fact, I have no personal knowledge of them, but I am in a better position to know they exist and that David and Watkins don't exaggerate. But I feel that if we take those conditions into account, and try and circumvent them by as much secrecy as is humanly possible, Mrs. Hubbard's plan has merit."

Mrs. Hubbard brightened visibly. She laughed gently. It was in these moments of capitulation that David discovered he could feel a sort of affectionate warmth toward her. "I know I'm an elderly idiot," she said. "I'm afraid far too few of us are aware of true conditions down there. You honestly think, Joe Klein, some such plan—modified, I realize—might work?"

"Yes. As you say, modified. There must be an approach geared to the general advancement of the civil rights movement. I doubt that it would be possible for anyone to walk into a southern town today and convince any but the younger and more progressively minded Negroes that even a semi-millennium was near. But with concrete evidence of progress the picture might be different. Although apathy born of deep-rooted, generations-old fear isn't going to be an easy obstacle to overcome."

We been frightened people. Gramp had voted in most elections, but he had never seen his *Tiger, Tiger.* David smiled at

Klein. "After we get every Negro on the registration rolls, I'm starting my own campaign to get 'em orchestra seats. Have I your support, Joe Klein?"

"Unqualified, David. See you next week—"

Isaiah left with him, and now, sitting in the coffee shop near the Common, David ate the last mouthful of his pie and looked at his watch. "Gotta go, 'Saiah."

"Hold up there, son. We'd ought to give some thought to what that woman was saying. 'Out of the mouths of babes'—"

"My God! She's no babe—"

"Sure she is, son. Being a chile's got nothing to do with years. And she ain't nothing but a chile, comes to living."

"Maybe so. Anyhow, what she was talking about sounded to me like recruiting a whole crew of John the Baptists to go crying in the wilderness, prophesying the coming of something that's a long way off—"

"Sure. But mebbe that's good."

"Do you think you could get more than a handful?"

Isaiah nodded. "Yes. You ain't been down there much lately, David. Things is working inside; fermenting, you might say. Young folks are beginning to think. The old folks are still backing away from trouble. But you get some of them young people fired up and we could get something going. Not but what there ain't too many of them looking for the quickest way out, looking to their own future and the hell with us what are left behind. But they's some that are thinking right. It'd take time, David. It'd take time. The old folks'd be a hindrance, but, shucks what else we had all our lives?" Isaiah had turned his chair around so that he was sitting sideways to the table. Now he rolled his eyes toward David, then away again. "Take quite a few people. And they'd have to be educated people what know the score."

"You could be right, 'Saiah." David grinned. "Dead right."

Isaiah grinned back. "That's all right, son. Lots of us going to be dead right before everything over."

"And a lot of them dead wrong. Stone-cold-daid-in-the-market wrong."

"Even your Gramp say that. Way back when you wuz just a chile he said it. Bloodshed."

"I know. Look, 'Saiah, I've got to go back for sure now. I'm way late. But I'll think about it. I'll come up with some ideas and some notes for a plan. At least, it'll be doing something besides yapping."

"That'll be fine, son."

47

ISAIAH WAS STAYING with relatives, and the next morning David dropped off at Klein's office the rough outline he had made. Isaiah would pick it up later in the day. When he reached his own office Dora said, "Mr. Willis wants you." She wrinkled her nose at him. "You aren't teacher's pet today, either."

"Can't you protect me any better than that, woman? If I had your gift for gathering scraps of important information, I'd never lose a case. What is it?"

"Go right on in. He's waiting."

Brad looked drawn and tired, the lines from nostril to mouth deeply etched, but when David entered he smiled. "Good morning, my learned colleague."

David grinned. "Just give me the facts. I've been warned."

"Let me give you some background, David. I want you to help a client who was a classmate of mine at Harvard for two years, before he decided to go all out for science. His name is Lloyd A. Litchfield. He looks a most unremarkable man, but he has a most remarkable scientific mind."

David said, "Something about space? There's a bell ringing in the back of my mind—"

"Yes. Research on a totally new kind of fuel. It got a few paragraphs in *Time* a while back. One of these days it will rate a cover story. To get back to the beginning—and don't interrupt. This is your first baptism in corporation law. Several years ago he started, with my help, the research firm of L. A. Litchfield and Associates. It inevitably became known as LaLa. Like a lot of artists, musicians, writers, and scientists with fuzzy fiscal minds, he prides himself on being a good businessman. Actually, he's a lousy one. His two associates aren't much better. One of them is a whiz in the electronics field, and they want to expand into manufacturing. They have already, in a small way, with a resultant foul-up that stood my hair on end. Now they want to go public. No one of them, believe me, knows a share of stock from a debenture, and I'm sure all of them think that 'convertible' is only a name for a car with a top that folds back. I'm turning the spadework over to you. He'll be in this afternoon at two o'clock."

"It might be a good idea if you checked with a man named Benford, my math professor, before turning this innocent character over to me."

"I'm not worrying. Naturally, you'll work closely with Lloyd's accountants. Lean on them whenever you feel at a loss. Just be sure that the firm is in top form for scrutiny to go public. I'll take it from there."

When Brad introduced Litchfield that afternoon he said: "David Champlin is the ideal lad for you, my friend. He has a gift so rare as to be almost nonexistent in young, fledgling lawyers—the gift of keeping it simple. For some reason he was never bitten by the 'whereas' bug. He drew up a complicated will the other day that left me gasping. Even the client understood it. She didn't ask a single question."

Litchfield was a small man, inconspicuously dressed, with shy dark eyes behind plain spectacles, and prematurely graying hair. After Brad had left them together in David's cubicle of an office, David took the top folder of the file Litchfield had brought with him, opened it, looked through its contents, and wondered why his feet weren't throbbing because they, sure as hell, were where his heart had landed. He closed the folder carefully, leaned back, tried to relax, and said: "Mr. Litchfield, suppose you start at the very beginning and give me the history of the firm until now. Then we'll go over these files and then meet with your accountants and your associates."

After two weeks David felt an almost paternal affection for Litchfield and, in a lesser degree, his two associates, protecting them from the occasional acerbity of the accountants, having a quiet drink with them at the firm's expense after the afternoon sessions, and explaining those points on which he felt they were confused. "In Mother Goose language," he told Brad.

On Thursday night of the third week of work on the case, Gramp called him at the apartment. He sensed instantly that Li'l Joe was troubled.

"You busy, son?"

"No, Gramp. Thinking about going to bed in a little bit. Just sitting here working on a case."

"I don't mean now. I means are you busy at your office?" Gramp never said "the office," always "your office" with a barely concealed pride, as though his grandson owned it lock, stock, and building.

"I—yes—well, sort of. What's wrong, Gramp? You sick?"

"It ain't me. It's the Prof. He's real bad."

"Gee, Gramp, I'm sorry—"

"He's been asking about you, son. His brother's here."

"Doc Knudsen? There? In New Orleans?" The Prof must really be sick to get Doc down there just at the start of the school year.

"He came down a couple of days ago. You reckon you could get away? You ain't got money enough to fly I can get it to you—"

"I've got enough, Gramp—"

Litchfield, Brad—the part of the job they were just getting to was the most important, with a meeting scheduled for the next day. And now the Prof—

"How bad is he, Gramp?"

" 'Bout as bad as a man can get. I seen him today."

"Is he in the hospital?"

"He was, but they sent him home. That's—that's what he wanted. He's got nurses—"

"Stick by the phone, Gramp. I'll call you back."

Brad, when David called, showed neither surprise nor displeasure. "I'll get in touch with Lloyd, David. Go down there. Charge the fare to the firm if you need to and we'll square things up later." It was almost, thought David as he hung up the receiver, as though Brad had been expecting it. Which, obviously, couldn't be true.

The next afternoon Ambrose Jefferson met him at the airport, as David had asked when he called Gramp back. The airport limousines wouldn't carry Negroes, and neither would the white cab companies. He was taking no chances on a two-hour wait for transportation to town such as he had once experienced.

"Li'l Joe says you might as well go direck to the Prof's," said Ambrose. "You give a ring when you're ready to leave, and I'll take you home. I'll take care of this here bag."

David opened the wrought-iron gate in front of the Professor's house and stood looking up at the spare, graceful façade that was as familiar to him as the little frame house across the river in Beauregard with its simple front porch built by Li'l Joe's own hands. He limped forward on the bricked path toward the side door. Old habits die hard, he thought; Gramp had cautioned him when he was a child about going to the front door. "It ain't that the Prof cares. Lawd! The Prof wouldn't have no one going to the side door. But we don't want the Prof being given no trouble by his neighbors, getting hisself talked about any more than what he is—"

As he approached the house the door opened and Karl Knudsen hurried down to meet him. The little man did not shake hands; instead he threw his arms around David's shoulders in the European embrace. He said something rapidly in Danish; then, hand on elbow, he guided David up the low steps and into the house, explaining, "I said 'God bless.' And God be thanked that you are here. Bjarne would not ask that we send for you, but he had talked of you constantly. Your grandfather told me you would be here, but I had to see you first before I was sure—"

As they entered, a nurse came down the hall from the rear of the house, a small tray with gauze-protected hypodermic on it in her hand. She stopped at the foot of the stairs, looking at David with shocked surprise. If they had been printed in large, easy-to-read type her thoughts could not have been easier to read: "I didn't know the person my patient talked about so much was colored." She must have been off duty when Gramp had been there, thought David, or surely she would have overheard something that would have prepared her. Suddenly he hated her; he hated the blossom whiteness of her skin, the sleek, neat blackness of her hair under its white cap, the dark coldness of her eyes. She had brought something into this house that had never been there before through all the years that it had been so familiar to him. There was a wall now, a high wall, between him and the man he had come to see, whom he loved greatly, and she was the wall. He knew the hate was in his eyes as he returned her look. And he knew from the sharp edge to Doc Knudsen's voice that, perhaps made sensitive by worry and fatigue, he sensed the situation.

"Mr. Champlin is going up to see my brother."

She looked at Knudsen, carrying the contempt in her eyes to him now. "It's time for his four o'clock injection. He needs the rest." Her upcountry drawl was as cold as her eyes.

"He needs to see this young man. That is what he needs. An extra fifteen minutes of rest does not matter now."

David, one foot already on the lowest stair, turned at the

words. It was one thing to feel fear; it was a cold something else to have that fear made real.

"You and I will talk later, David. Go now to Bjarne. You know the room? In a day or two we will have a good talk."

"In a day or two?"

Karl Knudsen nodded, not answering, and turned away. As David slowly mounted the staircase, he heard the whispering rustle of the nurse's skirts as she turned and walked angrily down the hall.

He knew where the Prof's room was; once, during his childhood the Prof had been laid up with some unremembered illness and had insisted that David's tutoring sessions continue just the same. The first time he had gone to the Prof's room it had been via the back stairs, led by the cook, a cousin of Ambrose and Pop Jefferson.

At the top of the staircase he turned and walked along the upper hallway to the front of the house and the corner room he had almost forgotten. The door to the room was closed. He stood for a long moment, not touching the door. Now it all seemed to have come too suddenly; there had been no time to prepare himself. The Prof had written months before, just after David returned to Boston, and said he was going into the hospital for surgery. "It is not to be worried about," he wrote. David had sent books, a humorous get-well card, and a lightly worded letter urging the Prof to get well quickly so he could attend the swearing-in of the first Negro Justice of the U.S. Soopreme Court. "I'm going to make a speech," he had written, "and tell them I owe it all to a Dane."

There had been no thought then that he would be standing so soon in the upper hallway of a house whose quiet was more shattering than the loudest roar the Prof had ever roared. It was a quiet broken by small, alien sounds that had no place there, that would have been inaudible in the presence of the immense vitality that, so short a time before, filled every room and hallway and remote corner.

He drew a deep breath and squared his shoulders, and his lips moved faintly. "Give me a hand, God—" Then he entered slowly, without knocking, the door opening soundlessly. Halfway across the room to the hospital-type bed that stood against the wall opposite the door he stopped, feeling the blood drain from his head, feeling his legs fail. The Professor lay quietly, head turned away, one arm stretched along the side of his body, the forefinger of the hand rising, falling, every few seconds. It was the only sign that life still existed within that gaunt, emaciated frame. The neatly trimmed beard seemed to grow out of bare bone; the eyes were closed within deep hollows above sharply outlined facial bones. The hands, the great, strong hands, were sallow skin lying loosely over bony protuberances.

"Christ!" breathed David, shock acting as heavy shackles on feet and legs and hands, as a choking gag in his mouth. He swallowed, trying to clear his throat for speech, closed his eyes against what he was seeing, and when he opened them the massive head was moving on the pillow, turning toward him, and then the blue fire of the eyes was blazing. David moved forward to take the hand that was slowly lifted from the counterpane.

"Prof—" What asinine, inadequate thing could he say next, even if he was able to master the emotion that was shaking him as a terrier shakes a rag toy. There was still strength in the hot, thin dryness of the hand that clasped his, but the voice seemed to be blown through the pale lips by the last, fading winds of the spirit.

"Ja," it said, and the lips moved in a smile. "I told them you would come. Not—not to send—"

"You were betting on a sure thing, Prof. You knew I'd be here."

"Is it afternoon, David?"

"Yes. Afternoon."

"Then it was this morning I dreamed about you. We were in a plane."

"I was in one just about then, Prof. Flying down here—"

The Prof was laughing, and David wanted to cry aloud to God at the sound of it.

"You think, my son, that I was making a little trip? Before the big one?"

"Knowing you, Prof, I think almost anything's possible." Anything except life; anything except living. David knew that he was smiling, could feel the effort of the muscles in his face to keep the smile alive and real.

"They have told you, yes? About me?"

"Only—only that you're graduating. *Cum laude.*"

Again the not quite soundless laugh. *"Cum laude?* Bah! *Summa cum laude!"*

Then the blue eyes were covered by the pale, veined lids, and the hand that David held grew slack. He laid it gently on the counterpane and drew forward a straight chair standing near so that he could sit quietly by the bed, watching the thin chest rise and fall. Even now the great body did not seem small and puny; there was a kind of majesty about it, and dignity still clothed the framework of its bones. David felt very young, was again the child who had giggled gleefully at the roaring laughter of this man, and, a few minutes later, frowned in concentration over a problem that, if left unsolved, would call forth another kind of roar.

As suddenly as they had closed down, the eyelids opened again, pale curtains rising on the ever-diminishing stage of Bjarne Knudsen's life.

"You are still here, my son. That is good."

"Yes. I—I won't go away."

"You must. It is not good for a boy to sit a death watch."

"I'm not a boy, Prof."

"I forget." His words came slower, now, the phrases spaced by spells of silence. "A few minutes ago I must have dreamed. . . . I thought you were here . . . as a child . . . and when I opened my eyes I would see you with your leg in a cast . . . and big scared eyes . . . And now you are here as a man. . . ." A quick, frown-like spasm moved the flesh of the Prof's forehead. "The pain I do not like. *Ja.* This is true. . . . Soon you will ring for the nurse because it is knocking at the door. . . . But it will hold off for a little. . . . Your hand, son."

David laid his hand over the unfleshed bones of the Prof's hand, closed strong fingers gently around it, waited, not able to speak.

"David. You have heard me say I believe in no God—"

"Yes, Prof. But—but it doesn't matter. Honestly it doesn't."

"Wait, son. . . . I do not know . . . yet. . . . I know only that when I—I . . ." He was silent for a long minute, gathering strength. "When I see . . . a child grow into a good man . . . then I must believe in—in something."

"When I see a good man like you, Prof, I don't believe. I know." He was watching the man in the bed closely. "Don't tire yourself, Prof."

"Bah!" There was a dim flash of the Prof of David's youth in the word. "If I tire myself . . . perhaps I will know . . . that much sooner."

"Prof—"

"Be quiet. . . . When I learn what this . . . something is . . . I will say to It that . . . that I have left here a son . . . a son of my mind . . . strong and fine. . . . That is good, David. . . . *Ja,* that is good." He was quiet again, eyes closed; then the hand under David's twitched, jerked involuntarily, and there was a strained, hoarse whisper, "The buzzer, David . . . over my head . . ."

A hospital-type bell, newly installed, was fastened by a safety pin around its cord to the mattress at the head of the bed. David tightened his fingers around the Prof's, and with the other hand pressed the button in the end of the bell. In less than a minute the nurse was in the room, going quickly to the other side of the bed, baring the loose flesh of the Professor's arm for the needle, saying, "You'll be all right in just a minute, Professor. Off to sleep—" She looked across at David, inclined her head sharply toward the door.

"I'll stay with him until he's asleep," said David.

"Certainly not. You will leave now."

"He will stay!" Where had the strength come from to shape those words so clearly? "Leave us, young woman. He does not like you and neither do I."

David's smile was genuine now. He focused it directly on the indignant nurse's face. "He's so right, Nurse," he said gently. "So right."

When she had left in wrathful silence, he said, "You knew I didn't like her, Prof. How?"

"Minds are alert . . . when they are going . . . they hear other minds. . . ."

"Try and sleep now, Prof." He stood up and went close to the bed, slipping a strong arm under the Prof's shoulders, raising the body from the bed, wincing at the lightness of his burden. With his other hand he turned and plumped the pillows up, smoothing the slips over them, then lowered the Professor gently back. He said again, "Try and sleep now—"

"A-a-ah. That is good. . . . My friend, Li'l Joe . . . he comes often. . . ."

"I know. He told me. He's thinking of you all the time, Prof."

"Ja." Again there was a long silence, and David sensed the drug-induced oblivion coming closer with every tick of the bedside clock. Before its mercy became absolute, the blue eyes opened again, vague and unfocused, then focused for the space of a few breaths on David's face. "My son," whispered the Prof. The eyes closed. "The son . . . of my mind . . . That is good; my God, that is good. . . ."

David waited ten minutes, his hand lying again over Bjarne

Knudsen's. Then he rose quietly and tiptoed from the room, although he knew the Prof was sleeping profoundly and would remain so for hours. There was nothing further that he could do until the Prof awakened, perhaps wanting to see him again. He would stay close to home where he could be reached. "My son," the Prof had said, and David knew it to be true. A part of David Champlin was drifting away in that narrow bed, and when it was gone it would not return and nothing would take its place. For the first time David Champlin realized that death, when it comes, takes more than just the life of him whose forehead it touches.

Karl Knudsen was standing in the doorway of the Professor's study, and David hurried over to him when he reached the lower floor. "What can I do to help, Doc? My God—it's—it's hell—"

"There is nothing, David. Except waiting. My wife will be here soon. A friend of Bjarne's will bring her from the airport. She will be glad, too, that you are here. Will you be at home?"

"I won't leave the house, Doc."

"Later, we will talk. Perhaps you could spend some time with us in Laurel?"

"I wish I could. But there's a case waiting—"

"I forgot. You are a lawyer now. And evidently a busy one. You cannot imagine, David, the happiness and pride my brother has known, realizing this. You could have given him nothing he would treasure more."

"It's not much to give a man who's done as much for me as the Prof—"

"Not much? It is everything, David; everything he could want in life."

David and his grandfather talked little that night. Conversations started and trailed off, ending nowhere. Part of the heavinesss of his heart came from his knowledge of how great Gramp's loneliness would be when the Prof died. After a late supper he said: "Gramp, I've got an idea. Why don't you come back with me for a while? Couple of weeks, maybe."

Gramp's face creased in the smile an older person gives a child. "I knows what you're getting at, son, and I appreciates it. But there ain't no sense in it. A man can't run away from what makes him feel bad. You don't know that yet, you going to learn it one of these days." The bright, dark eyes looked at David closely. "Reckon you found it out already, son."

It was the closest Gramp had ever come to putting a gentle finger on the wound David had hoped was so well hidden no one could see it. He did not answer for a minute; then a small smile flickered across his lips. "Know a lot, don't you, Gramp?"

"Know a lot I wish I didn't. Ain't nothing I got any business saying except God'll balance things up, give Him time."

David wasn't quite sure he knew what Gramp meant by that, but he did not press him for clarification. His first thought after Gramp's telephone call to Boston had been of Sara, all memory of their break momentarily wiped from his mind. He wanted to tell her of the Prof's illness, know her instantaneous identification with whatever concerned him, ask her advice about the trip. And then the realization had swept over him—there was no Sara he could reach out to, there was only a faraway figure in an unknown place. Just what it was Gramp meant God would balance up he did not know: the counterweight would have to be beyond his powers to imagine to offset the pain and loneliness of Sara's absence.

He carried the telephone into his room that night, and slept without resting. He was sitting on the edge of his bed drinking coffee at eight the next morning when the phone rang stridently. Hot liquid spilled over his hand as he jumped involuntarily, and picked up the receiver before it could ring again.

"David?" It was Doc Knudsen.

"Yes, Doc—"

"Bjarne is gone, David."

David asked mechanically, "When, Doc?"

"Early this morning. Eve and I were with him. He went in his sleep, David. He did not awaken again after you left him. I had thought it would be that way. He was waiting for you. You will tell your grandfather, or—or shall I?"

"I will, of course, Doc. I—I—we're both—hell, I don't know what to say—"

"There is nothing to be said, my boy. He loved you very much. Will you be at home this morning?"

"Certainly. What can I do?"

"Just let us come and sit with you and Li'l Joe and talk."

"Anytime, Doc. Come now and have breakfast with us."

Ambrose Jefferson drove Li'l Joe and David to the brief service in the chapel of the university and afterwards the Knudsens followed them back to Beauregard.

At supper, which Gramp had insisted be served in the dining room, Karl said: "Ah! I had almost forgotten. We have heard from our Sara. She spoke of you, David."

David kept his breathing slow and steady with an effort. He glanced down the table at Eve, saw her face flush with exasperation, and knew that if she could have reached the length of the table with a foot she would have kicked her husband without mercy. Knudsen, engrossed in the task of dismembering an artichoke, continued: "She is in Brussels for the time being. She says she is doing very well. There have been two paintings exhibited and both were sold. She is delighted, of course. She will do better now. An artist like Sara must have the feeling of communication, of giving something of herself to others, even if they are strangers and the gift is her art."

David had scarcely heard Knudsen's words after his, "She spoke of you, David." He would not ask what she had said, could only hope that Doc would not catch his wife's eye and the warning therein and stop before he had revealed whatever Sara had said. Then Eve, apparently resigned to her husband's blunder, and knowing it irrevocable, said, "In one of my letters I told her about Bjarne's illness, and that was why she wrote. She's a rotten poor correspondent. She addressed her letter to Karl. She said she knew how you would feel, David, as well as Karl. And, of course, that her sympathy was with you both."

Knudsen, the artichoke reduced to submission now, said, "Tell me, David, do you see Martin ever? And Sutherland? And Evans?"

David, living for a moment in a brighter world, a world made small enough for Sara to reach across it and touch him gently, replied almost automatically: "Sutherland is in his last year at med school, and married. Chuck Martin will be ordained in a few months as a—I think as a deacon—then a full-fledged minister, later. Tom is teaching at Bennington in Vermont."

Eve was laughing. "It's hard to picture Tom Evans as finally teaching. Sara always said he'd never last as a professor because all his students would fight to hold him on their laps."

David walked to the car with them and stood for a moment with his hand on the ledge of the door, leaning over to look in at them, loath suddenly to see them go.

"You will leave tomorrow morning, David?" asked Knudsen.

"I have to."

The car came to purring life under Knudsen's foot. "And you will remember that we want you with us for whatever time you can spare one of these days?"

"I'll sure remember, Doc."

Eve reached across her husband's body and laid her hand over David's. "Everything that's good to you, David. Keep in touch—"

He watched them drive off, his mind occupied by the memory of Eve's words about Sara. He wondered if Sara had thought, when she wrote, that the Knudsens would see him, if she had meant her words as a message destined to reach him eventually. He wanted to think that she had, and his step was lighter and quicker as he walked up the path to the little house whose lamps glowed warmly now through the open door.

48

As soon as he arrived at his apartment late in the afternoon of the next day, David called the office. Dora answered the telephone. "I missed you, David. I had time on my hands without you around to ask questions."

David laughed. "Remind me to tell Brad Willis that your presence in the office is incompetent, irrelevant, and irresponsible. Is he there?"

"No. He had to go to Dedham, poor dear. He left word that if you called I was to tell you to meet him in the lobby of the Bay State Hotel at eight o'clock tomorrow morning. He's taking you to breakfast."

"Eight o'clock!"

"Yup. And don't be late. I'm so sorry about your Wiking,

David. He was one of those people you can't think of as dying."

"He was one of those people who don't, Dora. They leave too much vitality and good behind them for anyone to ever think of them as dead."

Brad was ten minutes late the next morning, but smiling as he crossed the lobby.

"What in hell is going on?" asked David. "Breakfast here at eight, all this jazz. I've only been gone three days. Am I fired?"

"Good God, no! Have you been worrying, brat? I wanted to have you come to the house last night, but—well, I couldn't, that's all."

"I sort of figured that. It's why I didn't call. Things are rough?"

"Very. At the moment."

They followed a waiter through the dark-paneled, old-fashioned dining room to a small wall table. After they had ordered and the waiter had brought orange juice, Brad said: "Brace yourself, brat. This is the kind of talk that usually takes place in the hallowed sanctuary of a law office or a family living room after the services."

"Will you get going!"

"Do you remember when Professor Knudsen was here in the very early summer, and you came to the office one morning early and he was in conference with me?"

"Yes. I thought he was being Dr. Spock on David Champlin."

"He wasn't. You know what his feeling was for you, David. It shouldn't be too big a surprise to you to hear that he was discussing methods of expediting your receipt of a large portion—a third, to be exact—of his estate."

"A *third?* Of the Prof's estate?"

"Yes. You, his brother, and ALEC are residuary legatees, after expenses and some minor, but still generous, bequests to servants and friends. He also bequeathed you your choices of his books."

David sat without speaking, staring across the table at Brad. That the Prof might have remembered him in his will to a certain extent would have come as no surprise. This was a different thing entirely. He repeated stupidly, "A third? Brad, there's a mistake—"

"You know there isn't. He did not include your grandfather, he said, because he knew you would always take care of him. He specifically asked me to advise you—not that you need advice—on means of safeguarding Li'l Joe should you predecease him."

"He didn't forget anything, did he," said David, almost in a whisper.

"No. I wish I had known him for as many years as you did."

"It's hard to take in all at once."

"Aren't you going to ask how much?"

"I don't dare. Listen, Brad, I'm earning money today, and unless I really goof it'll increase. But I might be earning seventy-five cents an hour, even with a college education, driving a laundry truck or working as a janitor or God knows what if it hadn't been for a guy named Bjarne Knudsen and the cockeyed kind of luck that got me into his hands."

"Let's don't get into another argument about 'luck.' "

"O.K. But I feel that damned near everything I have the Prof left me."

"I think you'd have made it, somehow, on your own. But I'll go along that the Professor made it possible for you to get there on a first-class ticket. For some that might not have been good. But it did you no harm. For which, thank Gramp."

"We can't know I'd have made it. Not for sure."

"Let's leave the speculative, shall we? As for the extent of the estate, if you're interested—"

"Oh, hell, of course I am."

"We'll get into full detail back at the office. I doubt that anyone, even his brother, realized the full extent of the Professor's holdings. Even split three ways it will give you, carefully invested, an independent income of several thousand a year. Roughly, five. As times goes on, this will increase. If, as I say, if it is wisely handled."

"My God! And that's a third?"

"Yes."

"You," said David.

"I? What?"

"Take over. For God's sweet sake, take over. I'll make you my attorney-in-fact with absolute powers. We'll set it up somehow. So much each month to me, so much for Gramp. My God!"

"You're repeating yourself. And you're crazy besides. You're perfectly capable—"

"I'm not. Somebody else's maybe, not my own."

"We'll go into it later."

"It's decided."

"All right, all right. Eat, man! Time's a-wasting."

"Right."

When they arrived at the office, Brad told Dora he would take only important calls, rang for Lucy and more coffee, and took a copy of the last will and testament of Bjarne Knudsen from the wall safe, going over it quickly with David. It had been drawn up by a New Orleans attorney. "He wanted me to do it," said Brad, "but I explained that it should be done by a resident of the city in which he lived. That was why he had the idea of creating the trust for you before his death, naming me as trustee—what the hell had you been telling him about me, anyhow?—and having it become yours in its entirety, outright, on his death. He apparently didn't trust anyone down there."

"But—but no one said anything to me—"

"David, your 'Prof' knew when he was here that he was dying. He was told about it before he went to Europe, and it was confirmed by specialists there. He underwent a long and hideously unpleasant course of treatment there. And then he voluntarily discontinued it. He submitted to surgery in New Orleans more as an alleviation of pain and discomfort than as a therapeutic procedure. He knew it wouldn't be that."

"But I wish I'd known. I could have written oftener, been a hell of a lot more thoughtful than I was. I feel cheated out of the chance to have shown him—"

"Maybe that's why. Don't ever think the Prof doubted your affection for him. I think he simply did not want to make that affection a burden. Anyhow, he swore me to absolute secrecy."

"Good God! I still don't take it in. He didn't even tell Gramp. Or did he?"

"Said he didn't dare. Fond as he was of Li'l Joe, he said he was afraid Li'l Joe wouldn't have been able to keep quiet about this."

"And he wouldn't have been, even if he'd promised, and good as his word is."

"If the miracle had happened, he probably would have come out in the open and set up the trust anyhow."

"And I'd have raised a sand—"

"Exactly. He knew that. But he also knew how remote the possibility was. A few months did not matter."

A few months did not matter. The words brought the

Prof's death home to him more than anything that had happened during the past three days. Only a few months—and for much of that short time a sick and dying man had planned and worked out details for the future of David Champlin. And at the end there had been no shadow of things to come, of benefits to be gained, in that final poignant meeting.

He got up and prowled restlessly around the room until Brad's voice called him back to reality.

"Do you think you can manage to buckle down to what's left of the Litchfield mess now? Lloyd's all primed to come over this afternoon, if you're back."

David pulled his mind back to the office of Abernathy, Willis and Shea with an effort. "Sure, I'm ready. We ought to wind it up in about ten days. Then I'll rush out and put in an order for his first issue of stock."

It took three weeks instead of ten days to finish with Litchfield and get the final file on Brad's desk. The following week Brad came into his office and said, "Good going. Litchfield is delighted."

The next morning Brad called out to David as he heard him walk by the office. When David was standing beside the desk he said, "For God's sake, get a car."

"May I, daddy?"

"Shut up, you big ape. Treat your elders with more respect. You need one to run errands for the firm. Someone's got to make several trips to Dedham this week."

"It's up to you. I keep telling you that."

"No souped-up jobs, no swank. That you can't afford."

"No, sir. A modest, middle-income-type car for a modest, middle-income-type young lawyer. Of course, I've always hankered for a Jag—"

"No."

"Yes, sir. The modest, middle-income-type two-door. A little chrome, maybe?"

"A small amount. Beat it. Go out to Fenway Motors. I'll phone them, and we'll handle it until final settlement of the estate is made."

"Yes, sir." He grinned and started out the door, turned back at the threshold. "Radio and heater? It gets awful cold and lonesome—"

"Scram!"

"Right."

49

SARA KENT SWEPT HER London studio as though earthly time had run out to its last hour and eternal damnation awaited her who left behind an unswept floor. One reason was that she hated any form of housework and she wanted to put it behind her. Another reason was that on this particular morning she was tired, her mouth dry and fuzzy from too many cigarettes, her head aching from too much wine the night before, and her mood one of bitter self-analysis that she tried to sweep away along with the clutter and messiness left over from an informal studio party. It was a cool day for midsummer, drizzly and gray. She had rented the studio a month before, when she came over from Brussels and Copenhagen after more than a year away from the United States.

"It doesn't work, Sara Kent." She spoke out loud, pouncing on an empty cigarette package under an easel. "It doesn't work. Parties don't work, and kook friends don't work, and other men only make it worse, and trying to be cynical doesn't work. Nothing works. But work." She tossed the package onto a pile of swept-up debris in a corner just as there was a sharp knock at the door. That was the last thing she wanted—company. She hesitated before she said "Come in!" and braced herself to tell whoever it might be to get out and let her alone.

Then she was calling out "Hunter!" and suddenly wanting to cry, and finding it very good to hide her face against the lapel of his coat when he hugged her.

He walked farther into the studio, one arm still around her shoulders, looking over the room with unabashed curiosity. "You've got company?"

"No. Whatever made you think I had?"

"I heard you talking."

"To myself, luv. A lifelong habit."

"Before I came here I called that mausoleum."

"Mausoleum?"

"That great gray pile of fustiness where you—hell, I can't say 'live'—where you reside. Why for God's sake?"

"Because I like it, Hunter Travis. And you'll be careful, if you please, how you refer to one of London's oldest. It's quiet, and they're wonderful to me. The maids and porters and everyone else treat me as though I were their youngest and puniest."

"God knows you have to be their youngest. My mother tells me they keep a stock of collapsible wheelchairs behind the desk." He lowered himself to a cushion on the floor and sat cross-legged, looking up at her. "But why not save money and live here? Is it because you haven't any chairs? I'm sure the family has some, stashed away in storage—"

"No. And I do have chairs, two of them, over there in the corner. And a couch behind that screen where I can sleep if I want to work late."

"Or?"

" 'Or' nothing. Or—or nothing that matters. Hunter, go back where you came from if you're going to chivvy me."

"I'm not, ducks. Bed and breakfast at the mausoleum? And what they call food? Don't look at me like that. We stayed there once when I was a child, and ever after when I was naughty the family threatened me with dinner there again."

"Well, I don't mind. Sometimes they have treacle pudding—"

"My God!"

"I love it. Anyhow, as you well know, I hate to cook, especially makeshift studio cooking."

"You didn't exactly starve in Boston."

"I—I—" She stopped, unable to finish, and was pleased to see that Hunter's thin, expressive face showed embarrassment. She knew the slip had been careless and without intent to remind her that in Boston she had shared most of her meals with one David Champlin, a master cook since childhood, who would rather prepare a meal himself than take a chance on someone else's ignorance of the niceties of the art, a man whose strong, long-fingered hands had magic in them when they handled food. More than magic when they—

"Hunter. Tea? I can make it. Biscuits from a tin I can give you—"

"No. Having made a colossally stupid remark, I might as well follow through and not back away from it."

"No!"

He paid no attention to her protest, drew up his legs, folding long arms around them, resting his chin on a knee.

"You look like a blond satyr," said Sara.

"I have earlobes. I understand satyrs don't. Besides, who's ever heard of a Negro satyr?" His eyes narrowed to blue slits, showing no expression. "How you making it, young Kent?"

"Fine. Just fine and dandy and peachy-keen, you—you prying bastard!"

"I am, I know. The only reason I'm concerned is because—"

"I know, I know. Because you're fond of me. Keep your damned fondness! I don't mean that, Hunter; I don't, truly. But keep your concern. I'm not such an idiot I don't know that it takes time. And more time. And more—"

"With you and David time isn't the answer."

"Of course it is."

"No. Why'd you do it, Sara?"

"I didn't, Hunter. He did. For God's sake, why don't you mind your own business! How long will you be in London?"

Hunter laughed. "Are you hoping I'll say 'only a few minutes'? Sara, I don't blame you for blasting off. I saw Chuck Martin last week, and he says he's given David hell several times. Now I'm giving you hell. And to answer your question I'll be here two or three weeks. Then to the States again for a few weeks. And I repeat, why'd you do it?"

Sara walked to the end of the long, narrow studio, began fooling with brushes and a palette. Hunter watched her without speaking. When she took off the apron she was wearing and slipped into a paint-smeared smock, he said, "A hint?"

"Only if you'll stay in your own backyard and don't ask questions there aren't any answers to—"

"Like 'why did you do it?' "

Suddenly her mood changed. She tried desperately to cling to the exasperation that had been close to anger, felt it slipping away and giving over to an accustomed pain she could not hold back.

"We squabble so, Hunter, yet whenever I see you—and you always burst in unexpectedly—I go all mush inside with pleasure. So basically I suppose I think of you as one of my" —she hesitated, then went on determinedly—"no, one of *our* best friends. David's and mine. Hunter, listen, please. Please. *I didn't do it.* Yes, I'm the one who packed up and took off, but still I didn't do it. Can't you understand, Hunter? Do I have to—to put a fresh canvas on that easel and paint a picture for you?"

"No, baby." There was an unaccustomed softness in Hunter's voice. "It would show Sara being Sara, all loving and giving. And David being David, all loving and nongiving. And Sara being Sara, it's not good enough. And David being David, it's not good enough either, but he thinks the alternative would be worse. He's ambivalent, spoiled, mixed up, and very much in love with Sara Kent. . . . Don't look at me like that, baby; you blind me. . . . You haven't been doubting it?"

"After all this time? I wouldn't be human if I hadn't. At least now and then. A woman likes to *know* these things. Every day—oh, God, every hour!"

Hunter sighed. "Almost you convince me of love."

Sara smiled across the room at him. "You'll never be a real, honest-to-God cynic, my pet. Not about love. You grew up with it."

"You mean my mother and father?"

"Certainly."

He shrugged. "All right. Two exceptions. My mother and father. You and David. And I suppose there are some other examples too."

"Certainly there are."

"You know something, Sara? It's difficult to explain, but in that area it's a hell of a lot easier for a two-feet-on-the-ground, brown-skin, race-proud Negro like David than it is for the likes of me. Someday I'm going to get a mini-motion-picture camera and conceal it in my necktie just to catch, forever, the changing expressions on a woman's face when she discovers the guy she's attracted to is the son of a famous Negro statesman. Travis isn't such an unusual name that it's always spotted."

"Stupid nitwits." She laughed, a delighted giggle. "Hunter, oh, Hunter me darlin', I hope, hope, *hope* you don't tell 'em till the morning after!"

"You think I'm crazy? Sometimes I wait a whole week. But I always tell them, baby; I always tell them. Mind you, young Kent, a lot of these female characters would fall like a lead weight for a David Champlin, and be frustrated as all hell if he didn't reciprocate. At least to the extent of making a pass at them so they could put on an indignation act for their friends."

"There were two or three at Pengard—"

"The woods are full of them. And every Negro knows it. My drawback isn't that I'm part Negro. It's that I'm white part-Negro. They can't feel noble and self-sacrificing and liberal and all that; and they can't feel the thrill of nonconforming in a big way, and they can't satisfy their sexual curiosity. They're in a hell of a fix. They discover they've had an affair with a Negro with none of the advantages. And, mind you"—he shook his finger at her—"mind you, if they become furious because they've been deceived they brand themselves as bigots."

Sara was still grinning, and there was no sting in her words. "In your own twisted little way you have fun, don't you?"

"Yes, ma'am. Now I'd better go. You wanted to work."

"I did. Now the fire's gone out. It's not your fault. I'm just tired."

"Been living it up, luv?"

"Some. I—I—"

"It won't work."

"That's what you heard me telling myself when you were outside the door."

"How about showing me some of your stuff? I've been hearing good things, like exhibits and sales—"

Sara walked over to two canvasses tilted against a side wall, brought them back and leaned them against the legs of a large easel at one end of the room. "I don't know that I want to show them to you. You're a rough and knowing critic. I've never forgotten that 'pretty flower basket' crack. It was mean. I never painted one in my life."

"Sorry, luv."

"You were right. That's why I was mad—" She took a canvas showing a just-started picture from the easel and lifted one of the others to it, then stood back and watched Hunter nervously. After a moment he whistled softly, then turned to her, smiling. "You've grown up, baby. Did you do this on the Continent?"

"Yes. After I'd seen a monument to war dead."

The canvas showed an impressionistic, hazy blur of the spring greens and yellows of a quiet stretch of countryside with patches here and there of the brighter colors of wild flowers, and beneath the fields and low hills the rich brown earth from which the tangled roots of trees and meadow growth drew strength. Here and there were modern villas just enough distorted in outline to give the impression that they had been fashioned by the hands of a not too clever child who had then carelessly placed them wherever they could stand without toppling over. The stylized gardens that surrounded them were in sharp and jolting contrast to the vaguely outlined countryside. At first glance that was all. Then Hunter, assessing the nice balance of light and shade, the avoidance of the massing of any element, drew in his breath sharply. Now beneath the greens and soft spring colors and the crooked off-plumb villas could be seen, scattered throughout the dark, concealing earth as though tossed there by an idiot hand, the yellowing bones of men: skulls, rib cages, spines, long bones and knucklebones. And from the hollow eyes, the sockets of the joints, the interstices between the ribs, the disarticulated vertebrae grew the spidery roots of the trees and grass and field flowers, and the prim blossoms in the gardens of the villas. Barely discernible here and there were weapons and military equipment rotting with the bones. Some were modern, some obsolete, identifiable as such in spite of fragmentation. A long tangle of roots had crept around an arrow, and in one skull there was imbedded a Stone Age ax and what seemed at first to be hairlike root tendrils became on longer study the radiating lines of shattered bone.

After a long time Hunter said, "You've been eating meat, baby."

"Those aren't supposed to be the dead of any particular wars—"

"They're the dead of all time for no reason. One wonders why they died, because one can't somehow disassociate them from the crazy stupid little houses, with their crooked little windows and their silly little starched curtains. Who lives in those little houses, Sara?"

She shrugged. "Little people. Little women, little men—"

"The latter next in line for the boneyard? It's good, Sara." He didn't wait for her comment, said, "Give with the other picture, Kent."

She hesitated. "They're probably both real eighteen-karat corn—"

"The safe area between corn and pretentiousness is a narrow one. You have both feet planted on it very firmly." He walked over to her, tilted her chin up with a forefinger. "Listen, pet. Don't let what's happened to you as a woman destroy faith in yourself as an artist."

She placed the picture on the easel hurriedly, almost defiantly. Again Hunter stood quietly, without speaking, until she said, "Well, say something, Stoopid. Even if it's bad."

"Our little Sara," he said lightly.

"Oh, stop! If you can't be anything but patronizing—"

"God forbid!"

The second canvas was as cold and blue-white and devoid of color as the first had been warm and bright. It was a world of snow, and around its edges were the twisted, distorted shadows of unseen trees, yet there was no sun to cast them. They were nightmare shadows, their outlines exaggerated into the cruel, grasping claws and gaping, fang-filled mouths of beasts that lurked beyond sight. In a lower corner stood a tiny, defiant figure, naked and brown, that of a Negro boy-child. He stood facing the blue-white sweep of snow and the menacing shadows, chubby legs slightly spaced, one small foot advanced, half buried in the snow, little fists clenched in dimpled defensiveness. Again Sara had set definitely outlined form against an impressionistic background, and made the starkness of the form a head-on collision with reality. The eerie whiteness of the snow and the warm flesh tones of the child made Hunter shiver, his own flesh chilling and goose-pimpling.

"You may catch hell from the critics," he said. "You're not fashionable. But my God, they're good. Are you going to exhibit them?"

"I'm going to try. You've given me courage."

"I'd like that one—the little boy—for my father."

"You think he'd like it?"

"I think he'd flip. So would my mother."

"You're not just being good friend Hunter Travis?"

"No. If you want, I won't tell him about it, just wait till it's exhibited and take him to the gallery. I won't even tell him who did it. Now how about taking off that monstrosity you're wearing that makes you look nine months pregnant, and going to lunch with me? We might run by and see my mother afterward. She says you've only called once since you got here."

After lunch Hunter leaned back and lit a cigarette, waiting for coffee. Sara made a face at him from across the table. "You always look so damned elegant. You don't use a long cigarette holder, but you always manage to look as though you're using one."

Hunter sighed. "I'm overcompensating. Sara, you're in London to establish a root or two, aren't you?"

"I rather have to pick someplace, Hunter, and London's it. If they sneer at my foreign accent here, they're too polite to do it openly, in the French manner. And I love the city. My next choice is Copenhagen, but the language, Hunter! Besides, here I see people from home now and then."

"You still say 'home.' "

"I feel rootless there, too. Now. Did you know my father is going to marry again?"

"No. Mean old stepmother?"

"Real grand person. But. They plan to sell the house and buy a cooperative apartment. It's—God, Hunter, it's a desolate feeling."

"I can see how it would be. Now, mind if I talk about David for a minute?"

"I can't very well stop you. It's gratuitous—"

"Like hell it is. You're a living, quivering question mark from head to foot."

"I am not!"

"I'm learning to recognize it in both of you, that unspoken 'Have you seen him?' 'Have you seen her?' I wasn't born to be a middleman, but it's been thrust upon me. I may regard David Champlin as an advanced case of adult infantilism in certain areas of his thinking, but I'm fond of him—"

"He's in Boston?"

"Of course he's in Boston," said Hunter crossly. "Where did you think he'd be? I saw him about six weeks ago there. And did he ask about you?"

"I didn't ask—"

"To answer your question, no, he didn't exactly ask. But he managed to extract the information that you were in Denmark. Which you were, then. And which is, I suppose, where he thinks you are now. Sara, when you did that big renunciation bit, did you think that David might, just might, come trotting over here?"

"I knew he couldn't. And I knew I couldn't get back there without yelling for help to my family. And don't make nasty cracks like 'big renunciation bit.' It wasn't phony. If it had been, I'd have gone to New York or someplace where he could get to me."

"Well, he can now."

"How? Why now any more than then?"

"You knew Professor Knudsen died?"

"Aunt Eve wrote me about it."

"And left David a fairish—more than fairish—legacy?"

"Hunter! How wonderful!"

"I don't know whether it is or not. He's heading for Oxford in the fall, in a couple of months to be exact. Political science and international law. That jolts you?"

"Yes. I didn't dream—go on, Hunter."

"That's about it. I'm not sure about his motives. He thinks you're in Denmark—which is only a neighborly distance away. Unless he's going in for politics or diplomacy, he needs political science and international law at this point about as much as he needs an extra set of teeth. What he needs now is a couple of years sound, hard practice of law. So—I don't know. And to be honest, I don't think he knows himself."

"He's wanted to do that for a long time, Hunter."

"That doesn't prove anything. You've been coming over here for a long time. I become jittery, pet, when almost everything a guy wants, and far more than he could expect, falls into his lap."

"Almost?"

"Don't be coy. You. Perhaps losing you is the balance."

Sara reached across the table and pushed the check the waiter had left closer to Hunter's plate. "Pay it, sweetie, and let's go."

As they left the restaurant he looked down at her and said, "Shaken up?"

"A little. Hunter, give your mother my love and—and I think I'll go back to the hotel. Would she give me tea if I came by tomorrow afternoon?"

"Most assuredly. Pick you up about four?"

"Thanks, again."

She saw the street sign HIGH HOLBORN on a building and only then realized how far she had walked. A good brisk walk, she thought glumly, was supposed to clear a muddled mind. It had done nothing for hers. There had been the dizzying lift of spirit at Hunter's news, then a vortex of conflict within that dragged that spirit down into depths of indecision.

Just let it be enough that he's in England, she thought; just let that be enough. Her thoughts were close to prayers. Don't let me do what I've done before; don't let me hurt myself—and him—again. If it means going back to Europe, give me the strength to do it. David. David, forty miles away, an hour, two hours away. Just a little ride in a train through the countryside and then—David. Can I do it, can I go there, manage somehow just to see and not be seen? That will be enough, truly that will be enough before I go away again. David, David—she was halfway into the intersection at Southampton Row, not seeing the lights, stopping only at the blast of a horn, the sound of squealing brakes. She turned confusedly back to the curb, heedless of what the cabdriver had shouted, and waited now for the lights, trembling a little.

After she had crossed the intersection she hurried up Southampton Row to her hotel in Russell Square, thirsty now, and tired. She went directly into the big lounge, walked to a far corner, and sank into one of the big chairs, almost hidden by its hugeness, lonely all at once. She should have gone with Hunter to his mother's; it was better to be alone in sorrow, but not in this tumbling maelstrom of emotion. She ordered tea and toast from the lounge waiter absently. I'll let go, she told herself; I'll let go and not worry and not think about it until it happens, and then try to do what's right. And that will be to leave. Unless—unless—David—David—let me stay!

How could Hunter know that David was still in love with her? How could Hunter know? Hunter didn't know everything, not every damned thing there was to know. If David still cared anything at all about her, surely he would have been in touch with her. It would have been so very easy. The Knudsens, Tom Evans, Hunter, they all knew where to reach her. And there had been no word. Pride; perhaps it was pride. But she had been the aggrieved one, not David, he knew that. David—David—*Sometimes I'm frightened myself. . . . Of what, David? . . . Us. Sara.* And then, the day she had left—*But what about me?*

What about you, David—oh, my darling, what about you? For more than a year she had been crying silently, yet so loud was the cry within that it seemed everyone must hear it, those she passed on the street and sat beside in buses and cinemas and rode with in elevators. What about you, David my love—is it all right with you? That's all I want to know—is it all right with you?

And now she knew the answer, and was no happier.

"Two and six, madam."

She looked up, startled, to see the lounge waiter standing beside her chair. Tea and toast were on the small table in front of her.

"Two and six? But I didn't order—of course I did. I remember now." She fumbled in her purse for change, embarrassed, then decided that the waiter's opinion of her sanity didn't matter.

50

BRAD WILLIS LEANED BACK in the seat of the car beside David, twisting his head from side to side, massaging the back of his neck in an effort to relax the taut muscles that had followed weeks of strain.

David glanced sideways at him, hands on wheel. "Office?"

"God, no! At this point I never want to see it again. The logical thing for us to do is get drunk."

David laughed. "You're the boss. Sounds like a hell of a good idea to me."

"You don't have a drinking problem in the home. Peg's been doing fine for longer than usual. I can hardly stagger in plastered."

"Could be a good idea if you were plastered enough. Where to, Chief? East Cambridge doesn't have much to offer—"

"How about a run down to the North Shore for dinner? We'll pick up Peg." As they pulled away from the curb, Brad said: "I always have to spend a little time apologizing to my assistant after a murder trial. How big a son of a bitch was I this time?"

"Medium-sized. Of course, it was my first and I don't have any basis for comparison."

Brad grunted, stretched his legs, and sighed. "You did a good job, brat. I've got to learn to turn more of the trial work over."

"Thank God you didn't."

"Anyhow, we won." He sounded anything but victorious. "Yes, indeed, we won. Another damned soul spending a lifetime of nights looking at striped moons. I wonder if life—just life, just breathing and existing—is that important. But I'm damned if I'll hold still for cold-blooded, social murder in the name of punishment."

"Do you always have these letdowns?"

"Always. But don't let me pass this one on to you."

David, tired but not admitting it to the emotionally exhausted man beside him, drove slower than usual over the route he had traveled only a few years before with Bill Culbertson on that first visit to the Willis house, and as he drove his mind strayed back over the trial they had just completed.

There had never been any hope of acquittal for twenty-one-year-old Pete Martínez, the client they had just left at the Middlesex County Jail, awaiting transfer to State's prison. Their only hope had been a recommendation for life imprisonment instead of death, and that hope could only be realized by revealing to a jury the environmental pressures of his childhood and youth: poverty, slums, a bestial, drunken father who had once thrown him across a room after a brutal beating for bed-wetting. The resultant broken arm had been bungled in the setting by a neighborhood doctor and the too tight cast had left him with a semiparalyzed, stunted arm. The father had disappeared, and been followed by a procession of successors who were little better. The stay of these successors had slowly decreased from months to weeks and, finally, to hours.

Pete had been arrested less than two miles from the place where he and two companions had held up a gas station. The attendant had been shot and later died, and a witness, just coming out of the men's room of the station, identified Pete Martínez as the man who fired the gun when the attendant made a break for the telephone. The identification was more positive than that given by most eyewitnesses because of Pete's misshapen arm; the witness had mentioned it even before the police began detailed questioning.

David gave a little shiver now, remembering his interview with Pete's mother as soon as they received the case, unable to erase from his mind the smells and filth of the flat in which she lived. If she felt sorrow and concern over her son's plight, they were well hidden under a blanketing fog of self-pity. Brad had told David their only hope of a fee lay in her possession of some diamonds given to her during a drunken weekend by a merchant seaman whose tenure as a successor to her husband had lasted almost a year. She had clung to them tenaciously, refusing to sell them, pawning them when the need arose, but always managing to redeem them. Her son told Brad, "She'll see me burn before she'll sell 'em."

"No, she won't, Pete," Brad said quietly. "In the first place, you won't burn, and in the second place, she'll sell them. I'll take care of that. She owes you your defense."

For the purposes of that first, fact-finding interview David was instructed not to mention fee or the means of raising it. Yet it had obviously been on her mind. Toward the end of the interview she had broken down and cried, the weeping mean, shallow as dirty water running in a gutter, calling attention to her poverty. "You don't know how it is," she whined. "You don't know." She looked him over with swimming eyes. "You've had it good. Even if you are a nigger you've had it good—"

And then in a final obscene gesture of maudlin self-sacrifice she had offered her untidy, sated body, and when David ended the interview in stuttering haste and hurried down the stairs she screamed after him, "You black son of a bitch!"

When he described the incident to Brad he found disgust had added new life to his vocabulary. "I know I sound like a damned self-righteous phony, but I can't help it. I keep thinking of that guy—Pete. If he goes to the chair it won't be the jury that sent him there. With all the evil he's had going for him, how the hell could he come out much different?"

"Than being a killer? People do. He didn't. Anyhow, you had a good chance to see how the other half lives."

"Yeah. And how about the ofay bastards all over the country screaming about our low moral standards?"

"When she gets on the stand—"

"On the stand! You going to put that slut on the stand?"

"Yes. Yes, indeed. I look forward to it."

"They'll tear her apart on cross-examination."

"They won't cross-examine if they've got any sense."

During the next weeks, and especially during the trial, Brad was scarcely recognizable except in physical features. The speech slowed; the deep voice developed a cutting edge; the green eyes became shallow and expressionless. In the courtroom his deference to his opponents and the black-robed judge was different from the easy, sincere deference of Brad Willis appearing in a civil case or one in which a man's life was not the stake. It was an alert deference that made no effort to conceal a distrust of every man, even the man that sat on the bench above him. David, who liked things defined, tried to find a word for this attitude, and finally settled on "protective." He was like a lean and hungry mother cat, wary of all living creatures, vicious or slyly ingratiating as it suited her purpose, reflexes sharpened and made quicker by responsibility. Outside trial hours he showed unsheathed and unexpected claws, and David developed a catlike quickness of his own in dodging them.

Dora was both sympathetic and amused. "Never mind," she said soothingly one afternoon when he all but staggered into the office at the end of a trial day. "Remember the old saying, 'Even this shall pass away.' "

"How about swapping a cliché for a cup of coffee? Like now."

During the long hours waiting for the jury to come in, David was silently hoping there would never be another murder trial. It had been a year and a half, more or less, since he had first seen his own name on an office door. During that time only one capital case had come to the office, and that had been Mike Shea's, and Mike had unashamedly sought Brad's counsel. There was an undercurrent of excitement and tension in the office during the life of the case, and David had been secretly envious of the junior who assisted Mike. A "reasonable doubt" that had been strongly established brought an acquittal. Now David wondered why he had ever been envious of anyone who actively engaged in the rough-and-tumble, yet subtle and devious, tactics of a murder trial. He flinched from the sight and sound of a District Attorney who, acting on behalf of the "people," demanded of a jury the right of the State to take a man's life. The first time he had ever been in a fight Gramp had practically had to force him to go out and tackle the neighborhood bully; he didn't think he liked fighting any better today.

And in a murder trial you got yourself involved in ways that clouded your judgment. You found yourself thinking of a killer as a "good kid." At least, in this case that had just wound up, the guy had killed from fear, stupidly, not from hate. And that, damn it, was no grounds for tolerance, yet—after an hour in that sordid flat with the woman who had borne and reared Pete Martínez—it was no grounds for bitter condemnation either. He found himself wondering if he would ever—could ever—fight as hard to save from death a southern leader of a lynch mob, or a man such as the one Gramp told him had killed Gram's nephew, in cold blood, during a rape scare. "Going out and get me a nigger," the man had said, and blasted Gram's nephew's brains out with a shotgun just outside Mandeville. "Boy hadn't done a thing," Gramp had said. "Wasn't even walkin' on the sidewalk on the wrong side of the street." Could he ever base an advocacy for such a man on the evil influences of early environment, early pressures, the fact that he had been taught to hate, the intangibles on which Brad was basing his plea for mercy for a young killer named Pete Martínez?

The case went to the jury in midafternoon, and not until midmorning of the next day were he and Brad summoned to the courtroom from their uneasy coffee-drinking in the Cambridge Street restaurant. Brad's face was impassive as the foreman read the verdict, but David could feel himself grinning like a fool. Afterward Brad insisted upon going across the street to the jail to visit his client before he was transported to State's prison.

Pete, the specter of the electric chair no longer haunting him, seemed far easier and more relaxed than his attorneys. He thanked David, who said, "I didn't do much. There's the guy who really worked—"

"You worked like a son of a bitch." Pete's face flushed. "At first I didn't want no—" He stopped, embarrassed.

"Forget it, Pete. I'm used to that. As long as you don't feel that way now."

"Hell, no. Maybe you got something going for you instead of against you. Anyhow, thanks."

David caught the "Beat it!" signal in Brad's eyes, and walked down to the front office to wait. A trusty, mopping up the hallway, looked at David with a sort of curious contempt as he passed. David knew the man must be aware that the Negro he looked down on was one member of a team of two whose efforts had just saved a white man from death. Even up here, thought David, there are the likes of you, who'd spit on the hands that gave one of your people life—if the hands were black.

He talked for a moment with the sheriff while he waited. "That's a good lawyer you're working for, young fellow," said the sheriff. "Never misses coming over to see a client he's defended after the trial, even if he knows he's done all he can for him."

"It's my first capital case. Can't say I like 'em."

Brad came out, somber and slow-walking. "Ready, David?" He turned to the sheriff. "There was only one thing Martínez wanted. Or didn't want, I should say. Wanted to know if it could be fixed so his mother would stay the hell away from him."

"We can't fix it so she'll stay away, but I'll pass the word along that he doesn't want to see her. Can't anyone force him to see a visitor he doesn't want to see. Can't say I blame him after hearing her on the stand."

After Brad had put Rita Martínez on the stand, David realized it was this move that would have the greatest effect on the jury. Brad had been without semblance of mercy. There was not even a hint that he regarded her as a suffering, anxious mother, grief-stricken over what her son had done. He flirted dangerously with the possibility of a challenge that he was treating her as a hostile witness while he cut through the layers of self-pity like a surgeon cutting through layers of fat with a keen scalpel to get at vital organs; once the vital organs had been reached he revealed them as diseased and corrupt.

"Your son was identified by his stunted arm. Was this congenital? . . . Then how did it happen? . . . And the scar on his forehead. Was this injury also inflicted by his father? . . . Then if not his father, who was the man? . . . Please speak so the judge and jury can hear you. . . . Just a friend? Did you make no effort to save a small boy from these drunken beatings? . . . *Objection!* . . . Your honor, I am attempting . . ."

The prosecution had wisely avoided cross-examination, even though, as Brad pointed out to David, they might have brought out the fact that the boy was incorrigible. "Once upon a time it might have been possible to justify a broken arm and a head cut open by a belt buckle by pleading incorrigibility and the need for stern punishment. But not today. That's why I hung in there till I got a reasonably young jury with a better than average education. 'Child psychology' isn't a foreign phrase to them. A busted arm as the result of punishment for bed-wetting? They won't buy it."

While they had been sweating out the jury's deliberations, Brad said: "By the way, I've made arrangements for Rita Martínez to sell those diamonds. They're in our safe. I'll sit in on the sale."

"Yeah? How'd you do it?"

"Told her a few days ago I'd pull out of the case. Even Rita couldn't face what her conscience would do to her if she let her son burn so she could keep some jewels. She's too dumb to know I couldn't have done it in midtrial."

"Would you have? I mean if you could ethically?"
"Hell, no."

"Hey brat! Slow down and turn around; you just passed the house—"

Peg Willis must have already learned the verdict on the noon radio news and been waiting for them, because as David swung the car into a U-turn in front of the house she ran down the steps and across the sidewalk. It was when he saw Peg under circumstances like this, rather than when she had been drinking, that his sympathy for Brad was deepest. There was a kind of satisfaction in just looking at her tall handsomeness, the red-gold hair invariably swept back in loose waves from the broad forehead, the warm dark beauty of her eyes. At times like these there were few indications of the inner drives of tension.

Now she leaned through the open window of the car, and drew Brad's head close, her kiss landing on the corner of his eye. "It was grand! I just heard it—"

"Hey! You passing those out?" David leaned forward, laughing up at her.

"Come in for coffee and I will."

"Lobster?" said Brad.

"Idiot! I don't keep them on hand—"

"Want to drive down to Stickney's for some? We're starving and restless."

"Love it, darling. Give me four minutes."

David watched her hurry into the house, and said, "Any other woman would have to do a jillion things—makeup, change clothes—"

"She'll make it in less than four minutes." Brad tapped nervous fingers on the window ledge of the car door. After a moment he said, "There's got to be an answer somewhere, David."

"Sure there has. One of these days it will show itself."

"I wonder. I can't help feeling that somehow it has something to do with me."

"That's a lot of bull and you know it. The pattern was there when you were married. It goes back beyond the time Peg even knew you."

"I'll grant the cause does. I'm talking about the effect, and overcoming it."

"I don't believe there isn't an answer and that you won't find it—my God! Here she comes. Three minutes flat—"

"That's what I said—"

After dinner David walked out on the wide veranda of the old-fashioned hotel near Marblehead. Stickney's was a big, rambling building, weatherbeaten outside, shabbily comfortable inside. It was in the hands now of the third generation of Stickneys. The veranda ran around three sides of the building, its easterly end overlooking the tumbling chaos of giant rocks spilling from the headland to the sea. He was alone; inside, Brad and Peg were still in the wide hallway that served as a lobby, talking with friends who had waylaid them as they left the dining room.

He walked to the eastern railing, leaning on it with his hands, looking out across an angry sea and then below at the mountainous cresting swells that rushed toward land with silent fury, finding voice at last as they spent themselves on the rocks below in a dying shout and final show of white, defiant beauty.

Brad's letdown had come immediately, as soon as they had left Pete Martínez in the jail. His own was coming now, sweeping over him in waves that grew higher as they rolled in, like the waves of the rising tide below. For him the most poignant loneliness had always followed good fortune rather than bad. I can ride out disappointment alone, he thought. I can rassle with trouble better alone, we all can. He had kidded Peg when she ran to the car and kissed Brad, but within him there had been sharp pain. Would he always, he wondered, all his life, cry out instinctively, in times like this: "Sara! Good news! Let me tell you—" then hear the cry die within him, unspoken, in desperate futility?

He tried to let the sound of the surf drown the sound of her voice that at a time like this could be within his mind soft and quick and loving, and louder than any thunder.

A voice just behind him said, "Don't be so sad."

He turned quickly to smile at Peg. "How'd you know?"

"You looked as though doom had just reared its ugly head right in front of you—"

"Maybe it had, Peg. Here—I'll get some chairs together."

"We can sit here for a while before the storm breaks. I love it when it's like this. You boys can have a drink while I guzzle coffee."

"Don't you mind?"

"Not in the least. I usually start wanting a drink when

there isn't a drop within sight or reach. Right now it's repugnant."

Peg was being franker about what, for want of better identification, was known as her "problem" than David had ever known her to be.

"I just want a small, nonbulky drink," he said. He had been dreading for weeks any personal talks with Brad. The fact that Peg was there now he knew would not save him from a discussion of his contemplated trip to England. In fact, Brad might just be devious enough to bring it up because she was there, clearheaded and keen of judgment.

Brad came out carrying a tray with glasses and a cup of coffee. He set it down with a flourish on the wicker table in front of Peg and David. When David raised his eyebrows questioningly, Brad said, "I know they don't sell it here, but old man Stickney has his own ideas of hospitality. His compliments, by the way."

David sipped, grinned, and said, "Gosh!"

"You don't hardly ever taste brandy like that no more," said Brad.

"No more?" said David. "I never have. I didn't grow up in rare old brandy circles."

"Never mind the rare old brandy. You're flirting with a real menace. Warm beer."

"Warm beer? Since when?"

Peg answered, laughing: "In England. I prefer it myself. Brad doesn't mind it, but you'd have a hard time getting used to it."

"I don't think I could." He turned to Brad in an effort to change the subject. "Know something, Brad? I've learned more about trial work, rules of evidence, that sort of thing, in this last trial than in all the years at school, swear I have."

"David, you're trying to wiggle off the hook," said Peg. "Brad's been saying you'd like to go to England, Oxford. Why?"

"Well, look—" He stirred uneasily. "Isn't just a desire to learn more a valid reason? Who told me that the learning of law never ends? Guy named Bradford Willis."

"Not quite, David," said Brad sharply. "You're taking what I said out of context. If you'll recall correctly I said that the learning of law is progressive, from history through statutes, all that—on up—and I said 'up'—through its application in the courts, to the needs of the people. And I said that it holds just as true in a dry-as-dust civil case as in a criminal case. What were your struggles with Litchfield if they weren't a valiant effort to fit into the framework of the law the affairs of a delightful but fuzzy-minded man who would never knowingly violate the law or hurt his fellowman but must nevertheless be bound by it? Did you have any real concept of the words 'reasonable doubt' until Mike Shea won that acquittal? Did you have any real knowledge of how the 'eye for an eye' concept of law can have its fangs drawn until the verdict this morning?"

"No, I didn't. I know you're right. My God, you're both on my back, and I haven't even mentioned England!"

"No, but you would, brat," said Peg. "Sooner or later you'd have to. So why not now? We're doing you a favor, really. Saving you hours of dread about bringing it up."

"Gee, thanks," said David miserably. "Thanks a lot."

"Tut-tut," said Peg.

"I suppose Peg is right," said Brad. "She usually is. More brandy to fortify you?"

David shook his head. "I still have some. You've both had me too rattled to drink it."

"Poor lamb," said Peg. "No. I withdraw that. Sympathy's the last thing you need."

The ancient wicker chairs on which they sat creaked with each shift of their occupant's position. There was still no wind, only the alternating roar and crash and snarl of the surf below them, and the homey sound of pliant wicker complaining as it gave way to their bodies' movements. David leaned forward, one finger picking absently at a piece of broken reed in the skirt of the tabletop in front of him. He was quiet for a long time. Neither Brad nor Peg offered help by speaking.

At last he said: "I don't know why everyone's wondering about my motive. I know what Brad's getting at, but it's not for very long. Less than a year." He glanced up and sideways at Brad. "You don't think, do you, that I'm doing it as a sort of prestige thing? So that when I walk into a courtroom people will say 'There's a Negro who went to Oxford?' Like driving up to a real-estate office in a white Caddie knowing damned well they haven't got a house they'd show a Negro, but getting my licks in anyhow? Or maybe being able to thumb my nose at white lawyers— 'Yah-yah—anything you can do I can do better—' "

"Oh, God, of course we don't!" snapped Peg. "That's childish. After Brad told you about the legacy, we used to lie awake at night and picture you tossing on a bed of guilt. Another piece of 'luck' you'd figure you weren't entitled to. It wouldn't have surprised me if Brad had come home some night and told me you'd decided to give it away."

David laughed in spite of his mental discomfort. "Who, me? Give it away? But—but—hell, as long as I have the money what's wrong with using it to give myself all the leverage I can?"

Brad leaned back in his chair, hands clasped behind his head, his eyes on the weathered rafters of the veranda's roof. "It's only my opinion, of course, but I don't think that's the kind of leverage that's needed at this point. Unless you want to take the political route. And even then I think a little of the rough-and-tumble, homegrown politics with which the Commonwealth of Massachusetts is so rife would be helpful. I mean before you tackle the abstract realms of political science."

"Politics? God, no! I'd be lousy."

"Don't be so damned sure. You might need a Brad Willis and a Mike Shea—certainly a Mike Shea!—standing in the prompter's box at first. And to hand you a knife now and then—after you'd learned to use it. The climate's ripening for a young crusader like you."

"Complete with knife?" He grinned. "Anyhow, I'm no crusader."

"In your own simple way you're just that. If you'd get over this defeatism."

"I'm no defeatist either, damn it!"

"Perhaps not, basically. Or perhaps only occasionally. Anyhow, Klein agrees with me. Agrees with me, hell! He's the one who made me think about it. Mrs. Hubbard also agrees —and it was her husband who made her think about it. He's much taken with you."

"We've met three times—"

"He prides himself on omniscience. There are others who have their eyes on you, among them the district attorneys of Middlesex and Suffolk counties. You could rally a hell of a lot of quiet support, David, if you started laying the groundwork for a political career. Who prepared the brief for Klein to submit, the one that challenged the right of Federal legislators from the State of Alabama to hold office?"

David rose and walked to the railing of the veranda, looking for a moment at the surf and the lead-green of the sea. When he walked back to the table he said slowly: "Look,

Brad. Please, for God's sake, don't get mad. I know I've had damned near everything handed to me. Sure, I've had some rough spots because I'm a Negro, just as you have, but nothing like what most of us go up against. This may be the last thing I'll have handed to me, and as I said before, it's not for long. You think I'm going to stay over there, for gosh sake? I can't practice law in England. There's a law against it!"

"David, my dear, sit down and relax." Peg's eyes were warm and understanding. "How often have you said that the Prof used to hammer at you constantly about being honest with yourself? A lot of times. You'll feel a lot better if you admit right now why you're going."

Seated again, he looked over at her warily. "Why am I going, Mother Goose?"

"Sara's there."

"Peg!" Brad's tone was half admonition and half amused indulgence.

"You've been beating around the bush like a—a damned lawyer—for the past fifteen minutes. I'm a direct woman, who likes to come to the point. I don't think David resents it. Do you, David?"

I do, he thought; I resent it like hell, but it's only because you said something I wouldn't speculate about even with myself. And it isn't true; be damned to you both if it's true. But he said, "Of course I don't resent it. But it's not the reason. She—Sara's in Denmark."

Brad laughed softly. "Come off it, brat. Denmark's only a few hours from London, and last I heard she was in London."

He could find out, it would be easy to find out, where she would be staying, even if Hunter wouldn't tell him. It would be enough, he thought, enough just to see her; she needn't even know he was there. Perhaps by now she wouldn't even care. But there could be no harm in just finding out where she was, in managing somehow to see her and know for himself that all was well with her, be able at last to answer the question that seemed never to have left his mind in this past year and a half: Sara, smallest, is it all right with you? That's all I want to know, is it all right with you?

At last Peg's voice broke in on his thoughts: "David. Wake up, pet. I'm apologizing. Perhaps I should have kept quiet. I didn't mean to hurt you—"

He smiled at her, warmer and happier now than he had been in a long time. "You didn't, Peg. You couldn't." Instead of resentment, now he felt gratitude. She had been right to say what she had. It had opened the windows on his self-deceit. He wanted to go to England because Sara would be near. Not to join her again, just to see her. And if, in realizing his goal, he managed to get a crack at the best there was in graduate study, well, luck—luck—*Man pays for his luck. . . . You pay for your pretties. . . .*

He stood up abruptly, rubbed the knuckles of a clenched fist against Peg's chin. "That storm's getting too close for comfort. You two want to start back?"

51

THE THIRD AFTERNOON out from New York harbor, David ventured into the public lounges of H.M.S. *Carinthia* for the second time since boarding. He stood looking down at Hunter Travis sprawled out in a big chair in the smoking room. "You owe me at least five meals, you seagoing bastard."

"Six."

"Five. I made dinner the first night out."

"Something you ate then, no doubt."

"Something I ate then, hell! Something I did when I let you talk me into taking a ship."

"You'll love it in time. I swear it."

David sank into a chair next to Hunter, decided not to court further disaster, and shook his head at the smoking-room steward, who was hopefully awaiting a drink order. He shuddered, remembering the trials of the previous day and that morning, when Hunter had stood in the middle of his stateroom viewing him, if not with alarm, at least with concern.

"You're the Goddamndest color—" Hunter had said.

"Get lost."

"I've sent the room steward for the sister."

"Sister! What I need is the priest—"

"The nursing sister. In England 'sister' is the term for those in the higher echelons of nursing. And don't call her 'nurse.'

She'll give you a pill, and after that you'll sleep and when you wake up you'll be hungry."

"I'll never be hungry again."

But Hunter had been right. The sister had come, all crisp veil and motherly British authority, bullied him gently in a North of England accent, given him a pill, shooed Hunter out, and he had slept and then awakened in midafternoon, whole and healed.

It had taken an all-out effort on Hunter's part to persuade him to make the trip by sea, and he gave in without enthusiasm.

"My last chance at a vacation," said Hunter. "Maybe for years. I'll go to bat for you with Brad and get him to loosen up with enough for you so we can travel first class. The best sailing date is the *Carinthia*'s. She's not as big as the *Queens* or the *Mauretania,* but she's a loverly ship."

"Yes, but—"

"We'll land in Liverpool. You can go direct to Oxford and settle in, or come down to London for a couple of days with me. And you'll have a chance on the trip over to learn the language."

"Damn it, it's a whole week—oh, all right, all right—God help you if I'm seasick."

Now David grudgingly admitted to himself that sea travel had much to commend it. Hunter said, "I'll lower a lifeboat personally and row us back home if you see, hear, or smell Crow. I refer to ship's personnel. I won't speak for the passenger list." He snubbed out his cigarette. "Let's go topside. There's another lounge up there. And the last time I took this ship there was a piano."

David grinned. "Now I get all that sea-salesmanship. Figured you'd have a captive performer."

The big room on the uppermost deck was deserted, and although David religiously kept his eyes away from a horizon that rose and sank rhythmically and disturbingly, he could not hold back an exclamation at the sparkle of a white-flecked green sea under a westering sun. He walked over to the baby grand at the aft end of the room, smiling. "Even on tea I can play hell out of this baby." He flipped back the cover over the keys, then sat and rambled aimlessly through an improvised blues. In a chair nearby Hunter stretched out until he was resting on his spine, ankles crossed, one foot waggling with the beat, long fingers tapping it out on the table beside him. In five minutes David was lost in the music coming alive under his hands. Without looking toward Hunter he said, "I'll take requests from the audience—" When there was no reply he turned his head and then stopped playing abruptly. He was looking directly into the eyes of a stranger who was standing close to the piano, the almost dead blackness of the face broken by the gleam of large, dark eyes and white teeth revealed in a half-smile. After the first surprise David recognized the newcomer as an African. There was no mistaking the rounder head, the hair that had never been tampered with growing just slightly longer than that of the average American Negro, the dignity of the stance, the reserve of the smile.

"Well, hi—" he said lamely. "I didn't hear you come in."

Hunter pulled himself upright by sections and came over to the piano. "David, this is Mr. Jedediah Abikawai. I told you yesterday that he was aboard—"

"Anything you told me yesterday, pal—" David stood and came forward, holding out a hand to the newcomer. "Glad to meet you Mr.—Mr.—"

He recognized in the responsive laugh a muted echo of his own. "No one understands my name the first time. I do not mind if you call me Jed. It was what they called me at the university."

David had to strain to understand him. The soft, low voice combined with the English accent took getting used to; he had found that out at Harvard. He had also found out at Harvard that any idea he had previously entertained that there would be instant rapport between an American Negro and a blood brother from Africa was founded solely on wishful thinking. The aloofness of the ones he had met had been impregnable, and now he restrained himself warily.

"Won't you continue playing? It was very good." Jedediah Abikawai spoke with soft precision and formal phrasing, vowels broadened, the understated consonants almost liquid in sound.

"I was just getting warmed up." David looked over at Hunter. "And thirsty. I'm not scared now."

The bar at the forward end of the room was closed, and Hunter said: "I'll run down and see about drinks. I tipped Jed off that as soon as you healed I'd lead you to this piano. Be back in a minute."

Jedediah remained standing for a moment, a rather short figure with powerful but not heavy shoulders under a pale yellow shirt and matching cardigan. David moved to the chair Hunter had left, and watched Jedediah covertly as the other man walked to the chair opposite him. There were physical power there and catlike coordination, but more than either there was an immense dignity. He waited, without speaking, until Jedediah sat down and said, "You have known Hunter Travis a long time, Mr. Champlin?"

"We were in college together. Counting that, say, roughly, between nine and ten years all told."

"I had never met him before, but when we became acquainted yesterday we discovered that he and my father are old and good friends. They met first when I was very small and Mr. Travis visited my country, and they have met often since. Meeting his son this way, at sea, was like meeting an old friend."

David, mindful of previous experiences, did not ask questions; he was surprised at this volunteering of information on so short an acquaintance This character, he thought, is a damned likable guy, and if I don't come on too strong maybe he'll keep on unbending. He stretched and sighed. "Sure good to be up and out. This is my first day in circulation since we left."

Jedediah said "Brrr-rrr-rrr—" and shuddered. "You have my sympathy. I have been seasick, too. Not recently, but on earlier ocean trips."

"You have?" David realized he hadn't restrained the note of surprise in his own voice. Being seasick didn't jibe with this man's somber, dark strength, and that dignity; the circumstances were hard to picture.

"Yes, indeed. Oh, my God, yes. But I still return to sea travel. Until I was fourteen I saw only lakes and rivers. I fell in love with the sea then, and have never recovered: Though it slay me, yet will I trust in it—"

"I see now why your name is Jedediah."

"Yes. I went to school first in the mission school. The name I bear among my own people was difficult for them, so they named me Jedediah. I do not expect to live up to it. And there are other reasons."

"Were you in the mission school for long?" It seemed a harmless question.

"Until I was fourteen. Then my father sent me to public school in England. That was when I had my first bout of seasickness—on the way—"

Hunter, coming up the stairs a little later, stopped halfway, listening. David's laugh had brought students running from all directions at Pengard because, they said, their windows rattled. I missed out on that gift in my mixed heritage, he thought, the gift of deep and easy laughter; it was diluted out of existence, along with other gifts, so that I am a sitter-on-the-sidelines, never sharing fully in the mirth of those of the dark side of my heritage—or in the tears of either.

The laughter had subsided when he entered the lounge, but he said, "What were you two roaring about?"

"I guess it started with seasickness," said David.

Jedediah said: "I was telling David about my first sea trip, when I was fourteen, and how I lost my faith. It so happened that a pious young man, an instructor at the mission school, was returning to England at the same time, and my father put me in his care." He laughed, softly this time. "When the God of the Christians seemed to have deserted me in my hours of trial, I reverted to the gods and customs of my tribe as best I could. I was describing to David the reactions of the pious young man to my apostasy. He was also seasick. It is hard to be evangelical on a rough sea when one is feeling the motion violently."

An hour later, David looked at his watch. "Hey—another hour and we eat—"

Hunter said, "I have to shave—" He looked at Jedediah. "You're sitting alone, aren't you? So are we. Why don't we have the steward give us a table together?"

"Why not?" Jedediah's smile had the effect of making his skin glow.

David, instantly on the defensive said, "Why're you alone in the first place? Did they make you?"

There was a quick stiffening of the other man's shoulders, and the smile of a moment before might never have happened. "No. It was at my request." He relaxed, and the smile returned. "There were difficulties on my first transatlantic trip. I was only eighteen, and perhaps childish in my reactions. I was seated at a table where a couple from your Alabama were also seated."

"Oh, God, no!" said David. "A hell of an introduction. And don't call Alabama mine."

Jedediah shrugged. "It was good that I learned immediately. I played a childish game. I came to my meals early; they started coming late. Then I started coming late and they were forced to come early. They were discomfited and I was amused. Then I realized that I was being childish. The other couple at the table were delightful, from France. We became fast friends, talking only in their language. In the end it was the Americans who suffered. As I have found it usually is. However, since that time when I am on a ship which has the United States either as a starting point or home port, I always request a single table." He looked at David without smiling. "The tentacles of your country's prejudices reach a long way."

Hunter followed David into his stateroom when they reached A deck. David said, "Do I have to wear black tie and stuff? You swore I wouldn't."

"No. I do the second night out. Just to show I have one, I guess. And the night before the night before landing. Otherwise, an ordinary suit with white shirt and tie."

David sat on the edge of the bed and began unlacing his shoes. "I'm going to shower. Know something? I like that guy Jedediah. He's the first African I've met who seems all the way human."

"Perhaps because you're meeting him on foreign soil, not United States."

"He's colonialized British—"

"Not for long. Zambana gains its independence in less than a year. Don't you read the papers? His father's head man. Quite a person. The natives who have had English schooling call him Solomon. So does my father."

"That's what Jedediah meant when he said there were other reasons for giving him that name."

"Maybe I haven't had your advantages, but I don't see—"

"It's the name that was given to Solomon when he was a baby. Says so in the Bible, anyhow."

"Oh. Thanks. His father plans to make him minister of education. That's why the master's in education at Columbia."

"Yeah? We didn't get around to that this afternoon. Is that why he's been in the States?"

"Yes. His father told my father that his one hope was that the infant Zambana would remain stable, stay out of trouble long enough for them to put education within the reach of everyone. The way Solomon put it was: 'First the arrow and the bow so they will know they are men, then the knowledge.' All Solomon wants is the running start toward democracy that education will give the country. After that he's willing to hand the people the ball. And my father believes he is sincere in this. He's not a man who craves power."

"Do you suppose Jedediah cut his teeth on a bow and arrow?"

"He damned well better have. Notice those shoulders?"

"Hell, I sure wish Gramp was around. A real live bow-and-arrow African, even if he is up to his eyeballs in education. All Gramp's met have been seamen on the docks. And he had a hell of a time understanding them. A lot of them only spoke Portuguese or French, and it wasn't the French he grew up with. For an Afrophile like him, meeting Jedediah would be like taking part in the second coming."

For the next four days David, Jedediah, and Hunter talked, argued, laughed, and decided the world's fate in lounges, on decks, at meals, in smoking rooms, in staterooms, and on two mornings, exhausted, had watched the sun rise over a sea muted to a low murmur in the predawn quiet. Then they had returned to Jedediah's cabin to take up Plato's *Republic* where they had left it, and Hunter had fallen asleep on one of the beds, and left the field to David and Jed.

They set up straw governments for imaginary countries and blew them down, replaced them with other governments and made them work; they founded democracies and tried to shore up their weaknesses, and built republics that toppled because they had forgotten some key building block; David worked out constitutions and howled in anguish when the other two poked holes in them; they established economies and saw them crumble and rebuilt them and saw them prosper; they fought wars and negotiated peace pacts, and they wrestled with Plato and Aristotle and found fault with Athens. And every morning Jedediah walked around the deck twenty times before breakfast.

"Don't tell us," Hunter would say when Jed came to the table. "Don't, for God's sake, tell us."

And Jedediah would laugh aloud, his first greeting of the day to them, and say, "Twenty. How else can I clear my mind every morning and be able to take you both on?"

The night before landing, Jedediah said to David: "What will happen after we separate in Liverpool? We've left the world unfinished."

They were leaning on the rail of the ship. Hunter was below, finishing his packing. "Man, you know it," said David.

"You'll look me up when you come to London?" asked Jedediah. "I'll be there three or four months."

"Damn right I will. Hunter says he has a car. Can't you guys get up to where I'll be?"

"Easily." He turned to David almost shyly. "In my trunks in London I have a carving—a head—that is you. It's native work. Would you mind if I sent it to you?"

"Mind! Gosh, no. I'd be mighty proud to have it, as my grandfather would say."

"Your grandfather. You've talked so much about him and his interest in Africa. Would it please him if I wrote home and asked to have a native costume sent to him? A robe and—"

"The little round hat?"

"Yes, the little round hat, as you so disrespectfully call it. All in a very small size. You think it would please him?"

"Please him! Man, he'll flip. That's damned thoughtful of you, Jed. He'll have it on as soon—" He stopped abruptly, and a deckhand hurrying aft turned suddenly at the sound of David's laughter and stared a forbidden stare at the two passengers at the rail, the black man and the brown man, the brown man with his head thrown back and his laughter rolling down the deck and out over the water.

When he spoke at last, David said: "I'm sorry, Jed. If you knew Gramp you'd know why I laughed. Look, don't send it to him. Send it to me. I have to be there when he gets it. This I have to see. A wise brown mouse in a long white robe. Damn, Jed, I wish he could have met you."

"He'll probably live a long time, David. We have a saying that, roughly translated, means the less meat on the bones, the more years on the life. Perhaps, in fact quite possibly, I shall be able to get back to your country. Who knows? Perhaps he may get to mine. You will, I hope, most surely?"

"I'll try. I'll sure as hell try. I want to. Man, you know I want to."

Below in his cleared-out stateroom, bags stacked neatly beside David's in the passageway, Hunter Travis sat at his typewriter. He was sure his father would be stunned at receiving a letter from him written at sea. He would mail it before the ship docked and it would be back in New York, by air, no later than the following day. He could no longer hold back the idea that had been growing in strength almost since the first afternoon David and Jedediah Abikawai had met.

He ran paper into the typewriter and began. "Dear Chief,—Good trip. And an interesting fellow passenger. Jedediah Abikawai, son of Solomon of Zambana. He and David have become firm friends. I hope I'm not speaking out of turn, but if you keep to the schedule you had when I left you'll be in

Washington next week. After you've explained the facts of life to the President, how about having a talk with Abner Chittock about David? My thought is this—"

Twenty minutes later he sealed and stamped the letter, dropped it off in the library for mailing, and set out in search of David and Jed. He found them still on deck.

"What you been doing, man?" asked David.

"Packing."

"All this time?"

"All this time. When Travis packs he packs right."

Standing at the rail with Hunter and Jedediah again the next morning, watching the bustle of the Liverpool dock as the ship was maneuvered into position, David pointed, grinned, and said—"Look. England."

Hunter glanced sideways at him and then laughed. "You look like a kid who's just been handed a cream puff."

Jedediah said, "England is no cream puff. I can assure you of this."

"And a Zambanian is one who knows it," said Hunter. "But you'll part friends."

"We will part friends. With wisdom on both sides."

"Drop the politics, you guys," said David. "Here comes the gangplank."

"Listen, David—Jed and I will make a dash for the dock and round up all our luggage—his, yours, and mine—and an inspector. If we don't, that little bit of England you're seeing down there is damn all you will see of it for two or three hours. Take your time—"

David remained standing at the rail for a few minutes, letting the first group of impatient passengers crowd to the gangplank. A Liverpool dock, he decided, differed in no major point from a New Orleans or a New York dock. The sun had surprised all three of them when they had come on deck earlier. In David's mind there had always been a picture of England as a beautiful island, perpetually green under perpetually gray skies. Now he was standing with all of England, a new world, before him, with the sun warm enough on his shoulders so that before he started toward the gangplank he slipped off his light topcoat and carried it over his arm.

He had not been thinking of Sara, and then, suddenly, he was. All through the trip Sara had kept in the background, unobtrusive, making herself known only in those occasional moments when he had been alone, saying, "David, David—"

And now she was here, not a few hundred miles south but here, walking the deck beside him, her quick, half-running footsteps louder than the solid reality of the footsteps of the passengers hurrying to the gangplank.

There had been no questions asked of Hunter; he had gritted his teeth and determined not to ask them. But Hunter, on the first night out, before seasickness obscured everything but the joys of the hereafter, had said, "Oh, hell. I can't take it any longer."

"Can't take what?"

"That lost-dog look you get every now and then. Just like all the stray pups looking for a home that I picked up when I was a kid. Sara's in London."

"Oh?"

"Don't give me that wide-eyed 'Oh?' bit. I just answered a question that's been bugging you ever since I got back to the States five weeks ago. I'll even tell you where she's living. The Crown Hotel in Russell Square."

"My God, you don't have to get mad about it!"

"I'm not mad. Hell, yes, I suppose I am. It all seems so blasted stupid. Anyhow, there's your information. You're on your own now. I won't, God damn it, play cupid. You might try standing under the statue of Eros in Piccadilly and saying a few prayers."

"Hey, look. Cool off. I didn't ask—"

"You didn't. And Sara didn't. And you're both screaming it whenever I see you."

"Did she—"

"I told you. No. But find out for yourself."

"O.K., O.K., grampaw." He had smiled at the other's exasperation. "And thanks, pal."

52

DAVID HAD TAKEN IT for granted that Oxford would be a quiet backwater by the side of a pleasant river on which there was a good deal of boating, according to prints and

English novels, and that over its spires and ancient gray-walled colleges there would brood a deep, academic peace gently broken by the swish of black gowns and occasional low talk and equally low laughter.

After an initial period of adjustment to Oxford as it is, busy, noisy, bustling, traffic-jammed, he met the two tutors who would guide him through the term. The first, in international law, was a man who belonged in the fantasy Oxford of David's imagining; the second, in political science, was a man of forceful, outgoing personality who, except for his accent, might have stepped from the campus of any large American college. At least, he thought, one will relax me and the other will jar me. He found that they both jarred him, and for the first time in his life he had a full appreciation of what Bjarne Knudsen had done for him. It had been a long time since those sessions with the Prof, but now he could fall back on the conditioning they had given him for Oxford's academic approach. The Prof had never made him study—he had studied because the Prof had succeeded in sowing the seeds of a desire for knowledge. At Pengard there had been assigned work, and necessarily more discipline in spite of small classes and individual attention from instructors, and he had fallen into a different pattern of learning. He realized now that it had been, in a certain sense, a lazier pattern, and his mind at first responded slowly to the prodding of these dons, then began to assert itself as it had under the Prof's tutelage, when it had been, as it was now, first whetted, then pitted against another, more knowledgeable mind that was anxious that his own should match it. Of the two it was the quiet, quaint, and spectacled don who more often brought from him a gusty "Whe-ew!" of relief and exhaustion as he limped down the stairs from that gently spoken man's study, full of tea and law.

He knew that when he went to the city and saw the Travises again—especially Marcia—he would be expected to make enthusiastic sounds about Oxford. He could do that without dissembling when it came to certain aspects of it—the Bodleian, the scholastic challenge, the dons. But he could not turn faint with awe, as most Americans were reputed to do, at its great age, its hoary traditions. And why, he thought, should he? What did these have that would move an American Negro whose own traditions went no further back than a legendary great-grandfather, a good man dead of burning in an open field in the Deep South? Beyond the first David

Champlin—the dark. And this was something he would never be able to explain to anyone not of his own people, that there was no answering chord of Anglo-Saxon pride in him at the things that meant so much to others.

The best he could do, when he met white friends in England, would be to come on strong about the whole general scene, and stress those things that really moved him, such as the Bodleian, the dons, and the riverbank on a cool evening when there was a nip in the air and the sense of peace he had expected to find everywhere. And the pubs, and the unconcerned live-and-let-live friendliness. Someone had said—he thought it was Tom Evans on a quick trip to Boston—"You won't like it. Damned snobs—" Snobs they might be among themselves, he didn't give a damn; with him they had shown casual, easy friendliness, with no apparent thought to color.

Three weeks went by with unbelievable speed before he dared think of London. Hunter called and offered to come up with Jed and drive him down, but he put him off, not admitting to a childish desire to sample a British train; remembering scores of motion pictures with interesting people ducking in and out of cozy little compartments, the men all carrying briefcases loaded with important documents, the women invariably beautiful, the two coming together—the meetings always fraught with future love or dire peril—over sticking windows. And then, unexpectedly, there was a Friday ahead of him, and a tense mind and time to go to London on a train that would put him in Paddington Station late in the afternoon.

On Thursday he called Hunter, who said: "I'll meet you. We'll have dinner. . . . If we miss at the station call my mother. . . . Got the number and address? . . . Right . . . Or you can take a cab and go there. . . . You in funds? . . . Want to put up with me, or the family, or go to a hotel? I can fix you up with a reservation at one you'll like near Green Park. . . . Sure. Decide when you get here. . . . No problem this time of year . . ."

One picture sold at a pretty price: "Peace, 1960"; and another, the one of the small, defiant black boy facing a world of chill snow, was being held in reserve for Hunter's father. Sara tried to convince herself that it was silly to feel guilty because for a month she had been able to do no more than sketch stupid, meaningless scratches, not even worthy of a high-school art class, or daub meaningless blobs of color on canvas, blobs with no relation to anything in her mind, as though her brush had been held in the hand of a stranger. You could paint when you first came over, my girl, she told herself, when you were all shattered and hopeless; now you can't because a month ago David Champlin walked aboard a ship in New York and a week later walked ashore in England.

She knew that much because Hunter had said so, adding gratuitously that David had been seasick; other than that—nothing. The stinker, the sadistic, objective stinker . . . If you had any sense, Sara Kent, you'd head for the Continent. That's what you told yourself you'd do when he came over; that was the decision you made; only it wasn't, really. You decided you'd let go and do what seemed right when the time came, and that's what's right; only, I can't go because I'm weighted down, my feet and my heart and my life—they're weighted down with knowing David's in England. . . . God, where are my guts! All it takes is to walk into a travel bureau and say "Copenhagen." And the man behind the counter will say "Return?" And you'll say "Yes." You know you will.

The telephone rang, and the hand that held a brush, trying to bring a tricky color into line, jerked so uncontrollably that a three-inch streak of yellow sprawled across the canvas, ruining a morning's work.

Marcia Travis's voice said, "Sara, my dear. I got your message. Where in the world have you been?"

"Busy, Marcia—I mean, sort of—and feeling guilty about not having called. How are you?"

"Wet to the skin, pet. I just came in, and it's utterly foul outside. I'm going to change and then drink pots of hot tea. Join me?"

"I—I shouldn't. I just started—"

"Nonsense. Bundle up and get into a cab and come over. Do hurry. And don't for heaven's sake go out without your brolly. It's quite teeming out there."

She cleaned the canvas hurriedly, trying to erase the concrete evidence of taut nerves that for weeks had been short-circuiting her coordination and control. She had paid no attention to it before, but now she could hear the rain pounding on the skylight, sluicing off nearby roofs. If she was lucky—very lucky—there would be a cab in the rank outside a nearby hotel; if she wasn't she would have to stay at the studio. Even with raincoat and hat, umbrella and rubbers, this rain would defeat a Londoner as far as walking anywhere was concerned.

She was lucky. A cab had just drawn into the rank, and swung forward at her frantic arm wave. Ten minutes later, in spite of a sensation that she had been drowning in an upright position just walking across a sidewalk, she smiled, warmed and glad when Parsons opened the door of the Travis house. Sara had never doubted that Parsons had been picked by Marcia's father, never a stickler for tradition, as a conversation piece, and then kept on as an indispensable part of the family. He was a short, chubby, rosy-cheeked, chatty and beardless Santa, a non-butler type if she had ever seen one. His hair, at seventy, was luxurious and snowy and he exuded an air of boundless optimism at all times. His wife was several inches taller, angular and severe, with a repressed maternal instinct that embraced everyone connected with the family, even Marcia's younger sister, Ursula, excepting only Ursula's frequent husbands. "She couldn't abide any of 'em," Marcia had said once, lapsing into a New Englandism.

The tall narrow house in a short street just off Wigmore had been left to Marcia by her father, and the Parsons had never doubted that they went with it. "For which, thank God," said Marcia. The younger sister, of whom Sara was never able to recall anything but red hair and a mingled smell of cocktails and expensive perfume, used the house as headquarters between marriages and between mysterious trips to Paris, Rome, Madrid, Berlin, and once—no one ever found out why—to Moscow. It was kept open for her, with the Parsons in residence, whenever the Travises were in the States, or at some far-off corner of some geographically obscure but politically important country. Every inch of it was Marcia's, from the faded chintzes on the huge, comfortable chairs and couches in the ground-floor sitting room to the gracious eighteenth-century drawing room on the floor above.

Sara surrendered her outer clothing to a clucking and concerned Parsons. "Horrid weather," he said. "Horrid. Able to catch a cab, were you? . . . Lucky, I must say. . . . Never mind, can't last forever, you know. . . ." He hung her raincoat carefully on the old-fashioned umbrella-hat-stand in the small outer entrance hall, and took her rain hat away from her with gentle reproof when she started to cram it into the coat pocket. As though they were both platinum mink, no less, she thought. He preceded her to the door of the sitting room, and Sara noted with a grin that he was carrying her rubbers at arm's length, their final destination without doubt a spot near the kitchen stove to dry out their innards where water had intruded.

She sighed, beginning to relax, and moved gratefully to the sitting-room grate and its glowing coal fire. Her legs were damp and chilled, and she backed up to the blaze, hiking her skirts so the warmth could reach her thighs. She was able to smile almost gaily at Mrs. Parsons when she entered with a tray of tea things.

"Good afternoon, Miss Sara. Nice to see you. . . . You'd best take off those shoes, and I'll see you have some slippers. . . . Now, now, there'll be no one but you and Mrs. Travis. . . . We'll just sit them on the fender and they'll be warm in no time. . . . Nasty day, it's been; very nasty. . . ."

Sara submitted as she had once before when she had showed up for tea, flu-ridden, flushed with fever, and croaking dangerously. Mrs. Parsons had all but put her to bed bodily and for a week she had been babied and bullied, fed gruels and broths and custards and chops, until one afternoon, weakly recovering, she had lain back on her pillows after tea and wept silently, large tears of self-pity rolling down her cheeks at the realization of the vast desert of loneliness in which she had been living and to which she would return, and in which she would live out her life.

Mrs. Parsons stalked out, and she heard Marcia's steps on the stairway, then the ringing of a telephone. The footsteps came faster, and Marcia called, "I'll answer it, Dell—" and then she heard Marcia enter the study just behind the sitting room. The door was open slightly, and Marcia's words, clear and incisive, were audible. Sara squirmed uncomfortably; she hoped the call was not a personal one, perhaps her husband calling from the United States, something she knew he did frequently. She dropped her skirt over now warm thighs and put one stockinged foot forward to tiptoe over and close the study door, then stood, motionless, listening shamelessly.

". . . Who? Oh, Hunter! Dear, I can't hear you. . . . You're *where?* . . . I still didn't get it, but wherever you are you shouldn't be there in this weather. . . . Who? David Champlin? Of course. I'll be here, dear. . . . I'll tell him whatever you say. . . . Here, your flat, or a hotel? Whatever he decides? Right . . . Five-fifteen from Oxford, Paddington? I'll be waiting for the call. . . . Tell me again where you are. . . . Chillingsworth? But, darling, that's only four miles from the Burleighs. . . . Of course I don't mean for you to walk in this weather! I'll just get through to them, shall I, and see about rescue? A car or raft or something . . ."

By the time Marcia had said "Chillingsworth," Sara, fully shod, was in the hall, Marcia's words still audible. She narrowly avoided a collision with Mrs. Parsons, who was bearing down from the rear with a laden tray and a pair of soft slippers tucked into the pocket of her apron.

Sara dodged adroitly and gasped: "I have to go, Mrs. Parsons. I have to—I've forgotten something. Something dreadfully important. Please tell Mrs. Travis I'll call her right—right away—" She was in the small vestibule now, slipping into a cold damp raincoat, ramming the plastic rain hat down over her head.

"Miss Sara! You can't—"

"I have to—" The outer door was open now, the knob in her hand. If Mrs. Parsons had not been carrying a laden tray, Sara would not have put it beyond her to restrain her physically. As the door closed behind her and she entered a world of water and streaming pavements again, she heard an anguished, distant cry from Mrs. Parsons, "Your *rubbers!*—"

Mrs. Parsons and her mistress met in the middle of the sitting room, the housekeeper's hands shaking visibly as she put plates of sandwiches and cakes on the table in front of the fire. Marcia Travis, frowning in bewilderment, looked around the room and said, "Miss Sara? What happened? I know I heard her come in—"

"She ran off, madam. Like she was possessed. Said she'd forgotten something important—"

Marcia looked out the window at a wet and fast-darkening world. "In *that?*"

"Yes, madam. And without her rubbers. Something dreadfully important she said it was—"

"It's not like—" Marcia stopped, turned slowly, and looked at the door to the study, closed now. "Della, that door was open." She began to laugh softly. "Miss Sara didn't forget anything. Take back all but four of those cakes. I don't trust myself with them. And that other teacup. I'm quite sure I'll be toasting my toes and drinking tea alone today."

Whatever I do I mustn't get lost. . . . You could live in London twenty years and get lost in five minutes. . . . Thank God it's Paddington and not Euston. . . There's an underground near. . . . No, there isn't, and I don't dare take it if there is. . . . Or a bus. I can walk faster than a bus can go in this rain and traffic. . . . Cut through behind Wigmore Street, that's the way to do it. . . . Then Edgware Road. . . . More cabs on Edgware . . . then there's a Gardens. . . . What Gardens? Oh, God, what Gardens . . ."

A freshet of rain cascaded from her hat and down her neck, and she realized she had instinctively grabbed her umbrella—you're a real Londoner now, Sara—and hadn't even opened it. With the umbrella open she was even blinder than she had been before, and not much dryer. She stepped from a curb and felt water up to her ankle and as she crossed the street felt one low walking shoe full of water; the other matched it when she stepped up on the opposite sidewalk. There were taxis, hurrying, scurrying hordes of taxis, all occupied and most of them probably headed for Paddington too. She waved at them futilely. . . . Please, God, please let some compassionate soul take pity and offer me a lift. . . . No one did, and she knew she was wasting precious minutes. She tried to look at her wristwatch, but the tiny crystal was too wet and the light too poor to see it by. . . . It must be, had to be, later than four thirty.

You're a fool, Sara. . . . You're a damned fool . . . to go through all this just to see him. . . . Just to see *David?* No! . . . But you can't make it. . . . You'll be too late. . . . It's only Edgware now. . . . You'll be standing in the middle of that great cold station all alone like a drowning cat, looking, looking . . . and you've insulted Marcia. . . . She'll understand. I don't mind telling Marcia. . . . David, David, wait for me. . . . All I want, all I want is just to see you. . . .

"Sorry. I'm so sorry. Let me pick it up for you. There. I *was* looking where I was going only I couldn't *see* where I was going. I'm sorry."

A delay. A precious two minutes lost. . . . Damn the rain . . . damn, damn everything, including me. . . . Taxi! Oh, God, there's an empty one. . . . No, there's a stupid man in the back seat, and I hope his stupid moustache catches fire when he lights that stupid cigarette. . . . Edgware Road, miles of it, all of them wet and slippery. . . . God, I must be in Maida Vale by now. . . . The signs . . . I ought to look at the signs . . . Gardens . . . Sussex Gardens . . . I'm getting closer. . . . If I stopped and poured the water out of my shoes, I could run. . . .

"Yes! Here! Here, taxi!" This was a miracle, pure and simple. . . .

She tumbled into the cab, saw pools of water form on the floor, and felt a gust of wet air blow through the window behind the driver as he opened it. "Paddington, Miss?"

"Yes! Yes! Paddington Station."

"Naow, naow, miss. There's nothing to worry about. We'll myke it."

David, David, just at first you'll be lost in that station. . . . You'll have to stop and look around . . . look for Hunter, who won't be there. . . . That will make up for the time I lost when I bumped into that woman. . . . David, David . . .

His first British train was all that David had hoped for; only the lack of a seat that would recline as American train seats did bothered him. He gave the compartment he was riding in a figurative pat of approval, forgave its shortcomings, and lighted a cigarette. He tried to peer through the sheets of rain that blotted out everything but a narrow trackside strip of country, gave up, and after a quick, furtive look at his two fellow passengers—a woman knitting and a man reading a newspaper—he flipped open his copy of the overseas edition of *Time* and found that not a paragraph made sense. He closed it and fastened his gaze on the gray, rain-drenched world through which they were traveling. Hunter had told him about ewes with twin lambs in the fields, but there were no ewes and no lambs, twin or otherwise, visible under the pouring skies. Sara was getting closer to his thoughts; he could feel her wriggling into his mind, and once entrenched, a field full of twin lambs, each with two heads, would not be able to banish her.

Another confrontation with Sara I can't take, he thought. It seemed as though all the years of his life after leaving Pengard had been one heart-wrenching break from Sara after another, followed inevitably by a shattering, resolve-destroying confrontation. Yet he had survived those periods of being apart from her; more, he had survived and carried forward whatever he was doing. Let it be that way now; whatever his original motives in coming here, let it be that way now. For Sara's sake as well as his own, let it be that way now.

He would stay with Hunter, or at the Travis home instead of a hotel. He firmly put aside his previous decision to stay at a hotel where he would have more freedom of movement. He had been kidding himself about that "freedom of movement." A chance to go out, without anyone else's knowledge, find Russell Square and perhaps catch sight of Sara: that had been the "freedom of movement" he had wanted. Maybe he still wanted it, but he wasn't going to take it. Not now, after a quiet hour to think it over in and realize that he was no longer a damned kid, that he was, had to be, mature enough to fear another confrontation, more—to avoid one instead of taking a step that could only be defined as seeking one out. He'd taken Sara's absence now for a year and a half; in another year the feeling of loss would be lessened; a few more and it would become the vague background against which he would live out his life, free from the flood and ebb tides of happiness and pain. And that, he told himself, was a damned good analogy. Another flood could drown him; another ebb would be more than he could take. Let it be, he thought; let it be the way it is.

When he emerged into the dark, noisy cavern of London's western terminus his concern was mainly whether Hunter would be there. He had a confused feeling that everyone around him was speaking a foreign language, that only the signs were in English. Where in hell was Hunter? Nonchalant about a lot of things Hunter might be, but his old man had trained him to punctuality. In this rain, though, anything could happen, and traffic jams were a dead certainty; he'd give him ten minutes, then call the Travis home and hope to get Marcia.

He moved toward a newsstand, carrying his small bag, trying to get out of the way of hurrying, train-bound crowds, feeling in his pocket for his address book with the Travis address and phone number. It might be better to take a cab and go directly to the house without phoning if Hunter didn't show; there would be someone there, and Hunter would catch up with him eventually.

He was halfway to the newsstand, glancing back to the train gate he had just left, still looking for Hunter, when someone bumped—a rather solid bump—into his midsection. He moved aside quickly, said, "Beg your pardon—" looked down and said, "God! Good God—" while Paddington Station and London roared around the shores of the island on which he and Sara Kent stood alone.

"No. Not God. Sara. It's Sara, David—"

"I—I know—" His words came thickly, as though he were drunk; he had a baffled, lost feeling. Not now, he thought, not now—if it had to happen I needed time for defenses—"I—I know—" he said again, stupidly. "Sara." And saying her name, directly into her eyes, brought the world back around them, took them from an island and set them down in Paddington Station.

"Is that all you can say, David? Just 'I know—'?"

"I'm—well, I'm shook—" He was smiling now, but the words still came thickly, stupidly. "Where—where you headed for?" People came to stations to take trains. Hunter wouldn't have told her; this was nothing but an agonizing coincidence that couldn't happen in the largest city in the world and yet had happened.

"Paddington Station. That's where I was headed for. Where the trains from Oxford come in. Where students coming in from Oxford get off trains."

People also came to stations to meet people. He hadn't been the only Oxonian on that train. "You—you meeting the five-fifteen? It's—it's already in—"

Sara was laughing now, and as she laughed she reached up and pulled off her rain hat, shaking it so that little rivulets of water fell from its creases. "David! All that studying—it's made you teched in the haid—"

Suddenly he couldn't look at her any longer, not until he could quiet what was going on inside himself that would not let him talk sanely. He stooped to pick up his bag, saw tiny feet in what had once been smart walking shoes, shoes now so dark with water and a blackish slime they might be any color. From shoes to knees soaked stockings clung to slender legs, and at the knees the skirt of a wet, defeated raincoat hung soggily.

He straightened, said: "Your feet, Sara. My God, they're soaked! You're—well, you're soaked all over—" and his voice belonged to him again, and the words came clearly without stumbling through uncertain lips.

"I—I suppose I am—" She was moving back from him, and he had to restrain himself from reaching out to her. Then he realized she was moving away only to get a wider view of the station, and her hand was on his arm.

"Over there," she said. "Near the newspaper stand. Hot tea for my wet feet, David?"

"I—no—I—sure, Sara. Sure. Good gosh, you'll catch your damned death of cold—"

She walked beside him, footsteps half running, voice lilting, words tumbling: "No, I won't—not now, David. I won't catch anything bad or nasty or sick-making now—I couldn't, David; I couldn't—"

They found a table whose enamel top bore light tan puddles from previous tea drinkers. David scrubbed it carefully with a paper napkin while Sara giggled like a child, and he glared at her defensively. "Well, for gosh sake, it was dirty, wasn't it?"

They brought their tea to the table, and David said, frowning, "Sara, your feet. You're squishing when you walk—"

"David, *will* you stop talking about my feet! Damn my feet! My feet will be all right! Can't you think of anything else except my blasted feet! I run and run and run and panic and get soaked and finally get a cab and then run like hell through the station looking for you and then I find you and all you can talk about is my damned wet feet!"

He was quiet for a moment, looking at her, not wanting to speak, just wanting now to look at her, really see her, the glowing eyes, every line of face and throat and body. Then he smiled slowly.

"Little Sara. Smallest—"

"Go on, darling. David, my darling, go on—'little love—' "

"Little love—"

53

FOR SARA THERE WAS the joy of feeling whole again, and she tried to describe it to David. "As though I don't have any missing parts any more, like spark plugs and ignition switches, the bits and pieces that make something go."

But there was something other than the wholeness, something that marred that joy, and she kept silent about this, afraid that voicing it would give it strength. She had not felt it before, although she had sensed it in David and tried to convince him that it was false. Now she knew it was not false, that it was real and valid, and it came between them when she least wanted it, hovering over a table while they ate, her couch when they lay together, walking beside them as they strolled through a London park, her hand reaching up to tuck itself beneath his arm. Fear.

Sara Kent . . . the burnt child come back to the fire . . .

closer this time . . . and this time a hotter fire. . . . What will happen in the spring when David goes back home? . . . What will happen then? . . . Take what you have now and be happy with it. . . . It's time now to grow up, Sara. . . . Forget the spring. . . Forget the spring. . . .

During David's absences at Oxford she painted with a brush once again in her own hands and not the hands of a stranger, and on a morning when the rain was pounding on the skylight as forcefully as it had the afternoon she had raced to Paddington Station, she started her first abstraction, all yellows and blues and shades of rose, standing back from it every now and then to laugh delightedly. When Hunter Travis saw this one, a beautiful friendship would end with a bang. She started mental squabbles with Hunter about art—the only kind she ever really won were the mental ones—and considered giving the finished canvas to Marcia, who would love it and in sheer contrariness would hang it someplace where Hunter would be bound to see it every time he came to the house. Sara, squarest, she thought; that's you.

She showed it to David, who said, "What do you mean, 'square'? I'm the guy they invented the word for. I think it's real beeyootiful. . . ."

She tried to hug him, never completely successful at this because her arms would scarcely reach, and he picked her up and held her against his shoulder. "The better to kiss you, my dear." When he set her down he said, "Listen, where's the picture Hunter told me about that he wants you to save for his father to see? Don't I rate a look?"

She hesitated. From the moment she had started the painting of the little black boy she had known that on that particular canvas no one's judgment, amateur or expert, would count except David's. At that time she had thought he would never see it, that she would never know if she had somehow succeeded in translating fantasy into reality.

She walked to the storage cupboard, separated the black-boy canvas from several unfinished ones, and brought it to the easel. As she set it up she said: "I haven't named it yet. I don't know what to call it. Usually I know beforehand—"

He stood without speaking for so long that any thought she had that he might like it vanished and she steeled herself for criticism. At last he moved forward, closer to the picture, a smile she could not interpret disturbing the impassivity of his face.

When he spoke it was under his breath. "That's it, baby,"

he said. "Baby, that's *it.*" She could not tell whether he was speaking to her or the small black child on the canvas.

Later she grinned across a dinner table at him. "When I'm famous you can brag that you named a Kent canvas."

"How? What?"

" 'That's it, baby.' "

Sara was so delighted with Jedediah after they had met a few times that David told her he was jealous, and she laced her fingers through his as they walked along Southampton Row to Russell Square. "Not really, love?"

"Nope. Not really. Just enough to keep me interested." Then he frowned down at her, half smiling at the same time. He hadn't seen any adult Londoners skipping on the street, although he'd seen almost everything else.

"Ooops!" said Sara. "I'm being conspicuous. Sorry."

The weather was still drippy when he returned to Oxford after that first trip down, leaving a suddenly solemn and quiet Sara. "You're going away again, David—"

"Gosh, hon, I've got to. They won't move Oxford down here—"

"Of course not."

"Come on, baby, don't look like that."

"Like what?"

"As though you were seeing ghosts or something."

"I am. The ghosts of my own feelings, the way they were, the way they could be again—David, you're coming back?"

"No, I'm not. I'm going to stay up there and let the blues take over, die stone cold daid of loneliness every weekend. Honest. . . . There's time for one more kiss, sweet . . . two more . . . three . . ."

But on the journey back, through a countryside still gray, he remembered his conclusions on the first journey: that he would have to assume a maturity he had not shown yet in this situation that neither time nor distance had changed. He had understood Sara better than she realized when she said, "I feel whole again." His only problem, he thought, his only li'l piece of a problem wore a too familiar face: a choice that had been there from the beginning, from a spring evening in Laurel when he had first met a girl with one arm in a green silk sling: the choice between the spiritual disembodiment of separation or the facing of the new problem that would be created in marriage.

That new problem seemed dangerously simple of solution

here, four thousand miles away from home and the conditions that would create it. He had been forced to pull himself back time and again from the quicksands of complacency. A few more years, a few more Nottingham riots, a few more thousand black-skinned people on this little island—his inner laugh was a bitter one—and he would probably feel right at home, instead of free and identifiable as a person. But now, riding in an English train compartment, the polite, brief stares of his fellow passengers recognizable as those of curiosity and not of hate or repugnance, that marriage seemed right and possible, Chuck Martin's words, "Who are you, you self-righteous idiot, to look God's gifts in the teeth?" valid and understandable.

Gramp had said once, "There ain't nothing perfect. 'Cept maybe a new baby—"

It was all a long way off, even Gramp and Chop-bone and the little house in Beauregard and the Timmins kids across the road, and Isaiah and the Jeffersons. He had not merely come to Oxford, England; he had traveled through immeasurable reaches of space to another planet where he was as all men and he and Sara were as they had been created—male and female, and what had moved on the face of the waters and created life when the world was without form and void had been love.

. . . And it's not that simple . . . not now or here or anywhere, anytime. . . . Pull yourself together, Champlin. Here's your station. . . .

Identifying early spring in England, David decided, was a matter of bloodstream and bones, and the stirring of the spirit. "It's not just the contrast with that mess that came before. It's different," he told Marcia when she telephoned him one afternoon at Oxford.

"That it is, David. Our seasons explain us—"

"Come on, now. Nothing does that. A complex breed, the British—"

"Not at all. We'll argue it out one day. Right now I'm calling for my husband. He wants you for dinner Saturday night. Jedediah's father has come to London unexpectedly, and he wants you to meet him."

"Solomon of Zambana?"

"So biblical, isn't it? Like Saul of Tarsus, or Jehosaphat of Judah. And he's a bit of a biblical character. No beard, of course."

"Why 'of course'? I was thinking—"

"David Champlin, don't you dare!"

"All right, mum. I won't. What time? I'd sure like to meet him."

"Early; that is, for you. Lawrence wants to talk with you first."

"Have I done something I shouldn't?"

"No, pet. And it wouldn't be any of our business if you had. He just wants to discuss certain things with you. Around six?"

"Hunter—"

"Just you, my dear. Not even our dearly beloved son this time. Not even Sara."

"Gosh—"

"Sixish—?"

"I'll be running—"

Spring in London wasn't true; it was a miracle that couldn't possibly happen, yet it had, and David marveled, as a man does at miracles. Everything seemed illusionary: the blaze of yellow jonquils in the windowboxes of a huge, grime-blackened building wasn't the brightness of flowers, it was summer sun that had been stored within that building through the long gray winter and transplanted now to reassure the passersby that all was still ordered and well with God's plan for the seasons. In the parks the buds were a green mist against the sky and the brick and concrete, and in Trafalgar Square the lions basked, waiting for the summer the young sunlight promised.

On the Saturday he was to dine at the Travises', he and Sara ate lunch in Hyde Park, took undergrounds, and strolled through brighter streets than he had ever seen before. They shopped for clothes for Sara and a light blue pullover for him, and as they walked down Oxford Street he said: "Go ahead, honey chile. Skip. If I didn't have a gimpy leg I'd skip too."

"Like a young lamb gamboling on the green?"

"We-ell, not exactly." Then he said, "Don't say it."

"Say what?"

" 'O, Wind, If Winter comes'—"

"Stoopid. But six o'clock comes, and we have to get back so you can spruce up for whatever in the world it can be that Lawrence wants to talk to you about."

"It just about has to be some legal something or other he wants me to take up with Brad when I get back—"

He wondered as he walked toward the Travis house what a man was supposed to call the top guy in an African state. Chief? He'd heard that "Chief" was derived from European influences. Your Highness? Your Royal Highness? Mr. Abikawai?

With the Travis house just ahead now, he began to feel nervous. What in hell did Lawrence Travis want of him? Lawrence Travis and, for God's sake, a man called Solomon of Zambana? If it was legal matter, he wished he'd brought a notebook.

Parsons greeted him with a rosy smile. "Nice to see you, sir. . . . Lovely day it's been. . . . Mrs. Parsons and I were saying just last week 'O, Wind, If Winter comes' . . . I'll just hang it up for you. . . . Mr. Travis is in the study. . . ."

But Lawrence Travis had come out of the study to greet him and was standing in the center of the hall. "Glad you could make it early, David. What'll it be? A drink, tea, coffee? If Marcia was here it would be tea, ready or not. She'll be back for dinner, by the way—"

"Coffee. You-all don't know it yet, but the next time I come to England I'm moving in—just for that coffee."

Because there had never been a reason for a private talk with Lawrence Travis before, David had never been inside the study. As he entered he blinked at books so numerous that they had to be stacked on tables and even on chairs here and there. And, he remembered, there were fully as many in their apartment in New York.

"Gosh, the annex of the Bodleian—"

Travis laughed. "I could use that space, couldn't I? Wait—sorry, David, I'll have to clear that chair—" As he removed books and papers from the chair beside the fireplace and the coffee table in front of it, he said: "It's what comes of not getting inside a school until I was ten. . . . My grandmother was what the folks down there called a 'good reader.' . . . Her mother had learned from the people she belonged to as a slave. They'd be damned as liberals today. . . . Grandmother taught me until the year we got a horse as well as a mule. . . . The nearest colored school was eight miles—"

"And the nearest white?"

"Two. . . . Three. . . . Sit down, David. We'll need that

fire soon, spring or no spring." As David took his seat, Travis smiled across at him from his own seat on the other side of the grate. "Res' yo'se'f, man."

David chuckled, smiling contentedly. It was good to hear someone say something like that, unafraid of ridicule. He was at home. Always when he met his own kind of people in a world of whites there was this inner content, this sense of relaxation, of coming home; even, he had often thought, if he didn't happen to like the particular individual he was with.

"Y'all better stay 'way from that bandana-haid talk, Mr. Travis. You fixin' to get yourself read out of the race by us enlightened Negroes."

Travis laughed again, an easy, relaxed man here in his own study, still young looking, little gray in the dark hair, and showing no trace of the weight of the responsibilities he had carried, the crises he had weathered, the instant, agonizing judgments he had been forced to make in situations where not even his government could help him. A real great man, thought David, and here I am with him, the two of us like a couple of old friends sitting on the porch steps on a hot southern night.

"Enlightenment and forgetfulness of the past aren't necessarily the same," Travis was saying. "Forgetfulness of the dark areas of the heart and mind that existed before is not, in my opinion, a corollary of enlightenment. And, as far as that is concerned, how do you define enlightenment?"

"I don't. Not me. I know a lot of guys who think they can, but I'll pass that one."

"That's wisdom. By the way, Brad sends his best. So does Peg."

"Are they both all right? Brad writes once a month when he primes the pump. I sure miss him."

"He's fine. Peg—" Travis held out one hand, palm down, turning it from side to side. "It's a crying shame."

They talked through two cups of coffee, and David through four small sandwiches. "Sara and I went walking and shopping today. Makes you hungry," he said apologetically.

"I wish there weren't such long absences between our brief meetings, David. I always have the fear that the next time we meet you will have grown up."

"Gosh, I thought I had."

"Somewhat, David, somewhat. Not entirely. Wondering why you're here so early—by request?"

David remembered another night years before, when he

had heard Brad say, in almost that same tone, those same words: "Wondering why you're here?"

"Well," he answered, "I can't help being curious."

"In the Bible there's something about the last shall be first."

"Yes, sir."

"I'm no Bible student, in spite of having been brought up by a grandmother who knew it, so help me, from cover to cover, including the 'begats.' And she was great on prophecy. She said she was born with a veil."

"Are you serious, sir?"

"Hardly. For one thing she prophesied the end of the world once too often. Also the freedom of our people. Both were always just around the corner. It shook my faith. Besides, I'm enlightened, as you just remarked."

David laughed. "Anyhow, the State Department thinks so."

"David, if the people all over the world with whom I've negotiated and dealt in various ways, and have won over to our side, had one half the mother wit she had, I wouldn't be the 'esteemed Mr. Travis.' I'd be back where I came from, practicing law in Boston, Massachusetts, believe me."

"Believe you? Heck, I know it."

Travis absently poured more coffee into their cups. "Where was I?"

"The last was being boosted up to first. When a Negro says something like that, he's usually referring to his own people."

"I am. Africa."

"Africa!"

"Yes." Travis was deadly serious now. "The dark continent, some call it. In my opinion, and that of many others, the cradle of the future, just as it was the cradle of the far-distant past. Perhaps not the future of my generation, or of yours, or even your children, but the future of the world, nonetheless. And times a'wasting for it to start moving. There seems a strange parallel, perhaps unrelated but interesting to observe, in the emergence of Africa as a power to be reckoned with, and the stirrings in our South. And in our North, too, among our people. When I was at home this last trip I went to Atlanta and New Orleans—not by choice—"

"Gramp wrote me about it. Thanks for seeing him—"

"Don't thank me. You deserve the thanks. His gumbo, David! I thought I knew something about it—but I don't. It could win him a diplomatic post; it shows wisdom, judgment, and deviousness. However, what I am getting at is the general feeling in the South, the sense of ferment, of preparation. One can almost hear a bugler blowing softly just before he sounds 'Charge!' So it is in Africa, at the same moment in time."

"I agree it's interesting to think about."

"Africa will fly off in all directions at first, like the old woman with the wooden leg. But her people will learn. And by a circuitous route that brings me to you."

David grinned. "Anything I can do to add to the confusion—"

"It won't be exactly little, although it may not be world shaking. Still, one never knows. Last fall the suggestion came to me through—let's say a mutual friend, that I give some thought to proposing your name to the Department of State for a post in Africa."

David was conscious of no surprise; it had been obvious that Lawrence Travis had been leading up to something of the kind, but he could find no words. He was almost expecting what Travis said next.

"Zambana, to be exact. . . . You'll recall that Jedediah went home for a month just after he got to England? It dovetailed nicely."

"How do you mean?"

"That his father called me, asked me a great many questions about you, and has indicated that he would be pleased to have a young man, well versed in constitutional and international law, with good judgment and a level head, assigned to his country as an adviser to him. He of course can only express a desire. He is a tactful man. And a pragmatic one. And not at all ignorant of the fact that his country is wealthy —very wealthy—and strategic. Zambana's friendship, once the country is independent, which it will be in a few months, will be a damned juicy plum. He is hardheaded, dedicated, and won't play favorites. Still—"

It was coming too fast now; David wasn't taking it in; he knew he wasn't and he hesitated, trying not to let his mind jump ahead of Travis's words. "Mr. Travis—please—you're going too fast for me. You don't need to tell me that it was Hunter who made the first move. Let me kind of sort it out. You are thinking of proposing my name—David Champlin's —to the State Department—"

"Department of State—"

"Yes, sir—Department of State for some kind of advisory job in Zambana? When?"

"It's been done."

"Good God!"

"You must file a formal application, of course."

"But there's a hell of a lot of red tape and waiting, isn't there? Security check and so on—"

"Yes. In this instance the check is almost completed."

David was on his feet now, prowling the small room, winding up finally at a window in the side wall overlooking a passageway between this house and the next, a passageway that was half alley and half thoroughfare, where spring had not yet come. It was a far cry from the recreation hall at Pengard and the day Tom, Chuck, and Suds had angered him by taking over the reins of his life, practically cinching a job for him that he hadn't even known about. But in this situation any such resentment as he had felt then would be stupid. This was the way things were done in the echelons in which Travis moved. He supposed that the government would go ahead and throw a security check on a guy even if he only wanted to be a grocery clerk, if the right person asked for it. It wasn't a thought that exactly made for peace of mind.

When he turned back into the room his smile was bitter. "I can't," he said. "It's out. Let's forget it."

"Why, David?" Lawrence Travis's eyes were on his face and its bitter smile, and his voice was gentle, as gentle as the voice of the porter on the Humming Bird had been the first time he had taken a train, humiliated and sick-angry. "Why, David?" asked Travis again.

"Because I'm a Negro." There was no inflection in the voice, and David's eyes were without warmth, without anger, without any emotion whatever, flat and black.

"You're out of your mind, David." Travis said it quietly. "That has nothing to do with it. Actually—"

"Mr. Travis, I know what you're going to say. You know that when I was at Pengard I was Jim-Crowed in a unique way. The rumor was started by two southern gentlemen—one the real thing as our society judges gentlemen, the other a phony—that I was a homosexual. The Department of State wouldn't touch me with a barge pole. So—that's the ball game. And thanks—I mean, really thanks."

"David." Travis walked over to him, took his arm and led him back to his chair, almost forcing him into it. "I'm sending for drinks. They're called for right now. Do you think for one minute that I didn't make sure that this was thoroughly checked out? Have you forgotten the investigation and the report that Prentiss made? Those were available to the FBI. Even Clevenger was interviewed and said nothing harmful. Goodhue—" Travis chuckled—"said he didn't remember you except vaguely, that he was sure he would if there had been anything like that. You came out of that phase of the investigation with an absolutely clean bill of health."

David said nothing for a moment, then began to laugh. It was not what Chuck called his "blockbuster" laugh; it was a gentle laugh.

"Let me study about it, Mr. Travis. Just for a while."

Later, while Travis was greeting his friend Solomon Abikawai in the sitting room, David managed to whisper to Jedediah, "Man, am I glad to see you. I was scared you wouldn't be here." Before Jed could do more than smile reassuringly, Travis took David's arm and led him toward the man he had come to meet. "Biblical" had been a good word; Solomon was taller than his son; his skin had a more brownish cast, and the lines in his face were deeply grooved. He was a spare, stern man, with the powerful shoulders so noticeable in Jedediah. His eyes held more reserve than his son's; his voice was heavier and deeper. He wore native costume, a deep crimson robe over a long white undergarment, and David tried to convince himself it was a case of clothes making the man, that he was not really that sternly regal, but found himself awed and tongue-tied nonetheless. A formidable guy, he thought, and probably a damned astute one, and he wished this meeting was in actuality what it appeared to be on the surface—a purely social one, and not with himself as a specimen to be judged, because this man's judgments would be without tinge of emotion, impersonal, just, and, once made, not subject to appeal. Not even the surprising warmth of his smile reassured David; Solomon the Stern, that was this man. Not once was he aware of any direct scrutiny by Abikawai, only those casual glances any man gives another in a small, friendly gathering.

Sitting comfortably in front of a small fire after dinner, David's uneasiness lessened as he realized that the decision was as much his as it was Solomon Abikawai's and Travis's; he had not yet made up his own mind; even thinking of a move so drastic brought an awareness of the wrench it would be, the dislocation of his life and plans, and he was damned if he was going to sit like a scared child in a principal's office and worry about the judgments and opinions of others.

As he had expected, Solomon Abikawai initiated discussion almost immediately. He might have been asking a casual question of a tourist. "What do you know of my country, Mr. Champlin?"

"Mainly what your son has told me, sir, woven in with what I've read."

"Then you know more than most foreigners. It is generally known, of course, that we are a wealthy country in many respects. Our natural resources are enviable."

"And envied, sir." He had settled on "sir" as being respectful and not likely to be wrong.

"Yes." Abikawai's gaze was direct, ignoring the others. "And envied. As you say. Do you also know wherein we are vulnerable? Our weaknesses?"

"I should think that any Negro out of our South would be able to put his finger on several of them. I'd say one of the main ones would be the type of education that was made available under colonialism. It was bound to be an education aimed chiefly at increasing the value of the individual to the economic life of the country, at the same time maintaining his sense of inferiority and as far as possible erasing any sense of national pride." He stopped, afraid that he was talking too much, but Abikawai nodded slowly, and he went on. "In a country, as differentiated from a state in our Union, I suppose there would be exceptions. There would have to be a higher form of education encouraged for a certain group, an upper-echelon group, let's say, so there would be someone with whom at least to make a pretense of dealing." He stopped again, and again Abikawai nodded, not speaking, and he continued. "Isn't that what you have now? And will have when you become independent?"

Solomon's smile was so sudden and unexpected that David almost lost his train of thought. "Well put, Mr. Champlin. Given a reasonable world based on a reasonable system of ethics, these difficulties would not exist. Unfortunately, it is not a reasonable world. It is a civilized world." He smiled again. "As whites define civilization. Whether that civilization is good or evil we must leave undecided for the moment. What remains to be faced is that adaptation to that civilization is essential to survival. At least for the time being. The situation raises an interesting question for the defenders of that civilization to answer."

David had lost his self-conscious uneasiness completely now, no longer giving a damn whether Abikawai approved of him, thoughts crowding his mind that he wanted to voice whether or not this dark, compelling man agreed. "That sounds like a man who taught me when I was growing up—a Professor Knudsen."

"Bjarne Knudsen?" At David's surprised look Abikawai said: "Two of his books have been my most frequent reading. His conclusions are not comfortable for those who believe that the world can only progress through the triumph of what is called civilization today."

"He based a lot of his conclusions on comparative studies of African cultures and white cultures," said David.

It was like the starting gun for a football game; there was no longer a tête-à-tête between a young Champlin and an older, wiser Abikawai, but a four-sided debate, with Lawrence Travis jumping agilely from side to side verbally—supporting, opposing, whenever support or opposition would make the conversational blaze burn brighter. Every so often David turned to Jedediah, smiling, and said, "Hey, we missed that one on board ship." And Jedediah would remind him that they had been granted only a little less than a week; that they had agreed they had left the world unfinished.

Once Solomon Abikawai said: "As a pupil of Knudsen's you must know of the entirely different concept of land rights, for example, prevalent throughout much of Africa. In my country, for one, any concept of private ownership is difficult of achievement. Our lands were held—and still are in many of our clans—in continuity by the community, belonging to the community by right of descent from what has been best translated by others as a 'First Ancestor.' Conquest did not destroy this concept wholly. It was to the European a purely mystical concept, and as such, incomprehensible and unacceptable by those whose lives were lived by the standards of a cash economy, whose governments were founded on a cash economy. Because it could not be accepted by them, and was incomprehensible to them, it must be changed, translated into the cash economy both acceptable and understandable."

What Solomon was saying was not new to David. The Prof had guided him through the highways and byways of other civilizations, eyebrows bristling with interrogation. "This is bad, yes? Bah! It is not bad. What have we offered that has bettered it? Argue with me, David; argue with me—"

But never, he thought now, in his wildest imaginings, in his most involved arguments with the Prof, had he ever dreamed that any future that might lie before him, however unexpected, would involve him personally in those cultures they had discussed. In the world Solomon Abikawai was attempting to explicate, certain basic principles David Champlin had sweated to grasp through long nights of study were not necessarily the tools of enlightenment and progress; could be, instead, under certain conditions, tools of destruction. He attempted now, haltingly, to clarify this, to talk out his thoughts and ideas and conclusions, and he wondered at the man's apparently inexhaustible patience. Then he remembered from many years before something he had read in one of Gramp's books about Africa—the right of "palaver," the sacred right of palaver, the granting to every man at a meeting of the community the right to speak what was on his mind, even if it took many hours; even, he recalled, if the man was known to be the village idiot or a loquacious fool. Solomon Abikawai had not forgotten the ethical teachings of his youth. David stopped, embarrassed that he had taken up so much time, and finished by saying: "What it comes down to is pure democracy, sir. At least in my opinion. A democracy the rest of us couldn't handle if we had it. It would become corrupt in one century. One decade, perhaps I should say."

"Yes." Solomon's assent was simple, without embellishment. "I am afraid it is too late to save my country from that corruption, entirely. We can only hope to keep it at a minimum. For that reason we cannot accept help from those who seek control as the natural result of such help. We can only accept help selfishly, with no intent to repay in the coin of control. Wealth?" He shrugged. "I do not care if another country makes money from our riches if enough remains to us. Why should I? But I care that we be permitted to grow as our creator intended us to grow—to a peaceful maturity. Even if that maturity, when it is arrived at, seems to be a faulty one seen through eyes that cannot comprehend it."

He shifted his position in his chair, and David realized with a shock that for hours Solomon Abikawai had sat literally immobile, except for the muscles of eyes and face. He said: "We must start at the point of greatest weakness; a gap in our life that will destroy us even in the moment of birth. I refer to the gap between the educated élite of which you spoke and the people of the land, the communities and clans who, quite literally, are the country. Otherwise"—he smiled grimly—"we will become as other nations are becoming—the handwriting is on the wall—a country with airports on which few planes ever land, of great buildings that few people occupy, of traffic lights at corners where no traffic passes. Such a situation can spell dissolution or destruction; is spelling it in many places."

Jedediah stood up, walked to the fireplace, and stood with his back to it, looking down at David. "In the United States, David, I couldn't help noting a situation similar to the one my father speaks of as existing in Africa. Your so-called upper-class and middle-class Negro, your élite and near élite, have turned their faces away from those of their own people who have not had their advantages. The Negro leadership is too spotty, too varied in approach, in some instances too self-seeking, to be effective for all the people—the urban Negro, the rural Negro, and the many types in between. Do you agree?"

"Certainly. I'd be a fool not to when it's so evident."

"The disadvantaged Negro there, whether he likes it or not, must in the final analysis rely upon the whites in those areas of decision that affect his life and the lives of his children, decisions that either give or deny to him respect as a human being. There are outstanding exceptions, of course, and I have met several, but for the most part the members of his race who have—" He hesitated, groping for a phrase.

"Made it," supplied David.

"Yes. Made it. Those people want no part of him. We don't want this situation in Zambana, where there will be no white rule, where if any man is disadvantaged it will be by his own people."

"We will not have it in Zambana." Solomon Abikawai put no stress on any word; there was no deepening of his voice; it was a simple statement of fact, and a rebuke to his son, who had said "We do not want" instead of "We will not have."

David knew, looking at the man opposite him, that Lawrence Travis had been right: this man was no seeker of power; he was genuinely a seeker of light for his people, wanting power only as a means to bring this light.

At the end of the long evening, while Solomon and Lawrence Travis talked briefly in the central hallway, Jedediah drew David aside, looking up at him and smiling slightly. "I hope?" he said simply. He made no attempt to hide, now, his knowledge of the unspoken reason for the meeting.

"I don't know. I have to think about it. And besides, the whole thing could fall through in Washington. It's still in the 'if' stage. Very 'if.' " He returned Jed's smile. "One thing I understand. Your father's 'hands off' policy. It's got to be that way."

"We'll need watchdogs."

"Yes, but they'll have to be watchdogs with no masters of their own to protect. That's one of the problems. It's an ethical one. What would my government expect of me, *if*—"

Jedediah shrugged. "Of an 'adviser' only? I shouldn't think you would be expected to take an active part in furthering any political or material ambitions your government might have."

"Jed, damned if that isn't the first naïve remark I ever heard you make."

Not even love had been able to overcome the discomforts of two people occupying Sara's studio overnight, and when he came to the city David stayed at the "frightful great pile of gray stone" where Sara lived. Once in a while he was fortunate enough to be assigned a room on the same floor. Neither he nor Sara had been courageous enough to request this. "I can't," said Sara. "It's the watch pinned on that registration clerk's bosom that throws me."

On the weekend of the dinner at the Travises', David had been given a room two floors above Sara's. When he returned from the dinner he did not go to his room when the elevator reached his floor; instead he waited until its slow, creaking descent finally ended on the ground floor and he heard the doors clang shut; then he hurried down the wide staircase that flanked its shaft and along the corridor to her room. He knocked softly and started back in surprise when the door opened almost instantly. Sara pulled him inside quickly. "David, what happened? What happened? I'm busting. I knew, I knew all evening, that it was something important. I'd have died if you hadn't come down here—"

He kissed her, and for the first time since he had known her it was an absentminded kiss, then sat down on the edge of the bed.

"Crucial, baby," he said. "Crucial."

She stood in front of him, eyes shining, looking, in her pale blue tailored pajamas, like a small boy waiting to hear a story of the circus. "Go on, love. Go *on*—"

"There's so much to tell, and it's one o'clock—"

"I've got biscuits and cheese and instant coffee."

He wrinkled his nose. "Stale, cold biscuits?"

"Crackers, idiot. Crackers. You'll never learn—"

"Well, drag 'em out."

He took off coat, tie, and shoes, unbuttoned his collar, stacked pillows at the head of the bed and sat against them, long legs stretched out, toes wriggling in relaxed release. "My God!" he said. "My good, kind, beneficent, well-meaning God! You'll never believe it, pet—" His voice lost its lightness. "And I don't know what in hell to do."

She put a plate of crackers and cheese—*"Biscuits,"* she said—on his stomach, in spite of his protests, and two mugs of instant coffee on the bedside table, then climbed over his legs to curl against the pillows, beside his shoulder.

"Start, David. Now."

"At the beginning. Please let me start at the beginning. And please to shut up till I've finished—"

It was a long story, completed only after additional and frequent admonitions—"Wait, Sara, I'm getting there. . . . *Will* you shut up, sweetheart? . . . If you'll just wait till I get to it . . ." And then, "That's the story, baby. As I said, crucial."

He had expected a torrent of comment, of quick rushing questions, words tumbling. Instead the small figure pressed against his shoulder was silent, and when he raised his head to look down at her he saw that her eyes were closed. With a gentle finger he flicked a cracker crumb from the corner of the soft mouth, then bent and kissed first one closed eye and then the other. "Sara. Smallest—I didn't mean to strike you dumb. I didn't think anything could. You all right?"

Eyes still closed, she reached to encircle his neck with her arm, burying her face in the hollow between throat and shoulder. "Oh, God, David, why can't we know, why can't we know all the time that things will be all right? Why do we have to hurt like death, not knowing? It's right, I suppose; it's right because when it comes all of a sudden it's nondeath and living again and wonderful—"

He felt the warm moisture of tears on his skin, and slipped an arm beneath her body, raising her and himself until they were sitting, then released her gently and swung his feet to the floor. "Sara, honey, take it easy. It's not sure yet by a damned sight. A lot has to happen yet. And I'm not sure, either—"

She gave no sign that she had heard. Her lashes were wet, and she rubbed her eyes with the back of her hand, like a child; then, with a movement so quick he had no time to stop her, she was in the middle of the room, running toward the bureau, yanking open a drawer. She began to pull out airline folders, flipping through them, tossing them to the floor.

He watched her, bewildered. "Listen, hon. You don't understand. Nothing's settled. Not even my own mind."

"These blasted timetables with their God's-eye view of the world—how can you tell where any place is if you stand on the North Pole and look south or something. . . . Here's one . . . here's a map an ordinary, semiliterate college graduate can read—"

"But Sara, you know where Africa is—"

"I don't know where Zambana is. And as far as I'm concerned, that's all there is of Africa at this point." She sat beside him, map on knee, one finger trailing south through Europe. "Rome . . . Madrid . . . Madrid? Maybe . . . Lisbon. Lisbon? Probably . . . Aa-aah! Barcelona . . . It's wonderful . . . Now . . . Guinea—Rhodesia—Senegal—Zambana! There it is, God bless it! There's Zambana . . . Lisbon's best. Lisbon has better air service. . . ."

"Put that map away, nitwit. I'm not there yet. It hasn't even been decided on. I haven't even decided myself—"

The map slid to the floor from Sara's knees, and she stood slowly, so that she could face him, her eyes wide and frightened.

"You—haven't decided?"

"I—Sara, what's the matter? For God's sake, what's the matter?"

"If—if tomorrow—today—you knew they wanted you, if they told you today, you wouldn't say 'yes'? David—"

"I didn't say I wouldn't. I said I hadn't decided. That I don't know—"

"But David, there isn't anyone in the world better qualified. Your law—your studies here—"

He got to his feet, padding back and forth across the room, not answering her, not wanting to look at her, wanting above all else to take her into his arms and hide against his heart the fright in her eyes.

"David—a new country—a growing country—to be able to watch it and help it grow—all that you studied about constitutional law and government—David, they need you—"

"Sara, you're jumping all the guns. I—well—I didn't pick Harvard because it's the best in constitutional law so that I could make what I learned operative in Africa. That wasn't why—"

"You don't think people sometimes have opportunities to

go where they are needed just because they *are* needed? That maybe—"

"Sara, I'm not needed all that much. Solomon Abikawai is a brilliant man. And a wise one, well named. So is Jedediah. Good God, there are plenty of people they could get if I don't go. Better men than I am, with more experience. For that matter, they could get along fine without anyone."

"David—"

"I know that Africa's future is going to affect the entire world. And I know it would be the most damned interesting job any guy could be lucky enough to get. But—"

"But? But what, David?"

"I don't think I can explain. I don't even know exactly what I mean, myself. Commitments, and—well, a sort of debt—"

"What commitments? What debt?"

He stopped pacing and looked down at her and saw a woman waiting for a mortal blow—the blade of the guillotine, the drop from the gallows. What could Sara be expected to know of the deep inner commitment of a black man to his people, or of a debt owed a generous fate? *Homo vitae commodatus non donatus est.* The Prof had written that on the flyleaf of the book he had given him the day he left New Orleans for college: Man is lent, not given, life. Those words would have a different meaning for Sara Kent, to whom the good things of life had come as a matter of natural course, not as a kind of wide-ranging miracle. Sara, who loved him without reservation; Sara, whose life had been his since that first meeting; little Sara, who could not take her eyes from his face now, and into whose eyes he could no longer look; Sara, whom he felt he had loved since the day he was born, waiting now for words that would sustain her spirit—or destroy it.

At last she half whispered: "This is it, David. This is it—the whole thing—life—everything. Listen to me, David, because I won't say it again. If you accept this appointment it's us—you and I—David and Sara—living whole, getting married. It's me, perhaps in Lisbon while you're there, but together just the same. Maybe it's me there with you after a while. It's peace, David, peace—you won't have to worry about our marriage over here. Do you see? Do you understand?"

He dared not say he had not thought that far ahead, felt guilty that such a statement would be true. Now the look in her eyes was made clear, and what she was trying to say to him was clear, too: "This is it—life—everything—" And if he turned away now, he would be striking the mortal blow she feared—not only to her but to David Champlin as well, who would never in his lifetime know Sara Kent again. The chill certainty of this was in every taut line of Sara's body, in her eyes and face. This was not even the Sara Kent who had left him in Boston only to meet him in Paddington; this was a Sara Kent who would not return again.

"David." If he had not known it was Sara speaking, he would not have recognized her voice. "I'm not going to beg. Or try to persuade. I understand; I've always understood so much more than you've given me credit for. Not everything, but more than that. Who's to say you won't be fulfilling a commitment—paying a debt, helping your people—just because they are in Africa? What strengthens them anywhere strengthens them everywhere." She turned away from him, so that he could not see her face. "David, David. It's not that. I'm being a hypocrite. It's that I thought you'd want it—as I did—because of us. Not that you wouldn't know, couldn't decide. And I thought you'd know—the way I did, instantly—that it would mean—us, everything. And without some move like this there's only a future like the past, empty and lonely and awful—"

He walked slowly over to her and took her face between his hands, turning it toward him, the long dark strength of his fingers hiding all her tense paleness, only the forehead and the wide dark eyes and the straightly tiny nose and soft mouth and chin visible. He moved his index fingers so that they closed the lids over the stricken eyes. "Don't, baby; don't look like that." He bent and kissed her lips and felt her body go limp and he drew her toward him, his arms around her now, her face against him.

"David, don't ever frighten me like that again. Oh, my God, sweetheart, don't—"

54

Li'l Joe Champlin moved a small end table the better to sweep under it, and clucked disapprovingly as he picked up a crumpled, empty cigarette package from the floor. "You done that, Chop-bone. You stole that outa the wastebasket. You ain't been paying attention to what I been saying to you. David's coming home. It ain't right, me fussing at him about keeping things neat, an' you messing things up."

There had been times in the past year when the chores of housecleaning had seemed almost too much for him. Today, though, there was no tiredness or temptation to let things go until tomorrow, and hadn't been since David had called the day before, from Washington. He had expected the call from New York, not Washington, but starting with David's announcement that he was going over the water to go to college some more, Li'l Joe's capacity for surprise had lessened. He still couldn't figure out why the boy had to go so damned far away for more education; the Lord knew, he'd wanted the boy to get all the education he could, but it seemed like there were plenty good colleges in the United States where he could have gone. "Got a suspicion," he told himself, "got a mighty big suspicion that li'l bit of a white girl's mixed up in it somewheres." But even if he was right there wasn't much, at this point, that he could do about it. All he could do was pray that the Lord would show the boy what was right and then give him the strength to do it.

As he worked he thought about the visit the evening before of one of David's young white friends, his third visit since David had gone over the water. One of the nicest white boys he'd ever met, and a preacher at that. He remembered the first time he'd met the boy at Pengard he'd been thrown off by the accent. Took him a time to stop shying away from it, in spite of David's grinning, "Don't pay it no mind, Gramp. He doesn't think the way he talks." He still looked like a big overgrown country boy now, button-in-back collar and all. A nice, polite boy, a fine boy. Didn't always matter about color, as long as it was a man and not a woman.

He had driven up unexpectedly late in the afternoon the day before in a beat-up old car and grinned all over himself when he saw that Li'l Joe was at home. It was raining hard, and Li'l Joe stood in the doorway and called, "You-all better hurry. You going to get wet—" and when the greetings were over—"Sure glad you come, sure glad. I got news. David's back. He'll be coming home pretty soon."

"Gee, that's great! When?"

"Two, three days. He's in Washington now."

"Washington? What's he doing there?"

"He didn't say. Sit down, Reverend. Here—lemme res' your coat. Supper's coming up soon."

"I'm not about to share your supper if you call me 'reverend'."

Li'l Joe smiled. "It's them clothes. What David used to call 'threads' when he was a young un. Still does, I guess, now and then."

Later, when they were seated at the kitchen table, eating supper, Chuck said, "I'm going to be around these parts a lot more in the next few years, Li'l Joe."

"Sure glad to hear that, Chuck. What you going to be doing? Preaching?"

"No, not preaching. Oh, maybe some, here and there. The presiding bishop of my church has named six of us to go out into the field on a sort of double mission. Fact-finding, and an effort to consolidate the churches, all denominations, behind the civil rights movement. I'm the straw boss—I guess because I know the South. I get to do the most roaming around."

"Lawd!"

"You don't think it will work?"

"Ain't saying it won't. Coupla hundred years from now, mebbe. You just said it your ownself. You're from the South. You knows. It ain't going to be easy."

"Neither was Christianity, Li'l Joe. It didn't just happen. I haven't any high hopes of getting far fast. The others in the group have, but they're mostly Northerners. Still, here a church—there a church—here a minister—there a minister —like old MacDonald's farm. Things are stirring down here, Li'l Joe. If the churches aren't ready for it—"

"They won't be," said Li'l Joe grimly. "I ain't trying to discourage you, son, but you got rough going ahead. We fixin' for a mess of trouble right here come next fall if they tries this school integration like they say they going to. Real trouble."

"I suppose you are. I always thought of New Orleans, somehow, as being just a little further advanced, broader-minded. It ought to be, the mixture of races you've got here."

"Don't no one really know a place till they lives in it. Like you don't know a woman till you marries her. I was born here and so was my folks, and I figure to be buried here. And I'm saying it—we fixin' to have trouble."

"I believe you."

"You better believe it. Anyhow, David's going to be mighty happy about what you doing. He can give you some help, mebbe. He works real close with the ALEC people up there at headquarters in Boston, and down here, too. Here, push that cup outa the way so's I can give you a plate—rice now, beans—Lawd, boy! you wants more beans than that—David, he'd call them few just a teaser. Help yo'se'f now, to that cold chicken and the ham—"

"Lawd 'a' mercy! how you stay so thin, Gramp Champlin?"

Li'l Joe was already in bed when David's call came at eleven o'clock.

"Hi, Gramp! It's me again. Did I wake you up?"

"You knows I don't get to sleep till twelve, one o'clock. How come you calling again so soon, son? Something wrong?"

"No. Gosh, no, Gramp. When you going to stop worrying? I wanted to tell you I'll be home tomorrow about suppertime. I'm flying, not driving. You got red beans?"

"Always has. I'll fix us a gumbo and some crab."

"I have to be back here in Washington on Monday, but I'll be there for the weekend. Got a present for you."

"You has? What you got?"

"You'll see. You'll flip, Gramp."

"Don't let nothing hold you up now. Chop-bone, he's in your room, laying on the bed, keeping it warm for you—"

For a long time after he talked with his grandson, Li'l Joe sat up in bed, a light burning beside him, trying without success to concentrate on a magazine. He supposed he'd always start worrying, about this time of night, because most of his life, even when he was a kid, he'd gone to bed worrying about something or other. Now that there wasn't much to worry about he couldn't break the habit. Seemed almost like he felt guilty if he didn't worry. A man couldn't have the bad times he'd had when he was a kid, been all that poor, then forget about it when he was old, just because he knew where his next dollar was coming from. Man couldn't forget how hard his mother had worked, trying to take care of him; they'd been chicken-back, fishbone, peppergrass poor. Now, looking back, he didn't see how he'd made it, and sometimes he'd shake his head, thinking about it, wondering, remembering. Hadn't been till after him and Geneva took David things had begun to get better. First the job at Zeke Jones's, helping lay out corpses; and then a li'l job here and a li'l job there, putting up every penny they could; and then there was enough for a down payment on a house that wasn't nothing but framework, and then an inside toilet and then a bathtub and all—and right now there wasn't a nicer little house anywhere around, improving it like he'd done, every year, right up till now.

With everything going so good he was a damned fool to worry about something that hadn't happened, and looked like maybe it wouldn't happen after all this time fooling around —David maybe getting married with a white woman. It said in the Bible, didn't it, "sufficient unto the day is the evil thereof"? He'd better start thinking about the "good thereof." Wasn't right, worrying about something that hadn't happened yet, just when God was being so good to him.

Lawd! it would be good to hear the boy laugh again, and the sound of his uneven steps through the rooms. Sometimes Li'l Joe grew cold all over, thinking how he'd tried to persuade Geneva to give the baby up, send the child to its mother's folks in Mississippi. He wished now Geneva was with him, wished he could turn to her now, find her beside him, fussing at him about keeping the light on, talk to her about David and how fine he'd turned out, and how he hadn't ever forgotten his grandfather no matter what he was doing or how far away he went. All that he believed and had been taught to believe told him that she knew, but it would be nice to be sure.

He knew what would happen this weekend; David would stay home most of the time, wouldn't go traipsing off over the river; he'd stay home and tell his grandfather about all—or almost all—the things that had happened to him over the water, and when they both got talked out there were the piano and his banjo. Almost never was a time David wouldn't make a little music with him; he'd show the boy Li'l Joe Champlin wasn't so old he couldn't give a big grandson fits, playing that banjo; he'd make him sweat, trying to keep up.

On the plane back to Washington from his weekend in New Orleans, David startled the woman in the seat next to him by a sudden, involuntary chuckle. The woman was a white woman, and a tag on her tote bag gave a home address in a town in southern Louisiana; she gave him a startled sideways look as though the chuckle were the standard prelude to rape. It had been the only seat left in the plane, and David knew she thought he ought to be standing in the rear. What in hell these dumpy, pasty-faced women thought they had any Negro would want—and, for David's money, any white man—he couldn't figure out, never had been able. He chuckled again, this time on purpose, enjoying her uneasiness. The first chuckle had been at his memory of Gramp in the native costume Jedediah had sent. It hadn't been funny at the time and it wasn't funny now, in one sense. Behind the laugh then, when Gramp had put the costume on, and the chuckle now, there was a sort of ache, because Gramp's eyes had shone so brightly you could plug 'em in for lights, and when he had donned the robe there had come from somewhere inside that small, arrow-straight frame, a dignity and regality that made David remember Solomon of Zambana. He determined then that, come hell, highwater, or active warfare, Gramp was going to Zambana unless something went wrong with the appointment. The chance of this happening had prevented him from even hinting at it to Gramp; the whole thing would have to be a dead certainty before he'd risk disappointing him.

He had buried as best he could any misgivings he had about the decision made that night in Sara's room, although the burial was not complete. I suppose, he told himself, you're going to feel guilty about something or other all your life. But now, by God, if there was no other justification for his move there was the fact that it would enable him to give a gentle little brown man happiness, pressed down and running over, in his old age.

Lawrence Travis had bolstered his decision to say nothing about the possible appointment by advising that he remain silent, although, said Travis, there would probably be a leak. "There always is," he said. "It's positively spooky at times."

"How about mentioning it to Brad?" asked David.

"Certainly, certainly. That you should do. I'll write him myself."

When the expected leak came, David understood Lawrence's word "spooky." On a weekend in London, just before starting home, he went to a travel bureau to pick up his ticket for home, and found Hunter standing at the counter and with him a man David knew he had met, yet whose identity remained tantalizingly out of reach. Hunter, tucking an airline ticket into an inner coat pocket, joined him, while his companion remained at the counter.

"Where you going, man?" asked David.

"Nowhere. It's for my mother. To Paris."

David lowered his voice. "Who's the man you're with? Don't I know him?"

"Sure you do—"

He heard the man's voice then and snapped his fingers softly. "Sure. Sure. Barkeley. Christopher Barkeley. Republic Broadcasting guy."

"Right. Have a drink with us? We'll wait for you."

Barkeley came toward them in a moment, saw David, and greeted him with outstretched hand, smiling. "David Champlin."

Hunter said, "I've asked David to have a drink with us."

"By all means—"

They found a pub nearby—"I'm so damned sick of hotel bars and lounges," said Barkeley—and over drinks at a small table Barkeley said to David, "According to what is known in our circles as a 'reliable source,' your next trip away from the States will be a longer one."

David turned quickly to Hunter, half angry, but Hunter shook his head, his surprise obviously unfeigned.

"What do you mean?" David's question was guarded.

Barkeley looked at Hunter. "Have I put my foot in it? Doesn't he know?"

"Certainly he knows. But damn it, Chris, you're not supposed to know."

Barkeley sighed. "How not to make friends—"

"Nothing's settled," said David.

"You're wise to keep it quiet." Barkeley smiled, and David was struck then, as he had been years before, by the man's poise and a quality he supposed one would have to call charm, a word he didn't usually like, but in this case justified. "I wouldn't worry, Champlin," Barkeley continued. "You're pretty much an unknown—so far. It was your connection with the Boston law firm that made the item of interest. No one picked it up to use. I was interested because I remembered meeting you with so much pleasure. I'll be a prophet and say that ten years from now such small items about you will definitely be picked up."

55

ON THIS RETURN TRIP TO Washington his affairs continued to run as smoothly as they had the previous week, a circumstance he had not anticipated. Abner Chittock turned out to be an even easier person to deal with than Lawrence Travis had described; there had been several long talks in his office and over luncheons, and after each one David realized that another facet of his life had been exposed by the security check: his childhood, Gramp and Gram, the Prof, Pengard, Brad Willis. . . . They discussed his impending marriage, and he learned that Sara Kent's father and Chittock had been at college together, had practiced law at the same time in Chicago, and had frequently faced each other across the well of a courtroom. "He sneered, I glared," said Chittock. "Sometimes we reversed it, for variety."

He was given books and documents to read and told that there would be briefing sessions early in the fall and that a meeting would probably be arranged with two experts on African affairs in Geneva before he finally went into Zambana.

He had dreaded facing Brad more than anything else; it worried him through all the weeks prior to leaving England. He booked his ticket through to Boston, and was waiting in Brad's office for Brad to arrive, on the morning after landing. He should have been warmed and relieved at Brad's obvious happiness at having him back; instead he felt a sick feeling of guilt inside. Coolness or unspoken disapproval on Brad's part would have put him on the defensive; this left him helpless, and he realized as he had never done before the extent of the older man's affection for him. It wouldn't have made any difference what he had done—Brad's reaction to his return would have been as it was now.

Later, when they were drinking coffee at Brad's desk, Brad said: "Hell, brat, I'm not going to be a hypocrite and say I'm glad to see you go, give you a lot of static about 'whatever's best for you makes me happy.' I'm damned upset, selfishly upset, about it. So will everyone else be when they hear of it. Let me know when the last O.K. comes through so I can tell them."

"Did you tell Peg?"

Brad nodded. "Come what may, drinking or not, she's safe."

"How did she take it?" David shifted his eyes from Brad's face to the desk top. "Don't answer. I can tell by your face."

"I'm afraid she went pretty much overboard. I don't know exactly why. I never know, really, except that it is always something above and beyond—or below and behind—the actual incident that, on the surface, appears to be what triggered her off."

"Hell, Brad, I feel lousy about this. As though I was walking out on everyone. Like a damned dicty so-and-so who's let Oxford go to his head."

"Don't be a damned fool. By the way, vacations are already here. You going to be free to give us a hand for a while?"

"You know it."

There was a dinner with Brad and Peg just before he left that David wished had never happened. He was thankful that Chuck Martin and Tom Evans were both in town and that Brad included them in the invitation. At the end of the dinner he wondered if Brad had not done so purposely, because he thought it would be easier on the guest of honor. Usually, in a situation like this, Peg had sweet-talked him into coming early and cooking some special dish, even if it was only hot biscuits. This night she depended entirely on her own efforts and those of the housekeeper. She was tensely sober, as she had been the first time David met her, shying away from talk of his new work, encouraging him and Chuck and Tom to talk of days at Pengard. "This sounds more like a reunion than a goodbye affair," Brad said once, and David cried quickly, "Au revoir, for God's sake!"

They left early, Tom initiating the move on the plea of

having to catch an early-morning plane to Chicago, an excuse David knew was a lie. While the others walked slowly into the hall with Brad, Peg touched his arm and drew him into the dining room. She turned and faced him, standing very quiet, unsmiling, her eyes searching his face. "Why?" she said. *"Why?"*

He heard himself stammering. "Peg, I—what are you getting at?"

"I'm trying to get at you. What's inside you. What I thought was inside you—only, I was wrong. Guts."

He was too stunned to answer at first, then heard, gratefully, Tom's voice calling from the hall, and he turned away from Peg's eyes. "I—I wish you didn't feel that way, Peg. It hasn't been easy."

"No? I think it's been the easiest thing you ever did in your life, David Champlin."

Her eyes softened a little. He felt, and was sure he looked, like a favored dog who has come, tail wagging, to have its ears scratched, receiving a blow instead.

"That was rough, David," she said. "But I had to say it. We're here if you need us. Don't forget that."

"I won't," he mumbled. "Thanks." He hurried into the hall, Peg following slowly to say good night to her guests.

As they drove away in Chuck's car, Tom let out a long "Whee-eew! Is Peg like that often?"

"No," David said. "Not ever. Drunk or sober."

"Speaking of getting drunk—" said Tom.

"Chuck'll have to change clothes—"

"We can go to my room and talk and lubricate the vocal cords. Or—how about Sudsy's?"

"Hell, we'd wake the baby," snapped David.

"Let's go to Tom's room," said Chuck. "I'm at the same hotel."

When Brad came back into the living room, Peg was coming in from the dining room carrying a tray with a bowl of ice cubes and two fresh glasses. He had known it was coming, yet had hoped he would be able to forestall it, and he wanted to wrest the tray from her violently, shake her, beat her if necessary, into some semblance of sense, make her let go of what was eating her away inside. He stood, hands clenched in his pockets, fighting himself, knowing that fighting her would be worse than useless. A protest would do more harm than good, would make the hand that poured the drink from the decanter on the coffee table more generous, yet he could not stop himself.

"Peg!"

"Say when—"

"Oh, God, Peg! What's the matter?"

"I'm just going to have a couple tonight. Tomorrow, no. Just tonight."

"Peg, I know you hate to see David go. We both do. But he's on the way to great things. You wouldn't want—"

"Oh, shut up, Brad! You sound like a male PTA-er. Here, drink your drink."

He walked farther into the room slowly and took the drink, remembering what Mike Shea had said once: "Don't try to stop her, Brad. It will only make it worse. Just stand by and give her a hand when she's trying to stop."

He finished his drink standing, looking into the fireplace, and heard Peg set her empty glass down on the coffee table behind him. How long would it be this time? Days? Weeks? He supposed he'd have the stamina to go through another one; the strength had always come from somewhere, but there was a deep sadness within him. David gone, Peg—he turned quickly at her next words.

"The gutless wonder. Our brat. Our beautiful boy."

"Cut it out, Peg," he said wearily, but she did not seem to hear him.

"Zambana. That's the name of the damned place, isn't it? It gets its independence in January. I read all about it." Whiskey trickled over the ice cubes in her emptied glass, slowly, darkly, and her hand, as she poured it, was not quite steady. "De Lawd's done done it for Zambana—set His people free. And our David's going over there to help them. He's going to show them what to do with freedom." She began to laugh huskily, deep in her throat. "Our brat's going to show the Negroes in Zambana how to live as a free people, isn't he, dear? Oh, Christ!"

He took a step toward her, one hand held out, wanting to help her. "Peg, Peg, don't. I know what you're getting at—"

"Do you? Do you now?"

"I think so—for God's sake, Peg, take it easy with that whiskey—"

She held the now full glass up, looked at him through it. "Once in a lifetime, sweetheart. Just for the once-in-a-lifetime when a brat we love lets his people down—"

"He's not doing that, Peg—"

"He is, and he knows it." She rose and took his glass away from him, refilled it, and handed it back to him, then touched its rim with the rim of hers. She raised her glass, smiling. "To Sara," she said. And then, after a long moment, when she had taken the glass from her lips, "And I love her, too. That's why it's such hell, Brad. Can't you see? That's why it's such hell. People—two—turning their backs on people—millions. Drink your drink. Why don't you go to London and be best man?"

In the early fall David wound up his affairs in Boston and went to New York, staying at Hunter's apartment. Jedediah had written that one of his countrymen was at Columbia, and he made arrangements for some lessons in the Zambanian language. Before he left Boston he spent an evening with Suds and Rhoda. Suds was almost childlike in his delight at David's good fortune. "We'll miss you like hell, but we'll fill in the time bragging about you to our friends," he said. "And as soon as I finish my residency Rhoda and I are taking a long-delayed trip, before I start in at the clinic. We thought of Europe, leaving the offspring with my unfortunate parents. Maybe we'll see you and Sara—"

"If you make it the right time in November, why can't you be with us when we get married? It'll be in London, we decided. Hunter will be there—you could be witnesses—whatever they call them in England."

"You didn't do it for me, dad. Let me go through it alone, you did."

"Walla Walla, for gosh sake!"

Rhoda said: "Of course we can, David. We'd love it. Sara's going to need moral support."

David doubted that; Sara wouldn't need moral support if they got married in the middle of the veldt with two tigers and a lion on the sidelines crouched to spring. Suds, the same idea in mind, said: "The hell our Sara will need moral support. You don't know her as well as we do. But if you want us, David, we'll do our damnedest to make it."

In October, Sara came over to visit her father. "Now I don't mind visiting my family," she said. "Before it seemed awful. The old house gone, Father living in a modern apartment with a new wife. But now that I'm happy, it's all right. Selfish beasts, we humans. We can fly to London together,

David. Think of it—Christmas in Zambana. I can be with you then, don't you think? Perhaps that's when Gramp could come over."

When Sara telephoned him one night from her midtown hotel, after she returned from Chicago, and told him there had been a news item in the *Times* the day before about his appointment, and a gossip-column comment that day about their marriage, he said: "Lord, baby! I have to get down home, but quick. I haven't told Gramp yet, and 'Saiah Watkins takes the New York papers for the ALEC office. Gramp will die all over if he hears about it from someone else. I wasn't going until this weekend, but I'll go tomorrow now. Do some phoning for me, baby, to some people?"

"Of course. You won't be gone long, sweet?"

"Not more'n five years—"

"David!"

David knew the moment he saw his grandfather's face that he was too late: the news of his African appointment and his marriage had already been told to him by Isaiah or he had read it in the local Negro paper, picked up as a rewrite item from the New York papers. Surely he wasn't important enough to rate a wire-service dispatch. He was angry with himself for having postponed telling Gramp. No matter how well intentioned the planned delay had been, he shouldn't have taken a chance. Gramp must have had some damned bad hours after hearing about it—and every minute of them showed in his eyes and face as David hurried through the front door.

There had never been many outward demonstrations of affection between the two men but today David threw a long arm around the little man's shoulder, tightened it in a quick gesture of affectionate reassurance. "It's all right, Gramp. I wanted to tell you first, but some big-mouth got ahead of me, eh? Everything's going to be fine."

"You saying it, son, not me."

The memory of a night completely without sleep, of tossing restlessly in bed, then roaming uneasily through the house, of watching the little living room turn first gray, then light, in the early-morning hours was too vivid right now for Li'l Joe's mood to be lightened by his grandson's words. He was acquainted with grief and loneliness and sorrow, and had known all three in those dark night hours.

He knew the answer to sorrow; his mother had taught him that. Keep busy. Keep working. But when a man was getting on in years, the work wasn't always there. And even a young man gave way to it sometimes, had to let it carry him. He knew men, young men, who'd let pain and disappointment carry them too far, so far from life they couldn't get back to living it, wrapped themselves up in a cocoon of disappointment and defeat like fuzzy caterpillars, not caring if anyone called them shiftless and lazy. Better if they did call them that, so's nothing would be expected of them. Figured on coming out of that cocoon after they were in their graves, flying around on their wings after they were buried. He'd done that, after Geneva was taken, but, Lord! a man couldn't stay in a cocoon like that when there was a little chile to took after and an old lady who'd near killed herself to bring a son up, no matter how bad the grief was, how deep the darkness. And it had been dark, didn't anybody but God know how dark it had been after Geneva passed.

"And it ain't exactly light now," he said to himself, watching the thin grayness of dawn creep beneath the window shades.

Don't do no good, he told himself, don't do no good thinking how the boy's marrying up with a white woman. Lord's got to take care of that; He's sure got to take care of that because it ain't right, it's trouble, and Lord, if You can take his trouble away without hurting him too bad I sure wish You'd do it. The trouble would come more than likely when they had children, or when something come up that she'd see white and David would see colored, and there wouldn't be any way to bring them together so's they'd see it alike, never could be a way to bring two persons together, living as man and wife, when one of them was white and the other colored, when neither of them could remember one thing, scarce one thing, common from when they were children. "Jesus he'p him," Li'l Joe had murmured, half aloud. "Jesus he'p him. He's going to need it."

Those night hours had been too long for David's smile, his presence, his reassuring arm and words, to chase their memory away. And there were longer, lonelier ones ahead, and these were in his heart when he said, "You saying it, son, not me."

"Gramp, let's have a beer and then you let me talk and tell

you about it. Don't start feeling bad until I've finished, because then you won't feel bad—"

Li'l Joe wanted to say he'd already started, that feeling bad was part of him now. Instead he said, "Sure, son. There's plenty beer in the icebox."

It took almost an hour for David to tell the story, leaving nothing out, retracing his meeting and friendship with Jedediah and his later meeting with Solomon of Zambana; then the new story of Lawrence Travis and his efforts on his behalf, his meeting with Chittock of State—"That's why I was in Washington, Gramp—" and then hesitantly, defensively, the decision he and Sara had reached about their marriage now that they could live elsewhere and know peace. He had just started to tell Gramp of the plan to bring him to Africa when there was a familiar, thudding footstep on the porch, followed by a familiar knock.

" 'Saiah," said Gramp.

"Hell!" said David. "I was just getting—"

Then Isaiah was inside and there was more beer and more talk—Lord, thought David, how my people talk; You ought to do something about it—and he went over the story again, this time briefly and only in outline, mentioning his marriage only casually, in passing. He didn't mention the plan to have Gramp come to Africa because he wanted to be alone with Gramp when he told him.

The talk stopped all at once, and the sudden pause had an uncanny something about it. Isaiah took what was left of a well-smoked cigar from his mouth and laid it carefully in an ashtray. He looked stern and reproving, and when he cleared his throat the sternness and reproof became more marked. "You'd ought to be mighty proud, David," he said. "That's a big honor."

"Can't say that I see it exactly as an honor. It was more a case of meeting the right guy in the right place at the right time. I didn't go after it."

"Sure. Sure. And you ain't going to be there forever, don't suppose." He pulled another cigar from his pocket and studied it carefully, not looking at David. "After you get through helping the black man down there in Africa, maybe you can come back and help him here. Days of trouble coming. We could sure use an extra hand."

He stood up without waiting for an answer, said loudly, "Gotta go, Li'l Joe! Gotta go, David! Got a meeting at headquarters on this school mess that's coming up—"

After he had left, Gramp looked at David's back, as the boy stood in the doorway looking out, silent since Isaiah's barbed remark. "Don't take it hard, son. He's all wound up in this school trouble, people getting threats and all, and all the trouble stirring everywhere, can't think of nothing else. He's just what you calls 'needling.' A man goes where he's needed. I ain't happy about it, God knows I ain't, but a man goes where he's needed. Man's got something to give, God sends him where he can give it. Better there, where you're going, son, where you can get yourself a little peace inside. You got a woman you love, and you don't want no other. Don't guess you ever will, and I ain't even saying anything about that."

As Li'l Joe walked toward David, his grandson opened the door and the two men walked out on the front porch together and stood silently, leaning on the rail, watching Miz Timmins's grandchild playing in the yard across the road. At last Li'l Joe could keep silent no longer, and at the same time could not keep the pain from his voice.

"Don't look like you'll be coming back this way much again, David."

David turned so quickly that the little man gave a half-jump back. "What are you saying, Gramp?"

"You about finished here, son. Man has to go on. I said a long time ago, before you went away to collidge, that you'd be going away from here. I been lucky it ain't come sooner."

"Look, Gramp, is that what you've been thinking? Is that why you've been so brought down? Don't kid me, Gramp. I can tell. Now, listen to me—"

"That's what I been doing—"

"Just *listen,* will you! Anytime you need me, I can get here. I'm not exactly my own boss, but I know I can say that and back it up. Anytime you need me—twenty-four hours and I'm here. You haven't heard of airplanes?"

"What you saying! I been *on* 'em, ain't I?"

"Didn't waste any time, did they? Pretty soon they'll all be jets, too. Come on back inside and let's have another beer and sit down and I'll tell you what I've got in my mind—"

"Thought you had some damned thing in your head—" said Gramp as they sat down, beers at hand.

"Yup. Listen, Gramp—how'd you like to come to Africa, too, for a while? For as long as you want, as far as that's concerned. And no cracks about money. We can make it."

He thought Gramp would never answer. The mantel clock

Sara had sent Gramp on Christmas ticked more times than a man would want to count; the cat entrance-exit in the kitchen door squeaked softly as Chop-bone came in to check up on things; there was a soft plop-plop from the faucet in the kitchen Gramp said was acting up, and at last David said, "Well, Gramp?" The little man opposite was not looking at him now, and David knew he did not dare. Someday, David told himself for the millionth time since he'd been grown, he'd take time out and try to analyze what it was about Gramp, what in hell it was about Gramp that never left a guy.

Again David said, "Well, Gramp?" and Li'l Joe's silence finally gave way.

"Lawd! Africa!"

"And Europe, too. Sara can take over there. But Africa first, if you want it that way."

It was clear that Gramp was only half believing. "Look, son," he said. "You going to be on a honeymoon, sort of. You-ll don't want an old man trailing along—"

"Oh, for God's sake! Here we go again. Worrying. We'll have a honeymoon for a little while. It isn't as though we'd just met. Then, until I get my bearings in Zambana, Sara's going to stake out in southern Europe. By the time I send for you and you get there, I'll know plenty of people in Africa who'll welcome you with open arms."

"Lawd!" said Gramp again. "Lawd, Lawd, an old man—"

"You're not old. Shut up about being old."

"I ain't young. All my life, seems like, ever since I was a chile and used to listen to my grandma tell about what all she remembered about it, I been reading about where my people come from. Used to teach you—"

"To be proud of it, not run it down as most colored did in those days—"

"That's right. Been reading and studying. Lawd, don't know's I could stand it. I feels funny just thinking about it."

"You'll get over that."

"Reckon—reckon maybe we'd get to Senegal?"

"Senegal? I don't know. Why Senegal?"

"I done told you, Gawd knows how many times, that's where your Tant'Irene's mamma come from. Brought over on a slave ship when she was just a chile, eight year old—"

"I remember—"

"But it don't make no difference. If I get to Africa don't make no difference about getting there. S'pose we'll see any lions, tigers?"

"My God, I hope not! No, I don't. Maybe you can get to one of those big-game preserves where the lions come up to the car to get their ears scratched."

"Lawd!" said Gramp. He was silent again for a long time. Then, "I got to have a passport?"

"We'll start the wheels rolling tomorrow. And don't you let me hear you say again I won't be coming back this way. If you're here—and you need me—I'll be back so quick it'll make you dizzy."

"Guess I should have knowed that. Knowed you'd come back did I need you."

"I'll be back anyhow, whether you need me or not."

"Mebbe so. But I knows you'll come if I need you—" He got up, picked up their empty beer cans, and started for the kitchen. When he reached the dining room he stopped and did a quick shuffle dance step, looking back at David. "But I ain't going to be needing you. Feels like a young buck right now, a-snortin' and a-whuffin'—" He sighed what was for him a gusty sigh. "Lawd, I ain't gonna believe it till I sees the passport. Ain't gonna believe it then, not till I sets my feets—both of 'em—down on Africa."

56

LI'L JOE WAS RESTLESS. Seemed as though a man had a right to be, he thought; couldn't expect a man seventy years old to sit back and fold his hands when he had a passport to Africa in his pocket. David had warned him over and over: "Watch that passport, Gramp. Don't you go carrying it around with you. Ambrose's got a safe in his taxi office. Keep it in there." But he couldn't do that. How was a man going to convince folks he was really doing something like go to Africa unless he had something to show? He knew his people. "That's what Li'l Joe say—that's what he say—that he's going to Africa." They'd ought to have some of the needles the doctor at the health department had stuck into him, last week or two. Sick as a dog, a couple of them had made him. Man who hated needles bad as he did wasn't going through all that for nothing.

Li'l Joe thought that when he went to New York to take the plane, just before Christmas, he'd go by train. Get himself a roomette and take it easy, nothing to worry about; the Timminses were going to take care of Chop-bone, see that he stayed in the house at night, let him out in the morning, see he got fed and all. Maybe he'd even spend the money to put Chop-bone in one of these fancy cat kennels while he was gone. He didn't know just yet where he'd be landing over the water. David was taking care of that—David and Sara. He found he wasn't minding so much thinking about Sara. He wouldn't be able to bring her to his home, and that was bad, or their children. Li'l Joe wouldn't be seeing any great-grandchildren round the house; he supposed he'd have to go where they were. "There won't be any children," David had said. "That's me talking, and I mean it. If it was a hundred years from now—maybe. But not now. Sara doesn't feel that way about it, but she doesn't know the kind of hell we'd be letting them in for. After all, could be we might have to come back over to the United States and settle down—"

Li'l Joe grinned at Chop-bone, curled in one of his favorite places, beside the clock on the mantel. "David sure talks big," he said to the cat. "Boy sure talks big. I knows that girl. Does she want chilren—chilren's what they gonna have—"

Shucks, he couldn't stay home; even though he'd be leaving in a little bit more'n a month it was still an uneasy thing, knowing David was going so far away again tomorrow. He changed his clothes, gave his shoes a brisk polish, and put on a soft tan cashmere pullover that David had brought him, under his coat. Couldn't risk catching a fresh cold, not now. Might go into complications, just when he had to be feeling good for the trip.

He knew there was a lot of talk, a lot of worry, about the school trouble and the bad things that were happening, but he hadn't realized how much tension there would be everywhere he went; he could feel it even on the streets, where there seemed to be less people than usual. He listened to stories from his friends of some of the things that were happening because a little Negro girl was trying to enter a white school, and he knew the truth of them. He knew, too, that few, if any, of them would ever see print, and that was a damned shame. World ought to know, he thought, the whole world ought to know how some of these folks can treat a li'l chile just because she's black.

Not everyone he talked with was in agreement about the school trouble. Listening to them, he wondered if he'd have had the courage to send David to a white school, if the same situation had existed when David was a child. He didn't think he would have; it would be worse for a boy. A little boy, even if he was still chubby and round-eyed, would make the whites madder than what a little girl would. 'Saiah had been right when he'd used that old-fashioned phrase, "Days of trouble coming."

Over a beer, Li'l Joe told his favorite bartender: "I ain't going to live to see it, and you ain't either, but the time's coming it won't be like this. But there's going to be blood running first. I said it before and I says it again—"

And the bartender replied: "Don't do to talk that way, Li'l Joe, not right now. They got ears, those walls have. Can't even trust some of our own. You know that."

"Been knowing it—"

But there had been some who were glad to have something to talk about besides the school hassle, and he showed them his passport and they talked of his trip and what he would see and learn, and because he was Li'l Joe Champlin they wished him well and smiled without envy at his straight, slim back when he left them. "Sure glad for him," they said to each other. "No better man around than Li'l Joe. Sure glad—"

As he started for the bus stop, tired now, knowing he would sleep when he got home, he turned a block off his course; he'd drop in on Pop and Emma Jefferson for a cup of coffee, say hello to Ambrose if he was at his taxi office next door.

Just ahead was the building that used to be Guastella's bootleg club in the days of Prohibition and the depression. He seldom passed it he didn't remember the night years before when he had found ten dollars on the floor of the men's toilet, and how he'd gone home thinking about the things the ten dollars would buy that he and Geneva had needed so bad.

There hadn't been a night since Geneva had passed, all those years ago, he hadn't thought of her on his way home, half convincing himself a lot of times that she'd be there, just like tonight when he could almost see her, good as real, in the kitchen, happy in the new house, happy with the things he'd bought for her, smiling-happy with the boy, with David.

It was when he started across the street at the corner where Guastella's used to be that the footsteps behind him entered his conscious mind. That wasn't anything new. Lawd! some whites thought it was funny to follow a colored man, make him nervous, just, he supposed, so the colored man would know the whites were still around, watching everything he did. Best thing to do was stay near the curb, cross the street, and head for an all-colored bar and go inside and mingle till whoever it was had gone by; they'd be laughing, more'n likely.

But now, hearing the footsteps, remembering the stories he'd heard earlier, feeling the tension in the streets, he knew an old fear, and quickened his steps, his breathing faster, shorter, under the pressure of fear, the controlled hurry.

The footsteps did not stay behind him, came abreast of him, one on each side, and he rolled his eyes quickly from right to left and saw two young men in sports shirts, sweaters, and jeans, both fair-haired, fair-skinned, with duckwing haircuts, distinguishable from each other in Li'l Joe's eyes only because the one on the right was taller.

The taller one spoke first, over Li'l Joe's head, to the other. "He's a scrawny li'l ol' nigger—"

"Yeah. Too old to bother with—"

"Hell, man, we've got him. What'll we do with him?"

"Turn him loose. He's under the limit." They both laughed.

These boys were just trying to give him a bad time; Li'l Joe told himself that, knew it to be true; they were just acting smart, but there was fear in him tonight, so much had been happening, and the fear was a heaviness in his chest and belly, a weakness in his legs. He found words, fighting off the shortness of breath, the weakness. "Ain't you young uns got nothing better to do than bully an old man?"

"We ain't bullying you, boy. You come along with us—"

"Let him alone. People are looking—"

"Hell, no. We said we'd show these black bastards what we thought of 'em, didn't we?"

Li'l Joe heard a "snick," saw metal gleam in the taller boy's hand. They were getting closer now to Ambrose's; in a minute he'd risk the metal and make a break for it. "You coming along with us peaceable," the tall youth was saying. "Real peaceable." He snickered. "Hell, you ain't fit for much more than kindling wood. Not enough fat on those bones to make a good fire—nothing but spindly ol' kindling."

Somewhere inside Li'l Joe a child was screaming—"Ma! Ma!—My daddy didn't burn! Did he, Ma? Ma! Ma! *Mamma!*" and then the pain came, blotting out the little boy, tearing his chest in two, searing his arm and lancing into his mouth—came and went and came again, worse then, and he didn't have any legs, and the pavement rose and struck him and he lay there, gasping, while from somewhere a long way above him someone said, "Run! For Christ's sake, get going—" There was the sound of metal hitting the pavement beside him; then there were only the pain in his chest and the gasping struggle for the air that wasn't there. Strong arms cradled him, and a familiar voice said, "Li'l Joe. Li'l Joe!—Hey, you guys, call an ambulance! Li'l Joe, it's Ambrose. Can you hear me, Li'l Joe?"

Now he was forcing words out, each word a mountain to be pushed across a desert of hot pain: "David—David—tell David—needs—needs David—"

"All right, Li'l Joe; all right, now. Easy—easy—David'll come—*Christalmighty! He's gone*—"

But he hadn't gone, not for the space of another gasping breath, not for the length of time it took for the words to reach him through the fog of pain. "David'll come." What came after didn't matter because he couldn't hear the words as the pain gave over to peace.

57

"SARA," SAID DAVID. "Sara, baby, go home. Will you please for God's sake go home!"

"Why, sweet? Why—why—" She pirouetted in the center of the room in stockinged feet, one shoe in her hand, then stopped, arms wide, breasts high and small under the lacy top of her slip. Her eyes were glowing.

"Because, baby, I've got to pack. *I've got to pack*, that's why. Look, hon; look at this mess. And everything in sight has to get into a Val-Pak and an overnight bag. I should have done it this afternoon, woman."

"And I stopped you?" She was laughing now, perched cross-legged on a chair, jumping down to sit on the edge of the rumpled couch, searching for the missing shoe, then on her feet again, tiptoe. "Because I came to help you? That's why you didn't get it done? Poor David. Poor, dear, David. Oh, David, David, I love you so. What day is it? What day is it, David?"

"Monday. And it's night, damn it, Monday night."

She was dancing again, holding the single shoe in outstretched hand, kicking at it. "And what will it be a week from today? What day will it be then?"

David reached out and caught her with both hands on her waist, holding her still, looking down at her. "Wedding day, gal."

"David, it—I can't breathe when I think of it. Honestly, I can't breathe when I think of it. And I thought after all that's happened and we'd been together so much, and slept together, and cleaned our teeth together, eaten breakfast together—I thought it would be just like any other day. And now I can't breathe when I think of it. Kiss me, David."

"No! No, for God's sake. Sara, go home. I love you, Sara, but *I have to pack*. You want me to telephone the State Department in the morning and say, 'Sorry, sirs, Champlin unable to report for scheduled interviews due to unforeseen circumstances, to wit: a seduction.' After this afternoon, yet!"

"They won't know about this afternoon. Just tell them you were seduced tonight. Tell them it had been so long since you'd made love—two whole hours—that you couldn't—"

"Sara!"

"Sweet, I'm kidding. I'll go home now, and you'll pick me up in the morning and we'll fly into London town, and tomorrow night we'll be with Sudsy and Rhoda. And then you'll go to Geneva and I'll wait and die—just *die* while I'm waiting for you. David, will you stop loving me those four days you're in Geneva?"

"I haven't stopped loving you in ten years. Now, Sara, Smallest, please—"

"Say it again and I'll go, David. Oh, David, love can be hell when it's like this. The end of the world could be just around the corner. The end of the whole damned world. Kiss me and tell me again you haven't stopped loving me in ten years and then I'll go."

"Put your clothes on, baby. Your dress and your shoes and your coat and your hat. Then I'll kiss you and say anything you want."

"You're a beast." She spoke from behind the folds of her dress as she slipped it over her head. "A brown horrid beast and I hate you—" She was digging the other shoe from beneath the couch. "Hate you so bad I could eat you alive." She stood. "Zip me, darling. You don't zip as well as you unzip but you zip fairly—"

"Zip yourself, idiot! You've got two pretty little hands, and the zipper's in front—"

"As well you know, beast. Where's my coat? Where's my damned coat? And my damned hat—I have to go through this, he puts me through this, just to get a kiss. All right, David. All right, lover. I'm ready to be kissed."

David had been crouched, back to the room, searching for stray socks in the corners of the bottom drawer of the captain's chest. Now he rose and faced her where she stood, very still and quiet, in the center of the room, silly little hat set squarely on shining dark hair, eyes glowing still.

"God, yes," he said. "You are. You sure are."

He caught her in his arms, lifted her so that her feet swung clear of the floor, kissed her, and while he kissed her, carried her to the door. One arm still around her, he opened the door and at last set her on the other side of the threshold.

"Sara, Sara, run. Run like hell, and I'll see you in the morning. Early in the morning. Be ready."

"You'll be there, David? Early, early?"

" 'Neither snow, nor rain, nor heat'—"

" 'Nor gloom of night'—"

He reached out to her where she stood, just outside the threshold, touched her cheek gently with long brown fingers, drew his hand back and said, "Just for a little while, sweet."

She smiled almost shyly, almost as though he were a stranger, and he heard her whisper, "God bless." Then she turned and walked down the hall. He watched her until he felt her name welling up into his throat, crowding his lips, and shut the door quickly.

He stood for a long time looking at the closed door. "You lucky bastard," he said, half aloud. "You lucky, lucky bastard." *You pays for your luck somehow, one way or another.*

"This kind of luck you can't pay for, Gramp. This is right; this is life being right. It's more than luck."

He found himself grinning foolishly, standing there alone, and he turned to go back to his packing. He had not reached the captain's chest on the far side of the room before the telephone rang.

Pop Jefferson was waiting at the airport when David arrived in New Orleans. He was quiet, for Pop, saying little, putting an arm across David's shoulders and leading him through the half-light of dawn to the place where Ambrose was waiting with his ancient cab.

"Sure sorry about this, David," said Pop. "Sure sorry. Wasn't a better man in all New Orleans than your grandaddy. Been some kids it wouldn't have bothered me so much, but you and Li'l Joe was mighty close."

At the cab Ambrose reached out a hand, took David's, and mumbled something David could not catch but knew to be kind. Already the warm darkness of the world he had been born into was closing round him, the understanding of his people cradling his grief. Nothing of the quiet outer world through which they were passing intruded; they were a unit, the three men in the shabby taxi, the young man in his first real grief, the older men sharing it because they had been born, as he had, to a universal grief, had all felt and shared a larger, more impersonal pain throughout their lifetimes.

All of them were big men physically, and David sat in the back seat with his bag and typewriter, while Pop rode in front with Ambrose, half turned, one arm across the back of the seat, his cigar silhouetted against the windshield.

"You have a good trip, son?" he asked. "Good's it could be, I mean."

"Yes," said David. "Fine. Smooth all the way except for a little bit just before we landed."

It had been a relief to get on the plane. He remembered thinking as he walked down the aisle that this might be the last time he would make this trip. If he could clear up any business connected with Gramp's "li'l piece of property" before he returned to New York, there would be nothing left to bring him back. He would never have to leave Sara again except on trips connected with his work; there would be no need again to split himself into two persons emotionally, one drawn back to New Orleans by a man known as Li'l Joe Champlin, the other held back by a small vibrant girl like a bird whose heart was eternally in her eyes and who held his whole universe in warm, slender hands.

It might even be, he thought, that on this trip he would be seeing for the last time those festering sores that were the outer signs of the South's inner sickness, the signs "White" and "Colored." A circumstance, he thought grimly as he settled into his seat, that would in no way mean that he would forget them.

Chittock had been understanding when, by good luck and hard work on the part of the long-distance operator, he had been tracked down to a Washington restaurant.

Don't worry about it, Chittock said, and David knew the sympathy in his voice was genuine. God knew, the checking they had done on him had probably resulted in a detailed account even of Gramp and Tant'Irene teaching him how to use a knife and fork. Chittock had said he would get through to London and Geneva in the morning, set David's appointments up for later. "A week?" he asked, then, without waiting for an answer, "Ten days. I imagine there will be property to be settled."

The fight for composure had begun when he called Sara. At first there had been things to do: his plane reservation to London to cancel, another reservation to be made for a night plane to New Orleans, Chittock to be called. The fact that Gramp was gone did not sink into his consciousness. Chittock's words "property to be settled" were the first touch of the probe on the nerve of his grief.

"No!" cried Sara, in the first shock of the news. "Not Gramp!"

"I'm afraid so, baby. It had to come sooner or later. But I wish—God, how I wish—he could have made that trip."

"David, I'll be there in twenty minutes. Sooner if I can get a cab right away."

"Please, Sara, don't. I'll be leaving almost as soon as you could get here."

"David—David, I'm coming with you. You're feeling dreadfully—I can tell by your voice. I'm coming with you, or I'll meet you there tomorrow."

"No! Sara, no! For God's sake, you know better than that. You can't come to New Orleans with me. You couldn't even walk down the street with me. It will only be for a little while. Go on over to London, and I'll be there as soon as I can. Maybe by the end of the week."

She consented at last. "All right, David. If it will make it easier for you. Darling, I'm so sorry. Poor Gramp. Poor lamb. His whole life was in that trip, and now—"

"I know—"

"David, I love you. You know that. All that matters of me will be with you—"

"I know."

"I'll call you, dear. From London. I'll find out what time it is in that hellhole I can't go to with you, and when it's nine o'clock there Wednesday night, I'll call you."

"All right, sweet. Take care, baby. And—love me!"

"Yes. Oh, yes, yes, yes! Wait—David. Flowers. Red roses, the most beautiful you can find. 'With love to Gramp from Sara.' You won't forget?"

"Of course not. Wait for me, y'hear!"

"Stoopid! Where would I go—what would I do without you? I wouldn't even *be!*"

"God, I'm sorry, babe. I wouldn't—"

"David, David, dearest. Stop. You can't help it. You have to go to him now. This last time, when he needs you."

When he hung up, his head dropped until it rested on the hand that still gripped the receiver. He heard no sounds at all, not the swish of tires on the street outside, not the voices and laughter of the men and women passing above, nor the sound of their feet on the sidewalk. Something great and good had gone away from him and from the world, and he was alone in the vacuum left by its passing. *Makes a person sick, all that grief inside 'em, never coming out, like poison.*

He had lied to Sara; there was time, there were hours, that must pass before his plane left for New Orleans, but they must pass for him in a country of the heart where she could not follow. Had it been yesterday, the day before, ten years ago, that he had said to her, "There will be such wide areas in both our lives that we can't share, as though our spirits were each on another planet"?

What could Sara know, what could Sara ever know, of the wiry strength of thin brown arms picking a frightened child up in the night and gentling its crying? What could Sara—little love—know of a frightened brown boy sobbing in his grandmother's arms because he had heard for the first time the taunting insult of a white? What could Sara know of the man who had taken him from his grandmother's arms and set him on his feet and said in a voice the child had never heard before: "Stop it, son! You going to be crying all your life, you keep on like this. There ain't nothing you can do about it. Reckon me'n' Gram's got to teach you about God some more. Come on, little man, right now we goes and gets ourselfs an ice-cream cone"? The money, the hoard of nickels and dimes and pennies they had broached to still his crying, to make him forget everything but their love—what could Sara know of these things? Or of a man and his grandson making music in the steaming heat of a New Orleans night, in a little cottage in Beauregard, making their own music against the world? "I love you, Sara; I love you, but this is a different world. I'll never have to leave you and go to it again, be patient with me this one time."

Pop Jefferson had said—what had Pop said?—"He went real quick, David, real quick. God was good to him. Ambrose got to him and had him in his arms, and he only spoke once, son. Said your name. Said something like 'Need—needs David—' and then God took him; took right holt of his hand, son. He'd been seeing some of his friends, telling 'em about his trip. He had his passport in his pocket."

Then Pop had said: "Li'l Joe's at Jones's Funeral Home. We figured to wait till you got here to make arrangements. Figured you'd know what he'd want. We're fixing the parade, us lodge brothers, and the music. We know he wanted that. We're leaving the rest of it up to you."

He knew; he knew what Gramp wanted. They'd fixed it up a long time ago, the first summer he'd been home from Pengard.

"Look, son," said Gramp. "Come the time you got to bury me, there's a few things I wants done."

"Gramp, for gosh sake! You're not going to die. You're talking foolish."

"No, I ain't, son. Man's got to get shet of it all sometime. Every man. Black *and* white. Might as well have what he wants before they puts him away for good. I put it in writing, David, but I wants you to know about it from me. First thing, you keep that damfool Preacher Sims away from me, y'hear! Lawd! Preach a man right out of his coffin, Sims would. Besides, he ain't always strickly sober. Maybe I ain't either, but I don't want no cheap whiskey fumes blowing over my coffin. And I don't want a lot of talking, nohow."

"Listen, Gramp—"

"Hush up, son. You listen. I'll have the music going with me to the graveyard. 'Flee as a Bird' maybe, and 'Garden of Flowers.' Them's real pretty ones. On the way back I guess it don't matter so much, but I sure likes 'Walking with the

King.' George Lewis and his boys, they plays that like five hundred, and I'd like it, but I don't suppose it makes much difference what they plays on the way back."

(They'll play it, Gramp. I'll tell them to play it. Whatever you told me that night, whatever you told me, I'll do it.)

"And at the services I'd like a little music. If God don't call Emma Jefferson before He calls me, I'd like for Emma to play 'Take My Hand, Precious Lord' and 'Oh, Mary, Don't You Weep.' They was your Gram's favorites, and I sure like hearing 'Oh, Mary' when they sings it. And for sure I want the preacher—and you make sure it ain't Sims—to read the Ninety-first Psalm. I've got it all wrote out here. Look, David, you watch where I'm putting this piece of paper now, right here in the buffet under the forks. Mind you don't forget."

"All right, Gramp."

"Get the Bible, David. Been a long time since I heard the Ninety-first Psalm. Read it to me, son. And don't go showing no disrespeck."

David answered his grandfather's grin with one of his own; he knew what Li'l Joe meant. Gramp had decided there wasn't any better practice for a boy learning to read than the Bible, and he'd cut his reading teeth on it. The first time Gramp had asked for the Ninety-first Psalm and he'd come to the words "He shall cover thee with his feathers, and under his wings shalt thou trust," he had looked up and seen Gramp, head cocked on one side like a bird's, watching him and smiling, and suddenly he had snickered. Gramp had said: "What you snickering at, boy? If they's something funny, laugh like a man; don't go to snickering like an idiot. What's so funny?"

And David had told him, because he knew Gramp wouldn't mind, would even laugh with him. "When I was reading about the feathers and the wings and I looked up and you was looking at me like a sparrow and I seen you under a big wing, like an eagle's, a big, big wing, and you was peeking out and peeking out and smiling—"

And Gramp, as he'd known he would, was smiling with him and then he said: "Stop your foolishness now, boy, before you gets disrespeckful. Just keep on a-reading."

He heard the voice of the boy and the voice of the youth, now: "He that dwelleth in the secret place of the most High shall abide under the shadow of the Almighty. . . . He shall cover thee with his feathers, and under his wings shalt thou trust . . . Thou shalt not be afraid for the terror by night . . ."

David Champlin—Pengard, Harvard, Oxford—heard a new sound, the rasp of his own sob, and there in the noisy New York night he cried like a child for a gentle brown man who lay in a mortuary in New Orleans, little quieter when he slept in death than he had been when he slept in life and warm blood was in his veins.

He had his passport in his pocket.

58

AMBROSE DROVE THE CAB directly to Pop Jefferson's. It was not yet daylight, and the air was chill and damp. Lights were burning in the apartment of the old building; and when they entered, David heard Emma moving around in the kitchen. Without taking off his topcoat he walked back and surprised her at the stove, throwing a strong arm around her as he had done for years, saying, "Hiya, Sugar!"

She did not laugh this time as she usually did. "Lord, David!" she said. "It's sure fine to see you." He saw her eyes fill with tears.

He ate breakfast because it was put before him and because he could not destroy Emma's faith that good hot food would ease almost any ill of body or mind, including grief. After the meal he refused gently, because he did not want to hurt his feelings—Ambrose's offer to put himself and his cab at his disposal for the day, asked only that Ambrose drive him over the river to Beauregard and then back to Jones's Funeral Home. "There's something at the house I want to pick up," he said. "Gramp wrote out what he wanted done, and I want to make sure I don't forget anything."

At Jones's they set the funeral for the next afternoon, and he went over each point of Gramp's instructions with Hosea Jones, Zeke's son. David smiled when he said, "Gramp said, 'For Gawd's sake not Preacher Sims.' "

"Couldn't be," said Jones. "We buried Sims six months

ago. Wasn't anybody didn't expect him to start preaching his own funeral right from the coffin. You know Reverend Jackson?"

David shook his head.

"Him and your Gramp was acquainted. He's not much for talk. Li'l Joe liked him. We'll get him, and you can talk to him before the service. He'll go 'long with whatever you say."

David was able to reach Reverend Jackson only by telephone, but he was convinced the minister understood. He told him about the Ninety-first Psalm and he told Emma about the music at the services and Pop and Ambrose about the parade music, and by midafternoon everything was arranged and David was free.

There was little time for the emptiness of the cottage in Beauregard to get to him. The telephone rang continually. At six, Miz Timmins came over. "I come to carry you over to supper," she said. "You can't stay here, eating alone, with your grandaddy gone. You come over and eat with us like you used to. I still got the bib I used to make you wear."

David laughed. "I don't need it. I swear I don't, Miz Timmins." Miz Timmins had aged, he thought. He hadn't realized how much when he saw her on his last trip home, a couple of weeks before. The years of childbearing and hard work seemed to have been lying in wait for her and attacked her when she was defenseless. He saw the age, and he saw something else: his own grief mirrored in her eyes as it had been in the eyes of Pop and Emma and Ambrose, and old Zeke Jones when he had come in to greet him at the Funeral Home.

"I'd like that, Miz Timmins," he said.

After supper, back in the little house that was emptier, he thought, than any house must ever have been, the telephone rang again. For a moment, sandy-eyed from fatigue, he considered not answering it. When he did the sound of Chuck Martin's voice surprised him into complete wakefulness.

"Where are you, man!"

"Right here, David."

"You mean in New Orleans?"

"Right downtown. I came down yesterday. I heard about your grandfather this morning but I couldn't reach you. What can I do, David?"

"Nothing, Chuck. Everything's—I mean, it's just one of those things. Ain't nothin' no one kin do about it. You might—well, you might just sort of say something for Gramp."

Chuck's voice was low. "He doesn't need it now, David. He took care while he was here that he wouldn't need prayers when he was gone. But I'm sort of reminding the Lord about you, dad."

"Thanks. Listen, Chuck—what you doing here in New Orleans?"

"This school mess."

"School—" David's voice trailed off. He felt a quick shame. Although Pop and Emma and Miz Timmins had talked about it—Miz Timmins with frank disapproval of this "stirring up a whole mess of trouble"—the conversation had barely disturbed the periphery of his thinking, centered as his thoughts had been on his own loss, on the sorrow that it was too late for Gramp ever to see his *Tiger, Tiger*.

Now he said, regaining his composure, "School mess—helluva note, isn't it? But I still don't see why you're here."

"I'll tell you when I see you. Wait—there's another friend of yours here. Hang on—"

There was a pause, then someone said "David—" and before the voice could go on, David broke in with a startled exclamation. "Brad! Brad Willis! For God's sake! What in hell are *you* doing in New Orleans?"

"Tell you later. Is there anything I can do?"

David repeated what he had told Chuck.

"Are you alone there?" asked Brad.

"Yes."

"How about inviting your old boss over? Or would you rather—"

"God, yes! Where are you?"

"At ALEC headquarters. I don't know where I'll be later."

"You'll have to get a colored cab—"

"I'm ahead of you. Your friend Ambrose—my friend now—is here. I have to go to Baton Rouge tomorrow, then come back early Thursday morning. I'll be over as soon as Ambrose can get me there."

David had thought, before he talked with Brad, that he wanted to be alone. Now he knew he did not. Now he knew that no matter how tired he was, a night alone in the little house Gramp had left the day before, and to which he would never return, would be almost more than he could take. He walked to the door of Gramp's room and, head averted, closed it softly. Brad could have his room and he would sleep on the divan. He checked the refrigerator and found beer in plentiful supply. There was a nearly full fifth of bourbon in one cupboard.

Brad's handclasp was warm, but did not linger. He knows me well, thought David; he knows one kind word and I might break down like a blubbering kid.

"Got a razor?" asked Brad.

"Sure. Electric, no less."

"Pajamas?"

"Slews of them. Anything you need. Including beer. Or hard liquor, if that's the way your taste runs. It's—hell, it's good to see you."

"I don't mean to flatter myself, but I thought it might be. I mean—"

"I know what you mean. What'll it be? Beer or bourbon?"

"Bourbon. The first one straight, *if* you don't mind." He made a face. "Maybe it will kill the taste of this damned place."

"It's glamorous. It's cosmopolitan. It's picturesque. It stinks with history."

"It is also phony, corrupt, bigoted—and the history it stinks with I don't like. Did you think I would?"

"No. That's why I was so surprised when I heard your voice. The first time I met you—way back in East Cambridge—you said you'd never been here, never had any intention of being here." David motioned Brad to the divan, pushed the coffee table in front of him, and handed him his drink. He sat in Gramp's chair himself. When he put his drink on the end table beside it, he noticed that dust had gathered even since Gramp had left the house the evening before, and with a facial tissue from the box on the table he wiped it clean quickly, forgetting, forgetting completely that Li'l Joe Champlin would not see the dust now to "tsk-tsk" about, thinking, as he took the tissue from the box, Gramp's got the sniffles again.

Brad was saying: "You know how one always has a mental picture of places one's heard about? So help me, David, this is just as I had pictured it." He smiled. "I see now where you got your persnickety neatness."

"By hand," said David. "Believe me, I was brought up by hand to be neat. No cocoa and cookies at bedtime if there was so much as a toy train still on the floor."

Sitting in Li'l Joe Champlin's chair, with Li'l Joe lying in a mortuary across the river, with Li'l Joe no farther from him than his right hand, with Li'l Joe gone yet as close to him as the air he was breathing, David felt for the first time in his life the peculiar pride of ownership. In some strange way the pride seemed to come to him from Gramp, as though sitting in that chair he was somehow a part of Gramp and Gramp of him, and the little house of them both.

His own pennies and nickels and dimes, his own sweat and work, had not gone into this little house. "Sell it," he had said to Gramp. "Sell it and come north with me." Now he knew it was going to take all the guts he had to go to a real-estate agent tomorrow and say: I want to sell the property at 3020 St. Augustine Street. Lock, stock, and barrel. Sell it all: the new screen door, and the front porch Gramp had added on with his own hands; the kitchen with all the cupboards—*Neva's a terrible woman for a lot of cupboards*—where Tant'Irene had held him close the night Gram died; the roof from which Gramp had almost fallen, from which he had hung cussing, he said, like five hundred, till his friends rescued him. Sell it all, the room where he sat now, the piano in the dining room, the dining room where he had studied, where the portable typewriter Gramp had given him had taken his breath away; the bathroom in which Gramp had laid every tile; this house where he and Gramp had "made a little music" so many nights. Sell it all, including the bedroom with the closed door where Gramp had slept so quietly.

Get a good price for it, Mr. Agent, but sell it, sell it all. And if the folks who buy it hear small sounds in the night, tell them not to mind; that will be Gramp stirring round, seeing if a little boy is well tucked in. Sell it, Mr. Agent, sell it all.

He heard Brad say gently: "It's rough, David. It's damned rough. I know. And it's going to be rougher. Then it will ease off. But things won't ever be quite the same again."

David did not answer, and Brad went on, the blood of the dark people that flowed in his veins giving him the understanding, the wisdom about grief and the folly of burying it like a rotting bone, giving him the knowledge that it was clean and good when it was met face on.

"Years from now you'll find yourself still thinking, 'Gramp'll get a kick out of hearing about that,' then realizing he's gone. My mother died ten years ago, but it still happens to me. The people we love never really leave us."

When David spoke at last he said: "It's more than that, more than a personal thing, a personal loneliness. I felt it when the Prof died, too. He and my grandfather were the best men, the damnedest, *goodest* men I've ever known. Or ever will. There's a feeling of a vacuum in the world, a feeling of emptiness, when a man like Gramp leaves it."

"Yes, I know," said Brad. He held out his glass and smiled. "It's going to take a couple more of these to untie those knots, chum. I don't want you to drink alone."

As he took Brad's glass David said: "Come on, Brad. Let me show you the rest of the house. Gramp and his friends did it all except the bare framework."

Later, after Brad had showered and was sitting on the divan again in a pair of David's pajamas and one of his old flannel robes, David said: "All right, Brad. I've been a hell of a host, just talking about myself. What? Why? Brad Willis in New Orleans?"

"It gets bigger and better tomorrow. Brad Willis in Baton Rouge."

"Lord, yes! I remember now. Your cousin—"

"In the State Capitol. Attorney General's office. We had the same grandmother."

"I wouldn't bring the matter up if I were you."

"You mean I shouldn't rush into his office and say 'Hi, Cuz! How's it going? How about a drink?' I doubt that we meet."

"It doesn't seem likely." David smiled, remembering Goodhue at Pengard. "Pity. A great pity."

Brad looked into his drink for a moment, then spoke slowly, measuring his words like drops of acid from a medicine dropper.

"I weathered Little Rock," he said. "Yes, I weathered Little Rock just dandy, sitting at my nice mahogany desk in my nice Boston law office. Believe me, I held up bravely." David had heard anger and scorn in Brad's voice, never such mocking bitterness. "But I didn't take it lying down. No, indeed." Brad got to his feed, padded back and forth across the narrow room. "I acted. Yes, sir, I acted. It mustn't be said that while a white mob was screaming 'Lynch the black bitch!' at a nice teen-age colored girl, Bradford Willis didn't act. I sent two fat checks, one to ALEC and one to the N-double-ACP." He whirled, pointed a finger at David, and still without raising his voice from that bitter monotone, said: "And I did more. I fired letters off to the papers, boom-boom, just like that. And the *Globe* sent someone out to interview me. I told 'em. By God, I told 'em what Bradford Willis thought of Governor Faubus and the whole stinking state of Arkansas.

"And I did more than that. I told 'em what I thought of the Administration, too, from the President on down. Hell, there wasn't any feeling back of that show of force in Little Rock. Not a Goddamned word, not one lousy little word came out of Washington about it being an evil thing or even a not nice thing for children to walk through obscene mobs, risk their lives, to get to a school in the United States of America. All there was, all the hell there was, were high-sounding words about upholding the law of the land. You had the feeling that only great self-restraint prevented the word 'unfortunately' from being used. 'Unfortunately we must uphold the law.' Well, I told 'em about it; I told 'em all about it. Yes, indeed." He laughed abruptly. "That took courage, my boy. That took real courage. Even some of my Negro friends gave me hell for being so outspoken. You remember it, David—how up there in New England—cool, cool New England—the white people were more upset than the colored, at least as far as I could judge."

David, watching the slow deliberate pacing, listening to the low, biting voice, thought how fortunate it was for those accused of crime that Bradford Willis had elected to act for the defense and not the prosecution. These were the words, this the tone, of a hanging prosecutor.

"I felt virtuous as hell, David. Especially when I was criticized. I was, by God, in the forefront of the battle. I was, by God, hearing bullets whine. I went home and told Peg about it. She'd started on a whale of a bender, and all she'd say was, 'Come on, Buster. Have another drink.' She knows how brave I am; drunk or sober, God love her, Peg knows how brave I am."

Brad went back to the divan and sat down, looking tired and spent. David wanted to say something, groped mentally for words, could find none. Brad continued: "It was weeks afterward that I picked up an old news magazine in the press room of the courthouse in Boston. I don't know what one it was—*Life, Look, Newsweek, Time,* one of them. There was a picture in it of a girl, not a little girl or a big girl, just a girl in a pretty summer dress, wearing glasses, carrying schoolbooks. She was sitting on a bench, an ordinary wooden bench, the kind they put at bus stops. She was waiting for a bus. And ringed around her were beasts, slavering, filthy beasts, the kind you see in nightmares. She was all alone. *All alone, David.*

"While Bradford Willis was being brave, sending off fat

checks, making controversial remarks about a President whose voice was never heard, not even in a whisper, saying 'In the name of decency' but only saying 'In the name of the law'—this girl was sitting alone on a wooden bench listening to a mob of subhumans scream 'Lynch the black bitch!' Just a kid, David, just a damned sweet kid, all dressed up for her first day in high school."

David spoke at last. "I was being brave, too, Brad. Nice and comfortable in that Boston law office—sounding off at ALEC meetings."

"This isn't for you, David! For Christ's sake, no! You were stockpiling ammunition. You still are. Pengard, Harvard, practice, Oxford—you'll need them all."

He stood, started the slow pacing again, hands deep in the pockets of the robe. "That's it, the 'why' of Bradford Willis in New Orleans. Or part of it. The picture never left me, never left my mind. Every time I saw a wooden bench—any kind, anywhere, in a park, at a street corner—I felt as Pilate might have felt when he saw a cross after the Crucifixion. That girl was always sitting on that bench, David, wherever it was."

Were you there? Were you there when they crucified my Lord? Nehemiah was half screaming, half sobbing the words in the basement meeting room of the church in Laurel. *Must Jesus bear the cross alone and all the world go free?* His grandmother was singing the words in the church at the end of the road.

Brad's voice silenced the voices in his mind. "O'Shea was down here last week on an estate case. He told me all hell was brewing underneath. This time, David, it's the primary grades. It's a little girl, a very small girl with chubby brown legs, all dressed in her Sunday best, and frightened. But at least, at least she's not alone. There's someone to hold her hand. A United States Marshal. Not her mother, not her father; they'd stone them to death, so help me. *A United States Government official* to take the hand of a big-eyed, frightened little girl and lead her up the steps of a schoolhouse in America, past human spittle and the obscene screams of human beings with sewers for minds. She doesn't know what it's all about the way my girl on the bench must have known; she's too little. She's just a little kid. Just a baby! Jesus! Jesus Christ, David! She's my kid! She's the child of every Negro in this country!"

Suddenly the fire went out of Bradford Willis, and he sat

on the edge of the divan, drank what was left of his drink thirstily. "That's why I'm here," he said. "I'm a helluva good lawyer and I'd be the last to say I'm not. I offered my services to ALEC for field work. Right now ALEC's shorter staffed than the N-double-A. I can't leave everything up in the air in Boston, but gradually I'll be able to make myself more and more available. There's time, because it's not just here and it's not just now. It's tomorrow and next year, and the years to come until after they bury your grandchildren. Because I swear to you, David, all hell is going to break loose."

Lawrence Travis had said that too, just a short time ago. David told Brad of his talk with Travis, and what Travis had said after a recent trip South: a bugler practicing to sound reveille—and then—Charge!

"Yes," said Brad. "That's the way it is."

"But, Brad—it's not that simple. Are you suffering from the illusion that all the Negroes in the South are on our side of the fence?"

"Hell, no! On the bus today I overheard a colored woman talking to a friend. It was all just a mess of trouble, she said. First thing anyone knew there wouldn't be no colored have no jobs anywhere. Bunch of foolishness, and nothing but trouble coming out of it. No, I'm not so naïve I don't know there are *status quo* Negroes in the South as well as the 'Omi-god-isn't-it-a-shame-I'm-sure-glad-I'm-here' Negroes in the North. But standing in front of them there's a solid phalanx of youth. It only took me a day, sitting quietly as an observer in the ALEC office, to realize that."

The telephone had not rung for the better part of an hour, and now its sudden clamor startled them both. David glanced at his watch and said, "It might be important, calling this late." He answered it, then handed it to Brad. "Long distance. For Bradford Willis."

"Here?"

David saw the cringe of fear, knew Brad was thinking of Peg and some of her calls when she had been drinking, and tensed when the other man took the telephone and said, "Yes?" quietly.

David tactfully retired to the kitchen to refill their empty glasses, but the house was too small to take him out of the range of a normal voice, and Brad's followed him. There seemed to be no strain in it, no patient gentleness. Instead he heard a bantering affection. Maybe, he thought, it's not Peg;

maybe at last Brad has found someone to ease the tension—"apprehension" might be a better word—that living with Peg entailed. He heard Brad saying, "That's fine, hon. . . . Just getting back? . . . Fine. . . . Of course I'm all right. . . . Just take it easy, worry wart. . . . I'll call you tomorrow night. . . . You'll be all right, Babe. . . . Sure, wait. . . ." Brad called, "David!"

When David came into the room the expression on Brad's face warmed him. It was Peg, no doubt about that, and she must be sober. Brad's face was that of man who has been denied sex for a long time and then finds satisfaction. The deep vertical lines beside nose and mouth had smoothed out miraculously, and the eyes were clear with the clarity of inner release.

David heard Peg say, "Hi, David!" Her voice was the same, deep and husky, but there was no drink in it, and he smiled into the telephone. "I'm so sorry," she was saying. "We're all sorry about Gramp. There's nothing we can do, I know, and I'm not going to be a stupe and offer. But I'm thinking of you."

"Thanks, Peg."

"David."

"Yes?"

"That's quite a guy I've got, isn't it? Quite a guy."

"You mean that shyster ambulance chaser sitting here drinking my good liquor?"

"That's the lad. That's my boy. Imagine still being in love with a dope like that after thirteen years. Keep your eye on him, David. He's a good kid and he's in strange territory."

"Haven't you heard? They've repealed Louisiana's Black Code statutes for the duration of his visit. I heard there was talk of freeing the slaves. He's lunching at Chez François in Baton Rouge tomorrow with his cousin."

"That'll be the day. Let me speak to the dope again, David. And, remember—even though we chasten you now and then, we still love you."

"Thanks again, Peg. Here's the dope."

When he brought the drinks in from the kitchen, Brad was leaning back on the couch, his head on one of Tant'Irene's antimacassars. "God," he said, "that's a relief."

"She sounded fine. I didn't want to ask before—"

"I know. People don't. She was drinking when I left day before yesterday. For once I left anyhow. There wasn't anything I could do, and my being there seems to make it worse sometimes. Know where she's been tonight? An AA meeting. God knows, she's been before—plenty of times. But there's always the hope that this time it will work. Or that something will." He sighed deeply. "Let's drink our drinks and go to bed. We're both bushed."

59

JUST BEFORE THE FUNERAL services David was able to have a brief talk with Chuck Martin, who said only, "He ran a good race, David; don't wish him back."

"Just for that trip," said David. "That's all. I wish he could have had that."

It was obvious fifteen minutes before the scheduled time for the services that there would not be enough seats for all, that people would be standing in the back and out on the small roofed porch of the French Quarter church, the church where Geneva Champlin had sung in the choir and that Gramp had attended whenever his wife could exert enough influence to make him. Inside the building Emma Jefferson was playing the piano, runs and chords, no hymn in particular, not minor in key but to David inexpressibly sad. In Gramp's notes, under the forks in the buffet, had been the words: "Emma J.—piano" and the organ would remain silent.

He sent Chuck inside, afraid no seat would be available, and when Hosea Jones approached him to take him to the family entrance he shook his head and went in with others to a seat reserved for him beside Pop Jefferson. He had always said he had no use for funerals, and wished there could have been a private funeral service for Gramp, yet now the sight of the packed church brought a certain comfort. How did he know, who in hell was he to say Gramp was not drawing comfort from it too? One damn sure thing, he thought, if Gramp does know, he's proud, but he wished it were over. He could not shake the feeling that Li'l Joe Champlin would not be at rest, not really at rest, until all the people had gone away, even his grandson, and he was in the quiet of the cemetery, with the dark understanding earth over him; that not until then would Joseph Champlin go free.

Preacher Jackson looked a little like the pictures David had seen of Martin Luther King; he was of the generation just ahead of David's, with a round, open face that would have been no more than benign were it not for the eyes and the strength and fire behind them. Hosea Jones had been right: this was no old-time ranter, out to stir a congregation to a fever pitch of emotion and hysteria. He saw, when they met, why Gramp had liked him.

The service opened with one of the hymns Gramp had wanted: "Take My Hand, Precious Lord," and from where he sat he could see the tracks of tears on Emma Jefferson's face, the light from a window catching the moisture on the brown skin. In spite of himself he found the hymn getting to him, undermining his control. Then Jackson began to speak, and David sighed with relief at the opening words.

"Our beloved brother said he did not want a long talk at his funeral. That was like him. Joseph Champlin was a quiet man." The way he said "was a quiet man" made David's skin prickle. "But it would not be right to pay our last respects to a great and good man without a few words in parting." Keep it few, thought David; keep it few; don't cross Gramp and me up now, when we're helpless.

Sara's red roses were there, a glowing, crimson blanket over the coffin. He fixed his eyes on them now, remembering that he and Sara had once talked about the barbarism of funerals, the senselessness of a lot of claptrap over stiff cold clay; then he smiled inwardly at her understanding. Whatever she might feel, she had instinctively done the right thing, knowing Gramp set considerable store by funerals. Her card was tucked away among the roses—"To Gramp with love from Sara"—and when Gramp's friends had stood at the side of the coffin in the mortuary the night before, and when they had filed past before the start of the services, he had seen curious fingers turn it for a better view, caught puzzled expressions on all the faces.

He could hear the minister's voice in the background of his thoughts about Sara. Then, like a bugle, it was commanding his attention.

"It is not easy to bring comfort to those who are bereaved. But we can say to the young son—for he was more son than grandson—in the hour of his grief, 'You have been blessed by the Lord because in your infancy and youth you were in the care of a great and good man.' "

The minister's eyes were full on him, soft, compassionate, but behind the softness and compassion there was the flash of something like a sword.

" 'And Samuel said unto Jesse, Are here all thy children? And he said, There remaineth yet the youngest, and behold, he keepeth the sheep.' "

Preacher Jackson turned to the congregation. "That was David," he said, and then his voice dropped to a whisper, but the whisper could be heard in the far corners of the room: "That was David."

There was no sound from the people in the crowded little church. Before there had been punctuating cries of "Yes, Lord!" and "Yes, Jesus!" and "Amen!" Now there was silence.

"We know, brothers and sisters, what Jesse's son did. We know that when he stood before Saul and offered to slay the Philistine that the king armed him with a coat of mail and put upon his head a helmet of brass. And David put them off and said to the king, 'I cannot go with these; for I have not proved them.' And then the Bible tells us that 'he took his staff in his hand, and chose him five smooth stones out of the brook, and put them in a shepherd's bag which he had . . . and his sling was in his hand: and he drew near to the Philistine.'

"And then the Bible says that when the Philistine saw the boy he laughed at him and mocked him and cursed him by his gods. And then said David to the Philistine 'Thou comest to me with a sword, and with a spear, and with a shield: but I come to thee in the name of the Lord of hosts, the God of the armies of Israel, whom thou has defied. This day will the Lord deliver thee unto my hand . . .' "

What was he saying? What was he getting at, this man who had promised there would be no funeral oration? The preacher's voice went on, and now it was ringing like a deep-toned bell.

" '. . . and he fell upon his face to the earth. So David prevailed over the Philistine with a sling and with a stone . . . but there was no sword in the hand of David.' "

David Champlin passed a hand over his face and felt the fingers trembling on his cheek.

". . . the comfort we can bring now to his grandson is the knowledge that the last words that came from our brother's lips were of his need for the boy."

Need—needs David—that was what Pop Jefferson had told him on the telephone. *You need me, Gramp, I'll come back. You know that. I can make it in a day.*

Now the congregation found speech again, and the church was filled with the sounds of "Amen!" and "Yes, Jesus!" and "Lord, Lord!" and from somewhere there came the sound of a woman keening and more chanting: "Yes, Lord . . . Yes, Jesus . . . Yeyus, Jesus . . . Oooooooh, my Jesus."

"He did not call upon God because God was with him in his hour of fear, and I like to think he felt that hand of God."

The people were quiet now, and Jackson went on: "And I like to think—yes, I like to think that when our brother spoke the name of his beloved grandson he spoke not for himself alone but in the name of his father who died in the fire so many years ago, that he turned in his fear, as we must all turn, to our youth who carry in their hands the hopes of our deliverance. I like to think that Joseph Champlin cried aloud in the hour of his fear for *all* his people—" The black folds of the minister's gown were like dark wings as he spread his arms wide, and now it seemed that his words must carry far beyond the wooden framework of the church, must carry throughout the city, even to the steps of a schoolhouse —"Yes! In the name of *all* his people!"

He brought his arms forward, turned the palms outward to quiet the congregation: " 'Thus saith thy Lord and thy God . . . Behold, I have taken out of thine hand the cup of trembling, even the dregs of the cup of my fury; thou shalt no more drink it again.' " He was whispering as he repeated: " 'Thou shalt no more drink it again.' "

Now Jackson gripped the sides of the pulpit, bent his head, closed lids hiding the fire, the sword, behind the dark compassion of his eyes. "Let us say together the psalm our brother asked for, that sustained him in life, that promises us all life eternal, the Ninety-first Psalm: 'He that dwelleth in the secret place of the most High shall abide under the shadow of the Almighty. . . . He shall cover thee with his feathers, and under his wings shalt thou trust. . . .' "

Oh, God, Gramp, couldn't you have done without it, couldn't you have done without the Ninety-first? Because Gramp was there, very small and gentle, like a small brown mouse or a small bird, nestled in the soft down beneath a great wing peering out, and smiling, smiling. David turned his eyes from the minister, looked toward the window, seeing nothing through swimming eyes but a blur. He fumbled for a handkerchief, then realized he did not have to hide his tears, did not have to blow his nose to disguise his emotion, because he was among his own, where grief was natural and not weak, where a man could grieve aloud and not feel shamed.

He heard no more until Emma Jefferson's voice rose above the choir: " 'Oh, Mary, don't you weep—' " The minister's voice joined hers. There was the wide water, shimmering dark, and there on its banks were his people, all black, all singing, and he heard his own voice above the others—" 'Pharaoh's army got drownded—' "

60

It was all over. The body of Joseph Champlin was in its grave, beside Geneva's, and his grandson felt the release that comes with the easing of a heavy emotional burden. So long as that small, peaceful-looking scrap of brown clay had been above ground, looked at, exclaimed about in eerie whispers, David had felt that Gramp was still in bondage to the world. Now he was free. David could not explain why he felt this way, and did not try.

At the cemetery gate, as they were leaving, he turned to Pop. "Did you notice a tall, blond guy—white man, minister—around after the services?"

"He's around here somewhere, son, right around here. Seen him driving out, then seen him on foot after we got here. You don't want to come with me, I'll give you the keys to my car and go back with Ambrose."

"Thanks, Pop. I'd like to find this guy. See you later."

"You be there in time for supper, y'hear? Emma's counting on you."

The band was almost a block away now, and David gave an involuntary start at the sudden clear golden notes of the lead trumpet in an opening fanfare to "Walking with the King." The people along the sidewalks quickened their steps, and little brown and black and tan children ran to get closer. There was the sound of a motor revving up, and a motorcycle patrolman wheeled into the road, following the band, a check against disorder. David saw a white man with a camera in the crowd along the sidewalk, and swore under his breath. He told himself there was no point in going to jail for snatching the camera. The wonder of it was the guy hadn't come into the church, taken one of his Goddamned pictures of Gramp lying in the coffin.

" 'Sing hallelujah, I'm walking with the King, Praise His holy name—' " Someone in the crowd on the sidewalk was singing the words, and the sound of the band came back to him, clear, compelling, with a driving, syncopated up-tempo. They can play that, thought David. They can *really* play it. Ten years from now there wouldn't be any marches back from the cemetery, wouldn't be any second lines. Those were old men up there. There was a joyous, triumphant sound to the music. He supposed that in a certain sense it was cause for rejoicing, the march back from the cemetery; it was, in its way, a sort of freedom march, played for a brother whose slavery had never ended until then, to whom a man's name at the bottom of a Proclamation had been only a symbol of good intent.

He heard Chuck speak beside him and turned. "Hi, man! Sure nice of you to come."

"I wouldn't have not come; you know that. Say, is there anywhere around here we can go and have a cup of coffee? I mean together."

"Right across the road. I know them in there. Lots of whites go in there, curiosity seekers, photographers coming out here to get some shots of quaint Negro customs."

"Relax, chum."

Seated at a tiny table in the lunchroom, David looked across at Chuck. "Why are you here? Are you staying long?"

"I reckon I'm what you'd call on detached service, traveling round and about the South—because I'm a cracker myself, I guess—trying to pull our church and others into some sort of cohesive grouping, something that can speak with authority."

"You're not having any success." David made it a flat statement.

"You know it."

" 'Suffer little children'—"

"As long as they're white—"

David changed the subject abruptly. "Chuck, I've been puzzled ever since the services. That minister—"

"He did a fine job."

"All right, he did a fine job. But why go into all that business of 'David'? Embarrassed the hell out of me. And the business of Gramp being taken in the 'midst of his fear.' Why couldn't he leave all that out of it, at a funeral anyhow? I wish Gramp had stuck with Catholicism or been an Episcopalian. No talk at all at those funerals. All that about God's hand being on his shoulder. And about calling out for help in the name of all his people. It shook me up, and something—I can't put my finger on it—something about it puzzled me. Gramp went quickly, Ambrose said."

Chuck's round, open face looked thinner, even drawn, when he answered, "Perhaps he shouldn't have brought it up; at a funeral anyhow." He stirred his coffee slowly, absently, did not look at David. "Better to have kept away from it with all the tension there is here now. Your grandfather's fear couldn't have lasted long, seconds maybe. He must have known, even after the heart attack, that those hoodlums had run off."

The room and everything in it receded, vanished, and left him alone with Chuck. There was a ringing in his ears, in his head, like the brazen clanging of bells; then the bells were gone and he was in the midst of a great silence that was edged around with tiny sounds: the clatter of dishes, a laugh, the sound of a car's horn in the roadway outside, sounds that in no way intruded on the silence, were no louder than a tack hammer might be, tapping away in a great cathedral. His own voice was an echo from the center of the silence.

"What hoodlums?"

"The ones that came out of the alley that night and frightened your grandfather, of course. I suppose all they wanted to do was scare him, make him jump. Maybe the little rats—the little white rats—wouldn't have done it if they'd known about his heart, if they'd known that instead of just giving him a scare they'd—frighten him to death."

David was not conscious of getting to his feet.

"David—I thought you knew—"

Chuck saw a fine tremor in the brown hand that tossed coins on the table. He touched his friend's arm, felt it pull away, and was looking up into the face of a stranger. He rose and came round the table to stand beside the stranger, but he was too late. The voice that came back to him from the man limping through the door—"Sorry, Chuck"—was unrecognizable.

Pop Jefferson looked at the younger man standing in front of him. "Hell, David, it wouldn't have done no good to tell you."

Behind them, from the kitchen, they heard Emma's voice. "I told you, Pop Jefferson. I told you wasn't any use trying to keep it quiet. Told you there wasn't no such thing as a secret in New Orleans, the boy'd better get it from a friend."

Without turning or taking his eyes from Pop's face, David said, "I got it from a friend."

"You hush up, Emma. David, them white boys never laid a hand on Li'l Joe."

"They murdered him."

"Look, lemme fix you a drink. Sit down, son. Gawd's sake, sit down."

"No. What did they look like?"

"I didn't see 'em good. Not real good. Just a quick glimpse. They was running like striped-assed apes."

"Are you lying to me? You didn't tell me what happened, nobody told me. Not a Goddamned soul told me what happened to Gramp. That was lying. You let me think Gramp died a natural death. Are you lying to me now?"

"Swear to God I'm not, David. He did die a natural—"

"Who did see them? Someone saw them."

"David, you got to understand. Things was mighty mixed up and confused. Reckon maybe somebody may have seen 'em good, but I couldn't say who. Look, David, Li'l Joe wouldn't want you getting all upset—getting into—"

"Who was there? Who might have seen them good?"

"Lawd! I don't—"

Emma came to the doorway that led to the kitchen. "Rudy Lopez was there," she said. "Rudy run to Li'l Joe first before Pop and Ambrose got to him. Pop pushed him away a little so's Ambrose could get to your grandaddy. Ambrose got First Aid train—"

"Where's Rudy?" David turned and was looking at her now. "Where's Rudy living now?"

"I don't know—and that's God's truth, David. After his folks died and he got married he moved off somewhere. That's the first I seen of him in more'n three years—"

"Emma, will you shut up—"

"Let her talk. Let her tell me. Who else was there, Emma?"

"Ain't no one else I can call to mind—wait. Placide Smith. You know Placide?"

David shook his head.

"Li'l Joe's been knowing Placide a long time. Since they was kids, I guess. Placide's older'n your Gramp. I remember now, he come around the corner, looking back over his shoulder like maybe those white boys had bumped into him when they was running away. Then I heard Ambrose calling to get an ambulance, and I run for the house, and then the po-lice come. But Rudy Lopez, he picked up the knife before the law got there."

"Knife! What knife?"

"Look, David—" It was Pop, almost tearful, breathing heavily.

"What knife, Emma!"

Emma came into the living room now and stood by the table with the stiff crocheted doilie in the center and the leg trued up by a little pile of cardboard match clips. There was flour on her hands, and the rich, spicy smell of okra gumbo, coffee, and baking biscuits filled the house. "The knife one of them whites threw down when they started running." She tried to wipe the flour from her hands with a corner of her apron. "All I could figure was if the po-lice caught 'em they was going to say your Gramp pulled the knife on 'em. Any-how, Rudy, he snatched that knife up quicker'n a cat and put it in his pocket. I seen that myself. But Pop's right, David. They never laid a finger on him. Just jostled him and I guess talked bad to him, trying to scare him. All this trouble with the schools and all. Whites'll do anything once colored starts coming up."

Pop said, "Just a coupla punks, out to get a nigger. Half drunk."

"High-sperrited," said Emma. The bitterness of centuries was in her tone.

"They killed him."

"They never teched him, son."

"They killed him."

"Mebbe so," said Pop resignedly. "Mebbe in one way they did. Whites've been killing colored more'n a hundred years, never teching 'em. But it's done now, son. It's done now. F'Gawd sake—"

Emma and Pop Jefferson watched him go, helpless to stop him. As the quick, limping steps were heard on the banquette outside, then not heard because they had gone too far, Emma began to moan.

"Jesus have mercy!" It was not an exclamation. It was a prayer. "Oh, Lord Jesus, have mercy!"

Rampart, St. Anne, Ursuline, St. Peter, down one side, up the other. Bourbon, Burgundy, St. Philip, down by the waterfront and up to Canal, grief left behind, hate walking within him. Little neighborhood saloons, colored only; bigger saloons, colored screened off at one end of the bar, Coke shops and juke joints, restaurants and lunch wagons, and often when he entered there would be a sudden silence. In Cy's Place he heard a man say, "Lawd! Here comes trouble" and David walked to the cluttered table where he sat, recognizing him as someone Gramp had known. "Man, I don't know *nothing;* I was home eating supper—" and David left.

He went no place where there was not a friend of Li'l Joe Champlin's, no place Gramp wasn't known. Not all of them —Christ! not *all* of these people—could be a part of some nightmare conspiracy of silence; at some place some one of them must be able to answer the questions *"Did you see them?" "Do you know where I can find Rudy Lopez?"*

He did not walk off the hate and rage, but at last he banked their fires so that the glow of their flames did not show in his eyes, so that he could enter a bar and there would be no sudden silence—the talk would go on, and the noise. There were hate and rage on the streets and in the bars to match his own that night, but he was only vaguely conscious of it, only obscurely aware that the hate of those he met had fear for a running mate, until it came to him that this was the reason his questions went unanswered, and for the first time he realized that there were as great evils abroad as the one that had sent him on his blind search—greater.

On Burgundy Street he leaned for a moment, tired, against the corner of a building and felt in his pockets for cigarettes. A pair of policemen walked along the banquette toward him and looked at him with smoldering contempt. They slowed their steps, seemed about to stop, eyes alert and seeming almost hopeful that he would make an overt move; then they passed him slowly, a threat in every measured step. It must have been like this in Nazi Germany, thought David; it must have been like this in what the rest of the world liked to call "civilization's darkest hour." They were everywhere he looked that night, police in uniforms and men in plainclothes he knew to be police. "Ask them," he said to himself. "Ask them, David Champlin. You're a lawyer—and they're the servants of the people. Ask them. You went to Harvard. Remember? And Oxford. Remember? You're a Goddamned great lawyer, going to work for the Department of State of your country, going to show other countries how to do it, how to build a government, how to build a government so there'll be enough men to spare to take a little child to school, to protect a little child from spittle; you're going to show 'em, by God, you are! Ask the next cops you see. Tell 'em who you are, ask 'em if they know about the ofay bastards who left a little brown man named Joseph Champlin dying of fright in the street. Walk right up and tell 'em who you are and ask 'em." He began to laugh, not loudly, not the laughter that could be heard three courtyards away, but soundlessly.

He had drunk little; two or three whiskies at the most, spaced over the night. The others he had ordered were left on bars and tables when he had found himself cut off from communication, cut off by his own people, walled off as completely as though he had been white; faced by a blank, bland friendliness that had beneath it the wariness of the jungle animal who knows itself to be the prey of stronger creatures. Gramp would have done what these people had done: curled up in the hollow of the tree of his being, where it was deep and dark and secure, until the smell of danger was past.

He had not been to Hank's Place yet, and he limped down the banquette and around a corner, conscious of an ache of tiredness in his gimpy leg, made worse by the damp cold of the night. Hank's Place had changed since he was a child and Geneva had sent him scampering down there to fetch Gramp home for dinner or to answer a call for work. The original owner, who had so often given credit to Li'l Joe because he trusted him, was dead, and the new owner had enlarged the place, keeping its name. Although it was not crowded on this night, it gave the impression of being full, its blue, fuzzy atmosphere vibrant with sound: the blare of a jukebox, the laughter and loud talk of the young people milling around in its center, some dancing, some sitting at tables, some hanging around the jukebox. A woman was singing, and her voice had a flat, strident quality that hurt David's ears yet drove as true as a well-placed knife into his mind and heart. The big room smelled like the other places he had been that night—of stale smoke, beer, whiskey, and human bodies.

He cursed himself for not looking up Rudy on his trips home the last few years. He knew so few, almost no one now, of his own generation in New Orleans. The persons he recognized were either of Gramp's generation or their sons and daughters, old or middle-aged. No one of them knew where Rudy was; only a few even recognized the name, and they said, invariably, something like: "Stays someplace over the river, Beauregard, maybe, or Algiers . . . ain't seen him in a long time. . . . Mebbe he was over here the first of the week, like you say. I wouldn't know . . . ain't sure I'd know him if I seen him."

The bar in Hank's Place was in a recessed area at one side, and the quiet, older people sat there, the ones who had come to drink and talk. He slid onto a stool beside a copper-skinned man, an old man who, in spite of the nappiness of snow-white hair, could have passed for a southern European in the North. David could not remember ever seeing him before. He tried the same opening gambit he had tried with others earlier in the evening.

After he had ordered a drink he said, "I think we're acquainted." The man was obviously a Creole, and David chose a Creole name. "Aren't you Alcide Guesnon?"

The copper-skinned man smiled. The Creole accent was so thick David had difficulty understanding the rapid-fire words. He was not Alcide Guesnon, he said; his name was Placide Lafitte Smith.

"Got the name wrong," said David. (Placide Smith had been there the night Gramp died; Emma Jefferson had said so. Easy does it, David; take it slow and easy.) "Knew I'd seen you, though, with my grandaddy, Li'l Joe Champlin."

Two men were sitting on the other side of Smith, and David felt rather than saw them stir. Smith smiled and said, "I knew Li'l Joe. Heard about you."

A wrinkled black face like an aging crow's peered around the Creole's shoulder. "Lawd!" said the face's owner, "Li'l Joe's grandbaby. How you been, boy? Ain't seen you since one night on the ferry, long time ago. Had us a sing."

"Sure," said David. "Sure!" He knew that his lips were smiling. *When we get to Heaven gonna sing and shout*— That was the night Gramp gave him the typewriter. "I remember it well. How you been?"

"Fine. Fine. Getting older. Man's always getting older." He laughed a high, aged laugh. "You getting way up there. Li'l Joe told me about it." He turned the wrinkled blackness of his face to the man on the other side of him. "Was you acquainted with Li'l Joe Champlin?"

"You getting old, you sure getting old. I was here the night he come in, last week. I remember Li'l Joe from when I was a kid." The man had skin the color of light chocolate, and his eyes were gray.

David signaled the bartender, indicated the three men on his right. He did not want Placide Lafitte Smith to leave, but he knew he must not seem too anxious. A young Negro shouldered his way to the bar on David's left, jostling him, saying stridently, "The same identical only make it double."

The bartender said, "You want two? That chick you come in with ain't here no more."

"See a lot, don't you, Slats? See too damned much sometimes. Let her go and give me my drink. Whiskey one. Double. Now."

The bartender reached for a bottle, looking at David apologetically.

"It's O.K.," said David. "Fix it for him. It's on me."

The boy looked down at him. "What the hell!" he said. "What the hell? Much obliged."

David moved his shoulders uneasily under the light topcoat. There was a full awareness now in his mind and nerves, even his muscles, that every man and woman in that noisy room knew that he was Li'l Joe Champlin's grandson, come down from New York for his grandfather's funeral; knew how and why Li'l Joe had died. The youth did not take his drink back into the room, but stood at the bar nursing the glass in his hand, alone, isolated from the noise, the high-pitched, tearing laughter of the women, the loud voices of the men, the blaring of the jukebox.

He talked with the three seated men of the trouble in the schools, the tension in the streets and homes throughout the city, even those as far as the outer reaches of Canal Boulevard, lined with the residences of prosperous New Orleanians. The wife of the gray-eyed man worked in one of those homes. "Dagos," he said, and David winced. "And scared," the man went on. "First-generation Dagos, born over the water, and made the most of their money out of colored. Started with a li'l grocery store right here in the French

Quarter. Colored money put 'em in that house; now they don't want no colored going to school with their grand kids, can't no colored walk up their front steps."

"The hell they can't." The boy standing beside David seemed to feel that he was part of the conversation, although David had turned from him rather pointedly. He was staring into his drink. "The hell they can't. If there was enough of 'em, and they had the guts, they could." He laughed. "A colored man could walk up 'em fast enough if he had a scrub brush and pail in his hands. Any Negro in New Olreans can walk up a white man's front steps if he's going to scrub 'em."

Your Tant'Irene always said, 'Offer the work to God, son.' David started, almost spilling his drink, at the boy's next words. " 'A clean spittoon on the altar of the Lord. A clean bright spittoon all newly polished'—" The boy finished his drink in one swallow. *"Shit!"* he said. The glass made an ugly sound as he slammed it on the bar. "Tomorrow morning I'm going to get me a nice clean spittoon, all polished up, going to take it out to those white whores at the schoolhouse, going to give those ofay bastards something to spit at besides a little black kid."

David spoke quickly, to distract the youth. He sensed the bartender's fear and uneasiness at the rising note in the boy's voice. "You read Langston Hughes?" he asked the boy.

"Sure. Read 'em all. Wright, Hughes, Cullen, Baldwin. I like Wright. He's got blood in his mouth when he talks."

"Hughes hasn't?"

"Not exactly. It's like this, see. Hughes, now, he's got gall, like when you're cleaning a turkey and split the gallbaldder and don't know you've done it. The meat comes out of the oven as clean and nice looking as any meat you ever saw. You don't taste the gall till it gets on your tongue."

David signaled to the bartender, indicated the three men on his right and the boy on his left. He looked at the boy closely. The men would keep, even Placide, as long as another drink was coming up. His inner tensions were easing.

"You read a lot?" he asked the boy.

The youth said that, yes, he read a lot. Whenever he had chance. "Read," he said. "Read and think and get drunk and find a piece of tail somewhere. What the hell? Why not?"

Who was the boy like? David's eyes did not leave his face. Who was he like?

"You have a name?" asked David. "Or isn't it any of my business?"

"Sure, I've got a name." The boy turned and looked down at David, a quick smile consuming sullen bitterness in its warmth. "Luke. Luke Willis."

"Willis! Wait now—you got relatives up New England way?"

Luke shrugged. "Who knows? Maybe. One of my great-uncles went up that way, I heard. My grandfather's brother. Lucky bastard."

"If it's the same family I'm thinking of, you've got a relative nearer than that. On your grandma's side of the family. Creole name. Right up in Baton Rouge. A real pale relative."

Luke noded. "It's the same. And pale's not the word. Lily-white, that's what the bastard likes to think he is, lily-white and working like hell to keep the colored kids out of white schools, and he's got black blood-kin going to want into those schools. Wonder would he know 'em?"

"Not out loud," said David. "Would you like to meet one of your kin from New England? He's down this way now."

"Not if he's like—"

"He's not. He's a great guy. Give me your address and telephone number. I'll get in touch with you."

David knew now who stood beside him. It was David Champlin at eighteen; David Champlin without Gramp, without the Prof, with only—he learned after a few minutes of talk—a drunken father, his mother long since gone, no one knew where. Luke had finished high school that year; his father had retained enough authority to make him do that, but now his father was so far gone in drink that what Luke could bring in from odd jobs went for liquor and fines. It need only be a little while, thought David, only a little while—months, maybe weeks—before the odd jobs became jobs that would put him in jail, only a little while before the liquor he drank so expertly now became the substitute for everything his life lacked. All my people, he thought, all of us are sick unto dying from a slow poison, a radiation sickness no scientist ever unleashed.

"Thursday," said David to Luke. "I'll call you Thursday morning." Brad had said he would drive down early Thursday morning and go direct to ALEC headquarters; he'd call him there, arrange a meeting. He turned again to Placide and the others. "Another drink?" he asked.

Henry Clay cackled. "I'm buying, son. This time I'm buying."

"Right," said David. "You're buying."

"Ain't you drinking? Ain't that the same drink you set down with?"

"Sure I'm drinking. You just haven't been noticing, that's all. Doesn't take long to drink a straight one."

Behind them a fight broke out; a woman screamed shrilly. Slats ran around the end of the bar, and a jet-black man built like a fat inverted triangle, all shoulders and belly and no hips, appeared suddenly from the back. There was scuffling followed by loud hoarse obscenity and then comparative quiet, and Slats came back to his station. "Damn fools," he said. "Goddamned fools. Get in jail times like these, God know what'll happen to you."

David picked up his glass and took the drink in one searing swallow, backing it up with cold, clear ice water.

"Any of you fellows around when Li'l Joe took sick?" He asked the question casually.

"Placide was," said the man with the gray eyes. "Placide was right around the corner. Came a-runnin'."

"Too late to help any," said Placide. David had to strain to catch the words through the thick accent. "Ambrose had him when I got there."

"Somebody told me those two ofay bastards who roughed him up hang around the Bourbon Street joints." He was lying, trying to do it without emphasis, twirling his empty shot glass between his fingers.

"Wouldn't know about that." Henry Clay was equally casual, wiping foam from his lips with a thin, thick-veined hand. "Don't get around much."

The gray-eyed man with the light skin did not speak. David felt Placide gathering himself together to leave, pushing his glass to the back of the bar, taking his foot from the rail to push back his stool, picking up a half-smoked cigar from the ashtray. David tried not to sound urgent.

"They tell me one of 'em had a scar, bad scar, right across his forehead." (You're lying, Champlin, and leading the witness besides. Objection overruled!) "You notice the scar, Placide? Almost knocked you down, didn't they, running away?"

"Couldn't tell," Placide said. "Too dark." He was standing, relighting his cigar, then turning to edge his way between his stool and Clay's.

David spoke quickly, in Creole he thought he had forgotten: "The tongue has no bones, eh, old man?"

Placide turned and looked down at the younger man. He spoke in French. "Go home," he said. "Joseph Champlin is gone and at peace. Leave him at peace. Go home and get your rest. The scales are God's. Joseph Champlin was my friend." He laid a hand on David's shoulder. "Because of that you are my friend, too, and young."

David watched him leaving, a short, old man with heavy shoulders and white hair who had once been powerful and strong, was still powerful and strong enough to give a good day's work for a day's pay. He was lost for a moment in a group at the periphery of the crowd; then he was standing at the door. He turned and looked back at David, and David thought that with a toga and that head, that dignity, he could be a Roman senator. The old man smiled, and over the noise in the room David heard him call, "Au 'voir!"

O Lord! thought David. Lord, Lord, let thy people go! He stood, looked into the faces of the two men at his right, and saw nothing to give him comfort. The gray-eyed man said, "Better let it alone, son."

Henry Clay laughed his high, cackling laugh again, and this time it rasped along David's nerves like a fingernail on slate. "That's right, David. He's telling you right. Don't do no good. We got all the trouble we needs *all* the time; now we got more."

Only the voice of Luke, from where he stood beside him, saying under his breath, "I hope to Christ you find 'em, Champlin; I hope to Jesus Christ you find 'em," seemed the voice of a friend.

The words of the boy Luke were an echo in his ears as he walked, slowly now, toward Ambrose's taxi stand, an echo that sounded back and forth in the caverns of his mind as the echo of the laughter of a boy and girl had sounded back and forth across a lake years before. Echo. Hadn't Echo been a nymph who pined away for somebody until nothing was left but her voice? That was all that was left of his quest, the echo of the bitter voice of a friendly youth, wishing him well, wishing him success. He knew now that it was hopeless. Even his own people, those who had known and loved Joseph Champlin and had cause to hate that which had destroyed him, were lined against him; their fear was the wall from which the sound of Luke's voice rebounded, hollow and hopeless. Only Rudy might have been able to make that bitter "I hope to Jesus Christ you find them" come true, and Rudy, too, was hidden from him, buried beneath the fear and apathy of the silent ones.

He was too tired to take a bus and then walk from the bus stop. Ambrose's night relief was there, in the cubbyhole office, a surly, ill-spoken man whose surliness David welcomed because it meant he would not be expected to talk. He leaned back in the cab, elbow on the armrest, his hand covering eyes that were tired and smarting from too much smoke in too many bars. Tomorrow—God, don't let me think. Just for a few minutes, God, don't let me think—

He paid the driver before he got out of the cab, tipped him well, and was rewarded by something that could have been a smile, and the wheels of the car were turning before he got the door closed. When Ambrose drove, he always waited until he saw a fare enter the house after dark. "Can't never tell," he'd say. "Might be someone sneakin' around—" A car was parked just past the entrance to his yard, and he hoped wearily it wasn't company next door, and a loud party. When there was a sound on the porch, the sense of movement, a low voice, he froze, his hand still on the gate, heart pounding, his whole being mobilized for defense, wasting only the infinitely split second in which he thought that it was Gramp. God, he had realized within an hour after arriving in New Orleans, gives man no absolute acceptance of loss, of death—left for a while those poignant, infinitely split seconds when it wasn't true.

He heard his name, softly, "David—" from the porch, and moved forward warily.

"Who is it?" His voice was sharp with warning.

"It's me, man. Relax. It's Rudy, you dope—"

They met in midpath, and David's arm was around Rudy's shoulder as he unlocked the front door and they entered the house. "God damn, man, you have to scare a guy to death?"

"What else could I do? Sit on the steps and sing?"

"Man, am I glad to see you!"

"Been looking for me, I hear," said Rudy. The banter had gone from his voice, and it was slow and quiet.

David didn't answer, went to the kitchen, and Rudy followed, sitting at the old table in the center, low on his spine, hands in his pockets, watching David set out beer and glasses.

"My phone's been disconnected. I guess you found that out."

"Hell, I know."

"Hear you've been doing the bars, looking for me."

David sank into the chair opposite, heavily, like an old man, and Rudy said: "You're sure brought down, man. I'm sorry about Gramp. Guess I don't have to say it. I'd have been at the funeral but I got me a little job, first one in a long time—"

"They tell you why I was looking?"

"Yes." There was no elaboration. "They told me."

David waited. There was no sound in the room except the ticking of the clock on the shelf above the drainboard, then, sounding incongruously loud in the silence, the soft thud of four cat feet hitting the floor in David's room as Chop-bone came awake.

At last Rudy spoke. "Forget it."

"You know what you're saying?"

"I'm not saying anything that's not right. I'm saying it right. I'm not saying forget what happened. I sure as hell can't. I'm saying forget what you wanted me for."

"You saw it."

"Not all of it. Only the—well—"

"Only the end. Gramp dying—"

"Yes."

"You saw the guys who did it. Who frightened him to death."

"Only from the back. And the side for a minute. They were moving real fast, man."

"There was a knife."

"David, forget it."

"What about the knife?"

"It never came near Li'l Joe. One of the bastards threw it on the ground, I suppose to make it look as though Gramp had it. There's a few cops around would protect an old man, even if he was colored. They wanted to make it look as though Li'l Joe had pulled it on 'em, I guess. Hell! Not even the roughest French Quarter cop's going to believe Li'l Joe Champlin carried a switchblade."

Rudy reached deep into a trouser pocket, came up with something in his hand, and tossed it on the table in front of them where it showed stark against the scrubbed old boards. "There it is. There's a million like it in Louisiana. Or anywhere. Jesus, man. You're a lawyer. You got to know you can't trace a thing like that. Even with the police helping. And you know Goddamned well that isn't going to happen."

"I know that. It's why I was looking for you. But now—"

"Now you're getting a little sense in that skull?"

"You call it sense?"

"When it happened I didn't see anyone around but

Negroes. Supposing you'd found those two bastards, how many of those Negroes would rush up to the police station and tell about how they saw two white punks bullying a black man? You got any idea the kind of stuff been going on around here these last few days? You got any idea what's coming? The Citizens' Council's going to call for a mass march on the school board—I heard one of 'em say it was a 'total war.' And you think anyone's going to pay any attention to something like this? People likely to get dead around here next two, three days. How much help you think you're going to get, how many—even those that saw it—going to pop up and say what they saw? How many? Didn't you find out? Didn't you find out tonight?"

"I found out. Christ, yes, I found out."

"You know damned well you'll never find those two cats. And when you've cooled off you'll know you don't want to. But you'll find what licked you, baby; you'll find that. Fear. Scared shitless, everyone. Except some of the kids."

"I know. God, don't I know!" He got up and took two more bottles of beer from the refrigerator and handed one to Rudy. "There's two kinds of fear, Rudy. Ours—our people's—and theirs."

"You can talk sense when you feel like it. Jesus, man, I'm not a good man, like Gramp was. I'm just a fair-to-middlin' smart one. And I think when it says 'Thou shalt not kill' it's just good advice, and that's all. Because I'll be Goddamned if I'll go along that it's as bad to kill some of the ofay sons of bitches, like those guys, as it is to kill, well—"

"Gramp. And people like him."

"If it ever gets so we live in a reasonable world, if the time ever comes when killing one man's as bad as killing another, when a black corpse is as important as a white one, then—what the hell—there won't be any need running around looking for ofay bastards to kill quiet-like because they're going to think maybe three times before they go around making corpses out of Negroes."

David felt the sharp dig of claws as Chop-bone reached up, got a purchase on his thigh, then leaped to his lap, pressing against his chest, purring. "You think that'll ever come? A reasonable world?"

Rudy shrugged. Some trick of the overhead light made his skin seem darker and the freckles disappear, and the features and eyes were in that moment all Negro. "You ask me? You're the cat went away to college, studied law. Said the reason you went to Harvard, didn't you, was because it was the best in the country for constitutional law? You learn anything? Anything at all?"

David was silent for so long that Chop-bone had time to settle down comfortably and, drifting into sleep, let the purr in his throat die out. "Yes," he said. "I learned something. Learned a hell of a lot. A lot sometimes I wish I hadn't. Learned the Constitution doesn't mean a bloody thing as far as parts of the United States are concerned. And if it doesn't mean anything for part of it, it doesn't mean anything for any of it."

"Didn't learn it never will, did you?"

David hesitated. "No. I didn't learn that. I found out that things have got to be changed. Somehow. And I know, myself, without any law to tell me, that we've got the power to do it."

"How?"

"For God's sake, Rudy, some other time, huh? It would take all night. Laws, voting rights—" He looked at the knife that lay on the table, then over at Rudy. "Take the damned thing with you, Rudy. Get it out of my sight. I don't want it—"

Rudy reached forward, picked it up, and put it in his pocket. "I'll sell it. Know a guy who wants one—"

David's eyes had gone blank, looking inward; now he focused them on Rudy, frowning. "Sell it? You broke?"

"Down to penny one—"

"Jeez, I've been selfish, talking about myself, nothing else. What's with you?"

Rudy shrugged. "Sticking my neck out. Trying to be a pioneer. Or maybe a martyr. Me and Corrinne. We thought we'd try and register our oldest girl for school—integrated, that is. I went down and they told me to come back. That was on a morning. At two o'clock that afternoon—man, not more'n three hours later—I got fired."

"Jesus!"

"I found another job real quick. That same day. Rudy's got a good name as a mechanic. I figured I wouldn't even tell Corrinne I'd been fired; I'd let her think I made the move on my own. When I got home all the doors and windows were locked and she was inside, scared. I mean *scared*. Calls had started coming in by three in the afternoon. Half an hour after I got in, a rock came through the window. Missed the baby's crib by a foot. Next morning when I got to the new job—it was gone. Another guy had it. I guess the word had spread because by then I couldn't have gotten a job in all New Orleans. Even where I live, the garage wouldn't hire me. And it's all Negro, David. Negro-owned, Negro-managed. See what I mean? About fear?"

"Yes. Hell, yes."

"I looked all that day and the next, and that night when I got home Corrinne was packed. Everything. I got a nice little house, David. It's rented, but we've been saving to buy. There's a cement walk. Someone had covered it with dog crap they must have shoveled out of gutters and off lawns—God knows where. There were two more busted windows, and busted eggs all over the outside of the house. And the kids were cryin'-frightened. She took the money we'd been saving to buy—I gave it to her—to go to her sister's in California. She left the next morning. After that—they let the house alone." His laugh was not a pleasant one. "Wasn't any woman or any kids left to scare and I was out of a job—why the hell bother to bust any more windows or dirty up the place?"

David swore quietly and effectively, then said, "But look, fella, what're you going to do?"

"Christ knows. I kept enough money to eat on for a while. There wasn't enough dough to get us both back there. And just then I was fighting mad; I didn't want to go. Now? I think a lot of those kids, David. They're damned fine kids. And they sort of like their old man."

"Get out," said David. "Get out there with 'em. Get going, man. And money's what you ain't got, eh?"

"Yeah. Money's what I ain't got. I was figuring on selling the car and hitchhiking."

"No! You know something, Rudy? We've been hitchhiking for a couple of hundred years. I don't mean just on the roads. I mean all through our stinking lives. Hitchhike, balls! Take a train or a plane or a bus. Keep your car and drive. But don't hitchhike. Look, I haven't got a car here. Drive by tomorrow afternoon, latish. I'll have the dough—"

"No! Hell, no, David. You've got troubles too. Why should you—"

"Give me a reason, one reason why I shouldn't. You heard about the Prof?"

"Leaving you dough?"

"Yes. You know what would happen if I didn't give you a hand? A ha'nt, that's what would happen."

"I feel like I'm running away."

"Don't feel like that. Better your kids should have you. Too damned many kids without a father. Let 'em bust up your house. Don't let the sons of bitches bust up your life."

On his way to the gate with Rudy he said, "How'd you know for sure you'd find me here? That I'd get back?"

"David Champlin? Been knowing you a long time, man. We ran around together for a long time. Never saw li'l David when he didn't make it back home—"

He walked back into the kitchen, sat where he had been sitting before. Something of the pleasure he felt at being able to help Rudy lightened his mood, then passed, and the night of decision closed around him. He folded his arms on the table and laid his head on them, too tired now to sit upright and face what he knew he must: a future that could begin this day, could end God alone knew where—if he chose it. In the living room the telephone blared suddenly, and he did not stir except to raise his head and listen, his face tense with pain. "Tomorrow, baby," he whispered. "Tomorrow. For God's sake, stop now. I'll call tomorrow—I can't talk—I can't talk now—tomorrow I'll know—"

Eventually it stopped ringing.

The tension that was in the streets the next morning was like a sounding board for the uneven rhythm of his feet on the pavement. Clop-cloppity. He could smell the tension, almost touch it with his hands. The woman coming toward him, neatly, trimly dressed in starched work clothes, gray in the black of her hair: he knew her kind, she would say "Good morning" to a stranger—especially to a stranger—but this morning she did not speak. She was Gramp's kind of woman, Emma Jefferson's kind of woman, but today her eyes were on the pavement, and God alone knew where her thoughts were.

The offbeat rhythm of his own steps came to David's ears like the sound of another man walking. There was a woman standing on the stoop of a house just ahead, leaning on a broom and talking to a man on the sidewalk below her. She was a tall, spare woman, bright-skinned and with straight hair, but too dark to pass. The man was a red-bone Negro from the Cajun country.

The woman had a high-pitched, penetrating voice. "They'll be at it again," she said. The man, darker than she, older, said, "Sure will. Heered women're standing round now, waiting for that pore chile to get there."

David slowed his steps to pass the man, who was saying, "Heered there's a white family gonna send their kids there, put 'em in the school."

"Crazy," said the woman. "They're *sure* crazy."

"Trying mighty hard to learn what trouble is."

"They'll find out. What they doing to those women at the school? What's the law doing to 'em?"

"Shucks, I don't know. Spose they'll do like they done yestiddy. Run 'em off, pick 'em up. Saying right out loud they don't like it because they has to do it; don't like it having to protect a little chile."

Clop-cloppity. Clop-cloppity. They were behind him now, the half-white woman and the red-bone Negro. Two miles away a little child was hearing words she'd never heard before, was seeing red hate in the eyes of white women, white mothers. Even now, even as he walked along, the little girl might be mounting the steps of the schoolhouse, one small brown hand in the big white hand of a United States marshal, entering an echoing, empty building, where she would learn her lessons all alone.

What had her mother and father said to her before she left the house? "Don't cry, baby; whatever happens, baby, don't cry. You'll be crying all your life, you starts crying now." Something like that. How strong, how invincible must be the wall of love they had built around her.

He had heard talk last night that another little girl might enter the school this week. Two little girls in blue are we. . . .

Where are you now, Simmons? The days of the blues are over, eh, Simmons? Where are you now, Dunbar, blind, so damned blind and just as black as they are? Where are you now, Nehemiah? *Were you there when they crucified my Lord?* I'm here, Nehemiah. I'm here. *Were you there, Father? Were you? . . . Nehemiah, think! . . . You want me to think, Father? There's more harm done by just thinking than you knows of, Father.* Where are you now, Father McCartney, with your glib tongue and ready answers? Where? What was it you said, Nehemiah? *They crucify my Lord every day, in the streets, in the houses.* They're crucifying little children, Nehemiah, little girls in starched dresses, little girls in span-clean dresses, with little white gloves on chubby brown hands. Where are you, Nehemiah?

There in the warm kitchen the morning he came back to bury Gramp the voice of Emma Jefferson had been shaking with emotion: *Lady I work for says to me, "Oh, Emma, I hope the Negroes"—she don't ever say "nigra" and I never heered no one in that house say "nigger"—"I hope the Negroes know we aren't all like those dreadful people. That poor child. I hope the Negroes know there are lots of us want to see right done. It can't come overnight.* Two hundred years isn't overnight; two hundred years is a long time, hanging on a cross. *What I wants to know is what's she doing about it? What's her and all her lily-white friends doing about it? Moaning and groaning and carrying on about how dreadful it is.* Where are you now, white-lady-that-Emma-works for? *They talks about it all the time. Seems like they can't talk about nothing else, talking on the telephone, back and forth, saying it's so dreadful, saying how bad they making it out to be, worse than it is, in the papers up north and on the television, knowing all the time them pictures ain't lying.*

Where are you, friends-of-the-white-lady-Emma-works-for? Sitting at telephones, listening to the radio, watching television, talking, talking . . .

Clop-cloppity; clop-cloppity. Now he was facing the door of the building he sought. On the front of the door a square area lighter than the surrounding wood showed where there had been a sign. No need to wonder why it had been removed. When he opened the door the stairs that faced him were worn, uncarpeted. Voices above him were blurred by closed doors, and even in the small lower entry he could smell the smoke of cigars and cigarettes.

Can I go see the cartoon, Gramp? Can I, Gramp? Can I go see Popeye? . . . Reckon so, son. Reckon Gramp can get you up them steps. . . . I'll help you up them steps. . . . Don't act foolish, son; let Gramp help you. . . . You gonna hurt yourself, you don't let Li'l Joe help you. A big black man, his arms as hard and strong as oak boughs, had come along that day and picked him up and laughed as he carried him up the long stairway, Li'l Joe behind them. He could hear his own voice crowing with delighted laughter, see the whiteness of the cast on his leg, stiff and straight across the black man's arm. He could not remember why he was laughing that day, what the man had said that had made him laugh so loudly. The man had set him in a seat beside Gramp, way up high in the balcony, so high the figures on the screen were hard to see, and then the man had gone away, still laughing, and they had never seen him again.

I don't want to go back, Gramp. I can explain it to the Prof. He'll understand. There's other colleges, good ones, Howard, Dillard. . . . Whatever you say, son. You a man now. Many's the time, though, I've said: "Lord, I can't do it. I can't get down to them docks today. Lord, I'm a sick man." But I got there, and I could somehow. Man can do what he's got to do. Something helps him somehow.

He was walking up the stairs now, first the good foot, then the other following after. *I don't want Sudsy and Rhoda to meet us, David. I just want it to be us, David and Sara, coming into London town together. . . . You'll be there, David? Early, early . . . ? God bless.*

(Sara. Dear almighty God, Sara! Little love, smallest love. Wait for me, Sara. Wait for me, baby. Sara, little love. I'll be over for a day—an hour—just to see you. I'll make you understand. Sara, baby, love me.)

No one turned when he opened the door that bore on its ancient paneling the words "American League for Equal Citizenship." A girl whose creamy skin seemed lighter than it was because of the sleek, gleaming blackness of her hair sat at a desk facing the door behind a low railing that enclosed the central portion of the room. Even so early in the morning she looked harassed, tired, and there were purplish shadows under her eyes. She was speaking into a telephone, saying, "Keep trying, Operator; keep trying, please."

A blue-gray haze of smoke hung over the room, and every visible ashtray was filled to overflowing. The girl at the desk turned in her swivel chair and reached tiredly for the ashtray on an old oak desk behind her, emptied it into a wasebasket, and replaced it on the desk just in time to catch the stub of Isaiah Watkins's chewed cigar. Isaiah was half sitting, half standing, one massive haunch on the edge of the desk, talking to a tall, dark young Negro wearing black-rimmed glasses and a Brooks Brothers suit. A white man was standing off to one side, talking to another Negro, and although his words were indistinguishable David recognized the accents of New York. There was a window in the far wall, opposite the door, and silhouetted against its cloudy pane was the tall, spare figure of Brad Willis, talking to a man perched on its sill.

The girl at the desk noticed David at last and said, "Who did you want to see?" He shook his head. "I'll wait," he said. He walked to a window in the side wall at his right, and turned quickly at the sound of a familiar voice speaking his name.

"Chuck."

"Glad to see you, dad. Mighty glad. You had me worried plenty. Thought you were leaving—" Chuck looked at David's face, and the words trailed off.

David said, "Remember the church basement in Laurel?"

Chuck nodded. "Sure."

"And the meetings? And Father McCartney?"

"Sure. I hear he's still there."

"Remember Nehemiah?"

"Not likely to forget him."

David looked around the room, then back at Chuck. " 'Were you there?' " he said. "That's all I could think of on the way up here. 'Were you there?' "

"I know," said Chuck. "It's a question I can answer after this week. I can say, 'Yes.' "

David turned from him abruptly and looked out the window, not seeing the people passing on the sidewalk below, seeing only the small yard of a shabby house opposite, and two fat brown children tumbling on its earth, looking like the Timmins twins of years ago. The voices behind him seemed softened by the thick haze of smoke, as the face of an aging actress is softened by chiffon veiling. A white-haired, dark-skinned man had stopped at the gate, and the two babies were standing on fat brown legs, solemn round eyes fixed on the old man's face. *One thing makes me want to fight, just one thing now I'm old and come to my senses, and that's seeing somebody hurt a young un or an old person. . . .*

Now, below him, the children had forgotten their shyness, and the white-haired man was carrying them, a child in one arm, and one on his shoulder. He was laughing, and the fat fist of the child on his shoulder was tight in the curly white hair. They must have known him, thought David; must have known he had strong arms and shoulders and that he loved them, because they were laughing with him as he walked up the steps of the house and knocked at the door and then disappeared within it.

You don't need me to help you get down them steps, son. Just hang on and don't overbalance yourself. . . . Will you still love me, David, in that hellhole I can't go to with you? . . . You have to go to him now, this last time, when he needs you.

. . . And I like to think . . . that when our brother spoke

the name of his beloved grandson he spoke not for himself alone but in . . . the name of all his people. . . . "Thou shalt not be afraid for the terror by night . . ."

"This last time." There would never be a last time. Now he knew. Gramp, quiet in his grave, his heart stilled by fear, would need him always. Gramp had said, "Need—needs David—" Every dark-skinned man and woman, every Luke with crippled spirit, every small brown child, and every aging man and woman wherever they might be—on the streets of the southern cities, on the country roads, in the fields, and far into the bayou country and the swamps—each, each of them was Li'l Joe Champlin's need. Theirs were the feet in the muck, theirs the nostrils sickened by the stench, of putrefying white minds, the smell of hate. There in the spiritual filth and corruption of bigotry and oppression was the need of Li'l Joe Champlin, not across the water, not in far places.

Someone was calling to him, and he sensed the call had been repeated. He turned from the window and saw Isaiah walking toward him. As he limped to the railing he noticed that Brad had joined Chuck, and he heard their voices, low and serious.

He swung himself over the railing, took the big black hand Isaiah held out.

"David Champlin! Sure glad to see you. Sorry we kept you waiting. Whyn't you sing out you was here?"

"You were busy," said David. He could tell the other man's mind was on a hundred different things, that he was glad David had come, yet wished he hadn't; that with so many things pressing him there was no time, no heart, for the amenities.

"Thought you were long gone," Isaiah was saying. "Thought you was on a plane by now. Been so damned busy around here. Lawd!"

"I know," said David. "That's why I'm here. Heard you say a few weeks ago, didn't I, that you could use an extra hand?"

(Sara. Sara, baby. Smallest. Little love. Understand. For God's sweet sake, understand. Love me. Oh, my little love—)

Pharaoh's army got drownded—

Like hell it did. Like hell it did, Gramp; like hell it did, little girl on the schoolhouse steps. You can see its banners flying, hear its warriors shouting—everywhere. Like hell, like bloody hell it got drownded.

61

FOUR PEOPLE STOOD TALKING at one end of the big lounge in London's Crown Hotel in Russell Square—Hunter Travis, Dr. Clifton Sutherland and his wife, Rhoda, and a London doctor. Rhoda was saying: "It was good of you to come so quickly, Dr. Dutton. It wasn't actually an emergency."

"Not at all, Mrs. Sutherland. I'm delighted to help any friends of the Travises." The doctor turned to Suds. "There's precious little to be done, as you know, Dr. Sutherland. She must have sleep, of course, and certainly a little nourishment wouldn't do any harm either. The tonic I've prescribed ought to help that stomach. It's an old-fashioned mixture, but very effective."

"My wife and I have to return to the States very soon. We're glad she's in good hands."

"She's an extraordinarily healthy young woman. She'll land on her feet. It's difficult for any male, even a doctor, to put himself in the shoes of a young woman whose marriage has been called off abruptly and unexpectedly. I'll keep an eye on her for a while if she'll let me." He smiled at Hunter. "Your prescription was the best one, Hunter. Your mother. If you can persuade Miss Kent to stay with your family for a while, it would be splendid."

"The family will be back tonight," said Hunter. "I'll do my best."

"Excellent. There's a chemist at the corner. Run up and get these prescriptions filled like a good chap. She's to have the liquid before eating, two of the sleeping capsules tonight, then one a night for a while. You can explain to your mother. Miss Kent doesn't impress me as one who would remember to take medicine. And do try and get some tea and toast into her if nothing else—"

In the chemist's, Hunter fidgeted nervously, roaming the aisles, fingering bottles of mouthwash, boxes of facial tissue, finally buying two of the latter. Sooner or later Sara had to cry. Damn, she had to or she'd crack up completely. Maybe the sleeping tablets would do it, make her let go. He felt bruised and stunned. Emotional involvements were something he'd shied away from since boyhood. Now he was learning that the emotions, unused, could be like unused muscles—hurting like hell when exercising them could no longer be avoided.

Two items—capsules and a bottle of liquid. That was one thing he like about England. Medicine still came in liquid form. And most of it nasty. Gave a man a feeling of having his feet on the ground.

He hurried across the hotel lounge, said to Suds and Rhoda, "I'll bring these up to her—and make her take them."

Suds started to rise, and Hunter said: "Stay here, Suds. I think it would be better if I went alone."

The upstairs corridor looked ten miles long. He wished it were a hundred. Sara's door would be in front of him all too soon. He knocked, then opened it without waiting for a response.

Apparently she hadn't moved since they had gone downstairs with Dr. Dutton half an hour before. She sat like a statue in one of the big room's two armchairs. Like a statue, like a model posing for a painting, like a doll—like a dead woman, except for her eyes. He walked over to her, put a hand over one of her small ones that lay on the arm of the chair.

"Sara, luv—it's Dr. Travis."

"I know, Hunter." She moved now, stood up. "Sit here. It's the most comfortable." She walked to the bed with a curious stiffness, only her legs seeming to be in motion, then sat on the edge of it, straight and still again. She wore a downy cloud-blue robe, and the soft ruching of a blue nightgown showed at her throat.

He unwrapped the package, making a big thing of it, harrumphing and grunting like a cranky doctor, measuring out a teaspoon of the liquid into a glass, adding water, and putting it on the bedside table. "Drink hearty, me girl. It's good for those collywobbles." He picked up the telephone and ordered tea and toast.

"I don't want—"

"Quiet woman! Make that for two, please. Thank you."

"Sometimes you're so British, Hunter." Her voice had no inflection whatever; it was like soft fabric that had been gone over with a hot iron, all its softness made smooth and stiff and starchy. He wondered if she could hear it. If she could hear anything at all, even what he was saying, for the words that must have seared into her brain yesterday when David had called. "You're so British sometimes, and other times you're not." She laughed softly, and Hunter felt goose pimples start out on his flesh. "Tea." The laugh was a little louder now, and the goose pimples increased. "Tea. Oh, my God, Hunter, tea! God—God—God! Tea! Sudsy. Rhoda. That damned doctor. A nice cup of tea. That'll do it, old girl. A nice cup of tea and it all never happened."

He went closer, gripped her shoulders, shook her, not gently. "Stop it, Sara. It happened."

Suddenly her body went limp under his hands and she fell forward, her face against the rough tweed of his coat, her head heavy against him. "I know. I know." And still when she drew back and looked up at him her eyes were dry. "Why, Hunter? Why did it happen?"

He smiled down at her. "You want me to do what you ought to do? Break down and cry? I bloody well could, you know."

"Yes," she whispered. "Yes, I believe you could. You big phony."

He let go of her shoulders, frowning. "Drink that medicine, Sara Kent. It's horrid, judging by the smell. Do you good. Bound to."

He handed her the glass, and she held it in both hands, like a child, and drank it at last, wincing at the taste, then smiling for the first time. "Big bully, too."

Tea came and was set out on the table in front of the window, and when the door had closed behind the maid, Sara said, "Where are Suds and Rhoda?"

"Downstairs in the lounge."

"Thanks for keeping them there."

"Come over here and sit down, Sara. Drink this liquid in this pot. I won't name it, seeing as how it upsets you."

"Tea?" She walked to the table, still with that stiff, legs-only motion, and sat opposite him.

He poured her tea, adding cream and sugar, and she held the cup as she had the glass, in both hands, but did not drink until he said, "Sara, I'll count to five, then hold your nose and pour—"

"Big bully." But she took a swallow, then another. "All right, Hunter?"

"All right, infant. Only finish it. There's a lovely picture of Donald Duck on the bottom of the cup."

"Donald Duck's old hat. He was 'in' when I was a child. Was I ever, Hunter? I feel old. God, I feel old. A million years old."

He said nothing, uncovered the toast and handed her a piece, buttery and still warm. "Eat it."

"No—all right." She nibbled, then took a larger bite. "What was in that hell brew? I—it tastes good. The toast, I mean."

"Inasmuch as it's the first thing you've consented to bite into for twenty-four hours, and inasmuch as you upchucked half the night, I wouldn't give the medicine too much credit."

She did not speak again until she had drunk another cup of tea and eaten another piece of toast. Then she stood and walked to the window, looking down into the road below. She did not look at him when she said "Hunter, make Sudsy stop hating David."

"Sara! He doesn't—"

"Yes. Yes, he does. You know it. Yesterday—last night—he'd—I think he'd have strangled him if—if—"

"Suds is fond of you. We all are. It hurts him to see you hurt. Just as it does me and Rhoda. He's angry, yes. He'll get over it."

"No, he won't. I can tell. But he mustn't hate David. Because David's good. I don't know, Hunter. I don't know yet what—what happened. But I know David's goodness. No matter what things seem like. Sudsy mustn't hate him—" Her voice was shaking, and Hunter went over to her and took her arm.

"Sara, get over here and get into bed. Right now."

She let him lead her to the bed, and crawled into it.

"Here are two pills. Open wide—"

"No." She shook her head, and he knew he could not move her.

"Why not, luv?"

"Not until I know what happened. Hunter—all I heard—all I could hear was David saying he wouldn't—Hunter, he sounded as though he was crying—I never heard him like that—never, never—and then—then he hung up."

"You've been over it a thousand times, haven't you, pet?"

"A thousand thousand—"

"Did you think I wouldn't try and find out? I was on the phone half the night. I couldn't raise anyone, anywhere, couldn't get any word except that Brad Willis had left for

Boston." He looked at his watch. "I'm going to call again. Try him there. I'll call from downstairs, Sara. Not here."

"All right, that's all right. Just—for God's sake, find out. Please."

"Don't say 'please.' You know I will. And when I do, will you take your pills?"

"Yes." Her breath caught, and she sighed like a child whose fatigue has been unadmitted until then. "Yes. I'm tired now. But I can't sleep, Hunter, I can't—and then wake up still not knowing—"

"Tomorrow we want you to go to my family's house. For as long as you can—a week—a month—any time at all."

"Your mother wants me?"

"She'll be back tonight. You know she does."

"She's a love. Will she give me tea?"

"Pots and pots of it, I'm afraid."

"Bless her. But—I'm—I'm better alone—"

"I'll fetch you in the morning and now I'm going downstairs and call."

He left her sitting up in bed, her head on her knees, rocking gently back and forth like a mechanical doll, and still she had not wept.

When he went downstairs Suds and Rhoda were gone, and the lounge waiter told him they had left word that they would return by six o'clock. An hour later he was back at Sara's door. She had gotten up while he was gone and was sitting again in the big chair. He had the feeling that, if he had not come back, she would have sat there forever. This time he did not have to go to her, touch her, to bring her back to reality. She was running toward him. "Did you find out? Did you? Did you talk to him?"

He led her to the bed, forcing her to sit on its edge, holding both her hands tightly clasped in one of his. "Yes, I found out. I didn't talk to David, and I couldn't reach Brad in Boston. Only Peg. She sent her love, Sara."

"Go on—go on—"

"I reached Chuck Martin. He's in New Orleans, and he's been with David most of the time. David isn't there right now. Chuck told me—"

She did not speak while he told her the story until he described Gramp's death; then she swayed, whispered, "Oh, no! Please God, no. Not Gramp. Not Gramp—"

"Yes, Sara. Gramp. Li'l Joe Champlin, who never knowingly hurt a living soul." It was shock therapy, and he knew it was good because he could see life begin to return to her face. At last he said, "That's all I know. I think it's all there is to know."

She drew her hands away from his, covering her face with them, and Hunter was glad, because he hadn't thought it possible for eyes to hold more pain than Sara's had held. Her voice was muffled when she said, "Thank you, Hunter. You're so damned good and"—she dropped her hands to her lap and smiled shakily—"it upsets you like hell to hear it—"

"We are what we are, Sara." He smiled at her, tried to pull, as though by main force, another smile from her. "We do what we have to do, what we want to do. Will you take your pills now? I'll break your neck if you don't. You promised."

"Did I? All right. All right, Hunter. Whatever you say."

"And my mother's house tomorrow?"

"Let me think about—all right. Your mother's house tomorrow. I know now, I know about it now. You see, every once in a while I'd think it wasn't true. I'd think that if I could sit very still and not acknowledge it, I'd find out it wasn't true. But I know now. It is."

He handed her the pills and a glass of water and watched her as she swallowed them.

"One more thing—"

"Is it bad, Hunter? I can't take—"

"No. It's a message from Chuck to you. I'll give it verbatim; that's my kind of memory. He said: 'Tell Sara from me and from Brad that we're thinking of her. Me, I'm praying. And tell her for God's sake'—he wasn't being profane, Sara—'for God's sake to try and understand. And not to be angry. Above all, not to be angry. David is going through hell.' " When Sara did not speak, Hunter went on. " 'Ask her'—this is still Chuck talking, Sara—'ask her if she ever heard of Gethsemane—' "

She closed her eyes. "Yes. Yes, of course I have. It was—a garden—"

He stood up, threw back the covers of the bed, and made her lie down on the stacked pillows, covering her as he would a child. "Try to sleep, Sara. More water?"

"No, thanks. I'll—I'll sleep now. Hunter—Gramp! He had his passport and—and—"

"Want me to sit over here and read for a while, until you get to sleep?"

She had turned on her side and lay now with knees drawn

up, a very small mound under the blankets. One fist was pressed against her lips, and her words were difficult to hear: "No. Because I'm going to cry. Oh, God, Hunter, I'm going to cry—and I want to cry alone—"

"All right, Sara. I'll be downstairs. I'll see you're left alone, luv—"

In the lounge he ordered a double whiskey, drank it straight without putting the glass down, then swallowed water. He hadn't done that since they'd pulled him out of the wreck of his car on the Dover Road two years before. He leaned back, feeling as though he'd been running twenty miles with a full pack. This sort of thing, he thought, was supposed to be grist for a writer's mill. It damned well wasn't grist for his. His characters had better sense than to love the way Sara and David loved. Up to now he'd thought he'd made his characters too civilized. Now he wasn't sure. No woman, hurt as Sara had been hurt, had any business saying, "Don't let Suds hate David. . . ." Good God, she ought to be hating him herself! That would be normal. Saying "I know David's goodness—no matter what things seem like" wasn't.

Rhoda's voice roused him from an exhausted doze. "You seem to have another patient, Cliff."

Hunter straightened up, blinking.

Suds signaled to the waiter, ordered two whiskeys, and a coffee for Rhoda who asked sharply, "What about Sara?"

"What do you mean? She took her medicine like a good child. She must be sound asleep by now."

"Good," said Suds. "Well done, Hunter."

"Sit down, Rhoda, and I'll tell you both what I found out. I finally got the real gen from Chuck in New Orleans."

"Not yet. Did you leave her up there all alone? Where are the sleeping capsules?"

Hunter's eyes, usually cool and seldom wide, were wide now with astonishment. "Rhoda, you can't be serious! Do you honestly think she'd do what's called 'something drastic'? You're way off base."

"I don't care what you think, Hunter. You shouldn't have left her there alone. I'm going up—"

He jumped to his feet, took her arm. "Let her alone, Rhoda. I promised her we'd leave her alone."

"It was a very stupid thing to do. I'm going up—"

Hunter turned to Suds. "Don't let her."

Suds, unsmiling round face set and cold, said wearily:

"Don't wake her, Rhoda. She'll be dead asleep after two of those. Get the maid on the floor or the housekeeper to let you in and take the pills out if it will make you feel better." He looked at Hunter. "It could be a good idea."

Hunter shrugged. "All right. Only don't wake her. The pills are on the shelf in the bathroom. It never occurred to me, and I still think it's damned silly."

He watched Rhoda leave, and when she had walked through the archway into the lobby he said to Suds, "I have a message from Sara. For you."

"Yes?" This cold, detached man was a Suds that Hunter had never known.

"I am to tell you not to hate David. I'd like to put in my bit also. Don't."

" 'Hate' is a strong word. I'm sorry—but my understanding isn't all that elastic. I'd hardly call it 'hate' that I feel, though. Disgust, perhaps."

"Suds—listen—"

"Nothing justifies it, Hunter. You've seen Sara and been with her. Do you think anything in God's world can make it less than appalling to hurt a Sara Kent like that? What he has done is indefensible."

"It's easy to be angry, to hate someone you—"

"I told you 'hate' is a strong word."

"It's a murderous one in some places I could name. It was for Li'l Joe Champlin. Damn it, listen while I tell you what I learned—"

Rhoda rejoined them before he finished, and when the story had been told, he said: "Can't you see now, Suds? Understand? They killed more than just an old man. They killed what has made David tick. Good God, man, would you expect him to brush it off? Pick up his life and go on as if nothing had happened? What in hell did they teach you about shock?"

"Sara has already shown us all what shock can do. Even if it's only temporary, it's been unnecessary. One thing they taught me—avoid causing the patient unnecessary pain."

Hunter stood tiredly. "All right, Suds. Have it your own way. I hope to God that David never finds out how you feel. That would really do it for the poor devil."

"I'm afraid he will if I ever see him or talk to him."

"For God's sake, Suds, show a little compassion."

Suds ran a hand over his face, shivered. "I've used it all

up, Hunter. As Chuck would say, 'I've run plumb out.' I'm wrung dry."

Both Suds and Rhoda were standing now. Rhoda said: "I'm afraid I feel pretty much the same way Clifton does, Hunter. We're going up to our room and freshen up and then have dinner here. Join us?"

"No. Thank you, Rhoda. I'm going back to my flat and take a shower. It just might happen that I'll get drunk."

Before they started for the lobby, Rhoda asked, "Hunter, what made you so positive Sara wouldn't do—well, something rash?"

He looked down at her, then over to Suds. "Because Sara hasn't given up. Sara won't give up. Not on David. She asked me to say something else to you. That David is good, no matter how things may look. So—I've told you. And she won't give up. That's why I wasn't in the least worried. Shocked, grieved—yes. Defeated? Not our Sara." He turned and walked away from them, toward a door to a flanking side corridor, and said over his shoulder, "See you tomorrow—"

62

THE ONE INCONGRUOUS NOTE in Joseph Klein's otherwise modern offices in Boston was an old-fashioned desk lamp with a green glass shade that had belonged to his father. Its light was far more effective in warming the chill grayness of a late winter day than fluorescence would have been. When Mrs. Hubbard, shortly before her death, had insisted that she was going to donate new lighting to the office of ALEC's executive secretary, Klein said, "Nothing doing. It kept me honest in law, it's keeping me in touch with my ancestors now."

When David Champlin and Brad Willis came into the office late in the afternoon nine days after David's last meeting with Rudy Lopez, a last feeble glow of winter sunlight was touching the western window. When it was gone Klein lighted the green-shaded lamp and leaned back in his chair. "Before you two head back south you'll need more detailed briefing than we've been able to manage this afternoon." He opened a lower drawer in his desk and took out a bulging cardboard box. "This is the manuscript of the book by Gardner Pennoyer, the New York *Times* man, that I mentioned to you. He left it with me for corrections—dates, right names, that sort of thing. It needed damned little. It's a study of the South for the past decade with enough of the century to explain the decade. I'm sure Pennoyer would be glad to have you read it, especially if you'll use the information in the way he hopes it will be used. Just don't take it out of the office."

Brad said, "If we could brief it—"

David was leafing through the typed pages. "Give me some legal pads, a bottle of fountain-pen ink, and a Thermos of coffee and I'll get to it."

"Do it tomorrow," said Willis. "You're bushed. You're due home with me for dinner and the night." For three days he had been struggling to keep concern and paternalism out of his voice and attitude. David was a tired man; a man living with mental pain and suffering as he had lived with lameness, quietly; a man withdrawn from his fellow humans, remote, whipping his mind into frenzied activity, communicating with his mind only. Peg had said, "He gives me the creeps, Brad. I love him dearly, but he can't be touched—reached—at all."

"I know," answered Brad. "I've been with him for a week and I'm exhausted. Mind kissing me real hard, hon, so I can get back to reality?"

Now David said, "I'll do it tonight, Brad." Everything he said these days, thought Brad, was said with the same tone of finality. There was no "give" to him.

"You can't brief it all tonight, David," said Klein. "My God—"

"If I can't then I'll work on it tomorrow if you'll fix up a corner for me here. Now, let's get down to business—"

Hours after the night sounds of Boston's downtown streets had died away to silence, David sat at the desk in Klein's office, the green-shaded lamp throwing its circle of light over the manuscript before him and the yellow legal pad on which he was writing rapidly. Once he said aloud in the emptiness, "Thank *you,* Gardner Pennoyer. You deserve an easier name —" There could be no deadlier weapon, he thought, than fact welded to principle, and Pennoyer used that weapon with lethal accuracy. He stripped from the South—its moderates, its liberals, and its segregationists—every vestige of rationalization, held the segregationists' myth of Reconstruction's total blameworthiness up to the light of objectivity and fact. The "moderate" he left naked, blue and shivering, stripped by the cold winds of truth and analytical thinking. The "liberal" under Pennoyer's searching pen reminded one inevitably of the story of the Pharisee and the publican, and the Pharisee's loud-spoken gratitude to God that he was not as other men, while the publican stood quietly by with downcast eyes and said, "God, be merciful to me a sinner." If there was any lesson to be drawn from the book, David thought, it was that the country had need of those who could say, "Be merciful to me a sinner."

A century of death and terror walked through those pages of facts and figures, although they dealt specifically with but ten years of that century. The death and terror were made more horrible by the writer's calm acceptance of them; nor were the aberrations of death's human instruments treated with other than a calm acceptance of their being, because nothing else was possible.

David damned his hand for its slowness in writing, yet it was racing across the yellow pages. He felt ashamed that he must lean for his background on the work of a white man, realizing at last how far he had removed himself from the life of his people, how close he had come to removing himself from it entirely.

The Thermos had been empty for two hours when he laid down his pen, snapped his hand sharply at the wrist to start circulation in cramped fingers, and looked at his watch. Four o'clock. His mind was flagging now, tired and more liable to make mistakes, and he leaned back, rubbing his eyes with the heels of his palms.

He had been lost in his own country for nine hours, and he could not immediately bring himself back from that country, its cities and bayous and swamps, it red dust and redder clay, the stunted scrub oaks, the blue gum and cypress, the gray-green moss-fingers, the arid, lifeless stretches of its western reaches, the green, miasmic moistness of its most southern points . . . the rattlesnake coiled in cool dust beneath a rock on a Texas prairie, the 'gator sleeping by a riverbank. A black man from the South did not have to have walked each of its country roads and city streets; they were with him always. He could hear the cadence of black voices in the bar of a Birmingham slum, a Mississippi field, a South Carolina farm home, as clearly as he could hear its deep rhythms on the banquettes of the French Quarter.

Black boy, black boy, what do you hear? He thought someone had spoken the words, knew they had not, searched his mind for their origin, found it suddenly. A little boy on his grandmother's lap, crying over a mashed finger. He never knew whether it was a nursery rhyme or whether Gram had made it up.

She used to half-sing it: *Black boy, black boy, what do you hear?—I hear a little rabbit an' it's comin' mighty near. Black boy, black boy, what do you see?—I see a purple flower and a yellow bumblebee.* He would repeat it after her, mixing it up so that he could hear her laughter, feel it deep in her chest where his head rested: " 'I see a *yellow* flower and a *purple* bumblebee'—a *purple* bumblebee, Gram, a *purple* bumblebee—" and then they would be laughing, he and Gram—mashed finger, tears, forgotten in a purple bumblebee.

Black boy, black boy, what do you hear, all these years later? My own voice, that's what I hear, no better, no worse than the others, the voices of Birmingham and Mississippi and South Carolina and New Orleans. It had been a black voice in an Oxford pub, a Marblehead inn, a Pengard classroom, a Boston courtroom, and his own ears had been deaf to it. Now it would be a black voice among other black voices, sounding, please God, strong when strength was needed.

The eerie predawn quiet of the room, the relaxation after concentration, the lack of sleep—he knew they had combined to make him fanciful. A mind that should have been filled with neatly docketed dates and facts instead was peopled with monsters in khaki uniforms, and with dark-skinned men and women whose arms and hands, once outstretched and pleading, now were high above their heads, fists clenched—the men and women who had been dim singing presences along a riverbank in a little boy's dream—now turned from that river and running forward, their voices a deep roaring, like the rushing winds of a hurricane.

He tried to bring himself back to reality, reestablish himself in a dim and empty office above a sleeping Boston street. And found that he could not, because beyond the glow of the lamp on the desk there were still other people, silent ones, quiet, without voices, standing in the dimness, people whose eyes caught a fugitive ray from the light in a quick gleaming, whose teeth showed white in shadowed faces. Some had names, some were nameless; but he knew them all. Mack Charles Parker, Emmett Till, Thomas Foster, in his country's uniform, Joseph Champlin and his father, David—the known and the unknown, blood of his blood, mind of his mind, begotten, born, living, suffering, in a world that denied them humanity and in the end denied them life itself. Black boy, black boy, what do you see? Death.

He got to his feet abruptly. He'd managed to stay this side of the bend so far; he wasn't going around it now if he could help it. The hotel where he and Brad had breakfasted a long time ago, where he often stayed, was only two blocks away. He'd go there and get some sleep. It was too late to go clear out to Brad's and risk disturbing them. Once in bed the devils of the past would give way and the devils of the present would pluck at his eyeballs, different devils, the devils of sorrow and loneliness and the realization of what he had done and its immediate consequences, the devils of memories of Sara, and of Sudsy's voice on the telephone from London. *She's not at the Crown now. . . . I have no intention of telling you where she is. . . . I'm speaking, in a sense, as her medical adviser. . . . If she wants to, she'll get in touch with you. I hope to God she has better sense. . . .* Suds! Christ, not Suds, turning like that! Then Hunter, quiet, controlled. *You're spending too much dough on telephoning, dad. . . . Suds? . . . Yes, I know. I've tried to talk to him. . . . I think he'll snap out of it. . . . She's all right, David, but I agree with Suds. It would be better—for her, that is—if you didn't call her. . . . I know what you want to tell her. Hell, I already have. . . . She's all right. Couldn't be in better hands. You have my word for it. . . . Don't make it any rougher on her than it is by talking to her.*

These would be the ghosts that would crowd the room where he'd sleep tonight. They were with him now as his steps sounded unevenly in the cold darkness of Boylston Street. Would those others, the ghosts of the black men and women long dead, newly dead, the pain of their dying in their spectral eyes, be lying in wait for him in Klein's office tomorrow? They would lie in wait for him wherever he was.

Brad and David arrived at the ALEC office late the following morning. Klein was ready for them, desk cleared. "Give me as clear an idea as you can at this point what your plans are and your itineraries."

"I'm leaving tomorrow for New Orleans," said David.

"Some sessions with 'Saiah, and after that the northern part of the state, then Mississippi and then into Memphis to give Brad a hand there if he needs me."

"You, Brad?"

"New Orleans with David. I'm going to stick with him for a couple of weeks, for a sort of orientation course. I might get thrown in jail for using the wrong can."

"You won't," interrupted David. "They've got signs. Real clear. And in English, yet. Even our most illiterate blacks can read w-h-i-t-e o-n-l-y. Other kids learn how to spell 'cat' and 'dog' and 'house,' unimportant stuff like that, first. We learn 'white' and 'colored.' "

"I can hardly stand the waiting," said Brad. "Anyhow, I'll go to Memphis after New Orleans. Then some of the larger cities. At first I'll be guided by Watkins and you, Joe. And the brat here."

Klein laughed. "I wish you'd stop calling him the brat. You're not that much older."

"Granted. But I've lived with him professionally for a long time. Or so it seems."

David said: "Brad, my car. It's in storage, as you know. When I thought I was—was leaving the country I authorized the garage to find a buyer and arrange the sale with you. I've changed my mind."

"You going to drive it down there?"

"No. You think I'm crazy? You think I'd drive that honey in the Deep South? Sugar in the gas tank, sand in the transmission, nails in the tires—"

"How're you going to get around? Bicycle?"

"No. If Rudy Lopez hasn't left for California, I'm going to ask him to put that jalopy Chuck's driving into shape and I'll swap with Chuck. I wired Rudy this morning to stick around a few more days. Joe, will you take care of it for me?"

"Sure. But it'll break my heart. Your car makes me drool. Mine's eight years older. And I've seen that thing of Martin's, and spent hours wondering what holds it together."

"Rudy'll paste it together, don't worry. Put a new motor in it. When he gets through it will outlast mine. And still look like hell, if that's the way I want it. Chuck can drive mine back down there, reregister it in Louisiana. Massachusetts license plates could spell almost as much trouble as a brown skin."

"So. That's set," said Klein. "Now, David, give me some dope on this kid you want to take with you. You've only met him two or three times. Frankly, I'm leery. Even if he is a distant relative of Brad's. What's his name again? Luke Willis?"

"Right. I'll take the responsibility. You think I want any dead wood or potential troublemaker along? I think I've sized him up right. Brad agrees. I'll pay him enough—"

"Hold it!" said Brad sharply. "Remember me? The guy with a hand on the purse strings? You haven't got that kind of dough. What's been going to Gramp goes back in the kitty, and don't give me an argument. Emergencies happen."

Klein interrupted. "If you're both convinced he's O.K., ALEC'll put him on the payroll in a small way—the only way we can. We can do it, since David's being so blasted Quixotic about his own reimbursement."

David smiled. "Save my stipend for bail money. Luke won't need much. No travel expense for a while. I won't be sending him anywhere on his own, not until I've got him licked into shape a little, the sharp edges worn off. The main expense will be film and photographic supplies, developing, that sort of thing."

David was remembering the Luke Willis who had come to the house the afternoon after their meeting in Hank's Place. Brad had been there, and Rudy. Luke had been wary, almost sullen, watching Brad with something close to hostility. David ignored his attitude, treated him with casual friendliness, knowing too much warmth would scare the kid off. Gradually the wariness had left, the withdrawn, near hostility given way to interest. He had picked up a copy of a national news magazine on the table, become lost in a spread on slum conditions in Philadelphia, said, "Man! That's great stuff!"

Something in his tone made David say, "You interested in photography?"

"Sure am. I've got me a Leica—" and he had expounded for ten minutes on the subject.

When he managed to get a word in, David said: "Want to bring some of your stuff over? Maybe we can come up with something—a job of sorts—where you can use photography."

The photographs had been outstandingly good; an interior shot taken in Hank's Place was exceptional, the faces of the men and women, caught unaware and photographed by available light, stark and haunting. David offered to buy it, but Luke insisted on giving it to him. "Got all my negatives," he said proudly. "Fixed me up a fine file."

Klein was saying, "Where'd a kid without a job get a Leica? That's the kind of thing I was getting at."

"I didn't ask," said David. He'd known damned well the odds were high Luke hadn't gone in and bought a Leica—new, secondhand, or hocked—but even Joe Klein couldn't be expected to accept that fact as a matter of course.

Brad said quietly: "We'll get him to ditch it. They're damned easy to trace. I'm sure, though, from something he said, that the little miniature one is his own."

"I've been thinking while we were talking," said Klein. "When Pennoyer comes in to get that manuscript, I'll ask him how he feels about mapping out another book, using your reports and Luke's pictures. A more subjective treatment this time, with Luke supplying some behind-the-scenes stuff. God knows it's needed. Everyone in the United States knows now what a Negro boy looks like when he's prodded with an electric cattle goad, or a woman knocked down by a stream from a fire hose. How many know what that boy's home is like? How many know what a group of little black children looks like, watching white kids swimming in a tax-supported pool—from behind a fence. I saw that myself, and unfortunately I think I always will see it—"

"It's all right with me," said David. "It'd be a boost for Luke—"

"I'll talk it over with him." Klein looked at his watch. "Let's do a quick recap before we go to lunch. Now. ALEC, working partially from its own funds and partially from a legacy from Mrs. Augusta Hubbard, is sending out a task force to establish citizenship classes in the South and attempt to register voters, and gather concrete and documented evidence of interference with the voting rights of United States citizens. The wording of Mrs. Hubbard's will actually allows a little more latitude. I quote: 'and for such other educational endeavors among the Negroes in the South as ALEC deems necessary, etcetera, etcetera.' David Champlin to be in charge of this project under the general supervision of the New Orleans and Boston offices, and will undertake the job of surveying the rural areas and smaller towns, and instituting these classes and—or—educational endeavors. Brad Willis will do substantially the same thing in the larger towns and cities. You'll both have help, and you'll both work closely with the N-double-A to avoid duplication of effort. There's no question but what you'll be called on to act in a legal capacity, for the defense, many times. That chore goes along with it."

David said: "We're going to have to play it by ear, Joe, from day to day—or at least week to week. The red-neck is a predictable animal, and those predictions better take in lethal acts. You could set up your plan, and before you could implement it be high-tailing down a dirt road or through a swamp. Get this, friend, I'm no damned hero."

Klein laughed. "How do you know you're not?"

"Want to bet? Now, listen, Joe, don't hold your breath waiting for results. The very word 'vote' can start a stampede of running Negroes in some places down there. Because, man, that's a killing word. And I'm going to be working with the men and women who live in the little houses off the road, and thinking of how they feel when they hear a car slow down outside."

Klein drew his hand over his face. "Better you than me, David." He shivered, then straightened up in his chair and said: "There's another difficulty. The cloud-no-bigger-than-a man's-hand type of difficulty. An inevitable one, I suppose. Recently, within the past twelve months, I'd say, there have been definite stirrings of dissension among the different civil rights groups. It's not serious yet. It will be. I'll make that a flat statement."

"And I'll accept it," said David. "Chuck Martin will tell you the same thing. He's been around, really around, this past year."

"He already has told me," said Klein. "In the eyes of the younger and more militant groups, ALEC and the N-double-A are dragging their feet. Which is damned nonsense, of course. You'll be meeting a chap in Jackson, Mississippi, named Medgar Evers. An hour with him and you'll find out for yourself that it's damned nonsense. We're lawyers, we three, and we know that the heartbeat of freedom is the vote. And equal justice in the courts. But a seventeen-year-old, just coming into manhood, into self-realization—what the hell, you can't expect him to hold his fire while his elders futz around with legal technicalities. He wants to fight, and I say God bless and God help him. But things have been made damned tough on us a few times. And they're splitting up among themselves. And we've got too damned much work ahead of us down there to get involved in any intergroup warfare."

David said quietly: "Save your breath, Joe. You don't

have to defend the militant Negro to me. I think I'm perfectly capable of understanding how it feels to have it be your hand that holds the rock for a change."

"I was getting preachy, wasn't I? It's just that voting rights—"

"Now, don't get too starry-eyed over voting rights alone. Voting rights weren't the issue in Montgomery in fifty-five—but the Negro community bankrupted a whole transit system. Now we've got integrated buses in a hell of a lot of scared cities in the South. New Orleans, for one. And where was ALEC while Montgomery was happening? Looking out the window, watching empty buses rolling by. When we tackle the voting-rights situation in Montgomery, we'll probably have an easier time, because the blacks had guts back in fifty-five. What about those four college kids in North Carolina and their sit-ins? They started something, and you damned well know it. It's only just begun. What I'm getting at is, the things these kids are fighting for are essential forerunners. They'll mess up, sure, and they'll get fouled up, here and there, and make wrong moves, and that's the way it is, and we'll work with it as best we can. Help as much as we can. Our trouble, Joe—Brad—has been that we've wept and beaten our breasts about voting rights, thinking that if every Negro acquired the right, overnight all the other obscene oppressions would vanish. They wouldn't. They won't." He drew a deep breath. "For God's sake, someone take me off this soapbox. Brad?"

"I pass. All I am right now is a pilgrim and a stranger. Learning."

Klein said: "I'm agreeing with you, David. But I'm saying that these kids who are part of the revolution now are powerless and will be powerless for several years to get one lousy, crumby, prestige-bound, senile southern senator out of Washington. And as for the State legislatures! Take Virginia. Have you followed the actions of its state lawmakers over the past few years? They're appalling. Horrifying. Who knows about it? Damned few. That's part of our job, too. To get these barbaric legal atrocities, as well as the physical atrocities, before a thinking public."

"A *what?* If we had a thinking public, Virginia, Mississippi, the whole stinking, putrefying corpse of law in the South would have been buried a long time ago. Don't, for God's sake, give me that 'thinking public' routine."

"Then somehow they have to be made to think."

"Sure. These younger groups are doing that—insofar as it's possible to replace complacency with thought. I'm not so damned old yet that I can't know how they feel. Twenty-seven isn't senile. Anyhow—I'll guarantee one thing: Luke will get you the kind of stuff we need—he's got a feel for it. You know, even the complacent moderate may feel activity in his gray cells when he sees a picture of white kids pouring maple syrup on the head of a young Negro girl sitting at a lunch counter. That's more apt to produce the miracle of thought in those people than cops exercising their mandate to preserve law and order and attacking kids with dogs. God help us all, it's easier for people to identify with a scared, brutal cop than with a punk pouring syrup on a quiet girl. And that's a damned fact."

Brad said, "Are you two arguing or agreeing with each other?"

"Both," said Klein. "Sometimes Isaiah and I go on like this for hours." He looked at his watch. "Let's think about lunch. Remember Les Forsyte, David? You met him a couple of summers ago."

"Youngster? Or looks like one? He was at Columbia Law then."

"Right. He still looks like a youngster, but he has his degree now. He'll be headed for Memphis in a couple of weeks to work with Brad. And Fred Winters is lunching with us too."

"Fieldwork supervisor for the N-double-ACP? Attorney? He came to our house in Beauregard once with Isaiah. The quiet type, but I remember thinking he'd probably be damned effective."

"He can be murder. And he's a tremendous organizer and administrator. Yet if I saw him in a demonstration with my own eyes, I wouldn't believe it. But he has a cold courage in a courtroom that's particularly telling. Like Brad's. I sat in on a trial in southern Georgia with him once. He's like a rattlesnake, even though he knows he's licked before he walks in the door. Damned if even southern judges aren't leery of him. And it's sheer joy to watch him in a Federal court. He's due for his first U.S. Supreme Court appearance in a few weeks."

"His own people down there don't always understand him," said David. "Even 'Saiah has doubts at times."

"There's hardly an advance in any area where he's worked, or had workers, that doesn't have Fred Winters's name on the cornerstone. And precious little thanks he gets for it. Even as you and I." Klein stood up, stretched. "Wonder what we'll be hassling about next time we get together? Let's get moving, my learned colleagues—"

63

RAIN BLINDED HIM, ran in rivulets down his neck, whipped wet trouser legs against shins and calves, found its way into his shoes, and its pounding, perpendicular rivers obscured the light in the windows of the Timmins house, making its glow a distorted image seen through flawed glass.

David did not hurry up the uneven brick path to his own little white house; even in the short distance from car to gate he had become so wet that hurry wouldn't help, and he was too weary to call on the extra energy needed for a faster pace. He had the aggrieved feeling that rain had greeted him every time on his return home throughout the past two and a half years. On the porch he scraped mud from his feet, knocked the rain from his hat, slapping it against his leg, then unlocked the door and set his typewriter down inside.

The living room was dim, gray in the half-dusk, muggy from the early August heat. He turned on the gooseneck lamp on the table beside the big chair flanking the fireplace, then walked through the house, lighting each room as he passed through it, the dining room, the kitchen, his own room, even the bath. Only the door of the front bedroom remained closed, the room unlighted. He would open it for airing tomorrow, not acknowledging even to himself that even now he did not like to open it unless the sun was shining, and that he shied away from its emptiness when the house was dark or semidark.

He came back through the kitchen and lighted the water heater and released the hook on the cat entrance cut low in the door that led to the back porch. Miz Timmins or one of the children or grandchildren would see the lights and let Chop-bone out, and the cat would scamper home across the street through the rain. He'd never failed yet when David returned. "Come in, Chop-bone," David would say. "I'm in residence. You saw the flag?" Usually the cat would ignore him huffily for as much as an entire evening, reproaching him for his absence, but always, when it came time to go to bed, Chop-bone would forgive him and curl beside him while he slept.

David poured himself a drink from the bottle he always kept hidden where not even a curious Timmins could find it, and carried the drink to the table beside the big chair. When he sat down, the chair's back and arms were like an embrace, and he leaned his head against its worn upholstery, not sighing, not moving. In a little while he knew the ache in his ankle would subside; in a little while he could call up enough energy to take off his shoes. In a little while, an hour, a week, a year, a lifetime, the tiredness might abate and he would soak in a hot tub, letting the warm water on the outside and the whiskey on the inside do what they could for angry, screaming nerves, tired muscles, a mind and body at bay against the need to live.

He wanted the bath more than anything else, more than the food he had wired Miz Timmins to stock in for him, more than the drink at his side, more than the dim soft comfort of the familiar house. Thirty-four days in a stinking, rat-ridden, vermin-infested Jim Crow cellblock of a southern jail, and a bath had become an obsession. God damn them, he thought, and did not stir in his chair. And God damn, too, those three earnest workers who met him on his release and whirled him away, not to a bath, not to rest and respite, but another trouble spot a hundred miles away, riding over rutted, potholed roads, talking, talking, trouble, trouble. God damn them and God bless them and God keep 'em away from me just for tonight. Just for tonight let me rest, for no man can be so tired, yet live and function and fight.

He would soak in the tub, then lie down in his own bed, and he would sleep, please God, he would sleep, and then it would be morning and he would curse because it was morning, but he would acknowledge morning at last because he would have to, and he would broach the battlements of its gray horror with nerves sick as from a beating, a body heavy with fatigue, and a mind that worked in spite of that body, like the exposed mechanism of a shattered clock, still ticking,

ticking. He knew that was the way it would be because that was the way it had been for so long he could not remember any different beginning to a day.

At least tonight there would be no voices, unless the sound of those voices heard outside his cell night after night dwelt so deep in his brain that they would follow him here. They had followed him on his first three nights of freedom to small, hot rooms in motels or homes, but that was to be expected. They had come to him from the back seat of his car after he had gone back to the town where he was jailed and picked it up, and that was to be expected too. But not here. Not here in his own home, in his own bedroom, with a friendly cat purring beside him and an ancient calico tiger on the bureau. If Chop-bone couldn't exorcise them, the tiger would, and if the tiger couldn't, the bottle would, and he would suffer through a hell of belly pain tomorrow, but one way or another the voices would go.

When he had been alone on the road he had missed Luke whenever the boy was busy elsewhere, or was in the North, but here he missed no one, not now, not tonight. Later the loneliness would come, but now, at this moment, solitude was benediction.

Still, he couldn't help wondering where in hell the kid was. And Brad. And Chuck Martin. Hadn't they known about the thirty-day sentence with no reduction for four days served in the tank cell? He had been incommunicado—no mail, no newspapers, no letters, no messages, no visitors—and when he left there he had made only brief inquiries of the three white students who met him. "Where's Bradford Willis?" he had asked, and one had replied: "I heard he was in Boston. He might be in Cainsville. He's O.K." Chuck Martin, they said, was definitely in Cainsville, and they thought Luke Willis was also. "They've got some kind of a thing going there," said one of the boys. David didn't ask any more questions, certain the answers would be vague and inaccurate; these kids were so earnest, so Goddamned earnest, so Goddamned dedicated and so on fire with a sort of enraged enthusiasm that he couldn't trust them to give a simple answer to a simple question.

They said: "Look, we'll stop for food. Don't you want a steak? Something fit to eat? We won't force the issue of serving you. We'll bring it out to you."

He said, "No. Thanks. Milk." It was all he wanted: huge,

vast, white oceans of soothing milk, and he drank it in great greedy gulps wherever they could find it.

The trouble they were taking him to was over when they reached the town; the third bombing in a month, the boys said. It had happened two days after they arrived. Now the people were holding back, not willing to demonstrate.

"You want me to make them?" He snapped the words out.

"No. Of course not." They spoke soothingly, these youngsters, as though he were old and senile. "Only, well, this apathy is hard to take."

"It is not apathy. It's fear." He made a desperate effort to be patient. "Look. Let the thing rest for a while. Come back later with more support. It's not fair, you know. You come down here, there are reprisals, and for a while you're here to give some kind of protection. Then you have to leave, and the Negro is left alone with the men with the guns, God help him. The colored people in this town are old and settled—and afraid. There aren't enough young people to make any movement effective."

The boys were hurt and resentful when, dog-tired and half sick, he left by train for Heliopolis to pick up his car; Luke had stashed that away before he'd been arrested. The boys apparently had expected him, as God was his judge, to stay and defy a whole town single-handed. Which is what it would have amounted to with only their inexperienced help. He could do a better job alone or with Luke, working secretly among the people, talking to them, qualifying them, bringing them quietly to the courthouse to try to register them, with Luke standing by, looking as stupid as he could, a tiny tape recorder hidden under his voluminous sweatshirt, a mini-camera palmed in one hand.

Now that he was home and beginning to let down, he decided to wait until morning before he started tracking down Brad. He couldn't talk, not even to Brad, tonight. If he had known what was coming after that four days in the big tank cell he would have gotten a message out by one of the kids who had shared the cell with him, one of those who had been released early. Now he stirred in his chair, shook his shoulders as though trying to throw off a burden, remembering one hundred and fifty-odd youngsters in a cell designed for fifty. In one jail, he knew, in another city, three hundred and sixty-five had been crammed into a cell designed to hold sixty-five. They'd been lucky, he and Luke.

Luke had been arrested a day after his own arrest. He had been "loitering with intent." With intent to take pictures, the kind of pictures he'd been taking for the past three years. Obscene pictures, thought David; these were the genuinely obscene pictures. Naked bodies of lustful men and women, those were not the true obscenities; the true obscenities, the blasphemous obscenities, were women with pursed and cruel mouths turning away voters in a registrar's office, men with saps beating Negroes, a man clubbing a woman's head with the butt of a rifle. He'd give you obscenity, Luke would, the real thing. Pictures of young girls massed upright in a jail cell because there was no room to sit or lie, left there without blankets or toilet facilities; that had been a picture taken at the risk of his life. A picture of a nine-year-old boy being herded into a police wagon, looking up with wide dark eyes at the club held over him by his uniformed captor. What fun! What fun! Tour the South and bring your camera, get the pretty pictures of the lovely old plantations; never mind the slavery that made them so, it's all gone now. Don't miss the little children with the round dark eyes, forget—if you dare—the world those eyes will see. Get the pretty pictures of the smiling folk, white teeth gleaming; shoot your roll of film, you happy, happy tourist, shoot it all. Luke will give you more; Luke will give you all the pictures you can carry. Luke takes color pictures, Luke does, and red and brown are vivid, the one upon the other.

That first year with Luke after they left New Orleans together hadn't always been easy. David remembered sessions in hotel rooms, in dingy little restaurants and bars; sometimes Les Forsyte had been there, sometimes Brad, sometimes Chuck Martin. They worked the boy over with gentle, half-bullying affection, trying to make him understand that theirs was a work that would be weighed in the balances of the future, a future no longer unattainable but still definitely not a present, a "now." David had given him his head when it seemed wisest, let him blow off steam in demonstrations, sit-ins, freedom rides, bailed him out of jail a number of times. Sometimes Luke had his small camera tucked in an ingenious pocket in the belt band of his trousers, made for him by the clever hands of a woman in whose home they had stayed in northern Louisiana. "The kid has all the instincts of a pro," David told Chuck. "Last time he was jailed a deputy hit him in the belly with a club, trying to make him say 'I'm a nigger—' The third time he gave in. 'I kept thinking of that camera in my belt band, boss,' he said. You can't ask for more than that."

Several times David and the others had feared Luke's defection to one of the more militant groups. "I don't think he'd do it if the chips were down," was Brad's comment to David: "The boy thinks you're something close to the second coming. But, of course, he's young and hot-blooded. Actually, I think he's doing damned well."

He was doing more than well, thought David. He was making himself, without intent, close to indispensable. David did not like to think, even now, of what those long drives, hundreds of miles sometimes before they could find a place a Negro could sleep, would have been like without Luke's companionship. Without Luke, with only his own thoughts and the loneliness they bred, David wondered if his resolve would have held out.

Both he and Luke were never without the knowledge that behind them, beside them, and before them death waited for a wrong move. They joked about it because to do anything else would have been futile. The hatred that surrounded them was dependent on no act of theirs. It was a simple thing, like love, needing nothing more than the presence of its object to bring it to pulsating life.

That first year he had not even produced the one proud Mississippi voter he had mentioned to Joe Klein. One of his workers in rural Alabama reported—almost incredulously—that he had succeeded in getting one man registered. The man was a middle-aged farmer, with a better than average education, who had applied eleven times and been unable to pass the trumped-up tests. Yet he had never given up, spent every night with his books and his "readin'," determined to try again. Three days later, at the first opportunity he had, David drove to the town and was met by a grim-faced, sick-eyed youth of nineteen. The newly registered voter had disappeared.

"I shoulda known. God damn, I shoulda known. It was too easy. They done it on purpose—let him register so's they could make an example of him—"

"Any sign of a body, Jim?"

"No. And that's maybe good. His li'l piece of a car's gone. And his wife—she's gone. Their dog, he went over to the neighbors and they keeping care of him. Fine hound. He was crazy 'bout that dog. Neighbor's milking the cow, too. But they swear they don't know nothing. But nothing, man. Better not go out there, man; you likely to get run off."

"Any signs of trouble? Like a fight or struggle?"

"Nary one. I tell you, everything's like it would be if they'd took off right after supper straight up. Even the dishes wasn't washed, and that ain't like her."

"They got away, Jim."

"I hope to Christ they did. There was talk in the town about getting him. He musta heard it and got out. I hope he got out. I shoulda known."

"Don't blame yourself, Jim. Just find out what you can about where he might have gotten to, where he's got relatives and all that, and I'll start looking. We all will. He's got to be hurting for money."

"He been studying a long time. Been counting on it most of his life. Voting. He was mighty proud that day. So was we. He was the onlies' voter we had—"

Yet there was intangible progress that would eventually show up as tangible names on the registration rolls. More doors opened than would have opened a few years before; more Negroes listened, not turning away in fear. "You can see their faces now," David said to Luke. "Maybe you can't get what I mean, but you can see their faces because their heads are up. Maybe they aren't moving fast enough to suit you, but their heads are up, and a man sure as hell isn't going to move backward when he starts lifting his head."

He left field representatives in every area, and he knew that after he had done his own work and gone on, children would be sitting around tables in someone's home—learning; young people would be meeting in churches or social halls—learning; and older people would have hope living with their fear because these were their children who were learning.

Tents began to spring up here and there, the only shelter left to dispossessed Negroes who had revealed to the white man at last the faith and courage that had been lying dormant within them for a hundred years. Of the tent dwellers David said: "There's greatness in these people, Luke. Greatness. And don't forget it, just because they aren't marching."

Yet he still felt like a minnow trying to swim upstream against a torrential rush of water. Neither he nor Brad had won a case in court; most of the cases they had appeared in for the defendant were on appeal, a circumstance Les Forsyte and Fred Winters took for granted, but which Brad could not, just as he could not learn to take for granted the presence on southern benches of judges whose sole intent was circumvention of the law, to whom justice meant unthinkable surrender. "Relax, Chief," said David. "Save your energy to fight 'em all the way up."

He could afford to remember these things now, at the end of two and a half years, with his mind almost made up to return north, at least for a while, and work with Klein and Pennoyer, use the bitter knowledge he had gained to prepare legal defenses, administer fieldwork from there. The things he couldn't afford to remember, and which crept into his mind whenever he left the door ajar, were incidents like the one involving the little pharmacist in a small Alabama city. He was a small man, no bigger than Gramp, who had tried to register himself and his two sons, had been seen riding in a car with a CORE worker, a white woman, and was seen to tear the Confederate battle flags from the bumper of a car parked in front of his store. They had gotten him one night just as he was emptying trash into a barrel in the alley back of his store. Brad, Luke, and David were in the store, stocking up on toothpaste, shaving cream, and sundries for travel. Obadiah Brown had looked even smaller lying in the alley in the light from a streetlamp, his face a red-brown pulp, the bullet wounds only partially responsible for the blood in which he sprawled. Brad and David stood over the body, choking, and then Luke was with them, and Luke's camera recorded the battered face and almost every bullet hole. Not all, because some were in back.

The next day Luke found a Negro photographer and developed the films himself. That night they had their toughest time with him. By prearrangement Les Forsyte and Fred Winters arrived in town that morning, Les to confer with David and Brad, Fred down from New York to defend one of his field secretaries. And the three men did not return to the motel after dinner until late. Luke had preceded them, and they found him in the room he and David shared—packing. David saw Winter's face set in anger, but Forsyte took it in his stride. "Take it easy," he whispered to David. Brad eventually slowed Luke down, at least temporarily. Watching the scene, David thanked God that Luke was a guy who would listen once he had cooled down. Brad asked no questions, spoke quietly, suggested delay until he could line up transportation. The South, Brad said, had been a moral mess for two hundred years; it could go on being a mess for a couple of more days and Luke could wait those couple of days before saving it. "Come on, son. Shut that suitcase."

David watched Luke turn to the suitcase that lay open on a chair, bending to take out his shaving kit, and then he was across the room in two strides. He caught Luke from behind, one powerful arm around the youth's slender body, his free hand plunging into Luke's trouser pocket. He slackened his grip, and Luke whirled free, eyes blazing.

David stood looking at the gun he held in the palm of his hand. "What—the—hell—" he said slowly, then tossed the gun to the bed. "Perhaps I should have asked you for it," he said, still speaking slowly. "But I wasn't about to argue. You hadn't even learned how to protect it, you dope. A guy doesn't carry a gun so that any amateur can take it away from him. Or so a five-year-old could spot it from a block away." He was standing between Luke and the foot of the bed. "Leave it there, Luke. We'll wipe any prints off and throw it along the road after we leave tomorrow. You've got to have lifted it. Where?"

"Last week. In Chattanooga. In a hock shop where I was looking at cameras." He looked like a small boy, sullenly ashamed.

No one else had spoken since David made his move. Brad sat in a straight chair near the door, apparently relaxed and without concern. Fred Winters stood leaning against the doorjamb, looking cool and impeccably elegant in spite of a hard day, but there was fresh anger in his eyes. Les Forsyte stood at the side of the bed, looking at the gun. He spoke first, turning to Luke. "Where were you headed for? I mean, aside from the jailhouse?"

"Get off my back, all of you! What kind of a job is it when a guy sees people getting dead all around and all he's got to fight back with if they come after him is a lousy black box! God damn it, film ain't all we need. We need bullets! You see a guy lying dead in his own blood, in an alley, no nose, no teeth, full of holes. And what the hell do you do? You take a stinking picture of him! And then he's coming at you again in the dark room, coming up at you out of the developer, his face and his eyes, and them bullet holes, coming up at you slow-like, staring at you. And you knew the guy. You were talking to him five minutes before he got it. And you vomit, right there in the dark room, because you can't hold it in any longer, the way you felt when you run out that door and seen him lying there—"

David turned away, afraid that his face would show the same humanity that was in Luke, show that he wanted to give him back his gun, let him be a human being, make it possible for him to court destruction if need be in one final, instinctive act of self-preservation—and take his destroyer with him. Self-preservation. Self-defense. These meant self-destruction for the Lukes, the Brad Willises, the David Champlins— there was no plea of self-defense in the South when a Negro faced a white killer. Their lives were without value, defense of them indefensible. He felt sick and helpless, the high-pitched, ragged edge in Luke's voice scraping his nerves raw. Brad caught his eye and stood, and David saw the almost imperceptible movement of the head that meant "I'm taking over." He moved quietly away to stand in front of the window, near Fred Winters.

Brad walked over to Luke, stood leaning, then half sitting on the end of the bed. "Luke, no one's blaming you. I wish to God every Negro in the South had a gun. The picture would be different then. But they don't, and a lot of them wouldn't use them if they had them." He reached back and, with a skill that surprised David, unloaded the snub-nosed .38. "Learn all kinds of skills when you're a defense lawyer," he murmured, then tossed the gun back on the bed. "I'm not unloading this gun for your benefit, Luke. It's just that loaded guns scare the devil out of me. You can have the gun and the bullets any time you want them. You stole them fair and square from a white hock shop, and I don't hold that against you any more than I'd hold it against a man without a dime in his pocket if he stole penicillin because he thought he had a fatal infection penicillin would cure. But, Luke, suppose he steals the penicillin and finds out the infection won't respond to it? Some don't."

He threw the bullets on the bed, watched them roll over its lumpy surface and come to rest beside the gun. Brad repeated Les Forsyte's question. "Where were you headed for, Luke? You don't have to say if you don't want to."

"Atlanta." He muttered the word so low David could scarcely hear it.

"Atlanta! Martin Luther King?"

"God damn it, at least they're doing something—"

"Good God." Brad's exclamation was in the same low key. "You were going to present yourself to the King organization carrying a gun?"

"I'm not that stupid—"

"I didn't think so. Not even the Young People's Committee for Freedom would welcome you under those circumstances. You're a free agent, Luke. If it's going to make you feel happier and more fulfilled to line up with people nearer your age and get into this hassle on a more militant basis, none of us would try and stop you for any other reasons than that we need you, we're fond of you, and we'd hate to see you go. Only, for God's sake, if you're going to join one of these love-conquers-all groups don't do it with a gun in your pocket."

David, listening, was watching Luke. The boy had taken the suitcase off the chair and was sitting, elbows on knees, eyes on Brad. And that was good. He wasn't looking at the floor in sullen stubbornness. He was listening.

"Luke," said Brad. "You've taken part in a lot of demonstrations. Of all the damned fine pictures you've taken this year, the best one was the one you took of the woman with tears running down her cheeks, trying to patch up her boy's face after it had been laid open by a chain in that last freedom-rider melee. It's worth fifty bullets in fifty white bastards. I'll be damned if I can see Luke Willis kneeling in prayer with a cop dog's fangs an inch from his face. I'd rather see you kneeling to get a better focus of that dog's fangs and jaws with that camera under your shirt. You could caption it 'A Black Boy's View of the South.' "

That had done it. Luke's eyes had widened, he'd said, "He-e-ey—Mr. Willis! You got something there. You really got something. I'll bet I could do it—"

Les spoke up, interrupting: "Look, I don't want to seem nervous or anything like that. All that those red-necks in that big world out yonder want is an excuse to kill us. Nothing mean or petty. And if a gang of bastard cops with Confederate flags on their hats come busting in here—and they see that gun—you know how it is. They've got to defend themselves, haven't they?"

David laughed. "You chicken?"

"Man, yes! I'm so chicken I'd lay eggs if I was built right. Let's get the damned hell rid of this gun!"

"You've been quivering for the past hour, haven't you?" said Winters. "Anyone have a fresh idea about how to get rid of a stolen gun? Shall we advertise?"

"I'll go round back and bury it."

"The hell you will! It's past midnight. I've been hearing

cars go by on the road, real slow. You can't beat these crackers when it comes to rifle shooting—"

The bomb had landed then, the explosion rocking the room so that David, in front of the window, was thrown across the bed, and Winters was knocked to the floor. When the sound was gone there was the smell of burning on the damp breeze that came through the shattered window and billowed the sleazy draperies that hung beside it. Somewhere close at hand a woman screamed, not once but again and again, a series of insensate noises, and then there were running feet and the sound of a car's motor racing, then driving away, wide open, on the dark roadway that ran past the motel.

The force of the explosion had jammed the locked door, and Luke and David kicked and knocked glass out of the window so they could get outside. Les, David learned later, had dropped the gun in the toilet tank before he joined them. The manager of the motel, a heavy-set man, very dark, wall-eyed, and with patches of white on forehead and cheeks where the skin was losing its pigment, was running around aimlessly, punctuating his curses with, "Anybody hurt? Anybody hurt?"

The other guests were outside now, and flames were licking up the side of a cypress tree growing close to the front of the building. "Hose, man! Hose!" yelled Luke, and when the manager dragged garden hose over and turned it on he played the stream up and down the tree trunk, through the branches and over the roof and front of the building. The woman who had screamed was sitting on the ground in front of her room, wearing a transparent black nightgown. She was dull with shock now, and a man clad only in Roman-striped shorts was standing over her, holding a bottle of liquor to her mouth.

The manager, whose little office had been almost annihilated by the bomb, was still chanting, "Anybody hurt? Anybody hurt?" and David snapped irritably, "No! For God's sake, no! See if the phone's working. Call the police."

"What you saying man!" His voice was high and squeaky. "We ain't even in the city. You want the troopers? You want the sheriffs? Ain't a bomb enough? Say, man, you're hurt—man, you're bleeding—"

"Who? Me?" David put his hand on the back of his neck and shoulder, conscious of discomfort there now. When he drew the hand away he saw that it was covered with blood. He looked at it stupidly. "Be damned—"

Les ran over, stripped David's shirt from his shoulders, then whistled. "Looks like a razor job. Long, and"—he poked—"deep. Gotta be sewed up, pal. Must have been that window. Maybe there was a jagged piece left and you ripped yourself open—man, I mean *open*—getting through."

When the commotion died down and the few guests had been moved to undamaged rooms, Les announced that he was going to suture David's wound. David roared loudly. "The hell you are!"

"Sure am, sonny. My first love was medicine before I decided to save the human race. That's us. I took premed. . . . Luke, press that towel on there hard. Don't be afraid. It's not your neck. . . . I worked two summers and part-time winters in the emergency ward of a Harlem hospital. Rode the ambulance, too. Saw a lot like this, pal. You want to drive fifty miles to the nearest place where they'll put a stitch in brown skin?"

"What you think you're going to do this with, you bastard? Sewing needles?"

"Certainly, dad. Shut up, will you. Back in a few minutes. Stay with it, Luke."

Tired as he was now, and safe at home, he could still smile, remembering the scene in that shabby room, Les coming back from the kitchen of the motel carrying a small porcelain pie plate in which lay sterilized scissors, needles, and thread. In his other hand he carried the first-aid kit from his car. He was whistling the "Battle Hymn of the Republic" through his teeth. David said, "Look, you guys—Fred, Brad, Luke—get that bloodthirsty sadist the hell out of here! I'll get it fixed tomorrow."

"Now. Tonight. Immediately, baby. You can toss that towel on the floor of the can now, Luke. Somebody in Shakespeare said something about who'd have known someone had so much blood in 'em—"

"I'll die of staphylococcus—streptococcus—septicemia—"

"Not a chance, dad. After this a shot of penicillin. You allergic to it? No? O.K. I carry it as standard equipment, like a flashlight. Head forward a little more. Damn it, man, keep that hard head down—"

David let out exaggerated howls of pain at each stitch and broke down laughing in between them, addressing himself chiefly to a fascinated, if shaken, Luke, who was assisting.

"Luke, you sonofabitch, you're enjoying this—Ouch! How many more?"

"Two more should do it," said Les judiciously.

"Remind me to seduce those six sisters of yours next time I get north—one for each stitch—"

64

THE BOMBING OF THE MOTEL had been first blood. After that night his apparent immunity to reprisal and persecution vanished. Les Forsyte's neat sutures had still been in the flesh of neck and shoulder when he was picked up and jailed in the next town. His luck had not deserted him entirely, because a glancing blow from a policeman's club fell on the shoulder where there weren't any stitches. He could not remember now what the charge had been that first time. Two of many subsequent charges were in Brad's hands and, he supposed, would eventually work their way to the Supreme Court.

One circumstance he hadn't foreseen was the inevitable one of becoming known in the whole region, of having his picture sent from town to town, his activities watched with hostile eyes by police and state troopers, his plans spotted ahead of time through tapped telephone lines. It hadn't helped any when a national news magazine had run his picture in connection with a story about ALEC. After a while he insisted that workers in the various communities make all but the most trivial personal calls from pay telephones, and a different one whenever possible. Nowadays he planned to arrive in town at night when he could arrange it, and to keep out of sight during the day if it could be done, as much for the safety of the workers as for his own. And he was never without the knowledge, when he walked the southern streets and roads, that the companion who hadn't quite caught up with him yet was death.

He wasn't going to let it worry him now, and he stretched legs and arms and wriggled his body deeper into the worn upholstery of the familiar chair, groaning "Aa-a-ah—" at the sheer comfort of it. Luke, after he was released from jail, was scheduled to spend a few weeks with Brad. Pennoyer had suggested some courtroom shots, and Brad had a number of cases coming up. David hoped Luke had managed to get away with taking them. Chuck Martin was going to be with them part of the time, Luke said, and Chuck, under Luke's tutelage, had developed a knack with a camera and might have been able to take over if Luke got in trouble. He wouldn't put it beyond Luke by this time to risk taking a quick sneak shot in the U.S. Supreme Court itself. David decided it would be nice to have a picture of the Supreme Court while it reviewed a case against Champlin. It wasn't exactly what Suds Sutherland had meant when he had said, a long time ago, "The first Negro Justice of the Yew-nited States Soopreme Court," but it was closer to the Supreme Court than he would have been in Africa. Both cases had been considered newsworthy by press and wire services as well as broadcasters, and brought comment from columnists: "David Champlin, young Boston attorney who gave up a State Department career to join the civil rights struggle in the South—"

And now—Gramp would have added "if God spares"—he was going north. There might be other all-night sessions in Klein's office like the first one when he had briefed Pennoyer's book, and the men and women who had peopled the shadows of the room that night might return. But this time it would be as friends, with no silent reproaches. There would be more of them, and the newcomers would have names—Obadiah Brown, for one—and he would not shrink from them, because he had shared their peril now, faced, and been spared, their fate.

He forced both past and future out of his mind and tried to bring himself into the present and its practical problems. He would have to buy Luke a new camera, if Brad had not already done so. They had taken the one he was carrying when they arrested him that day in Heliopolis more than a month ago, and David would be amazed if they had returned it. It had not been, he was thankful, the miniature one; that one had been hidden in the car. There would probably be a letter from Luke in his mail at ALEC headquarters. He could see Luke now, the afternoon they threw him into the tank cell. He hadn't fallen; they were all packed in too solidly for anyone to fall. There were bruises on his face, blood on his forehead and trickling from nose and mouth, but he laughed when David and a sturdy fourteen-year-old steadied him. "Damned if it isn't the boss," he said. "What you doing in the nursery? You ain't even supposed to be in jail." David's laugh rang through the tank and turned every dark face toward him, and there was answering laughter; then a young voice in the background saying, "Man, what we laughing at? Man! We're in trouble and laughing! What the hell!"

He had smelled trouble even before he got into the actual town of Heliopolis, and when he spotted a running child carrying a "Light for Freedom" placard, had known he was headed for the middle of a Young People's Committee for Freedom demonstration. The child, a nine-year-old girl, was running away from town, crying in fright. The demonstration was ending in chaos and uproar when he got within three blocks of the main street, and he began to worry about Luke, who had preceded him the day before. The demonstrators were spilling over into the street where he parked his car, and he left the car and worked his way toward the center of town. He spotted Luke on a sidewalk and waved at him and turned back to his car, then began to run, hoping his gimpy leg would get him there before the crowd of teen-agers who were rushing toward the car could do it any damage. He waded into the group, shouting, "Hey, kids—that's my car!"

How in hell the police showed up so fast he'd never be able to figure out. He did not protest when they threw him roughly into a police wagon; he knew by then that it would be useless.

That was what Luke had meant when he said, "You ain't even supposed to be in jail."

"Can't you think of anything brighter to say, f'Christ's sake? Let's take a look at that face—what's left of it."

"It'll be O.K. I've seen it worse. Jeez! It stinks so bad in here you can hear yourself twice. The sound bounces back from the stink—"

David supposed he was thrown in the juvenile tank because all the other cells were full. Every time something happened, those four days that he was in it, the kids turned to him, and at night, squatting on the floor with his arms around his knees, he talked to them, and they sang together, there in the heat and the fetid air, the stench so strong they felt they had to raise their voices to cut through it. He helped them mop and clean up vomit from the skinny, frightened boy who crouched by himself in a corner, finally pulling the boy upright, cajoling, bullying, babying, almost forcing him into the circle with the others, keeping an arm around his shoulders until finally the lad joined their talk and song and the vomiting stopped.

The voices started about the second or third week after he was sentenced and put in a cell by himself, charged with incitement to riot and disturbing the peace. They came after dark, after the lights had been put out. They were pitched low, uninflected, drawling. They were slow, reflective, reasonable, seeming to be without passion or subjective emotion, and they were the most foully obscene sounds David had ever heard. At first he did not realize they were directed at him, and thought that the opening murmurs he heard were the beginning of a conversation between two of the guards. From the sound, they were standing near the cell door, in the corridor. He had the impression of two men leaning against the wall, passing a dark night hour together.

"Ain't no real reason for hatin' niggers." Those were the first words he distinguished. "Ain't never been hurt by no nigger. Main reason for keepin' clear of 'em is their habits—"

The voices went on for the better part of an hour, bandying obscenities, each man trying to outdo the other, with silence now and then as though the men were waiting. Then there was a return to the slow, thought-out filth. David's flesh crawled under sweat that made it damp and clammy; saliva filled his mouth as he fought off active nausea, making him spit into his handerchief silently, hoping they would think him asleep and not hearing them, yet knowing that his silence was useless, that they knew he was awake. He had never thought the white cracker mentality capable of this subtlety of method. One man had more to say than the other, describing the habits he deplored in niggers, while the second offered suggestions for overcoming those habits. They did not come every night; once there was a lapse of two nights, but on the third it was plain their inventive faculties had been sharpened by the layoff. Sleep was just as hard to come by on those silent nights; every sound that might be footsteps knotted David's stomach, brought the sweat out on his skin.

It was their fifth night of talking before he answered them, involuntarily, unable to stop himself, his mind a whirlpool of heat from lack of sleep, his nerves stretched to breaking point. He did not answer them in kind; he was outpowered in the profanity department, outdistanced in obscenity. Instead, he heard himself making a bitten-off wisecrack, sophomoric, useless; something about their lousy grammar, their ignorance.

And for his wit passed blood for three days.

They sent a doctor to him—he'd give the day guards credit for that—when they saw the blood they sent a doctor, and when the doctor asked him how it had happened, David told him, "All very simple and trivial, isn't it, Doctor?"

The doctor, spreading a white towel on the dirty blanket of a plank bed that let down from the wall on chains, did not look up. "We—all of us—must make allowances. For many things."

High-sperrited. Emma Jefferson, dead a year now, had said that of the boys who had sent a small brown man named Joseph Champlin to his death, said it bitterly. *High-sperrited.* He could hear her now, see her standing in the doorway of her kitchen, dark hands dusty with flour.

The doctor busied himself preparing two hypodermics, laying one on the towel, advancing with the other.

"What?" asked David.

The doctor laughed abruptly, without mirth. "Not cyanide. One is an antibiotic, the other, vitamins."

"My God, that's food. Don't tell the jailers."

"I can't defend them. But you are all making it difficult for us to have much sympathy. I am leaving you two sleeping tablets, one for tonight, one for tomorrow night. You obviously need sleep. The balance I shall leave with Sheriff Giddings to be given to you at night."

"Do you honestly think I'll ever get them?"

"I shall leave instructions."

Atta moderate! Atta fine, upstanding moderate! Give the poor Negro a sleeping pill so he won't hear the insults; give him morphia before you hang him, burn him, castrate him; let's keep our people happy, but never let them go. Leave instructions, oh, by all means leave instructions. There it was again, the thing he could not fight, the wall against which his people lunged until they fell, bleeding, wounded, dead: stupidity. The voices wouldn't miss a night. But don't reprimand the jailers, Doctor; they might think you were siding with the nigras.

"Thank you, Doctor; you've been kind." The doctor turned, something close to warmth in his eyes, and David caught them with his own eyes, saw the warmth die, saw the cheeks flush to scarlet, and the scarlet recede, leaving the skin chalk white.

The doctor did not say good bye, but left abruptly, and David heard his voice in the hall. "Harris, where is Sheriff Giddings? I want to leave medication for the prisoner with him." The voice did not quaver, but neither was it steady.

David loosened his belt and stripped his shirt off without rising from the big chair, then took off shoes and socks. He was being a damn fool, he thought, just a plain damned fool, dwelling on a petty incident in the past, with a mind too tired for discipline. That was the hell of this kind of fatigue. It had its own peculiar, subtle toxicity, undermining the brain's will, the mind's power, just as a physical poison would undermine the body's strength. He remembered how he had thought, the first night he met Luke Willis, that his people were sick, sick unto death, of a radiation sickness no scientist ever unleashed. If he had done nothing else, if he and Brad had done nothing else worthwhile, they had taken Luke before that sickness destroyed him, mind and body, put into his young hands an antidote for that poison, given a young and sickening mind the healing of honorable battle.

He wondered what Brad and Luke and Chuck were doing in the little city of Cainsville, scarcely legible on the map. In today's climate of violence the name itself was enough to give a man the horrors. There had been trouble there, before he had been jailed; demonstrations, blood and violence, but he had been busy elsewhere and had not found out much about it. "They've got something going there," the kids from Ohio had said. He would find out in the morning, when he talked to Brad.

There was a sound from the kitchen, the soft slap of the cat door, and he leaned forward. "Chop-bone?" he said softly. He didn't hear the black-and-white cat enter the room; it materialized. He watched it while it ignored him, disciplined him, withheld welcome from a human who had absented himself for weeks.

"You better be sweet to me, y'hear?"

Each time he came home, thought David, he planned to make it the last time, yet never did. There was no point in coming back. He could reach Boston by plane from the South almost as quickly, use his apartment there, handle business with Isaiah by telephone. "You, too," he said to Chop-bone. "They have nice metal boxes for cats to travel in on planes. Give 'em tranquilizers and cream every five hundred miles. You could live with Peg while I'm away. Or board."

This time. This time, after he was rested, he'd find a tenant or a buyer.

He soaped and scrubbed and soaked for half an hour; then, still not feeling wholly clean, showered the last of the jail from his body. He looked at himself in the mirror on the bathroom door, said, "Mmmm . . . *mmm.* You ain't thin, man; yore skinny. Damned if you don't look like Gramp from the neck down."

He found food in the refrigerator and suddenly was ravenous. His craving for milk was gone, his stomach quieter, and he brought out cold chicken, two cooked pork chops, rice, and food for Chop-bone, and blessed Miz Timmins silently. He and Chop-bone ate together companionably, and then, half blind with sleep, he stretched out on his bed and turned and sprawled on his belly, waiting for the voices to begin, but there was no sound except the soft fall of a diminishing rainstorm on roof and window and the low, sensuous purring of the cat beside him; then even those sounds were lost, and from a million miles away there was the sound of dark voices singing on a riverbank—"Pharaoh's army got drownded—" then oblivion.

65

BEFORE HE HAD BATHED the previous night he had filled the electric coffee maker and put it on the table beside his bed. When he woke early in the morning he turned it on, refusing to look at a gray world until the caffein's bite had bolstered his will to face it. Chop-bone asked to be let out, and he refused, explaining that there were the usual toilet facilities for cats behind a screen in the bathroom, glad to hear his own voice and glad that there was no answering voice except the cat's soft chirrup and, in a moment, urgent plea for breakfast.

At seven thirty he put in a call to the Willis house, hoping to find out from Peg where Brad could be reached. He smiled with pleasure when he heard Brad's voice, sharp and demanding. "David! In God's name, where are you?"

"New Orleans."

"Why haven't you called before?"

"How the hell could I, Brad? I've only been out four or five days, and some kids from Ohio State—"

"Out of where?"

"Jail, of course."

"Wait. Wait a minute. The same jail you were in about a month ago?"

"The very same. I was there thirty-four days. Didn't you know?"

"They told me you'd been released a few days after you were arrested. I've called New York, Chicago, New Orleans, God knows where else. No one knew anything."

"I was incommunicado. No mail, no visitors, no messages, no nothing. No outgoing mail, either. I wouldn't want to bet they didn't book me under a phony name just to keep me from being sprung."

"One of the hazards of fame, I suppose. What were you jailed for?"

"Breathing in and out. What else? Who told you I'd been released?"

"Fellow named Garnett. In Cainsville."

"Short, tubby, bald, brown-skin? Comes on with an accent like he'd just come out of the tall cotton?"

"Know him?"

"Yeah." He did not elaborate. Brad would get his meaning.

"Like that?"

"Yes. He keeps bobbing up."

"David, are you coming up here?"

"Hell, Brad, I'd like to stay put and rest a little while. And there are, well, there are things I want to do here at the house. Then I'll be up there. And I should get together with the ALEC people, tie up a lot of loose ends. How about you coming down here for a few days?"

"I could. I have to go back to Cainsville. It won't be easy. I may have to sneak out in the middle of the night when Peg's asleep. After what happened she doesn't want me out of her sight."

"What do you mean 'after what happened'? You make the bucket at last? It's high time, slacker—"

"I'll come down. There's too damned much catching up to do to try it by telephone. I was shot."

"Shot?"

"Sorry if I sounded annoyed when you first called. I'd been

wondering where the flowers and the calf's-foot jelly were."

David tried to speak and could not, could not even make his voice sound like a voice. He was shaking with inner tremors like an alcoholic in the early morning, and he cursed the battered nervous system that could bring them on.

"David?"

He cleared his throat, said: "Yes, Chief. I'm here. How bad was it? For God's sake, those damfool starry-eyed kids didn't tell me—"

"You know how it is. Shot on Monday, headlines Tuesday, forgotten Wednesday. Unless you die. Then it's headlines Tuesday and Wednesday, forgotten Thursday."

"How bad was it? I mean are 'all your wounds in front, out there'?"

"That's a stupid question if I ever heard one. Few of us have our wounds in front, as you damned well know. It was a slug from a trooper's gun. I was trying to get out of the way of a demonstration in a town near Cainsville. I had a Federal Court case coming up in a few days; the Williams case, if you recall. I couldn't do Williams any good behind bars."

"I asked you how bad it was—"

"Stop worrying, grandmaw. It caught me across the rib cage, from back to front. The hospital in Cainsville, the nearest one, is Crow, so they got me to Capitol City. I played dead, and someone picked me up. Look, if you're paying for this call—"

"I am, and it's O.K. Go on."

"Well, they took me to Capitol City in the Cainsville doctor's special ambulance for colored. The doctor is colored, and the ambulance is a beat-up station wagon with an oxygen tank in it. The doctor, incidentally, is damned good. Anyhow, after a few days I signed myself out of the county hospital there, and went on up to Boston. Some infection developed; I wound up in the hospital in Boston for a few days and I've been out about ten days now. And I'm O.K., perfectly O.K. Stop worrying. I can hear you worrying clear up here. I'll be down day after tomorrow. I'll fly from Capitol City, and wire you the time."

"Wait. Where's Luke?"

"Cainsville. He just got out of jail."

"Again! Where?"

"Maryland. For taking pictures of cops using gas on demonstrators. I don't know what the charge was, but that's the reason. I was in the hospital here. He got ten days, which was mild, but the fine will build them a whole new county road system. Incidentally, he's been offered a roving assignment job by *Today*. Expenses, pay, no spec about it."

"Great!" Things were working out, things were really working out, thought David. He had already begun to have a nagging worry about Luke. He wouldn't be able to keep an eye on him from Boston, and the kid wasn't quite seasoned enough, even yet, to go it alone.

"He won't take it if he thinks we need him."

"I know. I'll take care of it."

After Brad hung up, David sat, yogi-fashion, so long, so without motion, that the black-and-white cat gave up its bid for attention and settled on the rug in front of the door, eyes slitted in an alert doze, opening, round and yellow, at the sound of a voice from the bed.

"They shot a good man," the voice said. "A trooper's gun. It had to be a .45. You know what a .45 slug through the liver would do, Chop-bone? Through the lungs? Through the heart? That's what's under your rib cage, pal; your liver and your lights and your heart and some of your guts." The cat closed its eyes; there was nothing of interest to him in the words. "Death," said the voice.

The inner shakes had quieted, and David was glad to see that his hand was not shaking when he poured another cup of coffee. If Brad had been hit by a truck, died in a plane crash, succumbed to disease, there would have been grief, but it would have been clean grief. But if Brad had been ripped open by a slug from a red-neck trooper's gun— The thought of the nearness of that death, of the fraction of an inch of skin and bone that had stood between Brad and that shattering, gut-tearing impact brought the inner weakness back, turned the tremors loose again. "It didn't happen. God damn it, David Champlin, pull yourself together. It didn't happen. It's not the first narrow escape. It won't be the last. You're getting mental." He stretched out in bed, trying to gather his forces, to get his mind and body working as a unit again, understanding the alcoholic who, in fear and dread, starts his day with liquor to assure forgetfulness of nameless unknown things yet to happen.

66

IF HE LAY THERE a little longer, stretching, forcing himself to relax, he knew he'd eventually overcome the dread of what a new day would bring. It was not fear of the events of the day that brought that urge to bury himself somewhere where no one could find him; it was a new fear of his own reactions, a doubting of the wisdom of his own judgments. Once he had been able to assess a situation, judge its potentials, and act. He acknowledged that he hadn't always acted wisely, but there had been no such indecision as occasionally had plagued him lately. And that was sheer fatigue.

He and Luke had established a private routine. Each time one of them was released from jail he stayed in bed an extra hour the next morning. "Pampering ourselves," growled David. Luke said: "It ain't that, boss. When you stay in bed an extra hour you just lie there and worry and think up more trouble. Me, I sleep."

Luke had been right. Damned if he didn't feel guilty now if he wasn't worrying. There were a number of things to worry about this morning. Klein's two-months-old letter, still unanswered, received before he was jailed, outlining ALEC's financial troubles now that they had embarked on a program of demonstrations and fines were becoming a major problem; the knowledge that he must go to Washington soon and talk to officials there and the frustrated feeling that always gave him; the disorganized chaos in a number of communities and the realization that there must be others in the same situation, and the further realization that leadership had to be provided or gains would become losses overnight.

There was even, he reflected ruefully, a damned suspicious knock in the motor of the car that had once been Chuck's. It was entitled to a knock after the beating it had taken for two and a half years. He'd get rid of the car before he went north. That was a nice, comfortable worry, not calculated to bring on stomach cramps or knots in his belly. Maybe if he concentrated on that small worry he could manage to doze off again.

Or perhaps if he concentrated on the fact that there was one worry, unconcerned with his work, that he had not known for two and a half years—the worry over Brad and his difficulties with Peg's drinking. He was convinced, even more than Brad was, that Peg had at last found the key—rather, that the key had been handed to her when Brad made his decision and came to New Orleans. She had gone over the edge into alcoholism long ago, but David now had met too many alcoholics who could look back on a decade or more of sobriety not to believe that Peg would make it.

"I've got to be a little scared," Brad had said. "But I'm growing less so with time."

"I'm telling you, Chief, she'll make it. All the way. Wait and see. She's got something to be proud of. Like you."

"Yes. I was damned shortsighted for a long time. I suppose that's it."

David doubted that Brad could have carried the double burden of his work in the South, and the worry over the woman who had been Peg Willis for so many years. Now a few days at home and his nervous tension melted away and he came back refreshed and clearheaded. He was, reflected David, a lucky guy—after a hell of a long and patient wait. And Mike Shea, bless his Irishness, was probably calling it faith. And Mike Shea could just be right.

His immediate worry about Brad was the reference made to the man named Garnett. Whatever Brad was working on, he might run into trouble if Garnett was around. He was pretty certain Brad's instinct about people, his skill in handling them, would help him out if the woman named Sue-Ellen Moore was also around. Brad had a genius for slowing down and instilling forethought and reason into the minds of the overly impulsive. David did not have as much confidence in the older man's ability to spot at first glance, as he usually could, one of his people whose own neck was of greater importance than the collective neck of the Negroes.

Even without Isaiah Watkins's prior warning David would have recognized in Garnett an opportunist whose loyalty was bounded on all sides by his own interests. That Sue-Ellen Moore trusted him wasn't strange. For all her bitterness and apparent disillusionment she was, like many others of that temperament, inclined to judge quickly, on face values.

He had met Garnett before he met Sue-Ellen. It was early

morning when he entered the office-lobby of the small motel on the outskirts of a medium-sized southern city, grateful for these oases that were springing up in the desert of the South, offering shelter to traveling Negroes who otherwise might drive hundreds of miles before finding a place to sleep. This one was modern, well appointed, and with a restaurant-coffee shop. He was in the city for a series of conferences and to lay the groundwork for a later ALEC campaign—classes, demonstrations, a probable boycott. The morning of his arrival he was alone, Luke following with a group of ALEC volunteers from New Orleans.

Garnett had been turning away from the desk in the motel office, a battered Gladstone in one hand, a room key in the other. Instead of leaving the lobby, he lingered in the background while David registered, a short, tubby figure, bald and managing to look to David somehow damp, although the morning was dry and cool. The clerk behind the desk, in contrast, was tall and bony and, even at five o'clock in the morning, quick. He raised his eyebrows at David's signature and held out his hand. "Proud to meet you, Mr. Champlin. Been hearing 'bout you. Lemme bring you some coffee after you get to your room—"

"I'd sure appreciate it. Thanks. Say, has a young fellow named Willis checked in yet?"

"Ain't seen him."

"When he comes put him in another room and put it on my bill. O.K.?"

"Sure thing. You get along down there now. I'll be along with the coffee."

The motel parking lot was at the front of the building, and David had brought his suitcase in with him. His vague distaste for the chubby man became more positive as Garnett hurried across the lobby and held out his hand. David took the hand reluctantly, and, when the other man spoke, could not stop himself from drawing away. The accent was a mixture of urban North and cotton-field Deep South, as phony as a red-neck smile.

"Y'all David Champlin? Reckon all of us been hearin' 'bout you. Lemme make myse'f acquainted. Garnett's the name. Alonzo Garnett. Y'all jes fergit about the Alonzo. I tries to. Here, man, let me he'p you with that suitcase. I'll tote it—"

David had never been able to overcome an unreasonable irritation whenever he ran into anyone insensitive enough to offer to carry something for him because of his lameness. He knew he was overreacting but he couldn't help it. "I carry my own bags," he said.

Later the clerk who had been at the desk brought coffee and a warmed fried pie he'd "scrounged 'round for," and said, "You-all never met that fella was in the lobby? That fella Garnett?"

"No. Just call me lucky."

"He's with this here Young People's Committee for Freedom. Travels round most of the time with a woman named Moore. Sue-Ellen Moore. She's here now; he just j'ined up with her. They been all around these parts, organizing children and young folks for demonstrations. I ain't made up my mind 'bout that. Comes to kids I ain't so sure. Don't make no difference to the whites if it's jes a chile causin' trouble, if he's black. Got a few young uns myself."

"There are a couple of ways of looking at it."

David finished the last crumb of the fried pie, the last drop of coffee, and got into bed. He remembered most of what Isaiah Watkins had said to him about Sue-Ellen Moore, one day a few months before in Isaiah's office.

"She means well. Sure does. But she don't use what anyone could call good judgment. She ain't got what a lot of folks down here has got—mother wit. Down here we has to think ahead of ourselves. She ain't a patient woman and she don't know what the score is once she gets into the South. But she's in there pitchin,' just the same. Heads up that new Young People's Committee for Freedom. Biggest trouble with her is she goes off half cocked a lot of the time, louses the other guy's plans up. 'Course, sometimes she don't louse 'em up—she helps 'em out, them as were dragging their asses and needed someone to come along and give 'em a kick in the pants. But she ain't got much use—ain't got much respeck—for the older folks down here. Lot of the northern colored feels like that. She comes from San Francisco. Helluva fine-looking woman, I'll say that."

"I remember the name now. Luke was around in one city when she was staging some demonstrations. Said she had those kids really trained."

"Lawd! She does. Be better if a lot more of that was done. She's a nut on physical fitness. Trains them kids in classes like she was a Army drill sergeant. They loves it. But she don't seem to realize you can't lead the South to the Kingdom with just kids. The older folks down here been round a long time. Gonna be round a long time. The kids? Who knows. Most of them'll be cutting out. Besides, going to be a heap of time before some of them kids can vote, even when we gets the vote—"

When David was leaving the office, Isaiah had said, "Speaking of Sue-Ellen. There's a fellow hooked up with her group that'd bear watching. Name of Garnett. We had him in ALEC for a while 'fore you come down here; eased him out. Beats me why he's in the movement at all. My guess is he likes fame and thinks he's going to get fortune."

"I'll watch out—"

He slept until ten thirty, then showered and shaved and headed for the motel office to see if the coffee shop off the lobby was still open for breakfast. He didn't like to go too long without eating because when he did his stomach began cramping with pain. On every trip now he carried milk and sandwiches in the car. He'd noticed, though, that in spite of these in-between meal snacks he was having difficulty with clothes that were gradually becoming too big for him—coats hanging baggily from thinner shoulders, shorts too big around the waist, belts he sometimes had to put another notch in. When he came within two pounds of Luke, who was two inches shorter and naturally slender, he stopped weighing himself. If his trips North lasted more than a couple of days, he always started putting weight back on again.

He stopped at the desk to see if Luke had checked in, was told he'd arrived a half hour before. He delayed a moment to light a cigarette, glancing toward the glass doors of the coffee shop as he did so. What he saw made him purse his lips in a silent whistle. A young woman was standing in the doorway, evidently waiting for someone still inside. She wore tight-fitting blue Capri pants and a white silk blouse. What had Isaiah said—"Helluva fine-looking woman"? He'd understated it. He stood quietly, watching her. "Handsome" wasn't the word—she hadn't the height to carry "handsome." Neither was "beautiful" fitting, although "pretty" was unthinkable, and he was damned if he'd fall back on the shopworn "glamorous." Isaiah's word—"fine"—covered it nicely, and so did an expression of Tom Evans's that he remembered. Tom would have designated her as an "omigodder."

It wasn't her figure. His eye was as good as the next for figures, and hers lacked the curves necessary to call forth superlatives. Yet it was good; better than most: flat-stomached, long-legged, straight, whip-thin and supple, with small breasts that she disdained to augment artificially, and skin—what the hell was it like? Coffee-colored whipped cream? She wore her hair sleek and close on top, brushed up at the ends, so that it circled her head like a gleaming black half-halo.

She moved forward impatiently, letting the door close sharply behind her, tired of waiting, and turned toward the desk. Seen directly and not from an angle, her face was that of an Egyptian statue, full-lidded eyes and full lips of such perfection a sculptor would go out of his mind with delight in them. The planes of her face sloped sharply from high, well-defined cheekbones, and David wanted to tell her to band her hair back, draw it away from those bones, from a face that needed no embellishment.

She started toward him, and when she drew close, she smiled and her hand was outstretched. "I know you," she said. "You're David Champlin. I heard that you were here." Her grip was quick, firm.

"And you're Sue-Ellen Moore."

"Come now! You couldn't know. After all, I've seen pictures of you."

"I have friends with good powers of description."

"I hope they said pretty things—"

"What else could they say?"

He was conscious now that someone had come up behind her from the coffee shop, and saw Garnett standing a few feet away. She turned her head and said, "What kept you?" then turned back without waiting for an answer. She said to David, "I hope we'll meet again." She was as straightforward as a man, without apparent coquetry.

"I hope so. I'd hate to think we wouldn't."

She walked away then, toward the main door and he went into the coffee shop and picked a table by the window. Before the coffee came Luke strode into the room, grinning. He sat down opposite David, rubbing his palms together briskly. "Hi, boss! Man, what I just saw!"

"I think I know. Quit twitching."

"Who could help it!"

"Lay off, Luke," he said, then was annoyed at himself for being self-righteous and preachy again with the kid. He'd been riding the boy with a pretty tight rein.

"Yeah, I know. Man, you been telling me for two years—two years, man—if I hadda have a woman to pick a chick outside the movement. Don't mess with workers, white *or* black, you said. And that ain't been easy. But I made out, man, I made out. But if I'd of known we'd run into something like what I just saw I might of come up with what you maybe could call a case of galloping insubordination."

David grinned across the table. He had reason to suspect Luke wasn't being entirely truthful about never having anything to do with his female fellow workers. Still, considering his youth and temperament, Luke had been everything David could ask for, and maybe a bit more. His own biological urges had been more quiescent than at any time since adolescence. He supposed this could be attributed partly to physical fatigue, partly to unhealed emotional wounds, and partly to his ability to use horse sense and run like hell from a potential involvement. Only when he had been sure that no such involvement threatened had he slipped out from under the unrelenting drive and pressure he had imposed upon himself. And couldn't remember being particularly happy about it afterward.

"You know who she is?" asked Luke now.

"Yes. Her name's Sue-Ellen Moore. I thought you said you'd run across her. You said you were around once when she was heading up a demonstration."

"I didn't get to see her personally. Cop got in the way. Jeez, I thought she'd be an old battle-ax—or a young battle-ax, maybe. You know, all muscles and might. Who's the little fat character trails around after her?"

"Man named Garnett. Isaiah warned me to watch out for him. She seems to treat him like an errand boy. Can't say I spotted any evidence of any close relationship."

"Hell, that guy couldn't do a woman like her any good." Luke was smiling broadly. "Whyn't you make a try for it, boss?" When David returned the smile and shook his head, Luke said: "I dunno. Sometimes I get real worried about you, boss. I think mebbe if you were getting more you'd get rid of them cramps in your stomach."

David laughed. "Worry about your own self. I'll worry about me. And take it easy. It's only sex."

"Man, that's not *enough?*"

The next evening he met her again in the lobby, and suggested that they have dinner together. In the back of his mind was the thought that ALEC's own momentum could benefit by the help and cooperation of Sue-Ellen's committee, with its tie-ins with youth groups. There were several places he could think of where the local leadership troubled him by its lack of any dynamic drive. A Sue-Ellen might bring it to life.

Conversation at dinner was general. He had met no one with a more comprehensive or detailed knowledge of the activities of every civil rights group, South or North. He even learned things about his own organization he had not known. She could have been without sex as far as her general attitude was concerned. There were no meaningful glances or provocative gestures, no double entendres. She didn't need them, he thought, and she was one of those rare women with sense enough to know it.

She was objective—and abrasive—in her appraisal of civil rights activities in the South. But her criticisms, in David's opinion, were not valid because they were not based on any real understanding of the psychological factors involved. Isaiah had been right. She had no patience with the fears and misgivings of an older generation, one that had borne the burden of a lifetime in the white South and who at last were being shown some hope of the lightening of that burden—yet who remained unable to march with banners because of a very real and ever-present fear of a terrorism from which they had never been free. He tried to have for her the understanding she denied others, led her to talk about herself and her own background. She had been born and grown up in California, gone to college in Berkeley, and never been closer to the South than Arizona until she was past twenty. By that time, David realized, her bitterness against the white rule in both North and South was all-pervading. That bitterness became a searing hatred when she talked of white men, and she spoke with the frankness of a man about their inadequacies, mental, moral, emotional—and physical.

"Ask any whore in San Francisco if a Negro will pay to get into bed with her," she said. "He'll buy her the best meal in town, take her to a show, pay her for the income she lost while she was with him—and that's that. Pay to make love he won't."

"Don't blast me out of my chair if I say you seem pretty well informed."

"My kid sister is one—"

"Can't you get her out of it?"

"No. She won't leave. Why should she? Even with what she has to pay the Goddamned white pimp she's supporting, she still sees more money in a month than she'd see in a year with me." She shrugged. "I'm not blaming her. Just because I was lucky doesn't make me virtuous."

"Lucky?"

She laughed, and her eyes mocked him. "Lucky. The first man I knew was white. I'd made it to college still pure. He was a senior. We used to have lunch together in the cafeteria, have our goodies in an abandoned lab in the basement. I thought he had to go home every day after classes and take care of his poor invalid mother. Then I found out he was dating the white girls, taking them to dinner and the movies, taking them where he wouldn't take me—out in public. Then getting from me what they wouldn't give him. My kid sister had a similar experience in high school. She reacted one way, I reacted another. She's going to get all she can out of them. I'm going to get back at them."

"Why in hell did you come south?"

She shrugged again. "Because I'm a direct actionist. I'm no politician. The only weapon we have in the North, as you damned well know, is political. I tried for a while and couldn't stomach it. The white liberal politicians who suddenly find out they've got more bigots in their district than they realized, and cut your throat. Even our own people playing footsie with them. And I got really fed to the teeth when I read about the namby-pamby efforts, the same kind of thing, going on in the South. I could tell you about my family before they moved north, about what happened to my mother's husband, the man who should have been my father—"

"Your father was a white man." He made it a statement.

"Yes. And if I knew who the son of a bitch was, I'd kill him."

"I believe you." He had never believed anything more firmly in his life. He changed the subject as tactfully as he could. The words "my mother's husband—the man who should have been my father—" weren't words to dwell on.

He said: "I wish I could soften up your attitude about some things down here. Grant me the knowledge gained from growing up here."

"The knowledge? Or the handicap to your conscience as a Negro?"

"You take chances, don't you? I hate to think I look like a guy who would let that one get by, but I'm going to because I want to make you see the picture here as a whole. A middle-aged Negro walking into a registrar's office in a Mississippi county courthouse may not be militant, but he's showing a kind of guts I sometimes wonder if I'd have in his circumstances. Can't you see that as a valid move toward freedom?"

"No. Because it's useless. He knows it's useless. He's still just a funny, quaint character to the white—an object of ridicule—someone to dominate and intimidate."

"You're wrong, one hundred percent. If that was all he was to the whites, they'd hardly bother to go to the lengths they go to in reprisal. He's risking that black neck of his. Literally. Your kids are risking dog bites, beatings, goads, jails —and for a youngster who's been treated like a cute little black primate all his life that can be heady stuff. That man standing in front of a registrar's desk—his scars go deep."

She was wearing yellow Capri pants that night, and she stretched one slim leg out beyond the table and pointed to a fairly fresh scar just above the ankle. "Dog," she said. "And I love them. I used to take my Scottie everywhere I went until I realized I could be jailed for days, perhaps weeks, and God knew what would become of her."

"You must miss her. Is that why you got a substitute?" This would at least open up another combat area.

Instead of reacting resentfully, she laughed. "You mean Garnett? Alonzo? He's our radar. Our eyes and ears. He's quite harmless."

The hell he's harmless, thought David. He said: "I don't see him that way. Anyhow, you ought to tell him to ditch that phony corn-pone accent. You've been pretty outspoken about the shortcomings of our groups, ALEC, then N-double-ACP, others. You've even had the guts to imply we aren't sufficiently color-conscious, that's why we aren't militant on behalf of our race. Want me to tell you what's wrong with your approach?"

One of Sue-Ellen's strong points was that she did not anger easily. He wouldn't have wanted to be around when she did give way to anger, but he saw that in normal conversational give-and-take she was in complete control of her emotions.

Now she said, "There's nothing wrong with my committee's approach—but go ahead, tell me what you think is wrong."

"You're underestimating the intelligence of your people down here, underestimating it by a hell of a lot. I don't mean the young people. I can see why you're so successful in handling and organizing kids." He was smiling again. "Children and adolescents are very suspectible to beauty. I can remember when I was a kid in about the third grade having a hell of a crush on a pretty teacher. There was a man—a professor—who helped me because I had to miss a lot of school, and I used to wish he was pretty, like she was, instead of having a red beard."

"Red beard?"

"He was a Dane."

"You had white indoctrination early—"

His eyes darkened with anger. "You know better than to make a crack like that. My Dane is dead now, but if he were alive he'd be roaring in the streets with happiness over what's happening here—"

"I suppose so." She sounded uninterested. "It doesn't matter. What matters is to raise enough hell to get action."

He laughed, trying to keep the conversation on an even keel. "I'll bet you aren't the Southern Christian Leadership's pinup girl."

"I'm not. And I don't want to be. I happen to think this 'love' routine is futile. For God's sake, do you think these people mean it—praying in the streets for red-neck bastards who are itching to lynch them—talking about 'loving' them? Are you that big a fool?"

"I suppose I am. At least, they've made progress. They've made people think instead of react."

"What do you mean, 'made people think?' The whites here don't even know what the word 'think' means."

He moved in warily. "Sue-Ellen, we disagree like hell on almost everything. But we both—or maybe I should say our organizations—have something to offer. I think perhaps we could work together, ALEC and the YPCF. Without losing autonomy, of course."

She smiled at him. "Between rounds?"

"Between rounds. Yes. If you can organize kids into drill teams, you can organize them into classes. You damned well have to recognize the need for those."

"I do." She frowned thoughtfully. "We'd fight—"

"Yea, verily—"

"I'll think about it," she said after a moment.

"Keep an open mind?"

She laughed, and leaned back in her chair with a stretching movement that tightened her sweater over the small breasts, and her transformation from an argumentative and determined woman to just plain woman was so sudden it dazed him for a moment. She said: "I have a meeting at eight thirty. I'll give it some real thought when I get back. We can talk it over again before you leave—"

For a week he and Luke worked the community, David concentrating on the older people, Luke on the younger. Everywhere they went, even in remote rural areas, the evidences of a new spirit were as discernible as the first signs of spring in New England after a hard winter. Radio and television had brought the word to those whose reading was slight or non-existent. The knowledge that what had been "their gov'mint" might become "our gov'mint" in time, that their own children could conceivably face a future they would have a hand in shaping, was working a subtle alchemy, transmuting fear into hope, apathetic acceptance into courage.

"I'm surprised the whites haven't made it a crime for Negroes to own TV's or radios," said David. He and Luke had been in a crowded bar watching a TV news program showing scenes of an Alabama riot. The TV image was blurred by the thickness of the smoke that hung in the air, and the men and women in the room were quiet for the most part, but there was menace in the quiet. The volume was set high on the TV set, and the sounds of the riot were as clear as if the dogs and firehoses had been in the room. Now and then a man or woman, standing in the deep crowd in front of the bar, cursed, and the curse blended into the scene they were watching and became part of it, so that it seemed to come from someone in the mob. Once a woman who had been drunk when they came in, but who seemed sober now, cried out, "Ya ofay son of a bitch, git your hands off that boy! He ain't nothing' but a chile!" and a man's voice quieted her, and another woman's voice was raised: "She saying it right! They gonna roast in hell. Roast in hell, and I'm gonna be watching—"

The TV camera, concentrating now on the aftermath of the riot, swung to a Negro youth stretched along the heavy bough of a misshapen tree, high above the littered street. He must have eluded police, troopers, and volunteer white enforcers and escaped being caught in the mass arrests. But the reporters had seen him, and now, obviously unknown to him, he was squarely in the camera's focus. He was smiling. There was a cut on his forehead, and he had tied a handkerchief around his head to stop the blood from running into eyes that were looking from one end to the other of a block of buildings that had been transformed, in one flaming hour, to a shambles of broken glass, fire-damaged buildings, overturned cars. The smile never left his face. A man seated near David said softly, "I knows how he feels. Man, I knows how he feels." His companion laughed deep in his throat, softly. "Born again, man. That's how that boy feels. Born again."

He remembered that as he sat at the bar he thought again of the mass stupidity that passed as white thinking in the South, the ineptness that passed as white action in the North, and that he had felt as a warm and living thing his pride in his own dark skin, his pride in his people.

When he made his remark to Luke about whites forbidding Negroes access to TV or radio, Luke said: "They're not all that bright. I keep telling you, boss, these red-necks still—*still*—talking about their 'happy nigras.' "

"If they were any brighter we wouldn't be here. Educators, that's what we are, sonny boy, educators. And I'm not talking about citizenship classes for black people—"

During that week there had been only a few opportunities for another real talk with Sue-Ellen. They discussed methods of dovetailing the work of their organizations, arrived at a few tentative arrangements, argued, quarreled, and yet managed to establish an uncertain entente that David hoped would become stronger.

When he talked it over with Luke, whose opinion he was learning to respect more and more, Luke said: "She'd better get rid of the fat pussy-cat trails around after her. God knows, she's dedicated, but that guy's not dedicated to anything except himself."

"He's just the complete opportunist—"

"He ain't 'just' anything. You're taking chances, brushing him off like that. Right now he figures he's in the right spot. If he thought he'd be helping his own self, he'd cross that woman up quick as he would anyone else."

David grinned. "God help him if he ever does cross her up."

Luke shivered. "Wouldn't want to be around. No, man, wouldn't want to be around—"

"If we do get together it's not going to be easy." David ran his hand over his closely cropped head, digging his fingers into his scalp, frowning. "She's in the same groove, Luke, that a lot of northern Negroes are in. And a lot of the young militants down here. They're becoming almost a stereotype. They've got a damned 'thing' about the older Negro from—

or in—the South, a sort of contempt, and the more you try and make 'em see it any differently, the harder their heads get. They never stop to think what they owe their ancestors. They want to be born now. They never see the ones who came before them as anything but millstones around the neck of the race. Try and make them think and you're judged immediately, no trial, no jury, and found guilty of being an Uncle Tom. Hell, some of them are screaming because it's the National Association for the Advancement of Colored People, because 'colored' isn't right anymore. It ought to be the N double A *N* for 'Negro.' And a couple of generations ago 'Negro' was a word none of our people would use. Pretty soon 'Negro' won't be right. It'll have to be something else. And I'll be Goddamned if I want to be worried with it all."

"You think that explains this Sue-Ellen Moore?"

"Hell, ask a psychiatrist. Don't ask me. She's got something like contempt for the older generation. It comes close to an active hatred. She blames an ignorant, helpless, oppressed people for their own crippled status in society. She's dead right that the future lies with youth. But, God damn it, so does the future of every race, every country. That doesn't mean you have to relegate the people who've borne the brunt for a couple of hundred years to a sort of open grave of living dead. What I want to do is get 'em out of that grave so they can vote the freedom for these young people—get 'em out before they shovel the dirt in over 'em. Perhaps she doesn't even realize it, but she's shoveling that dirt now, she thinks she can march to an earthly Gloryland at the head of an army of militant kids—they tell me her groups never sing 'We Shall Overcome' in a demonstration—an army that doesn't represent one vote in its ranks, and that is getting 'trapped by the whites' into violence. It's a funny kind of war. She's fighting the whites, and damned if she isn't fighting a certain segment of her own people that she doesn't understand. I'm hoping we can give her some of that understanding."

They had been having a beer in the coffee shop, and David pushed his empty glass and beer bottle away, stood up. "Come on, Luke. I've got to go write to Klein. And you've got to get to town by five thirty and get film."

"What you doing tonight? Anything for me?"

"Not unless you want to go to a church prayer meeting. I'm going to one a few miles out, give a little talk."

"We-e-ell—I sort of had other ideas. I'm up to my ass in

church and prayer-meeting film now. I picked these other ideas up when we were here last month. Maybe I'll draw a blank. Maybe she's got another date—"

"What's been holding you up? Go on. Only, get the car back by seven thirty. You'll have to figure out your own transportation after that. Need money?"

"A five wouldn't hurt, boss."

"Here you are—now get the hell going—"

"This is your last night here." Sue-Ellen made the statement to David that night at dinner in the coffee shop.

"Unless something unexpected comes up."

"What are you doing with it?"

He looked at her, trying to keep his face serious. "Going to church. Want to come?"

"No! For God's sake, what church?"

"I believe it's called 'Holiness.' In brief. There's more to it. It's in that little town, Big Mountain, about five miles west."

He knew beforehand what her reaction would be, waited for its scornful contempt.

"And I suppose you'll shout and sing and witness and roll on the floor along with the rest of them—"

"Not quite. Might play piano and sing a hymn or two. It's the only chance I get outside of a bar here and there where there's a piano. I've got a couple of gospel numbers I can really shout—"

"Good Christ!"

"That's the general idea—"

He hadn't taken his eyes from her face, noting again that the beauty of its bone structure was the measure of its strength. He could tell by the way the cheekbones seemed to spring into greater prominence that his needling was getting to her.

"You can't be stupid enough, you can't, to be taken in by that mindless hysteria—"

"I didn't say I was." He was laughing at her now and he could see that anger, not ordinarily displayed, was mounting.

" 'Holiness Church'—"

"It's sanctified—"

"And that means something to you, Mr. Harvard-Oxford Champlin?"

"Its members are known as 'saints.' All members of 'sanctified' churches are known as 'saints.' I'll be speaking before the saints. Gosh, that ought to mean something—"

"Damn you, you think that's a sharp needle you carry, don't you? It isn't—"

"It seems to be drawing blood. I'll drop the needle and use an ax. I've tried everything else to make you see a little light—"

"You flatter yourself. I've been trying to make you see it."

"And we're both still in our own dark, eh?"

She pushed her soup plate away with a quick, impatient gesture, dismissing the subject abruptly. "Give me your itinerary again. Where does the bell ring for the next round?"

"That town called Heliopolis, I suppose. I've got a couple of brief stops between here and there, but that's the next project—"

"Heliopolis! You didn't tell me. Look, do you know that town?"

"I know enough about it to wish I could go in and out real fast. Real fast."

"You just might do that. Only you'd be going out stiff. *And* cold. You're not exactly unknown to the whites—"

"Is it true that every adult white Heliopolis male is reputed to be a member of the Citizens' Council?"

"Yes. Not 'reputed' to be, either. Is."

"All the more reason to go there—"

"David, do you honestly think you'll make any headway with your particular kind of program there?"

"You think you would with yours?"

"There's no other way."

"Oh, God! That's tripe, and you know it."

"I suppose you'll go in there and make friends with all the sisters and brethren and saints—and the preachers. Southern Negro preachers! Parasites, every damned one of them. Greedy opportunists, playing on the ignorance and primitive instincts of these poor people—"

"Climb down, babe—"

"You know damned well I'm right. They're no better than the plantation owners were. Ol' Massa dished out religion the way a doctor dishes out massive doses of sedation in the disturbed ward of a mental hospital. Perhaps the motives are different, but the results are the same."

"Sue-Ellen, honest to Gawd—and I'm taking my life in my hands when I say it—I've known whites with more understanding, more empathy if you will, for your people down here—dammit *your* people—than you have. Chap named Chuck Martin for one."

" 'Uncle Charlie.' Good old 'Chuck'—"

"Oh, hell, I might have known you'd say that. He can't help what his parents named him. He's got a middle name that's worse—Beauregard—so he's stuck with Charles."

"Take him—and lose him."

"You're itching to get back to flogging the preachers—"

"David, I'm on a lot of the same sucker mailing lists you must be on. Crap like a certain so-called bishop sends out—'Take a dollar bill, put it in Chapter So-and-So of the Bible, leave it there two days, then mail it to me.' Instant salvation."

"We've been over this before. *Ad nauseam.* I've told you that you underestimate your people here. *Your* people, God damn it. You've found out that down here education will get you nowhere in no time. You're still a nigra. Still a nigger in a town like Heliopolis. They haven't even gotten out of the slime as far as 'nigra.' And what are you up north?" She didn't reply, waiting for him to continue. "All right. Up north you're that 'beautiful Negro.' Graduate of a famous university. Brilliant. Wonderful, isn't it, what 'they' can do if they have the chance? You're still isolated as a human being. What makes you so Goddamn much better than people here? Education? That's not enough." He sighed, looking at her, knowing she was only becoming more annoyed, fretting under his words. "What do you know, actually *know*, of the faith, the suffering, the endurance, the hopelessness of these people? Your own experiences were bitter ones. What Negro's aren't? But have you lived every day, every hour, every Goddamned second, with what these people have lived with? And if you had, would you have what they've got? Faith. 'Primitive'! I ought to wash your beautiful superior mouth out with soap and water."

"Perhaps I didn't quite mean—"

"You did, babe, you did. I don't give a damn if a preacher's a charlatan or a saint at this point. If he's a charlatan his little flock are onto him. Don't think they aren't. But where else, how else, can they find release from pressures you can't seem to understand? They've got to have a rallying point for faith. Many of the early saints are great in my eyes because their faith was a lonely one, solitary."

"Faith! Honestly, David. What faith? In what? And why?"

David shrugged hopelessly, reached for the check. " ' 'Tis ye, 'tis your estrangèd faces—' " It was one of Sara's favorite poems, and he wished the words had not come to him just then. He was surprised to hear Sue-Ellen finish the verse:

" 'That miss the many-splendoured thing.' " She laughed. "You call it 'faith.' I call it a sort of mental anesthesia. The 'many-splendoured thing' in my book is freedom. And we'll never reach it with anesthetized minds."

"Good God! You seem to think faith is standing in the way. Damn it, woman, it's the blasted key! Maybe it won't do the trick all by itself, but without it you and I would be running around down here with our tongues hanging out—not getting anywhere. I mean *anywhere*. Even Luke's grasped that essential fact. So it came from the people in the Big House originally? So their descendants are having to reckon with it now. They're being beat over the head with their own weapon. And God help 'em. Them there angels with flapping wings these parasitic—your word, for Christ's sake, not mine!—preachers are telling them about just might carry these people to a ballot box before they carry 'em up yonder." He stood up, tired of trying to talk to her. "Let's go, Sister Moore."

She walked beside him to the cashier's desk and after he had paid the check laid her hand on his arm. "It's your last night here, David," she said. "Can't you get out of that meeting?"

He looked down at her, smiling to hide the irritation. "Sure I can."

"We could go—"

"But I don't intend to."

"I kept this evening free on purpose—"

"Sorry, Sue-Ellen. If I'd known that I would have gone to the Sunday-night service—"

"You should have thought of it. Men have no sentiment—"

He laughed down at her. "You aren't exactly loaded with it—"

"I'll see you when you come back?"

"If you're awake—"

"You could always wake me. Not everyone can."

"Thanks. That sounds like a compliment—"

He was relieved to get in the car and drive off. This was the first time he'd realized—perhaps he'd better say permitted himself to realize—that Sue-Ellen might have more than just an impersonal joining of forces in mind. An intimate involvement with Sue-Ellen Moore, or any woman like her, was the last damned thing he wanted. And he had too much respect for her as a person, her brains and dedication, to entertain any idea of a quick in-and-out-of-bed affair with her. Also, there was an uneasy feeling now that such a relationship wouldn't be possible with her, that it would mean more than momentary pleasure, that she would want it to be a continuing thing. A possessive Sue-Ellen—God help any man who got on that spot. Yet it could be that what she wanted—and needed—was some man to possess her, that under those circumstances she might become—Hell! let someone else experiment, Champlin. You aren't the type—

It had been more than two years, and he still could not throw himself into an affair as other men could. He must always remain apart from his own emotions in a sort of split-personality objectivity. For a long time now he had felt that he was watching himself, watching his own tired body push itself up to and beyond its limits, and this duality extended even to his emotional experiences. They did not happen within the man who stood apart, nor was the physical fatigue a part of that man. The body of the one seemed powered by the will of the other, fueled by it, driven. Only the deadening exhaustion of sheer physical strain brought them together, in one body, in sleep. And the man who stood apart was the repository of the memories, tried to hold them back from the other man whom he drove with such relentless cruelty along an uphill road.

"You gets here by the down road and you leaves by the up road." Those were the directions Elder Garrison had given David to reach the little church that sat back from the road, on the floor of a small valley.

"Sort of like life," David had said, and the church elder had laughed. "That's what I tells my people."

When David drove up, Garrison was standing just outside the church door, a heavy, handsome man with glowing brown skin and grizzled, white-black hair so effective it seemed to have been done by a makeup artist. They shook hands, and the elder introduced him to the people as they arrived—kindly, smiling people whose handclasps drew him into themselves, made him a part of their lives, trusting him because Garrison had brought him. This intangible something he could not describe—this sharing, however disparate their individual circumstances, of a common destiny, this reaching out, was an experience no white would ever know, no black could ever convey. Their loss, he had often thought. Yes, Lord, their loss.

"Guess the saints is all inside now," said Garrison, and together they entered the weatherbeaten, rickety frame building that was the house where the people worshiped God. Worn, patched-up, makeshift pews were supplemented by equally worn and patched-up chairs. The walls were bare boards, not even protected by plaster. David had never entered one of these little churches, either in country or town, without being deeply moved, without hearing a voice deep within himself crying in protest, and he could silence the voice only by the remembrance of the words, repeated over and over to himself until they brought peace—"Wherever two or three are gathered together in my name—"

He and Garrison talked for a few minutes behind the pulpit, and Garrison said: "Think we can get you to honor us with a song, Lawyer Champlin? And maybe play piano? Ain't much of a piano, but we hears tell you're a mighty fine singer and player—"

"Where did you hear a tall tale like that?" He asked the question from politeness; he was sure someone from another community must have visited Big Mountain and mentioned it.

"Little fella come see me the other day. Bald-headed little fella. I disremember his name. Working with ALEC. Least that what he say. You sit here, Lawyer Champlin. Soon's you hear your name you come up to the pulpit. That means I'm introducing you. After that we'll have a little music. You think that's a good way?"

"Sure. Anything you say." For a moment Garrison's disclosure about Garnett knocked his little planned speech out of his mind. The hell Garnett was working with ALEC. David doubted that Sue-Ellen had discussed any proposed coalition of activities with Garnett; whenever Garnett had been around she had treated him very definitely as a subordinate. She ought to be tipped off to the fact that Garnett had evidently sized up her group and ALEC, decided ALEC was the best bet and was going to try to worm his way back into ALEC's graces. She was asking for trouble if she kept him around, and any joint plan of action by the two groups was out until she got rid of him.

Garrison was talking now from the pulpit, had been for several minutes. ". . . and so we're privileged to have tonight this distinguished guest here, this fine young man who's come all the way down here to tell us 'bout something we been hearing about for a hundred years and ain't known nothing about yet—freedom. Lawyer Champlin—"

Driving the "up road" back to the motel, he decided first

to wait until morning to talk to Sue-Ellen, then changed his mind. He and Luke wanted to leave early; she might still be asleep, and he might as well get it over with while the feeling of accomplishment from the meeting he had just left was still with him. He was glad they were leaving in the morning; Sue-Ellen seemed perilously close to becoming a Problem.

He saw that there was a light in her room, a little beyond his. Luke apparently hadn't made out too well; the shades were drawn in their room, and a light was burning, indicating that Luke was probably there in bed reading. He'd tell her about his misgivings over Garnett as soon as he saw her, then get away fast and get a night's sleep.

He never had a chance. He had not taken more than three steps into the room when the blow landed on one cheek, openhanded but backed by the wiry strength of an enraged woman who believed in physical training. The blow was so hard, so unexpected, it sent him off-balance, one hand reaching out and grabbing the footboard of the bed. It also was so savage that it knocked out of him, for that moment, any anger, leaving him gaping in stunned amazement and shock at a finely sculptured face grown gaunt with rage, at eyes ink black with fury.

"Good God! What—"

"You bastard."

That was all. Why didn't she scream, curse—she wouldn't be half so dangerous as she was now, tight-lipped, speaking in a half-whispering snarl, deep in her throat. He looked quickly around for some sign of a weapon, saw none. This woman was killing mad. She moved toward him, and he saw that her fingers were curled, long nails clawlike. He grabbed her wrists before she could avoid him, held them and kept her at a distance, feeling, he thought later that night, much as he would have felt trying to hold an enraged mountain lion.

"Keep your hands off me." She did not struggle, and he loosened his grip. But only slightly.

"When you tell me why in hell you put one of yours on me I will. When someone hits me I want to know why. Right now."

"Let go of me." Still that low snarl.

"And lose an eye? You think I'm crazy?"

She twisted both arms suddenly in a downward arc, and the pressure was so strong on his thumbs that his loosened grip was broken and she was free. He couldn't get away from her without sidestepping or rolling backward over the bed.

The latter move he didn't let occupy his mind for more than a small fraction of a second. And if he tried to sidestep he wouldn't be quick enough. For some reason—shock, he supposed—he had no impulse to retaliate in kind. He knew she expected it, even wanted it.

Her breathing was short, heavy; with her eyes still fixed on him she reached sideways and snatched a newspaper clipping from the bureau. He would have expected her hand to be shaking with anger when she held the clipping out to him, but it was steady. And this was even more dangerous. God damn, what in hell ailed the woman? Maybe she was a manic-depressive, an honest-to-God mental case—yet he knew she wasn't. He couldn't read the clipping without taking his eyes off her. At the moment that seemed risky.

"Read it. Read it, you son of a bitch."

There was nothing to do but take a chance. He glanced down at the clipping in his hand. It was a gossip column from a New York paper. Every now and then the columnists ran a paragraph that was led into with the identifying words in boldface caps: "Torchbearers." In the text the names of individuals were also in boldface. The items were short, always in the same style: "So-and-So for that movie starlet who just married her producer. So-and-So for her ex, now living it up—or down?—at a Swiss ski resort with a famous Italian beauty." Vapid stuff that could have come strictly from the need to fill space, and out of the columnist's own sterile imagination.

Halfway down the paragraph his own name sprang out at him, and as he read the item there was the familiar feeling of tightening knots of tension in his belly, nerves crawling like snakes just under his skin. The item read: "David Champlin, former Boston attorney and State Department appointee, and Sara Kent, young American artist now getting kudos from European critics—for each other."

He wanted to run, leave Sue-Ellen and this small room, find a solitary place where he could battle with what the item had awakened in him.

The hoarse half-whisper broke through to him: "I didn't know. I was stupid. But Garnett knew. He gave me this. He told me who she is."

(Don't snarl at me. Let me alone. Let me the hell out of here—) "It's no one's—"

"Be quiet. Oh, be quiet, you son of a bitch. Do you think I'd have had anything to do with you if I'd known?"

There was no time now to kick himself for not getting the hell out of this situation before, for not seeing more clearly than he had that Sue-Ellen was not just becoming a Problem, but had become one.

This was a woman enraged by jealousy beyond all reason, her rage the more flaming because she had learned that he had been involved with a white woman—and the hint contained in the column that he was still involved emotionally. There was more than resentment in her, there was bitter fury, brought to life by the awakening of memories of her first lover, a white man. There was no "right thing" to say at the moment, only a multitude of wrong ones, and he said the first one that came into his head:

"You're acting like a three-year-old."

During the storm that rocked the room for the next few minutes his only thought was escape, but he was literally trapped, with Sue-Ellen standing now between him and the door. He wished again that she would curse; obscenity would be easier to take than the accusations she was hurling at him. The only answer seemed to be to knock her clear across the room, but he was damned if he wanted his first physical attack on a woman to be on this embittered, enraged embodiment of hate. She gave no signs of running down, of running out of either words or breath. A flash of memory brought to his mind the scene in a Boston kitchen when his landlady had launched a tirade of filth at him because she had seen Sara coming to his apartment. Then he thought of nothing but the need to duck as Sue-Ellen, in an incredibly swift movement, launched a heavy glass ashtray at his head, followed through with a vase, then started in a quick rush toward him. He heard the words, louder, far louder, than the previous torrent, "white woman's nigger—" and moved in.

Because she was moving he caught her off-balance, one arm around her waist, lifting her feet from the floor, one hand holding one of her wrists behind her. It was only a few feet to the shower, but by the time he made it he was out of breath. This was a powerful woman with—at last—a powerful voice. In the shower room he wrestled with her briefly, freeing her arm but holding her, still off the floor, tightly against him. With his free hand he opened the door of the shower stall, reached in, and turned on the cold water full force. Somehow he forced her to the floor of the stall, rolling her under the icy cascade, then shut the glass door of the shower. The door to the bedroom opened outward and he slammed it shut, wedging a heavy chest of drawers across it. Even as he hurried from the room, Sue-Ellen's screams following him, he thought what a damned shame it was to subject such physical perfection to such an ignoble and complete messing up.

The tiny screened window high up in the wall of the bathroom was open, and Sue-Ellen's screams for deliverance, he thought, must be heard by the occupants of every room in the place.

He ran the last few steps to the office. No man could have sent him fleeing at that speed, but Sue-Ellen was making him wish he had wings. When he thudded into the lobby her voice was still shatteringly audible, louder and more carrying even than it had been when she had first regained her breath. All he could see as he entered the lobby were the enormously wide eyes of the tall thin night clerk behind the desk.

"Man!" he gasped as David hurried toward him. "Man! You in trouble! You in *real* trouble—"

"Tell me something I don't know—" David fumbled for his wallet. "Give me our bill quick. Tell that kid Luke I'll call him from somewhere in the morning—"

The clerk was out from behind the desk, grasping his arm. "You ain't leaving. Where the hell you gonna go? Ain't nowheres nearer'n a hundred miles you can find a place to sleep." He was pulling David around the side of the counter. "Y'all come back here to my room. Gimme the keys to your car. I'll stash it away in a garage out back."

"No—"

"Y'all do like I say. Far's I know you done taken off, anybody asks. An' they sure as hell gonna ask—"

David found himself in a tiny bedroom in the rear, between kitchen and lobby. That chest of drawers he had wedged across the shower room door had been heavy, but sooner or later Sue-Ellen would be able to push her way out. He had to stay now. Too much time had been wasted. The clerk said: "I sleeps here when I works, and goes home weekends. I'll bring you a drink later." He put the old-fashioned key he carried in the keyhole. "You lock the door, y'hear. I'll get that woman out."

"No. Look, I can't let you—"

"Ain't no 'cain't' about it. You stays here. What that woman'd do to you, mad as she is, I don't want happenin' in my daddy's new motel. Gimme them car keys now—"

David handed over the keys. "I sure thank you." Then added piously, "And may God have mercy on your soul—"

Half an hour later there was a soft knock, followed by Luke's voice, low and a little unsteady: "It's me, boss. Luke." David unlocked the door, and Luke slid in sideways, then locked it again quickly. He was in pajamas and robe, barefoot. David, after a rough half hour during which many emotions had fought for ascendancy, had arrived at a state of suspension of all emotion. Until he saw Luke's face; then his body shook with his effort to control a reaction of wild laughter.

"Boss—" The awe in Luke's voice matched the awe in his eyes. "Boss, I didn't know you had it in you. Mr. Champlin, sir, do me the kindness to tell me what in hell happened—"

"You'll die wondering, kid. It's over. I hope."

"Yeah. I figured you'd say something like that. Like it says in the Bible, huh? Sufficient unto the day are the kicks thereof—"

"Did she come to our door?"

"Did she! You never heard? Scared the hell out of me. I thought I was next in line. That desk clerk, he hauled her away. I heard him tell her you'd taken off."

"You could hear all right from under the bed?"

"Under the bed! Man, I locked myself in the shower!"

"Look—go back and pack our stuff. I'll find out from that clerk how we can make it out in the morning. Then go back to sleep."

"Who can sleep?" He grinned. "You always said you didn't like to fight. Even when you were a kid—"

"I'm fighting now! Man, I'm running like a scalded cat. Give me a red-neck cop—damn it—pull your face in line. One laugh out of you—"

"Yes, sir, I hear you." Luke checked laughter with difficulty. "Always been a pleasure to work for you, sir. Sure been a pleasure. But damned if I ever thought it would be fun—hold it! Temper, temper! I gotta get out of here whole and get that guy to sneak me back home—"

He stretched, yawned, brought himself back to New Orleans gratefully; this was a hell of a way to spend one of those precious hours when he could sleep in, remembering a scene like that last one with Sue-Ellen Moore. His shock at the news of Brad's injury had worn off; his appetite was beginning to assert itself, and Chop-bone's was making itself known vocally. His feet thudded on the floor and he headed for the shower, saying, "Courage, cat. Food next—"

67

WHEN DAVID CALLED ALEC headquarters he was told that Isaiah Watkins was in Baton Rouge for the day. He was relieved to hear it and, still in robe and slippers, leaned back in the big chair, fighting an almost overwhelming impulse to crawl back into bed with a prayer to God to act intelligently for once, just once, and repudiate His handiwork: mankind and all its works.

When he finally looked up he said, "Food, Chop-bone," and rose slowly, stretching. There were still twinges in his back and in the rib area, but not, he supposed, as bad as the twinges Brad must feel in the scar tissue of a healing gunshot wound. He cooked scrambled eggs, bacon, and toast, but found that his appetite of the night before was gone, and he gave the eggs to a delighted cat. The bacon and toast he forced down, helping them along with more coffee.

Afterward he puttered around the house, fighting off what he knew was coming, holding it off with a tired mind, trying to build around that mind and the secret places of his emotions steel-strong walls, yet knowing that at last, like glass, they would shatter.

What brought him back to loneliness like this, time after time, a loneliness he felt nowhere else with such poignancy? That it was bad this time because he was physically and nervously depleted he acknowledged. Usually the worst of it passed after a couple of nights' sleep, a day or two of relaxation. This time he knew it would not.

He looked down at Chop-bone as he made the bed, and could hear Gramp's banjo and Gramp's singing, so husky and deep for so small a man, "Jesus gonna make up my dyin' bed—" and he responded softly to that ghostly voice, " 'Ya-ah, Jesus gonna make it up—' " tucking in sheets, squaring corners, smoothing the bright, striped counterpane.

"Whyn't you do the dishes, fat cat?" he asked Chop-bone when he went into the kitchen. He unlatched the cat door, and Chop-bone slithered through it. David stopped himself from calling the cat back. "You've had it, brother," he told himself. "Christ! You've really had it!" Wanting the cat's company because he needed something to talk to, because he felt self-conscious talking to himself without even Chop-bone there to hear the sound.

He washed and dried the dishes, put them away in the cupboard, then folded the dishtowel neatly and hung it on its bracket over the sink.

Darling, we'll never make it; never, never make it, sweet. You'll hate me in a week, following after me, hanging up dish towels, putting caps back on toothpaste tubes. Promise not to hate me, darling.

"Sara." The sound of the whisper and the thud of his fist on the sink's enamel edge seemed to echo through the house. His hands gripped the edge of the sink, and he bent over like a man retching with nausea. He let the pain carry him, convulse him, because to fight it only drove it to a corner, to return, renewed in strength, a little later. "Not again. Christ! Not again. God almighty, let the time come when it won't happen, won't ever happen again."

The pain would go, he knew that; if he could ride it out it would pass because it must if he was to keep on living. God would see to that, the God who let his people suffer the last full measure of pain and humiliation, pressed down and running over, that God would keep him living, and because he must keep living the pain would pass. And because he was alive, it would return; not all his pleas could hold it back.

It was here, in the little white house, that it lay in wait, an unconquerable army with spears of fire. But Sara had no part in the memories of this house, had never been here, could never be here; even if they had married she could never have been here. Yet in shabby motel rooms, in the poor homes of his people who took him in, or the well-to-do homes, in luxury hotels in New York, Chicago, San Francisco, even in his own apartment in Boston, the pain could be kept reasonably distant, Sara could be exorcised. Here, never. Here he could not order her from his side, still her voice in his mind.

It had to do with love, in some obscure, unanalyzable way; when the worst of the pain had abated he would tell himself this, that it was bound up somehow in the love that had permeated the house, that clung still to every board, each piece of furniture and knickknack and pot and pan, the love that had cradled the infant, taught the child, strengthened the youth. The love of Gram and Gramp and a huge red-bearded man who had said, "You are the son of my mind."

Benford had said, an aeon ago: "Within the four walls of whatever place we called home there was a security of love that passeth the understanding—" God help him, this was home, and he could never bring to it that which would make it whole again, and because of that the pain awaited him. Somehow, somehow, now, now on this trip, he must tear it from him, dismantle it, put it in its place in the past, bury it, bury it, bury it where it belonged, in the past with Gramp, and yellow cats and red-bearded men and the sound of music in a little room at night—and love of any kind.

David watched Brad walk from plane to terminal entrance, searching anxiously for any sign that the older man had been telling less than the truth when he said, "I'm O.K. now," found only a slowing of the walk that had always been more of a fast amble, a darkening of the skin beneath the eyes. "Satisfied?" asked Brad, and David grinned in reply.

They stopped at ALEC headquarters before crossing the bridge to Beauregard. On the way Brad had told David that Luke had been released a few days before; that the message about the job had reached him by telephone in Cainsville, and he had gone to New York. "He'll be here tonight or tomorrow," said Brad. "He'll be sticking with us for a while. In fact, he's hoping to make Cainsville his first series."

In Isaiah's office, while Isaiah was out hunting up beer, Brad said, "Damned if Isaiah doesn't look ten years younger than he did the first time I met him."

"He does, at that."

"I wish I could say the same of you, brat."

"You can't?"

"To the casual observer you still look the callow, untouched youth—"

"Get off my back. To the noncasual observer?"

"You look like hell," said Brad with a flat bluntness that raised David's eyebrows and brought a smile.

"Maybe I'm like the five-year-old who was told he was a fine, big boy and looked older than his age, and who said, 'I've thought a lot.' "

"Too damned much."

"Maybe I've crossed my last river, seen my last jail," said David.

"What do you mean?"

"Only that I think now I can be of more use in Boston, at national headquarters. My God, Brad, you have any idea of the damned mountain of legal paper work that's piling up?"

"Did you know Klein has had another heart attack?"

"No! When?"

"A few weeks ago. As a matter of fact, he was in the same hospital I was in. You brought it up, David. They'd like you to take over. I wasn't going to tell you till later."

"Hell, no, Chief. I've been out of touch too long for that. And it will take a hell of a long time just to get my own material in shape—"

"Fight it out with them. I'd like to see you do it. This year's going to be a big one, David; next year will be bigger. They need someone with front-line experience."

"Here's Isaiah—"

They talked a while of progress and nonprogress, discussed politics and the possibility of a civil rights bill and the handling of the trouble that would follow its passage. David told Isaiah of the need for organization and trained leadership, especially now that whites were coming down in groups. "They don't know what the score is," he said. "You can't expect them to; you can't expect a wide-eyed, white college kid who's never had anything worse than a campus curfew to contend with to understand fear and the apathy of fear. They'll catch on, only they need leadership and, well, call it education. And sometimes I think the young Negro needs it even more than the white. They don't have the tolerance, don't understand the psychology of their elders, tend to be contemptuous of the mental scars—"

He saw a gleam come into Isaiah's eyes. "How long you staying down here this time?"

"Middle of next week," said David.

"Fine, son, fine. You doing anything Sunday? You better not be. We've got our youth groups pretty well licked into shape. Sunday there's a big picnic, young folks, old folks, everyone. Over the lake, if it don't rain. They'd sure be proud if you'd give 'em a talk."

"God, no, 'Saiah. I'm no good at that sort of thing. And I hate making speeches, even though I've had to make a lot of 'em. Besides, you want someone who's better known—"

"What you saying! Better known! You think you ain't known around here? Negro press give you a mighty big play, son, when you give up that big gov'mint job to stay down around the South. Editorials and all that. They tell me the northern papers played it up, too, columnists and all. Li'l Joe Champlin's grandson stands mighty high around here, almighty high. Anyhow, it's just one day. Thought you might tell 'em about some of the snags they'll run into, some of the mistakes to steer clear of, keep 'em from making fools of theirselves when the time comes, getting theirselves in trouble—"

David shrugged. "O.K. So I make a speech and I give 'em the works on nonviolence—"

"Who said anything about a preachment on nonviolence?"

"I thought that was what you were getting at—the joys of law and order."

"Where's it going to get you with police dogs and cattle goads? You-all know what's been going on up around Plaquemine way?"

"I've heard," said David. He didn't want to talk about it. It made him sick, nauseated him, the memory of what he'd heard. Out of the corner of his eye he saw Brad shift in the wooden office chair, pull away from its back, rest his weight on one thigh, and said: "Give 'em rifle practice, too. Teach 'em to shoot straight."

"Lawd!" Isaiah's eyes widened. "Never thought I'd live to see the day. Li'l David Champlin, the kid his grandaddy said didn't like to fight. Never thought I'd ever live to see it."

"Me either," said David. He frowned at Brad. "Come on, Uncle Bradford. You're going to the house and get some rest." He turned to Isaiah. "Let me know where and when you want me Sunday. After that I'll be busy. So no more plans. O.K.?"

68

Luke came just before they started dinner, pounding up the path, knocking and then bursting in without waiting for an answer, saying "Hey, man!"—live, vital, bringing an almost tangible glow into the house.

"Charge!" said David, and grinned at Brad.

They called each other "jailbird" and other, less complimentary names, Luke giving David and Brad little chance to talk. "Can I use your shower, man? Man, five days out of the clink and the smell's still there. You got your phone connected, man? You got the water heater on? Must be half-dozen chicks in this town gonna sit up all night and cry, Luke don't let 'em know he's back, don't show 'em trouble hasn't changed him any. Man, what a trip! Out of the bucket and into the Ritz in five easy steps. Man, you hear about my job?"

"Slow down," said David. "Slow down. We're old men, remember? Listen, I've got hot water, telephone, and the divan bed's made up for you. But you've got to sleep in it alone, y'hear? And if you can hold still long enough to eat, we've got gumbo, beans, rice, chicken, and biscuits. If you want to tomcat around tonight, you can sleep tomorrow."

Luke grinned. "You mean I'm staying here?"

"Sure. Planned on it."

"And you do the cooking? Let the chicks wait. They'll be all the better for it. I've been out five days, four of 'em in New York, and Luke don't waste time. I can hold out. Lemme get us some drinking liquor before I start scrubbing the frame—"

David started to tell him there was plenty in the house, then stopped. The kid wanted to buy it himself, wanted to celebrate his new status, his new prestige. Brad said, "Put blinders on him and let him go—" and after the door had closed behind him, "My God, David, I never realized how much the boy had changed. The first time I saw him was right in this house. Remember? You sent for him. He was sulky, almost sullen. On the defensive, even with us."

"He's not the only one, Brad. Take Isaiah. You noticed it. And I've seen it all over. I don't mean just hotheaded kids; I mean older people, men I'd never seen before in my life, but I knew what they'd been like a few years back and I knew the change was there. Even while they were holding back, giving me a bad time, 'not wanting no trouble, son'; 'too old now to go looking for trouble, son,' the change was there, in back of their eyes."

"There's still fear," said Brad.

"Hell, yes, there's still fear. As my grandfather said once,

'We been frightened people, son.' But, Brad, fear without hope is one thing; fear with the leaven of hope is something else." He remembered a conversation with Gramp years before. "Jungle," he said. "Them antelopes sure learning fast."

Later, in the living room after dinner, as they were finishing the "drinking liquor" Luke had brought, David said: "Brad, come on with the Cainsville bit. Every time Luke's mentioned it you've shunted him off."

"You mean my interference with the course of a bullet? I've told you about it. That was in—"

"No, I don't mean that. I'm convinced now that you're in fair shape, loaded with luck. An ordinary guy, with ordinary, nigger luck would have bled to death on the way to the hospital. It's happened."

"Why don't you give him the scene, Brad? Why you holding back?" Luke freshened his drink and, swinging one leg along the length of the divan, leaned against its arm.

"Oh, hell." Brad was nursing his drink between the palms of his hands. "Why didn't you stay in jail, Luke? I've been holding back because I happen to be fond of this big ape. I'd like to see him out of the whole damned mess for a while, at least until he gets himself in shape again."

"How about talking to me instead of at me?" asked David. "You know, like I was in the same room."

"All right. Only I don't want you involved. Wait, that's not true. I'd give a good deal to have you with us there, but I'd give more to see you looking like a human being again, feeling like one."

"F'cris'sake, what makes you think I want to be involved, as you call it? If I want involvement there are other messes in other places; there are other jails. Unless you need me, man, I'm happy to stay away. And there's one whole hell of a lot of catching up to do in a nice quiet office in Boston, where the jailhouse is a long way off. That's my next stop. What's so special about Cainsville you've got to treat it like a top-secret bombsight? Just another crumby red-mud southern town—"

"Not now," said Brad. "Not quite. Do you know the Reverend Humboldt Sweeton?"

"Hummer? Yes. I met him more than a year ago, in Montgomery. A hell of a sweet guy. Well named. He's no Martin Luther King, but in his own way he's quite something. If he had King's grasp of reality, he'd be one of the best leaders we have. Is he in this Cainsville scene?"

"Very much so. ALEC just joined forces with him, unofficially, and secretly. Even Isaiah hasn't been told. The N-double-A and a couple of other groups are in the background, holding a watching brief. Fred Winters is there, and Les Forsyte."

Brad rose and took what had been a bowl of ice cubes and was now mostly water into the kitchen, and David, waiting, searched his memory for more details of the minister known as "Hummer" Sweeton. He had met him in a small wooden frame church hall on the edge of Montgomery, Alabama. The hall had been crowded that day with delegates to some kind of church convention. The local ALEC group had found David in New Orleans, asked him to come and speak before the general meeting. After the talk Hummer Sweeton came up to him and shook hands. "Can you get us some more like you down here?" he said. "That's what we need, young leaders with your kind of sense."

David shied away from the compliment, and Sweeton, smiling, said: "Sort of wasting your breath on the desert air sometimes, talking to the older folks. Not that they haven't done a fine job here, a mighty fine job, considering. But the young ones, they're rarin' to go, and every once in a while they gets led off in all directions, lots of times the wrong directions. Leastways, that's the way I see it."

Now David could see Sweeton clearly: a small man, very dark, not much bigger than Gramp had been, with a long face, thin and deeply lined; large eyes, set deep, the sockets almost black from fatigue. He looked like a man who slept little. He looked, too, like a solitary man, a man who would make few close friends. His smile, when he said goodbye and God bless, had been of such gentle sweetness, so free of the usual easy, ingratiating pretenses, that David, watching him move toward the door—stopped every few steps by well-wishers—had felt a familiar ache for Gramp awaken. "And God bless you, too," he murmured as he watched the small figure leave the building.

When Brad came back, David said: "I remember Hummer well now. There's a sort of otherworldly quality about him."

"He's sort of a kook." Luke swung his foot to the floor and tossed Brad a pillow so the older man could lean back.

"All right," said David. "He's sort of a kook. When you come right down to it, so was Jesus Christ."

Luke ran a finger over the rim of his glass, not looking up. "He laid me out once," he said. "I mean he *laid* me out. He brought me down so far I swear to God I went around all day feeling like I didn't have a stitch of clothes on." He sighed. "And he never even raised his voice. Swear he didn't speak as loud's I'm speaking now. And he didn't say more'n twenty-five words. That man can sure bring a guy down, somehow."

"And lift a crowd up," said Brad. "I don't know what it is. One meets it now and then. Hummer Sweeton is a man whose hatred of violence is as intense and deep-seated as his hatred of oppression. He's not so starry-eyed he doesn't realize its inevitability in certain situations; no one is. He lacks formal education. Grade school and the Bible, that was it. He differs radically from the general run of Negro preachers. He can sway a crowd, hold it, fire it up, and he can kneel beside a sick baby's bed all night and in the morning put his take from the previous night's prayer meeting on the table."

"You've got to be kidding," said David. "There ain't no such animal. Not even Hummer."

"No, David, I'm not kidding. Three months ago I made him—it wasn't easy—take a week's rest with us in Boston. We got to know him damned well. As you said, he lacks that touch with reality needed in a good leader, but he has other qualities just as important. One of them is the ability to inspire trust in a people who don't trust anyone, even each other. Another quality is the Goddamndest faith I ever ran across, a faith that quite literally passeth understanding. My understanding, anyhow."

"No cross, no crown?" said David. "Gramp—"

"No. Not the 'no cross, no crown' faith that's been the ruination of prior generations. No, not that. His is a fiery, Old Testament kind of faith, the faith of the Hebrews, made gentler and more acceptable by the teachings of Jesus. Damned if I can find exact words for it, and damned if an agnostic like me has any business trying to. I can explain the psychological motivations of a murderer. The faith of a Humboldt Sweeton is something else again."

"It's not unusual," said David. "It's—hell, Brad, you'd have had to be brought up in the South, lived with it, to know its strength. And when you leave the South, and look back on it, remember it, it—well, as you say, it passeth understanding."

"My grandmother," said Luke. "She was like that."

"Let's get to Cainsville," said David.

"Apparently Sweeton has had a dream for many years of a drastic nonviolent program, contradiction in terms though that may be. The elimination of the working Negro from the Southern way of life."

"My God, Brad, that's not new. We've all had that particular daydream."

"It's a lot more than a daydream to Hummer. He's been working on it, biding his time." Brad smiled. "I was one of the few he confided in. I'd run into him, here and there when he was moseying around the South, looking the territory over, preaching, and I'd say, 'How you doing, Reverend?' and he'd smile and say, 'So-so, Mr. Willis, so-so. Biding my time, tha's all, jes biding my time.' "

"And now his time has come? Or he thinks it has? In Cainsville?" David tried to keep the skepticism out of his voice.

"Actually, I think it has. Cainsville has more Negroes employed than many other places. Its whole economy is dependent on them in more ways than one. There is poverty, but not the abject poverty of so many southern Negro communities."

"Brad. Listen, man. Money. M-O-N-E-Y, money."

"It seems to be materializing."

"It can't be. At least, all that money. All the civil rights groups put together couldn't raise enough money to support a whole damned Negro community on a gone-fishing boycott of everything, including their own jobs. And even if they could, you must know what would happen. Pressure. Pressure by the whites on wholesalers, on banks, on loan companies. Good God, Brad, you of all people!"

"I've thought of them all, David. The first of the week, in Boston, I spent most of an afternoon dictating to Lucy a memo on possible retaliatory measures. I prepared it as carefully as I would an outline of the prosecution's probable case. After a while Lucy asked me please could she go home early, as soon as I'd finished, so she could throw up in private."

"Funny," broke in Luke. "Damned funny how hard it is for some of these so-called sympathetic whites to dig the Southerners. I've heard 'em say, 'Well, now the Supreme Court's decided so-and-so, there won't be so much trouble.' Bunch of starry-eyed assholes, if you ask me."

"I like that," said David judiciously. "Man, I like that. May I use it if I give you a credit line?"

"At least a name like that will give the whites something new to think about," said Brad.

Luke interrupted with a loud "Yah!" Then, anger mounting, was on his feet, eyes hot. "Who the hell cares what the whites think! For Christ's sake, who cares! There's fifty-eleven different kinds of colored in this damned country. There's Harlem colored who don't stop cutting throats—white *or* black—long enough to put the knife in their pocket, and who blames 'em! And there's Brad's kind of colored, who've had it pretty easy and still have a bone in their craw; and there's David's, brought up a hell of a lot better than most whites; and there's mine, all snarled up on a toboggan, going downhill; and there's colored like they got in Cainsville, good, decent colored, some of 'em scared shitless, and what the hell! We're all niggers to the whites. Man, you know it! We're all niggers. So what the hell difference does it make what the whites think!"

"Luke," said Brad gently. "I could drive an Army tank through that argument."

"Sure you could. You're fixin' to say there's just as many kinds of whites. You're fixin' to point to Chuck Martin and some of the others, like the students coming down here."

"Brad's just going at it from a pragmatic angle, Luke." Three years ago that "pragmatic" would have thrown Luke. Now it didn't.

"Sure. Sure. I'm not so damned dumb I don't know it hurts our cause when some little black kid pees on the wall inside a grocery story during a demonstration. But what you going to do? Train a hound dawg to kill cats, then shoot it when it kills your grandmaw's pet tabby? You think the whites are going to see anything but a nigger peeing on a wall?"

"Can't say I appreciate it myself," said Brad.

"Man, I'm not saying it's good. I'm just saying it don't make a damned bit of difference what the whites think, because they going to think the same thing no matter what we do. If we stand around singing hymns and talking love talk, they going to say, 'Ain't the nigras wonderful?' but they still ain't going to want us moving in next door, living near 'em, living in a house as good as theirs, sitting at the next table in a restaurant—"

"Marrying their sisters—" goaded David.

Luke whirled on him. "Who the hell wants to marry their Goddamned sisters! I don't even want to lay 'em. A few times is plenty, I mean *plenty*. Talk-talk-talk. Talk-talk-talk. They ain't all that good. My God, Luke Willis has got something better to do when he's in bed with a chick besides talk about race relations!"

David choked on his drink, didn't try to check the laugh. It had its usual effect, stopping argument, stopping discussion, filling the little house, spilling over through the open windows and the screen door. When it was spent and the sounds in the living room had come back to normal, he said, "Sorry, Luke. I guess I've got what they call a photographic mind."

Luke was still steaming, cooled off only slightly by the interruption. He pointed a finger at David and said: "You know what I'd like to see? You want to know, man? I'd like to see about ten big—and I mean *big*—black—and I mean *black*—bastards with nothing on but maybe a goatskin and maybe not even that, prancing up and down the aisles of Congress, steppin' high, peeing on every mush-mouthed southern congressman they got there, every damned one of them. And the whites wouldn't think any the worse of us than they do when we march down the street singing hymns. It don't make any difference *what* we do. We're still niggers."

It was Brad whose control snapped now, and he laughed, if not with the same overwhelming power of David, at least with as much spontaneity, his head against the back of the divan, eyes green slits, finally wiping away tears, shaking his head. "Same like David," he said. "Photographic mind. Certain fine, mealymouthed, old s'uthe'n gentlemen—"

"We're with you, Luke," said David. "We're ahead of you. But look, what happened to Cainsville? Sit down and cool it for a while, huh?"

"O.K., O.K." Luke sat, still fuming, but, David knew, feeling better, his mind clearer.

"You mentioned money, David," said Brad. "And economic retaliation. Remember, Hummer has rounded up an unbelievable amount of support. And Les Forsyte, who has a genius for organization and detail, is getting up a file consisting of a statement from everyone who will need help of just what their minimum requirements are for a two-week holdout. You'd be surprised at how little they've asked. A lot of these people could live off their land and stock indefinitely."

"Yes," said David thoughtfully. "I know. And there are a lot of us in the South, in business and in the professions, who are loaded, and willing to give. And a few whites who won't want to be identified—"

"Right. Forsyte has a projected figure of donations that, once the thing breaks into the open, would surprise you. The Negro storekeeper on the colored side of Main Street is the community leader. Fellow named Haskin. He's been quietly increasing his orders to the wholesalers for months. Dr. Anderson has stocked up on extra drugs and supplies, although he needed some help from ALEC. God knows, he may need 'em, because Hummer plans two demonstrations first. They'll be red herrings in a sense. If they work, and you know damned well they won't, we might have to change our plans."

"How closely is this Garnett guy working with you?"

"He's glommed on to Hummer, who's an exception to the rule and trusts everyone. Behind his back we call Garnett our gopher. You know, he 'goes fer' this and he 'goes fer' that; anything from a drink of water to a phone call. He's not in a position to hurt us."

"I doubt if he talks," said David. "So. What's the population ratio?"

"Sixty-forty, about. Sixty white, forty Negro. And vicious white, believe me. The first Negro has yet to be registered to vote."

"How's employment? Negro, I mean."

"High, such as it is. Which is one reason Hummer picked Cainsville. Pay is substandard, even for the South. There's a cigar factory, a paper box factory. Both finally had to employ Negroes. Of course, there are fieldworkers and tenant farmers."

David began ticking off work categories on his fingers, taking Brad's nods as answers: "Waiters? Dishwashers? Housemaids? House cooks? Day-work cleaning women? Gardeners? Cleaning women in the hospital? Store janitors? Hotel chambermaids? Hotel porters? Office building janitors? Ditch-digging-type laborers?"

Brad elaborated on his nod at the last category. "Definitely. The place is growing. There's a subdivision being laid out, roads. Ground has just been broken for another hospital."

"O.K. Elevator operators? If the town has buildings large enough."

"Hell, yes, three of them."

"Garbage collectors?"

"All of them."

"Any in what might be called public service? Besides garbage collectors. Policemen, firemen—"

"You out of your mind?" growled Luke.

"I'm just trying to find out what makes you guys think this would work. Brad, the supposedly cool legal mind; you, Luke, hotheaded, vindictive, and mean; man, really mean when you want to be—I swear I can't get it—"

Luke was on his feet again, anger rekindled. "Now wait! Wait a minute, dad! I'm just as mean and vindictive as I ever was. The only reason I'm for it is because it's going to hurt those lily-white sons of bitches on the other side of Main Street a hell of a lot worse than marching up and down a few streets, making muscles, singing hymns, or even, by God, busting windows, or shooting guns. If it works, it's going to get 'em right by the balls. That's the reason; that's all, dad. It's going to hurt 'em worse. I'm no Mahatma Gandhi. Not li'l Luke Willis. No, man! I'm for stringing 'em up by the balls over a slow fire. But I've grown a little sense these last couple of years, and that's *your* fault, dad."

"All right, kid, you're as mean as ever. But will you just sit down and stay sat? You're giving me fits."

After Luke had subsided David said to Brad, "What about Aunt Mattie?"

Brad frowned. "Aunt Mattie?"

"Lawd, you-all know Aunt Mattie! Deah ol' Aunt Mattie; she's the sweetest li'l ol' thing. Been working for us ever since my grandma was a little girl; she gave my mother her first spanking and ouah little Cynthia, too. We jus' love Aunt Mattie, and she loves us."

"Oh," said Brad. "We've got her too. But not too many of her. She's dying out."

"What about her husband, Uncle Mose; he must be around, too. Dying out maybe, but still there. I know. I've been running head on into Uncle Mose everywhere I've been these last years."

"I know that, David," said Brad quietly. "Aunt Mattie and Uncle Mose lost their individuality as something apart from their white families a long time ago. Not only their bodies but their minds were trained to servitude. But not so many of them live in now, and they may feel differently when they find themselves crossing Main Street all alone."

"God damn it, man, they won't be crossing Main Street alone. You think Cainsville's the only town in the whole damned South where they don't have white men's niggers? Cats who'd tie a rock around their own mother's necks and throw her in the river if they thought the whites would go easy on 'em? What about some poor devil with anywhere from five to fourteen kids scratching to make it every week, every day? If you think the expression 'bread' is some kind of modern slang, you're mistaken. I can remember my grandfather quoting his mother, who didn't use slang, as saying

'No man should be ashamed of the way he earns his bread.' Man, that bread on their own table is a hell of a lot more important to a lot of those guys than being able to break bread in a restaurant with whites."

"David, we don't expect one hundred percent participation. None of us expect that. But look back over your own experience in the field. Hasn't it been the man with a flock of children who's been as cooperative as he's dared? Haven't you found a number of people with the attitude of the old lady, hobbling along during the bus boycott—'I ain't walking for myself; I'm walking for my grandbabies'? Haven't you?"

David was silent for a long time, and neither Brad nor Luke disturbed his thoughts. At last he said slowly: "Yes. Yes, I have. And I've seen a lot of them lose their jobs, get foreclosed, have their credit cut off, their homes damaged. Hell, I've smelled lynching in the air." He was silent again, then looked at Luke. "Did you tell the magazine about this?"

"No. They've given me a free hand. They know something's cooking, I guess, but they didn't press me. They want some big-city stuff first, anyhow; what youth groups are doing in New Orleans, Atlanta, places like that. But I'm sticking as close to Cainsville as I can. I'll get that picnic Sunday, then go on to Memphis, but I'll be in touch. I ought to make it to Cainsville for a few days by the middle of the week."

"The minute the thing's ready to break, we'll notify the news media," said Brad.

"And I'll get some exclusives," said Luke. "Like Abraham Towers's nephew, Jim, sitting on his porch with a beer while the spittoons at the Grand Hotel stay full."

A clean spittoon on the altar of the Lord, a clean bright spittoon all newly polished. David wondered if Luke remembered saying that, the first night they met.

He had been sitting with one leg over the arm of the chair; now he put both feet on the floor. "I suppose it could work," he said. "I suppose it could. And if it did, Luke's right. You'd have 'em by the balls. But I don't know. I just don't know." He stood, stretching, and laughed shortly when Luke said, with an almost pleading note in his voice, "It's practical, boss."

"Cripes! Look who's talking about practicality. You hungry, kid? Must be all of two hours since you've eaten."

"Man, that's what I call *really* practical!"

While David was reheating gumbo, setting out plates, Brad leaned against the sink, his thin, tan face showing signs of fatigue now. "You know, David," he said, "we all know, the Emancipation Proclamation has never been really operative in the South. But there's still no law that says a policeman can go into a man's home and drag him out to work, yank a fishing pole out of his hand and put a shovel in its place."

"Right. But they can sure harass 'em."

"I remember we talked about it at your place one night. Peg was in New York. Your friend Tom Evans was down from Vermont, and Suds and Rhoda and Sara—"

He stopped, and David said evenly: "I remember. Later we all went to Marblehead for a shore dinner. Then came back and spent most of the night around the piano, drinking beer and singing. It was a long time ago. But my memory's good."

"Still like that, eh?"

David turned to him, eyes shadowed. "Your mother ever tell you that you were born with a veil?"

"If I haven't developed intuition in twenty years, I'm in the wrong racket."

"You seen Sara lately?"

"Two, maybe three, months ago. She was at the house for dinner with Suds and Rhoda. She was only in the U.S. a couple of weeks. She's in West Germany now, Düsseldorf. She went over to teach at some summer art classes. They ought to be over about now."

"Hunter Travis?"

"Why do you think I'm so well informed? He's still the faithful two-way channel for information."

"Does Sutherland still hate my guts?"

"Don't be an ass. He never did. And he's mellowed."

David carried rice from stove to drainboard. "I read something about an exhibit of Kent's—"

"At the Kershaw Gallery in London. In about two weeks. That's close to the top, very close—"

"Fine. That's fine. Hand me one of those soup plates, Chief."

David spooned rice into one side of the plate, filled the other side with steaming gumbo, and handed it to Brad, then did the same for Luke, who had been standing quietly in the background. "Let's eat it in the living room," he said. "It's cooler there."

On their way through the dining room Luke stopped and

pointed a finger. "Piano," he said. "There. Where's that guitar you had, man?"

"In the hall closet. After you've eaten you want to make a little music, kid?"

There was always some anodyne for pain there, in the ends of his fingers and the sounds they made.

69

ON SUNDAY MORNING LUKE APPEARED in the doorway of David's room dressed in tennis shoes, slacks, and a sports shirt of bilious green splashed with impressionistic orange flowers. David groaned, said: "Take it away. Take it outside. Take it off. Jeez! Take it away till I've had some coffee."

"You don't like this shirt? Man, it's a fine shirt. Cost me plenty. I got it in New York."

"I don't care where you got it. Just wear it someplace I'm not."

Luke grinned. "What makes you so conservative, boss? Look, I gotta go to a youth meeting. Take pictures. One of the churches on the other side of town. They're holding it after the service. Then I'll make the scene at the picnic."

David sat up, noted that the coffee maker beside the bed had stopped percolating, and poured coffee. "Want some? Get a cup."

"I've eaten, man. Coffee, eggs, bacon, toast, the works. I'd have had more only I'm hung over."

"You wash the dishes?"

"Me and the cat. Can I go now?"

"Yeah. And hurry. Out of my sight."

"Yes, *sir*. See you—"

David listened to Luke's feet padding through the house, heard the front door close and a car start up. It was a used car that Luke had acquired the day before after negotiations too complicated for even Brad or David to follow. His own car was a necessity for Luke now. Showering, shaving, David thought of how he'd miss the kid, of how dependent he had grown on Luke's need for him. It must be a little like seeing your child start off for school the first day. If there were only a few more years between us we'd be like three generations: Brad, me, and Luke, he thought. He knew he'd miss Luke, even when he was in Boston.

He was sitting at the kitchen table drinking coffee, wondering what a man had to do to get rested besides sleep, when Brad appeared in robe and slippers.

"I wasn't going to call you," said David. "Somebody in the joint ought to get rested. Luke's off and running, hung over some, and I feel like I've been digging ditches all night, and I haven't even had a drop."

"Comparatively speaking, then, I'm in fine shape."

"What time you planning on leaving for Cainsville?"

"One o'clock plane to Capitol City. I'll phone Chuck to meet me." He sat down, wincing, caught the expression on David's face, said: "It's all right. For God's sake, it's all right. It always stiffens up in the night, and wears off in an hour or so. Especially on a warm day. Forget it. If I mentioned breakfast would anything happen?"

"Breakfast. That's what would happen." David got up and walked to the pan cupboard. "Grits? . . . Eggs? . . . Ham? . . . Toast? . . . Look, don't you even know how to say 'no'!"

After he had eaten, Brad drew his coffee cup toward him, cradling it in his hands.

"Let's talk about real estate," he said.

"Talk about *what?*"

"Real estate."

David grinned. "Remember what old Higginbotham used to say to a new class on opening day?"

Brad laughed. "Yes. 'The ramifications, complications, involvements, and general cussedness of the laws governing real property are such that a man must either have great courage or be a damned fool to own it. Personally, I rent. Now, gentlemen—' "

"I agree. Why do we have to talk about real estate on a muggy Sunday morning?"

"Pour yourself another cup and listen. This real estate is in Cainsville. It belongs to an old lady named Towers. She's the only Negro I've run into there whom even the whites call by a last name. She's known as 'ol' Miz Towers' to everyone. She is, I believe, incredibly old to be so active. I've never asked her age because I knew I wouldn't believe what I was told. All estimates are in excess of ninety years. She has a son, Abraham, who lives with her. He is about fifty-four. His wife is dead and his children—four, I think, in the teen-age bracket—live with his sister."

"Who would be Miz Towers's daughter."

"Right. Said sister has a son of her own named Jim Towers. Lightish. His father is generally believed to be the man who is now chief of police. There's a touch of rape involved."

"That's not rape. That's the white man's privilege."

"I know. Anyhow, Jim works as porter at the Grand Hotel on Main Street."

"This is real estate?"

"Shut up and let me get on with it. Miz Towers owns the land her house, originally a cabin, stands on. She also owns a large piece of property to the west of it. We'll forget the land she lives on and that she and Abraham farm for themselves. It's not involved." Brad got up and walked to the desk that had replaced the buffet in the dining room, came back with a pencil and paper. "That's what I like about you, son. A place for everything and everything in its place. Like a damned old maid."

"Lay off. What about this west forty?"

"It's a lot more than forty." Brad was sketching as he talked. "The land is shaped like a pyramid with one straight side, with the base of the pyramid on the south, extending west. Actually, the boundary is roughly the road that runs to Heliopolis, and is a continuation of the southern boundary of the smaller piece of land. The lower, southern—I'd say eighth—of the land is nothing but an uncultivated field. The Negroes call it Flaming Meadows. There's some local superstition regarding it, and it's never been touched. It looks flat, but actually rises gently to a wooded area on the north. The rise becomes sharper there, continuing to the peak of the pyramid. Now. The eastern boundary is a river in the northern portion, Angel River. A little way south of the peak of the property there is a waterfall, quite a big one, and very beautiful. Below that, the river meets a diversion and splits, one branch of it running eastward, the other due south. The east branch doesn't concern us. The one that flows south is small, and it becomes known as Angel Creek. It seems wider than a creek to me, but only in California could it be called a river."

"Wait a minute. It's not actually a boundary after it reaches the Towers farm land? That land doesn't run as far north?"

"You're doing splendidly. It is not. It's merely a wide, flowing creek, or a narrow flowing river, whichever you prefer, passing through her property. There's an old-fashioned plank bridge over it in the roadway. If you're a good swimmer, it's grand on a hot day. The current's a little too strong for weaklings."

"Are you planning on building a resort or some such?"

"Quiet. I've just begun. Have some more coffee, and pour the old man some. Thanks. Now." David saw him draw a double line across the top of the lopsided pyramid he had sketched, then crosshatch it. "Railroad," said Brad. "A branch line of the A and C. They leased it while ol' Miz Towers's husband was alive. A ninety-nine-year lease. The money changed a one-room cabin into a house, bought stock, and made it possible for the old man to set Abraham up in his own auto-repair garage. He's been at it ever since. Naturally, they didn't get what it was worth, but the railroad wasn't too unfair, considering railroads."

Brad turned the sketch he had been working on around, pushed it across the table until it lay in front of David, then leaned back in his chair. "So!" he said.

David studied it a moment, and looked across at Brad. "All right. So. What am I supposed to say?"

"Look at it again. Doesn't anything jump out at you?"

David obeyed, said, "Nothing but those phony trees you've sketched into the wooded area." He frowned. "Wait!" He looked across at Brad, eyebrows raised. "Industry?"

"Congratulations."

"Don't be sarcastic. I'm growing old, slowing down. Somebody wants the land. Specifically, a white somebody. Or somebodies. Possibly acting as a front for a northern or eastern industry, or trying to buy it for a song and resell at a big price." He studied the sketch again. "The obvious question: If whites are involved, how good is the title?"

"It's perfect. Not even a southern court could upset it. The land was bought by the first Towers to be freed from slavery, passed from father to son, again to son, and then from that son, Miz Towers's husband, to her. She has left it to Abraham. I've even seen her will, drawn up by a man named Murfree, a white attorney whose practice has been wrecked, whose home has been stoned, and who is close to being driven out of town because of his outspoken defense of the Negro cause."

"Watch out, Chief—"

"The chips have been down a score of times, David. He's never backed off. He's another Chuck Martin."

"God help him. And I hope you're right."

Brad shrugged. "I'm beginning to understand the desperation back of the Negro saying 'Man's gotta trust someone.' It's not misplaced in this instance, David."

"All right, go on. Or shall I?"

"As it was in the beginning? When I used to insist on reviewing a case detail by detail, before trial, and put the screws on the starry-eyed young idiot—"

"I like Luke's phrase better."

"It's more imaginative, I'll give him that. You were right, of course. It's northern industry. But a group of white city and county officials and the town's leading banker have apparently—I say 'apparently' because I haven't a shred of proof—banded together to buy the property, or acquire it somehow, then sell it. And, again apparently, they have given the impression that they have, or are in the process of acquiring, title. And they probably think they are. My God, these people are stupid when they deal with Negroes!"

"I've said it for years, Brad. I mean years. Long before I ever went to college. Basically, it isn't the hate, it's the stupidity."

"Right. They're pressed for time. Any minute it might occur to the interested parties to search title for themselves. The local people want to make some move, put over some gimmick, that will put them in control."

"How about Miz Towers? Abraham?"

"So far she's been adamant, but the pressure's mounting. It's the reason I stopped off before coming here."

"I assume it's still in the benign phase? People she used to work for suddenly remembering her with little gifties, if they're kin to, or friends of, the locals involved. Abraham getting white business, maybe offers of an easy deal for new equipment, farm machinery, that kind of thing."

"That's about it. Abraham says when his mother dies he wouldn't mind 'being shet of' all that land. But he doesn't want to be cheated."

"Another question. How did you learn all this?"

"Jim Towers, Abraham's nephew. The Grand Hotel, where he works, is everything the name implies, used in the old sense. Old, built by slave labor, derived from Greek architecture, porticoed, pillared, still the luncheon and cocktail hangout for the town's leading business and professional men.

Rotary meets there, that sort of thing. It's even so old-fashioned they have a smoking room where ladies aren't allowed. That's where the spittoons are that Luke mentioned. The hotel is on Main Street, directly facing the colored section. A few months ago a man came down from the North and stayed at the new hotel uptown, but conferred frequently with the town's leading banker, a man named Spangler, at the Grand. Couple of weeks later he came back with two other men, and this time the luncheon and dinner conferences, the talks over drinks in the smoking room, were with the banker, the mayor, the city attorney, and a few other assorted local rascals. Practically everything that was said in the smoking room after a certain date got back to the dinner table in Jim's house, where Abraham eats every night, after the old lady goes to bed at sundown."

"You know, Brad, I don't know whether to pray, and I do sometimes, for my own people or the blasted whites."

"I know. I'm getting dry. More coffee? Jim probably wouldn't have paid any attention if it hadn't been for a crack by Spangler. Jim's not the curious type. All he wants is to get the day's work over, pick up a few tips, and get the hell out. One afternoon in the smoking room one of the outsiders reprimanded the local characters rather sharply. That room is usually deserted in midafternoon, and Jim picks that time to dust and tidy up for the cocktail period. On this day he was the only person in the room besides the aforementioned group. However, the reprimand was unmistakable; the man took them to task for discussing the project so freely in the presence of outsiders. Spangler looked around, said, 'But there's no one here,' and the visitor indicated Jim."

"And the banker said, 'Lord, that's only Jim. He don't count.' Or words to that effect."

"Yes. Jim moseyed on out through the curtains to the bar—Chuck says they still call them portieres—and naturally from that time on never missed a chance to listen. He said it riled him considerable. And, of course, after that they made it difficult for an eavesdropper. Jim even took to going through the wastebaskets after a meeting broke up. The only thing of value he found was an envelope with the return address of the man who had come down first. He brought that home. His mother, God help us, threw it out. No one seems to remember what was on it. Abraham says he remembered for a time, then disremembered.

"I had him trying to remember so hard he was losing

weight. Then I told him to put it out of his mind, as I would tell a witness, forget it, then someday I'd ask him and it would pop to the surface of his mind. Or it would do so spontaneously. So far it hasn't."

"There ought to be some way. If this man, Murfree, is such an upstanding liberal, couldn't he get at the register of the other hotel? Don't answer. He couldn't. They wouldn't give him a damn thing. No idea, no idea at all, what the whole thing is?"

"The gov'mint's involved, according to Jim. And, I gather, the reaches of outer space. Or maybe missiles. Hell, I don't know, except it's big, it's important, it's fairly secret and, Jim says, these outsiders seem to be becoming impatient. Which means the Cainsville syndicate is going to have to come up with the property soon." Brad stood up, sighed, and said: "I haven't talked this much since the last time I was in court. I'm going to shower and shave. Meanwhile, you can come up with the solution. Think."

He left the room, and David called after him. "It's easy—hey, Brad!"

He heard a voice from the bathroom call, "Think!" then the sound of the door closing and the rush of water in the shower.

Brad came back into the kitchen while David was washing up. "Ready, brat?"

"You mean to leave? It's too early."

"I mean with a solution to the problem of how to keep ol' Miz Towers's property and save her and Abraham from pressure."

"Oh, that," said David airily. "If you'd listened you'd have heard it half an hour ago. Option."

"That's what I told Abraham."

"You'd already thought of it. I should have known."

"Of course I had. I wanted you to come to the same conclusion. Abraham agrees. I explained it to him carefully, and he's waiting until his mother is in the right mood. Murfree can draw it up. Abraham trusts him, and trusts me, but not all of the colored trust me."

"That's the way it would be."

"I told him to tell his mother an option would be like a steel wall around the property. It would be better if someone who hasn't been connected with present activities took it. Only a nominal sum would be involved. Then we'd be in a position to deal directly with the principals, get a fair price for the old lady, if she changes her mind, or stymie the whole deal indefinitely."

"Options expire."

"And can be renewed. When she does die—"

"They'll have picked a site in Wyoming, and someone's left holding the option. Now I know it was your idea first, I'll shoot holes in it."

"You think if it's desirable enough for these people that others won't be interested? If that happens we'll be acting for Abraham."

David stopped wiping a plate and looked at Brad closely. "Listen, Chief, what's this 'we' routine you're sneaking into?" He laid the plate down on the drainboard with exaggerated care and said, "Why you low-down, conniving, illegitimate, legal son of a bitch!"

"I've heard you do better—"

David turned his head, called "Chop-bone!" There was an answering chirrup from the living room, and Chop-bone came padding rapidly into the kitchen. "Chop-bone, y'all want to be a cat of property? Y'all want about steen dozen acres to hunt mice in? Your old Uncle Bradford's real thoughtful that way."

"I'll put up the dough. You can see why, if it got out, my own motives in being there might not appear disinterested. You're so identified with ALEC now, they might think you were fronting for ALEC. Which would be all right. There's already been talk about ALEC building a school for social and governmental studies."

"All right, all right. I won't argue. You can even use my dough. I haven't spent any for more than a month. Just get me off the hook when the time comes. If there's one thing I don't want, it's real property in any place called Cainsville."

David returned the last plate to its allotted place in the cupboard over the drainboard.

"And furthermore," he went on, "after I get to Boston next week I don't want to leave for a long, long time."

"You really mean it, David?"

"This time, yes."

"My God, sense at last. I never thought it would come."

"You underestimate me, Chief. Me'n Chop-bone are taking off. If he doesn't like snow and ice, I'll get him a set of thermal underwear."

70

David drove to the picnic grounds from the airport, wishing heartily that Li'l Joe Champlin had not brought him up to such a keen sense of responsibility. "Any guy with any sense who feels the way I do would go home and watch a ball game on TV and go to bed," he told himself. Anyhow, it would be over eventually and he could go home, get another night's sleep and day's rest before he tackled the job of getting the house ready for renting or sale. He was grateful to Brad for making no attempt to get him up to Cainsville, although even Brad, trained to hide his emotions as he had been, had not been able to conceal the fact that in this particular fight, perhaps more than any other, he would have liked to have David with him.

As he neared the picnic grounds he could tell there was a good turnout in spite of the uncertain weather, the muggy heat and humidity. He parked under a tree about a hundred yards from the entrance and as he entered the grounds he sighed, contemplating the gregariousness of his people. There were probably only scores of children running around underfoot, but it looked like hundreds. Lunches had already been eaten by many of the people; Isaiah had told him it was a bring-your-own-lunch picnic instead of a community meal. Only the coffee had been prepared by Isaiah's wife to be served to everyone.

He stood, watching, searching for the Watkins family group whose lunch he had been invited to share. It seemed at first glance as though the shade of every tree that did not shelter a family sheltered a group of young people clustered around someone with a guitar. He thought of his speech. Should he tell them, he wondered, what half-a-hundred teenagers just like them looked like squatting on a pavement, arms linked, teeth bone white in dark faces, looking up at the bayonets in the hands of armed men in khaki? Somewhere near him a child raised a spoiled, whining cry. Should he tell them how the sound of the voice of a terrorized child sounded, a child who ran, screaming, not knowing where he was running, blinded and vomiting from gas?

He made a mighty effort to discipline a mind that was becoming more and more difficult to control these days. The smell of brewing coffee came to him and he saw that he was standing near the table where it was being served. That would do it, a cup of strong black coffee. He'd have coffee, find Isaiah, and talk a little with the family; he wanted no lunch, no food, until he could get home to peace and quiet, but he supposed that no matter how he felt the smell of freshly brewed coffee would always draw him. He remembered how, in jail, the guards used to make coffee in the night, and how its aroma cut through the rank smell of the cell blocks. He could tell them about that in his speech, he thought as he held the paper cup of steaming coffee in his hands; tell of the stench of a jail tank and what it was composed of, tell them of the cold feel of a filthy cement floor where the pools of liquid were not always water, where humans were crowded in like hens in a crate on the way to slaughter; tell them of a frightened boy, retching and vomiting in a corner, and of how sweet and deep had been that same boy's voice when at last he joined the rest, and sang with them. And he could tell them how one man felt about these things, how they tore at him and sickened him and would not leave him and how at last they had drained and defeated him.

And he wouldn't; he knew that these were the things he would not tell of, hint at perhaps, but not tell of in all their pristine horror. Somewhere someone once had said, "God help us, for we knew the worst too young—" These youngsters, here on the picnic ground, like the David Champlin of a thousand years ago, had not even touched the outermost edges of that worst; let them learn it for themselves.

His speech would be moderate, measured, objective. Because it was an ALEC-sponsored gathering the speech must, he knew, deal with citizenship, but it would not, while he was conscious, deal with the obligations of a citizen to his country, but instead with the obligations of a country to citizens who were expected to be generous with that "last full measure of devotion." He might even use that phrase. He'd bring in that battered overworked character, the first to die in the American Revolution, a Negro. And he'd bring in—oh, crap!

—he'd bring in taxation without representation, and then he'd tell them, tell those dark intent faces, that they must study hard like good little boys and girls so they could present literate, pleasant images of a black and stricken people. And it doesn't work that way; God knew, He knew full well, it didn't work that way.

A voice so close it startled him and made him spill his coffee sounded in his ear. He looked down into Isaiah's round and homely face, a face that was smiling, the eyes clear and happy.

"You a million miles away, son," said Isaiah.

"No, I wasn't. I was up there on that damned platform trying to make the right speech." He laid a hand on Isaiah's shoulder. "You'll be sorry you asked me, man."

"Give you odds," said Isaiah. They turned and walked slowly across the grass, Isaiah with the clumsy, lurching gait that threw his big buttocks almost in a half-circle with every other step; David, thinner, still graceful, limping on his one stiff ankle. "Been worried about you, son," said Isaiah. "Made 'em hold back on the food so's there'd be some for you. Everybody and his cousin's brought fried chicken, but Annie figured it was too damned hot for anything like that. She's got cold smoked turkey, and cold crab, and ham. Stuff like that. And beer—"

"I'm not hungry, 'Saiah. Just want to make my speech and get back home for some rest. I'll eat later."

"Anyone tell you you're looking mighty peaked, son? You better eat. You lost a hell of a lot of weight, and that's a fact. Got not much more flesh on your bones than what your grandaddy had; only, on him it looked natural. You go on home and get your rest after. I know you need it. We just beginning this fight."

David managed cold turkey and a beer, began to let down a little talking with Isaiah and Annie and some of their relatives, slipping into the easy, idle, relaxed talk of his people, letting its inconsequence and good humor carry him. Ambrose strolled over, greeted him warmly, and mentioned his brother, Pop Jefferson. "You seen him this trip, David?"

"Not yet," said David, and felt guilty.

"Sure is sad. Sure is a mighty sad thing, the way Pop's gone down. Seems like he don't take interest in nothing since Emma passed. Ev'ry day, ev'ry day you can see him going to the places they used to go together, down by the French Market, outside the place they used to drive to for ribs, sitting on his steps. Keeps the place she used to sit alongside of him clear; he's sitting there, someone comes along and he puts his hand down on the place she used to sit, you has to sit on the step below. It's sad, man, it's a sad sight. Seems like I lost a brother along with a sister-in-law."

"I'll go by there Tuesday," said David. He felt choked up, and wished, selfishly, that Ambrose would go away. Once he could have taken it; now everything that tore at his emotions was a certain threat to hard-fought-for equilibrium.

He got to his feet, said: "You-all mind if I find me a spot under a tree and make some notes for this speech? It ought to be coming up soon."

"Sure is," said Isaiah. "There goes Louis Grayson up now to play piano. There'll be some singing; then I'll make a little spiel and introduce you. You run along."

He looked for and found a tree where the nearby picnickers were strangers. He let himself down on the ground and leaned against its trunk, wondering about ants, knowing about mosquitoes. No notes were necessary for this speech, or at most just a one- or two-word "A,B,C" sequence reminder. He let his eyes roam over the crowd, seeking the color chaos of Luke's shirt. Some of the people had gathered in front of the stand and were singing; some had remained comfortably seated on the ground, listening, talking, a few of them also singing.

Then he saw the child, a boy in leg braces, using crutches, walking beside an older boy. Watching him he thought, Poor kid. It must have been polio rather than an injury. David thought that while it had been tough on him when he was a kid, it had not been as tough as this boy had known it, and would know it. The pair reached a small tree, and the older boy helped the child in braces to sit down, crutches beside him. David could sense what the older boy was saying before he started off: "Now you stay there, y'hear? I'll be right back."

David watched the younger boy for a moment, chuckling. As soon as the kid had known his older brother was far enough away he'd started fooling with the crutches. It was, thought David, exactly what he would have done himself. He remembered Gramp giving him fits when he had tried to get around too fast, too soon, on a walking cast. His difficulties, compared to this child's, had been minor. And, too, this boy was younger than he had been at the time of his injury; the boy's arms were still chubby, the backs of the hands padded with soft flesh. David sighed, rose, and went across to the boy; he couldn't let him hurt himself.

"Hi!" He dropped to one knee, and the child turned his head away shyly, began pulling at grass, no longer fooling with the crutches. "What's your name?"

The boy turned and looked at him directly, eyes enormous dark pools in a round face. "You—you Mr. Cham—Cham—"

"David. Me, David. You—?" He pointed a finger at the child's chest, and the child smiled a smile of such angelic and ineffable sweetness that David grinned, thinking such a smile could not be real, thinking also that he'd give odds this youngster was a heller around the house.

"Me, Billy," said the boy, and the clear peal of his laugh brought an answering laugh from David. "You going to talk."

"I'm going to try to talk."

The dark eyes fixed themselves intently on David's face. "I knows who you is—"

David laid a hand on the small knee. "Listen, son, don't go trying to hop off all by yourself. You listen to me. I know. I've got a bad leg too."

The boy nodded solemnly, the nod saying he'd noticed, and David realized the boy's parents must have pointed him out. "Did you have polio?"

David shook his head. "Nope. I had a truck, a big ol' truck, run right over my foot." He smiled, watching the young face, knowing the boy was thinking that it must be a lot more exciting to have a truck responsible for lameness than polio.

"Did it *hurt?*"

"Oh, I guess it did. It was a long time ago. Where's your mamma and daddy?"

"Mamma's working. Granny's here. Daddy's up there"—a nod toward the platform—"playing piano."

"Your daddy a musician?"

The black head rolled slowly from side to side. "Uh-*unh.* Not really and truly. He jus' plays at home and in church and if Mr. Isaiah wants him. Mr. Isaiah's gimpy too."

"By golly, so he is. Let's have a club. Billy and David and Mr. Isaiah. You can be president until you get rid of those crutches; then Mr. Isaiah can be president."

Again the head rolled slowly. "Uh-*unh.* You be president." Now the child was looking at him with a directness that made him uncomfortable. He realized that for some reason known only to the inscrutable God who fashioned children this boy was in the throes of an attack of hero worship. And I'm not even a cowboy, he thought; Isaiah must have been talking about me at the child's house, setting me up as some sort of damned celebrity among my people.

"O.K., I'll be president, you be vice-president, and Mr. Isaiah can be our big fat member and pay his dues every day so we can buy ice-cream cones and licorice whips." He hoped licorice whips were still in existence.

The boy gave a delighted crow of laughter. For a while they pursued the subject of what use they would make of Mr. Isaiah's dues; then the child changed the subject abruptly.

"Mr. Cham—Cham—"

"David."

Billy paused, but it was evident he couldn't quite encompass the full familiarity of a first name. He said, "Mr. David. You going to march?"

"March? Now? There isn't going to be a parade, Billy."

"Yes there is *too*. In Wash-ing-ton."

"Oh." David had forgotten the civ l rights parade in Washington scheduled for later in the month, although he had been talking it up, giving advice on plans in the towns and cities he had been working in. "It depends, Billy."

"My daddy's going. And my brother. With Mr Isaiah."

"Your mamma too?"

Again the solemn shake of the head. "She's 'fraid 'bout her job. Why, Mr. David?"

Why? Why? Why? How often had he, David Champlin, asked the question? How often received a dark and hurting answer, an answer he could not, if his life depended on it, give this round-eyed child?

"I don't know, Billy." And spoke, he thought, God's truth. "Look, Billy, did you ask your daddy to take you to the big parade?"

"He don't want to take me. Mr. David, I can walk. I can walk *good*."

"It's going to be a *long* walk, Billy. Even a little boy with strong legs would have a time."

The child's soft mouth set stubbornly. "I got a wheelchair."

David, looking down at the boy, wondered if he had been as stubborn when he was a child, and remembered that he had. "Why do you want to march, Billy? Just because your daddy and your big brother are going to?"

"Uh-*unh.*"

David, beginning to look for the solemn roll of the small head, held back a smile.

"Uh-*unh,*" said the child again. "So's little colored children everywhere can grow up same's everyone else. So's my daddy can get a good job. So's my mamma won't be 'fraid."

David had never had quite the feeling before that he had now, a cessation of all thought, his mind clear and light, like a limpid pool in which there are no images or shadows. When it began to stir with life again, he thought, "Rote." Coming from this child it had to be rote, learned at home, overheard. Yet it had not sounded like rote. Rote can be true, he thought; like formal prayers in a liturgical church, rote can be true. He was silent for a long time, and heard the boy say, "Mr. David?" from a distance, then more insistently, "Mr. David!"

"Yes, Billy?"

"Mr. David, you mad?"

One arm went round the child's shoulders, drawing him close. "No, Billy. No. Oh, my God, no!"

The singing by the people in front of the platform had stopped; he could hear Isaiah's high voice, and knew that in a moment he would hear his own name. He rose slowly, looking down at Billy.

"I'll talk to Mr. Isaiah, Billy. I'll ask him to tell your daddy to take you to Wash-ing-ton with him."

"Gee!"

"And I'll be there, Billy. I promise I'll be there, if God spares. And by golly, Billy, I'll find you and I'll push that wheelchair. We'll make it together, son."

The child's eyes shone so brightly that, as he had turned away from Gramp's eyes once because their light hurt him, he turned his head away now.

"They're waiting for me, Billy. Don't you go trying to hop around by yourself now before your brother gets back. If he's not back when I finish I'll take you to Granny. Be good now, y'hear!"

David stood with his foot on the first step of the wooden flight at the side of the platform until he heard Isaiah introduce him, then mounted quickly and stood quietly during the round of polite applause. He caught a flash of frantic color to his left, Luke jog-trotting across a clearing to the edge of the crowd, tossing a baseball mitt to a youth behind him. He smiled to himself. He'd thought the lad was under the bushes with a dame.

There was a lectern on the platform, and its presence annoyed him. Disregarding it, he launched into the talk he had planned. It differed from a score of other talks only in that today he was condensing as he went along. After the first few times when his talks had been broadcast, timing came easily to him. He wasn't, he thought, what singers called "in good voice." He could hear his voice sounding tired, strained, almost thready. His eyes, smarting from heat and glare, ranged over the quiet, intent crowd before him and he thought, as he had so often: God bless my people when they're an audience. Whatever our faults, we listen. And we hear. Through the years he had strengthened his ability to organize and give a talk with one part of his mind, observe with the other.

A young couple standing just below caught his eyes, held them, and he had to force himself to look away. They had moved forward quietly during the opening sentences of his speech and stood now, without moving, like statues. They were holding hands, standing close, their shoulders touching, the boy's head slightly above the girl's, both of them tall, straight, with a dark, brooding beauty in their eyes. They seemed without sex, although they were vital with a strength that reached up to him and gave new life to his own. The girl wore a blouse and tight stretch pants, and the contours of the brown flesh under them were rounded promises of pleasure. The youth beside her was more than youth, was a man now, shoulders broad, waist small, hips thin; the column of his throat rising from the open-necked sport shirt was a muscular cylinder of black power. Yet there was no sense of sex between them. The brown fingers of the girl's hand were interlaced with the fingers of the boy's without pressure, loosely.

It was not the first time during the past years that David had noted the young people of his race together, flesh touching flesh, yet without sensuality or desire or thought of coupling. They were like single individuals, these pairs, androgynous, the universal urge to bring forth the fruit of their bodies silenced for the moment, merged into a different urge, felt by both as one, the urge to create a world in which their seed could grow in freedom, could be children of men as well as of God, an urge stronger than sex, mightier than any instinct to lie together for an hour.

David missed the thread of his thought, snatched it back, half angry with himself, and rewove it into the pattern of his speech. He would not lose the couple standing so silently before him, he knew that. They would be with him wherever he went, had been with him wherever he had been. There would be no losing them; let his country take heed: there would be no losing them.

He reached that part of his talk about the only powerful Negro—the only Negro with real ability to influence the destiny of his people—being the voting Negro, but instead of making it the climax, as it had always been, he let it become a part of the preclimax buildup, and moved to the front of the platform.

"These things are important," he said. "These things that I have said." He knew the value of repetition when he spoke to his people, knew it to be the secret of his people's eloquence, the repetition of a phrase like the background beat of a drum lending rhythm to thought, making the subject matter of a speech a thing of the senses as well as the mind. "All the things that we have done are important, the boycotts, such as the one that brought about a victory for our people in Montgomery, the freedom rides, the demonstrations, the sit-ins, the pray-ins, all have left their mark. But what we have done is only a tiny shadow of what we will do, as, it has been said, the child is the shadow of the man. As we sit here today there are towns all over the South in which no Negro has ever entered a voting booth, towns in which Negroes still dare not walk on the white side of the street, towns from which Negroes still vanish, to be found, later, dead. That's how short a distance our shadow reaches."

David slipped one hand into a trouser pocket, smiled and gathered in the audience with the smile, not with intent but because in that moment its members had become real and close to him. His voice strengthened, lost its strained and thready quality.

"This morning," he said, "I was a man with a different mission than I have now. This morning I was making plans to leave the South, at least for a time, hide myself in a quiet office, behind a thick door, in our national headquarters in Boston. I would have been doing what I was trained to do: wrassling with the law, instead of with a red-neck bully."

They were listening intently, now that he had brought the talk down to a personal level.

"I have no shame," he continued, "for claiming on this day the prerogative of a woman. I have changed my mind. Tomorrow I will leave here for a town, or call it a small city, northeast of us, a town such as I mentioned a moment ago. There are others there before me, white and colored, working for our cause. I shall walk on the colored side of the street, live in the colored section of town, and pray that I don't vanish in the night. And perhaps when we leave that town we will leave behind us Negroes less afraid, Negroes walking with their heads up.

"What changed my mind? It happened here, right on this picnic ground. A little crippled boy told me how he wanted more than anything in the world to go, not to the circus or a ball game or the movies, but to go to Washington and march with his daddy later this month; march in a wheelchair if need be. And when I asked him why, he told me. He wanted to march, he said, and I will use his own words, 'so little colored children everywhere could live the same as everyone else,' so his daddy could get a good job, and so his mother need never be afraid of losing hers because she wanted to march for freedom for her family.

"And I realized then, as I had not realized before, that we have already accomplished a great and wonderful thing: a thing far greater than the right to eat in a white restaurant, greater than the right to ride in the front of the bus, greater than the right to worship God in a church in which He is a stranger. And it is so simple, so very simple, this accomplishment. It is this: We have made a lie out of what was once a statement of fact. We have changed the world we live in so that no child of our people need ever hear the words I heard as a child, the words your parents and your grandparents heard, the words that were the shackles of their minds: 'There ain't nothing you can do about it.' No dark-skinned child, hurt and humiliated, can look with tear-filled eyes into the face of an elder, and hear again those bitter words of oppression and defeat: 'There ain't nothing you can do about it.'

"That's why I'm staying in the front lines, leaving tomorrow for Cainsville instead of Boston, so that no child will ever hear those bitter words again. No child will ever hear those bitter words again: 'There ain't nothing you can do about it.' We've proved them a lie. Let's keep them a lie!"

Luke was waiting for him at the foot of the platform steps, his smile wide. David knew the smile had been on Luke's face, and in his mind, ever since the boy had heard the words, "I have changed my mind." There was no exuberance; it was as though David's speech had made him shy.

"Hi, boss." He spoke softly. "That was great. That was real great, man. Look, you weren't kidding? I mean when you said about going to Cainsville?"

"I wasn't kidding." David felt tiredness sucking at the very marrow of his bones. "Maybe you're all nuts, but it's worth a try. Christ! Anything's worth a try."

They were walking slowly across the grass to the roadway where David's car was parked. He looked for Billy, saw the child beneath a tree with a woman who must be his grandmother.

"Where you going now, boss?"

"Home," he said. "Home, and see if I can get some rest in what little time there is left for it."

71

THERE WAS NO DIFFICULTY in recognizing the land Brad had described as the Towers holdings. There was the broad, more or less flat, expanse known as—what had Brad said the people called it? Flaming Meadows?—and beyond it on the north the sharp high rise of a rocky, wooded hill. David pulled over to the shoulder of the rutted road and when he turned off the car's motor heard the cool sound of the wide flowing stream that ran along the eastern boundary, and beneath a plank bridge laid across the road just ahead of him, and his ears caught the distant sound of a waterfall, hypnotic in the quiet early-morning heat.

It was all very peaceful, he thought, very damned peaceful, the kind of peace that in time could cure a man's mind and bring rest to his body. But not to his, not under the circumstances that had brought him here, and now he damned those circumstances heartily. What in hell was wrong with him that he had let a small boy in leg braces crawl inside his mind, pull the strings that governed his actions? "You're not mature, Champlin," he told himself now. "That's it. Thirty years old and not mature." He could do as much in Boston as he could do here—more—and stay healthy in the bargain. But was he going to Boston? Not he, not li'l David Champlin; he was going to stay here because of some little kid he'd never seen before Sunday.

"Oh, hell, Champlin, go swimmin'!" He spoke aloud, and the sound of his own voice startled him in the hot, close confines of the car.

He pulled fresh shorts, socks, and cotton undershirt from his zipper overnight bag, took a clean yellow sports shirt and tan slacks from the hanger on the bracket behind him, and crossed the road, working his way through the bracken on the other side and down to the bank of the stream, looking for one of the spots Brad must have meant when he said the swimming was fine if you could handle the current. There was one not too far above the plank bridge, sheltered by a few scrub pine trees and high rank undergrowth, and he stripped and waded in. The water was shockingly cool at first on his sweaty, heated body, and he swam strongly against the current, then rested, floating on his back, letting the water carry him, turning and swimming against it when it threatened to take him too far. None of the baths he had taken in New Orleans in an obsession to wash away the intangible filth of the jail had cleansed him as this cool, clear water was cleansing him now. It was almost worth the trip, he thought, almost worth whatever lay ahead.

Out of the water he let the sun dry the moisture from his skin, pulled on the clean clothes, and made his way back to the car. He never minded his lameness as much on city streets or hard roads, even going up and down stairs, as he did on rough, uncertain footing like this.

As he got the car back on the road again, the heat closed in, and he knew that in a few minutes the fresh, clean clothes that had felt so good on cool skin would be moist and sticky with perspiration. He had been able to see the roof of a house on the other side of Angel Creek while he was swimming, and now, just as he crossed the plank bridge, it came into full view. It was a crazy quilt of a house. The oblong central portion must have been the original cabin; to this there had been added various rooms, at odd angles. The unrailed, roofed porch that ran across the front of the central portion was almost at ground level, reached by a single step. The curtains at the windows were stiffly starched, as clean and brave looking as the white sails of a catboat. The cushions on the ancient rocking chairs on the porch were gay in clean, bright chintz.

A house-proud woman lives in there, he thought, then saw her at the side, in the rear, wearing an ankle-length blue cotton dress, and carrying a pail, walking slowly toward a cluster of outbuildings that flanked the barnyard area in back. A building near the road, approached by a driveway wider than the road itself, had a weather-beaten sign over its double doors: TOWERS WIL-SAV-U GARAGE. He noticed that both house and garage had telephone and electricity, and he was almost sure there was indoor plumbing.

Brad had told him that with apologies to a long-dead essayist they named their headquarters building "Tether's End," and it came in sight a little more than a mile past the Towers house, on the left side of the road as it approached the town, recognizable by the number of cars parked around it, Brad's among them.

The building was frame, rickety, and only a few flakes of paint remained on its exterior. The porch and the three steps that led to it were sagging, but there were telephone and electricity lines and, gleaming incongruously, new screens at the windows and a new screen door. Brad, to whom mosquitoes were more than ordinary torment, would have done that.

The figures inside the house were only barely distinguishable through the screen door. He could hear voices and the whirring of an electric fan. From the back a voice that sounded like Chuck Martin's called loudly, "Hey! Somebody! Soap!"

Without knocking he opened the door and walked in, checking its close with a hand behind him because his nerves shrank from the idea of a loud bang. Humboldt Sweeton was standing facing him; Brad and Fred Winters were seated in battered wicker chairs, their backs to the door. Sweeton recognized him immediately, came forward with outstretched hand. "Well, Lord, Lord! If it ain't young David Champlin!" Away from the pulpit or platform his voice was low, close to a semiwhisper. My God, the man's tired, thought David; my God, he looks like hell. The great black eyes were even more sunken than they had been the time David had seen him in a Montgomery church hall; the bones of face and skull gave an effect of almost gleaming white through the dark skin. A slow smile put light into the deep pools of his eyes.

Brad had risen to his feet, saying softly, "I'll be damned, brat," the warm pleasure evident in his voice.

Winters, looking as trim and tailored as though Madison Avenue ran past their door instead of a red dirt southern road, smiled and said with obvious sincerity, "Good to see you, David."

"Beats me how you do it, Fred," said David. "For two dollars, Confederate, I'd muss you up." He remembered the time, a year or so before, when Winters had been jailed after considerable maneuvering by himself and members of his own group, who were concerned by the criticism within their ranks that the big shots managed to stay out of the reach of local law-enforcement bodies, that only the smaller fry and the locals took the raps. Three days later, when Fred was released, he had emerged, to David's envious surprise, looking as dapper and unruffled coming out the door as he had looked going in.

In an alcove kitchen at the side of the far end of the room he saw Les Forsyte, who came forward now to shake hands, the smooth tan face and round eyes looking as youthful as they had the first time David met him, years before, in New York.

Hummer Sweeton said, "Get the boy some lemonade, Les; reckon he's pretty warm. You been driving all night, son?"

"Nope," answered David. "Just two, three hours. Stayed at a motel the other side of Heliopolis. But you better believe I drove around the edges of that town. I don't need a rest all that bad."

Hummer took the lemonade from Les's hand, gave it to David, and fussed and clucked-clucked like a mother hen. "Going to jail for the cause is one thing; staying in it, that's something else again. Sit down, son; res' yo'self."

"Look—" said David, and stopped abruptly. Had anyone noticed the quaver in his voice? Brad had; he could not see Brad from where he was sitting, but he sensed Brad had noticed. "Good lemonade," he said, and drank deeply. What in the name of God did a grown man do when he found himself suddenly afflicted with the nervous system of a menopausal female? Get busy, he thought; get busy right now, beat it down, give it something to do; get busy, get busy—

"Hi ya, Stoopid!" Chuck Martin came pounding into the room from somewhere outside the kitchen, probably a lean-to, makeshift shower, David thought. The big bony frame was wrapped in a gray, knee-length seersucker robe, the bony shanks ending in bony feet wearing scuffs, the tow-colored hair standing upright in wet spikes. The warmth of Chuck's greeting and his wide-eyed, paternal concern almost embarrassed David. Chuck said, "Brad tells me you're a mite peaked." He looked more closely. "You seem O.K. to me, Stoopid." But his voice was without conviction and held an undertone of worry.

"Had breakfast, David?" Brad spoke quietly from behind him.

"Hell, no. Where'd you think I'd get breakfast? One of those white restaurants outside of Helio? Didn't look clean to me."

"Our vines grow sour grapes," said Winters. Les Forsyte headed for the kitchen, calling out, "One breakfast coming up! Grits, eggs, ham, corn bread—"

"You do yourselves damned well," said David.

"High on the hawg, son; high on the hawg." Hummer's smile had not left his face.

Brad said, "And everything home produced. Everything. My first experience. I don't believe we've even got a can opener in the joint."

"Bottle opener," said Winters. "The whites have the cornlikker monopoly. The still's in the hills on the other side of town."

Les Forsyte, busy in the kitchen, began to sing, improvising as he went along: "O-o-oh, the still's in the hills on the *oth*er side of town—" and David took the lead away from him, began singing the old song "I'm Movin' to the Outskirts of Town—" and Brad said, "Careful. Clergy present; take it easy." For no reason they all laughed, and David felt less like a menopausal female, more like a breakfastless male in sight of food after a sixty-mile drive and a swim in the early morning.

Chuck joined him at a card table that seemed to serve many purposes. While they waited for Les to bring breakfast, Brad said: "You know how damned glad I am that you're here, David. But I also disapprove strongly. You should have gone on to Boston. How come you changed your mind?"

David shrugged. "Call it the equivalent of your girl on the bench in Little Rock."

"Damn it, David, there isn't a mule in this state that can beat you for stubbornness and obstinacy when you want to be stubborn and obstinate. And there isn't a woman living who can beat you for changing your mind if your emotions get involved. Keeps a man guessing."

"It has its advantages," said David. "Anyhow, I thought an outside viewpoint, on the spot, even if it's a skeptical one, would be helpful."

"It will," said Brad. "Believe me, it will."

Chuck, busy now with ham and eggs, said, "We'd better brief you. I'm not supposed to be here. I don't mean in Cainsville; I mean on this side of Main Street." He looked speculatively at the plate of hot corn bread, took his third piece and spread it liberally with butter. "Ol' Miz Towers's butter. Hand churned by long-suffering great-grandchildren. Where was I? Oh, yes. This side of Main Street is, always has been, verboten to whites except those on business or errands of mercy to old-time servants. You get the picture."

"Without trying."

"Now the ban is even stricter, although, of course, it's not a legal one. They're beginning to smell something. I get here by devious routes, sneaking out the back door of the bus station across from the Grand, or I drive either north or south of town, make a swing around the side roads and come in the back way, the way you came this morning."

"For me it comes naturally. Back doors, back roads."

"All right. We're not kidding ourselves that the whites don't know about it. Hummer, you want to take over?"

"You're doing fine, Reverend, doing fine. You make a mistake, I'll stop you. You just keep a-going while I rests my voice."

"I don't know whether Brad told you, but we were planning one, perhaps two, demonstrations."

"Red herrings, as I understand it."

"Yes. Aimed, of course, at voter registration. But we want to keep them within the law. Not as a matter of principle but as a matter of expediency. Too much friction, any violence, could throw a monkey wrench in our more important project."

"A guy sitting in a jail cell saying he won't work isn't as effective as a man sitting on his porch saying the same thing."

"You still catch on quickly, don't you? Now, there's considerable profanity called for in this next bit, and I ought to let Brad or Fred take over, but I'll keep on and try and restrain myself. Day before yesterday, Sunday, there was a wildcat demonstration. It was just after sundown, close to dark. A torchlight parade, a 'Light of Freedom' parade, according to the placards."

"Wait," said David. "Wait, Chuck." A little crippled boy named Billy was a long way off now, and he was kicking himself mentally for ever having changed his plans to go to Boston. He was sure he knew what was coming. "YPCF? Mostly kids?"

"Nothing but. The dear, dedicated Young People's Committee for Freedom."

"Oh, God!" said David. "Why didn't I stay in bed!"

"I reckon it's because basically you haven't got good sense. Anyhow—"

"Chuck." Brad was walking back from the kitchen to the table, a cup of fresh coffee in his hand. "Let me pick it up here for a while. You see, David, we have no right to feel too angry. In a large measure it was our own damned fault. Hummer has had to be away every now and then, frying other fish—"

"At least, getting the fat ready," said Hummer. "But you still got no business faulting yourselves, Brad. I should of thought."

"Not of everything, Hummer," said Brad. "No man can. The point is that we failed to take one important factor into consideration. The young people. It's difficult to include kids too young to work in a project like this. If we'd been smart, we would have started a youth project, moving along with the other, perhaps a 'Future Voters' organization, something like that. These kids, as you well know, can't be left at loose ends now; some of them went to Heliopolis, took part in that demonstration you got caught up in. They've smelled action. Siege tactics don't appeal to them."

The telephone rang, and Hummer Sweeton answered it softly, and when he had finished talking, stood and touched Brad's shoulder gently. "I have to run along, Brad. You and Chuck's doing fine. If you need me, I'll be over at the Zion Church. They waiting for me there for a meeting with some young folks. I ain't too worried. I think we can get them young uns back in line."

Les Forsyte came in from the kitchen. "You're not going riding around this town alone, Reverend, the way things are. I'm coming along. One of you guys here can take over on the dishes."

"After that meeting you get some rest, Hummer," called Brad.

"Lawd! Who can rest!" Sweeton paused in the doorway and waved his hand, palm outward, the same quick wave David had seen in Montgomery. It was an infinitely gentle gesture, inexplicably touching. When he had left, Brad turned back to David.

"As I was saying: by the time we realized that we had slipped up it was damned near too late. These kids have been out of school since June; they're ripe for trouble, easily led—"

David leaned forward, pushing back plates and cup and saucer to assume his favorite position, arms splayed out, chin touching the knuckles of his clasped hands. "Brad. Hold on a minute. I have a question. When I talked to you on the telephone last week, before you came down to New Orleans, you mentioned Garnett. Has he been around?"

"Yes. He was here a while back, when we had the first demonstration; then he went to Heliopolis, and from there he went, I think, to Chicago. Then he came back here."

"When?"

"Last Friday. Two days before I did. To help the Reverend, he said."

"Sweeton?"

"Yes."

David looked across the table at Winters, who had been sitting quietly beside Chuck, listening. After a moment Winters shrugged. "I'm on a spot, Champlin. Officially, I'm not in this. You know our policy. Follow your own course, don't obstruct other groups, give, along with ALEC, all possible legal assistances—and above all, don't interfere. We've lost credit for a hell of a lot of things we've done, and been blamed for a lot we haven't. Right now one of the heaviest crosses we have to bear, in our relationships with our own people, is the way the whites pat us on the back." He sighed. "As for Garnett. We had him. And we told him to get lost. He's got an armor-plate hide either by nature or because it suits his purposes. Right now, for the time being, he's got Hummer Sweeton sold. I've tried warning Hummer, and Les is watching out, but Hummer's such a livin' saint himself—" Winters shrugged again.

"We can't put all the blame on this character," said Chuck. "There's someone else here. A woman named Sue-Ellen Moore."

"Jesus have moicy!" David laid his forehead on his clasped hands, and his shoulders shook with something that was both laugh and shudder.

Brad said, "You know her, too?"

David looked up. "Yeah, I know her." When he and Brad were alone he'd tell Brad of his last meeting with Sue-Ellen.

"Any suggestions?" asked Brad.

"No. Hell, no. Not at this point. What did they do to the demonstrators? And you don't need to tell me they were all kids, fifteen to seventeen. Or under."

"They jailed them, of course. They turned the youngest ones—and some of them were damned near babies—loose that night. The rest they fined heavily and turned loose the next morning and gave them an ultimatum. County juvenile detention home the next time."

"That something new?"

"Yes. Born of the present crisis. Crises, I should say. God forbid any child of mine should go there!"

"Sue-Ellen?"

"They didn't turn her loose till this morning."

"So there was no trouble last night."

"Let's say the natives were restless. Hummer took advantage of the situation to get it under control."

Fred Winters interrupted. "The night the kids were in jail they called an emergency council meeting, passed an emergency curfew ordinance. No one on the streets under the age of eighteen after seven o'clock at night. White or colored. The next day they built the stockade. You'll see it. There is—or was—a large parking lot between the jail and the City Hall. It's now a stockade, with cyclone fencing along the street side, and barbed wire along the top."

"David, what's this woman's general technique?" asked Brad.

"She doesn't have what you could call a technique. But she's very militant in her approach to the problem, and she thinks anyone older than twenty-one in the South has already had it, so she works entirely with the youngsters. From what I hear she often gets overzealous and goes ahead with her own plans, and more than once she's loused up some other group's project that had a wider-range goal. Trouble is, she means well, yet at the same time the result is often to place the whites in a position where it's easy to double-cross us."

"Is it ever difficult?" asked Brad.

"I know. Look, I'm not saying the Negro has any obligation whatsoever to adhere to any so-called code of ethics with the whites. We never learned one. No one ever practiced one on us. We weren't worth it. It's just more practical sometimes, that's all. Even my grandfather never taught me you had to play fair with the whites. What the hell! Our life's been a course in survival, not ethics. I'm not low-rating Sue-Ellen for that, or being moralistic about it." David looked over at Chuck who was silently setting up matchsticks in a geometric design on the table. "Sorry, Chuck," he said. "That's the way it is."

"I'm learning," said Chuck slowly. "I thought I knew a lot, but I didn't."

"All right," said Winters. "Let's not waste time on abstractions. What do you advise that we do about Sunshine Sue? Leave her to Hummer for handling by sweet reason?"

"Don't look to me for answers," said David. "I just came in to get warm. You fellows want to paralyze this town; use a sort of nerve gas, in a sense. I'm saying, quite honestly, that I have my doubts you'll be able to swing it. But it's worth chancing. The ordered massive demonstrations you're planning are the first step. But it's another something when someone makes it easy for teen-age youngsters to release their aggressions by heaving rocks through windows or at cops. Who hasn't, at one time or another, wanted to heave a rock through a window? Or at a cop? Most of these kids are doing it that way, for that reason; most of them in these parts are so poorly educated they can't tell you what the Bill of Rights really is. If you're going to throw rocks at cops or anything else, for God's sake know why you're doing it. I hate violence, always have, hate the sound and smell and sight of it. It makes me sick. But I've learned to accept its inevitability. Only—not for its own sake."

He was wandering, he knew that. And, worse, he was preaching. It was more than ironic, it was just damned bad luck, that he had come to Cainsville hoping for an off-chance victory that would not be Pyrrhic, that might focus the eyes of the South on the enraged Negro as more than a threat to life and property, as a very potent and dire threat to southern economy and material well-being. And what had he walked into? Sue-Ellen.

"David." Chuck spoke without looking up from his matchstick abstraction. "Until night before last we were in the right row to make a hundred. I'm convinced of that, plumb convinced. Where are we now?"

"I don't know. One thing's for damned sure. There's no time to waste."

Chuck stood up, long legs looking like knobbed stilts

below the short seersucker robe. "I'm going to get dressed and go back over there," he said. "Not that it will do any good. They look at me as though I had some loathsome social disease."

"You have," said David. "To them."

"So? Which one?"

"Belief in a universal God." David looked up at Chuck and smiled.

"We share it," said Chuck.

"But on you it looks better because it came harder."

"What do you mean?"

"You didn't grow up with it. The God of your childhood was a very pertickler and choosy gent. Mine wasn't."

"You win, Stoopid."

72

LATER IN THE DAY Brad asked David, "Care to do some sight-seeing?"

"I'd probably better. Then I'll know which way to run. Let's use my car."

"Calhoun Road's the one you came in on, the one that passes the Towers land, and comes on by here, then goes straight on into Main Street. It deadends there. Let's head that way first."

There was no need for Brad to point out Main Street when, after a little more than a mile of dusty, jolting travel they reached a slight rise about a quarter mile from it. The street ran like a wide river below them, a river that separated barren desert from fertile field, a selective river whose waters nourished but one side of its wide stream, leaving the other parched and dry.

"A lot more things than just Calhoun Road stop at Main Street," said David.

"True. The buildings on the north, on your left, across Main Street, are the paper-box factory, the cigar factory behind that, and still farther away and a little more to the north a bottling works. It employs a fair number of colored in unskilled capacities."

"Enough to hurt if they walked out?"

"I would say so, yes. Actually, that company's fairly sympathetic. They felt the pinch of a good-sized boycott a while back. Murfree tells me they're pleading for talks and get-togethers."

"When do you and this guy Murfree manage these little chats?"

"Cloak-and-dagger stuff. We meet up at the waterfall. Notes are passed by elevator operators. We've had to do it that way. He's got youngsters, and he's received some nasty threats."

"Where does this man Haskin have his store?"

"Right down there, at the very end of Calhoun, on the left. The side fence of his backyard—unloading area, actually—runs along this side of Main Street. His store and house face Calhoun. It's well away from the business center of our side of town, but it's still the main store; everyone over here gets there at least two or three times a week. I think it's because the store is somewhere to go for the nondrinkers and nonpool players. Also, he orders in larger quantities because of the volume, and his prices are lower." Brad was thoughtful for a moment, then said, "Until I came south, I never knew, never realized, how important two cents off on sugar could be, one cent off on apples, one cent off on bread."

"Yet you honestly think these people will give up earning those important pennies for two weeks?"

"Wait till you've been here a while before you pass judgment."

"Yes, sir. Sorry, Chief."

"Almost directly across Main Street from Haskin's store is the City Hall. You can see the cupola and the top of the upper floor. Go on down the road."

David drove on slowly, drew to the shoulder, and braked to a stop at a word from Brad.

"The stockade," said Brad. "See it?"

"It would be hard to miss."

The cyclone fencing stretched from the edge of the City Hall building to the edge of another, larger building that even from this distance could be identified as a police station and jail, a concrete building that managed to look gray and dirty, although it was obviously considerably newer than the white-frame City Hall. From where they were parked they could see the white, diagonal markings for cars on the black asphalt paving of the stockade. The back wall was an extension of the jail.

"Just on the other side of the jail is a street that runs east to the center of town. On the opposite corner of that street on the same side you can see the Grand Hotel. There are some offices in a couple of old, reconstructed residences next to that, then Third Street. That's the main drag of the city; it peters out here, but farther on, in town, it's the location of the principal stores and buildings."

"What happens to Main Street south of there?"

"It peters out, too, curves westward through the edges of the colored section. The paving ends, and in some places colored have moved over, without objections from the whites. A lot of the streets on this side of town end at Main Street, of course. Including Cottonwood Road, our principal business street. It runs parallel with Calhoun. Turn right at this little cross street just ahead and we'll go over that way. I'm supposed to see Dr. Anderson anyhow and get checked."

The houses in the area nearest Main Street were closer together and of better quality than the jerry-built homes and tar-paper-patched cabins that had straggled, widely spaced, along both sides of Calhoun Road; these had obviously once been the homes of whites. The lower end of Cottonwood Road, where it debouched into Main Street, still had a semblance of paving and sidewalks, and the stores and little restaurants were clean and well kept up.

"Zion Church, where Hummer went this morning, is west of here. There are several other churches scattered between here and Calhoun Road, and a big community hall known as Salvation Hall also lies between Cottonwood and Calhoun, about a quarter mile west."

They turned into a side street, and Brad directed David to stop in front of a house larger than any they had passed, a sample of pre-Victorian architecture whose beauty of line no shabbiness could hide.

"Anderson would fix the place up if he had more time. And money. He's the only Negro physician for miles around. I don't see how in hell he does it. He's poorly equipped. He has an old X-ray machine and a 'new' secondhand electrocardiograph machine of which he is mighty proud. Does his own laboratory work, of course."

They walked up the steps to the wide porch running across the front of the house, its roof supported by graceful pillars from which the paint was peeling in scrofulous patches. As they crossed the porch, the front door opened and a woman came out with her arm around the shoulders of a girl whom David judged to be about fourteen. One of the girl's eyes was almost obscured by a large bandage on her forehead. Behind them, in the doorway, stood a tall man with broad shoulders, wearing a starched white coat, who greeted Brad warmly. Brad indicated the woman and the girl with the bandaged forehead, who were now down the steps. "Sunday night?"

"Yes. I wonder if the time will ever come again when it will just be falling out of trees or getting hit by baseballs."

Brad introduced David, and the doctor said, "Come in, come in. Honored to have you here, Mr. Champlin."

Dr. Raymond Anderson had graying hair, abundant, and with wide waves. It had not been artificially straightened. His skin was dark from years of southern sunshine, but David knew that had he lived in the North the skin would have been lighter, and he could have passed for a native of some Mediterranean or Far Eastern country. He looked like a man who had adjusted to trouble, had subdued his devils but not eliminated them.

They sat in a cool, high-ceilinged office and drank lemonade brought by a thin, brown-skin woman in a nurse's uniform. There was a pin on the pocket of the uniform and a black velvet band on the wide-winged white cap. After she had passed the lemonade Anderson reached out and took her hand. "My wife, gentlemen. Also my surgical assistant, my anesthetist, my floor supervisor, and night and day nurse."

After he had checked Brad's wound and pronounced him in good shape, the doctor took them through the building. Upstairs three large rooms had been converted into four-bed wards, a male, female, and children's. The beds were old, some of them the standard hospital type, a few of them just cots. The other furnishings of the rooms were shabby, and some of the bedside tables were obviously handmade. Everything was scrupulously clean. A girl in a white uniform, but without cap, was making up a bed with fresh linen in the male ward.

"One of our Sunday-night casualties was just released," said Anderson. "A fifteen-year-old. He came here directly from jail with a broken wrist. He wasn't in very good shape, so we kept him overnight."

"Do you do any surgery?" asked David. He didn't want to talk about, think about, a fifteen-year-old boy with a broken wrist who "wasn't in very good shape" after spending the night in jail under conditions David knew only too well.

"Emergency only. Appendectomies, caesarians, things like that, when there isn't time to get the patient to the county hospital."

"And only you and Mrs. Anderson?"

"And the girl you just saw, plus a young lad who's going to enter Howard next month, and is hoping to take up medicine. I'm losing them both. The girl is going into nurse's training. Brad here is helping out on the scholarships for them."

They were downstairs again now, and David glanced at Brad, grinning. At least the Chief had the grace to look embarrassed at this revelation. "I didn't know," said David, and Brad snapped crossly, "There hasn't been time."

When they got in the car David said: "Tell me about him. I liked him."

"Born in Capitol City, made it to—and through—the University of Illinois, and then University of Michigan medical. Decided on California, interned, and then had a residency in a county hospital in the San Joaquin Valley. Dust bowl refugee country. Once it was all right, but each year it has received an increasing influx of Southerners. Now, I understand, it's not much better than some states in the South. His colleagues didn't give him any trouble, he says. It was the damned patients. It can't be very inspiring to a doctor to sweat it out trying to save the life of an ignorant white, and hear him say to a ward mate, 'That's the way the poor gets treated here: nigger doctors.' So he decided to come South, stick with his own people exclusively. His wife came with him."

"When you got it to do, you got it to do," said David.

"He's by way of being an authority on cardiac and hypertensive diseases. He's consulted frequently—on the phone, of course—by doctors on the other side of town. He tells me the Negro past a certain age in the Deep South who doesn't have hypertension is almost a novelty. That the first experiments in drugs designed to help high blood pressure were done in a clinic for Negroes in, I think, Mississippi."

"It figures," said David. "Any of the white doctors take colored?"

"A few. On an off-hours, in-the-side-door, basis. Why?"

"Because some of the people in the South, with a better than average doctor with a dark skin to consult, will go across town, go in side doors, be patronized, just because it's a white doctor."

"Yes. Why?"

David shrugged. "That's us." He glanced over at Brad, smiled. "Not criticizing, Chief, not criticizing. Just accepting."

They drove back to Calhoun Road and headed east, for Haskin's store. As the high fencing of the stockade came into view, David slowed to a crawl, watching the pedestrians on Main Street as they passed it. Almost all stopped to look. Two men stood together talking, then slapped each other on the back and laughed; one or two passed it looking straight ahead, the set of their heads showing they were as conscious of it as those who had stopped, but in a different way.

The motor of the car stalled just before they reached the Haskin store. David said, "Damn!" and Brad said, "Let's get moving. It's hot—" David reached for the ignition key but did not turn it. "Watch," he said. "Watch."

As they had drawn nearer to the stockade a wide gate, not discernible the first time he had seen the fence, became clear. Now a car drove along and parked in front of the gate. It was a green convertible, top down, about four or five years old. The stars and bars of the Confederacy flew from each side of the front bumper. The back seat held what appeared to be hunting gear, and two rifles were racked behind the front seat. The man driving the car was middle-aged, rangy, with a ruddy, thin-lipped face. He wore a green sport shirt. His passenger was a youth in jeans and green striped shirt, his tow-colored hair brush cut on top, swept back in duck wings on each side. As Brad and David watched, the younger man flung open the door of the car and ran to the stockade's gate, a large square of cardboard in one hand. When he turned to run back to the car the square of cardboard was fastened to the steel links of the gate, its message easily read by David and Brad: NIGGERS ONLY. The lettering was not crude, had been worked on carefully, and below it had been drawn the figure of a man hanging from the bough of a tree, head grotesquely bent, face painted black, kinky hair depicted by exaggerated scrolls.

When the youth returned to the car the green-shirted man gunned the motor, and the convertible sped out of sight, screaming around a curve just past City Hall.

Brad said at last: "There go two happy citizens. And the older is involved in the Towers land deal."

"Sweet Jesus!" breathed David.

"That driver," said Brad. "One of the Twelve Just Men."

"One of the *what*, for God's sake?"

"There's so much that's vile, one forgets." David had never heard so much emotion in Brad's voice. "To take vileness for granted, and forget it. Christ!"

"Brad," said David. "Snap out of it. Tell me about these —what did you call them? Twelve Just Men?"

Brad's voice was a monotone when he answered. "A while back, probably while you were in jail or you would have heard about it, a new organization was formed in this county. 'Conceived in liberty and dedicated to the proposition—' "

"Brad."

"All right, brat. It's a Klan-type thing, perhaps an offshoot of the Klan. They called themselves the Twelve Just Men because that was the number involved in its founding. It's spreading throughout the state. All of the original twelve wear green shirts, and don't ask me why green. I suppose black or brown or yellow didn't seem appropriate. Or red either. And blue's too damned wishy-washy. As I say, they wear green shirts, except of course the two or three who are state troopers. The junior members, like that kid we just saw, wear green somewhere, green stripes, tie, scarf, something." Brad laughed, a bitter sound. "Poor Haskin is stuck with a couple of dozen green shirts he ordered three months ago. Not a Negro would dare wear them."

David tried to keep it light. "Be sure and tell Luke so he'll get rid of that horror he wears."

"I will."

"Twelve Just Men." David scratched his head reflectively. "Sort of blasphemous, isn't it?"

"Now you mention it, yes. I hadn't thought of it in that light. The thing that struck me was its horrid parody of 'twelve good men and true.' It's so damned *adolescent*."

"That's what they said about Hitler." David was quiet for a moment. "Green. What a lousy stinking trick to play on the Irish."

73

As David crossed the long porch of the rectangular wooden building that housed Haskin's store, he noticed a structure on the other side of Main Street he had not seen before. It must once have been a huge barn, perhaps the barn of a large dairy; now it apparently was used as a warehouse. Under the sloping roof wide, closed doors indicated the former hayloft, and these doors overlooked the length of Main Street and the area in front of City Hall and the stockade. David remembered a novel he had read once, the scene laid in the time of World War I, and an incident that told of American soldiers entering a small French town and being picked off, one by one, by snipers in the loft of an abandoned barn. "Sure wish we could burn that place down," he said to Brad.

Now he had a clearer view of the Grand Hotel, where men who would have been lobby loungers on a cool or rainy day sat now in comfortable rockers on its wide veranda.

Inside the store the air was kept moving by a window fan set high in the wall above a counter behind which a short, slender dark-skinned man was wrapping a package for a stout gray-haired woman. When he gave her change, she put the coins in an old-fashioned coin purse that she snapped shut and dropped into a huge and shabby handbag. She turned from the counter, almost bumping into David, and smiled up at him. "Evenin', son. How you doin'—" and without waiting for an answer she bustled on, a stranger, still smiling, not knowing him but reaching out for a bright moment in the universal communion of his people. Steady, Champlin, he told himself. Steady. God, but he was shot, brought down, when for even a brief moment he could want above all things to follow a gray-haired kindly woman to whatever warm and shabby home she lived in, and there stay.

Brad, beside him, was leaning on the counter, and he heard the slender dark man behind it say, "Evenin', Lawyer Willis. How you making it?"

"Fine. Fine," answered Brad. "Everything all right here, Haskin?"

"Near's I can tell."

Brad introduced David, who saw immediately why Haskin was the community leader, why he had been selected as top man in the upcoming project. There was a sharp, discerning intelligence in the small dark eyes that, without being in the least shifty, seemed to move constantly, taking in everything that was happening in the big room. The grip of the wiry, thin hand was strong and sure; the lines in the middle-aged face were those of a man who has fought hard for a living, but fought clean. Enough Haskins, thought David, enough men like him, and we'll make it. All the way.

He stood to one side, waiting while Brad and Haskin talked between the demands of customers, enjoying the smell of the big room, a smell composed in part of old wood, beer, lunch meat, cheese, produce fresh from the earth, tobacco smoke, heat, and people. There was far more space in the Haskin General Department Store than there appeared to be from outside. Across the main room, opposite the counter against which he was leaning, half-open floor-length curtains hung in a double doorway, and through it David could see part of a smaller room with notion counters and dress racks. In the rear two doors led to what must be storerooms and the rear entrance.

The room was well filled, though not crowded, and suddenly he realized how quiet it was. What should have been the steady loudness of human voices was, instead, a low hum, and there were no familiar bursts of sudden laughter, deep from the men, shrill and exclamatory from the women. There should be some laughter; there was always its sound in a place like this at the end of the day, but now there was none.

He heard his name and turned to see Haskin leaning over the counter. "I was just tellin' Lawyer Willis we'd be mighty proud if you-all would have dinner with us. It ain't going to be fancy but it'll be good. Y'all like chittlins?"

"Sure do."

"Hog jowls?'" said Brad, and David turned wide surprised eyes toward him.

"You? Hog jowls? You told Peg? She'll dee-voce you."

"Well," said Brad defensively, "if you're going to eat part of a pig, you might as well—"

"Go whole hog? Forget it. I'll tell Peg you've gone native."

Haskin laughed. "He sure has. Ain't nothing we've had so far he don't eat like it was some fancy kind of restaurant food."

"It's probably a hell of a lot better," said David. "You fix those chittlins crisp?"

"Gracie does. That's my son's wife. Widow, I should say. She stays with us, her and the boy, keeps the house."

"Tell Gracie two more for dinner."

David found a seat on an upturned nail keg near the counter and sat quietly watching the people come and go, most of them hurrying now. Six thirty. He remembered the "emergency" seven o'clock curfew ordinance. That, he thought, was asking for trouble. Not even the strictest parents he had ever been acquainted with expected young people to stay at home after seven o'clock on a hot midsummer night. Could these people make their kids understand that right now it was important that they obey? Had Hummer gotten anywhere, really gotten anywhere, with them last night and this morning? Had someone else done a better job?

Almost in answer to his mental questions he saw the plump silhouette of a man entering the front door. It was unmistakably Garnett, the bald head tilted to one side like a fat bird's, the narrow, fleshy shoulders and, now that the light was no longer behind the other man, he could see the too quick smile.

"Lawd! If it ain't young Champlin!" If it had been on a woman his mouth would have been the best feature of the round face. Now it was smiling broadly. "How ya doin', man!"

David had been sitting with elbows on thighs, hands hanging slack between his knees, and he did not change his position. He said, without smiling, "Hi, Garnett. What are you doing here?"

"Didn't no one give you the word? I'm here with Hummer, with the Reverend Sweeton, he'ping him out. Man, we really got something going here. Too bad you ain't been in on it."

"Never too late. I'm here now." He saw the quick distress in Garnett's face, wanted to chuck him under the fat chin and say, "Wassa matter, baby? You-all hurtin' someplace?"

Garnett's laugh was nervous, close to a giggle. "Sue-Ellen's in town. Bet she don't even know you're here yet—"

"I know." He wished he didn't, and it would relieve his mind no end if he was sure Garnett would win his bet.

Garnett's stubby fingers gripped his shoulder, then massaged it, and he was glad when Brad came over and said: "Hello, Garnett. Let's go, David. Mrs. Haskin has already gone over and we're to go on in. Haskin will be along in a few minutes."

David wondered if Garnett would have the nerve to follow them to the house. Then Brad turned toward the front door and waved a hand in greeting, and David saw Hummer Sweeton and Les Forsyte entering. Garnett duck-waddled over to them, listened to something they were saying, nodded, and went out at a faster waddle.

Sweeton and Les joined them and they started for the house, which stood behind and a little to one side of the store. They passed through a rear door and into a yard that ran, on their right, to Main Street. Cyclone fencing enclosed this loading area, and on the Main Street side, a wide double gate served as entrance for laden trucks. There were a side door and small narrow porch at the side of the house that gave directly on this loading area. He could see the battered warehouse across the street even better from this point, its walls plastered with torn and peeling posters, and painted with soft-drink and patent-medicine ads.

The Haskin house had a large front living room that was entered directly from the front porch, a dining room behind it, and beyond that the kitchen and back porch. From the exterior David could tell that, like the Towers house, other rooms had been added on through the years.

Mrs. Haskin, a heavy, quick-spoken, smiling woman, greeted them, and as they passed through the kitchen on their way to wash up for dinner, introduced them to her daughter-in-law, Gracie. Gramp would have called Gracie "a fine woman, sure fine." When Gramp said "fine" about a woman he had generally been referring to figure and build. The word came back to David now. Gracie was a "fine" woman, and besides being fine she was, in spite of her youth, a comfortable woman. Few women as young and good looking as Gracie gave a man the feeling that she was mothering them, that even while he was looking upon her with more or less lustful intent he was at the same time resting his head on her shoulder.

A child stood beside her, and when she told him, "Say 'Good evenin' to the gentlemen," he hid his face in her skirt, then freed one round brown eye to peek at them. Haskin had entered the room now, and he picked the child up and carried him on his shoulder. "He's shy but he'll come out of it once he knows you. Name's Shadrach. Ain't that a shame! His mamma's grandmaw insisted on it and didn't none of us have the stren'th to fight the old lady. Pore li'l helpless chile. We calls him Shad."

They sat in the living room before dinner, David on the floor. He tried not to let his face reveal the inner uneasiness that kept him nervously turning a coin over and over in his fingers. He found he was not listening to the others, was listening to—no, for—something else. He knew when he spoke that he was rudely interrupting something Brad was saying, but he could not hold back the question. "What're you people doing about this curfew?"

"We're observing it," said Hummer. "If some of them young folks wants to break it and get in trouble, that's something we can't help. But at the church meeting this morning and in Salvation Hall this afternoon the word went out. Observe it, we says."

"Many at the meeting?" asked David.

"Lord, Lord, there was plenty. I mean *plenty* people."

"Older people or young folks?"

Les Forsyte answered, concern in his voice. "Mostly older. A lot of women. I'll say one thing, though. I had the feeling we've got them with us. And that's a lot in this matriarchal society."

"If only a small number go along on this work-stoppage deal, you just might face charges of vagrancy—and jail sentences."

"I thought of that," said Brad. "But a man in jail is still a nonproducer."

"And he's a damned vulnerable one," said David.

"Don't think that'll happen," said Hummer. "Nossir, don't think it will. And, like I say, the word's gone out to observe the curfew. 'Wise as serpents and harmless as doves—' " He smiled, and David smiled into the deep eyes, the trust in them, and the faith.

Haskin was on his feet headed for the door. "We're closing early," he said. "I'm going back over to the store and give the kid a hand. Don't you-all wait for me when dinner's ready."

David said to Sweeton, "There's a woman here now, name of Sue-Ellen Moore—"

"You know her, son?" Hummer smiled. "She's sort of hard to handle. But I'm not worrying myself about her, not now."

"If I were you I'd worry about her twenty-four hours a day," said David.

"We're not about to get in a fuss with any other organization. We gave her a job with us, training those young uns, teaching 'em how to protect theirselves, how to march so's the line'll be harder to break up, things like that. The whites give her twelve hours to get out of town, and can't none of us go for that. She's still here."

David would have felt a lot better without Hummer's last words. "Out of town" was where he would like Sue-Ellen to be permanently.

Gracie came in, telling them dinner was ready. While they were filing into the dining room, Haskin reentered the house, hurrying, his face dark and set.

"Town's crawling with po-lice," he said. "Plumb crawling with 'em. All of a sudden. Regular po-lice and special deputies with badges, and I swear to God I saw a trooper's uniform back of the old warehouse. They don't need all them po-lice just to enforce a curfew."

"Set down, Jim, set down," said Hummer. "They just looking for trouble, not finding it. They like a man squared off for a punch, and when he lets fly the other man ain't there."

"All of you set down," said Mrs. Haskin. "Eat your dinners. Worry don't do nothing but rile up the stomach." She hurried into the kitchen, and after they were seated Haskin, his face still showing the lines of worry and anxiety, said, "Pass your plates, folks."

"Daddy Jim." Gracie had entered from the kitchen. "You ain't asked the blessing yet."

"Lawd! So I ain't—" and there was sudden quiet in the room.

The blessing was long and earnest, and while Haskin's voice went on, David glanced across the table from under lowered eyelids and saw the solemn dark eyes of Shadrach fixed on him. He opened his own eyes wide, then closed one in a broad wink. Shad covered his mouth with a chubby hand; the eyes danced, then closed dutifully at a whispered reprimand from Gracie, sitting beside him.

It was then that David heard the sounds.

The sounds were not loud, but they were sharpened and made meaningful by a mind alert with apprehension: the steady thud of feet past the front of the house muffled but clearly audible, the same sound from the direction of Main Street barely distinguishable. Placing the heels of his palms against the table's edge, he pushed back his chair. "Trouble," he said, and walked quickly into the dining room. He heard Brad say, "David, what—" but did not slow down. When he reached the living-room window Brad and Haskin were just behind his shoulders, and he could hear the others hurrying from the dining room to join them. He thought, This is it again, Champlin! God! Here you go again—

Only the area in front of the house was clearly visible, but by twisting his neck he could see the dusty end of Calhoun Road, and the portion of Main Street in front of the stockade. Several white men were walking briskly along the sidewalk on the other side of Main Street. They wore khaki pants and white shirts and each had a revolver holstered on one hip. Four more were walking in Calhoun Road, two-by-two, in opposite directions. On these men the badges pinned on shirt pockets were clearly visible. He remembered seeing two of them in Heliopolis just before he was jailed.

"The store," said Haskin hoarsely. "We can see better from the store—"

David started on an uneven run for the side door, and when they reached the small side porch Brad's sudden grip on his arm threw him off balance so that he grabbed one of the roof supports to steady himself. He turned and was looking into Brad's eyes, icy, imperious.

"Stay out of this!" Brad's voice matched his eyes. "Stay out of it, damn you! We need you, *understand? We need you.* Don't be a damn martyr!"

"Turn me loose, Brad! For God's sake, you think I'm crazy?" The other men were ahead of them now, running across the rear yard. "Let's go, man, let's go!"

Haskin, just before he reached the rear door of the store, called: "Gracie! Gracie! Lock them doors and pull the shades! Keep the chile inside, y'hear! Keep the chile inside!"

(Oh, God, yes! Oh, God, yes! Keep the chile inside, Gracie; keep the small limbs and soft face inside; keep the young eyes and ears inside so they can't see or hear, so the chile won't wake screaming in the night because of what they've seen and heard.)

The front door of the store was already open, and a youth David knew must be Haskin's nephew was standing on the porch outside. There were the sound of sirens, and the edgy, shrill note of a police whistle. David and the others stood on the porch watching, stunned. Men in the uniforms of city police and sheriff's deputies were spotted every few yards on both sides of Main Street, and on the sidewalks men in khakis and green shirts were walking slowly, in couples, talking; even, God help him, laughing expectantly.

Hummer Sweeton was standing beside David now, and his eyes were those of a man who feels a deep inner sickness. He did not speak when David gripped his shoulder. Even in the shock of the moment David noted the thinness of that shoulder, the bone beneath too little flesh. He tried to keep his voice light when he said, "There ain't nothing we can do about it, Reverend, not just now—"

Hummer nodded without speaking, then after a moment said, "I know, I know. I been here before. But I didn't think —" and let the words trail off.

Les Forsyte said, "Nobody told us—but somebody must have tipped them. Some son of a bitch must have got the word out."

David did not answer because he was listening now to the sound of chanting in the distance. The heavy, humid heat that now held a threat of rain suddenly became almost too oppressive to bear, and he was conscious of the sweat that trickled down his temples and formed in beads on his forehead.

Now the source of the chanting came into view, at the far end of Main Street, rounding the curve that marked the end of the pavement and carried the street westward: a massed, orderly phalanx of marchers, six abreast, and when it reached the paved portion of the street the sound of marching feet became the background of the chanting, giving it reality, supporting it. When the last row of marchers rounded the curve, reinforcements from a large building on the west side of the street fell in line with ordered precision.

Sue-Ellen was marching in the front line, arms linked with those of a young boy and a girl. Just before the marchers reached Third Street the lines became uneven and the parade halted. Two young men, older than the bulk of the marchers, came out of the ranks and trotted down each side, straightening lines. There were few adults in those lines; at least two-thirds were young teen-agers.

Some of the deputized citizens started to move from in front of Calhoun Road and the stockade across the pavement, heading for the center of the street, and a man in the uniform of the city police barked: "Wait! Let 'em get to the police station! We got the dogs there—"

Men and women were already gathering below them on

Calhoun Road, some of them calling questions up to Haskin, who kept answering, "Gawd knows! We gotta wait and see—"

Two of the city police started up Calhoun from the intersection, swinging their clubs, ordering the people back to the side of the road or into the yards. David saw a truck rattle to a stop. It was loaded with regular high carpenter's sawhorses and others that were obviously the handiwork of local volunteers. Two of these latter were handed down from the truck to the two men at the intersection. They were waist-high for a tall man, made of heavy boards nailed across the top of two square uprights that were set into large, solid, sturdy wooden blocks. The two barriers reached across the end of Calhoun Road from the edge of a small warehouse in the front corner of Haskin's yard to a low board fence on the other side.

Les Forsyte said, "My God! They can't do that—"

"They're doing it," snapped David. "Stay here. Let 'em play with their damned Tinkertoys. We'll get our innings—"

The police who had been clearing the street were on their way back now, and as they passed the store they looked at the group on the porch.

"You niggers stay up there!" said one.

Brad's shoulder was brushing his, and David sensed the stiffening of the other man's entire body. He turned to speak and stopped, mouth half open, stunned at the naked, murderous rage he saw. He put a hand on Brad's arm. "Don't let 'em get to you, Chief," he said quietly. "For God's sake, don't let 'em get to you."

"Yes," said Brad. His lips scarcely moved. "Yes. I know. But for a minute—"

"You wanted to kill."

"I wanted to kill."

David kept his voice low, without emotion. "Remember me, Chief? I'm the starry-eyed idiot you used to lecture on the evils of getting angry at the opposition."

His eyes returned to the scene before him, and he saw a small boy he judged to be about five, holding the hand of a sturdy, fat-legged little girl who couldn't, he thought, be more than three years old. She was dressed in bright red corduroy overalls. The two were trotting as fast as the short legs of the little girl could go toward the barrier at the end of the road. As though, thought David, this was a parade where they'd get cotton candy.

"Haskin!" He did not even try to keep the irritation out of his voice. "Haskin! those two kids on the other side. Somebody get 'em back in!"

"Lawd!" Haskin ran down the steps, calling, "Patty! Patty! Bobby! Y'all git back here, y'hear!" Then he called to a group standing on the edge of a yard across the road: "Git Loretta out here! Tell her two of them kids done busted loose ag'in!"

A screen door banged in a house just beyond, and a woman ran out, eyes white-rimmed with fear, mouth open, calling, "Patty! Bobby!" as she started running down the steps, then stopping to scream at four children who had run out the door after her: "Git back in! Y'all stay in that house, or I'll bust you open!"

David turned away, forgetting them in the hell that was Main Street now.

The prearranged police strategy was simple. Law-enforcement officers had patrolled the west side of Main Street, and others had waited in ambush on the side streets on the east side, their greatest numbers concentrated south of Third Street. Now, as it moved again, the front line of the march was past the Grand Hotel, its rear ranks just passing Third Street. From the vantage point on the porch, aided by the slight southward slope of Main Street, David saw police and green shirts moving in at rear and sides. They were armed with hip-holstered guns, but the weapons they carried in their hands were cattle goads and clubs.

He heard the first high shriek of a goaded boy, could see, even at that distance, the flailing of clubs. The rear lines broke up in panic, the marchers who tried to break to the sides driven back to the center by goads and clubs. There was the sound of shots, and he knew they were fired into the air by trained troopers; these men were in no danger, these men were safe, and knew it.

There was only one way for the kids to run now, and that was forward, and the milling dark melee that had been the rear lines broke through the still orderly front ranks, the runners knocking some of their fellow demonstrators to the ground, the whole trapped mass pushed inexorably forward, toward the police station where men with dogs straining at leashes stood, toward a solid line of police that stretched across Main Street from the entrance to the City Hall to Haskin's fence, a line that moved forward now with cool intent, blocking any escape. The gate of the stockade had been opened, and at each side four men stood, waiting.

The area between City Hall and the police station was an inferno of black fantasy now, a hell the eye and ear could take in but that the sickening mind rejected.

At the corner of the porch Haskin's nephew stood, cursing steadily, monotonously. It was not the cursing of a Nehemiah, the easy blasphemy, the exhibitionist obscenity of habit; it was a cursing from the soul, not the cursing of a boy, but of a sick man suffering intolerable pain.

David heard Haskin call, "Willy! Willy!" and turned in time to see the storekeeper toss a key ring to the youth. "Take them keys and go round back and unlock the loading gate! Stay there! Maybe some of those young uns can break loose and git down there—" The boy ran off, silent now that there was something he could do.

The wailing of a child close at hand brought his attention back to Calhoun Road, and he saw the boy who, a few minutes before, had been holding the hand of the red-overalled little girl. He was running blindly through the crowd, screaming between wailing gasps, "Mamma! Mamma!" He was alone.

Brad's sharp, "David! David! Get back here!" came to him as he pounded down the steps and into the roadway. The mother of the boy was in front of him now, running toward the barricade, and he grabbed her roughly, half threw her into the arms of an old man standing, gape-mouthed and frightened, at the edge of the road. "Damn it, woman! You want to get your head split! Hold her, man!"

His eyes found what they had been searching for in the chaos of Main Street, the flash of a child's red corduroy overalls. The child was running, stopping, running again, sobbing; lost, bewildered, terrified, and disoriented. A trooper picked her up, carried her toward the barrier, set her on her feet and gave her a sharp pat on the bottom, then turned to grab the arm of a running girl and push her roughly back into the melee in front of the stockade.

As he drew closer David could hear the child's sobs, and he called out, "Patty! Patty! This way!" but the words did not penetrate her terror. Even in his anxiety he noticed the green shirt of the man running toward the edge of the crowd, a length of two-by-four in his hand. He called again, roaring, saw the child waver, then run blindly, saw the plump, red overalled figure strike one leg of the man in the green shirt. The man lost the cadence of his hurrying stride, regained it, not even stopping to see what had caused his stumble. In that moment David recognized him as the driver of the car that had stopped earlier in the day at the stockade gate.

The child's body hit the pavement face down, and for a split second she lay still, then raised her head. Blood ran from the small nose; the tiny mouth was open, gasping without sound. Around her the running, frantic feet of both whites and blacks were perilously close.

It was Fred Winters's voice he heard now—"Champlin! David!"—then he was sliding on his belly as he had slid so many times, years before, trying for a base in the Timminses' back lot, when his leg grew stronger and he could run for himself after a fashion. The slide took him under the barrier, and he crawled a few feet farther and encircled the baby's body with one arm, rolled over toward the barricade and half threw, half pushed her to the hands that were held out for her. He started to crawl back, keeping his body low, and heard a staccato, "Get that nigger on the ground!" He felt the blows on head and back, thought, God damn, both kidneys this time. These were not blows from a police club, but from a board with edges; the kicks could have come from any kind of boots that were heavy.

Someone was calling, "Clete! Clete!" and the blows stopped. David struggled to his knees, groggy, head ringing. They had brought dogs to this side now, and he could hear them close by. Straddled, khaki-clad legs were just in front of him, a tanned, sinewy hand still swung a length of two-by-four. Above the trousers he saw the green shirt, but did not look higher, at the face. He knew it. His doubled fist lashed upward with all the strength he could muster, and the legs that had been straddled over him were writhing on the pavement.

He dropped both hands to the ground again to finish his crawl to the barrier, sure that he would never reach it, sure that the next assault would knock him out, cripple him, possibly kill him. And then, miraculously, it did not come; no one had seen the blow, no one's attention had been anywhere but on the job of herding a hundred or so youngsters into stockade and jail. He looked sideways and saw someone dragging the man called Clete away, trying to help him. David heard himself laugh foolishly; at this point Clete wouldn't be saying anything, not for a few minutes.

He was almost at the barrier when a voice barked, "Someone get that nigger yonder on the ground!" and another voice said, "Hell, throw him back over! We got enough on our hands—" A booted foot struck viciously on his ribs; then he felt himself picked up by legs and shoulders, swung through the air and thrown over and clear of the wooden barricade. Though his fall was broken by the hands and arms of men on the other side, still his face slid into the dusty ruts of Calhoun Road.

Brad was beside him, swearing softly, and Hummer and Haskin and Les. He sat up and tried to wave them off. "O.K.," he said. "O.K." He was on one knee now. "Hell!" He had to throw an arm around Forsyte's shoulder in order to get to his feet because his legs were unsteady. "Hell, I'm O.K. —Christ, you guys, this is routine. This is just routine."

He walked painfully up the steps of Haskin's store between Brad and Hummer, and shook their support off when they reached the door, wondering as he walked if his kidneys had really had it again or just felt that way.

74

By ten thirty the only sounds from outside that seeped through the open windows of Haskin's house were those of singing from the stockade, the beat of patrolling feet, the occasional wail of sirens from police cars cruising through the west side, and the soft drumming of a steady, relentless rain.

David sat at one end of the big dining-room table, silent and still except for a hand that slapped softly, steadily, palm down, on the table, not varying its rhythm, slap-slap, slap-slap. He was looking straight ahead, eyes unfocused, hearing snatches of talk only as sounds without meaning. He did not see the owner of the dark hand that slid over his, quieting the slap-slap, lying softly firm on his own hand. He looked up, bringing life into focus again, and saw Gracie standing over him.

"Y'all relax, Mr. David," she said. "Y'all relax. Don't do no good staying all tensed up that way. Things'll work out. You'll see."

She was younger by years than he, but the ample breasts had already suckled a child. He wanted to lay his head on those breasts and close his eyes, never open them again; go to sleep with his face buried in the dark softness of those breasts and never wake up. He bit the inner surface of his lip until the pain brought him back to reality.

"Thanks, Gracie. Thanks. I'm all right."

She laughed and took her hand away from his. "Sure you are. You all right, 'cepting maybe for being banged up." She moved toward the kitchen. "Next time you gets in a state I'll get me a switch like I does for Shadrach—"

"You better not, Gracie. You better not get you a switch, old man like me—" He stopped at the sound of new voices in the living room. One was Chuck's, the other he did not know. It was a white voice, and young, the accent of the region noticeable but not marked, that of a Southerner whose education outside the South had left its imprint.

He heard Chuck say, "Where's David?" and got to his feet, wincing with the movement. "Here, Chuck." He limped to the archway between living room and dining room. Chuck was standing in the center of the room with another man. Brad, Sweeton, Winters, and Haskin were already there. Chuck's tall, big-boned frame made his companion seem smaller than he actually was. The man's hair was dark; his head and face were small and delicately boned. Emotion, not nature, had given his skin an almost dead-white pallor, and the thinned lips would, under different circumstances, have been full and sensitive. The eyes were large, and intensity made them seem coal black. But this was a white man, no passer, a white man from the white world, in a white suit, its shoulders sodden with rain.

Gracie edged past David gently as he stood in the archway. "You gentlemen better come in and set down round the table," she said. "There's plenty coffee and beer, and all the talking and planning you-all got to do needs a little lubrication."

Chuck took his arm as they went into the dining room. "What happened? I just heard about it."

"Tell you later, pal. I'm all right."

"Makes a man believe in the old-fashioned hell," said Chuck. "All these rehearsals for it—"

Hummer Sweeton did not sit down when they all went into the dining room; instead he stood with his back to the window, where Winters joined him. Several men David did not know seemed to materialize, drifting in from living room and side door; they stood leaning against the walls or sat on extra chairs brought in by Les Forsyte. Haskin, at the head of the table, scattered a pile of ashtrays down its length.

"You all acquainted with Lawyer Murfree? You ain't, Mr. Champlin. Lemme make you acquainted. Lawyer John Murfree, Lawyer David Champlin."

Murfree was on his feet before David. "Don't get up, Champlin. You must be hurting." But David was already standing, and their hands met across the table. "I've heard about you," said Murfree. "Brad Willis has told me a lot, and I've read a few things. I'm delighted to meet you."

So this was Murfree, the man from the other side of Main Street that Brad said could be counted on. David kept his eyes on Murfree's face, not caring that it might be rude, wanting to size him up, afraid of a snap judgment, distrusting, doubtful. He'd had a damned bellyful of "moderates." Left to his judgment no so-and-so-ing "moderate" would have been in this room tonight. Then the thought flicked through his mind that no "moderate" would have come there. If Murfree had been a southern "moderate," a small group would have been meeting in his office, listening to words of wisdom and sweet reason. For a moment he wished tiredly that all whites would either suddenly be missing or remain foes. Maybe, he thought, the Black Muslims have something after all. He was tired unto death of knowing that most white hands outstretched to his people wore gloves, that the grip of a white hand on his own was not so strong as the grip of that same hand on the knife handle of betrayal.

Murfree must have felt his gaze, for he turned his head now and their eyes met, and David had a squirmy feeling of embarrassment that the other man had read his thoughts. Murfree did not smile, and David sensed a flinching of the other's mind, as though from pain. "You'll have to take me on faith, Champlin."

David felt bewildered at his own reaction because when he spoke it was with intent to comfort, to reassure. "Of course. That's all any of us can do, isn't it? On either side."

Gracie set out coffee cups, cream and sugar, beer for those who wanted it, bread, crackers, and platters of sliced cheese and cold meats. Chuck, sitting in the next chair, laid a hand on David's knee.

"You-all sure you're all right?" Anxiety thickened his accent.

"Far as I know. Brad and Fred ran me over to Doc Anderson's. He says I'll live. Assorted bruises, bumps, contusions, abrasions. Maybe a couple of floating kidneys. Where were you when the lights went out?"

"God help me, in my own room. Asleep. I had what is known in these parts as a 'summer cold' coming on. I'd been up since before day, so I ate soup and ice cream about five, and a little later took a bath, a hot toddy, and some aspirin, and then died. Plumb died. Next thing I knew I was standing at the window looking at hell. Gives a man a shock."

David grinned. Chuck could always act on him like some kind of medicine taken for vertigo. "What'd you do?"

Chuck sighed. "Nothing. There wasn't anything I could do. By the time I could take it in, the boys with cattle goads and clubs were in full swing. There was no stopping any of it. All I could have done—and darned if I didn't start for the door—was stand on the steps and pray over 'em. All I had on was my pajama tops."

The effort to choke back the laugh was almost as painful to David's sore ribs and chest muscles as the laugh itself would have been. He was remembering a mass hysteria that had swept a mixed crowd in the quadrangle at Pengard the night of a fire in Chuck's dormitory, when Chuck, dead asleep, had been routed out by a fireman and had come tearing down the steps carrying a carton of milk and a bottle of beer—clad only in his pajama tops.

He swallowed the last quiver of his laugh as Hummer Sweeton's body was suddenly between them. He was leaning forward, his hands on the tabletop, the deep-set eyes seeming to take in everyone in the room.

"What we going to do about them chilren? *What we going to do about them?* You-all hear that rain, or you-all talking too much?"

The sound of talk stopped; even the blue haze of smoke that was beginning to cloud the room seemed to lift before the blast of Sweeton's words.

Murfree had been sitting quietly beside Haskin, arms folded on the table. He looked directly at Sweeton, without moving, and in spite of himself David found himself liking the look. It was intense, direct, without softness or compassion or phony "understanding."

"Chuck Martin and I have just come from City Hall, Reverend," said Murfree. "They released the children under ten—"

"Under ten!" Forsyte's interruption was explosive.

"There were a few, Les. They are home now. Those between ten and twelve will be released in the morning. They said. The others are being held for juvenile-court hearings. We did our best."

"That still don't answer my question," said Sweeton. "They going to stay where they are? Them chilren going to stay in that there stockade? Going to stay there like lambs in a slaughterhouse pen, all night, in the rain?"

Chuck said: "They've arranged shelter. A big tarp across the east end with flaps. The kids have the flaps back; that's why you can hear them singing. Some group is going to collect bedrolls and blankets from their families—"

"That's Goddamned kind of them!" David could feel his stomach knotting with sick, disgusted anger.

Murfree turned to David. "They think so," he said. "God help us all, they think so." He turned back to Hummer. "Mr. Sweeton, I don't know all of what happened tonight. I saw part of it, coming back from Otisville, driving south on Main Street. I was turned back just north of the old warehouse. I saw what happened to Champlin. Had there been anyone with me in the car—I travel alone these days—they would tell you that I was actively nauseated." The white face looked intolerably tired. "What I saw you do did me a world of good, Champlin."

David felt his defenses of doubt crumbling at Murfree's smile, faint though it was. He tried to shore them up, but knew they were not as strong as they had been when he first met this man. This was not the reaction of the true moderate, this rejoicing at a low blow to a white man's groin.

"The chilren," repeated Sweeton. "Them chilren—"

"Will be there for tonight. Tomorrow some of the adults will be released on bail. If, of course, they can raise the bail. Some of the kids are inside. I suppose as more space becomes available, they'll move the others in." He passed one hand over his face in a weary gesture. "I'm afraid my advocacy may have done more harm than good."

Haskin spoke for the first time. "Don't feel that way, Mr.

Murfree. Couldn't no one have got those kids turned loose. They aimin' to make an example of 'em, ship 'em off to that human cattle ranch they done built north of here. That dee-tention home."

"Yes," said Murfree. "They mentioned further talks in the morning. They said, and I quote, 'Their ringleaders will hear from us.' " He stirred in his chair and, watching him, David had the feeling that he was smarting from a recent humiliation. "Before I leave tonight, I do want to say one thing. I'm honored by your confidence." The dark, intense eyes ranged round the room, took in all its occupants. "There is no one on the other side of Main Street who, to my knowledge, knows your plans. Suspicion, yes. Knowledge, no. There is no knowing what tonight's fiasco has made of those plans. But let me point something out to all of you. Your opponents are not divided. They present a solid front. I am not completely alone in my thinking, only in my actions, but those of us in the background who share my feeling have about as much influence and weight at this time as a chapter of the Anti-Defamation League of the B'nai B'rith would have had in Nazi Germany."

The man's spoiling for a lynching, thought David; he's Klan bait pure and simple. What had happened between this man's birth and childhood, and now? Where had the break come? When had he first started swimming upstream, against the current, to clear headwaters, instead of drifting downstream to the swampy delta lands of his fellows?

The rumbles of assent to Murfree's talk rolled around the room, spent themselves, but before anyone could speak there was the sound of a door slamming, the thud of feet, and a breathless Garnett stood beneath the archway. David had not heard Fred Winters's voice until now, and the words crackled: "Where the hell have you been?"

"Man!" Garnett's familiar, high-pitched wail answered. "Man! Get off my back! They helt me back!"

"Who 'helt you back'?" David's voice did not crackle; it purred.

"Them guys over there in City Hall. They called me in after Lawyer Murfree and Chuck left. Man, I been in jail!"

"How come you was over there, Garnett?" Sweeton put the question.

"I'm tryin' to tell you. I got trapped. I was in that drugstore over there on Third getting me some stuff for my piles. It's the only place carries what I want. The guy's coming on with a lot of jazz about how there's something better, and then I looks out the window and I seen po-lice and people hurryin' toward Calhoun and I says 'Gimme what I ast for' and I pays for it and heads outa there runnin'. I never even got to Calhoun before they grabs me. Them kids was marching then, I mean *marching,* up that street."

David only half heard the remainder of Garnett's story. It wasn't worth trying to sort the lies from the truth when Garnett was talking anytime. The gist of it, the part that was capable of verification, was that he had sat out the demonstration in a jail cell. ("Man, I hadn't done *nothin'!*") Later, when it was over, they had taken him to City Hall. "Them kids, them pore kids in that stockade, having to walk right through 'em. Man, it was a shock."

"Never mind that," snapped Winters. "What happened in City Hall?"

When Garnett said, "They's something funny going on—" David had absorbed all he could take in silence. "Wait. Let me tell them, Garnett. You must be all worn out. Three hours in jail and piles and all." The plump face turned to him, and for a moment the anger was plain in the wide eyes; then the plump smile obscured it. Garnett said, "You wasn't there—" and David's voice knifed through the other's, cutting him short.

"I don't have to have been there. After Mr. Murfree and Chuck left, they brought you in. They wanted some nice reasonable talk-talks in the morning, and they wanted you to act as emissary."

Brad and Murfree and the man he had not yet met, Abraham Towers, as well as Mrs. Towers, had evidently done a good job in keeping quiet about the Towers land deal. He had no doubt whatever that any conciliatory move from the other side of Main Street was made with that in mind. Garnett's puzzlement, at least, was genuine. But they had ignored Murfree and Chuck, shown clear preference for dealing with Garnett, identifying him with Sweeton and the others.

It took the whites to spot some colored, he thought; took the whites to put them, in some cities, on police forces, help them get civil service jobs, even help them get elected to city councils, put on school boards, and, in red-necked towns like Cainsville, get steady jobs with more pay. It took the whites to see the yellow streak and take advantage of it, to know the meaning of *quid pro quo* and when the *quo* was the quieting of a troublemaking voice; took them to spot the sickest, most bruised psyches and offer balm. He'd give the whites credit for this much insight.

David turned painfully in his chair and saw Brad standing by the window alone. He couldn't trust his own control if he listened to Garnett any longer. There would be a loud spate of talk and argument for a while; let it run itself out. He got to his feet, and Brad started forward, frowning, motioning him back to his chair.

Garnett was talking again. "That's about it. They wants to talk to a committee in the morning."

"In the *morning*—" The words came from more than one person in the room.

"There ain't no use pushin' it tonight. All them big shots, the mayor and the po-lice chief and Banker Spangler—he was there—was going home when I left. They sent a po-liceman over with me—"

Had Garnett tried, even tried, to keep the puling, revealing pride out of his voice when he said, "They sent a po-liceman over with me—"?

Then he remembered Sue-Ellen. He caught Murfree's eye and said, "What about Sue-Ellen Moore? Do you know what happened to her?"

"She was one of the first picked up. Remember, she was in the front line."

"Hell!" He was surprised at the force of his own reaction to the news of Sue-Ellen's being jailed. She'd loused them up thoroughly, gotten a bunch of hot-headed kids in an open stockade and an overcrowded jail, but she'd done it because it seemed to her the right thing to do. The wrong things for the right reasons—that was Sue-Ellen, and he didn't like to think of her in jail for God knew how long. One damned sure thing, Sue-Ellen would see 'em all in hell before she'd do what Garnett had done. Which was why Garnett was free and smug and she was in jail. And without doubt, he reflected with some satisfaction, giving them all as bad a time as she knew how. Which would be bad.

"It's all right. I've stiffened up already, sitting so damned long. Better to move around." He joined Brad at the window. "Helluva mess, isn't it?"

Brad shrugged, looking tired. "I'm sorry you're in it, David. I should have kept my mouth shut."

"Nuts. I came. And you didn't bring me. You didn't ask for a damned thing except advice."

Brad said bitterly: "One lousy little town, in a crumby,

corrupt southern state, and all the evils of man contained in it. What have we got even if we win?"

"What the hell, Brad! Lay off that—"

"You could have been killed tonight—"

"I wasn't."

"No, but if you had been, somebody would probably have won a promotion. One troublemaking nigger less—"

"The guy who shot you was probably bucking for sergeant—"

"Win or lose, it's going to go on. And on—"

"And on. Trouble with you, Brad, is that you're too new to the South, even yet. You don't realize that one Negro having a cup of coffee at a counter in a white restaurant can almost be compared to Iwo Jima. He's the flag they put on top."

"A dead flag. That's good?"

"It's one hell of a lot better than none."

"You're . . ."

They both jumped involuntarily at a loud CRACK! behind them, wood hitting wood, and turned to see Haskin standing at the head of the table, a gavel in his hand. Sweeton was standing beside him; Murfree had risen and was standing against the wall with Winters and Les Forsyte.

"You-all quiet down!" There was valid authority in Haskin's voice. The sound of talk died out, and Haskin went on: "We agreed to send a committee over in the morning? Reverend Sweeton, Reverend Martin, Mr. Winters, Lawyer Willis, Lawyer Champlin—"

Garnett pushed his way through a group at the side of the table and stuck his head as far forward as his short neck would permit. "You can't do that!"

Haskin glared at the fat figure. "Why we can't?"

"They said they wouldn't talk to no outsiders. Said they'd only talk to Cainsville people."

David moved toward the table. "They wanted to talk to 'our nigras.' That's what they said, isn't it, Garnett?"

Garnett turned to him, and again David saw the anger in his eyes, and again the plump smile obscured it. "You got no call to say that, Davey-boy. That ain't what they said. Not in them words, anyhow. After all, ain't the people who lives over here the most concerned?"

A quiet courtroom Brad was coming forward now, speaking. "In many ways this resembles contract talks in a labor dispute. No responsible union will permit rank-and-file employees of a plant to sit around the bargaining table with management representatives. Too much pressure can be brought to bear. Joe Doaks received advances on salary when his wife had triplets; John Doe remembers the help he got when his kid was in an accident—or if he doesn't remember, he's reminded of it. Others may owe money to the credit union. A committee from the ranks is never advisable if you hope for real results."

"They ain't goin' to talk to anyone else." Garnett's face was set in stubborn immobility.

Now Murfree spoke, and when David looked at him he saw that the white man's eyes were looking directly at him. The message in the eyes and in the almost imperceptible nod of the head toward the kitchen was unmistakable: Go along with me, it said; we'll discuss it later.

"Mr. Willis is right," said Murfree. "In group negotiation between two opponents, frequently the weakest is the man with the most at stake."

Now David saw what was in Murfree's mind, and kicked himself mentally for not having thought of it himself. The men on the other side of Main Street had a lot at stake too; not the welfare of a hundred Negro children, but what to them was vastly more important: a deal that could bring them thousands upon thousands of dollars. Yet Murfree could not mention this, must present other arguments.

"However," continued Murfree, "in spite of pressure that will be brought to bear on a group of local Negroes—pressure from your own people and pressure from those on the other side—it is my opinion that it's worth a try. My advice is that no one on your committee have authority to make decisions without consulting with your legal experts, and believe me, you couldn't have finer. The main objective, as I see it, is to obtain release for those children. But don't let yourselves be stampeded. Or tricked. If I thought it would do any good, I would ask to sit in, but my welcome would be even less warm than would be extended to any of what they call the 'outsiders.' Actually, on this side of the street I am in the position of outsider. I hope you trust my sincerity."

Winters spoke quietly. "I don't believe any man who has suffered what you have suffered has the right to call himself an outsider."

Murfree smiled, the tension in his face lessening for a moment. "Thanks, Winters."

It did not take long to appoint the first three members of the committee: Haskin as chairman, a man named Al Williams who looked formidable and bitter to David, a man named Dexter Peters who was not present. "Home helping his wife mind the kids," said Haskin.

"I would suggest five," said David.

"How about two women?" asked Brad.

Haskin frowned thoughtfully, then slapped a hand on the table. "Damn! Damned if you ain't sayin' something! Womens been active other places, but they've sort of held back here. It'll give them guys over there a jolt." He listened to suggestions from the people present, and said: "There's one, Willy, there's one! That's a hell of a good one. Ella Simmons. We'll take Miz Simmons and—and—I got it. Liz Peters?" He looked around, saw his wife standing in the doorway to the kitchen. "What you think of Liz Peters for the committee, Ma?"

Mrs. Haskin's laugh must have been heard on the other side of the barriers. "Liz Peters? Lawd, man, you get Liz Peters along, and I only got one thing to say, jes' one thing: Gawd he'p the whites! I feels sorry for 'em, even bad as they're acting. I swear I do!"

Brad and David headed for the kitchen after Brad made arrangements to meet with Haskin's committee as soon as someone could bring the missing members to the house. "My wife'll stay with them Peters kids," said Al Williams.

Gracie was stooping over, reaching for something far back in a lower cupboard, amply rounded hips and buttocks outlined by her skirt, the brown smoothness of her thighs showing above stocking tops. She said something indistinguishable, then emerged and stood upright, a bottle of bourbon in her hand.

"Lawd Gawd!" said David. "Drinkin' liquor! Lemme at it—"

Gracie laughed. "Daddy Jim says it don't do to have hard stuff out, time like this. Trouble enough without it. We even went light on the beer—"

Brad poured and handed David a stiff one, and was pouring a second for himself when Murfree entered from the dining room, where a babble of talk was becoming more intense. "I'll have to go back in there in a minute—"

"No, you won't," said David. "That's good for a long time yet. You don't know our people if you don't know that. Join us? On the rocks?"

"Just straight, with some water on the side. Thanks." He

looked at Brad. "You're not pleased at the idea of a local committee, are you?"

"To be honest, no."

"You, Champlin?"

"No. But I think I see the point."

"If Brad briefs the committee properly, I can't see the harm. Incidentally, it's a good committee. I know them all. Mrs. Simmons has cause to be tough. Her oldest boy—he's left home now—has a stiff leg as the result—" he stopped, embarrassed.

David smiled. "It's all right. A truck ran over mine. When I was a kid." A sensitive guy, this, he thought.

"As for Liz Peters, she's a widow. Granted her husband was a no-account rascal and she was well rid of him, almost any woman would resent being widowed by a policeman's club. And she does. He died of a blood clot on the brain. Prompt hospitalization and surgery might have saved him, Dr. Anderson tells me."

Chuck Martin had come in quietly and was standing beside Brad. "Is this a private fight?" he asked.

"Definitely not," Brad said. "Drink?"

"It may wreck my image, but I could sure use one."

David had not taken his eyes from Murfree's face. He felt too damned tired to be polite, to play games, and he said now: "I'd like to ask you a question. Feel free to tell me to go to hell."

Murfree smiled. "Of course."

"It's this: Why are you over here? Instead of over there?"

For a moment the man in the white suit did not answer, but stood facing them, looking through the window behind them at the rain coursing down its panes, the drops caught in the light from the overhead fixture. One hand was in a trouser pocket; the other held his glass containing a half-finished drink.

When he spoke he said: "It would be easy to say 'I don't know.' Or, classically, 'I don't remember.' Do any of us know what makes us commit ourselves? Any of us remember the exact moment of our involvement?" The lips that had been thin and tense when he entered the house had relaxed now; the mouth was wide, sensitive, delicately shaped.

"I'm not as noble as one might think," he went on. "I'm striking my colors as soon as this is over. You heard me say 'I travel alone these days.' Last week my wife took our children and went to her mother's in Philadelphia. She is as committed as I am, but when little children become the targets for filth—am I boring you?"

"Good God, no," said Brad. "Go on."

"Our little girl's birthday was a week ago last Sunday. It happened to fall on the same day as her confirmation. Just before we left the house a boy rang the bell, handed our maid a package marked for our daughter, and ran off. My wife opened it on the spot. It was a doll. Handmade, at least in parts. A little black doll, naked, very—er—male and precocious, in an obscene posture. Attached to the doll was a card, 'Happy Birthday little nigger lover.' "

He finished his drink, handed his glass to Brad, and David noticed that Brad's hand was shaking when he took it. "My wife cracked. One can't wonder. The next day she packed and left. I've stayed on, to pull up stakes." He laughed shortly. "They've left precious few stakes for me to pull up."

Brad gave him a refilled glass, and he stood looking into it, not touching it at first. "That doesn't answer your question, Champlin; I was committed long before that. All it does is explain my continued commitment, my physical presence here tonight."

"Look," said David, "I shouldn't have asked. Forget it."

"I don't want to." Murfree smiled. "Do you mind? It's doing me good. I don't know why I'm talking to you like this, but it's satisfying a long-felt compulsion. My family were, and my wife and I are, Catholics."

"One strike against you to start with, in these parts," said Chuck.

"I know." Murfree looked at the big blond man who had hoisted himself up so that he sat now on the tiled counter, long legs dangling, a glass in his hand. The four men were alone in the room. Once Mrs. Haskin had hurried through the kitchen, clean bed linen over her arm, and gone through to the back porch. Murfree went on: "Strange, isn't it, Chuck? You've had your lumps, but they have not been as big as they would be if you had been of my faith. Yet, basically, where do we differ? You and I or those of any faith who believe that God is something more than an exterior force." Murfree took a swallow from his glass, shook his head at Brad's gesture toward the bottle. "Later, Brad. These things are difficult enough to sort out with a clear head. But one must sort them out sooner or later. There is endless talk, there are hundreds of thousands of words in writing, about the 'guilt complexes' of the white Southerner, his subconscious burdens and urges, his divided loyalties, his sexual and economic fears. I'll buy some of it, I'll buy a good deal of it. But, by God, I won't buy all of it."

"Well, hallelujah," said Chuck. "Excuse me, John."

"Quite all right, my friend. A noncontroversial interruption if I ever heard one. Of course, if one refuses to acknowledge anything but that which goes on within the finite mind of man, one can accept all the glib and complicated explanations of the theorists and those who attribute all commitments to humanity to subconscious motivations and enlightened self-interest. I happen to believe that there are other and equally valid reasons—'causes' may be a better word—for the involvement of a great many of us, white and black, Southerner and Northerner, in a movement that is concerned with something far deeper than merely civil rights."

David had pulled a high stool forward and was perched on it now. "May I interrupt?"

"Of course."

"'Merely civil rights.' I think I like that. I think I like it very much. What you are saying, in part, is that denying a fellow citizen the right to vote is more than a crime against established law, something our courts will eventually correct. Whether we live to see it or not." He waited for Murfree's nod, and went on: "And you're saying that the greater crime—sin, you would call it, perhaps—is the refusal to accept other men in—in—I don't know exactly how to say it—I'm no theologian—"

"The fellowship of the Holy Spirit?" said Chuck.

"Yes," said Murfree. "But by your phrasing you are narrowing it to Christianity, Chuck. A man called Brother Lawrence, back in the seventeenth century, a cook in a monastery, wrote as no one has ever written before or since, in my opinion, of what he called the 'practice of the presence of God.' He wrote within the frame of reference of his own religion, of course. But the same thoughts, the same spiritual truths, have been a part of all the great religions. That God is not the exterior entity which some people use as a crutch, but is a force which moves within us, sometimes unrecognized, unrealized, but which, once it is recognized, can never be ignored again. It goes by many different names, in many religions. I have to fall back on my own. We Catholics call it grace."

"Two cents worth, please," said Brad. It was the first time David had ever heard a note of tentativeness in Brad's voice;

deference, courtesy, puzzlement, but never tentativeness or uncertainty.

"A dime's worth if you want it." Color had come into Murfree's face now; he was smiling easily, warmly.

"What you're saying is—" Brad stopped and laughed. "We keep putting words in your mouth. Your point is one of first principles: two things cannot occupy the same space at the same time. This—this thing of the spirit you call God—and I thoroughly understand your differentiation between the exterior entity some people worship and the interior presence—cannot occupy the human soul at the same time that it is occupied by hatred. A simple matter of what might be called spiritual physics."

"You've managed to be a hell of a lot briefer and more succinct than I was. And you've made my point."

"Hold on," said Chuck. "Are you saying that all those who have been outspoken against—"

"Outspoken? No. I'm talking about commitment, involvement. Those who hear the voice behind them saying: 'This is the way; walk ye in it.' " He laid his empty glass down. "My God, how insufferably pious I sound. And yet, in spite of all I've been saying, I'm running away."

"No," said David. "After what happened? You have children. It wouldn't be right—"

"Right. Wrong. Who's to say where the difference lies in a case like this? Who's to say where wisdom ends and cowardice begins? At times they run courses that are close to parallel, and the ends and beginnings are hard to spot. Anyhow, Champlin, did I answer your question? I'm afraid not."

David did not reply immediately. When he did, he said: "My question was a rude one; it was about you, specifically; about John Murfree, white Southerner. That question you answered; My God, yes, you answered. But I don't think this particular finite mind is big enough to include, in that answer, all the phonies I've known: the Northerners who do not recognize that expediency is masking as conscience, or who want to feel all comfy warm inside; the southern moderates who may not hang you from a lower limb, as Gregory says, but who nevertheless hang you so that your toes just touch ground and you don't quite strangle to death. I'm afraid I'll have to reserve my opinion."

"That they are instruments—"

"Oh. That." David looked at Murfree directly. "Yes. I'll even go you one better. I'll concede the red-neck Ku Kluxer is an instrument. My grandfather used to say, 'Reckon God has to have something to work on and He sure got Hisself a mouthful in the whites. One of these days He's going to start giving 'em fits. You'll see.' "

Haskin, Brad, and Winters took over direction of the committee while David sat quietly, his chair against the wall, fighting off waves of sick fatigue. He spoke only to add emphasis to the repeated reminders to committee members that a deliberate violation of law was involved, that the young people could not be expected to be let off scot free, and that the main objective was to prevent them from being sent to what Haskin had called the "human cattle pen" of the emergency—and probably jerry-built—juvenile detention home. It seemed a hundred years ago to David, the days when he and Brad had taken for granted such things as immediate hearings, the rights of prisoners to be brought before a judge, taken as a matter of course the simple rights of citizens living in a country governed by consent of the people.

Mrs. Haskin gave no warning of her entrance, but suddenly was standing before him, hands on hips. "Mr. Champlin, you going to bed."

David's eyes widened in surprise. "In a—"

"Now. Dr. Anderson called, said you wasn't in the bed in half an hour I was to see to it you was. And I'm seeing to it."

There was a soft laugh behind her, and he turned and saw Gracie standing in the kitchen doorway, tall, straight, her face that was so darkly handsome when she was not smiling, softly pretty now that she was.

"You ask Dad Haskin what happens if you don't pay attention to Ma," she said.

Chuck and Winters had left their seats at the table and were standing beside him.

"Going quietly, Stoopid?" asked Chuck.

"Oh, go to hell," said David, but he was smiling when he crossed the kitchen with Mrs. Haskin.

They went out to the back porch and Mrs. Haskin opened the door to a room on their right. "I give you this room here by yourse'f so's you could get a good rest, get them aches and pains to bed where it's quiet."

For a long time after Mrs. Haskin left he sat on the edge of the three-quarter bed in the center of the little room. Now that the opportunity for sleep and rest was here, he was too keyed up to take advantage of it. The bed linen smelled fresh and sweet, as though it had been dried in sun and air before ironing. Only an occasional penetrating voice—he recognized one as Mrs. Peter's—came to him from the front of the house; then there was the unmistakable sound of a group of people breaking up, then footsteps within the house as people sought their rooms, then only the sound of the rain, lighter now, the storm subsiding reluctantly.

Listening, he wondered whether he would ever, this side of eternity, shake the feeling of disembodiment that had dogged him intermittently for so long; the standing outside himself, feeling pain and tiredness in another body, watching himself, and so damned tired of watching himself, wanting to merge the two bodies, the one that was tired and full of a pain that had no relation to the physical, and the one that watched it; and then to run, run like hell until, exhausted, he could fall down in some dim place that would be cool, silent as the sky is silent, or the grave.

The sleeping pill that Anderson had given him was in his shirt pocket and he took it out now and laid the little white envelope on the peeling varnish of the table beside the bed. That wouldn't do it, that wouldn't bring the peace he sought; it would only make the coming day a more formidable foe. With only a few hours left in which to sleep, if that sleep was artificial the awakening would be slow, leaden; his body would awaken, but his inner weapons of defense would be dulled and heavy and he would be without the strength to wield them.

He wondered if the stockade was quiet, or if the boys stirred and talked under their tarpaulin. "Them chilren," Hummer had said hoarsely. "Them chilren—" Mrs. Peters had said the girls had been taken into the jail building before she came to the meeting. When the rain stopped, as it would, for now it scarcely could be heard, would the singing start again? That would do it, he thought; that would really do it, the kids awake and singing in the gray and dreary hours before day broke. God, let them be asleep, he prayed, and bent his body forward, hands rubbing, fingers kneading, the tired, aching muscles of his neck and shoulders.

Gracie was standing in front of him before he realized she was in the room. He raised his head slowly, seeing first the straight, strong legs, then the hem of the fresh starched print, the fullness of the rounded thighs, the surprise of the slender waist and the soft heaviness of her breasts above it, their dark abundance spilling over the square neck of her dress. The skin of her face glowed in the weak rays of the table lamp as though the light were behind instead of in front of it. The dark smudges of fatigue beneath her eyes had not been there earlier, but the eyes were clear, moist and gleaming.

"I seen your light," she said softly. "Me'n the baby's sleeping in the room across the porch tonight. You ain't getting your rest like the doctor says you should."

He said, "Hi, Gracie—" not smiling, holding her eyes with his own. He knew what the glowing skin of her face would feel like against his cheek, knew the softness of breast and thighs would be warm velvet to his touch.

She came closer, the skirt of her dress brushing his arm and the cloth of his trousers. "You all nerved up." Her hand was on the back of his neck, replacing his; her firm warm fingers and palm kneaded the muscles of neck and shoulder, gently stroked the upper part of his spine. He had never felt strength like this in a woman's hand. "I does this all the time for Dad Haskin," she said. "Nights when he comes in all nerved up, people fussing at him all day." He could feel the blood coming into his neck, feel tenseness he had not realized was there giving way under her fingers. "All this trouble," she whispered. "All this trouble. Them muscles're like boards. Ain't no wonder you can't sleep."

She did not draw away when his arm encircled her waist, yet did not yield or come forward until his insistent strength drew her body against his. With his free hand he grasped the hand stroking his neck, drew it down and under his chin so that her body seemed to enfold his, laid his cheek against her breast, then turned and buried in his face in its softness.

"Gracie . . . Gracie . . . You don't mind. . . . Tell me you don't mind . . . Gracie . . ."

"I did . . . I did . . . I swear I did . . . but Lawd, I don't now. . . . Good Gawd, man! Turn me loose so's I can lock that door. . . . Give me time so's I can get out of these things. . . ."

"No . . . No, Gracie, no . . . Gracie, Gracie . . . you'll run away. . . ."

"I swear I won't. . . . Lawd, man! But you strong . . . I ain't running away. . . . Oh, Gawd! . . . Minute I seen you I says there's a man needs some lovin' . . . there's a man needs lovin'. . . . There ain't no harm . . . there ain't no harm in it. . . ."

Gracie's embrace was more than adequate for his physical need; deeply adequate for his spirit's need. There, in that small room for that small moment in time with Gracie, he was one person again, no longer two; at home, at peace even in the vortex of his passion, and when at last the vortex passed, gave way to an exhausted calm, he kept her body close to his, holding its warm softness gently, his face against her shoulder, plummeting into sleep at last with his hand cupping her breast.

75

SARA KENT TOLD HERSELF that it wasn't any hotter in Düsseldorf's Bahnhof than it would be in Grand Central in mid-August, nowhere nearly as hot as any one of Chicago's stations. She wiped the perspiration film from her face and throat, and wished that she could extend the operation to the rest of her clammy, moist body.

The train she had come to meet was in; she could tell by the increase in the number of hurrying individuals in the central lobby. Maybe Chris hadn't been able to make it, and that would be fine, would almost be a relief because it would give her another day to stiffen her resolves. The feeling of loneliness that swept over her at the thought that he might not have made it warned her of how badly those resolves needed stiffening.

Then there was Chris, coming toward her but not seeing her yet, covering ground rapidly, yet managing to seem unhurried, even deliberate. For God's sake, Sara, she told herself, for God's sake, smile; the man is tired and hot and has been under pressure and he'll need a smile and then some coffee or a drink.

"Sara! I hoped and it happened—"

She looked up at him, and the smile had been no effort. It was never any effort, when the time actually came, to smile at Chris, laugh with him. And that was why it was so hard, so damnably hard to face what she must do.

"What did you hope that happened?"

"You. Here. Meeting me." He stooped and kissed her lightly, quickly, on the forehead. "That was just for now," he said.

"It's hellishly hot, Chris. You'll wish you'd stayed in Switzerland."

"Don't be silly, Sara. You were here."

He shifted his attaché case and typewriter to one hand, slipped an arm around her shoulders, and spoke in near perfect German to the porter who was carrying his heavier bag.

"The gift of tongues!" said Sara as they walked toward the entrance of the station. "I was born without it. When I talk the Italians are amused, the Germans are patronizing, and the French sneer. Openly."

"Concentrate on accent and forget grammar, pet. The equivalent of 'I done it' in French is nowhere near the linguistic crime of saying 'Roo' for 'rue.' "

"Roo," said Sara. "Roo, roo, roo. I said it and I'm glad, glad, glad."

He drew her closer as they walked to the cab. "Sara, dear heart, I've missed you. My God, how I've missed you!"

"Only eight days."

"Only eight centuries, my beloved dope."

Did it have to hurt like this, she wondered; did the knowledge of another's imminent pain have to hurt like this? And knew the answer was "yes"; if you're Sara Kent it hurts like this, because you, Sara Kent, were cursed at birth with the dubious gift of empathy, and the only person who ever really understood its disadvantages in a world where everyone was hurting almost all the time in one way or another had been David. Yet David—she realized with a start that Chris had been speaking to her, there in the cab, that he was repeating a question she had not answered.

"Have you moved yet?"

"Moved?" It was the wrong answer; it was a stupid and childlike temporization, and she would have given much to be able to call it back.

"Yes, my dear: 'moved.' From the-hotel-where-you-are-staying to the-hotel-where-I-am-staying. We talked about it, remember? Rather at length, if I recall."

"I—I—no."

"Why?" His voice, which had been warm and close, was remote.

"It's—I—oh, it's been too damned hot for packing, Chris. And I'm a lazy baggage. You said so yourself."

"So I did." After a moment he continued: "Shall we go to my place first? I'll take a quick look at my mail, a quick wash; then we'll have a drink and dinner. Right?"

"Of course, Chris."

At the hotel desk he turned to her, key in hand. "Coming up?"

"It's cooler here in the lobby, but if you—"

She watched him cross the lobby to the elevators, a lean man, not above average height, with a lean head and face, the dark hair a smooth cap—"piped with gray" she had told him when she had first known him—the eyes startlingly blue. There was humor in the long upper lip; passion and sensitivity were in the fullness of the lower, and behind the high forehead a grave and penetrating intelligence. They had celebrated his forty-first birthday together in Rome; otherwise she would have thought him older.

She sat in a high-backed chair against the wall in the lobby, shunning the deep comfort of the lounge chairs because of the heat. She sat very straight, toes just touching the floor, her head resting against the red brocade of its back, her eyes closed. Chris will be all right, she told herself, and felt that she was pleading with herself to be convinced. He'll be all right; he has to be, he must be. Because he's wise and civilized, Christopher Barkeley will know that eventuall, it wouldn't work out, that a mind as keen as his, as fine hone l and analytical, would eventually tire of her own uncomplicated thinking, her emotionalism. All emotion, Sara, that's you, all emotion and intensity and a certain crazy loyalty—and still all another man's woman. And you're thinking rot, plain unadulterated rot and rationalization, because he won't know any such damned thing. She felt her throat tighten. Chris, Chris, you're so fine and wonderful, and millions of people hear your voice, see your face, every day, and read your words, and I wish to God I could love you and not hurt you; I do wish it, Chris, I do.

They had met prosaically enough, at an art gallery in London when Hunter Travis brought him in to see one of her exhibits. She recognized Barkeley immediately, and knew that when she heard his voice it would be as familiar to her as the voice of an old friend. "This is Christopher Barkeley, Republic Broadcasting System, saying 'good night' from Rome

—" or London or Bonn or Paris or Moscow. His book *Hours of Decision* had absorbed her because there had been no pontificating, and here and there he had mocked his own objectivity with sardonic humor, softened it by a wide, all-embracing compassion.

The next morning Chris called her, and the next afternoon they met in the lounge of her hotel and drank tea and ate buttered toast, and later had dinner at Simpson's. "I know it's touristy," Chris said. "And it's not the beef or mutton that draws me back either. It's the creamed tripe."

A month later she flew to Denmark with him. The hotel in Copenhagen gave them adjoining rooms, and she remembered the porter unlocking the connecting door, apparently as a matter of course, without asking. When Chris stood in the doorway she felt uncomfortable and more than a little resentful.

"They seem to know you well here," she said. "Your habits and customs."

His eyes clouded and his mouth set in a straight line, unsmiling. "You are mistaken, Sara Kent. This is neither habit nor custom with me—as Management will tell you. I merely asked for rooms on the same floor. A Dane, I'm afraid, takes it from there. I am a loner." The lips relaxed slightly. "Or have been," he added. He stood quietly, not coming into her room; then the smile returned. "Are you going to starve in lonely solitude, or shall we do something about lunch? Rather quickly, I'd suggest. I'm damned hungry."

At lunch, in the downstairs restaurant, they sat at a window table overlooking a canal, watching ships flying the flags of half a dozen countries, some she did not even recognize. Chris identified them for her, told her of the countries of their origin, and how they had come into being, told her why one little-known flag might someday fly over ships carrying more than half the world's oil supply, how another represented a country that might one day hold the balance of power in Africa.

Later, over coffee, she said, "The miracle of the loaves and fishes pales beside that of two hotel rooms in Europe in August. Just like that." She snapped her fingers.

"The company has an arrangement. They would have to when it's never certain where or when something will break." He was smiling. "I'm a very convenient guy to know. Even more convenient to travel with. I commend me to you."

She yawned suddenly, covered her mouth apologetically.

"Gosh, I'm sorry. Chris, I've got to nap. That was a cruel early start, my friend."

"I know. I should have qualified my commendation."

She had napped after lunch on the date of their first twenty-four hours together, and as she was dropping off to sleep heard the outer door of his room close and his steps going down the hall on his way out. He had not opened the door between their rooms again.

She thought now of the many ways in which Chris had been—and was still—different, disarmingly different. He had asked her to go to the Continent with him in hope— My God, of course he had hoped; the man was human, he was tremendously attracted to her, she would have been a fool not to see that. But he had not asked her to go with him in any firm expectation. How many, how nauseatingly many, had approached her during these last years, knowing of her love for and alliance with a man of another race, assuming that, per se, she was some kind of insatiable, thrill-seeking nymph. All of them stunned or hurt or angry, sometimes ugly, when she had driven them away with sick fury.

Chris knew Hunter Travis well; they were close friends; Hunter would have told him the true story. But whatever the reason, Chris had hoped, but not expected, had not taken her for granted.

The evening of that first day in Copenhagen they had dined on snails, then strolled through the Tivoli in the long late twilight of the North. Afterward they sat companionably in Chris's room, the only light that of the small lamp on the desk, looking across the canal at the sweep of Hans Christian Andersen Boulevard, watching the drawbridge below them as it imperiously halted all traffic by its rise to permit a ship to pass and graciously permitted the wheels to turn again once its duty was done.

"It may not have the grandeur of the Alps or the incredible beauty of Rio, but just sitting by the water in Copenhagen, watching ships and people, still remains my favorite pastime," said Chris.

Sara quoted sleepily," 'Believe me, my young friend, there is *nothing*—absolutely nothing—half so much worth doing as simply messing about in boats.' "

"You know it! I didn't realize that you and Water Rat were friends."

"Of long standing, I'll have you know. *The Wind in the Willows* was one of the nicest things about my childhood."

"Unfortunately, it came to me late in life. Comparatively speaking. My wife introduced me to it. I can remember wanting to sniffle, at the ripe age of twenty-seven, when they found Portly, the baby otter, at the feet of Pan. Do you remember what Water Rat said when Mole asked him if he was afraid of the being with the shaggy limbs and the hooked nose and the pan-pipes by his hand?"

" 'Afraid!' " replied Sara. " 'Afraid of *Him?* O, never, never!' "

"And the song Rat heard—'Lest limbs be reddened and rent—I spring the trap that is set— As I loose the snare you may glimpse me there—' How nice life can be with a fellow Wind in the Willowser." He was silent for a moment, then he said, "Do you also remember, Sara, the last great gift the demigod bestowed on those he had rescued from pain and fright?"

"Yes. Forgetfulness. 'Small waifs in the woodland wet—Strays I find in it, wounds I bind in it— Bidding them all forget!' "

"Yes." He rose and walked to the bell by the door. "I'm going to ring for a nightcap." When he returned to his chair he said, "I think the world and all the people in it have need of Pan—and of his gift."

"You don't sound like Chris Barkeley. You know, the man who says 'Now this is Christopher Barkeley saying 'good night'—"

"Nor you like Sara Kent. A bit brittle, I'd heard. And—forgive me, my dear—noticed."

There had been no urging that night after they drank their nightcap, no pleading, no sudden passionate rushing of any defenses she might have had, real or imagined; there had not even been the touch of his fingers on her hand or body. He had turned to her there in the half-light of the room, not quite smiling, eyebrows raised slightly. "Sara?" he had said.

"Chris—"

Strays I find in it, wounds I bind in it— Bidding them all forget!

She heard someone speaking and opened her eyes to see one of the hotel's elderly porters standing in front of her.

"Madam. The Herr Barkeley sends his apology. In the mail he has received a message that requires an overseas call. I am to bring you whatever you wish."

She shook her head. "Thank you. There is nothing."

"Madam will ring if there is?"

"Of course."

She rested her head again on the high back of the chair, closing her eyes against the bustle in the lobby. These delays had happened many times before, and she had never minded, calls during dinner, calls in the middle of the night, cables disrupting weekend plans. But tonight she minded because with every minute that passed the thing that she must do, the break she must make, seemed less inevitable, became closer and closer to impossible.

Why hadn't she had the good old-fashioned guts to say "no"? Not that first night in Copenhagen, but before, when Chris had asked her to make the trip with him. There was no answer except that there had been a hope within her that here, in this man, was something strong enough to hold her, something that would give her a lessening of pain and loneliness, perhaps, please God, eventual freedom from it. And there had been, but only for a while. She remembered waking that first morning in Copenhagen, with Chris gone to an early appointment, and thinking, as she sat in bed, breakfast tray on her knees, that he had mentioned his wife the night before. His wife, she knew from Hunter, had been dead for eight years. But she had felt no flicker of curiosity about his marriage. And, she told herself now, no normal female, be she ever so modern, is without curiosity about a man's marriage, does not want to delve and pry into a former intimacy. During the eight years he had been a widower there must have been other intimacies, and she had not been able to arouse in herself the slightest interest. Now she told herself, "You should have known then." Later she had learned from Hunter that Chris's wife's name had been Barbara and, by Chris's reticences more than anything he said, that he had loved her very much. Her only reaction had been then, and was now, the thought, You don't know, Chris, that there can be peace in the grief for someone who is dead; no peace, no letup in the grief for someone who is still alive and warm and vital, and very far away.

Now she, Sara Kent, was going to introduce him to the spiritual corrosion of that grief. Perhaps he won't mind; perhaps it won't give him all the pain you think it will; perhaps you overestimate—*Sara, dear heart, I've missed you. My God, how I've missed you!*

Again in Copenhagen they had lain late one morning after a night flight. He had scarcely spoken until after they heard a maid leave the breakfasts in his room. Then, in robe and slippers, he brought the tray in, setting his own coffee and pastry on the low coffee table, bringing the tray to her where she sat propped against pillows in bed.

After coffee and a cigarette he said: "Sara, we could make it, you and I. I think it would be something very damned special." And when she did not answer, added, "If." And while she still searched for words, said, "Half a loaf, Sara. Half a loaf has been a banquet these past six months. It scares me to think of what the whole loaf could be."

Christopher Barkeley wouldn't know how to plead, then or now, and he had kept his tone light when he said, "Perhaps in time, Sara?"

"Please, Chris. Please, my dear. I don't know. I just don't know."

"You must have loved him a hell of a lot. I met him, you know. Several years ago, with Hunter."

"Chris. You never told me."

"No. I'm not all that damned objective and detached. And you've never given me an opening. Prodding old wounds isn't exactly my idea of a good time." He was silent for a moment, sitting at the coffee table, busying himself with unwrapping the inevitable piece of Danish breakfast cheese. Without turning his head he said: "Old wounds. My choice of words was mistaken. Even now the wound is still fresh enough to bleed, isn't it." It was not a question.

"No. I mean—"

"Forget it, love. Forget I said it." Then he had come to the side of the bed and taken her in his arms, holding her close with a desperate sort of strength, hiding his face in the hollow of her throat and shoulder, saying roughly, "But only forget it for a while, my darling, only for a while."

She opened her eyes, feeling as though she were snapping them open, felt a whimper in her throat, and was looking into Chris's quiet, steady gaze. How long had he been there, looking at her, looking through her, looking into her?

"Sara," he said. His lips seemed not to move. "Sara. I don't think I have ever seen anyone look so unhappy, just sitting quietly with their eyes closed."

"I—I was dozing."

"No, you weren't. Shall we go? Dinner first, before I take you back to the hotel?"

No, she thought; not dinner. Let me go now. But she said,

"All right, Chris. If you'd like." Outside in the heavy early-evening heat they turned into Königsallee, stopped at a sidewalk café for an *apéritif*.

"Not shashlik tonight," he said. "It's too blasted hot and small and crowded in that place. Agreed?"

"Agreed."

"We'll go to the restaurant across from your hotel if you'd like. The cellars are cooler these nights. And the waiters there are old and remote and cranky and apparently hate all Americans. They won't hover warmly."

"Agreed also."

"You'll want *Bratkartoffelen?* You still like them?"

"You could hardly think my passion for *Bratkartoffelen* would cool in a week."

He paid the check and took her arm as they wove through tables to the sidewalk. "Home-fried potatoes to the rest of the world. Manna from heaven to you," he said lightly.

At the end of the meal he said: "Would you like a pastry? A cake? They have a wonderful touch here with things that come out of the oven."

Nothin' says lovin' like something from the oven, and Cha-a-amplin says it best. . . . Not here. Now now. David, go away. Go away. I don't want you here or anywhere, not unless we can see each other, and hear each other and touch each other. David, what did you make out of me, what kind of monster did you make out of me?

"Dessert, Sara? Come back to Düsseldorf."

"No! Nothing. I'm sorry. I sounded cross, didn't I? It's just—I mean, I can't eat any more."

Outside the restaurant there was the inevitable traffic jam in the narrow street as cars tried to park and other cars tried to pass them, engines growling like angry cats until they could move forward. The air was foul with exhaust smoke and the smell of hot pavement. Four young men, their voices loud in the evening heat, were running toward them, headed for the stage door of the theatre next to the restaurant. Chris drew her back quickly to avoid them, and they stood together in a doorway, facing each other.

"I won't cross over with you, Sara. That would be asking too much."

No questions; no searching, prying questions into her heart and mind; no pleading. He knew, and he had taken into his own hands the task she had dreaded, lifted from her the burden of telling, of explaining, even, perhaps, of comforting.

Thank you, Chris, thank you, and then she thought how old he looked, how chiseled out of marble his face seemed, with only the eyes alive and full of pain. No man so young should look so old. His eyes were steady, fixed on hers.

"Chris—"

"I know. I think I knew in the taxi when you said you had not moved, said it was too hot to pack. I was sure in the hotel when you didn't come up with me. Sara, don't look like that. It's all right."

"No. No, it's not all right. It's dreadful and horrible and it's tearing me to pieces—"

"Is it, Sara? Is it now?"

"Chris, don't—"

"That was unkind. I'm sorry. Sara, I love you. I love you with all that there is left in me to love a woman with. And I've learned during our year together that one of the strange things about love is that one can have more left over than one started with. I haven't put it well, but perhaps you'll learn it someday—"

"There's nothing left, Chris. Except not wanting to hurt someone—"

"You're quite a person, Sara. Quite a person. Don't change your mind. Don't change your mind, Sara. It would be hell. Sheer hell. For me. For you. Now go, Sara. Go, my dear, quickly."

She knew as she crossed the street, clear now for a moment, that he was not watching her, that he had turned toward Königsallee because he could not watch her, and was walking, very fast, away from where they had been standing together.

Russell Square was dusty green and mottled yellow in the noon heat. The cabbies in the taxi rank looked damp and uncomfortable, and it wasn't London at all, thought Sara; it never was London in the heat. It was any city anywhere, its people beaten down and oppressed by a blazing tyrant without mercy. She knew the hotel would be fairly comfortable; the thick old walls would have held back the heat; its high-ceilinged antiquity would give at least an illusion of more air, and she was glad she had been extravagant and leased a room with bath. A bath. Sleep. The racking emotion of the night before that had driven her to pack as though her very life depended on it had eased a little, leaving her exhausted, with smarting eyes and a throat made raw by chain smoking. It was fortunate that the only seat available had been on an early-morning plane. There would have been no sleep in the hotel in Düsseldorf, might even have been, God help her and God help Chris, a telephone call to Chris. She arrived at the airport a long two hours before the flight's departure.

Her room was musty-smelling and warm in spite of its high ceilings. She opened windows, started water for a bath, and while the tub was filling unpacked necessities. When she stepped out of the tub she dabbed lightly at her body with the big bath towel. *Cools you off better that way, honestly. It only makes you hotter if you rub. Here, let me show you—* Damn. Oh, damn, damn, *damn.* Go away, David, please for God's kind sake, go away.

She threw herself on the bed, naked, heedless that a cool breeze might come up and chill her overwarm body. She fell asleep almost at once.

The brassy tone of the telephone penetrated finally, and she groped for it on its shelf above her head, held the receiver a moment before answering, rubbing her face with her hand, trying to wake up.

"Sara. Sara. Are you there?"

"Hunter! Hunter Travis—"

"Who else, ducky—"

She shook her head, trying to clear it. "Bless you, Hunter. Wait. Wait. I haven't any clothes on. I just realized—"

"My God, what a woman! Doesn't even knew when she's nekkid—"

She rolled over on her back, noticed that the travel clock on the bedside table said four thirty, and flipped the light counterpane over her body. "There. Now I'm decent. I was asleep."

"Dinner, Sara?"

"How did you know I was here? No one knows—"

"A mutual acquaintance saw you totter into an airport bus this morning. Answer my question, young Kent. Dinner?"

"Give me a chance to wake up. I—let me think. Dinner? I don't think I've even had breakfast. Or lunch. Good grief, I haven't even had tea!"

"On a diet, luv?"

"No. Circumstances."

"Oh. Those."

"When I wake up I'll know it would be nice. What time?"

"Seven? Your lounge?"

"Fine. And—and—Hunter—I'm most awfully grateful—"

"You're *what?* Knock it off, sweetie. Order a drink. You're slipping—"

Hunter might not know why she was grateful, but she knew that it was because the first syllables of his voice had spelled home, had brought perspective. It was a sudden, present link with a sane and ordered past. It made her Sara Kent again, late of Chicago and New York and Pengard and Cincinnati.

Hunter was ten minutes early, but she was already in the lounge when he arrived. From where she was sitting she could see the entrance to the hotel, and when he came through the doorway she jumped to her feet, smiling. He looked astonishingly cool and handsome in a light gray suit, his linen crisp and fresh.

He gripped her shoulders, shook her gently, said, "None of your pecks on the cheek, my girl," and kissed her soundly. "Have you been sitting here guzzling alone?"

"Not even a sherry."

"We'll start now."

They went to a small restaurant near Picadilly for dinner. Sara liked it because the oysters and steaks were excellent, the waitresses friendly, and because it held no memories. There were pubs and restaurants and espresso bars and hotel lounges all over London whose entrances she could not face. Sudsy and Rhoda had understood, and so had Hunter. Friends and acquaintances whose suggestions for places to go for lunch or dinner or quiet drinking she had brushed off didn't matter. Hunter suggested Rule's once, and she had hesitated, then shaken her head. "Ghosts?" he said. She nodded and replied, "I can admit it to you. Others don't understand." He folded her hand in his, held it gently for a moment. "The hell with them," he said.

During dinner they talked around life, not of it; of Sara's exhibits, her students in Germany, of Hunter's father and of Hunter's latest book.

While they waited for brandy Hunter leaned back, eyes narrowing slightly. "How's Chris?"

She started to speak, hesitated, then said: "Unprovoked bombing attacks aren't fair. You didn't even ask if I'd seen him. You only said 'How's Chris?' What makes you think—"

"Sara. Sara, don't be coy. Not you. You've been over here enough to know that we live in a small town. The people you and I know move about. There are things called airplanes. Jets. Do you think you can be seen walking hand in hand on the Via Veneto in Rome, eating smorgasbord at the Europa in Copenhagen, drinking coffee together in Bonn and beer in Munich—and get away with a 'casual acquaintance' routine? I thought better of you."

Sara did not answer, kept her eyes on the package of cigarettes she was trying to line up with geometrical precision along the edge of the table.

Hunter went on relentlessly. "That's why you're here, isn't it? You've folded your tents. Again."

"Hunter, I don't want to talk about it."

"You're damned well going to. Or listen about it. I have two friends, Sara—male, that is—of whom I am very fond. One of them is Christopher Barkeley."

"Please—"

"My advice to you, my pet, is that you do one of two things. Legalize your biological urges—or hie thee to a nunnery."

"This from you!"

"I know. It's not advice I would usually hand out. But I'm talking about Sara Kent, who is aching all over for emotional security. And I'm not saying, God knows, that marriage usually brings it. But I'm also talking about Christopher Barkeley. And that makes it a different story. Chris isn't, never has been, a man who could feel comfortable for too long in an illicit liaison. Not when he loves. I know the guy. Better than you do, perhaps. Go back to him, Sara."

"I—I—God damn you, Hunter! No one asked your advice —no one asked—" She looked at him now, her eyes bright with anger.

"Temper!" he said. "Temper, temper. And stop gritting your teeth. Go back to Düsseldorf—"

"I—I can't. You're talking about something you don't know anything about. Chris doesn't want me. Not—not—"

"When you're still obsessively in love with another man. Whom you haven't seen in donkey's years."

"Please—"

"Please, my foot! I said I have two friends of whom I am very fond. The other is young Champlin. A spoiled brat, if ever there was one, but a lad who manages to make his friends knock themselves out for him. Without trying." He stopped and smiled. "Oh, hell, Sara. We're quarreling."

Sara's smile was small and uncertain. "We usually do, don't we? Eventually."

"I suppose we do, at that. But never for long, thank God."

His eyes warmed, his face softened. "There is, of course, another solution. A lousy one for you, perhaps. An excellent one for me, not requiring, maybe not deserving, as Chris does, all or nothing. Marry me."

Sara's eyes widened with almost comic suddenness.

"What—what— Hunter! What an—an incestuous suggestion."

"It is, isn't it? Unfortunately." He smiled at her bewilderment. "I just got tired of hiding the light of my nobility under a bushel of platonism. I shan't mention it again."

"Don't. Please. My God, Hunter, I'm upset enough—"

"Shattering, isn't it? To be a ninety-pound *femme fatale.*"

"What are you trying to do, Hunter, what are you trying to do? What's the point, what's the darned point of all this?"

"Actually, in spite of anything I may feel, I'm trying to drive you back to Chris. You see, Sara, you've never given up. Not for one second have you given up on David, even though you may think you have. What I'm saying is, for God's sake, give up. Now, before it's too late. I think, with Chris, you could at last let go, start looking somewhere besides backward. If I didn't think so I wouldn't be saying now, for about the tenth time—go back to Düsseldorf."

"It wouldn't work, I tell you. It wouldn't work. Not one small bit. I tell you, he doesn't want me. Hunter, listen please. Just listen and don't interrupt—" Not glibly but in short, halting phrases, uncertain sentences, she told him of her year with Chris, not sparing herself, watching his face, dreading to find judgment there, but not finding it. She finished her story at last with Chris's words, "Now go, Sara. Quickly." Then she said, "He's a pretty damned wonderful human, Hunter. Do you think I don't know it? He's a thousand, thousand years old; and wise, and disciplined and—and contained. And strong and vulnerable, all at once." Her voice became unsteady, and she stopped for a moment, then went on: "And I'm just a damned child, with a damned child's mind and emotions. I—I'm trying to grow up, but I'm not getting very far."

After a moment Hunter said, " 'He who knows and knows that he knows is wise, follow him.' " He reached for the check. "Lead me, Sara. Back to the hotel. We'll have a drink in the lounge."

They relaxed in the hotel lounge, sipping drinks, talking of small things, trivialities, in the low tones that so many old

London hotel lounges seem to call forth, as do musty ancient churches. It was Hunter who snatched the question that was at the back of both their minds out of the limbo where it hovered.

"You've been unusually patient." He sighed. "I know that every time I see you, I shall have to face a certain look. The 'have you heard?' look. All right, ducks, I have. As soon as Bill Holden told me he'd seen you at the airport, I got busy on the telephone, trying to track down Brad Willis. My father has a legal something going with his firm. It was a good excuse."

She leaned forward in her chair, unashamed of her eagerness, not trying to hide it. "Did you? Did you reach him?"

"Yes. It took time. Peg Willis sent me on a geographical treasure hunt from Boston to Beauregard, then over the river to New Orleans, then to some damned place that sounded like Heliopolis—it couldn't be, could it?—and finally to a place called Cainsville."

"Cainsville. What a—wait. There was trouble there a while ago. And in Heliopolis, too."

"You don't miss a thing, do you? Not a blow falls on an unprotected Negro head in the South you don't hear."

"It's—well, I suppose it's like having someone in the front lines in a war."

"Yes, and it's a hell of a comment on our times. Anyhow, the second place I tried in Cainsville I reached Brad. He answered the phone. By then it was four o'clock in the morning, their time. Everything's all right, Sara. All's well with our lad."

"That's not enough, Hunter. You know it isn't."

One of the reasons Lawrence Travis found such aid and comfort in his son's presence at meetings and conferences was the tape-recorder memory he had for conversations. Now Hunter could recall every word of his talk with Brad; it was as clear and distinct as Brad's voice had been when he answered the telephone at last.

"This is Bradford Willis."

"And high time. I've been all over the whole damned United States trying to find you."

"Hunter Travis! Good to hear you, boy."

"Don't 'boy' me, you bastard."

"Where are you?"

"London. What's going on back there."

"All hell."

"The press doesn't exaggerate?"

"That would be hard to do."

"Why Cainsville?"

"We've a little project going here. If I ever find time, I'll write you about it."

Hunter laughed. "The hell you will. I've heard that one before. Heard from David?"

"He's right here, in the same house. Sound asleep, I hope. He's pretty well beat."

"These days you have to ask: literally or figuratively?"

"Both, Hunter."

"Hell, no!"

"Yes. Acting like a damned hero in a riot when he should have been hiding under the porch. Or somewhere. He took a shellacking from a local red-neck. . . . Hunter . . . you still there?"

"Yes. I wonder why. To reverse Thoreau."

"Because it's where you belong. This mess isn't everyone's cup of tea."

"It takes guts, that's what you mean."

"Don't be an ass. That typewriter of yours can carry as much impact as a billy club."

"I don't type. I write with my own delicate nearly white damned hand. A pretty thing. Well shaped."

"Listen, son, did you call me at this hour to discuss the ethics of physical participation and nonparticipation? I say you're doing all right. Stay where you are and don't complicate matters further. Good God, I feel like a hen with too many chicks already—"

"David getting beat up—"

"It's not the first time. It won't be the last if he doesn't get the hell out of these parts. As a matter of fact, a few days ago he was planning to go back to Boston, get some rest, then dig into the legal work. I don't know exactly what changed his mind. He just showed up here this—no, yesterday morning. He was dead tired when he got here."

"You sound worried."

"I am. The edge he's on is too damned ragged to suit me. I'd call him, only—"

"Let him sleep, Brad. Give him my best."

"Right. If there are inquiries—"

"There will be. Loud, silent ones. Sara arrived in London early this morning, I hear. As soon as she's had a chance to get some sleep, I'm going to call her and have dinner with her if she's free."

"I'd go easy on the details—"

"Of course. You're not prettying it up, Brad? He is all right?"

"In general, yes. In particular, bruises, that sort of thing. That's all."

Hunter brought himself back to Sara, and Sara's impatient, questioning eyes and tense expectancy.

"What is it, Hunter? What's happened?"

"Nothing, Sara. David's O.K., Brad said. Tired, that's all. He's in Cainsville with Brad, but he's been planning to go back to Boston and rest and then devote his time to the legal work."

"But if he's really all right, why didn't you talk to him?"

"Sara, Sara. Because he was asleep. I told you it was four in the morning there. I wouldn't have called Brad except that I knew I'd have to face that look. You'll have to make do with that, my muffin."

"Thanks, Hunter. I mean, really thanks. I'm sorry to be so—so greedy. But it's all I have, these bits and pieces and scraps of news."

Hunter was standing now, looking down at her. "I know. I wish I could bring you more than news. Like, possibly, peace." He took her hands, drew her to her feet from the depths of the chair. "Get some more sleep, luv. Your eyes would be at home in a coma—"

She walked across the lobby toward the hotel entrance with him, but before they reached it he felt her small, strong hand on his arm, stopping him. She was looking up into his face with wide, troubled eyes. "Hunter. Have I done something wrong? In leaving Chris? Do you think I've done something horribly wrong? Do you, Hunter?"

"You ask me, of all people? How would I know, my dear? I'm the one who is constantly blasting at the concept of right and wrong, if you happen to have read the stuff I write that gets printed. You did what you had to do. Is anything right? And if it is, does that necessarily mean the opposing action is wrong? Stop thinking, Sara. Stop it. And get some sleep. Now."

When they reached the entrance, she squeezed his arm gently. "Thanks," she said. "Thanks again, Hunter. Good night. And God bless."

He touched her cheek lightly with the back of his hand. "Why?" and suddenly he saw the Sara Kent of years before, the tiny, intense girl who would desert the company of her classmates to slide belly-bumpus down a hill on a sled with the town children of Laurel. She grinned up at him. "Damned if I know, my friend. But sometimes God does seem to bless the most unlikely people."

76

Before six o'clock on the morning following the committee briefing, Brad Willis got up and dressed quietly. He had slept little and after Hunter Travis's call had lain half awake until daybreak.

He found David in the kitchen drinking coffee. "Feeling all right, brat?"

"So far. What do we do, just sit here and wait until they get damned good and ready to send over for the committee? Damn it, Brad, this whole thing is too lousy passive."

"There wasn't time to plan. Haskin is going to telephone the mayor's office at nine and tell them the committee will be over at ten o'clock."

" 'Here I come, ready or not—' like some fool kid game. There are people out there already, standing at the barriers."

"Any of them who have jobs over there?"

"Yes. It's the only bright spot in the picture. Mrs. Haskin has been out there already talking to some of them. She says a lot of them won't cross over as long as the kids are in the stockade or jail."

"Whether that's good or bad depends on a number of things. How many, for one."

"Couldn't tell you. She said it looked like a lot. She's already gone over to the store."

"Gracie?" Brad asked the question deliberately and noted the hesitation before David answered.

"Mrs. Haskin said she was letting her sleep in. She said

someone around here ought to get their rest if this was going to keep up. I made the coffee."

"And good, too." Brad turned away to replenish his cup. It was probably stupid to think David could tell anything by his face, but he didn't trust David's quick, almost intuitive, perceptions. He was remembering how, at two thirty that morning, restless and unable to sleep he had come into the kitchen to fix some whiskey and hot milk. The whiskey was gone, but he had taken milk from the refrigerator, heated it, and while he was drinking it heard a door close quietly on the back porch. Feet had padded softly across the creaking boards; there had been the sound of an old-fashioned latch lifting, then the sound of a second door closing. Which was just fine as far as he was concerned, thought Brad; best thing that could have happened to the guy. He wished to God he thought the incident might have some permanent emotional importance. For years he and Peg had wanted David to find someone warm and comfortable like Gracie, someone who could bring him the uncomplicated emotional peace he had never known, a peace whose healing he needed above all else.

"What's the next move, Chief?"

"I think we should head for Tether's End. I don't like leaving that place alone. We left correspondence, memos, everything. After this, stuff gets locked in car trunks or Haskin's safe."

"Yessir."

"The others can come along later. It's better if we keep that as headquarters. Safer. Les climbs the walls every night to make sure they aren't bugged. I suggest that you go on out to Miz Towers and pick up some supplies. I've got the list made out. You'll have a valid excuse for meeting her, and she'll have a chance to size you up. And don't think she won't do it. Abraham came in after you went to bed last night. He's going to call her this morning and tell her you're coming, also tell her something about you."

"You want me to mention the land deal?"

"If you can do it without forcing the issue. Abraham will have primed her. Don't let Tinker scare you."

"Who's Tinker?"

"The dog. You'll see. You go on out to Tether's End, see if everything's all right, then go on to Miz Towers' and get back to headquarters if you can by ten o'clock. Here's the supply list—and don't ask me why I haven't got beans on it because we've got closets full of them waiting for you. So. As soon as you leave I'll have to rouse Hummer and the others for a council of war. We may just have to do a wee bit of adjusting on our time schedule for the gone-fishing project. You know, like pushing it up a bit."

"There's not much time—"

"There's enough, I think. Hummer and Les know this town like a book. If they start out at seven, or send someone out, they can reach a hell of a lot of people who work over there, and who aren't in the group out front. If we need more time for talk, Haskin can take the committee over at eleven instead of ten."

"Nobody asked me what I thought, but I don't mind saying that for the first time since I heard of this project I feel good about it. Now these people have something more at stake than abstractions."

"And don't forget, the other side has leverage, too, that they didn't have before."

"Brad, get Chuck. Get him on the phone or something. Tell him to get in touch with all the press and radio and TV media he can. This situation can stand being aired to the public."

"Right. Another thing: we may be short on supplies, but not very much, and we'll get hell's own amount of support from outside under these circumstances."

"I'll go now—" David started again toward the door, and Brad called him back. "David!"

When David turned Brad said: "I almost forgot. Hunter Travis called this morning at four o'clock. You'd think, all the traveling he does, he would have learned about time zones."

"Whyn't you call me—"

"You were asleep, and needed to be. It wasn't anything special. A sort of routine inquiry. In anticipation of other routine inquiries."

"What inquiries?"

He knows damned well, thought Brad; knows damned well what inquiries. Suddenly he was sick of playing games. We spoil the guy, he thought; we all spoil him, men, women, all of us. Once in a while he would ask an outright question about Sara, as he had in New Orleans, but not often. Most of the time he'd wait, knowing someone would tell him. Why didn't he give up? Why didn't the poor damned unhappy devil give up? For a moment Brad forgot the pressing problems of Cainsville.

" 'What inquiries!' Don't be an ass. Sara got in from Düsseldorf, and Hunter hoped to have dinner with her."

"Oh. What did you tell him?"

"That you were all right."

"Thanks. Say, are you sore because he called or what? Because you're sure as hell sore about something."

"Hell, I'm not sore. I'm just disgusted, fed up with your gutlessness, David. Give up. Let go. Start living another life, one life. Pull that damned sore tooth out! It's the only way you'll stop biting on it."

"Well—I'll—be—God—damned." David spoke slowly, spacing the words, and Brad looked away, suddenly ashamed, yet angry at the weakness that made him ashamed.

"Get lost, youngster. I snapped because I'm tired of seeing you in pain, that's all. O.K.?"

"Sure," said David. He sounded like a hurt child, puzzled at an unprovoked slap from an adult. "Sure, I guess so. See you later—"

Brad listened to the uneven steps as David went down the short hall to the side door, heard the door close with exaggerated quiet, then heard the steps on porch and drive. "Hell," he said. "Damn it to hell." His own steps were slow, his face somber as he walked to a closed bedroom door and knocked. "Hummer. Hummer. You awake? It's Brad Willis. There's something important I want to talk to you and Les about."

There was a smaller double gate in the rear wall of Haskin's loading area, and David headed for it now in the car. It must, he figured, lead to some back road or drive that would take him away without having to face the people in front of the store, spare him possible questions that he couldn't answer. He was sensitive about his position as a newcomer, afraid they might look upon him as a possible instigator—or at the least, supporter—of the previous night's trouble.

The gate was open, and Haskin's nephew, the boy who had been standing on the porch the night before, cursing, was just inside, changing a tire on a pickup truck. He wore blue jeans and a blue-and-white-striped shirt. David slowed to a stop and leaned out. "Morning, Willy."

"Morning, Mr. Champlin. You feeling all right, Mr. Champlin? I heard what they did to you."

"Hell, yes, I'm all right. You've got to take things as they come, Willy. Don't let them get you."

"We just going to sit here and take it, Mr. Champlin?"

"No, Willy. But it's not going to help those kids if we all get our brains beat out. They can lick us that way. Just as long as they can beat our brains out, break our bones, keep us running, they've got the upper hand. Remember, Willy, they're the guys with the guns."

"What we doing now if it isn't running? Standing still can be running." He threw the tire iron to the ground with vicious strength. "I'd rather be shot than take it. If I had me a gun—"

David restarted the car's motor, but before he let his foot down on the accelerator, he said: "Look, Willy. I'm with you. But they'd be too well off dead. One dead white isn't going to do any good. Ten of 'em dead isn't going to, either. I'd rather see 'em sick and helpless. And that takes doing."

Willy spat on the ground, made an obscene gesture with one arm, spat again.

"That's what we're trying to do, son; that's what we're trying to do."

The talk with Willy had taken the edge off his reaction to Brad's surprising outburst, put the words in the back of his mind until he drove through the gate and turned left on what he supposed passed for a road. He knew he shouldn't be surprised or hurt at Brad's attitude. God knew, Brad had tried hard through the years to straighten him out emotionally, get him to stop doing what Brad called "living on two planets." Subtly, but not so subtly David couldn't spot it, he tried to urge on David the advantages of marriage, the stabilizing influence of a home and children. Once when he was being outspoken about it he said: "Maybe you wouldn't be split in two the way you are now. It takes a whole man to try and accomplish what you're after down here."

"Even if I could, Brad, even if it were possible to cut out the whole damned past like a worrisome appendix. I don't think I could go on from there the way you want. Know why?"

"No, I don't 'know why.' And I think any reason you give will be rationalization."

"That's a hell of an attitude for a supposedly astute attorney. The trouble is, Brad, I'm not an Ivy League Negro. I just look like one. I'm still nothing but the brown-skin grandson of Li'l Joe Champlin who happened to have the savvy to get through Pengard and Harvard and Oxford. With the help of a great guy from Denmark. I'm not screaming loud screams of self-pity. I'm a Negro, close to my roots, and proud of it. You'd damned well better be proud of it if Gramp brought you up. And what happens when some of the women of our world that I've met who have been seeing an Ivy League Negro suddenly discover what's underneath? Jeez! They go into shock. And when they find out I'd rather be what I am than what they've been thinking I am, that's it, brother. That's it. Li'l ol' Uncle Tom Champlin might as well go back to the tall cotton. And as for the whites! When they scratch that utterly-charming-young-Negro-lawyer-and-brilliant-my-dear, and find *me* it jolts the hell out of them. A sentimental brown-skin slob who likes old-time blues piano, who'll sing in a Negro church service at the drop of a hat—looks for 'em, by God—and who gets more feeling of accomplishment out of registering a middle-aged Negro sharecropper who's been scared witless all his life than he'll get out of arguing his first case before the U.S. Supreme Court—that guy they can't dig; *that* guy they can't dig."

"You poor devil," said Brad. "You just aren't sick enough."

77

Now as he drove out to Miz Towers, the memory of his conversation with Brad slipped away, replaced by a warmer one—that of Gracie.

He remembered waking in the night and finding her gone. She shouldn't have left him, he thought; shouldn't have taken her soft, all-encompassing comfort away from him. He had reached for her, there in the dark, and his groping hand had found only emptiness. He murmured, half asleep, "Gracie . . . Gracie . . ." and he remembered the impression he had that she was still in the room, standing somewhere in its darkness. When she had not answered, he had gone back to sleep to be half awakened later by the sound of a ringing telephone and then Brad's voice in the kitchen answering it, the words indistinguishable. He realized now that it must have been the call from Hunter. And even in that second awakening there had been loneliness and a hope that Gracie would return to lie beside him for what was left of the night.

He realized abruptly that he had passed the Towers house, was almost at the plank bridge across the stream, and he braked quickly, fought the skidding wheels into a full turn, and started back.

He was reaching over the gate for the hook fastening when he saw the dog come around the corner of the house. He drew his hand back slowly, let his arms hang loosely at his sides. Never, so help him, had he seen a more magnificent specimen. Or a bigger one. The damned dog's as big as a pony, he thought. It was all strong grace and swift muscle and power, the great granddaddy of all the German shepherds that had ever been whelped. I love dogs, he thought; yes, Lawd! I love dogs, but I'm no damned fool. The dog had stopped and was standing motionless, halfway between house and gate, and in the immobility of deep chest and sloping flanks there was still a flowing grace of motion and power, and the upright ears were evidence of complete awareness. David cleared his throat, said "Hi, Gorgeous!" There might have been a slight movement of the ears; he couldn't tell. He looked anxiously and saw that the fur along the back lay smooth and sleek, with no upright hackles. But, he thought, he couldn't see any movement of that damned great tail either. "If you think I'm not chicken enough to get back in that car, you're nuts, Gorgeous," he said and was rewarded by seeing the tail move slowly, back and forth, in a wide arc. Then its speed increased, and David looked beyond and saw Miz Towers step from the porch and start down the path. He remembered then. Tinker. That was the dog's name. He said, "Hello, Tinker. Good morning, Miz Towers." The dog did not move until she reached its side, then strode along with her, the lean, strong back almost level with her waist.

Past ninety, that was what Brad had said was the general estimate of her years. It couldn't be far wrong, and was probably accurate. The grizzled hair was controlled in tight, short braids pinned down on top of her head. The skin was almost blue-black. The eyes were far back in sockets rimmed with wrinkled skin, the upper lids drooping over their brightness, half veiling their alertness. Only the structure of the bones beneath the webbed seaminess of the skin gave indication of what she once had been; that and the full lower lip and the carriage of the head, straight and unbending over a body age had made shrunken, yet a body that refused to be slowed by time or by the thought or intimation of eventual dissolution.

As she drew closer David felt the familiar sense of humility that had come over him so often with so many of his people whose paths he had crossed through the years. "There's greatness in them," he had said to Luke once. "And don't you forget it, youngster. There's greatness in them."

"Morning, son. Morning! No call to be skeered of Tinker here—" She unhooked the gate for him, talking so rapidly and in such rich idiom and accent David had trouble catching all she said. As soon as he was inside the yard the dog greeted him, not graceful now, but clumsy in his joy at making a new friend, rearing his great body upright, resting enormous paws on David's chest, ears flat in ecstasy at David's mauling caresses.

"Tinker down! Git down, boy! Quit worrying the man, y'hear! Reckon you was skeered at that, you being strange and all. Ain't no one around here don't know Tinker ain't going to hurt no brown-skin man. Less'n I tells him to—" Her cracked laughter showed her age more than did the high quick speech. "You the young man my son spoke about? Called a bit ago . . . Y'all seen that boy, Abraham? He ain't been home in three days . . . ain't been in the bed or et a meal far's I know. . . . You see him when you gets back you tell him to git along home. . . ."

By the time they reached the house and went inside, David's mind was at full gallop, trying to keep up with her. She was evidently under the impression that he had already met her "boy" Abraham, and David said nothing to change that impression. She had not seemed to look directly at him since her first hooded, piercing appraisal at the gate, but David knew she had not missed a detail of his appearance or personality, that she was feeling him over with the fingers of her mind as she would a vegetable, seeking soft spots or rot, not trusting him for a moment until she felt she had reason to trust. When they entered the living room, she urged him to sit down, but he did not want to put himself in the position of a guest sitting on one of the best chairs in that seldom-used room, and ignoring her urging, he followed her into the kitchen.

He sat in a straight chair at a table by the west window, glancing out past the side yard to the smooth flowing waters of Angel Creek and the rough, wild greenness of Flaming Meadows beyond.

Miz Towers had poured coffee, given him a cup without asking. Now she was still talking, and David grinned down at Tinker, seated beside him, massive body pressed against his leg. It was beginning to seem as though he'd never hear the sound of his own voice again. "Abra'm sure thinks a heap o' that dog," she was saying. "Tinker's pappy, Abra'm say, he one of them dogs the po-lice got over in the town. Man what raises 'em, he stay over by Otisville, he give Abra'm the dog. Runt of the litter, he say. Ain't no runty li'l pup now, Tinker ain't."

"Sure ain't," said David. Man's got to make his voice heard once in a while, he thought, even in church. But how in hell was he going to check that spate of talk, the talk of the old and often lonely, long enough to discuss her land? He knew her kind too well to force the issue, thereby destroying any faint burgeonings of trust and confidence, seeds and all.

She did stop long enough for him to read off the list of items Brad had given him. She had anticipated most of them and was packing them into a carton on the table in front of him, gnarled and knobby hands extraordinarily deft and quick. She had put carrots in, although they hadn't been included on the list, and David reached into the carton and took one. "May I?"

"Go ahead, son. Seems like when my babies wuz growing up never wuz a time one of 'em wuzn't chomping on a carrot. We ain't had no boughten vegetable on the table since we had the flood, and that's way back."

"You've got a lot of land to grow them on, Miz Towers."

"You-all fixin' to talk about my land. I been waitin' for it—"

David checked a laugh and tied the grin he hadn't been able to check into his play with Tinker.

"Yes'm."

"Abra'm says you'd give me an understanding of it. Why them white folks wants it. Cain't see what good it would do 'em. They uses it now, hunting and fishing. Ain't no one going to stop 'em. And Flaming Meadows yonder, it cain't be no good to 'em. Ain't nothing going to grow there. Ain't nothing going to be let grow there."

"I sure feel lonesome, drinking coffee all by myself. Can't you get yourself a cup and sit with me, res' yourself a while? You been on your feet ever since I got here."

"Lawd, son, I don't mind. These bones wuzn't made for settin'. Too hard gettin' up again." Still she did as he asked, brought a full cup to the table and sat at the chair David pulled up for her, facing the window. She was looking at him directly now, something she had not done since after he had entered the gate. Deep in their sockets the eyes were black and bright, and he was acutely conscious that behind them lay the mother-wit and wisdom of nearly a century. Tinker went briefly to her side, glowed almost visibly at her touch, wagged an apology, and returned to David's side, laying a huge paw on his knee until ear-scratching began again.

"We owns this land legal," she said. "Been ownin' it since my daddy-in-law bought it after the war."

There had been only one "war" for the Miz Towerses of the land, David knew: the Civil War, the only war in which her people had a stake. The wars that had followed had been "their" wars. "They fixin' to get theirselves into another war," Gramp had said when Korea came along.

He was afraid that she would bog down in detail, but there was not too much of it. He learned that her name was Belle, that her husband's name had been Simon, and her father-in-law was called Zeb. She hadn't been "nothin' but a chile," she said, when she and Simon had gone to live together in the little cabin on Zeb Towers's new property. She guessed she'd been about fifteen, Simon maybe five years older. A year later Zeb's wife had died, and Zeb had come to live with them. "He wuz a good man," she said. "He wuz a mighty good man. Good to me as my own daddy. I never knew my daddy. Never even knew who he wuz." She and Simon had produced six children, three in the first three years of their marriage, with the firstborn dying in infancy, then, after a long time, three more. Abraham was her youngest, the man she still called her "boy" and who must be in his mid-fifties.

David began to worry about time, but he did not dare make the gesture of looking at his wristwatch or at the clock that ticked tantalizingly behind him on a shelf above the stove. He should have left after the supplies were ready and come back later to talk. God knew what was going on at the other end of Calhoun Road. Still, if they needed him, Brad could call. A question from Miz Towers brought him sharply back to attention.

"What they want with my daddy-in-law's land? You know?"

Now she was questioning him, and that was good; it

showed the establishment of a certain amount of trust. He outlined the situation carefully, not talking down to her, yet using phrases she would understand. Now that he had met her and could see for himself how adamant she was about not parting with the land, he questioned the necessity for their plan. Still, she had areas of vulnerability in Abraham, her grandchildren and great-grandchildren.

"Please understand, Miz Towers, no one is going to make any money on this, even if you sell the land. The only purpose is to protect you, make sure that you and Abra'm get a fair price. Not an outlandish one, with strings attached, but a decent, fair one. *If* you decide to sell. If you don't, we'll just keep the land optioned and there'll be no sense in anyone bothering you. We'll be the ones they'll turn the heat on."

"They ain't going to get it. What Abra'm do after I'm gone, tha's his business. But they keeps trying. Worries a person. First it wuz sweet talk and doing things for us, me 'n' Abra'm. Then a few days back they wuz *in*-spectors. They say they wuz from the fire department. Said as how Abra'm's shop there it didn't come up to the law." Her laughter crackled suddenly. "They thinks we fools. Shucks, them wan't no *in*-spectors." She laughed again. "Tinker run 'em off. All I has to do is wiggle me a hand jes so, and Tinker, he know what to do. They didn't even see me wiggle it. They wuz too busy lookin' at him walkin' stiff-legged down the path, hair riz' up straight on his back, all them teeth-showin'. All I'da had to do wuz say 'Go' an' that dog would have been right in amongst 'em."

"My own hair's riz' up thinking about it. You sit on your hands, ma'm, please, while I'm around."

"Lemme get you some lemonade, boy. Got it cold in the icebox."

"No, thanks, ma'm. You got buttermilk in there?"

"Lawd, it's the mos' thing I got."

He tried to forestall her and get it himself, but she was on her feet and walking toward the refrigerator she still called an icebox before he had a chance. When she came back with it, he said: "You study 'bout this land thing, Miz Towers. And you talk it over with Abra'm."

"I been studyin' about it. Me 'n' Abra'm's been talking 'bout it. Cain't see no harm in it, offhand. Like you say, they kin be powerful worrisome. Ain't nothin' they won't do does they see a chance to cheat colored and make theirselves some money."

He couldn't leave right away, and let her think all he was interested in was the land deal. He knew that fine hairline between trust and suspicion, and he settled back, hiding his restlessness as best he could.

He took a long swallow of the cold, fresh buttermilk and said, "Umm, good!" then, idly, "Why'd you say nothing would be 'let to grow' on that field over yonder—Flaming Meadows, I think it's called?"

She was seated again now, a glass of lemonade in front of her. He blinked at the directness of her answer.

"Ha'nt," she said. "Plenty people say they seen it."

There was a small bite of carrot left, and he chewed it now while he tried to think of what to say. All foolishness, Li'l Joe Champlin had said of ghosts and ha'ntings, all foolishness, but David smiled to himself, remembering that even as a kid he'd doubted if Gramp's words would have stood up to a test.

"Ain't you heered about Flaming Meadows?" Miz Towers called it "medders."

"I just got here yesterday. Guess there hasn't been time."

"You stays round here long enough, son, come the dark of the moon, mebbe you'll see it. You got the look of one who kin see ha'nts."

"Dark of the moon? I always thought ghosts walked in the full of the moon—"

"Mebbe so. Mebbe so. Reckon it depends when they come to be ha'nts." Then she was gone, from this day into countless yesterdays, gone so suddenly he almost felt she should have said goodbye. He could see the past in her sunken eyes and hear it in her voice, and he listened without speaking, interested in spite of his impatience to leave.

There had been no ha'nt when she and Simon Towers had gone there to live. The land known now as Flaming Meadows had been uncultivated, as it was today. Too small for cotton, too big to let lie fallow, Simon and his father, Zeb, had talked of planting it to corn and potatoes.

"I remembers it," said Belle Towers. "I remembers it good. They wuz talking 'bout building fences the day them two young mens come by, hongry. Fine young mens." She had told the story a hundred times, he knew, a thousand times perhaps, yet he felt that it had always been the same, not embellished with each telling. There was an eerie simplicity in her recountal; she told the tale as an unimaginative artist might paint a picture, the highlights harsh, the details clear as mirrored images.

"They wuz fine young mens," she said again. One of them had been big, black, soft-spoken, quick to laugh; the other had been smaller, brown-skin, laughing not so often, quiet and polite.

"Raised good, they wuz; anyone could see that." They had come from the Gulf region, riding the rods and flatcars because they had been told there was more and better work in the North. They had learned differently and now they were going home with what little money they had made in the fields and packinghouses.

"Must've been way long before your daddy's time. Must've been your granddaddy's time. I already had me two babies running round and one in the grave. Abra'm, he didn't come along till near fifteen years later. Had me two more girls before him."

Her father-in-law and her husband had asked the young men in, given them corn bread and chittlins and whatever else had been on their table. The house was only a three-room cabin then, the kitchen the focal point for the family.

"The big boy, he was bigger'n you, he set where you're settin' now; he'ped my husband mend the chair you're settin' on. He set there laughing, playing with them babies. I kin see him good as my hand," said Belle Towers. "He wuz crazy for them babies of mine. Set 'em on his shoulders an' pranced around playing he wuz a horse."

The big man had said: "Gonna have me one of these mighty soon. We been trying a long time and now we got one coming. Fixin' to get back so's I kin be the first to say howdy."

Belle Towers added, "He wuz a happy man, a real happy man, and laughing mos' of the time. And gentle. Real kind and gentle."

That afternoon the two men went hunting with her husband, and that night the Towerses bedded them down in a lean-to in the back, bringing them quilts and blankets because spring had not yet come and there was chill in the night air.

They planned to leave the next day, but Zeb Towers told them he was taking the mule and going to Heliopolis the day after that; if they waited, he said, and went with him they'd probably be able to hop a freight as soon as they got there. Walking would take two days.

She stopped speaking then for a moment, and her body

swayed back and forth. "God lef' us then," she said. "God lef' us then. There wouldn't be no ha'nt today if they'd gone on."

David reached a hand to Tinker's head, wanting to touch the warm life of it, the reality of it. His flesh felt cold in spite of the heat of the room.

"Simon, he went into Cainsville that day, and them boys, they figgered to go up yonder and get them a rabbit or two, mebbe a possum, bring 'em to us for dinner. Wan't no sun that day, and my daddy-in-law, he went to Angel Creek to get us some fish. They wuz a big cave there then, this side the creek; used to clean the fish there 'fore he brought 'em home, keep some of his gear there. It wuz hid real good with juniper, with a little sandy place in front. It ain't been there since the last flood. Didn't no one know 'bout that cave but us."

From the "little sandy place in front" Zeb Towers could look across the wide creek to the land it bordered, and northward to the scrubby woodland. He was cleaning fish when he heard the shouting and hoarse cries. They had already caught them; the whites had already caught the two young men the Towerses had befriended: the big, black man who laughed a lot and was gentle, and the smaller, brown-skin man, quiet and polite.

"He tried, my daddy-in-law tried, to tell us what happened; seemed like he couldn't give it no words, not for a long time. He wuzn't never the same after that day. He wuz always a good man, that don't change, but seemed like he wuz different after that."

Listening to the old woman, David Champlin felt the same cold fear in his belly that must have been in Zeb Towers's that day when there had been no sun and he had gone to catch fish for the family. He could see Zeb Towers slipping, a dark shadow not cast by any sun, behind the underbrush that hid the cave's mouth, then watching through branches not yet in spring bud, watching a horror he was powerless to stop. And praying. Zeb Towers would have been praying, and David cried silently, "To what God! To what God!"

"They wuz dragging the small man like he was a log, had him roped from his neck clear down to his feets so's he couldn't move. They wuz saving him for the last."

Like kids saving some of the icing on the cake so the sweetness would linger in their mouth; that was the way it would be with them.

The big man, the big, happy black man, said Miz Towers,

looked half dead, and they were dragging him too, by the arms, and he was bloody, all bloody in the head and back, but "he wuz putting up a fight, putting up a fight—"

David knew what was coming, knew it and wanted her voice to stop, but withheld his own voice, knowing it would not be heeded, back there where her mind was now.

They threw the smaller man to the side, on the bank of Angel Creek, and he lay there like a corpse, unmoving. He was so close that Zeb Towers could see the rope cutting into purpling flesh; then he saw the eyes roll, saw a quiver in the chest and knew the man was alive, that he was "froze up in fright, looking like a daid man 'cepting for his eyes."

Zeb must have been trembling, thought David, must have been shaking like a man with ague. He was surprised when he saw that his own hands were steady, one on the table, one on the dog's head resting on his knee.

They forgot the small trussed-up man lying on the bank of the stream and went about their business with the big black man, turned their backs and went away from that small figure, knowing he could not move. The big black man had bellowed, twice, like a bull in agony, and the sound had roared out over the voices of the white men. After that there had been no sound from where he lay on the ground, still living, more blood on his body now.

"We seen the fire from here, from out back, seen the smoke and heered the noise, heered 'em laughing, 'fore we run for kiver. White laughing it was, loud." Miz Towers waited, quiet for a moment in the terror of that day so long before. "Whites sure laugh at things wouldn't no colored laugh at, even wuz a white man burning alive."

Stop! Now can you stop! For Christ's sweet sake, stop! But the voice of Belle Towers went on, old and thin and cracked:

"My daddy-in-law he didn't get back till way late in the night. Me 'n' my husband and the babies, we wuz locked in the bedroom. Simon, after he come home from town, he didn't dast go hunting for his daddy. He knew it wouldn't do no good. Zeb Towers wuz either daid or he wuz alive and if he wuz alive he'd get back somehow. There wuzn't no moon that night, and when Zeb Towers come home, he wuz stark nekkid and he had that little man with him, slang over his shoulders like a sack of meal, the man they left on the bank."

The white men had been busy carrying the big man to the pile of logs that was in the middle of the field when Zeb Towers stripped off his clothes and crawled on his belly from behind the bushes that hid the cave's mouth. There was no more sound than a fish makes rising to the surface when his body slipped into the water, scarcely more when he reached the other side of the stream and grasped the trunk of a small sapling growing from the bank, steadying himself against the current. It had taken only a slight tug by his free hand to roll the trussed-up body of the small man over, start it down the bank. He slowed its descent so there would be no loud splash. Getting him across the stream had been easy for a man to whom a river had meant food and sport and a place for games in childhood.

More than courage, thought David; something more than courage had sent Zeb Towers alone and naked across that water to rescue a man he scarcely knew from under the noses of a mob of jeering whites, happy with their horror.

Zeb had never let the other man's body touch the ground until they reached the cave, Miz Towers said. Because the man had been wearing light clothes Zeb stripped him, too, and buried clothes and ropes in a hole he dug in the floor of the cave. Zeb heard the cursing of the whites when they found the body gone and realized their fun was ended. Someone saw the place where he had rolled down the bank to the water and he cursed the others loudly for their carelessness. They said the nigger must have drowned and been carried downstream, and Zeb listened, not daring to breathe, as the sound of feet tramping downstream came to him from the opposite bank, not daring to stir as long as he could hear voices. He waited until far into the night before he carried the small man home with him.

"The big black boy, he wuz daid in the fire," said Miz Towers. "Didn't no one dast go near it. The whites, they come back next day when there wuzn't no danger of burnin' theirselves, and they dug a grave up yonder and they threw his body, what was lef', in it and kivered it over. Cain't no one tell where it is now."

David's mouth felt parched, and he ran his tongue over dry lips. "The ha'nt—"

"Folks been saying they seen it ever since. I ain't never been there after that. They say it move slow and big and dark 'cross that field, laughing. But they say it don't laugh like no living man; they say they hears it from up yonder, when the wind's right, sounding like it come from the grave."

When the wind's right; it would be the sound of the wind coming from the darkness of the wood, blowing across the field. It had to be the sound of the wind. Now David was oblivious to the passage of time, to the ticking of the clock.

"We kep' that pore boy here," said Miz Towers. "We kep' him here a week, and for four days he never spoke no word, jes lay like he was daid. We fed him like he wuz a baby. When his voice come back he didn't talk like he wuz in his right senses, but after a while seemed like he come to hisself a little, and Zeb, he hid him under a load of vegetables in the mule cart and he carried him to where he could hop a freight. Zeb seen him catch the freight, and then Zeb come home. That night we prayed for him. Right y'ere in the kitchen on our knees, babies and all. He said he'd send word, but we ain't never heered from him again. Never knew did he make it."

It was alive and present to her. "We ain't never heered," she had said, as she would have if Zeb and Simon and the babies were still here. She said now: "They never done nothing. They found out later them boys never done nothing. A white chile, she live north of here then, she come running home one day crying, telling 'bout some black snake she seen in the woods. She wuz skeered she'd git a licking for going away from home. They put the words in her mouth, her daddy and a friend, about black men. After it was all over, she tol' her mamma wa'n't no black men around, tol' her mamma she wuzn't even in the woods. My sister, she cook for them; she heered it, she heered it all. But them white men, my sister say, didn't seem like they wuz sorry, seem like they wuz jes as glad, said a good lesson never done the niggers no harm, kep' 'em keerful—"

David did not even realize that she had gotten to her feet until she started walking across the kitchen with uneven, rickety speed. The room was unbearably hot and close. From somewhere beyond he could hear a sticking drawer being opened. It was the only sound except the groaning sigh of Tinker as he sank to his belly, then brought a smoky muzzle to rest sideways on crossed, tawny forepaws.

The packet Miz Towers carried when she came back had for an outer wrapping an oiled silk tobacco pouch, cracked and dry with age. "The big black boy, he lef' his coat here that day an' this wuz in the pocket—" She opened it when she sat down and took from it a cardboard folder that David knew contained a photograph. Before she could speak, he reached and gently took it from her hands, not opening it, letting it lie on the table before them, his fingers curled over its top.

"The brown-skin man made it, Miz Towers," he said. "He made it home. You didn't tell me his name, but I know. You named your youngest son for him, didn't you? Abraham."

"Lord Jesus! How you know? How you know?"

"Wait. There's nothing strange or spooky about it, Miz Towers. He lived in New Orleans, where I was born and grew up. It has to be the same man. He made it home. But that's all. Like you say, he wasn't in his right senses, and after a few days his mamma sent for a doctor. Abraham was sitting in the kitchen when the doctor came, and when he saw that white man come into the house he started to run. He never stopped, not even when he reached the river, and all the time he was running he was crying, 'I'm coming, Jesus! I'm coming, Jesus!' He ran into the river calling, 'Take me, Jesus!—' When I was a boy, there were still old folks who remembered. They used to say, 'Abra'm run to Jesus—' "

She was swaying again now, eyes closed, whispering. "Jesus done give him his res'. The good Lord Jesus done give him peace at las'—"

David put a hand on her wrinkled arm. "The big man, Miz Towers. The big, happy black man who laughed so much—"

Her eyes opened. "Y'all knows about him? You knows about him, too?"

"His name was David." He pressed her arm gently. "Wait, Miz Towers. Wait before you say anything." He curled his fingers between front and back covers of the folder, laid it open and looked at it, and Li'l Joe Champlin was beside him. *Never did get to see a picture of my daddy. Your Tant'Irene say the onlies' one they had he taken with him when he went away.* Now Li'l Joe Champlin's father was looking at his great-grandson, his namesake, from a faded photograph that was streaked and dim with age, in a close, stuffy kitchen on the outskirts of a small southern town, and the place where he had died in flames was just beyond the window, lying green and quiet under the morning sun. The chair on which he had sat, laughing, playing with the babies, was the chair on which his great-grandson sat now.

A big man, everyone said, and had not exaggerated. The camera techniques of the time had lightened the blackness of the skin, but in spite of the stiffly seated pose, the self-consciousness evident in the straightness of back and neck, the gentleness was there, in mouth and eyes, and the laughter.

Beside him stood his white-clad, veil-bedecked wife, a hand on her husband's shoulder. The sternness David remembered in Tant'Irene was not in that young face; in that face there was softness, even under the unaccustomed circumstance of being photographed, softness, and pride in the man she had chosen and now stood beside.

David freed the picture from the folder and turned it over, finding on its back what he knew would be there, the writing in Tant'Irene's clear hand, for years forgotten, remembered now:

Mr. and Mrs. David Champlin, October 10, 1885. "Whom God hath joined—"

He reached for his wallet, usually sure fingers fumbling and clumsy as he tried to unbutton the flap of the back pocket. He drew the wallet out at last and took a card from it. He laid the card on the back of the picture, beneath the inscription, edged his chair around until he was sitting beside Miz Towers, the picture in front of them. Carefully he spelled each name out for her, pointing with his forefinger first to the "D" of David on the picture, then to the same letter on the card, until he had gone through the entire name.

Her breathing was hoarse and loud as she listened, and she made small keening noises at the end of each exhalation. When he had finished she wrapped thin arms around her chest, rocking back and forth, a shrunken black figure, rocking, rocking. "Lord! Lord! An' you here carrying his name. Lord! Lord Jesus! A-a-a-ah, my Jesus!—"

78

DAVID WALKED SLOWLY down the path from Miz Towers's house to the gate, Tinker padding delightedly alongside. He was keenly conscious that the old lady who had shuff-shuffed to the edge of the porch with him was standing there now, watching him. He carried in his mind the image of the frame house with its ungainly appendages of tacked-on rooms, its front porch without foundation, its crisp curtains so white and clean and brave. And of a field that stretched wide and green and wild beyond it, a field his people in Cainsville called "Flaming Meadows."

Halfway down the path he turned to wave at her, and she called, "Y'all give my son that message, hear!"

"Yes, ma'am." He stood, smiling. She was like ol' Miz Speck, only brighter, less victimized by the years. "I'll get him out here. You'll remember what I told you, Miz Towers?"

"Sure will. Sure will and that's a fact. Don't you worry, son. I keeps my land. Even if they sends the law, I keeps my land less'n I talks with you and Abra'm."

He sighed with relief. She trusted him, and trust among his people, even of each other, could be hard to come by.

The reason she trusted him had shaken him inwardly so much that after its full significance hit him he found it almost impossible to talk any longer, even with her, and had to hurry his leave-taking. He needed time to do what he had learned in England to call "sort out" his tangled emotions.

Driving back he wondered how he could explain it all to Brad and Chuck. The facts were simple; he could give them those, tell about the faded old photograph of a young woman in a white wedding dress and veil, standing beside a big black man with happy eyes.

But his own reactions, his own shock, he could never explain to anyone—was having trouble trying to explain them to himself. He knew this much—those reactions, that shock, had something to do with all the things he had heard Gramp saying when Gramp had tried to tell him things about God. Not all the learning, the law, the experiences he had absorbed during the past years gave an answer, and he could not shake the feeling, and did not try, that somehow Li'l Joe Champlin would have found that answer.

He thought that the heat and dust, the rutted roadway he was traveling now toward Cainsville, had probably been much the same on that day nearly eighty years before when the old woman's father-in-law had let the first David Champlin and Abraham Jefferson wash themselves in clear cold water from his pump, had taken them into his home and given them something to eat—chittlins, had she said?—and then had let them bed down in the shed in the back, even bringing them quilts for comfort in the nip of the early spring night. The second David Champlin thought of these things and shook his head and said aloud, "Hell, it can't be true. It can't be."

He thought of novels he had read about the South and their so frequent preoccupation with its atmospheres of brooding malevolence. There had been nothing brooding or malevolent about Flaming Meadows, nothing but glaring heat, high grass unstirring in the humid air, and the sound of rushing water just above him where Angel Creek tumbled and sang over rocks, a creek as wide as a river and as deep. There should be malevolence, he thought, and a brooding sense of evil, not just here but everywhere. It was not more than a hundred miles from here that another Negro had been burned alive, more recently, and when the screams of his wife, heavy with his child, had disturbed the burners, she had been thrown on the fire to die with him. And not far from him a woman named Till must still remember a son named Emmett.

When he got out of the car at Tether's End he was soaked with perspiration, and he thanked God for the makeshift shower in the lean-to. He hitched up his khaki pants irritably, then tried to pull his belt in another notch and remembered it was already at the last one. He told himself for the thousandth time to buy and wear suspenders, at least until he got his weight back. The gnawing pain was in his belly again, and he was glad there was milk in the supplies Miz Towers had given him.

The heat in the building was stifling, the humidity like a fog, clogging lungs, slowing breath. Brad, stripped to the waist, was typing, *café-au-lait* skin gleaming with sweat. Chuck, sitting near him, was wearing his black trousers, but was down to a cotton undervest that was gradually becoming sodden. Garnett, fully clothed, was standing at the side door leaning against the jamb, Coke bottle in one pudgy hand. David flopped into the old wicker chair in front of the table, opposite Brad.

"The damndest thing," he said. "The Goddamndest thing has happened."

"Yes?" said Brad. "Now what? Never mind. Don't tell me, I'll tell you. The Ninth Brigade of the Ku Klux moved in last night. So what else is new?"

"Nuts. It's got nothing to do with this mess." He paused. "Or maybe it has. If you're interested in nonprogress and the ability of the human race to remain in *status quo*. Especially if the *status quo* is evil. Sometimes I wonder—Chuck, you ought to know the answer—why people think Jesus Christ ever bothered with it, ever bothered to be worried with the human race. You know the answer to that one, Chuck?"

"Don't needle me. It's all there was. I keep telling you, you oversimplify too much. Stop philosophizing and start talking, Stoopid."

"Out there at that house—" began David, and stopped at the rattling slam of the screen door. The man entering was heavy set, with brown skin, a powerful body, and a sternly lined patient face, and deep, patient eyes. He wore blue jeans, and his blue shirt was blotched with dark patches of sweat. "David," Brad said, "let me introduce you to Abra'm Towers."

David got to his feet, ignoring complaints of bruised muscles, and held out his hand. "I'm David. David Champlin. I've just come from your mother's house; got a message for you."

"Pleased to meet you," said Abra'm Towers. "We're mighty proud you come down here." His grip was hard, firm. "What's my ma worrying about now?"

"You."

"Lawd!"

"You aren't eating or sleeping, she says. You ain't been in the bed and you ain't had a good meal for two, three days. She says you better get on home and get you a good meal and some bed res' right quick before you sickens and dies."

Abra'm laughed. "Lawd!" he said again. "All we got going on here and it don't make no difference to her; she's got to worry about am I eating, am I sleeping. I'm eating. I'm eating fine. Long's a man eats good he don't need too much sleep. I'll go on out there soon's I leave here and ease her mind." He stopped and frowned. "Excuse me, sir, but what did you-all say is your name?"

"Sit down, Mr. Towers. Sit down and res' yourself. And listen."

Brad and Chuck sat quietly, without interrupting, while David told his story. Abraham Towers did not interrupt, but his interpolations were like exclamation points, the frequent "Well, I'll be!" and "Lawd!" and the hummed, amazed "Umm-ummmm. Ummm-*ummmm*."

When the story was finished, Abraham leaned forward. "My ma tell you about the ha'nt?"

"She mentioned it. You don't believe it, do you?"

Abraham averted his eyes, leaning back again. "Couldn't say. Don't know nothing about it myself. Never seen nothing. But then," he added, "I don't have no call to go 'cross there, to go round by there at night."

"Especially when the moon's dark."

"Not no time," said Abraham. "Not no time at *all*."

Brad said: "Abra'm, I wish you'd tell this around, you and your mother. There may be a certain feeling that we're outsiders, that we don't know enough about the problems here. If the people know that David's great-grandfather was burned alive only two miles away, it might help."

Abra'm smiled. "I don't know about you, Lawyer Willis. Mebbe a few of them feels that way about you. They'll get over it. They know about you getting shot, don't they? But this here young man"—he smiled at David—"shucks, he ain't no outsider. I knew the minute we spoke, even before he told us about his great-grandaddy, I knew he wasn't no outsider." Garnett put down his Coke bottle and went out the side door, saying something about working on his damned jalopy, and David watched him go, glad that he was leaving. Abra'm's eyes were also following the pudgy man, and when he was out of earshot Abra'm said, "Bear watching, that fella. Too full of big-mouth talk."

Relief swept over David. Garnett didn't have them fooled, at least not all of them.

"I wish Sweeton would wake up to him," said Chuck.

"Lawd! Reverend Sweeton, he trusts *every*one. *Every*one," said Abra'm. "Ain't never seen *no* colored person that trusting before. He'll wake up. You'll see."

Brad broke in. "One other thing, Abra'm, when you see your mother. Be sure, be sure to tell her not to weaken, not to agree to sell her land to anyone. Not now. Especially not now and especially not to anyone connected with the city."

"Like ol' Hoot'n' Holler?"

"Especially not your besotted mayor, ol' Hoot'n' Holler."

Abra'm turned to David. "You tell her anything?"

"I tried to give her the general idea. I'm pretty sure she trusts me. But it must come from you, too."

"What they want with that land, Mr. David? What they want with it? Plenty of other places where they can build 'em a factory." He began to laugh. "They cheats my ma outa that field, makes 'em a lot of money building a factory, I bet your great-grandaddy'll give 'em fits. Bet there'll be busted machinery and all kinds of trouble happening won't nobody be able to explain."

"Lay off, Abra'm. I've got goose pimples bad enough now. You're sure your mother'll hang tough?"

"She will if I tells her how and why they cheating her. My ma's powerful set against being cheated. Seen too much of it. We all has. This about the first chance we've had to get back at 'em."

Brad said, "Is Haskin related to you? Through your mother?"

"Distant," said Abra'm. "Distant."

"Could they get at her through him?"

"You mean in these here talks?" Abra'm grew thoughtful. "They could try," he said at last. "They could try. Sure could. But I don't think they will, don't think they got sense enough, not right now. Ol' Hoot'n' Holler, he won't want to tip his hand less he has to. And if he does, Haskin going to suspicion something. Mighty suspicious man, Haskin. Don't trust no one. That's one reason we picked him."

A new thought struck David, sending chills down his spine. "In Georgia," he said, "and some other states they're insisting on unencumbered real property, to secure bonds for demonstrator prisoners. It's one way to acquire real estate—cheap." He looked at Brad with a question in his eyes.

"Hell, David, the N-double-A and ALEC and CORE are going to be responsible for more damned new roads and courthouses and civic improvements in the South than they have towns in these lousy states. Add it all together and it's more than a million dollars, easily more. If it keeps up, their senators can quit asking for appropriations from Congress. This was bound to come. We're rebuilding the whole damned South." He frowned. "Wait a minute. What are you driving at? That they'll offer us the kids if the land's put up as bond?"

"Something like that," said David. "Something sweet and simple like that."

"Abra'm," said Brad, "if they should make that suggestion and your mother refuses and you back her it will turn the whole town—all your people—against you."

Abraham stood up. "Ain't no sense worrying 'bout that yet. Let's take the trouble when it comes, not 'fore it gets here."

David walked toward the door with him. "Damned if I know why I should worry at all. There's more damned common sense and mother-wit this side of those barricades than in that whole stinkhole of a town over there."

"We ain't all that smart, Mr. David. But them bastids don't give us credit for no sense at all. They still thinks like their grandaddies did, we nothing but a bunch of savages or something. Been a hell of shock to them, men like the Reverend King and Mr. Wilkins and Mr. Willis and you and all, coming down here. Ain't no wonder they say one thing they hates is an educated nigger. Hell, half-dozen educated colored running this town, it be a decent place to live in." They were at the door now, and Abra'm was still talking. "I've knowed a lot of colored, Mr. David, but I ain't never knowed *no* colored what'd treat a little chile bad, and I don't care what color the chile is. Maybe they is some, maybe they is, but I ain't never knowed 'em."

Brad's voice halted them as they started through the door: "Abra'm! You don't have any idea at all, any memory yet, of the name of the company that Holloway—Ol' Hoot'n' Holler—and Scoggins are dealing with on that land? You haven't remembered?"

"Said I disremembered earlier," said Abra'm. "But an inkling come to me a while ago while we were talking. Some big company way north of here, way north. Does a lot of work for the government. That's according to my nephew. Leech—Leechman—Leechwood—some such name."

Brad was on his feet, coming around the table toward them, his eyes the darkening green David had learned to recognize as a sign of inner excitement. "Litchfield? Was that it, Abra'm, Litchfield? Litchfield and Associates?"

"That's it! That's right. I can see the name now, good as a book, right on that envelope. Litchfield."

Brad stopped just in front of them, lean torso gleaming with sweat, ribs showing plainly under the skin, the purple-red of the bullet wound a surly scar. His breathing was quick and shallow. "You're sure, Abra'm? You're sure?"

"I'm positive, Mr. Willis. Why? You-all know them?"

"Know them!" breathed Brad. "*Know* them!"

David's own breathing had quickened, and when he lit a cigarette to cover his excitement he found that his hands were unsteady. He had seen Lloyd Litchfield only occasionally since those few weeks in Boston when he had tried to help him clear the jungle of red tape that surrounded the project of Litchfield and Associates going public. After he had returned to Boston following the Prof's death, Brad had invited him and Litchfield to dinner, and he learned then that the little scientist's mind was far from fuzzy when it came to human relationships, that he felt a deep emotional involvement in the Negro's struggle. They discussed at length the training program for Negroes set up by the Litchfield firm, and its three scholarships on scientific fields. "Abra'm," he said, "are you sure about something else? Are you sure your mother never signed a paper—I don't mean a bill of sale; I mean a paper of any kind, anything that might have been an option?"

"Sure I'm sure," said Abra'm. His own eyes had taken a spark from theirs and were glowing. "My ma never had no schooling. She knows to sign her name and that's all. Anytime she does that it's a big thing. My ma ever put her name to a piece of paper she'd tell me. Couldn't anyone make her put her name to a piece of paper anyhow she wouldn't ask me first."

The three men walked to the rickety, sagging porch, and David said, "Remember, Abra'm, you're to tell her not to sign anything, anything at all that anyone brings her. And she must trust us. You must trust us."

As Abra'm climbed into his pickup, David called after him, "Mind you don't stay out there! Mind you make your ma turn you loose, y'hear!"

As Abra'm's laughter, clear and rich and coming from deep inside, came back to him David thought how rare it had been, these last months, the sound of the deep, rich laughter of his people.

When they came back into the room, Chuck was standing, waiting for them. "You heard that, Chuck?" asked David.

Chuck nodded. "Sorry," he drawled, "but I've plumb got to say it: 'God works in mysterious ways,' you guys."

"He do," said David. "He do indeed. Where's Garnett?"

"Out back, working on his car. He couldn't hear anything."

Brad was at the telephone, his hand on the receiver. He withdrew it slowly. "I don't dare," he said. "God damn it, I don't dare use this phone for something like this. It's bugged as sure as I'm a foot high." He sighed. "I'll take a bullet any day over this kind of thing. Lloyd Litchfield is a hell of a person; he was one of my best friends at college, besides being one of our clients. But if I call him and start talking about tapped lines and acting like a phony hero in a cheap TV series he'll send the white coats after me."

"How about me phoning from Washington later?" asked Chuck. "I'm supposed to fiy there tonight for a conference with the rest of my group."

"If we have to, yes. But it should be me. Or David, for whom he has a high regard. Thinks he's a legal genius. Probably the best plan will be for me to drive to Heliopolis and call from that motel there."

"Wire first—" said Chuck, and Brad broke in. "Still naïve after all this time, Chuck? Scoggins would have the full text of the wire ten minutes after it was sent. It's not so much the text as it is the identity of the man it's going to."

"Stall and betray," said David slowly. "Stall and betray." Then, without preliminary smile or chuckle, laughter took hold of him and shook him like a gale; it threw his head back and doubled him over, shook the pain from his belly and the soreness from his body, and cleansed and healed him momentarily. It carried Chuck and Brad along with it, and when at last he could speak, Chuck said, "I'm damned forever; forever damned. Charles Beauregard Martin, an ordained minister of the Lord!" He sobered completely. "My people, my own people, have made a conniving so-and-so out of me—and I'm eating it up. Maybe its funny—and maybe it isn't."

79

TWENTY MINUTES LATER David came back from showering and shaving, bath towel around his middle. Winters and Les Forsyte were in the room now, talking to Chuck and Brad. It was evident there had been no developments downtown. He opened his suitcase in the dingy side bedroom, found clean shorts and khaki trousers, and slipped into them, and as he sloshed the clothes he had been wearing in a basin of suds at the sink he said to Winters, "Watchman, what of the night?"

Winters shrugged. "Still talking."

Garnett, back now at his self-appointed post at the side door, mopped his forehead and the top of his head with a handkerchief, then the back of his neck, finishing off with a swipe under his chin. "Those bastards must be really putting on the pressure," he muttered.

"God damn it!" Brad's voice was rough, sharp with exasperation. "Don't you trust your own people?"

Garnett whirled to face him, eyes hot with antagonism. "No, I don't. I'm not faulting them. There's not a Negro in that room in City Hall who isn't tied into the white economy, isn't dependent on some Goddamn' white for his income. Even Haskin with that little store of his. Day before yesterday the bank cut off his credit, you know that? Soon's they found out he was active in this. Cracked down on him on a loan."

"And just what in hell do you think keeps the white economy healthy?" David tried to keep his voice level, tried to turn Garnett's antagonism on himself and away from Brad. "Where would they be—where will they be without cheap labor, damned near slave labor, without Negro buying, without Negro bus fares? Remember Montgomery? Retail trade's already off fifty-six percent in a week here. That hurts." His eyes narrowed. "Maybe I just came in on this picture, but whose idea was it in the first place that we give in to them, keep outsiders out of the meeting, subject vulnerable people to pressure and threats? How did that setup in City Hall come about?"

"An outsider negotiator was something they wouldn't—" began Garnett, but David's voice, rasping with tension and suppressed anger, cut him off.

"Negotiate!" It was almost a snarl. "Negotiate! For Christ's sake, how often have I got to say it! You don't 'negotiate' rights! An American citizen doesn't 'negotiate' his right to vote, the right to use tax-supported facilities. Does the United States Government negotiate his right to pay taxes? His right to wear an Army uniform, his right to get shot to protect his second-class citizenship! 'Negotiate' hell! I wish you guys would quit using that word. Every time you do it weakens us."

"You got a better one?" Garnett used the question for an exit line, letting the front door slam behind him, then in a moment racing the motor of his car viciously, driving off with a squeal of brakes at the turn into the roadway.

David wrung out the now rinsed clothes and slapped them

down on the drainboard. It was too damned hot to get that angry. He spoke to the room at large. "Where's the reverend? I mean Hummer Sweeton."

Les Forsyte answered: "As soon as we got here I made him go into that little back room and take a nap. He's no youngster, and he looked like hell. Abra'm offered him a room at his mother's where he could get some good food and a little peace and quiet, but he turned it down."

"He would," said David. "No sense exposing an old lady to guns and bombs and arson. Save 'em for the kids in Sunday school." He pumped cold water into the washbasin and splashed his face and neck with it. "Christ, what in hell are we fighting? What in hell are we fighting? Berserk dinosaurs? Critters from another planet? Not humans, that's for certain."

A few minutes later, in the musty, airless bedroom, Chuck and David dressed. Chuck held up his newly washed, freshly starched white suit on its hanger and shook his head sadly. " 'So cool, so white, so fair,' " he said. "And in ten minutes— Still, I suppose I better wear 'em, turnaround collar, rabat and all."

"Sure had," said David. The blue cotton-mesh sport shirt he had put on had been, a year before, tight across his chest; now it fitted loosely. He had learned that crepe-soled sports shoes were cooler on his feet, and he slipped into a pair now and entered the front room in time to pick up the ringing telephone. It was Haskin.

"What's going on, Haskin?"

"Nothing much. They was an hour and a half late. They've been setting there, being kind, worrying about us and what we going to do, how we going to take care of our families and all if we keeps on like this, threatening we'd all get fired from our jobs."

"God damn them to hell," said David dispassionately. "Tell 'em to start worrying about how they're going to keep their stores open, keep their buses running with an economic boycott going on."

"Williams, he said something about that, and this city attorney guy what keeps coming in and out, Elmore's his name, Thomas Elmore, he says a boycott's a criminal conspiracy."

"Balls! Did you tell him that?"

"What you just said? You think I'm crazy!"

"How long will the lunch break be?"

"Dunno for sure. About two hours, I guess."

"Two hours!" The whole thing was going sour, thought

David. The whole lousy thing was going sour. The longer the kids were in the stockade and the jail in this heat, the harder it would be to control the crowd, the closer to the breaking point their men in City Hall would be. Stall and betray; stall and betray. It was the same old lily-white story. But he could not let Haskin sense for a moment the way he was feeling. "Keep the people cheered up if you can, Haskin. And listen. We'll be there in a few minutes. But if something delays us or we don't make it, here's what you must do. When you go back in there, stop talking. Don't bargain. Tell them to turn the youngsters loose, and we'll talk. Only one bargaining point, remember. Reasonable bail. That we have to go for. If they weasel on that—" He stopped. He had been going to say "Give 'em Article Eight of the Bill of Rights." Haskin probably did not even know it. He thought that if Garnett had been in the room he might conceivably have killed him. Someone should have been there with those men, someone who could cram facts down the stinking gullets of the Mayor's committee.

"You still there, Lawyer Champlin?"

"Yes, I'm here. Just sit tight and we'll be down there. You're doing fine, Just tell everybody who asks you that—wait a minute. Haskin, did anyone call you, anyone tell you to take a lunch break for two hours?"

"Sure. Reverend Sweeton."

"Reverend Sweeton? Hummer Sweeton? He's been here, asleep. Right here in this house."

"I dunno about that. Garnett, he telephoned just a bit ago and he said 'We'—that's what he say, 'We'—thought there ought to be a break for a couple of hours. Called me to the phone over there in City Hall. Seemed kinda funny to me, but then I thought mebbe there was something cooking over here on this side and he didn't want to say nothing 'bout it on the phone, so I went along."

"Sure," said David. "I can see how you would." His own voice came to him through a pounding of blood in his ears. "We'll be there soon. Just tell everyone you see that you've quit talking. That the next time you go over it'll be turn the kids loose, talk afterward."

He hung up the receiver and found Sweeton standing beside him. The minister's face seemed even more haggard than it had that morning. "Isn't that what they did?" he said. "Isn't that what they *did?*"

David shook his head. He concentrated on a small abrasion on the back of the hand that still held the receiver. He needed to think for a minute. Until now he hadn't been able to figure out exactly what the hell Garnett was up to. Now he was sure he knew. They had gotten to him when he was in jail. Now that David was reasonably sure of what was going on, the picture began to become clear, like one of Luke's photographs in the developing bath. He would never know the details for certain, but it must have been a case of turning Garnett loose, dropping the charges against him—trumped up though they had to have been. He could hear how they must have done it, kindly, reasonably, dealing in implied threats instead of actual brutality. They might have offered other inducements, a job perhaps, even though they knew he was an outsider. They would have told him they weren't really planning to keep the young people in the stockade any longer than was necessary but that everyone's welfare, and especially the Negroes', depended on the economic well-being of the entire community. They would have flattered him, and he would have known the flattery for what it was, being Negro—not even a Garnett could be fooled by a white's self-seeking flattery—but he would have pretended to swallow it, his eyes on the safety they offered. An indeterminate stretch in a Cainsville jail at the mercy of the Cainsville jailers and police would be more than Alonzo Garnett could face.

Now the telephone call purporting to be from Sweeton was understandable. Either by prearrangement or by getting word to him somehow they had asked him to call for a breathing spell. It was probably the reason for his abrupt leave-taking. The white committee's reasoning seemed clear enough: given a long morning of fruitless talk, then a long break with the young people still in the stockade, the pressures against the Negro committee from their own people would be so great they would give in on other points. It would also give the men on the other side of Main Street additional time to get their heads together and try to work out still greater leverage to apply on the Towers land deal.

This had to be the story. The counteraction would have to be taken by feeling their way, playing it by ear.

He became aware that Sweeton had been trying to get his attention and that his voice was becoming louder and more insistent. "I told them," he was saying, "I told them plain this morning they was to stay with it till they turned them young uns loose—"

Now David dared look up, control returning. "You told

Garnett," he said gently. "You told Garnett to tell them, didn't you?"

Sweeton nodded, not speaking, and David laid a hand on the thin shoulder. "Hummer, will you do something for us, for those kids, for the people here?"

"Whatever I can."

"Let Forstye take you back to the motel for an hour's more sleep." He saw the protest in Sweeton's eyes, but went on. "We need you, Hummer, need you like hell. What's happened so far Brad and I can handle, you know that. It's what may happen later that's worrying me. And that's when you'll be needed. You're damned close to collapse, man. It's not fair to us—to the kids—to the people—for you to take chances. I swear to you that if something comes up and you're wanted immediately, we'll get you."

"All right," said Sweeton. He turned away, and David knew it was to hide from him the look in his eyes of a man let down by someone he trusted. "Send Garnett to me," he said.

"We'll straighten him out, Hummer; we'll straighten him out." David raised his voice. "Les!"

"Front and center!"

"The Reverend Sweeton's under house arrest. Sleep's the sentence. Drive him to the motel for an hour's more rest."

"Right."

They left by the side door, and Sweeton did not speak again, did not turn back with his usual wave of the hand.

Brad came out of the bedroom, buttoning a drip-dry shirt. "All I do is wash clothes," he said.

"Let's get going," said David. "Where's Winters?"

"Getting ready to take a shower. He'll stay here to watch the phone and write some reports. You coming with us, Chuck? My God, you look pious in that outfit."

"Which is more than I can say for either of you," said Chuck. "I'm taking my own car. Going over to the enemy camp, see what I can spy out. Also, see what I can do."

"You can't," said David flatly. "They hate your guts worse than they do ours."

"Spitting on my grandfather's grave again, that's what," said Chuck. He walked, long-legged, big, lumbering, to the car that had been David's, and waved at them as he opened its door. "With my shield or on it!" he called back, and then clambered in, awkward as a young elephant.

80

AS THEY APPROACHED THE TOWN from the west, David and Brad saw people on the porches of the homes and in the yards, standing, sitting, leaning. Some of the people waved to Brad and he returned the wave; others stood or sat without moving, silent, watching them pass without apparent emotion, and in some of the faces David thought he saw hostility. Whether the hostility was for what they had done or what they had left undone there was no way of telling, or whether it was because they had moved too fast or too slowly. Some of these houses, most of them rundown, many of them little more than cabins, he knew were home to the children in the stockade and in the jail.

At the start of the straight unpaved stretch of Calhoun Road that led to the center of town, Brad slowed abruptly. "My God," he said, without emphasis. "My God."

David put a hand on his arm. "Stop here," he said. "Pull over into the weeds and turn it around and stop."

Brad obeyed without comment, and David stepped out, turning his back to the sun just beginning to slip to the west from overhead, catching the scene before him in the full heat and blaze of its rays. "Jesus!" he said. "Sweet Jesus!"

He saw no faces, only the backs of what seemed, in that first glimpse, to be thousands of quiet, waiting people, almost unmoving in their silent grimness. There were male backs in sweat-soaked shirts and blue jeans, khaki, T-shirts gray with dust and sweat; female backs in cotton dresses, sweat-soaked like the clothes of the men, once-bright prints dark with dampness. Here and there sunshades and umbrellas held back the sun, and scarves and old straw hats, and here and there bare heads took its full attack. The crowd was faceless because each man and woman looked toward the east and the stockade where their children waited.

David stood without advancing, his feet lead weights and his belly crawling, knotting with tension.

Brad came up to him and David jerked a thumb over his shoulder, westward. "I wanta go thataway," he said. "Way back yonder."

"You think I don't? At least we can admit it to each other."

David ran somber eyes over the crowd, the backs of the quiet people. "I wonder," he said. "I wonder if they know that in Leesburg, Georgia, twenty girls, young ones like those in that stockade, were kept for a month in a single jail room without bed or blankets? Do they know what's happened to kids like that in Jackson? In Planterstown? In Birmingham? In Maryland and Virginia? Do they?"

"Of course they do, David. What are you getting at?"

"Courage. That's what I'm getting at. Courage, for God's sake. After what we've seen, Brad, I'll spit in the eye of the first man or woman who gives me the 'self-preservation is the first law of nature' routine."

Brad started forward, but David remained standing, making no move. "There's no hurry, Brad. We've got fifty years; we've got a century." He smiled, and the teeth his lips parted over were clenched.

Brad turned, waiting. "We'd better get going and account for a day of it," he said.

For the first time there was a definable sound from the crowd, a woman's high-pitched, carrying "Yoo-hoo!" and near the front of the massed people a brown arm shot up, a brown hand waved, and David thought that he could hear, more faintly, from the direction of the stockade, an answering "Yoo-hoo!", like a distant echo. He moved forward then to join Brad.

They walked slowly. They both knew that to run or seem to hurry could mean trouble. There was no sound from the crowd in front of them now except that of moving feet, shuffling, shifting to ease strain. A man on the edge of the crowd looked over his shoulder, saw them, and came to meet them, a craggy black cliff of a man. He shook hands with Brad and without waiting for an introduction turned to David.

"How you feeling, young fella?"

"Who, me?" The inanity of his own response made him smile. "I'm fine." The man must have been in the crowd last night. "Been thrown out of a helluva lot of places lately. Getting used to it."

"You're Mr. Champlin, ain't you?" asked the man. "Lawyer fella?"

David nodded.

"We been hearing about you. Jenkins is my name. They calls me Topper. Topper Jenkins." They shook hands, and the man they called Topper turned and walked between them toward the crowd. "We're doing our best," he went on. "Yessir, doing our best. Trying to make it right, do it right, till the law helps us. The law of the land and the law of the Lord. That's what Reverend Sweeton says. Tired of waiting for the law of the land to catch up with the law of the Lord; got to give it a shove here and there. We sure appreciates it, you guys coming down here."

"Getting tossed on our cans," said David. He smiled and felt some of the tension going from him. The man who had come out of the crowd to join them had made the people real, made the crowd more than a massed symbol of dark and patient anger, had divided it into individuals, men and women like him who could say "How you feeling, young fella?" and "We're doing our best." Now that Topper Jenkins had joined them the crowd had broken down into men and women, become more—and less—than a silent, brooding menace.

As they drew nearer, Topper slowed almost to a stop, and David matched his step, his limp more pronounced as he involuntarily favored bruised muscles. They were joined by a small group of people he had seen crossing a vacant lot from the other side of the section. David shook hands all around, wishing he had not heard the note of pride in Topper's voice when he said "Lawyer Champlin." Topper, Abra'm, so many he had met in the past three years, were what he called in the inner places of his mind "Gramp-oriented Negroes"; men with black skins, denied their birthright yet possessing it none the less, staking indisputable claim to universal manhood by some divine authority, and proud—warmly, deeply proud—of those of their race who had "made it." The old feeling of guilt took over, the old feeling that nothing he had become really belonged to him, that it had all been luck, a feeling that he was in some way inferior to these quiet, patient people by very reason of what he was. And with the guilt, as always, came the shyness.

He heard one of the women saying, "You mighty young to have been doing all we hears about you, Lawyer Champlin."

"Yes'm," he said, and glanced at Brad and caught suppressed laughter in his eyes. "But I'm near thirty. I just look this way."

A man in the group said, "Where's Ruby Brown? Where'd that woman get to?"

"She's here," said Topper. "She's out there in the crowd. Seen her just a bit ago. We gets her to go over to Haskin's every now and again and lie down. Been here since daybreak. She's near crazy, worrying about that girl Effie of hers. Last she seen of Effie the girl was sitting on the ground, leaning up against the jailhouse wall, holding on to her stummick. Ruby's near crazy."

"Is the girl sick?" asked David.

The woman who had remarked on his youthfulness answered. "She *been* sick; she been sick more'n a week. Doc Anderson, he say she got appendix trouble. He was planning to drive her to the County Hospital yestiddy to get 'em X-rayed, get 'em out. Then all the trouble started. Her ma come home from work early, and Effie'd done got out of the bed and gone someplace. Next thing she knowed she seen the police pushing her down the street to the jailhouse. And talking filthy. Them po-lice *sure* talks filthy." She turned to the others. "Let's go see can we find Ruby."

"Wait a minute!" Brad stepped forward, lips thin and tight. "Wait a minute. Are you saying there's a girl in that jail with appendicitis—and she's had no medical attention?"

"That's what Doc Anderson say she's got," said the woman. "Haskin and Reverend Sweeton and Doc, they tried to get the law to turn loose of her, but the po-lice say she putting it on. She ain't, but they says that."

"Once upon a time," said David slowly, under his breath, though the words were audible, "there was a great big, wonderful country, with great big, wonderful laws. And the greatest of these was *habeas corpus*—"

Brad turned to him, his eyes green ice. "Washington?" he said. "Now? Without waiting?"

"I'll wire," said David bitterly. "Yessir, I'll wire. I can do it in my sleep by now. Saves time that way. What do you want me to say, boss? 'Send the Surgeon General down'? Or maybe those Army troops they've got stationed just over the state line—"

"You think they're still there?"

"They were yesterday, according to a guy I talked to in a

restaurant. They're still expecting more trouble at the university."

Brad lowered his voice so no one nearby could overhear. "Suppose she dies? She could."

David did not answer, merely turned toward the silent people massed before the barriers and nodded his head in their direction.

"We've got to do something, David."

"Yes?" said David. The bitterness of his tone had sharpened. "Yes? Right now I'm inclined to leave it up to them."

"Pull yourself together, David. I'm talking about saving one girl's life; you're talking about something that could mean the deaths of a hell of a lot more. You out of your mind?"

"After this, maybe." He plunged his hands into his pocket, gave his head a quick shake. "All right, Chief, all right. I was only sounding off. Call Washington. It won't matter if that call's tapped. If they can't do anything else, they can send an extra supply of polish for the troops' buttons; give 'em something to do while they're waiting around up there outside Capitol City."

"Take it easy, son. When this one's over you're going to take a long rest. Let's go. These roadside sessions won't look right to the others."

As they worked their way through the edge of the crowd, David felt that the pressure of emotion was almost more than he could bear. It was like being deep in the sea with immeasurable tons of dark water above and below him, pressing on every inch of his body, constricting him so that he felt actual physical symptoms; his arteries and veins and lungs seemed to be bursting, and he felt as though his eyeballs were starting from his head.

He reached the threshold of Haskin's store just behind Topper, and the noise that came from within the store deafened him momentarily after the quiet outside. At first he saw no one in the packed room who was not talking, and he remembered Gramp saying once: "Trouble with colored is they talks too damn much."

As he followed Topper to a doorway in the rear, he saw that there were some in the room who were silent, men and women both, and he feared the ugliness in their eyes. Brad was beside him, and he put his lips close to the other's ear: "We need Sweeton here."

In the back room there were not so many people, and only a few of them were talking, but even as it was men and women filled it wall to wall. They were facing Haskin, who sat on a straight chair against the far wall, flanked by two of the other committee members. Haskin looked smaller than he had the night before; the skin of his face seemed more taut, the lines in it black and deep. Garnett was standing in front of him, bald head beaded with sweat, and his voice was a high whine as he answered something Haskin had just said.

"That's what I thought he meant!" he was saying. "I told you right!"

"You lying!" It was the shrill voice of a woman. "You ain't told him right! Get them chilren outa there! How long you think their folks gonna wait? You don' want vi'lence, vi-'lence what you gonna get you don't get them kids outa there!"

"Amen!" It was a man's voice, and David's scalp prickled at the tone. The room seemed to be occupied now by a single rage-filled entity, and David knew that someone had to act, something had to be done to break that solid, massed anger, to scatter it, and then its fragments must be gathered together and welded into something other than what he had felt when he entered, a force that had seemed to push him bodily backward through the door.

He had not been conscious of any hostility toward himself in the outer room or outside the building; here it was as evident as though they had met him with fixed bayonets. Unsmiling, he limped directly toward the tableau at the far side of the room and stood behind Garnett for a moment, gathering his forces. He could not, no one of them could, admit to any mistake, not now, not during this period of intense emotionalism. To hold leadership, to keep the reins of control, to prevent a savage, tragic outbreak that might do their cause irreparable harm, he and the others could not appear in any light other than that of their own confidence, even though that confidence must be whistled up in the dark. And somewhere in the crowd, either inside or outside, was a woman who had gone thirty-six hours without sleep, a woman whose child was suffering and ill not more than a hundred yards away and to whom she could not go. He reached for the chair from which Haskin had risen, steadied it against the wall, and mounted it.

The first person he saw as he looked out over the room

from his stand on the chair was Brad, just inside the door on the far side of the room. There was no expression in the green eyes, but the gaze was so steady and strong he felt that he could almost lean on it physically, and it was like the cool, quick comfort of a drink at the end of a rough day. There had been no time to confer with Haskin; their telephone conversation was all that he knew of what had gone on that morning in the building across the road.

Although his throat felt choked with phlegm he did not clear it because to do so might be evidence of uncertainty. He remembered Brad advising him about relaxing throat and jaw and lip muscles, and even in his own ears his voice sounded full and clear when he spoke.

"In just a little while—" he said, and as he said it he glanced at his wristwatch because he knew the gesture would give a sense of more immediate action—"In just a little while your committee will cross that street outside again, the street the whites believe separates the sheep from the goats; the street we know to be the dividing line between good and evil." Someone must be with him, he thought, because he heard a man say, "Tha's *right.*" Now he dared clear his throat, and he felt someone steady the rickety chair beneath his feet and knew that it was Haskin, standing beside him. "Let's keep it that way!" he cried. "Let's keep the good and the decent on this side, and the evil on that side! Let's not let the evil spill over, crawl across that roadway like a snake, poison us with its venom! Let the rest of the country know what Main Street is today in Cainsville—the roadway that separates good from evil!"

More of them were with him now. From all directions in the room there were responses, and from the outer room too, its babel of talk quiet, its people crowding before the open doorway to the room where he stood. There had to be more with him, all of them had to be with him, or so many that those who held back would not count.

"When I came here yesterday I felt that many of you looked upon me as a stranger." There were scattered cries of "No! No!" and his eyes sought the ones who had said it, and he smiled. "But last night! Last night when they heaved me over those barricades out there I didn't hear anyone say 'Howdy, stranger!' "

There was, praise God, laughter now.

He lowered his voice. "No man, no woman of our people,

is a stranger to us now. We have known what it is to have dogs set upon us, to be shocked with electric goads like cattle, our young people have been clubbed and beaten—and our children have been blown to bits by bombs while they studied about God in a Sunday-school class! Strangers? No man with dark skin is stranger to another man with dark skin in our country today! Even those who betray us, even those who withhold their own black hands from our cause are not strangers. Leave them to their loneliness. When we've won this fight—and we will—and they share in the victory knowing they had no part in it, they'll be lonely and ashamed." He timed his pause like a veteran, then went on, his voice easy and conversational. He might have been talking with each of them individually, over a cup of coffee at a lunchroom counter. "For every Negro in this country who's saying today 'Deal me out,' there are ten thousand, a hundred thousand, a million, who are saying 'Deal me in!' They know we're going to win this hand. And we're going to win because we hold all the aces. We hold the legal aces, that we know. But we hold more important aces. We hold the spiritual aces! We hold aces we were dealt by the law of this land, and we hold aces we were dealt by God. We have aces in our hands and up our sleeves and down our necks and behind our backs. And we're going to play those aces. But we've got to play them one at a time. One at a time. When we need them most!"

He waited again, sensing the spirit of the people before him, feeling it draw closer to him, and when he felt that it was close enough he went on, his voice rising: "Right now there's been too much talk! When your committee crosses that roadway again it will not be to talk! No! Let's stop this foolishness about talk and 'negotiating.' Let's get our children home first!"

Now the spirit of the people was more than close to him. It was engulfing him. He slid a sweating hand into his pocket, fingered his change, his key ring, the oddments a man collects, waiting for the cries to die down. "Stranger!" he said. "Let me tell you how much of a stranger I am! This morning I walked across a field near here. You call it Flaming Meadows. The whites call it something else, but what they call it does not matter, because it is your field, and it is mine. More than seventy years ago a good man met his death there, a flaming death. And his best friend went out of his mind at what he saw. How do I know that the man who died in that field was a good man? Because I've been hearing about him all my life. Because down in the part of New Orleans where I come from he is a legend. When I was a boy there were still old people alive who remembered that man, knew him well, and loved him. One of those people was his wife, my great-grandmother! Abra'm Towers's old mother, who lives in the house on the edge of that field, has a picture of my great-grandmother and her husband, the first David Champlin, my great-grandfather. I guess most of you have seen it."

He had to wait longer now for the hubbub to die down. He held up his hand to silence it, and suddenly they were quiet, so quiet his own voice sounded louder than need be, and after the first words he lowered it:

"Yes, the man who died on Flaming Meadows was the first David Champlin, a good man, a kind and gentle man, whose firstborn was my grandfather—and he came into the world three weeks after his daddy was murdered. I don't believe it was an accident that sent me here! I don't believe in accidents of God! They tell me my great-grandaddy walks the field of Flaming Meadows at night when the moon is dark. I don't know about that. But I know who does walk that field at night and in the day. God walks that field, and in a few minutes God will walk Main Street in Cainsville! God is going to take the hands of your committee in His own and lead them across that street as he led the children of Israel across the Red Sea! And when they say, 'Give us back our children and then we will talk!' God will be talking on our side!"

The sound that swept through the room and the one beyond it was like a great hoarse sigh. David's voice broke into it, above the cries of "Yes! Yes, Lord!" and "Praise Jesus!" and "Amen!"

"Come on!" he cried, and one hand was high above his head. "Come on, let's send them over there with God!" His voice sang over their heads like a wind—" 'Oh, Mary, don't you weep, don't you moan—Pharaoh's army got drownded' "—and the sound of their voices ran before it like a gathering wave.

He stepped off the chair, weak from reaction, one hand on its back supporting him. The people were still singing, and he took Haskin's arm. "Some place we can talk a minute?" Haskin opened a door behind them and they entered a smaller storeroom, piled with unopened cartons of canned goods and cigarettes and beer. They closed the door, and when David looked at Haskin he saw that the other man was smiling, that the taut look was gone. "That was fine," said Haskin. "That was sure fine."

"Thanks. First time in my life I ever led the meeting! Haskin, have any of those men on that committee—the white committee—tried to talk with you privately? Tried to trick you into talking with them alone?"

Haskin scratched his head. "I couldn't prove it," he said. "I mean I couldn't say as how this one or that one come up to me and invited me out for a friendly cup of coffee, like maybe over to the ho-tel. But now you speaks of it—" He paused, and David waited without prompting him. "Now you speaks of it, it seemed like ol' Hoot'n' Holler was a mite chummier than what he usually is. Kept a-looking at me every time he said anything, seemed like he was trying to say 'You and me understands one another.' But you gets used to that. You know how it is. All the whites thinks they understands us better'n anyone." He paused thoughtfully, then frowned at David. It was evident he was on the defensive. "We picked our men and women careful, Lawyer Champlin. Real careful. We got white men's niggers here just like they got everywhere. But they ain't over there in that room with me, I'm telling you straight. I'm a suspicious man, Lawyer Champlin, and I swear to God I don't know how that fella Garnett took me in. I guess I jest figured if he was with Reverend Sweeton he was all right."

"Never mind, Haskin. Never mind that now. And I didn't mean for a minute that I thought your men couldn't be trusted. My God, no!" He hesitated, looked at Haskin closely, and hoped that his judgment was right: that this was a close-mouthed man. "Keep what I'm going to tell you under your hat. Don't tell the others." He briefed him quickly on the Towers land deal, then said: "That's why I say if he tries to get you alone, let him—except it would be better if you at least made an effort to have one of the others there, have a witness. But if he won't go for that, then talk with him alone. If he does this, stall. Stall, and get back to us with it. But leave him with the idea you'll see what you can do about getting cooperation from the Towerses. See?"

Haskin looked at David and smiled, and David was glad this man was on their side of the fence. "Sure I see," he said. "Sure I do."

"Now about Effie Brown. She's the first order of business."

"We been trying. They ain't about to budge."

"Try some more, Haskin. Try like hell. Mr. Willis may be able to get some pressure put on."

"We'll do our best. Effie's my sister's chile. You think I ain't trying?"

"I know you are."

"About this here other business. He makes a proposition and I comes back to you guys with it and meantime you got things fixed. Right?"

"I hope so."

"And then I go back and say as far as I know it's O.K., and they lets the kids out, mebbe a little bail money to save their faces, and *then*, after the kids is home—"

"That's it," said David. "That's it. And it won't be your fault. They can't blame you. If you keep your mouth shut."

Haskin's smile was one of genuine amusement now. "That's what I call a low punch, Lawyer Champlin. A real low punch. I'd a hell of a lot rather shoot 'em down, rush them stockades, but we got no choice. Man can't shoot without a gun; man can't fight odds like they got with his bare hands, not fair and square." He laughed. "They sure teaching us a lot, ain't they? About how to do business."

"We learn fast, once we start," said David.

After Haskin left, David walked to a side window and crossed his arms on the pile of cartons that half obscured it. Over the top of the pile he could see across Haskin's littered backyard to the roadway and across the roadway to City Hall and a corner of the stockade. The singing in the outer room had died down, and there was only a low murmur of voices. He suddenly gave way to the reaction he had been fighting off, laid his head on his forearms, not wanting to watch Haskin or the others cross the roadway, not wanting to see Al Williams look toward the stockade, perhaps wave or blow a kiss to his daughter who waited behind the heavy galvanized mesh with the barbed wire strung along its top. If I could just keep it a cause, he told himself. Just keep it a cause. But I can't. It's people, little people, big people, saints and sinners, good people and plain old-fashioned country sons of bitches; it's the white men's niggers and the men like Medgar Evers; it's the Effies and the no-count bastards like Garnett. And if I could just stop thinking about the people as individuals, lump 'em all into one, into the cause, it would be a hell of a lot easier.

He did not know that Brad had entered the room until he

heard him speak. He whirled, upset, embarrassed to have been caught in a moment of such weakness. "That was fine work," said Brad quietly. "I heard part of it between phone calls."

David shrugged. "Just call me Ne'miah," he said. He looked at Brad more closely and frowned in puzzlement. What in hell was going on? What in hell had happened? He'd never seen just that expression on Brad's face before, in his eyes. "You get hold of Washington?"

"Washington's at lunch."

"Whole damned city?"

"Whole damned government, anyway. 'Luncheon conference' is the word. Maybe it will be back at its desk by the time I get to Heliopolis."

"What's happened, Chief? You look strange-like."

"Don't 'Chief' me. I've passed that title on to you. Right now I'm going to get Abraham and go out to Tether's End in Haskin's station wagon, pick up my car and head for Miz Towers. When I leave there, I'll have an option on her land. Abraham can help on that. Now here's what I've done. I've called Peg. Seems strange but it won't in a minute. I asked her to call a friend of mine, Cass Adams, who was also a classmate of mine and of Lloyd Litchfield. Told her to ask him who I meant by 'Beansy.' She was to explain something of the emergency nature of the call, of course. 'Beansy' happens to be the unfortunate nickname Litchfield had at college. Then she and Cass were to try to get hold of Litchfield and alert him for a collect call from me from Heliopolis. I'll call her first, of course, and find out where he is. By doing it that way I didn't have to mention Litchfield's name on the telephone, and the time I spend on the way to Heliopolis she can be using tracking down Litchfield. Clever?"

"Sort of."

"Well, damn it, it took some thinking, brat. Another thing. We got rid of Garnett. He's left the area, rather rapidly, I'd say. Les went back to the motel with him to help him pack. Just to be sure."

"You mean leaving town, for Cripe's sake!"

"Would you stick around if more than a thousand of your people thought you'd betrayed them, proved yourself an ally of the whites if it was easier for you? Kept their kids in a jail and a stockade a minute more than was necessary—Les and I had a little woodshed session with him out back, and you can wipe that grin off your face because we never touched him.

He'd have dropped dead of fright on our hands if we had. He's the worst physical coward I ever ran into. Anyhow, he's out of this picture. He'll bob up somewhere else, of course, but that's not to worry about now."

"Busy little character, aren't you?"

"That's not all. I've seen Ruby Brown. That woman we talked to on the road was right. She's damned near demented." Brad gave an involuntary shudder. "Her eyes are something I won't forget for a hell of a long time. It seems that one of our committeemen told her that when they asked to have Effie released, or allow Dr. Anderson to see her, Scoggins told them the girl wasn't really sick, was just putting on. He sent a matron or some damned woman over last night, and she made Effie take castor oil; said it was just plain old-fashioned bellyache."

"Castor oil! With appendicitis!"

"That's why Ruby is almost out of her mind. Anderson had told her that whatever she did she was not to give the child a physic under any circumstances. I've sent someone to ask Anderson to come over and give her—Ruby, that is—something to quiet her."

"God! Sweet God! What—"

"There's no time for philosophizing or asking rhetorical questions, David. If nothing's happened in about an hour you're to call a Dr. Hendricks, on the other side of the barricades. He's chief of staff at the hospital—"

"Damned if I will."

"You will, David. You will. You know it. They tell me he's a moderate—"

"Now I know I won't! I'll be damned if I will!"

"Go see Ruby Brown. She's in Haskin's house. You'll call."

"Anderson—"

"He'll have been here by then. He'll talk to Hendricks also; give him the medical picture. I think even the A.M.A. would gag at the publicity if Hendricks won't interfere when he's called on—"

"They don't gag easy."

"All right, all right—but Hendricks throws a lot of weight in the town; quite a politician for a doctor, I judge."

"Why hasn't Anderson been in touch with him?"

"He's been trying all day. He can't get through. They say he's been in surgery. Maybe he has. I don't care who calls him. If you can get to Chuck, let him do it. But it seems advisable to have one of our group call him, in addition to Anderson. Just get it done, for God's sake!"

David was leaning against the piled-up cartons, hands in pockets, uncomfortably sure that he was acting—and looking—like a sulky child. He started to speak, but before he could get words out Brad was across the room, hitting one of his shoulders with a clenched fist, making him wince and cry, "Hey! I'm a sick man!"

"That's just the important stuff," cried Brad. "This is the world-shaker. We're going to have a baby!"

"Yeah? Who? What d'you mean 'we'?"

"You ape! You stupid ape. We—Peg and I—the Bradford Willises—she just told me—"

David let his body slide limp along the stacked cartons until he was sitting on the rolling, splintered floorboards. From there he looked up at Brad, knowing now what the expression on Brad's face when he first came in had meant. "Sweet Jesus—" he gasped.

Brad looked down at him, green eyes warm. "Get up, brat. Didn't you think we could do it?"

"You damned fool, of course I thought you could do it. But did you have to do it now—with all this— My God, Brad!" He was on his feet now, clapping the other man on the back, laughing with him. "Best damned news I've heard since sixty-three—eighteen, that is."

"All right," said Brad. "I've got to get going. Treat me with respect hereafter. I'm in an interesting condition." At the door he turned back, sober now. "Effie—" he said. "And that girl on the bench in Little Rock. Maybe this kid'll be a girl—"

"O.K., dad. I'll call your Goddamned ofay doctor if I have to. Don't worry about a thing except how many heads it'll have and whether it will look like you."

"If it's a boy we'll name it David Champlin Willis."

"I hope to God it's light-skinned—"

"You better hope so, you brown-skin so-and-so!"

"Love to Peg when you call—"

On his way to the door after Brad left, David peered behind another high stack of cartons opposite the window, then threw the door open, and called, "Couple of strong backs needed!"

With the help of the three men who responded, the stack

of cartons was moved and a battered, upright piano revealed in all its promise, complete with stool tucked under the keyboard. David flipped the cover up, struck A, then B-flat, then C-natural, and shuddered. One of the men laughed. "Nev' mind. It won't sound so bad outside."

"Will that porch hold it?"

"That porch got cee-ment foundations. It'll hold."

The piano was on casters, and they maneuvered it to one of the front corners of the porch, setting it at an angle so that when he sat at it David could see across Main Street to City Hall on one side, and the front ranks of the now restlessly stirring crowd on the other. He wished Sweeton were there to call a meeting in Salvation Hall on the other side of the section. Anything to move the people around, give them a new perspective; then they could return to their vigil. Yet Sweeton had been so close to collapse that he must be allowed, forced if necessary, to rest.

As he sat at the piano, chording tentatively, he realized for the first time in weeks how mind-weary, bone-weary, heart-weary he was. He had thought, less than a week ago down in New Orleans, that he had reached a peak of fatigue, knew it now to have been only a stopping place on the way to the peak. Mind and body had both been pushed past the limits of endurance, yet, he reflected, they were managing to cling together like two drunks supporting each other on the brink of a precipice. "Brinksmanship," he said to himself. "By God, now I know what it really means. We're the ones who know what the hell a brink really is."

The past weeks and months and years seemed as unreal as a nightmare dreamed by another man, not lived by a flesh-and-blood David Champlin. The real David Champlin had come to life again that morning, looking out a kitchen window across a wide green field called Flaming Meadows, remembering a gentle man who had been known as Li'l Joe Champlin.

Now that David Champlin sat at a scarred, out-of-tune piano on the porch of a general store in a town called, with uncanny foresight and accuracy, Cainsville, and felt on his shoulders the burdens of a hundred years, of millions of his people, feeling, under those burdens, as old as his race, with none of its spiritual strength, none of its power. He was conscious on the physical plane of bruises on a man-handled body he had not felt before because it had been the body of another man they scarred, the body of a man dreamed in a nightmare. That other man, who had been a character in a dream, had been somehow able to go on. The man sitting at the piano on the porch of Haskin's general store wondered if the flesh-and-blood David Champlin could.

Sweat drenched the blue cotton-mesh sport shirt. He wished he had thought to tell Brad to have Abraham bring back fresh clothes. Life and death, violence, horror, bloodshed, frightened children and a desperately ill girl in a crowded jail tank—and he wanted fresh clothes, felt them to be important. He supposed he should feel shame at himself but he could not; he felt nothing but the overwhelming weariness, the ache of fresh bruises and stiffening muscles, the clamminess of sweat trickling over sore ribs, and now the reawakening of a too familiar pain in the pit of his stomach. He rubbed wet palms across the front of his shirt in an instinctive gesture to soothe pain; then his hands fell on the keyboard. He cocked his head at the sound of the chord they struck, followed that chord with another, and another. People in the crowd were calling out to him, and he knew that word of the story he had told inside had spread to every man and woman out there, passed from one person to another, from group to group, exclaimed over, talked about, by the men and women standing in grim patience under a blazing sun.

The chords came more strongly now, and a woman in the front row began to sing. "Going home . . . going home . . ." and a man in the center of the crowd picked it up. "Shouldn't have played this," David told himself. "Should have played something up-tempo. This'll bring down our guys over there in City Hall."

He had been so absorbed in his own thoughts he had paid no attention to sounds behind him. Now he felt rather than heard the beat beneath his playing. He looked over his shoulder and saw a small man seated at the shabbiest set of drums he had ever seen, and for a moment he was startled at the drummer's resemblance to Nehemiah. David grinned, and his weariness receded a little. This was what he needed, someone to give him the beat, the beat for his music, the beat for his life; he had lost that somehow.

"Hi'ya, man!" he said. The drummer, hands apparently moving without volition, head nodding in unison with the floor pedal of his bass, smiled and said, "Let's go, man." David tapped the floorboards with his good foot, and suddenly the minor strains of "Going Home" became a call to arms. There was a bugle in the sound and a trumpet, and a dozen rhythms came to life, interwoven, held, and solidified by the drum and his piano, varied, syncopated in the clapping of hundreds of pairs of hands. The voice leads changed a score of times, and no man could tell where or when. The woman in the front of the crowd who had been the first to sing took over commandingly, and the others followed, their voices a turbulent sea of harmony, the high-rising single voices the white foam that capped its waves. "Thank you, God," said David, and scarcely knew he said it.

He did not give them time to fall silent at the end of the song but made a quick slashing run on the piano, tapped his foot again, struck a crashing chord and let his own voice roll out: " 'Just a little while to stay here . . . just a little while to wait . . . just a little more hard trouble . . .' "

The songs they were singing now had once been songs of defeat, in spite of the triumphant message of their words. They had been songs that invited death as the only way out, called to it, beckoned to it. Then they had been songs that meant freedom would come only when a great chariot came down from Heaven and carried them away to rest and release from soul burdens grown too hard to bear, to a place where they would be seemly in the eyes of a color-blind God. Now the songs had a different meaning; even to the ears of the old people they carried a different message.

He thought suddenly of Simmons and Dunbar, could almost see them standing in front of him, their faces looking at him over the top of the piano, blind faces with deaf ears tacked on them. Did they know, had they learned, that these of their people whom they despised had found new songs to sing in the same old words, with the same old compelling rhythms, songs with a new meaning that substituted life for death, that did not beckon to death but beckoned instead to a freedom that could come in life, need not wait for chariots from Heaven to carry them to it?

He knew the people on the other side of the barricades would not hear what he was hearing in the voices that must be coming to them, clear and strong. He saw the head of one of the troopers bobbing to the rhythm, and doubted that the man even knew he was doing it. If God had given them the ears to hear the music—and He had not, thought David—what they would be hearing now would send them running for the hills, like a mob running before rising, pursuing floodwaters.

Out of the past, out of a gray day when he had stood outside a cemetery in New Orleans, the music he wanted to play came to him, and he finished "Just a Little While," whirled on the piano stool and asked the drummer a question and, when the drummer nodded, he turned back to the keyboard, tapped his foot. The opening chords were like a fanfare from the lead trumpet of a marching band on its way back from releasing a brother to the freedom of eternity. He kept the opening verse clearly stated in melody and verse, because he did not know whether the song was familiar to them, but knew that give them one or two verses and it would be theirs as much as it would be if they had been singing it all their lives.

" 'Sing Hallelujah! I'm walking with the King. . . .' "

The drummer knew it, and his voice was filling in responses from behind, and the people in the crowd knew it because a man's voice rose rich and strong, making the air vibrate and tingle: " 'Praise His holy name. . . .' " and a woman's voice answered him, " 'Walking with the King!' "

Now they were with him in unison: " 'Oh, the devil tries to get me . . . But I'm walking with the King,' " broke away from him . . . " 'Praise His holy name . . .' " and were with him again, " 'Walking with the King!' "

And then they were not with him but he with them, walking with them on the highway, walking with the King, marching—marching—marching, and the ache of bruised muscles was gone, the soul-destroying weariness, the burdens of a hundred years and a million people, and he was walking with them, marching with them, invincible, walking with the King. There had been a day in church many years before when a child seated with his grandfather had soared high over the heads of the people to Gloryland as his grandmother sang. . . . Now the child was marching. . . . It was his own voice cutting into the harmony of the others: " 'Praise His holy name. . . .' " And then it was the voice of the unknown man and the unknown woman, " 'Walking with the King!' "

"That's right!" he called, and changed tempo, bringing it down just a little, the drummer following him without a falter, making the tempo easier for feet to follow that were marching on a long highway. . . . . " 'Walking with the King' " . . . Giving it the steady beat of a march, and the clapping of hundreds of pairs of hands was the sound of the marching feet.

He did not feel Topper's hand on his shoulder until the older man gripped it tightly, shook it. Then he looked up and saw, in Topper's eyes, trouble. Topper did not speak, only nodded his head in the direction of the store. David let the chords die out unobtrusively, quietly, left the people singing, and followed Topper.

"We got trouble," said Topper when they were inside. "We got trouble. And we got a little wiggle of life from over yonder. They going to let one of us go in with Reverend Chuck and talk with Scoggins about Effie."

"Thank God for that much," said David. "Now what kind of trouble you got for me?"

"Mr. Brad, he just called from Miz Towers'. They got held up."

"Car trouble?"

"You wait, son. It's worse'n that. Him and Abra'm got out to that house out there you-all call Tether's End and they found Winters in bad shape. I mean, it was real bad. Beat up till he was near dead; reckon them that done it thought he *was* dead. They seen a car driving off just as they come round the turn. Mr. Brad says they was two fellas and one of them had on some kind of green shirt and did I know who it might be. I got a hell of a good idea, but that ain't knowing. Anyhow the house was all tore up, including the telephone. They done ripped that out by the roots."

"Christ! Where's Winters now?"

"They took him to Doc Anderson's in the station wagon. Doc was over here with Ruby, but he went on back over there. Didn't you-all hear that old jalopy of his a-stompin' and a-snortin' up the road?"

(*Walking with the King* . . . I was walking with the King; hell, I didn't hear anything.)

"Anyhow, Mr. Brad says to tell you him and Abra'm just now got some kind of paper signed and he's going to burn up the road to Heliopolis. Abra'm's coming back here. He says to tell you he's going ahead with the plans you-all talked about and that he'd be back this evening." Topper scratched his head, frowned. "I guess that's all. Don't think I've forgot nothing."

"It's enough, Topper. Sweet Jesus, it's plenty!"

A few minutes later, as he slipped between two sawhorses and started across Main Street, he heard a trooper say: "That's the Oxford nigger. Ah mean Oxford, England." He heard the trooper's companion answer, "Yeah? Too bad you don't mean Mississippi. They know what they're doing there, comes to niggers—"

Behind him someone else had taken over at the piano, and the deep, muted voices of the people singing "We Shall Overcome" followed him for a few steps, then changed to the song he had led when he stood on a chair in Haskin's back room. (A wide river, he remembered, its banks lined with people, all black, all singing.)

" 'Pharaoh's army got drownded . . .' " they sang, and he turned and waved.

81

As he neared the opposite side of Main Street, he noted men clustered on the veranda of the Grand Hotel, and when one of them waved and shouted a greeting, he recognized them as representatives of various news media. It hadn't taken them long; they must have burned the highways from Capitol City after an earlier call by Chuck to tip them off. Chuck was mounting the steps of City Hall when David reached the sidewalk, and he wondered if there was some lingering hope in the minds of the whites inside that Chuck's apostasy from the cause they considered holy was one that he would desert, some hope that in the end he would be guided by the light that had guided his forefathers. The great white light, thought David, the light of their world—lead, kindly light, amidst encircling gloom. He smiled when he caught up with Chuck and Chuck's hand fell on his shoulder in friendly greeting. "They send for you, too?" he asked.

"Sure did," said Chuck.

"Bring your prayer book?"

"Nope. Takes too long to explain what it means to these characters."

"Do we just barge in? Like the white folks?"

The question was answered by a tall, sober man, still young enough for the sergeant's stripes on his police uniform to cause surprise. He opened the double entrance doors and said, "You-all come in and wait." His accent was as thick as Chuck's had been when David had first known him at Pengard when he had said that all he had to do was open his mouth and they sent for the N-double-A and ALEC and the ACLU on the double. The sergeant went ahead, limping noticeably on one foot, and David saw that the ankle appeared swollen under a pressure bandage.

"Our side's not the only one with walking wounded," he muttered to Chuck.

"Tsk, tsk. Mustn't be gleeful."

Two men past middle age, dressed in civilian khakis, were patrolling the hallway with restless imprecision. They wore badges pinned to shirt pockets and gun holsters slung around their hips. Both wore green neckties. David wished he could say to Chuck what he was thinking: that no human should look that vicious, that police departments paid money to buy and train dogs with that air of anticipatory alertness that revealed their eagerness to attack.

The young policeman stopped at a door in the left wall at the far end of the hall, knuckles raised to knock, then turned to Chuck. What the hell! David could feel himself frowning with surprise and puzzled suspicion. There was no viciousness in that young face; the eyes, lightish-brown under a thatch of hard-to-control mouse-colored hair, were almost appealing. Was he scared? Did he think that with his back turned they were going to rush him, there in that hot, dusty-smelling lobby, while two wolf-type humans prowled with their ears damned near visibly cocked?

"Look, Reverend," said the sergeant. "Look. Chief Scoggins is plenty upset—"

"I don't doubt it, Eddie," said Chuck. "Right now we aim to get a sick girl seen by a doctor and released if she's not all right. And to get to see her ourselves. Her mother's plenty upset, too. We don't aim to make trouble. We were sent for."

So Chuck knew this character. Chuck was talking to him in his own language; he'd ask Chuck about him later.

One of the men patrolling the hallway came closer, and the sergeant Chuck had called Eddie turned away and this time knocked on the door they were facing.

They all look alike, thought David when a man came to the doorway at last; they all look alike: fat, thin, tall, squatty, bald or brush-cut. They don't need bedsheets and hoods for disguise; their hate is a protective coloring that makes them an anonymous, universal entity, without individuality, even physical differences blurred. This man Scoggins was standard issue, short, fat, and mottled, but he might have been the tall rangy man in the green shirt David had seen at the stockade gate, whose arm later had swung the two-by-four when David lay on the ground in front of the barrier. In Scoggins there was an almost family resemblance to a bus driver remembered from many years ago. His belly bulged fatly over an elaborate belt buckle; he was sweating heavily, khaki shirt dark with moisture across shoulders and under arms. The skin of his face bore unhealthy patches of purplish veins, and the bald expanse of skull was red. He looked past Chuck, directly at David. His voice was high-pitched and nasal. "You can go back where you belong," he said. "Now."

"Just a minute, Chief." Chuck's voice brought the hot blueness of the chief's eyes, accentuated by the unhealthy flush, away from David. Straining to catch what was behind the eyes, David thought he sensed wariness.

"Just a minute," Chuck repeated. "You sent for us. And it is my understanding that you did so to discuss the immediate release of a sick girl in your jail or medical attention for her. We are also requesting that we be permitted to see her."

To himself, David said, "Whew!" at the dangerous deepening of the police chief's color. Going to have himself a stroke; sure as hell going to if he doesn't cool down. Can't have that, can't have the son of a bitch turn into a lousy martyr. But stroke or no stroke, it was going to take the combined efforts of Scoggins, Eddie, the hallway patrol, and anyone else Scoggins could call on to get him and Chuck out of that building before Effie's case was settled.

"Doctor's there," snapped Scoggins. "Dr. Hendricks got there more than half hour ago. And we sent for Anderson to keep the niggers happy. That satisfy you?"

"No," said Chuck quietly.

There was the wail of a siren from what David judged to be the east side of town, rising, then falling, and he saw Eddie turn and limp quickly into a room at the back of the hallway.

Scoggins had moved back, his hand on the edge of the open door preparatory to closing it, but Chuck's large and competent feet were planted firmly on the threshold. Now David could see beyond Scoggins into the room behind, where the committees were meeting. He caught Haskin's eye, but could not tell if the quick smile of recognition spelled encouragement, optimism, or patience at a stalemate. The two groups, white and colored, were seated on opposite sides of a long table with a white man, fat and perspiring, at its head.

This must be Ol' Hoot'n' Holler, the mayor; he looked ineffectual and frightened, and David wondered why.

He brought his attention back to Scoggins, who was well launched into a tirade, the sense of which David could have delivered from memory at any time.

". . . you and your kind, Martin. White niggers. You all come over here to talk about getting a doctor to a sick nigger in the jail, wanting to visit her. Well, the doctor's been got. Two doctors. So there's nothing to talk about. And if this nigger pal of yours don't get the hell back over where he belongs he'll be in jail too, and I ain't saying he won't need a doctor, My belly's full of you Goddamned Commies hiding what you're trying to do under a load of bullshit about wanting to help the niggers, just looking for new ways to start trouble—"

"Hold up, Chief." The man who had appeared at Scoggins' shoulder from somewhere inside the room was taller than the chief by more than a head. His narrow, angular body was topped by a narrow, angular face; snow-white hair was plastered to a high, narrow skull. The lower half of the face showed a lipless mouth that, when closed, looked like a scar and, when open, like a hatchet wound. "I am Thomas Elmore, city attorney." When he spoke it was evident that he had lips. "The taxpayers employ me to give legal advice and counsel." He looked down at Scoggins. "My advice is that you issue these two men passes to the jail at this time."

"You let me run my own Goddamned business, Elmore. You'll be let to run yours."

Elmore gave no evidence of hearing Scoggins other than a slight inclination of his head. He looked at Chuck. "We are releasing the occupants of the stockade and jail who were arrested last night. They will appear in court tomorrow morning for fining. Those who do not appear, do not pay fines, will be picked up by county juvenile authorities and taken to the detention home in Otisville. The necessary papers will be at the jail shortly."

David felt the rage start inside, begin to consume him, and he made a conscious effort to stiffen muscles, to stop the tremor he knew could follow the rage. He looked at Chuck, and for a moment Chuck became a part of the rage, Chuck smiling with pleasure, Chuck thinking they had won a victory. Was he so damned naïve he couldn't see what was back of this? Cruelly heavy fines, crippling fines, fines that would wipe out some of those families over there. And loans to meet the fines, loans levied on pay. Unless some organization paid the fines. It wasn't ALEC's responsibility, or the N-double-A's or any other group except the YPCF, and he knew they couldn't make out a check for a hundred dollars and be sure it wouldn't bounce. In the end ALEC would pay, and start their work-stoppage project with what might be a whopping five-figure outlay just in fines.

"Cattle goads and dogs are cleaner, Counselor." His voice came from the rage, but he held it low and steady.

Nothing stirred in the gray eyes and angular face that Elmore turned on David. "There were flagrant violations of the laws, and serious, very serious, breaches of the peace. We can hardly ignore them. The young people will be released a few at a time and taken home under guard."

"You gonna stand here and—and argue with—with a damned *nigger!*" Scoggins' color had risen to the danger mark again.

"No." The mouth became a deeper scar as he opened it now to call "Eddie!"

As they waited for Eddie to come, David said, "The young people will have legal representation in court."

Elmore shrugged. "If there is someone who will—"

"I was not asking a question. I was stating a fact. I will represent them. With my partner, Bradford Willis."

Elmore, who had turned away, turned back now. "What is your name?"

"David Champlin."

The name had obviously done more than ring the well-known bell, thought David; it had struck a spark, and the spark was hot enough to bring, for the first time, color into pallid cheeks, a flare into the cold eyes. There was a second's hesitation before Elmore said, "Ah. You are David Champlin, eh?"

"Yes. But I wouldn't rescind the passes on the strength of that if I were you."

"I don't intend to." He turned away again, and this time did not turn back. "Eddie, make out passes for the jail. Scoggins, cool down. We'll go to the mayor's office where it's private, and talk. Bring the passes there for signature, Eddie."

David followed Eddie and Chuck slowly to the back of the hall, and as Elmore and Scoggins started toward a door marked "Chief," he heard Elmore say in a scratchy undertone, "For God's sake, can't you see it's the only thing to do?"

There were two drinking fountains against the rear wall over which "White" and "Colored" signs were painted. The door through which the young police sergeant and Chuck had passed was a few feet to the right of the fountain for colored. David leaned against the wall between fountain and door, while the two armed patrolmen stood at the double-entrance front doorway, looking out. Occasionally one of them would glance back over his shoulder at David. Like a pitcher keeping the guy on first honest, thought David. They were like a couple of adolescent kids, obviously given the job to satisfy their urge to participate in what was going on now. David had no doubt that should another crisis occur they would be replaced instantly by younger men.

He didn't want to think about Elmore's disclosure until he could toss it back and forth with Brad and Fred Winters; then he remembered Topper's story of the beating Fred had received. He was looking for a pay-station telephone booth where he could call Mrs. Anderson and inquire about Fred when the voices in the room near him became distinct. Glancing at the door, he saw that the spring lock had failed to engage and that the door had swung slowly open. Eddie's voice came clearly. "But—but Reverend Martin, I got to talk to someone *now*. I'd rather it was you—"

"And I appreciate it. And I want you to talk freely with me. But can't we get together when you're off duty, after Mr. Champlin and I get this mess straightened out?"

"I dassent, Reverend. I just plumb dassent. It's my job if I do and—and right now that ain't none too sure—"

"I think I know what you want to say, Eddie." Chuck's drawl matched the younger man's now. "And I think it would be right nice if you'd let me call Mr. Champlin in while you say it. As a sort of representative of his people. If there are two doctors with Effie, we have time."

"No. I—I couldn't—all right, Reverend—"

When Chuck came to the door, David was concentrating heavily on the contents of a bulletin board hung between the two fountains. Without comment he went into the narrow room with its high, sloping, old-fashioned shelf-like desk beneath a rear window. Eddie did not look up from where he sat on a high stool in front of the desk, but picked up the pencil with which he had been making out the passes and began doodling on the soiled blotter. David heard the spring lock of the door click sharply behind him, and knew they were safe from an unannounced interruption.

"Listen, Chuck," he said. "Can't we hurry this up? Even if the doctors say Effie's O.K. I'd like to get over there as soon as possible—"

"She'll be all right," said Eddie.

"I heard a siren a bit ago. Would that be an ambulance?"

"Could be." Eddie was digging into the blotter with the point of the pencil now. It snapped suddenly, and he brushed the piece of lead from desk to floor with the edge of an open hand. He still did not look at the other two men, then clenched one fist and began pounding the edge of the desk with it in an unsteady, unrhythmic thudding.

"Look!" he blurted suddenly. "Look, Reverend! What's happened? I don't know, Reverend, I don't know. I don't want no part of this. No part. I never grew up hating colored people. I got a wife and baby, and last night when I told my wife about all that happened, she cried. It ain't right, Reverend, it ain't right. We've gone crazy. We've gone plumb crazy. It ain't the colored that's gone crazy. I didn't know, didn't anyone know, what was going on; didn't none of us know how the colored felt, and now we know and everyone's scared crazy."

David looked at Chuck, caught his eye, and sensed that he was about to speak. He shook his head, thinned his lips in a voiceless admonition to silence. Eddie's fist had stopped hitting the desk, and his breathing was short and heavy. He looked directly at David now, ignoring Chuck.

"I spent two years in the Army. Two years. Made sergeant. And even when I went in I didn't mind being integrated. Some of the guys did; some of the guys from up north, too. Captain of our outfit was colored. He was the spit of you. That wasn't easy, just at first; then it didn't make no difference. He was tough, tougher'n you, but couldn't anyone say he wasn't fair. Didn't anyone tell us that if a war come up and we took to fighting, them bullets was going to come marked 'White' and 'Colored.' Didn't anyone say the big bomb was Jim Crow. I saw what happened to you last night. I saw it, and it made me sick, plumb sick."

He got to his feet abruptly, swung one muscular leg up and laid his foot on the stool. He pulled up one leg of his khakis, then rolled his sock down to show an irregularly enlarged ankle snugly bound with an elastic bandage. He was talking to both of them when he said, "There ain't nothing wrong with that ankle, ain't a damned thing wrong with it." He hit the ankle with his hand, and David could tell it was hitting something other than flesh. "We got some of those things at the house the doctors use to look down your throat with. Tongue—tongue—"

"Depressors," supplied Chuck.

"Yeah. Tongue depressors. I got me some of them and I strapped 'em round my ankle and then I put on this bandage. And I told 'em this morning I sprained my ankle in the mess last night. That's goofing off. That's a real goof-off." He smiled an unamused smile. "That way I knew I'd have to limp. They've got it all planned for more trouble. They're loaded for trouble. They've got more'n a twelve-man mounted posse all ready back of here, and they got tear gas in this morning from the city." Now he was talking directly to Chuck, and David saw that his eyes were moist. "What am I going to do, Reverend? What am I going to *do?* I got no education like you and Lawyer Murfree. They've got him whupped, whupped good. He's cutting out. But I got no place to go with a wife and kid and all. And the colored people I grew up with and thought was my friends hating my guts all the time, and I didn't know, and now I'm taking orders to treat 'em like wild animals escaped from the zoo. If I was to kill one of them colored people I been knowing all my life there wouldn't anyone say a word to me. I'd—I'd—"

"Make captain," said David.

"I would, and that's a solid fact. Reverend, whatever am I going to *do?*"

Looking at Chuck's worried face, David mentally gave thanks he'd never felt a call to the ministry. Taking care of troubled souls must be a hell of a lot harder in some ways than fighting in the ranks for decency and justice. He'd be damned if he could see what Chuck could tell this tormented youth. Stall him, that was all he could do; stall him off until they could see Effie. Even if two doctors had seen her, even if the kids were all to be released soon, he'd feel better to get over there and find out for himself, offer to take her to Capitol City, to County Hospital, if it would help Anderson.

"Ride it out, Eddie," said Chuck quietly. "Ride it out on that phony limp and let me think about it. We'll manage somehow to get together and talk, even if you have to arrest me. There's always an answer, Eddie. Remember that. There's always an answer when a man wants to do what's right. Perhaps God doesn't make it easy, but He always makes it possible." Chuck laughed gently. "Just hop along on that homemade sprained ankle and get those passes signed so we can get in to see Effie, help her get out if she—"

It happened so quickly David felt nothing but blank shock for a second. Eddie turned from them, and his fist crashed to the desk; then he swung around, his face contorted, eyes wide and filled with moisture.

"Effie," he whispered. "Effie! God help us all, Reverend. That girl's dead. That pore girl's dead."

For an immeasurable moment in time following Eddie's broken whisper, there was a vacuum-like silence in the hot little room. Then Chuck, face dead white, made a run for the door. David did not rely on words, but on brute strength, pulling the big man back, holding his arm tightly. "Wait." He did not raise his voice. "Wait, Chuck. Wait."

He turned to Eddie, who was standing with his back to them, fighting for composure.

"When? When, Eddie? When did she die? For God's sake, answer me!"

When Eddie turned, his eyes begged for understanding and pity, found neither.

"Answer me! When did she die?"

"Just before you-all come over. I sent for the doctor myself without no orders when I saw how bad she was. She—she died just after he got there. She—she's got—she had what they call congenital heart trouble. Doc Anderson was trying to get her ma to let him fix it up somewhere in Philadelphia for an operation. I been knowing that little girl ever since she was a little brown tyke in pigtails coming to our house with her ma—"

"Never mind that! Who knows about this?"

"Only Scoggins and Elmore and the mayor, and the head jailer and the doctors. They put her in a separate cell in the adult section. I called the chief out of the meeting and told him, after the jailer called. He called the other two out. They ain't told the others. Reckon that's why they decided to turn the kids loose. Get 'em home and the people away from the barricades before they let anyone know about—about Effie. And Elmore, I suppose he figured you-all better go over there and help keep things quiet until—"

"Keep things quiet! For Christ's sake! That ambulance siren? They were coming to the back entrance for the body, weren't they? They'll carry a dead Negro, not a dying one. Right?"

Eddie nodded. "They were going to take her to the white mortuary, leave her there till the kids were out and things quieted down. I—I called over when I heard the siren. I didn't say right out the chief told me to, but I reckon they thought so. I—I told 'em to send the ambulance away. That white undertaker, he hates colored. I couldn't let—"

"It's too Goddamned bad you didn't come down with nobility earlier," snapped David. "You knew she was sick. Too damned bad risking your job didn't do somebody some good."

"Take it easy, David." Chuck's urgency was controlled now. "Eddie, you did what you could, what you had to do. Now get those passes signed so we can get over there."

Chuck closed the door after Eddie left and said, "David, suppose I go to the jail and you go back over and get hold of Hummer, tell him to find Ruby and stick close to her—"

"Better if I find him and tell him the truth, then ask him to get those people over to the back of town, into that big hall. They can take the kids there in trucks. He can take Ruby with him, let someone else take over at the hall, then get her home and tell her—"

"God help him," said Chuck.

Eddie, when he returned, gave David his pass first, not looking at him, and David said: "Thanks, Sergeant. I'm short-tempered right now. You've been swell."

"That's O.K." He handed Chuck his pass and said: "Look, Reverend. As soon as we turn the kids loose, I'm going home. Me and the wife will figure something out. And—and thanks—"

"I'll see you later, Eddie. At your house, maybe."

"Maybe." Suddenly Eddie smiled, and David saw the guy who'd made sergeant. "Maybe, Reverend. They make fine bombs in these parts. For amateurs—"

As they started out the door of City Hall, the two men with guns moved aside, as people must once have moved aside from lepers carrying bells. On the top step Chuck touched David's arm. "Let's give the situation a quick run-through, be sure we know what we're doing—"

There was no air stirring. The heat of the setting sun was as scorching as that of a noon sun. David looked across the street at the people still standing behind the barricades. Somewhere in the crowd an arm was raised, a hand waved in greeting. He raised his own arm in return. It was like lifting a dead weight.

He glanced toward Haskin's store and saw Abraham Towers with a group of men; then one of the group moved to the porch railing, waved, and shouted a greeting. It was Luke Willis. David felt an unreasonable sense of relief at the sight of the boy; whatever Luke's faults, he was always unquestioningly there when a job had to be done, and there would be many to be done before this day and night were over.

Below them, on the stoop of the police station, Dr. Anderson and a white man carrying a doctor's bag were standing. He started to speak to Chuck, to point them out, but Chuck did not give him a chance. "Cuss for me, chum. We're too late. Look—"

Across the street Hummer Sweeton was just straightening up after ducking under one of the barricades He stopped, spoke briefly to the policeman guarding it, and then was walking rapidly across the street on a diagonal course to the police station and jail. "Hummer!" called Chuck, and the little man slowed but did not stop. He smiled, waved, and hurried on. "He doesn't know," muttered David. "They've called him over to tell him. Who the hell—"

"Eddie," said Chuck. "The poor guy. He must have called after we left. He's burning his bridges. Doing all the wrong things for the right reasons—"

"We'd better get down there. No sense— Oh, God! Look now!"

A short, heavily-built woman had squeezed around one end of the barrier and was talking to the guard in a high-pitched, carrying voice. David caught the words "Reverend Sweeton," and saw the guard shrug and send her over with a jerk of his head. She began to run, trying to catch up with Sweeton, but she was short-legged and awkward and Sweeton was already on the stoop talking with Anderson and the other doctor before she was halfway across.

"Eddie may be getting right with God, but he sure as hell is messing things up," said David. "That's Ruby Brown. We both better go down there. Don't run. Take it slow and casual or those people over there will sense something."

They started down the steps, Chuck saying, "You think I grew up down here without knowing your people wouldn't sense something if we just walked along whistling. They know something's up already."

The heat seemed to have sucked all sound out of the air, but the whinny of a restless horse from somewhere back of City Hall came close and loud. Even the young people in the stockade, pressed close along the length of its fence, were quiet. A boy's voice cut the quiet, calling to them, "Hey, when we going to get out of here?"

Chuck called back, "Pretty soon, kid, pretty soon."

David did not take his eyes from the scene on the stoop of the police station; he spoke to Chuck without looking at him. "Hell's on its way again, Chuck, and these bastards over here are primed for it. Another week and we might have had a chance at— *Let's go!*" He started to run, Chuck outstripping him. He had seen Sweeton try to draw Ruby inside the building, seen her break away and run to Anderson, pound his chest with clenched fat fists, head thrown back to look at him, eyes white-rimmed and staring.

Ruby's first scream was a bayonet in his belly, stopping him, draining all thought and strength with its pain. The screams that followed were blinding, like forked lightning in a black, starless sky; deafening, like thunderbolts directly overhead. For an aeon there was nothing in the world but the screaming of Ruby Brown whose child lay dead in the jailhouse.

82

THE WORST OF IT WAS over just after dark. The tide of yelling humans that had roared through the barriers at Ruby's screams had receded. The horses were gone, and the men with clubs and whips who rode them into flesh and bone; the tear gas and the goads were gone, and the dogs. Soldiers, white and black, patrolled the sidewalks, and jeeps drove slowly through the dusty roads and along Main Street, their heedless wheels smearing and obliterating the thick dark patches that gleamed moistly under the lights. They had used a hose for what lay on the pavement between Haskin's store and City Hall, and David, standing on the store's porch, had cried out, "Let it be!" There had been a touch on his arm and Chuck's voice saying, "Come inside, David."

Now, after dark had fallen, he sat where he had more than

twenty-four hours before: at the end of the dining-room table in Haskin's dining room, one hand slapping steadily on the worn wood. But tonight no hand could quiet it, as Gracie's had then, not that of Gracie, who touched it lightly and turned away, defeated; not Brad's on his shoulder. He did not look at Chuck when he heard the low voice say, "Easy, chum. Take it easy. They've hanged themselves this time."

When he finally stopped the soft slap-slap, it was to cover his face with both hands, the table supporting his elbows, supporting him. Not all of what had happened was clear and sharp in his mind. He could not have told how many horses charged into Main Street from around the corner just above City Hall, and drove the people back from the area in front of City Hall, heedless of those who fell, nor how many there were in the second group that deployed along the eastern side, driving the people back, the riders slashing with whip and club, the horses rearing back from contact with soft, yielding flesh but goaded on by spurs.

Before the front runners of the Negro ranks from across Main Street had reached the eastern sidewalk, David saw Anderson pick Ruby Brown up bodily and carry her inside the jail, Hummer and the white doctor following. There was no chance now of reaching the jail. David feared for Chuck. Not all the Negroes could possibly know him, and the rocks and bottles being thrown now had only one general aim, whites. He kept his back to the stockade fence, his hand on Chuck's arm, said, "Back the way we came. We'll cut over above City Hall—" Then Eddie was there, running stiff-legged, wincing with real pain caused by the edges of the makeshift splint that were cutting into his flesh above the shoe top. This was not the fearful, agonizing youth of a few moments before, but a man in police uniform, one hand on the gun at his hip, the other carrying a regulation club, a man who had "made sergeant" at a younger age than most.

"You-all make a move to get into that mess and I'll wing you—"

The young prisoners in the stockade were screaming, massed at the fence where fingers were interlaced so thickly in its meshes they looked like clusters of brown grapes. One boy, shoes off, agile as any monkey, already had climbed close to the top, and was going to brave the barbed wire. Eddie stretched body and arm to their utmost, rapped sharply but not viciously on the knuckles of the clinging hand. "Get down from there, Jerry, y'hear! Y'all goin' to get hurt—" The boy stopped his climb, looked down at Eddie's upturned face, and spat.

The first contingent of horses came then, sweeping the people down from the City Hall area, then on their heels the second contingent, single-filing down the eastern sidewalk, a horse wheeling across from each intersection to charge into the crowd. There were people lying on the pavement now, some of them struggling to their feet again, others crawling toward the opposite side of the street. A young Negro in a striped shirt was running toward the Greyhound station, and when he saw that it was Willy Haskin, David gave a hoarse, involuntary shout of warning as he saw the horse that was following him. Willy was driven over the sidewalk, fell, and crawled into a corner by the station steps, and David saw the hoofs of the rearing horse plunge downward, saw the swinging whip in the rider's hand. A surging movement of the crowd obscured the scene for a moment, and when the steps were visible again horse and rider were charging back into the milling group in the center of the street. He saw Willy's hand reach up gropingly and grasp the edge of a step, saw him pull himself painfully half upright; then two men came from inside the building and lifted and supported him until they reached the inside of the station. The blood was clearly visible on face and body. He's alive, thought David. He's alive. And now he'll always fight like a cornered animal, always, wherever he is. More power to him, more power to him—

Main Street was comparatively quiet in the wake of the horses, all the pandemonium concentrated in the area below Calhoun, in front of the stockade and the police station and below. David could see that horses had followed Negroes who fled from them down the side streets, did not need to see to know that the horses would overtake many, some in their own yards, on their own porches.

The haunch of a wheeling horse just in front of them threw him against the stockade fence, knocking his breath from his lungs, and he needed Chuck's support for a moment as they edged along the fence, working their way back to the area in front of the City Hall.

"Where's Eddie?" asked Chuck. "Where is he?"

David leaned against the wall of the building, still fighting for breath. "Damned if I—" then pointed in the direction from which they had come. "There. Bleeding like a stuck pig."

By the time he reached them, Eddie had succeeded in slowing the flow of blood from a deep forehead gash. It had been made by a sharp-edged rock. David recognized the type of wound. Eddie said, "Stay where you are." David watched him mount the steps of City Hall, saw three men in khaki come forward. "Who's in charge here?" snapped one. A fourth stood quietly at the railing of the porch just above them.

"I am. Scoggins is down at the jail directing action."

"Want us to take care of those niggers you got there? Both of 'em? White and black?"

"Who sent for you?"

"No one. We're just li'l ol' taxpayers, keeping niggers off city property. There's more of us inside. We just took five niggers across the street. Them committee niggers. Elmore told us to. Son of a bitch if I ever thought I'd see the day I'd be giving safe conduct to a bunch of trouble-making niggers. We're sure getting soft."

David considered making a break for the other side of the street, but knew he'd be worse off than a sitting duck. Eddie was doing the best he could, keeping at his job because it suited his purpose at this time, following orders in his own way. David was sure Eddie had been on his way to the jail to deliver the release orders for the children when the riot had broken out and had realized it was out of the question for the time being.

Eddie was speaking again. "Never mind how you feel. Just don't forget, you're guarding property; you ain't here to start something new."

Looking up, David saw Eddie limp to the man standing at the railing just above them, heard him say, "How you like it, Underwood? How you-all like it now?"

The man called Underwood spoke so low it was difficult for David to catch the words. "I don't, son. I don't. Ruby Brown damned near raised our kids after my wife took sick. Get going, Eddie. I'll take over here."

Eddie turned, walked to the top step, and said quietly, "Underwood's in charge till I get back."

Hours later, sitting in the Haskin dining room, David remembered these things with reasonable clarity, the edges of the events blurred and made hazy by the sounds of the fighting and violence that were their background. But what had followed Eddie's quiet order was sharp and shatteringly clear in his mind, without merciful blurring or forgetfulness, and the sound of Ruby Brown's steady, monotonous sobbing had been the acid that etched the details into his brain. It came from behind him, and he turned and saw Hummer Sweeton and Dr. Anderson, Hummer supporting Ruby, who walked stumblingly between them. They were making their way along the sidewalk outside the stockade fence. Chuck said, "Couldn't they have sent her home by car, the back way—" and David growled, "When're you going to quit talking about these people as though they were human. She's lucky not to be in jail—" Beside the three an impassive trooper walked as escort. Before they reached David, they started across the road, and David saw Abraham Towers start down the steps of Haskin's store with Haskin, Mrs. Haskin, and Gracie just behind him. David walked quickly to Hummer, and the little preacher's sunken, tragedy-darkened eyes lighted. "David."

"What can I do to help, Hummer?"

Hummer shook his head, tightened his arm around Ruby. "Nothing, son. There's nothing anyone can do about it now. Doc's getting her over to the hospital." Ruby's sobs increased and, as her screams had done earlier, blocked from hearing the sounds below them.

"Come on," said the trooper. "It's dangerous here."

Hummer nodded and gently urged Ruby forward. Anderson's eyes met David's. They were bleak and cold, the devils behind them no longer subdued. "If you can, come over to the hospital later, David. Bring your boy, Luke." David nodded. There would be pictures for Luke in that hospital tonight, pretty pictures all in color.

Mrs. Haskin and Gracie ran past Abraham Towers, who, with Haskin, stood waiting at the edge of the pavement. "Let me," said Mrs. Haskin, and took Ruby into her arms, Gracie shielding them both as they made their way across. Anderson hurried after them. David turned and looked back at City Hall, trying to catch Eddie's eye, saw the young sergeant standing in the doorway with his back to them, talking to someone inside. When he turned back, Hummer was alone, the trooper dog-trotting toward a running group of Negroes, to herd them toward the west side of the street.

"We'll be over in a minute, Hummer," he said. "They were going to release the kids when this broke loose. We want to make sure there hasn't been any mind-changing." He wanted desperately to offer some word, some gesture of comfort to Hummer, but could only shake his head futilely. Hummer's smile was distilled sorrow as David and Chuck started away, and at the steps of City Hall David looked back and saw that the little preacher's walk had slowed. As though feeling David's eyes on his back, Hummer turned his face toward them, and lifted his hand in the familiar, gentle gesture that was half salute, half blessing.

Hummer's body did not crumple slowly to the ground, but struck the pavement as though he had fallen from a great height, and the crack of the gun that felled him came at the same instant.

It was all as clear now as an image seen in a flawless mirror, as sounds heard on stereophonic tape: Chuck's hoarse, half-crazed whisper at his side, "No, God; no, God; no, God; no, God—" and the way Hummer's blood had flowed slowly, not spurting, down and over one side of the dark forehead, filling the deep eye socket, the hollow of the cheek, flowing richly, redly, to the pavement. The gaping exit hole from which it spilled showed more than blood, showed splintered bone and the yellow-gray mucoid patches that had been Hummer's brains, and these things had splattered the pavement around his head in the brief instant of his fall.

David ran forward, but Abraham Towers was quicker, and when David reached the body Abraham was on his knees beside it, both hands on the pavement, Hummer's blood flowing, more slowly now, over black knuckles and fingers. David said "Abra'm—" but Abraham did not hear—or, if he heard, did not heed. The big man gathered Hummer's body into his arms, stood tall and straight and alone with his burden for a moment, his face a dark mask of pain and horror; then he moved toward those who waited, and Hummer's head rolled gently against his shoulder, the ruin of it hidden against the blue denim of his shirt. The exposed profile under the small red entrance hole in the temple was as peaceful and quiet and content as a tired child's, eyelid half open, waiting sleep.

His thoughts then were remembered now, in Haskin's dining room, in the same bitter sequence. The barn, the old barn turned warehouse, and the story of the World War I snipers. Where Hummer had been standing was in direct line with the doors of the former hayloft, and just after the shot David had looked up, backing away as he did so, and saw that they had been swung half open, saw the glint of the sun on a rifle barrel, and saw behind it, indistinct but unmistakable, the bright green of a man's shirt.

There was a second blast of gunfire, closer than the first, three shots this time, and a poster beside the hayloft doors advertising "Pep-U-Up" showed three holes in almost exact alignment. The angle of the rifle barrel behind the hayloft door changed, lost the glint of the sun as it was withdrawn slowly, eerily, by the unseen hand on its stock. On the porch of City Hall the man Eddie had called Underwood was holstering his gun. The three other men had moved away from him, and he stood alone in the center of the porch.

Chuck, gray and sick with shock, was waiting. Eddie had held him back with an expert grip, but now he released him, running up the steps, his voice rasping and harsh as he said, "You see, Underwood? You see now? You see what I mean—?"

"I see. Leave the trigger-happy son of a bitch to me, Eddie. I gave him notice to get the hell down. I'll talk to him when he—"

"Talk! *Talk* to him?"

David did not wait for any more, said to Chuck, "Let's go. We can't accomplish anything here now—"

They walked slowly, and David kept his eyes straight ahead, not looking at what he knew was on the pavement at his feet. As they drew near Calhoun he saw Haskin and Gracie half carrying Ruby Brown to Anderson's car. He could hear again the keening of her sobs, and said to Chuck through stiff lips, "Were you there, Chuck, were you there—"

"Yes, Lord, I'm here—"

He had heard someone, probably Gracie, place coffee on the table while he sat there, and he raised his head now and drew the cup toward him. When it came to a certain kind of chips-down guts, he thought, women have us all whipped. It had been Mrs. Haskin and Gracie who had stripped the sodden shirt and undershirt off Abraham Towers, washed Hummer's blood from the massive black chest, forced a powerful slug of whiskey on him, known best what to do when he broke and the shuddering cries had come from deep within him.

The call to Washington was made by Brad within minutes after his return from Heliopolis. "Two dead," he had said. "One of them Humboldt Sweeton. Numerous critical injuries and no adequate hospitalization . . . Snipers . . . Mounted posses . . . Uncontrollable rioting . . ." His voice had gone on, while David, leaning against the wall beside the telephone, had said, "Save your breath, Chief. Save your breath—"

But the jeeps had come, and the trucks, and the mobile hospital unit, but not before two Negro boys had been dragged from hiding and beaten to a bloody pulp on the City Hall porch while a young police sergeant named Eddie who had tried to interfere lay unconscious nearby; and not before David Champlin had crouched on the floor of a pickup truck beside the frighteningly quiet form of Luke Willis, calling to the driver, "Mind the bumps, Les; for God's sake take it slow and mind the bumps!"

Brad came into the room, a glass in each hand. He handed one to David, saying, "I can't get through to Anderson on the phone—"

"I know. It's a madhouse."

"I saw Hummer's body—"

"Well?"

Brad did not answer, and David said again, "Well? Aren't you going to say they can't get away with it?"

"No. They can."

"Effie. Hummer. Maybe Willy Haskin. And Fred. And another guy. Maybe our kid Luke—"

"What happened to Luke, David? I've only had a sketchy account."

"Ever watch a polo match where a man's head was the ball?"

"For God's sake, no!"

"The crazy bastard, the crazy, damfool bastard. He ran into the center of the street and focused on the horses, two of them, coming toward him hell-bent. He was running backward. He sidestepped the first horse, but not in time, and you could hear the crack of the club on his head clear over here. God knows why it didn't knock him cold, but it sent him staggering, and the guy on the second horse, coming up from behind, finished the job. He shouldn't have been moved, but we had to."

"Who's 'we'?"

"Haskin and someone else—I don't know who it was—and I. And a guy from the police department named Eddie. That was just before they knocked him out. Eddie, that is."

"Anyone see that happen?"

"Haskin says he did. Happened while we were getting Luke to Anderson's."

"Luke's camera?"

David gave a short bark of laughter. "Stupid. As I said before, they're stupid. It was still slung around his neck. It's in Anderson's safe. The film's intact, I'm sure. I'll get it and unload it and send it north in the morning. When Luke comes out of it, he'll give me hell for not getting it there tonight. On foot if necessary."

"When." Brad finished his drink with one swallow. "When Luke comes out of it. What does Anderson think?"

"He wouldn't say. That's why I have to go over, unless we can reach him by telephone."

"David, he may need brain surgery."

"For God's sake, you think I don't know! But where? How? By Anderson? With only his wife to assist? Or by a couple of interns at County in Capitol City?"

"A plane, David, a plane. Chartered. I understand that Fred and the other man who was in bad shape are both on their way to the Veterans Hospital in an Army ambulance."

"By God! By God, that's good! It's sure a wonderful thing to have worn a uniform! When the guys you wore it for damned near club your brains out while you're defenseless and alone as Fred was—you get to go to the hospital for free. Sure makes a guy feel good. Secure like."

"Easy, brat, easy."

David took his jacket from the back of a chair as Brad asked, "What about Willy Haskin?"

"Anderson says he can handle Willy's case there. Lucky he was hurt early. There was still a bed. Now the Army's here, they'll help with supplies and stuff, I imagine. They doing first aid?"

"Yes. All that we can channel to them. I suppose Anderson still has his hands full, though."

"About that plane?"

"I'll call Shea. I don't know what chance I'd have in Capitol City."

"Shea have 'em on tap?"

"No, but he's a fast worker when his Irish is up. And I'll get through to Luke's magazine, have them line up hospital and surgical care."

"I'll phone from Anderson's."

"Better take someone with you."

"I'll go alone."

"I wouldn't—"

"God damn it, I'll go alone!"

"Right, David." Brad spoke easily; only his eyes, as he watched David leave, showed worry.

The streets were quiet and dark, the yards and porches empty except for an occasional group talking at a gate or on a porch, but there was no laughter, and from open windows no music, only the stylized syllables of a radio reporter's voice, telling the rest of the country about the night's events in Cainsville. "Tell 'em about it, boy," muttered David. "Tell 'em about it. Tell 'em all about the southern way of life."

He was stopped three times by soldiers, explained his business and where he was going, and was waved on. Their faces were impassive, the not-to-reason-why impassivity of the trained military man. Only the Negro patrol who stopped him showed any sign of cognizance of the situation.

"Glad you're here," said David.

"Me, too. I come from Otisville, twenty miles north of here."

"The hell you say!"

"Man, this duty's doing my li'l black soul good. Really strengthifying it. Here's the Sarge. Get going, friend—"

There was more semblance of order in the hospital when he entered it now than there had been when they carried Luke in. Minor injuries were being cared for at a first-aid table set up in the waiting room by a young man in heavy horn-rimmed glasses wearing a blood-stained white doctor's coat over levis and cotton undershirt. The boy, thought David, must be the one who was headed for Howard, whom Brad was helping out on the scholarship. All of those with major injuries must have been put to bed by now, either upstairs or in the "front parlor" where Luke had been put because Anderson had not dared to have him carried up the stairs.

Mrs. Anderson came from the back of the house, face set and taut with strain, eyes preternaturally bright.

"Mr. Champlin—"

"I came to find out about Luke Willis."

"Doctor's dressing a bad bite wound now. He'll be free—"

"Mrs. Anderson, can't we forget the hospital-type formalities? The doctor-will-discuss-it-with-you routine? You must know as much as he does about it."

She nodded, and for a moment he saw weariness take over her body, saw the straight shoulders sag. Then she became taut again and walked past him toward the front room. "Let's go in and you can see him."

Luke lay on an Army cot in the dimly lit room, eyes closed in what might have been a deep sleep. David's throat tightened in fear and he pushed past Mrs. Anderson. Her hand on his arm stopped him before he reached the cot.

"He's alive, Mr. Champlin." She bent and took one slack wrist in her fingers, nodded, and straightened up.

"How bad?"

"Pretty bad. We're trying to think of some way—"

Outside the room a man called, "Ada!" and she hurried to the door. Anderson entered when she opened it, closed it carefully, then leaned against it, eyes closed. "That kid's leg, Ada. That kid's leg was bitten clear through. Muscles and all. And all he was doing was running, looking for his parents." He opened his eyes, saw David and said, "Hummer and that kid, the very young and the old. It doesn't matter, does it?"

"Not to them. But it does to us, Doctor. We've got a feeling for kids and old folks—"

Dr. Anderson shook his head violently, said, "Bah! It's just as well none of their wounded came here this night. If they had any."

"They did. A few. One of 'em was hurt by his own. Hit over the head, they tell me, when he tried to stop a half-dozen guys from beating up a couple of colored kids. Young police sergeant."

"Eddie? Hell, no! He was—never mind." Anderson walked to the cot where Luke lay, took the pulse as his wife had done, pulled back the lids of the eyes.

"Doctor, if he needs surgery, Brad Willis is getting a chartered-plane standby."

"There's no question about it. It may not be the only hope, but at the moment it seems to be."

"It will take a little time—"

"That's not even a calculated risk. It's an inevitable one."

"I'll go phone Brad and I'll go along to wherever they take him."

As Anderson walked to the front door with him a few minutes later, David asked, "How's Willy Haskin?"

"I think he'll do. There are internal injuries, but he and Luke have one good thing going for them. They're both young."

"Not now, Doctor. Not anymore—"

When he talked to Brad from Anderson's office, he told him he would go to Tether's End and pick up enough clothes to take north.

"You're going with Luke?" asked Brad.

"Yes. Till we see what's what." He thought he heard Brad say, "Thank God."

"Right. Can you get back here to Haskin's in, say, three quarters of an hour?"

"Sure. How we going to get Luke out of here?"

"Army ambulance, and the Army just told me there's an emergency field ten or fifteen miles east."

"You mean you've ordered the plane already?"

"Shea's going to. He'll either get one or the magazine will. Probably out of Capitol City."

"See you later. Good going—"

He drove slowly at first after he left the hospital, drawing the quiet of the night into his lungs, wondering if his bloodstream could distribute the quiet, like oxygen, to his jangled insides. Every house was lighted, and he could hear in his mind the endless talk behind the windows, in kitchens, and bedrooms, over coffee, over beer. With some the talk would be fearful, but not so fearful as it once would have been. With others, the talk would be angry, but not so angry as it once would have been, because now anger was no longer futile, a tortured, helpless thing, impotent. The chains had snapped tonight in Cainsville. Anger, freed, had brought men and women strength and hope. They had dead to bury, blood to staunch, but that night had shown them nothing they dared not face again, and thinking of it David felt his own being grow stronger, the sick weariness lessen.

At Tether's End he groaned aloud at the shambles that was the main room of the house, and at the blood that spattered floor and walls. Fred Winters, quiet, elegant Fred Winters, must have put up one hell of a fight, and David smiled in spite of his shock.

He gave up the idea of a quick shower; the homemade, tricky mechanism of that Rube Goldbergish arrangement in the lean-to might result in trouble and delay. Instead he satisfied himself with a once-over-lightly at the kitchen sink. There was fresh milk from Miz Towers's cow in the refrigerator, and he drank it slowly, knowing that in a few minutes the cramping pangs in his stomach would ease. As he changed clothes and packed the few things necessary for the trip, he thought again of the people of Cainsville, and of the new dimension of living into which they had traveled that night. They would not seek another horror such as the one they had just passed through, but they would meet it if it came. It had not been of their choice, had not, God knew, been planned. It had been set off by the young people, impatient at their elders, not knowing with any exactitude what they had been fighting for, any more than Billy, the wide-eyed boy at the picnic, had known because they had not lived the decades of oppression and poverty that their elders had. Yet, at the scream of a woman whose child lay dead of neglect and indifference, those faceless decades had been obliterated and the people who had poured in fury through the barriers had been human beings, no longer anonymous, no longer just "the nigras," but men and women made conscious of their birthright in the blinding, deafening sounds of a woman's screaming grief.

A Murfree, an Eddie; David wondered how many generations must be born, grow old, and die before there would be enough Murfrees and Eddies, and answered his own question without hesitation. There would never be enough, not in North or South, and the Negro who faced that fact, who, while acknowledging his debt to them, continued his fight in what would always be a climate of lonely alienation, was the strong Negro. He would always face an enemy; only the ranks of the enemy would change, grow less, become so weak by the infiltration of the Murfrees and the Eddies it could not hold him back. And that would take a hell of a long time. Not all of Pharaoh's army would be drownded; there would always be those who escaped the waters and lurked in the hills to wage guerrilla warfare from generation to generation.

There should be a new mind born, he thought as he walked down the steps and toward the car, a new mind for the human race; a clean new mind, oh, God, a fresh new mind on the altar of the Lord, a clean new mind all freshly polished—

He had not reached the car when he saw the headlights turn into the roadway from the south, and seconds later a searchlight blinded him. The first shot cut his legs from under him; the next slammed into his shoulder before he hit the ground, spinning him around. He fell face down, his one good arm outstretched, hand grabbing at the unyielding ground, trying to pull his body forward, toward the house, away from the running feet, the shouts, the insensate laughter. There was no pain yet from the bullets, but now there was pain from blows and kicks on head and spine and face, and there was rage at his own helplessness. Terror mingled with his rage at a new sound, the low, fury-filled snarling of dogs, very close. The shouts of the men took on new tones. There was a crashing blow on his skull, then darkness.

83

SARA SLEPT INTERMITTENTLY, with maddening indeterminate spells of half-wakefulness, thinking bitterly how easy it was for Hunter Travis to say "Get some more sleep, luv—" The city beyond her windows was taking form in gray light when she forced herself to full wakefulness, sitting up in bed, legs drawn up and held by tensely folded arms, chin on knees. She felt without identity: "an unidentified object in a waste place," she told herself. She knew she would have felt the same in Paris, New York, Rome, Chicago; she was in London, where she thought she had established a branch of her being and it made no difference. Düsseldorf? Would she be feeling the same if she were in Düsseldorf with Chris, a Chris whose eyes had not yet shown the pain and shock of her rejection of him? Was this feeling of complete aloneness, of being without living ties to the rest of the world and the people in it, one of simple loneliness that could be quickly, easily banished by a sleepy, maybe grumpy breakfast with a man who knew she wanted a little cream and lots of sugar in her coffee, whose only intrusion on her mood would be light words, a light kiss, because he loved her. "It would be hell," he had said. "Sheer hell. For me. For you . . . Go, my dear, quickly."

She rested her forehead on her knees, rocking her head back and forth. "Please, God, make it the right thing that happened, make it be the right thing. Make me know it was right and be content—" Yet how could she be content when no place was home; for the likes of you, she told herself, there is no home place; even a hungry alley kitten has a dark, secret hole where it feels secure, where it can tuck in its paws and rest. She had told herself this so often before, so damned often, and fought the self-pity off, fought back to reality and work.

Work. And more work. And the anodyne of creating. These would answer the needs of the moment, even if the greater need of a whole life remained unanswered.

While she was waiting for Hunter the afternoon before, she had telephoned the woman who cleaned her studio for her. She would meet her there at nine, and together they would tackle the job, sweeping, dusting, scrubbing, and before the day was over she would shop. She needed canvases. Itemizing things she needed always made her sleepy, and she straightened out in bed, punching the pillows as though they were bitter enemies, settling back. Canvas, cleansing cream, washing powder, shampoo, toothpaste—the kind Chris—Hell! Oh, hell!—toothpaste, the kind *she* liked, some of those sweet biscuits to nibble on in the studio—

The news was in the paper they brought with her tea at seven thirty, the headline snatching her attention from all else, a headline containing the words: "U.S."—"Riots"—"Dead."

Two known dead, the story said, in a racial disturbance in a small southern town, several more on the critical list, including a former Oxford student, David Champlin, who had given up a promising career with his country's State Department to aid in the struggle—

The cry her clenched fists tried to muffle at her lips was dry and hoarse. She could hear herself whimpering, feel her whole body trembling, and fought for control as she snatched the telephone receiver from its cradle on the shelf above her head. She seemed to be in some fourth dimension of fear, watching her own small body rocking back and forth, receiver at her ear, like someone in pain too great for voicing. "Sorry, Miss Kent, the Travel Bureau in the lobby will not be open for an hour and a half. . . . Yes, madam, I'll try the main office. . . . Sorry, madam, there seems to be no answer. . . . BOAC? Certainly, madam, I'll try. . . . TWA . . . ?"

"Never mind! Never mind. I—I'll be down—"

The whimpering, tearless sobs did not lessen as she packed frantically. It took only a little time; she had only unpacked necessities the day before. August. August, and every plane full. Damn all those who wanted to travel for fun and denied it to those who needed it in a race against death. Maybe it wasn't death. "Critical." Not "serious" but "critical." That was worse. The sharp point of a carelessly packed pair of scissors pierced her hand as she pressed the contents of a bag down, brought blood, but no more than annoyance at the pain. A no-show, a no-show, a no-show at the airport; God, let there be a no-show at the airport. Hunter. He could help. She wanted to scream aloud at the sound of the tinny, double-ring of the telephone in his empty apartment, repeated for what seemed hours.

In the elevator a commercial traveler from the North looked at her curiously, and she instinctively reached up to straighten whatever hat she had on her head. What hat had she grabbed? What clothes put on? It didn't matter. Keep your head, Sara; keep your head; what will I do with it, what will I do with my head and my heart and my mind and my life if David's gone? Coffee. Hot coffee in the dining room. No. I can't swallow it. Time. It would take ten minutes, and there wasn't ten minutes in all eternity she dared spare now. Money. Would they take a check? Would they take a check at the airport for a no-show or a cancellation? . . .

Three running steps from the elevator toward the desk, and Hunter's arm was around her. "Easy. Easy does it, Sara."

"Hunter! Oh, God, Hunter I'm so glad. Hunter, David's—"

"I know, Sara. I know all about it. I hoped you wouldn't hear till I could tell you. I was on my way to your room—"

"I'm packed, Hunter. All packed."

"Packed!"

"Help me get a plane seat, Hunter."

"No! Sara, my God, no! I didn't think you'd pull this. You can't do anything. Nothing is as bad as the press makes it—"

"You can't stop me. I'll wait for a no-show or a cancellation. At the airport—" Even Hunter was unreal, standing there looking down at her, not a loved friend now, but an obstacle. No one was real, nothing was real but the word "critical" and David Champlin, who was nowhere near, was three thousand miles away, yet who was the only reality.

Hunter's fingers bit into her shoulders. His eyes were stern on her face, trying to call her back; then he gave up, his hands loosened their grip, his eyes retreated from their attack.

"Coffee, Sara. Pots of it, in the dining room while I see what I can do."

"No. I don't—"

"Shut up, Stoopid! Old dad Travis is in charge."

In the dining room he forced her to sit, and ordered coffee

and toast. "The coffee immediately," he ordered. Sara felt his hands on her shoulders again. "Stay there. Drink that coffee. Pull yourself together."

"Can you get a seat for me, Hunter? Do you think you can? It's August—"

"I won't do a damned thing unless you drink that coffee, ducks. That's the girl. I'll be back. It may take time."

It took a thousand years, but when they had passed and she saw him coming toward her, he was smiling.

"Two," he said. "Two different ones. TWA to New York or BOAC to Boston and New York." He pulled out a chair and sat facing her. "You may drop my name anywhere if it will give you status. Two reservations. In mid-August. They had to be first class. Anything else was impossible, even for me. Which?"

"BOAC. To Boston. Oh, God, Hunter, but you're wonderful." Of course she wanted Boston, because it was David more than New York was, and it was Brad and Peg and Sudsy and Rhoda.

"I'll cable Peg," said Hunter. "Now sit still, for Pete's sake, while I get myself some hot coffee. There's time."

They sat, each in a corner of the cab, as it drove away from the hotel; then Hunter slid over beside her, took both her clenched hands in one of his.

"I tried to reach someone over there on the telephone, but I couldn't. I'll keep trying. Peg's been cabled. And I telephoned your studio and talked to the formidable Mrs. Fudge. I'll pay her when I get back from the airport."

"Hunter, what did the porter call you back for when I was getting into the cab?"

"It—it was the receptionist who wanted me. Suspicious, aren't you? It was about your messages."

"But I'd already told them to forward them to you. Was it bad news, Hunter? Was it? Was it bad news?"

"No! It was not bad news, Sara. I swear it." His hand tightened slightly on hers. "Sara, we're not rushed for time and we've a very conservative cabby who's taking it easy. It would be a splendid idea if you'd cry your damned eyes out on the way to the airport. Much as I loathe weeping females."

"I—I can't—"

"Yes, you can. Just look out the window at the weather. It's raining like hell—"

"Is it?"

"Yes. Here's a handkerchief and I have a pair of dark glasses in my pocket."

Later he said gently, "If I put that handkerchief in front of the gas heater, it shouldn't take more than all day to dry. Feeling better?"

"I—yes—no. I'm sorry to have been loathsome."

"Quite all right, my dear. You can think better now. Anything else you'd like me to do?"

He tried to keep his eyes focused on the gray wet world ahead of them, a dim place of driving rain, slickly gleaming pavements, open umbrellas, and frustrated drivers. Looking at her was sharp pain, her pain and his own mingled. He knew she was sitting with both hands pressing the handkerchief to nose and mouth, eyes no longer streaming but breath catching like a child's on the echoes of spent sobs. He thought: I'm not in love with her; it's not in me to be in love with anyone, but if she had said "yes" last night, something good would have happened to me, inside. And thank God she didn't, because if she had, today would have hurt unbearably.

He heard a muffled sound he took to be a question. "Don't mumble your words, child."

"Hunter, can you pray?"

"Good God, Sara! I don't know. I suppose I can try, but it's a lot to ask of a guy who's on record as saying that existentialism is the modern opiate of the people. Besides, I don't fancy being snubbed by strangers—"

"David does."

"Pray, you mean? He damned well better. If he didn't, Li'l Joe Champlin would come back and beat hell out of him with an ectoplasmic club. Damn it, Sara, I'm sorry. I didn't mean to be flip."

"It's—it's never done any good before. This is a sort of last chance—"

"A challenge to the Almighty? I'll try, sweetie. Though I must say I doubt that the voice of Hunter Travis, the objective modernist, the teller of tales of frustrated heels, the guy who acknowledges the human psyche as the only force, would be heard after all these years. . . . We're there, Sara. . . . Pull up your socks, kiddie; we'll head for a drink and the plane. . . ."

As he watched the group of which she was a part go through the doorway and make its way to the bus that would take them planeside, he kicked himself mentally for not noticing what hat she was wearing. It was usually the only way one could pick Sara out of a crowd, by what was on top of her head. He finally glimpsed the brown head, damp with rain, and some small and ridiculous green object atop that would be a Sara hat. Then the group broke apart at the bus door and he saw her completely, walking very straight and firm, shoulders squared, five feet tall, and not looking back.

He stood alone by a window, watching the bus cross the field in the driving downpour. " 'I can try,' " he muttered. " 'I can try,' I told her. Listen, God, don't let her do some damn-fool thing like go to Cainsville; don't let Sara go to Cainsville if you have to arrange for a broken leg. Sara and David, David and Sara, in Cainsville. If you ever want to hear from me again, don't let it happen. It's not a hell of a lot to ask—"

He turned away, slipping his hands into his pockets, and his fingers touched a crumpled scrap of paper. He drew it out slowly, hearing again the overcultivated, affected accents of the receptionist at the desk of Sara's hotel after the porter had called him back: "I'm frightfully sorry, Mr. Travis. I thought Miss Kent had left. It's a call for her from Germany. Düssseldorf. The telephonist told the operator she had left. Perhaps she can return the call from the airport? I'm ever so sorry—"

Standing alone in the air terminal, Hunter looked at the pink scrap of paper, saw the words again he had read in the hotel lobby: "Düsseldorf" and "Christopher Barkeley" and a number. Then the words and the number gave way to Sara walking through the rain, straight and tiny, yet towering above all those around her, little Sara, going home.

84

First there was one pain, grinding, huge, circumscribed, identifiable at last as in a shoulder. This, in the blackness, was all there was at first. Then there was another, and this was in a leg and was somehow familiar, had happened before, had been known a long time ago. There was pain, too, a dull aching pain, in his head, and something was holding it in, a something around his forehead, and that was all there was, just the pain and the blackness until he sensed movement at the periphery of the encompassing pain. Something touched his cheek gently, and he heard a man groan. The touch came again, light and soft, and again he heard a man groan, and knew it for his own voice. He had not meant it to be a groan, had meant it to be a word: "No." He fought the tide that was bringing him back to consciousness, and this, too, had happened before. Gramp had been there that other time, Gramp had touched his cheek. "So-so, little man." But that had been a long time ago, and Gramp had gone away. Gramp couldn't have touched his cheek because Gramp was gone, and with that realization the tide swept him to life and beached him, pain and all, on a strange bed, in a strange room, and in a moment he would open his eyes, but he did not want to yet because he was afraid.

Now a voice joined the sound of movement at the edge of the pain that walled him in. It was familiar; he knew the voice, and the fear receded. "He's coming round," it said. There were fingers on his wrist, and the voice said, very slowly and distinctly, "David. You are all right."

He tried to open his eyes, but the lids were leaden and the effort splintered the dull ache in his head into sharp, agonizing barbs. He tried to speak, but his lips were made of rubber and moving them took more strength than he could muster.

"Don't try to talk, dad," the voice said, and it was Sudsy's and the knowledge cut through the pain and darkness, and at last he managed to open his lids to a slit, but the light was more painful than the blackness, and he closed them again.

"It's Suds, David. You're in the hospital in Boston. There's nothing to worry about. My father and I are taking care of you. You're going back to sleep now. When you wake up, we'll tell you all about it."

There was something he had to tell someone; it was vital and urgent, and he could not sleep until he had told whatever it was, and then the edges of the pain that pressed in on him softened, the sounds could not be heard although they were still there in his consciousness, and then blackness obliterated thought and feeling and he let it carry him.

The second time he awakened, the pain crept through the darkness, moving slowly, pushing at his mind until it propelled him into consciousness. This time there was no fear, but he could not remember why there should be no fear, although there was still the sense of urgency. A woman's voice at a great distance said, "Call Dr. Sutherland. The patient's coming round again."

A year or more passed while consciousness receded and returned, receded and returned, like the ebb and flow of a tide on a rocky beach. There was a memory of the pain of light when he opened his eyes before, and he kept them closed, not opening them even when he heard Sudsy's low, "Hi, dad."

There was strength enough now to force the rubber lips to move. "Effie," he said.

"We know, David. Quiet now, huh?"

"Effie's dead."

"Yes. No talking, David."

"Hummer—"

A woman saying, "Shh-shh-"

"Bastards—"

"Later, dad—"

There was a firm hand on his arm, a sharp sting and a brisk rub.

"Suds. They let Effie die—"

"Take it easy, dad—"

"Little girl. Nothing but a chile—"

"Sleep a little more, David."

"Brad—Brad—"

"He's fine. He's O.K." The darkness was returning now, and he could not fight it off. He sighed, and realized for the first time that his body was bound round with something hard that would not let him move; then that one arm would move but that the other, where the pain was, lay cramped and stiff and immobile and that the pain in his leg was trapped as it had been so long ago in a hospital in New Orleans, by plaster. He managed to say, "Suds—" but the darkness obscured the answer.

Chuck Martin was waiting in the corridor outside Room 21 in Boston's new Endicott Memorial Hospital when Dr. Clifton Sutherland came out. "How's it going, Suds?"

Sutherland did not look directly at the other man. He crossed the hall and stood for a moment looking down into a patio-like courtyard where ambulatory patients sat basking in the sun. Chuck came and stood beside him. At last Sutherland said, "I think he'll be all right, if nothing unforeseen develops, and if there aren't injuries we haven't been able to spot. And I doubt that."

"So do I," said Chuck. "How many is it you've got on the job by now?"

"Six. Not counting me. There'll be more surgery. A hell of a lot of pain. A hell of a lot of time here. A lot of crippling in that leg. The good one. Or what was the good one. The fractured vertebrae should be O.K. in time and, of course, the facial injuries and the ribs and lung." He fell silent until Chuck moved closer and shook him gently by one shoulder.

"Stop torturing yourself, Suds. David never held it against you. He understood."

"But I didn't. I didn't understand one God-damned thing. Stupid, self-righteous, obnoxious—"

"Forget it. You're making up for it now."

"Am I?" He turned to Chuck. "Hell, until now, until I saw what they brought off that plane on a stretcher, dedication was just a word in the dictionary."

"You couldn't be expected to know, Suds. The only reason I understood was because I'd grown up with what he had to fight."

"Nuts. The reason you understood was because you're a better man than I am, any day. Any day, dad."

"That's a lot of you-damned-well-know-what, Suds."

"Remember what he did at Pengard? For me? Compared to this it was trivial. But I'm speaking relatively. Stuck his neck out ten miles, and damned near got his head cut off. Just as we thought, at first, we might have to do to that leg. Don't pull that 'forget it' routine on me."

"All right, Suds. Remember it, then, if it makes you feel better. But it doesn't make sense; you're only hurting yourself. When he gets all his senses back, he'll forget it."

"I hope so. I hope he does—"

"Come on, Suds. Sara and Brad are waiting in the lounge—"

The planners of the Endicott Memorial Hospital had taken thought for the usually forgotten visitor; each floor had, besides a sun lounge for patients, a waiting lounge with deep chairs and small sofas. Brad, Peg, and Sara were sitting on one of the small sofas, and Sara was on her feet and running to Suds before they crossed the threshold. He took her hand in both of his and said, "Everything's all right, Sara."

"Is it, Suds? Is it really? Are you telling me the truth?"

"Yes, Sara. There's nothing to be gained by lying in a situation like this. We think he's turned the corner." He looked over her head at Brad and Peg. "I was whistling in the dark before; we all were, including my father. He has a long way to go yet, but—oh, good God!—" He was looking down, not at Sara's face, but at the top of a small head with a close-cut cap of brown hair. The face was buried on his shoulder. Peg was hurrying forward, but Suds grinned at her and shook his head, then led Sara to the sofa, forcing her to sit. "Cry, Sara."

"I'm going to. I'm—I'm damned well going to. I couldn't have stood it, Suds, I couldn't—"

Suds beckoned to Chuck over her shoulder. "See if you can rustle up a nurse—"

When the nurse appeared, Suds gave a brief order, and in a moment she returned with a half-filled paper cup.

"Just stop blubbering long enough to drink this, Sara. Come on. Doctor's orders—"

The hand that took the cup was shaking, but between them, they got it to her mouth. She drank, drew a deep breath, shuddered, then looked at Suds with brimming eyes. "Whiskey," she said. "You won—wonderful man."

"What else? You were expecting champagne, maybe?"

She gave an exhausted sigh, hiccoughed, and said, "Now may I see him, Suds?"

Sutherland looked across at Brad for help, then at Chuck. "Not now, Sara. Later."

"Let Peg take you back to the hotel now, Sara," said Brad. "It must be three days since you've really slept."

Sara did not turn her head, but kept her eyes on Sudsy's face. "Why not? Why not, Suds? You—you let me see him the other day. You let me look at him. I even touched him. Why not now?"

"He's asleep—"

"Then it's all right. I can just peek—"

"Sara, even yesterday we weren't sure. Now he's really beginning to rally. The next time he wakes, I think it will be to a pretty complete awareness. And Sara, pet, it is absolutely necessary that he be kept quiet, that he see no one for a little while, that nothing disturb or excite him."

"You damned doctors! Just a peek. I'll just peek around the screen."

Suds sighed and stood up. "You will, anyhow, even if you have to sneak back. You might as well do it legally. Come on, Stoopid. Meet us at the elevator, Peg?"

"If I can walk that far." Peg put her arm around Brad and

leaned against him, smiling. "We're shook, dear Doctor. We're shook up as hell. Sara's not the only one who wants to bawl with relief."

"Let's all bawl," said Brad. "While Chuck prays."

Chuck grinned at him. "There's an appalling amount of disrespect for the clergy around here." They were walking to the door. "Show me anyone in this room who hasn't been. Praying, that is. Even you, you blasted heathen."

"Even I," said Brad quietly, and took Sara's hand as they walked down the corridor.

At the door of David's room Suds said, "One toot and you're oot—"

"I promise."

He made her wait while he went into the room and around the folding screen just inside the door, then came back and motioned her forward. She stood beside him just inside the screen, and he heard her catch her breath. A nurse who had stood when they entered smiled reassuringly at them. There was a feather-light touch on his arm, and he looked down. Sara was looking up at him, and he turned away from her eyes, nodded helplessly and watched her tiptoe slowly forward, almost like someone who is afraid. She stood beside the bed for a long minute, then stooped and touched David's bruised and swollen cheek softly with her lips. So light was the touch that even had he been awake it would scarcely have been felt. She turned and tiptoed past Sudsy and into the hall, and he closed the door gently behind them.

Peg was waiting at the elevator. "Come on, hon. Brad and Chuck have gone on. Bed for you. Orders, Doctor?"

"Yes," said Suds. "A warm bath, tea and graveyard stew sent up, no calls, and one of the pills I'll have the pharmacy deliver. If you're not asleep in an hour, take the second one." He tried to glare authoritatively at Sara, was defeated utterly by her smile, and said, "Beat it, you guys. I've got work to do."

Each time she had entered the hotel room since her arrival, she had given thanks for Peg Willis's understanding. "Brad wanted you with us," Peg had said. "But I told him I knew you better than he did. There's a room waiting for you at the Sheraton-Plaza. All paid for. And no back talk. No one can fussbudget over you. And I throw up every morning."

Sara knew now what Peg's warm, confident smile at the airport must have cost in effort. "David's here," had been her first words. "At the Endicott Hospital. The Sutherland Clinic and every specialist available have taken over."

"Is he going to die, Peg?" She remembered now she hadn't even said "Hello" or "Glad to see you."

"Not if a whole damned squad of the best doctors and surgeons in the country can help it—"

"Surgeons! Peg, Peg—"

"We're due at Sudsy's father's office as soon as we check you in at the hotel. Suds arranged it. He'll brief you."

But Sudsy's father hadn't been there; he'd been in surgery at Endicott Hospital with David.

She told herself now not to think about the all-night vigil in the lounge on the second floor. It's over, she told herself, it's over; and knew it would never be over in her mind, that she could never dismiss it. The nurses who didn't know anything or if they knew would not say; the coffee they brought throughout the night; Brad arriving and he and Chuck going and returning every few minutes to answer telephone calls until someone brought a portable phone with a polite, hellishly irritating buzz instead of a ring, and plugged it into a wall connection in the lounge. The calls from New Orleans that Brad took, and from Atlanta and Montgomery and New York. A call from Hunter Travis in London; the person-to-person call to her from Vermont, and Tom Evans's voice, "Sara. What happened? How is he? What can I do? I can start down now—" She broke then, and Chuck took the telephone from her gently. "Tom. Chuck here. We don't know much yet. . . . We thought you were in Mississippi. . . . I'll call you later tomorrow . . . I mean today. . . ."

She remembered saying stupidly when Chuck hung up, "Mississippi?"

"He took a group of students down there this summer to help rebuild bombed Negro churches and homes. He came back a few days ago to make some speeches and pick up more recruits."

"Oh. Of course." It had seemed natural then, as though she should have known it. "I've been away so damned long. Really away—"

She remembered the electric moment when a nurse passing the door had said to someone down the hall, "Is twenty-one ready for the patient?" Brad's grip on her arm and around her waist when he overtook her at the door was painfully hard and tight. She did not try to free herself, because her body suddenly became limp and unmanageable and she leaned against him, trembling, while Chuck stood quietly beside them.

All that was David on the gurney that rolled past the door had been a long, strong brown arm stretched beside a swaddled form, a tube leading from a vein in the crook of the elbow to a bottle held high by an orderly, the hand lax and quiet. All the rest was white, distorted, except for the bruised chin and battered lips, the whole a nightmare figure of bandages and plaster and tubes, tubes, tubes, and a cloth over the eyes. She heard herself say, "He's not breathing. God in heaven, Brad, he's not breathing!" and heard Brad answer in a whisper, "Yes, he is, my dear. Of course he is. I think there's a body cast—"

Suds came in then, in sneakers and limp, green, pajama-like suit, gray-faced, drinking black coffee in great greedy gulps, too exhausted to smile, saying as he set the cup down: "So far, so good, chums. Two nurses, each shift, around the clock for twenty-four hours. We'll know more then." A Sudsy Sutherland grown old looked at Chuck and said, "We've done everything humanly possible—"

It was all right to remember it now, lying in a tepid bath, all right to remember these last few days because she had known when she stood by David's bed an hour ago that he would live. And that was all that mattered, that and the knowledge that he was near, that her thoughts did not have to reach across a continent, a great sea, to touch him; he was no longer in some corner of hell, some dark inferno; he was near, and if she wanted, she could go now and stand outside the door of a room in which he lay, alive and near. Suddenly, she was crying again, not the racking sobs that had torn at her in the cab with Hunter, or in Sudsy's arms at the hospital, not sobs at all, really, just warm tears coursing down her cheeks, healing her.

Consciousness began to sort itself into segments of time, day and night, then divisions of day: morning, noon, and night; then hours. Pain and consciousness were one entity at first, then became separate, and consciousness was the master, the pain something that an effort of will could keep subordinate. There were nurses, orderlies, an exhausting succession of doctors, and a quiet, authoritative Sudsy he had never known before, a Sudsy who seemed omnipresent, who only when they were alone was the hesitantly earnest, diffident, unconsciously humorous companion of years before.

They told him not to talk, and he obeyed because he was too tired to talk except to answer necessary questions; the urgency to communicate he had felt when consciousness first returned was gone. He knew there must be extensive trouble in his pain-racked body, but was content for a while to let the various short, tall, fat, lean, warm, cool, competent men who came in each day worry about it.

He did not keep track of the days because measured time was unimportant. He was mildly surprised the first morning the nurse fed him boiled egg and bits of toast to realize that he had felt no hunger but that the food was good in a way food had never been good before. It was that morning Sudsy came in and nodded at the nurse, who was gone with a quiet rustle, leaving them alone.

"By God," said Suds. "You've got brown eyes. First time we've really been able to see 'em. I'd almost forgotten."

"Yeah. And I can talk."

"Sure you can. All that breakfast. A whole egg, dad, and a piece of toast. The nurse is ecstatic."

"Suds, what the hell—"

"Just because you're able to talk doesn't mean you have to go overboard and chatter—" Suds moved from the foot of the bed, and standing by the side, took David's wrist between his fingers.

"For God's sake, leave my pulse alone. It's worn out—"

"It's good, chum, all things considered; it's damned good."

"You want to tell me what the hell's going on below my neck or keep it a secret?"

"If I could do that I would, but it's better to know than to wonder. As I used to tell all the gals. First, David, it's not as bad as it will sound. You'll be O.K."

"Say 'patience' and I'll punch you in the eye the first day up—"

"Feisty, aren't you? And therefore improving. Your leg, David—"

"My good one, damn it—"

"Your good one. It took a slug in the knee. Later there'll have to be more surgery to lessen the stiffness. Maybe an artificial kneecap. We thought at first it was a goner."

"Hell."

"Pretty much so, pal. I tried to fob this job of telling you off on my father, but he wouldn't have any part of it. Your shoulder also took a slug. Which you know, of course. You won't pitch any no-hitters, dad—"

"I never did."

"You always talked a good one. Anyhow, we can't tell yet whether we're through with the shoulder or not. There were some busted ribs, and a lung puncture—"

"Is that why I hurt when I breathe?"

"Yup. And there was kidney damage—"

"You mean I've still got kidneys? They're about ten-time losers—"

"Will you shut up! There were two fractured vertebrae—wait, David. Don't panic. Actually, except for the body cast, they're the least serious. It always scares people to tell 'em they have a broken back, but there was no spinal cord or nerve damage. Just bear in mind you wouldn't be having all that pain in your leg if there had been."

"Well, goody." David was quiet for a long time, his eyes closed, and Sudsy did not speak. Then David said, "Those guys that jumped me; it'll break their hearts." After another long silent minute he said, "That all? Because if it is, I've got something—"

"Not quite all. You have a skull fracture, but not too bad a one. You've lost two teeth. Those can be taken care of while you're in the hospital."

Now David opened his eyes and looked directly at Suds. "How long, dad?"

"Before you're well?"

"I don't dare ask that. Before I'm out."

"We don't know. For sure, that is. Weeks, let's say."

David tried to laugh, winced, and said, "Weeks, hell! Months, pal, and you damned well know it."

"I'm afraid I do, David." Suds left the side of the bed, walked to the window, then stood at the bureau, leafing through a stack of telegrams and mail, not looking at David. "Lots of telegrams and mail, dad, when you're up to it." His words were mumbled, close to indistinct. When he turned at last to the bed, he saw a man lying very quietly, eyes open and fixed on the distant wall, no expression on a face that still bore bruises and swellings.

"David," he said gently, "if there was anything in God's world I could do, anything, I would." The other's eyes did not move, nor did the head turn, and Suds went on, hesitantly, slowly. "I remember, a long time ago, a real great character saying to me, 'Jesus have moicy! How can one sorry little piece of a guy have so much stupidness in him!' That was me, by God, Clifton Sutherland, the sorry little piece of a guy who's managed to prove the stupidity these last few years. It's been rough, finding that out this past week, David—"

Now the head turned slowly on the pillow, and Suds was looking down into eyes that carried the smile the swollen lips could not manage.

"What the hell you talking about, Stoopid! Go heal the sick, and tell 'em out there I want more than one lousy li'l ol' egg for lunch—"

Just as Suds was leaving, David said, "Brad?"

"Brad's in Cainsville. You'll see him as soon as he gets back. I'm ordering a shot for you now, for sleep. To be administered after an egg and a half for lunch."

"Bastard. Listen, Suds."

"No more talk now—"

"Damn it, listen. I've got something else wrong with me."

Hand on the doorknob, Sudsy turned. "You can't have—"

"The hell I can't. I've got a stomach ulcer."

Sudsy came to the foot of the bed, stood glaring down at his patient. "Why in the name of heaven didn't you tell—"

"Maybe it's duodenal. And how could I—"

"We'll fix you, sonny boy; we'll fix you. My father's old-fashioned about handling ulcers. Graveyard stew—"

"What's—"

"Custards, puréed vegetables, no seasonings—I told you not to talk. See what it's got you."

"Double bastard. Gumbo tomorrow? Tell Peg."

"Maybe, pal. Maybe. As a special treat. Now shut up before I find out you've got coccidioidomycosis or something—"

85

THE DRS. SUTHERLAND, father and son, remained chary of visitor privileges for their patient, and it was not until the day after Sudsy's disclosure of his many injuries that David woke from a fitful, image-filled nap to find Brad standing quietly at the foot of the bed, looking down at him.

"Hi, Chief!" His lips were manageable now, almost normal, and his eyes no longer near-slits surrounded by puffed flesh.

"Hi, brat." Brad's smile was gentle. "Don't get up. I'll find a chair."

"Jokes, yet. Practically at a guy's deathbed. Damn, I'm glad to see you.'"

"Must have been like solitary confinement." Brad pulled the room's one armchair close to the bed and sat, stretching long legs. "You're not tó talk much. Sudsy's orders. You feel pretty tough?"

"Not too bad. I hurt like hell, if that's what you mean."

Brad winced. "God! I can imagine."

"Keep it there, in your imagination. Damn it, I'm glad to see you. I've already said that, haven't I?"

"I can do with hearing it a hell of a lot of times, son. Peg's acting up rough because she can't hear it, too. She's down the line a way on the waiting list. Suds said I could come and ease your mind about all that happened. If—"

"You didn't upset me. F'cris'sake, tell me all there is and upset the hell out of me. Now I'm getting better I'm getting curious. At first I didn't give a damn."

"Just being alive was probably enough—"

"And that wasn't such a much, brother, believe me."

"Did Suds tell you Luke's going to be O.K.?"

"Yes. Couple of years ago, it seems like. I was sort of coming in and out of the fog every so often and I heard him say, 'Brad says to tell you Luke's all right.' "

"He's in New York Medical Center. Wait. You've used up your quota of talk. I'll start at the beginning. Do you have any amnesia for what preceded the attack?"

"I wish to God I did. The last I remember they set the dogs on me when I was lying on the ground."

"No, they didn't. Now, once and for all, be quiet. You can ask questions another time. First, the U.S. Army was damned near breathtaking in its efficiency. They had an ambulance—the one that took Fred Winters to Veterans Hospital—at Dr. Anderson's right after you left. You were headed for Tether's End, and there wasn't any telephone there anymore. Just after I finished talking to Anderson, we got word that there were two or three cars prowling around the outskirts of the town with three or four whites in each car with rifles. I got the wind up and notified the Army, and asked them to check Tether's End while they were scouting and send you the hell back to town. You were a damned fool to go—never mind. I'll bawl you out when you're better. We come now to the dogs."

"Now? So soon?"

"Or almost now. Early in the evening Abraham Towers called his nephew and told him to get Miz Towers down to their house if they had to carry her. Now, one doesn't take Miz Towers anywhere that Tinker doesn't go too. I'd hate to be the one to argue the point with him. Once she's safe inside and bedded down, he relaxes and gets reacquainted with his daughter."

"His what?"

"Daughter. Half red-bone hound, half Tinker. A noble beast, if strange and fearful looking. Jim's wife won't have dogs in the house, so Tinker sleeps on the porch. Every time the old lady's been there—not many—he waits till everything's quiet and then takes off for a quick run home and a look-see that everything's all right there. Then comes back. He's got sense enough to know the old lady's safe. The night you got it, his daughter, Sheba, decided to go along."

"Man! This is doing me more good than every damned pill they've given me—"

"I rather thought it would. The men in the Army jeep said they heard the shots. They were headed out Calhoun. The dogs went by them like a couple of hares. Then they saw the headlights of the car just west of Tether's End. When they were close enough, just at the top of that little rise in the road, they saw what was going on. Dogs, men, yells, shouts, then men running and dogs after them and you lying on the ground, a bloody mess. They literally, for a minute, didn't know whom to rescue."

"Wait, Brad. The hell with what Suds said. They didn't hurt Tinker, did they? Those sons of bitches that jumped me?"

"They didn't have time. Calhoun Road isn't exactly the Indianapolis Speedway, but the jeep was doing a good job, I gather. Shots were fired, but the men made their car and took off, and Tinker was back waiting for the jeep. Then Sheba was back, and they gave the troops a bad time at first. One of the soldiers was colored, and he says he 'gentled' them. Also, Jim Towers got there about then. He'd heard the shots. He helped with the dogs."

"You mean that dog saved my life?"

"I won't go that far, but he helped. The Army would have busted them up anyhow. But Tinker helped. And both dogs left their marks. There was blood on the road between you and their car, and the grapevine has it that a white man was treated for a badly torn arm and another for a chewed-up leg at the hospital on the other side of town."

"Lawd!" said David. "Lawd! Lawd! You sho' been good to me—"

Brad looked closely at the man on the bed, put his hands on the arm of the chair, and started to rise. "My time's about up. You're beginning to look tired—"

"No, for God's sake! You've got to get me off the ground. You left me there a bloody mess—"

"So I did. The Army handled the immediate medical work. You were in shock, and they did what was necessary so that when you got to the hospital it wouldn't be a dead-on-arrival. Plasma, control of bleeding, antibiotics, that sort of thing. You made the plane with Luke eventually. Mrs. Anderson went with you along with Chuck. She kept up the treatment—"

"How'd Anderson manage?"

"He traded her in temporarily for a couple of Army corpsmen. They touched down in New York, where Luke's magazine had everything set up at the Medical Center. Chuck says he doesn't think the landing-gear wheels even stopped rolling. Then they brought you here. Suds met the plane. Incidentally, they operated on Luke. Blood clot. The only after-effect so far is amnesia covering about an hour before it happened."

"Brad." David was quiet for a moment. "Brad, it's not right. Luke and I. If we'd been someone like Jim Haskin or Abr'am, we'd be dead now. But just because we knew the right people—or something. That's just too damned much luck, Brad, too damned much—"

"Is that all you've got to worry about? It just happened that way. My grandmother used to say if you're born to be hanged you'll never drown."

The door opened, and a nurse with red hair and freckles and an obvious effort to look stern came in and said, "Time's up—"

"Please," said David. "Please, he's doing me good. Just a few more minutes, huh?"

Brad covered his mouth with a quick hand to hide a smile

at the expression of warm indulgence on her face as she said hesitantly, "We-e-ell—"

"Be sweet, now—"

"Just a few minutes. And don't tell Dr. Sutherland—"

"No, ma'am. God forbid—"

She left, and Brad shook his head. "How do you do it? How the hell do you do it? Eating out of your hand. Shot, beaten half to death, and spoiled rotten all at once. You could ask for the moon here, and I have not the slightest doubt you'd get it. With butter and jam."

David did not look at him, kept his eyes on the screen in front of the door. "Know something, Chief? I'd trade it in, whatever the hell it is you're talking about, for something I'll never have again. One good leg. Just one."

Brad said. "Hell, I know—" and David turned his head to face him. "Forget it, Chief. Look—you and Chuck away, Fred, I suppose, still out of the picture, and Hummer—he's gone. Who in hell's minding the store?"

"Les, Haskin, Abraham. And doing a fine job. If, on next Monday morning, more than fifteen Negroes cross Main Street to go to work I'll join the Klan. I'm going back there tonight. I'm just up for a day or so. Mainly to check on you."

"The kids?"

"Fifty-dollar fines. That's all."

"You're lying for sure!"

"No. I stayed down until the next noon, and if you think that was any fun with you and Luke possibly listening to harp tune-ups, you're crazy. As it turned out, I didn't need to stay. I stood by and let Les handle the defense, and nicely he did it. But I am quite certain that the interested spectators in the courtroom accounted for the moderate fines. Army, press, and two United States marshals. It was all over in an hour and a half, and I made the one o'clock plane from Capitol City and arrived here while you were in surgery."

Brad came closer to the bed, hand outstretched, and David grasped it with his free left hand.

"If I behave and go now, perhaps they'll give both Chuck and me a chance to see you tomorrow before I leave. And any fool can tell you're tired."

"So I'm tired. It's something different anyhow. At least it doesn't hurt. And thanks, Chief."

"What for?"

"Damned if I know. I'll study about it and tell you tomorrow. Ask 'em to push Peg's name up on the list so I can see her soon."

"Right." Brad released David's hand and started for the door. Before he reached the screen he stopped at the low voice behind him.

"I thought you'd break down and tell me before you left. What're you holding back, Chief?"

He turned. "Nothing. What's eating you? Nothing. You're getting fanciful."

"Think so? After watching you hold out on surprise testimony as often as I have? I don't know when you're holding back?"

"If I am, I don't know it. It's in my subconscious and I'll have to rout it out in my sleep and tell you tomorrow. Is that O.K.?"

"No. But I'll settle for it for now."

Ten days later Brad Willis and Suds Sutherland had coffee in the hospital coffee shop while they waited for Chuck Martin.

"Do they give this coffee to the patients, Doctor?" asked Brad.

"No. Theirs is better."

"I was just thinking of our boy. This stuff could set him back where he was when they scraped him off the road."

He stirred his coffee, then looked at the entrance door with obvious relief. "Here's Chuck—"

Chuck, looking no more dignified and ministerial in his clericals than he had when he was in duffel coat and corduroys at Pengard, but with his hair slicked down in temporary subjection, sat beside Brad and said, "How's it going?"

"So far, very well," said Suds.

"I would say he's as well taken care of and spoiled a patient as Endicott Memorial has ever had," said Brad.

"Everyone loves the guy," said Suds. Chuck's eyebrows rose slowly, and Suds added, "That is a gross exaggeration, of course. There must be a million or so who hate him. Obviously. Thank God only three or four of them caught up with him." He added cream and sugar to his second cup of coffee, sipped it, and said morosely: "It must be hell. Day and night, not knowing anything for sure except that you're surrounded by hate and disgust and that somewhere near you, always, there are those who would kill you without even calling it murder. And go scot-free." He pushed his cup away from him, plump face grim. "Can you keep him out of there, Brad, after this? You, Chuck?"

"No," said Brad quietly. "I can't and Chuck can't. He may elect to stay out of there, but it will be David Champlin who's staying out by his own decision. Hell, Suds, he was all set to come back here two weeks ago. And stay. At least for a good while. The next thing I knew he was walking through the door of our headquarters in Cainsville. Something had triggered him off."

"We haven't had a chance yet to find out what," said Chuck.

Brad said, "His nerves—" and Suds interrupted him. "You think I don't know? Thin as a damned scarecrow. Probably an ulcer, although it hasn't bothered him here, but from what he says it's been giving him a bad time for quite a while. Now this. I don't think he can take another bout of it after this."

"He'll try," said Chuck. "Sure as I'm sitting here, he'll try, eventually."

"We have months, perhaps a year or more to worry about that in," said Brad. "He's not so quixotic that he'll leave here as long as he's under treatment. Or, poor devil, having periodic surgery. I've a more pressing problem at the moment."

"Concerning David?" asked Suds.

"Very much so. And Sara. I think you're going to have to let her see him, Suds. This business of not letting him get emotionally upset is fine, but he's definitely aware of something. He accused me yesterday of holding out on him. I denied it. And how much longer can you hold the lid on Sara?"

"Indefinitely. Which has been one of the great surprises of my life. Brad, we're taking chances. I don't want him put through any emotional pulling and hauling."

Chuck said: "Suds, will you let me tell him? It's not a job I relish, but I think I can handle it. If, of course, you think it's safe." He made a quick hand movement toward his hair, then checked himself, grinning. "Trying to keep it civilized." He waited a moment then prodded, "How about it, Suds?"

"It's 'safe' enough. It won't endanger his life, if that's what you thought I meant. But I'm shying away from adding emotional wounds—or opening old ones—with a guy as sick and suffering as he is."

"I've had some experience with human beings myself, Suds. And a lot with David."

"Why don't we wait till he asks?"

"He won't," said Brad. "Not because he's too stubborn or proud but because if he really wants to see her he'll be too afraid of being hurt."

"All right," said Suds. "I'm not convinced, but all right. Nothing sudden, Chuck. Sound him out. No sudden, gladsome whoops of joy, no 'Goody, goody, Sara's here!' stuff."

"You blasted imbecile! Do you think I'm that stupid? When can I go up?"

"In about an hour, after rounds. If they do anything cute like mess with the knee through the cast window, I'll page you and call you off. Call everyone off." Suds got to his feet slowly. "What a damned stinking mess the world is—"

Chuck looked up at the unimposing, tubby, troubled figure of Suds Sutherland. "I wouldn't say that, dad. I honest-to-God wouldn't. Not as long as there are guys like David who can be 'triggered off.' That's what counts, not what happens afterward."

Suds reached a short arm out, brought his hand across Chuck's head from front to back, as he had done years before at Pengard, smiled at the wrath on Chuck's face, at the hair so rudely freed from subjection.

"You win, Reverend; you win."

The nurse wheeled the bed-table so that it stretched across the bed a little way below David's chin and laid a pile of opened telegrams and cards on it. "Read what you can," she said, "until you get tired. Reading is more tiring than talking when you've been sick."

"Thanks for the past tense. Hey! Here's one from the U.S. Attorney General!"

"And a lot of good it does," she observed tartly.

"Mustn't be like that." He picked up another wire, but before he read it, he said, "We could use your disposition down there. How's about joining the fight?"

"I'd kill 'em all, Mr. Champlin. If I couldn't shoot 'em I'd —I'd needle 'em to death."

"And that's the truth." He squinted his eyes at blurring print. "This one's from—damned if it isn't from Beany Benford—" There was a sound, and he looked toward the door as Chuck's head appeared around the screen, the face solemn and concerned.

"Pax," said the face.

"Be damned! Pax yourself, Reverend! Man, come in! Pull up a chair. Res' yo'se'f!"

After they had shaken hands, Chuck flexed his fingers and looked at them doubtfully. "They said you'd been sick."

"Just have to stay off my feet, that's all. Fallen arches."

The nurse smiled a red-haired, freckle-faced young smile as she left, and said, "No wrestling, now."

Chuck settled back in the big chair, and David said, "How long did they give you? Ten and a half minutes?"

"No one said. The way they're watching over your battered hulk, they'll throw me out when the time comes."

David looked at the big blond man sitting quietly beside him and could find no words. What was there about the guy, he wondered, that always made something inside himself feel warm and good, a guy so naïve in some ways, so wise in others, so far removed from reality at times, yet at other times so close to the suffering of every man that his own pain called for comforting? David could remember times when Chuck had irritated him almost past control, as he had when the hatchet-faced man, Elmore, said the kids in the stockade would only be fined. And he could remember times when Chuck's strength and understanding had been like a strong arm holding him upright.

He found himself saying inanely: "What're you all dressed up for? A wedding or something? I'm not used to it—"

"Who me? Dressed up?" Chuck grinned. "It's my hair. And no thanks to a young quack named Sutherland they permit to roam these halls. I've reformed. I'm trying to civilize this stuff on my head."

David touched the thick, no longer closely cropped nappiness of his own hair and said, "You reckon I could get me a barber?"

"Why not, chum?"

"No white ones. For gosh sake, no white barbers. They don't know what to do with this stuff."

"I'll get Brad on it. You want some of Peg's old stockings for caps?"

"You'd have made a swell Negro, Chuck. Sometimes I wonder—"

"The universal mind, that's me—"

Chuck talked quietly for a while, filling him in on details Brad had forgotten, telling him in low, uninflected tones that the man who had gone to the Veterans Administration Hospital with Fred Winters had been named Jason Patterson, that he had been a young man whose first child was just two weeks old, and that he had died before noon the next day. "Suds will scalp me," he said.

"It's all right. What Suds doesn't realize, because he can't, is that the telling and hearing can never equal the reality. If we lived through Hummer's death and didn't lose our minds, Chuck—"

"Right."

"Eddie, Chuck?"

Chuck shifted his weight uneasily in the big chair before he spoke. "They bombed his house four or five days ago. No serious injuries. His wife and baby had some minor cuts from flying glass. He's going to Philadelphia, too. Murfree's going to give him a hand in getting a job."

"They must think this brotherly-love bit is more than skin deep. Why Philadelphia? It's no shining example—"

"Murfree's in-laws are there. It's not completely strange to him. Remember, chum, they're both white."

"It makes a difference. Luck to 'em both—"

"Here's something else, David, only it's not bad. Ol' Miz Towers—" Chuck paused, shook his head and grinned over at David.

"What about her? She all right?"

"Bright-eyed and lively as a collie pup. I think she thrives on this sort of thing now. What really threw her, though, was what happened to you. Abr'am had a time with her, David. She made him call here three times a day, and hang the expense. She's going to deed that piece of land known as Flaming Meadows over to you."

"Oh, my God!" David closed his eyes, opened them, and tried not to laugh. "I don't want it. For gosh sake, stop her, Chuck! What in hell do I want with thirty acres of ground in the middle of nowhere! I was afraid I'd get stuck with it when we worked out that option deal. Stop her if you can."

"How you talk. Stop that old lady when her mind's made up? The last thing our friend John Murfree did before he moved to Philadelphia, day before yesterday, was fix up a codicil to her will leaving it to you. Then she decided she wanted to live to see you own it. She says it's yours by right. Says once you own it that ha'nt will be at peace. Says that ha'nt's been waiting for you. You can't reason with her, David. She just knows what she wants and sticks to it. And she thinks you ought to own that land, and do something with it. What, she didn't say. Just, 'Tha's his land by rights—!' "

David gave a short, strange laugh that came from somewhere no deeper than his throat. "If I could take a deep breath I'd sing it: '. . . Land where my fathers died'—"

After a moment Chuck said: "Did Brad tell you there was a goodly amount of mail with contributions for you? One postmarked Cainsville, absolutely anonymous, five one-hundred-dollar bills, in a heavy envelope."

"Good God!"

"Exactly."

"We can't keep it, Chuck. Give it to Effie's mother. Maybe that's what Brad was—no, it can't be."

"What can't be what?"

"I had the feeling he was holding something back, not telling me something. I didn't get the impression it was anything bad, but it's been bugging me." David was silent again, eyes closed. Chuck waited, letting him rest, knowing that in a minute he would tell him about Sara. This man was strong. He knew David, and in spite of trauma, suffering, the knowledge of crippling, in spite of the years of fighting a bitter, cruel evil, this was still the David Champlin—basically and so far as his mental well-being was concerned—who had eaten his first meal at Pengard at a card table across from him. The man is indestructible, he thought. There is that in him that will not be destroyed; there is in him that core of indestructible spirit that has brought his people to an unflinching confrontation of their dark history and has given them the strength and power to lay the foundations of a new and brighter one.

Chuck rose quietly and came to the foot of the bed, and David opened his eyes. "Don't go now," said David. "I just became a southern landowner. You better stick around and get to work on my soul."

"There's something else, David."

"Something else? That I can't take. I'll report you to Suds."

"I think you can take it, David. But I want you to tell me the truth, so help you God. Will you?"

"What the hell—of course I will."

"Then listen, David. Within a few hours after she heard about you, Sara Kent was on a plane to Boston, from London. She sweated out the night with us when you were in surgery. Suds let her see you twice while you were unconscious. After that, he refused to let her see you again because he was afraid, and rightly, of any emotional shock for you. David, the chips are pretty much down. Whatever has happened in the past must not happen again. I would pick Sara up bodily and put her on the first plane leaving the country if I thought that you would refuse her commitment again now. You've had more strain and suffering than God usually calls on one person to take. But so has she, David. So has Sara. And she didn't choose the path that led to it as you did. She's waiting. She's been waiting a long time with a love and devotion as patient and unselfish as any I've ever seen. May I tell Suds to call her and ask her to come to you? Do you want to see her?"

After an interminable pause, a pause so quiet the faint whirring of the small electric clock on the bedside table could be heard distinctly, Chuck turned slowly to leave. Sudsy had been right, and he had been wrong. Damage was possible, and he—blundering, well-meaning Chuck Martin—had done it. Only at the sound of Chuck's movement did David speak. Chuck looked down at the dark head turned away from him now, at the closed eyes in the tired face.

"Yes," whispered David. "Yes. Oh, dear God, yes."

She wouldn't be running when she came down the corridor, not even Sara would run down a hospital corridor, but he would know her step. "After three o'clock," the nurse said. "Cryptic, isn't it? Mr. Martin telephoned and just said 'Tell him after three o'clock.' " Chuck would have done that, timed it for after the nurse had left.

There was only one special nurse now, the red-haired one, and she would be through the next day. "Can you leave the door open when you go off duty, Miss Riley? So I can hear the rest of the world go by?" (So you can hear Sara's steps coming closer, know that much sooner, those few seconds sooner, that she's here.)

"I can't, Mr. Champlin. People go popping into the wrong rooms by mistake, and some people are just plain nosey, and we fought reporters off for a week, and one of those might be lurking. Like the photographer who walked in and got your picture with me sitting right here."

There were times when he could get around her and times when he couldn't. This was one of the latter. He submitted docilely to being fed his lunch, and being settled down for another Goddamned "nice nap, now" which he had no intention of taking and which, at quarter of three, he realized with astonishment he had taken.

"The door?" he said to the nurse as she was leaving.

"No." She smiled at him. "After tomorrow perhaps, when I'm not here. Now, no."

After five minutes his eyes felt dry and stary. He had not taken them from the door, and he closed them for a moment, which was why, when he opened them, he first saw Sara standing by the screen, the door closing silently behind her.

She was so still, so quiet, she seemed to be a statue of warm flesh, a tiny statue with dark, shining eyes. She was like a small and hesitant child, half afraid, not running or appearing to run now, but waiting like a child at a strange door. He saw her lips move and saw the sound defeated by the emotion that was crowding her eyes.

His own voice failed him, and he had to call on it twice before it came out, cracked and faltering.

"Sara."

Those were hours that were passing as she came forward slowly, almost as though she would turn at every step and run back and through the door, hours before his outstretched hand could take hers, feel the smallness of it lost in his, feel her lift their joined hands and hold them against her heart.

"Sara. Smallest. Little love—"

86

SUDS SUTHERLAND ALTERNATELY clucked over and bullied his patient, rationing visitors with care, telling them "If you haven't anything cheerful to say, stay home" until David protested. "Look, Stoopid, the whole damned world hasn't changed just because I've got a cracked skull. There has to be something bad going on—rape, arson, murder, epidemics, muggings, race riots—stuff like that there. Interesting stuff—"

"Sure there is. Only not for you. It's not your skull. That'll take anything. It's your nerves and your stomach ulcer. I'm trying out a theory—"

"F'cris'sake! I'm sorry I told you. Better a bellyache than a vacuum."

A week after Sara's first visit, Hunter tiptoed into the room with the obviously cheerful expression any patient's visitor assumes to cover concern. David greeted him with the loudest "Hey!" he could manage. Hunter, after releasing his hand from David's grip, dropped into the chair beside the bed, saying, "I ought to belt you right in the nose—"

"What in hell—"

"Who believes a doctor, even if he is a good friend, when he says someone who's got everything wrong you have is O.K.? For three weeks every time your name's been mentioned around the family scatter it's been in hushed tones—"

"Past tense?"

"Almost. Jedediah's been in town. London, that is. He's practically turned my color from worry and general shock. He'll be over here next week."

"For God's sake cable him he'll be in plenty of time for the services. It'll be fine to see him."

"I'm headed for New York, but I came here first, straight from the airport. I was all set to stand beside the bed with moist eyes and whisper to Suds about you. And what happens? Damn you, you look fine!"

"You wouldn't say that if I didn't have this cast on, by God, you wouldn't!"

Hunter changed the subject, sobering. "Sara's here. That's good, pal. Very damned good."

"Yes." David cleared his throat, spoke in an embarrassed tone. "Look, thanks, huh? For sort of keeping the lines open, stuff like that—"

"Hell of a strain on my self-control, believe me. Thank God, it's over." There was a soft knock on the door, the faint swush of its opening, a light step, and Hunter said, "And here she is. Hi, infant!"

David lay quietly, letting them talk, not trying to talk himself. He had learned to do this in the past days, reserving his small store of strength, needing it for the night hours when pain became a husky adversary. After a few minutes Sara said: "Brad's back from that dreadful place down there, and he's due here soon. Suds said he could give you the story about everything now."

"Yeah?" David's eyes brightened. "Sure nice of ol' Suds to let me join the world again—"

"I'm glad," said Sara gently. "I'm so glad about Suds—and you. I—I worried, didn't I, Hunter?"

Hunter looked at her and smiled, remembering. He felt very much alone. *Make Sudsy stop hating David. . . . He mustn't hate David. Because David's good. . . . I don't know yet what happened. But I know David's goodness.* Could it have been more than a few weeks ago, months at the most, that he had heard those words? Yet it had been well over two years since he had sat in that hotel room in London with Sara and tried by sheer force of his own will to hold off the onslaughts of grief and sorrow that were shattering her. And there had been a night, and that night in all truth had been less than a month ago, when he had sat across a table from her in a small restaurant near Picadilly, and said *You've never given up on David.* He could still hear the quiver in her voice—*I'm just a damned child, with a damned child's mind and emotions. I'm trying to grow up but I'm not getting very far.*

Sara, the child. Sara, the wise. He stood up so abruptly that David started, wincing from the pain of the involuntary movement.

"Kiddies, Uncle Hunter's leaving. It's known as 'jet fatigue' these days."

"Heck, man, don't go. Wait for Brad. This'll be worth hearing—"

"You can tell me tomorrow. I'll be back then." He took David's outstretched hand and smiled as he flexed his fingers after their handshake. "You're in fine shape, dad. Let no one tell you otherwise. You'll be taking over in no time, right where you left off. I'm going to drown some of this fatigue—"

"Take it easy—"

Hunter nodded, dropped a light kiss on the top of Sara's head as he passed her chair, and left without turning back.

"What gives with Hunter?" asked David. "Did I say something I shouldn't? And—what's the matter with you, pet? Has something bad happened no one's supposed to tell me about?"

Sara shook her head. She did not look directly at him. "It's—well, I think Hunter's caught up with Hunter, sort of. You can't know, David, you can't possibly know, how wonderful Hunter's been to me. I couldn't begin to tell anyone. I guess now he feels sort of lost—" She dug into her purse, came up with a crumpled piece of facial tissue, and blew her nose.

Brad came in then, arms piled high with files and magazines. "Here it is, brat. The day-by-day, blow-by-blow story of the first complete Negro work stoppage in a southern city. That blasted Sutherland kid wouldn't let me bring this to you before. And besides, I haven't been here—"

"He's just a youngster starting out. Be kind to him," said

David. "Some damned bigmouth told him I had a stomach ulcer—"

Brad, having meticulously arranged magazines and folders in what David assumed was chronological order, never looked at the files again. David grinned, watching him; he had worked days—weeks—at a time preparing cases for Brad only to see the same thing happen once the defense opened.

They had waited, Brad said, until everyone was out of jail. The children had been released the day after the riots but some of the adults were still being held. "One of them," said Brad, "was Sue-Ellen Moore. We put up bail and will handle her appeal. Then I took her for a long drive one day and talked to her. We wound up at the waterfall. And I convinced her. God damn, I actually convinced her that as far as Cainsville was concerned we were on the right track. It wasn't all that hard—she was with Effie Brown when Effie died. She saw the scene with Ruby Brown and she saw Hummer murdered—standing at a window in the jail. After she was released I told her the only repayment we wanted for getting her out, putting up bail, was that she attend—merely as a spectator—some of our meetings on this thing. I don't say there was a great transformation—but I do say she started to think and to see the situation more as a whole. Our fingers are crossed. But she went to work, organized kids into clean-up gangs. We had a hell of a lot better trash and garbage pickup service than the whites did. Burned the trash, buried the garbage."

"What about financing?" David wanted to steer Brad away from the subject of Sue-Ellen before Sara asked questions. Later he'd try to analyze the feeling of warm gratefulness that had come over him when Brad described Sue-Ellen's change of heart, however temporary. If she ever saw the problem whole, instead of just one segment of it, Sue-Ellen Moore could be one of the most dynamic and worthwhile leaders in the movement.

"Financing?" said Brad. "It wasn't as bad as it might have been. I'd overlooked a good bet. We all had. Man named Lapham, Curtis Lapham, from Chicago. Know him?"

David frowned. "Negro banker? Loaded with the stuff? He was never active that I ever heard. I crossed him off one list and put him on another a long time ago."

"Too soon. Damned if he wasn't born in Cainsville. Got out early, but not so early he doesn't remember. Something about our project stirred him up. Chuck's the one who told him about it. He came down, took over our credit setup. He and Haskin worked about thirty hours straight. A sort of trade and barter system sprang up spontaneously. Another generous contributor was Lloyd Litchfield. I didn't know he was capable of the anger he showed when he found out how close he had come—and by what means—to being sucked into the white establishment. He really blew. You know what that mild, fuzzy-minded little scientist offered? Besides money?"

"Guided missiles?"

"He would have if we could have used them. Guns. Rifles—"

"Good God! Little Litchfield!"

"Right. And while you were still on the critical list he tried to reach me by telephone, couldn't, and sent Mike Shea a telegram with blisters on it demanding to pay your hospital and surgical bill."

"Good guy. But can't I make it without putting my hand out?"

"Sure. But it's good to know there are people like that. We didn't let Litchfield buy guns, but we rounded up all we could lay our hands on, and saw to it that they were displayed casual-like along with fishing gear, stuff like that, on porches and propped up against walls. I've lived such a sheltered life I never realized what a powerful aid to second-thinking a good twelve-gauge shotgun can be. Next to a boycott—"

"How'd that go?"

"Splendidly. Just about the only stores you could find a Negro in on the other side were the pharmacies—and then only occasionally. They were getting prescriptions. I suggested that Litchfield use the money he would have used for guns to stock Anderson up on prescription drugs. He was jubilant over the idea. So jubilant he also bought Anderson a new refrigerator and some lab equipment. Chuck took the pickup and brought the stuff back from Capitol City. He said it was like running a blockade. The whole place, both sides of Main Street, was crawling with green shirts and imported Klansmen and civilian deputies. He said it was probably only his imagination, but he was certain every man of 'em had his finger on a trigger and the gun was pointed at him—"

"Imagination? The guy was probably right—"

A small voice from the corner of the room halted the conversation. "David—Brad—how can ordinary people like me—ever understand? I thought I understood—I bragged to

David that I did—but—when it comes as close as this, how can I?"

Brad turned to her. "You can't, Sara, when the Negroes themselves can't. They see the hate. That's enough. They know how quickly 'kindness' and patronage can turn to hate if they make the wrong move. To hate a man, a whole people, for what they are and not for anything they've done is a form of mass psychosis, the same mass psychosis that ruled Germany under Nazism. And the average mind finds difficulty in understanding the psychotic mind. Actually, I don't suppose it can be done. When the Negro hates the whites it's because of what the whites have done. There's nothing psychotic about it. You read the words 'crazed Negroes' in a riot story. Good God! What's crazy about revolt? The crazy, the insane, the psychotic character is the white—"

"You're not helping much," said Sara. "Not one damned bit, in fact."

"Can't we get back to the work stoppage?" asked David. "When did it take off?"

"Eight days after your little mishap. And I don't think the whites ever did really know what was brewing until it started. Not even the colored who wouldn't go along gave it away."

"Were there many of those?"

"Damned few," said Brad grimly. "Damned few. And those that welched didn't cross Main Street. They went way round the north end of town. Remember how some of the farmers send buses to pick up field workers? Abraham and a few others went to the bus pickup spots and sat there and watched the buses waiting. They were also all set to 'reason' with anyone who wanted to take one. Had a real enjoyable morning, they said. He was also responsible for seeing to it that the kids had a supply of fresh milk from those of our people who had cows. What he couldn't get of fresh milk Haskin supplied in the form of dried and condensed and evaporated. After the second day parties of green shirts stopped the milk trucks from farms in the east from delivering milk on our side of the street." Brad grinned, looked as boyish as David had ever seen him look. "Hell, we didn't give a damn."

"Well, thank you, Jesus!" said David.

"Whatever you say. Anyhow, here we are with the dawn about to rise over the first nearly complete Negro work stoppage. Complete, as far as our purposes were concerned.

Curt Lapham, Les and I were staying at the Haskins'. By early morning we were all punchy. We hauled all the rocking chairs we could find out on the porch and sat there, Mrs. Haskin, Gracie, Les, Lapham, and I. Haskin was in the store. Les got a bright idea, brought out straws from a broom for us to chew on. 'Twas a pretty sight. Take it easy, brat. You can't laugh. Lapham alternated his cigar with the straw. Gracie suggested we each get a gun, aim it at the road, ready for the first rat fink who came along toward Main Street."

"Damn—we should have gotten Tom Evans's old man, Bull, down there—"

"He'd have enjoyed it mightily. Along about seven thirty, three or four men came down the road, and Lapham and Les and I used language. But when they got to the house they turned in. One was Jim Towers. They wanted to borrow some fishing gear—some stuff they didn't have—and a Thermos. Mrs. Haskin let out a squeal, and Les said 'God damn, we're in!' " Brad paused for dramatic effect. "And, God damn, we were!"

No one said anything for a moment. David spoke first. "I hope Hummer knows. I sure hope Hummer knows."

"Yes," said Brad. "So do I. No Negro crossed Main Street that day. As I told you, a few made it into town around the northern end, beyond the factories. The hell with them too. They didn't hurt us a bit. And the boycott is still on. It was worth everything I've been through including a .45 slug across the ribs. They were hurting over there. At first they didn't believe it. Haskin's phone rang constantly, whites asking him to find out about a no-show employee. Finally he'd just say, 'He—or she—ain't comin' to work today,' and hang up. After a while they caught on. Still, they didn't think it would last more than a day. And in all honesty, David, I wasn't too damned sure myself. But it is. Monday is garbage pickup day, and by Wednesday it was beginning to loom as a problem. I use the word 'loom' advisedly. Doctors with offices on the third and fourth floors were either running elevators themselves for their cardiac patients or their secretaries were trying to. The whites they hired proved undependable, it seems. Everyone was being very Brave in the Hour of Trial. The spittoons at the Grand—"

"Brad—" David interrupted. "Does Luke know about it all?"

"Not all, no. I'll see him in New York on my way back tomorrow."

"'A clean bright spittoon on the altar of the Lord—' That's one of the first things I ever heard Luke say."

"There wasn't a clean bright spittoon in town. On the altar of the Lord or the floor of a bar. Chuck came over with the story that there were signs in all of 'em—'If you have to spit, go outside.' When I think of all those terbaccer-chawin' crackers—"

"Any effort to recruit workers from Heliopolis?"

"Some. We got a lot of support from the N-double-ACP man there—Clinton. He saw to it that word got round even before the stoppage. Maybe twenty or thirty went along with the recruiters. No more. Not enough to matter. And there wasn't too much solidarity between the Heliopolis whites and the Cainsville whites after a couple of days. They didn't want the same thing to happen there. And it very likely will—I hope."

David was looking at the wall over Brad's head, grinning. "Cooks, laborers, clean-up men, houseworkers, garbage men, day laborers, porters, caddies—by God, I bet those golfers were suffering—elevator operators, gardeners, field hands—and me laid up here like a damned corpse!" He brought his eyes back to Brad, sobering. "And none of it matters a damned bit if you can't come up with a decent answer to this one: Did we get anywhere?"

Brad was silent for a moment, frowning. "Yes, we did, I think. I'm not going to make it a flat, triumphant 'yes.' What has been promised—apprenticeship training programs, quicker action on the schools, noninterference in voter registration, other things—will result in betrayal. You know that. Except we may have a chance to get apprentice programs because that bottling company has experienced a region-wide boycott and been hurt. But—and it's a big one, David—Chuck has been in Washington, and there's a strong consensus that both a civil rights bill and a voting rights bill are inevitable. With another work stoppage possible, and Federal enforcement procedures that are tough enough, we'll make it. And if they go back on every promise—well, whatever our people learned of betrayal we learned from them. I think we're on our way in one of the outposts of bigotry, anyhow. We may not make it by morning but we're on our way—"

"I'll bet Peg's busting at the seams with pride—"

"She is. And you should hear Abraham. He was laughing for the first time since he picked Hummer's body off the pavement. 'And we ain't done nothing, Lawyer Willis. Ain't that a beauty? We ain't done nothing. We ain't fired a gun; we ain't heaved a rock; we ain't even marched. And we ain't even prayed. Out loud, that is. And we got 'em crying like babies. Cain't no one point a finger at us, and we got that town daid, plumb daid. Be sure now you tell Mr. David, y'hear?' We can do it again, David. By God, we can."

A nurse came to the door, looked around the screen, frowned at David, then smiled. "All out," she said. "Patient has to rest. Doctor's orders—"

"Hell—" said David, then smiled up at Sara, who had come to the side of the bed. He laid his hand over hers where it lay on the cast over his chest.

"I'm glad they didn't put you on a rotisserie spit," she said. "It's easier to kiss you this way—"

"Rotisserie spit!"

Brad was laughing. "It's a new method for treating spinal fractures. No cast. Suds will tell you about it—"

"Don't mention it to him, for God's sake. Or that bone man. Maybe they forgot about it." He drew Sara's hand to his cheek, then across his lips. "You'll come back tonight, sweet?"

"Of course—"

"You can look through those files after you've had your little nappie," said Brad, and ducked at David's growl. "The news media went all out."

"Thanks, Brad. Thanks for livin'—"

At the door he heard Brad stop, saw his head come around the screen. "I'll be back for a few minutes tomorrow morning. Then after Cainsville I'm going to New Orleans. My car's there. I'm bringing Chop-bone back with me. Sara's making me. Write me an order for release to custody to show Miz Timmins, huh?"

David listened to their footsteps die away down the corridor, and closed his eyes. He was very tired now. Sleep was going to come almost immediately. "Them there antelopes, Gramp," he murmured. "They're learning. Them there antelopes are sure closing in."

87

All morning he had been looking forward with the delight of a child to spending part of the afternoon in the hospital's sun lounge. When the nurse and orderly maneuvered the bed through the wide doorway, he felt as he had the first day he set foot on a Liverpool dock and entered a new world. On his right he could see half-a-dozen white-uniformed nurses at the chart desk, and a patient in a wheelchair, all watching. The nurses waved, and the patient, a young woman, smiled. "I feel like a guy who's just hit a home run in the bottom of the ninth and won the game," he said to the nurse. "Whole darned team comes out." He grinned widely and waved back at the nurses with his good arm; then his bed was turned and wheeled away from them, toward the lounge at the far end of the corridor.

Sunlight engulfed him as they entered, warmed him, was bright to the point of pain, and very beautiful. "Man!" he breathed.

"Nice, isn't it?" said the nurse.

"Very nice," said David. "Oh, very, very nice."

He closed his eyes against the sudden brilliance. When he opened them they were filled with the glowing red and russet and gold of a tree whose topmost branches were level with the wide window before him. There had been sun in his room in the morning, whenever the sun was visible anywhere, for weeks—God, it must have been years!—but not this sun. That had been another sun that just shone in windows and said "Good morning" and went away. This sun that greeted him now was an everlasting sun, the sun that warmed the world and powered it. The red and gold and russet leaves of the tree outside the window danced obeisance to it, and he understood their worship.

The nurse and the orderly placed his bed so that the rays of this almighty sun would fall across it and not shine directly in his eyes. As the nurse left she patted the plaster cast that encased his body and said, "No gymnastics now."

His was the only bed in the lounge. On the far side of the room were three patients in wheelchairs, and a man in bathrobe and slippers sat reading in a big chair, back to a window. One of the wheelchair patients, an elderly man, raised a hand in greeting, then turned and said something to the others, and their heads swung toward David. He lifted his hand and returned the old man's greeting, and smiled. The man propelled himself across the room to the side of David's bed.

"Hell of a thing," said the man. "Glad to see you out."

"Thanks," said David.

"I've only been here a week," said the other. "Damned prostate. I was home when all that trouble was going on down there. The wife and I watched the papers every day to see how you were getting along. Never thought then I'd be meeting you. Want the wife to meet you too, next time she comes. You'll make it all right. All it takes is gumption, and you've got that to spare."

"Yes, sir," said David. The man in the big chair by the window lifted his head and looked across the room with eyes that held no more than cold curiosity, then returned to his reading. The old man in the wheelchair winked a faded blue eye. "Takes all kinds," he said. "Guess you know that."

A nurse came in, smiled at David and said, "Hi, Tiger!" then walked to the back of the old man's wheelchair. "Doctor's here, Mr. Gilman." As she pushed him past David's bed he said, "Play cribbage?" and, when David nodded, smiled delightedly. "Take you on next time," he called as the nurse wheeled him through the door.

I'm alive again, thought David; an old man wants to play cribbage with me and another man hates my guts clear through the damned plaster cast, and the world is all around me once more. He closed his eyes for a moment and opened them in time to catch, full on his face, the eyes of the man who had been sitting in the big chair. He was walking to the door and turned his head away quickly, but not so quickly that David did not catch on his face an expression that seemed like wondering distaste, and a puzzlement at the will of an inscrutable Almighty that would permit the recovery of a Negro guilty of—what? What was he supposed to be guilty of? The hell with it. David closed his eyes again, the better to enjoy the feeling of the warm sun on his skin, and carried into the darkness behind his lids the picture of the gay, bright leaves that danced outside his window.

Damn it, he was tired. A journey of maybe seventy feet

down a corridor, a few words with a stranger, and he might have been wrassling bales of cotton on a dock. He remembered the elder Dr. Sutherland's words when he had asked that rotund character how long it would be before he could resume at least halfway normal activities, tackle the mounds of paper work, the complaints to be briefed, Luke's pictures to be captioned and sorted, the strategy meetings to attend. "You've a way to go yet," the doctor had said.

That was true, but not as Sutherland had meant it, because Sutherland knew nothing of the distance a man must travel on a battlefield. It was a distance not to be measured by time, by the days and weeks and months it would take shattered bones to knit, or an exhausted body and mind to mend, to build reserves. It was a distance to be measured only by the strength of the spirit; as far as that strength would take you, as far and beyond, that was the distance you had to go.

He could wait. He could wait until his body caught up with that spirit, would have to, if going from one room to another, wheeled like a baby in a crib, could tire him.

He did not want to be tired when Sara came. She would be there soon and would know that he was tired even before he had a chance to speak. She would stand beside his bed, laughing down at him with her eyes, loving him, knowing how he felt before a word was spoken.

If he kept his eyes closed he knew he would doze for a few minutes, perhaps sleep, and afterward the tiredness would be gone. He felt himself drifting away from the big lounge and the sun, into a friendly darkness. Then the darkness was made less by a shimmer of light on a wide river; and the sound of the voices of the people on its banks was like hearing old friends, not seen for many years but always dear.

When he awakened it was with the feeling that he was returning from a long journey home. Gramp had been there, and Gram, and even Tant'Irene. The sun was still warm and comforting on his body, and he lay quiet, eyes on the autumn glory of the tree outside his window. He was almost afraid to breathe; even that movement might dispel the knowledge he had brought back from his dream, and it must be captured—captured quickly or it would be gone.

It had not been an ordinary dream, in which people are seen and heard and places recognized. It had been a mere sensing of place and presences, a dream of feeling, utterly subjective—and then he had it in his grasp and did not let it go. It was so simple; as simple as an old man standing in the doorway of a French Quarter bistro saying, "Au 'voir!" He had returned, when he awakened, from a journey home and had felt no sadness because he had not said "Goodbye" at the end of the journey; he had said, and brought back with him the feeling of the words, "Au 'voir!"

Now he could breathe, deeply, drawing a certainty into his mind and heart with the breath. There would be no end to going home. The thoughts and feelings of the years since he had first left New Orleans—Gramp's typewriter in his hand and the Prof's book in his pocket—that the time would come when he would not have to return, these thoughts and feelings were gone so completely they might never have been a part of him.

And he had brought back something more from that short, deep sleep: the knowledge that he was no longer afraid, that he no longer feared his luck and an inevitable reckoning for it. There would always be an account owing to life, but now he could pay it. He would never know when a payment on that account would fall due, but the funds would be there, although there would never be a receipt marked "Paid in Full."

Brad and Chuck and Hunter and Sudsy—they had been so sure, so loving sure, when they had said, each in his own way: "You've had it, dad. Now you can relax and stay up here and work. You're not damned fool enough—not even David Champlin is damned fool enough—to go back now."

They had not known what he knew now, finally and unequivocally, that when he had been at Pengard, in Boston, in Oxford, when Europe and Africa had lain just ahead of him, even when the plane that brought his shattered, unconscious body here was high above the earth—that he had never left; he had only been away.

He and Sara would be married and their marriage would be a good one, but it would not be like other marriages, rounded, whole. He had run from this imperfect marriage, wanting the perfect, wanting the impossible. Now he accepted its inevitability, and with new insight realized that Sara had always accepted it, had not run from it but toward it, not wanting the perfect, the impossible, wanting only love.

There would be loneliness for them both, buried, unspoken. "Needs—needs David," Gramp had said. It would always be a need he would have to answer, as he had answered it the morning he said to Isaiah Watkins, "Heard you say, didn't I, that you could use an extra hand?"

There was no place in all the country where Gramp's need was not present, and there would be those of his race to serve the need in the North, the East, the West. But Gramp had died with an unused passport in his pocket; he had never seen his *Tiger, Tiger*. This was the need that Li'l Joe Champlin's grandson must answer. God giving him the strength and time, he must do what he could to put in the hands of his people their passports, their tickets to a downstairs seat at *Tiger, Tiger*—there, in the region of his birth. These were the men and women who lined the banks of a wide river, singing; of them Gramp had said, "I know my people's voices."

Now he accepted and did not fear that he must break himself in two time and again to return to the little white house in Beauregard with its funny narrow living room where a shabby divan still had antimacassars pinned to threadbare upholstery. Now he knew he would climb, again and again—with a cane to help what would be then a labored, doubly crippled step—the worn stairway that led to a room where dedicated men and women mapped strategy and laid plans for the freeing of his people.

Sara would be here soon. When he heard her steps far down the corridor, he would see her in his mind's eye, half walking, half running, to him. Her eyes would be bright and soft when she saw him, her touch on his cheek gentle. "So thin," she would say, smiling. "So thin. Such a thin, thin love he is!"

Sara, little love, hurry! Sara, baby, come a-running! We must hoard every minute of every day together; they're the bright and shining coins with which to make the payments on a debt that will always be due; they'll be my strength and power in that world you cannot enter with me. He closed his eyes again, and he did not know whether the words that came to him were in a dream or whether he spoke them to himself:

"You'll have but one home, David Champlin—the one that's part of you, has always been and always will be. You cannot tear it or its people out of you; not even Sara can take it from you or replace it with another. There will be many payments on your luck; make this one without whimpering—whenever you go home, you will always go home alone."

88

Sara Champlin broke five eggs into a bowl, seasoned them, and began beating them vigorously with a fork. "Always use a fork," David had said. "Those damned electric mixers are all right I suppose for mashed potatoes and cake batter, but they're pure murder on scrambled eggs." Even so, she knew that when she had finished they wouldn't come within a mile of tasting as good as David's always did.

"Maybe," she murmured to herself, "if I could get closer to the stove—" then smiled at her own irrelevance because she knew there must be thousands, perhaps millions, of pregnant women just about at term, all over the country who could, at any given moment, whip up a decent panful of scrambled eggs.

In a minute she would have to call David if he didn't show up because he hated to hurry through breakfast. "You spoil the big ape," Brad had said. "So I spoil him," she had answered. "Some people gamble, some people drink, some people sniff glue. I spoil David. What else can you do with a character like that? It's compulsive."

She was glad now that Brad and Peg had urged them to wait before buying a place, because they had just learned that a family who lived near the Willises was moving sometime within a year, and they had taken an option on the house. Renting for the interim period hadn't been easy. Plenty of people were willing to sell; few were willing to rent to a mixed couple. She walked away from these places, cheeks flaming with anger, beside a calm and philosophical David. "I hate it for you," he said once. "I suppose I can take it because I can remember the time—and plenty of places—when I wouldn't have been stupid enough even to ask."

The apartment they finally found was in a neighborhood in transit from white to colored. In size and arrangement it was more nearly ideal than they had dared anticipate. There were a large living room, a dining room, bedroom, kitchen with breakfast nook, and a bath. They bought a bed-divan for the living room so they could put up Chuck or Luke or anyone else they wanted, and settled in while Sara, wondering if such happiness was quite decent, simultaneously searched for and found a studio.

She savored these memories now, in present happiness, remembering the years of loneliness and alienation with a sort of shrinking wonderment that she had survived to grasp and make whole the life that had been restored to her that afternoon in David's hospital room. It had been such a damned silly afternoon of little words and little phrases, of laughing and being told by David not to make him laugh, of saying finally: "Fifteen minutes, David. I have to go; they'll make me. Do you want—you—David, you won't send me away? I'll come tomorrow?" And he hadn't heard her. "Don't be late tomorrow, Smallest. Don't—" and as she was going out the door, he had called, "Sara! Sara! Wait! there's a hotel near here. Much, much nearer. Chuck stays there. After a while they'll let you come morning and afternoon and night. I'll make them—"

That same night she had called Chuck Martin and asked, "How did you know, way back there in college, Who it is that runs things?"

A voice said, "Don't beat those eggs to death, hon," and she turned as quickly as her ungainliness would permit and made a face at the man in the doorway.

"Hi, sweet."

He stood tall, still thin, leaning on a cane, bones showing in his face that had not shown years before, eyes clear and smiling. The open neck of the green robe showed the wide, deep chest, the strong symmetry of the dark throat where it sloped to the shoulders.

"Hi, Smallest."

"Smallest, my foot! Not Smallest now. Maybe next week."

He limped over to her, his cane thudding on the floor, and put his arm around her. "It better be sooner than that."

She rose on her toes and kissed him gently, pulling his head down to her lips, one hand soft and still on his cheek. "We're in dreadful shape, aren't we? You can't bend your back far enough over yet to kiss me, and I can't get close enough to you to kiss you properly because of the baby."

He laughed. "We seem to be doing all right. Want me to take over on the eggs?"

"Gosh, yes. Please. Just so they'll be the way you like 'em—"

Usually when they ate in the breakfast nook, David sat with his back against the wall window, the leg with the injured knee stretched out along the bench. Today he sat facing her squarely, the leg, knee slightly bent, extended along the floor beside the table. He looked at the knee, wagged the leg, and said, "It bendeth."

"It will bendeth more after Moore has another go at it, Sudsy says."

"One more river to cross. Only let's not even talk about it, huh? Let's wait till we get over this baby-having deal."

"Till you get over it, you mean."

"All right. Till I get over it, pet." Toast popped up in the toaster beside him, and he took a piece. A sound brought his eyes to the chair at the end of the table, and he saw two small black, pink-lined ears and two round yellow eyes just clearing the table's edge.

"Sara."

"Don't be a meanie."

"Sara, I know I've always been a damned fool about that cat. But I never, I swear I never let him sit at the table."

"Don't blame Chop-bone. And don't make him get down. He won't be top dog—top cat—much longer." She took a small scrap of bacon and laid it near the edge of the table and grinned delightedly when a white-tipped black paw snaked out, speared it, and brought it to a pink and dainty mouth.

"Do you suppose our son will be that smart? Relatively speaking, of course," she asked.

When David did not respond she said, "David, you're not going to mind terribly, are you, I mean really mind, if we have a boy?"

He broke off a small piece of toast, buttered it with careful deliberation, his eyes on the knife, the butter, the toast, miles from Sara.

"David."

He did not look up. "I'm not going to 'really mind,' as you put it, anything if you'll just hurry up and have the baby so I can stop worrying."

"That's not an answer. And I've told you and Suds has told you and Dr. Frye has told you I'm going to be all right."

"What the hell do they know about it?"

"A fair amount, I'd say. Anyhow, look at Peg. Ten years older than I am."

"And twice your size. Besides, she had a Caesarean."

"So will I if anything goes haywire. It won't. David, I think it's going to be a boy. And so does Dr. Frye."

"He's only guessing. Only person I ever knew who could tell beforehand was an old, old lady in the French Quarter. Black as jet, and folks said she practiced voodoo. She was never known to miss. . . ." He broke off another piece of toast, began the slow buttering process again. "She's dead now."

Some women, thought Sara, some women would throw that specially softened butter right smack in his face. And win custody of the child, the cat, and both bank accounts. She drew a deep breath and said, "You mustn't, David; you simply must not mind having a baby, me having a baby, and it's being a boy."

He looked at her now and saw a troubled, anxious face.

"Sweet, let's not go all through it again, huh? There sure as hell isn't anything we can do about it. I know when I'm licked. I even gave in on naming him David. Let's just concentrate on bringing the baby into a world that doesn't particularly want him—or her."

"David. It's not—" She stopped, started to resume speaking twice before she finally managed. "We're in one of those 'areas' again, aren't we? The kind you've talked about. Your area and my area and never the twain and stuff."

"I'm afraid we are."

She remembered their past discussion of the subject, sitting where they were sitting now, late at night, drinking beer, eating cheese and crackers. She wasn't even sure about her pregnancy that time, only hopeful. And she was more than hopeful that David, once he thought they were going to have a baby, would change his stubborn attitude of "no children, for God's sake." His reaction to the news of her possible pregnancy had been the most jolting hurt of her marriage.

"No!" he said. "Go see Suds or an obstetrician or someone tomorrow. You could be mistaken. Lots of times—"

"I've already made an appointment." She was almost whispering. "I made it today. David, I was so happy about it." She sat upright suddenly, stiff and straight and defiant. "And if it's true, David, I'm not going to do anything about it. Not for you or for anything in the world. So don't even mention it."

"I know better than to do that." He smiled across the table at her, and she could tell he was trying to soothe the hurt. "I'll just put in an order for a girl."

"Girl? I've already spoken for a boy. Most men—"

"Sara, love, I've told you this before. I don't want a baby, any kind of baby, because it's too damned rough on any human who has to go through life living in two worlds. It's rough to have one white parent and be called a nigger. It's rough to have two black parents and be called a nigger, but of the two, I'll take two black parents and the word 'nigger' and know pride in my skin. It takes a lot of doing, Sara, for two people to instill pride of race into a child half white, half black. I was born black, lived black, but on my mother's side I must have had white ancestors. You think I'm proud of it? Christ no! Remember Jedediah? There's a proud man. Real pride, I'm talking about. The right kind of pride."

He had gotten up and gone to the refrigerator for more beer. His limp was more pronounced then, and she knew the leg was often painful, but the doctor had said, "Don't try to spare him moderate walking, Mrs. Champlin," and she held herself back from the quick jump to bring him what he wanted, to push things closer to him, her own inner pain greater than his outer pain.

When he came back to the table he said, "I happen to believe that the mixed-race girl has a little better chance. Let's say a less lousy chance."

He poured beer, then smiled at her over the glass, and she knew he was trying to change the course of their talk. "Besides, if this baby we don't know whether we're producing or not is a girl, it might look like you."

"David, if he's a boy—and don't call a baby 'it'—I want him to look like you. Only it doesn't work that way usually. Daughters look like fathers, sons like mothers."

"My God, a midget!"

Sara knew she was being stubborn and female but refused to be diverted. "You've got so much, David, so damned much to offer a son—"

Only when they were in what he'd called "those areas" did David explode with a change of mood so sudden it frightened her. It was as though a word, a phrase not thought out beforehand, acted on the stored memories in his mind like a torch to dynamite.

"What? For Christ's sake, what! A heritage of horror, that's what. One ancestor burned alive, his son dying of fright on a city street when he was an old man, that man's son killed hopping a freight trying to make a living for his family in a white man's world, and his own father missing death from lynching by minutes, permanently crippled. I'll offer him a Champlin coat of arms, I'll draw it—a noose, symbolizing his people; a bonfire, crossed rifles, and a wolf dog rampant."

"David. Don't! You've never talked quite this way before."

"Maybe I've never faced being a parent before."

"But David, that's downright silly. That's not pride of race. It's not what happened to them that's important. It's what they were. Good, fine men, every one of them. You've always said so. And I can speak for Gramp. David, wouldn't you rather point to a dozen ancestors who were lynched than one —just one—who'd taken part in a lynching? Wouldn't you?"

"Of course I would! Of course I would! But how can a man explain that to his son when the kid hears himself called 'nigger' for the first time—a kid who's only half nigger at that? What does he say? Does he say: 'Listen, son, don't let it upset you. Your old man's folks were O.K., they were black. But your mother's folks were stinkers, they were white, and they hung and burned and shot and castrated and enslaved and oppressed your old man's people for two hundred years.' And they'll still be doing it! Even while you're talking to the poor little tyke, they'll still be doing it!"

And I can't do anything about it, she thought; no one can do anything about those deep and hidden areas of stored-up agony and humiliation; no one, no one, no matter how much they love. If only I could bear this baby secretly, without having it show, have it suddenly, not let him know until it is alive and his—and mine. He'd love it, oh, most surely he must love his own as he did other children.

She said, "Billy. You know, the little boy in New Orleans you told me about—"

"He'd already been born! He was already here and in the world, and of it—"

"And fighting. Isaiah told us when he was here that he's the youngest member of ALEC, that he gives a nickel a week to ALEC, out of what little he has. Do you think if you had a son he'd just sit back and feel sorry for himself, let himself be licked? Not David Champlin's son."

It ended then, with David behind the wall she could never stretch tall enough to peer over, even his voice different when it came from the other side of that battlement. "Maybe," he said lightly, "I'd rather a girl because I like girls best—" and she had remained silent because of the bitter knowledge that now, at this moment, when a man and a woman should be closest, she and David were two different lifetimes apart.

They had not discussed it again during the nine months just past, David's shrinking from the fact of the child apparently swallowed up in his inordinate worry about her. She told Peg, "Honestly, there's not a single thing that can go wrong with a pregnancy or delivery that he doesn't wake up in the night worrying about."

"As long as you don't do that, it'll be a breeze—"

"I don't care if it's a breeze or a hurricane, Peg. I just can't seem to be anything but brainless and happy about the whole thing—"

Now, in what might be only a matter of days or even hours before the child was born that he had said he didn't want, she drew back from getting any deeper into one of the "areas" that held pain for them both.

She refilled their cups, sugared David's generously, and held her own in both hands, looking at him over its rim.

"You know when this baby was conceived, David? I mean, really conceived?"

He grinned at her. "We could turn the problem over to a computer—"

"Please. I'm serious, David. I hoped you'd know, but I imagine it's one of those only-female things. And maybe you won't even understand. It was a long time ago. It was on a spring night in Laurel, Ohio, when a kid named David Champlin came to a door and a girl with her arm in a green silk sling opened it and loved him like hell from then on in. That's when it was."

Looking at her, he felt his throat constrict. What could a man say when his wife came out with something as completely woman as that; what say that wouldn't be clumsy or flip or sound as if he was making fun? He took her hand and rolled the fingers in, closing his own hand over the tiny fist.

"Maybe you're right, hon. But we're a long way out there, in the realms of metaphysics, and predestination, and theology and God knows what. It wasn't nearly as much fun standing in the door as depending on the good old way—"

"You—you thing, you." She grinned at him. "No soul."

"One damned sure thing. Our child wasn't conceived when we thought it was. The infant would be three weeks old now and I'd be sleeping better. Viper."

"Who's a viper?"

"You are, honey chile. Lawd, yes! Losing count, not taking your pill on the right days—"

"Judge, the defendant called my client a viper and a liar

and accused her of deceit and treachery and we hereby petition this honorable court—"

"Brad'll handle it, baby."

He stood up slowly, taking his cane from where it was hooked over the back of the bench. "I have to get dressed and beat it." He scratched behind Chop-bone's ears, and the cat, settled now in elderly complacency on the seat of the chair, paws tucked in, responded with dignified thanks. As David limped toward the bedroom, Sara watched him, thinking how much faster he was getting around now, how his body had adjusted to the new handicaps and managed somehow to keep its grace, noting the wide spread of the shoulders and how almost undetectable was the stiffness of one. She remembered the long hours he had spent at the piano, forcing his right shoulder to guide his arm, playing more treble than she had ever heard. "Gramp always said he didn't give a hoot how good a man's right hand was, that it wasn't worth a damn if he couldn't back it up with a solid left. But damned if he meant the left hand to do it all."

After she had cleared the table, she followed David to the bedroom and began making the bed.

"Don't," he said. "Just smooth it up."

"This from you!"

"I'm scared to have you stoop over."

"I won't tuck in."

"See you don't." He was standing in front of the mirror, chin up, making fearful grimaces as he knotted his tie.

"Sara."

"What? Go on. Don't just stand there making faces."

"Are you going to raise a sand if I take that trip to Cainsville with Brad? I mean, after the baby's born."

She was pulling up the plaid bedspread, and stood holding it in her hand. "Raise a sand? I haven't before, have I? I don't when you go to New Orleans. And I didn't when you went to Selma, did I?"

He was watching her in the mirror, and now, smoothing the ends of his tie, he laughed. "Baby, you never said a word, you never made a sound, when I went to Selma. But you screamed to high heaven just the same."

She sighed. "Probably I did. I didn't mean to. You won't go alone?"

"There'll be Brad, and Luke if he can make it."

"And only for a day?"

"Early plane in the morning, rent a car in Capitol City,

plane to Washington late that evening with a good connection to Boston that night."

"I'd be a dope to mind, wouldn't I? Or worry."

"That's not saying you won't, but honest-to-God, Sara, it will be all right. A couple of deaths too long delayed have helped."

"That poisonous little puff adder, Scoggins—"

"Stone-cold daid in the market. Apoplexy. As you know."

"I know."

"And the mayor. Mowed down in his prime, he was, by his own tractor, on his own farm. A squashy character he looked, even alive. He must have—"

"Ick!—"

"Sorry. I forgot your usually strong stomach has weakened—"

He slipped into his coat, walked over to her and drew her close, his arm around her. "It hasn't been easy for you, Smallest. Married to me."

"Or for you—to me."

"Sorry?"

"Stoopid! You don't know, you just don't know, what it was like all that long time—"

"I don't? Sara. Sara." His arm tightened; then he released her, and she walked beside him to the front door.

"Today? Think you can manage to produce today, elephant girl?"

"Elephant girl!"

"I stood in that doorway a hell of a long time ago—"

"So you did, sweet, so you did—"

At four o'clock that afternoon David Champlin thumped into the third-floor lounge of Endicott Hospital's maternity wing, Brad just behind him, and glared at Peg Willis. "Why didn't you call me this morning!"

She took his arm, her husky voice deeper than usual with amusement. "Everything's fine, kid. All systems go—"

"She's been here all day!"

"She wouldn't let me." Peg turned to Brad. "What'll we do with the guy, Brad?" then back to David. "She said she could labor and bring forth for one but she was damned if she could do it for two. I see what she meant. She had me call as soon as your offspring seemed more imminent—"

"The last damned minute—"

"By the time I got to the telephone, called, and came back

up, they were taking her to the delivery room. Things were happening that fast."

"That can be bad, can't it?"

"No! My God! Brad, rustle up some coffee—"

For an hour David prowled the room, sat, stood up, growled when spoken to and growled when not spoken to, finally retreating into tense silence. He was standing by a center table leafing through a magazine, seeing nothing, when Suds came into the room, pink and beaming.

"Congratulations, dad! It's a boy, six seven, and Sara's fine!"

David dropped the magazine to the table and leaned forward, resting his weight on his hands. Sudsy's hand hit him between the shoulders. "Did you hear me?"

"Sure. Sure I heard you. You're not kidding? About Sara?"

Peg ran over, hugged him and kissed him resoundingly on his cheek. "Of course he's not. I tried to tell you, dope. It's wonderful!"

David looked uncomprehendingly at Suds. "Six seven?"

"Weight. Pounds and ounces. What did you think it was, height? Or quantity?"

"Can I go up now?"

"Wait for half an hour. She'll be wide awake then. That lad was in a hurry, a real hurry. Frye had to slow things down a bit. I promised Sara I'd run over from the office for the big moment, and I barely made it."

David said, "I'm going up now—"

"There's no point—Wait, here's the boss of the project."

Dr. Anthony Frye entered, and David thought he had never seen a more incompetent-looking man. There was only a thin veil over the hostility in David's eyes when he looked at the doctor. For a moment, his thoughts left Sara as he tried to read the other man's face. What was the smug-looking bastard thinking now, breaking the news of a son to the black husband of the white woman who had borne that son? What was he thinking, this man who could be the archetype of the ordered, conventional white world into which he brought God knew how many babies each year to lead ordered, conventional white lives? There was no answer in the smiling face that, David had to admit, did not bear at that moment any evidence of giving the matter even superficial thought.

"Mr. Champlin, you can relax now." The doctor's eyes were bright. "I'll turn you over to young Dr. Sutherland here for care and treatment. Everything is one hundred percent. The boy, the mother, the friends." He laughed a practiced laugh. "Everyone's fine except the father, eh?"

"I'm all right. I want to see her now—"

"Wait a bit. Your son was in quite a hurry, Mr. Champlin. I don't think I've ever run as fast, comparatively speaking, to catch a train. We had to put your wife under to slow things a bit. And there was a little repair work—" He held up a hand reassuringly. "Bound to be. Makes for discomfort, nothing worse, and no fooling around with surgery later." He spoke to Suds now. "The whole thing was rather amazing, wasn't it, Doctor?"

"Great," said Suds.

"Once in a while," said Frye, his eyes on David again, "one finds an obstetrical case in which the patient is, quite literally, in a state we can only call euphoria, without drugs. It is not too unusual. It's almost a state of ecstasy. Your wife was angry because we had to put her under."

Peg said, "I've been trying to tell him—"

"I believe I told you when we first met that I follow the in-room policy? Your baby will be in the room with his mother. They'll have a chance to get acquainted. And while some obstetricians send their patients home practically from the delivery room, I keep my patients hospitalized five days. A little rest and coddling does no harm. She'll be up and have bathroom privileges in the morning. I'll talk to you both before she goes home." The doctor walked over, held out his hand, and David looked at it dazedly for a minute, then shook it, grinning. Best obstretrician in New England, Suds had said, and by God, he'd been right. Not a bad guy, either.

"Thanks, Doctor," said David. "Thanks a million."

The doctor hurried out, and Brad lit a cigarette and said, "Would anyone like to know that I'm here?" He looked at David, his eyes quiet and unsmiling, affection deep within them. "You know how I feel, brat. Everything's going to be fine."

David smiled his thanks and turned to Suds. "I want to see her the minute she's awake. Tell her I'm glad it's a boy."

"You will. As if she didn't know, Stoopid."

"She doesn't," said David. He went to one of the room's big armchairs and let himself down into it with a thud. "Suds, my wife—"

"Sara?"

"Quit clowning, for God's sake. This is serious. Maybe a matter of life and death. Sara told me you once rustled up a drink for her here. Man, I could sure use one—"

89

DAVID ALWAYS TRIED TO handle with tact his knowledge of Brad's dislike of flying. When he could take a train, Brad did so and reveled in the trip; when time pressed he flew. And suffered, thought David, settling himself in the aisle seat beside the older man, trying to bring his stiff leg as far under the seat in front as he could so the stewardesses wouldn't trip over it. If his stiff leg had done nothing else, it had provided him with a valid excuse for spending the money to travel first class. Which he had always done anyhow when he was alone, putting up the extra money when he checked in at the ticket counter, thereby preventing reprimands. Brad's first experience with travel hadn't been on a southern bus with a redneck driver; his own reaction was still adolescent, he knew, but he got a lot of satisfaction out of it. And, he reflected, so did his legs, both of them.

He glanced sideways at Brad, trying to decide whether this was one of the times when he would welcome distracting conversation or one of the times when he wanted to be let alone to turn green in peace. Their plane trip always started with a stock phrase from Brad. "No statistics, please."

David let his seat back a notch and said, "What you ought to do is take a nice long trip in a bus, southern route. You'd be yelling for a plane."

"Hrrmph."

If I talk to him I won't, so help me God, I won't mention the baby again. The poor guy's had it. David took a newspaper from his pocket, flipped it open.

"Been a long time since anyone could say there's nothing in the paper. Vietnam, South America, Louisiana. Ever been in Bogalusa? I have. Remind me to call Isaiah from Cainsville. . . . That five-day hospital stay worked out fine. I wouldn't have left Sara alone at home with the baby, that's for sure. . . ."

"You certainly underestimate that young woman. . . . We're taking off—"

"I was trying to keep it from you. . . . How the devil do they manage to get them so perfect? Hands and feet, right number of toes and fingers, ears. . . . It's early to say, but I think he's going to be about your complexion . . . Hell, I forgot to cable Hunter. . . . Remind me to call Isaiah Watkins from Cainsville, huh? . . . Did I tell you Sara's going to nurse the baby? Says maybe she'll finally get a figure. . . . It's a lot better for the baby, Frye says. . . . Oh, God, I wasn't going to mention the baby again. . . . Here comes the gal with the breakfast. You want?"

"No. Yes. Just coffee. You can have the food. Go on, talk about young David. I gave you the routine for months after we had Carolyne."

David looked at his tray and drew a deep breath. He couldn't remember having an appetite like this since he'd been at Pengard. It had started with Sudsy's drink in the hospital and grown inordinately ever since. "That tray bothering you, Chief? I'll call her and have her take it—"

"There's nothing wrong with me two feet on the ground won't cure. I'm not airsick. Just hurry up and finish your tray and then take mine and I can get some work done on this table thing."

David choked back a laugh and tackled his breakfast. If he'd stop thinking about the baby, he'd stop talking about him. "Remember that psychiatrist Cloninger we had on the Sampson case? He told me that every time he got on a plane he froze solid."

"Just proves it's not true that psychiatrists need their own therapy."

The stewardess poured more coffee, and David said, "I've always gotten a bang out of flying. But I don't believe I'll encourage young David to take it up as a career—"

"Eat."

"Yes, sir. Sorry, sir."

What had changed his attitude, he wondered? The change hadn't come about all at once, when he had first seen his son. He had been far too limp with reaction, too preoccupied with the most beautiful woman he had ever seen. That night he and Brad and Suds had gotten fairly well polluted and he had been asleep almost before he got into bed, yet the change had taken place by the next day when he sweet-talked his way upstairs outside visiting hours and found Sara's bed empty, with the sound of a shower coming from the bathroom, and the laughter of two women, Sara and a nurse.

He stood by the bassinet, looking down at the baby, not touching or wanting to touch, afraid to touch, just wanting to communicate, knowing he couldn't, but willing it with his mind so hard he thought the words must be audible and comprehensible even to a mind just eighteen hours old. "We'll make out, kid. I can't do it the way Gramp did, but I'll try. That's a promise. It's too bad you had to miss out on Gramp. He'd have known the answers to a lot of questions you'll ask." *Reckon me'n' Gram's got to teach you about God some more. Come on, li'l man, right now we gets ourselves some ice cream.* Now David reached out and touched a soft cheek with a gentle finger. "Your mother won't always understand. And I won't either. But don't you ever forget, youngster, we love you." He smiled suddenly and whispered aloud, "Sorry, son, about not wanting you before."

Sara had come in then, smiling, glowing, wincing with funny little grimaces as she walked, "David, darling—"

In about two seconds now he'd be talking about his son to Brad again, and he resolutely pulled his mind away from the bassinet in the third-floor room at Endicott Hospital. There were half-a-dozen things he should be thinking about, problems that his thinking and planning could affect materially, and that small scrap of male humanity back in Boston could —damn! When the stewardess picked up the trays he let his seat back to the last notch. Sleep was never far when he was on a plane, was very close when he had had to get up at five thirty in order to catch it. There had been little enough of it the night before, waking what seemed like every hour on the hour, something within him shouting: "You've got a son! You've got a son! You and Sara have a son—" Turning, twisting, punching pillows, he said to himself: "Sunday morning I'll go to Roxbury before I get Sara and the baby. Go to church, do a little singing. Yes, Lawd! They'll know I'm there Sunday. . . . Damn, why can't I sleep?"

He had left the bedroom door open, and sometime during the night he felt Chop-bone's quiet, considerate jump to the bed, the soft maneuverings as the cat settled down beside him. "Don't stomp," he'd said. "And stay off my back—"

In the plane he stretched a little more and settled his head more comfortably on the back of the seat. When he awakened he did not open his eyes at first and as he sat there quietly a memory dislodged itself from somewhere and floated to the surface of his mind and he saw an enraged, humiliated, sickened boy taking his first train trip and the porter who had known so well how to handle him. *Shucks. Couldn't let Li'l Joe Champlin's grandson go hongry in my car. . . . Thought I knowed you when I seen you. . . . Soon's I seen you smile I was sure. . . . Stretch out now, son, and get your res'.*

Good people, he thought; my people are good people, with quick eyes to see and quick hands to help another's hurt, and how could their own in other places let them down, how isolate themselves within the cocoon of their own bitterness and frustration until they could neither see nor comprehend the warm and secret comradeship that had drawn their forefathers together and given them strength? The handkerchiefs were coming off the heads now; even grizzled, gray heads were held a little higher, uncovered; and aged, rheumy eyes held a vision of the future of their race they had never held before. Each trip home that he had made since he had been well enough, each visit to a smaller town, had lifted his heart. Selma, Alabama, had sent him home silent and remote for days, the far horizons he had seen filling him with an awed wonderment, giving him strength for the harder, more grueling struggle he knew lay just ahead before those horizons could be reached. Lord! he thought now, and his lips moved in a half-smile, Lord, you better let my people go, because if You don't, they're going anyhow.

He glanced sideways at Brad, and the half-smile became a full one at the expression of determined concentration on the thin face bending over the contents of a Manila folder. The Chief wasn't going to let a li'l ol' airplane bug him. The cover of the folder was marked "Hospital," and he felt he ought to discuss the contents with Brad, then decided against it. Maybe the guy was really engrossed, and conversation would bring him back to the unpleasant realization that he was thirty thousand feet up.

He didn't want to become too involved in the hospital project that had been started by Lloyd Litchfield when Litchfield, breathing fire, had visited him while he was still in Endicott Memorial. Brad and Chuck had been there, and during a general discussion of the use of the land he had said, "Whyn't you take that meadow off my hands anyhow, Lloyd? I can't give it away—or sell it. Old Miz Towers would die of a broken heart. I can lease it to you—ninety-nine-year lease—for free, if you want."

Chuck had leaned forward in his chair suddenly. "Hospital," he said, beaming, and before any of them had realized it, Litchfield had talked to architects, had plans drawn up, and launched—with Chuck and Brad's help—a full-fledged campaign for the building of a hospital on Flaming Meadows. Money had come almost unasked in the aftermath of the publicity the Cainsville troubles had received. It would be a hospital that would serve the whole area, without discrimination, with a large children's annex. "Call it the Effie Brown Memorial Annex," said David.

Plans for this trip to Cainsville had been made when Brad said ol' Miz Towers had been dead set on giving David the deed to the land with her own hands. "Says she won't die until she does it. And even Miz Towers doesn't want to live forever. That deed represents the land to her now, in a sort of transubstantive way."

And David had understood, and known, and agreed to come. "O.K., Chief. We'll go after the baby's born, eh?"

Brad was closing the folder now, looking gingerly out the window. "Say, David! That's ground down there."

"Well, hallelujah! Don't worry about a thing. We'll hit it slow and easy, on wheels."

90

IT WAS LIKE COMING BACK to a place in which he had spent a long time. Surely more than two days had passed on that first experience of Cainsville; surely a larger part of his lifetime had been spent among these familiar buildings, these familiar rooms, these friendly faces.

There was still an upturned nail keg near the counter in Haskin's store, and he awkwardly lowered his body to sit on it as he had the afternoon of his first day there. He could see few changes, none significant; even the smell was the same—old wood, beer, lunch meet, cheese, vegetables fresh from the earth, tobacco smoke, and people. Only the feel of the humid heat of that August day was missing.

As it had been then, the room was well filled, but not crowded. And if there was nothing absent that had been there then except the heat, there was something added: the sound of easy laughter, of the lightning-quick banter of his people when there is no outsider present, the sound, the feel of the vital rhythm of their being.

The greetings between him and Haskin were over and he waited now, as he had waited that first time, for the storekeeper to finish with his counter customers, relaxed, letting the feel of the place take over his mind, responding to the warmth of the inevitable, innumerable handclasps; feeling himself grow slower, easier, answering in kind the familiar phrases of welcome and concern, knowing himself as whole and not divided, his body loose and easy, his mind content, at peace.

His eyes lighted as he noticed a stout gray-haired woman at the front counter, and he watched her and waited for Haskin to give her change, sure she would put the coins in an old-fashioned change purse, snap it shut, then drop it into the huge, shabby bag she carried, the same bag she had carried on that other afternoon. This time she did not see him on her way out because he was seated, and as she passed him he said, "Morning, ma'am—" and she looked down at him and smiled. "Mornin', son, mornin'. How you doin'?" then hurried on, still smiling, reaching out to him today, as she had then, for a bright moment in the universal communion of his people. He did not need to steady himself today, as he had needed to then, against an almost overwhelming urge to follow her to whatever warm and shabby home she lived in, there to stay. Today he would have liked to follow her, to stop a while with her in the home he could visualize so well, sit and drink the lemonade or soft drink sure to be stored in her icebox. But it was not the sick longing of a spent mind and tortured soul. He had seen her once, and then again, and now she was gone, and it might well be he would never see her in the future, but he had known her all his life. He had heard her voice among the voices of the people who had lined the banks of the wide river of his childhood's fantasy, had known her in the friendly corner stores of New Orelans' Vieux Carré, kind to a little boy, watched her bustle down the aisle in the small weather-beaten church Gramp took him to in Beauregard, seen her sit, talking to Gram, in their kitchen.

He did not realize Brad had come over and was standing close to him until he heard, "David. Wake up. Onward and upward—" He pulled himself to his feet with the help of his cane. All around him there were dark eyes, warm with compassion, but no tactless move to help him.

Drinking beer in Haskin's kitchen later, he learned that Gracie and Shad had gone to California to visit her sister and that she was settling there for good; that Willy was in Chicago, had been there, since a couple of months after leaving Anderson's hospital.

"How's he doing?" asked David.

"Says he's doing fine," said Haskin. And added, "That's what he say."

That's us, thought David; got to see it, hear it, touch it, smell it, know it by our own senses to believe it—if it's good. But if it's bad—it's true. He had heard it so often, the story of another's good fortune tagged with "That's what he say." It was one of the paradoxes of that "Negro character" others mouthed about so freely, a reaction part jealousy, part antagonism toward his own race; one of the imponderables that made the Negro wary always, yet in spite of that wariness bound to his fellows, with bonds of common suffering, bonds whose very strength sometimes bred secret hatred of such humiliating fetters. Yet his race had given to its people a Martin Luther King, a Hummer Sweeton, a Dick Gregory, a Mahalia Jackson, because there was a greatness in its blood and bone and heart. Where was the greatness beneath the pettiness, the all-too-frequent sabotage? Where was it in the lost and lonely defiance of the ghetto-born, the bitter aloofness of the intellectual? Crushed, twisted, broken, racked; still, it survived in all his people more often than it died; it was there for all the world to see and take account of in the massed thousands of a march on Washington, the singing hundreds on the road from Selma to Montgomery; immortalized, witnessed to by the corpses of the Medgar Everses, the Hummer Sweetons, the shattered, tortured body of a brown youth found beneath an embankment.

Now, in retrospect, he asked himself if it had been the knowledge of his people's need that had kept him with them, or an instinctive homage to an emergent greatness impossible to turn from. It did not matter; he would never know the answer, just as he would never know the answer to the riddle of the paradoxes of his people—of himself.

He jumped, startled, at Mrs. Haskin's voice. "Penny," she said. "Penny for your thoughts."

"Gosh, I'm sorry, Mrs. Haskin!"

Jim Haskin looked at him closely. "Ain't upset, are you? Coming back down here after all that happened?"

"Lord, no! I'm glad to be here. I was thinking, back there in the store, that I'd only been here two days on that other trip, yet I felt as though I was back with old friends."

"You are. You sure are and that's a fact—"

Later, said Haskin, when Brad and David had finished their business with Miz Towers, they could come back for supper and talk about the present situation and future plans. "Voting rights bill, it'll get us registered now," said Haskin. "But it ain't got us in the ballot booths yet. Not by a long sight, it ain't. We got a ways to go yet—"

He and Brad were leaving for the Towers house when Luke Willis called, long distance, for David.

"Hi, boss! Congratulations!"

"Thanks, kid. Where you calling from?"

"New York. I couldn't make it down there. Man, it seems like a year since I saw you."

"Two months."

"Yeah. And now you're a daddy. When you sending him to school?"

"Next week."

"Be seeing you then maybe. I'll be down your way. Just wanted to call today and send my regards to the folks there, and congratulate you."

"Thanks, kid."

"See you soon, boss. Hey, wait—does the baby look like you or Sara?"

"Who can tell! Looks like a baby to me. A real fine one—"

"See you—"

As Brad and David drove away, Brad said, "We'll come back the long way round and stop for a minute to see Anderson and his wife, maybe bring them back with us to Haskin's. Mrs. Haskin would rather, I swear, she'd rather cook for a dozen than a few."

"Listen, Chief, there's one thing that absolutely must not get loused up. Anderson's to be top dog on this hospital thing. You got that straight with Litchfield?"

"Don't worry. We're keeping control. Anderson may give some of the white doctors who are volunteering a bad time."

"You think so?"

Brad shrugged. "He's a bitter man now, David. He's never gotten over Effie Brown, and the things that happened the night you were hurt." He swung the car around a chuckhole and continued on slowly. "If it sickens laymen, decent laymen, to see people die for lack of care, to know the color of a man's skin opened the pearly gates for him, mustn't it be hell for a doctor?"

"Up till now it hasn't been hell for most of the ofay doctors in these lily-white southern hospitals." David gave a short laugh. "On the other hand, maybe it has, and they just feel at home there."

After a few jolting moments they came to the house that had been Tether's End. David noticed that the yard was strewn with battered toys, the house occupied now that ALEC had taken over a back room in Haskin's store.

"It must be just about here that Tinker did his bit for his country," said Brad.

"Notice this package I'm carrying? Juicy soupbones."

Suddenly his mood changed, and bitterness mingled sourly with remembered terror; he felt again the sickening blows on spine and head, his own prone helplessness, heard again the shouted obscenities and sadistic laughter, the vicious snarls of unseen dogs, not known then as rescuers.

Tinker was on Miz Towers's porch when they parked outside the gate, and came slowly toward them, stopping and sitting, motionless, at the halfway mark of the path. David said, "Hiya, gorgeous; hiya, Tinker," softly, and the powerful body came bounding toward them. David handed the soupbone package hastily to Brad, steadied himself on his cane, saying "Down, Tinker, down," as the big paws hit his chest. Brad said, "My God, he's a fearsome thing at first sight. Scared the hell out of me even now."

Miz Towers was on the porch as they approached the house, brought there by Tinker's heralding barks. David saw marks of age that had not been there before, even the two years had bent the shoulders, put a tremor in the gnarled black hands, sunk the eyes even deeper into dark sockets, yet left untouched the life behind the eyes. She talked as she had before, incessantly, as she led them into house and kitchen and there, for the first time, seemed to take in David's limp and cane. "Lord Jesus!" she said. "They hurted you bad—"

"A cup of your coffee, Miz Towers, and another raw carrot and I'll forget about it—"

They were sitting at the table by the window when Abraham came in. "Man, it's sure fine to see you," he said. "You looking good, man!"

"Considering," said David, and grinned up at Abraham. "Don't look so bad yourself."

"You-all heard? I'm a citizen now."

"God's sake! I missed out on that." David told the lie easily. Brad had told him about it, but he knew that Abraham wanted to tell him about it himself.

"I ain't saying we didn't have a time. There was eighty-five of us the first time we went up to register. Les Forsyte and some folks from ALEC in New Orleans, they took us over. Five of us made it, and I was one, and twenty made the jailhouse. But five's better'n none. Next time they was ten of us made it. But Ma, here, I don't reckon she stopped praying from sunup to sundown that first time till I come home all in one piece. Man could get hisself kilt even thinking about registering to vote fer as long as she can remember." He was pouring coffee from the pot on the stove, brought his cup to the table now. "This town sure got its belly full of quiet back there, nothing but a handful of colored crossing to the other side to work. Didn't make humans out of 'em, but they ain't hankering for another dose of it. Hear it's working good other places, too. This here boycott, that'll help, too—"

"Don't relax, Abraham," said David. He heard Miz Towers slip up beside him, saw a gnarled black hand holding a folded legal document and a photograph. He took them from her, and she said: "Mighty proud to put these in your hands, son. They been waitin' for you."

"Thanks." He did not look directly at her or at the others either, not wanting to show the emotion that was threatening his composure. "Thanks again, Miz Towers—" He slipped the photograph and the deed into the inner pocket of his coat, patting the coat lightly afterward, then looked directly into her wise, hooded old eyes, and smiled.

Abraham's voice broke the silence. "We all knows better than to lay back now. Ain't none of us doing anything that foolish. Registering ain't voting. Always did say that would be the day of reckoning. Always did say it. Still, times is changing. Even Ma notices it. Times is changing—"

As David maneuvered himself into the car after leaving the Towers house, he handed the deed to Brad. "Please. In your briefcase, Chief." When the motor started he said: "Look, Chief, run on down the road a bit, will you? We can spare five minutes. I've been hatching an idea. That wide place in the creek where I went swimming—I've been wondering if they could build a dam up above, or divert the stream or something like that, make a natural swimming hole for the kids who are ambulatory or who need it for therapy. Like a kid I know in New Orleans named Billy—"

"Still spoiling you, brat," said Brad and backed the car into the driveway of Abraham's garage, turning it westward. He pulled to the side of the road just short of the plank bridge that crossed the stream. "You aren't getting out, are you?"

"Sure I am."

Brad reached for the door handle beside him, and David said, "Get off my back, Grandmaw! I'm O.K. I can make it alone. It's not all that rough—"

He limped slowly away from the car, his cane making a hollow thudding sound on the worn planks of the bridge. Without turning, he waved his free hand at Brad when he heard the older man call, "Take it easy!"

Now he stood on the far side of the bridge, more than ankle deep in the spiky, coarse grass that lined the rutted roadway. The late-afternoon hush lay over Flaming Meadows, and no breeze stirred its lush greenness; there were no ripples now to change its colors in subtle movement. The only sound was that of swiftly running Angel Creek brawling against its bonds, hurtling over fallen branches, chuckling over rocks. David Champlin, standing there in the quiet, tried to take in, to make his own, the knowledge that here, where once had been flaming horror, there would be healing; here, where in fear-inspired fantasies imaginative minds heard the windblown eerie laughter of a "ha'nt," there would be the human sound of the voices of men and women and children who would come for help to a place once known as Flaming Meadows.

The words of a hymn he had last heard in the church in Roxbury came to him—"Lord, don't let my running be in vain"—and he began to hum softly; then the words and the melody were obscured by the wide river of his childhood's half-dream, its bank lined with people, all black, all singing —and his voice became more than a hum, became a song, the words low and vibrant. It felt good to sing here in the open, in the quiet before dusk. "Pharaoh's army got drownded—"

The tree on the low hill that rose gently from the edge of Flaming Meadows was small and sturdy. One of its branches was of just the right height to give comfortable support to the folded arms of the tall, thin man in the green shirt, and he leaned on them now, waiting. Now and then he reached down to touch the rifle propped against the tree's trunk, making sure that it was steady, and twice he raised it to his shoulder and sighted experimentally at some distant object. When he did this the wide thin lips curled upward, parted just enough to show the edges of tobacco-stained teeth. Get a rabbit from here easy, he thought; a nigger ought to be duck soup.

He had a good feeling about it; folks could laugh, but he'd always known when things were going to go right for him, when his luck had changed and things were really going his way. He'd had it that noon when someone at City Hall told him the nigger they'd tried to get two years ago was back in town. If he'd been along the night they set out to get him, the nigger wouldn't be back; he wouldn't have bitched the job up the way those punk kids had. And they wouldn't bitch it up now; they'd been trained good now. But they'd sure bitched it up then.

He'd got the scrawny little preacher, everyone knew that, and those folks that hadn't congratulated him had kept their mouths shut. Even if they caught him for getting this one, he wasn't worried; maybe a little while in the jailhouse till his friends brought bail, but nothing serious. But it was a hell of a note when a God-fearing white man in the South even had to think about a spell in the jailhouse for getting a trouble-making nigger, a hell of a note when a man couldn't get credit, fair and square and in the open, for doing his duty by his people.

But those kids should have gotten this nigger that night they went after him; he had a personal score to settle with the black bastard. Wasn't no white man could get away with hitting ol' Clete in the balls, and this black son of a bitch had sent him sprawling, moaning, on the pavement. He mighta been hurt, lying there, all them folks running, not seeing where they was going.

And that wasn't all. He swore obscenely, thinking about how it wasn't all. This black ape had gone back north and married a white woman, come back down here from a white woman's bed—been in the papers, been on the radio, hadn't it, about his marrying some white bitch who'd ought to be turned over to the Klan? By God, ol' Clete was doing his Christian duty, that's what he was doing, his Christian duty, killing the black bastard.

He shifted his weight, muscles tiring now. That must have been their car, in front of the Towers place—and that was something else. Him and his mongrel friend, coming down here, buying land, tricking decent white people out of it. That must have been their car in front of the Towers house, and from where he stood he could see the house, the yard, and the car. Sooner or later they'd come out, and he was sure, certain sure, they'd drive down a piece to see the land the nigger had come back here and bought.

He straightened as the sound of a car starting came to him clearly in that tranquil twilight hush. He turned his head and saw the car in front of the Towers house pull away and travel down the road, stop at the edge of the plank bridge. He'd been right; his hunch had been right. He saw the big dark man climb awkwardly out of the car, thought fleetingly that even if the kids had bitched the job up two years ago they'd given the nigger something to remember them by. The man was limping across the bridge now, using a cane, then stopping in the grass beside the roadside, looking upstream.

He raised his rifle, brought the dark head to dead center in the cross hairs of his sight. It was a damned shame, a God-damned shame, to have to kill a bad nigger quick like this. It ought to be done slow, so's the son of a bitch would know what was happening, slow so's the other niggers would know, when they found out, how he must have screamed and prayed. The bastards always prayed. This kind of hunting was for deer, for animals; it was too good, too quick for uppity niggers. It used to be different, in the old days when the South was let to be what God meant it to be, white man's country. Things were getting worse in the South, getting worse. Times were changing—things were getting bad—times were changing—

The dark head had moved, but now it was dead center again, thrown back a little, and he thought he saw the nigger's lips moving, could hear, faintly, his voice. Black bastard must be singing, the way the sound carried. There was no breeze to calculate; the cold eyes looking through the sight were keen; the finger on the trigger was steady. When the sound of the shot died out, he waited for the space of four breaths before turning away. Just to be sure. Just to be dead sure.

91

DR. CLIFTON SUTHERLAND stumbled into an unoccupied room in the maternity ward of Endicott Memorial Hospital. He closed the door quickly behind him and leaned against it, fighting for control. There had been no time to think, to take the news fully into his consciousness when they had called him at home. "Dr. Frye is in surgery. Can you come immediately?" the nurse had said, and behind her voice he heard Sara's. He did what it lay within his power to do, gave her a few kind hours of oblivion, then checked and rechecked, calling desperately to Brad's office, to wire services, to radio and TV news editors. It had to be an unspeakable, macabre joke, the call to Sara, an obscenity of such horror the mind could not accept it, and then, at last, his mind was forced to accept it, and he almost stumbled down the corridor to the haven of the empty room, seeking solitude, like a wounded animal. Some one of those who gathered now in a knot at the chart desk, their low tones charged with shock and pity, might have touched him, he thought, might have said, "It's terrible. You were such good friends." Some other doctor might have put an arm across his shoulder, his father even, and there was already an arm across his shoulder. It was a strong, brown arm, and he was back in Laurel, in the cold gray bleakness of a winter afternoon, coughing, coughing, then standing, weak and shaken, feeling that strong arm, hearing a deep laugh, a deep young voice saying, "You tell your father you want David Champlin with you—" He was in a room, the only damned student's room on the whole damned campus with a fireplace, and that same voice was saying, "You think you've got the plague? There's millions of us were born with it," and then he was outside again in the bleak gray cold, and the strength of another's body was supporting him, and he could feel the strong and steady rhythm of the other's heart—the strong and steady rhythm of David's heart—Suds Sutherland, alone, leaned his head against the door, and tears ran unchecked down plump cheeks, gray now with shock and grief.

It was ten strides from one end to the other of the bricked terrace outside Beanie Benford's classroom. Ten strides, and he had made them a hundred times since his telephone had rung an hour before, and he heard Karl Knudsen's shaken voice. "We are sure now," said Knudsen. "I did not call to tell you until I was sure." Benford thought: I would not have doubted; I would have known the truth of it, but that is because I am black and you are white.

"For one thing only I am thankful," said Knudsen. "For one thing only. That my brother Bjarne did not live to know of this. David was—he called him his—the son of his mind—"

"Yes," said Benford. "Yes. Thank you, Karl, for calling."

And so he had walked, back and forth, while the shadowy form of a stunned, proud youth stood by the parapet and watched. The sound of his own voice talking to that youth came back to him now, but he could not remember the words he had said, except that he had meant them to bring comfort and strength, but he would not forget the look on the young face, the set of the wide shoulders, the hurt in the dark eyes—or the words: "One thing, Professor. One thing I'm not going to do is pack. I'm not going to pack."

Benford searched his mind again for his own words on that day; they might bring him the comfort and strength he had sought to give the boy. There had been something about courage, and the evils of becoming torpid, and about love and, somehow, about God. But all that came back to his mind today were the words he had whispered inaudibly as David Champlin limped, straight and tall, down the path away from him: "Lawd Jesus, he'p him; he ain't nothing but a chile."

The lounge of the London hotel where the former Dean Goodhue of Pengard College and his wife had been staying for two months had the hushed quietude of one of the city's older and fustier clubs. They chose the hotel because it was a favorite in those academic circles where Goodhue moved and tried to have his being. Today the outside fog made its dim interior seem almost warmly inviting. "Shabby old place," Goodhue would say. "But we enjoy it; feel more at home there, don't you know. And they serve a really proper tea."

Elacoya Goodhue was presiding over one of what her husband called the "really proper" teas, and with them, more by accident than design, were an angular professor from a Midlands university and a rounder, plumper one from nearby London University. The angular professor accepted a cup of tea from Elacoya, selected a sandwich, and said, "Shocking thing, eh Goodhue? Murder of that young man. Graduate of your college, wasn't he?"

Goodhue fumbled through pockets, one hand eventually emerging with pipe, the other with tobacco pouch. "I believe he was eventually graduated. After I left there. Yes, I believe it must have been after that."

"My son knew him at Oxford," said the plump professor. "Good friends, actually. Haven't talked to him yet, but his mother tells me he's quite shaken up by it."

Elacoya Goodhue said, "Hot water, Professor?" and the man who had just spoken passed his cup absently. "Seems a bit hard to understand, things like that happening. All of us supposedly civilized, eh?"

"May I remind you, there is also racial tension here," said Goodhue. He tamped tobacco down, put the pipe in his mouth, began the first attempt to light it.

"Quite a bit different," said the angular professor. "Here we are contending with the economic fears of the workingmen. Fears of loss of jobs, lower pay scales. Frankly, I can't recall a case of cold-blooded, calculated murder."

"There are many facets to the situation," said Goodhue. "Many problems we—er—are perhaps better equipped to understand over there. One doesn't condone these things, of course. This boy was, well, difficult, shall we say. Bit of a troublemaker—"

"Married Sara Kent, the artist," said the plump man. "Or so my son tells me. Classmates, weren't they?"

The puffs came faster from Goodhue's pipe. "Kent—Kent. Ah, yes. I believe they were. It was quite a while ago, you understand—"

"'Murder most foul,'" said the angular man abruptly. "Mark of Cain, eh? Hardly the solution for a troublemaker. Most of our great men were troublemakers in their youth. Difficult, all of them."

"Chap was an outstanding scholar, my son tells me. Always regretted I didn't meet him," said the plump man.

"Shot from ambush, I heard," said the other. "One of your southern communities. Incredible."

"More tea, dear?" asked Elacoya of her husband.

"As I said, problems," said Goodhue. "Rather complex ones. Problems we must not let defeat us—ah, yes, thank you, my dear—"

"Shocking thing, just the same," said the angular man.

"Frightful," said the other.

It might have been Sunday at ALEC headquarters in New Orleans. The few people there talked in sudden bursts, then were silent. The receptionist-typist sat quietly, only her dark eyes, blazing in the honey-colored face, showed emotion. Isaiah Watkins had been in his office, alone, the door closed for a long time; how long he could not have told.

Man had to be alone sometimes. Even if it meant remembering a young man with haunted eyes and a quiet voice saying, "Heard you say you could use an extra hand here—" Even if it meant remembering, with equal clarity and pain, a small, gentle man, eyes glowing with love and the pride he would not voice, the pride in his grandson, first the baby, then the boy, and finally the man, who had given him the passport he carried in his pocket on the night he died.

"Don't gimme any calls; don't let anyone in," Isaiah had told the receptionist, but now the door opened squeakily, and he turned his chair from the window to face it. Ambrose Jefferson stood just inside, and Isaiah Watkins thought: Ambrose's an old man. He's an old man now, and was conscious of surprise.

"Don't do no good brooding, 'Saiah," said Ambrose. "Don't do no good. Like I tries to tell Pop, don't do no good grieving. It ain't never brought no one back."

Isaiah did not answer, and Ambrose lowered himself slowly to a chair. "Li'l Joe," said Ambrose. "Li'l Joe Champlin. I keeps thinking of him. I keeps thinking of him more than David. Seems like I ain't taken it in yet, about David. I keeps thinking on Li'l Joe."

After a long time Isaiah brought his gaze from the window, let it rest on Ambrose's face. "What we going to do?" he asked and Ambrose Jefferson, looking at him, thought: 'Saiah's an old man now. Never give it much thought before, but 'Saiah's an old man now.

Aloud he said: "Reckon we got to wait and see. See what his wife wants. He'd oughta lie with Li'l Joe and Geneva."

"Even if he don't, we ought to have a service."

"Memorial service," said Ambrose. "And the music. Seems to me we got to have that. Li'l Joe would want us to have that for the boy, like he had it. Reckon the boy would too. Been thinking we ought to have Preacher Jackson, like he had for his grandaddy."

"Seems somehow like we all coming back to where we started," said Isaiah. "Seems like we ain't getting nowhere." He was silent again for a long time, and his voice was still lifeless, without timbre, when he spoke. "You reckon it's all true, Ambrose? Things we was taught about meeting up with our folks after we've passed? God and all that?"

"We got to, 'Saiah. Don't nothing make sense if we don't. You-all better get busy, 'Saiah. Brooding don't do no good."

"Li'l Joe was mighty proud of that boy, Ambrose. David was Li'l Joe's heart. It was a long time ago, but I remember it as good as if it was yesterday. Li'l Joe was mighty proud of that boy."

"You think he ain't now, 'Saiah? You think he ain't now?"

The small package on the desk was marked "Gift" and partially addressed with the name only. Within it lay a blanket, so light and soft Hunter Travis had said to his mother when they selected it, "I could blow it across the room with one puff."

"Better get it off quickly," she had said. "You do procrastinate sometimes, you know—"

Beside the package lay two cables. One was smooth and lay flat on the rich mahogany of the desk top. It read: "It's a boy. Three days old now. Everyone fine. David." The other was crumpled, torn as a man in a frenzy would crumple and tear the cause of his frenzy. It had come last night, eight hours after the first, and bore the same date, and was signed "Chuck Martin," and through an endless London night, into a gray, fog-shrouded London day, Hunter Travis had sought, not verification, but denial, some word that it was a mistake, a night and a day filled with unreal telephone calls, made and received in a waking nightmare, yet from them, pieced together, there had emerged a truth more fearful than any nightmare, less credible than any delirium.

"Can you pray? . . . David does. . . ." Sara had said that, in a cab, driving through the rain, frightened. And he had answered something about not liking to be rebuffed by strangers, something about not thinking words from Hunter Travis would be too well received by the Almighty. To what God can you pray now, little Sara? To what God? To what God had David's unseeing eyes been turned, lying at the edge of a southern field in the spring twilight?

There could be no God for the living, because life was chaos, a thing of whirling forces powered by a universal mind gone mad. But let there be a God for the dead, because David was dead; a remote and kindly God, unconcerned with the evil that was life. And if he could not now or ever pray, he could weep and when his eyes were clear again finish the address on the package that still bore only a name. His mother had said that Sara—little Sara, oh, Christ! little Sara—would be pleased when her son received a present addressed to his small self in person: "Master David Champlin."

The room in the little undertaking establishment in the Negro section of Cainsville was hot and stuffy, without life or movement. Brad Willis stood beside a simple wooden casket with metal handles, clenched fists resting on the closed lid, head bowed. Not for more than fragmentary moments since he had dropped to his knees in the blood-soaked grass of Flaming Meadows, by the body of David Champlin, had the sound of his own inhuman cry faded from his mind. What had to be done he had done, not knowing grief at first, but only the consuming rage that had given life to that first cry that surged from his throat. In a little while details would clamor for attention, but after the details, after the hell that would be the next few days, there would be an emptiness, a desk swept clean, the moments of forgetting and the quick turning to someone who would not be there. And in the years to come there would be the courts and the people—his people, David's people—and in the well of the court a shadowy advocate he alone would see. But here in the land where that advocate's roots had been, there would be many who would see a tall brave man whose laughter had been deep and loud, who had fought, and sung, not for them or to them, but with them. And who had died as his ancestors had, because he was one of them.

Brad had learned long ago that tears were no weakness in a man; he had seen too many weep, in joy, in grief, in fear, in remorse. Chuck Martin had broken down like a child when Brad had finally reached him in Chicago, and Brad had envied him. Perhaps the soundless cry of agony that had lived within him since he had knelt by David Champlin's body—brat, brat, brat!—would fade, be washed away if he could call on the release of the tears that would not come, and then came and brought their healing at the sound of a low voice—"Brad, Brad, my dear, my dear—" the closeness of Peg, the strength in the pressure of her hands on his shoulders.

Later, when he raised his head, she said, "Brad, come away now."

"I didn't know you were coming. How—"

"I flew, dear. Your friend Jim Haskin met me. I couldn't reach you. And I had to come to you—"

"Peg, Peg."

"Things are all arranged. I've finished the loose ends for you. You can come with me now—"

"Sara?"

"She needs us, Brad."

Before he left, he laid a hand again on the wooden casket, touched the burnished metal handle. "The brat—" he said.

"Yes, my dear. Our brat, our boy. Safe now. Please, Brad—"

"Coming, Peg."

"What time would be best for me to see her, Suds?" Chuck Martin spaced his words slowly and deliberately. He had the feeling that this was the only way they would reach the mind of the man across the desk.

"Any time, Chuck. Only don't waken her if she's sleeping. We tried not to overdo sedation, but the shock had to be cushioned. It seems—apparently it happens all over again when she first wakes up."

"I know," said Chuck. "It's been happening to me."

Suds Sutherland stood, walked from desk to door and back to desk, remained standing, hands gripping the back of his swivel chair. It was the fifth time he had done this in the fifteen minutes Chuck had been in the office. Chuck rose slowly to his feet. "Some of your own medicine, Suds. That's what I'd prescribe."

Suds gave no sign of having heard, leaned forward, bearing his weight on hands that were white-knuckled from their grip on the chairback. "Chuck, what manner of person could do this! I don't mean David. I don't mean David. I mean Sara. Another woman. God almighty, Chuck! It was another woman who made that call. A woman calling another woman, the mother of a three-day-old son—mouthing filth, saying she was glad—Christ, Chuck! These things don't happen!"

"They do. How did it get through?"

"The call? The telephone operator at the hospital took a person-to-person from Cainsville. She thought nothing of it, of course. Chuck, it's unbelievable—"

"I wish it were."

"Sara screamed and ran out of her room and down the corridor, screaming. No one knew what had happened. She was like a madwoman. They got her back to her room and reached me. I—I—God help me, Chuck, I hadn't even heard about it myself. David hadn't been dead an hour. How did they know? How did that she-devil know where to call?"

"The baby's birth was on all the wire services, Suds, with the name of the hospital. And radio and TV carried it."

Suds Sutherland gave the chair he was gripping a violent shove that sent it thudding against the desk.

"What are you going to say to her, Reverend Charles Martin?" he asked slowly. "What are you going to say to our kid? Are you going to pray? Are you going to tell her about the love of God? The will of a good, kind God? Make her feel better?"

Chuck stopped, halfway to the door. "Suds—"

"And after you've seen her, are you going forth and preach the Gospel? Are you going to spread the Gospel, Chuck? After you've seen the casket they won't open because —because— Chuck, what God are you going to tell them about? Answer me that! After this—after this—you'll spread the word of God?"

"Suds, that's why. Can't you see—that's why—"

But Clifton Sutherland was no longer looking at him. His elbows rested on the desk top; the heels of his palms were pressed against his cheekbones, his hands covering his eyes, the short, stubby fingers kneading skin of forehead and scalp. "Go on, Chuck. Go see Sara. Tell her we all love her—"

Chuck stopped, one hand on the knob of the door to the outer office. He stretched the other hand, big-boned, big-knuckled, toward Suds in a clumsy gesture, started to speak, let the words die unuttered, and left, closing the door behind him gently.

Sara was awake when Chuck came into the room, propped half sitting, eyes enormous. He saw no trace of recent tears, thought not of some Biblical text or pat prayer, but of the words, "I like a look of agony because I know it's true—"

"Chuck. I—we've been waiting for you—"

He hesitated, taking in the meaning of the "we," and walked to the crib against the wall and smiled down at the sleeping child, then walked to the bed and took Sara's hand.

"I came as fast as I could, Sara."

Her hand stirred within his, and he tightened his grip a little, then opened his hand so that hers lay against his palm. Hunter had said to him once, "Sara Kent can be ten feet tall—" After his talk with Suds, he had been prepared—steeled—for tears, for hysteria, for a frantic cry against what Fate had dealt her. This quietude was harder to take. It robbed him of words, left him feeling inadequate and helpless; she was encased in an armor of quiet he could not pierce. She had turned her head away, and he waited, thinking her stillness might be sleep, but in a moment she turned back and her eyes were open, clear. When he glimpsed their depths, he looked away, down at the small hand in the palm of his, the fingers, like a child's, gripping his.

"You know?" she said. "You know about it? All about—everything?"

"Yes, Sara. Suds told me. And Brad."

"I—I—oh, God! Oh, God, Chuck! It's so lonely. That woman doesn't matter, Chuck; she doesn't matter. I don't want you to think—Chuck—it's always going to be so lonely, always—forever—"

He waited till the storm passed, saw that earlier storms had exhausted her so that this one spent itself soon.

"Not forever, Sara. It's not the evil and grief that's forever. Try—"

She had gone away again, and he could see only the small, fine-featured profile on the pillow, but this was not sedation; there were no signs of sedation in eyes or voice.

"Sara."

When she faced him again her eyes were closed; there was no flicker of the lids. "Chuck."

"Yes, Sara. I'm here."

"Chuck. You were at Gramp's funeral."

He checked the start of surprise. "Yes."

"You remember it? All of it?"

"Most of it, my dear."

Her eyes opened, looked into his directly, burning his with their intensity.

"I've been trying to think." Her fingers tightened on his. "To remember. The minister said something, Chuck, that upset David." She spoke the name firmly, as though only by firmness could the pain of it be vanquished. "It was a quotation from the Bible, from the Old Testament. Do you remember, Chuck? Do you? I know it—but—but not just right—"

"I think I know, Sara." He waited a moment, steadying himself. "It was from Samuel: 'And Samuel said unto Jesse, Are here all thy children? And he said, There remaineth yet the youngest, and, behold, he keepeth the sheep.' "

Sara lay quietly, her eyes distant. The hungry wail from the baby sounded loud in the room.

"Yes," Sara whispered. "Yes. 'There remaineth yet the youngest. And he keepeth the sheep.' That was David, Chuck—"

The wail grew stronger, and her eyes sought the crib where David Champlin lay, waking noisily.

"David—"

ABOUT THE AUTHOR

ANN FAIRBAIRN was born in Cambridge, Mass. but spent several of her childhood years in the deep South. She has worked as a newspaper reporter and feature director of a television station. For more than ten years she handled the tours of George Lewis, the New Orleans clarinetist, and his band throughout the United States, Great Britain and Europe. Her first book, a biography of Lewis entitled *Call Him George,* was published in London in 1962. Miss Fairbairn, a widow with no children, now lives in the Monterey Peninsula in California.